I0819849

Daniel Defoe Collection

By

Daniel Defoe

Cover Photograph: lyng883

ISBN: 978-1-78139-327-7

Contents

THE LIFE AND ADVENTURES OF ROBINSON CRUSOE

THE FURTHER ADVENTURES OF ROBINSON CRUSOE

THE FORTUNES & MISFORTUNES OF THE FAMOUS MOLL FLANDERS

A JOURNAL OF THE PLAGUE YEAR

ROXANA

THE LIFE AND ADVENTURES OF ROBINSON CRUSOE

Chapter I—START IN LIFE

I was born in the year 1632, in the city of York, of a good family, though not of that country, my father being a foreigner of Bremen, who settled first at Hull. He got a good estate by merchandise, and leaving off his trade, lived afterwards at York, from whence he had married my mother, whose relations were named Robinson, a very good family in that country, and from whom I was called Robinson Kreutznaer; but, by the usual corruption of words in England, we are now called—nay we call ourselves and write our name—Crusoe; and so my companions always called me.

I had two elder brothers, one of whom was lieutenant-colonel to an English regiment of foot in Flanders, formerly commanded by the famous Colonel Lockhart, and was killed at the battle near Dunkirk against the Spaniards. What became of my second brother I never knew, any more than my father or mother knew what became of me.

Being the third son of the family and not bred to any trade, my head began to be filled very early with rambling thoughts. My father, who was very ancient, had given me a competent share of learning, as far as house-education and a country free school generally go, and designed me for the law; but I would be satisfied with nothing but going to sea; and my inclination to this led me so strongly against the will, nay, the commands of my father, and against all the entreaties and persuasions of my mother and other friends, that there seemed to be something fatal in that propensity of nature, tending directly to the life of misery which was to befall me.

My father, a wise and grave man, gave me serious and excellent counsel against what he foresaw was my design. He called me one morning into his chamber, where he was confined by the gout, and expostulated very warmly with me upon this subject. He asked me what reasons, more than a mere wandering inclination, I had for leaving father's house and my native country, where I might be well introduced, and had a prospect of raising my fortune by application and industry, with a life of ease and pleasure. He told me it was men of desperate fortunes on one hand, or of aspiring, superior fortunes on the other, who went abroad upon adventures, to rise by enterprise, and make themselves famous in undertakings of a nature out of the common road; that these things were all either too far above me or too far below me; that mine was the middle state, or what might be called the upper station of low life, which he had found, by long experience, was the best state in the world, the most suited to human happiness, not exposed to the miseries and hardships, the labour and sufferings of the mechanic part of mankind, and not embarrassed with the pride, luxury, ambition, and envy of the upper part of mankind. He told me I might judge of the happiness of this state by this one thing—viz. that this was the state of life which all other people envied; that kings have frequently lamented the miserable consequence of being born to great things, and wished they had been placed in the middle of the two extremes, between the mean and the great; that the wise man gave his testimony to this, as the standard of felicity, when he prayed to have neither poverty nor riches.

He bade me observe it, and I should always find that the calamities of life were shared among the upper and lower part of mankind, but that the middle station had the fewest disasters, and was not exposed to so many vicissitudes as the higher or lower part of mankind; nay, they were not subjected to so many distempers and uneasinesses, either of body or mind, as those were who, by vicious living, luxury, and extravagances on the one hand, or by hard labour, want of necessaries, and mean or insufficient diet on the other hand, bring distemper upon themselves by the natural consequences of their way of living; that the middle station of life was calculated for all kind of virtue and all kind of enjoyments; that peace and plenty were the handmaids of a middle fortune; that temperance, moderation, quietness, health, society, all agreeable diversions, and all desirable pleasures, were the blessings attending the middle station of life; that this way men went silently and smoothly through the world, and comfortably out of it, not embarrassed with the labours of the hands or of the head, not sold to a life of slavery for daily bread, nor harassed with perplexed circumstances, which rob the soul of peace and the body of rest, nor enraged with the passion of envy, or the secret burning lust of ambition for great things; but, in easy circumstances, sliding gently through the world, and sensibly tasting the sweets of living, without the bitter; feeling that they are happy, and learning by every day's experience to know it more sensibly.

After this he pressed me earnestly, and in the most affectionate manner, not to play the young man, nor to precipitate myself into miseries which nature, and the station of life I was born in, seemed to have provided against; that I was under no necessity of seeking my bread; that he would do well for me, and endeavour to enter me fairly into the station of life which he had just been recommending to me; and that if I was not very easy and happy in the world, it must be my mere fate or fault that must hinder it; and that he should have nothing to answer for, having thus discharged his duty in warning me against measures which he knew would be to my hurt; in a word, that as he would do very kind things for me if I would stay and settle at home as he directed, so he would not have so much hand in my misfortunes as to give me any encouragement to go away; and to close all, he told me I had my elder brother for an example, to whom he had used the same earnest persuasions to keep him from going into the Low Country wars, but could not prevail, his young desires prompting him to run into the army, where he was killed; and though he said he would not cease to pray for me, yet he would venture to say to me, that if I did take this foolish step, God would not bless me, and I should have leisure hereafter to reflect upon having neglected his counsel when there might be none to assist in my recovery.

I observed in this last part of his discourse, which was truly prophetic, though I suppose my father did not know it to be so himself—I say, I observed the tears run down his face very plentifully, especially when he spoke of my brother who was killed: and that when he spoke of my having leisure to repent, and none to assist me, he was so moved that he broke off the discourse, and told me his heart was so full he could say no more to me.

I was sincerely affected with this discourse, and, indeed, who could be otherwise? and I resolved not to think of going abroad any more, but to settle at home according to my father's desire. But alas! a few days wore it all off; and, in short, to prevent any of my father's further importunities, in a few weeks after I resolved to run quite away from him. However, I did not act quite so hastily as the first heat of my resolution prompted; but I took my mother at a time when I thought her a little more pleasant than ordinary, and told her that my thoughts were so entirely bent upon seeing the world that I should never settle to anything with resolution enough to go through with it, and my father had better give me his consent than force me to go without it; that I was now eighteen years old, which was too late to go apprentice to a trade or clerk to an attorney; that I was sure if I did I should never serve out my time, but I should certainly run away from my master before my time was out, and go to sea; and if she would speak to my father to let me go one voyage abroad, if I came home again, and did not like it, I would go no more; and I would promise, by a double diligence, to recover the time that I had lost.

This put my mother into a great passion; she told me she knew it would be to no purpose to speak to my father upon any such subject; that he knew too well what was my interest to give his consent to anything so much for my hurt; and that she wondered how I could think of any such thing after the discourse I had had with my father, and such kind and tender expressions as she knew my father had used to me; and that, in short, if I would ruin myself, there was no help for me; but I might depend I should never have their consent to it; that for her part she would not have so much hand in my destruction; and I should never have it to say that my mother was willing when my father was not.

Though my mother refused to move it to my father, yet I heard afterwards that she reported all the discourse to him, and that my father, after showing a great concern at it, said to her, with a sigh, "That boy might be happy if he would stay at home; but if he goes abroad, he will be the most miserable wretch that ever was born: I can give no consent to it."

It was not till almost a year after this that I broke loose, though, in the meantime, I continued obstinately deaf to all proposals of settling to business, and frequently expostulated with my father and mother about their being so positively determined against what they knew my inclinations prompted me to. But being one day at Hull, where I went casually, and without any purpose of making an elopement at that time; but, I say, being there, and one of my companions being about to sail to London in his father's ship, and prompting me to go with them with the common allurement of seafaring men, that it should cost me nothing for my passage, I consulted neither father nor mother any more, nor so much as sent them word of it; but leaving them to hear of it as they might, without asking God's blessing or my father's, without any consideration of circumstances or consequences, and in an ill hour, God knows, on the 1st of September 1651, I went on board a ship bound for London. Never any young adventurer's misfortunes, I believe, began sooner, or continued longer than mine. The ship was no sooner out of the Humber than the wind began to blow and the sea to rise in a most frightful manner; and, as I had never been at sea before, I was most inexpressibly sick in body and terrified in mind. I began now seriously to reflect upon what I had done, and how justly I was overtaken by the judgment of Heaven for my wicked leaving my father's house, and abandoning my duty. All the good counsels of my parents, my father's tears and my mother's entreaties, came now fresh into my mind; and my conscience, which was not yet come to the pitch of hardness to which it has since, reproached me with the contempt of advice, and the breach of my duty to God and my father.

All this while the storm increased, and the sea went very high, though nothing like what I have seen many times since; no, nor what I saw a few days after; but it was enough to affect me then, who was but a young sailor, and had never known anything of the matter. I expected every wave would have swallowed us up, and that every time the ship fell down, as I thought it did, in the trough or hollow of the sea, we should never rise more; in this agony of mind, I made many vows and resolutions that if it would please God to spare my life in this one voyage, if ever I got once my foot upon dry land again, I would go directly home to my father, and never set it into a ship again while I lived; that I would take his advice, and never run myself into such miseries as these any more. Now I saw plainly the goodness of his observations about the middle station of life, how easy, how comfortably he had lived all his days, and never had been exposed to tempests at sea or troubles on shore; and I resolved that I would, like a true repenting prodigal, go home to my father.

These wise and sober thoughts continued all the while the storm lasted, and indeed some time after; but the next day the wind was abated, and the sea calmer, and I began to be a little inured to it; however, I was very grave for all that day, being also a little sea-sick still; but towards night the weather cleared up, the wind was quite over, and a charming fine evening followed; the sun went down perfectly clear, and rose so the next morning; and having little or no wind, and a smooth sea, the sun shining upon it, the sight was, as I thought, the most delightful that ever I saw.

I had slept well in the night, and was now no more sea-sick, but very cheerful, looking with wonder upon the sea that was so rough and terrible the day before, and could be so calm and so pleasant in so little a time after. And now, lest my good resolutions should continue, my companion, who had enticed me away, comes to me; "Well, Bob," says he, clapping me upon the shoulder, "how do you do after it? I warrant you were frighted, wer'n't you, last night, when it blew but a capful of wind?" "A capful d'you call it?" said I; "'twas a terrible storm." "A storm, you fool you," replies he; "do you call that a storm? why, it was nothing at all; give us but a good ship and sea-room, and we think nothing of such a squall of wind as that; but you're but a fresh-water sailor, Bob. Come, let us make a bowl of punch, and we'll forget all that; d'ye see what charming weather 'tis now?" To make short this sad part of my story, we went the way of all sailors; the punch was made and I was made half drunk with it: and in that one night's wickedness I drowned all my repentance, all my reflections upon my past conduct, all my resolutions for the future. In a word, as the sea was returned to its smoothness of surface and settled calmness by the abatement of that storm, so the hurry of my thoughts being over, my fears and apprehensions of being swallowed up by the sea being forgotten, and the current of my former desires returned, I entirely forgot the vows and promises that I made in my distress. I found, indeed, some intervals of reflection; and the serious thoughts did, as it were, endeavour to return again sometimes; but I shook them off, and roused myself from them as it were from a distemper, and applying myself to drinking and company, soon mastered the return of those fits—for so I called them; and I had in five or six days got as complete a victory over conscience as any young fellow that resolved not to be troubled with it could desire. But I was to have another trial for it still; and Providence, as in such cases generally it does, resolved to leave me entirely without excuse; for if I would not take this for a deliverance, the next was to be such a one as the worst and most hardened wretch among us would confess both the danger and the mercy of.

The sixth day of our being at sea we came into Yarmouth Roads; the wind having been contrary and the weather calm, we had made but little way since the storm. Here we were obliged to come to an anchor, and here we lay, the wind continuing contrary—viz. at south-west—for seven or eight days, during which time a great many ships from Newcastle came into the same Roads, as the common harbour where the ships might wait for a wind for the river.

We had not, however, rid here so long but we should have tided it up the river, but that the wind blew too fresh, and after we had lain four or five days, blew very hard. However, the Roads being reckoned as good as a harbour, the anchorage good, and our ground-tackle very strong, our men were unconcerned, and not in the least apprehensive of danger, but spent the time in rest and mirth, after the manner of the sea; but the eighth day, in the morning, the wind increased, and we had all hands at work to strike our topmasts, and make everything snug and close, that the ship might ride as easy as possible. By noon the sea went very high indeed, and our ship rode forecastle in, shipped several seas, and we thought once or twice our anchor had come home; upon which our master ordered out the sheet-anchor, so that we rode with two anchors ahead, and the cables veered out to the bitter end.

By this time it blew a terrible storm indeed; and now I began to see terror and amazement in the faces even of the seamen themselves. The master, though vigilant in the business of preserving the ship, yet as he went in and out of his cabin by me, I could hear him softly to himself say, several times, "Lord be merciful to us! we shall be all lost! we shall be all undone!" and the like. During these first hurries I was stupid, lying still in my cabin, which was in the steerage, and cannot describe my temper: I could ill resume the first penitence which I had so apparently trampled upon and hardened myself against: I thought the bitterness of death had been past, and that this would be nothing like the first; but when the master himself came by me, as I said just now, and said we should be all lost, I was dreadfully frighted. I got up out of my cabin and looked out; but such a dismal sight I never saw: the sea ran mountains high, and broke upon us every three or four minutes; when I could look about, I could see nothing but distress round us; two ships that rode near us, we found, had cut their masts by the board, being deep laden; and our men cried out that a ship which rode about a mile ahead of us was foundered. Two more ships, being driven from their anchors, were run out of the Roads to sea, at all adventures, and that with not a mast standing. The light ships fared the best, as not so much labouring in the sea; but two or three of them drove, and came close by us, running away with only their spritsail out before the wind.

Towards evening the mate and boatswain begged the master of our ship to let them cut away the fore-mast, which he was very unwilling to do; but the boatswain protesting to him that if he did not the ship would founder, he consented; and when they had cut away the fore-mast, the main-mast stood so loose, and shook the ship so much, they were obliged to cut that away also, and make a clear deck.

Any one may judge what a condition I must be in at all this, who was but a young sailor, and who had been in such a fright before at but a little. But if I can express at this distance the thoughts I had about me at that time, I was in tenfold more horror of mind upon account of my former convictions, and the having returned from them to the resolutions I had wickedly taken at first, than I was at death itself; and these, added to the terror of the storm, put me into such a condition that I can by no words describe it. But the worst was not come yet; the storm continued with such fury that the seamen themselves acknowledged they had never seen a worse. We had a good ship, but she was deep laden, and wallowed in the sea, so that the seamen every now and then cried out she would founder. It was my advantage in one respect, that I did not know what they meant by *founder* till I inquired. However, the storm was so violent that I saw, what is not often seen, the master, the boatswain, and some others more sensible than the rest, at their prayers, and expecting every moment when the ship would go to the bottom. In the middle of the night, and under all the rest of our distresses, one of the men that had been down to see cried out we had sprung a leak; another said there was four feet water in the hold. Then all hands were called to the pump. At that word, my heart, as I thought, died within me: and I fell backwards upon the side of my bed where I sat, into the cabin. However, the men roused me, and told me that I, that was able to do nothing before, was as well able to pump as another; at which I stirred up and went to the pump, and worked very heartily. While this was doing the master, seeing some light colliers, who, not able to ride out the storm were obliged to slip and run away to sea, and would come near us, ordered to fire a gun as a signal of distress. I, who knew nothing what they meant, thought the ship had broken, or some dreadful thing happened. In a word, I was so surprised that I fell down in a swoon. As this was a time when everybody had his own life to think of, nobody minded me, or what was become of me; but another man stepped up to the pump, and thrusting me aside with his foot, let me lie, thinking I had been dead; and it was a great while before I came to myself.

We worked on; but the water increasing in the hold, it was apparent that the ship would founder; and though the storm began to abate a little, yet it was not possible she could swim till we might run into any port; so the master continued firing guns for help; and a light ship, who had rid it out just ahead of us, ventured a boat out to help us. It was with the utmost hazard the boat came near us; but it was impossible for us to get on board, or for the boat to lie near the ship's side, till at last the men rowing very heartily, and venturing their lives to save ours, our men cast them a rope over the stern with a buoy to it, and then veered it out a great length, which they, after much labour and hazard, took hold of, and we hauled them close under our stern, and got all into their boat. It was to no purpose for them or us, after we were in the boat, to think of reaching their own ship; so all agreed to let her drive, and only to pull her in towards shore as much as we could; and our master promised them, that if the boat was staved upon shore, he would make it good to their master: so partly rowing and partly driving, our boat went away to the northward, sloping towards the shore almost as far as Winterton Ness.

We were not much more than a quarter of an hour out of our ship till we saw her sink, and then I understood for the first time what was meant by a ship foundering in the sea. I must acknowledge I had hardly eyes to look up when the seamen told me she was sinking; for from the moment that they rather put me into the boat than that I might be said to go in, my heart was, as it were, dead within me, partly with fright, partly with horror of mind, and the thoughts of what was yet before me.

While we were in this condition—the men yet labouring at the oar to bring the boat near the shore—we could see (when, our boat mounting the waves, we were able to see the shore) a great many people running along the strand to assist us when we should come near; but we made but slow way towards the shore; nor were we able to reach the shore till, being past the lighthouse at Winterton, the shore falls off to the westward towards Cromer, and so the land broke off a little the violence of the wind. Here we got in, and though not without much difficulty, got all safe on shore, and walked afterwards on foot to Yarmouth, where, as unfortunate men, we were used with great humanity, as well by the magistrates of the town, who assigned us good quarters, as by particular merchants and owners of ships, and had money given us sufficient to carry us either to London or back to Hull as we thought fit.

Had I now had the sense to have gone back to Hull, and have gone home, I had been happy, and my father, as in our blessed Saviour's parable, had even killed the fatted calf for me; for hearing the ship I went away in was cast away in Yarmouth Roads, it was a great while before he had any assurances that I was not drowned.

But my ill fate pushed me on now with an obstinacy that nothing could resist; and though I had several times loud calls from my reason and my more composed judgment to go home, yet I had no power to do it. I know not what to call this, nor will I urge that it is a secret overruling decree, that hurries us on to be the instruments of our own destruction, even though it be before us, and that we rush upon it with our eyes open. Certainly, nothing but some such decreed unavoidable misery, which it was impossible for me to escape, could have pushed me forward against the calm reasonings and persuasions of my most retired thoughts, and against two such visible instructions as I had met with in my first attempt.

My comrade, who had helped to harden me before, and who was the master's son, was now less forward than I. The first time he spoke to me after we were at Yarmouth, which was not till two or three days, for we were separated in the town to several quarters; I say, the first time he saw me, it appeared his tone was altered; and, looking very melancholy, and shaking his head, he asked me how I did, and telling his father who I was, and how I had come this voyage only for a trial, in order to go further abroad, his father, turning to me with a very grave and concerned tone "Young man," says he, "you ought never to go to sea any more; you ought to take this for a plain and visible token that you are not to be a seafaring man." "Why, sir," said I, "will you go to sea no more?" "That is another case," said he; "it is my calling, and therefore my duty; but as you made this voyage on trial, you see what a taste Heaven has given you of what you are to expect if you persist. Perhaps this has all befallen us on your account, like Jonah in the ship of Tarshish. Pray," continues he, "what are you; and on what account did you go to sea?" Upon that I told him some of my story; at the end of which he burst out into a strange kind of passion: "What had I done," says he, "that such an unhappy wretch should come into my ship? I would not set my foot in the same ship with thee again for a thousand pounds." This indeed was, as I said, an excursion of his spirits, which were yet agitated by the sense of his loss, and was farther than he could have authority to go. However, he afterwards talked very gravely to me, exhorting me to go back to my father, and not tempt Providence to my ruin, telling me I might see a visible hand of Heaven against me. "And, young man," said he, "depend upon it, if you do not go back, wherever you go, you will meet with nothing but disasters and disappointments, till your father's words are fulfilled upon you."

We parted soon after; for I made him little answer, and I saw him no more; which way he went I knew not. As for me, having some money in my pocket, I travelled to London by land; and there, as well as on the road, had many struggles with myself what course of life I should take, and whether I should go home or to sea.

As to going home, shame opposed the best motions that offered to my thoughts, and it immediately occurred to me how I should be laughed at among the neighbours, and should be ashamed to see, not my father and mother only, but even everybody else; from whence I have since often observed, how incongruous and irrational the common temper of mankind is, especially of youth, to that reason which ought to guide them in such cases—viz. that they are not ashamed to sin, and yet are ashamed to repent; not ashamed of the action for which they ought justly to be esteemed fools, but are ashamed of the returning, which only can make them be esteemed wise men.

In this state of life, however, I remained some time, uncertain what measures to take, and what course of life to lead. An irresistible reluctance continued to going home; and as I stayed away a while, the remembrance of the distress I had been in wore off, and as that abated, the little motion I had in my desires to return wore off with it, till at last I quite laid aside the thoughts of it, and looked out for a voyage.

Chapter II—SLAVERY AND ESCAPE

That evil influence which carried me first away from my father's house—which hurried me into the wild and indigested notion of raising my fortune, and that impressed those conceits so forcibly upon me as to make me deaf to all good advice, and to the entreaties and even the commands of my father—I say, the same influence, whatever it was, presented the most unfortunate of all enterprises to my view; and I went on board a vessel bound to the coast of Africa; or, as our sailors vulgarly called it, a voyage to Guinea.

It was my great misfortune that in all these adventures I did not ship myself as a sailor; when, though I might indeed have worked a little harder than ordinary, yet at the same time I should have learnt the duty and office of a fore-mast man, and in time might have qualified myself for a mate or lieutenant, if not for a master. But as it was always my fate to choose for the worse, so I did here; for having money in my pocket and good clothes upon my back, I would always go on board in the habit of a gentleman; and so I neither had any business in the ship, nor learned to do any.

It was my lot first of all to fall into pretty good company in London, which does not always happen to such loose and misguided young fellows as I then was; the devil generally not omitting to lay some snare for them very early; but it was not so with me. I first got acquainted with the master of a ship who had been on the coast of Guinea; and who, having had very good success there, was resolved to go again. This captain taking a fancy to my conversation, which was not at all disagreeable at that time, hearing me say I had a mind to see the world, told me if I would go the voyage with him I should be at no expense; I should be his messmate and his companion; and if I could carry anything with me, I should have all the advantage of it that the trade would admit; and perhaps I might meet with some encouragement.

I embraced the offer; and entering into a strict friendship with this captain, who was an honest, plain-dealing man, I went the voyage with him, and carried a small adventure with me, which, by the disinterested honesty of my friend the captain, I increased very considerably; for I carried about £40 in such toys and trifles as the captain directed me to buy. These £40 I had mustered together by the assistance of some of my relations whom I corresponded with; and who, I believe, got my father, or at least my mother, to contribute so much as that to my first adventure.

This was the only voyage which I may say was successful in all my adventures, which I owe to the integrity and honesty of my friend the captain; under whom also I got a competent knowledge of the mathematics and the rules of navigation, learned how to keep an account of the ship's course, take an observation, and, in short, to understand some things that were needful to be understood by a sailor; for, as he took delight to instruct me, I took delight to learn; and, in a word, this voyage made me both a sailor and a merchant; for I brought home five pounds nine ounces of gold-dust for my adventure, which yielded me in London, at my return, almost £300; and this filled me with those aspiring thoughts which have since so completed my ruin.

Yet even in this voyage I had my misfortunes too; particularly, that I was continually sick, being thrown into a violent calenture by the excessive heat of the climate; our principal trading being upon the coast, from latitude of 15 degrees north even to the line itself.

I was now set up for a Guinea trader; and my friend, to my great misfortune, dying soon after his arrival, I resolved to go the same voyage again, and I embarked in the same vessel with one who was his mate in the former voyage, and had now got the command of the ship. This was the unhappiest voyage that ever man made; for though I did not carry quite £100 of my new-gained wealth, so that I had £200 left, which I had lodged with my friend's widow, who was very just to me, yet I fell into terrible misfortunes. The first was this: our ship making her course towards the Canary Islands, or rather between those islands and the African shore, was surprised in the grey of the morning by a Turkish rover of Sallee, who gave chase to us with all the sail she could make. We crowded also as much canvas as our yards would spread, or our masts carry, to get clear; but finding the pirate gained upon us, and would certainly come up with us in a few hours, we prepared to fight; our ship having twelve guns, and the rogue eighteen. About three in the afternoon he came up with us, and bringing to, by mistake, just athwart our quarter, instead of athwart our stern, as he intended, we brought eight of our guns to bear on that side, and poured in a broadside upon him, which made him sheer off again, after returning our fire, and pouring in also his small shot from near two hundred men which he had on board. However, we had not a man touched, all our men keeping close. He prepared to attack us again, and we to defend ourselves. But laying us on board the next time upon our other quarter, he entered sixty men upon our decks, who immediately fell to cutting and hacking the sails and rigging. We plied them with small shot, half-pikes, powder-chests, and such like, and cleared our deck of them twice. However, to cut short this melancholy part of our story, our ship being disabled, and three of our men killed, and eight wounded, we were obliged to yield, and were carried all prisoners into Sallee, a port belonging to the Moors.

The usage I had there was not so dreadful as at first I apprehended; nor was I carried up the country to the emperor's court, as the rest of our men were, but was kept by the captain of the rover as his proper prize, and made his slave, being young and nimble, and fit for his business. At this surprising change of my circumstances, from a merchant to a miserable slave, I was perfectly overwhelmed; and now I looked back upon my father's prophetic discourse to me, that I should be miserable and have none to relieve me, which I thought was now so effectually brought to pass that I could not be worse; for now the hand of Heaven had overtaken me, and I was undone without redemption; but, alas! this was but a taste of the misery I was to go through, as will appear in the sequel of this story.

As my new patron, or master, had taken me home to his house, so I was in hopes that he would take me with him when he went to sea again, believing that it would some time or other be his fate to be taken by a Spanish or Portugal man-of-war; and that then I should be set at liberty. But this hope of mine was soon taken away; for when he went to sea, he left me on shore to look after his little garden, and do the common drudgery of slaves about his house; and when he came home again from his cruise, he ordered me to lie in the cabin to look after the ship.

Here I meditated nothing but my escape, and what method I might take to effect it, but found no way that had the least probability in it; nothing presented to make the supposition of it rational; for I had nobody to communicate it to that would embark with me—no fellow-slave, no Englishman, Irishman, or Scotchman there but myself; so that for two years, though I often pleased myself with the imagination, yet I never had the least encouraging prospect of putting it in practice.

After about two years, an odd circumstance presented itself, which put the old thought of making some attempt for my liberty again in my head. My patron lying at home longer than usual without fitting out his ship, which, as I heard, was for want of money, he used constantly, once or twice a week, sometimes oftener if the weather was fair, to take the ship's pinnace and go out into the road a-fishing; and as he always took me and young Maresco with him to row the boat, we made him very merry, and I proved very dexterous in catching fish; insomuch that sometimes he would send me with a Moor, one of his kinsmen, and the youth—the Maresco, as they called him—to catch a dish of fish for him.

It happened one time, that going a-fishing in a calm morning, a fog rose so thick that, though we were not half a league from the shore, we lost sight of it; and rowing we knew not whither or which way, we laboured all day, and all the next night; and when the morning came we found we had pulled off to sea instead of pulling in for the shore; and that we were at least two leagues from the shore. However, we got well in again, though with a great deal of labour and some danger; for the wind began to blow pretty fresh in the morning; but we were all very hungry.

But our patron, warned by this disaster, resolved to take more care of himself for the future; and having lying by him the longboat of our English ship that he had taken, he resolved he would not go a-fishing any more without a compass and some provision; so he ordered the carpenter of his ship, who also was an English slave, to build a little state-room, or cabin, in the middle of the long-boat, like that of a barge, with a place to stand behind it to steer, and haul home the main-sheet; the room before for a hand or two to stand and work the sails. She sailed with what we call a shoulder-of-mutton sail; and the boom jibed over the top of the cabin, which lay very snug and low, and had in it room for him to lie, with a slave or two, and a table to eat on, with some small lockers to put in some bottles of such liquor as he thought fit to drink; and his bread, rice, and coffee.

We went frequently out with this boat a-fishing; and as I was most dexterous to catch fish for him, he never went without me. It happened that he had appointed to go out in this boat, either for pleasure or for fish, with two or three Moors of some distinction in that place, and for whom he had provided extraordinarily, and had, therefore, sent on board the boat overnight a larger store of provisions than ordinary; and had ordered me to get ready three fusees with powder and shot, which were on board his ship, for that they designed some sport of fowling as well as fishing.

I got all things ready as he had directed, and waited the next morning with the boat washed clean, her ancient and pendants out, and everything to accommodate his guests; when by-and-by my patron came on board alone, and told me his guests had put off going from some business that fell out, and ordered me, with the man and boy, as usual, to go out with the boat and catch them some fish, for that his friends were to sup at his house, and commanded that as soon as I got some fish I should bring it home to his house; all which I prepared to do.

This moment my former notions of deliverance darted into my thoughts, for now I found I was likely to have a little ship at my command; and my master being gone, I prepared to furnish myself, not for fishing business, but for a voyage; though I knew not, neither did I so much as consider, whither I should steer—anywhere to get out of that place was my desire.

My first contrivance was to make a pretence to speak to this Moor, to get something for our subsistence on board; for I told him we must not presume to eat of our patron's bread. He said that was true; so he brought a large basket of rusk or biscuit, and three jars of fresh water, into the boat. I knew where my patron's case of bottles stood, which it was evident, by the make, were taken out of some English prize, and I conveyed them into the boat while the Moor was on shore, as if they had been there before for our master. I conveyed also a great lump of beeswax into the boat, which weighed about half a hundred-weight, with a parcel of twine or thread, a hatchet, a saw, and a hammer, all of which were of great use to us afterwards, especially the wax, to make candles. Another trick I tried upon him, which he innocently came into also: his name was Ismael, which they call Muley, or Moely; so I called to him—"Moely," said I, "our patron's guns are on board the boat; can you not get a little powder and shot? It may be we may kill some alcamies (a fowl like our curlews) for ourselves, for I know he keeps the gunner's stores in the ship." "Yes," says he, "I'll bring some;" and accordingly he brought a great leather pouch, which held a pound and a half of powder, or rather more; and another with shot, that had five or six pounds, with some bullets, and put all into the boat. At the same time I had found some powder of my master's in the great cabin, with which I filled one of the large bottles in the case, which was almost empty, pouring what was in it into another; and thus furnished with everything needful, we sailed out of the port to fish. The castle, which is at the entrance of the port, knew who we were, and took no notice of us; and we were not above a mile out of the port before we hauled in our sail and set us down to fish. The wind blew from the N.N.E., which was contrary to my desire, for had it blown southerly I had been sure to have made the coast of Spain, and at least reached to the bay of Cadiz; but my resolutions were, blow which way it would, I would be gone from that horrid place where I was, and leave the rest to fate.

After we had fished some time and caught nothing—for when I had fish on my hook I would not pull them up, that he might not see them—I said to the Moor, "This will not do; our master will not be thus served; we must stand farther off." He, thinking no harm, agreed, and being in the head of the boat, set the sails; and, as I had the helm, I ran the boat out near a league farther, and then brought her to, as if I would fish; when, giving the boy the helm, I stepped forward to where the Moor was, and making as if I stooped for something behind him, I took him by surprise with my arm under his waist, and tossed him clear overboard into the sea. He rose immediately, for he swam like a cork, and called to me, begged to be taken in, told me he would go all over the world with me. He swam so strong after the boat that he would have reached me very quickly, there being but little wind; upon which I stepped into the cabin, and fetching one of the fowling-pieces, I presented it at him, and told him I had done him no hurt, and if he would be quiet I would do him none. "But," said I, "you swim well enough to reach to the shore, and the sea is calm; make the best of your way to shore, and I will do you no harm; but if you come near the boat I'll shoot you through the head, for I am resolved to have my liberty;" so he turned himself about, and swam for the shore, and I make no doubt but he reached it with ease, for he was an excellent swimmer.

I could have been content to have taken this Moor with me, and have drowned the boy, but there was no venturing to trust him. When he was gone, I turned to the boy, whom they called Xury, and said to him, "Xury, if you will be faithful to me, I'll make you a great man; but if you will not stroke your face to be true to me"—that is, swear by Mahomet and his father's beard—"I must throw you into the sea too." The boy smiled in my face, and spoke so innocently that I could not distrust him, and swore to be faithful to me, and go all over the world with me.

While I was in view of the Moor that was swimming, I stood out directly to sea with the boat, rather stretching to windward, that they might think me gone towards the Straits' mouth (as indeed any one that had been in their wits must have been supposed to do): for who would have supposed we were sailed on to the southward, to the truly Barbarian coast, where whole nations of negroes were sure to surround us with their canoes and destroy us; where we could not go on shore but we should be devoured by savage beasts, or more merciless savages of human kind.

But as soon as it grew dusk in the evening, I changed my course, and steered directly south and by east, bending my course a little towards the east, that I might keep in with the shore; and having a fair, fresh gale of wind, and a smooth, quiet sea, I made such sail that I believe by the next day, at three o'clock in the afternoon, when I first made the land, I could not be less than one hundred and fifty miles south of Sallee; quite beyond the Emperor of Morocco's dominions, or indeed of any other king thereabouts, for we saw no people.

Yet such was the fright I had taken of the Moors, and the dreadful apprehensions I had of falling into their hands, that I would not stop, or go on shore, or come to an anchor; the wind continuing fair till I had sailed in that manner five days; and then the wind shifting to the southward, I concluded also that if any of our vessels were in chase of me, they also would now give over; so I ventured to make to the coast, and came to an anchor in the mouth of a little river, I knew not what, nor where, neither what latitude, what country, what nation, or what river. I neither saw, nor desired to see any people; the principal thing I wanted was fresh water. We came into this creek in the evening, resolving to swim on shore as soon as it was dark, and discover the country; but as soon as it was quite dark, we heard such dreadful noises of the barking, roaring, and howling of wild creatures, of we knew not what kinds, that the poor boy was ready to die with fear, and begged of me not to go on shore till day. "Well, Xury," said I, "then I won't; but it may be that we may see men by day, who will be as bad to us as those lions." "Then we give them the shoot gun," says Xury, laughing, "make them run wey." Such English Xury spoke by conversing among us slaves. However, I was glad to see the boy so cheerful, and I gave him a dram (out of our patron's case of bottles) to cheer him up. After all, Xury's advice was good, and I took it; we dropped our little anchor, and lay still all night; I say still, for we slept none; for in two or three hours we saw vast great creatures (we knew not what to call them) of many sorts, come down to the sea-shore and run into the water, wallowing and washing themselves for the pleasure of cooling themselves; and they made such hideous howlings and yellings, that I never indeed heard the like.

Xury was dreadfully frighted, and indeed so was I too; but we were both more frighted when we heard one of these mighty creatures come swimming towards our boat; we could not see him, but we might hear him by his blowing to be a monstrous huge and furious beast. Xury said it was a lion, and it might be so for aught I know; but poor Xury cried to me to weigh the anchor and row away; "No," says I, "Xury; we can slip our cable, with the buoy to it, and go off to sea; they cannot follow us far." I had no sooner said so, but I perceived the creature (whatever it was) within two oars' length, which something surprised me; however, I immediately stepped to the cabin door, and taking up my gun, fired at him; upon which he immediately turned about and swam towards the shore again.

But it is impossible to describe the horrid noises, and hideous cries and howlings that were raised, as well upon the edge of the shore as higher within the country, upon the noise or report of the gun, a thing I have some reason to believe those creatures had never heard before: this convinced me that there was no going on shore for us in the night on that coast, and how to venture on shore in the day was another question too; for to have fallen into the hands of any of the savages had been as bad as to have fallen into the hands of the lions and tigers; at least we were equally apprehensive of the danger of it.

Be that as it would, we were obliged to go on shore somewhere or other for water, for we had not a pint left in the boat; when and where to get to it was the point. Xury said, if I would let him go on shore with one of the jars, he would find if there was any water, and bring some to me. I asked him why he would go? why I should not go, and he stay in the boat? The boy answered with so much affection as made me love him ever after. Says he, "If wild mans come, they eat me, you go wey." "Well, Xury," said I, "we will both go and if the wild mans come, we will kill them, they shall eat neither of us." So I gave Xury a piece of rusk bread to eat, and a dram out of our patron's case of bottles which I mentioned before; and we hauled the boat in as near the shore as we thought was proper, and so waded on shore, carrying nothing but our arms and two jars for water.

I did not care to go out of sight of the boat, fearing the coming of canoes with savages down the river; but the boy seeing a low place about a mile up the country, rambled to it, and by-and-by I saw him come running towards me. I thought he was pursued by some savage, or frighted with some wild beast, and I ran forward towards him to help him; but when I came nearer to him I saw something hanging over his shoulders, which was a creature that he had shot, like a hare, but different in colour, and longer legs; however, we were very glad of it, and it was very good meat; but the great joy that poor Xury came with, was to tell me he had found good water and seen no wild mans.

But we found afterwards that we need not take such pains for water, for a little higher up the creek where we were we found the water fresh when the tide was out, which flowed but a little way up; so we filled our jars, and feasted on the hare he had killed, and prepared to go on our way, having seen no footsteps of any human creature in that part of the country.

As I had been one voyage to this coast before, I knew very well that the islands of the Canaries, and the Cape de Verde Islands also, lay not far off from the coast. But as I had no instruments to take an observation to know what latitude we were in, and not exactly knowing, or at least remembering, what latitude they were in, I knew not where to look for them, or when to stand off to sea towards them; otherwise I might now easily have found some of these islands. But my hope was, that if I stood along this coast till I came to that part where the English traded, I should find some of their vessels upon their usual design of trade, that would relieve and take us in.

By the best of my calculation, that place where I now was must be that country which, lying between the Emperor of Morocco's dominions and the negroes, lies waste and uninhabited, except by wild beasts; the negroes having abandoned it and gone farther south for fear of the Moors, and the Moors not thinking it worth inhabiting by reason of its barrenness; and indeed, both forsaking it because of the prodigious number of tigers, lions, leopards, and other furious creatures which harbour there; so that the Moors use it for their hunting only, where they go like an army, two or three thousand men at a time; and indeed for near a hundred miles together upon this coast we saw nothing but a waste, uninhabited country by day, and heard nothing but howlings and roaring of wild beasts by night.

Once or twice in the daytime I thought I saw the Pico of Teneriffe, being the high top of the Mountain Teneriffe in the Canaries, and had a great mind to venture out, in hopes of reaching thither; but having tried twice, I was forced in again by contrary winds, the sea also going too high for my little vessel; so, I resolved to pursue my first design, and keep along the shore.

Several times I was obliged to land for fresh water, after we had left this place; and once in particular, being early in morning, we came to an anchor under a little point of land, which was pretty high; and the tide beginning to flow, we lay still to go farther in. Xury, whose eyes were more about him than it seems mine were, calls softly to me, and tells me that we had best go farther off the shore; "For," says he, "look, yonder lies a dreadful monster on the side of that hillock, fast asleep." I looked where he pointed, and saw a dreadful monster indeed, for it was a terrible, great lion that lay on the side of the shore, under the shade of a piece of the hill that hung as it were a little over him. "Xury," says I, "you shall on shore and kill him." Xury, looked frighted, and said, "Me kill! he eat me at one mouth!"—one mouthful he meant. However, I said no more to the boy, but bade him lie still, and I took our biggest gun, which was almost musket-bore, and loaded it with a good charge of powder, and with two slugs, and laid it down; then I loaded another gun with two bullets; and the third (for we had three pieces) I loaded with five smaller bullets. I took the best aim I could with the first piece to have shot him in the head, but he lay so with his leg raised a little above his nose, that the slugs hit his leg about the knee and broke the bone. He started up, growling at first, but finding his leg broken, fell down again; and then got upon three legs, and gave the most hideous roar that ever I heard. I was a little surprised that I had not hit him on the head; however, I took up the second piece immediately, and though he began to move off, fired again, and shot him in the head, and had the pleasure to see him drop and make but little noise, but lie struggling for life. Then Xury took heart, and would have me let him go on shore. "Well, go," said I: so the boy jumped into the water and taking a little gun in one hand, swam to shore with the other hand, and coming close to the creature, put the muzzle of the piece to his ear, and shot him in the head again, which despatched him quite.

This was game indeed to us, but this was no food; and I was very sorry to lose three charges of powder and shot upon a creature that was good for nothing to us. However, Xury said he would have some of him; so he comes on board, and asked me to give him the hatchet. "For what, Xury?" said I. "Me cut off his head," said he. However, Xury could not cut off his head, but he cut off a foot, and brought it with him, and it was a monstrous great one.

I bethought myself, however, that, perhaps the skin of him might, one way or other, be of some value to us; and I resolved to take off his skin if I could. So

Xury and I went to work with him; but Xury was much the better workman at it, for I knew very ill how to do it. Indeed, it took us both up the whole day, but at last we got off the hide of him, and spreading it on the top of our cabin, the sun effectually dried it in two days' time, and it afterwards served me to lie upon.

Chapter III—WRECKED ON A DESERT ISLAND

After this stop, we made on to the southward continually for ten or twelve days, living very sparingly on our provisions, which began to abate very much, and going no oftener to the shore than we were obliged to for fresh water. My design in this was to make the river Gambia or Senegal, that is to say anywhere about the Cape de Verde, where I was in hopes to meet with some European ship; and if I did not, I knew not what course I had to take, but to seek for the islands, or perish there among the negroes. I knew that all the ships from Europe, which sailed either to the coast of Guinea or to Brazil, or to the East Indies, made this cape, or those islands; and, in a word, I put the whole of my fortune upon this single point, either that I must meet with some ship or must perish.

When I had pursued this resolution about ten days longer, as I have said, I began to see that the land was inhabited; and in two or three places, as we sailed by, we saw people stand upon the shore to look at us; we could also perceive they were quite black and naked. I was once inclined to have gone on shore to them; but Xury was my better counsellor, and said to me, "No go, no go." However, I hauled in nearer the shore that I might talk to them, and I found they ran along the shore by me a good way. I observed they had no weapons in their hand, except one, who had a long slender stick, which Xury said was a lance, and that they could throw them a great way with good aim; so I kept at a distance, but talked with them by signs as well as I could; and particularly made signs for something to eat: they beckoned to me to stop my boat, and they would fetch me some meat. Upon this I lowered the top of my sail and lay by, and two of them ran up into the country, and in less than half-an-hour came back, and brought with them two pieces of dried flesh and some corn, such as is the produce of their country; but we neither knew what the one or the other was; however, we were willing to accept it, but how to come at it was our next dispute, for I would not venture on shore to them, and they were as much afraid of us; but they took a safe way for us all, for they brought it to the shore and laid it down, and went and stood a great way off till we fetched it on board, and then came close to us again.

We made signs of thanks to them, for we had nothing to make them amends; but an opportunity offered that very instant to oblige them wonderfully; for while we were lying by the shore came two mighty creatures, one pursuing the other (as we took it) with great fury from the mountains towards the sea; whether it was the male pursuing the female, or whether they were in sport or in rage, we could not tell, any more than we could tell whether it was usual or strange, but I believe it was the latter; because, in the first place, those ravenous creatures seldom appear but in the night; and, in the second place, we found the people terribly frighted, especially the women. The man that had the lance or dart did not fly from them, but the rest did; however, as the two creatures ran directly into the water, they did not offer to fall upon any of the negroes, but plunged themselves into the sea, and swam about, as if they had come for their diversion; at last one of them began to come nearer our boat than at first I expected; but I lay ready for him, for I had loaded my gun with all possible expedition, and bade Xury load both the others. As soon as he came fairly within my reach, I fired, and shot him directly in the head; immediately he sank down into the water, but rose instantly, and plunged up and down, as if he were struggling for life, and so indeed he was; he immediately made to the shore; but between the wound, which was his mortal hurt, and the strangling of the water, he died just before he reached the shore.

It is impossible to express the astonishment of these poor creatures at the noise and fire of my gun: some of them were even ready to die for fear, and fell down as dead with the very terror; but when they saw the creature dead, and sunk in the water, and that I made signs to them to come to the shore, they took heart and came, and began to search for the creature. I found him by his blood staining the water; and by the help of a rope, which I slung round him, and gave the negroes to haul, they dragged him on shore, and found that it was a most curious leopard, spotted, and fine to an admirable degree; and the negroes held up their hands with admiration, to think what it was I had killed him with.

The other creature, frighted with the flash of fire and the noise of the gun, swam on shore, and ran up directly to the mountains from whence they came; nor could I, at that distance, know what it was. I found quickly the negroes wished to eat the flesh of this creature, so I was willing to have them take it as a favour from me; which, when I made signs to them that they might take him, they were very thankful for. Immediately they fell to work with him; and though they had no knife, yet, with a sharpened piece of wood, they took off his skin as readily, and much more readily, than we could have done with a knife. They offered me some of the flesh, which I declined, pointing out that I would give it them; but made signs for the skin, which they gave me very freely, and brought me a great deal more of their provisions, which, though I did not understand, yet I accepted. I then made signs to them for some water, and held out one of my jars to them, turning it bottom upward, to show that it was empty, and that I wanted to have it filled. They called immediately to some of their friends, and there came two women, and brought a great vessel made of earth, and burnt, as I supposed, in the sun, this they set down to me, as before, and I sent Xury on shore with my jars, and filled them all three. The women were as naked as the men.

I was now furnished with roots and corn, such as it was, and water; and leaving my friendly negroes, I made forward for about eleven days more, without offering to go near the shore, till I saw the land run out a great length into the sea, at about the distance of four or five leagues before me; and the sea being very calm, I kept a large offing to make this point. At length, doubling the point, at about two leagues from the land, I saw plainly land on the other side, to seaward; then I concluded, as it was most certain indeed, that this was the Cape de Verde, and those the islands called, from thence, Cape de Verde Islands. However, they were at a great distance, and I could not well tell what I had best to do; for if I should be taken with a fresh of wind, I might neither reach one or other.

In this dilemma, as I was very pensive, I stepped into the cabin and sat down, Xury having the helm; when, on a sudden, the boy cried out, "Master, master, a ship with a sail!" and the foolish boy was frighted out of his wits, thinking it must needs be some of his master's ships sent to pursue us, but I knew we were far enough out of their reach. I jumped out of the cabin, and immediately saw, not only the ship, but that it was a Portuguese ship; and, as I thought, was bound to the coast of Guinea, for negroes. But, when I observed the course she steered, I was soon convinced they were bound some other way, and did not design to come any nearer to the shore; upon which I stretched out to sea as much as I could, resolving to speak with them if possible.

With all the sail I could make, I found I should not be able to come in their way, but that they would be gone by before I could make any signal to them: but after I had crowded to the utmost, and began to despair, they, it seems, saw by the help of their glasses that it was some European boat, which they supposed must belong to some ship that was lost; so they shortened sail to let me come up. I was encouraged with this, and as I had my patron's ancient on board, I made a waft of it to them, for a signal of distress, and fired a gun, both which they saw; for they told me they saw the smoke, though they did not hear the gun. Upon these signals they very kindly brought to, and lay by for me; and in about three hours; time I came up with them.

They asked me what I was, in Portuguese, and in Spanish, and in French, but I understood none of them; but at last a Scotch sailor, who was on board, called to me: and I answered him, and told him I was an Englishman, that I had made my escape out of slavery from the Moors, at Sallee; they then bade me come on board, and very kindly took me in, and all my goods.

It was an inexpressible joy to me, which any one will believe, that I was thus delivered, as I esteemed it, from such a miserable and almost hopeless condition as I was in; and I immediately offered all I had to the captain of the ship, as a return for my deliverance; but he generously told me he would take nothing from me, but that all I had should be delivered safe to me when I came to the Brazils. "For," says he, "I have saved your life on no other terms than I would be glad to be saved myself: and it may, one time or other, be my lot to be taken up in the same condition. Besides," said he, "when I carry you to the Brazils, so great a way from your own country, if I should take from you what you have, you will be starved there, and then I only take away that life I have given. No, no," says he: "Seignior Inglese" (Mr. Englishman), "I will carry you thither in charity, and those things will help to buy your subsistence there, and your passage home again."

As he was charitable in this proposal, so he was just in the performance to a tittle; for he ordered the seamen that none should touch anything that I had: then he took everything into his own possession, and gave me back an exact inventory of them, that I might have them, even to my three earthen jars.

As to my boat, it was a very good one; and that he saw, and told me he would buy it of me for his ship's use; and asked me what I would have for it? I told him he had been so generous to me in everything that I could not offer to make any price of the boat, but left it entirely to him: upon which he told me he would give me a note of hand to pay me eighty pieces of eight for it at Brazil; and when it came there, if any one offered to give more, he would make it up. He offered me also sixty pieces of eight more for my boy Xury, which I was loth to take; not that I was unwilling to let the captain have him, but I was very loth to sell the poor boy's liberty, who had assisted me so faithfully in procuring my own. However, when I let him know my reason, he owned it to be just, and offered me this medium, that he would give the boy an obligation to set him free in ten years, if he turned Christian: upon this, and Xury saying he was willing to go to him, I let the captain have him.

We had a very good voyage to the Brazils, and I arrived in the Bay de Todos los Santos, or All Saints' Bay, in about twenty-two days after. And now I was once more delivered from the most miserable of all conditions of life; and what to do next with myself I was to consider.

The generous treatment the captain gave me I can never enough remember: he would take nothing of me for my passage, gave me twenty ducats for the leopard's skin, and forty for the lion's skin, which I had in my boat, and caused everything I had in the ship to be punctually delivered to me; and what I was willing to sell he bought of me, such as the case of bottles, two of my guns, and a piece of the lump of beeswax—for I had made candles of the rest: in a word, I made about two hundred and twenty pieces of eight of all my cargo; and with this stock I went on shore in the Brazils.

I had not been long here before I was recommended to the house of a good honest man like himself, who had an *ingenio*, as they call it (that is, a plantation and a sugar-house). I lived with him some time, and acquainted myself by that means with the manner of planting and making of sugar; and seeing how well the planters lived, and how they got rich suddenly, I resolved, if I could get a licence to settle there, I would turn planter among them: resolving in the meantime to find out some way to get my money, which I had left in London, remitted to me. To this purpose, getting a kind of letter of naturalisation, I purchased as much land that was uncured as my money would reach, and formed a plan for my plantation and settlement; such a one as might be suitable to the stock which I proposed to myself to receive from England.

I had a neighbour, a Portuguese, of Lisbon, but born of English parents, whose name was Wells, and in much such circumstances as I was. I call him my neighbour, because his plantation lay next to mine, and we went on very sociably together. My stock was but low, as well as his; and we rather planted for food than anything else, for about two years. However, we began to increase, and our land began to come into order; so that the third year we planted some tobacco, and made each of us a large piece of ground ready for planting canes in the year to come. But we both wanted help; and now I found, more than before, I had done wrong in parting with my boy Xury.

But, alas! for me to do wrong that never did right, was no great wonder. I hail no remedy but to go on: I had got into an employment quite remote to my genius, and directly contrary to the life I delighted in, and for which I forsook my father's house, and broke through all his good advice. Nay, I was coming into the very middle station, or upper degree of low life, which my father advised me to before, and which, if I resolved to go on with, I might as well have stayed at home, and never have fatigued myself in the world as I had done; and I used often to say to myself, I could have done this as well in England, among my friends, as have gone five thousand miles off to do it among strangers and savages, in a wilderness, and at such a distance as never to hear from any part of the world that had the least knowledge of me.

In this manner I used to look upon my condition with the utmost regret. I had nobody to converse with, but now and then this neighbour; no work to be done, but by the labour of my hands; and I used to say, I lived just like a man cast away upon some desolate island, that had nobody there but himself. But how just has it been—and how should all men reflect, that when they compare their present conditions with others that are worse, Heaven may oblige them to make the exchange, and be convinced of their former felicity by their experience—I say, how just has it been, that the truly solitary life I reflected on, in an island of mere desolation, should be my lot, who had so often unjustly compared it with the life which I then led, in which, had I continued, I had in all probability been exceeding prosperous and rich.

I was in some degree settled in my measures for carrying on the plantation before my kind friend, the captain of the ship that took me up at sea, went back—for the ship remained there, in providing his lading and preparing for his voyage, nearly three months—when telling him what little stock I had left behind me in London, he gave me this friendly and sincere advice:—"Seignior Inglese," says he (for so he always called me), "if you will give me letters, and a procuration in form to me, with orders to the person who has your money in London to send your effects to Lisbon, to such persons as I shall direct, and in such goods as are proper for this country, I will bring you the produce of them, God willing, at my return; but, since human affairs are all subject to changes and disasters, I would have you give orders but for one hundred pounds sterling, which, you say, is half your stock, and let the hazard be run for the first; so that, if it come safe, you may order the rest the same way, and, if it miscarry, you may have the other half to have recourse to for your supply."

This was so wholesome advice, and looked so friendly, that I could not but be convinced it was the best course I could take; so I accordingly prepared letters to the gentlewoman with whom I had left my money, and a procuration to the Portuguese captain, as he desired.

I wrote the English captain's widow a full account of all my adventures—my slavery, escape, and how I had met with the Portuguese captain at sea, the humanity of his behaviour, and what condition I was now in, with all other necessary directions for my supply; and when this honest captain came to Lisbon, he found means, by some of the English merchants there, to send over, not the order only, but a full account of my story to a merchant in London, who represented it effectually to her; whereupon she not only delivered the money, but out of her own pocket sent the Portugal captain a very handsome present for his humanity and charity to me.

The merchant in London, vesting this hundred pounds in English goods, such as the captain had written for, sent them directly to him at Lisbon, and he brought them all safe to me to the Brazils; among which, without my direction (for I was too young in my business to think of them), he had taken care to have all sorts of tools, ironwork, and utensils necessary for my plantation, and which were of great use to me.

When this cargo arrived I thought my fortune made, for I was surprised with the joy of it; and my stood steward, the captain, had laid out the five pounds, which my friend had sent him for a present for himself, to purchase and bring me over a servant, under bond for six years' service, and would not accept of any consideration, except a little tobacco, which I would have him accept, being of my own produce.

Neither was this all; for my goods being all English manufacture, such as cloths, stuffs, baize, and things particularly valuable and desirable in the country, I found means to sell them to a very great advantage; so that I might say I had more than four times the value of my first cargo, and was now infinitely beyond my poor neighbour—I mean in the advancement of my plantation; for the first thing I did, I bought me a negro slave, and an European servant also—I mean another besides that which the captain brought me from Lisbon.

But as abused prosperity is oftentimes made the very means of our greatest adversity, so it was with me. I went on the next year with great success in my plantation: I raised fifty great rolls of tobacco on my own ground, more than I had disposed of for necessaries among my neighbours; and these fifty rolls, being each of above a hundredweight, were well cured, and laid by against the return of the fleet from Lisbon: and now increasing in business and wealth, my head began to be full of projects and undertakings beyond my reach; such as are, indeed, often the ruin of the best heads in business. Had I continued in the station I was now in, I had room for all the happy things to have yet befallen me for which my father so earnestly recommended a quiet, retired life, and of which he had so sensibly described the middle station of life to be full of; but other things attended me, and I was still to be the wilful agent of all my own miseries; and particularly, to increase my fault, and double the reflections upon myself, which in my future sorrows I should have leisure to make, all these miscarriages were procured by my apparent obstinate adhering to my foolish inclination of wandering abroad, and pursuing that inclination, in contradiction to the clearest views of doing myself good in a fair and plain pursuit of those prospects, and those measures of life, which nature and Providence concurred to present me with, and to make my duty.

As I had once done thus in my breaking away from my parents, so I could not be content now, but I must go and leave the happy view I had of being a rich and thriving man in my new plantation, only to pursue a rash and immoderate desire of rising faster than the nature of the thing admitted; and thus I cast myself down again into the deepest gulf of human misery that ever man fell into, or perhaps could be consistent with life and a state of health in the world.

To come, then, by the just degrees to the particulars of this part of my story. You may suppose, that having now lived almost four years in the Brazils, and beginning to thrive and prosper very well upon my plantation, I had not only learned the language, but had contracted acquaintance and friendship among my fellow-planters, as well as among the merchants at St. Salvador, which was our port; and that, in my discourses among them, I had frequently given them an account of my two voyages to the coast of Guinea: the manner of trading with the negroes there, and how easy it was to purchase upon the coast for trifles—such as beads, toys, knives, scissors, hatchets, bits of glass, and the like—not only gold-dust, Guinea grains, elephants' teeth, &c., but negroes, for the service of the Brazils, in great numbers.

They listened always very attentively to my discourses on these heads, but especially to that part which related to the buying of negroes, which was a trade at that time, not only not far entered into, but, as far as it was, had been carried on by assientos, or permission of the kings of Spain and Portugal, and engrossed in the public stock: so that few negroes were bought, and these excessively dear.

It happened, being in company with some merchants and planters of my acquaintance, and talking of those things very earnestly, three of them came to me next morning, and told me they had been musing very much upon what I had discoursed with them of the last night, and they came to make a secret proposal to me; and, after enjoining me to secrecy, they told me that they had a mind to fit out a ship to go to Guinea; that they had all plantations as well as I, and were straitened for nothing so much as servants; that as it was a trade that could not be carried on, because they could not publicly sell the negroes when they came home, so they desired to make but one voyage, to bring the negroes on shore privately, and divide them among their own plantations; and, in a word, the question was whether I would go their supercargo in the ship, to manage the trading part upon the coast of Guinea; and they offered me that I should have my equal share of the negroes, without providing any part of the stock.

This was a fair proposal, it must be confessed, had it been made to any one that had not had a settlement and a plantation of his own to look after, which was in a fair way of coming to be very considerable, and with a good stock upon it;

but for me, that was thus entered and established, and had nothing to do but to go on as I had begun, for three or four years more, and to have sent for the other hundred pounds from England; and who in that time, and with that little addition, could scarce have failed of being worth three or four thousand pounds sterling, and that increasing too—for me to think of such a voyage was the most preposterous thing that ever man in such circumstances could be guilty of.

But I, that was born to be my own destroyer, could no more resist the offer than I could restrain my first rambling designs when my father' good counsel was lost upon me. In a word, I told them I would go with all my heart, if they would undertake to look after my plantation in my absence, and would dispose of it to such as I should direct, if I miscarried. This they all engaged to do, and entered into writings or covenants to do so; and I made a formal will, disposing of my plantation and effects in case of my death, making the captain of the ship that had saved my life, as before, my universal heir, but obliging him to dispose of my effects as I had directed in my will; one half of the produce being to himself, and the other to be shipped to England.

In short, I took all possible caution to preserve my effects and to keep up my plantation. Had I used half as much prudence to have looked into my own interest, and have made a judgment of what I ought to have done and not to have done, I had certainly never gone away from so prosperous an undertaking, leaving all the probable views of a thriving circumstance, and gone upon a voyage to sea, attended with all its common hazards, to say nothing of the reasons I had to expect particular misfortunes to myself.

But I was hurried on, and obeyed blindly the dictates of my fancy rather than my reason; and, accordingly, the ship being fitted out, and the cargo furnished, and all things done, as by agreement, by my partners in the voyage, I went on board in an evil hour, the 1st September 1659, being the same day eight years that I went from my father and mother at Hull, in order to act the rebel to their authority, and the fool to my own interests.

Our ship was about one hundred and twenty tons burden, carried six guns and fourteen men, besides the master, his boy, and myself. We had on board no large cargo of goods, except of such toys as were fit for our trade with the negroes, such as beads, bits of glass, shells, and other trifles, especially little looking-glasses, knives, scissors, hatchets, and the like.

The same day I went on board we set sail, standing away to the northward upon our own coast, with design to stretch over for the African coast when we came about ten or twelve degrees of northern latitude, which, it seems, was the manner of course in those days. We had very good weather, only excessively hot, all the way upon our own coast, till we came to the height of Cape St. Augustino; from whence, keeping further off at sea, we lost sight of land, and steered as if we were bound for the isle Fernando de Noronha, holding our course N.E. by N., and leaving those isles on the east. In this course we passed the line in about twelve days' time, and were, by our last observation, in seven degrees twenty-two minutes northern latitude, when a violent tornado, or hurricane, took us quite out of our knowledge. It began from the south-east, came about to the north-west, and then settled in the north-east; from whence it blew in such a terrible manner, that for twelve days together we could do nothing but drive, and, scudding away before it, let it carry us whither fate and the fury of the winds directed; and, during these twelve days, I need not say that I expected every day to be swallowed up; nor, indeed, did any in the ship expect to save their lives.

In this distress we had, besides the terror of the storm, one of our men die of the calenture, and one man and the boy washed overboard. About the twelfth day, the weather abating a little, the master made an observation as well as he could, and found that he was in about eleven degrees north latitude, but that he was twenty-two degrees of longitude difference west from Cape St. Augustino; so that he found he was upon the coast of Guiana, or the north part of Brazil, beyond the river Amazon, toward that of the river Orinoco, commonly called the Great River; and began to consult with me what course he should take, for the ship was leaky, and very much disabled, and he was going directly back to the coast of Brazil.

I was positively against that; and looking over the charts of the sea-coast of America with him, we concluded there was no inhabited country for us to have recourse to till we came within the circle of the Caribbee Islands, and therefore resolved to stand away for Barbadoes; which, by keeping off at sea, to avoid the indraft of the Bay or Gulf of Mexico, we might easily perform, as we hoped, in about fifteen days' sail; whereas we could not possibly make our voyage to the coast of Africa without some assistance both to our ship and to ourselves.

With this design we changed our course, and steered away N.W. by W., in order to reach some of our English islands, where I hoped for relief. But our voyage was otherwise determined; for, being in the latitude of twelve degrees eighteen minutes, a second storm came upon us, which carried us away with the same impetuosity westward, and drove us so out of the way of all human commerce, that, had all our lives been saved as to the sea, we were rather in danger of being devoured by savages than ever returning to our own country.

In this distress, the wind still blowing very hard, one of our men early in the morning cried out, "Land!" and we had no sooner run out of the cabin to look out, in hopes of seeing whereabouts in the world we were, than the ship struck upon a sand, and in a moment her motion being so stopped, the sea broke over her in such a manner that we expected we should all have perished immediately; and we were immediately driven into our close quarters, to shelter us from the very foam and spray of the sea.

It is not easy for any one who has not been in the like condition to describe or conceive the consternation of men in such circumstances. We knew nothing where we were, or upon what land it was we were driven—whether an island or the main, whether inhabited or not inhabited. As the rage of the wind was still great, though rather less than at first, we could not so much as hope to have the ship hold many minutes without breaking into pieces, unless the winds, by a kind of miracle, should turn immediately about. In a word, we sat looking upon one another, and expecting death every moment, and every man, accordingly, preparing for another world; for there was little or nothing more for us to do in this. That which was our present comfort, and all the comfort we had, was that, contrary to our expectation, the ship did not break yet, and that the master said the wind began to abate.

Now, though we thought that the wind did a little abate, yet the ship having thus struck upon the sand, and sticking too fast for us to expect her getting off, we were in a dreadful condition indeed, and had nothing to do but to think of saving our lives as well as we could. We had a boat at our stern just before the storm, but she was first staved by dashing against the ship's rudder, and in the next place she broke away, and either sunk or was driven off to sea; so there was no hope from her. We had another boat on board, but how to get her off into the sea was a doubtful thing. However, there was no time to debate, for we fancied that the ship would break in pieces every minute, and some told us she was actually broken already.

In this distress the mate of our vessel laid hold of the boat, and with the help of the rest of the men got her slung over the ship's side; and getting all into her, let go, and committed ourselves, being eleven in number, to God's mercy and the wild sea; for though the storm was abated considerably, yet the sea ran dreadfully high upon the shore, and might be well called *den wild zee*, as the Dutch call the sea in a storm.

And now our case was very dismal indeed; for we all saw plainly that the sea went so high that the boat could not live, and that we should be inevitably drowned. As to making sail, we had none, nor if we had could we have done anything with it; so we worked at the oar towards the land, though with heavy hearts, like men going to execution; for we all knew that when the boat came near the shore she would be dashed in a thousand pieces by the breach of the sea. However, we committed our souls to God in the most earnest manner; and the wind driving us towards the shore, we hastened our destruction with our own hands, pulling as well as we could towards land.

What the shore was, whether rock or sand, whether steep or shoal, we knew not. The only hope that could rationally give us the least shadow of expectation was, if we might find some bay or gulf, or the mouth of some river, where by great chance we might have run our boat in, or got under the lee of the land, and perhaps made smooth water. But there was nothing like this appeared; but as we made nearer and nearer the shore, the land looked more frightful than the sea.

After we had rowed, or rather driven about a league and a half, as we reckoned it, a raging wave, mountain-like, came rolling astern of us, and plainly bade us expect the *coup de grâce*. It took us with such a fury, that it overset the boat at once; and separating us as well from the boat as from one another, gave us no time to say, "O God!" for we were all swallowed up in a moment.

Nothing can describe the confusion of thought which I felt when I sank into the water; for though I swam very well, yet I could not deliver myself from the waves so as to draw breath, till that wave having driven me, or rather carried me, a vast way on towards the shore, and having spent itself, went back, and left me upon the land almost dry, but half dead with the water I took in. I had so much presence of mind, as well as breath left, that seeing myself nearer the mainland than I expected, I got upon my feet, and endeavoured to make on towards the land as fast as I could before another wave should return and take me up again; but I soon found it was impossible to avoid it; for I saw the sea come after me as high as a great hill, and as furious as an enemy, which I had no means or strength to contend with: my business was to hold my breath, and raise myself upon the water if I could; and so, by swimming, to preserve my breathing, and pilot myself towards the shore, if possible, my greatest concern now being that the sea, as it would carry me a great way towards the shore when it came on, might not carry me back again with it when it gave back towards the sea.

The wave that came upon me again buried me at once twenty or thirty feet deep in its own body, and I could feel myself carried with a mighty force and swiftness towards the shore—a very great way; but I held my breath, and assisted myself to swim still forward with all my might. I was ready to burst with holding my breath, when, as I felt myself rising up, so, to my immediate relief, I found my head and hands shoot out above the surface of the water; and though it was not two seconds of time that I could keep myself so, yet it relieved me greatly, gave me breath, and new courage. I was covered again with water a good while, but not so long but I held it out; and finding the water had spent itself, and began to return, I struck forward against the return of the waves, and felt ground again with my feet. I stood still a few moments to recover breath, and till the waters went from me, and then took to my heels and ran with what strength I had further towards the shore. But neither would this deliver me from the fury of the sea, which came pouring in after me again; and twice more I was lifted up by the waves and carried forward as before, the shore being very flat.

The last time of these two had well-nigh been fatal to me, for the sea having hurried me along as before, landed me, or rather dashed me, against a piece of rock, and that with such force, that it left me senseless, and indeed helpless, as to my own deliverance; for the blow taking my side and breast, beat the breath as it were quite out of my body; and had it returned again immediately, I must have been strangled in the water; but I recovered a little before the return of the waves, and seeing I should be covered again with the water, I resolved to hold fast by a piece of the rock, and so to hold my breath, if possible, till the wave went back. Now, as the waves were not so high as at first, being nearer land, I held my hold till the wave abated, and then fetched another run, which brought me so near the shore that the next wave, though it went over me, yet did not so swallow me up as to carry me away; and the next run I took, I got to the mainland, where, to my great comfort, I clambered up the cliffs of the shore and sat me down upon the grass, free from danger and quite out of the reach of the water.

I was now landed and safe on shore, and began to look up and thank God that my life was saved, in a case wherein there was some minutes before scarce any room to hope. I believe it is impossible to express, to the life, what the ecstasies and transports of the soul are, when it is so saved, as I may say, out of the very grave: and I do not wonder now at the custom, when a malefactor, who has the halter about his neck, is tied up, and just going to be turned off, and has a reprieve brought to him—I say, I do not wonder that they bring a surgeon with it, to let him blood that very moment they tell him of it, that the surprise may not drive the animal spirits from the heart and overwhelm him.

"For sudden joys, like griefs, confound at first."

I walked about on the shore lifting up my hands, and my whole being, as I may say, wrapped up in a contemplation of my deliverance; making a thousand gestures and motions, which I cannot describe; reflecting upon all my comrades that were drowned, and that there should not be one soul saved but myself; for, as for them, I never saw them afterwards, or any sign of them, except three of their hats, one cap, and two shoes that were not fellows.

I cast my eye to the stranded vessel, when, the breach and froth of the sea being so big, I could hardly see it, it lay so far of; and considered, Lord! how was it possible I could get on shore?

After I had solaced my mind with the comfortable part of my condition, I began to look round me, to see what kind of place I was in, and what was next to be done; and I soon found my comforts abate, and that, in a word, I had a dreadful deliverance; for I was wet, had no clothes to shift me, nor anything either to eat or drink to comfort me; neither did I see any prospect before me but that of perishing with hunger or being devoured by wild beasts; and that which was particularly afflicting to me was, that I had no weapon, either to hunt and kill any creature for my sustenance, or to defend myself against any other creature that might desire to kill me for theirs. In a word, I had nothing about me but a knife, a tobacco-pipe, and a little tobacco in a box. This was all my provisions; and this threw me into such terrible agonies of mind, that for a while I ran about like a madman. Night coming upon me, I began with a heavy heart to consider what would be my lot if there were any ravenous beasts in that country, as at night they always come abroad for their prey.

All the remedy that offered to my thoughts at that time was to get up into a thick bushy tree like a fir, but thorny, which grew near me, and where I resolved to sit all night, and consider the next day what death I should die, for as yet I saw no prospect of life. I walked about a furlong from the shore, to see if I could find any fresh water to drink, which I did, to my great joy; and having drank, and put a little tobacco into my mouth to prevent hunger, I went to the tree, and getting up into it, endeavoured to place myself so that if I should sleep I might not fall. And having cut me a short stick, like a truncheon, for my defence, I took up my lodging; and having been excessively fatigued, I fell fast asleep, and slept as comfortably as, I believe, few could have done in my condition, and found myself more refreshed with it than, I think, I ever was on such an occasion.

Chapter IV—FIRST WEEKS ON THE ISLAND

When I waked it was broad day, the weather clear, and the storm abated, so that the sea did not rage and swell as before. But that which surprised me most was, that the ship was lifted off in the night from the sand where she lay by the swelling of the tide, and was driven up almost as far as the rock which I at first mentioned, where I had been so bruised by the wave dashing me against it. This being within about a mile from the shore where I was, and the ship seeming to stand upright still, I wished myself on board, that at least I might save some necessary things for my use.

When I came down from my apartment in the tree, I looked about me again, and the first thing I found was the boat, which lay, as the wind and the sea had tossed her up, upon the land, about two miles on my right hand. I walked as far as I could upon the shore to have got to her; but found a neck or inlet of water between me and the boat which was about half a mile broad; so I came back for the present, being more intent upon getting at the ship, where I hoped to find something for my present subsistence.

A little after noon I found the sea very calm, and the tide ebbed so far out that I could come within a quarter of a mile of the ship. And here I found a fresh renewing of my grief; for I saw evidently that if we had kept on board we had been all safe—that is to say, we had all got safe on shore, and I had not been so miserable as to be left entirety destitute of all comfort and company as I now was. This forced tears to my eyes again; but as there was little relief in that, I resolved, if possible, to get to the ship; so I pulled off my clothes—for the weather was hot to extremity—and took the water. But when I came to the ship my difficulty was still greater to know how to get on board; for, as she lay aground, and high out of the water, there was nothing within my reach to lay hold of. I swam round her twice, and the second time I spied a small piece of rope, which I wondered I did not see at first, hung down by the fore-chains so low, as that with great difficulty I got hold of it, and by the help of that rope I got up into the forecastle of the ship. Here I found that the ship was bulged, and had a great deal of water in her hold, but that she lay so on the side of a bank of hard sand, or, rather earth, that her stern lay lifted up upon the bank, and her head low, almost to the water. By this means all her quarter was free, and all that was in that part was dry; for you may be sure my first work was to search, and to see what was spoiled and what was free. And, first, I found that all the ship's provisions were dry and untouched by the water, and being very well disposed to eat, I went to the bread room and filled my pockets with biscuit, and ate it as I went about other things, for I had no time to lose. I also found some rum in the great cabin, of which I took a large dram, and which I had, indeed, need enough of to spirit me for what was before me. Now I wanted nothing but a boat to furnish myself with many things which I foresaw would be very necessary to me.

It was in vain to sit still and wish for what was not to be had; and this extremity roused my application. We had several spare yards, and two or three large spars of wood, and a spare topmast or two in the ship; I resolved to fall to work with these, and I flung as many of them overboard as I could manage for their weight, tying every one with a rope, that they might not drive away. When this was done I went down the ship's side, and pulling them to me, I tied four of them together at both ends as well as I could, in the form of a raft, and laying two or three short pieces of plank upon them crossways, I found I could walk upon it very well, but that it was not able to bear any great weight, the pieces being too light. So I went to work, and with a carpenter's saw I cut a spare topmast into three lengths, and added them to my raft, with a great deal of labour and pains. But the hope of furnishing myself with necessaries encouraged me to go beyond what I should have been able to have done upon another occasion.

My raft was now strong enough to bear any reasonable weight. My next care was what to load it with, and how to preserve what I laid upon it from the surf of the sea; but I was not long considering this. I first laid all the planks or boards upon it that I could get, and having considered well what I most wanted, I got three of the seamen's chests, which I had broken open, and emptied, and lowered them down upon my raft; the first of these I filled with provisions—viz. bread, rice, three Dutch cheeses, five pieces of dried goat's flesh (which we lived much upon), and a little remainder of European corn, which had been laid by for some fowls which we brought to sea with us, but the fowls were killed. There had been some barley and wheat together; but, to my great disappointment, I found afterwards that the rats had eaten or spoiled it all. As for liquors, I found several, cases of bottles belonging to our skipper, in which were some cordial waters; and, in all, about five or six gallons of rack. These I stowed by themselves, there being no need to put them into the chest, nor any room for them. While I was doing this, I found the tide begin to flow, though very calm; and I had the mortification to see my coat, shirt, and waistcoat, which I had left on the shore, upon the sand, swim away. As for my breeches, which were only linen, and open-kneed, I swam on board in them and my stockings. However, this set me on rummaging for clothes, of which I found enough, but took no more than I wanted for present use, for I had others things which my eye was more upon—as, first, tools to work with on shore. And it was after long searching that I found out the carpenter's chest, which was, indeed, a very useful prize to me, and much more valuable than a shipload of gold would have been at that time. I got it down to my raft, whole as it was, without losing time to look into it, for I knew in general what it contained.

My next care was for some ammunition and arms. There were two very good fowling-pieces in the great cabin, and two pistols. These I secured first, with some powder-horns and a small bag of shot, and two old rusty swords. I knew there were three barrels of powder in the ship, but knew not where our gunner had stowed them; but with much search I found them, two of them dry and good, the third had taken water. Those two I got to my raft with the arms. And now I thought myself pretty well freighted, and began to think how I should get to shore with them, having neither sail, oar, nor rudder; and the least capful of wind would have overset all my navigation.

I had three encouragements—1st, a smooth, calm sea; 2ndly, the tide rising, and setting in to the shore; 3rdly, what little wind there was blew me towards the land. And thus, having found two or three broken oars belonging to the boat—and, besides the tools which were in the chest, I found two saws, an axe, and a hammer; with this cargo I put to sea. For a mile or thereabouts my raft went very well, only that I found it drive a little distant from the place where I had landed before; by which I perceived that there was some indraft of the water, and consequently I hoped to find some creek or river there, which I might make use of as a port to get to land with my cargo.

As I imagined, so it was. There appeared before me a little opening of the land, and I found a strong current of the tide set into it; so I guided my raft as well as I could, to keep in the middle of the stream.

But here I had like to have suffered a second shipwreck, which, if I had, I think verily would have broken my heart; for, knowing nothing of the coast, my raft ran aground at one end of it upon a shoal, and not being aground at the other end, it wanted but a little that all my cargo had slipped off towards the end that was afloat, and to fallen into the water. I did my utmost, by setting my back against the chests, to keep them in their places, but could not thrust off the raft with all my strength; neither durst I stir from the posture I was in; but holding up the chests with all my might, I stood in that manner near half-an-hour, in which time the rising of the water brought me a little more upon a level; and a little after, the water still-rising, my raft floated again, and I thrust her off with the oar I had into the channel, and then driving up higher, I at length found myself in the mouth of a little river, with land on both sides, and a strong current of tide running up. I looked on both sides for a proper place to get to shore, for I was not willing to be driven too high up the river: hoping in time to see some ships at sea, and therefore resolved to place myself as near the coast as I could.

At length I spied a little cove on the right shore of the creek, to which with great pain and difficulty I guided my raft, and at last got so near that, reaching ground with my oar, I could thrust her directly in. But here I had like to have dipped all my cargo into the sea again; for that shore lying pretty steep—that is to say sloping—there was no place to land, but where one end of my float, if it ran on shore, would lie so high, and the other sink lower, as before, that it would endanger my cargo again. All that I could do was to wait till the tide was at the highest, keeping the raft with my oar like an anchor, to hold the side of it fast to the shore, near a flat piece of ground, which I expected the water would flow over; and so it did. As soon as I found water enough—for my raft drew about a foot of water—I thrust her upon that flat piece of ground, and there fastened or moored her, by sticking my two broken oars into the ground, one on one side near one end, and one on the other side near the other end; and thus I lay till the water ebbed away, and left my raft and all my cargo safe on shore.

My next work was to view the country, and seek a proper place for my habitation, and where to stow my goods to secure them from whatever might happen. Where I was, I yet knew not; whether on the continent or on an island; whether inhabited or not inhabited; whether in danger of wild beasts or not. There was a hill not above a mile from me, which rose up very steep and high, and which seemed to overtop some other hills, which lay as in a ridge from it northward. I took out one of the fowling-pieces, and one of the pistols, and a horn of powder; and thus armed, I travelled for discovery up to the top of that hill, where, after I had with great labour and difficulty got to the top, I saw my fate, to my great affliction—viz. that I was in an island environed every way with the sea: no land to be seen except some rocks, which lay a great way off; and two small islands, less than this, which lay about three leagues to the west.

I found also that the island I was in was barren, and, as I saw good reason to believe, uninhabited except by wild beasts, of whom, however, I saw none. Yet I saw abundance of fowls, but knew not their kinds; neither when I killed them could I tell what was fit for food, and what not. At my coming back, I shot at a great bird which I saw sitting upon a tree on the side of a great wood. I believe it was the first gun that had been fired there since the creation of the world. I had no sooner fired, than from all parts of the wood there arose an innumerable number of fowls, of many sorts, making a confused screaming and crying, and every one according to his usual note, but not one of them of any kind that I knew. As for the creature I killed, I took it to be a kind of hawk, its colour and beak resembling it, but it had no talons or claws more than common. Its flesh was carrion, and fit for nothing.

Contented with this discovery, I came back to my raft, and fell to work to bring my cargo on shore, which took me up the rest of that day. What to do with myself at night I knew not, nor indeed where to rest, for I was afraid to lie down on the ground, not knowing but some wild beast might devour me, though, as I afterwards found, there was really no need for those fears.

However, as well as I could, I barricaded myself round with the chest and boards that I had brought on shore, and made a kind of hut for that night's lodging. As for food, I yet saw not which way to supply myself, except that I had seen two or three creatures like hares run out of the wood where I shot the fowl.

I now began to consider that I might yet get a great many things out of the ship which would be useful to me, and particularly some of the rigging and sails, and such other things as might come to land; and I resolved to make another voyage on board the vessel, if possible. And as I knew that the first storm that blew must necessarily break her all in pieces, I resolved to set all other things apart till I had got everything out of the ship that I could get. Then I called a council—that is to say in my thoughts—whether I should take back the raft; but this appeared impracticable: so I resolved to go as before, when the tide was down; and I did so, only that I stripped before I went from my hut, having nothing on but my chequered shirt, a pair of linen drawers, and a pair of pumps on my feet.

I got on board the ship as before, and prepared a second raft; and, having had experience of the first, I neither made this so unwieldy, nor loaded it so hard, but yet I brought away several things very useful to me; as first, in the carpenters stores I found two or three bags full of nails and spikes, a great screw-jack, a dozen or two of hatchets, and, above all, that most useful thing called a grindstone. All these I secured, together with several things belonging to the gunner, particularly two or three iron crows, and two barrels of musket bullets, seven muskets, another fowling-piece, with some small quantity of powder more; a large bagful of small shot, and a great roll of sheet-lead; but this last was so heavy, I could not hoist it up to get it over the ship's side.

Besides these things, I took all the men's clothes that I could find, and a spare fore-topsail, a hammock, and some bedding; and with this I loaded my second raft, and brought them all safe on shore, to my very great comfort.

I was under some apprehension, during my absence from the land, that at least my provisions might be devoured on shore: but when I came back I found no sign of any visitor; only there sat a creature like a wild cat upon one of the chests, which, when I came towards it, ran away a little distance, and then stood still. She sat very composed and unconcerned, and looked full in my face, as if she had a mind to be acquainted with me. I presented my gun at her, but, as she did not understand it, she was perfectly unconcerned at it, nor did she offer to stir away; upon which I tossed her a bit of biscuit, though by the way, I was not very free of it, for my store was not great: however, I spared her a bit, I say, and she went to it, smelled at it, and ate it, and looked (as if pleased) for more; but I thanked her, and could spare no more: so she marched off.

Having got my second cargo on shore—though I was fain to open the barrels of powder, and bring them by parcels, for they were too heavy, being large casks—I went to work to make me a little tent with the sail and some poles which I cut for that purpose: and into this tent I brought everything that I knew would spoil either with rain or sun; and I piled all the empty chests and casks up in a circle round the tent, to fortify it from any sudden attempt, either from man or beast.

When I had done this, I blocked up the door of the tent with some boards within, and an empty chest set up on end without; and spreading one of the beds upon the ground, laying my two pistols just at my head, and my gun at length by me, I went to bed for the first time, and slept very quietly all night, for I was very weary and heavy; for the night before I had slept little, and had laboured very hard all day to fetch all those things from the ship, and to get them on shore.

I had the biggest magazine of all kinds now that ever was laid up, I believe, for one man: but I was not satisfied still, for while the ship sat upright in that posture, I thought I ought to get everything out of her that I could; so every day at low water I went on board, and brought away something or other; but particularly the third time I went I brought away as much of the rigging as I could, as also all the small ropes and rope-twine I could get, with a piece of spare canvas, which was to mend the sails upon occasion, and the barrel of wet gunpowder. In a word, I brought away all the sails, first and last; only that I was fain to cut them in pieces, and bring as much at a time as I could, for they were no more useful to be sails, but as mere canvas only.

But that which comforted me more still, was, that last of all, after I had made five or six such voyages as these, and thought I had nothing more to expect from the ship that was worth my meddling with—I say, after all this, I found a great hogshead of bread, three large runlets of rum, or spirits, a box of sugar, and a barrel of fine flour; this was surprising to me, because I had given over expecting any more provisions, except what was spoiled by the water. I soon emptied the hogshead of the bread, and wrapped it up, parcel by parcel, in pieces of the sails, which I cut out; and, in a word, I got all this safe on shore also.

The next day I made another voyage, and now, having plundered the ship of what was portable and fit to hand out, I began with the cables. Cutting the great cable into pieces, such as I could move, I got two cables and a hawser on shore, with all the ironwork I could get; and having cut down the spritsail-yard, and the mizzen-yard, and everything I could, to make a large raft, I loaded it with all these heavy goods, and came away. But my good luck began now to leave me; for this raft was so unwieldy, and so overladen, that, after I had entered the little cove where I had landed the rest of my goods, not being able to guide it so handily as I did the other, it overset, and threw me and all my cargo into the water. As for myself, it was no great harm, for I was near the shore; but as to my cargo, it was a great part of it lost, especially the iron, which I expected would have been of great use to me; however, when the tide was out, I got most of the pieces of the cable ashore, and some of the iron, though with infinite labour; for I was fain to dip for it into the water, a work which fatigued me very much. After this, I went every day on board, and brought away what I could get.

I had been now thirteen days on shore, and had been eleven times on board the ship, in which time I had brought away all that one pair of hands could well be supposed capable to bring; though I believe verily, had the calm weather held, I should have brought away the whole ship, piece by piece. But preparing the twelfth time to go on board, I found the wind began to rise: however, at low water I went on board, and though I thought I had rummaged the cabin so effectually that nothing more could be found, yet I discovered a locker with drawers in it, in one of which I found two or three razors, and one pair of large scissors, with some ten or a dozen of good knives and forks: in another I found about thirty-six pounds value in money—some European coin, some Brazil, some pieces of eight, some gold, and some silver.

I smiled to myself at the sight of this money: "O drug!" said I, aloud, "what art thou good for? Thou art not worth to me—no, not the taking off the ground; one of those knives is worth all this heap; I have no manner of use for thee—e'en remain where thou art, and go to the bottom as a creature whose life is not worth saying." However, upon second thoughts I took it away; and wrapping all this in a piece of canvas, I began to think of making another raft; but while I was preparing this, I found the sky overcast, and the wind began to rise, and in a quarter of an hour it blew a fresh gale from the shore. It presently occurred to me that it was in vain to pretend to make a raft with the wind offshore; and that it was my business to be gone before the tide of flood began, otherwise I might not be able to reach the shore at all. Accordingly, I let myself down into the water, and swam across the channel, which lay between the ship and the sands, and even that with difficulty enough, partly with the weight of the things I had about me, and partly the roughness of the water; for the wind rose very hastily, and before it was quite high water it blew a storm.

But I had got home to my little tent, where I lay, with all my wealth about me, very secure. It blew very hard all night, and in the morning, when I looked out, behold, no more ship was to be seen! I was a little surprised, but recovered myself with the satisfactory reflection that I had lost no time, nor abated any diligence, to get everything out of her that could be useful to me; and that, indeed, there was little left in her that I was able to bring away, if I had had more time.

I now gave over any more thoughts of the ship, or of anything out of her, except what might drive on shore from her wreck; as, indeed, divers pieces of her afterwards did; but those things were of small use to me.

My thoughts were now wholly employed about securing myself against either savages, if any should appear, or wild beasts, if any were in the island; and I had many thoughts of the method how to do this, and what kind of dwelling to make—whether I should make me a cave in the earth, or a tent upon the earth; and, in short, I resolved upon both; the manner and description of which, it may not be improper to give an account of.

I soon found the place I was in was not fit for my settlement, because it was upon a low, moorish ground, near the sea, and I believed it would not be wholesome, and more particularly because there was no fresh water near it; so I resolved to find a more healthy and more convenient spot of ground.

I consulted several things in my situation, which I found would he proper for me: 1st, health and fresh water, I just now mentioned; 2ndly, shelter from the heat of the sun; 3rdly, security from ravenous creatures, whether man or beast; 4thly, a view to the sea, that if God sent any ship in sight, I might not lose any advantage for my deliverance, of which I was not willing to banish all my expectation yet.

In search of a place proper for this, I found a little plain on the side of a rising hill, whose front towards this little plain was steep as a house-side, so that nothing could come down upon me from the top. On the one side of the rock there was a hollow place, worn a little way in, like the entrance or door of a cave but there was not really any cave or way into the rock at all.

On the flat of the green, just before this hollow place, I resolved to pitch my tent. This plain was not above a hundred yards broad, and about twice as long, and lay like a green before my door; and, at the end of it, descended irregularly every way down into the low ground by the seaside. It was on the N.N.W. side of the hill; so that it was sheltered from the heat every day, till it came to a W. and by S. sun, or thereabouts, which, in those countries, is near the setting.

Before I set up my tent I drew a half-circle before the hollow place, which took in about ten yards in its semi-diameter from the rock, and twenty yards in its diameter from its beginning and ending.

In this half-circle I pitched two rows of strong stakes, driving them into the ground till they stood very firm like piles, the biggest end being out of the ground above five feet and a half, and sharpened on the top. The two rows did not stand above six inches from one another.

Then I took the pieces of cable which I had cut in the ship, and laid them in rows, one upon another, within the circle, between these two rows of stakes, up to the top, placing other stakes in the inside, leaning against them, about two feet and a half high, like a spur to a post; and this fence was so strong, that neither man nor beast could get into it or over it. This cost me a great deal of time and labour, especially to cut the piles in the woods, bring them to the place, and drive them into the earth.

The entrance into this place I made to be, not by a door, but by a short ladder to go over the top; which ladder, when I was in, I lifted over after me; and so I was completely fenced in and fortified, as I thought, from all the world, and consequently slept secure in the night, which otherwise I could not have done; though, as it appeared afterwards, there was no need of all this caution from the enemies that I apprehended danger from.

Into this fence or fortress, with infinite labour, I carried all my riches, all my provisions, ammunition, and stores, of which you have the account above; and I made a large tent, which to preserve me from the rains that in one part of the year are very violent there, I made double—one smaller tent within, and one larger tent above it; and covered the uppermost with a large tarpaulin, which I had saved among the sails.

And now I lay no more for a while in the bed which I had brought on shore, but in a hammock, which was indeed a very good one, and belonged to the mate of the ship.

Into this tent I brought all my provisions, and everything that would spoil by the wet; and having thus enclosed all my goods, I made up the entrance, which till now I had left open, and so passed and repassed, as I said, by a short ladder.

When I had done this, I began to work my way into the rock, and bringing all the earth and stones that I dug down out through my tent, I laid them up within my fence, in the nature of a terrace, so that it raised the ground within about a foot and a half; and thus I made me a cave, just behind my tent, which served me like a cellar to my house.

It cost me much labour and many days before all these things were brought to perfection; and therefore I must go back to some other things which took up some of my thoughts. At the same time it happened, after I had laid my scheme for the setting up my tent, and making the cave, that a storm of rain falling from a thick, dark cloud, a sudden flash of lightning happened, and after that a great clap of thunder, as is naturally the effect of it. I was not so much surprised with the lightning as I was with the thought which darted into my mind as swift as the lightning itself—Oh, my powder! My very heart sank within me when I thought that, at one blast, all my powder might be destroyed; on which, not my defence only, but the providing my food, as I thought, entirely depended. I was nothing near so anxious about my own danger, though, had the powder took fire, I should never have known who had hurt me.

Such impression did this make upon me, that after the storm was over I laid aside all my works, my building and fortifying, and applied myself to make bags and boxes, to separate the powder, and to keep it a little and a little in a parcel, in the hope that, whatever might come, it might not all take fire at once; and to keep it so apart that it should not be possible to make one part fire another. I finished this work in about a fortnight; and I think my powder, which in all was about two hundred and forty pounds weight, was divided in not less than a hundred parcels. As to the barrel that had been wet, I did not apprehend any danger from that; so I placed it in my new cave, which, in my fancy, I called my kitchen; and the rest I hid up and down in holes among the rocks, so that no wet might come to it, marking very carefully where I laid it.

In the interval of time while this was doing, I went out once at least every day with my gun, as well to divert myself as to see if I could kill anything fit for food; and, as near as I could, to acquaint myself with what the island produced. The first time I went out, I presently discovered that there were goats in the island, which was a great satisfaction to me; but then it was attended with this misfortune to me—viz. that they were so shy, so subtle, and so swift of foot, that it was the most difficult thing in the world to come at them; but I was not discouraged at this, not doubting but I might now and then shoot one, as it soon happened; for after I had found their haunts a little, I laid wait in this manner for them: I observed if they saw me in the valleys, though they were upon the rocks, they would run away, as in a terrible fright; but if they were feeding in the valleys, and I was upon the rocks, they took no notice of me; from whence I concluded that, by the position of their optics, their sight was so directed downward that they did not readily see objects that were above them; so afterwards I took this method—I always climbed the rocks first, to get above them, and then had frequently a fair mark.

The first shot I made among these creatures, I killed a she-goat, which had a little kid by her, which she gave suck to, which grieved me heartily; for when the old one fell, the kid stood stock still by her, till I came and took her up; and not only so, but when I carried the old one with me, upon my shoulders, the kid followed me quite to my enclosure; upon which I laid down the dam, and took the kid in my arms, and carried it over my pale, in hopes to have bred it up tame; but it would not eat; so I was forced to kill it and eat it myself. These two supplied me with flesh a great while, for I ate sparingly, and saved my provisions, my bread especially, as much as possibly I could.

Having now fixed my habitation, I found it absolutely necessary to provide a place to make a fire in, and fuel to burn: and what I did for that, and also how I enlarged my cave, and what conveniences I made, I shall give a full account of in its place; but I must now give some little account of myself, and of my thoughts about living, which, it may well be supposed, were not a few.

I had a dismal prospect of my condition; for as I was not cast away upon that island without being driven, as is said, by a violent storm, quite out of the course of our intended voyage, and a great way, viz. some hundreds of leagues, out of the ordinary course of the trade of mankind, I had great reason to consider it as a determination of Heaven, that in this desolate place, and in this desolate manner, I should end my life. The tears would run plentifully down my face when I made these reflections; and sometimes I would expostulate with myself why Providence should thus completely ruin His creatures, and render them so absolutely miserable; so without help, abandoned, so entirely depressed, that it could hardly be rational to be thankful for such a life.

But something always returned swift upon me to check these thoughts, and to reprove me; and particularly one day, walking with my gun in my hand by the seaside, I was very pensive upon the subject of my present condition, when reason, as it were, expostulated with me the other way, thus: "Well, you are in a desolate condition, it is true; but, pray remember, where are the rest of you? Did not you come, eleven of you in the boat? Where are the ten? Why were they not saved, and you lost? Why were you singled out? Is it better to be here or there?" And then I pointed to the sea. All evils are to be considered with the good that is in them, and with what worse attends them.

Then it occurred to me again, how well I was furnished for my subsistence, and what would have been my case if it had not happened (which was a hundred thousand to one) that the ship floated from the place where she first struck, and was driven so near to the shore that I had time to get all these things out of her; what would have been my case, if I had been forced to have lived in the condition in which I at first came on shore, without necessaries of life, or necessaries to supply and procure them? "Particularly," said I, aloud (though to myself), "what should I have done without a gun, without ammunition, without any tools to make anything, or to work with, without clothes, bedding, a tent, or any manner of covering?" and that now I had all these to sufficient quantity, and was in a fair way to provide myself in such a manner as to live without my gun, when my ammunition was spent: so that I had a tolerable view of subsisting, without any want, as long as I lived; for I considered from the beginning how I would provide for the accidents that might happen, and for the time that was to come, even not only after my ammunition should be spent, but even after my health and strength should decay.

I confess I had not entertained any notion of my ammunition being destroyed at one blast—I mean my powder being blown up by lightning; and this made the thoughts of it so surprising to me, when it lightened and thundered, as I observed just now.

Chapter IV—FIRST WEEKS ON THE ISLAND

And now being about to enter into a melancholy relation of a scene of silent life, such, perhaps, as was never heard of in the world before, I shall take it from its beginning, and continue it in its order. It was by my account the 30th of September, when, in the manner as above said, I first set foot upon this horrid island; when the sun, being to us in its autumnal equinox, was almost over my head; for I reckoned myself, by observation, to be in the latitude of nine degrees twenty-two minutes north of the line.

After I had been there about ten or twelve days, it came into my thoughts that I should lose my reckoning of time for want of books, and pen and ink, and should even forget the Sabbath days; but to prevent this, I cut with my knife upon a large post, in capital letters—and making it into a great cross, I set it up on the shore where I first landed—"I came on shore here on the 30th September 1659."

Upon the sides of this square post I cut every day a notch with my knife, and every seventh notch was as long again as the rest, and every first day of the month as long again as that long one; and thus I kept my calendar, or weekly, monthly, and yearly reckoning of time.

In the next place, we are to observe that among the many things which I brought out of the ship, in the several voyages which, as above mentioned, I made to it, I got several things of less value, but not at all less useful to me, which I omitted setting down before; as, in particular, pens, ink, and paper, several parcels in the captain's, mate's, gunner's and carpenter's keeping; three or four compasses, some mathematical instruments, dials, perspectives, charts, and books of navigation, all which I huddled together, whether I might want them or no; also, I found three very good Bibles, which came to me in my cargo from England, and which I had packed up among my things; some Portuguese books also; and among them two or three Popish prayer-books, and several other books, all which I carefully secured. And I must not forget that we had in the ship a dog and two cats, of whose eminent history I may have occasion to say something in its place; for I carried both the cats with me; and as for the dog, he jumped out of the ship of himself, and swam on shore to me the day after I went on shore with my first cargo, and was a trusty servant to me many years; I wanted nothing that he could fetch me, nor any company that he could make up to me; I only wanted to have him talk to me, but that would not do. As I observed before, I found pens, ink, and paper, and I husbanded them to the utmost; and I shall show that while my ink lasted, I kept things very exact, but after that was gone I could not, for I could not make any ink by any means that I could devise.

And this put me in mind that I wanted many things notwithstanding all that I had amassed together; and of these, ink was one; as also a spade, pickaxe, and shovel, to dig or remove the earth; needles, pins, and thread; as for linen, I soon learned to want that without much difficulty.

This want of tools made every work I did go on heavily; and it was near a whole year before I had entirely finished my little pale, or surrounded my habitation. The piles, or stakes, which were as heavy as I could well lift, were a long time in cutting and preparing in the woods, and more, by far, in bringing home; so that I spent sometimes two days in cutting and bringing home one of those posts, and a third day in driving it into the ground; for which purpose I got a heavy piece of wood at first, but at last bethought myself of one of the iron crows; which, however, though I found it, made driving those posts or piles very laborious and tedious work. But what need I have been concerned at the tediousness of anything I had to do, seeing I had time enough to do it in? nor had I any other employment, if that had been over, at least that I could foresee, except the ranging the island to seek for food, which I did, more or less, every day.

I now began to consider seriously my condition, and the circumstances I was reduced to; and I drew up the state of my affairs in writing, not so much to leave them to any that were to come after me—for I was likely to have but few heirs—as to deliver my thoughts from daily poring over them, and afflicting my mind; and as my reason began now to master my despondency, I began to comfort myself as well as I could, and to set the good against the evil, that I might have something to distinguish my case from worse; and I stated very impartially, like debtor and creditor, the comforts I enjoyed against the miseries I suffered, thus:—

Evil.	*Good.*
I am cast upon a horrible, desolate island, void of all hope of recovery.	But I am alive; and not drowned, as all my ship's company were.
I am singled out and separated, as it were, from all the world, to be miserable.	But I am singled out, too, from all the ship's crew, to be spared from death; and He that miraculously saved me from death can deliver me from this condition.
I am divided from mankind—a solitaire; one banished from human society.	But I am not starved, and perishing on a barren place, affording no sustenance.
I have no clothes to cover me.	But I am in a hot climate, where, if I had clothes, I could hardly wear them.
I am without any defence, or means to resist any violence of man or beast.	But I am cast on an island where I see no wild beasts to hurt me, as I saw on the coast of Africa; and what if I had been shipwrecked there?
I have no soul to speak to or relieve me.	But God wonderfully sent the ship in near enough to the shore, that I have got out as many necessary things as will either supply my wants or enable me to supply myself, even as long as I live.

Upon the whole, here was an undoubted testimony that there was scarce any condition in the world so miserable but there was something negative or something positive to be thankful for in it; and let this stand as a direction from the experience of the most miserable of all conditions in this world: that we may always find in it something to comfort ourselves from, and to set, in the description of good and evil, on the credit side of the account.

Having now brought my mind a little to relish my condition, and given over looking out to sea, to see if I could spy a ship—I say, giving over these things, I began to apply myself to arrange my way of living, and to make things as easy to me as I could.

I have already described my habitation, which was a tent under the side of a rock, surrounded with a strong pale of posts and cables: but I might now rather call it a wall, for I raised a kind of wall up against it of turfs, about two feet thick on the outside; and after some time (I think it was a year and a half) I raised rafters from it, leaning to the rock, and thatched or covered it with boughs of trees, and such things as I could get, to keep out the rain; which I found at some times of the year very violent.

I have already observed how I brought all my goods into this pale, and into the cave which I had made behind me. But I must observe, too, that at first this was a confused heap of goods, which, as they lay in no order, so they took up all my place; I had no room to turn myself: so I set myself to enlarge my cave, and work farther into the earth; for it was a loose sandy rock, which yielded easily to the labour I bestowed on it: and so when I found I was pretty safe as to beasts of prey, I worked sideways, to the right hand, into the rock; and then, turning to the right again, worked quite out, and made me a door to come out on the outside of my pale or fortification. This gave me not only egress and regress, as it was a back way to my tent and to my storehouse, but gave me room to store my goods.

And now I began to apply myself to make such necessary things as I found I most wanted, particularly a chair and a table; for without these I was not able to enjoy the few comforts I had in the world; I could not write or eat, or do several things, with so much pleasure without a table: so I went to work. And here I must needs observe, that as reason is the substance and origin of the mathematics, so by stating and squaring everything by reason, and by making the most rational judgment of things, every man may be, in time, master of every mechanic art. I had never handled a tool in my life; and yet, in time, by labour, application, and contrivance, I found at last that I wanted nothing but I could have made it, especially if I had had tools. However, I made abundance of things, even without tools; and some with no more tools than an adze and a hatchet, which perhaps were never made that way before, and that with infinite labour. For example, if I wanted a board, I had no other way but to cut down a tree, set it on an edge before me, and hew it flat on either side with my axe, till I brought it to be thin as a plank, and then dub it smooth with my adze. It is true, by this method I could make but one board out of a whole tree; but this I had no remedy for but patience, any more than I had for the prodigious deal of time and labour which it took me up to make a plank or board: but my time or labour was little worth, and so it was as well employed one way as another.

However, I made me a table and a chair, as I observed above, in the first place; and this I did out of the short pieces of boards that I brought on my raft from the ship. But when I had wrought out some boards as above, I made large shelves, of the breadth of a foot and a half, one over another all along one side of my cave, to lay all my tools, nails and ironwork on; and, in a word, to separate everything at large into their places, that I might come easily at them. I knocked pieces into the wall of the rock to hang my guns and all things that would hang up; so that, had my cave been to be seen, it looked like a general magazine of all necessary things; and had everything so ready at my hand, that it was a great pleasure to me to see all my goods in such order, and especially to find my stock of all necessaries so great.

And now it was that I began to keep a journal of every day's employment; for, indeed, at first I was in too much hurry, and not only hurry as to labour, but in too much discomposure of mind; and my journal would have been full of many dull things; for example, I must have said thus: "30*th.*—After I had got to shore, and escaped drowning, instead of being thankful to God for my deliverance, having first vomited, with the great quantity of salt water which had got into my stomach, and recovering myself a little, I ran about the shore wringing my hands and beating my head and face, exclaiming at my misery, and crying out, 'I was undone, undone!' till, tired and faint, I was forced to lie down on the ground to repose, but durst not sleep for fear of being devoured."

Some days after this, and after I had been on board the ship, and got all that I could out of her, yet I could not forbear getting up to the top of a little mountain and looking out to sea, in hopes of seeing a ship; then fancy at a vast distance I spied a sail, please myself with the hopes of it, and then after looking steadily, till I was almost blind, lose it quite, and sit down and weep like a child, and thus increase my misery by my folly.

But having gotten over these things in some measure, and having settled my household staff and habitation, made me a table and a chair, and all as handsome about me as I could, I began to keep my journal; of which I shall here give you the copy (though in it will be told all these particulars over again) as long as it lasted; for having no more ink, I was forced to leave it off.

Chapter V—BUILDS A HOUSE—THE JOURNAL

September 30, 1659.—I, poor miserable Robinson Crusoe, being shipwrecked during a dreadful storm in the offing, came on shore on this dismal, unfortunate island, which I called "The Island of Despair"; all the rest of the ship's company being drowned, and myself almost dead.

All the rest of the day I spent in afflicting myself at the dismal circumstances I was brought to—viz. I had neither food, house, clothes, weapon, nor place to fly to; and in despair of any relief, saw nothing but death before me—either that I should be devoured by wild beasts, murdered by savages, or starved to death for want of food. At the approach of night I slept in a tree, for fear of wild creatures; but slept soundly, though it rained all night.

October 1.—In the morning I saw, to my great surprise, the ship had floated with the high tide, and was driven on shore again much nearer the island; which, as it was some comfort, on one hand—for, seeing her set upright, and not broken to pieces, I hoped, if the wind abated, I might get on board, and get some food and necessaries out of her for my relief—so, on the other hand, it renewed my grief at the loss of my comrades, who, I imagined, if we had all stayed on board, might have saved the ship, or, at least, that they would not have been all drowned as they were; and that, had the men been saved, we might perhaps have built us a boat out of the ruins of the ship to have carried us to some other part of the world. I spent great part of this day in perplexing myself on these things; but at length, seeing the ship almost dry, I went upon the sand as near as I could, and then swam on board. This day also it continued raining, though with no wind at all.

From the 1st of October to the 24th.—All these days entirely spent in many several voyages to get all I could out of the ship, which I brought on shore every tide of flood upon rafts. Much rain also in the days, though with some intervals of fair weather; but it seems this was the rainy season.

Oct. 20.—I overset my raft, and all the goods I had got upon it; but, being in shoal water, and the things being chiefly heavy, I recovered many of them when the tide was out.

Oct. 25.—It rained all night and all day, with some gusts of wind; during which time the ship broke in pieces, the wind blowing a little harder than before, and was no more to be seen, except the wreck of her, and that only at low water. I spent this day in covering and securing the goods which I had saved, that the rain might not spoil them.

Oct. 26.—I walked about the shore almost all day, to find out a place to fix my habitation, greatly concerned to secure myself from any attack in the night, either from wild beasts or men. Towards night, I fixed upon a proper place, under a rock, and marked out a semicircle for my encampment; which I resolved to strengthen with a work, wall, or fortification, made of double piles, lined within with cables, and without with turf.

From the 26th to the 30th I worked very hard in carrying all my goods to my new habitation, though some part of the time it rained exceedingly hard.

The 31st, in the morning, I went out into the island with my gun, to seek for some food, and discover the country; when I killed a she-goat, and her kid followed me home, which I afterwards killed also, because it would not feed.

November 1.—I set up my tent under a rock, and lay there for the first night; making it as large as I could, with stakes driven in to swing my hammock upon.

Nov. 2.—I set up all my chests and boards, and the pieces of timber which made my rafts, and with them formed a fence round me, a little within the place I had marked out for my fortification.

Nov. 3.—I went out with my gun, and killed two fowls like ducks, which were very good food. In the afternoon went to work to make me a table.

Nov. 4.—This morning I began to order my times of work, of going out with my gun, time of sleep, and time of diversion—viz. every morning I walked out with my gun for two or three hours, if it did not rain; then employed myself to work till about eleven o'clock; then eat what I had to live on; and from twelve to two I lay down to sleep, the weather being excessively hot; and then, in the evening, to work again. The working part of this day and of the next were wholly employed in making my table, for I was yet but a very sorry workman, though time and necessity made me a complete natural mechanic soon after, as I believe they would do any one else.

Nov. 5.—This day went abroad with my gun and my dog, and killed a wild cat; her skin pretty soft, but her flesh good for nothing; every creature that I killed I took of the skins and preserved them. Coming back by the sea-shore, I saw many sorts of sea-fowls, which I did not understand; but was surprised, and almost frightened, with two or three seals, which, while I was gazing at, not well knowing what they were, got into the sea, and escaped me for that time.

Nov. 6.—After my morning walk I went to work with my table again, and finished it, though not to my liking; nor was it long before I learned to mend it.

Nov. 7.—Now it began to be settled fair weather. The 7th, 8th, 9th, 10th, and part of the 12th (for the 11th was Sunday) I took wholly up to make me a chair, and with much ado brought it to a tolerable shape, but never to please me; and even in the making I pulled it in pieces several times.

Note.—I soon neglected my keeping Sundays; for, omitting my mark for them on my post, I forgot which was which.

Nov. 13.—This day it rained, which refreshed me exceedingly, and cooled the earth; but it was accompanied with terrible thunder and lightning, which frightened me dreadfully, for fear of my powder. As soon as it was over, I resolved to separate my stock of powder into as many little parcels as possible, that it might not be in danger.

Nov. 14, 15, 16.—These three days I spent in making little square chests, or boxes, which might hold about a pound, or two pounds at most, of powder; and so, putting the powder in, I stowed it in places as secure and remote from one another as possible. On one of these three days I killed a large bird that was good to eat, but I knew not what to call it.

Nov. 17.—This day I began to dig behind my tent into the rock, to make room for my further conveniency.

Note.—Three things I wanted exceedingly for this work—viz. a pickaxe, a shovel, and a wheelbarrow or basket; so I desisted from my work, and began to consider how to supply that want, and make me some tools. As for the pickaxe, I made use of the iron crows, which were proper enough, though heavy; but the next thing was a shovel or spade; this was so absolutely necessary, that, indeed, I could do nothing effectually without it; but what kind of one to make I knew not.

Nov. 18.—The next day, in searching the woods, I found a tree of that wood, or like it, which in the Brazils they call the iron-tree, for its exceeding hardness. Of this, with great labour, and almost spoiling my axe, I cut a piece, and brought it home, too, with difficulty enough, for it was exceeding heavy. The excessive hardness of the wood, and my having no other way, made me a long while upon this machine, for I worked it effectually by little and little into the form of a shovel or spade; the handle exactly shaped like ours in England, only that the board part having no iron shod upon it at bottom, it would not last me so long; however, it served well enough for the uses which I had occasion to put it to; but never was a shovel, I believe, made after that fashion, or so long in making.

I was still deficient, for I wanted a basket or a wheelbarrow. A basket I could not make by any means, having no such things as twigs that would bend to make wicker-ware—at least, none yet found out; and as to a wheelbarrow, I fancied I could make all but the wheel; but that I had no notion of; neither did I know how to go about it; besides, I had no possible way to make the iron gudgeons for the spindle or axis of the wheel to run in; so I gave it over, and so, for carrying away the earth which I dug out of the cave, I made me a thing like a hod which the labourers carry mortar in when they serve the bricklayers. This was not so difficult to me as the making the shovel: and yet this and the shovel, and the attempt which I made in vain to make a wheelbarrow, took me up no less than four days—I mean always excepting my morning walk with my gun, which I seldom failed, and very seldom failed also bringing home something fit to eat.

Nov. 23.—My other work having now stood still, because of my making these tools, when they were finished I went on, and working every day, as my strength and time allowed, I spent eighteen days entirely in widening and deepening my cave, that it might hold my goods commodiously.

Note.—During all this time I worked to make this room or cave spacious enough to accommodate me as a warehouse or magazine, a kitchen, a dining-room, and a cellar. As for my lodging, I kept to the tent; except that sometimes, in the wet season of the year, it rained so hard that I could not keep myself dry, which caused me afterwards to cover all my place within my pale with long poles, in the form of rafters, leaning against the rock, and load them with flags and large leaves of trees, like a thatch.

December 10.—I began now to think my cave or vault finished, when on a sudden (it seems I had made it too large) a great quantity of earth fell down from the top on one side; so much that, in short, it frighted me, and not without reason, too, for if I had been under it, I had never wanted a gravedigger. I had now a great deal of work to do over again, for I had the loose earth to carry out; and, which was of more importance, I had the ceiling to prop up, so that I might be sure no more would come down.

Dec. 11.—This day I went to work with it accordingly, and got two shores or posts pitched upright to the top, with two pieces of boards across over each post; this I finished the next day; and setting more posts up with boards, in about a week more I had the roof secured, and the posts, standing in rows, served me for partitions to part off the house.

Dec. 17.—From this day to the 20th I placed shelves, and knocked up nails on the posts, to hang everything up that could be hung up; and now I began to be in some order within doors.

Dec. 20.—Now I carried everything into the cave, and began to furnish my house, and set up some pieces of boards like a dresser, to order my victuals upon; but boards began to be very scarce with me; also, I made me another table.

Dec. 24.—Much rain all night and all day. No stirring out.

Dec. 25.—Rain all day.

Dec. 26.—No rain, and the earth much cooler than before, and pleasanter.

Dec. 27.—Killed a young goat, and lamed another, so that I caught it and led it home in a string; when I had it at home, I bound and splintered up its leg, which was broke.

N.B.—I took such care of it that it lived, and the leg grew well and as strong as ever; but, by my nursing it so long, it grew tame, and fed upon the little green at my door, and would not go away. This was the first time that I entertained a thought of breeding up some tame creatures, that I might have food when my powder and shot was all spent.

Dec. 28,29,30,31.—Great heats, and no breeze, so that there was no stirring abroad, except in the evening, for food; this time I spent in putting all my things in order within doors.

January 1.—Very hot still: but I went abroad early and late with my gun, and lay still in the middle of the day. This evening, going farther into the valleys which lay towards the centre of the island, I found there were plenty of goats, though exceedingly shy, and hard to come at; however, I resolved to try if I could not bring my dog to hunt them down.

Jan. 2.—Accordingly, the next day I went out with my dog, and set him upon the goats, but I was mistaken, for they all faced about upon the dog, and he knew his danger too well, for he would not come near them.

Jan. 3.—I began my fence or wall; which, being still jealous of my being attacked by somebody, I resolved to make very thick and strong.

N.B.—This wall being described before, I purposely omit what was said in the journal; it is sufficient to observe, that I was no less time than from the 2nd of January to the 14th of April working, finishing, and perfecting this wall, though it was no more than about twenty-four yards in length, being a half-circle from one place in the rock to another place, about eight yards from it, the door of the cave being in the centre behind it.

All this time I worked very hard, the rains hindering me many days, nay, sometimes weeks together; but I thought I should never be perfectly secure till this wall was finished; and it is scarce credible what inexpressible labour everything was done with, especially the bringing piles out of the woods and driving them into the ground; for I made them much bigger than I needed to have done.

When this wall was finished, and the outside double fenced, with a turf wall raised up close to it, I perceived myself that if any people were to come on shore there, they would not perceive anything like a habitation; and it was very well I did so, as may be observed hereafter, upon a very remarkable occasion.

During this time I made my rounds in the woods for game every day when the rain permitted me, and made frequent discoveries in these walks of something or other to my advantage; particularly, I found a kind of wild pigeons, which build, not as wood-pigeons in a tree, but rather as house-pigeons, in the holes of the rocks; and taking some young ones, I endeavoured to breed them up tame, and did so; but when they grew older they flew away, which perhaps was at first for want of feeding them, for I had nothing to give them; however, I frequently found their nests, and got their young ones, which were very good meat. And now, in the managing my household affairs, I found myself wanting in many things, which I thought at first it was impossible for me to make; as, indeed, with some of them it was: for instance, I could never make a cask to be hooped. I had a small runlet or two, as I observed before; but I could never arrive at the capacity of making one by them, though I spent many weeks about it; I could neither put in the heads, or join the staves so true to one another as to make them hold water; so I gave that also over. In the next place, I was at a great loss for candles; so that as soon as ever it was dark, which was generally by seven o'clock, I was obliged to go to bed. I remembered the lump of beeswax with which I made candles in my African adventure; but I had none of that now; the only remedy I had was, that when I had killed a goat I saved the tallow, and with a little dish made of clay, which I baked in the sun, to which I added a wick of some oakum, I made me a lamp; and this gave me light, though not a clear, steady light, like a candle. In the middle of all my labours it happened that, rummaging my things, I found a little bag which, as I hinted before, had been filled with corn for the feeding of poultry—not for this voyage, but before, as I suppose, when the ship came from Lisbon. The little remainder of corn that had been in the bag was all devoured by the rats, and I saw nothing in the bag but husks and dust; and being willing to have the bag for some other use (I think it was to put powder in, when I divided it for fear of the lightning, or some such use), I shook the husks of corn out of it on one side of my fortification, under the rock.

It was a little before the great rains just now mentioned that I threw this stuff away, taking no notice, and not so much as remembering that I had thrown anything there, when, about a month after, or thereabouts, I saw some few stalks of something green shooting out of the ground, which I fancied might be some plant I had not seen; but I was surprised, and perfectly astonished, when, after a little longer time, I saw about ten or twelve ears come out, which were perfect green barley, of the same kind as our European—nay, as our English barley.

It is impossible to express the astonishment and confusion of my thoughts on this occasion. I had hitherto acted upon no religious foundation at all; indeed, I had very few notions of religion in my head, nor had entertained any sense of anything that had befallen me otherwise than as chance, or, as we lightly say, what pleases God, without so much as inquiring into the end of Providence in these things, or His order in governing events for the world. But after I saw barley grow there, in a climate which I knew was not proper for corn, and especially that I knew not how it came there, it startled me strangely, and I began to suggest that God had miraculously caused His grain to grow without any help of seed sown, and that it was so directed purely for my sustenance on that wild, miserable place.

This touched my heart a little, and brought tears out of my eyes, and I began to bless myself that such a prodigy of nature should happen upon my account; and this was the more strange to me, because I saw near it still, all along by the side of the rock, some other straggling stalks, which proved to be stalks of rice, and which I knew, because I had seen it grow in Africa when I was ashore there.

I not only thought these the pure productions of Providence for my support, but not doubting that there was more in the place, I went all over that part of the island, where I had been before, peering in every corner, and under every rock, to see for more of it, but I could not find any. At last it occurred to my thoughts that I shook a bag of chickens' meat out in that place; and then the wonder began to cease; and I must confess my religious thankfulness to God's providence began to abate, too, upon the discovering that all this was nothing but what was common; though I ought to have been as thankful for so strange and unforeseen a providence as if it had been miraculous; for it was really the work of Providence to me, that should order or appoint that ten or twelve grains of corn should remain unspoiled, when the rats had destroyed all the rest, as if it had been dropped from heaven; as also, that I should throw it out in that particular place, where, it being in the shade of a high rock, it sprang up immediately; whereas, if I had thrown it anywhere else at that time, it had been burnt up and destroyed.

I carefully saved the ears of this corn, you may be sure, in their season, which was about the end of June; and, laying up every corn, I resolved to sow them all again, hoping in time to have some quantity sufficient to supply me with bread. But it was not till the fourth year that I could allow myself the least grain of this corn to eat, and even then but sparingly, as I shall say afterwards, in its order; for I lost all that I sowed the first season by not observing the proper time; for I sowed it just before the dry season, so that it never came up at all, at least not as it would have done; of which in its place.

Besides this barley, there were, as above, twenty or thirty stalks of rice, which I preserved with the same care and for the same use, or to the same purpose—to make me bread, or rather food; for I found ways to cook it without baking, though I did that also after some time.

But to return to my Journal.

I worked excessive hard these three or four months to get my wall done; and the 14th of April I closed it up, contriving to go into it, not by a door but over the wall, by a ladder, that there might be no sign on the outside of my habitation.

April 16.—I finished the ladder; so I went up the ladder to the top, and then pulled it up after me, and let it down in the inside. This was a complete enclosure to me; for within I had room enough, and nothing could come at me from without, unless it could first mount my wall.

The very next day after this wall was finished I had almost had all my labour overthrown at once, and myself killed. The case was thus: As I was busy in the inside, behind my tent, just at the entrance into my cave, I was terribly frighted with a most dreadful, surprising thing indeed; for all on a sudden I found the earth come crumbling down from the roof of my cave, and from the edge of the hill over my head, and two of the posts I had set up in the cave cracked in a frightful manner. I was heartily scared; but thought nothing of what was really the cause, only thinking that the top of my cave was fallen in, as some of it had done before: and for fear I should be buried in it I ran forward to my ladder, and not thinking myself safe there neither, I got over my wall for fear of the pieces of the hill, which I expected might roll down upon me. I had no sooner stepped do ground, than I plainly saw it was a terrible earthquake, for the ground I stood on shook three times at about eight minutes' distance, with three such shocks as would have overturned the strongest building that could be supposed to have stood on the earth; and a great piece of the top of a rock which stood about half a mile from me next the sea fell down with such a terrible noise as I never heard in all my life. I perceived also the very sea was put into violent motion by it; and I believe the shocks were stronger under the water than on the island.

I was so much amazed with the thing itself, having never felt the like, nor discoursed with any one that had, that I was like one dead or stupefied; and the motion of the earth made my stomach sick, like one that was tossed at sea; but the noise of the falling of the rock awakened me, as it were, and rousing me from the stupefied condition I was in, filled me with horror; and I thought of nothing then but the hill falling upon my tent and all my household goods, and burying all at once; and this sunk my very soul within me a second time.

After the third shock was over, and I felt no more for some time, I began to take courage; and yet I had not heart enough to go over my wall again, for fear of being buried alive, but sat still upon the ground greatly cast down and disconsolate, not knowing what to do. All this while I had not the least serious religious thought; nothing but the common "Lord have mercy upon me!" and when it was over that went away too.

While I sat thus, I found the air overcast and grow cloudy, as if it would rain. Soon after that the wind arose by little and little, so that in less than half-an-hour it blew a most dreadful hurricane; the sea was all on a sudden covered over with foam and froth; the shore was covered with the breach of the water, the trees were torn up by the roots, and a terrible storm it was. This held about three hours, and then began to abate; and in two hours more it was quite calm, and began to rain very hard. All this while I sat upon the ground very much terrified and dejected; when on a sudden it came into my thoughts, that these winds and rain being the consequences of the earthquake, the earthquake itself was spent and over, and I might venture into my cave again. With this thought my spirits began to revive; and the rain also helping to persuade me, I went in and sat down in my tent. But the rain was so violent that my tent was ready to be beaten down with it; and I was forced to go into my cave, though very much afraid and uneasy, for fear it should fall on my head. This violent rain forced me to a new work—viz. to cut a hole through my new fortification, like a sink, to let the water go out, which would else have flooded my cave. After I had been in my cave for some time, and found still no more shocks of the earthquake follow, I began to be more composed. And now, to support my spirits, which indeed wanted it very much, I went to my little store, and took a small sup of rum; which, however, I did then and always very sparingly, knowing I could have no more when that was gone. It continued raining all that night and great part of the next day, so that I could not stir abroad; but my mind being more composed, I began to think of what I had best do; concluding that if the island was subject to these earthquakes, there would be no living for me in a cave, but I must consider of building a little hut in an open place which I might surround with a wall, as I had done here, and so make myself secure from wild beasts or men; for I concluded, if I stayed where I was, I should certainly one time or other be buried alive.

With these thoughts, I resolved to remove my tent from the place where it stood, which was just under the hanging precipice of the hill; and which, if it should be shaken again, would certainly fall upon my tent; and I spent the two next days, being the 19th and 20th of April, in contriving where and how to remove my habitation. The fear of being swallowed up alive made me that I never slept in quiet; and yet the apprehension of lying abroad without any fence was almost equal to it; but still, when I looked about, and saw how everything was put in order, how pleasantly concealed I was, and how safe from danger, it made me very loath to remove. In the meantime, it occurred to me that it would require a vast deal of time for me to do this, and that I must be contented to venture where I was, till I had formed a camp for myself, and had secured it so as to remove to it.

So with this resolution I composed myself for a time, and resolved that I would go to work with all speed to build me a wall with piles and cables, &c., in a circle, as before, and set my tent up in it when it was finished; but that I would venture to stay where I was till it was finished, and fit to remove. This was the 21st.

April 22.—The next morning I begin to consider of means to put this resolve into execution; but I was at a great loss about my tools. I had three large axes, and abundance of hatchets (for we carried the hatchets for traffic with the Indians); but with much chopping and cutting knotty hard wood, they were all full of notches, and dull; and though I had a grindstone, I could not turn it and grind my tools too. This cost me as much thought as a statesman would have bestowed upon a grand point of politics, or a judge upon the life and death of a man. At length I contrived a wheel with a string, to turn it with my foot, that I might have both my hands at liberty. *Note.*—I had never seen any such thing in England, or at least, not to take notice how it was done, though since I have observed, it is very common there; besides that, my grindstone was very large and heavy. This machine cost me a full week's work to bring it to perfection.

April 28, 29.—These two whole days I took up in grinding my tools, my machine for turning my grindstone performing very well.

April 30.—Having perceived my bread had been low a great while, now I took a survey of it, and reduced myself to one biscuit cake a day, which made my heart very heavy.

May 1.—In the morning, looking towards the sea side, the tide being low, I saw something lie on the shore bigger than ordinary, and it looked like a cask; when I came to it, I found a small barrel, and two or three pieces of the wreck of the ship, which were driven on shore by the late hurricane; and looking towards the wreck itself, I thought it seemed to lie higher out of the water than it used to do. I examined the barrel which was driven on shore, and soon found it was a barrel of gunpowder; but it had taken water, and the powder was caked as hard as a stone; however, I rolled it farther on shore for the present, and went on upon the sands, as near as I could to the wreck of the ship, to look for more.

Chapter VI—ILL AND CONSCIENCE-STRICKEN

When I came down to the ship I found it strangely removed. The forecastle, which lay before buried in sand, was heaved up at least six feet, and the stern, which was broke in pieces and parted from the rest by the force of the sea, soon after I had left rummaging her, was tossed as it were up, and cast on one side; and the sand was thrown so high on that side next her stern, that whereas there was a great place of water before, so that I could not come within a quarter of a mile of the wreck without swimming I could now walk quite up to her when the tide was out. I was surprised with this at first, but soon concluded it must be done by the earthquake; and as by this violence the ship was more broke open than formerly, so many things came daily on shore, which the sea had loosened, and which the winds and water rolled by degrees to the land.

This wholly diverted my thoughts from the design of removing my habitation, and I busied myself mightily, that day especially, in searching whether I could make any way into the ship; but I found nothing was to be expected of that kind, for all the inside of the ship was choked up with sand. However, as I had learned not to despair of anything, I resolved to pull everything to pieces that I could of the ship, concluding that everything I could get from her would be of some use or other to me.

May 3.—I began with my saw, and cut a piece of a beam through, which I thought held some of the upper part or quarter-deck together, and when I had cut it through, I cleared away the sand as well as I could from the side which lay highest; but the tide coming in, I was obliged to give over for that time.

May 4.—I went a-fishing, but caught not one fish that I durst eat of, till I was weary of my sport; when, just going to leave off, I caught a young dolphin. I had made me a long line of some rope-yarn, but I had no hooks; yet I frequently caught fish enough, as much as I cared to eat; all which I dried in the sun, and ate them dry.

May 5.—Worked on the wreck; cut another beam asunder, and brought three great fir planks off from the decks, which I tied together, and made to float on shore when the tide of flood came on.

May 6.—Worked on the wreck; got several iron bolts out of her and other pieces of ironwork. Worked very hard, and came home very much tired, and had thoughts of giving it over.

May 7.—Went to the wreck again, not with an intent to work, but found the weight of the wreck had broke itself down, the beams being cut; that several pieces of the ship seemed to lie loose, and the inside of the hold lay so open that I could see into it; but it was almost full of water and sand.

May 8.—Went to the wreck, and carried an iron crow to wrench up the deck, which lay now quite clear of the water or sand. I wrenched open two planks, and brought them on shore also with the tide. I left the iron crow in the wreck for next day.

May 9.—Went to the wreck, and with the crow made way into the body of the wreck, and felt several casks, and loosened them with the crow, but could not break them up. I felt also a roll of English lead, and could stir it, but it was too heavy to remove.

May 10–14.—Went every day to the wreck; and got a great many pieces of timber, and boards, or plank, and two or three hundredweight of iron.

May 15.—I carried two hatchets, to try if I could not cut a piece off the roll of lead by placing the edge of one hatchet and driving it with the other; but as it lay about a foot and a half in the water, I could not make any blow to drive the hatchet.

May 16.—It had blown hard in the night, and the wreck appeared more broken by the force of the water; but I stayed so long in the woods, to get pigeons for food, that the tide prevented my going to the wreck that day.

May 17.—I saw some pieces of the wreck blown on shore, at a great distance, near two miles off me, but resolved to see what they were, and found it was a piece of the head, but too heavy for me to bring away.

May 24.—Every day, to this day, I worked on the wreck; and with hard labour I loosened some things so much with the crow, that the first flowing tide several casks floated out, and two of the seamen's chests; but the wind blowing from the shore, nothing came to land that day but pieces of timber, and a hogshead, which had some Brazil pork in it; but the salt water and the sand had spoiled it. I continued this work every day to the 15th of June, except the time necessary to get food, which I always appointed, during this part of my employment, to be when the tide was up, that I might be ready when it was ebbed out; and by this time I had got timber and plank and ironwork enough to have built a good boat, if I had known how; and also I got, at several times and in several pieces, near one hundredweight of the sheet lead.

June 16.—Going down to the seaside, I found a large tortoise or turtle. This was the first I had seen, which, it seems, was only my misfortune, not any defect of the place, or scarcity; for had I happened to be on the other side of the island, I might have had hundreds of them every day, as I found afterwards; but perhaps had paid dear enough for them.

June 17.—I spent in cooking the turtle. I found in her three-score eggs; and her flesh was to me, at that time, the most savoury and pleasant that ever I tasted in my life, having had no flesh, but of goats and fowls, since I landed in this horrid place.

June 18.—Rained all day, and I stayed within. I thought at this time the rain felt cold, and I was something chilly; which I knew was not usual in that latitude.

June 19.—Very ill, and shivering, as if the weather had been cold.

June 20.—No rest all night; violent pains in my head, and feverish.

June 21.—Very ill; frighted almost to death with the apprehensions of my sad condition—to be sick, and no help. Prayed to God, for the first time since the storm off Hull, but scarce knew what I said, or why, my thoughts being all confused.

June 22.—A little better; but under dreadful apprehensions of sickness.

June 23.—Very bad again; cold and shivering, and then a violent headache.

June 24.—Much better.

June 25.—An ague very violent; the fit held me seven hours; cold fit and hot, with faint sweats after it.

June 26.—Better; and having no victuals to eat, took my gun, but found myself very weak. However, I killed a she-goat, and with much difficulty got it home, and broiled some of it, and ate, I would fain have stewed it, and made some broth, but had no pot.

June 27.—The ague again so violent that I lay a-bed all day, and neither ate nor drank. I was ready to perish for thirst; but so weak, I had not strength to stand up, or to get myself any water to drink. Prayed to God again, but was light-headed; and when I was not, I was so ignorant that I knew not what to say; only I lay and cried, "Lord, look upon me! Lord, pity me! Lord, have mercy upon me!" I suppose I did nothing else for two or three hours; till, the fit wearing off, I fell asleep, and did not wake till far in the night. When I awoke, I found myself much refreshed, but weak, and exceeding thirsty. However, as I had no water in my habitation, I was forced to lie till morning, and went to sleep again. In this second sleep I had this terrible dream: I thought that I was sitting on the ground, on the outside of my wall, where I sat when the storm blew after the earthquake, and that I saw a man descend from a great black cloud, in a bright flame of fire, and light upon the ground. He was all over as bright as a flame, so that I could but just bear to look towards him; his countenance was most inexpressibly dreadful, impossible for words to describe. When he stepped upon the ground with his feet, I thought the earth trembled, just as it had done before in the earthquake, and all the air looked, to my apprehension, as if it had been filled with flashes of fire. He was no sooner landed upon the earth, but he moved forward towards me, with a long spear or weapon in his hand, to kill me; and when he came to a rising ground, at some distance, he spoke to me—or I heard a voice so terrible that it is impossible to express the terror of it. All that I can say I understood was this: "Seeing all these things have not brought thee to repentance, now thou shalt die;" at which words, I thought he lifted up the spear that was in his hand to kill me.

No one that shall ever read this account will expect that I should be able to describe the horrors of my soul at this terrible vision. I mean, that even while it was a dream, I even dreamed of those horrors. Nor is it any more possible to describe the impression that remained upon my mind when I awaked, and found it was but a dream.

I had, alas! no divine knowledge. What I had received by the good instruction of my father was then worn out by an uninterrupted series, for eight years, of seafaring wickedness, and a constant conversation with none but such as were, like myself, wicked and profane to the last degree. I do not remember that I had, in all that time, one thought that so much as tended either to looking upwards towards God, or inwards towards a reflection upon my own ways; but a certain stupidity of soul, without desire of good, or conscience of evil, had entirely overwhelmed me; and I was all that the most hardened, unthinking, wicked creature among our common sailors can be supposed to be; not having the least sense, either of the fear of God in danger, or of thankfulness to God in deliverance.

In the relating what is already past of my story, this will be the more easily believed when I shall add, that through all the variety of miseries that had to this day befallen me, I never had so much as one thought of it being the hand of God, or that it was a just punishment for my sin—my rebellious behaviour against my father—or my present sins, which were great—or so much as a punishment for the general course of my wicked life. When I was on the desperate expedition on the desert shores of Africa, I never had so much as one thought of what would become of me, or one wish to God to direct me whither I should go, or to keep me from the danger which apparently surrounded me, as well from voracious creatures as cruel savages. But I was merely thoughtless of a God or a Providence, acted like a mere brute, from the principles of nature, and by the dictates of common sense only, and, indeed, hardly that. When I was delivered and taken up at sea by the Portugal captain, well used, and dealt justly and honourably with, as well as charitably, I had not the least thankfulness in my thoughts. When, again, I was shipwrecked, ruined, and in danger of drowning on this island, I was as far from remorse, or looking on it as a judgment. I only said to myself often, that I was an unfortunate dog, and born to be always miserable.

It is true, when I got on shore first here, and found all my ship's crew drowned and myself spared, I was surprised with a kind of ecstasy, and some transports of soul, which, had the grace of God assisted, might have come up to true thankfulness; but it ended where it began, in a mere common flight of joy, or, as I may say, being glad I was alive, without the least reflection upon the distinguished goodness of the hand which had preserved me, and had singled me out to be preserved when all the rest were destroyed, or an inquiry why Providence had been thus merciful unto me. Even just the same common sort of joy which seamen generally have, after they are got safe ashore from a shipwreck, which they drown all in the next bowl of punch, and forget almost as soon as it is over; and all the rest of my life was like it. Even when I was afterwards, on due consideration, made sensible of my condition, how I was cast on this dreadful place, out of the reach of human kind, out of all hope of relief, or prospect of redemption, as soon as I saw but a prospect of living and that I should not starve and perish for hunger, all the sense of my affliction wore off; and I began to be very easy, applied myself to the works proper for my preservation and supply, and was far enough from being afflicted at my condition, as a judgment from heaven, or as the hand of God against me: these were thoughts which very seldom entered my head.

The growing up of the corn, as is hinted in my Journal, had at first some little influence upon me, and began to affect me with seriousness, as long as I thought it had something miraculous in it; but as soon as ever that part of the thought was removed, all the impression that was raised from it wore off also, as I have noted already. Even the earthquake, though nothing could be more terrible in its nature, or more immediately directing to the invisible Power which alone directs such things, yet no sooner was the first fright over, but the impression it had made went off also. I had no more sense of God or His judgments—much less of the present affliction of my circumstances being from His hand—than if I had been in the most prosperous condition of life. But now, when I began to be sick, and a leisurely view of the miseries of death came to place itself before me; when my spirits began to sink under the burden of a strong distemper, and nature was exhausted with the violence of the fever; conscience, that had slept so long, began to awake, and I began to reproach myself with my past life, in which I had so evidently, by uncommon wickedness, provoked the justice of God to lay me under uncommon strokes, and to deal with me in so vindictive a manner. These reflections oppressed me for the second or third day of my distemper; and in the violence, as well of the fever as of the dreadful reproaches of my conscience, extorted some words from me like praying to God, though I cannot say they were either a prayer attended with desires or with hopes: it was rather the voice of mere fright and distress. My thoughts were confused, the convictions great upon my mind, and the horror of dying in such a miserable condition raised vapours into my head with the mere apprehensions; and in these hurries of my soul I knew not what my tongue might express. But it was rather exclamation, such as, "Lord, what a miserable creature am I! If I should be sick, I shall certainly die for want of help; and what will become of me!" Then the tears burst out of my eyes, and I could say no more for a good while. In this interval the good advice of my father came to my mind, and presently his prediction, which I mentioned at the beginning of this story—viz. that if I did take this foolish step, God would not bless me, and I would have leisure hereafter to reflect upon having neglected his counsel when there might be none to assist in my recovery. "Now," said I, aloud, "my dear father's words are come to pass; God's justice has overtaken me, and I have none to help or hear me. I rejected the voice of Providence, which had mercifully put me in a posture or station of life wherein I might have been happy and easy; but I would neither see it myself nor learn to know the blessing of it from my parents. I left them to mourn over my folly, and now I am left to mourn under the consequences of it. I abused their help and assistance, who would have lifted me in the world, and would have made everything easy to me; and now I have difficulties to struggle with, too great for even nature itself to support, and no assistance, no help, no comfort, no advice." Then I cried out, "Lord, be my help, for I am in great distress." This was the first prayer, if I may call it so, that I had made for many years.

But to return to my Journal.

June 28.—Having been somewhat refreshed with the sleep I had had, and the fit being entirely off, I got up; and though the fright and terror of my dream was very great, yet I considered that the fit of the ague would return again the next day, and now was my time to get something to refresh and support myself when I should be ill; and the first thing I did, I filled a large square case-bottle with water, and set it upon my table, in reach of my bed; and to take off the chill or aguish disposition of the water, I put about a quarter of a pint of rum into it, and mixed them together. Then I got me a piece of the goat's flesh and broiled it on the coals, but could eat very little. I walked about, but was very weak, and withal very sad and heavy-hearted under a sense of my miserable condition, dreading, the return of my distemper the next day. At night I made my supper of three of the turtle's eggs, which I roasted in the ashes, and ate, as we call it, in the shell, and this was the first bit of meat I had ever asked God's blessing to, that I could remember, in my whole life. After I had eaten I tried to walk, but found myself so weak that I could hardly carry a gun, for I never went out without that; so I went but a little way, and sat down upon the ground, looking out upon the sea, which was just before me, and very calm and smooth. As I sat here some such thoughts as these occurred to me: What is this earth and sea, of which I have seen so much? Whence is it produced? And what am I, and all the other creatures wild and tame, human and brutal? Whence are we? Sure we are all made by some secret Power, who formed the earth and sea, the air and sky. And who is that? Then it followed most naturally, it is God that has made all. Well, but then it came on strangely, if God has made all these things, He guides and governs them all, and all things that concern them; for the Power that could make all things must certainly have power to guide and direct them. If so, nothing can happen in the great circuit of His works, either without His knowledge or appointment.

And if nothing happens without His knowledge, He knows that I am here, and am in this dreadful condition; and if nothing happens without His appointment, He has appointed all this to befall me. Nothing occurred to my thought to contradict any of these conclusions, and therefore it rested upon me with the greater force, that it must needs be that God had appointed all this to befall me; that I was brought into this miserable circumstance by His direction, He having the sole power, not of me only, but of everything that happened in the world. Immediately it followed: Why has God done this to me? What have I done to be thus used? My conscience presently checked me in that inquiry, as if I had blasphemed, and methought it spoke to me like a voice: "Wretch! dost *thou* ask what thou hast done? Look back upon a dreadful misspent life, and ask thyself what thou hast *not* done? Ask, why is it that thou wert not long ago destroyed? Why wert thou not drowned in Yarmouth Roads; killed in the fight when the ship was taken by the Sallee man-of-war; devoured by the wild beasts on the coast of Africa; or drowned *here*, when all the crew perished but thyself? Dost *thou* ask, what have I done?" I was struck dumb with these reflections, as one astonished, and had not a word to say—no, not to answer to myself, but rose up pensive and sad, walked back to my retreat, and went up over my wall, as if I had been going to bed; but my thoughts were sadly disturbed, and I had no inclination to sleep; so I sat down in my chair, and lighted my lamp, for it began to be dark. Now, as the apprehension of the return of my distemper terrified me very much, it occurred to my thought that the Brazilians take no physic but their tobacco for almost all distempers, and I had a piece of a roll of tobacco in one of the chests, which was quite cured, and some also that was green, and not quite cured.

I went, directed by Heaven no doubt; for in this chest I found a cure both for soul and body. I opened the chest, and found what I looked for, the tobacco; and as the few books I had saved lay there too, I took out one of the Bibles which I mentioned before, and which to this time I had not found leisure or inclination to look into. I say, I took it out, and brought both that and the tobacco with me to the table. What use to make of the tobacco I knew not, in my distemper, or whether it was good for it or no: but I tried several experiments with it, as if I was resolved it should hit one way or other. I first took a piece of leaf, and chewed it in my mouth, which, indeed, at first almost stupefied my brain, the tobacco being green and strong, and that I had not been much used to. Then I took some and steeped it an hour or two in some rum, and resolved to take a dose of it when I lay down; and lastly, I burnt some upon a pan of coals, and held my nose close over the smoke of it as long as I could bear it, as well for the heat as almost for suffocation. In the interval of this operation I took up the Bible and began to read; but my head was too much disturbed with the tobacco to bear reading, at least at that time; only, having opened the book casually, the first words that occurred to me were these, "Call on Me in the day of trouble, and I will deliver thee, and thou shalt glorify Me." These words were very apt to my case, and made some impression upon my thoughts at the time of reading them, though not so much as they did afterwards; for, as for being *delivered*, the word had no sound, as I may say, to me; the thing was so remote, so impossible in my apprehension of things, that I began to say, as the children of Israel did when they were promised flesh to eat, "Can God spread a table in the wilderness?" so I began to say, "Can God Himself deliver me from this place?" And as it was not for many years that any hopes appeared, this prevailed very often upon my thoughts; but, however, the words made a great impression upon me, and I mused upon them very often. It grew now late, and the tobacco had, as I said, dozed my head so much that I inclined to sleep; so I left my lamp burning in the cave, lest I should want anything in the night, and went to bed. But before I lay down, I did what I never had done in all my life—I kneeled down, and prayed to God to fulfil the promise to me, that if I called upon Him in the day of trouble, He would deliver me. After my broken and imperfect prayer was over, I drank the rum in which I had steeped the tobacco, which was so strong and rank of the tobacco that I could scarcely get it down; immediately upon this I went to bed. I found presently it flew up into my head violently; but I fell into a sound sleep, and waked no more till, by the sun, it must necessarily be near three o'clock in the afternoon the next day—nay, to this hour I am partly of opinion that I slept all the next day and night, and till almost three the day after; for otherwise I know not how I should lose a day out of my reckoning in the days of the week, as it appeared some years after I had done; for if I had lost it by crossing and recrossing the line, I should have lost more than one day; but certainly I lost a day in my account, and never knew which way. Be that, however, one way or the other, when I awaked I found myself exceedingly refreshed, and my spirits lively and cheerful; when I got up I was stronger than I was the day before, and my stomach better, for I was hungry; and, in short, I had no fit the next day, but continued much altered for the better. This was the 29th.

The 30th was my well day, of course, and I went abroad with my gun, but did not care to travel too far. I killed a sea-fowl or two, something like a brandgoose, and brought them home, but was not very forward to eat them; so I ate some more of the turtle's eggs, which were very good. This evening I renewed the medicine, which I had supposed did me good the day before—the tobacco steeped in rum; only I did not take so much as before, nor did I chew any of the leaf, or hold my head over the smoke; however, I was not so well the next day, which was the first of July, as I hoped I should have been; for I had a little spice of the cold fit, but it was not much.

July 2.—I renewed the medicine all the three ways; and dosed myself with it as at first, and doubled the quantity which I drank.

July 3.—I missed the fit for good and all, though I did not recover my full strength for some weeks after. While I was thus gathering strength, my thoughts ran exceedingly upon this Scripture, "I will deliver thee"; and the impossibility of my deliverance lay much upon my mind, in bar of my ever expecting it; but as I was discouraging myself with such thoughts, it occurred to my mind that I pored so much upon my deliverance from the main affliction, that I disregarded the deliverance I had received, and I was as it were made to ask myself such questions as these—viz. Have I not been delivered, and wonderfully too, from sickness—from the most distressed condition that could be, and that was so frightful to me? and what notice had I taken of it? Had I done my part? God had delivered me, but I had not glorified Him—that is to say, I had not owned and been thankful for that as a deliverance; and how could I expect greater deliverance? This touched my heart very much; and immediately I knelt down and gave God thanks aloud for my recovery from my sickness.

July 4.—In the morning I took the Bible; and beginning at the New Testament, I began seriously to read it, and imposed upon myself to read a while every morning and every night; not tying myself to the number of chapters, but long as my thoughts should engage me. It was not long after I set seriously to this work till I found my heart more deeply and sincerely affected with the wickedness of my past life. The impression of my dream revived; and the words, "All these things have not brought thee to repentance," ran seriously through my thoughts. I was earnestly begging of God to give me repentance, when it happened providentially, the very day, that, reading the Scripture, I came to these words: "He is exalted a Prince and a Saviour, to give repentance and to give remission." I threw down the book; and with my heart as well as my hands lifted up to heaven, in a kind of ecstasy of joy, I cried out aloud, "Jesus, thou son of David! Jesus, thou exalted Prince and Saviour! give me repentance!" This was the first time I could say, in the true sense of the words, that I prayed in all my life; for now I prayed with a sense of my condition, and a true Scripture view of hope, founded on the encouragement of the Word of God; and from this time, I may say, I began to hope that God would hear me.

Now I began to construe the words mentioned above, "Call on Me, and I will deliver thee," in a different sense from what I had ever done before; for then I had no notion of anything being called *deliverance*, but my being delivered from the captivity I was in; for though I was indeed at large in the place, yet the island was certainly a prison to me, and that in the worse sense in the world. But now I learned to take it in another sense: now I looked back upon my past life with such horror, and my sins appeared so dreadful, that my soul sought nothing of God but deliverance from the load of guilt that bore down all my comfort. As for my solitary life, it was nothing. I did not so much as pray to be delivered from it or think of it; it was all of no consideration in comparison to this. And I add this part here, to hint to whoever shall read it, that whenever they come to a true sense of things, they will find deliverance from sin a much greater blessing than deliverance from affliction.

But, leaving this part, I return to my Journal.

My condition began now to be, though not less miserable as to my way of living, yet much easier to my mind: and my thoughts being directed, by a constant reading the Scripture and praying to God, to things of a higher nature, I had a great deal of comfort within, which till now I knew nothing of; also, my health and strength returned, I bestirred myself to furnish myself with everything that I wanted, and make my way of living as regular as I could.

From the 4th of July to the 14th I was chiefly employed in walking about with my gun in my hand, a little and a little at a time, as a man that was gathering up his strength after a fit of sickness; for it is hardly to be imagined how low I was, and to what weakness I was reduced. The application which I made use of was perfectly new, and perhaps which had never cured an ague before; neither can I recommend it to any to practise, by this experiment: and though it did carry off the fit, yet it rather contributed to weakening me; for I had frequent convulsions in my nerves and limbs for some time. I learned from it also this, in particular, that being abroad in the rainy season was the most pernicious thing to my health that could be, especially in those rains which came attended with storms and hurricanes of wind; for as the rain which came in the dry season was almost always accompanied with such storms, so I found that rain was much more dangerous than the rain which fell in September and October.

Chapter VII—AGRICULTURAL EXPERIENCE

I had now been in this unhappy island above ten months. All possibility of deliverance from this condition seemed to be entirely taken from me; and I firmly believe that no human shape had ever set foot upon that place. Having now secured my habitation, as I thought, fully to my mind, I had a great desire to make a more perfect discovery of the island, and to see what other productions I might find, which I yet knew nothing of.

It was on the 15th of July that I began to take a more particular survey of the island itself. I went up the creek first, where, as I hinted, I brought my rafts on shore. I found after I came about two miles up, that the tide did not flow any higher, and that it was no more than a little brook of running water, very fresh and good; but this being the dry season, there was hardly any water in some parts of it—at least not enough to run in any stream, so as it could be perceived. On the banks of this brook I found many pleasant savannahs or meadows, plain, smooth, and covered with grass; and on the rising parts of them, next to the higher grounds, where the water, as might be supposed, never overflowed, I found a great deal of tobacco, green, and growing to a great and very strong stalk. There were divers other plants, which I had no notion of or understanding about, that might, perhaps, have virtues of their own, which I could not find out. I searched for the cassava root, which the Indians, in all that climate, make their bread of, but I could find none. I saw large plants of aloes, but did not understand them. I saw several sugar-canes, but wild, and, for want of cultivation, imperfect. I contented myself with these discoveries for this time, and came back, musing with myself what course I might take to know the virtue and goodness of any of the fruits or plants which I should discover, but could bring it to no conclusion; for, in short, I had made so little observation while I was in the Brazils, that I knew little of the plants in the field; at least, very little that might serve to any purpose now in my distress.

The next day, the sixteenth, I went up the same way again; and after going something further than I had gone the day before, I found the brook and the savannahs cease, and the country become more woody than before. In this part I found different fruits, and particularly I found melons upon the ground, in great abundance, and grapes upon the trees. The vines had spread, indeed, over the trees, and the clusters of grapes were just now in their prime, very ripe and rich.

This was a surprising discovery, and I was exceeding glad of them; but I was warned by my experience to eat sparingly of them; remembering that when I was ashore in Barbary, the eating of grapes killed several of our Englishmen, who were slaves there, by throwing them into fluxes and fevers. But I found an excellent use for these grapes; and that was, to cure or dry them in the sun, and keep them as dried grapes or raisins are kept, which I thought would be, as indeed they were, wholesome and agreeable to eat when no grapes could be had.

I spent all that evening there, and went not back to my habitation; which, by the way, was the first night, as I might say, I had lain from home. In the night, I took my first contrivance, and got up in a tree, where I slept well; and the next morning proceeded upon my discovery; travelling nearly four miles, as I might judge by the length of the valley, keeping still due north, with a ridge of hills on the south and north side of me. At the end of this march I came to an opening where the country seemed to descend to the west; and a little spring of fresh water, which issued out of the side of the hill by me, ran the other way, that is, due east; and the country appeared so fresh, so green, so flourishing, everything being in a constant verdure or flourish of spring that it looked like a planted garden. I descended a little on the side of that delicious vale, surveying it with a secret kind of pleasure, though mixed with my other afflicting thoughts, to think that this was all my own; that I was king and lord of all this country indefensibly, and had a right of possession; and if I could convey it, I might have it in inheritance as completely as any lord of a manor in England. I saw here abundance of cocoa trees, orange, and lemon, and citron trees; but all wild, and very few bearing any fruit, at least not then. However, the green limes that I gathered were not only pleasant to eat, but very wholesome; and I mixed their juice afterwards with water, which made it very wholesome, and very cool and refreshing. I found now I had business enough to gather and carry home; and I resolved to lay up a store as well of grapes as limes and lemons, to furnish myself for the wet season, which I knew was approaching. In order to do this, I gathered a great heap of grapes in one place, a lesser heap in another place, and a great parcel of limes and lemons in another place; and taking a few of each with me, I travelled homewards; resolving to come again, and bring a bag or sack, or what I could make, to carry the rest home. Accordingly, having spent three days in this journey, I came home (so I must now call my tent and my cave); but before I got thither the grapes were spoiled; the richness of the fruit and the weight of the juice having broken them and bruised them, they were good for little or nothing; as to the limes, they were good, but I could bring but a few.

The next day, being the nineteenth, I went back, having made me two small bags to bring home my harvest; but I was surprised, when coming to my heap of grapes, which were so rich and fine when I gathered them, to find them all spread about, trod to pieces, and dragged about, some here, some there, and abundance eaten and devoured. By this I concluded there were some wild creatures thereabouts, which had done this; but what they were I knew not. However, as I found there was no laying them up on heaps, and no carrying them away in a sack, but that one way they would be destroyed, and the other way they would be crushed with their own weight, I took another course; for I gathered a large quantity of the grapes, and hung upon the out-branches of the trees, that they might cure and dry in the sun; and as for the limes and lemons, I carried as many back as I could well stand under.

When I came home from this journey, I contemplated with great pleasure the fruitfulness of that valley, and the pleasantness of the situation; the security from storms on that side of the water, and the wood: and concluded that I had pitched upon a place to fix my abode which was by far the worst part of the country. Upon the whole, I began to consider of removing my habitation, and looking out for a place equally safe as where now I was situate, if possible, in that pleasant, fruitful part of the island.

This thought ran long in my head, and I was exceeding fond of it for some time, the pleasantness of the place tempting me; but when I came to a nearer view of it, I considered that I was now by the seaside, where it was at least possible that something might happen to my advantage, and, by the same ill fate that brought me hither might bring some other unhappy wretches to the same place; and though it was scarce probable that any such thing should ever happen, yet to enclose myself among the hills and woods in the centre of the island was to anticipate my bondage, and to render such an affair not only improbable, but impossible; and that therefore I ought not by any means to remove. However, I was so enamoured of this place, that I spent much of my time there for the whole of the remaining part of the month of July; and though upon second thoughts, I resolved not to remove, yet I built me a little kind of a bower, and surrounded it at a distance with a strong fence, being a double hedge, as high as I could reach, well staked and filled between with brushwood; and here I lay very secure, sometimes two or three nights together; always going over it with a ladder; so that I fancied now I had my country house and my sea-coast house; and this work took me up to the beginning of August.

I had but newly finished my fence, and began to enjoy my labour, when the rains came on, and made me stick close to my first habitation; for though I had made me a tent like the other, with a piece of a sail, and spread it very well, yet I had not the shelter of a hill to keep me from storms, nor a cave behind me to retreat into when the rains were extraordinary.

About the beginning of August, as I said, I had finished my bower, and began to enjoy myself. The 3rd of August, I found the grapes I had hung up perfectly dried, and, indeed, were excellent good raisins of the sun; so I began to take them down from the trees, and it was very happy that I did so, for the rains which followed would have spoiled them, and I had lost the best part of my winter food; for I had above two hundred large bunches of them. No sooner had I taken them all down, and carried the most of them home to my cave, than it began to rain; and from hence, which was the 14th of August, it rained, more or less, every day till the middle of October; and sometimes so violently, that I could not stir out of my cave for several days.

In this season I was much surprised with the increase of my family; I had been concerned for the loss of one of my cats, who ran away from me, or, as I thought, had been dead, and I heard no more tidings of her till, to my astonishment, she came home about the end of August with three kittens. This was the more strange to me because, though I had killed a wild cat, as I called it, with my gun, yet I thought it was quite a different kind from our European cats; but the young cats were the same kind of house-breed as the old one; and both my cats being females, I thought it very strange. But from these three cats I afterwards came to be so pestered with cats that I was forced to kill them like vermin or wild beasts, and to drive them from my house as much as possible.

From the 14th of August to the 26th, incessant rain, so that I could not stir, and was now very careful not to be much wet. In this confinement, I began to be straitened for food: but venturing out twice, I one day killed a goat; and the last day, which was the 26th, found a very large tortoise, which was a treat to me, and my food was regulated thus: I ate a bunch of raisins for my breakfast; a piece of the goat's flesh, or of the turtle, for my dinner, broiled—for, to my great misfortune, I had no vessel to boil or stew anything; and two or three of the turtle's eggs for my supper.

During this confinement in my cover by the rain, I worked daily two or three hours at enlarging my cave, and by degrees worked it on towards one side, till I came to the outside of the hill, and made a door or way out, which came beyond my fence or wall; and so I came in and out this way. But I was not perfectly easy at lying so open; for, as I had managed myself before, I was in a perfect enclosure; whereas now I thought I lay exposed, and open for anything to come in upon me; and yet I could not perceive that there was any living thing to fear, the biggest creature that I had yet seen upon the island being a goat.

Sept. 30.—I was now come to the unhappy anniversary of my landing. I cast up the notches on my post, and found I had been on shore three hundred and sixty-five days. I kept this day as a solemn fast, setting it apart for religious exercise, prostrating myself on the ground with the most serious humiliation, confessing my sins to God, acknowledging His righteous judgments upon me, and praying to Him to have mercy on me through Jesus Christ; and not having tasted the least refreshment for twelve hours, even till the going down of the sun, I then ate a biscuit-cake and a bunch of grapes, and went to bed, finishing the day as I began it. I had all this time observed no Sabbath day; for as at first I had no sense of religion upon my mind, I had, after some time, omitted to distinguish the weeks, by making a longer notch than ordinary for the Sabbath day, and so did not really know what any of the days were; but now, having cast up the days as above, I found I had been there a year; so I divided it into weeks, and set apart every seventh day for a Sabbath; though I found at the end of my account I had lost a day or two in my reckoning. A little after this, my ink began to fail me, and so I contented myself to use it more sparingly, and to write down only the most remarkable events of my life, without continuing a daily memorandum of other things.

Chapter VII—AGRICULTURAL EXPERIENCE

The rainy season and the dry season began now to appear regular to me, and I learned to divide them so as to provide for them accordingly; but I bought all my experience before I had it, and this I am going to relate was one of the most discouraging experiments that I made.

I have mentioned that I had saved the few ears of barley and rice, which I had so surprisingly found spring up, as I thought, of themselves, and I believe there were about thirty stalks of rice, and about twenty of barley; and now I thought it a proper time to sow it, after the rains, the sun being in its southern position, going from me. Accordingly, I dug up a piece of ground as well as I could with my wooden spade, and dividing it into two parts, I sowed my grain; but as I was sowing, it casually occurred to my thoughts that I would not sow it all at first, because I did not know when was the proper time for it, so I sowed about two-thirds of the seed, leaving about a handful of each. It was a great comfort to me afterwards that I did so, for not one grain of what I sowed this time came to anything: for the dry months following, the earth having had no rain after the seed was sown, it had no moisture to assist its growth, and never came up at all till the wet season had come again, and then it grew as if it had been but newly sown. Finding my first seed did not grow, which I easily imagined was by the drought, I sought for a moister piece of ground to make another trial in, and I dug up a piece of ground near my new bower, and sowed the rest of my seed in February, a little before the vernal equinox; and this having the rainy months of March and April to water it, sprung up very pleasantly, and yielded a very good crop; but having part of the seed left only, and not daring to sow all that I had, I had but a small quantity at last, my whole crop not amounting to above half a peck of each kind. But by this experiment I was made master of my business, and knew exactly when the proper season was to sow, and that I might expect two seed-times and two harvests every year.

While this corn was growing I made a little discovery, which was of use to me afterwards. As soon as the rains were over, and the weather began to settle, which was about the month of November, I made a visit up the country to my bower, where, though I had not been some months, yet I found all things just as I left them. The circle or double hedge that I had made was not only firm and entire, but the stakes which I had cut out of some trees that grew thereabouts were all shot out and grown with long branches, as much as a willow-tree usually shoots the first year after lopping its head. I could not tell what tree to call it that these stakes were cut from. I was surprised, and yet very well pleased, to see the young trees grow; and I pruned them, and led them up to grow as much alike as I could; and it is scarce credible how beautiful a figure they grew into in three years; so that though the hedge made a circle of about twenty-five yards in diameter, yet the trees, for such I might now call them, soon covered it, and it was a complete shade, sufficient to lodge under all the dry season. This made me resolve to cut some more stakes, and make me a hedge like this, in a semi-circle round my wall (I mean that of my first dwelling), which I did; and placing the trees or stakes in a double row, at about eight yards distance from my first fence, they grew presently, and were at first a fine cover to my habitation, and afterwards served for a defence also, as I shall observe in its order.

I found now that the seasons of the year might generally be divided, not into summer and winter, as in Europe, but into the rainy seasons and the dry seasons, which were generally thus:—The half of February, the whole of March, and the half of April—rainy, the sun being then on or near the equinox.

The half of April, the whole of May, June, and July, and the half of August—dry, the sun being then to the north of the line.

The half of August, the whole of September, and the half of October—rainy, the sun being then come back.

The half of October, the whole of November, December, and January, and the half of February—dry, the sun being then to the south of the line.

The rainy seasons sometimes held longer or shorter as the winds happened to blow, but this was the general observation I made. After I had found by experience the ill consequences of being abroad in the rain, I took care to furnish myself with provisions beforehand, that I might not be obliged to go out, and I sat within doors as much as possible during the wet months. This time I found much employment, and very suitable also to the time, for I found great occasion for many things which I had no way to furnish myself with but by hard labour and constant application; particularly I tried many ways to make myself a basket, but all the twigs I could get for the purpose proved so brittle that they would do nothing. It proved of excellent advantage to me now, that when I was a boy, I used to take great delight in standing at a basket-maker's, in the town where my father lived, to see them make their wicker-ware; and being, as boys usually are, very officious to help, and a great observer of the manner in which they worked those things, and sometimes lending a hand, I had by these means full knowledge of the methods of it, and I wanted nothing but the materials, when it came into my mind that the twigs of that tree from whence I cut my stakes that grew might possibly be as tough as the sallows, willows, and osiers in England, and I resolved to try. Accordingly, the next day I went to my country house, as I called it, and cutting some of the smaller twigs, I found them to my purpose as much as I could desire; whereupon I came the next time prepared with a hatchet to cut down a quantity, which I soon found, for there was great plenty of them. These I set up to dry within my circle or hedge, and when they were fit for use I carried them to my cave; and here, during the next season, I employed myself in making, as well as I could, a great many baskets, both to carry earth or to carry or lay up anything, as I had occasion; and though I did not finish them very handsomely, yet I made them sufficiently serviceable for my purpose; thus, afterwards, I took care never to be without them; and as my wicker-ware decayed, I made more, especially strong, deep baskets to place my corn in, instead of sacks, when I should come to have any quantity of it.

Having mastered this difficulty, and employed a world of time about it, I bestirred myself to see, if possible, how to supply two wants. I had no vessels to hold anything that was liquid, except two runlets, which were almost full of rum, and some glass bottles—some of the common size, and others which were case bottles, square, for the holding of water, spirits, &c. I had not so much as a pot to boil anything, except a great kettle, which I saved out of the ship, and which was too big for such as I desired it—viz. to make broth, and stew a bit of meat by itself. The second thing I fain would have had was a tobacco-pipe, but it was impossible to me to make one; however, I found a contrivance for that, too, at last. I employed myself in planting my second rows of stakes or piles, and in this wicker-working all the summer or dry season, when another business took me up more time than it could be imagined I could spare.

Chapter VIII—SURVEYS HIS POSITION

I mentioned before that I had a great mind to see the whole island, and that I had travelled up the brook, and so on to where I built my bower, and where I had an opening quite to the sea, on the other side of the island. I now resolved to travel quite across to the sea-shore on that side; so, taking my gun, a hatchet, and my dog, and a larger quantity of powder and shot than usual, with two biscuit-cakes and a great bunch of raisins in my pouch for my store, I began my journey. When I had passed the vale where my bower stood, as above, I came within view of the sea to the west, and it being a very clear day, I fairly descried land—whether an island or a continent I could not tell; but it lay very high, extending from the W. to the W.S.W. at a very great distance; by my guess it could not be less than fifteen or twenty leagues off.

I could not tell what part of the world this might be, otherwise than that I knew it must be part of America, and, as I concluded by all my observations, must be near the Spanish dominions, and perhaps was all inhabited by savages, where, if I had landed, I had been in a worse condition than I was now; and therefore I acquiesced in the dispositions of Providence, which I began now to own and to believe ordered everything for the best; I say I quieted my mind with this, and left off afflicting myself with fruitless wishes of being there.

Besides, after some thought upon this affair, I considered that if this land was the Spanish coast, I should certainly, one time or other, see some vessel pass or repass one way or other; but if not, then it was the savage coast between the Spanish country and Brazils, where are found the worst of savages; for they are cannibals or men-eaters, and fail not to murder and devour all the human bodies that fall into their hands.

With these considerations, I walked very leisurely forward. I found that side of the island where I now was much pleasanter than mine—the open or savannah fields sweet, adorned with flowers and grass, and full of very fine woods. I saw abundance of parrots, and fain I would have caught one, if possible, to have kept it to be tame, and taught it to speak to me. I did, after some painstaking, catch a young parrot, for I knocked it down with a stick, and having recovered it, I brought it home; but it was some years before I could make him speak; however, at last I taught him to call me by name very familiarly. But the accident that followed, though it be a trifle, will be very diverting in its place.

Chapter VIII—SURVEYS HIS POSITION

I was exceedingly diverted with this journey. I found in the low grounds hares (as I thought them to be) and foxes; but they differed greatly from all the other kinds I had met with, nor could I satisfy myself to eat them, though I killed several. But I had no need to be venturous, for I had no want of food, and of that which was very good too, especially these three sorts, viz. goats, pigeons, and turtle, or tortoise, which added to my grapes, Leadenhall market could not have furnished a table better than I, in proportion to the company; and though my case was deplorable enough, yet I had great cause for thankfulness that I was not driven to any extremities for food, but had rather plenty, even to dainties.

I never travelled in this journey above two miles outright in a day, or thereabouts; but I took so many turns and re-turns to see what discoveries I could make, that I came weary enough to the place where I resolved to sit down all night; and then I either reposed myself in a tree, or surrounded myself with a row of stakes set upright in the ground, either from one tree to another, or so as no wild creature could come at me without waking me.

As soon as I came to the sea-shore, I was surprised to see that I had taken up my lot on the worst side of the island, for here, indeed, the shore was covered with innumerable turtles, whereas on the other side I had found but three in a year and a half. Here was also an infinite number of fowls of many kinds, some which I had seen, and some which I had not seen before, and many of them very good meat, but such as I knew not the names of, except those called penguins.

I could have shot as many as I pleased, but was very sparing of my powder and shot, and therefore had more mind to kill a she-goat if I could, which I could better feed on; and though there were many goats here, more than on my side the island, yet it was with much more difficulty that I could come near them, the country being flat and even, and they saw me much sooner than when I was on the hills.

I confess this side of the country was much pleasanter than mine; but yet I had not the least inclination to remove, for as I was fixed in my habitation it became natural to me, and I seemed all the while I was here to be as it were upon a journey, and from home. However, I travelled along the shore of the sea towards the east, I suppose about twelve miles, and then setting up a great pole upon the shore for a mark, I concluded I would go home again, and that the next journey I took should be on the other side of the island east from my dwelling, and so round till I came to my post again.

I took another way to come back than that I went, thinking I could easily keep all the island so much in my view that I could not miss finding my first dwelling by viewing the country; but I found myself mistaken, for being come about two or three miles, I found myself descended into a very large valley, but so surrounded with hills, and those hills covered with wood, that I could not see which was my way by any direction but that of the sun, nor even then, unless I knew very well the position of the sun at that time of the day. It happened, to my further misfortune, that the weather proved hazy for three or four days while I was in the valley, and not being able to see the sun, I wandered about very uncomfortably, and at last was obliged to find the seaside, look for my post, and come back the same way I went: and then, by easy journeys, I turned homeward, the weather being exceeding hot, and my gun, ammunition, hatchet, and other things very heavy.

In this journey my dog surprised a young kid, and seized upon it; and I, running in to take hold of it, caught it, and saved it alive from the dog. I had a great mind to bring it home if I could, for I had often been musing whether it might not be possible to get a kid or two, and so raise a breed of tame goats, which might supply me when my powder and shot should be all spent. I made a collar for this little creature, and with a string, which I made of some rope-yam, which I always carried about me, I led him along, though with some difficulty, till I came to my bower, and there I enclosed him and left him, for I was very impatient to be at home, from whence I had been absent above a month.

I cannot express what a satisfaction it was to me to come into my old hutch, and lie down in my hammock-bed. This little wandering journey, without settled place of abode, had been so unpleasant to me, that my own house, as I called it to myself, was a perfect settlement to me compared to that; and it rendered everything about me so comfortable, that I resolved I would never go a great way from it again while it should be my lot to stay on the island.

I reposed myself here a week, to rest and regale myself after my long journey; during which most of the time was taken up in the weighty affair of making a cage for my Poll, who began now to be a mere domestic, and to be well acquainted with me. Then I began to think of the poor kid which I had penned in within my little circle, and resolved to go and fetch it home, or give it some food; accordingly I went, and found it where I left it, for indeed it could not get out, but was almost starved for want of food. I went and cut boughs of trees, and branches of such shrubs as I could find, and threw it over, and having fed it, I tied it as I did before, to lead it away; but it was so tame with being hungry, that I had no need to have tied it, for it followed me like a dog: and as I continually fed it, the creature became so loving, so gentle, and so fond, that it became from that time one of my domestics also, and would never leave me afterwards.

The rainy season of the autumnal equinox was now come, and I kept the 30th of September in the same solemn manner as before, being the anniversary of my landing on the island, having now been there two years, and no more prospect of being delivered than the first day I came there, I spent the whole day in humble and thankful acknowledgments of the many wonderful mercies which my solitary condition was attended with, and without which it might have been infinitely more miserable. I gave humble and hearty thanks that God had been pleased to discover to me that it was possible I might be more happy in this solitary condition than I should have been in the liberty of society, and in all the pleasures of the world; that He could fully make up to me the deficiencies of my solitary state, and the want of human society, by His presence and the communications of His grace to my soul; supporting, comforting, and encouraging me to depend upon His providence here, and hope for His eternal presence hereafter.

Chapter VIII—SURVEYS HIS POSITION

It was now that I began sensibly to feel how much more happy this life I now led was, with all its miserable circumstances, than the wicked, cursed, abominable life I led all the past part of my days; and now I changed both my sorrows and my joys; my very desires altered, my affections changed their gusts, and my delights were perfectly new from what they were at my first coming, or, indeed, for the two years past.

Before, as I walked about, either on my hunting or for viewing the country, the anguish of my soul at my condition would break out upon me on a sudden, and my very heart would die within me, to think of the woods, the mountains, the deserts I was in, and how I was a prisoner, locked up with the eternal bars and bolts of the ocean, in an uninhabited wilderness, without redemption. In the midst of the greatest composure of my mind, this would break out upon me like a storm, and make me wring my hands and weep like a child. Sometimes it would take me in the middle of my work, and I would immediately sit down and sigh, and look upon the ground for an hour or two together; and this was still worse to me, for if I could burst out into tears, or vent myself by words, it would go off, and the grief, having exhausted itself, would abate.

But now I began to exercise myself with new thoughts: I daily read the word of God, and applied all the comforts of it to my present state. One morning, being very sad, I opened the Bible upon these words, "I will never, never leave thee, nor forsake thee." Immediately it occurred that these words were to me; why else should they be directed in such a manner, just at the moment when I was mourning over my condition, as one forsaken of God and man? "Well, then," said I, "if God does not forsake me, of what ill consequence can it be, or what matters it, though the world should all forsake me, seeing on the other hand, if I had all the world, and should lose the favour and blessing of God, there would be no comparison in the loss?"

From this moment I began to conclude in my mind that it was possible for me to be more happy in this forsaken, solitary condition than it was probable I should ever have been in any other particular state in the world; and with this thought I was going to give thanks to God for bringing me to this place. I know not what it was, but something shocked my mind at that thought, and I durst not speak the words. "How canst thou become such a hypocrite," said I, even audibly, "to pretend to be thankful for a condition which, however thou mayest endeavour to be contented with, thou wouldst rather pray heartily to be delivered from?" So I stopped there; but though I could not say I thanked God for being there, yet I sincerely gave thanks to God for opening my eyes, by whatever afflicting providences, to see the former condition of my life, and to mourn for my wickedness, and repent. I never opened the Bible, or shut it, but my very soul within me blessed God for directing my friend in England, without any order of mine, to pack it up among my goods, and for assisting me afterwards to save it out of the wreck of the ship.

Thus, and in this disposition of mind, I began my third year; and though I have not given the reader the trouble of so particular an account of my works this year as the first, yet in general it may be observed that I was very seldom idle, but having regularly divided my time according to the several daily employments that were before me, such as: first, my duty to God, and the reading the Scriptures, which I constantly set apart some time for thrice every day; secondly, the going abroad with my gun for food, which generally took me up three hours in every morning, when it did not rain; thirdly, the ordering, cutting, preserving, and cooking what I had killed or caught for my supply; these took up great part of the day. Also, it is to be considered, that in the middle of the day, when the sun was in the zenith, the violence of the heat was too great to stir out; so that about four hours in the evening was all the time I could be supposed to work in, with this exception, that sometimes I changed my hours of hunting and working, and went to work in the morning, and abroad with my gun in the afternoon.

To this short time allowed for labour I desire may be added the exceeding laboriousness of my work; the many hours which, for want of tools, want of help, and want of skill, everything I did took up out of my time. For example, I was full two and forty days in making a board for a long shelf, which I wanted in my cave; whereas, two sawyers, with their tools and a saw-pit, would have cut six of them out of the same tree in half a day.

My case was this: it was to be a large tree which was to be cut down, because my board was to be a broad one. This tree I was three days in cutting down, and two more cutting off the boughs, and reducing it to a log or piece of timber. With inexpressible hacking and hewing I reduced both the sides of it into chips till it began to be light enough to move; then I turned it, and made one side of it smooth and flat as a board from end to end; then, turning that side downward, cut the other side til I brought the plank to be about three inches thick, and smooth on both sides. Any one may judge the labour of my hands in such a piece of work; but labour and patience carried me through that, and many other things. I only observe this in particular, to show the reason why so much of my time went away with so little work—viz. that what might be a little to be done with help and tools, was a vast labour and required a prodigious time to do alone, and by hand. But notwithstanding this, with patience and labour I got through everything that my circumstances made necessary to me to do, as will appear by what follows.

I was now, in the months of November and December, expecting my crop of barley and rice. The ground I had manured and dug up for them was not great; for, as I observed, my seed of each was not above the quantity of half a peck, for I had lost one whole crop by sowing in the dry season. But now my crop promised very well, when on a sudden I found I was in danger of losing it all again by enemies of several sorts, which it was scarcely possible to keep from it; as, first, the goats, and wild creatures which I called hares, who, tasting the sweetness of the blade, lay in it night and day, as soon as it came up, and eat it so close, that it could get no time to shoot up into stalk.

This I saw no remedy for but by making an enclosure about it with a hedge; which I did with a great deal of toil, and the more, because it required speed. However, as my arable land was but small, suited to my crop, I got it totally well fenced in about three weeks' time; and shooting some of the creatures in the daytime, I set my dog to guard it in the night, tying him up to a stake at the gate, where he would stand and bark all night long; so in a little time the enemies forsook the place, and the corn grew very strong and well, and began to ripen apace.

But as the beasts ruined me before, while my corn was in the blade, so the birds were as likely to ruin me now, when it was in the ear; for, going along by the place to see how it throve, I saw my little crop surrounded with fowls, of I know not how many sorts, who stood, as it were, watching till I should be gone. I immediately let fly among them, for I always had my gun with me. I had no sooner shot, but there rose up a little cloud of fowls, which I had not seen at all, from among the corn itself.

This touched me sensibly, for I foresaw that in a few days they would devour all my hopes; that I should be starved, and never be able to raise a crop at all; and what to do I could not tell; however, I resolved not to lose my corn, if possible, though I should watch it night and day. In the first place, I went among it to see what damage was already done, and found they had spoiled a good deal of it; but that as it was yet too green for them, the loss was not so great but that the remainder was likely to be a good crop if it could be saved.

I stayed by it to load my gun, and then coming away, I could easily see the thieves sitting upon all the trees about me, as if they only waited till I was gone away, and the event proved it to be so; for as I walked off, as if I was gone, I was no sooner out of their sight than they dropped down one by one into the corn again. I was so provoked, that I could not have patience to stay till more came on, knowing that every grain that they ate now was, as it might be said, a peck-loaf to me in the consequence; but coming up to the hedge, I fired again, and killed three of them. This was what I wished for; so I took them up, and served them as we serve notorious thieves in England—hanged them in chains, for a terror to others. It is impossible to imagine that this should have such an effect as it had, for the fowls would not only not come at the corn, but, in short, they forsook all that part of the island, and I could never see a bird near the place as long as my scarecrows hung there. This I was very glad of, you may be sure, and about the latter end of December, which was our second harvest of the year, I reaped my corn.

I was sadly put to it for a scythe or sickle to cut it down, and all I could do was to make one, as well as I could, out of one of the broadswords, or cutlasses, which I saved among the arms out of the ship. However, as my first crop was but small, I had no great difficulty to cut it down; in short, I reaped it in my way, for I cut nothing off but the ears, and carried it away in a great basket which I had made, and so rubbed it out with my hands; and at the end of all my harvesting, I found that out of my half-peck of seed I had near two bushels of rice, and about two bushels and a half of barley; that is to say, by my guess, for I had no measure at that time.

However, this was a great encouragement to me, and I foresaw that, in time, it would please God to supply me with bread. And yet here I was perplexed again, for I neither knew how to grind or make meal of my corn, or indeed how to clean it and part it; nor, if made into meal, how to make bread of it; and if how to make it, yet I knew not how to bake it. These things being added to my desire of having a good quantity for store, and to secure a constant supply, I resolved not to taste any of this crop but to preserve it all for seed against the next season; and in the meantime to employ all my study and hours of working to accomplish this great work of providing myself with corn and bread.

It might be truly said, that now I worked for my bread. I believe few people have thought much upon the strange multitude of little things necessary in the providing, producing, curing, dressing, making, and finishing this one article of bread.

I, that was reduced to a mere state of nature, found this to my daily discouragement; and was made more sensible of it every hour, even after I had got the first handful of seed-corn, which, as I have said, came up unexpectedly, and indeed to a surprise.

First, I had no plough to turn up the earth—no spade or shovel to dig it. Well, this I conquered by making me a wooden spade, as I observed before; but this did my work but in a wooden manner; and though it cost me a great many days to make it, yet, for want of iron, it not only wore out soon, but made my work the harder, and made it be performed much worse. However, this I bore with, and was content to work it out with patience, and bear with the badness of the performance. When the corn was sown, I had no harrow, but was forced to go over it myself, and drag a great heavy bough of a tree over it, to scratch it, as it may be called, rather than rake or harrow it. When it was growing, and grown, I have observed already how many things I wanted to fence it, secure it, mow or reap it, cure and carry it home, thrash, part it from the chaff, and save it. Then I wanted a mill to grind it sieves to dress it, yeast and salt to make it into bread, and an oven to bake it; but all these things I did without, as shall be observed; and yet the corn was an inestimable comfort and advantage to me too. All this, as I said, made everything laborious and tedious to me; but that there was no help for. Neither was my time so much loss to me, because, as I had divided it, a certain part of it was every day appointed to these works; and as I had resolved to use none of the corn for bread till I had a greater quantity by me, I had the next six months to apply myself wholly, by labour and invention, to furnish myself with utensils proper for the performing all the operations necessary for making the corn, when I had it, fit for my use.

Chapter IX—A BOAT

But first I was to prepare more land, for I had now seed enough to sow above an acre of ground. Before I did this, I had a week's work at least to make me a spade, which, when it was done, was but a sorry one indeed, and very heavy, and required double labour to work with it. However, I got through that, and sowed my seed in two large flat pieces of ground, as near my house as I could find them to my mind, and fenced them in with a good hedge, the stakes of which were all cut off that wood which I had set before, and knew it would grow; so that, in a year's time, I knew I should have a quick or living hedge, that would want but little repair. This work did not take me up less than three months, because a great part of that time was the wet season, when I could not go abroad. Within-doors, that is when it rained and I could not go out, I found employment in the following occupations—always observing, that all the while I was at work I diverted myself with talking to my parrot, and teaching him to speak; and I quickly taught him to know his own name, and at last to speak it out pretty loud, "Poll," which was the first word I ever heard spoken in the island by any mouth but my own. This, therefore, was not my work, but an assistance to my work; for now, as I said, I had a great employment upon my hands, as follows: I had long studied to make, by some means or other, some earthen vessels, which, indeed, I wanted sorely, but knew not where to come at them. However, considering the heat of the climate, I did not doubt but if I could find out any clay, I might make some pots that might, being dried in the sun, be hard enough and strong enough to bear handling, and to hold anything that was dry, and required to be kept so; and as this was necessary in the preparing corn, meal, &c., which was the thing I was doing, I resolved to make some as large as I could, and fit only to stand like jars, to hold what should be put into them.

It would make the reader pity me, or rather laugh at me, to tell how many awkward ways I took to raise this paste; what odd, misshapen, ugly things I made; how many of them fell in and how many fell out, the clay not being stiff enough to bear its own weight; how many cracked by the over-violent heat of the sun, being set out too hastily; and how many fell in pieces with only removing, as well before as after they were dried; and, in a word, how, after having laboured hard to find the clay—to dig it, to temper it, to bring it home, and work it—I could not make above two large earthen ugly things (I cannot call them jars) in about two months' labour.

However, as the sun baked these two very dry and hard, I lifted them very gently up, and set them down again in two great wicker baskets, which I had made on purpose for them, that they might not break; and as between the pot and the basket there was a little room to spare, I stuffed it full of the rice and barley straw; and these two pots being to stand always dry I thought would hold my dry corn, and perhaps the meal, when the corn was bruised.

Though I miscarried so much in my design for large pots, yet I made several smaller things with better success; such as little round pots, flat dishes, pitchers, and pipkins, and any things my hand turned to; and the heat of the sun baked them quite hard.

But all this would not answer my end, which was to get an earthen pot to hold what was liquid, and bear the fire, which none of these could do. It happened after some time, making a pretty large fire for cooking my meat, when I went to put it out after I had done with it, I found a broken piece of one of my earthenware vessels in the fire, burnt as hard as a stone, and red as a tile. I was agreeably surprised to see it, and said to myself, that certainly they might be made to burn whole, if they would burn broken.

This set me to study how to order my fire, so as to make it burn some pots. I had no notion of a kiln, such as the potters burn in, or of glazing them with lead, though I had some lead to do it with; but I placed three large pipkins and two or three pots in a pile, one upon another, and placed my firewood all round it, with a great heap of embers under them. I plied the fire with fresh fuel round the outside and upon the top, till I saw the pots in the inside red-hot quite through, and observed that they did not crack at all. When I saw them clear red, I let them stand in that heat about five or six hours, till I found one of them, though it did not crack, did melt or run; for the sand which was mixed with the clay melted by the violence of the heat, and would have run into glass if I had gone on; so I slacked my fire gradually till the pots began to abate of the red colour; and watching them all night, that I might not let the fire abate too fast, in the morning I had three very good (I will not say handsome) pipkins, and two other earthen pots, as hard burnt as could be desired, and one of them perfectly glazed with the running of the sand.

After this experiment, I need not say that I wanted no sort of earthenware for my use; but I must needs say as to the shapes of them, they were very indifferent, as any one may suppose, when I had no way of making them but as the children make dirt pies, or as a woman would make pies that never learned to raise paste.

No joy at a thing of so mean a nature was ever equal to mine, when I found I had made an earthen pot that would bear the fire; and I had hardly patience to stay till they were cold before I set one on the fire again with some water in it to boil me some meat, which it did admirably well; and with a piece of a kid I made some very good broth, though I wanted oatmeal, and several other ingredients requisite to make it as good as I would have had it been.

Chapter IX—A BOAT

My next concern was to get me a stone mortar to stamp or beat some corn in; for as to the mill, there was no thought of arriving at that perfection of art with one pair of hands. To supply this want, I was at a great loss; for, of all the trades in the world, I was as perfectly unqualified for a stone-cutter as for any whatever; neither had I any tools to go about it with. I spent many a day to find out a great stone big enough to cut hollow, and make fit for a mortar, and could find none at all, except what was in the solid rock, and which I had no way to dig or cut out; nor indeed were the rocks in the island of hardness sufficient, but were all of a sandy, crumbling stone, which neither would bear the weight of a heavy pestle, nor would break the corn without filling it with sand. So, after a great deal of time lost in searching for a stone, I gave it over, and resolved to look out for a great block of hard wood, which I found, indeed, much easier; and getting one as big as I had strength to stir, I rounded it, and formed it on the outside with my axe and hatchet, and then with the help of fire and infinite labour, made a hollow place in it, as the Indians in Brazil make their canoes. After this, I made a great heavy pestle or beater of the wood called the iron-wood; and this I prepared and laid by against I had my next crop of corn, which I proposed to myself to grind, or rather pound into meal to make bread.

My next difficulty was to make a sieve or searce, to dress my meal, and to part it from the bran and the husk; without which I did not see it possible I could have any bread. This was a most difficult thing even to think on, for to be sure I had nothing like the necessary thing to make it—I mean fine thin canvas or stuff to searce the meal through. And here I was at a full stop for many months; nor did I really know what to do. Linen I had none left but what was mere rags; I had goat's hair, but neither knew how to weave it or spin it; and had I known how, here were no tools to work it with. All the remedy that I found for this was, that at last I did remember I had, among the seamen's clothes which were saved out of the ship, some neckcloths of calico or muslin; and with some pieces of these I made three small sieves proper enough for the work; and thus I made shift for some years: how I did afterwards, I shall show in its place.

The baking part was the next thing to be considered, and how I should make bread when I came to have corn; for first, I had no yeast. As to that part, there was no supplying the want, so I did not concern myself much about it. But for an oven I was indeed in great pain. At length I found out an experiment for that also, which was this: I made some earthen-vessels very broad but not deep, that is to say, about two feet diameter, and not above nine inches deep. These I burned in the fire, as I had done the other, and laid them by; and when I wanted to bake, I made a great fire upon my hearth, which I had paved with some square tiles of my own baking and burning also; but I should not call them square.

When the firewood was burned pretty much into embers or live coals, I drew them forward upon this hearth, so as to cover it all over, and there I let them lie till the hearth was very hot. Then sweeping away all the embers, I set down my loaf or loaves, and whelming down the earthen pot upon them, drew the embers all round the outside of the pot, to keep in and add to the heat; and thus as well as in the best oven in the world, I baked my barley-loaves, and became in little time a good pastrycook into the bargain; for I made myself several cakes and puddings of the rice; but I made no pies, neither had I anything to put into them supposing I had, except the flesh either of fowls or goats.

It need not be wondered at if all these things took me up most part of the third year of my abode here; for it is to be observed that in the intervals of these things I had my new harvest and husbandry to manage; for I reaped my corn in its season, and carried it home as well as I could, and laid it up in the ear, in my large baskets, till I had time to rub it out, for I had no floor to thrash it on, or instrument to thrash it with.

And now, indeed, my stock of corn increasing, I really wanted to build my barns bigger; I wanted a place to lay it up in, for the increase of the corn now yielded me so much, that I had of the barley about twenty bushels, and of the rice as much or more; insomuch that now I resolved to begin to use it freely; for my bread had been quite gone a great while; also I resolved to see what quantity would be sufficient for me a whole year, and to sow but once a year.

Upon the whole, I found that the forty bushels of barley and rice were much more than I could consume in a year; so I resolved to sow just the same quantity every year that I sowed the last, in hopes that such a quantity would fully provide me with bread, &c.

All the while these things were doing, you may be sure my thoughts ran many times upon the prospect of land which I had seen from the other side of the island; and I was not without secret wishes that I were on shore there, fancying that, seeing the mainland, and an inhabited country, I might find some way or other to convey myself further, and perhaps at last find some means of escape.

But all this while I made no allowance for the dangers of such an undertaking, and how I might fall into the hands of savages, and perhaps such as I might have reason to think far worse than the lions and tigers of Africa: that if I once came in their power, I should run a hazard of more than a thousand to one of being killed, and perhaps of being eaten; for I had heard that the people of the Caribbean coast were cannibals or man-eaters, and I knew by the latitude that I could not be far from that shore. Then, supposing they were not cannibals, yet they might kill me, as many Europeans who had fallen into their hands had been served, even when they had been ten or twenty together—much more I, that was but one, and could make little or no defence; all these things, I say, which I ought to have considered well; and did come into my thoughts afterwards, yet gave me no apprehensions at first, and my head ran mightily upon the thought of getting over to the shore.

Now I wished for my boy Xury, and the long-boat with shoulder-of-mutton sail, with which I sailed above a thousand miles on the coast of Africa; but this was in vain: then I thought I would go and look at our ship's boat, which, as I have said, was blown up upon the shore a great way, in the storm, when we were first cast away. She lay almost where she did at first, but not quite; and was turned, by the force of the waves and the winds, almost bottom upward, against a high ridge of beachy, rough sand, but no water about her. If I had had hands to have refitted her, and to have launched her into the water, the boat would have done well enough, and I might have gone back into the Brazils with her easily enough; but I might have foreseen that I could no more turn her and set her upright upon her bottom than I could remove the island; however, I went to the woods, and cut levers and rollers, and brought them to the boat resolving to try what I could do; suggesting to myself that if I could but turn her down, I might repair the damage she had received, and she would be a very good boat, and I might go to sea in her very easily.

I spared no pains, indeed, in this piece of fruitless toil, and spent, I think, three or four weeks about it; at last finding it impossible to heave it up with my little strength, I fell to digging away the sand, to undermine it, and so to make it fall down, setting pieces of wood to thrust and guide it right in the fall.

But when I had done this, I was unable to stir it up again, or to get under it, much less to move it forward towards the water; so I was forced to give it over; and yet, though I gave over the hopes of the boat, my desire to venture over for the main increased, rather than decreased, as the means for it seemed impossible.

This at length put me upon thinking whether it was not possible to make myself a canoe, or periagua, such as the natives of those climates make, even without tools, or, as I might say, without hands, of the trunk of a great tree. This I not only thought possible, but easy, and pleased myself extremely with the thoughts of making it, and with my having much more convenience for it than any of the negroes or Indians; but not at all considering the particular inconveniences which I lay under more than the Indians did—viz. want of hands to move it, when it was made, into the water—a difficulty much harder for me to surmount than all the consequences of want of tools could be to them; for what was it to me, if when I had chosen a vast tree in the woods, and with much trouble cut it down, if I had been able with my tools to hew and dub the outside into the proper shape of a boat, and burn or cut out the inside to make it hollow, so as to make a boat of it—if, after all this, I must leave it just there where I found it, and not be able to launch it into the water?

One would have thought I could not have had the least reflection upon my mind of my circumstances while I was making this boat, but I should have immediately thought how I should get it into the sea; but my thoughts were so intent upon my voyage over the sea in it, that I never once considered how I should get it off the land: and it was really, in its own nature, more easy for me to guide it over forty-five miles of sea than about forty-five fathoms of land, where it lay, to set it afloat in the water.

I went to work upon this boat the most like a fool that ever man did who had any of his senses awake. I pleased myself with the design, without determining whether I was ever able to undertake it; not but that the difficulty of launching my boat came often into my head; but I put a stop to my inquiries into it by this foolish answer which I gave myself—"Let me first make it; I warrant I will find some way or other to get it along when it is done."

This was a most preposterous method; but the eagerness of my fancy prevailed, and to work I went. I felled a cedar-tree, and I question much whether Solomon ever had such a one for the building of the Temple of Jerusalem; it was five feet ten inches diameter at the lower part next the stump, and four feet eleven inches diameter at the end of twenty-two feet; after which it lessened for a while, and then parted into branches. It was not without infinite labour that I felled this tree; I was twenty days hacking and hewing at it at the bottom; I was fourteen more getting the branches and limbs and the vast spreading head cut off, which I hacked and hewed through with axe and hatchet, and inexpressible labour; after this, it cost me a month to shape it and dub it to a proportion, and to something like the bottom of a boat, that it might swim upright as it ought to do. It cost me near three months more to clear the inside, and work it out so as to make an exact boat of it; this I did, indeed, without fire, by mere mallet and chisel, and by the dint of hard labour, till I had brought it to be a very handsome periagua, and big enough to have carried six-and-twenty men, and consequently big enough to have carried me and all my cargo.

When I had gone through this work I was extremely delighted with it. The boat was really much bigger than ever I saw a canoe or periagua, that was made of one tree, in my life. Many a weary stroke it had cost, you may be sure; and had I gotten it into the water, I make no question, but I should have begun the maddest voyage, and the most unlikely to be performed, that ever was undertaken.

But all my devices to get it into the water failed me; though they cost me infinite labour too. It lay about one hundred yards from the water, and not more; but the first inconvenience was, it was up hill towards the creek. Well, to take away this discouragement, I resolved to dig into the surface of the earth, and so make a declivity: this I began, and it cost me a prodigious deal of pains (but who grudge pains who have their deliverance in view?); but when this was worked through, and this difficulty managed, it was still much the same, for I could no more stir the canoe than I could the other boat. Then I measured the distance of ground, and resolved to cut a dock or canal, to bring the water up to the canoe, seeing I could not bring the canoe down to the water. Well, I began this work; and when I began to enter upon it, and calculate how deep it was to be dug, how broad, how the stuff was to be thrown out, I found that, by the number of hands I had, being none but my own, it must have been ten or twelve years before I could have gone through with it; for the shore lay so high, that at the upper end it must have been at least twenty feet deep; so at length, though with great reluctancy, I gave this attempt over also.

This grieved me heartily; and now I saw, though too late, the folly of beginning a work before we count the cost, and before we judge rightly of our own strength to go through with it.

In the middle of this work I finished my fourth year in this place, and kept my anniversary with the same devotion, and with as much comfort as ever before; for, by a constant study and serious application to the Word of God, and by the assistance of His grace, I gained a different knowledge from what I had before. I entertained different notions of things. I looked now upon the world as a thing remote, which I had nothing to do with, no expectations from, and, indeed, no desires about: in a word, I had nothing indeed to do with it, nor was ever likely to have, so I thought it looked, as we may perhaps look upon it hereafter—viz. as a place I had lived in, but was come out of it; and well might I say, as Father Abraham to Dives, "Between me and thee is a great gulf fixed."

In the first place, I was removed from all the wickedness of the world here; I had neither the lusts of the flesh, the lusts of the eye, nor the pride of life. I had nothing to covet, for I had all that I was now capable of enjoying; I was lord of the whole manor; or, if I pleased, I might call myself king or emperor over the whole country which I had possession of: there were no rivals; I had no competitor, none to dispute sovereignty or command with me: I might have raised shiploadings of corn, but I had no use for it; so I let as little grow as I thought enough for my occasion. I had tortoise or turtle enough, but now and then one was as much as I could put to any use: I had timber enough to have built a fleet of ships; and I had grapes enough to have made wine, or to have cured into raisins, to have loaded that fleet when it had been built.

But all I could make use of was all that was valuable: I had enough to eat and supply my wants, and what was all the rest to me? If I killed more flesh than I could eat, the dog must eat it, or vermin; if I sowed more corn than I could eat, it must be spoiled; the trees that I cut down were lying to rot on the ground; I could make no more use of them but for fuel, and that I had no occasion for but to dress my food.

In a word, the nature and experience of things dictated to me, upon just reflection, that all the good things of this world are no farther good to us than they are for our use; and that, whatever we may heap up to give others, we enjoy just as much as we can use, and no more. The most covetous, griping miser in the world would have been cured of the vice of covetousness if he had been in my case; for I possessed infinitely more than I knew what to do with. I had no room for desire, except it was of things which I had not, and they were but trifles, though, indeed, of great use to me. I had, as I hinted before, a parcel of money, as well gold as silver, about thirty-six pounds sterling. Alas! there the sorry, useless stuff lay; I had no more manner of business for it; and often thought with myself that I would have given a handful of it for a gross of tobacco-pipes; or for a hand-mill to grind my corn; nay, I would have given it all for a sixpenny-worth of turnip and carrot seed out of England, or for a handful of peas and beans, and a bottle of ink. As it was, I had not the least advantage by it or benefit from it; but there it lay in a drawer, and grew mouldy with the damp of the cave in the wet seasons; and if I had had the drawer full of diamonds, it had been the same case—they had been of no manner of value to me, because of no use.

I had now brought my state of life to be much easier in itself than it was at first, and much easier to my mind, as well as to my body. I frequently sat down to meat with thankfulness, and admired the hand of God's providence, which had thus spread my table in the wilderness. I learned to look more upon the bright side of my condition, and less upon the dark side, and to consider what I enjoyed rather than what I wanted; and this gave me sometimes such secret comforts, that I cannot express them; and which I take notice of here, to put those discontented people in mind of it, who cannot enjoy comfortably what God has given them, because they see and covet something that He has not given them. All our discontents about what we want appeared to me to spring from the want of thankfulness for what we have.

Another reflection was of great use to me, and doubtless would be so to any one that should fall into such distress as mine was; and this was, to compare my present condition with what I at first expected it would be; nay, with what it would certainly have been, if the good providence of God had not wonderfully ordered the ship to be cast up nearer to the shore, where I not only could come at her, but could bring what I got out of her to the shore, for my relief and comfort; without which, I had wanted for tools to work, weapons for defence, and gunpowder and shot for getting my food.

I spent whole hours, I may say whole days, in representing to myself, in the most lively colours, how I must have acted if I had got nothing out of the ship. How I could not have so much as got any food, except fish and turtles; and that, as it was long before I found any of them, I must have perished first; that I should have lived, if I had not perished, like a mere savage; that if I had killed a goat or a fowl, by any contrivance, I had no way to flay or open it, or part the flesh from the skin and the bowels, or to cut it up; but must gnaw it with my teeth, and pull it with my claws, like a beast.

These reflections made me very sensible of the goodness of Providence to me, and very thankful for my present condition, with all its hardships and misfortunes; and this part also I cannot but recommend to the reflection of those who are apt, in their misery, to say, "Is any affliction like mine?" Let them consider how much worse the cases of some people are, and their case might have been, if Providence had thought fit.

I had another reflection, which assisted me also to comfort my mind with hopes; and this was comparing my present situation with what I had deserved, and had therefore reason to expect from the hand of Providence. I had lived a dreadful life, perfectly destitute of the knowledge and fear of God. I had been well instructed by father and mother; neither had they been wanting to me in their early endeavours to infuse a religious awe of God into my mind, a sense of my duty, and what the nature and end of my being required of me. But, alas! falling early into the seafaring life, which of all lives is the most destitute of the fear of God, though His terrors are always before them; I say, falling early into the seafaring life, and into seafaring company, all that little sense of religion which I had entertained was laughed out of me by my messmates; by a hardened despising of dangers, and the views of death, which grew habitual to me by my long absence from all manner of opportunities to converse with anything but what was like myself, or to hear anything that was good or tended towards it.

Chapter IX—A BOAT

So void was I of everything that was good, or the least sense of what I was, or was to be, that, in the greatest deliverances I enjoyed—such as my escape from Sallee; my being taken up by the Portuguese master of the ship; my being planted so well in the Brazils; my receiving the cargo from England, and the like—I never had once the words "Thank God!" so much as on my mind, or in my mouth; nor in the greatest distress had I so much as a thought to pray to Him, or so much as to say, "Lord, have mercy upon me!" no, nor to mention the name of God, unless it was to swear by, and blaspheme it.

I had terrible reflections upon my mind for many months, as I have already observed, on account of my wicked and hardened life past; and when I looked about me, and considered what particular providences had attended me since my coming into this place, and how God had dealt bountifully with me—had not only punished me less than my iniquity had deserved, but had so plentifully provided for me—this gave me great hopes that my repentance was accepted, and that God had yet mercy in store for me.

With these reflections I worked my mind up, not only to a resignation to the will of God in the present disposition of my circumstances, but even to a sincere thankfulness for my condition; and that I, who was yet a living man, ought not to complain, seeing I had not the due punishment of my sins; that I enjoyed so many mercies which I had no reason to have expected in that place; that I ought never more to repine at my condition, but to rejoice, and to give daily thanks for that daily bread, which nothing but a crowd of wonders could have brought; that I ought to consider I had been fed even by a miracle, even as great as that of feeding Elijah by ravens, nay, by a long series of miracles; and that I could hardly have named a place in the uninhabitable part of the world where I could have been cast more to my advantage; a place where, as I had no society, which was my affliction on one hand, so I found no ravenous beasts, no furious wolves or tigers, to threaten my life; no venomous creatures, or poisons, which I might feed on to my hurt; no savages to murder and devour me. In a word, as my life was a life of sorrow one way, so it was a life of mercy another; and I wanted nothing to make it a life of comfort but to be able to make my sense of God's goodness to me, and care over me in this condition, be my daily consolation; and after I did make a just improvement on these things, I went away, and was no more sad. I had now been here so long that many things which I had brought on shore for my help were either quite gone, or very much wasted and near spent.

My ink, as I observed, had been gone some time, all but a very little, which I eked out with water, a little and a little, till it was so pale, it scarce left any appearance of black upon the paper. As long as it lasted I made use of it to minute down the days of the month on which any remarkable thing happened to me; and first, by casting up times past, I remembered that there was a strange concurrence of days in the various providences which befell me, and which, if I had been superstitiously inclined to observe days as fatal or fortunate, I might have had reason to have looked upon with a great deal of curiosity.

First, I had observed that the same day that I broke away from my father and friends and ran away to Hull, in order to go to sea, the same day afterwards I was taken by the Sallee man-of-war, and made a slave; the same day of the year that I escaped out of the wreck of that ship in Yarmouth Roads, that same day-year afterwards I made my escape from Sallee in a boat; the same day of the year I was born on—viz. the 30th of September, that same day I had my life so miraculously saved twenty-six years after, when I was cast on shore in this island; so that my wicked life and my solitary life began both on a day.

The next thing to my ink being wasted was that of my bread—I mean the biscuit which I brought out of the ship; this I had husbanded to the last degree, allowing myself but one cake of bread a-day for above a year; and yet I was quite without bread for near a year before I got any corn of my own, and great reason I had to be thankful that I had any at all, the getting it being, as has been already observed, next to miraculous.

My clothes, too, began to decay; as to linen, I had had none a good while, except some chequered shirts which I found in the chests of the other seamen, and which I carefully preserved; because many times I could bear no other clothes on but a shirt; and it was a very great help to me that I had, among all the men's clothes of the ship, almost three dozen of shirts. There were also, indeed, several thick watch-coats of the seamen's which were left, but they were too hot to wear; and though it is true that the weather was so violently hot that there was no need of clothes, yet I could not go quite naked—no, though I had been inclined to it, which I was not—nor could I abide the thought of it, though I was alone. The reason why I could not go naked was, I could not bear the heat of the sun so well when quite naked as with some clothes on; nay, the very heat frequently blistered my skin: whereas, with a shirt on, the air itself made some motion, and whistling under the shirt, was twofold cooler than without it. No more could I ever bring myself to go out in the heat of the sun without a cap or a hat; the heat of the sun, beating with such violence as it does in that place, would give me the headache presently, by darting so directly on my head, without a cap or hat on, so that I could not bear it; whereas, if I put on my hat it would presently go away.

Upon these views I began to consider about putting the few rags I had, which I called clothes, into some order; I had worn out all the waistcoats I had, and my business was now to try if I could not make jackets out of the great watch-coats which I had by me, and with such other materials as I had; so I set to work, tailoring, or rather, indeed, botching, for I made most piteous work of it. However, I made shift to make two or three new waistcoats, which I hoped would serve me a great while: as for breeches or drawers, I made but a very sorry shift indeed till afterwards.

I have mentioned that I saved the skins of all the creatures that I killed, I mean four-footed ones, and I had them hung up, stretched out with sticks in the sun, by which means some of them were so dry and hard that they were fit for little, but others were very useful. The first thing I made of these was a great cap for my head, with the hair on the outside, to shoot off the rain; and this I performed so well, that after I made me a suit of clothes wholly of these skins—that is to say, a waistcoat, and breeches open at the knees, and both loose, for they were rather wanting to keep me cool than to keep me warm. I must not omit to acknowledge that they were wretchedly made; for if I was a bad carpenter, I was a worse tailor. However, they were such as I made very good shift with, and when I was out, if it happened to rain, the hair of my waistcoat and cap being outermost, I was kept very dry.

After this, I spent a great deal of time and pains to make an umbrella; I was, indeed, in great want of one, and had a great mind to make one; I had seen them made in the Brazils, where they are very useful in the great heats there, and I felt the heats every jot as great here, and greater too, being nearer the equinox; besides, as I was obliged to be much abroad, it was a most useful thing to me, as well for the rains as the heats. I took a world of pains with it, and was a great while before I could make anything likely to hold: nay, after I had thought I had hit the way, I spoiled two or three before I made one to my mind: but at last I made one that answered indifferently well: the main difficulty I found was to make it let down. I could make it spread, but if it did not let down too, and draw in, it was not portable for me any way but just over my head, which would not do. However, at last, as I said, I made one to answer, and covered it with skins, the hair upwards, so that it cast off the rain like a pent-house, and kept off the sun so effectually, that I could walk out in the hottest of the weather with greater advantage than I could before in the coolest, and when I had no need of it could close it, and carry it under my arm.

Thus I lived mighty comfortably, my mind being entirely composed by resigning myself to the will of God, and throwing myself wholly upon the disposal of His providence. This made my life better than sociable, for when I began to regret the want of conversation I would ask myself, whether thus conversing mutually with my own thoughts, and (as I hope I may say) with even God Himself, by ejaculations, was not better than the utmost enjoyment of human society in the world?

Chapter X—TAMES GOATS

I cannot say that after this, for five years, any extraordinary thing happened to me, but I lived on in the same course, in the same posture and place, as before; the chief things I was employed in, besides my yearly labour of planting my barley and rice, and curing my raisins, of both which I always kept up just enough to have sufficient stock of one year's provisions beforehand; I say, besides this yearly labour, and my daily pursuit of going out with my gun, I had one labour, to make a canoe, which at last I finished: so that, by digging a canal to it of six feet wide and four feet deep, I brought it into the creek, almost half a mile. As for the first, which was so vastly big, for I made it without considering beforehand, as I ought to have done, how I should be able to launch it, so, never being able to bring it into the water, or bring the water to it, I was obliged to let it lie where it was as a memorandum to teach me to be wiser the next time: indeed, the next time, though I could not get a tree proper for it, and was in a place where I could not get the water to it at any less distance than, as I have said, near half a mile, yet, as I saw it was practicable at last, I never gave it over; and though I was near two years about it, yet I never grudged my labour, in hopes of having a boat to go off to sea at last.

However, though my little periagua was finished, yet the size of it was not at all answerable to the design which I had in view when I made the first; I mean of venturing over to the *terra firma*, where it was above forty miles broad; accordingly, the smallness of my boat assisted to put an end to that design, and now I thought no more of it. As I had a boat, my next design was to make a cruise round the island; for as I had been on the other side in one place, crossing, as I have already described it, over the land, so the discoveries I made in that little journey made me very eager to see other parts of the coast; and now I had a boat, I thought of nothing but sailing round the island.

For this purpose, that I might do everything with discretion and consideration, I fitted up a little mast in my boat, and made a sail too out of some of the pieces of the ship's sails which lay in store, and of which I had a great stock by me. Having fitted my mast and sail, and tried the boat, I found she would sail very well; then I made little lockers or boxes at each end of my boat, to put provisions, necessaries, ammunition, &c., into, to be kept dry, either from rain or the spray of the sea; and a little, long, hollow place I cut in the inside of the boat, where I could lay my gun, making a flap to hang down over it to keep it dry.

I fixed my umbrella also in the step at the stern, like a mast, to stand over my head, and keep the heat of the sun off me, like an awning; and thus I every now and then took a little voyage upon the sea, but never went far out, nor far from the little creek. At last, being eager to view the circumference of my little kingdom, I resolved upon my cruise; and accordingly I victualled my ship for the voyage, putting in two dozen of loaves (cakes I should call them) of barley-bread, an earthen pot full of parched rice (a food I ate a good deal of), a little bottle of rum, half a goat, and powder and shot for killing more, and two large watch-coats, of those which, as I mentioned before, I had saved out of the seamen's chests; these I took, one to lie upon, and the other to cover me in the night.

It was the 6th of November, in the sixth year of my reign—or my captivity, which you please—that I set out on this voyage, and I found it much longer than I expected; for though the island itself was not very large, yet when I came to the east side of it, I found a great ledge of rocks lie out about two leagues into the sea, some above water, some under it; and beyond that a shoal of sand, lying dry half a league more, so that I was obliged to go a great way out to sea to double the point.

When I first discovered them, I was going to give over my enterprise, and come back again, not knowing how far it might oblige me to go out to sea; and above all, doubting how I should get back again: so I came to an anchor; for I had made a kind of an anchor with a piece of a broken grappling which I got out of the ship.

Having secured my boat, I took my gun and went on shore, climbing up a hill, which seemed to overlook that point where I saw the full extent of it, and resolved to venture.

In my viewing the sea from that hill where I stood, I perceived a strong, and indeed a most furious current, which ran to the east, and even came close to the point; and I took the more notice of it because I saw there might be some danger that when I came into it I might be carried out to sea by the strength of it, and not be able to make the island again; and indeed, had I not got first upon this hill, I believe it would have been so; for there was the same current on the other side the island, only that it set off at a further distance, and I saw there was a strong eddy under the shore; so I had nothing to do but to get out of the first current, and I should presently be in an eddy.

I lay here, however, two days, because the wind blowing pretty fresh at ESE., and that being just contrary to the current, made a great breach of the sea upon the point: so that it was not safe for me to keep too close to the shore for the breach, nor to go too far off, because of the stream.

The third day, in the morning, the wind having abated overnight, the sea was calm, and I ventured: but I am a warning to all rash and ignorant pilots; for no sooner was I come to the point, when I was not even my boat's length from the shore, but I found myself in a great depth of water, and a current like the sluice of a mill; it carried my boat along with it with such violence that all I could do could not keep her so much as on the edge of it; but I found it hurried me farther and farther out from the eddy, which was on my left hand. There was no wind stirring to help me, and all I could do with my paddles signified nothing: and now I began to give myself over for lost; for as the current was on both sides of the island, I knew in a few leagues distance they must join again, and then I was irrecoverably gone; nor did I see any possibility of avoiding it; so that I had no prospect before me but of perishing, not by the sea, for that was calm enough, but of starving from hunger. I had, indeed, found a tortoise on the shore, as big almost as I could lift, and had tossed it into the boat; and I had a great jar of fresh water, that is to say, one of my earthen pots; but what was all this to being driven into the vast ocean, where, to be sure, there was no shore, no mainland or island, for a thousand leagues at least?

And now I saw how easy it was for the providence of God to make even the most miserable condition of mankind worse. Now I looked back upon my desolate, solitary island as the most pleasant place in the world and all the happiness my heart could wish for was to be but there again. I stretched out my hands to it, with eager wishes—"O happy desert!" said I, "I shall never see thee more. O miserable creature! whither am going?" Then I reproached myself with my unthankful temper, and that I had repined at my solitary condition; and now what would I give to be on shore there again! Thus, we never see the true state of our condition till it is illustrated to us by its contraries, nor know how to value what we enjoy, but by the want of it. It is scarcely possible to imagine the consternation I was now in, being driven from my beloved island (for so it appeared to me now to be) into the wide ocean, almost two leagues, and in the utmost despair of ever recovering it again. However, I worked hard till, indeed, my strength was almost exhausted, and kept my boat as much to the northward, that is, towards the side of the current which the eddy lay on, as possibly I could; when about noon, as the sun passed the meridian, I thought I felt a little breeze of wind in my face, springing up from SSE. This cheered my heart a little, and especially when, in about half-an-hour more, it blew a pretty gentle gale. By this time I had got at a frightful distance from the island, and had the least cloudy or hazy weather intervened, I had been undone another way, too; for I had no compass on board, and should never have known how to have steered towards the island, if I had but once lost sight of it; but the weather continuing clear, I applied myself to get up my mast again, and spread my sail, standing away to the north as much as possible, to get out of the current.

Just as I had set my mast and sail, and the boat began to stretch away, I saw even by the clearness of the water some alteration of the current was near; for where the current was so strong the water was foul; but perceiving the water clear, I found the current abate; and presently I found to the east, at about half a mile, a breach of the sea upon some rocks: these rocks I found caused the current to part again, and as the main stress of it ran away more southerly, leaving the rocks to the north-east, so the other returned by the repulse of the rocks, and made a strong eddy, which ran back again to the north-west, with a very sharp stream.

They who know what it is to have a reprieve brought to them upon the ladder, or to be rescued from thieves just going to murder them, or who have been in such extremities, may guess what my present surprise of joy was, and how gladly I put my boat into the stream of this eddy; and the wind also freshening, how gladly I spread my sail to it, running cheerfully before the wind, and with a strong tide or eddy underfoot.

This eddy carried me about a league on my way back again, directly towards the island, but about two leagues more to the northward than the current which carried me away at first; so that when I came near the island, I found myself open to the northern shore of it, that is to say, the other end of the island, opposite to that which I went out from.

When I had made something more than a league of way by the help of this current or eddy, I found it was spent, and served me no further. However, I found that being between two great currents—viz. that on the south side, which had hurried me away, and that on the north, which lay about a league on the other side; I say, between these two, in the wake of the island, I found the water at least still, and running no way; and having still a breeze of wind fair for me, I kept on steering directly for the island, though not making such fresh way as I did before.

About four o'clock in the evening, being then within a league of the island, I found the point of the rocks which occasioned this disaster stretching out, as is described before, to the southward, and casting off the current more southerly, had, of course, made another eddy to the north; and this I found very strong, but not directly setting the way my course lay, which was due west, but almost full north. However, having a fresh gale, I stretched across this eddy, slanting northwest; and in about an hour came within about a mile of the shore, where, it being smooth water, I soon got to land.

When I was on shore, God I fell on my knees and gave God thanks for my deliverance, resolving to lay aside all thoughts of my deliverance by my boat; and refreshing myself with such things as I had, I brought my boat close to the shore, in a little cove that I had spied under some trees, and laid me down to sleep, being quite spent with the labour and fatigue of the voyage.

I was now at a great loss which way to get home with my boat! I had run so much hazard, and knew too much of the case, to think of attempting it by the way I went out; and what might be at the other side (I mean the west side) I knew not, nor had I any mind to run any more ventures; so I resolved on the next morning to make my way westward along the shore, and to see if there was no creek where I might lay up my frigate in safety, so as to have her again if I wanted her. In about three miles or thereabouts, coasting the shore, I came to a very good inlet or bay, about a mile over, which narrowed till it came to a very little rivulet or brook, where I found a very convenient harbour for my boat, and where she lay as if she had been in a little dock made on purpose for her. Here I put in, and having stowed my boat very safe, I went on shore to look about me, and see where I was.

I soon found I had but a little passed by the place where I had been before, when I travelled on foot to that shore; so taking nothing out of my boat but my gun and umbrella, for it was exceedingly hot, I began my march. The way was comfortable enough after such a voyage as I had been upon, and I reached my old bower in the evening, where I found everything standing as I left it; for I always kept it in good order, being, as I said before, my country house.

I got over the fence, and laid me down in the shade to rest my limbs, for I was very weary, and fell asleep; but judge you, if you can, that read my story, what a surprise I must be in when I was awaked out of my sleep by a voice calling me by my name several times, "Robin, Robin, Robin Crusoe: poor Robin Crusoe! Where are you, Robin Crusoe? Where are you? Where have you been?"

I was so dead asleep at first, being fatigued with rowing, or part of the day, and with walking the latter part, that I did not wake thoroughly; but dozing thought I dreamed that somebody spoke to me; but as the voice continued to repeat, "Robin Crusoe, Robin Crusoe," at last I began to wake more perfectly, and was at first dreadfully frightened, and started up in the utmost consternation; but no sooner were my eyes open, but I saw my Poll sitting on the top of the hedge; and immediately knew that it was he that spoke to me; for just in such bemoaning language I had used to talk to him and teach him; and he had learned it so perfectly that he would sit upon my finger, and lay his bill close to my face and cry, "Poor Robin Crusoe! Where are you? Where have you been? How came you here?" and such things as I had taught him.

However, even though I knew it was the parrot, and that indeed it could be nobody else, it was a good while before I could compose myself. First, I was amazed how the creature got thither; and then, how he should just keep about the place, and nowhere else; but as I was well satisfied it could be nobody but honest Poll, I got over it; and holding out my hand, and calling him by his name, "Poll," the sociable creature came to me, and sat upon my thumb, as he used to do, and continued talking to me, "Poor Robin Crusoe! and how did I come here? and where had I been?" just as if he had been overjoyed to see me again; and so I carried him home along with me.

I had now had enough of rambling to sea for some time, and had enough to do for many days to sit still and reflect upon the danger I had been in. I would have been very glad to have had my boat again on my side of the island; but I knew not how it was practicable to get it about. As to the east side of the island, which I had gone round, I knew well enough there was no venturing that way; my very heart would shrink, and my very blood run chill, but to think of it; and as to the other side of the island, I did not know how it might be there; but supposing the current ran with the same force against the shore at the east as it passed by it on the other, I might run the same risk of being driven down the stream, and carried by the island, as I had been before of being carried away from it: so with these thoughts, I contented myself to be without any boat, though it had been the product of so many months' labour to make it, and of so many more to get it into the sea.

In this government of my temper I remained near a year; and lived a very sedate, retired life, as you may well suppose; and my thoughts being very much composed as to my condition, and fully comforted in resigning myself to the dispositions of Providence, I thought I lived really very happily in all things except that of society.

I improved myself in this time in all the mechanic exercises which my necessities put me upon applying myself to; and I believe I should, upon occasion, have made a very good carpenter, especially considering how few tools I had.

Besides this, I arrived at an unexpected perfection in my earthenware, and contrived well enough to make them with a wheel, which I found infinitely easier and better; because I made things round and shaped, which before were filthy things indeed to look on. But I think I was never more vain of my own performance, or more joyful for anything I found out, than for my being able to make a tobacco-pipe; and though it was a very ugly, clumsy thing when it was done, and only burned red, like other earthenware, yet as it was hard and firm, and would draw the smoke, I was exceedingly comforted with it, for I had been always used to smoke; and there were pipes in the ship, but I forgot them at first, not thinking there was tobacco in the island; and afterwards, when I searched the ship again, I could not come at any pipes.

In my wicker-ware also I improved much, and made abundance of necessary baskets, as well as my invention showed me; though not very handsome, yet they were such as were very handy and convenient for laying things up in, or fetching things home. For example, if I killed a goat abroad, I could hang it up in a tree, flay it, dress it, and cut it in pieces, and bring it home in a basket; and the like by a turtle; I could cut it up, take out the eggs and a piece or two of the flesh, which was enough for me, and bring them home in a basket, and leave the rest behind me. Also, large deep baskets were the receivers of my corn, which I always rubbed out as soon as it was dry and cured, and kept it in great baskets.

I began now to perceive my powder abated considerably; this was a want which it was impossible for me to supply, and I began seriously to consider what I must do when I should have no more powder; that is to say, how I should kill any goats. I had, as is observed in the third year of my being here, kept a young kid, and bred her up tame, and I was in hopes of getting a he-goat; but I could not by any means bring it to pass, till my kid grew an old goat; and as I could never find in my heart to kill her, she died at last of mere age.

But being now in the eleventh year of my residence, and, as I have said, my ammunition growing low, I set myself to study some art to trap and snare the goats, to see whether I could not catch some of them alive; and particularly I wanted a she-goat great with young. For this purpose I made snares to hamper them; and I do believe they were more than once taken in them; but my tackle was not good, for I had no wire, and I always found them broken and my bait devoured. At length I resolved to try a pitfall; so I dug several large pits in the earth, in places where I had observed the goats used to feed, and over those pits I placed hurdles of my own making too, with a great weight upon them; and several times I put ears of barley and dry rice without setting the trap; and I could easily perceive that the goats had gone in and eaten up the corn, for I could see the marks of their feet. At length I set three traps in one night, and going the next morning I found them, all standing, and yet the bait eaten and gone; this was very discouraging. However, I altered my traps; and not to trouble you with particulars, going one morning to see my traps, I found in one of them a large old he-goat; and in one of the others three kids, a male and two females.

As to the old one, I knew not what to do with him; he was so fierce I durst not go into the pit to him; that is to say, to bring him away alive, which was what I wanted. I could have killed him, but that was not my business, nor would it answer my end; so I even let him out, and he ran away as if he had been frightened out of his wits. But I did not then know what I afterwards learned, that hunger will tame a lion. If I had let him stay three or four days without food, and then have carried him some water to drink and then a little corn, he would have been as tame as one of the kids; for they are mighty sagacious, tractable creatures, where they are well used.

However, for the present I let him go, knowing no better at that time: then I went to the three kids, and taking them one by one, I tied them with strings together, and with some difficulty brought them all home.

It was a good while before they would feed; but throwing them some sweet corn, it tempted them, and they began to be tame. And now I found that if I expected to supply myself with goats' flesh, when I had no powder or shot left, breeding some up tame was my only way, when, perhaps, I might have them about my house like a flock of sheep. But then it occurred to me that I must keep the tame from the wild, or else they would always run wild when they grew up; and the only way for this was to have some enclosed piece of ground, well fenced either with hedge or pale, to keep them in so effectually, that those within might not break out, or those without break in.

This was a great undertaking for one pair of hands yet, as I saw there was an absolute necessity for doing it, my first work was to find out a proper piece of ground, where there was likely to be herbage for them to eat, water for them to drink, and cover to keep them from the sun.

Those who understand such enclosures will think I had very little contrivance when I pitched upon a place very proper for all these (being a plain, open piece of meadow land, or savannah, as our people call it in the western colonies), which had two or three little drills of fresh water in it, and at one end was very woody—I say, they will smile at my forecast, when I shall tell them I began by enclosing this piece of ground in such a manner that, my hedge or pale must have been at least two miles about. Nor was the madness of it so great as to the compass, for if it was ten miles about, I was like to have time enough to do it in; but I did not consider that my goats would be as wild in so much compass as if they had had the whole island, and I should have so much room to chase them in that I should never catch them.

My hedge was begun and carried on, I believe, about fifty yards when this thought occurred to me; so I presently stopped short, and, for the beginning, I resolved to enclose a piece of about one hundred and fifty yards in length, and one hundred yards in breadth, which, as it would maintain as many as I should have in any reasonable time, so, as my stock increased, I could add more ground to my enclosure.

This was acting with some prudence, and I went to work with courage. I was about three months hedging in the first piece; and, till I had done it, I tethered the three kids in the best part of it, and used them to feed as near me as possible, to make them familiar; and very often I would go and carry them some ears of barley, or a handful of rice, and feed them out of my hand; so that after my enclosure was finished and I let them loose, they would follow me up and down, bleating after me for a handful of corn.

This answered my end, and in about a year and a half I had a flock of about twelve goats, kids and all; and in two years more I had three-and-forty, besides several that I took and killed for my food. After that, I enclosed five several pieces of ground to feed them in, with little pens to drive them to take them as I wanted, and gates out of one piece of ground into another.

But this was not all; for now I not only had goat's flesh to feed on when I pleased, but milk too—a thing which, indeed, in the beginning, I did not so much as think of, and which, when it came into my thoughts, was really an agreeable surprise, for now I set up my dairy, and had sometimes a gallon or two of milk in a day. And as Nature, who gives supplies of food to every creature, dictates even naturally how to make use of it, so I, that had never milked a cow, much less a goat, or seen butter or cheese made only when I was a boy, after a great many essays and miscarriages, made both butter and cheese at last, also salt (though I found it partly made to my hand by the heat of the sun upon some of the rocks of the sea), and never wanted it afterwards. How mercifully can our Creator treat His creatures, even in those conditions in which they seemed to be overwhelmed in destruction! How can He sweeten the bitterest providences, and give us cause to praise Him for dungeons and prisons! What a table was here spread for me in the wilderness, where I saw nothing at first but to perish for hunger!

Chapter XI—FINDS PRINT OF MAN'S FOOT ON THE SAND

It would have made a Stoic smile to have seen me and my little family sit down to dinner. There was my majesty the prince and lord of the whole island; I had the lives of all my subjects at my absolute command; I could hang, draw, give liberty, and take it away, and no rebels among all my subjects. Then, to see how like a king I dined, too, all alone, attended by my servants! Poll, as if he had been my favourite, was the only person permitted to talk to me. My dog, who was now grown old and crazy, and had found no species to multiply his kind upon, sat always at my right hand; and two cats, one on one side of the table and one on the other, expecting now and then a bit from my hand, as a mark of especial favour.

But these were not the two cats which I brought on shore at first, for they were both of them dead, and had been interred near my habitation by my own hand; but one of them having multiplied by I know not what kind of creature, these were two which I had preserved tame; whereas the rest ran wild in the woods, and became indeed troublesome to me at last, for they would often come into my house, and plunder me too, till at last I was obliged to shoot them, and did kill a great many; at length they left me. With this attendance and in this plentiful manner I lived; neither could I be said to want anything but society; and of that, some time after this, I was likely to have too much.

I was something impatient, as I have observed, to have the use of my boat, though very loath to run any more hazards; and therefore sometimes I sat contriving ways to get her about the island, and at other times I sat myself down contented enough without her. But I had a strange uneasiness in my mind to go down to the point of the island where, as I have said in my last ramble, I went up the hill to see how the shore lay, and how the current set, that I might see what I had to do: this inclination increased upon me every day, and at length I resolved to travel thither by land, following the edge of the shore. I did so; but had any one in England met such a man as I was, it must either have frightened him, or raised a great deal of laughter; and as I frequently stood still to look at myself, I could not but smile at the notion of my travelling through Yorkshire with such an equipage, and in such a dress. Be pleased to take a sketch of my figure, as follows.

I had a great high shapeless cap, made of a goat's skin, with a flap hanging down behind, as well to keep the sun from me as to shoot the rain off from running into my neck, nothing being so hurtful in these climates as the rain upon the flesh under the clothes.

I had a short jacket of goat's skin, the skirts coming down to about the middle of the thighs, and a pair of open-kneed breeches of the same; the breeches were made of the skin of an old he-goat, whose hair hung down such a length on either side that, like pantaloons, it reached to the middle of my legs; stockings and shoes I had none, but had made me a pair of somethings, I scarce knew what to call them, like buskins, to flap over my legs, and lace on either side like spatterdashes, but of a most barbarous shape, as indeed were all the rest of my clothes.

I had on a broad belt of goat's skin dried, which I drew together with two thongs of the same instead of buckles, and in a kind of a frog on either side of this, instead of a sword and dagger, hung a little saw and a hatchet, one on one side and one on the other. I had another belt not so broad, and fastened in the same manner, which hung over my shoulder, and at the end of it, under my left arm, hung two pouches, both made of goat's skin too, in one of which hung my powder, in the other my shot. At my back I carried my basket, and on my shoulder my gun, and over my head a great clumsy, ugly, goat's-skin umbrella, but which, after all, was the most necessary thing I had about me next to my gun. As for my face, the colour of it was really not so mulatto-like as one might expect from a man not at all careful of it, and living within nine or ten degrees of the equinox. My beard I had once suffered to grow till it was about a quarter of a yard long; but as I had both scissors and razors sufficient, I had cut it pretty short, except what grew on my upper lip, which I had trimmed into a large pair of Mahometan whiskers, such as I had seen worn by some Turks at Sallee, for the Moors did not wear such, though the Turks did; of these moustachios, or whiskers, I will not say they were long enough to hang my hat upon them, but they were of a length and shape monstrous enough, and such as in England would have passed for frightful.

But all this is by-the-bye; for as to my figure, I had so few to observe me that it was of no manner of consequence, so I say no more of that. In this kind of dress I went my new journey, and was out five or six days. I travelled first along the seashore, directly to the place where I first brought my boat to an anchor to get upon the rocks; and having no boat now to take care of, I went over the land a nearer way to the same height that I was upon before, when, looking forward to the points of the rocks which lay out, and which I was obliged to double with my boat, as is said above, I was surprised to see the sea all smooth and quiet—no rippling, no motion, no current, any more there than in other places. I was at a strange loss to understand this, and resolved to spend some time in the observing it, to see if nothing from the sets of the tide had occasioned it; but I was presently convinced how it was—viz. that the tide of ebb setting from the west, and joining with the current of waters from some great river on the shore, must be the occasion of this current, and that, according as the wind blew more forcibly from the west or from the north, this current came nearer or went farther from the shore; for, waiting thereabouts till evening, I went up to the rock again, and then the tide of ebb being made, I plainly saw the current again as before, only that it ran farther off, being near half a league from the shore, whereas in my case it set close upon the shore, and hurried me and my canoe along with it, which at another time it would not have done.

This observation convinced me that I had nothing to do but to observe the ebbing and the flowing of the tide, and I might very easily bring my boat about the island again; but when I began to think of putting it in practice, I had such terror upon my spirits at the remembrance of the danger I had been in, that I could not think of it again with any patience, but, on the contrary, I took up another resolution, which was more safe, though more laborious—and this was, that I would build, or rather make, me another periagua or canoe, and so have one for one side of the island, and one for the other.

You are to understand that now I had, as I may call it, two plantations in the island—one my little fortification or tent, with the wall about it, under the rock, with the cave behind me, which by this time I had enlarged into several apartments or caves, one within another. One of these, which was the driest and largest, and had a door out beyond my wall or fortification—that is to say, beyond where my wall joined to the rock—was all filled up with the large earthen pots of which I have given an account, and with fourteen or fifteen great baskets, which would hold five or six bushels each, where I laid up my stores of provisions, especially my corn, some in the ear, cut off short from the straw, and the other rubbed out with my hand.

As for my wall, made, as before, with long stakes or piles, those piles grew all like trees, and were by this time grown so big, and spread so very much, that there was not the least appearance, to any one's view, of any habitation behind them.

Near this dwelling of mine, but a little farther within the land, and upon lower ground, lay my two pieces of corn land, which I kept duly cultivated and sowed, and which duly yielded me their harvest in its season; and whenever I had occasion for more corn, I had more land adjoining as fit as that.

Besides this, I had my country seat, and I had now a tolerable plantation there also; for, first, I had my little bower, as I called it, which I kept in repair—that is to say, I kept the hedge which encircled it in constantly fitted up to its usual height, the ladder standing always in the inside. I kept the trees, which at first were no more than stakes, but were now grown very firm and tall, always cut, so that they might spread and grow thick and wild, and make the more agreeable shade, which they did effectually to my mind. In the middle of this I had my tent always standing, being a piece of a sail spread over poles, set up for that purpose, and which never wanted any repair or renewing; and under this I had made me a squab or couch with the skins of the creatures I had killed, and with other soft things, and a blanket laid on them, such as belonged to our sea-bedding, which I had saved; and a great watch-coat to cover me. And here, whenever I had occasion to be absent from my chief seat, I took up my country habitation.

Adjoining to this I had my enclosures for my cattle, that is to say my goats, and I had taken an inconceivable deal of pains to fence and enclose this ground. I was so anxious to see it kept entire, lest the goats should break through, that I never left off till, with infinite labour, I had stuck the outside of the hedge so full of small stakes, and so near to one another, that it was rather a pale than a hedge, and there was scarce room to put a hand through between them; which afterwards, when those stakes grew, as they all did in the next rainy season, made the enclosure strong like a wall, indeed stronger than any wall.

This will testify for me that I was not idle, and that I spared no pains to bring to pass whatever appeared necessary for my comfortable support, for I considered the keeping up a breed of tame creatures thus at my hand would be a living magazine of flesh, milk, butter, and cheese for me as long as I lived in the place, if it were to be forty years; and that keeping them in my reach depended entirely upon my perfecting my enclosures to such a degree that I might be sure of keeping them together; which by this method, indeed, I so effectually secured, that when these little stakes began to grow, I had planted them so very thick that I was forced to pull some of them up again.

In this place also I had my grapes growing, which I principally depended on for my winter store of raisins, and which I never failed to preserve very carefully, as the best and most agreeable dainty of my whole diet; and indeed they were not only agreeable, but medicinal, wholesome, nourishing, and refreshing to the last degree.

As this was also about half-way between my other habitation and the place where I had laid up my boat, I generally stayed and lay here in my way thither, for I used frequently to visit my boat; and I kept all things about or belonging to her in very good order. Sometimes I went out in her to divert myself, but no more hazardous voyages would I go, scarcely ever above a stone's cast or two from the shore, I was so apprehensive of being hurried out of my knowledge again by the currents or winds, or any other accident. But now I come to a new scene of my life. It happened one day, about noon, going towards my boat, I was exceedingly surprised with the print of a man's naked foot on the shore, which was very plain to be seen on the sand. I stood like one thunderstruck, or as if I had seen an apparition. I listened, I looked round me, but I could hear nothing, nor see anything; I went up to a rising ground to look farther; I went up the shore and down the shore, but it was all one; I could see no other impression but that one. I went to it again to see if there were any more, and to observe if it might not be my fancy; but there was no room for that, for there was exactly the print of a foot—toes, heel, and every part of a foot. How it came thither I knew not, nor could I in the least imagine; but after innumerable fluttering thoughts, like a man perfectly confused and out of myself, I came home to my fortification, not feeling, as we say, the ground I went on, but terrified to the last degree, looking behind me at every two or three steps, mistaking every bush and tree, and fancying every stump at a distance to be a man. Nor is it possible to describe how many various shapes my affrighted imagination represented things to me in, how many wild ideas were found every moment in my fancy, and what strange, unaccountable whimsies came into my thoughts by the way.

When I came to my castle (for so I think I called it ever after this), I fled into it like one pursued. Whether I went over by the ladder, as first contrived, or went in at the hole in the rock, which I had called a door, I cannot remember; no, nor could I remember the next morning, for never frightened hare fled to cover, or fox to earth, with more terror of mind than I to this retreat.

I slept none that night; the farther I was from the occasion of my fright, the greater my apprehensions were, which is something contrary to the nature of such things, and especially to the usual practice of all creatures in fear; but I was so embarrassed with my own frightful ideas of the thing, that I formed nothing but dismal imaginations to myself, even though I was now a great way off. Sometimes I fancied it must be the devil, and reason joined in with me in this supposition, for how should any other thing in human shape come into the place? Where was the vessel that brought them? What marks were there of any other footstep? And how was it possible a man should come there? But then, to think that Satan should take human shape upon him in such a place, where there could be no manner of occasion for it, but to leave the print of his foot behind him, and that even for no purpose too, for he could not be sure I should see it—this was an amusement the other way. I considered that the devil might have found out abundance of other ways to have terrified me than this of the single print of a foot; that as I lived quite on the other side of the island, he would never have been so simple as to leave a mark in a place where it was ten thousand to one whether I should ever see it or not, and in the sand too, which the first surge of the sea, upon a high wind, would have defaced entirely. All this seemed inconsistent with the thing itself and with all the notions we usually entertain of the subtlety of the devil.

Abundance of such things as these assisted to argue me out of all apprehensions of its being the devil; and I presently concluded then that it must be some more dangerous creature—viz. that it must be some of the savages of the mainland opposite who had wandered out to sea in their canoes, and either driven by the currents or by contrary winds, had made the island, and had been on shore, but were gone away again to sea; being as loath, perhaps, to have stayed in this desolate island as I would have been to have had them.

While these reflections were rolling in my mind, I was very thankful in my thoughts that I was so happy as not to be thereabouts at that time, or that they did not see my boat, by which they would have concluded that some inhabitants had been in the place, and perhaps have searched farther for me. Then terrible thoughts racked my imagination about their having found out my boat, and that there were people here; and that, if so, I should certainly have them come again in greater numbers and devour me; that if it should happen that they should not find me, yet they would find my enclosure, destroy all my corn, and carry away all my flock of tame goats, and I should perish at last for mere want.

Thus my fear banished all my religious hope, all that former confidence in God, which was founded upon such wonderful experience as I had had of His goodness; as if He that had fed me by miracle hitherto could not preserve, by His power, the provision which He had made for me by His goodness. I reproached myself with my laziness, that would not sow any more corn one year than would just serve me till the next season, as if no accident could intervene to prevent my enjoying the crop that was upon the ground; and this I thought so just a reproof, that I resolved for the future to have two or three years' corn beforehand; so that, whatever might come, I might not perish for want of bread.

How strange a chequer-work of Providence is the life of man! and by what secret different springs are the affections hurried about, as different circumstances present! To-day we love what to-morrow we hate; to-day we seek what to-morrow we shun; to-day we desire what to-morrow we fear, nay, even tremble at the apprehensions of. This was exemplified in me, at this time, in the most lively manner imaginable; for I, whose only affliction was that I seemed banished from human society, that I was alone, circumscribed by the boundless ocean, cut off from mankind, and condemned to what I call silent life; that I was as one whom Heaven thought not worthy to be numbered among the living, or to appear among the rest of His creatures; that to have seen one of my own species would have seemed to me a raising me from death to life, and the greatest blessing that Heaven itself, next to the supreme blessing of salvation, could bestow; I say, that I should now tremble at the very apprehensions of seeing a man, and was ready to sink into the ground at but the shadow or silent appearance of a man having set his foot in the island.

Such is the uneven state of human life; and it afforded me a great many curious speculations afterwards, when I had a little recovered my first surprise. I considered that this was the station of life the infinitely wise and good providence of God had determined for me; that as I could not foresee what the ends of Divine wisdom might be in all this, so I was not to dispute His sovereignty; who, as I was His creature, had an undoubted right, by creation, to govern and dispose of me absolutely as He thought fit; and who, as I was a creature that had offended Him, had likewise a judicial right to condemn me to what punishment He thought fit; and that it was my part to submit to bear His indignation, because I had sinned against Him. I then reflected, that as God, who was not only righteous but omnipotent, had thought fit thus to punish and afflict me, so He was able to deliver me: that if He did not think fit to do so, it was my unquestioned duty to resign myself absolutely and entirely to His will; and, on the other hand, it was my duty also to hope in Him, pray to Him, and quietly to attend to the dictates and directions of His daily providence.

These thoughts took me up many hours, days, nay, I may say weeks and months: and one particular effect of my cogitations on this occasion I cannot omit. One morning early, lying in my bed, and filled with thoughts about my danger from the appearances of savages, I found it discomposed me very much; upon which these words of the Scripture came into my thoughts, "Call upon Me in the day of trouble, and I will deliver thee, and thou shalt glorify Me." Upon this, rising cheerfully out of my bed, my heart was not only comforted, but I was guided and encouraged to pray earnestly to God for deliverance: when I had done praying I took up my Bible, and opening it to read, the first words that presented to me were, "Wait on the Lord, and be of good cheer, and He shall strengthen thy heart; wait, I say, on the Lord." It is impossible to express the comfort this gave me. In answer, I thankfully laid down the book, and was no more sad, at least on that occasion.

In the middle of these cogitations, apprehensions, and reflections, it came into my thoughts one day that all this might be a mere chimera of my own, and that this foot might be the print of my own foot, when I came on shore from my boat: this cheered me up a little, too, and I began to persuade myself it was all a delusion; that it was nothing else but my own foot; and why might I not come that way from the boat, as well as I was going that way to the boat? Again, I considered also that I could by no means tell for certain where I had trod, and where I had not; and that if, at last, this was only the print of my own foot, I had played the part of those fools who try to make stories of spectres and apparitions, and then are frightened at them more than anybody.

Now I began to take courage, and to peep abroad again, for I had not stirred out of my castle for three days and nights, so that I began to starve for provisions; for I had little or nothing within doors but some barley-cakes and water; then I knew that my goats wanted to be milked too, which usually was my evening diversion: and the poor creatures were in great pain and inconvenience for want of it; and, indeed, it almost spoiled some of them, and almost dried up their milk. Encouraging myself, therefore, with the belief that this was nothing but the print of one of my own feet, and that I might be truly said to start at my own shadow, I began to go abroad again, and went to my country house to milk my flock: but to see with what fear I went forward, how often I looked behind me, how I was ready every now and then to lay down my basket and run for my life, it would have made any one have thought I was haunted with an evil conscience, or that I had been lately most terribly frightened; and so, indeed, I had. However, I went down thus two or three days, and having seen nothing, I began to be a little bolder, and to think there was really nothing in it but my own imagination; but I could not persuade myself fully of this till I should go down to the shore again, and see this print of a foot, and measure it by my own, and see if there was any similitude or fitness, that I might be assured it was my own foot: but when I came to the place, first, it appeared evidently to me, that when I laid up my boat I could not possibly be on shore anywhere thereabouts; secondly, when I came to measure the mark with my own foot, I found my foot not so large by a great deal. Both these things filled my head with new imaginations, and gave me the vapours again to the highest degree, so that I shook with cold like one in an ague; and I went home again, filled with the belief that some man or men had been on shore there; or, in short, that the island was inhabited, and I might be surprised before I was aware; and what course to take for my security I knew not.

Oh, what ridiculous resolutions men take when possessed with fear! It deprives them of the use of those means which reason offers for their relief. The first thing I proposed to myself was, to throw down my enclosures, and turn all my tame cattle wild into the woods, lest the enemy should find them, and then frequent the island in prospect of the same or the like booty: then the simple thing of digging up my two corn-fields, lest they should find such a grain there, and still be prompted to frequent the island: then to demolish my bower and tent, that they might not see any vestiges of habitation, and be prompted to look farther, in order to find out the persons inhabiting.

These were the subject of the first night's cogitations after I was come home again, while the apprehensions which had so overrun my mind were fresh upon me, and my head was full of vapours. Thus, fear of danger is ten thousand times more terrifying than danger itself, when apparent to the eyes; and we find the burden of anxiety greater, by much, than the evil which we are anxious about: and what was worse than all this, I had not that relief in this trouble that from the resignation I used to practise I hoped to have. I looked, I thought, like Saul, who complained not only that the Philistines were upon him, but that God had forsaken him; for I did not now take due ways to compose my mind, by crying to God in my distress, and resting upon His providence, as I had done before, for my defence and deliverance; which, if I had done, I had at least been more cheerfully supported under this new surprise, and perhaps carried through it with more resolution.

This confusion of my thoughts kept me awake all night; but in the morning I fell asleep; and having, by the amusement of my mind, been as it were tired, and my spirits exhausted, I slept very soundly, and waked much better composed than I had ever been before. And now I began to think sedately; and, upon debate with myself, I concluded that this island (which was so exceedingly pleasant, fruitful, and no farther from the mainland than as I had seen) was not so entirely abandoned as I might imagine; that although there were no stated inhabitants who lived on the spot, yet that there might sometimes come boats off from the shore, who, either with design, or perhaps never but when they were driven by cross winds, might come to this place; that I had lived there fifteen years now and had not met with the least shadow or figure of any people yet; and that, if at any time they should be driven here, it was probable they went away again as soon as ever they could, seeing they had never thought fit to fix here upon any occasion; that the most I could suggest any danger from was from any casual accidental landing of straggling people from the main, who, as it was likely, if they were driven hither, were here against their wills, so they made no stay here, but went off again with all possible speed; seldom staying one night on shore, lest they should not have the help of the tides and daylight back again; and that, therefore, I had nothing to do but to consider of some safe retreat, in case I should see any savages land upon the spot.

Now, I began sorely to repent that I had dug my cave so large as to bring a door through again, which door, as I said, came out beyond where my fortification joined to the rock: upon maturely considering this, therefore, I resolved to draw me a second fortification, in the manner of a semicircle, at a distance from my wall, just where I had planted a double row of trees about twelve years before, of which I made mention: these trees having been planted so thick before, they wanted but few piles to be driven between them, that they might be thicker and stronger, and my wall would be soon finished. So that I had now a double wall; and my outer wall was thickened with pieces of timber, old cables, and everything I could think of, to make it strong; having in it seven little holes, about as big as I might put my arm out at. In the inside of this I thickened my wall to about ten feet thick with continually bringing earth out of my cave, and laying it at the foot of the wall, and walking upon it; and through the seven holes I contrived to plant the muskets, of which I took notice that I had got seven on shore out of the ship; these I planted like my cannon, and fitted them into frames, that held them like a carriage, so that I could fire all the seven guns in two minutes' time; this wall I was many a weary month in finishing, and yet never thought myself safe till it was done.

When this was done I stuck all the ground without my wall, for a great length every way, as full with stakes or sticks of the osier-like wood, which I found so apt to grow, as they could well stand; insomuch that I believe I might set in near twenty thousand of them, leaving a pretty large space between them and my wall, that I might have room to see an enemy, and they might have no shelter from the young trees, if they attempted to approach my outer wall.

Thus in two years' time I had a thick grove; and in five or six years' time I had a wood before my dwelling, growing so monstrously thick and strong that it was indeed perfectly impassable: and no men, of what kind soever, could ever imagine that there was anything beyond it, much less a habitation. As for the way which I proposed to myself to go in and out (for I left no avenue), it was by setting two ladders, one to a part of the rock which was low, and then broke in, and left room to place another ladder upon that; so when the two ladders were taken down no man living could come down to me without doing himself mischief; and if they had come down, they were still on the outside of my outer wall.

Thus I took all the measures human prudence could suggest for my own preservation; and it will be seen at length that they were not altogether without just reason; though I foresaw nothing at that time more than my mere fear suggested to me.

Chapter XII—A CAVE RETREAT

While this was doing, I was not altogether careless of my other affairs; for I had a great concern upon me for my little herd of goats: they were not only a ready supply to me on every occasion, and began to be sufficient for me, without the expense of powder and shot, but also without the fatigue of hunting after the wild ones; and I was loath to lose the advantage of them, and to have them all to nurse up over again.

For this purpose, after long consideration, I could think of but two ways to preserve them: one was, to find another convenient place to dig a cave underground, and to drive them into it every night; and the other was to enclose two or three little bits of land, remote from one another, and as much concealed as I could, where I might keep about half-a-dozen young goats in each place; so that if any disaster happened to the flock in general, I might be able to raise them again with little trouble and time: and this though it would require a good deal of time and labour, I thought was the most rational design.

Accordingly, I spent some time to find out the most retired parts of the island; and I pitched upon one, which was as private, indeed, as my heart could wish: it was a little damp piece of ground in the middle of the hollow and thick woods, where, as is observed, I almost lost myself once before, endeavouring to come back that way from the eastern part of the island. Here I found a clear piece of land, near three acres, so surrounded with woods that it was almost an enclosure by nature; at least, it did not want near so much labour to make it so as the other piece of ground I had worked so hard at.

I immediately went to work with this piece of ground; and in less than a month's time I had so fenced it round that my flock, or herd, call it which you please, which were not so wild now as at first they might be supposed to be, were well enough secured in it: so, without any further delay, I removed ten young she-goats and two he-goats to this piece, and when they were there I continued to perfect the fence till I had made it as secure as the other; which, however, I did at more leisure, and it took me up more time by a great deal. All this labour I was at the expense of, purely from my apprehensions on account of the print of a man's foot; for as yet I had never seen any human creature come near the island; and I had now lived two years under this uneasiness, which, indeed, made my life much less comfortable than it was before, as may be well imagined by any who know what it is to live in the constant snare of the fear of man. And this I must observe, with grief, too, that the discomposure of my mind had great impression also upon the religious part of my thoughts; for the dread and terror of falling into the hands of savages and cannibals lay so upon my spirits, that I seldom found myself in a due temper for application to my Maker; at least, not with the sedate calmness and resignation of soul which I was wont to do: I rather prayed to God as under great affliction and pressure of mind, surrounded with danger, and in expectation every night of being murdered and devoured before morning; and I must testify, from my experience, that a temper of peace, thankfulness, love, and affection, is much the more proper frame for prayer than that of terror and discomposure: and that under the dread of mischief impending, a man is no more fit for a comforting performance of the duty of praying to God than he is for a repentance on a sick-bed; for these discomposures affect the mind, as the others do the body; and the discomposure of the mind must necessarily be as great a disability as that of the body, and much greater; praying to God being properly an act of the mind, not of the body.

But to go on. After I had thus secured one part of my little living stock, I went about the whole island, searching for another private place to make such another deposit; when, wandering more to the west point of the island than I had ever done yet, and looking out to sea, I thought I saw a boat upon the sea, at a great distance. I had found a perspective glass or two in one of the seamen's chests, which I saved out of our ship, but I had it not about me; and this was so remote that I could not tell what to make of it, though I looked at it till my eyes were not able to hold to look any longer; whether it was a boat or not I do not know, but as I descended from the hill I could see no more of it, so I gave it over; only I resolved to go no more out without a perspective glass in my pocket. When I was come down the hill to the end of the island, where, indeed, I had never been before, I was presently convinced that the seeing the print of a man's foot was not such a strange thing in the island as I imagined: and but that it was a special providence that I was cast upon the side of the island where the savages never came, I should easily have known that nothing was more frequent than for the canoes from the main, when they happened to be a little too far out at sea, to shoot over to that side of the island for harbour: likewise, as they often met and fought in their canoes, the victors, having taken any prisoners, would bring them over to this shore, where, according to their dreadful customs, being all cannibals, they would kill and eat them; of which hereafter.

When I was come down the hill to the shore, as I said above, being the SW. point of the island, I was perfectly confounded and amazed; nor is it possible for me to express the horror of my mind at seeing the shore spread with skulls, hands, feet, and other bones of human bodies; and particularly I observed a place where there had been a fire made, and a circle dug in the earth, like a cockpit, where I supposed the savage wretches had sat down to their human feastings upon the bodies of their fellow-creatures.

Chapter XII—A CAVE RETREAT

I was so astonished with the sight of these things, that I entertained no notions of any danger to myself from it for a long while: all my apprehensions were buried in the thoughts of such a pitch of inhuman, hellish brutality, and the horror of the degeneracy of human nature, which, though I had heard of it often, yet I never had so near a view of before; in short, I turned away my face from the horrid spectacle; my stomach grew sick, and I was just at the point of fainting, when nature discharged the disorder from my stomach; and having vomited with uncommon violence, I was a little relieved, but could not bear to stay in the place a moment; so I got up the hill again with all the speed I could, and walked on towards my own habitation.

When I came a little out of that part of the island I stood still awhile, as amazed, and then, recovering myself, I looked up with the utmost affection of my soul, and, with a flood of tears in my eyes, gave God thanks, that had cast my first lot in a part of the world where I was distinguished from such dreadful creatures as these; and that, though I had esteemed my present condition very miserable, had yet given me so many comforts in it that I had still more to give thanks for than to complain of: and this, above all, that I had, even in this miserable condition, been comforted with the knowledge of Himself, and the hope of His blessing: which was a felicity more than sufficiently equivalent to all the misery which I had suffered, or could suffer.

In this frame of thankfulness I went home to my castle, and began to be much easier now, as to the safety of my circumstances, than ever I was before: for I observed that these wretches never came to this island in search of what they could get; perhaps not seeking, not wanting, or not expecting anything here; and having often, no doubt, been up the covered, woody part of it without finding anything to their purpose. I knew I had been here now almost eighteen years, and never saw the least footsteps of human creature there before; and I might be eighteen years more as entirely concealed as I was now, if I did not discover myself to them, which I had no manner of occasion to do; it being my only business to keep myself entirely concealed where I was, unless I found a better sort of creatures than cannibals to make myself known to. Yet I entertained such an abhorrence of the savage wretches that I have been speaking of, and of the wretched, inhuman custom of their devouring and eating one another up, that I continued pensive and sad, and kept close within my own circle for almost two years after this: when I say my own circle, I mean by it my three plantations—viz. my castle, my country seat (which I called my bower), and my enclosure in the woods: nor did I look after this for any other use than an enclosure for my goats; for the aversion which nature gave me to these hellish wretches was such, that I was as fearful of seeing them as of seeing the devil himself. I did not so much as go to look after my boat all this time, but began rather to think of making another; for I could not think of ever making any more attempts to bring the other boat round the island to me, lest I should meet with some of these creatures at sea; in which case, if I had happened to have fallen into their hands, I knew what would have been my lot.

Time, however, and the satisfaction I had that I was in no danger of being discovered by these people, began to wear off my uneasiness about them; and I began to live just in the same composed manner as before, only with this difference, that I used more caution, and kept my eyes more about me than I did before, lest I should happen to be seen by any of them; and particularly, I was more cautious of firing my gun, lest any of them, being on the island, should happen to hear it. It was, therefore, a very good providence to me that I had furnished myself with a tame breed of goats, and that I had no need to hunt any more about the woods, or shoot at them; and if I did catch any of them after this, it was by traps and snares, as I had done before; so that for two years after this I believe I never fired my gun once off, though I never went out without it; and what was more, as I had saved three pistols out of the ship, I always carried them out with me, or at least two of them, sticking them in my goat-skin belt. I also furbished up one of the great cutlasses that I had out of the ship, and made me a belt to hang it on also; so that I was now a most formidable fellow to look at when I went abroad, if you add to the former description of myself the particular of two pistols, and a broadsword hanging at my side in a belt, but without a scabbard.

Things going on thus, as I have said, for some time, I seemed, excepting these cautions, to be reduced to my former calm, sedate way of living. All these things tended to show me more and more how far my condition was from being miserable, compared to some others; nay, to many other particulars of life which it might have pleased God to have made my lot. It put me upon reflecting how little repining there would be among mankind at any condition of life if people would rather compare their condition with those that were worse, in order to be thankful, than be always comparing them with those which are better, to assist their murmurings and complainings.

As in my present condition there were not really many things which I wanted, so indeed I thought that the frights I had been in about these savage wretches, and the concern I had been in for my own preservation, had taken off the edge of my invention, for my own conveniences; and I had dropped a good design, which I had once bent my thoughts upon, and that was to try if I could not make some of my barley into malt, and then try to brew myself some beer. This was really a whimsical thought, and I reproved myself often for the simplicity of it: for I presently saw there would be the want of several things necessary to the making my beer that it would be impossible for me to supply; as, first, casks to preserve it in, which was a thing that, as I have observed already, I could never compass: no, though I spent not only many days, but weeks, nay months, in attempting it, but to no purpose. In the next place, I had no hops to make it keep, no yeast to make it work, no copper or kettle to make it boil; and yet with all these things wanting, I verily believe, had not the frights and terrors I was in about the savages intervened, I had undertaken it, and perhaps brought it to pass too; for I seldom gave anything over without accomplishing it, when once I had it in my head to began it. But my invention now ran quite another way; for night and day I could think of nothing but how I might destroy some of the monsters in their cruel, bloody entertainment, and if possible save the victim they should bring hither to destroy. It would take up a larger volume than this whole work is intended to be to set down all the contrivances I hatched, or rather brooded upon, in my thoughts, for the destroying these creatures, or at least frightening them so as to prevent their coming hither any more: but all this was abortive; nothing could be possible to take effect, unless I was to be there to do it myself: and what could one man do among them, when perhaps there might be twenty or thirty of them together with their darts, or their bows and arrows, with which they could shoot as true to a mark as I could with my gun?

Sometimes I thought if digging a hole under the place where they made their fire, and putting in five or six pounds of gunpowder, which, when they kindled their fire, would consequently take fire, and blow up all that was near it: but as, in the first place, I should be unwilling to waste so much powder upon them, my store being now within the quantity of one barrel, so neither could I be sure of its going off at any certain time, when it might surprise them; and, at best, that it would do little more than just blow the fire about their ears and fright them, but not sufficient to make them forsake the place: so I laid it aside; and then proposed that I would place myself in ambush in some convenient place, with my three guns all double-loaded, and in the middle of their bloody ceremony let fly at them, when I should be sure to kill or wound perhaps two or three at every shot; and then falling in upon them with my three pistols and my sword, I made no doubt but that, if there were twenty, I should kill them all. This fancy pleased my thoughts for some weeks, and I was so full of it that I often dreamed of it, and, sometimes, that I was just going to let fly at them in my sleep. I went so far with it in my imagination that I employed myself several days to find out proper places to put myself in ambuscade, as I said, to watch for them, and I went frequently to the place itself, which was now grown more familiar to me; but while my mind was thus filled with thoughts of revenge and a bloody putting twenty or thirty of them to the sword, as I may call it, the horror I had at the place, and at the signals of the barbarous wretches devouring one another, abetted my malice. Well, at length I found a place in the side of the hill where I was satisfied I might securely wait till I saw any of their boats coming; and might then, even before they would be ready to come on shore, convey myself unseen into some thickets of trees, in one of which there was a hollow large enough to conceal me entirely; and there I might sit and observe all their bloody doings, and take my full aim at their heads, when they were so close together as that it would be next to impossible that I should miss my shot, or that I could fail wounding three or four of them at the first shot. In this place, then, I resolved to fulfil my design; and accordingly I prepared two muskets and my ordinary fowling-piece. The two muskets I loaded with a brace of slugs each, and four or five smaller bullets, about the size of pistol bullets; and the fowling-piece I loaded with near a handful of swan-shot of the largest size; I also loaded my pistols with about four bullets each; and, in this posture, well provided with ammunition for a second and third charge, I prepared myself for my expedition.

After I had thus laid the scheme of my design, and in my imagination put it in practice, I continually made my tour every morning to the top of the hill, which was from my castle, as I called it, about three miles or more, to see if I could observe any boats upon the sea, coming near the island, or standing over towards it; but I began to tire of this hard duty, after I had for two or three months constantly kept my watch, but came always back without any discovery; there having not, in all that time, been the least appearance, not only on or near the shore, but on the whole ocean, so far as my eye or glass could reach every way.

As long as I kept my daily tour to the hill, to look out, so long also I kept up the vigour of my design, and my spirits seemed to be all the while in a suitable frame for so outrageous an execution as the killing twenty or thirty naked savages, for an offence which I had not at all entered into any discussion of in my thoughts, any farther than my passions were at first fired by the horror I conceived at the unnatural custom of the people of that country, who, it seems, had been suffered by Providence, in His wise disposition of the world, to have no other guide than that of their own abominable and vitiated passions; and consequently were left, and perhaps had been so for some ages, to act such horrid things, and receive such dreadful customs, as nothing but nature, entirely abandoned by Heaven, and actuated by some hellish degeneracy, could have run them into. But now, when, as I have said, I began to be weary of the fruitless excursion which I had made so long and so far every morning in vain, so my opinion of the action itself began to alter; and I began, with cooler and calmer thoughts, to consider what I was going to engage in; what authority or call I had to pretend to be judge and executioner upon these men as criminals, whom Heaven had thought fit for so many ages to suffer unpunished to go on, and to be as it were the executioners of His judgments one upon another; how far these people were offenders against me, and what right I had to engage in the quarrel of that blood which they shed promiscuously upon one another. I debated this very often with myself thus: "How do I know what God Himself judges in this particular case? It is certain these people do not commit this as a crime; it is not against their own consciences reproving, or their light reproaching them; they do not know it to be an offence, and then commit it in defiance of divine justice, as we do in almost all the sins we commit. They think it no more a crime to kill a captive taken in war than we do to kill an ox; or to eat human flesh than we do to eat mutton."

When I considered this a little, it followed necessarily that I was certainly in the wrong; that these people were not murderers, in the sense that I had before condemned them in my thoughts, any more than those Christians were murderers who often put to death the prisoners taken in battle; or more frequently, upon many occasions, put whole troops of men to the sword, without giving quarter, though they threw down their arms and submitted. In the next place, it occurred to me that although the usage they gave one another was thus brutish and inhuman, yet it was really nothing to me: these people had done me no injury: that if they attempted, or I saw it necessary, for my immediate preservation, to fall upon them, something might be said for it: but that I was yet out of their power, and they really had no knowledge of me, and consequently no design upon me; and therefore it could not be just for me to fall upon them; that this would justify the conduct of the Spaniards in all their barbarities practised in America, where they destroyed millions of these people; who, however they were idolators and barbarians, and had several bloody and barbarous rites in their customs, such as sacrificing human bodies to their idols, were yet, as to the Spaniards, very innocent people; and that the rooting them out of the country is spoken of with the utmost abhorrence and detestation by even the Spaniards themselves at this time, and by all other Christian nations of Europe, as a mere butchery, a bloody and unnatural piece of cruelty, unjustifiable either to God or man; and for which the very name of a Spaniard is reckoned to be frightful and terrible, to all people of humanity or of Christian compassion; as if the kingdom of Spain were particularly eminent for the produce of a race of men who were without principles of tenderness, or the common bowels of pity to the miserable, which is reckoned to be a mark of generous temper in the mind.

These considerations really put me to a pause, and to a kind of a full stop; and I began by little and little to be off my design, and to conclude I had taken wrong measures in my resolution to attack the savages; and that it was not my business to meddle with them, unless they first attacked me; and this it was my business, if possible, to prevent: but that, if I were discovered and attacked by them, I knew my duty. On the other hand, I argued with myself that this really was the way not to deliver myself, but entirely to ruin and destroy myself; for unless I was sure to kill every one that not only should be on shore at that time, but that should ever come on shore afterwards, if but one of them escaped to tell their country-people what had happened, they would come over again by thousands to revenge the death of their fellows, and I should only bring upon myself a certain destruction, which, at present, I had no manner of occasion for. Upon the whole, I concluded that I ought, neither in principle nor in policy, one way or other, to concern myself in this affair: that my business was, by all possible means to conceal myself from them, and not to leave the least sign for them to guess by that there were any living creatures upon the island—I mean of human shape. Religion joined in with this prudential resolution; and I was convinced now, many ways, that I was perfectly out of my duty when I was laying all my bloody schemes for the destruction of innocent creatures—I mean innocent as to me. As to the crimes they were guilty of towards one another, I had nothing to do with them; they were national, and I ought to leave them to the justice of God, who is the Governor of nations, and knows how, by national punishments, to make a just retribution for national offences, and to bring public judgments upon those who offend in a public manner, by such ways as best please Him. This appeared so clear to me now, that nothing was a greater satisfaction to me than that I had not been suffered to do a thing which I now saw so much reason to believe would have been no less a sin than that of wilful murder if I had committed it; and I gave most humble thanks on my knees to God, that He had thus delivered me from blood-guiltiness; beseeching Him to grant me the protection of His providence, that I might not fall into the hands of the barbarians, or that I might not lay my hands upon them, unless I had a more clear call from Heaven to do it, in defence of my own life.

In this disposition I continued for near a year after this; and so far was I from desiring an occasion for falling upon these wretches, that in all that time I never once went up the hill to see whether there were any of them in sight, or to know whether any of them had been on shore there or not, that I might not be tempted to renew any of my contrivances against them, or be provoked by any advantage that might present itself to fall upon them; only this I did: I went and removed my boat, which I had on the other side of the island, and carried it down to the east end of the whole island, where I ran it into a little cove, which I found under some high rocks, and where I knew, by reason of the currents, the savages durst not, at least would not, come with their boats upon any account whatever. With my boat I carried away everything that I had left there belonging to her, though not necessary for the bare going thither—viz. a mast and sail which I had made for her, and a thing like an anchor, but which, indeed, could not be called either anchor or grapnel; however, it was the best I could make of its kind: all these I removed, that there might not be the least shadow for discovery, or appearance of any boat, or of any human habitation upon the island. Besides this, I kept myself, as I said, more retired than ever, and seldom went from my cell except upon my constant employment, to milk my she-goats, and manage my little flock in the wood, which, as it was quite on the other part of the island, was out of danger; for certain, it is that these savage people, who sometimes haunted this island, never came with any thoughts of finding anything here, and consequently never wandered off from the coast, and I doubt not but they might have been several times on shore after my apprehensions of them had made me cautious, as well as before. Indeed, I looked back with some horror upon the thoughts of what my condition would have been if I had chopped upon them and been discovered before that; when, naked and unarmed, except with one gun, and that loaded often only with small shot, I walked everywhere, peeping and peering about the island, to see what I could get; what a surprise should I have been in if, when I discovered the print of a man's foot, I had, instead of that, seen fifteen or twenty savages, and found them pursuing me, and by the swiftness of their running no possibility of my escaping them! The thoughts of this sometimes sank my very soul within me, and distressed my mind so much that I could not soon recover it, to think what I should have done, and how I should not only have been unable to resist them, but even should not have had presence of mind enough to do what I might have done; much less what now, after so much consideration and preparation, I might be able to do. Indeed, after serious thinking of these things, I would be melancholy, and sometimes it would last a great while; but I resolved it all at last into thankfulness to that Providence which had delivered me from so many unseen dangers, and had kept me from those mischiefs which I could have no way been the agent in delivering myself from, because I had not the least notion of any such thing depending, or the least supposition of its being possible. This renewed a contemplation which often had come into my thoughts in former times, when first I began to see the merciful dispositions of Heaven, in the dangers we run through in this life; how wonderfully we are delivered when we know nothing of it; how, when we are in a quandary as we call it, a doubt or hesitation whether to go this way or that way, a secret hint shall direct us this way, when we intended to go that way: nay, when sense, our own inclination, and perhaps business has called us to go the other way, yet a strange impression upon the mind, from we know not what springs, and by we know not what power, shall overrule us to go this way; and it shall afterwards appear that had we gone that way, which we should have gone, and even to our imagination ought to have gone, we should have been ruined and lost. Upon these and many like reflections I afterwards made it a certain rule with me, that whenever I found those secret hints or pressings of mind to doing or not doing anything that presented, or going this way or that way, I never failed to obey the secret dictate; though I knew no other reason for it than such a pressure or such a hint hung upon my mind. I could give many examples of the success of this conduct in the course of my life, but more especially in the latter part of my inhabiting this unhappy island; besides many occasions which it is very likely I might have taken notice of, if I had seen with the same eyes then that I see with now. But it is never too late to be wise; and I cannot but advise all considering men, whose lives are attended with such extraordinary incidents as mine, or even though not so extraordinary, not to slight such secret intimations of Providence, let them come from what invisible intelligence they will. That I shall not discuss, and perhaps cannot account for; but certainly they are a proof of the converse of spirits, and a secret communication between those embodied and those unembodied, and such a proof as can never be withstood; of which I shall have occasion to give some remarkable instances in the remainder of my solitary residence in this dismal place.

I believe the reader of this will not think it strange if I confess that these anxieties, these constant dangers I lived in, and the concern that was now upon me, put an end to all invention, and to all the contrivances that I had laid for my future accommodations and conveniences. I had the care of my safety more now upon my hands than that of my food. I cared not to drive a nail, or chop a stick of wood now, for fear the noise I might make should be heard: much less would I fire a gun for the same reason: and above all I was intolerably uneasy at making any fire, lest the smoke, which is visible at a great distance in the day, should betray me. For this reason, I removed that part of my business which required fire, such as burning of pots and pipes, &c., into my new apartment in the woods; where, after I had been some time, I found, to my unspeakable consolation, a mere natural cave in the earth, which went in a vast way, and where, I daresay, no savage, had he been at the mouth of it, would be so hardy as to venture in; nor, indeed, would any man else, but one who, like me, wanted nothing so much as a safe retreat.

The mouth of this hollow was at the bottom of a great rock, where, by mere accident (I would say, if I did not see abundant reason to ascribe all such things now to Providence), I was cutting down some thick branches of trees to make charcoal; and before I go on I must observe the reason of my making this charcoal, which was this—I was afraid of making a smoke about my habitation, as I said before; and yet I could not live there without baking my bread, cooking my meat, &c.; so I contrived to burn some wood here, as I had seen done in England, under turf, till it became chark or dry coal: and then putting the fire out, I preserved the coal to carry home, and perform the other services for which fire was wanting, without danger of smoke. But this is by-the-bye. While I was cutting down some wood here, I perceived that, behind a very thick branch of low brushwood or underwood, there was a kind of hollow place: I was curious to look in it; and getting with difficulty into the mouth of it, I found it was pretty large, that is to say, sufficient for me to stand upright in it, and perhaps another with me: but I must confess to you that I made more haste out than I did in, when looking farther into the place, and which was perfectly dark, I saw two broad shining eyes of some creature, whether devil or man I knew not, which twinkled like two stars; the dim light from the cave's mouth shining directly in, and making the reflection. However, after some pause I recovered myself, and began to call myself a thousand fools, and to think that he that was afraid to see the devil was not fit to live twenty years in an island all alone; and that I might well think there was nothing in this cave that was more frightful than myself. Upon this, plucking up my courage, I took up a firebrand, and in I rushed again, with the stick flaming in my hand: I had not gone three steps in before I was almost as frightened as before; for I heard a very loud sigh, like that of a man in some pain, and it was followed by a broken noise, as of words half expressed, and then a deep sigh again. I stepped back, and was indeed struck with such a surprise that it put me into a cold sweat, and if I had had a hat on my head, I will not answer for it that my hair might not have lifted it off. But still plucking up my spirits as well as I could, and encouraging myself a little with considering that the power and presence of God was everywhere, and was able to protect me, I stepped forward again, and by the light of the firebrand, holding it up a little over my head, I saw lying on the ground a monstrous, frightful old he-goat, just making his will, as we say, and gasping for life, and, dying, indeed, of mere old age. I stirred him a little to see if I could get him out, and he essayed to get up, but was not able to raise himself; and I thought with myself he might even lie there—for if he had frightened me, so he would certainly fright any of the savages, if any of them should be so hardy as to come in there while he had any life in him.

I was now recovered from my surprise, and began to look round me, when I found the cave was but very small—that is to say, it might be about twelve feet over, but in no manner of shape, neither round nor square, no hands having ever been employed in making it but those of mere Nature. I observed also that there was a place at the farther side of it that went in further, but was so low that it required me to creep upon my hands and knees to go into it, and whither it went I knew not; so, having no candle, I gave it over for that time, but resolved to go again the next day provided with candles and a tinder-box, which I had made of the lock of one of the muskets, with some wildfire in the pan.

Accordingly, the next day I came provided with six large candles of my own making (for I made very good candles now of goat's tallow, but was hard set for candle-wick, using sometimes rags or rope-yarn, and sometimes the dried rind of a weed like nettles); and going into this low place I was obliged to creep upon all-fours as I have said, almost ten yards—which, by the way, I thought was a venture bold enough, considering that I knew not how far it might go, nor what was beyond it. When I had got through the strait, I found the roof rose higher up, I believe near twenty feet; but never was such a glorious sight seen in the island, I daresay, as it was to look round the sides and roof of this vault or cave—the wall reflected a hundred thousand lights to me from my two candles. What it was in the rock—whether diamonds or any other precious stones, or gold which I rather supposed it to be—I knew not. The place I was in was a most delightful cavity, or grotto, though perfectly dark; the floor was dry and level, and had a sort of a small loose gravel upon it, so that there was no nauseous or venomous creature to be seen, neither was there any damp or wet on the sides or roof. The only difficulty in it was the entrance—which, however, as it was a place of security, and such a retreat as I wanted; I thought was a convenience; so that I was really rejoiced at the discovery, and resolved, without any delay, to bring some of those things which I was most anxious about to this place: particularly, I resolved to bring hither my magazine of powder, and all my spare arms—viz. two fowling-pieces—for I had three in all—and three muskets—for of them I had eight in all; so I kept in my castle only five, which stood ready mounted like pieces of cannon on my outmost fence, and were ready also to take out upon any expedition. Upon this occasion of removing my ammunition I happened to open the barrel of powder which I took up out of the sea, and which had been wet, and I found that the water had penetrated about three or four inches into the powder on every side, which caking and growing hard, had preserved the inside like a kernel in the shell, so that I had near sixty pounds of very good powder in the centre of the cask. This was a very agreeable discovery to me at that time; so I carried all away thither, never keeping above two or three pounds of powder with me in my castle, for fear of a surprise of any kind; I also carried thither all the lead I had left for bullets.

I fancied myself now like one of the ancient giants who were said to live in caves and holes in the rocks, where none could come at them; for I persuaded myself, while I was here, that if five hundred savages were to hunt me, they could never find me out—or if they did, they would not venture to attack me here. The old goat whom I found expiring died in the mouth of the cave the next day after I made this discovery; and I found it much easier to dig a great hole there, and throw him in and cover him with earth, than to drag him out; so I interred him there, to prevent offence to my nose.

Chapter XIII—WRECK OF A SPANISH SHIP

I was now in the twenty-third year of my residence in this island, and was so naturalised to the place and the manner of living, that, could I but have enjoyed the certainty that no savages would come to the place to disturb me, I could have been content to have capitulated for spending the rest of my time there, even to the last moment, till I had laid me down and died, like the old goat in the cave. I had also arrived to some little diversions and amusements, which made the time pass a great deal more pleasantly with me than it did before—first, I had taught my Poll, as I noted before, to speak; and he did it so familiarly, and talked so articulately and plain, that it was very pleasant to me; and he lived with me no less than six-and-twenty years. How long he might have lived afterwards I know not, though I know they have a notion in the Brazils that they live a hundred years. My dog was a pleasant and loving companion to me for no less than sixteen years of my time, and then died of mere old age. As for my cats, they multiplied, as I have observed, to that degree that I was obliged to shoot several of them at first, to keep them from devouring me and all I had; but at length, when the two old ones I brought with me were gone, and after some time continually driving them from me, and letting them have no provision with me, they all ran wild into the woods, except two or three favourites, which I kept tame, and whose young, when they had any, I always drowned; and these were part of my family. Besides these I always kept two or three household kids about me, whom I taught to feed out of my hand; and I had two more parrots, which talked pretty well, and would all call "Robin Crusoe," but none like my first; nor, indeed, did I take the pains with any of them that I had done with him. I had also several tame sea-fowls, whose name I knew not, that I caught upon the shore, and cut their wings; and the little stakes which I had planted before my castle-wall being now grown up to a good thick grove, these fowls all lived among these low trees, and bred there, which was very agreeable to me; so that, as I said above, I began to be very well contented with the life I led, if I could have been secured from the dread of the savages. But it was otherwise directed; and it may not be amiss for all people who shall meet with my story to make this just observation from it: How frequently, in the course of our lives, the evil which in itself we seek most to shun, and which, when we are fallen into, is the most dreadful to us, is oftentimes the very means or door of our deliverance, by which alone we can be raised again from the affliction we are fallen into. I could give many examples of this in the course of my unaccountable life; but in nothing was it more particularly remarkable than in the circumstances of my last years of solitary residence in this island.

It was now the month of December, as I said above, in my twenty-third year; and this, being the southern solstice (for winter I cannot call it), was the particular time of my harvest, and required me to be pretty much abroad in the fields, when, going out early in the morning, even before it was thorough daylight, I was surprised with seeing a light of some fire upon the shore, at a distance from me of about two miles, toward that part of the island where I had observed some savages had been, as before, and not on the other side; but, to my great affliction, it was on my side of the island.

I was indeed terribly surprised at the sight, and stopped short within my grove, not daring to go out, lest I might be surprised; and yet I had no more peace within, from the apprehensions I had that if these savages, in rambling over the island, should find my corn standing or cut, or any of my works or improvements, they would immediately conclude that there were people in the place, and would then never rest till they had found me out. In this extremity I went back directly to my castle, pulled up the ladder after me, and made all things without look as wild and natural as I could.

Then I prepared myself within, putting myself in a posture of defence. I loaded all my cannon, as I called them—that is to say, my muskets, which were mounted upon my new fortification—and all my pistols, and resolved to defend myself to the last gasp—not forgetting seriously to commend myself to the Divine protection, and earnestly to pray to God to deliver me out of the hands of the barbarians. I continued in this posture about two hours, and began to be impatient for intelligence abroad, for I had no spies to send out. After sitting a while longer, and musing what I should do in this case, I was not able to bear sitting in ignorance longer; so setting up my ladder to the side of the hill, where there was a flat place, as I observed before, and then pulling the ladder after me, I set it up again and mounted the top of the hill, and pulling out my perspective glass, which I had taken on purpose, I laid me down flat on my belly on the ground, and began to look for the place. I presently found there were no less than nine naked savages sitting round a small fire they had made, not to warm them, for they had no need of that, the weather being extremely hot, but, as I supposed, to dress some of their barbarous diet of human flesh which they had brought with them, whether alive or dead I could not tell.

They had two canoes with them, which they had hauled up upon the shore; and as it was then ebb of tide, they seemed to me to wait for the return of the flood to go away again. It is not easy to imagine what confusion this sight put me into, especially seeing them come on my side of the island, and so near to me; but when I considered their coming must be always with the current of the ebb, I began afterwards to be more sedate in my mind, being satisfied that I might go abroad with safety all the time of the flood of tide, if they were not on shore before; and having made this observation, I went abroad about my harvest work with the more composure.

As I expected, so it proved; for as soon as the tide made to the westward I saw them all take boat and row (or paddle as we call it) away. I should have observed, that for an hour or more before they went off they were dancing, and I could easily discern their postures and gestures by my glass. I could not perceive, by my nicest observation, but that they were stark naked, and had not the least covering upon them; but whether they were men or women I could not distinguish.

As soon as I saw them shipped and gone, I took two guns upon my shoulders, and two pistols in my girdle, and my great sword by my side without a scabbard, and with all the speed I was able to make went away to the hill where I had discovered the first appearance of all; and as soon as I get thither, which was not in less than two hours (for I could not go quickly, being so loaded with arms as I was), I perceived there had been three canoes more of the savages at that place; and looking out farther, I saw they were all at sea together, making over for the main. This was a dreadful sight to me, especially as, going down to the shore, I could see the marks of horror which the dismal work they had been about had left behind it—viz. the blood, the bones, and part of the flesh of human bodies eaten and devoured by those wretches with merriment and sport. I was so filled with indignation at the sight, that I now began to premeditate the destruction of the next that I saw there, let them be whom or how many soever. It seemed evident to me that the visits which they made thus to this island were not very frequent, for it was above fifteen months before any more of them came on shore there again—that is to say, I neither saw them nor any footsteps or signals of them in all that time; for as to the rainy seasons, then they are sure not to come abroad, at least not so far. Yet all this while I lived uncomfortably, by reason of the constant apprehensions of their coming upon me by surprise: from whence I observe, that the expectation of evil is more bitter than the suffering, especially if there is no room to shake off that expectation or those apprehensions.

During all this time I was in a murdering humour, and spent most of my hours, which should have been better employed, in contriving how to circumvent and fall upon them the very next time I should see them—especially if they should be divided, as they were the last time, into two parties; nor did I consider at all that if I killed one party—suppose ten or a dozen—I was still the next day, or week, or month, to kill another, and so another, even *ad infinitum*, till I should be, at length, no less a murderer than they were in being man-eaters—and perhaps much more so. I spent my days now in great perplexity and anxiety of mind, expecting that I should one day or other fall, into the hands of these merciless creatures; and if I did at any time venture abroad, it was not without looking around me with the greatest care and caution imaginable. And now I found, to my great comfort, how happy it was that I had provided a tame flock or herd of goats, for I durst not upon any account fire my gun, especially near that side of the island where they usually came, lest I should alarm the savages; and if they had fled from me now, I was sure to have them come again with perhaps two or three hundred canoes with them in a few days, and then I knew what to expect. However, I wore out a year and three months more before I ever saw any more of the savages, and then I found them again, as I shall soon observe. It is true they might have been there once or twice; but either they made no stay, or at least I did not see them; but in the month of May, as near as I could calculate, and in my four-and-twentieth year, I had a very strange encounter with them; of which in its place.

The perturbation of my mind during this fifteen or sixteen months' interval was very great; I slept unquietly, dreamed always frightful dreams, and often started out of my sleep in the night. In the day great troubles overwhelmed my mind; and in the night I dreamed often of killing the savages and of the reasons why I might justify doing it.

But to waive all this for a while. It was in the middle of May, on the sixteenth day, I think, as well as my poor wooden calendar would reckon, for I marked all upon the post still; I say, it was on the sixteenth of May that it blew a very great storm of wind all day, with a great deal of lightning and thunder, and; a very foul night it was after it. I knew not what was the particular occasion of it, but as I was reading in the Bible, and taken up with very serious thoughts about my present condition, I was surprised with the noise of a gun, as I thought, fired at sea. This was, to be sure, a surprise quite of a different nature from any I had met with before; for the notions this put into my thoughts were quite of another kind. I started up in the greatest haste imaginable; and, in a trice, clapped my ladder to the middle place of the rock, and pulled it after me; and mounting it the second time, got to the top of the hill the very moment that a flash of fire bid me listen for a second gun, which, accordingly, in about half a minute I heard; and by the sound, knew that it was from that part of the sea where I was driven down the current in my boat. I immediately considered that this must be some ship in distress, and that they had some comrade, or some other ship in company, and fired these for signals of distress, and to obtain help. I had the presence of mind at that minute to think, that though I could not help them, it might be that they might help me; so I brought together all the dry wood I could get at hand, and making a good handsome pile, I set it on fire upon the hill. The wood was dry, and blazed freely; and, though the wind blew very hard, yet it burned fairly out; so that I was certain, if there was any such thing as a ship, they must needs see it. And no doubt they did; for as soon as ever my fire blazed up, I heard another gun, and after that several others, all from the same quarter. I plied my fire all night long, till daybreak: and when it was broad day, and the air cleared up, I saw something at a great distance at sea, full east of the island, whether a sail or a hull I could not distinguish—no, not with my glass: the distance was so great, and the weather still something hazy also; at least, it was so out at sea.

I looked frequently at it all that day, and soon perceived that it did not move; so I presently concluded that it was a ship at anchor; and being eager, you may be sure, to be satisfied, I took my gun in my hand, and ran towards the south side of the island to the rocks where I had formerly been carried away by the current; and getting up there, the weather by this time being perfectly clear, I could plainly see, to my great sorrow, the wreck of a ship, cast away in the night upon those concealed rocks which I found when I was out in my boat; and which rocks, as they checked the violence of the stream, and made a kind of counter-stream, or eddy, were the occasion of my recovering from the most desperate, hopeless condition that ever I had been in in all my life. Thus, what is one man's safety is another man's destruction; for it seems these men, whoever they were, being out of their knowledge, and the rocks being wholly under water, had been driven upon them in the night, the wind blowing hard at ENE. Had they seen the island, as I must necessarily suppose they did not, they must, as I thought, have endeavoured to have saved themselves on shore by the help of their boat; but their firing off guns for help, especially when they saw, as I imagined, my fire, filled me with many thoughts. First, I imagined that upon seeing my light they might have put themselves into their boat, and endeavoured to make the shore: but that the sea running very high, they might have been cast away. Other times I imagined that they might have lost their boat before, as might be the case many ways; particularly by the breaking of the sea upon their ship, which many times obliged men to stave, or take in pieces, their boat, and sometimes to throw it overboard with their own hands. Other times I imagined they had some other ship or ships in company, who, upon the signals of distress they made, had taken them up, and carried them off. Other times I fancied they were all gone off to sea in their boat, and being hurried away by the current that I had been formerly in, were carried out into the great ocean, where there was nothing but misery and perishing: and that, perhaps, they might by this time think of starving, and of being in a condition to eat one another.

As all these were but conjectures at best, so, in the condition I was in, I could do no more than look on upon the misery of the poor men, and pity them; which had still this good effect upon my side, that it gave me more and more cause to give thanks to God, who had so happily and comfortably provided for me in my desolate condition; and that of two ships' companies, who were now cast away upon this part of the world, not one life should be spared but mine. I learned here again to observe, that it is very rare that the providence of God casts us into any condition so low, or any misery so great, but we may see something or other to be thankful for, and may see others in worse circumstances than our own. Such certainly was the case of these men, of whom I could not so much as see room to suppose any were saved; nothing could make it rational so much as to wish or expect that they did not all perish there, except the possibility only of their being taken up by another ship in company; and this was but mere possibility indeed, for I saw not the least sign or appearance of any such thing. I cannot explain, by any possible energy of words, what a strange longing I felt in my soul upon this sight, breaking out sometimes thus: "Oh that there had been but one or two, nay, or but one soul saved out of this ship, to have escaped to me, that I might but have had one companion, one fellow-creature, to have spoken to me and to have conversed with!" In all the time of my solitary life I never felt so earnest, so strong a desire after the society of my fellow-creatures, or so deep a regret at the want of it.

There are some secret springs in the affections which, when they are set a-going by some object in view, or, though not in view, yet rendered present to the mind by the power of imagination, that motion carries out the soul, by its impetuosity, to such violent, eager embracings of the object, that the absence of it is insupportable. Such were these earnest wishings that but one man had been saved. I believe I repeated the words, "Oh that it had been but one!" a thousand times; and my desires were so moved by it, that when I spoke the words my hands would clinch together, and my fingers would press the palms of my hands, so that if I had had any soft thing in my hand I should have crushed it involuntarily; and the teeth in my head would strike together, and set against one another so strong, that for some time I could not part them again. Let the naturalists explain these things, and the reason and manner of them. All I can do is to describe the fact, which was even surprising to me when I found it, though I knew not from whence it proceeded; it was doubtless the effect of ardent wishes, and of strong ideas formed in my mind, realising the comfort which the conversation of one of my fellow-Christians would have been to me. But it was not to be; either their fate or mine, or both, forbade it; for, till the last year of my being on this island, I never knew whether any were saved out of that ship or no; and had only the affliction, some days after, to see the corpse of a drowned boy come on shore at the end of the island which was next the shipwreck. He had no clothes on but a seaman's waistcoat, a pair of open-kneed linen drawers, and a blue linen shirt; but nothing to direct me so much as to guess what nation he was of. He had nothing in his pockets but two pieces of eight and a tobacco pipe—the last was to me of ten times more value than the first.

It was now calm, and I had a great mind to venture out in my boat to this wreck, not doubting but I might find something on board that might be useful to me. But that did not altogether press me so much as the possibility that there might be yet some living creature on board, whose life I might not only save, but might, by saving that life, comfort my own to the last degree; and this thought clung so to my heart that I could not be quiet night or day, but I must venture out in my boat on board this wreck; and committing the rest to God's providence, I thought the impression was so strong upon my mind that it could not be resisted—that it must come from some invisible direction, and that I should be wanting to myself if I did not go.

Under the power of this impression, I hastened back to my castle, prepared everything for my voyage, took a quantity of bread, a great pot of fresh water, a compass to steer by, a bottle of rum (for I had still a great deal of that left), and a basket of raisins; and thus, loading myself with everything necessary. I went down to my boat, got the water out of her, got her afloat, loaded all my cargo in her, and then went home again for more. My second cargo was a great bag of rice, the umbrella to set up over my head for a shade, another large pot of water, and about two dozen of small loaves, or barley cakes, more than before, with a bottle of goat's milk and a cheese; all which with great labour and sweat I carried to my boat; and praying to God to direct my voyage, I put out, and rowing or paddling the canoe along the shore, came at last to the utmost point of the island on the north-east side. And now I was to launch out into the ocean, and either to venture or not to venture. I looked on the rapid currents which ran constantly on both sides of the island at a distance, and which were very terrible to me from the remembrance of the hazard I had been in before, and my heart began to fail me; for I foresaw that if I was driven into either of those currents, I should be carried a great way out to sea, and perhaps out of my reach or sight of the island again; and that then, as my boat was but small, if any little gale of wind should rise, I should be inevitably lost.

These thoughts so oppressed my mind that I began to give over my enterprise; and having hauled my boat into a little creek on the shore, I stepped out, and sat down upon a rising bit of ground, very pensive and anxious, between fear and desire, about my voyage; when, as I was musing, I could perceive that the tide was turned, and the flood come on; upon which my going was impracticable for so many hours. Upon this, presently it occurred to me that I should go up to the highest piece of ground I could find, and observe, if I could, how the sets of the tide or currents lay when the flood came in, that I might judge whether, if I was driven one way out, I might not expect to be driven another way home, with the same rapidity of the currents. This thought was no sooner in my head than I cast my eye upon a little hill which sufficiently overlooked the sea both ways, and from whence I had a clear view of the currents or sets of the tide, and which way I was to guide myself in my return. Here I found, that as the current of ebb set out close by the south point of the island, so the current of the flood set in close by the shore of the north side; and that I had nothing to do but to keep to the north side of the island in my return, and I should do well enough.

Encouraged by this observation, I resolved the next morning to set out with the first of the tide; and reposing myself for the night in my canoe, under the watch-coat I mentioned, I launched out. I first made a little out to sea, full north, till I began to feel the benefit of the current, which set eastward, and which carried me at a great rate; and yet did not so hurry me as the current on the south side had done before, so as to take from me all government of the boat; but having a strong steerage with my paddle, I went at a great rate directly for the wreck, and in less than two hours I came up to it. It was a dismal sight to look at; the ship, which by its building was Spanish, stuck fast, jammed in between two rocks. All the stern and quarter of her were beaten to pieces by the sea; and as her forecastle, which stuck in the rocks, had run on with great violence, her mainmast and foremast were brought by the board—that is to say, broken short off; but her bowsprit was sound, and the head and bow appeared firm. When I came close to her, a dog appeared upon her, who, seeing me coming, yelped and cried; and as soon as I called him, jumped into the sea to come to me. I took him into the boat, but found him almost dead with hunger and thirst. I gave him a cake of my bread, and he devoured it like a ravenous wolf that had been starving a fortnight in the snow; I then gave the poor creature some fresh water, with which, if I would have let him, he would have burst himself. After this I went on board; but the first sight I met with was two men drowned in the cook-room, or forecastle of the ship, with their arms fast about one another. I concluded, as is indeed probable, that when the ship struck, it being in a storm, the sea broke so high and so continually over her, that the men were not able to bear it, and were strangled with the constant rushing in of the water, as much as if they had been under water. Besides the dog, there was nothing left in the ship that had life; nor any goods, that I could see, but what were spoiled by the water. There were some casks of liquor, whether wine or brandy I knew not, which lay lower in the hold, and which, the water being ebbed out, I could see; but they were too big to meddle with. I saw several chests, which I believe belonged to some of the seamen; and I got two of them into the boat, without examining what was in them. Had the stern of the ship been fixed, and the forepart broken off, I am persuaded I might have made a good voyage; for by what I found in those two chests I had room to suppose the ship had a great deal of wealth on board; and, if I may guess from the course she steered, she must have been bound from Buenos Ayres, or the Rio de la Plata, in the south part of America, beyond the Brazils to the Havannah, in the Gulf of Mexico, and so perhaps to Spain. She had, no doubt, a great treasure in her, but of no use, at that time, to anybody; and what became of the crew I then knew not.

I found, besides these chests, a little cask full of liquor, of about twenty gallons, which I got into my boat with much difficulty. There were several muskets in the cabin, and a great powder-horn, with about four pounds of powder in it; as for the muskets, I had no occasion for them, so I left them, but took the powder-horn. I took a fire-shovel and tongs, which I wanted extremely, as also two little brass kettles, a copper pot to make chocolate, and a gridiron; and with this cargo, and the dog, I came away, the tide beginning to make home again—and the same evening, about an hour within night, I reached the island again, weary and fatigued to the last degree. I reposed that night in the boat and in the morning I resolved to harbour what I had got in my new cave, and not carry it home to my castle. After refreshing myself, I got all my cargo on shore, and began to examine the particulars. The cask of liquor I found to be a kind of rum, but not such as we had at the Brazils; and, in a word, not at all good; but when I came to open the chests, I found several things of great use to me—for example, I found in one a fine case of bottles, of an extraordinary kind, and filled with cordial waters, fine and very good; the bottles held about three pints each, and were tipped with silver. I found two pots of very good succades, or sweetmeats, so fastened also on the top that the salt-water had not hurt them; and two more of the same, which the water had spoiled. I found some very good shirts, which were very welcome to me; and about a dozen and a half of white linen handkerchiefs and coloured neckcloths; the former were also very welcome, being exceedingly refreshing to wipe my face in a hot day. Besides this, when I came to the till in the chest, I found there three great bags of pieces of eight, which held about eleven hundred pieces in all; and in one of them, wrapped up in a paper, six doubloons of gold, and some small bars or wedges of gold; I suppose they might all weigh near a pound. In the other chest were some clothes, but of little value; but, by the circumstances, it must have belonged to the gunner's mate; though there was no powder in it, except two pounds of fine glazed powder, in three flasks, kept, I suppose, for charging their fowling-pieces on occasion. Upon the whole, I got very little by this voyage that was of any use to me; for, as to the money, I had no manner of occasion for it; it was to me as the dirt under my feet, and I would have given it all for three or four pair of English shoes and stockings, which were things I greatly wanted, but had had none on my feet for many years. I had, indeed, got two pair of shoes now, which I took off the feet of two drowned men whom I saw in the wreck, and I found two pair more in one of the chests, which were very welcome to me; but they were not like our English shoes, either for ease or service, being rather what we call pumps than shoes. I found in this seaman's chest about fifty pieces of eight, in rials, but no gold: I supposed this belonged to a poorer man than the other, which seemed to belong to some officer. Well, however, I lugged this money home to my cave, and laid it up, as I had done that before which I had brought from our own ship; but it was a great pity, as I said, that the other part of this ship had not come to my share: for I am satisfied I might have loaded my canoe several times over with money; and, thought I, if I ever escape to England, it might lie here safe enough till I come again and fetch it.

Chapter XIV—A DREAM REALISED

Having now brought all my things on shore and secured them, I went back to my boat, and rowed or paddled her along the shore to her old harbour, where I laid her up, and made the best of my way to my old habitation, where I found everything safe and quiet. I began now to repose myself, live after my old fashion, and take care of my family affairs; and for a while I lived easy enough, only that I was more vigilant than I used to be, looked out oftener, and did not go abroad so much; and if at any time I did stir with any freedom, it was always to the east part of the island, where I was pretty well satisfied the savages never came, and where I could go without so many precautions, and such a load of arms and ammunition as I always carried with me if I went the other way. I lived in this condition near two years more; but my unlucky head, that was always to let me know it was born to make my body miserable, was all these two years filled with projects and designs how, if it were possible, I might get away from this island: for sometimes I was for making another voyage to the wreck, though my reason told me that there was nothing left there worth the hazard of my voyage; sometimes for a ramble one way, sometimes another—and I believe verily, if I had had the boat that I went from Sallee in, I should have ventured to sea, bound anywhere, I knew not whither. I have been, in all my circumstances, a memento to those who are touched with the general plague of mankind, whence, for aught I know, one half of their miseries flow: I mean that of not being satisfied with the station wherein God and Nature hath placed them—for, not to look back upon my primitive condition, and the excellent advice of my father, the opposition to which was, as I may call it, my *original sin*, my subsequent mistakes of the same kind had been the means of my coming into this miserable condition; for had that Providence which so happily seated me at the Brazils as a planter blessed me with confined desires, and I could have been contented to have gone on gradually, I might have been by this time—I mean in the time of my being in this island—one of the most considerable planters in the Brazils—nay, I am persuaded, that by the improvements I had made in that little time I lived there, and the increase I should probably have made if I had remained, I might have been worth a hundred thousand moidores—and what business had I to leave a settled fortune, a well-stocked plantation, improving and increasing, to turn supercargo to Guinea to fetch negroes, when patience and time would have so increased our stock at home, that we could have bought them at our own door from those whose business it was to fetch them? and though it had cost us something more, yet the difference of that price was by no means worth saving at so great a hazard. But as this is usually the fate of young heads, so reflection upon the folly of it is as commonly the exercise of more years, or of the dear-bought experience of time—so it was with me now; and yet so deep had the mistake taken root in my temper, that I could not satisfy myself in my station, but was continually poring upon the means and possibility of my escape from this place; and that I may, with greater pleasure to the reader, bring on the remaining part of my story, it may not be improper to give some account of my first conceptions on the subject of this foolish scheme for my escape, and how, and upon what foundation, I acted.

I am now to be supposed retired into my castle, after my late voyage to the wreck, my frigate laid up and secured under water, as usual, and my condition restored to what it was before: I had more wealth, indeed, than I had before, but was not at all the richer; for I had no more use for it than the Indians of Peru had before the Spaniards came there.

It was one of the nights in the rainy season in March, the four-and-twentieth year of my first setting foot in this island of solitude, I was lying in my bed or hammock, awake, very well in health, had no pain, no distemper, no uneasiness of body, nor any uneasiness of mind more than ordinary, but could by no means close my eyes, that is, so as to sleep; no, not a wink all night long, otherwise than as follows: It is impossible to set down the innumerable crowd of thoughts that whirled through that great thoroughfare of the brain, the memory, in this night's time. I ran over the whole history of my life in miniature, or by abridgment, as I may call it, to my coming to this island, and also of that part of my life since I came to this island. In my reflections upon the state of my case since I came on shore on this island, I was comparing the happy posture of my affairs in the first years of my habitation here, with the life of anxiety, fear, and care which I had lived in ever since I had seen the print of a foot in the sand. Not that I did not believe the savages had frequented the island even all the while, and might have been several hundreds of them at times on shore there; but I had never known it, and was incapable of any apprehensions about it; my satisfaction was perfect, though my danger was the same, and I was as happy in not knowing my danger as if I had never really been exposed to it. This furnished my thoughts with many very profitable reflections, and particularly this one: How infinitely good that Providence is, which has provided, in its government of mankind, such narrow bounds to his sight and knowledge of things; and though he walks in the midst of so many thousand dangers, the sight of which, if discovered to him, would distract his mind and sink his spirits, he is kept serene and calm, by having the events of things hid from his eyes, and knowing nothing of the dangers which surround him.

After these thoughts had for some time entertained me, I came to reflect seriously upon the real danger I had been in for so many years in this very island, and how I had walked about in the greatest security, and with all possible tranquillity, even when perhaps nothing but the brow of a hill, a great tree, or the casual approach of night, had been between me and the worst kind of destruction—viz. that of falling into the hands of cannibals and savages, who would have seized on me with the same view as I would on a goat or turtle; and have thought it no more crime to kill and devour me than I did of a pigeon or a curlew. I would unjustly slander myself if I should say I was not sincerely thankful to my great Preserver, to whose singular protection I acknowledged, with great humanity, all these unknown deliverances were due, and without which I must inevitably have fallen into their merciless hands.

When these thoughts were over, my head was for some time taken up in considering the nature of these wretched creatures, I mean the savages, and how it came to pass in the world that the wise Governor of all things should give up any of His creatures to such inhumanity—nay, to something so much below even brutality itself—as to devour its own kind: but as this ended in some (at that time) fruitless speculations, it occurred to me to inquire what part of the world these wretches lived in? how far off the coast was from whence they came? what they ventured over so far from home for? what kind of boats they had? and why I might not order myself and my business so that I might be able to go over thither, as they were to come to me?

I never so much as troubled myself to consider what I should do with myself when I went thither; what would become of me if I fell into the hands of these savages; or how I should escape them if they attacked me; no, nor so much as how it was possible for me to reach the coast, and not to be attacked by some or other of them, without any possibility of delivering myself: and if I should not fall into their hands, what I should do for provision, or whither I should bend my course: none of these thoughts, I say, so much as came in my way; but my mind was wholly bent upon the notion of my passing over in my boat to the mainland. I looked upon my present condition as the most miserable that could possibly be; that I was not able to throw myself into anything but death, that could be called worse; and if I reached the shore of the main I might perhaps meet with relief, or I might coast along, as I did on the African shore, till I came to some inhabited country, and where I might find some relief; and after all, perhaps I might fall in with some Christian ship that might take me in: and if the worst came to the worst, I could but die, which would put an end to all these miseries at once. Pray note, all this was the fruit of a disturbed mind, an impatient temper, made desperate, as it were, by the long continuance of my troubles, and the disappointments I had met in the wreck I had been on board of, and where I had been so near obtaining what I so earnestly longed for—somebody to speak to, and to learn some knowledge from them of the place where I was, and of the probable means of my deliverance. I was agitated wholly by these thoughts; all my calm of mind, in my resignation to Providence, and waiting the issue of the dispositions of Heaven, seemed to be suspended; and I had as it were no power to turn my thoughts to anything but to the project of a voyage to the main, which came upon me with such force, and such an impetuosity of desire, that it was not to be resisted.

When this had agitated my thoughts for two hours or more, with such violence that it set my very blood into a ferment, and my pulse beat as if I had been in a fever, merely with the extraordinary fervour of my mind about it, Nature—as if I had been fatigued and exhausted with the very thoughts of it—threw me into a sound sleep. One would have thought I should have dreamed of it, but I did not, nor of anything relating to it, but I dreamed that as I was going out in the morning as usual from my castle, I saw upon the shore two canoes and eleven savages coming to land, and that they brought with them another savage whom they were going to kill in order to eat him; when, on a sudden, the savage that they were going to kill jumped away, and ran for his life; and I thought in my sleep that he came running into my little thick grove before my fortification, to hide himself; and that I seeing him alone, and not perceiving that the others sought him that way, showed myself to him, and smiling upon him, encouraged him: that he kneeled down to me, seeming to pray me to assist him; upon which I showed him my ladder, made him go up, and carried him into my cave, and he became my servant; and that as soon as I had got this man, I said to myself, "Now I may certainly venture to the mainland, for this fellow will serve me as a pilot, and will tell me what to do, and whither to go for provisions, and whither not to go for fear of being devoured; what places to venture into, and what to shun." I waked with this thought; and was under such inexpressible impressions of joy at the prospect of my escape in my dream, that the disappointments which I felt upon coming to myself, and finding that it was no more than a dream, were equally extravagant the other way, and threw me into a very great dejection of spirits.

Upon this, however, I made this conclusion: that my only way to go about to attempt an escape was, to endeavour to get a savage into my possession: and, if possible, it should be one of their prisoners, whom they had condemned to be eaten, and should bring hither to kill. But these thoughts still were attended with this difficulty: that it was impossible to effect this without attacking a whole caravan of them, and killing them all; and this was not only a very desperate attempt, and might miscarry, but, on the other hand, I had greatly scrupled the lawfulness of it to myself; and my heart trembled at the thoughts of shedding so much blood, though it was for my deliverance. I need not repeat the arguments which occurred to me against this, they being the same mentioned before; but though I had other reasons to offer now—viz. that those men were enemies to my life, and would devour me if they could; that it was self-preservation, in the highest degree, to deliver myself from this death of a life, and was acting in my own defence as much as if they were actually assaulting me, and the like; I say though these things argued for it, yet the thoughts of shedding human blood for my deliverance were very terrible to me, and such as I could by no means reconcile myself to for a great while. However, at last, after many secret disputes with myself, and after great perplexities about it (for all these arguments, one way and another, struggled in my head a long time), the eager prevailing desire of deliverance at length mastered all the rest; and I resolved, if possible, to get one of these savages into my hands, cost what it would. My next thing was to contrive how to do it, and this, indeed, was very difficult to resolve on; but as I could pitch upon no probable means for it, so I resolved to put myself upon the watch, to see them when they came on shore, and leave the rest to the event; taking such measures as the opportunity should present, let what would be.

With these resolutions in my thoughts, I set myself upon the scout as often as possible, and indeed so often that I was heartily tired of it; for it was above a year and a half that I waited; and for great part of that time went out to the west end, and to the south-west corner of the island almost every day, to look for canoes, but none appeared. This was very discouraging, and began to trouble me much, though I cannot say that it did in this case (as it had done some time before) wear off the edge of my desire to the thing; but the longer it seemed to be delayed, the more eager I was for it: in a word, I was not at first so careful to shun the sight of these savages, and avoid being seen by them, as I was now eager to be upon them. Besides, I fancied myself able to manage one, nay, two or three savages, if I had them, so as to make them entirely slaves to me, to do whatever I should direct them, and to prevent their being able at any time to do me any hurt. It was a great while that I pleased myself with this affair; but nothing still presented itself; all my fancies and schemes came to nothing, for no savages came near me for a great while.

About a year and a half after I entertained these notions (and by long musing had, as it were, resolved them all into nothing, for want of an occasion to put them into execution), I was surprised one morning by seeing no less than five canoes all on shore together on my side the island, and the people who belonged to them all landed and out of my sight. The number of them broke all my measures; for seeing so many, and knowing that they always came four or six, or sometimes more in a boat, I could not tell what to think of it, or how to take my measures to attack twenty or thirty men single-handed; so lay still in my castle, perplexed and discomforted. However, I put myself into the same position for an attack that I had formerly provided, and was just ready for action, if anything had presented. Having waited a good while, listening to hear if they made any noise, at length, being very impatient, I set my guns at the foot of my ladder, and clambered up to the top of the hill, by my two stages, as usual; standing so, however, that my head did not appear above the hill, so that they could not perceive me by any means. Here I observed, by the help of my perspective glass, that they were no less than thirty in number; that they had a fire kindled, and that they had meat dressed. How they had cooked it I knew not, or what it was; but they were all dancing, in I know not how many barbarous gestures and figures, their own way, round the fire.

While I was thus looking on them, I perceived, by my perspective, two miserable wretches dragged from the boats, where, it seems, they were laid by, and were now brought out for the slaughter. I perceived one of them immediately fall; being knocked down, I suppose, with a club or wooden sword, for that was their way; and two or three others were at work immediately, cutting him open for their cookery, while the other victim was left standing by himself, till they should be ready for him. In that very moment this poor wretch, seeing himself a little at liberty and unbound, Nature inspired him with hopes of life, and he started away from them, and ran with incredible swiftness along the sands, directly towards me; I mean towards that part of the coast where my habitation was. I was dreadfully frightened, I must acknowledge, when I perceived him run my way; and especially when, as I thought, I saw him pursued by the whole body: and now I expected that part of my dream was coming to pass, and that he would certainly take shelter in my grove; but I could not depend, by any means, upon my dream, that the other savages would not pursue him thither and find him there. However, I kept my station, and my spirits began to recover when I found that there was not above three men that followed him; and still more was I encouraged, when I found that he outstripped them exceedingly in running, and gained ground on them; so that, if he could but hold out for half-an-hour, I saw easily he would fairly get away from them all.

There was between them and my castle the creek, which I mentioned often in the first part of my story, where I landed my cargoes out of the ship; and this I saw plainly he must necessarily swim over, or the poor wretch would be taken there; but when the savage escaping came thither, he made nothing of it, though the tide was then up; but plunging in, swam through in about thirty strokes, or thereabouts, landed, and ran with exceeding strength and swiftness. When the three persons came to the creek, I found that two of them could swim, but the third could not, and that, standing on the other side, he looked at the others, but went no farther, and soon after went softly back again; which, as it happened, was very well for him in the end. I observed that the two who swam were yet more than twice as strong swimming over the creek as the fellow was that fled from them. It came very warmly upon my thoughts, and indeed irresistibly, that now was the time to get me a servant, and, perhaps, a companion or assistant; and that I was plainly called by Providence to save this poor creature's life. I immediately ran down the ladders with all possible expedition, fetched my two guns, for they were both at the foot of the ladders, as I observed before, and getting up again with the same haste to the top of the hill, I crossed towards the sea; and having a very short cut, and all down hill, placed myself in the way between the pursuers and the pursued, hallowing aloud to him that fled, who, looking back, was at first perhaps as much frightened at me as at them; but I beckoned with my hand to him to come back; and, in the meantime, I slowly advanced towards the two that followed; then rushing at once upon the foremost, I knocked him down with the stock of my piece. I was loath to fire, because I would not have the rest hear; though, at that distance, it would not have been easily heard, and being out of sight of the smoke, too, they would not have known what to make of it. Having knocked this fellow down, the other who pursued him stopped, as if he had been frightened, and I advanced towards him: but as I came nearer, I perceived presently he had a bow and arrow, and was fitting it to shoot at me: so I was then obliged to shoot at him first, which I did, and killed him at the first shot. The poor savage who fled, but had stopped, though he saw both his enemies fallen and killed, as he thought, yet was so frightened with the fire and noise of my piece that he stood stock still, and neither came forward nor went backward, though he seemed rather inclined still to fly than to come on. I hallooed again to him, and made signs to come forward, which he easily understood, and came a little way; then stopped again, and then a little farther, and stopped again; and I could then perceive that he stood trembling, as if he had been taken prisoner, and had just been to be killed, as his two enemies were. I beckoned to him again to come to me, and gave him all the signs of encouragement that I could think of; and he came nearer and nearer, kneeling down every ten or twelve steps, in token of acknowledgment for saving his life. I smiled at him, and looked pleasantly, and beckoned to him to come still nearer; at length he came close to me; and then he kneeled down again, kissed the ground, and laid his head upon the ground, and taking me by the foot, set my foot upon his head; this, it seems, was in token of swearing to be my slave for ever. I took him up and made much of him, and encouraged him all I could. But there was more work to do yet; for I perceived the savage whom I had knocked down was not killed, but stunned with the blow, and began to come to himself: so I pointed to him, and showed him the savage, that he was not dead; upon this he spoke some words to me, and though I could not understand them, yet I thought they were pleasant to hear; for they were the first sound of a man's voice that I had heard, my own excepted, for above twenty-five years. But there was no time for such reflections now; the savage who was knocked down recovered himself so far as to sit up upon the ground, and I perceived that my savage began to be afraid; but when I saw that, I presented my other piece at the man, as if I would shoot him: upon this my savage, for so I call him now, made a motion to me to lend him my sword, which hung naked in a belt by my side, which I did. He no sooner had it, but he runs to his enemy, and at one blow cut off his head so cleverly, no executioner in Germany could have done it sooner or better; which I thought very strange for one who, I had reason to believe, never saw a sword in his life before, except their own wooden swords: however, it seems, as I learned afterwards, they make their wooden swords so sharp, so heavy, and the wood is so hard, that they will even cut off heads with them, ay, and arms, and that at one blow, too. When he had done this, he comes laughing to me in sign of triumph, and brought me the sword again, and with abundance of gestures which I did not understand, laid it down, with the head of the savage that he had killed, just before me. But that which astonished him most was to know how I killed the other Indian so far off; so, pointing to him, he made signs to me to let him go to him; and I bade him go, as well as I could. When he came to him, he stood like one amazed, looking at him, turning him first on one side, then on the other; looked at the wound the bullet had made, which it seems was just in his breast, where it had made a hole, and no great quantity of blood had followed; but he had bled inwardly, for he was quite dead. He took up his bow and arrows, and came back; so I turned to go away, and beckoned him to follow me, making signs to him that more might come after them. Upon this he made signs to me that he should bury them with sand, that they might not be seen by the rest, if they followed; and so I made signs to him again to do so. He fell to work; and in an instant he had scraped a hole in the sand with his hands big enough to bury the first in, and then dragged him into it, and covered him; and did so by the other also; I believe he had him buried them both in a quarter of an hour. Then, calling away, I carried him, not to my castle, but quite away to my cave, on the farther part of the island: so I did not let my dream come to pass in that part, that he came into my grove for shelter. Here I gave him bread and a bunch of raisins to eat, and a draught of water, which I found he was indeed in great distress for, from his running: and having refreshed him, I made signs for him to go and lie down to sleep, showing him a place where I had laid some rice-straw, and a blanket upon it, which I used to sleep upon myself sometimes; so the poor creature lay down, and went to sleep.

He was a comely, handsome fellow, perfectly well made, with straight, strong limbs, not too large; tall, and well-shaped; and, as I reckon, about twenty-six years of age. He had a very good countenance, not a fierce and surly aspect, but seemed to have something very manly in his face; and yet he had all the sweetness and softness of a European in his countenance, too, especially when he smiled. His hair was long and black, not curled like wool; his forehead very high and large; and a great vivacity and sparkling sharpness in his eyes. The colour of his skin was not quite black, but very tawny; and yet not an ugly, yellow, nauseous tawny, as the Brazilians and Virginians, and other natives of America are, but of a bright kind of a dun olive-colour, that had in it something very agreeable, though not very easy to describe. His face was round and plump; his nose small, not flat, like the negroes; a very good mouth, thin lips, and his fine teeth well set, and as white as ivory.

After he had slumbered, rather than slept, about half-an-hour, he awoke again, and came out of the cave to me: for I had been milking my goats which I had in the enclosure just by: when he espied me he came running to me, laying himself down again upon the ground, with all the possible signs of an humble, thankful disposition, making a great many antic gestures to show it. At last he lays his head flat upon the ground, close to my foot, and sets my other foot upon his head, as he had done before; and after this made all the signs to me of subjection, servitude, and submission imaginable, to let me know how he would serve me so long as he lived. I understood him in many things, and let him know I was very well pleased with him. In a little time I began to speak to him; and teach him to speak to me: and first, I let him know his name should be Friday, which was the day I saved his life: I called him so for the memory of the time. I likewise taught him to say Master; and then let him know that was to be my name: I likewise taught him to say Yes and No and to know the meaning of them. I gave him some milk in an earthen pot, and let him see me drink it before him, and sop my bread in it; and gave him a cake of bread to do the like, which he quickly complied with, and made signs that it was very good for him. I kept there with him all that night; but as soon as it was day I beckoned to him to come with me, and let him know I would give him some clothes; at which he seemed very glad, for he was stark naked. As we went by the place where he had buried the two men, he pointed exactly to the place, and showed me the marks that he had made to find them again, making signs to me that we should dig them up again and eat them. At this I appeared very angry, expressed my abhorrence of it, made as if I would vomit at the thoughts of it, and beckoned with my hand to him to come away, which he did immediately, with great submission. I then led him up to the top of the hill, to see if his enemies were gone; and pulling out my glass I looked, and saw plainly the place where they had been, but no appearance of them or their canoes; so that it was plain they were gone, and had left their two comrades behind them, without any search after them.

But I was not content with this discovery; but having now more courage, and consequently more curiosity, I took my man Friday with me, giving him the sword in his hand, with the bow and arrows at his back, which I found he could use very dexterously, making him carry one gun for me, and I two for myself; and away we marched to the place where these creatures had been; for I had a mind now to get some further intelligence of them. When I came to the place my very blood ran chill in my veins, and my heart sunk within me, at the horror of the spectacle; indeed, it was a dreadful sight, at least it was so to me, though Friday made nothing of it. The place was covered with human bones, the ground dyed with their blood, and great pieces of flesh left here and there, half-eaten, mangled, and scorched; and, in short, all the tokens of the triumphant feast they had been making there, after a victory over their enemies. I saw three skulls, five hands, and the bones of three or four legs and feet, and abundance of other parts of the bodies; and Friday, by his signs, made me understand that they brought over four prisoners to feast upon; that three of them were eaten up, and that he, pointing to himself, was the fourth; that there had been a great battle between them and their next king, of whose subjects, it seems, he had been one, and that they had taken a great number of prisoners; all which were carried to several places by those who had taken them in the fight, in order to feast upon them, as was done here by these wretches upon those they brought hither.

I caused Friday to gather all the skulls, bones, flesh, and whatever remained, and lay them together in a heap, and make a great fire upon it, and burn them all to ashes. I found Friday had still a hankering stomach after some of the flesh, and was still a cannibal in his nature; but I showed so much abhorrence at the very thoughts of it, and at the least appearance of it, that he durst not discover it: for I had, by some means, let him know that I would kill him if he offered it.

When he had done this, we came back to our castle; and there I fell to work for my man Friday; and first of all, I gave him a pair of linen drawers, which I had out of the poor gunner's chest I mentioned, which I found in the wreck, and which, with a little alteration, fitted him very well; and then I made him a jerkin of goat's skin, as well as my skill would allow (for I was now grown a tolerably good tailor); and I gave him a cap which I made of hare's skin, very convenient, and fashionable enough; and thus he was clothed, for the present, tolerably well, and was mighty well pleased to see himself almost as well clothed as his master. It is true he went awkwardly in these clothes at first: wearing the drawers was very awkward to him, and the sleeves of the waistcoat galled his shoulders and the inside of his arms; but a little easing them where he complained they hurt him, and using himself to them, he took to them at length very well.

The next day, after I came home to my hutch with him, I began to consider where I should lodge him: and that I might do well for him and yet be perfectly easy myself, I made a little tent for him in the vacant place between my two fortifications, in the inside of the last, and in the outside of the first. As there was a door or entrance there into my cave, I made a formal framed door-case, and a door to it, of boards, and set it up in the passage, a little within the entrance; and, causing the door to open in the inside, I barred it up in the night, taking in my ladders, too; so that Friday could no way come at me in the inside of my innermost wall, without making so much noise in getting over that it must needs awaken me; for my first wall had now a complete roof over it of long poles, covering all my tent, and leaning up to the side of the hill; which was again laid across with smaller sticks, instead of laths, and then thatched over a great thickness with the rice-straw, which was strong, like reeds; and at the hole or place which was left to go in or out by the ladder I had placed a kind of trap-door, which, if it had been attempted on the outside, would not have opened at all, but would have fallen down and made a great noise—as to weapons, I took them all into my side every night. But I needed none of all this precaution; for never man had a more faithful, loving, sincere servant than Friday was to me: without passions, sullenness, or designs, perfectly obliged and engaged; his very affections were tied to me, like those of a child to a father; and I daresay he would have sacrificed his life to save mine upon any occasion whatsoever—the many testimonies he gave me of this put it out of doubt, and soon convinced me that I needed to use no precautions for my safety on his account.

This frequently gave me occasion to observe, and that with wonder, that however it had pleased God in His providence, and in the government of the works of His hands, to take from so great a part of the world of His creatures the best uses to which their faculties and the powers of their souls are adapted, yet that He has bestowed upon them the same powers, the same reason, the same affections, the same sentiments of kindness and obligation, the same passions and resentments of wrongs, the same sense of gratitude, sincerity, fidelity, and all the capacities of doing good and receiving good that He has given to us; and that when He pleases to offer them occasions of exerting these, they are as ready, nay, more ready, to apply them to the right uses for which they were bestowed than we are. This made me very melancholy sometimes, in reflecting, as the several occasions presented, how mean a use we make of all these, even though we have these powers enlightened by the great lamp of instruction, the Spirit of God, and by the knowledge of His word added to our understanding; and why it has pleased God to hide the like saving knowledge from so many millions of souls, who, if I might judge by this poor savage, would make a much better use of it than we did. From hence I sometimes was led too far, to invade the sovereignty of Providence, and, as it were, arraign the justice of so arbitrary a disposition of things, that should hide that sight from some, and reveal it to others, and yet expect a like duty from both; but I shut it up, and checked my thoughts with this conclusion: first, that we did not know by what light and law these should be condemned; but that as God was necessarily, and by the nature of His being, infinitely holy and just, so it could not be, but if these creatures were all sentenced to absence from Himself, it was on account of sinning against that light which, as the Scripture says, was a law to themselves, and by such rules as their consciences would acknowledge to be just, though the foundation was not discovered to us; and secondly, that still as we all are the clay in the hand of the potter, no vessel could say to him, "Why hast thou formed me thus?"

But to return to my new companion. I was greatly delighted with him, and made it my business to teach him everything that was proper to make him useful, handy, and helpful; but especially to make him speak, and understand me when I spoke; and he was the aptest scholar that ever was; and particularly was so merry, so constantly diligent, and so pleased when he could but understand me, or make me understand him, that it was very pleasant for me to talk to him. Now my life began to be so easy that I began to say to myself that could I but have been safe from more savages, I cared not if I was never to remove from the place where I lived.

Chapter XV—FRIDAY'S EDUCATION

After I had been two or three days returned to my castle, I thought that, in order to bring Friday off from his horrid way of feeding, and from the relish of a cannibal's stomach, I ought to let him taste other flesh; so I took him out with me one morning to the woods. I went, indeed, intending to kill a kid out of my own flock; and bring it home and dress it; but as I was going I saw a she-goat lying down in the shade, and two young kids sitting by her. I catched hold of Friday. "Hold," said I, "stand still;" and made signs to him not to stir: immediately I presented my piece, shot, and killed one of the kids. The poor creature, who had at a distance, indeed, seen me kill the savage, his enemy, but did not know, nor could imagine how it was done, was sensibly surprised, trembled, and shook, and looked so amazed that I thought he would have sunk down. He did not see the kid I shot at, or perceive I had killed it, but ripped up his waistcoat to feel whether he was not wounded; and, as I found presently, thought I was resolved to kill him: for he came and kneeled down to me, and embracing my knees, said a great many things I did not understand; but I could easily see the meaning was to pray me not to kill him.

I soon found a way to convince him that I would do him no harm; and taking him up by the hand, laughed at him, and pointing to the kid which I had killed, beckoned to him to run and fetch it, which he did: and while he was wondering, and looking to see how the creature was killed, I loaded my gun again. By-and-by I saw a great fowl, like a hawk, sitting upon a tree within shot; so, to let Friday understand a little what I would do, I called him to me again, pointed at the fowl, which was indeed a parrot, though I thought it had been a hawk; I say, pointing to the parrot, and to my gun, and to the ground under the parrot, to let him see I would make it fall, I made him understand that I would shoot and kill that bird; accordingly, I fired, and bade him look, and immediately he saw the parrot fall. He stood like one frightened again, notwithstanding all I had said to him; and I found he was the more amazed, because he did not see me put anything into the gun, but thought that there must be some wonderful fund of death and destruction in that thing, able to kill man, beast, bird, or anything near or far off; and the astonishment this created in him was such as could not wear off for a long time; and I believe, if I would have let him, he would have worshipped me and my gun. As for the gun itself, he would not so much as touch it for several days after;

but he would speak to it and talk to it, as if it had answered him, when he was by himself; which, as I afterwards learned of him, was to desire it not to kill him. Well, after his astonishment was a little over at this, I pointed to him to run and fetch the bird I had shot, which he did, but stayed some time; for the parrot, not being quite dead, had fluttered away a good distance from the place where she fell: however, he found her, took her up, and brought her to me; and as I had perceived his ignorance about the gun before, I took this advantage to charge the gun again, and not to let him see me do it, that I might be ready for any other mark that might present; but nothing more offered at that time: so I brought home the kid, and the same evening I took the skin off, and cut it out as well as I could; and having a pot fit for that purpose, I boiled or stewed some of the flesh, and made some very good broth. After I had begun to eat some I gave some to my man, who seemed very glad of it, and liked it very well; but that which was strangest to him was to see me eat salt with it. He made a sign to me that the salt was not good to eat; and putting a little into his own mouth, he seemed to nauseate it, and would spit and sputter at it, washing his mouth with fresh water after it: on the other hand, I took some meat into my mouth without salt, and I pretended to spit and sputter for want of salt, as much as he had done at the salt; but it would not do; he would never care for salt with meat or in his broth; at least, not for a great while, and then but a very little.

Having thus fed him with boiled meat and broth, I was resolved to feast him the next day by roasting a piece of the kid: this I did by hanging it before the fire on a string, as I had seen many people do in England, setting two poles up, one on each side of the fire, and one across the top, and tying the string to the cross stick, letting the meat turn continually. This Friday admired very much; but when he came to taste the flesh, he took so many ways to tell me how well he liked it, that I could not but understand him: and at last he told me, as well as he could, he would never eat man's flesh any more, which I was very glad to hear.

The next day I set him to work beating some corn out, and sifting it in the manner I used to do, as I observed before; and he soon understood how to do it as well as I, especially after he had seen what the meaning of it was, and that it was to make bread of; for after that I let him see me make my bread, and bake it too; and in a little time Friday was able to do all the work for me as well as I could do it myself.

I began now to consider, that having two mouths to feed instead of one, I must provide more ground for my harvest, and plant a larger quantity of corn than I used to do; so I marked out a larger piece of land, and began the fence in the same manner as before, in which Friday worked not only very willingly and very hard, but did it very cheerfully: and I told him what it was for; that it was for corn to make more bread, because he was now with me, and that I might have enough for him and myself too. He appeared very sensible of that part, and let me know that he thought I had much more labour upon me on his account than I had for myself; and that he would work the harder for me if I would tell him what to do.

This was the pleasantest year of all the life I led in this place. Friday began to talk pretty well, and understand the names of almost everything I had occasion to call for, and of every place I had to send him to, and talked a great deal to me; so that, in short, I began now to have some use for my tongue again, which, indeed, I had very little occasion for before. Besides the pleasure of talking to him, I had a singular satisfaction in the fellow himself: his simple, unfeigned honesty appeared to me more and more every day, and I began really to love the creature; and on his side I believe he loved me more than it was possible for him ever to love anything before.

I had a mind once to try if he had any inclination for his own country again; and having taught him English so well that he could answer me almost any question, I asked him whether the nation that he belonged to never conquered in battle? At which he smiled, and said—"Yes, yes, we always fight the better;" that is, he meant always get the better in fight; and so we began the following discourse:—

Master.—You always fight the better; how came you to be taken prisoner, then, Friday?

Friday.—My nation beat much for all that.

Master.—How beat? If your nation beat them, how came you to be taken?

Friday.—They more many than my nation, in the place where me was; they take one, two, three, and me: my nation over-beat them in the yonder place, where me no was; there my nation take one, two, great thousand.

Master.—But why did not your side recover you from the hands of your enemies, then?

Friday.—They run, one, two, three, and me, and make go in the canoe; my nation have no canoe that time.

Master.—Well, Friday, and what does your nation do with the men they take? Do they carry them away and eat them, as these did?

Friday.—Yes, my nation eat mans too; eat all up.

Master.—Where do they carry them?

Friday.—Go to other place, where they think.

Master.—Do they come hither?

Friday.—Yes, yes, they come hither; come other else place.

Master.—Have you been here with them?

Friday.—Yes, I have been here (points to the NW. side of the island, which, it seems, was their side).

By this I understood that my man Friday had formerly been among the savages who used to come on shore on the farther part of the island, on the same man-eating occasions he was now brought for; and some time after, when I took the courage to carry him to that side, being the same I formerly mentioned, he presently knew the place, and told me he was there once, when they ate up twenty men, two women, and one child; he could not tell twenty in English, but he numbered them by laying so many stones in a row, and pointing to me to tell them over.

I have told this passage, because it introduces what follows: that after this discourse I had with him, I asked him how far it was from our island to the shore, and whether the canoes were not often lost. He told me there was no danger, no canoes ever lost: but that after a little way out to sea, there was a current and wind, always one way in the morning, the other in the afternoon. This I understood to be no more than the sets of the tide, as going out or coming in; but I afterwards understood it was occasioned by the great draft and reflux of the mighty river Orinoco, in the mouth or gulf of which river, as I found afterwards, our island lay; and that this land, which I perceived to be W. and NW., was the great island Trinidad, on the north point of the mouth of the river. I asked Friday a thousand questions about the country, the inhabitants, the sea, the coast, and what nations were near; he told me all he knew with the greatest openness imaginable. I asked him the names of the several nations of his sort of people, but could get no other name than Caribs; from whence I easily understood that these were the Caribbees, which our maps place on the part of America which reaches from the mouth of the river Orinoco to Guiana, and onwards to St. Martha. He told me that up a great way beyond the moon, that was beyond the setting of the moon, which must be west from their country, there dwelt white bearded men, like me, and pointed to my great whiskers, which I mentioned before; and that they had killed much mans, that was his word: by all which I understood he meant the Spaniards, whose cruelties in America had been spread over the whole country, and were remembered by all the nations from father to son.

I inquired if he could tell me how I might go from this island, and get among those white men. He told me, "Yes, yes, you may go in two canoe." I could not understand what he meant, or make him describe to me what he meant by two canoe, till at last, with great difficulty, I found he meant it must be in a large boat, as big as two canoes. This part of Friday's discourse I began to relish very well; and from this time I entertained some hopes that, one time or other, I might find an opportunity to make my escape from this place, and that this poor savage might be a means to help me.

During the long time that Friday had now been with me, and that he began to speak to me, and understand me, I was not wanting to lay a foundation of religious knowledge in his mind; particularly I asked him one time, who made him. The creature did not understand me at all, but thought I had asked who was his father—but I took it up by another handle, and asked him who made the sea, the ground we walked on, and the hills and woods. He told me, "It was one Benamuckee, that lived beyond all;" he could describe nothing of this great person, but that he was very old, "much older," he said, "than the sea or land, than the moon or the stars." I asked him then, if this old person had made all things, why did not all things worship him? He looked very grave, and, with a perfect look of innocence, said, "All things say O to him." I asked him if the people who die in his country went away anywhere? He said, "Yes; they all went to Benamuckee." Then I asked him whether those they eat up went thither too. He said, "Yes."

From these things, I began to instruct him in the knowledge of the true God; I told him that the great Maker of all things lived up there, pointing up towards heaven; that He governed the world by the same power and providence by which He made it; that He was omnipotent, and could do everything for us, give everything to us, take everything from us; and thus, by degrees, I opened his eyes. He listened with great attention, and received with pleasure the notion of Jesus Christ being sent to redeem us; and of the manner of making our prayers to God, and His being able to hear us, even in heaven. He told me one day, that if our God could hear us, up beyond the sun, he must needs be a greater God than their Benamuckee, who lived but a little way off, and yet could not hear till they went up to the great mountains where he dwelt to speak to them. I asked him if ever he went thither to speak to him. He said, "No; they never went that were young men; none went thither but the old men," whom he called their Oowokakee; that is, as I made him explain to me, their religious, or clergy; and that they went to say O (so he called saying prayers), and then came back and told them what Benamuckee said. By this I observed, that there is priestcraft even among the most blinded, ignorant pagans in the world; and the policy of making a secret of religion, in order to preserve the veneration of the people to the clergy, not only to be found in the Roman, but, perhaps, among all religions in the world, even among the most brutish and barbarous savages.

I endeavoured to clear up this fraud to my man Friday; and told him that the pretence of their old men going up to the mountains to say O to their god Benamuckee was a cheat; and their bringing word from thence what he said was much more so; that if they met with any answer, or spake with any one there, it must be with an evil spirit; and then I entered into a long discourse with him about the devil, the origin of him, his rebellion against God, his enmity to man, the reason of it, his setting himself up in the dark parts of the world to be worshipped instead of God, and as God, and the many stratagems he made use of to delude mankind to their ruin; how he had a secret access to our passions and to our affections, and to adapt his snares to our inclinations, so as to cause us even to be our own tempters, and run upon our destruction by our own choice.

I found it was not so easy to imprint right notions in his mind about the devil as it was about the being of a God. Nature assisted all my arguments to evidence to him even the necessity of a great First Cause, an overruling, governing Power, a secret directing Providence, and of the equity and justice of paying homage to Him that made us, and the like; but there appeared nothing of this kind in the notion of an evil spirit, of his origin, his being, his nature, and above all, of his inclination to do evil, and to draw us in to do so too; and the poor creature puzzled me once in such a manner, by a question merely natural and innocent, that I scarce knew what to say to him. I had been talking a great deal to him of the power of God, His omnipotence, His aversion to sin, His being a consuming fire to the workers of iniquity; how, as He had made us all, He could destroy us and all the world in a moment; and he listened with great seriousness to me all the while. After this I had been telling him how the devil was God's enemy in the hearts of men, and used all his malice and skill to defeat the good designs of Providence, and to ruin the kingdom of Christ in the world, and the like. "Well," says Friday, "but you say God is so strong, so great; is He not much strong, much might as the devil?" "Yes, yes," says I, "Friday; God is stronger than the devil—God is above the devil, and therefore we pray to God to tread him down under our feet, and enable us to resist his temptations and quench his fiery darts." "But," says he again, "if God much stronger, much might as the wicked devil, why God no kill the devil, so make him no more do wicked?" I was strangely surprised at this question; and, after all, though I was now an old man, yet I was but a young doctor, and ill qualified for a casuist or a solver of difficulties; and at first I could not tell what to say; so I pretended not to hear him, and asked him what he said; but he was too earnest for an answer to forget his question, so that he repeated it in the very same broken words as above. By this time I had recovered myself a little, and I said, "God will at last punish him severely; he is reserved for the judgment, and is to be cast into the bottomless pit, to dwell with everlasting fire." This did not satisfy Friday; but he returns upon me, repeating my words, "'*Reserve at last*!' me no understand—but why not kill the devil now; not kill great ago?" "You may as well ask me," said I, "why God does not kill you or me, when we do wicked things here that offend Him—we are preserved to repent and be pardoned." He mused some time on this. "Well, well," says he, mighty affectionately, "that well—so you, I, devil, all wicked, all preserve, repent, God pardon all." Here I was run down again by him to the last degree; and it was a testimony to me, how the mere notions of nature, though they will guide reasonable creatures to the knowledge of a God, and of a worship or homage due to the supreme being of God, as the consequence of our nature, yet nothing but divine revelation can form the knowledge of Jesus Christ, and of redemption purchased for us; of a Mediator of the new covenant, and of an Intercessor at the footstool of God's throne; I say, nothing but a revelation from Heaven can form these in the soul; and that, therefore, the gospel of our Lord and Saviour Jesus Christ, I mean the Word of God, and the Spirit of God, promised for the guide and sanctifier of His people, are the absolutely necessary instructors of the souls of men in the saving knowledge of God and the means of salvation.

I therefore diverted the present discourse between me and my man, rising up hastily, as upon some sudden occasion of going out; then sending him for something a good way off, I seriously prayed to God that He would enable me to instruct savingly this poor savage; assisting, by His Spirit, the heart of the poor ignorant creature to receive the light of the knowledge of God in Christ, reconciling him to Himself, and would guide me so to speak to him from the Word of God that his conscience might be convinced, his eyes opened, and his soul saved. When he came again to me, I entered into a long discourse with him upon the subject of the redemption of man by the Saviour of the world, and of the doctrine of the gospel preached from Heaven, viz. of repentance towards God, and faith in our blessed Lord Jesus. I then explained to him as well as I could why our blessed Redeemer took not on Him the nature of angels but the seed of Abraham;

and how, for that reason, the fallen angels had no share in the redemption; that He came only to the lost sheep of the house of Israel, and the like.

I had, God knows, more sincerity than knowledge in all the methods I took for this poor creature's instruction, and must acknowledge, what I believe all that act upon the same principle will find, that in laying things open to him, I really informed and instructed myself in many things that either I did not know or had not fully considered before, but which occurred naturally to my mind upon searching into them, for the information of this poor savage; and I had more affection in my inquiry after things upon this occasion than ever I felt before: so that, whether this poor wild wretch was better for me or no, I had great reason to be thankful that ever he came to me; my grief sat lighter, upon me; my habitation grew comfortable to me beyond measure: and when I reflected that in this solitary life which I have been confined to, I had not only been moved to look up to heaven myself, and to seek the Hand that had brought me here, but was now to be made an instrument, under Providence, to save the life, and, for aught I knew, the soul of a poor savage, and bring him to the true knowledge of religion and of the Christian doctrine, that he might know Christ Jesus, in whom is life eternal; I say, when I reflected upon all these things, a secret joy ran through every part of My soul, and I frequently rejoiced that ever I was brought to this place, which I had so often thought the most dreadful of all afflictions that could possibly have befallen me.

I continued in this thankful frame all the remainder of my time; and the conversation which employed the hours between Friday and me was such as made the three years which we lived there together perfectly and completely happy, if any such thing as complete happiness can be formed in a sublunary state. This savage was now a good Christian, a much better than I; though I have reason to hope, and bless God for it, that we were equally penitent, and comforted, restored penitents. We had here the Word of God to read, and no farther off from His Spirit to instruct than if we had been in England. I always applied myself, in reading the Scripture, to let him know, as well as I could, the meaning of what I read; and he again, by his serious inquiries and questionings, made me, as I said before, a much better scholar in the Scripture knowledge than I should ever have been by my own mere private reading. Another thing I cannot refrain from observing here also, from experience in this retired part of my life, viz. how infinite and inexpressible a blessing it is that the knowledge of God, and of the doctrine of salvation by Christ Jesus, is so plainly laid down in the Word of God, so easy to be received and understood, that, as the bare reading the Scripture made me capable of understanding enough of my duty to carry me directly on to the great work of sincere repentance for my sins, and laying hold of a Saviour for life and salvation, to a stated reformation in practice, and obedience to all God's commands, and this without any teacher or instructor, I mean human; so the same plain instruction sufficiently served to the enlightening this savage creature, and bringing him to be such a Christian as I have known few equal to him in my life.

As to all the disputes, wrangling, strife, and contention which have happened in the world about religion, whether niceties in doctrines or schemes of church government, they were all perfectly useless to us, and, for aught I can yet see, they have been so to the rest of the world. We had the sure guide to heaven, viz. the Word of God; and we had, blessed be God, comfortable views of the Spirit of God teaching and instructing by His word, leading us into all truth, and making us both willing and obedient to the instruction of His word. And I cannot see the least use that the greatest knowledge of the disputed points of religion, which have made such confusion in the world, would have been to us, if we could have obtained it. But I must go on with the historical part of things, and take every part in its order.

After Friday and I became more intimately acquainted, and that he could understand almost all I said to him, and speak pretty fluently, though in broken English, to me, I acquainted him with my own history, or at least so much of it as related to my coming to this place: how I had lived there, and how long; I let him into the mystery, for such it was to him, of gunpowder and bullet, and taught him how to shoot. I gave him a knife, which he was wonderfully delighted with; and I made him a belt, with a frog hanging to it, such as in England we wear hangers in; and in the frog, instead of a hanger, I gave him a hatchet, which was not only as good a weapon in some cases, but much more useful upon other occasions.

I described to him the country of Europe, particularly England, which I came from; how we lived, how we worshipped God, how we behaved to one another, and how we traded in ships to all parts of the world. I gave him an account of the wreck which I had been on board of, and showed him, as near as I could, the place where she lay; but she was all beaten in pieces before, and gone. I showed him the ruins of our boat, which we lost when we escaped, and which I could not stir with my whole strength then; but was now fallen almost all to pieces. Upon seeing this boat, Friday stood, musing a great while, and said nothing. I asked him what it was he studied upon. At last says he, "Me see such boat like come to place at my nation." I did not understand him a good while; but at last, when I had examined further into it, I understood by him that a boat, such as that had been, came on shore upon the country where he lived: that is, as he explained it, was driven thither by stress of weather. I presently imagined that some European ship must have been cast away upon their coast, and the boat might get loose and drive ashore; but was so dull that I never once thought of men making their escape from a wreck thither, much less whence they might come: so I only inquired after a description of the boat.

Friday described the boat to me well enough; but brought me better to understand him when he added with some warmth, "We save the white mans from drown." Then I presently asked if there were any white mans, as he called them, in the boat. "Yes," he said; "the boat full of white mans." I asked him how many. He told upon his fingers seventeen. I asked him then what became of them. He told me, "They live, they dwell at my nation."

This put new thoughts into my head; for I presently imagined that these might be the men belonging to the ship that was cast away in the sight of my island, as I now called it; and who, after the ship was struck on the rock, and they saw her inevitably lost, had saved themselves in their boat, and were landed upon that wild shore among the savages. Upon this I inquired of him more critically what was become of them. He assured me they lived still there; that they had been there about four years; that the savages left them alone, and gave them victuals to live on. I asked him how it came to pass they did not kill them and eat them. He said, "No, they make brother with them;" that is, as I understood him, a truce; and then he added, "They no eat mans but when make the war fight;" that is to say, they never eat any men but such as come to fight with them and are taken in battle.

It was after this some considerable time, that being upon the top of the hill at the east side of the island, from whence, as I have said, I had, in a clear day, discovered the main or continent of America, Friday, the weather being very serene, looks very earnestly towards the mainland, and, in a kind of surprise, falls a jumping and dancing, and calls out to me, for I was at some distance from him. I asked him what was the matter. "Oh, joy!" says he; "Oh, glad! there see my country, there my nation!" I observed an extraordinary sense of pleasure appeared in his face, and his eyes sparkled, and his countenance discovered a strange eagerness, as if he had a mind to be in his own country again. This observation of mine put a great many thoughts into me, which made me at first not so easy about my new man Friday as I was before; and I made no doubt but that, if Friday could get back to his own nation again, he would not only forget all his religion but all his obligation to me, and would be forward enough to give his countrymen an account of me, and come back, perhaps with a hundred or two of them, and make a feast upon me, at which he might be as merry as he used to be with those of his enemies when they were taken in war. But I wronged the poor honest creature very much, for which I was very sorry afterwards. However, as my jealousy increased, and held some weeks, I was a little more circumspect, and not so familiar and kind to him as before: in which I was certainly wrong too; the honest, grateful creature having no thought about it but what consisted with the best principles, both as a religious Christian and as a grateful friend, as appeared afterwards to my full satisfaction.

While my jealousy of him lasted, you may be sure I was every day pumping him to see if he would discover any of the new thoughts which I suspected were in him; but I found everything he said was so honest and so innocent, that I could find nothing to nourish my suspicion; and in spite of all my uneasiness, he made me at last entirely his own again; nor did he in the least perceive that I was uneasy, and therefore I could not suspect him of deceit.

One day, walking up the same hill, but the weather being hazy at sea, so that we could not see the continent, I called to him, and said, "Friday, do not you wish yourself in your own country, your own nation?" "Yes," he said, "I be much O glad to be at my own nation." "What would you do there?" said I. "Would you turn wild again, eat men's flesh again, and be a savage as you were before?" He looked full of concern, and shaking his head, said, "No, no, Friday tell them to live good; tell them to pray God; tell them to eat corn-bread, cattle flesh, milk; no eat man again." "Why, then," said I to him, "they will kill you." He looked grave at that, and then said, "No, no, they no kill me, they willing love learn." He meant by this, they would be willing to learn. He added, they learned much of the bearded mans that came in the boat. Then I asked him if he would go back to them. He smiled at that, and told me that he could not swim so far. I told him I would make a canoe for him. He told me he would go if I would go with him. "I go!" says I; "why, they will eat me if I come there." "No, no," says he, "me make they no eat you; me make they much love you." He meant, he would tell them how I had killed his enemies, and saved his life, and so he would make them love me. Then he told me, as well as he could, how kind they were to seventeen white men, or bearded men, as he called them who came on shore there in distress.

From this time, I confess, I had a mind to venture over, and see if I could possibly join with those bearded men, who I made no doubt were Spaniards and Portuguese; not doubting but, if I could, we might find some method to escape from thence, being upon the continent, and a good company together, better than I could from an island forty miles off the shore, alone and without help. So, after some days, I took Friday to work again by way of discourse, and told him I would give him a boat to go back to his own nation; and, accordingly, I carried him to my frigate, which lay on the other side of the island, and having cleared it of water (for I always kept it sunk in water), I brought it out, showed it him, and we both went into it. I found he was a most dexterous fellow at managing it, and would make it go almost as swift again as I could. So when he was in, I said to him, "Well, now, Friday, shall we go to your nation?" He looked very dull at my saying so; which it seems was because he thought the boat was too small to go so far. I then told him I had a bigger; so the next day I went to the place where the first boat lay which I had made, but which I could not get into the water. He said that was big enough; but then, as I had taken no care of it, and it had lain two or three and twenty years there, the sun had so split and dried it, that it was rotten. Friday told me such a boat would do very well, and would carry "much enough vittle, drink, bread;" this was his way of talking.

Chapter XVI—RESCUE OF PRISONERS FROM CANNIBALS

Upon the whole, I was by this time so fixed upon my design of going over with him to the continent that I told him we would go and make one as big as that, and he should go home in it. He answered not one word, but looked very grave and sad. I asked him what was the matter with him. He asked me again, "Why you angry mad with Friday?—what me done?" I asked him what he meant. I told him I was not angry with him at all. "No angry!" says he, repeating the words several times; "why send Friday home away to my nation?" "Why," says I, "Friday, did not you say you wished you were there?" "Yes, yes," says he, "wish we both there; no wish Friday there, no master there." In a word, he would not think of going there without me. "I go there, Friday?" says I; "what shall I do there?" He turned very quick upon me at this. "You do great deal much good," says he; "you teach wild mans be good, sober, tame mans; you tell them know God, pray God, and live new life." "Alas, Friday!" says I, "thou knowest not what thou sayest; I am but an ignorant man myself." "Yes, yes," says he, "you teachee me good, you teachee them good." "No, no, Friday," says I, "you shall go without me; leave me here to live by myself, as I did before." He looked confused again at that word; and running to one of the hatchets which he used to wear, he takes it up hastily, and gives it to me. "What must I do with this?" says I to him. "You take kill Friday," says he. "What must kill you for?" said I again. He returns very quick—"What you send Friday away for? Take kill Friday, no send Friday away." This he spoke so earnestly that I saw tears stand in his eyes. In a word, I so plainly discovered the utmost affection in him to me, and a firm resolution in him, that I told him then and often after, that I would never send him away from me if he was willing to stay with me.

Upon the whole, as I found by all his discourse a settled affection to me, and that nothing could part him from me, so I found all the foundation of his desire to go to his own country was laid in his ardent affection to the people, and his hopes of my doing them good; a thing which, as I had no notion of myself, so I had not the least thought or intention, or desire of undertaking it. But still I found a strong inclination to attempting my escape, founded on the supposition gathered from the discourse, that there were seventeen bearded men there; and therefore, without any more delay, I went to work with Friday to find out a great tree proper to fell, and make a large periagua, or canoe, to undertake the voyage. There were trees enough in the island to have built a little fleet, not of periaguas or canoes, but even of good, large vessels; but the main thing I looked at was, to get one so near the water that we might launch it when it was made, to avoid the mistake I committed at first. At last Friday pitched upon a tree; for I found he knew much better than I what kind of wood was fittest for it; nor can I tell to this day what wood to call the tree we cut down, except that it was very like the tree we call fustic, or between that and the Nicaragua wood, for it was much of the same colour and smell. Friday wished to burn the hollow or cavity of this tree out, to make it for a boat, but I showed him how to cut it with tools; which, after I had showed him how to use, he did very handily; and in about a month's hard labour we finished it and made it very handsome; especially when, with our axes, which I showed him how to handle, we cut and hewed the outside into the true shape of a boat. After this, however, it cost us near a fortnight's time to get her along, as it were inch by inch, upon great rollers into the water; but when she was in, she would have carried twenty men with great ease.

When she was in the water, though she was so big, it amazed me to see with what dexterity and how swift my man Friday could manage her, turn her, and paddle her along. So I asked him if he would, and if we might venture over in her. "Yes," he said, "we venture over in her very well, though great blow wind." However I had a further design that he knew nothing of, and that was, to make a mast and a sail, and to fit her with an anchor and cable. As to a mast, that was easy enough to get; so I pitched upon a straight young cedar-tree, which I found near the place, and which there were great plenty of in the island, and I set Friday to work to cut it down, and gave him directions how to shape and order it. But as to the sail, that was my particular care. I knew I had old sails, or rather pieces of old sails, enough; but as I had had them now six-and-twenty years by me, and had not been very careful to preserve them, not imagining that I should ever have this kind of use for them, I did not doubt but they were all rotten; and, indeed, most of them were so. However, I found two pieces which appeared pretty good, and with these I went to work; and with a great deal of pains, and awkward stitching, you may be sure, for want of needles, I at length made a three-cornered ugly thing, like what we call in England a shoulder-of-mutton sail, to go with a boom at bottom, and a little short sprit at the top, such as usually our ships' long-boats sail with, and such as I best knew how to manage, as it was such a one as I had to the boat in which I made my escape from Barbary, as related in the first part of my story.

I was near two months performing this last work, viz. rigging and fitting my masts and sails; for I finished them very complete, making a small stay, and a sail, or foresail, to it, to assist if we should turn to windward; and, what was more than all, I fixed a rudder to the stern of her to steer with. I was but a bungling shipwright, yet as I knew the usefulness and even necessity of such a thing, I applied myself with so much pains to do it, that at last I brought it to pass; though, considering the many dull contrivances I had for it that failed, I think it cost me almost as much labour as making the boat.

After all this was done, I had my man Friday to teach as to what belonged to the navigation of my boat; though he knew very well how to paddle a canoe, he knew nothing of what belonged to a sail and a rudder; and was the most amazed when he saw me work the boat to and again in the sea by the rudder, and how the sail jibed, and filled this way or that way as the course we sailed changed; I say when he saw this he stood like one astonished and amazed. However, with a little use, I made all these things familiar to him, and he became an expert sailor, except that of the compass I could make him understand very little. On the other hand, as there was very little cloudy weather, and seldom or never any fogs in those parts, there was the less occasion for a compass, seeing the stars were always to be seen by night, and the shore by day, except in the rainy seasons, and then nobody cared to stir abroad either by land or sea.

I was now entered on the seven-and-twentieth year of my captivity in this place; though the three last years that I had this creature with me ought rather to be left out of the account, my habitation being quite of another kind than in all the rest of the time. I kept the anniversary of my landing here with the same thankfulness to God for His mercies as at first: and if I had such cause of acknowledgment at first, I had much more so now, having such additional testimonies of the care of Providence over me, and the great hopes I had of being effectually and speedily delivered; for I had an invincible impression upon my thoughts that my deliverance was at hand, and that I should not be another year in this place. I went on, however, with my husbandry; digging, planting, and fencing as usual. I gathered and cured my grapes, and did every necessary thing as before.

The rainy season was in the meantime upon me, when I kept more within doors than at other times. We had stowed our new vessel as secure as we could, bringing her up into the creek, where, as I said in the beginning, I landed my rafts from the ship; and hauling her up to the shore at high-water mark, I made my man Friday dig a little dock, just big enough to hold her, and just deep enough to give her water enough to float in; and then, when the tide was out, we made a strong dam across the end of it, to keep the water out; and so she lay, dry as to the tide from the sea: and to keep the rain off we laid a great many boughs of trees, so thick that she was as well thatched as a house; and thus we waited for the months of November and December, in which I designed to make my adventure.

When the settled season began to come in, as the thought of my design returned with the fair weather, I was preparing daily for the voyage. And the first thing I did was to lay by a certain quantity of provisions, being the stores for our voyage; and intended in a week or a fortnight's time to open the dock, and launch out our boat. I was busy one morning upon something of this kind, when I called to Friday, and bid him to go to the sea-shore and see if he could find a turtle or a tortoise, a thing which we generally got once a week, for the sake of the eggs as well as the flesh. Friday had not been long gone when he came running back, and flew over my outer wall or fence, like one that felt not the ground or the steps he set his foot on; and before I had time to speak to him he cries out to me, "O master! O master! O sorrow! O bad!"—"What's the matter, Friday?" says I. "O yonyonder there," says he, "one, two, three canoes; one, two, three!" By this way of speaking I concluded there were six; but on inquiry I found there were but three. "Well, Friday," says I, "do not be frightened." So I heartened him up as well as I could. However, I saw the poor fellow was most terribly scared, for nothing ran in his head but that they were come to look for him, and would cut him in pieces and eat him; and the poor fellow trembled so that I scarcely knew what to do with him. I comforted him as well as I could, and told him I was in as much danger as he, and that they would eat me as well as him. "But," says I, "Friday, we must resolve to fight them. Can you fight, Friday?" "Me shoot," says he, "but there come many great number." "No matter for that," said I again; "our guns will fright them that we do not kill." So I asked him whether, if I resolved to defend him, he would defend me, and stand by me, and do just as I bid him. He said, "Me die when you bid die, master." So I went and fetched a good dram of rum and gave him; for I had been so good a husband of my rum that I had a great deal left. When we had drunk it, I made him take the two fowling-pieces, which we always carried, and loaded them with large swan-shot, as big as small pistol-bullets. Then I took four muskets, and loaded them with two slugs and five small bullets each; and my two pistols I loaded with a brace of bullets each. I hung my great sword, as usual, naked by my side, and gave Friday his hatchet. When I had thus prepared myself, I took my perspective glass, and went up to the side of the hill, to see what I could discover; and I found quickly by my glass that there were one-and-twenty savages, three prisoners, and three canoes; and that their whole business seemed to be the triumphant banquet upon these three human bodies: a barbarous feast, indeed! but nothing more than, as I had observed, was usual with them. I observed also that they had landed, not where they had done when Friday made his escape, but nearer to my creek, where the shore was low, and where a thick wood came almost close down to the sea. This, with the abhorrence of the inhuman errand these wretches came about, filled me with such indignation that I came down again to Friday, and told him I was resolved to go down to them and kill them all; and asked him if he would stand by me. He had now got over his fright, and his spirits being a little raised with the dram I had given him, he was very cheerful, and told me, as before, he would die when I bid die.

In this fit of fury I divided the arms which I had charged, as before, between us; I gave Friday one pistol to stick in his girdle, and three guns upon his shoulder, and I took one pistol and the other three guns myself; and in this posture we marched out. I took a small bottle of rum in my pocket, and gave Friday a large bag with more powder and bullets; and as to orders, I charged him to keep close behind me, and not to stir, or shoot, or do anything till I bid him, and in the meantime not to speak a word. In this posture I fetched a compass to my right hand of near a mile, as well to get over the creek as to get into the wood, so that I could come within shot of them before I should be discovered, which I had seen by my glass it was easy to do.

While I was making this march, my former thoughts returning, I began to abate my resolution: I do not mean that I entertained any fear of their number, for as they were naked, unarmed wretches, it is certain I was superior to them—nay, though I had been alone. But it occurred to my thoughts, what call, what occasion, much less what necessity I was in to go and dip my hands in blood, to attack people who had neither done or intended me any wrong? who, as to me, were innocent, and whose barbarous customs were their own disaster, being in them a token, indeed, of God's having left them, with the other nations of that part of the world, to such stupidity, and to such inhuman courses, but did not call me to take upon me to be a judge of their actions, much less an executioner of His justice—that whenever He thought fit He would take the cause into His own hands, and by national vengeance punish them as a people for national crimes, but that, in the meantime, it was none of my business—that it was true Friday might justify it, because he was a declared enemy and in a state of war with those very particular people, and it was lawful for him to attack them—but I could not say the same with regard to myself. These things were so warmly pressed upon my thoughts all the way as I went, that I resolved I would only go and place myself near them that I might observe their barbarous feast, and that I would act then as God should direct; but that unless something offered that was more a call to me than yet I knew of, I would not meddle with them.

With this resolution I entered the wood, and, with all possible wariness and silence, Friday following close at my heels, I marched till I came to the skirts of the wood on the side which was next to them, only that one corner of the wood lay between me and them. Here I called softly to Friday, and showing him a great tree which was just at the corner of the wood, I bade him go to the tree, and bring me word if he could see there plainly what they were doing. He did so, and came immediately back to me, and told me they might be plainly viewed there—that they were all about their fire, eating the flesh of one of their prisoners, and that another lay bound upon the sand a little from them, whom he said they would kill next; and this fired the very soul within me. He told me it was not one of their nation, but one of the bearded men he had told me of, that came to their country in the boat. I was filled with horror at the very naming of the white bearded man; and going to the tree, I saw plainly by my glass a white man, who lay upon the beach of the sea with his hands and his feet tied with flags, or things like rushes, and that he was an European, and had clothes on.

There was another tree and a little thicket beyond it, about fifty yards nearer to them than the place where I was, which, by going a little way about, I saw I might come at undiscovered, and that then I should be within half a shot of them; so I withheld my passion, though I was indeed enraged to the highest degree; and going back about twenty paces, I got behind some bushes, which held all the way till I came to the other tree, and then came to a little rising ground, which gave me a full view of them at the distance of about eighty yards.

I had now not a moment to lose, for nineteen of the dreadful wretches sat upon the ground, all close huddled together, and had just sent the other two to butcher the poor Christian, and bring him perhaps limb by limb to their fire, and they were stooping down to untie the bands at his feet. I turned to Friday. "Now, Friday," said I, "do as I bid thee." Friday said he would. "Then, Friday," says I, "do exactly as you see me do; fail in nothing." So I set down one of the muskets and the fowling-piece upon the ground, and Friday did the like by his, and with the other musket I took my aim at the savages, bidding him to do the like; then asking him if he was ready, he said, "Yes." "Then fire at them," said I; and at the same moment I fired also.

Friday took his aim so much better than I, that on the side that he shot he killed two of them, and wounded three more; and on my side I killed one, and wounded two. They were, you may be sure, in a dreadful consternation: and all of them that were not hurt jumped upon their feet, but did not immediately know which way to run, or which way to look, for they knew not from whence their destruction came. Friday kept his eyes close upon me, that, as I had bid him, he might observe what I did; so, as soon as the first shot was made, I threw down the piece, and took up the fowling-piece, and Friday did the like; he saw me cock and present; he did the same again. "Are you ready, Friday?" said I. "Yes," says he. "Let fly, then," says I, "in the name of God!" and with that I fired again among the amazed wretches, and so did Friday; and as our pieces were now loaded with what I call swan-shot, or small pistol-bullets, we found only two drop; but so many were wounded that they ran about yelling and screaming like mad creatures, all bloody, and most of them miserably wounded; whereof three more fell quickly after, though not quite dead.

"Now, Friday," says I, laying down the discharged pieces, and taking up the musket which was yet loaded, "follow me," which he did with a great deal of courage; upon which I rushed out of the wood and showed myself, and Friday close at my foot. As soon as I perceived they saw me, I shouted as loud as I could, and bade Friday do so too, and running as fast as I could, which, by the way, was not very fast, being loaded with arms as I was, I made directly towards the poor victim, who was, as I said, lying upon the beach or shore, between the place where they sat and the sea. The two butchers who were just going to work with him had left him at the surprise of our first fire, and fled in a terrible fright to the seaside, and had jumped into a canoe, and three more of the rest made the same way. I turned to Friday, and bade him step forwards and fire at them; he understood me immediately, and running about forty yards, to be nearer them, he shot at them; and I thought he had killed them all, for I saw them all fall of a heap into the boat, though I saw two of them up again quickly; however, he killed two of them, and wounded the third, so that he lay down in the bottom of the boat as if he had been dead.

While my man Friday fired at them, I pulled out my knife and cut the flags that bound the poor victim; and loosing his hands and feet, I lifted him up, and asked him in the Portuguese tongue what he was. He answered in Latin, Christianus;

but was so weak and faint that he could scarce stand or speak. I took my bottle out of my pocket and gave it him, making signs that he should drink, which he did; and I gave him a piece of bread, which he ate. Then I asked him what countryman he was: and he said, Espagniole; and being a little recovered, let me know, by all the signs he could possibly make, how much he was in my debt for his deliverance. "Seignior," said I, with as much Spanish as I could make up, "we will talk afterwards, but we must fight now: if you have any strength left, take this pistol and sword, and lay about you." He took them very thankfully; and no sooner had he the arms in his hands, but, as if they had put new vigour into him, he flew upon his murderers like a fury, and had cut two of them in pieces in an instant; for the truth is, as the whole was a surprise to them, so the poor creatures were so much frightened with the noise of our pieces that they fell down for mere amazement and fear, and had no more power to attempt their own escape than their flesh had to resist our shot; and that was the case of those five that Friday shot at in the boat; for as three of them fell with the hurt they received, so the other two fell with the fright.

I kept my piece in my hand still without firing, being willing to keep my charge ready, because I had given the Spaniard my pistol and sword: so I called to Friday, and bade him run up to the tree from whence we first fired, and fetch the arms which lay there that had been discharged, which he did with great swiftness; and then giving him my musket, I sat down myself to load all the rest again, and bade them come to me when they wanted. While I was loading these pieces, there happened a fierce engagement between the Spaniard and one of the savages, who made at him with one of their great wooden swords, the weapon that was to have killed him before, if I had not prevented it. The Spaniard, who was as bold and brave as could be imagined, though weak, had fought the Indian a good while, and had cut two great wounds on his head; but the savage being a stout, lusty fellow, closing in with him, had thrown him down, being faint, and was wringing my sword out of his hand; when the Spaniard, though undermost, wisely quitting the sword, drew the pistol from his girdle, shot the savage through the body, and killed him upon the spot, before I, who was running to help him, could come near him.

Friday, being now left to his liberty, pursued the flying wretches, with no weapon in his hand but his hatchet: and with that he despatched those three who as I said before, were wounded at first, and fallen, and all the rest he could come up with: and the Spaniard coming to me for a gun, I gave him one of the fowling-pieces, with which he pursued two of the savages, and wounded them both; but as he was not able to run, they both got from him into the wood, where Friday pursued them, and killed one of them, but the other was too nimble for him; and though he was wounded, yet had plunged himself into the sea, and swam with all his might off to those two who were left in the canoe; which three in the canoe, with one wounded, that we knew not whether he died or no, were all that escaped our hands of one-and-twenty. The account of the whole is as follows: Three killed at our first shot from the tree; two killed at the next shot; two killed by Friday in the boat; two killed by Friday of those at first wounded; one killed by Friday in the wood; three killed by the Spaniard; four killed, being found dropped here and there, of the wounds, or killed by Friday in his chase of them; four escaped in the boat, whereof one wounded, if not dead—twenty-one in all.

Those that were in the canoe worked hard to get out of gun-shot, and though Friday made two or three shots at them, I did not find that he hit any of them. Friday would fain have had me take one of their canoes, and pursue them; and indeed I was very anxious about their escape, lest, carrying the news home to their people, they should come back perhaps with two or three hundred of the canoes and devour us by mere multitude; so I consented to pursue them by sea, and running to one of their canoes, I jumped in and bade Friday follow me: but when I was in the canoe I was surprised to find another poor creature lie there, bound hand and foot, as the Spaniard was, for the slaughter, and almost dead with fear, not knowing what was the matter; for he had not been able to look up over the side of the boat, he was tied so hard neck and heels, and had been tied so long that he had really but little life in him.

I immediately cut the twisted flags or rushes which they had bound him with, and would have helped him up; but he could not stand or speak, but groaned most piteously, believing, it seems, still, that he was only unbound in order to be killed. When Friday came to him I bade him speak to him, and tell him of his deliverance; and pulling out my bottle, made him give the poor wretch a dram, which, with the news of his being delivered, revived him, and he sat up in the boat. But when Friday came to hear him speak, and look in his face, it would have moved any one to tears to have seen how Friday kissed him, embraced him, hugged him, cried, laughed, hallooed, jumped about, danced, sang; then cried again, wrung his hands, beat his own face and head; and then sang and jumped about again like a distracted creature. It was a good while before I could make him speak to me or tell me what was the matter; but when he came a little to himself he told me that it was his father.

It is not easy for me to express how it moved me to see what ecstasy and filial affection had worked in this poor savage at the sight of his father, and of his being delivered from death; nor indeed can I describe half the extravagances of his affection after this: for he went into the boat and out of the boat a great many times: when he went in to him he would sit down by him, open his breast, and hold his father's head close to his bosom for many minutes together, to nourish it; then he took his arms and ankles, which were numbed and stiff with the binding, and chafed and rubbed them with his hands; and I, perceiving what the case was, gave him some rum out of my bottle to rub them with, which did them a great deal of good.

This affair put an end to our pursuit of the canoe with the other savages, who were now almost out of sight; and it was happy for us that we did not, for it blew so hard within two hours after, and before they could be got a quarter of their way, and continued blowing so hard all night, and that from the north-west, which was against them, that I could not suppose their boat could live, or that they ever reached their own coast.

But to return to Friday; he was so busy about his father that I could not find in my heart to take him off for some time; but after I thought he could leave him a little, I called him to me, and he came jumping and laughing, and pleased to the highest extreme: then I asked him if he had given his father any bread. He shook his head, and said, "None; ugly dog eat all up self." I then gave him a cake of bread out of a little pouch I carried on purpose; I also gave him a dram for himself; but he would not taste it, but carried it to his father. I had in my pocket two or three bunches of raisins, so I gave him a handful of them for his father. He had no sooner given his father these raisins but I saw him come out of the boat, and run away as if he had been bewitched, for he was the swiftest fellow on his feet that ever I saw: I say, he ran at such a rate that he was out of sight, as it were, in an instant; and though I called, and hallooed out too after him, it was all one—away he went; and in a quarter of an hour I saw him come back again, though not so fast as he went; and as he came nearer I found his pace slacker, because he had something in his hand. When he came up to me I found he had been quite home for an earthen jug or pot, to bring his father some fresh water, and that he had got two more cakes or loaves of bread: the bread he gave me, but the water he carried to his father; however, as I was very thirsty too, I took a little of it. The water revived his father more than all the rum or spirits I had given him, for he was fainting with thirst.

When his father had drunk, I called to him to know if there was any water left. He said, "Yes"; and I bade him give it to the poor Spaniard, who was in as much want of it as his father; and I sent one of the cakes that Friday brought to the Spaniard too, who was indeed very weak, and was reposing himself upon a green place under the shade of a tree; and whose limbs were also very stiff, and very much swelled with the rude bandage he had been tied with. When I saw that upon Friday's coming to him with the water he sat up and drank, and took the bread and began to eat, I went to him and gave him a handful of raisins. He looked up in my face with all the tokens of gratitude and thankfulness that could appear in any countenance; but was so weak, notwithstanding he had so exerted himself in the fight, that he could not stand up upon his feet—he tried to do it two or three times, but was really not able, his ankles were so swelled and so painful to him; so I bade him sit still, and caused Friday to rub his ankles, and bathe them with rum, as he had done his father's.

I observed the poor affectionate creature, every two minutes, or perhaps less, all the while he was here, turn his head about to see if his father was in the same place and posture as he left him sitting; and at last he found he was not to be seen; at which he started up, and, without speaking a word, flew with that swiftness to him that one could scarce perceive his feet to touch the ground as he went; but when he came, he only found he had laid himself down to ease his limbs, so Friday came back to me presently; and then I spoke to the Spaniard to let Friday help him up if he could, and lead him to the boat, and then he should carry him to our dwelling, where I would take care of him. But Friday, a lusty, strong fellow, took the Spaniard upon his back, and carried him away to the boat, and set him down softly upon the side or gunnel of the canoe, with his feet in the inside of it; and then lifting him quite in, he set him close to his father; and presently stepping out again, launched the boat off, and paddled it along the shore faster than I could walk, though the wind blew pretty hard too; so he brought them both safe into our creek, and leaving them in the boat, ran away to fetch the other canoe. As he passed me I spoke to him, and asked him whither he went. He told me, "Go fetch more boat;" so away he went like the wind, for sure never man or horse ran like him; and he had the other canoe in the creek almost as soon as I got to it by land; so he wafted me over, and then went to help our new guests out of the boat, which he did; but they were neither of them able to walk; so that poor Friday knew not what to do.

To remedy this, I went to work in my thought, and calling to Friday to bid them sit down on the bank while he came to me, I soon made a kind of hand-barrow to lay them on, and Friday and I carried them both up together upon it between us.

But when we got them to the outside of our wall, or fortification, we were at a worse loss than before, for it was impossible to get them over, and I was resolved not to break it down; so I set to work again, and Friday and I, in about two hours' time, made a very handsome tent, covered with old sails, and above that with boughs of trees, being in the space without our outward fence and between that and the grove of young wood which I had planted; and here we made them two beds of such things as I had—viz. of good rice-straw, with blankets laid upon it to lie on, and another to cover them, on each bed.

My island was now peopled, and I thought myself very rich in subjects; and it was a merry reflection, which I frequently made, how like a king I looked. First of all, the whole country was my own property, so that I had an undoubted right of dominion. Secondly, my people were perfectly subjected—I was absolutely lord and lawgiver—they all owed their lives to me, and were ready to lay down their lives, if there had been occasion for it, for me. It was remarkable, too, I had but three subjects, and they were of three different religions—my man Friday was a Protestant, his father was a Pagan and a cannibal, and the Spaniard was a Papist. However, I allowed liberty of conscience throughout my dominions. But this is by the way.

As soon as I had secured my two weak, rescued prisoners, and given them shelter, and a place to rest them upon, I began to think of making some provision for them; and the first thing I did, I ordered Friday to take a yearling goat, betwixt a kid and a goat, out of my particular flock, to be killed; when I cut off the hinder-quarter, and chopping it into small pieces, I set Friday to work to boiling and stewing, and made them a very good dish, I assure you, of flesh and broth; and as I cooked it without doors, for I made no fire within my inner wall, so I carried it all into the new tent, and having set a table there for them, I sat down, and ate my own dinner also with them, and, as well as I could, cheered them and encouraged them. Friday was my interpreter, especially to his father, and, indeed, to the Spaniard too; for the Spaniard spoke the language of the savages pretty well.

After we had dined, or rather supped, I ordered Friday to take one of the canoes, and go and fetch our muskets and other firearms, which, for want of time, we had left upon the place of battle; and the next day I ordered him to go and bury the dead bodies of the savages, which lay open to the sun, and would presently be offensive. I also ordered him to bury the horrid remains of their barbarous feast, which I could not think of doing myself; nay, I could not bear to see them if I went that way; all which he punctually performed, and effaced the very appearance of the savages being there; so that when I went again, I could scarce know where it was, otherwise than by the corner of the wood pointing to the place.

I then began to enter into a little conversation with my two new subjects; and, first, I set Friday to inquire of his father what he thought of the escape of the savages in that canoe, and whether we might expect a return of them, with a power too great for us to resist. His first opinion was, that the savages in the boat never could live out the storm which blew that night they went off, but must of necessity be drowned, or driven south to those other shores, where they were as sure to be devoured as they were to be drowned if they were cast away; but, as to what they would do if they came safe on shore, he said he knew not; but it was his opinion that they were so dreadfully frightened with the manner of their being attacked, the noise, and the fire, that he believed they would tell the people they were all killed by thunder and lightning, not by the hand of man; and that the two which appeared—viz. Friday and I—were two heavenly spirits, or furies, come down to destroy them, and not men with weapons. This, he said, he knew; because he heard them all cry out so, in their language, one to another; for it was impossible for them to conceive that a man could dart fire, and speak thunder, and kill at a distance, without lifting up the hand, as was done now: and this old savage was in the right; for, as I understood since, by other hands, the savages never attempted to go over to the island afterwards, they were so terrified with the accounts given by those four men (for it seems they did escape the sea), that they believed whoever went to that enchanted island would be destroyed with fire from the gods. This, however, I knew not; and therefore was under continual apprehensions for a good while, and kept always upon my guard, with all my army: for, as there were now four of us, I would have ventured upon a hundred of them, fairly in the open field, at any time.

Chapter XVII—VISIT OF MUTINEERS

In a little time, however, no more canoes appearing, the fear of their coming wore off; and I began to take my former thoughts of a voyage to the main into consideration; being likewise assured by Friday's father that I might depend upon good usage from their nation, on his account, if I would go. But my thoughts were a little suspended when I had a serious discourse with the Spaniard, and when I understood that there were sixteen more of his countrymen and Portuguese, who having been cast away and made their escape to that side, lived there at peace, indeed, with the savages, but were very sore put to it for necessaries, and, indeed, for life. I asked him all the particulars of their voyage, and found they were a Spanish ship, bound from the Rio de la Plata to the Havanna, being directed to leave their loading there, which was chiefly hides and silver, and to bring back what European goods they could meet with there; that they had five Portuguese seamen on board, whom they took out of another wreck; that five of their own men were drowned when first the ship was lost, and that these escaped through infinite dangers and hazards, and arrived, almost starved, on the cannibal coast, where they expected to have been devoured every moment. He told me they had some arms with them, but they were perfectly useless, for that they had neither powder nor ball, the washing of the sea having spoiled all their powder but a little, which they used at their first landing to provide themselves with some food.

I asked him what he thought would become of them there, and if they had formed any design of making their escape. He said they had many consultations about it; but that having neither vessel nor tools to build one, nor provisions of any kind, their councils always ended in tears and despair. I asked him how he thought they would receive a proposal from me, which might tend towards an escape; and whether, if they were all here, it might not be done. I told him with freedom, I feared mostly their treachery and ill-usage of me, if I put my life in their hands; for that gratitude was no inherent virtue in the nature of man, nor did men always square their dealings by the obligations they had received so much as they did by the advantages they expected. I told him it would be very hard that I should be made the instrument of their deliverance, and that they should afterwards make me their prisoner in New Spain, where an Englishman was certain to be made a sacrifice, what necessity or what accident soever brought him thither;

and that I had rather be delivered up to the savages, and be devoured alive, than fall into the merciless claws of the priests, and be carried into the Inquisition. I added that, otherwise, I was persuaded, if they were all here, we might, with so many hands, build a barque large enough to carry us all away, either to the Brazils southward, or to the islands or Spanish coast northward; but that if, in requital, they should, when I had put weapons into their hands, carry me by force among their own people, I might be ill-used for my kindness to them, and make my case worse than it was before.

He answered, with a great deal of candour and ingenuousness, that their condition was so miserable, and that they were so sensible of it, that he believed they would abhor the thought of using any man unkindly that should contribute to their deliverance; and that, if I pleased, he would go to them with the old man, and discourse with them about it, and return again and bring me their answer; that he would make conditions with them upon their solemn oath, that they should be absolutely under my direction as their commander and captain; and they should swear upon the holy sacraments and gospel to be true to me, and go to such Christian country as I should agree to, and no other; and to be directed wholly and absolutely by my orders till they were landed safely in such country as I intended, and that he would bring a contract from them, under their hands, for that purpose. Then he told me he would first swear to me himself that he would never stir from me as long as he lived till I gave him orders; and that he would take my side to the last drop of his blood, if there should happen the least breach of faith among his countrymen. He told me they were all of them very civil, honest men, and they were under the greatest distress imaginable, having neither weapons nor clothes, nor any food, but at the mercy and discretion of the savages; out of all hopes of ever returning to their own country; and that he was sure, if I would undertake their relief, they would live and die by me.

Upon these assurances, I resolved to venture to relieve them, if possible, and to send the old savage and this Spaniard over to them to treat. But when we had got all things in readiness to go, the Spaniard himself started an objection, which had so much prudence in it on one hand, and so much sincerity on the other hand, that I could not but be very well satisfied in it; and, by his advice, put off the deliverance of his comrades for at least half a year. The case was thus: he had been with us now about a month, during which time I had let him see in what manner I had provided, with the assistance of Providence, for my support; and he saw evidently what stock of corn and rice I had laid up; which, though it was more than sufficient for myself, yet it was not sufficient, without good husbandry, for my family, now it was increased to four; but much less would it be sufficient if his countrymen, who were, as he said, sixteen, still alive, should come over; and least of all would it be sufficient to victual our vessel, if we should build one, for a voyage to any of the Christian colonies of America; so he told me he thought it would be more advisable to let him and the other two dig and cultivate some more land, as much as I could spare seed to sow, and that we should wait another harvest, that we might have a supply of corn for his countrymen, when they should come; for want might be a temptation to them to disagree, or not to think themselves delivered, otherwise than out of one difficulty into another. "You know," says he, "the children of Israel, though they rejoiced at first for their being delivered out of Egypt, yet rebelled even against God Himself, that delivered them, when they came to want bread in the wilderness."

His caution was so seasonable, and his advice so good, that I could not but be very well pleased with his proposal, as well as I was satisfied with his fidelity; so we fell to digging, all four of us, as well as the wooden tools we were furnished with permitted; and in about a month's time, by the end of which it was seed-time, we had got as much land cured and trimmed up as we sowed two-and-twenty bushels of barley on, and sixteen jars of rice, which was, in short, all the seed we had to spare: indeed, we left ourselves barely sufficient, for our own food for the six months that we had to expect our crop; that is to say reckoning from the time we set our seed aside for sowing; for it is not to be supposed it is six months in the ground in that country.

Having now society enough, and our numbers being sufficient to put us out of fear of the savages, if they had come, unless their number had been very great, we went freely all over the island, whenever we found occasion; and as we had our escape or deliverance upon our thoughts, it was impossible, at least for me, to have the means of it out of mine. For this purpose I marked out several trees, which I thought fit for our work, and I set Friday and his father to cut them down; and then I caused the Spaniard, to whom I imparted my thoughts on that affair, to oversee and direct their work. I showed them with what indefatigable pains I had hewed a large tree into single planks, and I caused them to do the like, till they made about a dozen large planks, of good oak, near two feet broad, thirty-five feet long, and from two inches to four inches thick: what prodigious labour it took up any one may imagine.

At the same time I contrived to increase my little flock of tame goats as much as I could; and for this purpose I made Friday and the Spaniard go out one day, and myself with Friday the next day (for we took our turns), and by this means we got about twenty young kids to breed up with the rest; for whenever we shot the dam, we saved the kids, and added them to our flock. But above all, the season for curing the grapes coming on, I caused such a prodigious quantity to be hung up in the sun, that, I believe, had we been at Alicant, where the raisins of the sun are cured, we could have filled sixty or eighty barrels; and these, with our bread, formed a great part of our food—very good living too, I assure you, for they are exceedingly nourishing.

It was now harvest, and our crop in good order: it was not the most plentiful increase I had seen in the island, but, however, it was enough to answer our end; for from twenty-two bushels of barley we brought in and thrashed out above two hundred and twenty bushels; and the like in proportion of the rice; which was store enough for our food to the next harvest, though all the sixteen Spaniards had been on shore with me; or, if we had been ready for a voyage, it would very plentifully have victualled our ship to have carried us to any part of the world; that is to say, any part of America. When we had thus housed and secured our magazine of corn, we fell to work to make more wicker-ware, viz. great baskets, in which we kept it; and the Spaniard was very handy and dexterous at this part, and often blamed me that I did not make some things for defence of this kind of work; but I saw no need of it.

And now, having a full supply of food for all the guests I expected, I gave the Spaniard leave to go over to the main, to see what he could do with those he had left behind him there. I gave him a strict charge not to bring any man who would not first swear in the presence of himself and the old savage that he would in no way injure, fight with, or attack the person he should find in the island, who was so kind as to send for them in order to their deliverance; but that they would stand by him and defend him against all such attempts, and wherever they went would be entirely under and subjected to his command; and that this should be put in writing, and signed in their hands. How they were to have done this, when I knew they had neither pen nor ink, was a question which we never asked. Under these instructions, the Spaniard and the old savage, the father of Friday, went away in one of the canoes which they might be said to have come in, or rather were brought in, when they came as prisoners to be devoured by the savages. I gave each of them a musket, with a firelock on it, and about eight charges of powder and ball, charging them to be very good husbands of both, and not to use either of them but upon urgent occasions.

This was a cheerful work, being the first measures used by me in view of my deliverance for now twenty-seven years and some days. I gave them provisions of bread and of dried grapes, sufficient for themselves for many days, and sufficient for all the Spaniards—for about eight days' time; and wishing them a good voyage, I saw them go, agreeing with them about a signal they should hang out at their return, by which I should know them again when they came back, at a distance, before they came on shore. They went away with a fair gale on the day that the moon was at full, by my account in the month of October; but as for an exact reckoning of days, after I had once lost it I could never recover it again; nor had I kept even the number of years so punctually as to be sure I was right; though, as it proved when I afterwards examined my account, I found I had kept a true reckoning of years.

It was no less than eight days I had waited for them, when a strange and unforeseen accident intervened, of which the like has not, perhaps, been heard of in history. I was fast asleep in my hutch one morning, when my man Friday came running in to me, and called aloud, "Master, master, they are come, they are come!" I jumped up, and regardless of danger I went, as soon as I could get my clothes on, through my little grove, which, by the way, was by this time grown to be a very thick wood; I say, regardless of danger I went without my arms, which was not my custom to do; but I was surprised when, turning my eyes to the sea, I presently saw a boat at about a league and a half distance, standing in for the shore, with a shoulder-of-mutton sail, as they call it, and the wind blowing pretty fair to bring them in: also I observed, presently, that they did not come from that side which the shore lay on, but from the southernmost end of the island. Upon this I called Friday in, and bade him lie close, for these were not the people we looked for, and that we might not know yet whether they were friends or enemies. In the next place I went in to fetch my perspective glass to see what I could make of them; and having taken the ladder out, I climbed up to the top of the hill, as I used to do when I was apprehensive of anything, and to take my view the plainer without being discovered. I had scarce set my foot upon the hill when my eye plainly discovered a ship lying at anchor, at about two leagues and a half distance from me, SSE., but not above a league and a half from the shore. By my observation it appeared plainly to be an English ship, and the boat appeared to be an English long-boat.

I cannot express the confusion I was in, though the joy of seeing a ship, and one that I had reason to believe was manned by my own countrymen, and consequently friends, was such as I cannot describe; but yet I had some secret doubts hung about me—I cannot tell from whence they came—bidding me keep upon my guard. In the first place, it occurred to me to consider what business an English ship could have in that part of the world, since it was not the way to or from any part of the world where the English had any traffic; and I knew there had been no storms to drive them in there in distress; and that if they were really English it was most probable that they were here upon no good design; and that I had better continue as I was than fall into the hands of thieves and murderers.

Let no man despise the secret hints and notices of danger which sometimes are given him when he may think there is no possibility of its being real. That such hints and notices are given us I believe few that have made any observation of things can deny; that they are certain discoveries of an invisible world, and a converse of spirits, we cannot doubt; and if the tendency of them seems to be to warn us of danger, why should we not suppose they are from some friendly agent (whether supreme, or inferior and subordinate, is not the question), and that they are given for our good?

The present question abundantly confirms me in the justice of this reasoning; for had I not been made cautious by this secret admonition, come it from whence it will, I had been done inevitably, and in a far worse condition than before, as you will see presently. I had not kept myself long in this posture till I saw the boat draw near the shore, as if they looked for a creek to thrust in at, for the convenience of landing; however, as they did not come quite far enough, they did not see the little inlet where I formerly landed my rafts, but ran their boat on shore upon the beach, at about half a mile from me, which was very happy for me; for otherwise they would have landed just at my door, as I may say, and would soon have beaten me out of my castle, and perhaps have plundered me of all I had. When they were on shore I was fully satisfied they were Englishmen, at least most of them; one or two I thought were Dutch, but it did not prove so; there were in all eleven men, whereof three of them I found were unarmed and, as I thought, bound; and when the first four or five of them were jumped on shore, they took those three out of the boat as prisoners: one of the three I could perceive using the most passionate gestures of entreaty, affliction, and despair, even to a kind of extravagance; the other two, I could perceive, lifted up their hands sometimes, and appeared concerned indeed, but not to such a degree as the first. I was perfectly confounded at the sight, and knew not what the meaning of it should be. Friday called out to me in English, as well as he could, "O master! you see English mans eat prisoner as well as savage mans." "Why, Friday," says I, "do you think they are going to eat them, then?" "Yes," says Friday, "they will eat them." "No no," says I, "Friday; I am afraid they will murder them, indeed; but you may be sure they will not eat them."

All this while I had no thought of what the matter really was, but stood trembling with the horror of the sight, expecting every moment when the three prisoners should be killed; nay, once I saw one of the villains lift up his arm with a great cutlass, as the seamen call it, or sword, to strike one of the poor men; and I expected to see him fall every moment; at which all the blood in my body seemed to run chill in my veins. I wished heartily now for the Spaniard, and the savage that had gone with him, or that I had any way to have come undiscovered within shot of them, that I might have secured the three men, for I saw no firearms they had among them; but it fell out to my mind another way. After I had observed the outrageous usage of the three men by the insolent seamen, I observed the fellows run scattering about the island, as if they wanted to see the country. I observed that the three other men had liberty to go also where they pleased; but they sat down all three upon the ground, very pensive, and looked like men in despair. This put me in mind of the first time when I came on shore, and began to look about me; how I gave myself over for lost; how wildly I looked round me; what dreadful apprehensions I had; and how I lodged in the tree all night for fear of being devoured by wild beasts. As I knew nothing that night of the supply I was to receive by the providential driving of the ship nearer the land by the storms and tide, by which I have since been so long nourished and supported; so these three poor desolate men knew nothing how certain of deliverance and supply they were, how near it was to them, and how effectually and really they were in a condition of safety, at the same time that they thought themselves lost and their case desperate. So little do we see before us in the world, and so much reason have we to depend cheerfully upon the great Maker of the world, that He does not leave His creatures so absolutely destitute, but that in the worst circumstances they have always something to be thankful for, and sometimes are nearer deliverance than they imagine; nay, are even brought to their deliverance by the means by which they seem to be brought to their destruction.

It was just at high-water when these people came on shore; and while they rambled about to see what kind of a place they were in, they had carelessly stayed till the tide was spent, and the water was ebbed considerably away, leaving their boat aground. They had left two men in the boat, who, as I found afterwards, having drunk a little too much brandy, fell asleep; however, one of them waking a little sooner than the other and finding the boat too fast aground for him to stir it, hallooed out for the rest, who were straggling about: upon which they all soon came to the boat: but it was past all their strength to launch her, the boat being very heavy, and the shore on that side being a soft oozy sand, almost like a quicksand. In this condition, like true seamen, who are, perhaps, the least of all man-mankind given to forethought, they gave it over, and away they strolled about the country again; and I heard one of them say aloud to another, calling them off from the boat, "Why, let her alone, Jack, can't you? she'll float next tide;" by which I was fully confirmed in the main inquiry of what countrymen they were. All this while I kept myself very close, not once daring to stir out of my castle any farther than to my place of observation near the top of the hill: and very glad I was to think how well it was fortified. I knew it was no less than ten hours before the boat could float again, and by that time it would be dark, and I might be at more liberty to see their motions, and to hear their discourse, if they had any. In the meantime I fitted myself up for a battle as before, though with more caution, knowing I had to do with another kind of enemy than I had at first. I ordered Friday also, whom I had made an excellent marksman with his gun, to load himself with arms. I took myself two fowling-pieces, and I gave him three muskets. My figure, indeed, was very fierce; I had my formidable goat-skin coat on, with the great cap I have mentioned, a naked sword by my side, two pistols in my belt, and a gun upon each shoulder.

It was my design, as I said above, not to have made any attempt till it was dark; but about two o'clock, being the heat of the day, I found that they were all gone straggling into the woods, and, as I thought, laid down to sleep. The three poor distressed men, too anxious for their condition to get any sleep, had, however, sat down under the shelter of a great tree, at about a quarter of a mile from me, and, as I thought, out of sight of any of the rest. Upon this I resolved to discover myself to them, and learn something of their condition; immediately I marched as above, my man Friday at a good distance behind me, as formidable for his arms as I, but not making quite so staring a spectre-like figure as I did. I came as near them undiscovered as I could, and then, before any of them saw me, I called aloud to them in Spanish, "What are ye, gentlemen?" They started up at the noise, but were ten times more confounded when they saw me, and the uncouth figure that I made. They made no answer at all, but I thought I perceived them just going to fly from me, when I spoke to them in English. "Gentlemen," said I, "do not be surprised at me; perhaps you may have a friend near when you did not expect it." "He must be sent directly from heaven then," said one of them very gravely to me, and pulling off his hat at the same time to me; "for our condition is past the help of man." "All help is from heaven, sir," said I, "but can you put a stranger in the way to help you? for you seem to be in some great distress. I saw you when you landed; and when you seemed to make application to the brutes that came with you, I saw one of them lift up his sword to kill you."

The poor man, with tears running down his face, and trembling, looking like one astonished, returned, "Am I talking to God or man? Is it a real man or an angel?" "Be in no fear about that, sir," said I; "if God had sent an angel to relieve you, he would have come better clothed, and armed after another manner than you see me; pray lay aside your fears; I am a man, an Englishman, and disposed to assist you; you see I have one servant only; we have arms and ammunition; tell us freely, can we serve you? What is your case?" "Our case, sir," said he, "is too long to tell you while our murderers are so near us; but, in short, sir, I was commander of that ship—my men have mutinied against me; they have been hardly prevailed on not to murder me, and, at last, have set me on shore in this desolate place, with these two men with me—one my mate, the other a passenger—where we expected to perish, believing the place to be uninhabited, and know not yet what to think of it." "Where are these brutes, your enemies?" said I; "do you know where they are gone? There they lie, sir," said he, pointing to a thicket of trees; "my heart trembles for fear they have seen us and heard you speak; if they have, they will certainly murder us all." "Have they any firearms?" said I. He answered, "They had only two pieces, one of which they left in the boat." "Well, then," said I, "leave the rest to me; I see they are all asleep; it is an easy thing to kill them all; but shall we rather take them prisoners?" He told me there were two desperate villains among them that it was scarce safe to show any mercy to; but if they were secured, he believed all the rest would return to their duty. I asked him which they were. He told me he could not at that distance distinguish them, but he would obey my orders in anything I would direct. "Well," says I, "let us retreat out of their view or hearing, lest they awake, and we will resolve further." So they willingly went back with me, till the woods covered us from them.

"Look you, sir," said I, "if I venture upon your deliverance, are you willing to make two conditions with me?" He anticipated my proposals by telling me that both he and the ship, if recovered, should be wholly directed and commanded by me in everything; and if the ship was not recovered, he would live and die with me in what part of the world soever I would send him; and the two other men said the same. "Well," says I, "my conditions are but two; first, that while you stay in this island with me, you will not pretend to any authority here; and if I put arms in your hands, you will, upon all occasions, give them up to me, and do no prejudice to me or mine upon this island, and in the meantime be governed by my orders; secondly, that if the ship is or may be recovered, you will carry me and my man to England passage free."

He gave me all the assurances that the invention or faith of man could devise that he would comply with these most reasonable demands, and besides would owe his life to me, and acknowledge it upon all occasions as long as he lived. "Well, then," said I, "here are three muskets for you, with powder and ball; tell me next what you think is proper to be done." He showed all the testimonies of his gratitude that he was able, but offered to be wholly guided by me. I told him I thought it was very hard venturing anything; but the best method I could think of was to fire on them at once as they lay, and if any were not killed at the first volley, and offered to submit, we might save them, and so put it wholly upon God's providence to direct the shot. He said, very modestly, that he was loath to kill them if he could help it; but that those two were incorrigible villains, and had been the authors of all the mutiny in the ship, and if they escaped, we should be undone still, for they would go on board and bring the whole ship's company, and destroy us all. "Well, then," says I, "necessity legitimates my advice, for it is the only way to save our lives." However, seeing him still cautious of shedding blood, I told him they should go themselves, and manage as they found convenient.

In the middle of this discourse we heard some of them awake, and soon after we saw two of them on their feet. I asked him if either of them were the heads of the mutiny? He said, "No." "Well, then," said I, "you may let them escape; and Providence seems to have awakened them on purpose to save themselves. Now," says I, "if the rest escape you, it is your fault." Animated with this, he took the musket I had given him in his hand, and a pistol in his belt, and his two comrades with him, with each a piece in his hand; the two men who were with him going first made some noise, at which one of the seamen who was awake turned about, and seeing them coming, cried out to the rest; but was too late then, for the moment he cried out they fired—I mean the two men, the captain wisely reserving his own piece. They had so well aimed their shot at the men they knew, that one of them was killed on the spot, and the other very much wounded; but not being dead, he started up on his feet, and called eagerly for help to the other; but the captain stepping to him, told him it was too late to cry for help, he should call upon God to forgive his villainy, and with that word knocked him down with the stock of his musket, so that he never spoke more; there were three more in the company, and one of them was slightly wounded. By this time I was come; and when they saw their danger, and that it was in vain to resist, they begged for mercy. The captain told them he would spare their lives if they would give him an assurance of their abhorrence of the treachery they had been guilty of, and would swear to be faithful to him in recovering the ship, and afterwards in carrying her back to Jamaica, from whence they came. They gave him all the protestations of their sincerity that could be desired; and he was willing to believe them, and spare their lives, which I was not against, only that I obliged him to keep them bound hand and foot while they were on the island.

While this was doing, I sent Friday with the captain's mate to the boat with orders to secure her, and bring away the oars and sails, which they did; and by-and-by three straggling men, that were (happily for them) parted from the rest, came back upon hearing the guns fired; and seeing the captain, who was before their prisoner, now their conqueror, they submitted to be bound also; and so our victory was complete.

It now remained that the captain and I should inquire into one another's circumstances. I began first, and told him my whole history, which he heard with an attention even to amazement—and particularly at the wonderful manner of my being furnished with provisions and ammunition; and, indeed, as my story is a whole collection of wonders, it affected him deeply. But when he reflected from thence upon himself, and how I seemed to have been preserved there on purpose to save his life, the tears ran down his face, and he could not speak a word more. After this communication was at an end, I carried him and his two men into my apartment, leading them in just where I came out, viz. at the top of the house, where I refreshed them with such provisions as I had, and showed them all the contrivances I had made during my long, long inhabiting that place.

All I showed them, all I said to them, was perfectly amazing; but above all, the captain admired my fortification, and how perfectly I had concealed my retreat with a grove of trees, which having been now planted nearly twenty years, and the trees growing much faster than in England, was become a little wood, so thick that it was impassable in any part of it but at that one side where I had reserved my little winding passage into it. I told him this was my castle and my residence, but that I had a seat in the country, as most princes have, whither I could retreat upon occasion, and I would show him that too another time; but at present our business was to consider how to recover the ship. He agreed with me as to that, but told me he was perfectly at a loss what measures to take, for that there were still six-and-twenty hands on board, who, having entered into a cursed conspiracy, by which they had all forfeited their lives to the law, would be hardened in it now by desperation, and would carry it on, knowing that if they were subdued they would be brought to the gallows as soon as they came to England, or to any of the English colonies, and that, therefore, there would be no attacking them with so small a number as we were.

I mused for some time on what he had said, and found it was a very rational conclusion, and that therefore something was to be resolved on speedily, as well to draw the men on board into some snare for their surprise as to prevent their landing upon us, and destroying us. Upon this, it presently occurred to me that in a little while the ship's crew, wondering what was become of their comrades and of the boat, would certainly come on shore in their other boat to look for them, and that then, perhaps, they might come armed, and be too strong for us: this he allowed to be rational. Upon this, I told him the first thing we had to do was to stave the boat which lay upon the beach, so that they might not carry her of, and taking everything out of her, leave her so far useless as not to be fit to swim. Accordingly, we went on board, took the arms which were left on board out of her, and whatever else we found there—which was a bottle of brandy, and another of rum, a few biscuit-cakes, a horn of powder, and a great lump of sugar in a piece of canvas (the sugar was five or six pounds): all which was very welcome to me, especially the brandy and sugar, of which I had had none left for many years.

When we had carried all these things on shore (the oars, mast, sail, and rudder of the boat were carried away before), we knocked a great hole in her bottom, that if they had come strong enough to master us, yet they could not carry off the boat. Indeed, it was not much in my thoughts that we could be able to recover the ship; but my view was, that if they went away without the boat, I did not much question to make her again fit to carry as to the Leeward Islands, and call upon our friends the Spaniards in my way, for I had them still in my thoughts.

Chapter XVIII—THE SHIP RECOVERED

While we were thus preparing our designs, and had first, by main strength, heaved the boat upon the beach, so high that the tide would not float her off at high-water mark, and besides, had broke a hole in her bottom too big to be quickly stopped, and were set down musing what we should do, we heard the ship fire a gun, and make a waft with her ensign as a signal for the boat to come on board—but no boat stirred; and they fired several times, making other signals for the boat. At last, when all their signals and firing proved fruitless, and they found the boat did not stir, we saw them, by the help of my glasses, hoist another boat out and row towards the shore; and we found, as they approached, that there were no less than ten men in her, and that they had firearms with them.

As the ship lay almost two leagues from the shore, we had a full view of them as they came, and a plain sight even of their faces; because the tide having set them a little to the east of the other boat, they rowed up under shore, to come to the same place where the other had landed, and where the boat lay; by this means, I say, we had a full view of them, and the captain knew the persons and characters of all the men in the boat, of whom, he said, there were three very honest fellows, who, he was sure, were led into this conspiracy by the rest, being over-powered and frightened; but that as for the boatswain, who it seems was the chief officer among them, and all the rest, they were as outrageous as any of the ship's crew, and were no doubt made desperate in their new enterprise; and terribly apprehensive he was that they would be too powerful for us. I smiled at him, and told him that men in our circumstances were past the operation of fear; that seeing almost every condition that could be was better than that which we were supposed to be in, we ought to expect that the consequence, whether death or life, would be sure to be a deliverance. I asked him what he thought of the circumstances of my life, and whether a deliverance were not worth venturing for? "And where, sir," said I, "is your belief of my being preserved here on purpose to save your life, which elevated you a little while ago? For my part," said I, "there seems to be but one thing amiss in all the prospect of it." "What is that?" say he. "Why," said I, "it is, that as you say there are three or four honest fellows among them which should be spared, had they been all of the wicked part of the crew I should have thought God's providence had singled them out to deliver them into your hands; for depend upon it, every man that comes ashore is our own, and shall die or live as they behave to us." As I spoke this with a raised voice and cheerful countenance, I found it greatly encouraged him; so we set vigorously to our business.

We had, upon the first appearance of the boat's coming from the ship, considered of separating our prisoners; and we had, indeed, secured them effectually. Two of them, of whom the captain was less assured than ordinary, I sent with Friday, and one of the three delivered men, to my cave, where they were remote enough, and out of danger of being heard or discovered, or of finding their way out of the woods if they could have delivered themselves. Here they left them bound, but gave them provisions; and promised them, if they continued there quietly, to give them their liberty in a day or two; but that if they attempted their escape they should be put to death without mercy. They promised faithfully to bear their confinement with patience, and were very thankful that they had such good usage as to have provisions and light left them; for Friday gave them candles (such as we made ourselves) for their comfort; and they did not know but that he stood sentinel over them at the entrance.

The other prisoners had better usage; two of them were kept pinioned, indeed, because the captain was not able to trust them; but the other two were taken into my service, upon the captain's recommendation, and upon their solemnly engaging to live and die with us; so with them and the three honest men we were seven men, well armed; and I made no doubt we should be able to deal well enough with the ten that were coming, considering that the captain had said there were three or four honest men among them also. As soon as they got to the place where their other boat lay, they ran their boat into the beach and came all on shore, hauling the boat up after them, which I was glad to see, for I was afraid they would rather have left the boat at an anchor some distance from the shore, with some hands in her to guard her, and so we should not be able to seize the boat. Being on shore, the first thing they did, they ran all to their other boat; and it was easy to see they were under a great surprise to find her stripped, as above, of all that was in her, and a great hole in her bottom. After they had mused a while upon this, they set up two or three great shouts, hallooing with all their might, to try if they could make their companions hear; but all was to no purpose. Then they came all close in a ring, and fired a volley of their small arms, which indeed we heard, and the echoes made the woods ring. But it was all one; those in the cave, we were sure, could not hear; and those in our keeping, though they heard it well enough, yet durst give no answer to them. They were so astonished at the surprise of this, that, as they told us afterwards, they resolved to go all on board again to their ship, and let them know that the men were all murdered, and the long-boat staved; accordingly, they immediately launched their boat again, and got all of them on board.

The captain was terribly amazed, and even confounded, at this, believing they would go on board the ship again and set sail, giving their comrades over for lost, and so he should still lose the ship, which he was in hopes we should have recovered; but he was quickly as much frightened the other way.

They had not been long put off with the boat, when we perceived them all coming on shore again; but with this new measure in their conduct, which it seems they consulted together upon, viz. to leave three men in the boat, and the rest to go on shore, and go up into the country to look for their fellows. This was a great disappointment to us, for now we were at a loss what to do, as our seizing those seven men on shore would be no advantage to us if we let the boat escape; because they would row away to the ship, and then the rest of them would be sure to weigh and set sail, and so our recovering the ship would be lost. However we had no remedy but to wait and see what the issue of things might present. The seven men came on shore, and the three who remained in the boat put her off to a good distance from the shore, and came to an anchor to wait for them; so that it was impossible for us to come at them in the boat. Those that came on shore kept close together, marching towards the top of the little hill under which my habitation lay; and we could see them plainly, though they could not perceive us. We should have been very glad if they would have come nearer us, so that we might have fired at them, or that they would have gone farther off, that we might come abroad. But when they were come to the brow of the hill where they could see a great way into the valleys and woods, which lay towards the north-east part, and where the island lay lowest, they shouted and hallooed till they were weary; and not caring, it seems, to venture far from the shore, nor far from one another, they sat down together under a tree to consider it. Had they thought fit to have gone to sleep there, as the other part of them had done, they had done the job for us; but they were too full of apprehensions of danger to venture to go to sleep, though they could not tell what the danger was they had to fear.

The captain made a very just proposal to me upon this consultation of theirs, viz. that perhaps they would all fire a volley again, to endeavour to make their fellows hear, and that we should all sally upon them just at the juncture when their pieces were all discharged, and they would certainly yield, and we should have them without bloodshed. I liked this proposal, provided it was done while we were near enough to come up to them before they could load their pieces again. But this event did not happen; and we lay still a long time, very irresolute what course to take. At length I told them there would be nothing done, in my opinion, till night; and then, if they did not return to the boat, perhaps we might find a way to get between them and the shore, and so might use some stratagem with them in the boat to get them on shore. We waited a great while, though very impatient for their removing; and were very uneasy when, after long consultation, we saw them all start up and march down towards the sea; it seems they had such dreadful apprehensions of the danger of the place that they resolved to go on board the ship again, give their companions over for lost, and so go on with their intended voyage with the ship.

As soon as I perceived them go towards the shore, I imagined it to be as it really was that they had given over their search, and were going back again; and the captain, as soon as I told him my thoughts, was ready to sink at the apprehensions of it; but I presently thought of a stratagem to fetch them back again, and which answered my end to a tittle. I ordered Friday and the captain's mate to go over the little creek westward, towards the place where the savages came on shore, when Friday was rescued, and so soon as they came to a little rising round, at about half a mile distant, I bid them halloo out, as loud as they could, and wait till they found the seamen heard them; that as soon as ever they heard the seamen answer them, they should return it again; and then, keeping out of sight, take a round, always answering when the others hallooed, to draw them as far into the island and among the woods as possible, and then wheel about again to me by such ways as I directed them.

They were just going into the boat when Friday and the mate hallooed; and they presently heard them, and answering, ran along the shore westward, towards the voice they heard, when they were stopped by the creek, where the water being up, they could not get over, and called for the boat to come up and set them over; as, indeed, I expected. When they had set themselves over, I observed that the boat being gone a good way into the creek, and, as it were, in a harbour within the land, they took one of the three men out of her, to go along with them, and left only two in the boat, having fastened her to the stump of a little tree on the shore. This was what I wished for; and immediately leaving Friday and the captain's mate to their business, I took the rest with me; and, crossing the creek out of their sight, we surprised the two men before they were aware—one of them lying on the shore, and the other being in the boat. The fellow on shore was between sleeping and waking, and going to start up; the captain, who was foremost, ran in upon him, and knocked him down; and then called out to him in the boat to yield, or he was a dead man. They needed very few arguments to persuade a single man to yield, when he saw five men upon him and his comrade knocked down: besides, this was, it seems, one of the three who were not so hearty in the mutiny as the rest of the crew, and therefore was easily persuaded not only to yield, but afterwards to join very sincerely with us. In the meantime, Friday and the captain's mate so well managed their business with the rest that they drew them, by hallooing and answering, from one hill to another, and from one wood to another, till they not only heartily tired them, but left them where they were, very sure they could not reach back to the boat before it was dark; and, indeed, they were heartily tired themselves also, by the time they came back to us.

We had nothing now to do but to watch for them in the dark, and to fall upon them, so as to make sure work with them. It was several hours after Friday came back to me before they came back to their boat; and we could hear the foremost of them, long before they came quite up, calling to those behind to come along; and could also hear them answer, and complain how lame and tired they were, and not able to come any faster: which was very welcome news to us. At length they came up to the boat: but it is impossible to express their confusion when they found the boat fast aground in the creek, the tide ebbed out, and their two men gone. We could hear them call one to another in a most lamentable manner, telling one another they were got into an enchanted island; that either there were inhabitants in it, and they should all be murdered, or else there were devils and spirits in it, and they should be all carried away and devoured. They hallooed again, and called their two comrades by their names a great many times; but no answer. After some time we could see them, by the little light there was, run about, wringing their hands like men in despair, and sometimes they would go and sit down in the boat to rest themselves: then come ashore again, and walk about again, and so the same thing over again. My men would fain have had me give them leave to fall upon them at once in the dark; but I was willing to take them at some advantage, so as to spare them, and kill as few of them as I could; and especially I was unwilling to hazard the killing of any of our men, knowing the others were very well armed. I resolved to wait, to see if they did not separate; and therefore, to make sure of them, I drew my ambuscade nearer, and ordered Friday and the captain to creep upon their hands and feet, as close to the ground as they could, that they might not be discovered, and get as near them as they could possibly before they offered to fire.

They had not been long in that posture when the boatswain, who was the principal ringleader of the mutiny, and had now shown himself the most dejected and dispirited of all the rest, came walking towards them, with two more of the crew; the captain was so eager at having this principal rogue so much in his power, that he could hardly have patience to let him come so near as to be sure of him, for they only heard his tongue before: but when they came nearer, the captain and Friday, starting up on their feet, let fly at them. The boatswain was killed upon the spot: the next man was shot in the body, and fell just by him, though he did not die till an hour or two after; and the third ran for it. At the noise of the fire I immediately advanced with my whole army, which was now eight men, viz. myself, generalissimo; Friday, my lieutenant-general; the captain and his two men, and the three prisoners of war whom we had trusted with arms. We came upon them, indeed, in the dark, so that they could not see our number; and I made the man they had left in the boat, who was now one of us, to call them by name, to try if I could bring them to a parley, and so perhaps might reduce them to terms; which fell out just as we desired: for indeed it was easy to think, as their condition then was, they would be very willing to capitulate. So he calls out as loud as he could to one of them, "Tom Smith! Tom Smith!" Tom Smith answered immediately, "Is that Robinson?" for it seems he knew the voice. The other answered, "Ay, ay; for God's sake, Tom Smith, throw down your arms and yield, or you are all dead men this moment." "Who must we yield to? Where are they?" says Smith again. "Here they are," says he; "here's our captain and fifty men with him, have been hunting you these two hours; the boatswain is killed; Will Fry is wounded, and I am a prisoner; and if you do not yield you are all lost." "Will they give us quarter, then?" says Tom Smith, "and we will yield." "I'll go and ask, if you promise to yield," said Robinson: so he asked the captain, and the captain himself then calls out, "You, Smith, you know my voice; if you lay down your arms immediately and submit, you shall have your lives, all but Will Atkins."

Upon this Will Atkins cried out, "For God's sake, captain, give me quarter; what have I done? They have all been as bad as I:" which, by the way, was not true; for it seems this Will Atkins was the first man that laid hold of the captain when they first mutinied, and used him barbarously in tying his hands and giving him injurious language. However, the captain told him he must lay down his arms at discretion, and trust to the governor's mercy: by which he meant me, for they all called me governor. In a word, they all laid down their arms and begged their lives; and I sent the man that had parleyed with them, and two more, who bound them all; and then my great army of fifty men, which, with those three, were in all but eight, came up and seized upon them, and upon their boat; only that I kept myself and one more out of sight for reasons of state.

Our next work was to repair the boat, and think of seizing the ship: and as for the captain, now he had leisure to parley with them, he expostulated with them upon the villainy of their practices with him, and upon the further wickedness of their design, and how certainly it must bring them to misery and distress in the end, and perhaps to the gallows. They all appeared very penitent, and begged hard for their lives. As for that, he told them they were not his prisoners, but the commander's of the island; that they thought they had set him on shore in a barren, uninhabited island; but it had pleased God so to direct them that it was inhabited, and that the governor was an Englishman; that he might hang them all there, if he pleased; but as he had given them all quarter, he supposed he would send them to England, to be dealt with there as justice required, except Atkins, whom he was commanded by the governor to advise to prepare for death, for that he would be hanged in the morning.

Though this was all but a fiction of his own, yet it had its desired effect; Atkins fell upon his knees to beg the captain to intercede with the governor for his life; and all the rest begged of him, for God's sake, that they might not be sent to England.

It now occurred to me that the time of our deliverance was come, and that it would be a most easy thing to bring these fellows in to be hearty in getting possession of the ship; so I retired in the dark from them, that they might not see what kind of a governor they had, and called the captain to me; when I called, at a good distance, one of the men was ordered to speak again, and say to the captain, "Captain, the commander calls for you;" and presently the captain replied, "Tell his excellency I am just coming." This more perfectly amazed them, and they all believed that the commander was just by, with his fifty men. Upon the captain coming to me, I told him my project for seizing the ship, which he liked wonderfully well, and resolved to put it in execution the next morning. But, in order to execute it with more art, and to be secure of success, I told him we must divide the prisoners, and that he should go and take Atkins, and two more of the worst of them, and send them pinioned to the cave where the others lay. This was committed to Friday and the two men who came on shore with the captain. They conveyed them to the cave as to a prison: and it was, indeed, a dismal place, especially to men in their condition. The others I ordered to my bower, as I called it, of which I have given a full description: and as it was fenced in, and they pinioned, the place was secure enough, considering they were upon their behaviour.

To these in the morning I sent the captain, who was to enter into a parley with them; in a word, to try them, and tell me whether he thought they might be trusted or not to go on board and surprise the ship. He talked to them of the injury done him, of the condition they were brought to, and that though the governor had given them quarter for their lives as to the present action, yet that if they were sent to England they would all be hanged in chains; but that if they would join in so just an attempt as to recover the ship, he would have the governor's engagement for their pardon.

Any one may guess how readily such a proposal would be accepted by men in their condition; they fell down on their knees to the captain, and promised, with the deepest imprecations, that they would be faithful to him to the last drop, and that they should owe their lives to him, and would go with him all over the world; that they would own him as a father to them as long as they lived. "Well," says the captain, "I must go and tell the governor what you say, and see what I can do to bring him to consent to it." So he brought me an account of the temper he found them in, and that he verily believed they would be faithful. However, that we might be very secure, I told him he should go back again and choose out those five, and tell them, that they might see he did not want men, that he would take out those five to be his assistants, and that the governor would keep the other two, and the three that were sent prisoners to the castle (my cave), as hostages for the fidelity of those five; and that if they proved unfaithful in the execution, the five hostages should be hanged in chains alive on the shore. This looked severe, and convinced them that the governor was in earnest; however, they had no way left them but to accept it; and it was now the business of the prisoners, as much as of the captain, to persuade the other five to do their duty.

Our strength was now thus ordered for the expedition: first, the captain, his mate, and passenger; second, the two prisoners of the first gang, to whom, having their character from the captain, I had given their liberty, and trusted them with arms; third, the other two that I had kept till now in my bower, pinioned, but on the captain's motion had now released; fourth, these five released at last; so that there were twelve in all, besides five we kept prisoners in the cave for hostages.

I asked the captain if he was willing to venture with these hands on board the ship; but as for me and my man Friday, I did not think it was proper for us to stir, having seven men left behind; and it was employment enough for us to keep them asunder, and supply them with victuals. As to the five in the cave, I resolved to keep them fast, but Friday went in twice a day to them, to supply them with necessaries; and I made the other two carry provisions to a certain distance, where Friday was to take them.

When I showed myself to the two hostages, it was with the captain, who told them I was the person the governor had ordered to look after them; and that it was the governor's pleasure they should not stir anywhere but by my direction; that if they did, they would be fetched into the castle, and be laid in irons: so that as we never suffered them to see me as governor, I now appeared as another person, and spoke of the governor, the garrison, the castle, and the like, upon all occasions.

The captain now had no difficulty before him, but to furnish his two boats, stop the breach of one, and man them. He made his passenger captain of one, with four of the men; and himself, his mate, and five more, went in the other; and they contrived their business very well, for they came up to the ship about midnight. As soon as they came within call of the ship, he made Robinson hail them, and tell them they had brought off the men and the boat, but that it was a long time before they had found them, and the like, holding them in a chat till they came to the ship's side; when the captain and the mate entering first with their arms, immediately knocked down the second mate and carpenter with the butt-end of their muskets, being very faithfully seconded by their men; they secured all the rest that were upon the main and quarter decks, and began to fasten the hatches, to keep them down that were below; when the other boat and their men, entering at the forechains, secured the forecastle of the ship, and the scuttle which went down into the cook-room, making three men they found there prisoners. When this was done, and all safe upon deck, the captain ordered the mate, with three men, to break into the round-house, where the new rebel captain lay, who, having taken the alarm, had got up, and with two men and a boy had got firearms in their hands; and when the mate, with a crow, split open the door, the new captain and his men fired boldly among them, and wounded the mate with a musket ball, which broke his arm, and wounded two more of the men, but killed nobody. The mate, calling for help, rushed, however, into the round-house, wounded as he was, and, with his pistol, shot the new captain through the head, the bullet entering at his mouth, and came out again behind one of his ears, so that he never spoke a word more: upon which the rest yielded, and the ship was taken effectually, without any more lives lost.

As soon as the ship was thus secured, the captain ordered seven guns to be fired, which was the signal agreed upon with me to give me notice of his success, which, you may be sure, I was very glad to hear, having sat watching upon the shore for it till near two o'clock in the morning. Having thus heard the signal plainly, I laid me down; and it having been a day of great fatigue to me, I slept very sound, till I was surprised with the noise of a gun; and presently starting up, I heard a man call me by the name of "Governor! Governor!" and presently I knew the captain's voice; when, climbing up to the top of the hill, there he stood, and, pointing to the ship, he embraced me in his arms, "My dear friend and deliverer," says he, "there's your ship; for she is all yours, and so are we, and all that belong to her." I cast my eyes to the ship, and there she rode, within little more than half a mile of the shore; for they had weighed her anchor as soon as they were masters of her, and, the weather being fair, had brought her to an anchor just against the mouth of the little creek; and the tide being up, the captain had brought the pinnace in near the place where I had first landed my rafts, and so landed just at my door. I was at first ready to sink down with the surprise; for I saw my deliverance, indeed, visibly put into my hands, all things easy, and a large ship just ready to carry me away whither I pleased to go. At first, for some time, I was not able to answer him one word; but as he had taken me in his arms I held fast by him, or I should have fallen to the ground. He perceived the surprise, and immediately pulled a bottle out of his pocket and gave me a dram of cordial, which he had brought on purpose for me. After I had drunk it, I sat down upon the ground; and though it brought me to myself, yet it was a good while before I could speak a word to him. All this time the poor man was in as great an ecstasy as I, only not under any surprise as I was; and he said a thousand kind and tender things to me, to compose and bring me to myself; but such was the flood of joy in my breast, that it put all my spirits into confusion: at last it broke out into tears, and in a little while after I recovered my speech; I then took my turn, and embraced him as my deliverer, and we rejoiced together. I told him I looked upon him as a man sent by Heaven to deliver me, and that the whole transaction seemed to be a chain of wonders; that such things as these were the testimonies we had of a secret hand of Providence governing the world, and an evidence that the eye of an infinite Power could search into the remotest corner of the world, and send help to the miserable whenever He pleased. I forgot not to lift up my heart in thankfulness to Heaven; and what heart could forbear to bless Him, who had not only in a miraculous manner provided for me in such a wilderness, and in such a desolate condition, but from whom every deliverance must always be acknowledged to proceed.

When we had talked a while, the captain told me he had brought me some little refreshment, such as the ship afforded, and such as the wretches that had been so long his masters had not plundered him of. Upon this, he called aloud to the boat, and bade his men bring the things ashore that were for the governor; and, indeed, it was a present as if I had been one that was not to be carried away with them, but as if I had been to dwell upon the island still. First, he had brought me a case of bottles full of excellent cordial waters, six large bottles of Madeira wine (the bottles held two quarts each), two pounds of excellent good tobacco, twelve good pieces of the ship's beef, and six pieces of pork, with a bag of peas, and about a hundred-weight of biscuit; he also brought me a box of sugar, a box of flour, a bag full of lemons, and two bottles of lime-juice, and abundance of other things. But besides these, and what was a thousand times more useful to me, he brought me six new clean shirts, six very good neckcloths, two pair of gloves, one pair of shoes, a hat, and one pair of stockings, with a very good suit of clothes of his own, which had been worn but very little: in a word, he clothed me from head to foot. It was a very kind and agreeable present, as any one may imagine, to one in my circumstances, but never was anything in the world of that kind so unpleasant, awkward, and uneasy as it was to me to wear such clothes at first.

After these ceremonies were past, and after all his good things were brought into my little apartment, we began to consult what was to be done with the prisoners we had; for it was worth considering whether we might venture to take them with us or no, especially two of them, whom he knew to be incorrigible and refractory to the last degree; and the captain said he knew they were such rogues that there was no obliging them, and if he did carry them away, it must be in irons, as malefactors, to be delivered over to justice at the first English colony he could come to; and I found that the captain himself was very anxious about it. Upon this, I told him that, if he desired it, I would undertake to bring the two men he spoke of to make it their own request that he should leave them upon the island. "I should be very glad of that," says the captain, "with all my heart." "Well," says I, "I will send for them up and talk with them for you." So I caused Friday and the two hostages, for they were now discharged, their comrades having performed their promise; I say, I caused them to go to the cave, and bring up the five men, pinioned as they were, to the bower, and keep them there till I came. After some time, I came thither dressed in my new habit; and now I was called governor again. Being all met, and the captain with me, I caused the men to be brought before me, and I told them I had got a full account of their villainous behaviour to the captain, and how they had run away with the ship, and were preparing to commit further robberies, but that Providence had ensnared them in their own ways, and that they were fallen into the pit which they had dug for others. I let them know that by my direction the ship had been seized; that she lay now in the road; and they might see by-and-by that their new captain had received the reward of his villainy, and that they would see him hanging at the yard-arm; that, as to them, I wanted to know what they had to say why I should not execute them as pirates taken in the fact, as by my commission they could not doubt but I had authority so to do.

One of them answered in the name of the rest, that they had nothing to say but this, that when they were taken the captain promised them their lives, and they humbly implored my mercy. But I told them I knew not what mercy to show them; for as for myself, I had resolved to quit the island with all my men, and had taken passage with the captain to go to England; and as for the captain, he could not carry them to England other than as prisoners in irons, to be tried for mutiny and running away with the ship; the consequence of which, they must needs know, would be the gallows; so that I could not tell what was best for them, unless they had a mind to take their fate in the island. If they desired that, as I had liberty to leave the island, I had some inclination to give them their lives, if they thought they could shift on shore. They seemed very thankful for it, and said they would much rather venture to stay there than be carried to England to be hanged. So I left it on that issue.

However, the captain seemed to make some difficulty of it, as if he durst not leave them there. Upon this I seemed a little angry with the captain, and told him that they were my prisoners, not his; and that seeing I had offered them so much favour, I would be as good as my word; and that if he did not think fit to consent to it I would set them at liberty, as I found them: and if he did not like it he might take them again if he could catch them. Upon this they appeared very thankful, and I accordingly set them at liberty, and bade them retire into the woods, to the place whence they came, and I would leave them some firearms, some ammunition, and some directions how they should live very well if they thought fit. Upon this I prepared to go on board the ship; but told the captain I would stay that night to prepare my things, and desired him to go on board in the meantime, and keep all right in the ship, and send the boat on shore next day for me; ordering him, at all events, to cause the new captain, who was killed, to be hanged at the yard-arm, that these men might see him.

When the captain was gone I sent for the men up to me to my apartment, and entered seriously into discourse with them on their circumstances. I told them I thought they had made a right choice; that if the captain had carried them away they would certainly be hanged. I showed them the new captain hanging at the yard-arm of the ship, and told them they had nothing less to expect.

When they had all declared their willingness to stay, I then told them I would let them into the story of my living there, and put them into the way of making it easy to them. Accordingly, I gave them the whole history of the place, and of my coming to it; showed them my fortifications, the way I made my bread, planted my corn, cured my grapes; and, in a word, all that was necessary to make them easy. I told them the story also of the seventeen Spaniards that were to be expected, for whom I left a letter, and made them promise to treat them in common with themselves. Here it may be noted that the captain, who had ink on board, was greatly surprised that I never hit upon a way of making ink of charcoal and water, or of something else, as I had done things much more difficult.

I left them my firearms—viz. five muskets, three fowling-pieces, and three swords. I had above a barrel and a half of powder left; for after the first year or two I used but little, and wasted none. I gave them a description of the way I managed the goats, and directions to milk and fatten them, and to make both butter and cheese. In a word, I gave them every part of my own story; and told them I should prevail with the captain to leave them two barrels of gunpowder more, and some garden-seeds, which I told them I would have been very glad of. Also, I gave them the bag of peas which the captain had brought me to eat, and bade them be sure to sow and increase them.

Chapter XIX—RETURN TO ENGLAND

Having done all this I left them the next day, and went on board the ship. We prepared immediately to sail, but did not weigh that night. The next morning early, two of the five men came swimming to the ship's side, and making the most lamentable complaint of the other three, begged to be taken into the ship for God's sake, for they should be murdered, and begged the captain to take them on board, though he hanged them immediately. Upon this the captain pretended to have no power without me; but after some difficulty, and after their solemn promises of amendment, they were taken on board, and were, some time after, soundly whipped and pickled; after which they proved very honest and quiet fellows.

Some time after this, the boat was ordered on shore, the tide being up, with the things promised to the men; to which the captain, at my intercession, caused their chests and clothes to be added, which they took, and were very thankful for. I also encouraged them, by telling them that if it lay in my power to send any vessel to take them in, I would not forget them.

When I took leave of this island, I carried on board, for relics, the great goatskin cap I had made, my umbrella, and one of my parrots; also, I forgot not to take the money I formerly mentioned, which had lain by me so long useless that it was grown rusty or tarnished, and could hardly pass for silver till it had been a little rubbed and handled, as also the money I found in the wreck of the Spanish ship. And thus I left the island, the 19th of December, as I found by the ship's account, in the year 1686, after I had been upon it eight-and-twenty years, two months, and nineteen days; being delivered from this second captivity the same day of the month that I first made my escape in the long-boat from among the Moors of Sallee. In this vessel, after a long voyage, I arrived in England the 11th of June, in the year 1687, having been thirty-five years absent.

When I came to England I was as perfect a stranger to all the world as if I had never been known there. My benefactor and faithful steward, whom I had left my money in trust with, was alive, but had had great misfortunes in the world; was become a widow the second time, and very low in the world. I made her very easy as to what she owed me, assuring her I would give her no trouble; but, on the contrary, in gratitude for her former care and faithfulness to me, I relieved her as my little stock would afford; which at that time would, indeed, allow me to do but little for her; but I assured her I would never forget her former kindness to me;

nor did I forget her when I had sufficient to help her, as shall be observed in its proper place. I went down afterwards into Yorkshire; but my father was dead, and my mother and all the family extinct, except that I found two sisters, and two of the children of one of my brothers; and as I had been long ago given over for dead, there had been no provision made for me; so that, in a word, I found nothing to relieve or assist me; and that the little money I had would not do much for me as to settling in the world.

I met with one piece of gratitude indeed, which I did not expect; and this was, that the master of the ship, whom I had so happily delivered, and by the same means saved the ship and cargo, having given a very handsome account to the owners of the manner how I had saved the lives of the men and the ship, they invited me to meet them and some other merchants concerned, and all together made me a very handsome compliment upon the subject, and a present of almost £200 sterling.

But after making several reflections upon the circumstances of my life, and how little way this would go towards settling me in the world, I resolved to go to Lisbon, and see if I might not come at some information of the state of my plantation in the Brazils, and of what was become of my partner, who, I had reason to suppose, had some years past given me over for dead. With this view I took shipping for Lisbon, where I arrived in April following, my man Friday accompanying me very honestly in all these ramblings, and proving a most faithful servant upon all occasions. When I came to Lisbon, I found out, by inquiry, and to my particular satisfaction, my old friend, the captain of the ship who first took me up at sea off the shore of Africa. He was now grown old, and had left off going to sea, having put his son, who was far from a young man, into his ship, and who still used the Brazil trade. The old man did not know me, and indeed I hardly knew him. But I soon brought him to my remembrance, and as soon brought myself to his remembrance, when I told him who I was.

After some passionate expressions of the old acquaintance between us, I inquired, you may be sure, after my plantation and my partner. The old man told me he had not been in the Brazils for about nine years; but that he could assure me that when he came away my partner was living, but the trustees whom I had joined with him to take cognisance of my part were both dead: that, however, he believed I would have a very good account of the improvement of the plantation; for that, upon the general belief of my being cast away and drowned, my trustees had given in the account of the produce of my part of the plantation to the procurator-fiscal, who had appropriated it, in case I never came to claim it, one-third to the king, and two-thirds to the monastery of St. Augustine, to be expended for the benefit of the poor, and for the conversion of the Indians to the Catholic faith: but that, if I appeared, or any one for me, to claim the inheritance, it would be restored; only that the improvement, or annual production, being distributed to charitable uses, could not be restored: but he assured me that the steward of the king's revenue from lands, and the providore, or steward of the monastery, had taken great care all along that the incumbent, that is to say my partner, gave every year a faithful account of the produce, of which they had duly received my moiety. I asked him if he knew to what height of improvement he had brought the plantation, and whether he thought it might be worth looking after; or whether, on my going thither, I should meet with any obstruction to my possessing my just right in the moiety. He told me he could not tell exactly to what degree the plantation was improved; but this he knew, that my partner was grown exceeding rich upon the enjoying his part of it; and that, to the best of his remembrance, he had heard that the king's third of my part, which was, it seems, granted away to some other monastery or religious house, amounted to above two hundred moidores a year: that as to my being restored to a quiet possession of it, there was no question to be made of that, my partner being alive to witness my title, and my name being also enrolled in the register of the country; also he told me that the survivors of my two trustees were very fair, honest people, and very wealthy; and he believed I would not only have their assistance for putting me in possession, but would find a very considerable sum of money in their hands for my account, being the produce of the farm while their fathers held the trust, and before it was given up, as above; which, as he remembered, was for about twelve years.

I showed myself a little concerned and uneasy at this account, and inquired of the old captain how it came to pass that the trustees should thus dispose of my effects, when he knew that I had made my will, and had made him, the Portuguese captain, my universal heir, &c.

He told me that was true; but that as there was no proof of my being dead, he could not act as executor until some certain account should come of my death; and, besides, he was not willing to intermeddle with a thing so remote: that it was true he had registered my will, and put in his claim; and could he have given any account of my being dead or alive, he would have acted by procuration, and taken possession of the ingenio (so they call the sugar-house), and have given his son, who was now at the Brazils, orders to do it. "But," says the old man, "I have one piece of news to tell you, which perhaps may not be so acceptable to you as the rest; and that is, believing you were lost, and all the world believing so also, your partner and trustees did offer to account with me, in your name, for the first six or eight years' profits, which I received. There being at that time great disbursements for increasing the works, building an ingenio, and buying slaves, it did not amount to near so much as afterwards it produced; however," says the old man, "I shall give you a true account of what I have received in all, and how I have disposed of it."

After a few days' further conference with this ancient friend, he brought me an account of the first six years' income of my plantation, signed by my partner and the merchant-trustees, being always delivered in goods, viz. tobacco in roll, and sugar in chests, besides rum, molasses, &c., which is the consequence of a sugar-work; and I found by this account, that every year the income considerably increased; but, as above, the disbursements being large, the sum at first was small: however, the old man let me see that he was debtor to me four hundred and seventy moidores of gold, besides sixty chests of sugar and fifteen double rolls of tobacco, which were lost in his ship; he having been shipwrecked coming home to Lisbon, about eleven years after my having the place. The good man then began to complain of his misfortunes, and how he had been obliged to make use of my money to recover his losses, and buy him a share in a new ship. "However, my old friend," says he, "you shall not want a supply in your necessity; and as soon as my son returns you shall be fully satisfied." Upon this he pulls out an old pouch, and gives me one hundred and sixty Portugal moidores in gold; and giving the writings of his title to the ship, which his son was gone to the Brazils in, of which he was quarter-part owner, and his son another, he puts them both into my hands for security of the rest.

I was too much moved with the honesty and kindness of the poor man to be able to bear this; and remembering what he had done for me, how he had taken me up at sea, and how generously he had used me on all occasions, and particularly how sincere a friend he was now to me, I could hardly refrain weeping at what he had said to me; therefore I asked him if his circumstances admitted him to spare so much money at that time, and if it would not straiten him? He told me he could not say but it might straiten him a little; but, however, it was my money, and I might want it more than he.

Everything the good man said was full of affection, and I could hardly refrain from tears while he spoke; in short, I took one hundred of the moidores, and called for a pen and ink to give him a receipt for them: then I returned him the rest, and told him if ever I had possession of the plantation I would return the other to him also (as, indeed, I afterwards did); and that as to the bill of sale of his part in his son's ship, I would not take it by any means; but that if I wanted the money, I found he was honest enough to pay me; and if I did not, but came to receive what he gave me reason to expect, I would never have a penny more from him.

When this was past, the old man asked me if he should put me into a method to make my claim to my plantation. I told him I thought to go over to it myself. He said I might do so if I pleased, but that if I did not, there were ways enough to secure my right, and immediately to appropriate the profits to my use: and as there were ships in the river of Lisbon just ready to go away to Brazil, he made me enter my name in a public register, with his affidavit, affirming, upon oath, that I was alive, and that I was the same person who took up the land for the planting the said plantation at first. This being regularly attested by a notary, and a procuration affixed, he directed me to send it, with a letter of his writing, to a merchant of his acquaintance at the place; and then proposed my staying with him till an account came of the return.

Never was anything more honourable than the proceedings upon this procuration; for in less than seven months I received a large packet from the survivors of my trustees, the merchants, for whose account I went to sea, in which were the following, particular letters and papers enclosed:—

First, there was the account-current of the produce of my farm or plantation, from the year when their fathers had balanced with my old Portugal captain, being for six years; the balance appeared to be one thousand one hundred and seventy-four moidores in my favour.

Secondly, there was the account of four years more, while they kept the effects in their hands, before the government claimed the administration, as being the effects of a person not to be found, which they called civil death; and the balance of this, the value of the plantation increasing, amounted to nineteen thousand four hundred and forty-six crusadoes, being about three thousand two hundred and forty moidores.

Thirdly, there was the Prior of St. Augustine's account, who had received the profits for above fourteen years; but not being able to account for what was disposed of by the hospital, very honestly declared he had eight hundred and seventy-two moidores not distributed, which he acknowledged to my account: as to the king's part, that refunded nothing.

There was a letter of my partner's, congratulating me very affectionately upon my being alive, giving me an account how the estate was improved, and what it produced a year; with the particulars of the number of squares, or acres that it contained, how planted, how many slaves there were upon it: and making two-and-twenty crosses for blessings, told me he had said so many *Ave Marias* to thank the Blessed Virgin that I was alive; inviting me very passionately to come over and take possession of my own, and in the meantime to give him orders to whom he should deliver my effects if I did not come myself; concluding with a hearty tender of his friendship, and that of his family; and sent me as a present seven fine leopards' skins, which he had, it seems, received from Africa, by some other ship that he had sent thither, and which, it seems, had made a better voyage than I. He sent me also five chests of excellent sweetmeats, and a hundred pieces of gold uncoined, not quite so large as moidores. By the same fleet my two merchant-trustees shipped me one thousand two hundred chests of sugar, eight hundred rolls of tobacco, and the rest of the whole account in gold.

I might well say now, indeed, that the latter end of Job was better than the beginning. It is impossible to express the flutterings of my very heart when I found all my wealth about me; for as the Brazil ships come all in fleets, the same ships which brought my letters brought my goods: and the effects were safe in the river before the letters came to my hand. In a word, I turned pale, and grew sick; and, had not the old man run and fetched me a cordial, I believe the sudden surprise of joy had overset nature, and I had died upon the spot: nay, after that I continued very ill, and was so some hours, till a physician being sent for, and something of the real cause of my illness being known, he ordered me to be let blood; after which I had relief, and grew well: but I verily believe, if I had not been eased by a vent given in that manner to the spirits, I should have died.

I was now master, all on a sudden, of above five thousand pounds sterling in money, and had an estate, as I might well call it, in the Brazils, of above a thousand pounds a year, as sure as an estate of lands in England: and, in a word, I was in a condition which I scarce knew how to understand, or how to compose myself for the enjoyment of it. The first thing I did was to recompense my original benefactor, my good old captain, who had been first charitable to me in my distress, kind to me in my beginning, and honest to me at the end. I showed him all that was sent to me; I told him that, next to the providence of Heaven, which disposed all things, it was owing to him; and that it now lay on me to reward him, which I would do a hundred-fold: so I first returned to him the hundred moidores I had received of him; then I sent for a notary, and caused him to draw up a general release or discharge from the four hundred and seventy moidores, which he had acknowledged he owed me, in the fullest and firmest manner possible. After which I caused a procuration to be drawn, empowering him to be the receiver of the annual profits of my plantation: and appointing my partner to account with him, and make the returns, by the usual fleets, to him in my name; and by a clause in the end, made a grant of one hundred moidores a year to him during his life, out of the effects, and fifty moidores a year to his son after him, for his life: and thus I requited my old man.

I had now to consider which way to steer my course next, and what to do with the estate that Providence had thus put into my hands; and, indeed, I had more care upon my head now than I had in my state of life in the island where I wanted nothing but what I had, and had nothing but what I wanted; whereas I had now a great charge upon me, and my business was how to secure it. I had not a cave now to hide my money in, or a place where it might lie without lock or key, till it grew mouldy and tarnished before anybody would meddle with it; on the contrary, I knew not where to put it, or whom to trust with it. My old patron, the captain, indeed, was honest, and that was the only refuge I had. In the next place, my interest in the Brazils seemed to summon me thither; but now I could not tell how to think of going thither till I had settled my affairs, and left my effects in some safe hands behind me. At first I thought of my old friend the widow, who I knew was honest, and would be just to me; but then she was in years, and but poor, and, for aught I knew, might be in debt: so that, in a word, I had no way but to go back to England myself and take my effects with me.

It was some months, however, before I resolved upon this; and, therefore, as I had rewarded the old captain fully, and to his satisfaction, who had been my former benefactor, so I began to think of the poor widow, whose husband had been my first benefactor, and she, while it was in her power, my faithful steward and instructor. So, the first thing I did, I got a merchant in Lisbon to write to his correspondent in London, not only to pay a bill, but to go find her out, and carry her, in money, a hundred pounds from me, and to talk with her, and comfort her in her poverty, by telling her she should, if I lived, have a further supply: at the same time I sent my two sisters in the country a hundred pounds each, they being, though not in want, yet not in very good circumstances; one having been married and left a widow; and the other having a husband not so kind to her as he should be. But among all my relations or acquaintances I could not yet pitch upon one to whom I durst commit the gross of my stock, that I might go away to the Brazils, and leave things safe behind me; and this greatly perplexed me.

I had once a mind to have gone to the Brazils and have settled myself there, for I was, as it were, naturalised to the place; but I had some little scruple in my mind about religion, which insensibly drew me back. However, it was not religion that kept me from going there for the present; and as I had made no scruple of being openly of the religion of the country all the while I was among them, so neither did I yet; only that, now and then, having of late thought more of it than formerly, when I began to think of living and dying among them, I began to regret having professed myself a Papist, and thought it might not be the best religion to die with.

But, as I have said, this was not the main thing that kept me from going to the Brazils, but that really I did not know with whom to leave my effects behind me; so I resolved at last to go to England, where, if I arrived, I concluded that I should make some acquaintance, or find some relations, that would be faithful to me; and, accordingly, I prepared to go to England with all my wealth.

In order to prepare things for my going home, I first (the Brazil fleet being just going away) resolved to give answers suitable to the just and faithful account of things I had from thence; and, first, to the Prior of St. Augustine I wrote a letter full of thanks for his just dealings, and the offer of the eight hundred and seventy-two moidores which were undisposed of, which I desired might be given, five hundred to the monastery, and three hundred and seventy-two to the poor, as the prior should direct; desiring the good padre's prayers for me, and the like. I wrote next a letter of thanks to my two trustees, with all the acknowledgment that so much justice and honesty called for: as for sending them any present, they were far above having any occasion of it. Lastly, I wrote to my partner, acknowledging his industry in the improving the plantation, and his integrity in increasing the stock of the works; giving him instructions for his future government of my part, according to the powers I had left with my old patron, to whom I desired him to send whatever became due to me, till he should hear from me more particularly; assuring him that it was my intention not only to come to him, but to settle myself there for the remainder of my life. To this I added a very handsome present of some Italian silks for his wife and two daughters, for such the captain's son informed me he had; with two pieces of fine English broadcloth, the best I could get in Lisbon, five pieces of black baize, and some Flanders lace of a good value.

Having thus settled my affairs, sold my cargo, and turned all my effects into good bills of exchange, my next difficulty was which way to go to England: I had been accustomed enough to the sea, and yet I had a strange aversion to go to England by the sea at that time, and yet I could give no reason for it, yet the difficulty increased upon me so much, that though I had once shipped my baggage in order to go, yet I altered my mind, and that not once but two or three times.

It is true I had been very unfortunate by sea, and this might be one of the reasons; but let no man slight the strong impulses of his own thoughts in cases of such moment: two of the ships which I had singled out to go in, I mean more particularly singled out than any other, having put my things on board one of them, and in the other having agreed with the captain; I say two of these ships miscarried. One was taken by the Algerines, and the other was lost on the Start, near Torbay, and all the people drowned except three; so that in either of those vessels I had been made miserable.

Having been thus harassed in my thoughts, my old pilot, to whom I communicated everything, pressed me earnestly not to go by sea, but either to go by land to the Groyne, and cross over the Bay of Biscay to Rochelle, from whence it was but an easy and safe journey by land to Paris, and so to Calais and Dover; or to go up to Madrid, and so all the way by land through France. In a word, I was so prepossessed against my going by sea at all, except from Calais to Dover, that I resolved to travel all the way by land; which, as I was not in haste, and did not value the charge, was by much the pleasanter way: and to make it more so, my old captain brought an English gentleman, the son of a merchant in Lisbon, who was willing to travel with me; after which we picked up two more English merchants also, and two young Portuguese gentlemen, the last going to Paris only; so that in all there were six of us and five servants; the two merchants and the two Portuguese, contenting themselves with one servant between two, to save the charge; and as for me, I got an English sailor to travel with me as a servant, besides my man Friday, who was too much a stranger to be capable of supplying the place of a servant on the road.

In this manner I set out from Lisbon; and our company being very well mounted and armed, we made a little troop, whereof they did me the honour to call me captain, as well because I was the oldest man, as because I had two servants, and, indeed, was the origin of the whole journey.

As I have troubled you with none of my sea journals, so I shall trouble you now with none of my land journals; but some adventures that happened to us in this tedious and difficult journey I must not omit.

When we came to Madrid, we, being all of us strangers to Spain, were willing to stay some time to see the court of Spain, and what was worth observing; but it being the latter part of the summer, we hastened away, and set out from Madrid about the middle of October; but when we came to the edge of Navarre, we were alarmed, at several towns on the way, with an account that so much snow was falling on the French side of the mountains, that several travellers were obliged to come back to Pampeluna, after having attempted at an extreme hazard to pass on.

When we came to Pampeluna itself, we found it so indeed; and to me, that had been always used to a hot climate, and to countries where I could scarce bear any clothes on, the cold was insufferable; nor, indeed, was it more painful than surprising to come but ten days before out of Old Castile, where the weather was not only warm but very hot, and immediately to feel a wind from the Pyrenean Mountains so very keen, so severely cold, as to be intolerable and to endanger benumbing and perishing of our fingers and toes.

Poor Friday was really frightened when he saw the mountains all covered with snow, and felt cold weather, which he had never seen or felt before in his life. To mend the matter, when we came to Pampeluna it continued snowing with so much violence and so long, that the people said winter was come before its time; and the roads, which were difficult before, were now quite impassable; for, in a word, the snow lay in some places too thick for us to travel, and being not hard frozen, as is the case in the northern countries, there was no going without being in danger of being buried alive every step. We stayed no less than twenty days at Pampeluna; when (seeing the winter coming on, and no likelihood of its being better, for it was the severest winter all over Europe that had been known in the memory of man) I proposed that we should go away to Fontarabia, and there take shipping for Bordeaux, which was a very little voyage. But, while I was considering this, there came in four French gentlemen, who, having been stopped on the French side of the passes, as we were on the Spanish, had found out a guide, who, traversing the country near the head of Languedoc, had brought them over the mountains by such ways that they were not much incommoded with the snow; for where they met with snow in any quantity, they said it was frozen hard enough to bear them and their horses. We sent for this guide, who told us he would undertake to carry us the same way, with no hazard from the snow, provided we were armed sufficiently to protect ourselves from wild beasts; for, he said, in these great snows it was frequent for some wolves to show themselves at the foot of the mountains, being made ravenous for want of food, the ground being covered with snow. We told him we were well enough prepared for such creatures as they were, if he would insure us from a kind of two-legged wolves, which we were told we were in most danger from, especially on the French side of the mountains. He satisfied us that there was no danger of that kind in the way that we were to go; so we readily agreed to follow him, as did also twelve other gentlemen with their servants, some French, some Spanish, who, as I said, had attempted to go, and were obliged to come back again.

Accordingly, we set out from Pampeluna with our guide on the 15th of November; and indeed I was surprised when, instead of going forward, he came directly back with us on the same road that we came from Madrid, about twenty miles; when, having passed two rivers, and come into the plain country, we found ourselves in a warm climate again, where the country was pleasant, and no snow to be seen; but, on a sudden, turning to his left, he approached the mountains another way; and though it is true the hills and precipices looked dreadful, yet he made so many tours, such meanders, and led us by such winding ways, that we insensibly passed the height of the mountains without being much encumbered with the snow; and all on a sudden he showed us the pleasant and fruitful provinces of Languedoc and Gascony, all green and flourishing, though at a great distance, and we had some rough way to pass still.

We were a little uneasy, however, when we found it snowed one whole day and a night so fast that we could not travel; but he bid us be easy; we should soon be past it all: we found, indeed, that we began to descend every day, and to come more north than before; and so, depending upon our guide, we went on.

It was about two hours before night when, our guide being something before us, and not just in sight, out rushed three monstrous wolves, and after them a bear, from a hollow way adjoining to a thick wood; two of the wolves made at the guide, and had he been far before us, he would have been devoured before we could have helped him; one of them fastened upon his horse, and the other attacked the man with such violence, that he had not time, or presence of mind enough, to draw his pistol, but hallooed and cried out to us most lustily. My man Friday being next me, I bade him ride up and see what was the matter. As soon as Friday came in sight of the man, he hallooed out as loud as the other, "O master! O master!" but like a bold fellow, rode directly up to the poor man, and with his pistol shot the wolf in the head that attacked him.

It was happy for the poor man that it was my man Friday; for, having been used to such creatures in his country, he had no fear upon him, but went close up to him and shot him; whereas, any other of us would have fired at a farther distance, and have perhaps either missed the wolf or endangered shooting the man.

But it was enough to have terrified a bolder man than I; and, indeed, it alarmed all our company, when, with the noise of Friday's pistol, we heard on both sides the most dismal howling of wolves; and the noise, redoubled by the echo of the mountains, appeared to us as if there had been a prodigious number of them; and perhaps there was not such a few as that we had no cause of apprehension: however, as Friday had killed this wolf, the other that had fastened upon the horse left him immediately, and fled, without doing him any damage, having happily fastened upon his head, where the bosses of the bridle had stuck in his teeth. But the man was most hurt; for the raging creature had bit him twice, once in the arm, and the other time a little above his knee; and though he had made some defence, he was just tumbling down by the disorder of his horse, when Friday came up and shot the wolf.

It is easy to suppose that at the noise of Friday's pistol we all mended our pace, and rode up as fast as the way, which was very difficult, would give us leave, to see what was the matter. As soon as we came clear of the trees, which blinded us before, we saw clearly what had been the case, and how Friday had disengaged the poor guide, though we did not presently discern what kind of creature it was he had killed.

Chapter XX—FIGHT BETWEEN FRIDAY AND A BEAR

But never was a fight managed so hardily, and in such a surprising manner as that which followed between Friday and the bear, which gave us all, though at first we were surprised and afraid for him, the greatest diversion imaginable. As the bear is a heavy, clumsy creature, and does not gallop as the wolf does, who is swift and light, so he has two particular qualities, which generally are the rule of his actions; first, as to men, who are not his proper prey (he does not usually attempt them, except they first attack him, unless he be excessively hungry, which it is probable might now be the case, the ground being covered with snow), if you do not meddle with him, he will not meddle with you; but then you must take care to be very civil to him, and give him the road, for he is a very nice gentleman; he will not go a step out of his way for a prince; nay, if you are really afraid, your best way is to look another way and keep going on; for sometimes if you stop, and stand still, and look steadfastly at him, he takes it for an affront; but if you throw or toss anything at him, though it were but a bit of stick as big as your finger, he thinks himself abused, and sets all other business aside to pursue his revenge, and will have satisfaction in point of honour—that is his first quality: the next is, if he be once affronted, he will never leave you, night or day, till he has his revenge, but follows at a good round rate till he overtakes you.

My man Friday had delivered our guide, and when we came up to him he was helping him off his horse, for the man was both hurt and frightened, when on a sudden we espied the bear come out of the wood; and a monstrous one it was, the biggest by far that ever I saw. We were all a little surprised when we saw him; but when Friday saw him, it was easy to see joy and courage in the fellow's countenance. "O! O! O!" says Friday, three times, pointing to him; "O master, you give me te leave, me shakee te hand with him; me makee you good laugh."

I was surprised to see the fellow so well pleased. "You fool," says I, "he will eat you up."—"Eatee me up! eatee me up!" says Friday, twice over again; "me eatee him up; me makee you good laugh; you all stay here, me show you good laugh." So down he sits, and gets off his boots in a moment, and puts on a pair of pumps (as we call the flat shoes they wear, and which he had in his pocket), gives my other servant his horse, and with his gun away he flew, swift like the wind.

The bear was walking softly on, and offered to meddle with nobody, till Friday coming pretty near, calls to him, as if the bear could understand him. "Hark ye, hark ye," says Friday, "me speakee with you." We followed at a distance, for now being down on the Gascony side of the mountains, we were entered a vast forest, where the country was plain and pretty open, though it had many trees in it scattered here and there. Friday, who had, as we say, the heels of the bear, came up with him quickly, and took up a great stone, and threw it at him, and hit him just on the head, but did him no more harm than if he had thrown it against a wall; but it answered Friday's end, for the rogue was so void of fear that he did it purely to make the bear follow him, and show us some laugh as he called it. As soon as the bear felt the blow, and saw him, he turns about and comes after him, taking very long strides, and shuffling on at a strange rate, so as would have put a horse to a middling gallop; away reins Friday, and takes his course as if he ran towards us for help; so we all resolved to fire at once upon the bear, and deliver my man; though I was angry at him for bringing the bear back upon us, when he was going about his own business another way; and especially I was angry that he had turned the bear upon us, and then ran away; and I called out, "You dog! is this your making us laugh? Come away, and take your horse, that we may shoot the creature." He heard me, and cried out, "No shoot, no shoot; stand still, and you get much laugh:" and as the nimble creature ran two feet for the bear's one, he turned on a sudden on one side of us, and seeing a great oak-tree fit for his purpose, he beckoned to us to follow; and doubling his pace, he got nimbly up the tree, laying his gun down upon the ground, at about five or six yards from the bottom of the tree. The bear soon came to the tree, and we followed at a distance: the first thing he did he stopped at the gun, smelt at it, but let it lie, and up he scrambles into the tree, climbing like a cat, though so monstrous heavy. I was amazed at the folly, as I thought it, of my man, and could not for my life see anything to laugh at, till seeing the bear get up the tree, we all rode near to him.

When we came to the tree, there was Friday got out to the small end of a large branch, and the bear got about half-way to him. As soon as the bear got out to that part where the limb of the tree was weaker, "Ha!" says he to us, "now you see me teachee the bear dance:" so he began jumping and shaking the bough, at which the bear began to totter, but stood still, and began to look behind him, to see how he should get back; then, indeed, we did laugh heartily. But Friday had not done with him by a great deal; when seeing him stand still, he called out to him again, as if he had supposed the bear could speak English, "What, you come no farther? pray you come farther;" so he left jumping and shaking the tree; and the bear, just as if he understood what he said, did come a little farther; then he began jumping again, and the bear stopped again. We thought now was a good time to knock him in the head, and called to Friday to stand still and we should shoot the bear: but he cried out earnestly, "Oh, pray! Oh, pray! no shoot, me shoot by and then:" he would have said by-and-by. However, to shorten the story, Friday danced so much, and the bear stood so ticklish, that we had laughing enough, but still could not imagine what the fellow would do: for first we thought he depended upon shaking the bear off; and we found the bear was too cunning for that too; for he would not go out far enough to be thrown down, but clung fast with his great broad claws and feet, so that we could not imagine what would be the end of it, and what the jest would be at last. But Friday put us out of doubt quickly: for seeing the bear cling fast to the bough, and that he would not be persuaded to come any farther, "Well, well," says Friday, "you no come farther, me go; you no come to me, me come to you;" and upon this he went out to the smaller end, where it would bend with his weight, and gently let himself down by it, sliding down the bough till he came near enough to jump down on his feet, and away he ran to his gun, took it up, and stood still. "Well," said I to him, "Friday, what will you do now? Why don't you shoot him?" "No shoot," says Friday, "no yet; me shoot now, me no kill; me stay, give you one more laugh:" and, indeed, so he did; for when the bear saw his enemy gone, he came back from the bough, where he stood, but did it very cautiously, looking behind him every step, and coming backward till he got into the body of the tree, then, with the same hinder end foremost, he came down the tree, grasping it with his claws, and moving one foot at a time, very leisurely. At this juncture, and just before he could set his hind foot on the ground, Friday stepped up close to him, clapped the muzzle of his piece into his ear, and shot him dead. Then the rogue turned about to see if we did not laugh; and when he saw we were pleased by our looks, he began to laugh very loud. "So we kill bear in my country," says Friday. "So you kill them?" says I; "why, you have no guns."—"No," says he, "no gun, but shoot great much long arrow." This was a good diversion to us; but we were still in a wild place, and our guide very much hurt, and what to do we hardly knew; the howling of wolves ran much in my head; and, indeed, except the noise I once heard on the shore of Africa, of which I have said something already, I never heard anything that filled me with so much horror.

These things, and the approach of night, called us off, or else, as Friday would have had us, we should certainly have taken the skin of this monstrous creature off, which was worth saving; but we had near three leagues to go, and our guide hastened us; so we left him, and went forward on our journey.

The ground was still covered with snow, though not so deep and dangerous as on the mountains; and the ravenous creatures, as we heard afterwards, were come down into the forest and plain country, pressed by hunger, to seek for food, and had done a great deal of mischief in the villages, where they surprised the country people, killed a great many of their sheep and horses, and some people too. We had one dangerous place to pass, and our guide told us if there were more wolves in the country we should find them there; and this was a small plain, surrounded with woods on every side, and a long, narrow defile, or lane, which we were to pass to get through the wood, and then we should come to the village where we were to lodge. It was within half-an-hour of sunset when we entered the wood, and a little after sunset when we came into the plain: we met with nothing in the first wood, except that in a little plain within the wood, which was not above two furlongs over, we saw five great wolves cross the road, full speed, one after another, as if they had been in chase of some prey, and had it in view; they took no notice of us, and were gone out of sight in a few moments. Upon this, our guide, who, by the way, was but a fainthearted fellow, bid us keep in a ready posture, for he believed there were more wolves a-coming. We kept our arms ready, and our eyes about us; but we saw no more wolves till we came through that wood, which was near half a league, and entered the plain. As soon as we came into the plain, we had occasion enough to look about us. The first object we met with was a dead horse; that is to say, a poor horse which the wolves had killed, and at least a dozen of them at work, we could not say eating him, but picking his bones rather; for they had eaten up all the flesh before. We did not think fit to disturb them at their feast, neither did they take much notice of us. Friday would have let fly at them, but I would not suffer him by any means; for I found we were like to have more business upon our hands than we were aware of. We had not gone half over the plain when we began to hear the wolves howl in the wood on our left in a frightful manner, and presently after we saw about a hundred coming on directly towards us, all in a body, and most of them in a line, as regularly as an army drawn up by experienced officers. I scarce knew in what manner to receive them, but found to draw ourselves in a close line was the only way; so we formed in a moment; but that we might not have too much interval, I ordered that only every other man should fire, and that the others, who had not fired, should stand ready to give them a second volley immediately, if they continued to advance upon us; and then that those that had fired at first should not pretend to load their fusees again, but stand ready, every one with a pistol, for we were all armed with a fusee and a pair of pistols each man; so we were, by this method, able to fire six volleys, half of us at a time; however, at present we had no necessity; for upon firing the first volley, the enemy made a full stop, being terrified as well with the noise as with the fire. Four of them being shot in the head, dropped; several others were wounded, and went bleeding off, as we could see by the snow. I found they stopped, but did not immediately retreat; whereupon, remembering that I had been told that the fiercest creatures were terrified at the voice of a man, I caused all the company to halloo as loud as they could; and I found the notion not altogether mistaken; for upon our shout they began to retire and turn about. I then ordered a second volley to be fired in their rear, which put them to the gallop, and away they went to the woods. This gave us leisure to charge our pieces again; and that we might lose no time, we kept going; but we had but little more than loaded our fusees, and put ourselves in readiness, when we heard a terrible noise in the same wood on our left, only that it was farther onward, the same way we were to go.

The night was coming on, and the light began to be dusky, which made it worse on our side; but the noise increasing, we could easily perceive that it was the howling and yelling of those hellish creatures; and on a sudden we perceived three troops of wolves, one on our left, one behind us, and one in our front, so that we seemed to be surrounded with them: however, as they did not fall upon us, we kept our way forward, as fast as we could make our horses go, which, the way being very rough, was only a good hard trot. In this manner, we came in view of the entrance of a wood, through which we were to pass, at the farther side of the plain; but we were greatly surprised, when coming nearer the lane or pass, we saw a confused number of wolves standing just at the entrance. On a sudden, at another opening of the wood, we heard the noise of a gun, and looking that way, out rushed a horse, with a saddle and a bridle on him, flying like the wind, and sixteen or seventeen wolves after him, full speed: the horse had the advantage of them; but as we supposed that he could not hold it at that rate, we doubted not but they would get up with him at last: no question but they did.

But here we had a most horrible sight; for riding up to the entrance where the horse came out, we found the carcasses of another horse and of two men, devoured by the ravenous creatures; and one of the men was no doubt the same whom we heard fire the gun, for there lay a gun just by him fired off; but as to the man, his head and the upper part of his body was eaten up. This filled us with horror, and we knew not what course to take; but the creatures resolved us soon, for they gathered about us presently, in hopes of prey; and I verily believe there were three hundred of them. It happened, very much to our advantage, that at the entrance into the wood, but a little way from it, there lay some large timber-trees, which had been cut down the summer before, and I suppose lay there for carriage. I drew my little troop in among those trees, and placing ourselves in a line behind one long tree, I advised them all to alight, and keeping that tree before us for a breastwork, to stand in a triangle, or three fronts, enclosing our horses in the centre. We did so, and it was well we did; for never was a more furious charge than the creatures made upon us in this place. They came on with a growling kind of noise, and mounted the piece of timber, which, as I said, was our breastwork, as if they were only rushing upon their prey; and this fury of theirs, it seems, was principally occasioned by their seeing our horses behind us. I ordered our men to fire as before, every other man; and they took their aim so sure that they killed several of the wolves at the first volley; but there was a necessity to keep a continual firing, for they came on like devils, those behind pushing on those before.

When we had fired a second volley of our fusees, we thought they stopped a little, and I hoped they would have gone off, but it was but a moment, for others came forward again; so we fired two volleys of our pistols; and I believe in these four firings we had killed seventeen or eighteen of them, and lamed twice as many, yet they came on again. I was loth to spend our shot too hastily; so I called my servant, not my man Friday, for he was better employed, for, with the greatest dexterity imaginable, he had charged my fusee and his own while we were engaged—but, as I said, I called my other man, and giving him a horn of powder, I had him lay a train all along the piece of timber, and let it be a large train. He did so, and had but just time to get away, when the wolves came up to it, and some got upon it, when I, snapping an unchanged pistol close to the powder, set it on fire; those that were upon the timber were scorched with it, and six or seven of them fell; or rather jumped in among us with the force and fright of the fire; we despatched these in an instant, and the rest were so frightened with the light, which the night—for it was now very near dark—made more terrible that they drew back a little; upon which I ordered our last pistols to be fired off in one volley, and after that we gave a shout; upon this the wolves turned tail, and we sallied immediately upon near twenty lame ones that we found struggling on the ground, and fell to cutting them with our swords, which answered our expectation, for the crying and howling they made was better understood by their fellows; so that they all fled and left us.

We had, first and last, killed about threescore of them, and had it been daylight we had killed many more. The field of battle being thus cleared, we made forward again, for we had still near a league to go. We heard the ravenous creatures howl and yell in the woods as we went several times, and sometimes we fancied we saw some of them; but the snow dazzling our eyes, we were not certain. In about an hour more we came to the town where we were to lodge, which we found in a terrible fright and all in arms; for, it seems, the night before the wolves and some bears had broken into the village, and put them in such terror that they were obliged to keep guard night and day, but especially in the night, to preserve their cattle, and indeed their people.

The next morning our guide was so ill, and his limbs swelled so much with the rankling of his two wounds, that he could go no farther; so we were obliged to take a new guide here, and go to Toulouse, where we found a warm climate, a fruitful, pleasant country, and no snow, no wolves, nor anything like them; but when we told our story at Toulouse, they told us it was nothing but what was ordinary in the great forest at the foot of the mountains, especially when the snow lay on the ground; but they inquired much what kind of guide we had got who would venture to bring us that way in such a severe season, and told us it was surprising we were not all devoured. When we told them how we placed ourselves and the horses in the middle, they blamed us exceedingly, and told us it was fifty to one but we had been all destroyed, for it was the sight of the horses which made the wolves so furious, seeing their prey, and that at other times they are really afraid of a gun; but being excessively hungry, and raging on that account, the eagerness to come at the horses had made them senseless of danger, and that if we had not by the continual fire, and at last by the stratagem of the train of powder, mastered them, it had been great odds but that we had been torn to pieces; whereas, had we been content to have sat still on horseback, and fired as horsemen, they would not have taken the horses so much for their own, when men were on their backs, as otherwise; and withal, they told us that at last, if we had stood altogether, and left our horses, they would have been so eager to have devoured them, that we might have come off safe, especially having our firearms in our hands, being so many in number. For my part, I was never so sensible of danger in my life; for, seeing above three hundred devils come roaring and open-mouthed to devour us, and having nothing to shelter us or retreat to, I gave myself over for lost; and, as it was, I believe I shall never care to cross those mountains again: I think I would much rather go a thousand leagues by sea, though I was sure to meet with a storm once a-week.

I have nothing uncommon to take notice of in my passage through France—nothing but what other travellers have given an account of with much more advantage than I can. I travelled from Toulouse to Paris, and without any considerable stay came to Calais, and landed safe at Dover the 14th of January, after having had a severe cold season to travel in.

I was now come to the centre of my travels, and had in a little time all my new-discovered estate safe about me, the bills of exchange which I brought with me having been currently paid.

My principal guide and privy-counsellor was my good ancient widow, who, in gratitude for the money I had sent her, thought no pains too much nor care too great to employ for me; and I trusted her so entirely that I was perfectly easy as to the security of my effects; and, indeed, I was very happy from the beginning, and now to the end, in the unspotted integrity of this good gentlewoman.

And now, having resolved to dispose of my plantation in the Brazils, I wrote to my old friend at Lisbon, who, having offered it to the two merchants, the survivors of my trustees, who lived in the Brazils, they accepted the offer, and remitted thirty-three thousand pieces of eight to a correspondent of theirs at Lisbon to pay for it.

In return, I signed the instrument of sale in the form which they sent from Lisbon, and sent it to my old man, who sent me the bills of exchange for thirty-two thousand eight hundred pieces of eight for the estate, reserving the payment of one hundred moidores a year to him (the old man) during his life, and fifty moidores afterwards to his son for his life, which I had promised them, and which the plantation was to make good as a rent-charge. And thus I have given the first part of a life of fortune and adventure—a life of Providence's chequer-work, and of a variety which the world will seldom be able to show the like of; beginning foolishly, but closing much more happily than any part of it ever gave me leave so much as to hope for.

Any one would think that in this state of complicated good fortune I was past running any more hazards—and so, indeed, I had been, if other circumstances had concurred; but I was inured to a wandering life, had no family, nor many relations; nor, however rich, had I contracted fresh acquaintance; and though I had sold my estate in the Brazils, yet I could not keep that country out of my head, and had a great mind to be upon the wing again; especially I could not resist the strong inclination I had to see my island, and to know if the poor Spaniards were in being there. My true friend, the widow, earnestly dissuaded me from it, and so far prevailed with me, that for almost seven years she prevented my running abroad, during which time I took my two nephews, the children of one of my brothers, into my care; the eldest, having something of his own, I bred up as a gentleman, and gave him a settlement of some addition to his estate after my decease. The other I placed with the captain of a ship; and after five years, finding him a sensible, bold, enterprising young fellow, I put him into a good ship, and sent him to sea; and this young fellow afterwards drew me in, as old as I was, to further adventures myself.

In the meantime, I in part settled myself here; for, first of all, I married, and that not either to my disadvantage or dissatisfaction, and had three children, two sons and one daughter; but my wife dying, and my nephew coming home with good success from a voyage to Spain, my inclination to go abroad, and his importunity, prevailed, and engaged me to go in his ship as a private trader to the East Indies; this was in the year 1694.

In this voyage I visited my new colony in the island, saw my successors the Spaniards, had the old story of their lives and of the villains I left there; how at first they insulted the poor Spaniards, how they afterwards agreed, disagreed, united, separated, and how at last the Spaniards were obliged to use violence with them; how they were subjected to the Spaniards, how honestly the Spaniards used them—a history, if it were entered into, as full of variety and wonderful accidents as my own part—particularly, also, as to their battles with the Caribbeans, who landed several times upon the island, and as to the improvement they made upon the island itself, and how five of them made an attempt upon the mainland, and brought away eleven men and five women prisoners, by which, at my coming, I found about twenty young children on the island.

Here I stayed about twenty days, left them supplies of all necessary things, and particularly of arms, powder, shot, clothes, tools, and two workmen, which I had brought from England with me, viz. a carpenter and a smith.

Besides this, I shared the lands into parts with them, reserved to myself the property of the whole, but gave them such parts respectively as they agreed on; and having settled all things with them, and engaged them not to leave the place, I left them there.

From thence I touched at the Brazils, from whence I sent a bark, which I bought there, with more people to the island; and in it, besides other supplies, I sent seven women, being such as I found proper for service, or for wives to such as would take them. As to the Englishmen, I promised to send them some women from England, with a good cargo of necessaries, if they would apply themselves to planting—which I afterwards could not perform. The fellows proved very honest and diligent after they were mastered and had their properties set apart for them. I sent them, also, from the Brazils, five cows, three of them being big with calf, some sheep, and some hogs, which when I came again were considerably increased.

But all these things, with an account how three hundred Caribbees came and invaded them, and ruined their plantations, and how they fought with that whole number twice, and were at first defeated, and one of them killed; but at last, a storm destroying their enemies' canoes, they famished or destroyed almost all the rest, and renewed and recovered the possession of their plantation, and still lived upon the island.

All these things, with some very surprising incidents in some new adventures of my own, for ten years more, I shall give a farther account of in the Second Part of my Story.

THE FURTHER ADVENTURES OF ROBINSON CRUSOE

Chapter I—REVISITS ISLAND

That homely proverb, used on so many occasions in England, viz. "That what is bred in the bone will not go out of the flesh," was never more verified than in the story of my Life. Any one would think that after thirty-five years' affliction, and a variety of unhappy circumstances, which few men, if any, ever went through before, and after near seven years of peace and enjoyment in the fulness of all things; grown old, and when, if ever, it might be allowed me to have had experience of every state of middle life, and to know which was most adapted to make a man completely happy; I say, after all this, any one would have thought that the native propensity to rambling which I gave an account of in my first setting out in the world to have been so predominant in my thoughts, should be worn out, and I might, at sixty one years of age, have been a little inclined to stay at home, and have done venturing life and fortune any more.

Nay, farther, the common motive of foreign adventures was taken away in me, for I had no fortune to make; I had nothing to seek: if I had gained ten thousand pounds I had been no richer; for I had already sufficient for me, and for those I had to leave it to; and what I had was visibly increasing; for, having no great family, I could not spend the income of what I had unless I would set up for an expensive way of living, such as a great family, servants, equipage, gaiety, and the like, which were things I had no notion of, or inclination to; so that I had nothing, indeed, to do but to sit still, and fully enjoy what I had got, and see it increase daily upon my hands. Yet all these things had no effect upon me, or at least not enough to resist the strong inclination I had to go abroad again, which hung about me like a chronic distemper. In particular, the desire of seeing my new plantation in the island, and the colony I left there, ran in my head continually. I dreamed of it all night, and my imagination ran upon it all day: it was uppermost in all my thoughts, and my fancy worked so steadily and strongly upon it that I talked of it in my sleep; in short, nothing could remove it out of my mind: it even broke so violently into all my discourses that it made my conversation tiresome, for I could talk of nothing else; all my discourse ran into it, even to impertinence; and I saw it myself.

I have often heard persons of good judgment say that all the stir that people make in the world about ghosts and apparitions is owing to the strength of imagination, and the powerful operation of fancy in their minds; that there is no such thing as a spirit appearing, or a ghost walking; that people's poring affectionately upon the past conversation of their deceased friends so realises it to them that they are capable of fancying, upon some extraordinary circumstances, that they see them, talk to them, and are answered by them, when, in truth, there is nothing but shadow and vapour in the thing, and they really know nothing of the matter.

For my part, I know not to this hour whether there are any such things as real apparitions, spectres, or walking of people after they are dead; or whether there is anything in the stories they tell us of that kind more than the product of vapours, sick minds, and wandering fancies: but this I know, that my imagination worked up to such a height, and brought me into such excess of vapours, or what else I may call it, that I actually supposed myself often upon the spot, at my old castle, behind the trees; saw my old Spaniard, Friday's father, and the reprobate sailors I left upon the island; nay, I fancied I talked with them, and looked at them steadily, though I was broad awake, as at persons just before me; and this I did till I often frightened myself with the images my fancy represented to me. One time, in my sleep, I had the villainy of the three pirate sailors so lively related to me by the first Spaniard, and Friday's father, that it was surprising: they told me how they barbarously attempted to murder all the Spaniards, and that they set fire to the provisions they had laid up, on purpose to distress and starve them; things that I had never heard of, and that, indeed, were never all of them true in fact: but it was so warm in my imagination, and so realised to me, that, to the hour I saw them, I could not be persuaded but that it was or would be true; also how I resented it, when the Spaniard complained to me; and how I brought them to justice, tried them, and ordered them all three to be hanged. What there was really in this shall be seen in its place; for however I came to form such things in my dream, and what secret converse of spirits injected it, yet there was, I say, much of it true. I own that this dream had nothing in it literally and specifically true; but the general part was so true—the base; villainous behaviour of these three hardened rogues was such, and had been so much worse than all I can describe, that the dream had too much similitude of the fact; and as I would afterwards have punished them severely, so, if I had hanged them all, I had been much in the right, and even should have been justified both by the laws of God and man.

But to return to my story. In this kind of temper I lived some years; I had no enjoyment of my life, no pleasant hours, no agreeable diversion but what had something or other of this in it; so that my wife, who saw my mind wholly bent upon it, told me very seriously one night that she believed there was some secret, powerful impulse of Providence upon me, which had determined me to go thither again; and that she found nothing hindered me going but my being engaged to a wife and children. She told me that it was true she could not think of parting with me: but as she was assured that if she was dead it would be the first thing I would do, so, as it seemed to her that the thing was determined above, she would not be the only obstruction; for, if I thought fit and resolved to go—[Here she found me very intent upon her words, and that I looked very earnestly at her, so that it a little disordered her, and she stopped. I asked her why she did not go on, and say out what she was going to say? But I perceived that her heart was too full, and some tears stood in her eyes.] "Speak out, my dear," said I; "are you willing I should go?"—"No," says she, very affectionately, "I am far from willing; but if you are resolved to go," says she, "rather than I would be the only hindrance, I will go with you: for though I think it a most preposterous thing for one of your years, and in your condition, yet, if it must be," said she, again weeping, "I would not leave you; for if it be of Heaven you must do it, there is no resisting it; and if Heaven make it your duty to go, He will also make it mine to go with you, or otherwise dispose of me, that I may not obstruct it."

This affectionate behaviour of my wife's brought me a little out of the vapours, and I began to consider what I was doing; I corrected my wandering fancy, and began to argue with myself sedately what business I had after threescore years, and after such a life of tedious sufferings and disasters, and closed in so happy and easy a manner; I, say, what business had I to rush into new hazards, and put myself upon adventures fit only for youth and poverty to run into?

With those thoughts I considered my new engagement; that I had a wife, one child born, and my wife then great with child of another; that I had all the world could give me, and had no need to seek hazard for gain; that I was declining in years, and ought to think rather of leaving what I had gained than of seeking to increase it; that as to what my wife had said of its being an impulse from Heaven, and that it should be my duty to go, I had no notion of that; so, after many of these cogitations, I struggled with the power of my imagination, reasoned myself out of it, as I believe people may always do in like cases if they will: in a word, I conquered it, composed myself with such arguments as occurred to my thoughts, and which my present condition furnished me plentifully with; and particularly, as the most effectual method, I resolved to divert myself with other things, and to engage in some business that might effectually tie me up from any more excursions of this kind; for I found that thing return upon me chiefly when I was idle, and had nothing to do, nor anything of moment immediately before me. To this purpose, I bought a little farm in the county of Bedford, and resolved to remove myself thither. I had a little convenient house upon it, and the land about it, I found, was capable of great improvement; and it was many ways suited to my inclination, which delighted in cultivating, managing, planting, and improving of land; and particularly, being an inland country, I was removed from conversing among sailors and things relating to the remote parts of the world. I went down to my farm, settled my family, bought ploughs, harrows, a cart, waggon-horses, cows, and sheep, and, setting seriously to work, became in one half-year a mere country gentleman. My thoughts were entirely taken up in managing my servants, cultivating the ground, enclosing, planting, &c.; and I lived, as I thought, the most agreeable life that nature was capable of directing, or that a man always bred to misfortunes was capable of retreating to.

I farmed upon my own land; I had no rent to pay, was limited by no articles; I could pull up or cut down as I pleased; what I planted was for myself, and what I improved was for my family; and having thus left off the thoughts of wandering, I had not the least discomfort in any part of life as to this world. Now I thought, indeed, that I enjoyed the middle state of life which my father so earnestly recommended to me, and lived a kind of heavenly life, something like what is described by the poet, upon the subject of a country life:—

> "Free from vices, free from care,
> Age has no pain, and youth no snare."

But in the middle of all this felicity, one blow from unseen Providence unhinged me at once; and not only made a breach upon me inevitable and incurable, but drove me, by its consequences, into a deep relapse of the wandering disposition, which, as I may say, being born in my very blood, soon recovered its hold of me; and, like the returns of a violent distemper, came on with an irresistible force upon me. This blow was the loss of my wife. It is not my business here to write an elegy upon my wife, give a character of her particular virtues, and make my court to the sex by the flattery of a funeral sermon. She was, in a few words, the stay of all my affairs; the centre of all my enterprises; the engine that, by her prudence, reduced me to that happy compass I was in, from the most extravagant and ruinous project that filled my head, and did more to guide my rambling genius than a mother's tears, a father's instructions, a friend's counsel, or all my own reasoning powers could do. I was happy in listening to her, and in being moved by her entreaties; and to the last degree desolate and dislocated in the world by the loss of her.

When she was gone, the world looked awkwardly round me. I was as much a stranger in it, in my thoughts, as I was in the Brazils, when I first went on shore there; and as much alone, except for the assistance of servants, as I was in my island. I knew neither what to think nor what to do. I saw the world busy around me: one part labouring for bread, another part squandering in vile excesses or empty pleasures, but equally miserable because the end they proposed still fled from them; for the men of pleasure every day surfeited of their vice, and heaped up work for sorrow and repentance; and the men of labour spent their strength in daily struggling for bread to maintain the vital strength they laboured with: so living in a daily circulation of sorrow, living but to work, and working but to live, as if daily bread were the only end of wearisome life, and a wearisome life the only occasion of daily bread.

This put me in mind of the life I lived in my kingdom, the island; where I suffered no more corn to grow, because I did not want it; and bred no more goats, because I had no more use for them; where the money lay in the drawer till it grew mouldy, and had scarce the favour to be looked upon in twenty years. All these things, had I improved them as I ought to have done, and as reason and religion had dictated to me, would have taught me to search farther than human enjoyments for a full felicity; and that there was something which certainly was the reason and end of life superior to all these things, and which was either to be possessed, or at least hoped for, on this side of the grave.

But my sage counsellor was gone; I was like a ship without a pilot, that could only run afore the wind. My thoughts ran all away again into the old affair; my head was quite turned with the whimsies of foreign adventures; and all the pleasant, innocent amusements of my farm, my garden, my cattle, and my family, which before entirely possessed me, were nothing to me, had no relish, and were like music to one that has no ear, or food to one that has no taste. In a word, I resolved to leave off housekeeping, let my farm, and return to London; and in a few months after I did so.

When I came to London, I was still as uneasy as I was before; I had no relish for the place, no employment in it, nothing to do but to saunter about like an idle person, of whom it may be said he is perfectly useless in God's creation, and it is not one farthing's matter to the rest of his kind whether he be dead or alive. This also was the thing which, of all circumstances of life, was the most my aversion, who had been all my days used to an active life; and I would often say to myself, "A state of idleness is the very dregs of life;" and, indeed, I thought I was much more suitably employed when I was twenty-six days making a deal board.

It was now the beginning of the year 1693, when my nephew, whom, as I have observed before, I had brought up to the sea, and had made him commander of a ship, was come home from a short voyage to Bilbao, being the first he had made. He came to me, and told me that some merchants of his acquaintance had been proposing to him to go a voyage for them to the East Indies, and to China, as private traders. "And now, uncle," says he, "if you will go to sea with me, I will engage to land you upon your old habitation in the island; for we are to touch at the Brazils."

Nothing can be a greater demonstration of a future state, and of the existence of an invisible world, than the concurrence of second causes with the idea of things which we form in our minds, perfectly reserved, and not communicated to any in the world.

My nephew knew nothing how far my distemper of wandering was returned upon me, and I knew nothing of what he had in his thought to say, when that very morning, before he came to me, I had, in a great deal of confusion of thought, and revolving every part of my circumstances in my mind, come to this resolution, that I would go to Lisbon, and consult with my old sea-captain; and if it was rational and practicable, I would go and see the island again, and what was become of my people there. I had pleased myself with the thoughts of peopling the place, and carrying inhabitants from hence, getting a patent for the possession and I know not what; when, in the middle of all this, in comes my nephew, as I have said, with his project of carrying me thither in his way to the East Indies.

I paused a while at his words, and looking steadily at him, "What devil," said I, "sent you on this unlucky errand?" My nephew stared as if he had been frightened at first; but perceiving that I was not much displeased at the proposal, he recovered himself. "I hope it may not be an unlucky proposal, sir," says he. "I daresay you would be pleased to see your new colony there, where you once reigned with more felicity than most of your brother monarchs in the world." In a word, the scheme hit so exactly with my temper, that is to say, the prepossession I was under, and of which I have said so much, that I told him, in a few words, if he agreed with the merchants, I would go with him; but I told him I would not promise to go any further than my own island. "Why, sir," says he, "you don't want to be left there again, I hope?" "But," said I, "can you not take me up again on your return?" He told me it would not be possible to do so; that the merchants would never allow him to come that way with a laden ship of such value, it being a month's sail out of his way, and might be three or four. "Besides, sir, if I should miscarry," said he, "and not return at all, then you would be just reduced to the condition you were in before."

This was very rational; but we both found out a remedy for it, which was to carry a framed sloop on board the ship, which, being taken in pieces, might, by the help of some carpenters, whom we agreed to carry with us, be set up again in the island, and finished fit to go to sea in a few days. I was not long resolving, for indeed the importunities of my nephew joined so effectually with my inclination that nothing could oppose me; on the other hand, my wife being dead, none concerned themselves so much for me as to persuade me one way or the other, except my ancient good friend the widow, who earnestly struggled with me to consider my years, my easy circumstances, and the needless hazards of a long voyage; and above all, my young children. But it was all to no purpose, I had an irresistible desire for the voyage; and I told her I thought there was something so uncommon in the impressions I had upon my mind, that it would be a kind of resisting Providence if I should attempt to stay at home; after which she ceased her expostulations, and joined with me, not only in making provision for my voyage, but also in settling my family affairs for my absence, and providing for the education of my children. In order to do this, I made my will, and settled the estate I had in such a manner for my children, and placed in such hands, that I was perfectly easy and satisfied they would have justice done them, whatever might befall me; and for their education, I left it wholly to the widow, with a sufficient maintenance to herself for her care: all which she richly deserved; for no mother could have taken more care in their education, or understood it better; and as she lived till I came home, I also lived to thank her for it.

My nephew was ready to sail about the beginning of January 1694-5; and I, with my man Friday, went on board, in the Downs, the 8th; having, besides that sloop which I mentioned above, a very considerable cargo of all kinds of necessary things for my colony, which, if I did not find in good condition, I resolved to leave so.

First, I carried with me some servants whom I purposed to place there as inhabitants, or at least to set on work there upon my account while I stayed, and either to leave them there or carry them forward, as they should appear willing; particularly, I carried two carpenters, a smith, and a very handy, ingenious fellow, who was a cooper by trade, and was also a general mechanic; for he was dexterous at making wheels and hand-mills to grind corn, was a good turner and a good pot-maker; he also made anything that was proper to make of earth or of wood: in a word, we called him our Jack-of-all-trades. With these I carried a tailor, who had offered himself to go a passenger to the East Indies with my nephew, but afterwards consented to stay on our new plantation, and who proved a most necessary handy fellow as could be desired in many other businesses besides that of his trade; for, as I observed formerly, necessity arms us for all employments.

My cargo, as near as I can recollect, for I have not kept account of the particulars, consisted of a sufficient quantity of linen, and some English thin stuffs, for clothing the Spaniards that I expected to find there; and enough of them, as by my calculation might comfortably supply them for seven years; if I remember right, the materials I carried for clothing them, with gloves, hats, shoes, stockings, and all such things as they could want for wearing, amounted to about two hundred pounds, including some beds, bedding, and household stuff, particularly kitchen utensils, with pots, kettles, pewter, brass, &c.; and near a hundred pounds more in ironwork, nails, tools of every kind, staples, hooks, hinges, and every necessary thing I could think of.

I carried also a hundred spare arms, muskets, and fusees; besides some pistols, a considerable quantity of shot of all sizes, three or four tons of lead, and two pieces of brass cannon; and, because I knew not what time and what extremities I was providing for, I carried a hundred barrels of powder, besides swords, cutlasses, and the iron part of some pikes and halberds. In short, we had a large magazine of all sorts of store; and I made my nephew carry two small quarter-deck guns more than he wanted for his ship, to leave behind if there was occasion; so that when we came there we might build a fort and man it against all sorts of enemies. Indeed, I at first thought there would be need enough for all, and much more, if we hoped to maintain our possession of the island, as shall be seen in the course of that story.

I had not such bad luck in this voyage as I had been used to meet with, and therefore shall have the less occasion to interrupt the reader, who perhaps may be impatient to hear how matters went with my colony; yet some odd accidents, cross winds and bad weather happened on this first setting out, which made the voyage longer than I expected it at first; and I, who had never made but one voyage, my first voyage to Guinea, in which I might be said to come back again, as the voyage was at first designed, began to think the same ill fate attended me, and that I was born to be never contented with being on shore, and yet to be always unfortunate at sea. Contrary winds first put us to the northward, and we were obliged to put in at Galway, in Ireland, where we lay wind-bound two-and-twenty days; but we had this satisfaction with the disaster, that provisions were here exceeding cheap, and in the utmost plenty; so that while we lay here we never touched the ship's stores, but rather added to them. Here, also, I took in several live hogs, and two cows with their calves, which I resolved, if I had a good passage, to put on shore in my island; but we found occasion to dispose otherwise of them.

We set out on the 5th of February from Ireland, and had a very fair gale of wind for some days. As I remember, it might be about the 20th of February in the evening late, when the mate, having the watch, came into the round-house and told us he saw a flash of fire, and heard a gun fired; and while he was telling us of it, a boy came in and told us the boatswain heard another. This made us all run out upon the quarter-deck, where for a while we heard nothing; but in a few minutes we saw a very great light, and found that there was some very terrible fire at a distance; immediately we had recourse to our reckonings, in which we all agreed that there could be no land that way in which the fire showed itself, no, not for five hundred leagues, for it appeared at WNW. Upon this, we concluded it must be some ship on fire at sea; and as, by our hearing the noise of guns just before, we concluded that it could not be far off, we stood directly towards it, and were presently satisfied we should discover it, because the further we sailed, the greater the light appeared; though, the weather being hazy, we could not perceive anything but the light for a while. In about half-an-hour's sailing, the wind being fair for us, though not much of it, and the weather clearing up a little, we could plainly discern that it was a great ship on fire in the middle of the sea.

I was most sensibly touched with this disaster, though not at all acquainted with the persons engaged in it; I presently recollected my former circumstances, and what condition I was in when taken up by the Portuguese captain; and how much more deplorable the circumstances of the poor creatures belonging to that ship must be, if they had no other ship in company with them. Upon this I immediately ordered that five guns should be fired, one soon after another, that, if possible, we might give notice to them that there was help for them at hand and that they might endeavour to save themselves in their boat; for though we could see the flames of the ship, yet they, it being night, could see nothing of us.

We lay by some time upon this, only driving as the burning ship drove, waiting for daylight; when, on a sudden, to our great terror, though we had reason to expect it, the ship blew up in the air; and in a few minutes all the fire was out, that is to say, the rest of the ship sunk. This was a terrible, and indeed an afflicting sight, for the sake of the poor men, who, I concluded, must be either all destroyed in the ship, or be in the utmost distress in their boat, in the middle of the ocean; which, at present, as it was dark, I could not see. However, to direct them as well as I could, I caused lights to be hung out in all parts of the ship where we could, and which we had lanterns for, and kept firing guns all the night long, letting them know by this that there was a ship not far off.

About eight o'clock in the morning we discovered the ship's boats by the help of our perspective glasses, and found there were two of them, both thronged with people, and deep in the water. We perceived they rowed, the wind being against them; that they saw our ship, and did their utmost to make us see them. We immediately spread our ancient, to let them know we saw them, and hung a waft out, as a signal for them to come on board, and then made more sail, standing directly to them. In little more than half-an-hour we came up with them; and took them all in, being no less than sixty-four men, women, and children; for there were a great many passengers.

Upon inquiry we found it was a French merchant ship of three-hundred tons, home-bound from Quebec. The master gave us a long account of the distress of his ship; how the fire began in the steerage by the negligence of the steersman, which, on his crying out for help, was, as everybody thought, entirely put out; but they soon found that some sparks of the first fire had got into some part of the ship so difficult to come at that they could not effectually quench it; and afterwards getting in between the timbers, and within the ceiling of the ship, it proceeded into the hold, and mastered all the skill and all the application they were able to exert.

They had no more to do then but to get into their boats, which, to their great comfort, were pretty large; being their long-boat, and a great shallop, besides a small skiff, which was of no great service to them, other than to get some fresh water and provisions into her, after they had secured their lives from the fire. They had, indeed, small hopes of their lives by getting into these boats at that distance from any land; only, as they said, that they thus escaped from the fire, and there was a possibility that some ship might happen to be at sea, and might take them in. They had sails, oars, and a compass; and had as much provision and water as, with sparing it so as to be next door to starving, might support them about twelve days, in which, if they had no bad weather and no contrary winds, the captain said he hoped he might get to the banks of Newfoundland, and might perhaps take some fish, to sustain them till they might go on shore. But there were so many chances against them in all these cases, such as storms, to overset and founder them; rains and cold, to benumb and perish their limbs; contrary winds, to keep them out and starve them; that it must have been next to miraculous if they had escaped.

In the midst of their consternation, every one being hopeless and ready to despair, the captain, with tears in his eyes, told me they were on a sudden surprised with the joy of hearing a gun fire, and after that four more: these were the five guns which I caused to be fired at first seeing the light. This revived their hearts, and gave them the notice, which, as above, I desired it should, that there was a ship at hand for their help. It was upon the hearing of these guns that they took down their masts and sails: the sound coming from the windward, they resolved to lie by till morning. Some time after this, hearing no more guns, they fired three muskets, one a considerable while after another; but these, the wind being contrary, we never heard. Some time after that again they were still more agreeably surprised with seeing our lights, and hearing the guns, which, as I have said, I caused to be fired all the rest of the night. This set them to work with their oars, to keep their boats ahead, at least that we might the sooner come up with them; and at last, to their inexpressible joy, they found we saw them.

It is impossible for me to express the several gestures, the strange ecstasies, the variety of postures which these poor delivered people ran into, to express the joy of their souls at so unexpected a deliverance. Grief and fear are easily described: sighs, tears, groans, and a very few motions of the head and hands, make up the sum of its variety; but an excess of joy, a surprise of joy, has a thousand extravagances in it. There were some in tears; some raging and tearing themselves, as if they had been in the greatest agonies of sorrow; some stark raving and downright lunatic; some ran about the ship stamping with their feet, others wringing their hands; some were dancing, some singing, some laughing, more crying, many quite dumb, not able to speak a word; others sick and vomiting; several swooning and ready to faint; and a few were crossing themselves and giving God thanks.

I would not wrong them either; there might be many that were thankful afterwards; but the passion was too strong for them at first, and they were not able to master it: then were thrown into ecstasies, and a kind of frenzy, and it was but a very few that were composed and serious in their joy. Perhaps also, the case may have some addition to it from the particular circumstance of that nation they belonged to: I mean the French, whose temper is allowed to be more volatile, more passionate, and more sprightly, and their spirits more fluid than in other nations. I am not philosopher enough to determine the cause; but nothing I had ever seen before came up to it. The ecstasies poor Friday, my trusty savage, was in when he found his father in the boat came the nearest to it; and the surprise of the master and his two companions, whom I delivered from the villains that set them on shore in the island, came a little way towards it; but nothing was to compare to this, either that I saw in Friday, or anywhere else in my life.

It is further observable, that these extravagances did not show themselves in that different manner I have mentioned, in different persons only; but all the variety would appear, in a short succession of moments, in one and the same person. A man that we saw this minute dumb, and, as it were, stupid and confounded, would the next minute be dancing and hallooing like an antic; and the next moment be tearing his hair, or pulling his clothes to pieces, and stamping them under his feet like a madman; in a few moments after that we would have him all in tears, then sick, swooning, and, had not immediate help been had, he would in a few moments have been dead. Thus it was, not with one or two, or ten or twenty, but with the greatest part of them; and, if I remember right, our surgeon was obliged to let blood of about thirty persons.

There were two priests among them: one an old man, and the other a young man; and that which was strangest was, the oldest man was the worst. As soon as he set his foot on board our ship, and saw himself safe, he dropped down stone dead to all appearance. Not the least sign of life could be perceived in him; our surgeon immediately applied proper remedies to recover him, and was the only man in the ship that believed he was not dead. At length he opened a vein in his arm, having first chafed and rubbed the part, so as to warm it as much as possible. Upon this the blood, which only dropped at first, flowing freely, in three minutes after the man opened his eyes; a quarter of an hour after that he spoke, grew better, and after the blood was stopped, he walked about, told us he was perfectly well, and took a dram of cordial which the surgeon gave him. About a quarter of an hour after this they came running into the cabin to the surgeon, who was bleeding a Frenchwoman that had fainted, and told him the priest was gone stark mad. It seems he had begun to revolve the change of his circumstances in his mind, and again this put him into an ecstasy of joy. His spirits whirled about faster than the vessels could convey them, the blood grew hot and feverish, and the man was as fit for Bedlam as any creature that ever was in it. The surgeon would not bleed him again in that condition, but gave him something to doze and put him to sleep; which, after some time, operated upon him, and he awoke next morning perfectly composed and well. The younger priest behaved with great command of his passions, and was really an example of a serious, well-governed mind. At his first coming on board the ship he threw himself flat on his face, prostrating himself in thankfulness for his deliverance, in which I unhappily and unseasonably disturbed him, really thinking he had been in a swoon; but he spoke calmly, thanked me, told me he was giving God thanks for his deliverance, begged me to leave him a few moments, and that, next to his Maker, he would give me thanks also. I was heartily sorry that I disturbed him, and not only left him, but kept others from interrupting him also. He continued in that posture about three minutes, or little more, after I left him, then came to me, as he had said he would, and with a great deal of seriousness and affection, but with tears in his eyes, thanked me, that had, under God, given him and so many miserable creatures their lives. I told him I had no need to tell him to thank God for it, rather than me, for I had seen that he had done that already; but I added that it was nothing but what reason and humanity dictated to all men, and that we had as much reason as he to give thanks to God, who had blessed us so far as to make us the instruments of His mercy to so many of His creatures. After this the young priest applied himself to his countrymen, and laboured to compose them: he persuaded, entreated, argued, reasoned with them, and did his utmost to keep them within the exercise of their reason; and with some he had success, though others were for a time out of all government of themselves.

I cannot help committing this to writing, as perhaps it may be useful to those into whose hands it may fall, for guiding themselves in the extravagances of their passions; for if an excess of joy can carry men out to such a length beyond the reach of their reason, what will not the extravagances of anger, rage, and a provoked mind carry us to? And, indeed, here I saw reason for keeping an exceeding watch over our passions of every kind, as well those of joy and satisfaction as those of sorrow and anger.

We were somewhat disordered by these extravagances among our new guests for the first day; but after they had retired to lodgings provided for them as well as our ship would allow, and had slept heartily—as most of them did, being fatigued and frightened—they were quite another sort of people the next day. Nothing of good manners, or civil acknowledgments for the kindness shown them, was wanting; the French, it is known, are naturally apt enough to exceed that way. The captain and one of the priests came to me the next day, and desired to speak with me and my nephew; the commander began to consult with us what should be done with them; and first, they told us we had saved their lives, so all they had was little enough for a return to us for that kindness received. The captain said they had saved some money and some things of value in their boats, caught hastily out of the flames, and if we would accept it they were ordered to make an offer of it all to us; they only desired to be set on shore somewhere in our way, where, if possible, they might get a passage to France. My nephew wished to accept their money at first word, and to consider what to do with them afterwards; but I overruled him in that part, for I knew what it was to be set on shore in a strange country; and if the Portuguese captain that took me up at sea had served me so, and taken all I had for my deliverance, I must have been starved, or have been as much a slave at the Brazils as I had been at Barbary, the mere being sold to a Mahometan excepted; and perhaps a Portuguese is not a much better master than a Turk, if not in some cases much worse.

I therefore told the French captain that we had taken them up in their distress, it was true, but that it was our duty to do so, as we were fellow-creatures; and we would desire to be so delivered if we were in the like or any other extremity; that we had done nothing for them but what we believed they would have done for us if we had been in their case and they in ours; but that we took them up to save them, not to plunder them; and it would be a most barbarous thing to take that little from them which they had saved out of the fire, and then set them on shore and leave them; that this would be first to save them from death, and then kill them ourselves: save them from drowning, and abandon them to starving; and therefore I would not let the least thing be taken from them. As to setting them on shore, I told them indeed that was an exceeding difficulty to us, for that the ship was bound to the East Indies; and though we were driven out of our course to the westward a very great way, and perhaps were directed by Heaven on purpose for their deliverance, yet it was impossible for us wilfully to change our voyage on their particular account; nor could my nephew, the captain, answer it to the freighters, with whom he was under charter to pursue his voyage by way of Brazil; and all I knew we could do for them was to put ourselves in the way of meeting with other ships homeward bound from the West Indies, and get them a passage, if possible, to England or France.

The first part of the proposal was so generous and kind they could not but be very thankful for it; but they were in very great consternation, especially the passengers, at the notion of being carried away to the East Indies; they then entreated me that as I was driven so far to the westward before I met with them, I would at least keep on the same course to the banks of Newfoundland, where it was probable I might meet with some ship or sloop that they might hire to carry them back to Canada.

I thought this was but a reasonable request on their part, and therefore I inclined to agree to it; for indeed I considered that to carry this whole company to the East Indies would not only be an intolerable severity upon the poor people, but would be ruining our whole voyage by devouring all our provisions; so I thought it no breach of charter-party, but what an unforeseen accident made absolutely necessary to us, and in which no one could say we were to blame; for the laws of God and nature would have forbid that we should refuse to take up two boats full of people in such a distressed condition; and the nature of the thing, as well respecting ourselves as the poor people, obliged us to set them on shore somewhere or other for their deliverance. So I consented that we would carry them to Newfoundland, if wind and weather would permit: and if not, I would carry them to Martinico, in the West Indies.

The wind continued fresh easterly, but the weather pretty good; and as the winds had continued in the points between NE. and SE. a long time, we missed several opportunities of sending them to France; for we met several ships bound to Europe, whereof two were French, from St. Christopher's, but they had been so long beating up against the wind that they durst take in no passengers, for fear of wanting provisions for the voyage, as well for themselves as for those they should take in; so we were obliged to go on. It was about a week after this that we made the banks of Newfoundland; where, to shorten my story, we put all our French people on board a bark, which they hired at sea there, to put them on shore, and afterwards to carry them to France, if they could get provisions to victual themselves with. When I say all the French went on shore, I should remember that the young priest I spoke of, hearing we were bound to the East Indies, desired to go the voyage with us, and to be set on shore on the coast of Coromandel; which I readily agreed to, for I wonderfully liked the man, and had very good reason, as will appear afterwards; also four of the seamen entered themselves on our ship, and proved very useful fellows.

From hence we directed our course for the West Indies, steering away S. and S. by E. for about twenty days together, sometimes little or no wind at all; when we met with another subject for our humanity to work upon, almost as deplorable as that before.

Chapter II—INTERVENING HISTORY OF COLONY

It was in the latitude of 27 degrees 5 minutes N., on the 19th day of March 1694-95, when we spied a sail, our course SE. and by S. We soon perceived it was a large vessel, and that she bore up to us, but could not at first know what to make of her, till, after coming a little nearer, we found she had lost her main-topmast, fore-mast, and bowsprit; and presently she fired a gun as a signal of distress. The weather was pretty good, wind at NNW. a fresh gale, and we soon came to speak with her. We found her a ship of Bristol, bound home from Barbadoes, but had been blown out of the road at Barbadoes a few days before she was ready to sail, by a terrible hurricane, while the captain and chief mate were both gone on shore; so that, besides the terror of the storm, they were in an indifferent case for good mariners to bring the ship home. They had been already nine weeks at sea, and had met with another terrible storm, after the hurricane was over, which had blown them quite out of their knowledge to the westward, and in which they lost their masts. They told us they expected to have seen the Bahama Islands, but were then driven away again to the south-east, by a strong gale of wind at NNW., the same that blew now: and having no sails to work the ship with but a main course, and a kind of square sail upon a jury fore-mast, which they had set up, they could not lie near the wind, but were endeavouring to stand away for the Canaries.

But that which was worst of all was, that they were almost starved for want of provisions, besides the fatigues they had undergone; their bread and flesh were quite gone—they had not one ounce left in the ship, and had had none for eleven days. The only relief they had was, their water was not all spent, and they had about half a barrel of flour left; they had sugar enough; some succades, or sweetmeats, they had at first, but these were all devoured; and they had seven casks of rum. There was a youth and his mother and a maid-servant on board, who were passengers, and thinking the ship was ready to sail, unhappily came on board the evening before the hurricane began; and having no provisions of their own left, they were in a more deplorable condition than the rest: for the seamen being reduced to such an extreme necessity themselves, had no compassion, we may be sure, for the poor passengers; and they were, indeed, in such a condition that their misery is very hard to describe.

I had perhaps not known this part, if my curiosity had not led me, the weather being fair and the wind abated, to go on board the ship. The second mate, who upon this occasion commanded the ship, had been on board our ship, and he told me they had three passengers in the great cabin that were in a deplorable condition. "Nay," says he, "I believe they are dead, for I have heard nothing of them for above two days; and I was afraid to inquire after them," said he, "for I had nothing to relieve them with." We immediately applied ourselves to give them what relief we could spare; and indeed I had so far overruled things with my nephew, that I would have victualled them though we had gone away to Virginia, or any other part of the coast of America, to have supplied ourselves; but there was no necessity for that.

But now they were in a new danger; for they were afraid of eating too much, even of that little we gave them. The mate, or commander, brought six men with him in his boat; but these poor wretches looked like skeletons, and were so weak that they could hardly sit to their oars. The mate himself was very ill, and half starved; for he declared he had reserved nothing from the men, and went share and share alike with them in every bit they ate. I cautioned him to eat sparingly, and set meat before him immediately, but he had not eaten three mouthfuls before he began to be sick and out of order; so he stopped a while, and our surgeon mixed him up something with some broth, which he said would be to him both food and physic; and after he had taken it he grew better. In the meantime I forgot not the men. I ordered victuals to be given them, and the poor creatures rather devoured than ate it: they were so exceedingly hungry that they were in a manner ravenous, and had no command of themselves; and two of them ate with so much greediness that they were in danger of their lives the next morning. The sight of these people's distress was very moving to me, and brought to mind what I had a terrible prospect of at my first coming on shore in my island, where I had not the least mouthful of food, or any prospect of procuring any; besides the hourly apprehensions I had of being made the food of other creatures. But all the while the mate was thus relating to me the miserable condition of the ship's company, I could not put out of my thought the story he had told me of the three poor creatures in the great cabin, viz. the mother, her son, and the maid-servant, whom he had heard nothing of for two or three days, and whom, he seemed to confess, they had wholly neglected, their own extremities being so great; by which I understood that they had really given them no food at all, and that therefore they must be perished, and be all lying dead, perhaps, on the floor or deck of the cabin.

As I therefore kept the mate, whom we then called captain, on board with his men, to refresh them, so I also forgot not the starving crew that were left on board, but ordered my own boat to go on board the ship, and, with my mate and twelve men, to carry them a sack of bread, and four or five pieces of beef to boil. Our surgeon charged the men to cause the meat to be boiled while they stayed, and to keep guard in the cook-room, to prevent the men taking it to eat raw, or taking it out of the pot before it was well boiled, and then to give every man but a very little at a time: and by this caution he preserved the men, who would otherwise have killed themselves with that very food that was given them on purpose to save their lives.

At the same time I ordered the mate to go into the great cabin, and see what condition the poor passengers were in; and if they were alive, to comfort them, and give them what refreshment was proper: and the surgeon gave him a large pitcher, with some of the prepared broth which he had given the mate that was on board, and which he did not question would restore them gradually. I was not satisfied with this; but, as I said above, having a great mind to see the scene of misery which I knew the ship itself would present me with, in a more lively manner than I could have it by report, I took the captain of the ship, as we now called him, with me, and went myself, a little after, in their boat.

I found the poor men on board almost in a tumult to get the victuals out of the boiler before it was ready; but my mate observed his orders, and kept a good guard at the cook-room door, and the man he placed there, after using all possible persuasion to have patience, kept them off by force; however, he caused some biscuit-cakes to be dipped in the pot, and softened with the liquor of the meat, which they called brewis, and gave them every one some to stay their stomachs, and told them it was for their own safety that he was obliged to give them but little at a time. But it was all in vain; and had I not come on board, and their own commander and officers with me, and with good words, and some threats also of giving them no more, I believe they would have broken into the cook-room by force, and torn the meat out of the furnace—for words are indeed of very small force to a hungry belly; however, we pacified them, and fed them gradually and cautiously at first, and the next time gave them more, and at last filled their bellies, and the men did well enough.

But the misery of the poor passengers in the cabin was of another nature, and far beyond the rest; for as, first, the ship's company had so little for themselves, it was but too true that they had at first kept them very low, and at last totally neglected them: so that for six or seven days it might be said they had really no food at all, and for several days before very little. The poor mother, who, as the men reported, was a woman of sense and good breeding, had spared all she could so affectionately for her son, that at last she entirely sank under it; and when the mate of our ship went in, she sat upon the floor on deck, with her back up against the sides, between two chairs, which were lashed fast, and her head sunk between her shoulders like a corpse, though not quite dead. My mate said all he could to revive and encourage her, and with a spoon put some broth into her mouth. She opened her lips, and lifted up one hand, but could not speak: yet she understood what he said, and made signs to him, intimating, that it was too late for her, but pointed to her child, as if she would have said they should take care of him. However, the mate, who was exceedingly moved at the sight, endeavoured to get some of the broth into her mouth, and, as he said, got two or three spoonfuls down—though I question whether he could be sure of it or not; but it was too late, and she died the same night.

The youth, who was preserved at the price of his most affectionate mother's life, was not so far gone; yet he lay in a cabin bed, as one stretched out, with hardly any life left in him. He had a piece of an old glove in his mouth, having eaten up the rest of it; however, being young, and having more strength than his mother, the mate got something down his throat, and he began sensibly to revive; though by giving him, some time after, but two or three spoonfuls extraordinary, he was very sick, and brought it up again.

But the next care was the poor maid: she lay all along upon the deck, hard by her mistress, and just like one that had fallen down in a fit of apoplexy, and struggled for life. Her limbs were distorted; one of her hands was clasped round the frame of the chair, and she gripped it so hard that we could not easily make her let it go; her other arm lay over her head, and her feet lay both together, set fast against the frame of the cabin table: in short, she lay just like one in the agonies of death, and yet she was alive too. The poor creature was not only starved with hunger, and terrified with the thoughts of death, but, as the men told us afterwards, was broken-hearted for her mistress, whom she saw dying for two or three days before, and whom she loved most tenderly. We knew not what to do with this poor girl; for when our surgeon, who was a man of very great knowledge and experience, had, with great application, recovered her as to life, he had her upon his hands still; for she was little less than distracted for a considerable time after.

Whoever shall read these memorandums must be desired to consider that visits at sea are not like a journey into the country, where sometimes people stay a week or a fortnight at a place. Our business was to relieve this distressed ship's crew, but not lie by for them; and though they were willing to steer the same course with us for some days, yet we could carry no sail to keep pace with a ship that had no masts. However, as their captain begged of us to help him to set up a main-topmast, and a kind of a topmast to his jury fore-mast, we did, as it were, lie by him for three or four days; and then, having given him five barrels of beef, a barrel of pork, two hogsheads of biscuit, and a proportion of peas, flour, and what other things we could spare; and taking three casks of sugar, some rum, and some pieces of eight from them for satisfaction, we left them, taking on board with us, at their own earnest request, the youth and the maid, and all their goods.

The young lad was about seventeen years of age, a pretty, well-bred, modest, and sensible youth, greatly dejected with the loss of his mother, and also at having lost his father but a few months before, at Barbadoes. He begged of the surgeon to speak to me to take him out of the ship; for he said the cruel fellows had murdered his mother: and indeed so they had, that is to say, passively; for they might have spared a small sustenance to the poor helpless widow, though it had been but just enough to keep her alive; but hunger knows no friend, no relation, no justice, no right, and therefore is remorseless, and capable of no compassion.

The surgeon told him how far we were going, and that it would carry him away from all his friends, and put him, perhaps, in as bad circumstances almost as those we found him in, that is to say, starving in the world. He said it mattered not whither he went, if he was but delivered from the terrible crew that he was among; that the captain (by which he meant me, for he could know nothing of my nephew) had saved his life, and he was sure would not hurt him; and as for the maid, he was sure, if she came to herself, she would be very thankful for it, let us carry them where we would. The surgeon represented the case so affectionately to me that I yielded, and we took them both on board, with all their goods, except eleven hogsheads of sugar, which could not be removed or come at; and as the youth had a bill of lading for them, I made his commander sign a writing, obliging himself to go, as soon as he came to Bristol, to one Mr. Rogers, a merchant there, to whom the youth said he was related, and to deliver a letter which I wrote to him, and all the goods he had belonging to the deceased widow; which, I suppose, was not done, for I could never learn that the ship came to Bristol, but was, as is most probable, lost at sea, being in so disabled a condition, and so far from any land, that I am of opinion the first storm she met with afterwards she might founder, for she was leaky, and had damage in her hold when we met with her.

I was now in the latitude of 19 degrees 32 minutes, and had hitherto a tolerable voyage as to weather, though at first the winds had been contrary. I shall trouble nobody with the little incidents of wind, weather, currents, &c., on the rest of our voyage; but to shorten my story, shall observe that I came to my old habitation, the island, on the 10th of April 1695. It was with no small difficulty that I found the place; for as I came to it and went to it before on the south and east side of the island, coming from the Brazils, so now, coming in between the main and the island, and having no chart for the coast, nor any landmark, I did not know it when I saw it, or, know whether I saw it or not. We beat about a great while, and went on shore on several islands in the mouth of the great river Orinoco, but none for my purpose; only this I learned by my coasting the shore, that I was under one great mistake before, viz. that the continent which I thought I saw from the island I lived in was really no continent, but a long island, or rather a ridge of islands, reaching from one to the other side of the extended mouth of that great river; and that the savages who came to my island were not properly those which we call Caribbees, but islanders, and other barbarians of the same kind, who inhabited nearer to our side than the rest.

In short, I visited several of these islands to no purpose; some I found were inhabited, and some were not; on one of them I found some Spaniards, and thought they had lived there; but speaking with them, found they had a sloop lying in a small creek hard by, and came thither to make salt, and to catch some pearl-mussels if they could; but that they belonged to the Isle de Trinidad, which lay farther north, in the latitude of 10 and 11 degrees.

Thus coasting from one island to another, sometimes with the ship, sometimes with the Frenchman's shallop, which we had found a convenient boat, and therefore kept her with their very good will, at length I came fair on the south side of my island, and presently knew the very countenance of the place: so I brought the ship safe to an anchor, broadside with the little creek where my old habitation was. As soon as I saw the place I called for Friday, and asked him if he knew where he was? He looked about a little, and presently clapping his hands, cried, "Oh yes, Oh there, Oh yes, Oh there!" pointing to our old habitation, and fell dancing and capering like a mad fellow; and I had much ado to keep him from jumping into the sea to swim ashore to the place.

"Well, Friday," says I, "do you think we shall find anybody here or no? and do you think we shall see your father?" The fellow stood mute as a stock a good while; but when I named his father, the poor affectionate creature looked dejected, and I could see the tears run down his face very plentifully. "What is the matter, Friday? are you troubled because you may see your father?" "No, no," says he, shaking his head, "no see him more: no, never more see him again." "Why so, Friday? how do you know that?" "Oh no, Oh no," says Friday, "he long ago die, long ago; he much old man." "Well, well, Friday, you don't know; but shall we see any one else, then?" The fellow, it seems, had better eyes than I, and he points to the hill just above my old house; and though we lay half a league off, he cries out, "We see! we see! yes, we see much man there, and there, and there." I looked, but I saw nobody, no, not with a perspective glass, which was, I suppose, because I could not hit the place: for the fellow was right, as I found upon inquiry the next day; and there were five or six men all together, who stood to look at the ship, not knowing what to think of us.

As soon as Friday told me he saw people, I caused the English ancient to be spread, and fired three guns, to give them notice we were friends; and in about a quarter of an hour after we perceived a smoke arise from the side of the creek; so I immediately ordered the boat out, taking Friday with me, and hanging out a white flag, I went directly on shore, taking with me the young friar I mentioned, to whom I had told the story of my living there, and the manner of it, and every particular both of myself and those I left there, and who was on that account extremely desirous to go with me. We had, besides, about sixteen men well armed, if we had found any new guests there which we did not know of; but we had no need of weapons.

As we went on shore upon the tide of flood, near high water, we rowed directly into the creek; and the first man I fixed my eye upon was the Spaniard whose life I had saved, and whom I knew by his face perfectly well: as to his habit, I shall describe it afterwards. I ordered nobody to go on shore at first but myself; but there was no keeping Friday in the boat, for the affectionate creature had spied his father at a distance, a good way off the Spaniards, where, indeed, I saw nothing of him; and if they had not let him go ashore, he would have jumped into the sea. He was no sooner on shore, but he flew away to his father like an arrow out of a bow. It would have made any man shed tears, in spite of the firmest resolution, to have seen the first transports of this poor fellow's joy when he came to his father: how he embraced him, kissed him, stroked his face, took him up in his arms, set him down upon a tree, and lay down by him; then stood and looked at him, as any one would look at a strange picture, for a quarter of an hour together; then lay down on the ground, and stroked his legs, and kissed them, and then got up again and stared at him; one would have thought the fellow bewitched. But it would have made a dog laugh the next day to see how his passion ran out another way: in the morning he walked along the shore with his father several hours, always leading him by the hand, as if he had been a lady; and every now and then he would come to the boat to fetch something or other for him, either a lump of sugar, a dram, a biscuit, or something or other that was good. In the afternoon his frolics ran another way; for then he would set the old man down upon the ground, and dance about him, and make a thousand antic gestures; and all the while he did this he would be talking to him, and telling him one story or another of his travels, and of what had happened to him abroad to divert him. In short, if the same filial affection was to be found in Christians to their parents in our part of the world, one would be tempted to say there would hardly have been any need of the fifth commandment.

But this is a digression: I return to my landing. It would be needless to take notice of all the ceremonies and civilities that the Spaniards received me with. The first Spaniard, whom, as I said, I knew very well, was he whose life I had saved. He came towards the boat, attended by one more, carrying a flag of truce also; and he not only did not know me at first, but he had no thoughts, no notion of its being me that was come, till I spoke to him. "Seignior," said I, in Portuguese, "do you not know me?" At which he spoke not a word, but giving his musket to the man that was with him, threw his arms abroad, saying something in Spanish that I did not perfectly hear, came forward and embraced me, telling me he was inexcusable not to know that face again that he had once seen, as of an angel from heaven sent to save his life; he said abundance of very handsome things, as a well-bred Spaniard always knows how, and then, beckoning to the person that attended him, bade him go and call out his comrades. He then asked me if I would walk to my old habitation, where he would give me possession of my own house again, and where I should see they had made but mean improvements. I walked along with him, but, alas! I could no more find the place than if I had never been there; for they had planted so many trees, and placed them in such a position, so thick and close to one another, and in ten years' time they were grown so big, that the place was inaccessible, except by such windings and blind ways as they themselves only, who made them, could find.

I asked them what put them upon all these fortifications; he told me I would say there was need enough of it when they had given me an account how they had passed their time since their arriving in the island, especially after they had the misfortune to find that I was gone. He told me he could not but have some pleasure in my good fortune, when he heard that I was gone in a good ship, and to my satisfaction; and that he had oftentimes a strong persuasion that one time or other he should see me again, but nothing that ever befell him in his life, he said, was so surprising and afflicting to him at first as the disappointment he was under when he came back to the island and found I was not there.

As to the three barbarians (so he called them) that were left behind, and of whom, he said, he had a long story to tell me, the Spaniards all thought themselves much better among the savages, only that their number was so small: "And," says he, "had they been strong enough, we had been all long ago in purgatory;" and with that he crossed himself on the breast. "But, sir," says he, "I hope you will not be displeased when I shall tell you how, forced by necessity, we were obliged for our own preservation to disarm them, and make them our subjects, as they would not be content with being moderately our masters, but would be our murderers." I answered I was afraid of it when I left them there, and nothing troubled me at my parting from the island but that they were not come back, that I might have put them in possession of everything first, and left the others in a state of subjection, as they deserved; but if they had reduced them to it I was very glad, and should be very far from finding any fault with it; for I knew they were a parcel of refractory, ungoverned villains, and were fit for any manner of mischief.

While I was saying this, the man came whom he had sent back, and with him eleven more. In the dress they were in it was impossible to guess what nation they were of; but he made all clear, both to them and to me. First, he turned to me, and pointing to them, said, "These, sir, are some of the gentlemen who owe their lives to you;" and then turning to them, and pointing to me, he let them know who I was; upon which they all came up, one by one, not as if they had been sailors, and ordinary fellows, and the like, but really as if they had been ambassadors or noblemen, and I a monarch or great conqueror: their behaviour was, to the last degree, obliging and courteous, and yet mixed with a manly, majestic gravity, which very well became them; and, in short, they had so much more manners than I, that I scarce knew how to receive their civilities, much less how to return them in kind.

The history of their coming to, and conduct in, the island after my going away is so very remarkable, and has so many incidents which the former part of my relation will help to understand, and which will in most of the particulars, refer to the account I have already given, that I cannot but commit them, with great delight, to the reading of those that come after me.

In order to do this as intelligibly as I can, I must go back to the circumstances in which I left the island, and the persons on it, of whom I am to speak. And first, it is necessary to repeat that I had sent away Friday's father and the Spaniard (the two whose lives I had rescued from the savages) in a large canoe to the main, as I then thought it, to fetch over the Spaniard's companions that he left behind him, in order to save them from the like calamity that he had been in, and in order to succour them for the present; and that, if possible, we might together find some way for our deliverance afterwards. When I sent them away I had no visible appearance of, or the least room to hope for, my own deliverance, any more than I had twenty years before—much less had I any foreknowledge of what afterwards happened, I mean, of an English ship coming on shore there to fetch me off; and it could not be but a very great surprise to them, when they came back, not only to find that I was gone, but to find three strangers left on the spot, possessed of all that I had left behind me, which would otherwise have been their own.

The first thing, however, which I inquired into, that I might begin where I left off, was of their own part; and I desired the Spaniard would give me a particular account of his voyage back to his countrymen with the boat, when I sent him to fetch them over. He told me there was little variety in that part, for nothing remarkable happened to them on the way, having had very calm weather and a smooth sea. As for his countrymen, it could not be doubted, he said, but that they were overjoyed to see him (it seems he was the principal man among them, the captain of the vessel they had been shipwrecked in having been dead some time): they were, he said, the more surprised to see him, because they knew that he was fallen into the hands of the savages, who, they were satisfied, would devour him as they did all the rest of their prisoners; that when he told them the story of his deliverance, and in what manner he was furnished for carrying them away, it was like a dream to them, and their astonishment, he said, was somewhat like that of Joseph's brethren when he told them who he was, and the story of his exaltation in Pharaoh's court; but when he showed them the arms, the powder, the ball, the provisions that he brought them for their journey or voyage, they were restored to themselves, took a just share of the joy of their deliverance, and immediately prepared to come away with him.

Their first business was to get canoes; and in this they were obliged not to stick so much upon the honesty of it, but to trespass upon their friendly savages, and to borrow two large canoes, or periaguas, on pretence of going out a-fishing, or for pleasure. In these they came away the next morning. It seems they wanted no time to get themselves ready; for they had neither clothes nor provisions, nor anything in the world but what they had on them, and a few roots to eat, of which they used to make their bread. They were in all three weeks absent; and in that time, unluckily for them, I had the occasion offered for my escape, as I mentioned in the other part, and to get off from the island, leaving three of the most impudent, hardened, ungoverned, disagreeable villains behind me that any man could desire to meet with—to the poor Spaniards' great grief and disappointment.

The only just thing the rogues did was, that when the Spaniards came ashore, they gave my letter to them, and gave them provisions, and other relief, as I had ordered them to do; also they gave them the long paper of directions which I had left with them, containing the particular methods which I took for managing every part of my life there; the way I baked my bread, bred up tame goats, and planted my corn; how I cured my grapes, made my pots, and, in a word, everything I did. All this being written down, they gave to the Spaniards (two of them understood English well enough): nor did they refuse to accommodate the Spaniards with anything else, for they agreed very well for some time. They gave them an equal admission into the house or cave, and they began to live very sociably; and the head Spaniard, who had seen pretty much of my methods, together with Friday's father, managed all their affairs; but as for the Englishmen, they did nothing but ramble about the island, shoot parrots, and catch tortoises; and when they came home at night, the Spaniards provided their suppers for them.

The Spaniards would have been satisfied with this had the others but let them alone, which, however, they could not find in their hearts to do long: but, like the dog in the manger, they would not eat themselves, neither would they let the others eat. The differences, nevertheless, were at first but trivial, and such as are not worth relating, but at last it broke out into open war: and it began with all the rudeness and insolence that can be imagined—without reason, without provocation, contrary to nature, and indeed to common sense; and though, it is true, the first relation of it came from the Spaniards themselves, whom I may call the accusers, yet when I came to examine the fellows they could not deny a word of it.

But before I come to the particulars of this part, I must supply a defect in my former relation; and this was, I forgot to set down among the rest, that just as we were weighing the anchor to set sail, there happened a little quarrel on board of our ship, which I was once afraid would have turned to a second mutiny; nor was it appeased till the captain, rousing up his courage, and taking us all to his assistance, parted them by force, and making two of the most refractory fellows prisoners, he laid them in irons: and as they had been active in the former disorders, and let fall some ugly, dangerous words the second time, he threatened to carry them in irons to England, and have them hanged there for mutiny and running away with the ship. This, it seems, though the captain did not intend to do it, frightened some other men in the ship; and some of them had put it into the head of the rest that the captain only gave them good words for the present, till they should come to same English port, and that then they should be all put into gaol, and tried for their lives. The mate got intelligence of this, and acquainted us with it, upon which it was desired that I, who still passed for a great man among them, should go down with the mate and satisfy the men, and tell them that they might be assured, if they behaved well the rest of the voyage, all they had done for the time past should be pardoned. So I went, and after passing my honour's word to them they appeared easy, and the more so when I caused the two men that were in irons to be released and forgiven.

But this mutiny had brought us to an anchor for that night; the wind also falling calm next morning, we found that our two men who had been laid in irons had stolen each of them a musket and some other weapons (what powder or shot they had we knew not), and had taken the ship's pinnace, which was not yet hauled up, and run away with her to their companions in roguery on shore. As soon as we found this, I ordered the long-boat on shore, with twelve men and the mate, and away they went to seek the rogues; but they could neither find them nor any of the rest, for they all fled into the woods when they saw the boat coming on shore. The mate was once resolved, in justice to their roguery, to have destroyed their plantations, burned all their household stuff and furniture, and left them to shift without it; but having no orders, he let it all alone, left everything as he found it, and bringing the pinnace way, came on board without them.

These two men made their number five; but the other three villains were so much more wicked than they, that after they had been two or three days together they turned the two newcomers out of doors to shift for themselves, and would have nothing to do with them; nor could they for a good while be persuaded to give them any food: as for the Spaniards, they were not yet come.

When the Spaniards came first on shore, the business began to go forward: the Spaniards would have persuaded the three English brutes to have taken in their countrymen again, that, as they said, they might be all one family; but they would not hear of it, so the two poor fellows lived by themselves; and finding nothing but industry and application would make them live comfortably, they pitched their tents on the north shore of the island, but a little more to the west, to be out of danger of the savages, who always landed on the east parts of the island. Here they built them two huts, one to lodge in, and the other to lay up their magazines and stores in; and the Spaniards having given them some corn for seed, and some of the peas which I had left them, they dug, planted, and enclosed, after the pattern I had set for them all, and began to live pretty well. Their first crop of corn was on the ground; and though it was but a little bit of land which they had dug up at first, having had but a little time, yet it was enough to relieve them, and find them with bread and other eatables; and one of the fellows being the cook's mate of the ship, was very ready at making soup, puddings, and such other preparations as the rice and the milk, and such little flesh as they got, furnished him to do.

They were going on in this little thriving position when the three unnatural rogues, their own countrymen too, in mere humour, and to insult them, came and bullied them, and told them the island was theirs: that the governor, meaning me, had given them the possession of it, and nobody else had any right to it; and that they should build no houses upon their ground unless they would pay rent for them. The two men, thinking they were jesting at first, asked them to come in and sit down, and see what fine houses they were that they had built, and to tell them what rent they demanded; and one of them merrily said if they were the ground-landlords, he hoped if they built tenements upon their land, and made improvements, they would, according to the custom of landlords, grant a long lease: and desired they would get a scrivener to draw the writings. One of the three, cursing and raging, told them they should see they were not in jest; and going to a little place at a distance, where the honest men had made a fire to dress their victuals, he takes a firebrand, and claps it to the outside of their hut, and set it on fire: indeed, it would have been all burned down in a few minutes if one of the two had not run to the fellow, thrust him away, and trod the fire out with his feet, and that not without some difficulty too.

The fellow was in such a rage at the honest man's thrusting him away, that he returned upon him, with a pole he had in his hand, and had not the man avoided the blow very nimbly, and run into the hut, he had ended his days at once. His comrade, seeing the danger they were both in, ran after him, and immediately they came both out with their muskets, and the man that was first struck at with the pole knocked the fellow down that began the quarrel with the stock of his musket, and that before the other two could come to help him; and then, seeing the rest come at them, they stood together, and presenting the other ends of their pieces to them, bade them stand off.

The others had firearms with them too; but one of the two honest men, bolder than his comrade, and made desperate by his danger, told them if they offered to move hand or foot they were dead men, and boldly commanded them to lay down their arms. They did not, indeed, lay down their arms, but seeing him so resolute, it brought them to a parley, and they consented to take their wounded man with them and be gone: and, indeed, it seems the fellow was wounded sufficiently with the blow. However, they were much in the wrong, since they had the advantage, that they did not disarm them effectually, as they might have done, and have gone immediately to the Spaniards, and given them an account how the rogues had treated them; for the three villains studied nothing but revenge, and every day gave them some intimation that they did so.

Chapter III—FIGHT WITH CANNIBALS

But not to crowd this part with an account of the lesser part of the rogueries with which they plagued them continually, night and day, it forced the two men to such a desperation that they resolved to fight them all three, the first time they had a fair opportunity. In order to do this they resolved to go to the castle (as they called my old dwelling), where the three rogues and the Spaniards all lived together at that time, intending to have a fair battle, and the Spaniards should stand by to see fair play: so they got up in the morning before day, and came to the place, and called the Englishmen by their names telling a Spaniard that answered that they wanted to speak with them.

It happened that the day before two of the Spaniards, having been in the woods, had seen one of the two Englishmen, whom, for distinction, I called the honest men, and he had made a sad complaint to the Spaniards of the barbarous usage they had met with from their three countrymen, and how they had ruined their plantation, and destroyed their corn, that they had laboured so hard to bring forward, and killed the milch-goat and their three kids, which was all they had provided for their sustenance, and that if he and his friends, meaning the Spaniards, did not assist them again, they should be starved. When the Spaniards came home at night, and they were all at supper, one of them took the freedom to reprove the three Englishmen, though in very gentle and mannerly terms, and asked them how they could be so cruel, they being harmless, inoffensive fellows: that they were putting themselves in a way to subsist by their labour, and that it had cost them a great deal of pains to bring things to such perfection as they were then in.

One of the Englishmen returned very briskly, "What had they to do there? that they came on shore without leave; and that they should not plant or build upon the island; it was none of their ground." "Why," says the Spaniard, very calmly, "Seignior Inglese, they must not starve." The Englishman replied, like a rough tarpaulin, "They might starve; they should not plant nor build in that place." "But what must they do then, seignior?" said the Spaniard. Another of the brutes returned, "Do? they should be servants, and work for them." "But how can you expect that of them?" says the Spaniard; "they are not bought with your money; you have no right to make them servants." The Englishman answered, "The island was theirs; the governor had given it to them, and no man had anything to do there but themselves;" and with that he swore that he would go and burn all their new huts; they should build none upon their land. "Why, seignior," says the Spaniard, "by the same rule, we must be your servants, too." "Ay," returned the bold dog, "and so you shall, too, before we have done with you;" mixing two or three oaths in the proper intervals of his speech. The Spaniard only smiled at that, and made him no answer. However, this little discourse had heated them; and starting up, one says to the other. (I think it was he they called Will Atkins), "Come, Jack, let's go and have t'other brush with them; we'll demolish their castle, I'll warrant you; they shall plant no colony in our domin-dominions."

Upon this they were all trooping away, with every man a gun, a pistol, and a sword, and muttered some insolent things among themselves of what they would do to the Spaniards, too, when opportunity offered; but the Spaniards, it seems, did not so perfectly understand them as to know all the particulars, only that in general they threatened them hard for taking the two Englishmen's part. Whither they went, or how they bestowed their time that evening, the Spaniards said they did not know; but it seems they wandered about the country part of the night, and them lying down in the place which I used to call my bower, they were weary and overslept themselves. The case was this: they had resolved to stay till midnight, and so take the two poor men when they were asleep, and as they acknowledged afterwards, intended to set fire to their huts while they were in them, and either burn them there or murder them as they came out. As malice seldom sleeps very sound, it was very strange they should not have been kept awake. However, as the two men had also a design upon them, as I have said, though a much fairer one than that of burning and murdering, it happened, and very luckily for them all, that they were up and gone abroad before the bloody-minded rogues came to their huts.

When they came there, and found the men gone, Atkins, who it seems was the forwardest man, called out to his comrade, "Ha, Jack, here's the nest, but the birds are flown." They mused a while, to think what should be the occasion of their being gone abroad so soon, and suggested presently that the Spaniards had given them notice of it; and with that they shook hands, and swore to one another that they would be revenged of the Spaniards. As soon as they had made this bloody bargain they fell to work with the poor men's habitation; they did not set fire, indeed, to anything, but they pulled down both their houses, and left not the least stick standing, or scarce any sign on the ground where they stood; they tore all their household stuff in pieces, and threw everything about in such a manner, that the poor men afterwards found some of their things a mile off. When they had done this, they pulled up all the young trees which the poor men had planted; broke down an enclosure they had made to secure their cattle and their corn; and, in a word, sacked and plundered everything as completely as a horde of Tartars would have done.

The two men were at this juncture gone to find them out, and had resolved to fight them wherever they had been, though they were but two to three; so that, had they met, there certainly would have been blood shed among them, for they were all very stout, resolute fellows, to give them their due.

But Providence took more care to keep them asunder than they themselves could do to meet; for, as if they had dogged one another, when the three were gone thither, the two were here; and afterwards, when the two went back to find them, the three were come to the old habitation again: we shall see their different conduct presently. When the three came back like furious creatures, flushed with the rage which the work they had been about had put them into, they came up to the Spaniards, and told them what they had done, by way of scoff and bravado; and one of them stepping up to one of the Spaniards, as if they had been a couple of boys at play, takes hold of his hat as it was upon his head, and giving it a twirl about, fleering in his face, says to him, “And you, Seignior Jack Spaniard, shall have the same sauce if you do not mend your manners.” The Spaniard, who, though a quiet civil man, was as brave a man as could be, and withal a strong, well-made man, looked at him for a good while, and then, having no weapon in his hand, stepped gravely up to him, and, with one blow of his fist, knocked him down, as an ox is felled with a pole-axe; at which one of the rogues, as insolent as the first, fired his pistol at the Spaniard immediately; he missed his body, indeed, for the bullets went through his hair, but one of them touched the tip of his ear, and he bled pretty much. The blood made the Spaniard believe he was more hurt than he really was, and that put him into some heat, for before he acted all in a perfect calm; but now resolving to go through with his work, he stooped, and taking the fellow’s musket whom he had knocked down, was just going to shoot the man who had fired at him, when the rest of the Spaniards, being in the cave, came out, and calling to him not to shoot, they stepped in, secured the other two, and took their arms from them.

When they were thus disarmed, and found they had made all the Spaniards their enemies, as well as their own countrymen, they began to cool, and giving the Spaniards better words, would have their arms again; but the Spaniards, considering the feud that was between them and the other two Englishmen, and that it would be the best method they could take to keep them from killing one another, told them they would do them no harm, and if they would live peaceably, they would be very willing to assist and associate with them as they did before; but that they could not think of giving them their arms again, while they appeared so resolved to do mischief with them to their own countrymen, and had even threatened them all to make them their servants.

The rogues were now quite deaf to all reason, and being refused their arms, they raved away like madmen, threatening what they would do, though they had no firearms. But the Spaniards, despising their threatening, told them they should take care how they offered any injury to their plantation or cattle; for if they did they would shoot them as they would ravenous beasts, wherever they found them; and if they fell into their hands alive, they should certainly be hanged. However, this was far from cooling them, but away they went, raging and swearing like furies. As soon as they were gone, the two men came back, in passion and rage enough also, though of another kind; for having been at their plantation, and finding it all demolished and destroyed, as above mentioned, it will easily be supposed they had provocation enough. They could scarce have room to tell their tale, the Spaniards were so eager to tell them theirs: and it was strange enough to find that three men should thus bully nineteen, and receive no punishment at all.

The Spaniards, indeed, despised them, and especially, having thus disarmed them, made light of their threatenings; but the two Englishmen resolved to have their remedy against them, what pains soever it cost to find them out. But the Spaniards interposed here too, and told them that as they had disarmed them, they could not consent that they (the two) should pursue them with firearms, and perhaps kill them. "But," said the grave Spaniard, who was their governor, "we will endeavour to make them do you justice, if you will leave it to us: for there is no doubt but they will come to us again, when their passion is over, being not able to subsist without our assistance. We promise you to make no peace with them without having full satisfaction for you; and upon this condition we hope you will promise to use no violence with them, other than in your own defence." The two Englishmen yielded to this very awkwardly, and with great reluctance; but the Spaniards protested that they did it only to keep them from bloodshed, and to make them all easy at last. "For," said they, "we are not so many of us; here is room enough for us all, and it is a great pity that we should not be all good friends." At length they did consent, and waited for the issue of the thing, living for some days with the Spaniards; for their own habitation was destroyed.

In about five days' time the vagrants, tired with wandering, and almost starved with hunger, having chiefly lived on turtles' eggs all that while, came back to the grove; and finding my Spaniard, who, as I have said, was the governor, and two more with him, walking by the side of the creek, they came up in a very submissive, humble manner, and begged to be received again into the society. The Spaniards used them civilly, but told them they had acted so unnaturally to their countrymen, and so very grossly to themselves, that they could not come to any conclusion without consulting the two Englishmen and the rest; but, however, they would go to them and discourse about it, and they should know in half-an-hour. It may be guessed that they were very hard put to it; for, as they were to wait this half-hour for an answer, they begged they would send them out some bread in the meantime, which they did, sending at the same time a large piece of goat's flesh and a boiled parrot, which they ate very eagerly.

After half-an-hour's consultation they were called in, and a long debate ensued, their two countrymen charging them with the ruin of all their labour, and a design to murder them; all which they owned before, and therefore could not deny now. Upon the whole, the Spaniards acted the moderators between them; and as they had obliged the two Englishmen not to hurt the three while they were naked and unarmed, so they now obliged the three to go and rebuild their fellows' two huts, one to be of the same and the other of larger dimensions than they were before; to fence their ground again, plant trees in the room of those pulled up, dig up the land again for planting corn, and, in a word, to restore everything to the same state as they found it, that is, as near as they could.

Well, they submitted to all this; and as they had plenty of provisions given them all the while, they grew very orderly, and the whole society began to live pleasantly and agreeably together again; only that these three fellows could never be persuaded to work—I mean for themselves—except now and then a little, just as they pleased. However, the Spaniards told them plainly that if they would but live sociably and friendly together, and study the good of the whole plantation, they would be content to work for them, and let them walk about and be as idle as they pleased; and thus, having lived pretty well together for a month or two, the Spaniards let them have arms again, and gave them liberty to go abroad with them as before.

It was not above a week after they had these arms, and went abroad, before the ungrateful creatures began to be as insolent and troublesome as ever. However, an accident happened presently upon this, which endangered the safety of them all, and they were obliged to lay by all private resentments, and look to the preservation of their lives.

It happened one night that the governor, the Spaniard whose life I had saved, who was now the governor of the rest, found himself very uneasy in the night, and could by no means get any sleep: he was perfectly well in body, only found his thoughts tumultuous; his mind ran upon men fighting and killing one another; but he was broad awake, and could not by any means get any sleep; in short, he lay a great while, but growing more and more uneasy, he resolved to rise. As they lay, being so many of them, on goat-skins laid thick upon such couches and pads as they made for themselves, so they had little to do, when they were willing to rise, but to get upon their feet, and perhaps put on a coat, such as it was, and their pumps, and they were ready for going any way that their thoughts guided them. Being thus got up, he looked out; but being dark, he could see little or nothing, and besides, the trees which I had planted, and which were now grown tall, intercepted his sight, so that he could only look up, and see that it was a starlight night, and hearing no noise, he returned and lay down again; but to no purpose; he could not compose himself to anything like rest; but his thoughts were to the last degree uneasy, and he knew not for what. Having made some noise with rising and walking about, going out and coming in, another of them waked, and asked who it was that was up. The governor told him how it had been with him. "Say you so?" says the other Spaniard; "such things are not to be slighted, I assure you; there is certainly some mischief working near us;" and presently he asked him, "Where are the Englishmen?" "They are all in their huts," says he, "safe enough." It seems the Spaniards had kept possession of the main apartment, and had made a place for the three Englishmen, who, since their last mutiny, were always quartered by themselves, and could not come at the rest. "Well," says the Spaniard, "there is something in it, I am persuaded, from my own experience. I am satisfied that our spirits embodied have a converse with and receive intelligence from the spirits unembodied, and inhabiting the invisible world; and this friendly notice is given for our advantage, if we knew how to make use of it. Come, let us go and look abroad; and if we find nothing at all in it to justify the trouble, I'll tell you a story to the purpose, that shall convince you of the justice of my proposing it."

They went out presently to go up to the top of the hill, where I used to go; but they being strong, and a good company, nor alone, as I was, used none of my cautions to go up by the ladder, and pulling it up after them, to go up a second stage to the top, but were going round through the grove unwarily, when they were surprised with seeing a light as of fire, a very little way from them, and hearing the voices of men, not of one or two, but of a great number.

Among the precautions I used to take on the savages landing on the island, it was my constant care to prevent them making the least discovery of there being any inhabitant upon the place: and when by any occasion they came to know it, they felt it so effectually that they that got away were scarce able to give any account of it; for we disappeared as soon as possible, nor did ever any that had seen me escape to tell any one else, except it was the three savages in our last encounter who jumped into the boat; of whom, I mentioned, I was afraid they should go home and bring more help. Whether it was the consequence of the escape of those men that so great a number came now together, or whether they came ignorantly, and by accident, on their usual bloody errand, the Spaniards could not understand; but whatever it was, it was their business either to have concealed themselves or not to have seen them at all, much less to have let the savages have seen there were any inhabitants in the place; or to have fallen upon them so effectually as not a man of them should have escaped, which could only have been by getting in between them and their boats; but this presence of mind was wanting to them, which was the ruin of their tranquillity for a great while.

We need not doubt but that the governor and the man with him, surprised with this sight, ran back immediately and raised their fellows, giving them an account of the imminent danger they were all in, and they again as readily took the alarm; but it was impossible to persuade them to stay close within where they were, but they must all run out to see how things stood. While it was dark, indeed, they were safe, and they had opportunity enough for some hours to view the savages by the light of three fires they had made at a distance from one another; what they were doing they knew not, neither did they know what to do themselves. For, first, the enemy were too many; and secondly, they did not keep together, but were divided into several parties, and were on shore in several places.

The Spaniards were in no small consternation at this sight; and, as they found that the fellows went straggling all over the shore, they made no doubt but, first or last, some of them would chop in upon their habitation, or upon some other place where they would see the token of inhabitants; and they were in great perplexity also for fear of their flock of goats, which, if they should be destroyed, would have been little less than starving them. So the first thing they resolved upon was to despatch three men away before it was light, two Spaniards and one Englishman, to drive away all the goats to the great valley where the cave was, and, if need were, to drive them into the very cave itself. Could they have seen the savages all together in one body, and at a distance from their canoes, they were resolved, if there had been a hundred of them, to attack them; but that could not be done, for they were some of them two miles off from the other, and, as it appeared afterwards, were of two different nations.

After having mused a great while on the course they should take, they resolved at last, while it was still dark, to send the old savage, Friday's father, out as a spy, to learn, if possible, something concerning them, as what they came for, what they intended to do, and the like. The old man readily undertook it; and stripping himself quite naked, as most of the savages were, away he went. After he had been gone an hour or two, he brings word that he had been among them undiscovered, that he found they were two parties, and of two several nations, who had war with one another, and had a great battle in their own country; and that both sides having had several prisoners taken in the fight, they were, by mere chance, landed all on the same island, for the devouring their prisoners and making merry; but their coming so by chance to the same place had spoiled all their mirth—that they were in a great rage at one another, and were so near that he believed they would fight again as soon as daylight began to appear; but he did not perceive that they had any notion of anybody being on the island but themselves. He had hardly made an end of telling his story, when they could perceive, by the unusual noise they made, that the two little armies were engaged in a bloody fight. Friday's father used all the arguments he could to persuade our people to lie close, and not be seen; he told them their safety consisted in it, and that they had nothing to do but lie still, and the savages would kill one another to their hands, and then the rest would go away; and it was so to a tittle. But it was impossible to prevail, especially upon the Englishmen; their curiosity was so importunate that they must run out and see the battle. However, they used some caution too: they did not go openly, just by their own dwelling, but went farther into the woods, and placed themselves to advantage, where they might securely see them manage the fight, and, as they thought, not be seen by them; but the savages did see them, as we shall find hereafter.

The battle was very fierce, and, if I might believe the Englishmen, one of them said he could perceive that some of them were men of great bravery, of invincible spirit, and of great policy in guiding the fight. The battle, they said, held two hours before they could guess which party would be beaten; but then that party which was nearest our people's habitation began to appear weakest, and after some time more some of them began to fly; and this put our men again into a great consternation, lest any one of those that fled should run into the grove before their dwelling for shelter, and thereby involuntarily discover the place; and that, by consequence, the pursuers would also do the like in search of them. Upon this, they resolved that they would stand armed within the wall, and whoever came into the grove, they resolved to sally out over the wall and kill them, so that, if possible, not one should return to give an account of it; they ordered also that it should be done with their swords, or by knocking them down with the stocks of their muskets, but not by shooting them, for fear of raising an alarm by the noise.

As they expected it fell out; three of the routed army fled for life, and crossing the creek, ran directly into the place, not in the least knowing whither they went, but running as into a thick wood for shelter. The scout they kept to look abroad gave notice of this within, with this comforting addition, that the conquerors had not pursued them, or seen which way they were gone; upon this the Spanish governor, a man of humanity, would not suffer them to kill the three fugitives, but sending three men out by the top of the hill, ordered them to go round, come in behind them, and surprise and take them prisoners, which was done. The residue of the conquered people fled to their canoes, and got off to sea; the victors retired, made no pursuit, or very little, but drawing themselves into a body together, gave two great screaming shouts, most likely by way of triumph, and so the fight ended; the same day, about three o'clock in the afternoon, they also marched to their canoes. And thus the Spaniards had the island again free to themselves, their fright was over, and they saw no savages for several years after.

After they were all gone, the Spaniards came out of their den, and viewing the field of battle, they found about two-and-thirty men dead on the spot; some were killed with long arrows, which were found sticking in their bodies; but most of them were killed with great wooden swords, sixteen or seventeen of which they found in the field of battle, and as many bows, with a great many arrows. These swords were strange, unwieldy things, and they must be very strong men that used them; most of those that were killed with them had their heads smashed to pieces, as we may say, or, as we call it in English, their brains knocked out, and several their arms and legs broken; so that it is evident they fight with inexpressible rage and fury. We found not one man that was not stone dead; for either they stay by their enemy till they have killed him, or they carry all the wounded men that are not quite dead away with them.

This deliverance tamed our ill-disposed Englishmen for a great while; the sight had filled them with horror, and the consequences appeared terrible to the last degree, especially upon supposing that some time or other they should fall into the hands of those creatures, who would not only kill them as enemies, but for food, as we kill our cattle; and they professed to me that the thoughts of being eaten up like beef and mutton, though it was supposed it was not to be till they were dead, had something in it so horrible that it nauseated their very stomachs, made them sick when they thought of it, and filled their minds with such unusual terror, that they were not themselves for some weeks after. This, as I said, tamed even the three English brutes I have been speaking of; and for a great while after they were tractable, and went about the common business of the whole society well enough—planted, sowed, reaped, and began to be all naturalised to the country. But some time after this they fell into such simple measures again as brought them into a great deal of trouble.

They had taken three prisoners, as I observed; and these three being stout young fellows, they made them servants, and taught them to work for them, and as slaves they did well enough; but they did not take their measures as I did by my man Friday, viz. to begin with them upon the principle of having saved their lives, and then instruct them in the rational principles of life; much less did they think of teaching them religion, or attempt civilising and reducing them by kind usage and affectionate arguments. As they gave them their food every day, so they gave them their work too, and kept them fully employed in drudgery enough; but they failed in this by it, that they never had them to assist them and fight for them as I had my man Friday, who was as true to me as the very flesh upon my bones.

But to come to the family part. Being all now good friends—for common danger, as I said above, had effectually reconciled them—they began to consider their general circumstances; and the first thing that came under consideration was whether, seeing the savages particularly haunted that side of the island, and that there were more remote and retired parts of it equally adapted to their way of living, and manifestly to their advantage, they should not rather move their habitation, and plant in some more proper place for their safety, and especially for the security of their cattle and corn.

Upon this, after long debate, it was concluded that they would not remove their habitation; because that, some time or other, they thought they might hear from their governor again, meaning me; and if I should send any one to seek them, I should be sure to direct them to that side, where, if they should find the place demolished, they would conclude the savages had killed us all, and we were gone, and so our supply would go too. But as to their corn and cattle, they agreed to remove them into the valley where my cave was, where the land was as proper for both, and where indeed there was land enough. However, upon second thoughts they altered one part of their resolution too, and resolved only to remove part of their cattle thither, and part of their corn there; so that if one part was destroyed the other might be saved. And one part of prudence they luckily used: they never trusted those three savages which they had taken prisoners with knowing anything of the plantation they had made in that valley, or of any cattle they had there, much less of the cave at that place, which they kept, in case of necessity, as a safe retreat; and thither they carried also the two barrels of powder which I had sent them at my coming away. They resolved, however, not to change their habitation; yet, as I had carefully covered it first with a wall or fortification, and then with a grove of trees, and as they were now fully convinced their safety consisted entirely in their being concealed, they set to work to cover and conceal the place yet more effectually than before. For this purpose, as I planted trees, or rather thrust in stakes, which in time all grew up to be trees, for some good distance before the entrance into my apartments, they went on in the same manner, and filled up the rest of that whole space of ground from the trees I had set quite down to the side of the creek, where I landed my floats, and even into the very ooze where the tide flowed, not so much as leaving any place to land, or any sign that there had been any landing thereabouts: these stakes also being of a wood very forward to grow, they took care to have them generally much larger and taller than those which I had planted. As they grew apace, they planted them so very thick and close together, that when they had been three or four years grown there was no piercing with the eye any considerable way into the plantation. As for that part which I had planted, the trees were grown as thick as a man's thigh, and among them they had placed so many other short ones, and so thick, that it stood like a palisado a quarter of a mile thick, and it was next to impossible to penetrate it, for a little dog could hardly get between the trees, they stood so close.

But this was not all; for they did the same by all the ground to the right hand and to the left, and round even to the side of the hill, leaving no way, not so much as for themselves, to come out but by the ladder placed up to the side of the hill, and then lifted up, and placed again from the first stage up to the top: so that when the ladder was taken down, nothing but what had wings or witchcraft to assist it could come at them. This was excellently well contrived: nor was it less than what they afterwards found occasion for, which served to convince me, that as human prudence has the authority of Providence to justify it, so it has doubtless the direction of Providence to set it to work; and if we listened carefully to the voice of it, I am persuaded we might prevent many of the disasters which our lives are now, by our own negligence, subjected to.

They lived two years after this in perfect retirement, and had no more visits from the savages. They had, indeed, an alarm given them one morning, which put them into a great consternation; for some of the Spaniards being out early one morning on the west side or end of the island (which was that end where I never went, for fear of being discovered), they were surprised with seeing about twenty canoes of Indians just coming on shore. They made the best of their way home in hurry enough; and giving the alarm to their comrades, they kept close all that day and the next, going out only at night to make their observation: but they had the good luck to be undiscovered, for wherever the savages went, they did not land that time on the island, but pursued some other design.

Chapter IV—RENEWED INVASION OF SAVAGES

And now they had another broil with the three Englishmen; one of whom, a most turbulent fellow, being in a rage at one of the three captive slaves, because the fellow had not done something right which he bade him do, and seemed a little untractable in his showing him, drew a hatchet out of a frog-belt which he wore by his side, and fell upon the poor savage, not to correct him, but to kill him. One of the Spaniards who was by, seeing him give the fellow a barbarous cut with the hatchet, which he aimed at his head, but stuck into his shoulder, so that he thought he had cut the poor creature's arm off, ran to him, and entreating him not to murder the poor man, placed himself between him and the savage, to prevent the mischief. The fellow, being enraged the more at this, struck at the Spaniard with his hatchet, and swore he would serve him as he intended to serve the savage; which the Spaniard perceiving, avoided the blow, and with a shovel, which he had in his hand (for they were all working in the field about their corn land), knocked the brute down. Another of the Englishmen, running up at the same time to help his comrade, knocked the Spaniard down; and then two Spaniards more came in to help their man, and a third Englishman fell in upon them. They had none of them any firearms or any other weapons but hatchets and other tools, except this third Englishman; he had one of my rusty cutlasses, with which he made at the two last Spaniards, and wounded them both. This fray set the whole family in an uproar, and more help coming in they took the three Englishmen prisoners. The next question was, what should be done with them? They had been so often mutinous, and were so very furious, so desperate, and so idle withal, they knew not what course to take with them, for they were mischievous to the highest degree, and cared not what hurt they did to any man; so that, in short, it was not safe to live with them.

The Spaniard who was governor told them, in so many words, that if they had been of his own country he would have hanged them; for all laws and all governors were to preserve society, and those who were dangerous to the society ought to be expelled out of it; but as they were Englishmen, and that it was to the generous kindness of an Englishman that they all owed their preservation and deliverance, he would use them with all possible lenity, and would leave them to the judgment of the other two Englishmen, who were their countrymen. One of the two honest Englishmen stood up, and said they desired it might not be left to them. "For," says he, "I am sure we ought to sentence them to the gallows;" and with that he gives an account how Will Atkins, one of the three, had proposed to have all the five Englishmen join together and murder all the Spaniards when they were in their sleep.

When the Spanish governor heard this, he calls to Will Atkins, "How, Seignior Atkins, would you murder us all? What have you to say to that?" The hardened villain was so far from denying it, that he said it was true, and swore they would do it still before they had done with them. "Well, but Seignior Atkins," says the Spaniard, "what have we done to you that you will kill us? What would you get by killing us? And what must we do to prevent you killing us? Must we kill you, or you kill us? Why will you put us to the necessity of this, Seignior Atkins?" says the Spaniard very calmly, and smiling. Seignior Atkins was in such a rage at the Spaniard's making a jest of it, that, had he not been held by three men, and withal had no weapon near him, it was thought he would have attempted to kill the Spaniard in the middle of all the company. This hare-brained carriage obliged them to consider seriously what was to be done. The two Englishmen and the Spaniard who saved the poor savage were of the opinion that they should hang one of the three for an example to the rest, and that particularly it should be he that had twice attempted to commit murder with his hatchet; indeed, there was some reason to believe he had done it, for the poor savage was in such a miserable condition with the wound he had received that it was thought he could not live. But the governor Spaniard still said No; it was an Englishman that had saved all their lives, and he would never consent to put an Englishman to death, though he had murdered half of them; nay, he said if he had been killed himself by an Englishman, and had time left to speak, it should be that they should pardon him.

This was so positively insisted on by the governor Spaniard, that there was no gainsaying it; and as merciful counsels are most apt to prevail where they are so earnestly pressed, so they all came into it. But then it was to be considered what should be done to keep them from doing the mischief they designed; for all agreed, governor and all, that means were to be used for preserving the society from danger. After a long debate, it was agreed that they should be disarmed, and not permitted to have either gun, powder, shot, sword, or any weapon; that they should be turned out of the society, and left to live where they would and how they would, by themselves; but that none of the rest, either Spaniards or English, should hold any kind of converse with them, or have anything to do with them; that they should be forbid to come within a certain distance of the place where the rest dwelt; and if they offered to commit any disorder, so as to spoil, burn, kill, or destroy any of the corn, plantings, buildings, fences, or cattle belonging to the society, they should die without mercy, and they would shoot them wherever they could find them.

The humane governor, musing upon the sentence, considered a little upon it; and turning to the two honest Englishmen, said, "Hold; you must reflect that it will be long ere they can raise corn and cattle of their own, and they must not starve; we must therefore allow them provisions." So he caused to be added, that they should have a proportion of corn given them to last them eight months, and for seed to sow, by which time they might be supposed to raise some of their own; that they should have six milch-goats, four he-goats, and six kids given them, as well for present subsistence as for a store; and that they should have tools given them for their work in the fields, but they should have none of these tools or provisions unless they would swear solemnly that they would not hurt or injure any of the Spaniards with them, or of their fellow-Englishmen.

Thus they dismissed them the society, and turned them out to shift for themselves. They went away sullen and refractory, as neither content to go away nor to stay: but, as there was no remedy, they went, pretending to go and choose a place where they would settle themselves; and some provisions were given them, but no weapons. About four or five days after, they came again for some victuals, and gave the governor an account where they had pitched their tents, and marked themselves out a habitation and plantation; and it was a very convenient place indeed, on the remotest part of the island, NE., much about the place where I providentially landed in my first voyage, when I was driven out to sea in my foolish attempt to sail round the island.

Here they built themselves two handsome huts, and contrived them in a manner like my first habitation, being close under the side of a hill, having some trees already growing on three sides of it, so that by planting others it would be very easily covered from the sight, unless narrowly searched for. They desired some dried goat-skins for beds and covering, which were given them; and upon giving their words that they would not disturb the rest, or injure any of their plantations, they gave them hatchets, and what other tools they could spare; some peas, barley, and rice, for sowing; and, in a word, anything they wanted, except arms and ammunition.

They lived in this separate condition about six months, and had got in their first harvest, though the quantity was but small, the parcel of land they had planted being but little. Indeed, having all their plantation to form, they had a great deal of work upon their hands; and when they came to make boards and pots, and such things, they were quite out of their element, and could make nothing of it; therefore when the rainy season came on, for want of a cave in the earth, they could not keep their grain dry, and it was in great danger of spoiling. This humbled them much: so they came and begged the Spaniards to help them, which they very readily did; and in four days worked a great hole in the side of the hill for them, big enough to secure their corn and other things from the rain: but it was a poor place at best compared to mine, and especially as mine was then, for the Spaniards had greatly enlarged it, and made several new apartments in it.

About three quarters of a year after this separation, a new frolic took these rogues, which, together with the former villainy they had committed, brought mischief enough upon them, and had very near been the ruin of the whole colony. The three new associates began, it seems, to be weary of the laborious life they led, and that without hope of bettering their circumstances: and a whim took them that they would make a voyage to the continent, from whence the savages came, and would try if they could seize upon some prisoners among the natives there, and bring them home, so as to make them do the laborious part of the work for them.

The project was not so preposterous, if they had gone no further. But they did nothing, and proposed nothing, but had either mischief in the design, or mischief in the event. And if I may give my opinion, they seemed to be under a blast from Heaven: for if we will not allow a visible curse to pursue visible crimes, how shall we reconcile the events of things with the divine justice? It was certainly an apparent vengeance on their crime of mutiny and piracy that brought them to the state they were in; and they showed not the least remorse for the crime, but added new villanies to it, such as the piece of monstrous cruelty of wounding a poor slave because he did not, or perhaps could not, understand to do what he was directed, and to wound him in such a manner as made him a cripple all his life, and in a place where no surgeon or medicine could be had for his cure; and, what was still worse, the intentional murder, for such to be sure it was, as was afterwards the formed design they all laid to murder the Spaniards in cold blood, and in their sleep.

The three fellows came down to the Spaniards one morning, and in very humble terms desired to be admitted to speak with them. The Spaniards very readily heard what they had to say, which was this: that they were tired of living in the manner they did, and that they were not handy enough to make the necessaries they wanted, and that having no help, they found they should be starved; but if the Spaniards would give them leave to take one of the canoes which they came over in, and give them arms and ammunition proportioned to their defence, they would go over to the main, and seek their fortunes, and so deliver them from the trouble of supplying them with any other provisions.

The Spaniards were glad enough to get rid of them, but very honestly represented to them the certain destruction they were running into; told them they had suffered such hardships upon that very spot, that they could, without any spirit of prophecy, tell them they would be starved or murdered, and bade them consider of it. The men replied audaciously, they should be starved if they stayed here, for they could not work, and would not work, and they could but be starved abroad; and if they were murdered, there was an end of them; they had no wives or children to cry after them; and, in short, insisted importunately upon their demand, declaring they would go, whether they gave them any arms or not.

The Spaniards told them, with great kindness, that if they were resolved to go they should not go like naked men, and be in no condition to defend themselves; and that though they could ill spare firearms, not having enough for themselves, yet they would let them have two muskets, a pistol, and a cutlass, and each man a hatchet, which they thought was sufficient for them. In a word, they accepted the offer; and having baked bread enough to serve them a month given them, and as much goats' flesh as they could eat while it was sweet, with a great basket of dried grapes, a pot of fresh water, and a young kid alive, they boldly set out in the canoe for a voyage over the sea, where it was at least forty miles broad. The boat, indeed, was a large one, and would very well have carried fifteen or twenty men, and therefore was rather too big for them to manage; but as they had a fair breeze and flood-tide with them, they did well enough. They had made a mast of a long pole, and a sail of four large goat-skins dried, which they had sewed or laced together; and away they went merrily together. The Spaniards called after them "*Bon voyajo*;" and no man ever thought of seeing them any more.

The Spaniards were often saying to one another, and to the two honest Englishmen who remained behind, how quietly and comfortably they lived, now these three turbulent fellows were gone. As for their coming again, that was the remotest thing from their thoughts that could be imagined; when, behold, after two-and-twenty days' absence, one of the Englishmen being abroad upon his planting work, sees three strange men coming towards him at a distance, with guns upon their shoulders.

Away runs the Englishman, frightened and amazed, as if he was bewitched, to the governor Spaniard, and tells him they were all undone, for there were strangers upon the island, but he could not tell who they were. The Spaniard, pausing a while, says to him, "How do you mean—you cannot tell who? They are the savages, to be sure." "No, no," says the Englishman, "they are men in clothes, with arms." "Nay, then," says the Spaniard, "why are you so concerned! If they are not savages they must be friends; for there is no Christian nation upon earth but will do us good rather than harm." While they were debating thus, came up the three Englishmen, and standing without the wood, which was new planted, hallooed to them. They presently knew their voices, and so all the wonder ceased. But now the admiration was turned upon another question—What could be the matter, and what made them come back again?

It was not long before they brought the men in, and inquiring where they had been, and what they had been doing, they gave them a full account of their voyage in a few words: that they reached the land in less than two days, but finding the people alarmed at their coming, and preparing with bows and arrows to fight them, they durst not go on, shore, but sailed on to the northward six or seven hours, till they came to a great opening, by which they perceived that the land they saw from our island was not the main, but an island: that upon entering that opening of the sea they saw another island on the right hand north, and several more west; and being resolved to land somewhere, they put over to one of the islands which lay west, and went boldly on shore; that they found the people very courteous and friendly to them; and they gave them several roots and some dried fish, and appeared very sociable; and that the women, as well as the men, were very forward to supply them with anything they could get for them to eat, and brought it to them a great way, on their heads. They continued here for four days, and inquired as well as they could of them by signs, what nations were this way, and that way, and were told of several fierce and terrible people that lived almost every way, who, as they made known by signs to them, used to eat men;

but, as for themselves, they said they never ate men or women, except only such as they took in the wars; and then they owned they made a great feast, and ate their prisoners.

The Englishmen inquired when they had had a feast of that kind; and they told them about two moons ago, pointing to the moon and to two fingers; and that their great king had two hundred prisoners now, which he had taken in his war, and they were feeding them to make them fat for the next feast. The Englishmen seemed mighty desirous of seeing those prisoners; but the others mistaking them, thought they were desirous to have some of them to carry away for their own eating. So they beckoned to them, pointing to the setting of the sun, and then to the rising; which was to signify that the next morning at sunrising they would bring some for them; and accordingly the next morning they brought down five women and eleven men, and gave them to the Englishmen to carry with them on their voyage, just as we would bring so many cows and oxen down to a seaport town to victual a ship.

As brutish and barbarous as these fellows were at home, their stomachs turned at this sight, and they did not know what to do. To refuse the prisoners would have been the highest affront to the savage gentry that could be offered them, and what to do with them they knew not. However, after some debate, they resolved to accept of them: and, in return, they gave the savages that brought them one of their hatchets, an old key, a knife, and six or seven of their bullets; which, though they did not understand their use, they seemed particularly pleased with; and then tying the poor creatures' hands behind them, they dragged the prisoners into the boat for our men.

The Englishmen were obliged to come away as soon as they had them, or else they that gave them this noble present would certainly have expected that they should have gone to work with them, have killed two or three of them the next morning, and perhaps have invited the donors to dinner. But having taken their leave, with all the respect and thanks that could well pass between people, where on either side they understood not one word they could say, they put off with their boat, and came back towards the first island; where, when they arrived, they set eight of their prisoners at liberty, there being too many of them for their occasion. In their voyage they endeavoured to have some communication with their prisoners; but it was impossible to make them understand anything. Nothing they could say to them, or give them, or do for them, but was looked upon as going to murder them. They first of all unbound them; but the poor creatures screamed at that, especially the women, as if they had just felt the knife at their throats; for they immediately concluded they were unbound on purpose to be killed. If they gave them thing to eat, it was the same thing; they then concluded it was for fear they should sink in flesh, and so not be fat enough to kill. If they looked at one of them more particularly, the party presently concluded it was to see whether he or she was fattest, and fittest to kill first; nay, after they had brought them quite over, and began to use them kindly, and treat them well, still they expected every day to make a dinner or supper for their new masters.

When the three wanderers had give this unaccountable history or journal of their voyage, the Spaniard asked them where their new family was; and being told that they had brought them on shore, and put them into one of their huts, and were come up to beg some victuals for them, they (the Spaniards) and the other two Englishmen, that is to say, the whole colony, resolved to go all down to the place and see them; and did so, and Friday's father with them. When they came into the hut, there they sat, all bound; for when they had brought them on shore they bound their hands that they might not take the boat and make their escape; there, I say, they sat, all of them stark naked. First, there were three comely fellows, well shaped, with straight limbs, about thirty to thirty-five years of age; and five women, whereof two might be from thirty to forty, two more about four or five and twenty; and the fifth, a tall, comely maiden, about seventeen. The women were well-favoured, agreeable persons, both in shape and features, only tawny; and two of them, had they been perfect white, would have passed for very handsome women, even in London, having pleasant countenances, and of a very modest behaviour; especially when they came afterwards to be clothed and dressed, though that dress was very indifferent, it must be confessed.

The sight, you may be sure, was something uncouth to our Spaniards, who were, to give them a just character, men of the most calm, sedate tempers, and perfect good humour, that ever I met with: and, in particular, of the utmost modesty: I say, the sight was very uncouth, to see three naked men and five naked women, all together bound, and in the most miserable circumstances that human nature could be supposed to be, viz. to be expecting every moment to be dragged out and have their brains knocked out, and then to be eaten up like a calf that is killed for a dainty.

The first thing they did was to cause the old Indian, Friday's father, to go in, and see first if he knew any of them, and then if he understood any of their speech. As soon as the old man came in, he looked seriously at them, but knew none of them; neither could any of them understand a word he said, or a sign he could make, except one of the women. However, this was enough to answer the end, which was to satisfy them that the men into whose hands they were fallen were Christians; that they abhorred eating men or women; and that they might be sure they would not be killed. As soon as they were assured of this, they discovered such a joy, and by such awkward gestures, several ways, as is hard to describe; for it seems they were of several nations. The woman who was their interpreter was bid, in the next place, to ask them if they were willing to be servants, and to work for the men who had brought them away, to save their lives; at which they all fell a-dancing; and presently one fell to taking up this, and another that, anything that lay next, to carry on their shoulders, to intimate they were willing to work.

The governor, who found that the having women among them would presently be attended with some inconvenience, and might occasion some strife, and perhaps blood, asked the three men what they intended to do with these women, and how they intended to use them, whether as servants or as wives? One of the

Englishmen answered, very boldly and readily, that they would use them as both; to which the governor said: "I am not going to restrain you from it—you are your own masters as to that; but this I think is but just, for avoiding disorders and quarrels among you, and I desire it of you for that reason only, viz. that you will all engage, that if any of you take any of these women as a wife, he shall take but one; and that having taken one, none else shall touch her; for though we cannot marry any one of you, yet it is but reasonable that, while you stay here, the woman any of you takes shall be maintained by the man that takes her, and should be his wife—I mean," says he, "while he continues here, and that none else shall have anything to do with her." All this appeared so just, that every one agreed to it without any difficulty.

Then the Englishmen asked the Spaniards if they designed to take any of them? But every one of them answered "No." Some of them said they had wives in Spain, and the others did not like women that were not Christians; and all together declared that they would not touch one of them, which was an instance of such virtue as I have not met with in all my travels. On the other hand, the five Englishmen took them every one a wife, that is to say, a temporary wife; and so they set up a new form of living; for the Spaniards and Friday's father lived in my old habitation, which they had enlarged exceedingly within. The three servants which were taken in the last battle of the savages lived with them; and these carried on the main part of the colony, supplied all the rest with food, and assisted them in anything as they could, or as they found necessity required.

But the wonder of the story was, how five such refractory, ill-matched fellows should agree about these women, and that some two of them should not choose the same woman, especially seeing two or three of them were, without comparison, more agreeable than the others; but they took a good way enough to prevent quarrelling among themselves, for they set the five women by themselves in one of their huts, and they went all into the other hut, and drew lots among them who should choose first.

Him that drew to choose first went away by himself to the hut where the poor naked creatures were, and fetched out her he chose; and it was worth observing, that he that chose first took her that was reckoned the homeliest and oldest of the five, which made mirth enough amongst the rest; and even the Spaniards laughed at it; but the fellow considered better than any of them, that it was application and business they were to expect assistance in, as much as in anything else; and she proved the best wife of all the parcel.

When the poor women saw themselves set in a row thus, and fetched out one by one, the terrors of their condition returned upon them again, and they firmly believed they were now going to be devoured. Accordingly, when the English sailor came in and fetched out one of them, the rest set up a most lamentable cry, and hung about her, and took their leave of her with such agonies and affection as would have grieved the hardest heart in the world: nor was it possible for the Englishmen to satisfy them that they were not to be immediately murdered, till they fetched the old man, Friday's father, who immediately let them know that the five men, who were to fetch them out one by one, had chosen them for their wives. When they had done, and the fright the women were in was a little over, the men went to work, and the Spaniards came and helped them: and in a few hours they had built them every one a new hut or tent for their lodging apart; for those they had already were crowded with their tools, household stuff, and provisions. The three wicked ones had pitched farthest off, and the two honest ones nearer, but both on the north shore of the island, so that they continued separated as before; and thus my island was peopled in three places, and, as I might say, three towns were begun to be built.

And here it is very well worth observing that, as it often happens in the world (what the wise ends in God's providence are, in such a disposition of things, I cannot say), the two honest fellows had the two worst wives; and the three reprobates, that were scarce worth hanging, that were fit for nothing, and neither seemed born to do themselves good nor any one else, had three clever, careful, and ingenious wives; not that the first two were bad wives as to their temper or humour, for all the five were most willing, quiet, passive, and subjected creatures, rather like slaves than wives; but my meaning is, they were not alike capable, ingenious, or industrious, or alike cleanly and neat. Another observation I must make, to the honour of a diligent application on one hand, and to the disgrace of a slothful, negligent, idle temper on the other, that when I came to the place, and viewed the several improvements, plantings, and management of the several little colonies, the two men had so far out-gone the three, that there was no comparison. They had, indeed, both of them as much ground laid out for corn as they wanted, and the reason was, because, according to my rule, nature dictated that it was to no purpose to sow more corn than they wanted; but the difference of the cultivation, of the planting, of the fences, and indeed, of everything else, was easy to be seen at first view.

The two men had innumerable young trees planted about their huts, so that, when you came to the place, nothing was to be seen but a wood; and though they had twice had their plantation demolished, once by their own countrymen, and once by the enemy, as shall be shown in its place, yet they had restored all again, and everything was thriving and flourishing about them; they had grapes planted in order, and managed like a vineyard, though they had themselves never seen anything of that kind; and by their good ordering their vines, their grapes were as good again as any of the others. They had also found themselves out a retreat in the thickest part of the woods, where, though there was not a natural cave, as I had found, yet they made one with incessant labour of their hands, and where, when the mischief which followed happened, they secured their wives and children so as they could never be found; they having, by sticking innumerable stakes and poles of the wood which, as I said, grew so readily, made the grove impassable, except in some places, when they climbed up to get over the outside part, and then went on by ways of their own leaving.

As to the three reprobates, as I justly call them, though they were much civilised by their settlement compared to what they were before, and were not so quarrelsome, having not the same opportunity; yet one of the certain companions of a profligate mind never left them, and that was their idleness. It is true, they planted corn and made fences; but Solomon's words were never better verified than in them, "I went by the vineyard of the slothful, and it was all overgrown with thorns": for when the Spaniards came to view their crop they could not see it in some places for weeds, the hedge had several gaps in it, where the wild goats had got in and eaten up the corn; perhaps here and there a dead bush was crammed in, to stop them out for the present, but it was only shutting the stable-door after the steed was stolen. Whereas, when they looked on the colony of the other two, there was the very face of industry and success upon all they did; there was not a weed to be seen in all their corn, or a gap in any of their hedges; and they, on the other hand, verified Solomon's words in another place, "that the diligent hand maketh rich"; for everything grew and thrived, and they had plenty within and without; they had more tame cattle than the others, more utensils and necessaries within doors, and yet more pleasure and diversion too.

It is true, the wives of the three were very handy and cleanly within doors; and having learned the English ways of dressing, and cooking from one of the other Englishmen, who, as I said, was a cook's mate on board the ship, they dressed their husbands' victuals very nicely and well; whereas the others could not be brought to understand it; but then the husband, who, as I say, had been cook's mate, did it himself. But as for the husbands of the three wives, they loitered about, fetched turtles' eggs, and caught fish and birds: in a word, anything but labour; and they fared accordingly. The diligent lived well and comfortably, and the slothful hard and beggarly; and so, I believe, generally speaking, it is all over the world.

But I now come to a scene different from all that had happened before, either to them or to me; and the origin of the story was this: Early one morning there came on shore five or six canoes of Indians or savages, call them which you please, and there is no room to doubt they came upon the old errand of feeding upon their slaves; but that part was now so familiar to the Spaniards, and to our men too, that they did not concern themselves about it, as I did: but having been made sensible, by their experience, that their only business was to lie concealed, and that if they were not seen by any of the savages they would go off again quietly, when their business was done, having as yet not the least notion of there being any inhabitants in the island; I say, having been made sensible of this, they had nothing to do but to give notice to all the three plantations to keep within doors, and not show themselves, only placing a scout in a proper place, to give notice when the boats went to sea again.

This was, without doubt, very right; but a disaster spoiled all these measures, and made it known among the savages that there were inhabitants there; which was, in the end, the desolation of almost the whole colony. After the canoes with the savages were gone off, the Spaniards peeped abroad again; and some of them had the curiosity to go to the place where they had been, to see what they had been doing. Here, to their great surprise, they found three savages left behind, and lying fast asleep upon the ground. It was supposed they had either been so gorged with their inhuman feast, that, like beasts, they were fallen asleep, and would not stir when the others went, or they had wandered into the woods, and did not come back in time to be taken in.

The Spaniards were greatly surprised at this sight and perfectly at a loss what to do. The Spaniard governor, as it happened, was with them, and his advice was asked, but he professed he knew not what to do. As for slaves, they had enough already; and as to killing them, there were none of them inclined to do that: the Spaniard governor told me they could not think of shedding innocent blood; for as to them, the poor creatures had done them no wrong, invaded none of their property, and they thought they had no just quarrel against them, to take away their lives. And here I must, in justice to these Spaniards, observe that, let the accounts of Spanish cruelty in Mexico and Peru be what they will, I never met with seventeen men of any nation whatsoever, in any foreign country, who were so universally modest, temperate, virtuous, so very good-humoured, and so courteous, as these Spaniards: and as to cruelty, they had nothing of it in their very nature; no inhumanity, no barbarity, no outrageous passions; and yet all of them men of great courage and spirit. Their temper and calmness had appeared in their bearing the insufferable usage of the three Englishmen; and their justice and humanity appeared now in the case of the savages above. After some consultation they resolved upon this; that they would lie still a while longer, till, if possible, these three men might be gone. But then the governor recollected that the three savages had no boat; and if they were left to rove about the island, they would certainly discover that there were inhabitants in it; and so they should be undone that way. Upon this, they went back again, and there lay the fellows fast asleep still, and so they resolved to awaken them, and take them prisoners; and they did so. The poor fellows were strangely frightened when they were seized upon and bound; and afraid, like the women, that they should be murdered and eaten: for it seems those people think all the world does as they do, in eating men's flesh; but they were soon made easy as to that, and away they carried them.

It was very happy for them that they did not carry them home to the castle, I mean to my palace under the hill; but they carried them first to the bower, where was the chief of their country work, such as the keeping the goats, the planting the corn, &c.; and afterward they carried them to the habitation of the two Englishmen. Here they were set to work, though it was not much they had for them to do; and whether it was by negligence in guarding them, or that they thought the fellows could not mend themselves, I know not, but one of them ran away, and, taking to the woods, they could never hear of him any more. They had good reason to believe he got home again soon after in some other boats or canoes of savages who came on shore three or four weeks afterwards, and who, carrying on their revels as usual, went off in two days' time. This thought terrified them exceedingly; for they concluded, and that not without good cause indeed, that if this fellow came home safe among his comrades, he would certainly give them an account that there were people in the island, and also how few and weak they were; for this savage, as observed before, had never been told, and it was very happy he had not, how many there were or where they lived; nor had he ever seen or heard the fire of any of their guns, much less had they shown him any of their other retired places; such as the cave in the valley, or the new retreat which the two Englishmen had made, and the like.

The first testimony they had that this fellow had given intelligence of them was, that about two months after this six canoes of savages, with about seven, eight, or ten men in a canoe, came rowing along the north side of the island, where they never used to come before, and landed, about an hour after sunrise, at a convenient place, about a mile from the habitation of the two Englishmen, where this escaped man had been kept. As the chief Spaniard said, had they been all there the damage would not have been so much, for not a man of them would have escaped; but the case differed now very much, for two men to fifty was too much odds. The two men had the happiness to discover them about a league off, so that it was

above an hour before they landed; and as they landed a mile from their huts, it was some time before they could come at them. Now, having great reason to believe that they were betrayed, the first thing they did was to bind the two slaves which were left, and cause two of the three men whom they brought with the women (who, it seems, proved very faithful to them) to lead them, with their two wives, and whatever they could carry away with them, to their retired places in the woods, which I have spoken of above, and there to bind the two fellows hand and foot, till they heard farther. In the next place, seeing the savages were all come on shore, and that they had bent their course directly that way, they opened the fences where the milch cows were kept, and drove them all out; leaving their goats to straggle in the woods, whither they pleased, that the savages might think they were all bred wild; but the rogue who came with them was too cunning for that, and gave them an account of it all, for they went directly to the place.

When the two poor frightened men had secured their wives and goods, they sent the other slave they had of the three who came with the women, and who was at their place by accident, away to the Spaniards with all speed, to give them the alarm, and desire speedy help, and, in the meantime, they took their arms and what ammunition they had, and retreated towards the place in the wood where their wives were sent; keeping at a distance, yet so that they might see, if possible, which way the savages took. They had not gone far but that from a rising ground they could see the little army of their enemies come on directly to their habitation, and, in a moment more, could see all their huts and household stuff flaming up together, to their great grief and mortification; for this was a great loss to them, irretrievable, indeed, for some time. They kept their station for a while, till they found the savages, like wild beasts, spread themselves all over the place, rummaging every way, and every place they could think of, in search of prey; and in particular for the people, of whom now it plainly appeared they had intelligence.

The two Englishmen seeing this, thinking themselves not secure where they stood, because it was likely some of the wild people might come that way, and they might come too many together, thought it proper to make another retreat about half a mile farther; believing, as it afterwards happened, that the further they strolled, the fewer would be together. Their next halt was at the entrance into a very thick-grown part of the woods, and where an old trunk of a tree stood, which was hollow and very large; and in this tree they both took their standing, resolving to see there what might offer. They had not stood there long before two of the savages appeared running directly that way, as if they had already had notice where they stood, and were coming up to attack them; and a little way farther they espied three more coming after them, and five more beyond them, all coming the same way; besides which, they saw seven or eight more at a distance, running another way; for in a word, they ran every way, like sportsmen beating for their game.

The poor men were now in great perplexity whether they should stand and keep their posture or fly; but after a very short debate with themselves, they considered that if the savages ranged the country thus before help came, they might perhaps find their retreat in the woods, and then all would be lost; so they resolved to stand them there, and if they were too many to deal with, then they would get up to the top of the tree, from whence they doubted not to defend themselves, fire excepted, as long as their ammunition lasted, though all the savages that were landed, which was near fifty, were to attack them.

Having resolved upon this, they next considered whether they should fire at the first two, or wait for the three, and so take the middle party, by which the two and the five that followed would be separated; at length they resolved to let the first two pass by, unless they should spy them the tree, and come to attack them. The first two savages confirmed them also in this resolution, by turning a little from them towards another part of the wood; but the three, and the five after them, came forward directly to the tree, as if they had known the Englishmen were there. Seeing them come so straight towards them, they resolved to take them in a line as they came: and as they resolved to fire but one at a time, perhaps the first shot might hit them all three; for which purpose the man who was to fire put three or four small bullets into his piece; and having a fair loophole, as it were, from a broken hole in the tree, he took a sure aim, without being seen, waiting till they were within about thirty yards of the tree, so that he could not miss.

While they were thus waiting, and the savages came on, they plainly saw that one of the three was the runaway savage that had escaped from them; and they both knew him distinctly, and resolved that, if possible, he should not escape, though they should both fire; so the other stood ready with his piece, that if he did not drop at the first shot, he should be sure to have a second. But the first was too good a marksman to miss his aim; for as the savages kept near one another, a little behind in a line, he fired, and hit two of them directly; the foremost was killed outright, being shot in the head; the second, which was the runaway Indian, was shot through the body, and fell, but was not quite dead; and the third had a little scratch in the shoulder, perhaps by the same ball that went through the body of the second; and being dreadfully frightened, though not so much hurt, sat down upon the ground, screaming and yelling in a hideous manner.

The five that were behind, more frightened with the noise than sensible of the danger, stood still at first; for the woods made the sound a thousand times bigger than it really was, the echoes rattling from one side to another, and the fowls rising from all parts, screaming, and every sort making a different noise, according to their kind; just as it was when I fired the first gun that perhaps was ever shot off in the island.

However, all being silent again, and they not knowing what the matter was, came on unconcerned, till they came to the place where their companions lay in a condition miserable enough. Here the poor ignorant creatures, not sensible that they were within reach of the same mischief, stood all together over the wounded man, talking, and, as may be supposed, inquiring of him how he came to be hurt; and who, it is very rational to believe, told them that a flash of fire first, and immediately after that thunder from their gods, had killed those two and wounded him. This, I say, is rational; for nothing is more certain than that, as they saw no man near them, so they had never heard a gun in all their lives, nor so much as heard of a gun; neither knew they anything of killing and wounding at a distance with fire and bullets: if they had, one might reasonably believe they would not have stood so unconcerned to view the fate of their fellows, without some apprehensions of their own.

Our two men, as they confessed to me, were grieved to be obliged to kill so many poor creatures, who had no notion of their danger; yet, having them all thus in their power, and the first having loaded his piece again, resolved to let fly both together among them; and singling out, by agreement, which to aim at, they shot together, and killed, or very much wounded, four of them; the fifth, frightened even to death, though not hurt, fell with the rest; so that our men, seeing them all fall together, thought they had killed them all.

The belief that the savages were all killed made our two men come boldly out from the tree before they had charged their guns, which was a wrong step; and they were under some surprise when they came to the place, and found no less than four of them alive, and of them two very little hurt, and one not at all. This obliged them to fall upon them with the stocks of their muskets; and first they made sure of the runaway savage, that had been the cause of all the mischief, and of another that was hurt in the knee, and put them out of their pain; then the man that was not hurt at all came and kneeled down to them, with his two hands held up, and made piteous moans to them, by gestures and signs, for his life, but could not say one word to them that they could understand. However, they made signs to him to sit down at the foot of a tree hard by; and one of the Englishmen, with a piece of rope-yarn, which he had by great chance in his pocket, tied his two hands behind him, and there they left him; and with what speed they could made after the other two, which were gone before, fearing they, or any more of them, should find way to their covered place in the woods, where their wives, and the few goods they had left, lay. They came once in sight of the two men, but it was at a great distance; however, they had the satisfaction to see them cross over a valley towards the sea, quite the contrary way from that which led to their retreat, which they were afraid of; and being satisfied with that, they went back to the tree where they left their prisoner, who, as they supposed, was delivered by his comrades, for he was gone, and the two pieces of rope-yarn with which they had bound him lay just at the foot of the tree.

They were now in as great concern as before, not knowing what course to take, or how near the enemy might be, or in what number; so they resolved to go away to the place where their wives were, to see if all was well there, and to make them easy. These were in fright enough, to be sure; for though the savages were their own countrymen, yet they were most terribly afraid of them, and perhaps the more for the knowledge they had of them. When they came there, they found the savages had been in the wood, and very near that place, but had not found it; for it was indeed inaccessible, from the trees standing so thick, unless the persons seeking it had been directed by those that knew it, which these did not: they found, therefore, everything very safe, only the women in a terrible fright. While they were here they had the comfort to have seven of the Spaniards come to their assistance; the other ten, with their servants, and Friday's father, were gone in a body to defend their bower, and the corn and cattle that were kept there, in case the savages should have roved over to that side of the country, but they did not spread so far. With the seven Spaniards came one of the three savages, who, as I said, were their prisoners formerly; and with them also came the savage whom the Englishmen had left bound hand and foot at the tree; for it seems they came that way, saw the slaughter of the seven men, and unbound the eighth, and brought him along with them; where, however, they were obliged to bind again, as they had the two others who were left when the third ran away.

The prisoners now began to be a burden to them; and they were so afraid of their escaping, that they were once resolving to kill them all, believing they were under an absolute necessity to do so for their own preservation. However, the chief of the Spaniards would not consent to it, but ordered, for the present, that they should be sent out of the way to my old cave in the valley, and be kept there, with two Spaniards to guard them, and have food for their subsistence, which was done; and they were bound there hand and foot for that night.

When the Spaniards came, the two Englishmen were so encouraged, that they could not satisfy themselves to stay any longer there; but taking five of the Spaniards, and themselves, with four muskets and a pistol among them, and two stout quarter-staves, away they went in quest of the savages. And first they came to the tree where the men lay that had been killed; but it was easy to see that some more of the savages had been there, for they had attempted to carry their dead men away, and had dragged two of them a good way, but had given it over. From thence they advanced to the first rising ground, where they had stood and seen their camp destroyed, and where they had the mortification still to see some of the smoke; but neither could they here see any of the savages. They then resolved, though with all possible caution, to go forward towards their ruined plantation; but, a little before they came thither, coming in sight of the sea-shore, they saw plainly the savages all embarked again in their canoes, in order to be gone. They seemed sorry at first that there was no way to come at them, to give them a parting blow; but, upon the whole, they were very well satisfied to be rid of them.

The poor Englishmen being now twice ruined, and all their improvements destroyed, the rest all agreed to come and help them to rebuild, and assist them with needful supplies. Their three countrymen, who were not yet noted for having the least inclination to do any good, yet as soon as they heard of it (for they, living remote eastward, knew nothing of the matter till all was over), came and offered their help and assistance, and did, very friendly, work for several days to restore their habitation and make necessaries for them. And thus in a little time they were set upon their legs again.

About two days after this they had the farther satisfaction of seeing three of the savages' canoes come driving on shore, and, at some distance from them, two drowned men, by which they had reason to believe that they had met with a storm at sea, which had overset some of them; for it had blown very hard the night after they went off. However, as some might miscarry, so, on the other hand, enough of them escaped to inform the rest, as well of what they had done as of what had happened to them; and to whet them on to another enterprise of the same nature, which they, it seems, resolved to attempt, with sufficient force to carry all before them; for except what the first man had told them of inhabitants, they could say little of it of their own knowledge, for they never saw one man; and the fellow being killed that had affirmed it, they had no other witness to confirm it to, them.

Chapter V—A GREAT VICTORY

It was five or six months after this before they heard any more of the savages, in which time our men were in hopes they had either forgot their former bad luck, or given over hopes of better; when, on a sudden, they were invaded with a most formidable fleet of no less than eight-and-twenty canoes, full of savages, armed with bows and arrows, great clubs, wooden swords, and such like engines of war; and they brought such numbers with them, that, in short, it put all our people into the utmost consternation.

As they came on shore in the evening, and at the easternmost side of the island, our men had that night to consult and consider what to do. In the first place, knowing that their being entirely concealed was their only safety before and would be much more so now, while the number of their enemies would be so great, they resolved, first of all, to take down the huts which were built for the two Englishmen, and drive away their goats to the old cave; because they supposed the savages would go directly thither, as soon as it was day, to play the old game over again, though they did not now land within two leagues of it. In the next place, they drove away all the flocks of goats they had at the old bower, as I called it, which belonged to the Spaniards; and, in short, left as little appearance of inhabitants anywhere as was possible; and the next morning early they posted themselves, with all their force, at the plantation of the two men, to wait for their coming. As they guessed, so it happened: these new invaders, leaving their canoes at the east end of the island, came ranging along the shore, directly towards the place, to the number of two hundred and fifty, as near as our men could judge. Our army was but small indeed; but, that which was worse, they had not arms for all their number. The whole account, it seems, stood thus: first, as to men, seventeen Spaniards, five Englishmen, old Friday, the three slaves taken with the women, who proved very faithful, and three other slaves, who lived with the Spaniards. To arm these, they had eleven muskets, five pistols, three fowling-pieces, five muskets or fowling-pieces which were taken by me from the mutinous seamen whom I reduced, two swords, and three old halberds.

To their slaves they did not give either musket or fusee; but they had each a halberd, or a long staff, like a quarter-staff, with a great spike of iron fastened into each end of it, and by his side a hatchet; also every one of our men had a hatchet. Two of the women could not be prevailed upon but they would come into the fight, and they had bows and arrows, which the Spaniards had taken from the savages when the first action happened, which I have spoken of, where the Indians fought with one another; and the women had hatchets too.

The chief Spaniard, whom I described so often, commanded the whole; and Will Atkins, who, though a dreadful fellow for wickedness, was a most daring, bold fellow, commanded under him. The savages came forward like lions; and our men, which was the worst of their fate, had no advantage in their situation; only that Will Atkins, who now proved a most useful fellow, with six men, was planted just behind a small thicket of bushes as an advanced guard, with orders to let the first of them pass by and then fire into the middle of them, and as soon as he had fired, to make his retreat as nimbly as he could round a part of the wood, and so come in behind the Spaniards, where they stood, having a thicket of trees before them.

When the savages came on, they ran straggling about every way in heaps, out of all manner of order, and Will Atkins let about fifty of them pass by him; then seeing the rest come in a very thick throng, he orders three of his men to fire, having loaded their muskets with six or seven bullets apiece, about as big as large pistol-bullets. How many they killed or wounded they knew not, but the consternation and surprise was inexpressible among the savages; they were frightened to the last degree to hear such a dreadful noise, and see their men killed, and others hurt, but see nobody that did it; when, in the middle of their fright, Will Atkins and his other three let fly again among the thickest of them; and in less than a minute the first three, being loaded again, gave them a third volley.

Had Will Atkins and his men retired immediately, as soon as they had fired, as they were ordered to do, or had the rest of the body been at hand to have poured in their shot continually, the savages had been effectually routed; for the terror that was among them came principally from this, that they were killed by the gods with thunder and lightning, and could see nobody that hurt them. But Will Atkins, staying to load again, discovered the cheat: some of the savages who were at a distance spying them, came upon them behind; and though Atkins and his men fired at them also, two or three times, and killed above twenty, retiring as fast as they could, yet they wounded Atkins himself, and killed one of his fellow-Englishmen with their arrows, as they did afterwards one Spaniard, and one of the Indian slaves who came with the women. This slave was a most gallant fellow, and fought most desperately, killing five of them with his own hand, having no weapon but one of the armed staves and a hatchet.

Our men being thus hard laid at, Atkins wounded, and two other men killed, retreated to a rising ground in the wood; and the Spaniards, after firing three volleys upon them, retreated also; for their number was so great, and they were so desperate, that though above fifty of them were killed, and more than as many wounded, yet they came on in the teeth of our men, fearless of danger, and shot their arrows like a cloud; and it was observed that their wounded men, who were not quite disabled, were made outrageous by their wounds, and fought like madmen.

When our men retreated, they left the Spaniard and the Englishman that were killed behind them: and the savages, when they came up to them, killed them over again in a wretched manner, breaking their arms, legs, and heads, with their clubs and wooden swords, like true savages; but finding our men were gone, they did not seem inclined to pursue them, but drew themselves up in a ring, which is, it seems, their custom, and shouted twice, in token of their victory; after which, they had the mortification to see several of their wounded men fall, dying with the mere loss of blood.

The Spaniard governor having drawn his little body up together upon a rising ground, Atkins, though he was wounded, would have had them march and charge again all together at once: but the Spaniard replied, "Seignior Atkins, you see how their wounded men fight; let them alone till morning; all the wounded men will be stiff and sore with their wounds, and faint with the loss of blood; and so we shall have the fewer to engage." This advice was good: but Will Atkins replied merrily, "That is true, seignior, and so shall I too; and that is the reason I would go on while I am warm." "Well, Seignior Atkins," says the Spaniard, "you have behaved gallantly, and done your part; we will fight for you if you cannot come on; but I think it best to stay till morning:" so they waited.

But as it was a clear moonlight night, and they found the savages in great disorder about their dead and wounded men, and a great noise and hurry among them where they lay, they afterwards resolved to fall upon them in the night, especially if they could come to give them but one volley before they were discovered, which they had a fair opportunity to do; for one of the Englishmen in whose quarter it was where the fight began, led them round between the woods and the seaside westward, and then turning short south, they came so near where the thickest of them lay, that before they were seen or heard eight of them fired in among them, and did dreadful execution upon them; in half a minute more eight others fired after them, pouring in their small shot in such a quantity that abundance were killed and wounded; and all this while they were not able to see who hurt them, or which way to fly.

The Spaniards charged again with the utmost expedition, and then divided themselves into three bodies, and resolved to fall in among them all together. They had in each body eight persons, that is to say, twenty-two men and the two women, who, by the way, fought desperately. They divided the firearms equally in each party, as well as the halberds and staves. They would have had the women kept back, but they said they were resolved to die with their husbands. Having thus formed their little army, they marched out from among the trees, and came up to the teeth of the enemy, shouting and hallooing as loud as they could; the savages stood all together, but were in the utmost confusion, hearing the noise of our men shouting from three quarters together. They would have fought if they had seen us; for as soon as we came near enough to be seen, some arrows were shot, and poor old Friday was wounded, though not dangerously. But our men gave them no time, but running up to them, fired among them three ways, and then fell in with the butt-ends of their muskets, their swords, armed staves, and hatchets, and laid about them so well that, in a word, they set up a dismal screaming and howling, flying to save their lives which way soever they could.

Our men were tired with the execution, and killed or mortally wounded in the two fights about one hundred and eighty of them; the rest, being frightened out of their wits, scoured through the woods and over the hills, with all the speed that fear and nimble feet could help them to; and as we did not trouble ourselves much to pursue them, they got all together to the seaside, where they landed, and where their canoes lay. But their disaster was not at an end yet; for it blew a terrible storm of wind that evening from the sea, so that it was impossible for them to go off; nay, the storm continuing all night, when the tide came up their canoes were most of them driven by the surge of the sea so high upon the shore that it required infinite toil to get them off; and some of them were even dashed to pieces against the beach. Our men, though glad of their victory, yet got little rest that night; but having refreshed themselves as well as they could, they resolved to march to that part of the island where the savages were fled, and see what posture they were in. This necessarily led them over the place where the fight had been, and where they found several of the poor creatures not quite dead, and yet past recovering life; a sight disagreeable enough to generous minds, for a truly great man though obliged by the law of battle to destroy his enemy, takes no delight in his misery. However, there was no need to give any orders in this case; for their own savages, who were their servants, despatched these poor creatures with their hatchets.

At length they came in view of the place where the more miserable remains of the savages' army lay, where there appeared about a hundred still; their posture was generally sitting upon the ground, with their knees up towards their mouth, and the head put between the two hands, leaning down upon the knees. When our men came within two musket-shots of them, the Spaniard governor ordered two muskets to be fired without ball, to alarm them; this he did, that by their countenance he might know what to expect, whether they were still in heart to fight, or were so heartily beaten as to be discouraged, and so he might manage accordingly. This stratagem took: for as soon as the savages heard the first gun, and saw the flash of the second, they started up upon their feet in the greatest consternation imaginable; and as our men advanced swiftly towards them, they all ran screaming and yelling away, with a kind of howling noise, which our men did not understand, and had never heard before; and thus they ran up the hills into the country.

At first our men had much rather the weather had been calm, and they had all gone away to sea: but they did not then consider that this might probably have been the occasion of their coming again in such multitudes as not to be resisted, or, at least, to come so many and so often as would quite desolate the island, and starve them. Will Atkins, therefore, who notwithstanding his wound kept always with them, proved the best counsellor in this case: his advice was, to take the advantage that offered, and step in between them and their boats, and so deprive them of the capacity of ever returning any more to plague the island. They consulted long about this; and some were against it for fear of making the wretches fly to the woods and live there desperate, and so they should have them to hunt like wild beasts, be afraid to stir out about their business, and have their plantations continually rifled, all their tame goats destroyed, and, in short, be reduced to a life of continual distress.

Will Atkins told them they had better have to do with a hundred men than with a hundred nations; that, as they must destroy their boats, so they must destroy the men, or be all of them destroyed themselves. In a word, he showed them the necessity of it so plainly that they all came into it; so they went to work immediately with the boats, and getting some dry wood together from a dead tree, they tried to set some of them on fire, but they were so wet that they would not burn; however, the fire so burned the upper part that it soon made them unfit for use at sea.

When the Indians saw what they were about, some of them came running out of the woods, and coming as near as they could to our men, kneeled down and cried, "Oa, Oa, Waramokoa," and some other words of their language, which none of the others understood anything of; but as they made pitiful gestures and strange noises, it was easy to understand they begged to have their boats spared, and that they would be gone, and never come there again. But our men were now satisfied that they had no way to preserve themselves, or to save their colony, but effectually to prevent any of these people from ever going home again; depending upon this, that if even so much as one of them got back into their country to tell the story, the colony was undone; so that, letting them know that they should not have any mercy, they fell to work with their canoes, and destroyed every one that the storm had not destroyed before; at the sight of which, the savages raised a hideous cry in the woods, which our people heard plain enough, after which they ran about the island like distracted men, so that, in a word, our men did not really know what at first to do with them. Nor did the Spaniards, with all their prudence, consider that while they made those people thus desperate, they ought to have kept a good guard at the same time upon their plantations; for though it is true they had driven away their cattle, and the Indians did not find out their main retreat, I mean my old castle at the hill, nor the cave in the valley, yet they found out my plantation at the bower, and pulled it all to pieces, and all the fences and planting about it; trod all the corn under foot, tore up the vines and grapes, being just then almost ripe, and did our men inestimable damage, though to themselves not one farthing's worth of service.

Though our men were able to fight them upon all occasions, yet they were in no condition to pursue them, or hunt them up and down; for as they were too nimble of foot for our people when they found them single, so our men durst not go abroad single, for fear of being surrounded with their numbers. The best was they had no weapons; for though they had bows, they had no arrows left, nor any materials to make any; nor had they any edge-tool among them. The extremity and distress they were reduced to was great, and indeed deplorable; but, at the same time, our men were also brought to very bad circumstances by them, for though their retreats were preserved, yet their provision was destroyed, and their harvest spoiled, and what to do, or which way to turn themselves, they knew not. The only refuge they had now was the stock of cattle they had in the valley by the cave, and some little corn which grew there, and the plantation of the three Englishmen. Will Atkins and his comrades were now reduced to two; one of them being killed by an arrow, which struck him on the side of his head, just under the temple, so that he never spoke more; and it was very remarkable that this was the same barbarous fellow that cut the poor savage slave with his hatchet, and who afterwards intended to have murdered the Spaniards.

I looked upon their case to have been worse at this time than mine was at any time, after I first discovered the grains of barley and rice, and got into the manner of planting and raising my corn, and my tame cattle; for now they had, as I may say, a hundred wolves upon the island, which would devour everything they could come at, yet could be hardly come at themselves.

When they saw what their circumstances were, the first thing they concluded was, that they would, if possible, drive the savages up to the farther part of the island, south-west, that if any more came on shore they might not find one another; then, that they would daily hunt and harass them, and kill as many of them as they could come at, till they had reduced their number; and if they could at last tame them, and bring them to anything, they would give them corn, and teach them how to plant, and live upon their daily labour. In order to do this, they so followed them, and so terrified them with their guns, that in a few days, if any of them fired a gun at an Indian, if he did not hit him, yet he would fall down for fear. So dreadfully frightened were they that they kept out of sight farther and farther; till at last our men followed them, and almost every day killing or wounding some of them, they kept up in the woods or hollow places so much, that it reduced them to the utmost misery for want of food; and many were afterwards found dead in the woods, without any hurt, absolutely starved to death.

When our men found this, it made their hearts relent, and pity moved them, especially the generous-minded Spaniard governor; and he proposed, if possible, to take one of them alive and bring him to understand what they meant, so far as to be able to act as interpreter, and go among them and see if they might be brought to some conditions that might be depended upon, to save their lives and do us no harm.

It was some while before any of them could be taken; but being weak and half-starved, one of them was at last surprised and made a prisoner. He was sullen at first, and would neither eat nor drink; but finding himself kindly used, and victuals given to him, and no violence offered him, he at last grew tractable, and came to himself. They often brought old Friday to talk to him, who always told him how kind the others would be to them all; that they would not only save their lives, but give them part of the island to live in, provided they would give satisfaction that they would keep in their own bounds, and not come beyond it to injure or prejudice others; and that they should have corn given them to plant and make it grow for their bread, and some bread given them for their present subsistence; and old Friday bade the fellow go and talk with the rest of his country-countrymen, and see what they said to it; assuring them that, if they did not agree immediately, they should be all destroyed.

The poor wretches, thoroughly humbled, and reduced in number to about thirty-seven, closed with the proposal at the first offer, and begged to have some food given them; upon which twelve Spaniards and two Englishmen, well armed, with three Indian slaves and old Friday, marched to the place where they were. The three Indian slaves carried them a large quantity of bread, some rice boiled up to cakes and dried in the sun, and three live goats; and they were ordered to go to the side of a hill, where they sat down, ate their provisions very thankfully, and were the most faithful fellows to their words that could be thought of; for, except when they came to beg victuals and directions, they never came out of their bounds; and there they lived when I came to the island and I went to see them. They had taught them both to plant corn, make bread, breed tame goats, and milk them: they wanted nothing but wives in order for them soon to become a nation. They were confined to a neck of land, surrounded with high rocks behind them, and lying plain towards the sea before them, on the south-east corner of the island. They had land enough, and it was very good and fruitful; about a mile and a half broad, and three or four miles in length. Our men taught them to make wooden spades, such as I made for myself, and gave among them twelve hatchets and three or four knives; and there they lived, the most subjected, innocent creatures that ever were heard of.

After this the colony enjoyed a perfect tranquillity with respect to the savages, till I came to revisit them, which was about two years after; not but that, now and then, some canoes of savages came on shore for their triumphal, unnatural feasts; but as they were of several nations, and perhaps had never heard of those that came before, or the reason of it, they did not make any search or inquiry after their countrymen; and if they had, it would have been very hard to have found them out.

Thus, I think, I have given a full account of all that happened to them till my return, at least that was worth notice. The Indians were wonderfully civilised by them, and they frequently went among them; but they forbid, on pain of death, any one of the Indians coming to them, because they would not have their settlement betrayed again. One thing was very remarkable, viz. that they taught the savages to make wicker-work, or baskets, but they soon outdid their masters: for they made abundance of ingenious things in wicker-work, particularly baskets, sieves, bird-cages, cupboards, &c.; as also chairs, stools, beds, couches, being very ingenious at such work when they were once put in the way of it.

My coming was a particular relief to these people, because we furnished them with knives, scissors, spades, shovels, pick-axes, and all things of that kind which they could want. With the help of those tools they were so very handy that they came at last to build up their huts or houses very handsomely, raddling or working it up like basket-work all the way round. This piece of ingenuity, although it looked very odd, was an exceeding good fence, as well against heat as against all sorts of vermin; and our men were so taken with it that they got the Indians to come and do the like for them; so that when I came to see the two Englishmen's colonies, they looked at a distance as if they all lived like bees in a hive.

As for Will Atkins, who was now become a very industrious, useful, and sober fellow, he had made himself such a tent of basket-work as I believe was never seen; it was one hundred and twenty paces round on the outside, as I measured by my steps; the walls were as close worked as a basket, in panels or squares of thirty-two in number, and very strong, standing about seven feet high; in the middle was another not above twenty-two paces round, but built stronger, being octagon in its form, and in the eight corners stood eight very strong posts; round the top of which he laid strong pieces, knit together with wooden pins, from which he raised a pyramid for a handsome roof of eight rafters, joined together very well, though he had no nails, and only a few iron spikes, which he made himself, too, out of the old iron that I had left there. Indeed, this fellow showed abundance of ingenuity in several things which he had no knowledge of: he made him a forge, with a pair of wooden bellows to blow the fire; he made himself charcoal for his work; and he formed out of the iron crows a middling good anvil to hammer upon: in this manner he made many things, but especially hooks, staples, and spikes, bolts and hinges. But to return to the house: after he had pitched the roof of his innermost tent, he worked it up between the rafters with basket-work, so firm, and thatched that over again so ingeniously with rice-straw, and over that a large leaf of a tree, which covered the top, that his house was as dry as if it had been tiled or slated. He owned, indeed, that the savages had made the basket-work for him. The outer circuit was covered as a lean-to all round this inner apartment, and long rafters lay from the thirty-two angles to the top posts of the inner house, being about twenty feet distant, so that there was a space like a walk within the outer wicker-wall, and without the inner, near twenty feet wide.

The inner place he partitioned off with the same wickerwork, but much fairer, and divided into six apartments, so that he had six rooms on a floor, and out of every one of these there was a door: first into the entry, or coming into the main tent, another door into the main tent, and another door into the space or walk that was round it; so that walk was also divided into six equal parts, which served not only for a retreat, but to store up any necessaries which the family had occasion for. These six spaces not taking up the whole circumference, what other apartments the outer circle had were thus ordered: As soon as you were in at the door of the outer circle you had a short passage straight before you to the door of the inner house; but on either side was a wicker partition and a door in it, by which you went first into a large room or storehouse, twenty feet wide and about thirty feet long, and through that into another not quite so long; so that in the outer circle were ten handsome rooms, six of which were only to be come at through the apartments of the inner tent, and served as closets or retiring rooms to the respective chambers of the inner circle; and four large warehouses, or barns, or what you please to call them, which went through one another, two on either hand of the passage, that led through the outer door to the inner tent. Such a piece of basket-work, I believe, was never seen in the world, nor a house or tent so neatly contrived, much less so built. In this great bee-hive lived the three families, that is to say, Will Atkins and his companion; the third was killed, but his wife remained with three children, and the other two were not at all backward to give the widow her full share of everything, I mean as to their corn, milk, grapes, &c., and when they killed a kid, or found a turtle on the shore; so that they all lived well enough; though it was true they were not so industrious as the other two, as has been observed already.

One thing, however, cannot be omitted, viz. that as for religion, I do not know that there was anything of that kind among them; they often, indeed, put one another in mind that there was a God, by the very common method of seamen, swearing by His name: nor were their poor ignorant savage wives much better for having been married to Christians, as we must call them; for as they knew very little of God themselves, so they were utterly incapable of entering into any discourse with their wives about a God, or to talk anything to them concerning religion.

The utmost of all the improvement which I can say the wives had made from them was, that they had taught them to speak English pretty well; and most of their children, who were near twenty in all, were taught to speak English too, from their first learning to speak, though they at first spoke it in a very broken manner, like their mothers. None of these children were above six years old when I came thither, for it was not much above seven years since they had fetched these five savage ladies over; they had all children, more or less: the mothers were all a good sort of well-governed, quiet, laborious women, modest and decent, helpful to one another, mighty observant, and subject to their masters (I cannot call them husbands), and lacked nothing but to be well instructed in the Christian religion, and to be legally married; both of which were happily brought about afterwards by my means, or at least in consequence of my coming among them.

Chapter VI—THE FRENCH CLERGYMAN'S COUNSEL

Having thus given an account of the colony in general, and pretty much of my runagate Englishmen, I must say something of the Spaniards, who were the main body of the family, and in whose story there are some incidents also remarkable enough.

I had a great many discourses with them about their circumstances when they were among the savages. They told me readily that they had no instances to give of their application or ingenuity in that country; that they were a poor, miserable, dejected handful of people; that even if means had been put into their hands, yet they had so abandoned themselves to despair, and were so sunk under the weight of their misfortune, that they thought of nothing but starving. One of them, a grave and sensible man, told me he was convinced they were in the wrong; that it was not the part of wise men to give themselves up to their misery, but always to take hold of the helps which reason offered, as well for present support as for future deliverance: he told me that grief was the most senseless, insignificant passion in the world, for that it regarded only things past, which were generally impossible to be recalled or to be remedied, but had no views of things to come, and had no share in anything that looked like deliverance, but rather added to the affliction than proposed a remedy; and upon this he repeated a Spanish proverb, which, though I cannot repeat in the same words that he spoke it in, yet I remember I made it into an English proverb of my own, thus:—

"In trouble to be troubled,
Is to have your trouble doubled."

He then ran on in remarks upon all the little improvements I had made in my solitude: my unwearied application, as he called it; and how I had made a condition, which in its circumstances was at first much worse than theirs, a thousand times more happy than theirs was, even now when they were all together. He told me it was remarkable that Englishmen had a greater presence of mind in their distress than any people that ever he met with; that their unhappy nation and the Portuguese were the worst men in the world to struggle with misfortunes; for that their first step in dangers, after the common efforts were over, was to despair, lie down under it, and die, without rousing their thoughts up to proper remedies for escape.

I told him their case and mine differed exceedingly; that they were cast upon the shore without necessaries, without supply of food, or present sustenance till they could provide for it; that, it was true, I had this further disadvantage and discomfort, that I was alone; but then the supplies I had providentially thrown into my hands, by the unexpected driving of the ship on the shore, was such a help as would have encouraged any creature in the world to have applied himself as I had done. "Seignior," says the Spaniard, "had we poor Spaniards been in your case, we should never have got half those things out of the ship, as you did: nay," says he, "we should never have found means to have got a raft to carry them, or to have got the raft on shore without boat or sail: and how much less should we have done if any of us had been alone!" Well, I desired him to abate his compliments, and go on with the history of their coming on shore, where they landed. He told me they unhappily landed at a place where there were people without provisions; whereas, had they had the common sense to put off to sea again, and gone to another island a little further, they had found provisions, though without people: there being an island that way, as they had been told, where there were provisions, though no people—that is to say, that the Spaniards of Trinidad had frequently been there, and had filled the island with goats and hogs at several times, where they had bred in such multitudes, and where turtle and sea-fowls were in such plenty, that they could have been in no want of flesh, though they had found no bread; whereas, here they were only sustained with a few roots and herbs, which they understood not, and which had no substance in them, and which the inhabitants gave them sparingly enough; and they could treat them no better, unless they would turn cannibals and eat men's flesh.

They gave me an account how many ways they strove to civilise the savages they were with, and to teach them rational customs in the ordinary way of living, but in vain; and how they retorted upon them as unjust that they who came there for assistance and support should attempt to set up for instructors to those that gave them food; intimating, it seems, that none should set up for the instructors of others but those who could live without them. They gave me dismal accounts of the extremities they were driven to; how sometimes they were many days without any food at all, the island they were upon being inhabited by a sort of savages that lived more indolent, and for that reason were less supplied with the necessaries of life, than they had reason to believe others were in the same part of the world; and yet they found that these savages were less ravenous and voracious than those who had better supplies of food. Also, they added, they could not but see with what demonstrations of wisdom and goodness the governing providence of God directs the events of things in this world, which, they said, appeared in their circumstances: for if, pressed by the hardships they were under, and the barrenness of the country where they were, they had searched after a better to live in, they had then been out of the way of the relief that happened to them by my means.

They then gave me an account how the savages whom they lived amongst expected them to go out with them into their wars; and, it was true, that as they had firearms with them, had they not had the disaster to lose their ammunition, they could have been serviceable not only to their friends, but have made themselves terrible both to friends and enemies; but being without powder and shot, and yet in a condition that they could not in reason decline to go out with their landlords to their wars; so when they came into the field of battle they were in a worse condition than the savages themselves, for they had neither bows nor arrows, nor could they use those the savages gave them. So they could do nothing but stand still and be wounded with arrows, till they came up to the teeth of the enemy; and then, indeed, the three halberds they had were of use to them; and they would often drive a whole little army before them with those halberds, and sharpened sticks put into the muzzles of their muskets. But for all this they were sometimes surrounded with multitudes, and in great danger from their arrows, till at last they found the way to make themselves large targets of wood, which they covered with skins of wild beasts, whose names they knew not, and these covered them from the arrows of the savages: that, notwithstanding these, they were sometimes in great danger; and five of them were once knocked down together with the clubs of the savages, which was the time when one of them was taken prisoner—that is to say, the Spaniard whom I relieved. At first they thought he had been killed; but when they afterwards heard he was taken prisoner, they were under the greatest grief imaginable, and would willingly have all ventured their lives to have rescued him.

They told me that when they were so knocked down, the rest of their company rescued them, and stood over them fighting till they were come to themselves, all but him whom they thought had been dead; and then they made their way with their halberds and pieces, standing close together in a line, through a body of above a thousand savages, beating down all that came in their way, got the victory over their enemies, but to their great sorrow, because it was with the loss of their friend, whom the other party finding alive, carried off with some others, as I gave an account before. They described, most affectionately, how they were surprised with joy at the return of their friend and companion in misery, who they thought had been devoured by wild beasts of the worst kind—wild men; and yet, how more and more they were surprised with the account he gave them of his errand, and that there was a Christian in any place near, much more one that was able, and had humanity enough, to contribute to their deliverance.

They described how they were astonished at the sight of the relief I sent them, and at the appearance of loaves of bread—things they had not seen since their coming to that miserable place; how often they crossed it and blessed it as bread sent from heaven; and what a reviving cordial it was to their spirits to taste it, as also the other things I had sent for their supply; and, after all, they would have told me something of the joy they were in at the sight of a boat and pilots, to carry them away to the person and place from whence all these new comforts came. But it was impossible to express it by words, for their excessive joy naturally driving them to unbecoming extravagances, they had no way to describe them but by telling me they bordered upon lunacy, having no way to give vent to their passions suitable to the sense that was upon them; that in some it worked one way and in some another; and that some of them, through a surprise of joy, would burst into tears, others be stark mad, and others immediately faint. This discourse extremely affected me, and called to my mind Friday's ecstasy when he met his father, and the poor people's ecstasy when I took them up at sea after their ship was on fire; the joy of the mate of the ship when he found himself delivered in the place where he expected to perish; and my own joy, when, after twenty-eight years' captivity, I found a good ship ready to carry me to my own country. All these things made me more sensible of the relation of these poor men, and more affected with it.

Having thus given a view of the state of things as I found them, I must relate the heads of what I did for these people, and the condition in which I left them. It was their opinion, and mine too, that they would be troubled no more with the savages, or if they were, they would be able to cut them off, if they were twice as many as before; so they had no concern about that. Then I entered into a serious discourse with the Spaniard, whom I call governor, about their stay in the island; for as I was not come to carry any of them off, so it would not be just to carry off some and leave others, who, perhaps, would be unwilling to stay if their strength was diminished. On the other hand, I told them I came to establish them there, not to remove them; and then I let them know that I had brought with me relief of sundry kinds for them; that I had been at a great charge to supply them with all things necessary, as well for their convenience as their defence; and that I had such and such particular persons with me, as well to increase and recruit their number, as by the particular necessary employments which they were bred to, being artificers, to assist them in those things in which at present they were in want.

They were all together when I talked thus to them; and before I delivered to them the stores I had brought, I asked them, one by one, if they had entirely forgot and buried the first animosities that had been among them, and would shake hands with one another, and engage in a strict friendship and union of interest, that so there might be no more misunderstandings and jealousies.

Will Atkins, with abundance of frankness and good humour, said they had met with affliction enough to make them all sober, and enemies enough to make them all friends; that, for his part, he would live and die with them, and was so far from designing anything against the Spaniards, that he owned they had done nothing to him but what his own mad humour made necessary, and what he would have done, and perhaps worse, in their case; and that he would ask them pardon, if I desired it, for the foolish and brutish things he had done to them, and was very willing and desirous of living in terms of entire friendship and union with them, and would do anything that lay in his power to convince them of it; and as for going to England, he cared not if he did not go thither these twenty years.

The Spaniards said they had, indeed, at first disarmed and excluded Will Atkins and his two countrymen for their ill conduct, as they had let me know, and they appealed to me for the necessity they were under to do so; but that Will Atkins had behaved himself so bravely in the great fight they had with the savages, and on several occasions since, and had showed himself so faithful to, and concerned for, the general interest of them all, that they had forgotten all that was past, and thought he merited as much to be trusted with arms and supplied with necessaries as any of them; that they had testified their satisfaction in him by committing the command to him next to the governor himself; and as they had entire confidence in him and all his countrymen, so they acknowledged they had merited that confidence by all the methods that honest men could merit to be valued and trusted; and they most heartily embraced the occasion of giving me this assurance, that they would never have any interest separate from one another.

Upon these frank and open declarations of friendship, we appointed the next day to dine all together; and, indeed, we made a splendid feast. I caused the ship's cook and his mate to come on shore and dress our dinner, and the old cook's mate we had on shore assisted. We brought on shore six pieces of good beef and four pieces of pork, out of the ship's provisions, with our punch-bowl and materials to fill it; and in particular I gave them ten bottles of French claret, and ten bottles of English beer; things that neither the Spaniards nor the English had tasted for many years, and which it may be supposed they were very glad of. The Spaniards added to our feast five whole kids, which the cooks roasted; and three of them were sent, covered up close, on board the ship to the seamen, that they might feast on fresh meat from on shore, as we did with their salt meat from on board.

After this feast, at which we were very innocently merry, I brought my cargo of goods; wherein, that there might be no dispute about dividing, I showed them that there was a sufficiency for them all, desiring that they might all take an equal quantity, when made up, of the goods that were for wearing. As, first, I distributed linen sufficient to make every one of them four shirts, and, at the Spaniard's request, afterwards made them up six; these were exceeding comfortable to them, having been what they had long since forgot the use of, or what it was to wear them. I allotted the thin English stuffs, which I mentioned before, to make every one a light coat, like a frock, which I judged fittest for the heat of the season, cool and loose; and ordered that whenever they decayed, they should make more, as they thought fit; the like for pumps, shoes, stockings, hats, &c. I cannot express what pleasure sat upon the countenances of all these poor men when they saw the care I had taken of them, and how well I had furnished them. They told me I was a father to them; and that having such a correspondent as I was in so remote a part of the world, it would make them forget that they were left in a desolate place; and they all voluntarily engaged to me not to leave the place without my consent.

Then I presented to them the people I had brought with me, particularly the tailor, the smith, and the two carpenters, all of them most necessary people; but, above all, my general artificer, than whom they could not name anything that was more useful to them; and the tailor, to show his concern for them, went to work immediately, and, with my leave, made them every one a shirt, the first thing he did; and, what was still more, he taught the women not only how to sew and stitch, and use the needle, but made them assist to make the shirts for their husbands, and for all the rest. As to the carpenters, I scarce need mention how useful they were; for they took to pieces all my clumsy, unhandy things, and made clever convenient tables, stools, bedsteads, cupboards, lockers, shelves, and everything they wanted of that kind. But to let them see how nature made artificers at first, I carried the carpenters to see Will Atkins' basket-house, as I called it; and they both owned they never saw an instance of such natural ingenuity before, nor anything so regular and so handily built, at least of its kind; and one of them, when he saw it, after musing a good while, turning about to me, "I am sure," says he, "that man has no need of us; you need do nothing but give him tools."

Then I brought them out all my store of tools, and gave every man a digging-spade, a shovel, and a rake, for we had no barrows or ploughs; and to every separate place a pickaxe, a crow, a broad axe, and a saw; always appointing, that as often as any were broken or worn out, they should be supplied without grudging out of the general stores that I left behind. Nails, staples, hinges, hammers, chisels, knives, scissors, and all sorts of ironwork, they had without reserve, as they required; for no man would take more than he wanted, and he must be a fool that would waste or spoil them on any account whatever; and for the use of the smith I left two tons of unwrought iron for a supply.

My magazine of powder and arms which I brought them was such, even to profusion, that they could not but rejoice at them; for now they could march as I used to do, with a musket upon each shoulder, if there was occasion; and were able to fight a thousand savages, if they had but some little advantages of situation, which also they could not miss, if they had occasion.

I carried on shore with me the young man whose mother was starved to death, and the maid also; she was a sober, well-educated, religious young woman, and behaved so inoffensively that every one gave her a good word; she had, indeed, an unhappy life with us, there being no woman in the ship but herself, but she bore it with patience. After a while, seeing things so well ordered, and in so fine a way of thriving upon my island, and considering that they had neither business nor acquaintance in the East Indies, or reason for taking so long a voyage, both of them came to me and desired I would give them leave to remain on the island, and be entered among my family, as they called it. I agreed to this readily; and they had a little plot of ground allotted to them, where they had three tents or houses set up, surrounded with a basket-work, palisadoed like Atkins's, adjoining to his plantation. Their tents were contrived so that they had each of them a room apart to lodge in, and a middle tent like a great storehouse to lay their goods in, and to eat and to drink in. And now the other two Englishmen removed their habitation to the same place; and so the island was divided into three colonies, and no more—viz. the Spaniards, with old Friday and the first servants, at my habitation under the hill, which was, in a word, the capital city, and where they had so enlarged and extended their works, as well under as on the outside of the hill, that they lived, though perfectly concealed, yet full at large.

Never was there such a little city in a wood, and so hid, in any part of the world; for I verify believe that a thousand men might have ranged the island a month, and, if they had not known there was such a thing, and looked on purpose for it, they would not have found it. Indeed the trees stood so thick and so close, and grew so fast woven one into another, that nothing but cutting them down first could discover the place, except the only two narrow entrances where they went in and out could be found, which was not very easy; one of them was close down at the water's edge, on the side of the creek, and it was afterwards above two hundred yards to the place; and the other was up a ladder at twice, as I have already described it; and they had also a large wood, thickly planted, on the top of the hill, containing above an acre, which grew apace, and concealed the place from all discovery there, with only one narrow place between two trees, not easily to be discovered, to enter on that side.

The other colony was that of Will Atkins, where there were four families of Englishmen, I mean those I had left there, with their wives and children; three savages that were slaves, the widow and children of the Englishman that was killed, the young man and the maid, and, by the way, we made a wife of her before we went away. There were besides the two carpenters and the tailor, whom I brought with me for them: also the smith, who was a very necessary man to them, especially as a gunsmith, to take care of their arms; and my other man, whom I called Jack-of-all-trades, who was in himself as good almost as twenty men; for he was not only a very ingenious fellow, but a very merry fellow, and before I went away we married him to the honest maid that came with the youth in the ship I mentioned before.

And now I speak of marrying, it brings me naturally to say something of the French ecclesiastic that I had brought with me out of the ship's crew whom I took up at sea. It is true this man was a Roman, and perhaps it may give offence to some hereafter if I leave anything extraordinary upon record of a man whom, before I begin, I must (to set him out in just colours) represent in terms very much to his disadvantage, in the account of Protestants; as, first, that he was a Papist; secondly, a Popish priest; and thirdly, a French Popish priest. But justice demands of me to give him a due character; and I must say, he was a grave, sober, pious, and most religious person; exact in his life, extensive in his charity, and exemplary in almost everything he did. What then can any one say against being very sensible of the value of such a man, notwithstanding his profession? though it may be my opinion perhaps, as well as the opinion of others who shall read this, that he was mistaken.

The first hour that I began to converse with him after he had agreed to go with me to the East Indies, I found reason to delight exceedingly in his conversation; and he first began with me about religion in the most obliging manner imaginable. "Sir," says he, "you have not only under God" (and at that he crossed his breast) "saved my life, but you have admitted me to go this voyage in your ship, and by your obliging civility have taken me into your family, giving me an opportunity of free conversation. Now, sir, you see by my habit what my profession is, and I guess by your nation what yours is; I may think it is my duty, and doubtless it is so, to use my utmost endeavours, on all occasions, to bring all the souls I can to the knowledge of the truth, and to embrace the Catholic doctrine; but as I am here under your permission, and in your family, I am bound, in justice to your kindness as well as in decency and good manners, to be under your government; and therefore I shall not, without your leave, enter into any debate on the points of religion in which we may not agree, further than you shall give me leave."

I told him his carriage was so modest that I could not but acknowledge it; that it was true we were such people as they call heretics, but that he was not the first Catholic I had conversed with without falling into inconveniences, or carrying the questions to any height in debate; that he should not find himself the worse used for being of a different opinion from us, and if we did not converse without any dislike on either side, it should be his fault, not ours.

He replied that he thought all our conversation might be easily separated from disputes; that it was not his business to cap principles with every man he conversed with; and that he rather desired me to converse with him as a gentleman than as a religionist; and that, if I would give him leave at any time to discourse upon religious subjects, he would readily comply with it, and that he did not doubt but I would allow him also to defend his own opinions as well as he could; but that without my leave he would not break in upon me with any such thing. He told me further, that he would not cease to do all that became him, in his office as a priest, as well as a private Christian, to procure the good of the ship, and the safety of all that was in her; and though, perhaps, we would not join with him, and he could not pray with us, he hoped he might pray for us, which he would do upon all occasions. In this manner we conversed; and as he was of the most obliging, gentlemanlike behaviour, so he was, if I may be allowed to say so, a man of good sense, and, as I believe, of great learning.

He gave me a most diverting account of his life, and of the many extraordinary events of it; of many adventures which had befallen him in the few years that he had been abroad in the world; and particularly, it was very remarkable, that in the voyage he was now engaged in he had had the misfortune to be five times shipped and unshipped, and never to go to the place whither any of the ships he was in were at first designed. That his first intent was to have gone to Martinico, and that he went on board a ship bound thither at St. Malo; but being forced into Lisbon by bad weather, the ship received some damage by running aground in the mouth of the river Tagus, and was obliged to unload her cargo there; but finding a Portuguese ship there bound for the Madeiras, and ready to sail, and supposing he should meet with a ship there bound to Martinico, he went on board, in order to sail to the Madeiras; but the master of the Portuguese ship being but an indifferent mariner, had been out of his reckoning, and they drove to Fayal; where, however, he happened to find a very good market for his cargo, which was corn, and therefore resolved not to go to the Madeiras, but to load salt at the Isle of May, and to go away to Newfoundland. He had no remedy in this exigence but to go with the ship, and had a pretty good voyage as far as the Banks (so they call the place where they catch the fish), where, meeting with a French ship bound from France to Quebec, and from thence to Martinico, to carry provisions, he thought he should have an opportunity to complete his first design, but when he came to Quebec, the master of the ship died, and the vessel proceeded no further; so the next voyage he shipped himself for France, in the ship that was burned when we took them up at sea, and then shipped with us for the East Indies, as I have already said. Thus he had been disappointed in five voyages; all, as I may call it, in one voyage, besides what I shall have occasion to mention further of him.

But I shall not make digression into other men's stories which have no relation to my own; so I return to what concerns our affair in the island. He came to me one morning (for he lodged among us all the while we were upon the island), and it happened to be just when I was going to visit the Englishmen's colony, at the furthest part of the island; I say, he came to me, and told me, with a very grave countenance, that he had for two or three days desired an opportunity of some discourse with me, which he hoped would not be displeasing to me, because he thought it might in some measure correspond with my general design, which was the prosperity of my new colony, and perhaps might put it, at least more than he yet thought it was, in the way of God's blessing.

I looked a little surprised at the last of his discourse, and turning a little short, "How, sir," said I, "can it be said that we are not in the way of God's blessing, after such visible assistances and deliverances as we have seen here, and of which I have given you a large account?" "If you had pleased, sir," said he, with a world of modesty, and yet great readiness, "to have heard me, you would have found no room to have been displeased, much less to think so hard of me, that I should suggest that you have not had wonderful assistances and deliverances; and I hope, on your behalf, that you are in the way of God's blessing, and your design is exceeding good, and will prosper. But, sir, though it were more so than is even possible to you, yet there may be some among you that are not equally right in their actions: and you know that in the story of the children of Israel, one Achan in the camp removed God's blessing from them, and turned His hand so against them, that six-and-thirty of them, though not concerned in the crime, were the objects of divine vengeance, and bore the weight of that punishment."

I was sensibly touched with this discourse, and told him his inference was so just, and the whole design seemed so sincere, and was really so religious in its own nature, that I was very sorry I had interrupted him, and begged him to go on; and, in the meantime, because it seemed that what we had both to say might take up some time, I told him I was going to the Englishmen's plantations, and asked him to go with me, and we might discourse of it by the way. He told me he would the more willingly wait on me thither, because there partly the thing was acted which he desired to speak to me about; so we walked on, and I pressed him to be free and plain with me in what he had to say.

"Why, then, sir," said he, "be pleased to give me leave to lay down a few propositions, as the foundation of what I have to say, that we may not differ in the general principles, though we may be of some differing opinions in the practice of particulars. First, sir, though we differ in some of the doctrinal articles of religion (and it is very unhappy it is so, especially in the case before us, as I shall show afterwards), yet there are some general principles in which we both agree—that there is a God; and that this God having given us some stated general rules for our service and obedience, we ought not willingly and knowingly to offend Him, either by neglecting to do what He has commanded, or by doing what He has expressly forbidden. And let our different religions be what they will, this general principle is readily owned by us all, that the blessing of God does not ordinarily follow presumptuous sinning against His command; and every good Christian will be affectionately concerned to prevent any that are under his care living in a total neglect of God and His commands. It is not your men being Protestants, whatever my opinion may be of such, that discharges me from being concerned for their souls, and from endeavouring, if it lies before me, that they should live in as little distance from enmity with their Maker as possible, especially if you give me leave to meddle so far in your circuit."

I could not yet imagine what he aimed at, and told him I granted all he had said, and thanked him that he would so far concern himself for us: and begged he would explain the particulars of what he had observed, that like Joshua, to take his own parable, I might put away the accursed thing from us.

"Why, then, sir," says he, "I will take the liberty you give me; and there are three things, which, if I am right, must stand in the way of God's blessing upon your endeavours here, and which I should rejoice, for your sake and their own, to see removed. And, sir, I promise myself that you will fully agree with me in them all, as soon as I name them; especially because I shall convince you, that every one of them may, with great ease, and very much to your satisfaction, be remedied. First, sir," says he, "you have here four Englishmen, who have fetched women from among the savages, and have taken them as their wives, and have had many children by them all, and yet are not married to them after any stated legal manner, as the laws of God and man require. To this, sir, I know, you will object that there was no clergyman or priest of any kind to perform the ceremony; nor any pen and ink, or paper, to write down a contract of marriage, and have it signed between them. And I know also, sir, what the Spaniard governor has told you, I mean of the agreement that he obliged them to make when they took those women, viz. that they should choose them out by consent, and keep separately to them; which, by the way, is nothing of a marriage, no agreement with the women as wives, but only an agreement among themselves, to keep them from quarrelling. But, sir, the essence of the sacrament of matrimony" (so he called it, being a Roman) "consists not only in the mutual consent of the parties to take one another as man and wife, but in the formal and legal obligation that there is in the contract to compel the man and woman, at all times, to own and acknowledge each other; obliging the man to abstain from all other women, to engage in no other contract while these subsist; and, on all occasions, as ability allows, to provide honestly for them and their children; and to oblige the women to the same or like conditions, on their side. Now, sir," says he, "these men may, when they please, or when occasion presents, abandon these women, disown their children, leave them to perish, and take other women, and marry them while these are living;" and here he added, with some warmth, "How, sir, is God honoured in this unlawful liberty? And how shall a blessing succeed your endeavours in this place, however good in themselves, and however sincere in your design, while these men, who at present are your subjects, under your absolute government and dominion, are allowed by you to live in open adultery?"

I confess I was struck with the thing itself, but much more with the convincing arguments he supported it with; but I thought to have got off my young priest by telling him that all that part was done when I was not there: and that they had lived so many years with them now, that if it was adultery, it was past remedy; nothing could be done in it now.

"Sir," says he, "asking your pardon for such freedom, you are right in this, that, it being done in your absence, you could not be charged with that part of the crime; but, I beseech you, flatter not yourself that you are not, therefore, under an obligation to do your utmost now to put an end to it. You should legally and effectually marry them; and as, sir, my way of marrying may not be easy to reconcile them to, though it will be effectual, even by your own laws, so your way may be as well before God, and as valid among men. I mean by a written contract signed by both man and woman, and by all the witnesses present, which all the laws of Europe would decree to be valid."

I was amazed to see so much true piety, and so much sincerity of zeal, besides the unusual impartiality in his discourse as to his own party or church, and such true warmth for preserving people that he had no knowledge of or relation to from transgressing the laws of God. But recollecting what he had said of marrying them by a written contract, which I knew he would stand to, I returned it back upon him, and told him I granted all that he had said to be just, and on his part very kind; that I would discourse with the men upon the point now, when I came to them; and I knew no reason why they should scruple to let him marry them all, which I knew well enough would be granted to be as authentic and valid in England as if they were married by one of our own clergymen.

I then pressed him to tell me what was the second complaint which he had to make, acknowledging that I was very much his debtor for the first, and thanking him heartily for it. He told me he would use the same freedom and plainness in the second, and hoped I would take it as well; and this was, that notwithstanding these English subjects of mine, as he called them, had lived with these women almost seven years, had taught them to speak English, and even to read it, and that they were, as he perceived, women of tolerable understanding, and capable of instruction, yet they had not, to this hour, taught them anything of the Christian religion—no, not so much as to know there was a God, or a worship, or in what manner God was to be served, or that their own idolatry, and worshipping they knew not whom, was false and absurd. This he said was an unaccountable neglect, and what God would certainly call them to account for, and perhaps at last take the work out of their hands. He spoke this very affectionately and warmly.

"I am persuaded," says he, "had those men lived in the savage country whence their wives came, the savages would have taken more pains to have brought them to be idolaters, and to worship the devil, than any of these men, so far as I can see, have taken with them to teach the knowledge of the true God. Now, sir," said he, "though I do not acknowledge your religion, or you mine, yet we would be glad to see the devil's servants and the subjects of his kingdom taught to know religion; and that they might, at least, hear of God and a Redeemer, and the resurrection, and of a future state—things which we all believe; that they might, at least, be so much nearer coming into the bosom of the true Church than they are now in the public profession of idolatry and devil-worship."

I could hold no longer: I took him in my arms and embraced him eagerly. "How far," said I to him, "have I been from understanding the most essential part of a Christian, viz. to love the interest of the Christian Church, and the good of other men's souls! I scarce have known what belongs to the being a Christian."—"Oh, sir! do not say so," replied he; "this thing is not your fault."—"No," said I; "but why did I never lay it to heart as well as you?"—"It is not too late yet," said he; "be not too forward to condemn yourself."—"But what can be done now?" said I: "you see I am going away."—"Will you give me leave to talk with these poor men about it?"—"Yes, with all my heart," said I: "and oblige them to give heed to what you say too."—"As to that," said he, "we must leave them to the mercy of Christ; but it is your business to assist them, encourage them, and instruct them; and if you give me leave, and God His blessing, I do not doubt but the poor ignorant souls shall be brought home to the great circle of Christianity, if not into the particular faith we all embrace, and that even while you stay here." Upon this I said, "I shall not only give you leave, but give you a thousand thanks for it."

I now pressed him for the third article in which we were to blame. "Why, really," says he, "it is of the same nature. It is about your poor savages, who are, as I may say, your conquered subjects. It is a maxim, sir, that is or ought to be received among all Christians, of what church or pretended church soever, that the Christian knowledge ought to be propagated by all possible means and on all possible occasions. It is on this principle that our Church sends missionaries into Persia, India, and China; and that our clergy, even of the superior sort, willingly engage in the most hazardous voyages, and the most dangerous residence amongst murderers and barbarians, to teach them the knowledge of the true God, and to bring them over to embrace the Christian faith. Now, sir, you have such an opportunity here to have six or seven and thirty poor savages brought over from a state of idolatry to the knowledge of God, their Maker and Redeemer, that

I wonder how you can pass such an occasion of doing good, which is really worth the expense of a man's whole life."

I was now struck dumb indeed, and had not one word to say. I had here the spirit of true Christian zeal for God and religion before me. As for me, I had not so much as entertained a thought of this in my heart before, and I believe I should not have thought of it; for I looked upon these savages as slaves, and people whom, had we not had any work for them to do, we would have used as such, or would have been glad to have transported them to any part of the world; for our business was to get rid of them, and we would all have been satisfied if they had been sent to any country, so they had never seen their own. I was confounded at his discourse, and knew not what answer to make him.

He looked earnestly at me, seeing my confusion. "Sir," says he, "I shall be very sorry if what I have said gives you any offence."—"No, no," said I, "I am offended with nobody but myself; but I am perfectly confounded, not only to think that I should never take any notice of this before, but with reflecting what notice I am able to take of it now. You know, sir," said I, "what circumstances I am in; I am bound to the East Indies in a ship freighted by merchants, and to whom it would be an insufferable piece of injustice to detain their ship here, the men lying all this while at victuals and wages on the owners' account. It is true, I agreed to be allowed twelve days here, and if I stay more, I must pay three pounds sterling *per diem* demurrage; nor can I stay upon demurrage above eight days more, and I have been here thirteen already; so that I am perfectly unable to engage in this work unless I would suffer myself to be left behind here again; in which case, if this single ship should miscarry in any part of her voyage, I should be just in the same condition that I was left in here at first, and from which I have been so wonderfully delivered." He owned the case was very hard upon me as to my voyage; but laid it home upon my conscience whether the blessing of saving thirty-seven souls was not worth venturing all I had in the world for. I was not so sensible of that as he was. I replied to him thus: "Why, sir, it is a valuable thing, indeed, to be an instrument in God's hand to convert thirty-seven heathens to the knowledge of Christ: but as you are an ecclesiastic, and are given over to the work, so it seems so naturally to fall in the way of your profession; how is it, then, that you do not rather offer yourself to undertake it than to press me to do it?"

Upon this he faced about just before me, as he walked along, and putting me to a full stop, made me a very low bow. "I most heartily thank God and you, sir," said he, "for giving me so evident a call to so blessed a work; and if you think yourself discharged from it, and desire me to undertake it, I will most readily do it, and think it a happy reward for all the hazards and difficulties of such a broken, disappointed voyage as I have met with, that I am dropped at last into so glorious a work."

I discovered a kind of rapture in his face while he spoke this to me; his eyes sparkled like fire; his face glowed, and his colour came and went; in a word, he was fired with the joy of being embarked in such a work. I paused a considerable while before I could tell what to say to him; for I was really surprised to find a man of such sincerity, and who seemed possessed of a zeal beyond the ordinary rate of men. But after I had considered it a while, I asked him seriously if he was in earnest, and that he would venture, on the single consideration of an attempt to convert those poor people, to be locked up in an unplanted island for perhaps his life, and at last might not know whether he should be able to do them good or not? He turned short upon me, and asked me what I called a venture? "Pray, sir," said he, "what do you think I consented to go in your ship to the East Indies for?"—"ay," said I, "that I know not, unless it was to preach to the Indians."—"Doubtless it was," said he; "and do you think, if I can convert these thirty-seven men to the faith of Jesus Christ, it is not worth my time, though I should never be fetched off the island again?—nay, is it not infinitely of more worth to save so many souls than my life is, or the life of twenty more of the same profession? Yes, sir," says he, "I would give God thanks all my days if I could be made the happy instrument of saving the souls of those poor men, though I were never to get my foot off this island or see my native country any more. But since you will honour me with putting me into this work, for which I will pray for you all the days of my life, I have one humble petition to you besides."—"What is that?" said I.—"Why," says he, "it is, that you will leave your man Friday with me, to be my interpreter to them, and to assist me; for without some help I cannot speak to them, or they to me."

I was sensibly touched at his requesting Friday, because I could not think of parting with him, and that for many reasons: he had been the companion of my travels; he was not only faithful to me, but sincerely affectionate to the last degree; and I had resolved to do something considerable for him if he out-lived me, as it was probable he would. Then I knew that, as I had bred Friday up to be a Protestant, it would quite confound him to bring him to embrace another religion; and he would never, while his eyes were open, believe that his old master was a heretic, and would be damned; and this might in the end ruin the poor fellow's principles, and so turn him back again to his first idolatry. However, a sudden thought relieved me in this strait, and it was this: I told him I could not say that I was willing to part with Friday on any account whatever, though a work that to him was of more value than his life ought to be of much more value than the keeping or parting with a servant. On the other hand, I was persuaded that Friday would by no means agree to part with me; and I could not force him to it without his consent, without manifest injustice; because I had promised I would never send him away, and he had promised and engaged that he would never leave me, unless I sent him away.

He seemed very much concerned at it, for he had no rational access to these poor people, seeing he did not understand one word of their language, nor they one of his. To remove this difficulty, I told him Friday's father had learned Spanish, which I found he also understood, and he should serve him as an interpreter. So he was much better satisfied, and nothing could persuade him but he would stay and endeavour to convert them; but Providence gave another very happy turn to all this.

I come back now to the first part of his objections. When we came to the Englishmen, I sent for them all together, and after some account given them of what I had done for them, viz. what necessary things I had provided for them, and how they were distributed, which they were very sensible of, and very thankful for, I began to talk to them of the scandalous life they led, and gave them a full account of the notice the clergyman had taken of it; and arguing how unchristian and irreligious a life it was, I first asked them if they were married men or bachelors? They soon explained their condition to me, and showed that two of them were widowers, and the other three were single men, or bachelors. I asked them with what conscience they could take these women, and call them their wives, and have so many children by them, and not be lawfully married to them? They all gave me the answer I expected, viz. that there was nobody to marry them; that they agreed before the governor to keep them as their wives, and to maintain them and own them as their wives; and they thought, as things stood with them, they were as legally married as if they had been married by a parson and with all the formalities in the world.

I told them that no doubt they were married in the sight of God, and were bound in conscience to keep them as their wives; but that the laws of men being otherwise, they might desert the poor women and children hereafter; and that their wives, being poor desolate women, friendless and moneyless, would have no way to help themselves. I therefore told them that unless I was assured of their honest intent, I could do nothing for them, but would take care that what I did should be for the women and children without them; and that, unless they would give me some assurances that they would marry the women, I could not think it was convenient they should continue together as man and wife; for that it was both scandalous to men and offensive to God, who they could not think would bless them if they went on thus.

All this went on as I expected; and they told me, especially Will Atkins, who now seemed to speak for the rest, that they loved their wives as well as if they had been born in their own native country, and would not leave them on any account whatever; and they did verily believe that their wives were as virtuous and as modest, and did, to the utmost of their skill, as much for them and for their children, as any woman could possibly do: and they would not part with them on any account. Will Atkins, for his own particular, added that if any man would take him away, and offer to carry him home to England, and make him captain of the best man-of-war in the navy, he would not go with him if he might not carry his wife and children with him; and if there was a clergyman in the ship, he would be married to her now with all his heart.

This was just as I would have it. The priest was not with me at that moment, but he was not far off; so to try him further, I told him I had a clergyman with me, and, if he was sincere, I would have him married next morning, and bade him consider of it, and talk with the rest. He said, as for himself, he need not consider of it at all, for he was very ready to do it, and was glad I had a minister with me, and he believed they would be all willing also. I then told him that my friend, the minister, was a Frenchman, and could not speak English, but I would act the clerk between them. He never so much as asked me whether he was a Papist or Protestant, which was, indeed, what I was afraid of. We then parted, and I went back to my clergyman, and Will Atkins went in to talk with his companions. I desired the French gentleman not to say anything to them till the business was thoroughly ripe; and I told him what answer the men had given me.

Before I went from their quarter they all came to me and told me they had been considering what I had said; that they were glad to hear I had a clergyman in my company, and they were very willing to give me the satisfaction I desired, and to be formally married as soon as I pleased; for they were far from desiring to part with their wives, and that they meant nothing but what was very honest when they chose them. So I appointed them to meet me the next morning; and, in the meantime, they should let their wives know the meaning of the marriage law; and that it was not only to prevent any scandal, but also to oblige them that they should not forsake them, whatever might happen.

The women were easily made sensible of the meaning of the thing, and were very well satisfied with it, as, indeed, they had reason to be: so they failed not to attend all together at my apartment next morning, where I brought out my clergyman; and though he had not on a minister's gown, after the manner of England, or the habit of a priest, after the manner of France, yet having a black vest something like a cassock, with a sash round it, he did not look very unlike a minister; and as for his language, I was his interpreter. But the seriousness of his behaviour to them, and the scruples he made of marrying the women, because they were not baptized and professed Christians, gave them an exceeding reverence for his person; and there was no need, after that, to inquire whether he was a clergyman or not. Indeed, I was afraid his scruples would have been carried so far as that he would not have married them at all; nay, notwithstanding all I was able to say to him, he resisted me, though modestly, yet very steadily, and at last refused absolutely to marry them, unless he had first talked with the men and the women too; and though at first I was a little backward to it, yet at last I agreed to it with a good will, perceiving the sincerity of his design.

When he came to them he let them know that I had acquainted him with their circumstances, and with the present design; that he was very willing to perform that part of his function, and marry them, as I had desired; but that before he could do it, he must take the liberty to talk with them. He told them that in the sight of all indifferent men, and in the sense of the laws of society, they had lived all this while in a state of sin; and that it was true that nothing but the consenting to marry, or effectually separating them from one another, could now put an end to it; but there was a difficulty in it, too, with respect to the laws of Christian matrimony, which he was not fully satisfied about, that of marrying one that is a professed Christian to a savage, an idolater, and a heathen—one that is not baptized; and yet that he did not see that there was time left to endeavour to persuade the women to be baptized, or to profess the name of Christ, whom they had, he doubted, heard nothing of, and without which they could not be baptized. He told them he doubted they were but indifferent Christians themselves; that they had but little knowledge of God or of His ways, and, therefore, he could not expect that they had said much to their wives on that head yet; but that unless they would promise him to use their endeavours with their wives to persuade them to become Christians, and would, as well as they could, instruct them in the knowledge and belief of God that made them, and to worship Jesus Christ that redeemed them, he could not marry them; for he would have no hand in joining Christians with savages, nor was it consistent with the principles of the Christian religion, and was, indeed, expressly forbidden in God's law.

They heard all this very attentively, and I delivered it very faithfully to them from his mouth, as near his own words as I could; only sometimes adding something of my own, to convince them how just it was, and that I was of his mind; and I always very carefully distinguished between what I said from myself and what were the clergyman's words. They told me it was very true what the gentleman said, that they were very indifferent Christians themselves, and that they had never talked to their wives about religion. "Lord, sir," says Will Atkins, "how should we teach them religion? Why, we know nothing ourselves; and besides, sir," said he, "should we talk to them of God and Jesus Christ, and heaven and hell, it would make them laugh at us, and ask us what we believe ourselves. And if we should tell them that we believe all the things we speak of to them, such as of good people going to heaven, and wicked people to the devil, they would ask us where we intend to go ourselves, that believe all this, and are such wicked fellows as we indeed are? Why, sir; 'tis enough to give them a surfeit of religion at first hearing; folks must have some religion themselves before they begin to teach other people."—"Will Atkins," said I to him, "though I am afraid that what you say has too much truth in it, yet can you not tell your wife she is in the wrong; that there is a God and a religion better than her own; that her gods are idols; that they can neither hear nor speak; that there is a great Being that made all things, and that can destroy all that He has made; that He rewards the good and punishes the bad; and that we are to be judged by Him at last for all we do here? You are not so ignorant but even nature itself will teach you that all this is true; and I am satisfied you know it all to be true, and believe it yourself."—"That is true, sir," said Atkins; "but with what face can I say anything to my wife of all this, when she will tell me immediately it cannot be true?"—"Not true!" said I; "what do you mean by that?"—"Why, sir," said he, "she will tell me it cannot be true that this God I shall tell her of can be just, or can punish or reward, since I am not punished and sent to the devil, that have been such a wicked creature as she knows I have been, even to her, and to everybody else; and that I should be suffered to live, that have been always acting so contrary to what I must tell her is good, and to what I ought to have done."—"Why, truly, Atkins," said I, "I am afraid thou speakest too much truth;" and with that I informed the clergyman of what Atkins had said, for he was impatient to know. "Oh," said the priest, "tell him there is one thing will make him the best minister in the world to his wife, and that is repentance; for none teach repentance like true penitents. He wants nothing but to repent, and then he will be so much the better qualified to instruct his wife; he will then be able to tell her that there is not only a God, and that He is the just rewarder of good and evil, but that He is a merciful Being, and with infinite goodness and long-suffering forbears to punish those that offend; waiting to be gracious, and willing not the death of a sinner, but rather that he should return and live; and even reserves damnation to the general day of retribution; that it is a clear evidence of God and of a future state that righteous men receive not their reward, or wicked men their punishment, till they come into another world; and this will lead him to teach his wife the doctrine of the resurrection and of the last judgment. Let him but repent himself, he will be an excellent preacher of repentance to his wife."

I repeated all this to Atkins, who looked very serious all the while, and, as we could easily perceive, was more than ordinarily affected with it; when being eager, and hardly suffering me to make an end, "I know all this, master," says he, "and a great deal more; but I have not the impudence to talk thus to my wife, when God and my conscience know, and my wife will be an undeniable evidence against me, that I have lived as if I had never heard of a God or future state, or anything about it; and to talk of my repenting, alas!" (and with that he fetched a deep sigh, and I could see that the tears stood in his eyes) "'tis past all that with me."—"Past it, Atkins?" said I: "what dost thou mean by that?"—"I know well enough what I mean," says he; "I mean 'tis too late, and that is too true."

I told the clergyman, word for word, what he said, and this affectionate man could not refrain from tears; but, recovering himself, said to me, "Ask him but one question. Is he easy that it is too late; or is he troubled, and wishes it were not so?" I put the question fairly to Atkins; and he answered with a great deal of passion, "How could any man be easy in a condition that must certainly end in eternal destruction? that he was far from being easy; but that, on the contrary, he believed it would one time or other ruin him."—"What do you mean by that?" said I.—"Why," he said, "he believed he should one time or other cut his throat, to put an end to the terror of it."

The clergyman shook his head, with great concern in his face, when I told him all this; but turning quick to me upon it, says, "If that be his case, we may assure him it is not too late; Christ will give him repentance. But pray," says he, "explain this to him: that as no man is saved but by Christ, and the merit of His passion procuring divine mercy for him, how can it be too late for any man to receive mercy? Does he think he is able to sin beyond the power or reach of divine mercy? Pray tell him there may be a time when provoked mercy will no longer strive, and when God may refuse to hear, but that it is never too late for men to ask mercy; and we, that are Christ's servants, are commanded to preach mercy at all times, in the name of Jesus Christ, to all those that sincerely repent: so that it is never too late to repent."

I told Atkins all this, and he heard me with great earnestness; but it seemed as if he turned off the discourse to the rest, for he said to me he would go and have some talk with his wife; so he went out a while, and we talked to the rest. I perceived they were all stupidly ignorant as to matters of religion, as much as I was when I went rambling away from my father; yet there were none of them backward to hear what had been said; and all of them seriously promised that they would talk with their wives about it, and do their endeavours to persuade them to turn Christians.

The clergyman smiled upon me when I reported what answer they gave, but said nothing a good while; but at last, shaking his head, "We that are Christ's servants," says he, "can go no further than to exhort and instruct: and when men comply, submit to the reproof, and promise what we ask, 'tis all we can do; we are bound to accept their good words; but believe me, sir," said he, "whatever you may have known of the life of that man you call Will Atkin's, I believe he is the only sincere convert among them: I will not despair of the rest; but that man is apparently struck with the sense of his past life, and I doubt not, when he comes to talk of religion to his wife, he will talk himself effectually into it: for attempting to teach others is sometimes the best way of teaching ourselves. If that poor Atkins begins but once to talk seriously of Jesus Christ to his wife, he will assuredly talk himself into a thorough convert, make himself a penitent, and who knows what may follow."

Upon this discourse, however, and their promising, as above, to endeavour to persuade their wives to embrace Christianity, he married the two other couple; but Will Atkins and his wife were not yet come in. After this, my clergyman, waiting a while, was curious to know where Atkins was gone, and turning to me, said, "I entreat you, sir, let us walk out of your labyrinth here and look; I daresay we shall find this poor man somewhere or other talking seriously to his wife, and teaching her already something of religion." I began to be of the same mind; so we went out together, and I carried him a way which none knew but myself, and where the trees were so very thick that it was not easy to see through the thicket of leaves, and far harder to see in than to see out: when, coming to the edge of the wood, I saw Atkins and his tawny wife sitting under the shade of a bush, very eager in discourse: I stopped short till my clergyman came up to me, and then having showed him where they were, we stood and looked very steadily at them a good while. We observed him very earnest with her, pointing up to the sun, and to every quarter of the heavens, and then down to the earth, then out to the sea, then to himself, then to her, to the woods, to the trees. "Now," says the clergyman, "you see my words are made good, the man preaches to her; mark him now, he is telling her that our God has made him, her, and the heavens, the earth, the sea, the woods, the trees, &c."—"I believe he is," said I. Immediately we perceived Will Atkins start upon his feet, fall down on his knees, and lift up both his hands. We supposed he said something, but we could not hear him; it was too far for that. He did not continue kneeling half a minute, but comes and sits down again by his wife, and talks to her again; we perceived then the woman very attentive, but whether she said anything to him we could not tell. While the poor fellow was upon his knees I could see the tears run plentifully down my clergyman's cheeks, and I could hardly forbear myself; but it was a great affliction to us both that we were not near enough to hear anything that passed between them. Well, however, we could come no nearer for fear of disturbing them: so we resolved to see an end of this piece of still conversation, and it spoke loud enough to us without the help of voice. He sat down again, as I have said, close by her, and talked again earnestly to her, and two or three times we could see him embrace her most passionately; another time we saw him take out his handkerchief and wipe her eyes, and then kiss her again with a kind of transport very unusual; and after several of these things, we saw him on a sudden jump up again, and lend her his hand to help her up, when immediately leading her by the hand a step or two, they both kneeled down together, and continued so about two minutes.

My friend could bear it no longer, but cries out aloud, "St. Paul! St. Paul! behold he prayeth." I was afraid Atkins would hear him, therefore I entreated him to withhold himself a while, that we might see an end of the scene, which to me, I must confess, was the most affecting that ever I saw in my life. Well, he strove with himself for a while, but was in such raptures to think that the poor heathen woman was become a Christian, that he was not able to contain himself; he wept several times, then throwing up his hands and crossing his breast, said over several things ejaculatory, and by the way of giving God thanks for so miraculous a testimony of the success of our endeavours. Some he spoke softly, and I could not well hear others; some things he said in Latin, some in French; then two or three times the tears would interrupt him, that he could not speak at all; but I begged that he would contain himself, and let us more narrowly and fully observe what was before us, which he did for a time, the scene not being near ended yet; for after the poor man and his wife were risen again from their knees, we observed he stood talking still eagerly to her, and we observed her motion, that she was greatly affected with what he said, by her frequently lifting up her hands, laying her hand to her breast, and such other postures as express the greatest seriousness and attention; this continued about half a quarter of an hour, and then they walked away, so we could see no more of them in that situation.

I took this interval to say to the clergyman, first, that I was glad to see the particulars we had both been witnesses to; that, though I was hard enough of belief in such cases, yet that I began to think it was all very sincere here, both in the man and his wife, however ignorant they might both be, and I hoped such a beginning would yet have a more happy end. "But, my friend," added I, "will you give me leave to start one difficulty here? I cannot tell how to object the least thing against that affectionate concern which you show for the turning of the poor people from their paganism to the Christian religion; but how does this comfort you, while these people are, in your account, out of the pale of the Catholic Church, without which you believe there is no salvation? so that you esteem these but heretics, as effectually lost as the pagans themselves."

To this he answered, with abundance of candour, thus: "Sir, I am a Catholic of the Roman Church, and a priest of the order of St. Benedict, and I embrace all the principles of the Roman faith; but yet, if you will believe me, and that I do not speak in compliment to you, or in respect to my circumstances and your civilities; I say nevertheless, I do not look upon you, who call yourselves reformed, without some charity. I dare not say (though I know it is our opinion in general) that you cannot be saved; I will by no means limit the mercy of Christ so far as think that He cannot receive you into the bosom of His Church, in a manner to us unperceivable; and I hope you have the same charity for us: I pray daily for you being all restored to Christ's Church, by whatsoever method He, who is all-wise, is pleased to direct. In the meantime, surely you will allow it consists with me as a Roman to distinguish far between a Protestant and a pagan; between one that calls on Jesus Christ, though in a way which I do not think is according to the true faith, and a savage or a barbarian, that knows no God, no Christ, no Redeemer; and if you are not within the pale of the Catholic Church, we hope you are nearer being restored to it than those who know nothing of God or of His Church: and I rejoice, therefore, when I see this poor man, who you say has been a profligate, and almost a murderer kneel down and pray to Jesus Christ, as we suppose he did, though not fully enlightened; believing that God, from whom every such work proceeds, will sensibly touch his heart, and bring him to the further knowledge of that truth in His own time; and if God shall influence this poor man to convert and instruct the ignorant savage, his wife, I can never believe that he shall be cast away himself. And have I not reason, then, to rejoice, the nearer any are brought to the knowledge of Christ, though they may not be brought quite home into the bosom of the Catholic Church just at the time when I desire it, leaving it to the goodness of Christ to perfect His work in His own time, and in his own way? Certainly, I would rejoice if all the savages in America were brought, like this poor woman, to pray to God, though they were all to be Protestants at first, rather than they should continue pagans or heathens; firmly believing, that He that had bestowed the first light on them would farther illuminate them with a beam of His heavenly grace, and bring them into the pale of His Church when He should see good."

Chapter VII—CONVERSATION BETWIXT WILL ATKINS AND HIS WIFE

I was astonished at the sincerity and temper of this pious Papist, as much as I was oppressed by the power of his reasoning; and it presently occurred to my thoughts, that if such a temper was universal, we might be all Catholic Christians, whatever Church or particular profession we joined in; that a spirit of charity would soon work us all up into right principles; and as he thought that the like charity would make us all Catholics, so I told him I believed, had all the members of his Church the like moderation, they would soon all be Protestants. And there we left that part; for we never disputed at all. However, I talked to him another way, and taking him by the hand, "My friend," says I, "I wish all the clergy of the Romish Church were blessed with such moderation, and had an equal share of your charity. I am entirely of your opinion; but I must tell you that if you should preach such doctrine in Spain or Italy, they would put you into the Inquisition."—"It may be so," said he; "I know not what they would do in Spain or Italy; but I will not say they would be the better Christians for that severity; for I am sure there is no heresy in abounding with charity."

Well, as Will Atkins and his wife were gone, our business there was over, so we went back our own way; and when we came back, we found them waiting to be called in. Observing this, I asked my clergyman if we should discover to him that we had seen him under the bush or not; and it was his opinion we should not, but that we should talk to him first, and hear what he would say to us; so we called him in alone, nobody being in the place but ourselves, and I began by asking him some particulars about his parentage and education. He told me frankly enough that his father was a clergyman who would have taught him well, but that he, Will Atkins, despised all instruction and correction; and by his brutish conduct cut the thread of all his father's comforts and shortened his days, for that he broke his heart by the most ungrateful, unnatural return for the most affectionate treatment a father ever gave.

In what he said there seemed so much sincerity of repentance, that it painfully affected me. I could not but reflect that I, too, had shortened the life of a good, tender father by my bad conduct and obstinate self-will. I was, indeed, so surprised with what he had told me, that I thought, instead of my going about to teach and instruct him, the man was made a teacher and instructor to me in a most unexpected manner.

I laid all this before the young clergyman, who was greatly affected with it, and said to me, "Did I not say, sir, that when this man was converted he would preach to us all? I tell you, sir, if this one man be made a true penitent, there will be no need of me; he will make Christians of all in the island."—But having a little composed myself, I renewed my discourse with Will Atkins. "But, Will," said I, "how comes the sense of this matter to touch you just now?"

W.A.—Sir, you have set me about a work that has struck a dart though my very soul; I have been talking about God and religion to my wife, in order, as you directed me, to make a Christian of her, and she has preached such a sermon to me as I shall never forget while I live.

R.C.—No, no, it is not your wife has preached to you; but when you were moving religious arguments to her, conscience has flung them back upon you.

W.A.—Ay, sir, with such force as is not to be resisted.

R.C.—Pray, Will, let us know what passed between you and your wife; for I know something of it already.

W.A.—Sir, it is impossible to give you a full account of it; I am too full to hold it, and yet have no tongue to express it; but let her have said what she will, though I cannot give you an account of it, this I can tell you, that I have resolved to amend and reform my life.

R.C.—But tell us some of it: how did you begin, Will? For this has been an extraordinary case, that is certain. She has preached a sermon, indeed, if she has wrought this upon you.

W.A.—Why, I first told her the nature of our laws about marriage, and what the reasons were that men and women were obliged to enter into such compacts as it was neither in the power of one nor other to break; that otherwise, order and justice could not be maintained, and men would run from their wives, and abandon their children, mix confusedly with one another, and neither families be kept entire, nor inheritances be settled by legal descent.

R.C.—You talk like a civilian, Will. Could you make her understand what you meant by inheritance and families? They know no such things among the savages, but marry anyhow, without regard to relation, consanguinity, or family; brother and sister, nay, as I have been told, even the father and the daughter, and the son and the mother.

W.A.—I believe, sir, you are misinformed, and my wife assures me of the contrary, and that they abhor it; perhaps, for any further relations, they may not be so exact as we are; but she tells me never in the near relationship you speak of.

R.C.—Well, what did she say to what you told her?

W.A.—She said she liked it very well, as it was much better than in her country.

R.C.—But did you tell her what marriage was?

W.A.—Ay, ay, there began our dialogue. I asked her if she would be married to me our way. She asked me what way that was; I told her marriage was appointed by God; and here we had a strange talk together, indeed, as ever man and wife had, I believe.

N.B.—This dialogue between Will Atkins and his wife, which I took down in writing just after he told it me, was as follows:—

Wife.—Appointed by your God!—Why, have you a God in your country?

W.A.—Yes, my dear, God is in every country.

Wife.—No your God in my country; my country have the great old Benamuckee God.

W.A.—Child, I am very unfit to show you who God is; God is in heaven and made the heaven and the earth, the sea, and all that in them is.

Wife.—No makee de earth; no you God makee all earth; no makee my country.

[Will Atkins laughed a little at her expression of God not making her country.]

Wife.—No laugh; why laugh me? This no ting to laugh.

[He was justly reproved by his wife, for she was more serious than he at first.]

W.A.—That's true, indeed; I will not laugh any more, my dear.

Wife.—Why you say you God makee all?

W.A.—Yes, child, our God made the whole world, and you, and me, and all things; for He is the only true God, and there is no God but Him. He lives for ever in heaven.

Wife.—Why you no tell me long ago?

W.A.—That's true, indeed; but I have been a wicked wretch, and have not only forgotten to acquaint thee with anything before, but have lived without God in the world myself.

Wife.—What, have you a great God in your country, you no know Him? No say O to Him? No do good ting for Him? That no possible.

W.A.—It is true; though, for all that, we live as if there was no God in heaven, or that He had no power on earth.

Wife.—But why God let you do so? Why He no makee you good live?

W.A.—It is all our own fault.

Wife.—But you say me He is great, much great, have much great power; can makee kill when He will: why He no makee kill when you no serve Him? no say O to Him? no be good mans?

W.A.—That is true, He might strike me dead; and I ought to expect it, for I have been a wicked wretch, that is true; but God is merciful, and does not deal with us as we deserve.

Wife.—But then do you not tell God thankee for that too?

W. A.—No, indeed, I have not thanked God for His mercy, any more than I have feared God from His power.

Wife.—Then you God no God; me no think, believe He be such one, great much power, strong: no makee kill you, though you make Him much angry.

W.A.—What, will my wicked life hinder you from believing in God? What a dreadful creature am I! and what a sad truth is it, that the horrid lives of Christians hinder the conversion of heathens!

Wife.—How me tink you have great much God up there [she points up to heaven], and yet no do well, no do good ting? Can He tell? Sure He no tell what you do?

W.A.—Yes, yes, He knows and sees all things; He hears us speak, sees what we do, knows what we think though we do not speak.

Wife.—What! He no hear you curse, swear, speak de great damn?

W.A.—Yes, yes, He hears it all.

Wife.—Where be then the much great power strong?

W.A.—He is merciful, that is all we can say for it; and this proves Him to be the true God; He is God, and not man, and therefore we are not consumed.

[Here Will Atkins told us he was struck with horror to think how he could tell his wife so clearly that God sees, and hears, and knows the secret thoughts of the heart, and all that we do, and yet that he had dared to do all the vile things he had done.]

Wife.—Merciful! What you call dat?

W.A.—He is our Father and Maker, and He pities and spares us.

Wife.—So then He never makee kill, never angry when you do wicked; then He no good Himself, or no great able.

W.A.—Yes, yes, my dear, He is infinitely good and infinitely great, and able to punish too; and sometimes, to show His justice and vengeance, He lets fly His anger to destroy sinners and make examples; many are cut off in their sins.

Wife.—But no makee kill you yet; then He tell you, maybe, that He no makee you kill: so you makee the bargain with Him, you do bad thing, He no be angry at you when He be angry at other mans.

W.A.—No, indeed, my sins are all presumptions upon His goodness; and He would be infinitely just if He destroyed me, as He has done other men.

Wife.—Well, and yet no kill, no makee you dead: what you say to Him for that? You no tell Him thankee for all that too?

W.A.—I am an unthankful, ungrateful dog, that is true.

Wife.—Why He no makee you much good better? you say He makee you.

W.A.—He made me as He made all the world: it is I have deformed myself and abused His goodness, and made myself an abominable wretch.

Wife.—I wish you makee God know me. I no makee Him angry—I no do bad wicked thing.

[Here Will Atkins said his heart sunk within him to hear a poor untaught creature desire to be taught to know God, and he such a wicked wretch, that he could not say one word to her about God, but what the reproach of his own carriage would make most irrational to her to believe; nay, that already she had told him that she could not believe in God, because he, that was so wicked, was not destroyed.]

W.A.—My dear, you mean, you wish I could teach you to know God, not God to know you; for He knows you already, and every thought in your heart.

Wife.—Why, then, He know what I say to you now: He know me wish to know Him. How shall me know who makee me?

W.A.—Poor creature, He must teach thee: I cannot teach thee. I will pray to Him to teach thee to know Him, and forgive me, that am unworthy to teach thee.

[The poor fellow was in such an agony at her desiring him to make her know God, and her wishing to know Him, that he said he fell down on his knees before her, and prayed to God to enlighten her mind with the saving knowledge of Jesus Christ, and to pardon his sins, and accept of his being the unworthy instrument of instructing her in the principles of religion: after which he sat down by her again, and their dialogue went on. This was the time when we saw him kneel down and hold up his hands.]

Wife.—What you put down the knee for? What you hold up the hand for? What you say? Who you speak to? What is all that?

W.A.—My dear, I bow my knees in token of my submission to Him that made me: I said O to Him, as you call it, and as your old men do to their idol Benamuckee; that is, I prayed to Him.

Wife.—What say you O to Him for?

W.A.—I prayed to Him to open your eyes and your understanding, that you may know Him, and be accepted by Him.

Wife.—Can He do that too?

W.A.—Yes, He can: He can do all things.

Wife.—But now He hear what you say?

W.A.—Yes, He has bid us pray to Him, and promised to hear us.

Wife.—Bid you pray? When He bid you? How He bid you? What you hear Him speak?

W.A.—No, we do not hear Him speak; but He has revealed Himself many ways to us.

[Here he was at a great loss to make her understand that God has revealed Himself to us by His word, and what His word was; but at last he told it to her thus.]

W.A.—God has spoken to some good men in former days, even from heaven, by plain words; and God has inspired good men by His Spirit; and they have written all His laws down in a book.

Wife.—Me no understand that; where is book?

W.A.—Alas! my poor creature, I have not this book; but I hope I shall one time or other get it for you, and help you to read it.

[Here he embraced her with great affection, but with inexpressible grief that he had not a Bible.]

Wife.—But how you makee me know that God teachee them to write that book?

W.A.—By the same rule that we know Him to be God.

Wife.—What rule? What way you know Him?

W.A.—Because He teaches and commands nothing but what is good, righteous, and holy, and tends to make us perfectly good, as well as perfectly happy; and because He forbids and commands us to avoid all that is wicked, that is evil in itself, or evil in its consequence.

Wife.—That me would understand, that me fain see; if He teachee all good thing, He makee all good thing, He give all thing, He hear me when I say O to Him, as you do just now; He makee me good if I wish to be good; He spare me, no makee kill me, when I no be good: all this you say He do, yet He be great God; me take, think, believe Him to be great God; me say O to Him with you, my dear.

Here the poor man could forbear no longer, but raised her up, made her kneel by him, and he prayed to God aloud to instruct her in the knowledge of Himself, by His Spirit; and that by some good providence, if possible, she might, some time or other, come to have a Bible, that she might read the word of God, and be taught by it to know Him. This was the time that we saw him lift her up by the hand, and saw him kneel down by her, as above.

They had several other discourses, it seems, after this; and particularly she made him promise that, since he confessed his own life had been a wicked, abominable course of provocations against God, that he would reform it, and not make God angry any more, lest He should make him dead, as she called it, and then she would be left alone, and never be taught to know this God better; and lest he should be miserable, as he had told her wicked men would be after death.

This was a strange account, and very affecting to us both, but particularly to the young clergyman; he was, indeed, wonderfully surprised with it, but under the greatest affliction imaginable that he could not talk to her, that he could not speak English to make her understand him; and as she spoke but very broken English, he could not understand her; however, he turned himself to me, and told me that he believed that there must be more to do with this woman than to marry her. I did not understand him at first; but at length he explained himself, viz. that she ought to be baptized. I agreed with him in that part readily, and wished it to be done presently. "No, no; hold, sir," says he; "though I would have her be baptized, by all means, for I must observe that Will Atkins, her husband, has indeed brought her, in a wonderful manner, to be willing to embrace a religious life, and has given her just ideas of the being of a God; of His power, justice, and mercy: yet I desire to know of him if he has said anything to her of Jesus Christ, and of the salvation of sinners; of the nature of faith in Him, and redemption by Him; of the Holy Spirit, the resurrection, the last judgment, and the future state."

I called Will Atkins again, and asked him; but the poor fellow fell immediately into tears, and told us he had said something to her of all those things, but that he was himself so wicked a creature, and his own conscience so reproached him with his horrid, ungodly life, that he trembled at the apprehensions that her knowledge of him should lessen the attention she should give to those things, and make her rather contemn religion than receive it; but he was assured, he said, that her mind was so disposed to receive due impressions of all those things, and that if I would but discourse with her, she would make it appear to my satisfaction that my labour would not be lost upon her.

Accordingly I called her in, and placing myself as interpreter between my religious priest and the woman, I entreated him to begin with her; but sure such a sermon was never preached by a Popish priest in these latter ages of the world; and as I told him, I thought he had all the zeal, all the knowledge, all the sincerity of a Christian, without the error of a Roman Catholic; and that I took him to be such a clergyman as the Roman bishops were before the Church of Rome assumed spiritual sovereignty over the consciences of men. In a word, he brought the poor woman to embrace the knowledge of Christ, and of redemption by Him, not with wonder and astonishment only, as she did the first notions of a God, but with joy and faith; with an affection, and a surprising degree of understanding, scarce to be imagined, much less to be expressed; and, at her own request, she was baptized.

When he was preparing to baptize her, I entreated him that he would perform that office with some caution, that the man might not perceive he was of the Roman Church, if possible, because of other ill consequences which might attend a difference among us in that very religion which we were instructing the other in. He told me that as he had no consecrated chapel, nor proper things for the office, I should see he would do it in a manner that I should not know by it that he was a Roman Catholic myself, if I had not known it before; and so he did; for saying only some words over to himself in Latin, which I could not understand, he poured a whole dishful of water upon the woman's head, pronouncing in French, very loud, "Mary" (which was the name her husband desired me to give her, for I was her godfather), "I baptize thee in the name of the Father, and of the Son, and of the Holy Ghost;" so that none could know anything by it what religion he was of. He gave the benediction afterwards in Latin, but either Will Atkins did not know but it was French, or else did not take notice of it at that time.

As soon as this was over we married them; and after the marriage was over, he turned to Will Atkins, and in a very affectionate manner exhorted him, not only to persevere in that good disposition he was in, but to support the convictions that were upon him by a resolution to reform his life: told him it was in vain to say he repented if he did not forsake his crimes; represented to him how God had honoured him with being the instrument of bringing his wife to the knowledge of the Christian religion, and that he should be careful he did not dishonour the grace of God; and that if he did, he would see the heathen a better Christian than himself; the savage converted, and the instrument cast away. He said a great many good things to them both; and then, recommending them to God's goodness, gave them the benediction again, I repeating everything to them in English; and thus ended the ceremony. I think it was the most pleasant and agreeable day to me that ever I passed in my whole life. But my clergyman had not done yet: his thoughts hung continually upon the conversion of the thirty-seven savages, and fain be would have stayed upon the island to have undertaken it; but I convinced him, first, that his undertaking was impracticable in itself; and, secondly, that perhaps I would put it into a way of being done in his absence to his satisfaction.

Having thus brought the affairs of the island to a narrow compass, I was preparing to go on board the ship, when the young man I had taken out of the famished ship's company came to me, and told me he understood I had a clergyman with me, and that I had caused the Englishmen to be married to the savages; that he had a match too, which he desired might be finished before I went, between two Christians, which he hoped would not be disagreeable to me.

I knew this must be the young woman who was his mother's servant, for there was no other Christian woman on the island: so I began to persuade him not to do anything of that kind rashly, or because be found himself in this solitary circumstance. I represented to him that he had some considerable substance in the world, and good friends, as I understood by himself, and the maid also; that the maid was not only poor, and a servant, but was unequal to him, she being six or seven and twenty years old, and he not above seventeen or eighteen; that he might very probably, with my assistance, make a remove from this wilderness, and come into his own country again; and that then it would be a thousand to one but he would repent his choice, and the dislike of that circumstance might be disadvantageous to both. I was going to say more, but he interrupted me, smiling, and told me, with a great deal of modesty, that I mistook in my guesses—that he had nothing of that kind in his thoughts; and he was very glad to hear that I had an intent of putting them in a way to see their own country again; and nothing should have made him think of staying there, but that the voyage I was going was so exceeding long and hazardous, and would carry him quite out of the reach of all his friends; that he had nothing to desire of me but that I would settle him in some little property in the island where he was, give him a servant or two, and some few necessaries, and he would live here like a planter, waiting the good time when, if ever I returned to England, I would redeem him. He hoped I would not be unmindful of him when I came to England: that he would give me some letters to his friends in London, to let them know how good I had been to him, and in what part of the world and what circumstances I had left him in: and he promised me that whenever I redeemed him, the plantation, and all the improvements he had made upon it, let the value be what it would, should be wholly mine.

His discourse was very prettily delivered, considering his youth, and was the more agreeable to me, because he told me positively the match was not for himself. I gave him all possible assurances that if I lived to come safe to England, I would deliver his letters, and do his business effectually; and that he might depend I should never forget the circumstances I had left him in. But still I was impatient to know who was the person to be married; upon which he told me it was my Jack-of-all-trades and his maid Susan. I was most agreeably surprised when he named the match; for, indeed, I thought it very suitable. The character of that man I have given already; and as for the maid, she was a very honest, modest, sober, and religious young woman: had a very good share of sense, was agreeable enough in her person, spoke very handsomely and to the purpose, always with decency and good manners, and was neither too backward to speak when requisite, nor impertinently forward when it was not her business; very handy and housewifely, and an excellent manager; fit, indeed, to have been governess to the whole island; and she knew very well how to behave in every respect.

The match being proposed in this manner, we married them the same day; and as I was father at the altar, and gave her away, so I gave her a portion; for I appointed her and her husband a handsome large space of ground for their plantation; and indeed this match, and the proposal the young gentleman made to give him a small property in the island, put me upon parcelling it out amongst them, that they might not quarrel afterwards about their situation.

This sharing out the land to them I left to Will Atkins, who was now grown a sober, grave, managing fellow, perfectly reformed, exceedingly pious and religious; and, as far as I may be allowed to speak positively in such a case, I verily believe he was a true penitent. He divided things so justly, and so much to every one's satisfaction, that they only desired one general writing under my hand for the whole, which I caused to be drawn up, and signed and sealed, setting out the bounds and situation of every man's plantation, and testifying that I gave them thereby severally a right to the whole possession and inheritance of the respective plantations or farms, with their improvements, to them and their heirs, reserving all the rest of the island as my own property, and a certain rent for every particular plantation after eleven years, if I, or any one from me, or in my name, came to demand it, producing an attested copy of the same writing. As to the government and laws among them, I told them I was not capable of giving them better rules than they were able to give themselves; only I made them promise me to live in love and good neighbourhood with one another; and so I prepared to leave them.

One thing I must not omit, and that is, that being now settled in a kind of commonwealth among themselves, and having much business in hand, it was odd to have seven-and-thirty Indians live in a nook of the island, independent, and, indeed, unemployed; for except the providing themselves food, which they had difficulty enough to do sometimes, they had no manner of business or property to manage. I proposed, therefore, to the governor Spaniard that he should go to them, with Friday's father, and propose to them to remove, and either plant for themselves, or be taken into their several families as servants to be maintained for their labour, but without being absolute slaves; for I would not permit them to make them slaves by force, by any means; because they had their liberty given them by capitulation, as it were articles of surrender, which they ought not to break.

They most willingly embraced the proposal, and came all very cheerfully along with him: so we allotted them land and plantations, which three or four accepted of, but all the rest chose to be employed as servants in the several families we had settled. Thus my colony was in a manner settled as follows: The Spaniards possessed my original habitation, which was the capital city, and extended their plantations all along the side of the brook, which made the creek that I have so often described, as far as my bower; and as they increased their culture, it went always eastward. The English lived in the north-east part, where Will Atkins and his comrades began, and came on southward and south-west, towards the back part of the Spaniards; and every plantation had a great addition of land to take in, if they found occasion, so that they need not jostle one another for want of room. All the east end of the island was left uninhabited, that if any of the savages should come on shore there only for their customary barbarities, they might come and go; if they disturbed nobody, nobody would disturb them: and no doubt but they were often ashore, and went away again; for I never heard that the planters were ever attacked or disturbed any more.

Chapter VIII—SAILS FROM THE ISLAND FOR THE BRAZILS

It now came into my thoughts that I had hinted to my friend the clergyman that the work of converting the savages might perhaps be set on foot in his absence to his satisfaction, and I told him that now I thought that it was put in a fair way; for the savages, being thus divided among the Christians, if they would but every one of them do their part with those which came under their hands, I hoped it might have a very good effect.

He agreed presently in that, if they did their part. "But how," says he, "shall we obtain that of them?" I told him we would call them all together, and leave it in charge with them, or go to them, one by one, which he thought best; so we divided it—he to speak to the Spaniards, who were all Papists, and I to speak to the English, who were all Protestants; and we recommended it earnestly to them, and made them promise that they would never make any distinction of Papist or Protestant in their exhorting the savages to turn Christians, but teach them the general knowledge of the true God, and of their Saviour Jesus Christ; and they likewise promised us that they would never have any differences or disputes one with another about religion.

When I came to Will Atkins's house, I found that the young woman I have mentioned above, and Will Atkins's wife, were become intimates; and this prudent, religious young woman had perfected the work Will Atkins had begun; and though it was not above four days after what I have related, yet the new-baptized savage woman was made such a Christian as I have seldom heard of in all my observation or conversation in the world. It came next into my mind, in the morning before I went to them, that amongst all the needful things I had to leave with them I had not left them a Bible, in which I showed myself less considering for them than my good friend the widow was for me when she sent me the cargo of a hundred pounds from Lisbon, where she packed up three Bibles and a Prayer-book. However, the good woman's charity had a greater extent than ever she imagined, for they were reserved for the comfort and instruction of those that made much better use of them than I had done.

I took one of the Bibles in my pocket, and when I came to Will Atkins's tent, or house, and found the young woman and Atkins's baptized wife had been discoursing of religion together—for Will Atkins told it me with a great deal of joy—I asked if they were together now, and he said, "Yes"; so I went into the house, and he with me, and we found them together very earnest in discourse. "Oh, sir," says Will Atkins, "when God has sinners to reconcile to Himself, and aliens to bring home, He never wants a messenger; my wife has got a new instructor: I knew I was unworthy, as I was incapable of that work; that young woman has been sent hither from heaven—she is enough to convert a whole island of savages." The young woman blushed, and rose up to go away, but I desired her to sit-still; I told her she had a good work upon her hands, and I hoped God would bless her in it.

We talked a little, and I did not perceive that they had any book among them, though I did not ask; but I put my hand into my pocket, and pulled out my Bible. "Here," said I to Atkins, "I have brought you an assistant that perhaps you had not before." The man was so confounded that he was not able to speak for some time; but, recovering himself, he takes it with both his hands, and turning to his wife, "Here, my dear," says he, "did not I tell you our God, though He lives above, could hear what we have said? Here's the book I prayed for when you and I kneeled down under the bush; now God has heard us and sent it." When he had said so, the man fell into such passionate transports, that between the joy of having it, and giving God thanks for it, the tears ran down his face like a child that was crying.

The woman was surprised, and was like to have run into a mistake that none of us were aware of; for she firmly believed God had sent the book upon her husband's petition. It is true that providentially it was so, and might be taken so in a consequent sense; but I believe it would have been no difficult matter at that time to have persuaded the poor woman to have believed that an express messenger came from heaven on purpose to bring that individual book. But it was too serious a matter to suffer any delusion to take place, so I turned to the young woman, and told her we did not desire to impose upon the new convert in her first and more ignorant understanding of things, and begged her to explain to her that God may be very properly said to answer our petitions, when, in the course of His providence, such things are in a particular manner brought to pass as we petitioned for; but we did not expect returns from heaven in a miraculous and particular manner, and it is a mercy that it is not so.

This the young woman did afterwards effectually, so that there was no priestcraft used here; and I should have thought it one of the most unjustifiable frauds in the world to have had it so. But the effect upon Will Atkins is really not to be expressed; and there, we may be sure, was no delusion. Sure no man was ever more thankful in the world for anything of its kind than he was for the Bible, nor, I believe, never any man was glad of a Bible from a better principle; and though he had been a most profligate creature, headstrong, furious, and desperately wicked, yet this man is a standing rule to us all for the well instructing children, viz. that parents should never give over to teach and instruct, nor ever despair of the success of their endeavours, let the children be ever so refractory, or to appearance insensible to instruction; for if ever God in His providence touches the conscience of such, the force of their education turns upon them, and the early instruction of parents is not lost, though it may have been many years laid asleep, but some time or other they may find the benefit of it. Thus it was with this poor man: however ignorant he was of religion and Christian knowledge, he found he had some to do with now more ignorant than himself, and that the least part of the instruction of his good father that now came to his mind was of use to him.

Among the rest, it occurred to him, he said, how his father used to insist so much on the inexpressible value of the Bible, and the privilege and blessing of it to nations, families, and persons; but he never entertained the least notion of the worth of it till now, when, being to talk to heathens, savages, and barbarians, he wanted the help of the written oracle for his assistance. The young woman was glad of it also for the present occasion, though she had one, and so had the youth, on board our ship among their goods, which were not yet brought on shore. And now, having said so many things of this young woman, I cannot omit telling one story more of her and myself, which has something in it very instructive and remarkable.

I have related to what extremity the poor young woman was reduced; how her mistress was starved to death, and died on board that unhappy ship we met at sea, and how the whole ship's company was reduced to the last extremity. The gentlewoman, and her son, and this maid, were first hardly used as to provisions, and at last totally neglected and starved—that is to say, brought to the last extremity of hunger. One day, being discoursing with her on the extremities they suffered, I asked her if she could describe, by what she had felt, what it was to starve, and how it appeared? She said she believed she could, and told her tale very distinctly thus:—

"First, we had for some days fared exceedingly hard, and suffered very great hunger; but at last we were wholly without food of any kind except sugar, and a little wine and water. The first day after I had received no food at all, I found myself towards evening, empty and sick at the stomach, and nearer night much inclined to yawning and sleep. I lay down on the couch in the great cabin to sleep, and slept about three hours, and awaked a little refreshed, having taken a glass of wine when I lay down; after being about three hours awake, it being about five o'clock in the morning, I found myself empty, and my stomach sickish, and lay down again, but could not sleep at all, being very faint and ill; and thus I continued all the second day with a strange variety—first hungry, then sick again, with retchings to vomit. The second night, being obliged to go to bed again without any food more than a draught of fresh water, and being asleep, I dreamed I was at Barbadoes, and that the market was mightily stocked with provisions; that I bought some for my mistress, and went and dined very heartily. I thought my stomach was full after this, as it would have been after a good dinner; but when I awaked I was exceedingly sunk in my spirits to find myself in the extremity of family. The last glass of wine we had I drank, and put sugar in it, because of its having some spirit to supply nourishment; but there being no substance in the stomach for the digesting office to work upon, I found the only effect of the wine was to raise disagreeable fumes from the stomach into the head; and I lay, as they told me, stupid and senseless, as one drunk, for some time. The third day, in the morning, after a night of strange, confused, and inconsistent dreams, and rather dozing than sleeping, I awaked ravenous and furious with hunger; and I question, had not my understanding returned and conquered it, whether if I had been a mother, and had had a little child with me, its life would have been safe or not. This lasted about three hours, during which time I was twice raging mad as any creature in Bedlam, as my young master told me, and as he can now inform you.

"In one of these fits of lunacy or distraction I fell down and struck my face against the corner of a pallet-bed, in which my mistress lay, and with the blow the blood gushed out of my nose; and the cabin-boy bringing me a little basin, I sat down and bled into it a great deal; and as the blood came from me I came to myself, and the violence of the flame or fever I was in abated, and so did the ravenous part of the hunger. Then I grew sick, and retched to vomit, but could not, for I had nothing in my stomach to bring up. After I had bled some time I swooned, and they all believed I was dead; but I came to myself soon after, and then had a most dreadful pain in my stomach not to be described—not like the colic, but a gnawing, eager pain for food; and towards night it went off with a kind of earnest wishing or longing for food. I took another draught of water with sugar in it; but my stomach loathed the sugar and brought it all up again; then I took a draught of water without sugar, and that stayed with me; and I laid me down upon the bed, praying most heartily that it would please God to take me away; and composing my mind in hopes of it, I slumbered a while, and then waking, thought myself dying, being light with vapours from an empty stomach. I recommended my soul then to God, and then earnestly wished that somebody would throw me into the into the sea.

"All this while my mistress lay by me, just, as I thought, expiring, but she bore it with much more patience than I, and gave the last bit of bread she had left to her child, my young master, who would not have taken it, but she obliged him to eat it; and I believe it saved his life. Towards the morning I slept again, and when I awoke I fell into a violent passion of crying, and after that had a second fit of violent hunger. I got up ravenous, and in a most dreadful condition; and once or twice I was going to bite my own arm. At last I saw the basin in which was the blood I had bled at my nose the day before: I ran to it, and swallowed it with such haste, and such a greedy appetite, as if I wondered nobody had taken it before, and afraid it should be taken from me now. After it was down, though the thoughts of it filled me with horror, yet it checked the fit of hunger, and I took another draught of water, and was composed and refreshed for some hours after. This was the fourth day; and this I kept up till towards night, when, within the compass of three hours, I had all the several circumstances over again, one after another, viz. sick, sleepy, eagerly hungry, pain in the stomach, then ravenous again, then sick, then lunatic, then crying, then ravenous again, and so every quarter of an hour, and my strength wasted exceedingly; at night I lay me down, having no comfort but in the hope that I should die before morning.

"All this night I had no sleep; but the hunger was now turned into a disease; and I had a terrible colic and griping, by wind instead of food having found its way into the bowels; and in this condition I lay till morning, when I was surprised by the cries and lamentations of my young master, who called out to me that his mother was dead. I lifted myself up a little, for I had not strength to rise, but found she was not dead, though she was able to give very little signs of life. I had then such convulsions in my stomach, for want of some sustenance, as I cannot describe; with such frequent throes and pangs of appetite as nothing but the tortures of death can imitate; and in this condition I was when I heard the seamen above cry out, 'A sail! a sail!' and halloo and jump about as if they were distracted. I was not able to get off from the bed, and my mistress much less; and my young master was so sick that I thought he had been expiring; so we could not open the cabin door, or get any account what it was that occasioned such confusion; nor had we had any conversation with the ship's company for twelve days, they having told us that they had not a mouthful of anything to eat in the ship; and this they told us afterwards—they thought we had been dead. It was this dreadful condition we were in when you were sent to save our lives; and how you found us, sir, you know as well as I, and better too."

This was her own relation, and is such a distinct account of starving to death, as, I confess, I never met with, and was exceeding instructive to me. I am the rather apt to believe it to be a true account, because the youth gave me an account of a good part of it; though I must own, not so distinct and so feeling as the maid; and the rather, because it seems his mother fed him at the price of her own life: but the poor maid, whose constitution was stronger than that of her mistress, who was in years, and a weakly woman too, might struggle harder with it; nevertheless she might be supposed to feel the extremity something sooner than her mistress, who might be allowed to keep the last bit something longer than she parted with any to relieve her maid. No question, as the case is here related, if our ship or some other had not so providentially met them, but a few days more would have ended all their lives. I now return to my disposition of things among the people. And, first, it is to be observed here, that for many reasons I did not think fit to let them know anything of the sloop I had framed, and which I thought of setting up among them; for I found, at least at my first coming, such seeds of division among them, that I saw plainly, had I set up the sloop, and left it among them, they would, upon every light disgust, have separated, and gone away from one another; or perhaps have turned pirates, and so made the island a den of thieves, instead of a plantation of sober and religious people, as I intended it; nor did I leave the two pieces of brass cannon that I had on board, or the extra two quarter-deck guns that my nephew had provided, for the same reason. I thought it was enough to qualify them for a defensive war against any that should invade them, but not to set them up for an offensive war, or to go abroad to attack others; which, in the end, would only bring ruin and destruction upon them. I reserved the sloop, therefore, and the guns, for their service another way, as I shall observe in its place.

Having now done with the island, I left them all in good circumstances and in a flourishing condition, and went on board my ship again on the 6th of May, having been about twenty-five days among them: and as they were all resolved to stay upon the island till I came to remove them, I promised to send them further relief from the Brazils, if I could possibly find an opportunity. I particularly promised to send them some cattle, such as sheep, hogs, and cows: as to the two cows and calves which I brought from England, we had been obliged, by the length of our voyage, to kill them at sea, for want of hay to feed them.

The next day, giving them a salute of five guns at parting, we set sail, and arrived at the bay of All Saints in the Brazils in about twenty-two days, meeting nothing remarkable in our passage but this: that about three days after we had sailed, being becalmed, and the current setting strong to the ENE., running, as it were, into a bay or gulf on the land side, we were driven something out of our course, and once or twice our men cried out, "Land to the eastward!" but whether it was the continent or islands we could not tell by any means. But the third day, towards evening, the sea smooth, and the weather calm, we saw the sea as it were covered towards the land with something very black; not being able to discover what it was till after some time, our chief mate, going up the main shrouds a little way, and looking at them with a perspective, cried out it was an army. I could not imagine what he meant by an army, and thwarted him a little hastily. "Nay, sir," says he, "don't be angry, for 'tis an army, and a fleet too: for I believe there are a thousand canoes, and you may see them paddle along, for they are coming towards us apace."

I was a little surprised then, indeed, and so was my nephew the captain; for he had heard such terrible stories of them in the island, and having never been in those seas before, that he could not tell what to think of it, but said, two or three times, we should all be devoured. I must confess, considering we were becalmed, and the current set strong towards the shore, I liked it the worse; however, I bade them not be afraid, but bring the ship to an anchor as soon as we came so near as to know that we must engage them. The weather continued calm, and they came on apace towards us, so I gave orders to come to an anchor, and furl all our sails; as for the savages, I told them they had nothing to fear but fire, and therefore they should get their boats out, and fasten them, one close by the head and the other by the stern, and man them both well, and wait the issue in that posture: this I did, that the men in the boats might he ready with sheets and buckets to put out any fire these savages might endeavour to fix to the outside of the ship.

In this posture we lay by for them, and in a little while they came up with us; but never was such a horrid sight seen by Christians; though my mate was much mistaken in his calculation of their number, yet when they came up we reckoned about a hundred and twenty-six canoes; some of them had sixteen or seventeen men in them, and some more, and the least six or seven. When they came nearer to us, they seemed to be struck with wonder and astonishment, as at a sight which doubtless they had never seen before; nor could they at first, as we afterwards understood, know what to make of us; they came boldly up, however, very near to us, and seemed to go about to row round us; but we called to our men in the boats not to let them come too near them. This very order brought us to an engagement with them, without our designing it; for five or six of the large canoes came so near our long-boat, that our men beckoned with their hands to keep them back, which they understood very well, and went back: but at their retreat about fifty arrows came on board us from those boats, and one of our men in the long-boat was very much wounded. However, I called to them not to fire by any means; but we handed down some deal boards into the boat, and the carpenter presently set up a kind of fence, like waste boards, to cover them from the arrows of the savages, if they should shoot again.

About half-an-hour afterwards they all came up in a body astern of us, and so near that we could easily discern what they were, though we could not tell their design; and I easily found they were some of my old friends, the same sort of savages that I had been used to engage with. In a short time more they rowed a little farther out to sea, till they came directly broadside with us, and then rowed down straight upon us, till they came so near that they could hear us speak; upon this, I ordered all my men to keep close, lest they should shoot any more arrows, and made all our guns ready; but being so near as to be within hearing, I made Friday go out upon the deck, and call out aloud to them in his language, to know what they meant. Whether they understood him or not, that I knew not; but as soon as he had called to them, six of them, who were in the foremost or nighest boat to us, turned their canoes from us, and stooping down, showed us their naked backs; whether this was a defiance or challenge we knew not, or whether it was done in mere contempt, or as a signal to the rest; but immediately Friday cried out they were going to shoot, and, unhappily for him, poor fellow, they let fly about three hundred of their arrows, and to my inexpressible grief, killed poor Friday, no other man being in their sight. The poor fellow was shot with no less than three arrows, and about three more fell very near him; such unlucky marksmen they were!

I was so annoyed at the loss of my old trusty servant and companion, that I immediately ordered five guns to be loaded with small shot, and four with great, and gave them such a broadside as they had never heard in their lives before. They were not above half a cable's length off when we fired; and our gunners took their aim so well, that three or four of their canoes were overset, as we had reason to believe, by one shot only. The ill manners of turning up their bare backs to us gave us no great offence; neither did I know for certain whether that which would pass for the greatest contempt among us might be understood so by them or not; therefore, in return, I had only resolved to have fired four or five guns at them with powder only, which I knew would frighten them sufficiently: but when they shot at us directly with all the fury they were capable of, and especially as they had killed my poor Friday, whom I so entirely loved and valued, and who, indeed, so well deserved it, I thought myself not only justifiable before God and man, but would have been very glad if I could have overset every canoe there, and drowned every one of them.

I can neither tell how many we killed nor how many we wounded at this broadside, but sure such a fright and hurry never were seen among such a multitude; there were thirteen or fourteen of their canoes split and overset in all, and the men all set a-swimming: the rest, frightened out of their wits, scoured away as fast as they could, taking but little care to save those whose boats were split or spoiled with our shot; so I suppose that many of them were lost; and our men took up one poor fellow swimming for his life, above an hour after they were all gone. The small shot from our cannon must needs kill and wound a great many; but, in short, we never knew how it went with them, for they fled so fast, that in three hours or thereabouts we could not see above three or four straggling canoes, nor did we ever see the rest any more; for a breeze of wind springing up the same evening, we weighed and set sail for the Brazils.

We had a prisoner, indeed, but the creature was so sullen that he would neither cat nor speak, and we all fancied he would starve himself to death. But I took a way to cure him: for I had made them take him and turn him into the long-boat, and make him believe they would toss him into the sea again, and so leave him where they found him, if he would not speak; nor would that do, but they really did throw him into the sea, and came away from him. Then he followed them, for he swam like a cork, and called to them in his tongue, though they knew not one word of what he said; however at last they took him in again., and then he began to be more tractable: nor did I ever design they should drown him.

We were now under sail again, but I was the most disconsolate creature alive for want of my man Friday, and would have been very glad to have gone back to the island, to have taken one of the rest from thence for my occasion, but it could not be: so we went on. We had one prisoner, as I have said, and it was a long time before we could make him understand anything; but in time our men taught him some English, and he began to be a little tractable. Afterwards, we inquired what country he came from; but could make nothing of what he said; for his speech was so odd, all gutturals, and he spoke in the throat in such a hollow, odd manner, that we could never form a word after him; and we were all of opinion that they might speak that language as well if they were gagged as otherwise; nor could we perceive that they had any occasion either for teeth, tongue, lips, or palate, but formed their words just as a hunting-horn forms a tune with an open throat. He told us, however, some time after, when we had taught him to speak a little English, that they were going with their kings to fight a great battle. When he said kings, we asked him how many kings? He said they were five nation (we could not make him understand the plural 's), and that they all joined to go against two nation. We asked him what made them come up to us? He said, "To makee te great wonder look." Here it is to be observed that all those natives, as also those of Africa when they learn English, always add two e's at the end of the words where we use one; and they place the accent upon them, as makée, takée, and the like; nay, I could hardly make Friday leave it off, though at last he did.

And now I name the poor fellow once more, I must take my last leave of him. Poor honest Friday! We buried him with all the decency and solemnity possible, by putting him into a coffin, and throwing him into the sea; and I caused them to fire eleven guns for him. So ended the life of the most grateful, faithful, honest, and most affectionate servant that ever man had.

We went now away with a fair wind for Brazil; and in about twelve days' time we made land, in the latitude of five degrees south of the line, being the north-easternmost land of all that part of America. We kept on S. by E., in sight of the shore four days, when we made Cape St. Augustine, and in three days came to an anchor off the bay of All Saints, the old place of my deliverance, from whence came both my good and evil fate. Never ship came to this port that had less business than I had, and yet it was with great difficulty that we were admitted to hold the least correspondence on shore: not my partner himself, who was alive, and made a great figure among them, not my two merchant-trustees, not the fame of my wonderful preservation in the island, could obtain me that favour. My partner, however, remembering that I had given five hundred moidores to the prior of the monastery of the Augustines, and two hundred and seventy-two to the poor, went to the monastery, and obliged the prior that then was to go to the governor, and get leave for me personally, with the captain and one more, besides eight seamen, to come on shore, and no more; and this upon condition, absolutely capitulated for, that we should not offer to land any goods out of the ship, or to carry any person away without licence. They were so strict with us as to landing any goods, that it was with extreme difficulty that I got on shore three bales of English goods, such as fine broadcloths, stuffs, and some linen, which I had brought for a present to my partner.

He was a very generous, open-hearted man, although he began, like me, with little at first. Though he knew not that I had the least design of giving him anything, he sent me on board a present of fresh provisions, wine, and sweetmeats, worth about thirty moidores, including some tobacco, and three or four fine medals of gold: but I was even with him in my present, which, as I have said, consisted of fine broadcloth, English stuffs, lace, and fine holland; also, I delivered him about the value of one hundred pounds sterling in the same goods, for other uses; and I obliged him to set up the sloop, which I had brought with me from England, as I have said, for the use of my colony, in order to send the refreshments I intended to my plantation.

Accordingly, he got hands, and finished the sloop in a very few days, for she was already framed; and I gave the master of her such instructions that he could not miss the place; nor did he, as I had an account from my partner afterwards. I got him soon loaded with the small cargo I sent them; and one of our seamen, that had been on shore with me there, offered to go with the sloop and settle there, upon my letter to the governor Spaniard to allot him a sufficient quantity of land for a plantation, and on my giving him some clothes and tools for his planting work, which he said he understood, having been an old planter at Maryland, and a buccaneer into the bargain. I encouraged the fellow by granting all he desired; and, as an addition, I gave him the savage whom we had taken prisoner of war to be his slave, and ordered the governor Spaniard to give him his share of everything he wanted with the rest.

When we came to fit this man out, my old partner told me there was a certain very honest fellow, a Brazil planter of his acquaintance, who had fallen into the displeasure of the Church. "I know not what the matter is with him," says he, "but, on my conscience, I think he is a heretic in his heart, and he has been obliged to conceal himself for fear of the Inquisition." He then told me that he would be very glad of such an opportunity to make his escape, with his wife and two daughters; and if I would let them go to my island, and allot them a plantation, he would give them a small stock to begin with—for the officers of the Inquisition had seized all his effects and estate, and he had nothing left but a little household stuff and two slaves; "and," adds he, "though I hate his principles, yet I would not have him fall into their hands, for he will be assuredly burned alive if he does." I granted this presently, and joined my Englishman with them: and we concealed the man, and his wife and daughters, on board our ship, till the sloop put out to go to sea; and then having put all their goods on board some time before, we put them on board the sloop after she was got out of the bay. Our seaman was mightily pleased with this new partner; and their stocks, indeed, were much alike, rich in tools, in preparations, and a farm—but nothing to begin with, except as above: however, they carried over with them what was worth all the rest, some materials for planting sugar-canes, with some plants of canes, which he, I mean the Brazil planter, understood very well.

Among the rest of the supplies sent to my tenants in the island, I sent them by the sloop three milch cows and five calves; about twenty-two hogs, among them three sows; two mares, and a stone-horse. For my Spaniards, according to my promise, I engaged three Brazil women to go, and recommended it to them to marry them, and use them kindly. I could have procured more women, but I remembered that the poor persecuted man had two daughters, and that there were but five of the Spaniards that wanted partners; the rest had wives of their own, though in another country. All this cargo arrived safe, and, as you may easily suppose, was very welcome to my old inhabitants, who were now, with this addition, between sixty and seventy people, besides little children, of which there were a great many. I found letters at London from them all, by way of Lisbon, when I came back to England.

I have now done with the island, and all manner of discourse about it: and whoever reads the rest of my memorandums would do well to turn his thoughts entirely from it, and expect to read of the follies of an old man, not warned by his own harms, much less by those of other men, to beware; not cooled by almost forty years' miseries and disappointments—not satisfied with prosperity beyond expectation, nor made cautious by afflictions and distress beyond example.

Chapter IX—DREADFUL OCCURRENCES IN MADAGASCAR

I had no more business to go to the East Indies than a man at full liberty has to go to the turnkey at Newgate, and desire him to lock him up among the prisoners there, and starve him. Had I taken a small vessel from England and gone directly to the island; had I loaded her, as I did the other vessel, with all the necessaries for the plantation and for my people; taken a patent from the government here to have secured my property, in subjection only to that of England; had I carried over cannon and ammunition, servants and people to plant, and taken possession of the place, fortified and strengthened it in the name of England, and increased it with people, as I might easily have done; had I then settled myself there, and sent the ship back laden with good rice, as I might also have done in six months' time, and ordered my friends to have fitted her out again for our supply—had I done this, and stayed there myself, I had at least acted like a man of common sense. But I was possessed of a wandering spirit, and scorned all advantages: I pleased myself with being the patron of the people I placed there, and doing for them in a kind of haughty, majestic way, like an old patriarchal monarch, providing for them as if I had been father of the whole family, as well as of the plantation. But I never so much as pretended to plant in the name of any government or nation, or to acknowledge any prince, or to call my people subjects to any one nation more than another; nay, I never so much as gave the place a name, but left it as I found it, belonging to nobody, and the people under no discipline or government but my own, who, though I had influence over them as a father and benefactor, had no authority or power to act or command one way or other, further than voluntary consent moved them to comply. Yet even this, had I stayed there, would have done well enough; but as I rambled from them, and came there no more, the last letters I had from any of them were by my partner's means, who afterwards sent another sloop to the place, and who sent me word, though I had not the letter till I got to London, several years after it was written, that they went on but poorly; were discontented with their long stay there; that Will Atkins was dead; that five of the Spaniards were come away; and though they had not been much molested by the savages, yet they had had some skirmishes with them; and that they begged of him to write to me to think of the promise I had made to fetch them away, that they might see their country again before they died.

But I was gone a wildgoose chase indeed, and they that will have any more of me must be content to follow me into a new variety of follies, hardships, and wild adventures, wherein the justice of Providence may be duly observed; and we may see how easily Heaven can gorge us with our own desires, make the strongest of our wishes be our affliction, and punish us most severely with those very things which we think it would be our utmost happiness to be allowed to possess. Whether I had business or no business, away I went: it is no time now to enlarge upon the reason or absurdity of my own conduct, but to come to the history—I was embarked for the voyage, and the voyage I went.

I shall only add a word or two concerning my honest Popish clergyman, for let their opinion of us, and all other heretics in general, as they call us, be as uncharitable as it may, I verily believe this man was very sincere, and wished the good of all men: yet I believe he used reserve in many of his expressions, to prevent giving me offence; for I scarce heard him once call on the Blessed Virgin, or mention St. Jago, or his guardian angel, though so common with the rest of them. However, I say I had not the least doubt of his sincerity and pious intentions; and I am firmly of opinion, if the rest of the Popish missionaries were like him, they would strive to visit even the poor Tartars and Laplanders, where they have nothing to give them, as well as covet to flock to India, Persia, China, &c., the most wealthy of the heathen countries; for if they expected to bring no gains to their Church by it, it may well be admired how they came to admit the Chinese Confucius into the calendar of the Christian saints.

A ship being ready to sail for Lisbon, my pious priest asked me leave to go thither; being still, as he observed, bound never to finish any voyage he began. How happy it had been for me if I had gone with him. But it was too late now; all things Heaven appoints for the best: had I gone with him I had never had so many things to be thankful for, and the reader had never heard of the second part of the travels and adventures of Robinson Crusoe: so I must here leave exclaiming at myself, and go on with my voyage. From the Brazils we made directly over the Atlantic Sea to the Cape of Good Hope, and had a tolerably good voyage, our course generally south-east, now and then a storm, and some contrary winds; but my disasters at sea were at an end—my future rubs and cross events were to befall me on shore, that it might appear the land was as well prepared to be our scourge as the sea.

Our ship was on a trading voyage, and had a supercargo on board, who was to direct all her motions after she arrived at the Cape, only being limited to a certain number of days for stay, by charter-party, at the several ports she was to go to. This was none of my business, neither did I meddle with it; my nephew, the captain, and the supercargo adjusting all those things between them as they thought fit. We stayed at the Cape no longer than was needful to take in-fresh water, but made the best of our way for the coast of Coromandel. We were, indeed, informed that a French man-of-war, of fifty guns, and two large merchant ships, were gone for the Indies; and as I knew we were at war with France, I had some apprehensions of them; but they went their own way, and we heard no more of them.

I shall not pester the reader with a tedious description of places, journals of our voyage, variations of the compass, latitudes, trade-winds, &c.; it is enough to name the ports and places which we touched at, and what occurred to us upon our passages from one to another. We touched first at the island of Madagascar, where, though the people are fierce and treacherous, and very well armed with lances and bows, which they use with inconceivable dexterity, yet we fared very well with them a while. They treated us very civilly; and for some trifles which we gave them, such as knives, scissors, &c., they brought us eleven good fat bullocks, of a middling size, which we took in, partly for fresh provisions for our present spending, and the rest to salt for the ship's use.

We were obliged to stay here some time after we had furnished ourselves with provisions; and I, who was always too curious to look into every nook of the world wherever I came, went on shore as often as I could. It was on the east side of the island that we went on shore one evening: and the people, who, by the way, are very numerous, came thronging about us, and stood gazing at us at a distance. As we had traded freely with them, and had been kindly used, we thought ourselves in no danger; but when we saw the people, we cut three boughs out of a tree, and stuck them up at a distance from us; which, it seems, is a mark in that country not only of a truce and friendship, but when it is accepted the other side set up three poles or boughs, which is a signal that they accept the truce too; but then this is a known condition of the truce, that you are not to pass beyond their three poles towards them, nor they to come past your three poles or boughs towards you; so that you are perfectly secure within the three poles, and all the space between your poles and theirs is allowed like a market for free converse, traffic, and commerce. When you go there you must not carry your weapons with you; and if they come into that space they stick up their javelins and lances all at the first poles, and come on unarmed; but if any violence is offered them, and the truce thereby broken, away they run to the poles, and lay hold of their weapons, and the truce is at an end.

It happened one evening, when we went on shore, that a greater number of their people came down than usual, but all very friendly and civil; and they brought several kinds of provisions, for which we satisfied them with such toys as we had; the women also brought us milk and roots, and several things very acceptable to us, and all was quiet; and we made us a little tent or hut of some boughs or trees, and lay on shore all night. I know not what was the occasion, but I was not so well satisfied to lie on shore as the rest; and the boat riding at an anchor at about a stone's cast from the land, with two men in her to take care of her, I made one of them come on shore; and getting some boughs of trees to cover us also in the boat, I spread the sail on the bottom of the boat, and lay under the cover of the branches of the trees all night in the boat.

About two o'clock in the morning we heard one of our men making a terrible noise on the shore, calling out, for God's sake, to bring the boat in and come and help them, for they were all like to be murdered; and at the same time I heard the fire of five muskets, which was the number of guns they had, and that three times over; for it seems the natives here were not so easily frightened with guns as the savages were in America, where I had to do with them. All this while, I knew not what was the matter, but rousing immediately from sleep with the noise, I caused the boat to be thrust in, and resolved with three fusees we had on board to land and assist our men. We got the boat soon to the shore, but our men were in too much haste; for being come to the shore, they plunged into the water, to get to the boat with all the expedition they could, being pursued by between three and four hundred men. Our men were but nine in all, and only five of them had fusees with them; the rest had pistols and swords, indeed, but they were of small use to them.

We took up seven of our men, and with difficulty enough too, three of them being very ill wounded; and that which was still worse was, that while we stood in the boat to take our men in, we were in as much danger as they were in on shore; for they poured their arrows in upon us so thick that we were glad to barricade the side of the boat up with the benches, and two or three loose boards which, to our great satisfaction, we had by mere accident in the boat. And yet, had it been daylight, they are, it seems, such exact marksmen, that if they could have seen but the least part of any of us, they would have been sure of us. We had, by the light of the moon, a little sight of them, as they stood pelting us from the shore with darts and arrows; and having got ready our firearms, we gave them a volley that we could hear, by the cries of some of them, had wounded several; however, they stood thus in battle array on the shore till break of day, which we supposed was that they might see the better to take their aim at us.

In this condition we lay, and could not tell how to weigh our anchor, or set up our sail, because we must needs stand up in the boat, and they were as sure to hit us as we were to hit a bird in a tree with small shot. We made signals of distress to the ship, and though she rode a league off, yet my nephew, the captain, hearing our firing, and by glasses perceiving the posture we lay in, and that we fired towards the shore, pretty well understood us; and weighing anchor with all speed, he stood as near the shore as he durst with the ship, and then sent another boat with ten hands in her, to assist us. We called to them not to come too near, telling them what condition we were in; however, they stood in near to us, and one of the men taking the end of a tow-line in his hand, and keeping our boat between him and the enemy, so that they could not perfectly see him, swam on board us, and made fast the line to the boat: upon which we slipped out a little cable, and leaving our anchor behind, they towed us out of reach of the arrows; we all the while lying close behind the barricade we had made. As soon as we were got from between the ship and the shore, that we could lay her side to the shore, she ran along just by them, and poured in a broadside among them, loaded with pieces of iron and lead, small bullets, and such stuff, besides the great shot, which made a terrible havoc among them.

When we were got on board and out of danger, we had time to examine into the occasion of this fray; and indeed our supercargo, who had been often in those parts, put me upon it; for he said he was sure the inhabitants would not have touched us after we had made a truce, if we had not done something to provoke them to it. At length it came out that an old woman, who had come to sell us some milk, had brought it within our poles, and a young woman with her, who also brought us some roots or herbs; and while the old woman (whether she was mother to the young woman or no they could not tell) was selling us the milk, one of our men offered some rudeness to the girl that was with her, at which the old woman made a great noise: however, the seaman would not quit his prize, but carried her out of the old woman's sight among the trees, it being almost dark; the old woman went away without her, and, as we may suppose, made an outcry among the people she came from; who, upon notice, raised that great army upon us in three or four hours, and it was great odds but we had all been destroyed.

One of our men was killed with a lance thrown at him just at the beginning of the attack, as he sallied out of the tent they had made; the rest came off free, all but the fellow who was the occasion of all the mischief, who paid dear enough for his brutality, for we could not hear what became of him for a great while. We lay upon the shore two days after, though the wind presented, and made signals for him, and made our boat sail up shore and down shore several leagues, but in vain; so we were obliged to give him over; and if he alone had suffered for it, the loss had been less. I could not satisfy myself, however, without venturing on shore once more, to try if I could learn anything of him or them; it was the third night after the action that I had a great mind to learn, if I could by any means, what mischief we had done, and how the game stood on the Indians' side. I was careful to do it in the dark, lest we should be attacked again: but I ought indeed to have been sure that the men I went with had been under my command, before I engaged in a thing so hazardous and mischievous as I was brought into by it, without design.

We took twenty as stout fellows with us as any in the ship, besides the supercargo and myself, and we landed two hours before midnight, at the same place where the Indians stood drawn up in the evening before. I landed here, because my design, as I have said, was chiefly to see if they had quitted the field, and if they had left any marks behind them of the mischief we had done them, and I thought if we could surprise one or two of them, perhaps we might get our man again, by way of exchange.

We landed without any noise, and divided our men into two bodies, whereof the boatswain commanded one and I the other. We neither saw nor heard anybody stir when we landed: and we marched up, one body at a distance from another, to the place. At first we could see nothing, it being very dark; till by-and-by our boatswain, who led the first party, stumbled and fell over a dead body. This made them halt a while; for knowing by the circumstances that they were at the place where the Indians had stood, they waited for my coming up there. We concluded to halt till the moon began to rise, which we knew would be in less than an hour, when we could easily discern the havoc we had made among them. We told thirty-two bodies upon the ground, whereof two were not quite dead; some had an arm and some a leg shot off, and one his head; those that were wounded, we supposed, they had carried away. When we had made, as I thought, a full discovery of all we could come to the knowledge of, I resolved on going on board; but the boatswain and his party sent me word that they were resolved to make a visit to the Indian town, where these dogs, as they called them, dwelt, and asked me to go along with them; and if they could find them, as they still fancied they should, they did not doubt of getting a good booty; and it might be they might find Tom Jeffry there: that was the man's name we had lost.

Had they sent to ask my leave to go, I knew well enough what answer to have given them; for I should have commanded them instantly on board, knowing it was not a hazard fit for us to run, who had a ship and ship-loading in our charge, and a voyage to make which depended very much upon the lives of the men; but as they sent me word they were resolved to go, and only asked me and my company to go along with them, I positively refused it, and rose up, for I was sitting on the ground, in order to go to the boat. One or two of the men began to importune me to go; and when I refused, began to grumble, and say they were not under my command, and they would go. "Come, Jack," says one of the men, "will you go with me? I'll go for one." Jack said he would—and then another—and, in a word, they all left me but one, whom I persuaded to stay, and a boy left in the boat. So the supercargo and I, with the third man, went back to the boat, where we told them we would stay for them, and take care to take in as many of them as should be left; for I told them it was a mad thing they were going about, and supposed most of them would have the fate of Tom Jeffry.

They told me, like seamen, they would warrant it they would come off again, and they would take care, &c.; so away they went. I entreated them to consider the ship and the voyage, that their lives were not their own, and that they were entrusted with the voyage, in some measure; that if they miscarried, the ship might be lost for want of their help, and that they could not answer for it to God or man. But I might as well have talked to the mainmast of the ship: they were mad upon their journey; only they gave me good words, and begged I would not be angry; that they did not doubt but they would be back again in about an hour at furthest; for the Indian town, they said, was not above half-a mile off, though they found it above two miles before they got to it.

Well, they all went away, and though the attempt was desperate, and such as none but madmen would have gone about, yet, to give them their due, they went about it as warily as boldly; they were gallantly armed, for they had every man a fusee or musket, a bayonet, and a pistol; some of them had broad cutlasses, some of them had hangers, and the boatswain and two more had poleaxes; besides all which they had among them thirteen hand grenadoes. Bolder fellows, and better provided, never went about any wicked work in the world. When they went out their chief design was plunder, and they were in mighty hopes of finding gold there; but a circumstance which none of them were aware of set them on fire with revenge, and made devils of them all.

When they came to the few Indian houses which they thought had been the town, which was not above half a mile off, they were under great disappointment, for there were not above twelve or thirteen houses, and where the town was, or how big, they knew not. They consulted, therefore, what to do, and were some time before they could resolve; for if they fell upon these, they must cut all their throats; and it was ten to one but some of them might escape, it being in the night, though the moon was up; and if one escaped, he would run and raise all the town, so they should have a whole army upon them; on the other hand, if they went away and left those untouched, for the people were all asleep, they could not tell which way to look for the town; however, the last was the best advice, so they resolved to leave them, and look for the town as well as they could. They went on a little way, and found a cow tied to a tree; this, they presently concluded, would be a good guide to them; for, they said, the cow certainly belonged to the town before them, or the town behind them, and if they untied her, they should see which way she went: if she went back, they had nothing to say to her; but if she went forward, they would follow her. So they cut the cord, which was made of twisted flags, and the cow went on before them, directly to the town; which, as they reported, consisted of above two hundred houses or huts, and in some of these they found several families living together.

Here they found all in silence, as profoundly secure as sleep could make them: and first, they called another council, to consider what they had to do; and presently resolved to divide themselves into three bodies, and so set three houses on fire in three parts of the town; and as the men came out, to seize them and bind them (if any resisted, they need not be asked what to do then), and so to search the rest of the houses for plunder: but they resolved to march silently first through the town, and see what dimensions it was of, and if they might venture upon it or no.

They did so, and desperately resolved that they would venture upon them: but while they were animating one another to the work, three of them, who were a little before the rest, called out aloud to them, and told them that they had found—Tom Jeffry: they all ran up to the place, where they found the poor fellow hanging up naked by one arm, and his throat cut. There was an Indian house just by the tree, where they found sixteen or seventeen of the principal Indians, who had been concerned in the fray with us before, and two or three of them wounded with our shot; and our men found they were awake, and talking one to another in that house, but knew not their number.

The sight of their poor mangled comrade so enraged them, as before, that they swore to one another that they would be revenged, and that not an Indian that came into their hands should have any quarter; and to work they went immediately, and yet not so madly as might be expected from the rage and fury they were in. Their first care was to get something that would soon take fire, but, after a little search, they found that would be to no purpose; for most of the houses were low, and thatched with flags and rushes, of which the country is full; so they presently made some wildfire, as we call it, by wetting a little powder in the palm of their hands, and in a quarter of an hour they set the town on fire in four or five places, and particularly that house where the Indians were not gone to bed.

As soon as the fire begun to blaze, the poor frightened creatures began to rush out to save their lives, but met with their fate in the attempt; and especially at the door, where they drove them back, the boatswain himself killing one or two with his poleaxe. The house being large, and many in it, he did not care to go in, but called for a hand grenado, and threw it among them, which at first frightened them, but, when it burst, made such havoc among them that they cried out in a hideous manner. In short, most of the Indians who were in the open part of the house were killed or hurt with the grenado, except two or three more who pressed to the door, which the boatswain and two more kept, with their bayonets on the muzzles of their pieces, and despatched all that came in their way; but there was another apartment in the house, where the prince or king, or whatever he was, and several others were; and these were kept in till the house, which was by this time all in a light flame, fell in upon them, and they were smothered together.

All this while they fired not a gun, because they would not waken the people faster than they could master them; but the fire began to waken them fast enough, and our fellows were glad to keep a little together in bodies; for the fire grew so raging, all the houses being made of light combustible stuff, that they could hardly bear the street between them. Their business was to follow the fire, for the surer execution: as fast as the fire either forced the people out of those houses which were burning, or frightened them out of others, our people were ready at their doors to knock them on the head, still calling and hallooing one to another to remember Tom Jeffry.

While this was doing, I must confess I was very uneasy, and especially when I saw the flames of the town, which, it being night, seemed to be close by me. My nephew, the captain, who was roused by his men seeing such a fire, was very uneasy, not knowing what the matter was, or what danger I was in, especially hearing the guns too, for by this time they began to use their firearms; a thousand thoughts oppressed his mind concerning me and the supercargo, what would become of us; and at last, though he could ill spare any more men, yet not knowing what exigence we might be in, he took another boat, and with thirteen men and himself came ashore to me.

He was surprised to see me and the supercargo in the boat with no more than two men; and though he was glad that we were well, yet he was in the same impatience with us to know what was doing; for the noise continued, and the flame increased; in short, it was next to an impossibility for any men in the world to restrain their curiosity to know what had happened, or their concern for the safety of the men: in a word, the captain told me he would go and help his men, let what would come. I argued with him, as I did before with the men, the safety of the ship, the danger of the voyage, the interests of the owners and merchants, &c.,

and told him I and the two men would go, and only see if we could at a distance learn what was likely to be the event, and come back and tell him. It was in vain to talk to my nephew, as it was to talk to the rest before; he would go, he said; and he only wished he had left but ten men in the ship, for he could not think of having his men lost for want of help: he had rather lose the ship, the voyage, and his life, and all; and away he went.

I was no more able to stay behind now than I was to persuade them not to go; so the captain ordered two men to row back the pinnace, and fetch twelve men more, leaving the long-boat at an anchor; and that, when they came back, six men should keep the two boats, and six more come after us; so that he left only sixteen men in the ship: for the whole ship's company consisted of sixty-five men, whereof two were lost in the late quarrel which brought this mischief on.

Being now on the march, we felt little of the ground we trod on; and being guided by the fire, we kept no path, but went directly to the place of the flame. If the noise of the guns was surprising to us before, the cries of the poor people were now quite of another nature, and filled us with horror. I must confess I was never at the sacking a city, or at the taking a town by storm. I had heard of Oliver Cromwell taking Drogheda, in Ireland, and killing man, woman, and child; and I had read of Count Tilly sacking the city of Magdeburg and cutting the throats of twenty-two thousand of all sexes; but I never had an idea of the thing itself before, nor is it possible to describe it, or the horror that was upon our minds at hearing it. However, we went on, and at length came to the town, though there was no entering the streets of it for the fire. The first object we met with was the ruins of a hut or house, or rather the ashes of it, for the house was consumed; and just before it, plainly now to be seen by the light of the fire, lay four men and three women, killed, and, as we thought, one or two more lay in the heap among the fire; in short, there were such instances of rage, altogether barbarous, and of a fury something beyond what was human, that we thought it impossible our men could be guilty of it; or, if they were the authors of it, we thought they ought to be every one of them put to the worst of deaths. But this was not all: we saw the fire increase forward, and the cry went on just as the fire went on; so that we were in the utmost confusion. We advanced a little way farther, and behold, to our astonishment, three naked women, and crying in a most dreadful manner, came flying as if they had wings, and after them sixteen or seventeen men, natives, in the same terror and consternation, with three of our English butchers in the rear, who, when they could not overtake them, fired in among them, and one that was killed by their shot fell down in our sight. When the rest saw us, believing us to be their enemies, and that we would murder them as well as those that pursued them, they set up a most dreadful shriek, especially the women; and two of them fell down, as if already dead, with the fright.

My very soul shrunk within me, and my blood ran chill in my veins, when I saw this; and, I believe, had the three English sailors that pursued them come on, I had made our men kill them all; however, we took some means to let the poor flying creatures know that we would not hurt them; and immediately they came up to us, and kneeling down, with their hands lifted up, made piteous lamentation to us to save them, which we let them know we would: whereupon they crept all together in a huddle close behind us, as for protection. I left my men drawn up together, and, charging them to hurt nobody, but, if possible, to get at some of our people, and see what devil it was possessed them, and what they intended to do, and to command them off; assuring them that if they stayed till daylight they would have a hundred thousand men about their ears: I say I left them, and went among those flying people, taking only two of our men with me; and there was, indeed, a piteous spectacle among them. Some of them had their feet terribly burned with trampling and running through the fire; others their hands burned; one of the women had fallen down in the fire, and was very much burned before she could get out again; and two or three of the men had cuts in their backs and thighs, from our men pursuing; and another was shot through the body and died while I was there.

I would fain have learned what the occasion of all this was; but I could not understand one word they said; though, by signs, I perceived some of them knew not what was the occasion themselves. I was so terrified in my thoughts at this outrageous attempt that I could not stay there, but went back to my own men, and resolved to go into the middle of the town, through the fire, or whatever might be in the way, and put an end to it, cost what it would; accordingly, as I came back to my men, I told them my resolution, and commanded them to follow me, when, at the very moment, came four of our men, with the boatswain at their head, roving over heaps of bodies they had killed, all covered with blood and dust, as if they wanted more people to massacre, when our men hallooed to them as loud as they could halloo; and with much ado one of them made them hear, so that they knew who we were, and came up to us.

As soon as the boatswain saw us, he set up a halloo like a shout of triumph, for having, as he thought, more help come; and without waiting to hear me, "Captain," says he, "noble captain! I am glad you are come; we have not half done yet. Villainous hell-hound dogs! I'll kill as many of them as poor Tom has hairs upon his head: we have sworn to spare none of them; we'll root out the very nation of them from the earth;" and thus he ran on, out of breath, too, with action, and would not give us leave to speak a word. At last, raising my voice that I might silence him a little, "Barbarous dog!" said I, "what are you doing! I won't have one creature touched more, upon pain of death; I charge you, upon your life, to stop your hands, and stand still here, or you are a dead man this minute."—"Why, sir," says he, "do you know what you do, or what they have done? If you want a reason for what we have done, come hither;" and with that he showed me the poor fellow hanging, with his throat cut.

I confess I was urged then myself, and at another time would have been forward enough; but I thought they had carried their rage too far, and remembered Jacob's words to his sons Simeon and Levi: "Cursed be their anger, for it was fierce; and their wrath, for it was cruel." But I had now a new task upon my hands; for when the men I had carried with me saw the sight, as I had done, I had as much to do to restrain them as I should have had with the others; nay, my nephew himself fell in with them, and told me, in their hearing, that he was only concerned for fear of the men being overpowered; and as to the people, he thought not one of them ought to live; for they had all glutted themselves with the murder of the poor man, and that they ought to be used like murderers. Upon these words, away ran eight of my men, with the boatswain and his crew, to complete their bloody work; and I, seeing it quite out of my power to restrain them, came away pensive and sad; for I could not bear the sight, much less the horrible noise and cries of the poor wretches that fell into their hands.

I got nobody to come back with me but the supercargo and two men, and with these walked back to the boat. It was a very great piece of folly in me, I confess, to venture back, as it were, alone; for as it began now to be almost day, and the alarm had run over the country, there stood about forty men armed with lances and boughs at the little place where the twelve or thirteen houses stood, mentioned before: but by accident I missed the place, and came directly to the seaside, and by the time I got to the seaside it was broad day: immediately I took the pinnace and went on board, and sent her back to assist the men in what might happen. I observed, about the time that I came to the boat-side, that the fire was pretty well out, and the noise abated; but in about half-an-hour after I got on board, I heard a volley of our men's firearms, and saw a great smoke. This, as I understood afterwards, was our men falling upon the men, who, as I said, stood at the few houses on the way, of whom they killed sixteen or seventeen, and set all the houses on fire, but did not meddle with the women or children.

By the time the men got to the shore again with the pinnace our men began to appear; they came dropping in, not in two bodies as they went, but straggling here and there in such a manner, that a small force of resolute men might have cut them all off. But the dread of them was upon the whole country; and the men were surprised, and so frightened, that I believe a hundred of them would have fled at the sight of but five of our men. Nor in all this terrible action was there a man that made any considerable defence: they were so surprised between the terror of the fire and the sudden attack of our men in the dark, that they knew not which way to turn themselves; for if they fled one way they were met by one party, if back again by another, so that they were everywhere knocked down; nor did any of our men receive the least hurt, except one that sprained his foot, and another that had one of his hands burned.

Chapter X—HE IS LEFT ON SHORE

I was very angry with my nephew, the captain, and indeed with all the men, but with him in particular, as well for his acting so out of his duty as a commander of the ship, and having the charge of the voyage upon him, as in his prompting, rather than cooling, the rage of his blind men in so bloody and cruel an enterprise. My nephew answered me very respectfully, but told me that when he saw the body of the poor seaman whom they had murdered in so cruel and barbarous a manner, he was not master of himself, neither could he govern his passion; he owned he should not have done so, as he was commander of the ship; but as he was a man, and nature moved him, he could not bear it. As for the rest of the men, they were not subject to me at all, and they knew it well enough; so they took no notice of my dislike. The next day we set sail, so we never heard any more of it. Our men differed in the account of the number they had killed; but according to the best of their accounts, put all together, they killed or destroyed about one hundred and fifty people, men, women, and children, and left not a house standing in the town. As for the poor fellow Tom Jeffry, as he was quite dead (for his throat was so cut that his head was half off), it would do him no service to bring him away; so they only took him down from the tree, where he was hanging by one hand.

However just our men thought this action, I was against them in it, and I always, after that time, told them God would blast the voyage; for I looked upon all the blood they shed that night to be murder in them. For though it is true that they had killed Tom Jeffry, yet Jeffry was the aggressor, had broken the truce, and had ill-used a young woman of theirs, who came down to them innocently, and on the faith of the public capitulation.

The boatswain defended this quarrel when we were afterwards on board. He said it was true that we seemed to break the truce, but really had not; and that the war was begun the night before by the natives themselves, who had shot at us, and killed one of our men without any just provocation; so that as we were in a capacity to fight them now, we might also be in a capacity to do ourselves justice upon them in an extraordinary manner; that though the poor man had taken a little liberty with the girl, he ought not to have been murdered, and that in such a villainous manner: and that they did nothing but what was just and what the laws of God allowed to be done to murderers. One would think this should have been enough to have warned us against going on shore amongst the heathens and barbarians; but it is impossible to make mankind wise but at their own expense, and their experience seems to be always of most use to them when it is dearest bought.

We were now bound to the Gulf of Persia, and from thence to the coast of Coromandel, only to touch at Surat; but the chief of the supercargo's design lay at the Bay of Bengal, where, if he missed his business outward-bound, he was to go out to China, and return to the coast as he came home. The first disaster that befell us was in the Gulf of Persia, where five of our men, venturing on shore on the Arabian side of the gulf, were surrounded by the Arabians, and either all killed or carried away into slavery; the rest of the boat's crew were not able to rescue them, and had but just time to get off their boat. I began to upbraid them with the just retribution of Heaven in this case; but the boatswain very warmly told me, he thought I went further in my censures than I could show any warrant for in Scripture; and referred to Luke xiii. 4, where our Saviour intimates that those men on whom the Tower of Siloam fell were not sinners above all the Galileans; but that which put me to silence in the case was, that not one of these five men who were now lost were of those who went on shore to the massacre of Madagascar, so I always called it, though our men could not bear to hear the word *massacre* with any patience.

But my frequent preaching to them on this subject had worse consequences than I expected; and the boatswain, who had been the head of the attempt, came up boldly to me one time, and told me he found that I brought that affair continually upon the stage; that I made unjust reflections upon it, and had used the men very ill on that account, and himself in particular; that as I was but a passenger, and had no command in the ship, or concern in the voyage, they were not obliged to bear it; that they did not know but I might have some ill-design in my head, and perhaps to call them to an account for it when they came to England; and that, therefore, unless I would resolve to have done with it, and also not to concern myself any further with him, or any of his affairs, he would leave the ship; for he did not think it safe to sail with me among them.

I heard him patiently enough till he had done, and then told him that I confessed I had all along opposed the massacre of Madagascar, and that I had, on all occasions, spoken my mind freely about it, though not more upon him than any of the rest; that as to having no command in the ship, that was true; nor did I exercise any authority, only took the liberty of speaking my mind in things which publicly concerned us all; and what concern I had in the voyage was none of his business; that I was a considerable owner in the ship. In that claim I conceived I had a right to speak even further than I had done, and would not be accountable to him or any one else, and began to be a little warm with him. He made but little reply to me at that time, and I thought the affair had been over. We were at this time in the road at Bengal; and being willing to see the place, I went on shore with the supercargo in the ship's boat to divert myself; and towards evening was preparing to go on board, when one of the men came to me, and told me he would not have me trouble myself to come down to the boat, for they had orders not to carry me on board any more. Any one may guess what a surprise I was in at so insolent a message; and I asked the man who bade him deliver that message to me? He told me the coxswain.

I immediately found out the supercargo, and told him the story, adding that I foresaw there would be a mutiny in the ship; and entreated him to go immediately on board and acquaint the captain of it. But I might have spared this intelligence, for before I had spoken to him on shore the matter was effected on board. The boatswain, the gunner, the carpenter, and all the inferior officers, as soon as I was gone off in the boat, came up, and desired to speak with the captain; and then the boatswain, making a long harangue, and repeating all he had said to me, told the captain that as I was now gone peaceably on shore, they were loath to use any violence with me, which, if I had not gone on shore, they would otherwise have done, to oblige me to have gone. They therefore thought fit to tell him that as they shipped themselves to serve in the ship under his command, they would perform it well and faithfully; but if I would not quit the ship, or the captain oblige me to quit it, they would all leave the ship, and sail no further with him; and at that word *all* he turned his face towards the main-mast, which was, it seems, a signal agreed on, when the seamen, being got together there, cried out, "*One and all*! *one and all*!"

My nephew, the captain, was a man of spirit, and of great presence of mind; and though he was surprised, yet he told them calmly that he would consider of the matter, but that he could do nothing in it till he had spoken to me about it. He used some arguments with them, to show them the unreasonableness and injustice of the thing, but it was all in vain; they swore, and shook hands round before his face, that they would all go on shore unless he would engage to them not to suffer me to come any more on board the ship.

This was a hard article upon him, who knew his obligation to me, and did not know how I might take it. So he began to talk smartly to them; told them that I was a very considerable owner of the ship, and that if ever they came to England again it would cost them very dear; that the ship was mine, and that he could not put me out of it; and that he would rather lose the ship, and the voyage too, than disoblige me so much: so they might do as they pleased. However, he would go on shore and talk with me, and invited the boatswain to go with him, and perhaps they might accommodate the matter with me. But they all rejected the proposal, and said they would have nothing to do with me any more; and if I came on board they would all go on shore. "Well," said the captain, "if you are all of this mind, let me go on shore and talk with him." So away he came to me with this account, a little after the message had been brought to me from the coxswain.

I was very glad to see my nephew, I must confess; for I was not without apprehensions that they would confine him by violence, set sail, and run away with the ship; and then I had been stripped naked in a remote country, having nothing to help myself; in short, I had been in a worse case than when I was alone in the island. But they had not come to that length, it seems, to my satisfaction; and when my nephew told me what they had said to him, and how they had sworn and shook hands that they would, one and all, leave the ship if I was suffered to come on board, I told him he should not be concerned at it at all, for I would stay on shore. I only desired he would take care and send me all my necessary things on shore, and leave me a sufficient sum of money, and I would find my way to England as well as I could. This was a heavy piece of news to my nephew, but there was no way to help it but to comply; so, in short, he went on board the ship again, and satisfied the men that his uncle had yielded to their importunity, and had sent for his goods from on board the ship; so that the matter was over in a few hours, the men returned to their duty, and I began to consider what course I should steer.

I was now alone in a most remote part of the world, for I was near three thousand leagues by sea farther off from England than I was at my island; only, it is true, I might travel here by land over the Great Mogul's country to Surat, might go from thence to Bassora by sea, up the Gulf of Persia, and take the way of the caravans, over the desert of Arabia, to Aleppo and Scanderoon; from thence by sea again to Italy, and so overland into France. I had another way before me, which was to wait for some English ships, which were coming to Bengal from Achin, on the island of Sumatra, and get passage on board them from England. But as I came hither without any concern with the East Indian Company, so it would be difficult to go from hence without their licence, unless with great favour of the captains of the ships, or the company's factors: and to both I was an utter stranger.

Here I had the mortification to see the ship set sail without me; however, my nephew left me two servants, or rather one companion and one servant; the first was clerk to the purser, whom he engaged to go with me, and the other was his own servant. I then took a good lodging in the house of an Englishwoman, where several merchants lodged, some French, two Italians, or rather Jews, and one Englishman. Here I stayed above nine months, considering what course to take. I had some English goods with me of value, and a considerable sum of money; my nephew furnishing me with a thousand pieces of eight, and a letter of credit for more if I had occasion, that I might not be straitened, whatever might happen. I quickly disposed of my goods to advantage; and, as I originally intended, I bought here some very good diamonds, which, of all other things, were the most proper for me in my present circumstances, because I could always carry my whole estate about me.

During my stay here many proposals were made for my return to England, but none falling out to my mind, the English merchant who lodged with me, and whom I had contracted an intimate acquaintance with, came to me one morning, saying: "Countryman, I have a project to communicate, which, as it suits with my thoughts, may, for aught I know, suit with yours also, when you shall have thoroughly considered it. Here we are posted, you by accident and I by my own choice, in a part of the world very remote from our own country; but it is in a country where, by us who understand trade and business, a great deal of money is to be got. If you will put one thousand pounds to my one thousand pounds, we will hire a ship here, the first we can get to our minds. You shall be captain, I'll be merchant, and we'll go a trading voyage to China; for what should we stand still for? The whole world is in motion; why should we be idle?"

I liked this proposal very well; and the more so because it seemed to be expressed with so much goodwill. In my loose, unhinged circumstances, I was the fitter to embrace a proposal for trade, or indeed anything else. I might perhaps say with some truth, that if trade was not my element, rambling was; and no proposal for seeing any part of the world which I had never seen before could possibly come amiss to me. It was, however, some time before we could get a ship to our minds, and when we had got a vessel, it was not easy to get English sailors—that is to say, so many as were necessary to govern the voyage and manage the sailors which we should pick up there. After some time we got a mate, a boatswain, and a gunner, English; a Dutch carpenter, and three foremast men. With these we found we could do well enough, having Indian seamen, such as they were, to make up.

When all was ready we set sail for Achin, in the island of Sumatra, and from thence to Siam, where we exchanged some of our wares for opium and some arrack; the first a commodity which bears a great price among the Chinese, and which at that time was much wanted there. Then we went up to Saskan, were eight months out, and on our return to Bengal I was very well satisfied with my adventure. Our people in England often admire how officers, which the company send into India, and the merchants which generally stay there, get such very great estates as they do, and sometimes come home worth sixty or seventy thousand pounds at a time; but it is little matter for wonder, when we consider the innumerable ports and places where they have a free commerce; indeed, at the ports where the English ships come there is such great and constant demands for the growth of all other countries, that there is a certain vent for the returns, as well as a market abroad for the goods carried out.

I got so much money by my first adventure, and such an insight into the method of getting more, that had I been twenty years younger, I should have been tempted to have stayed here, and sought no farther for making my fortune; but what was all this to a man upwards of threescore, that was rich enough, and came abroad more in obedience to a restless desire of seeing the world than a covetous desire of gaining by it? A restless desire it really was, for when I was at home I was restless to go abroad; and when I was abroad I was restless to be at home. I say, what was this gain to me? I was rich enough already, nor had I any uneasy desires about getting more money; therefore the profit of the voyage to me was of no great force for the prompting me forward to further undertakings. Hence, I thought that by this voyage I had made no progress at all, because I was come back, as I might call it, to the place from whence I came, as to a home: whereas, my eye, like that which Solomon speaks of, was never satisfied with seeing. I was come into a part of the world which I was never in before, and that part, in particular, which I heard much of, and was resolved to see as much of it as I could: and then I thought I might say I had seen all the world that was worth seeing.

But my fellow-traveller and I had different notions: I acknowledge his were the more suited to the end of a merchant's life: who, when he is abroad upon adventures, is wise to stick to that, as the best thing for him, which he is likely to get the most money by. On the other hand, mine was the notion of a mad, rambling boy, that never cares to see a thing twice over. But this was not all: I had a kind of impatience upon me to be nearer home, and yet an unsettled resolution which way to go. In the interval of these consultations, my friend, who was always upon the search for business, proposed another voyage among the Spice Islands, to bring home a loading of cloves from the Manillas, or thereabouts.

We were not long in preparing for this voyage; the chief difficulty was in bringing me to come into it. However, at last, nothing else offering, and as sitting still, to me especially, was the unhappiest part of life, I resolved on this voyage too, which we made very successfully, touching at Borneo and several other islands, and came home in about five months, when we sold our spices, with very great profit, to the Persian merchants, who carried them away to the Gulf. My friend, when we made up this account, smiled at me: "Well, now," said he, with a sort of friendly rebuke on my indolent temper, "is not this better than walking about here, like a man with nothing to do, and spending our time in staring at the nonsense and ignorance of the Pagans?"—"Why, truly," said I, "my friend, I think it is, and I begin to be a convert to the principles of merchandising; but I must tell you, by the way, you do not know what I am doing; for if I once conquer my backwardness, and embark heartily, old as I am, I shall harass you up and down the world till I tire you; for I shall pursue it so eagerly, I shall never let you lie still."

Chapter XI—WARNED OF DANGER BY A COUNTRYMAN

A little while after this there came in a Dutch ship from Batavia; she was a coaster, not an European trader, of about two hundred tons burden; the men, as they pretended, having been so sickly that the captain had not hands enough to go to sea with, so he lay by at Bengal; and having, it seems, got money enough, or being willing, for other reasons, to go for Europe, he gave public notice he would sell his ship. This came to my ears before my new partner heard of it, and I had a great mind to buy it; so I went to him and told him of it. He considered a while, for he was no rash man neither; and at last replied, "She is a little too big—however, we will have her." Accordingly, we bought the ship, and agreeing with the master, we paid for her, and took possession. When we had done so we resolved to engage the men, if we could, to join with those we had, for the pursuing our business; but, on a sudden, they having received not their wages, but their share of the money, as we afterwards learned, not one of them was to be found; we inquired much about them, and at length were told that they were all gone together by land to Agra, the great city of the Mogul's residence, to proceed from thence to Surat, and then go by sea to the Gulf of Persia.

Nothing had so much troubled me a good while as that I should miss the opportunity of going with them; for such a ramble, I thought, and in such company as would both have guarded and diverted me, would have suited mightily with my great design; and I should have both seen the world and gone homeward too. But I was much better satisfied a few days after, when I came to know what sort of fellows they were; for, in short, their history was, that this man they called captain was the gunner only, not the commander; that they had been a trading voyage, in which they had been attacked on shore by some of the Malays, who had killed the captain and three of his men; and that after the captain was killed, these men, eleven in number, having resolved to run away with the ship, brought her to Bengal, leaving the mate and five men more on shore.

Well, let them get the ship how they would, we came honestly by her, as we thought, though we did not, I confess, examine into things so exactly as we ought; for we never inquired anything of the seamen, who would certainly have faltered in their account, and contradicted one another. Somehow or other we should have had reason to have suspected, them; but the man showed us a bill of sale for the ship, to one Emanuel Clostershoven, or some such name, for I suppose it was all a forgery, and called himself by that name, and we could not contradict him: and withal, having no suspicion of the thing, we went through with our bargain. We picked up some more English sailors here after this, and some Dutch, and now we resolved on a second voyage to the south-east for cloves, &c.—that is to say, among the Philippine and Malacca isles. In short, not to fill up this part of my story with trifles when what is to come is so remarkable, I spent, from first to last, six years in this country, trading from port to port, backward and forward, and with very good success, and was now the last year with my new partner, going in the ship above mentioned, on a voyage to China, but designing first to go to Siam to buy rice.

In this voyage, being by contrary winds obliged to beat up and down a great while in the Straits of Malacca and among the islands, we were no sooner got clear of those difficult seas than we found our ship had sprung a leak, but could not discover where it was. This forced us to make some port; and my partner, who knew the country better than I did, directed the captain to put into the river of Cambodia; for I had made the English mate, one Mr. Thompson, captain, not being willing to take the charge of the ship upon myself. This river lies on the north side of the great bay or gulf which goes up to Siam. While we were here, and going often on shore for refreshment, there comes to me one day an Englishman, a gunner's mate on board an English East India ship, then riding in the same river. "Sir," says he, addressing me, "you are a stranger to me, and I to you; but I have something to tell you that very nearly concerns you. I am moved by the imminent danger you are in, and, for aught I see, you have no knowledge of it."—"I know no danger I am in," said I, "but that my ship is leaky, and I cannot find it out; but I intend to lay her aground to-morrow, to see if I can find it."—"But, sir," says he, "leaky or not leaky, you will be wiser than to lay your ship on shore to-morrow when you hear what I have to say to you. Do you know, sir," said he, "the town of Cambodia lies about fifteen leagues up the river; and there are two large English ships about five leagues on this side, and three Dutch?"—"Well," said I, "and what is that to me?"—"Why, sir," said be, "is it for a man that is upon such adventures as you are to come into a port, and not examine first what ships there are there, and whether he is able to deal with them? I suppose you do not think you are a match for them?" I could not conceive what he meant; and I turned short upon him, and said: "I wish you would explain yourself; I cannot imagine what reason I have to be afraid of any of the company's ships, or Dutch ships. I am no interloper. What can they have to say to me?"—"Well, sir," says he, with a smile, "if you think yourself secure you must take your chance; but take my advice, if you do not put to sea immediately, you will the very next tide be attacked by five longboats full of men, and perhaps if you are taken you will be hanged for a pirate, and the particulars be examined afterwards. I thought, sir," added he, "I should have met with a better reception than this for doing you a piece of service of such importance."—"I can never be ungrateful," said I, "for any service, or to any man that offers me any kindness; but it is past my comprehension what they should have such a design upon me for: however, since you say there is no time to be lost, and that there is some villainous design on hand against me, I will go on board this minute, and put to sea immediately, if my men can stop the leak; but, sir," said I, "shall I go away ignorant of the cause of all this? Can you give me no further light into it?"

"I can tell you but part of the story, sir," says he; "but I have a Dutch seaman here with me, and I believe I could persuade him to tell you the rest; but there is scarce time for it. But the short of the story is this—the first part of which I suppose you know well enough—that you were with this ship at Sumatra; that there your captain was murdered by the Malays, with three of his men; and that you, or some of those that were on board with you, ran away with the ship, and are since turned pirates. This is the sum of the story, and you will all be seized as pirates, I can assure you, and executed with very little ceremony; for you know merchant ships show but little law to pirates if they get them into their power."—"Now you speak plain English," said I, "and I thank you; and though I know nothing that we have done like what you talk of, for I am sure we came honestly and fairly by the ship; yet seeing such a work is doing, as you say, and that you seem to mean honestly, I will be upon my guard."—"Nay, sir," says he, "do not talk of being upon your guard; the best defence is to be out of danger. If you have any regard for your life and the lives of all your men, put to sea without fail at high-water; and as you have a whole tide before you, you will be gone too far out before they can come down; for they will come away at high-water, and as they have twenty miles to come, you will get near two hours of them by the difference of the tide, not reckoning the length of the way: besides, as they are only boats, and not ships, they will not venture to follow you far out to sea, especially if it blows."—"Well," said I, "you have been very kind in this: what shall I do to make you amends?"—"Sir," says he, "you may not be willing to make me any amends, because you may not be convinced of the truth of it. I will make an offer to you: I have nineteen months' pay due to me on board the ship ---, which I came out of England in; and the Dutchman that is with me has seven months' pay due to him. If you will make good our pay to us we will go along with you; if you find nothing more in it we will desire no more; but if we do convince you that we have saved your lives, and the ship, and the lives of all the men in her, we will leave the rest to you."

I consented to this readily, and went immediately on board, and the two men with me. As soon as I came to the ship's side, my partner, who was on board, came out on the quarter-deck, and called to me, with a great deal of joy, "We have stopped the leak—we have stopped the leak!"—"Say you so?" said I; "thank God; but weigh anchor, then, immediately."—"Weigh!" says he; "what do you mean by that? What is the matter?"—"Ask no questions," said I; "but set all hands to work, and weigh without losing a minute." He was surprised; however, he called the captain, and he immediately ordered the anchor to be got up; and though the tide was not quite down, yet a little land-breeze blowing, we stood out to sea. Then I called him into the cabin, and told him the story; and we called in the men, and they told us the rest of it; but as it took up a great deal of time, before we had done a seaman comes to the cabin door, and called out to us that the captain bade him tell us we were chased by five sloops, or boats, full of men. “Very well,” said I, “then it is apparent there is something in it.” I then ordered all our men to be called up, and told them there was a design to seize the ship, and take us for pirates, and asked them if they would stand by us, and by one another; the men answered cheerfully, one and all, that they would live and die with us. Then I asked the captain what way he thought best for us to manage a fight with them; for resist them I was resolved we would, and that to the last drop. He said readily, that the way was to keep them off with our great shot as long as we could, and then to use our small arms, to keep them from boarding us; but when neither of these would do any longer, we would retire to our close quarters, for perhaps they had not materials to break open our bulkheads, or get in upon us.

The gunner had in the meantime orders to bring two guns, to bear fore and aft, out of the steerage, to clear the deck, and load them with musket-bullets, and small pieces of old iron, and what came next to hand. Thus we made ready for fight; but all this while we kept out to sea, with wind enough, and could see the boats at a distance, being five large longboats, following us with all the sail they could make.

Two of those boats (which by our glasses we could see were English) outsailed the rest, were near two leagues ahead of them, and gained upon us considerably, so that we found they would come up with us; upon which we fired a gun without ball, to intimate that they should bring to: and we put out a flag of truce, as a signal for parley: but they came crowding after us till within shot, when we took in our white flag, they having made no answer to it, and hung out a red flag, and fired at them with a shot. Notwithstanding this, they came on till they were near enough to call to them with a speaking-trumpet, bidding them keep off at their peril.

It was all one; they crowded after us, and endeavoured to come under our stern, so as to board us on our quarter; upon which, seeing they were resolute for mischief, and depended upon the strength that followed them, I ordered to bring the ship to, so that they lay upon our broadside; when immediately we fired five guns at them, one of which had been levelled so true as to carry away the stern of the hindermost boat, and we then forced them to take down their sail, and to run all to the head of the boat, to keep her from sinking; so she lay by, and had enough of it; but seeing the foremost boat crowd on after us, we made ready to fire at her in particular. While this was doing one of the three boats that followed made up to the boat which we had disabled, to relieve her, and we could see her take out the men. We then called again to the foremost boat, and offered a truce, to parley again, and to know what her business was with us; but had no answer, only she crowded close under our stern. Upon this, our gunner who was a very dexterous fellow ran out his two case-guns, and fired again at her, but the shot missing, the men in the boat shouted, waved their caps, and came on. The gunner, getting quickly ready again, fired among them a second time, one shot of which, though it missed the boat itself, yet fell in among the men, and we could easily see did a great deal of mischief among them. We now wore the ship again, and brought our quarter to bear upon them, and firing three guns more, we found the boat was almost split to pieces; in particular, her rudder and a piece of her stern were shot quite away; so they handed her sail immediately, and were in great disorder. To complete their misfortune, our gunner let fly two guns at them again; where he hit them we could not tell, but we found the boat was sinking, and some of the men already in the water: upon this, I immediately manned out our pinnace, with orders to pick up some of the men if they could, and save them from drowning, and immediately come on board ship with them, because we saw the rest of the boats began to come up. Our men in the pinnace followed their orders, and took up three men, one of whom was just drowning, and it was a good while before we could recover him. As soon as they were on board we crowded all the sail we could make, and stood farther out to the sea; and we found that when the other boats came up to the first, they gave over their chase.

Being thus delivered from a danger which, though I knew not the reason of it, yet seemed to be much greater than I apprehended, I resolved that we should change our course, and not let any one know whither we were going; so we stood out to sea eastward, quite out of the course of all European ships, whether they were bound to China or anywhere else, within the commerce of the European nations. When we were at sea we began to consult with the two seamen, and inquire what the meaning of all this should be; and the Dutchman confirmed the gunner's story about the false sale of the ship and of the murder of the captain, and also how that he, this Dutchman, and four more got into the woods, where they wandered about a great while, till at length he made his escape, and swam off to a Dutch ship, which was sailing near the shore in its way from China.

He then told us that he went to Batavia, where two of the seamen belonging to the ship arrived, having deserted the rest in their travels, and gave an account that the fellow who had run away with the ship, sold her at Bengal to a set of pirates, who were gone a-cruising in her, and that they had already taken an English ship and two Dutch ships very richly laden. This latter part we found to concern us directly, though we knew it to be false; yet, as my partner said, very justly, if we had fallen into their hands, and they had had such a prepossession against us beforehand, it had been in vain for us to have defended ourselves, or to hope for any good quarter at their hands; especially considering that our accusers had been our judges, and that we could have expected nothing from them but what rage would have dictated, and an ungoverned passion have executed. Therefore it was his opinion we should go directly back to Bengal, from whence we came, without putting in at any port whatever—because where we could give a good account of ourselves, could prove where we were when the ship put in, of whom we bought her, and the like; and what was more than all the rest, if we were put upon the necessity of bringing it before the proper judges, we should be sure to have some justice, and not to be hanged first and judged afterwards.

I was some time of my partner's opinion; but after a little more serious thinking, I told him I thought it was a very great hazard for us to attempt returning to Bengal, for that we were on the wrong side of the Straits of Malacca, and that if the alarm was given, we should be sure to be waylaid on every side—that if we should be taken, as it were, running away, we should even condemn ourselves, and there would want no more evidence to destroy us. I also asked the English sailor's opinion, who said he was of my mind, and that we certainly should be taken. This danger a little startled my partner and all the ship's company, and we immediately resolved to go away to the coast of Tonquin, and so on to the coast of China—and pursuing the first design as to trade, find some way or other to dispose of the ship, and come back in some of the vessels of the country such as we could get. This was approved of as the best method for our security, and accordingly we steered away NNE., keeping above fifty leagues off from the usual course to the eastward. This, however, put us to some inconvenience: for, first, the winds, when we came that distance from the shore, seemed to be more steadily against us, blowing almost trade, as we call it, from the E. and ENE., so that we were a long while upon our voyage, and we were but ill provided with victuals for so long a run; and what was still worse, there was some danger that those English and Dutch ships whose boats pursued us, whereof some were bound that way, might have got in before us, and if not, some other ship bound to China might have information of us from them, and pursue us with the same vigour.

I must confess I was now very uneasy, and thought myself, including the late escape from the longboats, to have been in the most dangerous condition that ever I was in through my past life; for whatever ill circumstances I had been in, I was never pursued for a thief before; nor had I ever done anything that merited the name of dishonest or fraudulent, much less thievish. I had chiefly been my own enemy, or, as I may rightly say, I had been nobody's enemy but my own; but now I was woefully embarrassed: for though I was perfectly innocent, I was in no condition to make that innocence appear; and if I had been taken, it had been under a supposed guilt of the worst kind. This made me very anxious to make an escape, though which way to do it I knew not, or what port or place we could go to. My partner endeavoured to encourage me by describing the several ports of that coast, and told me he would put in on the coast of Cochin China, or the bay of Tonquin, intending afterwards to go to Macao, where a great many European families resided, and particularly the missionary priests, who usually went thither in order to their going forward to China.

Hither then we resolved to go; and, accordingly, though after a tedious course, and very much straitened for provisions, we came within sight of the coast very early in the morning; and upon reflection on the past circumstances of danger we were in, we resolved to put into a small river, which, however, had depth enough of water for us, and to see if we could, either overland or by the ship's pinnace, come to know what ships were in any port thereabouts. This happy step was, indeed, our deliverance: for though we did not immediately see any European ships in the bay of Tonquin, yet the next morning there came into the bay two Dutch ships; and a third without any colours spread out, but which we believed to be a Dutchman, passed by at about two leagues' distance, steering for the coast of China; and in the afternoon went by two English ships steering the same course; and thus we thought we saw ourselves beset with enemies both one way and the other. The place we were in was wild and barbarous, the people thieves by occupation; and though it is true we had not much to seek of them, and, except getting a few provisions, cared not how little we had to do with them, yet it was with much difficulty that we kept ourselves from being insulted by them several ways. We were in a small river of this country, within a few leagues of its utmost limits northward; and by our boat we coasted north-east to the point of land which opens the great bay of Tonquin; and it was in this beating up along the shore that we discovered we were surrounded with enemies. The people we were among were the most barbarous of all the inhabitants of the coast; and among other customs they have this one: that if any vessel has the misfortune to be shipwrecked upon their coast, they make the men all prisoners or slaves; and it was not long before we found a spice of their kindness this way, on the occasion following.

I have observed above that our ship sprung a leak at sea, and that we could not find it out; and it happened that, as I have said, it was stopped unexpectedly, on the eve of our being pursued by the Dutch and English ships in the bay of Siam; yet, as we did not find the ship so perfectly tight and sound as we desired, we resolved while we were at this place to lay her on shore, and clean her bottom, and, if possible, to find out where the leaks were. Accordingly, having lightened the ship, and brought all our guns and other movables to one side, we tried to bring her down, that we might come at her bottom; but, on second thoughts, we did not care to lay her on dry ground, neither could we find out a proper place for it.

Chapter XII—THE CARPENTER'S WHIMSICAL CONTRIVANCE

The inhabitants came wondering down the shore to look at us; and seeing the ship lie down on one side in such a manner, and heeling in towards the shore, and not seeing our men, who were at work on her bottom with stages, and with their boats on the off-side, they presently concluded that the ship was cast away, and lay fast on the ground. On this supposition they came about us in two or three hours' time with ten or twelve large boats, having some of them eight, some ten men in a boat, intending, no doubt, to have come on board and plundered the ship, and if they found us there, to have carried us away for slaves.

When they came up to the ship, and began to row round her, they discovered us all hard at work on the outside of the ship's bottom and side, washing, and graving, and stopping, as every seafaring man knows how. They stood for a while gazing at us, and we, who were a little surprised, could not imagine what their design was; but being willing to be sure, we took this opportunity to get some of us into the ship, and others to hand down arms and ammunition to those that were at work, to defend themselves with if there should be occasion. And it was no more than need: for in less than a quarter of an hour's consultation, they agreed, it seems, that the ship was really a wreck, and that we were all at work endeavouring to save her, or to save our lives by the help of our boats; and when we handed our arms into the boat, they concluded, by that act, that we were endeavouring to save some of our goods. Upon this, they took it for granted we all belonged to them, and away they came directly upon our men, as if it had been in a line-of-battle.

Our men, seeing so many of them, began to be frightened, for we lay but in an ill posture to fight, and cried out to us to know what they should do. I immediately called to the men that worked upon the stages to slip them down, and get up the side into the ship, and bade those in the boat to row round and come on board. The few who were on board worked with all the strength and hands we had to bring the ship to rights; however, neither the men upon the stages nor those in the boats could do as they were ordered before the Cochin Chinese were upon them, when two of their boats boarded our longboat, and began to lay hold of the men as their prisoners.

The first man they laid hold of was an English seaman, a stout, strong fellow, who having a musket in his hand, never offered to fire it, but laid it down in the boat, like a fool, as I thought; but he understood his business better than I could teach him, for he grappled the Pagan, and dragged him by main force out of their boat into ours, where, taking him by the ears, he beat his head so against the boat's gunnel that the fellow died in his hands. In the meantime, a Dutchman, who stood next, took up the musket, and with the butt-end of it so laid about him, that he knocked down five of them who attempted to enter the boat. But this was doing little towards resisting thirty or forty men, who, fearless because ignorant of their danger, began to throw themselves into the longboat, where we had but five men in all to defend it; but the following accident, which deserved our laughter, gave our men a complete victory.

Our carpenter being prepared to grave the outside of the ship, as well as to pay the seams where he had caulked her to stop the leaks, had got two kettles just let down into the boat, one filled with boiling pitch, and the other with rosin, tallow, and oil, and such stuff as the shipwrights use for that work; and the man that attended the carpenter had a great iron ladle in his hand, with which he supplied the men that were at work with the hot stuff. Two of the enemy's men entered the boat just where this fellow stood in the foresheets; he immediately saluted them with a ladle full of the stuff, boiling hot which so burned and scalded them, being half-naked that they roared out like bulls, and, enraged with the fire, leaped both into the sea. The carpenter saw it, and cried out, "Well done, Jack! give them some more of it!" and stepping forward himself, takes one of the mops, and dipping it in the pitch-pot, he and his man threw it among them so plentifully that, in short, of all the men in the three boats, there was not one that escaped being scalded in a most frightful manner, and made such a howling and crying that I never heard a worse noise.

I was never better pleased with a victory in my life; not only as it was a perfect surprise to me, and that our danger was imminent before, but as we got this victory without any bloodshed, except of that man the seaman killed with his naked hands, and which I was very much concerned at. Although it maybe a just thing, because necessary (for there is no necessary wickedness in nature), yet I thought it was a sad sort of life, when we must be always obliged to be killing our fellow-creatures to preserve ourselves; and, indeed, I think so still; and I would even now suffer a great deal rather than I would take away the life even of the worst person injuring me; and I believe all considering people, who know the value of life, would be of my opinion, if they entered seriously into the consideration of it.

All the while this was doing, my partner and I, who managed the rest of the men on board, had with great dexterity brought the ship almost to rights, and having got the guns into their places again, the gunner called to me to bid our boat get out of the way, for he would let fly among them. I called back again to him, and bid him not offer to fire, for the carpenter would do the work without him; but bid him heat another pitch-kettle, which our cook, who was on broad, took care of. However, the enemy was so terrified with what they had met with in their first attack, that they would not come on again; and some of them who were farthest off, seeing the ship swim, as it were, upright, began, as we suppose, to see their mistake, and gave over the enterprise, finding it was not as they expected. Thus we got clear of this merry fight; and having got some rice and some roots and bread, with about sixteen hogs, on board two days before, we resolved to stay here no longer, but go forward, whatever came of it; for we made no doubt but we should be surrounded the next day with rogues enough, perhaps more than our pitch-kettle would dispose of for us. We therefore got all our things on board the same evening, and the next morning were ready to sail: in the meantime, lying at anchor at some distance from the shore, we were not so much concerned, being now in a fighting posture, as well as in a sailing posture, if any enemy had presented. The next day, having finished our work within board, and finding our ship was perfectly healed of all her leaks, we set sail. We would have gone into the bay of Tonquin, for we wanted to inform ourselves of what was to be known concerning the Dutch ships that had been there; but we durst not stand in there, because we had seen several ships go in, as we supposed, but a little before; so we kept on NE. towards the island of Formosa, as much afraid of being seen by a Dutch or English merchant ship as a Dutch or English merchant ship in the Mediterranean is of an Algerine man-of-war.

When we were thus got to sea, we kept on NE., as if we would go to the Manillas or the Philippine Islands; and this we did that we might not fall into the way of any of the European ships; and then we steered north, till we came to the latitude of 22 degrees 30 seconds, by which means we made the island of Formosa directly, where we came to an anchor, in order to get water and fresh provisions, which the people there, who are very courteous in their manners, supplied us with willingly, and dealt very fairly and punctually with us in all their agreements and bargains. This is what we did not find among other people, and may be owing to the remains of Christianity which was once planted here by a Dutch missionary of Protestants, and it is a testimony of what I have often observed, viz. that the Christian religion always civilises the people, and reforms their manners, where it is received, whether it works saving effects upon them or no.

From thence we sailed still north, keeping the coast of China at an equal distance, till we knew we were beyond all the ports of China where our European ships usually come; being resolved, if possible, not to fall into any of their hands, especially in this country, where, as our circumstances were, we could not fail of being entirely ruined. Being now come to the latitude of 30 degrees, we resolved to put into the first trading port we should come at; and standing in for the shore, a boat came of two leagues to us with an old Portuguese pilot on board, who, knowing us to be an European ship, came to offer his service, which, indeed, we were glad of and took him on board; upon which, without asking us whither we would go, he dismissed the boat he came in, and sent it back. I thought it was now so much in our choice to make the old man carry us whither we would, that I began to talk to him about carrying us to the Gulf of Nankin, which is the most northern part of the coast of China. The old man said he knew the Gulf of Nankin very well; but smiling, asked us what we would do there? I told him we would sell our cargo and purchase China wares, calicoes, raw silks, tea, wrought silks, &c.; and so we would return by the same course we came. He told us our best port would have been to put in at Macao, where we could not have failed of a market for our opium to our satisfaction, and might for our money have purchased all sorts of China goods as cheap as we could at Nankin.

Not being able to put the old man out of his talk, of which he was very opinionated or conceited, I told him we were gentlemen as well as merchants, and that we had a mind to go and see the great city of Pekin, and the famous court of the monarch of China. "Why, then," says the old man, "you should go to Ningpo, where, by the river which runs into the sea there, you may go up within five leagues of the great canal. This canal is a navigable stream, which goes through the heart of that vast empire of China, crosses all the rivers, passes some considerable hills by the help of sluices and gates, and goes up to the city of Pekin, being in length near two hundred and seventy leagues."—"Well," said I, "Seignior Portuguese, but that is not our business now; the great question is, if you can carry us up to the city of Nankin, from whence we can travel to Pekin afterwards?" He said he could do so very well, and that there was a great Dutch ship gone up that way just before. This gave me a little shock, for a Dutch ship was now our terror, and we had much rather have met the devil, at least if he had not come in too frightful a figure; and we depended upon it that a Dutch ship would be our destruction, for we were in no condition to fight them; all the ships they trade with into those parts being of great burden, and of much greater force than we were.

The old man found me a little confused, and under some concern when he named a Dutch ship, and said to me, "Sir, you need be under no apprehensions of the Dutch; I suppose they are not now at war with your nation?"—"No," said I, "that's true; but I know not what liberties men may take when they are out of the reach of the laws of their own country."—"Why," says he, "you are no pirates; what need you fear? They will not meddle with peaceable merchants, sure." These words put me into the greatest disorder and confusion imaginable; nor was it possible for me to conceal it so, but the old man easily perceived it.

"Sir," says he, "I find you are in some disorder in your thoughts at my talk: pray be pleased to go which way you think fit, and depend upon it, I'll do you all the service I can." Upon this we fell into further discourse, in which, to my alarm and amazement, he spoke of the villainous doings of a certain pirate ship that had long been the talk of mariners in those seas; no other, in a word, than the very ship he was now on board of, and which we had so unluckily purchased. I presently saw there was no help for it but to tell him the plain truth, and explain all the danger and trouble we had suffered through this misadventure, and, in particular, our earnest wish to be speedily quit of the ship altogether; for which reason we had resolved to carry her up to Nankin.

The old man was amazed at this relation, and told us we were in the right to go away to the north; and that, if he might advise us, it should be to sell the ship in China, which we might well do, and buy, or build another in the country; adding that I should meet with customers enough for the ship at Nankin, that a Chinese junk would serve me very well to go back again, and that he would procure me people both to buy one and sell the other. "Well, but, seignior," said I, "as you say they know the ship so well, I may, perhaps, if I follow your measures, be instrumental to bring some honest, innocent men into a terrible broil; for wherever they find the ship they will prove the guilt upon the men, by proving this was the ship."—"Why," says the old man, "I'll find out a way to prevent that; for as I know all those commanders you speak of very well, and shall see them all as they pass by, I will be sure to set them to rights in the thing, and let them know that they had been so much in the wrong; that though the people who were on board at first might run away with the ship, yet it was not true that they had turned pirates; and that, in particular, these were not the men that first went off with the ship, but innocently bought her for their trade; and I am persuaded they will so far believe me as at least to act more cautiously for the time to come."

In about thirteen days' sail we came to an anchor, at the south-west point of the great Gulf of Nankin; where I learned by accident that two Dutch ships were gone the length before me, and that I should certainly fall into their hands. I consulted my partner again in this exigency, and he was as much at a loss as I was. I then asked the old pilot if there was no creek or harbour which I might put into and pursue my business with the Chinese privately, and be in no danger of the enemy. He told me if I would sail to the southward about forty-two leagues, there was a little port called Quinchang, where the fathers of the mission usually landed from Macao, on their progress to teach the Christian religion to the Chinese, and where no European ships ever put in; and if I thought to put in there, I might consider what further course to take when I was on shore. He confessed, he said, it was not a place for merchants, except that at some certain times they had a kind of a fair there, when the merchants from Japan came over thither to buy Chinese merchandises. The name of the port I may perhaps spell wrong, having lost this, together with the names of many other places set down in a little pocket-book, which was spoiled by the water by an accident; but this I remember, that the Chinese merchants we corresponded with called it by a different name from that which our Portuguese pilot gave it, who pronounced it Quinchang. As we were unanimous in our resolution to go to this place, we weighed the next day, having only gone twice on shore where we were, to get fresh water; on both which occasions the people of the country were very civil, and brought abundance of provisions to sell to us; but nothing without money.

We did not come to the other port (the wind being contrary) for five days; but it was very much to our satisfaction, and I was thankful when I set my foot on shore, resolving, and my partner too, that if it was possible to dispose of ourselves and effects any other way, though not profitably, we would never more set foot on board that unhappy vessel. Indeed, I must acknowledge, that of all the circumstances of life that ever I had any experience of, nothing makes mankind so completely miserable as that of being in constant fear. Well does the Scripture say, "The fear of man brings a snare"; it is a life of death, and the mind is so entirely oppressed by it, that it is capable of no relief.

Nor did it fail of its usual operations upon the fancy, by heightening every danger; representing the English and Dutch captains to be men incapable of hearing reason, or of distinguishing between honest men and rogues; or between a story calculated for our own turn, made out of nothing, on purpose to deceive, and a true, genuine account of our whole voyage, progress, and design; for we might many ways have convinced any reasonable creatures that we were not pirates; the goods we had on board, the course we steered, our frankly showing ourselves, and entering into such and such ports; and even our very manner, the force we had, the number of men, the few arms, the little ammunition, short provisions; all these would have served to convince any men that we were no pirates. The opium and other goods we had on board would make it appear the ship had been at Bengal. The Dutchmen, who, it was said, had the names of all the men that were in the ship, might easily see that we were a mixture of English, Portuguese, and Indians, and but two Dutchmen on board. These, and many other particular circumstances, might have made it evident to the understanding of any commander, whose hands we might fall into, that we were no pirates.

But fear, that blind, useless passion, worked another way, and threw us into the vapours; it bewildered our understandings, and set the imagination at work to form a thousand terrible things that perhaps might never happen. We first supposed, as indeed everybody had related to us, that the seamen on board the English and Dutch ships, but especially the Dutch, were so enraged at the name of a pirate, and especially at our beating off their boats and escaping, that they would not give themselves leave to inquire whether we were pirates or no, but would execute us off-hand, without giving us any room for a defence. We reflected that there really was so much apparent evidence before them, that they would scarce inquire after any more; as, first, that the ship was certainly the same, and that some of the seamen among them knew her, and had been on board her; and, secondly, that when we had intelligence at the river of Cambodia that they were coming down to examine us, we fought their boats and fled. Therefore we made no doubt but they were as fully satisfied of our being pirates as we were satisfied of the contrary; and, as I often said, I know not but I should have been apt to have taken those circumstances for evidence, if the tables were turned, and my case was theirs; and have made no scruple of cutting all the crew to pieces, without believing, or perhaps considering, what they might have to offer in their defence.

But let that be how it will, these were our apprehensions; and both my partner and I scarce slept a night without dreaming of halters and yard-arms; of fighting, and being taken; of killing, and being killed: and one night I was in such a fury in my dream, fancying the Dutchmen had boarded us, and I was knocking one of their seamen down, that I struck my doubled fist against the side of the cabin I lay in with such a force as wounded my hand grievously, broke my knuckles, and cut and bruised the flesh, so that it awaked me out of my sleep. Another apprehension I had was, the cruel usage we might meet with from them if we fell into their hands; then the story of Amboyna came into my head, and how the Dutch might perhaps torture us, as they did our countrymen there, and make some of our men, by extremity of torture, confess to crimes they never were guilty of, or own themselves and all of us to be pirates, and so they would put us to death with a formal appearance of justice; and that they might be tempted to do this for the gain of our ship and cargo, worth altogether four or five thousand pounds. We did not consider that the captains of ships have no authority to act thus; and if we had surrendered prisoners to them, they could not answer the destroying us, or torturing us, but would be accountable for it when they came to their country. However, if they were to act thus with us, what advantage would it be to us that they should be called to an account for it?—or if we were first to be murdered, what satisfaction would it be to us to have them punished when they came home?

I cannot refrain taking notice here what reflections I now had upon the vast variety of my particular circumstances; how hard I thought it that I, who had spent forty years in a life of continual difficulties, and was at last come, as it were, to the port or haven which all men drive at, viz. to have rest and plenty, should be a volunteer in new sorrows by my own unhappy choice, and that I, who had escaped so many dangers in my youth, should now come to be hanged in my old age, and in so remote a place, for a crime which I was not in the least inclined to, much less guilty of. After these thoughts something of religion would come in; and I would be considering that this seemed to me to be a disposition of immediate Providence, and I ought to look upon it and submit to it as such. For, although I was innocent as to men, I was far from being innocent as to my Maker; and I ought to look in and examine what other crimes in my life were most obvious to me, and for which Providence might justly inflict this punishment as a retribution; and thus I ought to submit to this, just as I would to a shipwreck, if it had pleased God to have brought such a disaster upon me.

In its turn natural courage would sometimes take its place, and then I would be talking myself up to vigorous resolutions; that I would not be taken to be barbarously used by a parcel of merciless wretches in cold blood; that it were much better to have fallen into the hands of the savages, though I were sure they would feast upon me when they had taken me, than those who would perhaps glut their rage upon me by inhuman tortures and barbarities; that in the case of the savages, I always resolved to die fighting to the last gasp, and why should I not do so now? Whenever these thoughts prevailed, I was sure to put myself into a kind of fever with the agitation of a supposed fight; my blood would boil, and my eyes sparkle, as if I was engaged, and I always resolved to take no quarter at their hands; but even at last, if I could resist no longer, I would blow up the ship and all that was in her, and leave them but little booty to boast of.

Chapter XIII—ARRIVAL IN CHINA

The greater weight the anxieties and perplexities of these things were to our thoughts while we were at sea, the greater was our satisfaction when we saw ourselves on shore; and my partner told me he dreamed that he had a very heavy load upon his back, which he was to carry up a hill, and found that he was not able to stand longer under it; but that the Portuguese pilot came and took it off his back, and the hill disappeared, the ground before him appearing all smooth and plain: and truly it was so; they were all like men who had a load taken off their backs. For my part I had a weight taken off from my heart that it was not able any longer to bear; and as I said above we resolved to go no more to sea in that ship. When we came on shore, the old pilot, who was now our friend, got us a lodging, together with a warehouse for our goods; it was a little hut, with a larger house adjoining to it, built and also palisadoed round with canes, to keep out pilferers, of which there were not a few in that country: however, the magistrates allowed us a little guard, and we had a soldier with a kind of half-pike, who stood sentinel at our door, to whom we allowed a pint of rice and a piece of money about the value of three-pence per day, so that our goods were kept very safe.

The fair or mart usually kept at this place had been over some time; however, we found that there were three or four junks in the river, and two ships from Japan, with goods which they had bought in China, and were not gone away, having some Japanese merchants on shore.

The first thing our old Portuguese pilot did for us was to get us acquainted with three missionary Romish priests who were in the town, and who had been there some time converting the people to Christianity; but we thought they made but poor work of it, and made them but sorry Christians when they had done. One of these was a Frenchman, whom they called Father Simon; another was a Portuguese; and a third a Genoese. Father Simon was courteous, and very agreeable company; but the other two were more reserved, seemed rigid and austere, and applied seriously to the work they came about, viz. to talk with and insinuate themselves among the inhabitants wherever they had opportunity. We often ate and drank with those men; and though I must confess the conversion, as they call it, of the Chinese to Christianity is so far from the true conversion required to bring heathen people to the faith of Christ, that it seems to amount to little more than letting them know the name of Christ, and say some prayers to the Virgin

Mary and her Son, in a tongue which they understood not, and to cross themselves, and the like; yet it must be confessed that the religionists, whom we call missionaries, have a firm belief that these people will be saved, and that they are the instruments of it; and on this account they undergo not only the fatigue of the voyage, and the hazards of living in such places, but oftentimes death itself, and the most violent tortures, for the sake of this work.

Father Simon was appointed, it seems, by order of the chief of the mission, to go up to Pekin, and waited only for another priest, who was ordered to come to him from Macao, to go along with him. We scarce ever met together but he was inviting me to go that journey; telling me how he would show me all the glorious things of that mighty empire, and, among the rest, Pekin, the greatest city in the world: "A city," said he, "that your London and our Paris put together cannot be equal to." But as I looked on those things with different eyes from other men, so I shall give my opinion of them in a few words, when I come in the course of my travels to speak more particularly of them.

Dining with Father Simon one day, and being very merry together, I showed some little inclination to go with him; and he pressed me and my partner very hard to consent. "Why, father," says my partner, "should you desire our company so much? you know we are heretics, and you do not love us, nor cannot keep us company with any pleasure."—"Oh," says he, "you may perhaps be good Catholics in time; my business here is to convert heathens, and who knows but I may convert you too?"—"Very well, father," said I, "so you will preach to us all the way?"—"I will not be troublesome to you," says he; "our religion does not divest us of good manners; besides, we are here like countrymen; and so we are, compared to the place we are in; and if you are Huguenots, and I a Catholic, we may all be Christians at last; at least, we are all gentlemen, and we may converse so, without being uneasy to one another." I liked this part of his discourse very well, and it began to put me in mind of my priest that I had left in the Brazils; but Father Simon did not come up to his character by a great deal; for though this friar had no appearance of a criminal levity in him, yet he had not that fund of Christian zeal, strict piety, and sincere affection to religion that my other good ecclesiastic had.

But to leave him a little, though he never left us, nor solicited us to go with him; we had something else before us at first, for we had all this while our ship and our merchandise to dispose of, and we began to be very doubtful what we should do, for we were now in a place of very little business. Once I was about to venture to sail for the river of Kilam, and the city of Nankin; but Providence seemed now more visibly, as I thought, than ever to concern itself in our affairs; and I was encouraged, from this very time, to think I should, one way or other, get out of this entangled circumstance, and be brought home to my own country again, though I had not the least view of the manner. Providence, I say, began here to clear up our way a little; and the first thing that offered was, that our old Portuguese pilot brought a Japan merchant to us, who inquired what goods we had: and, in the first place, he bought all our opium, and gave us a very good price for it, paying us in gold by weight, some in small pieces of their own coin, and some in small wedges, of about ten or twelves ounces each. While we were dealing with him for our opium, it came into my head that he might perhaps deal for the ship too, and I ordered the interpreter to propose it to him. He shrunk up his shoulders at it when it was first proposed to him; but in a few days after he came to me, with one of the missionary priests for his interpreter, and told me he had a proposal to make to me, which was this: he had bought a great quantity of our goods, when he had no thoughts of proposals made to him of buying the ship; and that, therefore, he had not money to pay for the ship: but if I would let the same men who were in the ship navigate her, he would hire the ship to go to Japan; and would send them from thence to the Philippine Islands with another loading, which he would pay the freight of before they went from Japan: and that at their return he would buy the ship. I began to listen to his proposal, and so eager did my head still run upon rambling, that I could not but begin to entertain a notion of going myself with him, and so to set sail from the Philippine Islands away to the South Seas; accordingly, I asked the Japanese merchant if he would not hire us to the Philippine Islands and discharge us there. He said No, he could not do that, for then he could not have the return of his cargo; but he would discharge us in Japan, at the ship's return. Well, still I was for taking him at that proposal, and going myself; but my partner, wiser than myself, persuaded me from it, representing the dangers, as well of the seas as of the Japanese, who are a false, cruel, and treacherous people; likewise those of the Spaniards at the Philippines, more false, cruel, and treacherous than they.

But to bring this long turn of our affairs to a conclusion; the first thing we had to do was to consult with the captain of the ship, and with his men, and know if they were willing to go to Japan. While I was doing this, the young man whom my nephew had left with me as my companion came up, and told me that he thought that voyage promised very fair, and that there was a great prospect of advantage, and he would be very glad if I undertook it; but that if I would not, and would give him leave, he would go as a merchant, or as I pleased to order him; that if ever he came to England, and I was there and alive, he would render me a faithful account of his success, which should be as much mine as I pleased. I was loath to part with him; but considering the prospect of advantage, which really was considerable, and that he was a young fellow likely to do well in it, I inclined to let him go; but I told him I would consult my partner, and give him an answer the next day. I discoursed about it with my partner, who thereupon made a most generous offer: "You know it has been an unlucky ship," said he, "and we both resolve not to go to sea in it again; if your steward" (so he called my man) "will venture the voyage, I will leave my share of the vessel to him, and let him make the best of it; and if we live to meet in England, and he meets with success abroad, he shall account for one half of the profits of the ship's freight to us; the other shall be his own."

If my partner, who was no way concerned with my young man, made him such an offer, I could not do less than offer him the same; and all the ship's company being willing to go with him, we made over half the ship to him in property, and took a writing from him, obliging him to account for the other, and away he went to Japan. The Japan merchant proved a very punctual, honest man to him: protected him at Japan, and got him a licence to come on shore, which the Europeans in general have not lately obtained. He paid him his freight very punctually; sent him to the Philippines loaded with Japan and China wares, and a supercargo of their own, who, trafficking with the Spaniards, brought back European goods again, and a great quantity of spices; and there he was not only paid his freight very well, and at a very good price, but not being willing to sell the ship, then the merchant furnished him goods on his own account; and with some money, and some spices of his own which he brought with him, he went back to the Manillas, where he sold his cargo very well. Here, having made a good acquaintance at Manilla, he got his ship made a free ship, and the governor of Manilla hired him to go to Acapulco, on the coast of America, and gave him a licence to land there, and to travel to Mexico, and to pass in any Spanish ship to Europe with all his men. He made the voyage to Acapulco very happily, and there he sold his ship: and having there also obtained allowance to travel by land to Porto Bello, he found means to get to Jamaica, with all his treasure, and about eight years after came to England exceeding rich.

But to return to our particular affairs, being now to part with the ship and ship's company, it came before us, of course, to consider what recompense we should give to the two men that gave us such timely notice of the design against us in the river Cambodia. The truth was, they had done us a very considerable service, and deserved well at our hands; though, by the way, they were a couple of rogues, too; for, as they believed the story of our being pirates, and that we had really run away with the ship, they came down to us, not only to betray the design that was formed against us, but to go to sea with us as pirates. One of them confessed afterwards that nothing else but the hopes of going a-roguing brought him to do it: however, the service they did us was not the less, and therefore, as I had promised to be grateful to them, I first ordered the money to be paid them which they said was due to them on board their respective ships: over and above that, I gave each of them a small sum of money in gold, which contented them very well. I then made the Englishman gunner in the ship, the gunner being now made second mate and purser; the Dutchman I made boatswain; so they were both very well pleased, and proved very serviceable, being both able seamen, and very stout fellows.

We were now on shore in China; if I thought myself banished, and remote from my own country at Bengal, where I had many ways to get home for my money, what could I think of myself now, when I was about a thousand leagues farther off from home, and destitute of all manner of prospect of return? All we had for it was this: that in about four months' time there was to be another fair at the place where we were, and then we might be able to purchase various manufactures of the country, and withal might possibly find some Chinese junks from Tonquin for sail, that would carry us and our goods whither we pleased. This I liked very well, and resolved to wait; besides, as our particular persons were not obnoxious, so if any English or Dutch ships came thither, perhaps we might have an opportunity to load our goods, and get passage to some other place in India nearer home. Upon these hopes we resolved to continue here; but, to divert ourselves, we took two or three journeys into the country.

First, we went ten days' journey to Nankin, a city well worth seeing; they say it has a million of people in it: it is regularly built, and the streets are all straight, and cross one another in direct lines. But when I come to compare the miserable people of these countries with ours, their fabrics, their manner of living, their government, their religion, their wealth, and their glory, as some call it, I must confess that I scarcely think it worth my while to mention them here. We wonder at the grandeur, the riches, the pomp, the ceremonies, the government, the manufactures, the commerce, and conduct of these people; not that there is really any matter for wonder, but because, having a true notion of the barbarity of those countries, the rudeness and the ignorance that prevail there, we do not expect to find any such thing so far off. Otherwise, what are their buildings to the palaces and royal buildings of Europe? What their trade to the universal commerce of England, Holland, France, and Spain? What are their cities to ours, for wealth, strength, gaiety of apparel, rich furniture, and infinite variety? What are their ports, supplied with a few junks and barks, to our navigation, our merchant fleets, our large and powerful navies? Our city of London has more trade than half their mighty empire: one English, Dutch, or French man-of-war of eighty guns would be able to fight almost all the shipping belonging to China: but the greatness of their wealth, their trade, the power of their government, and the strength of their armies, may be a little surprising to us, because, as I have said, considering them as a barbarous nation of pagans, little better than savages, we did not expect such things among them. But all the forces of their empire, though they were to bring two millions of men into the field together, would be able to do nothing but ruin the country and starve themselves; a million of their foot could not stand before one embattled body of our infantry, posted so as not to be surrounded, though they were not to be one to twenty in number; nay, I do not boast if I say that thirty thousand German or English foot, and ten thousand horse, well managed, could defeat all the forces of China. Nor is there a fortified town in China that could hold out one month against the batteries and attacks of an European army. They have firearms, it is true, but they are awkward and uncertain in their going off; and their powder has but little strength. Their armies are badly disciplined, and want skill to attack, or temper to retreat; and therefore, I must confess, it seemed strange to me, when I came home, and heard our people say such fine things of the power, glory, magnificence, and trade of the Chinese; because, as far as I saw, they appeared to be a contemptible herd or crowd of ignorant, sordid slaves, subjected to a government qualified only to rule such a people; and were not its distance inconceivably, great from Muscovy, and that empire in a manner as rude, impotent, and ill governed as they, the Czar of Muscovy might with ease drive them all out of their country, and conquer them in one campaign; and had the Czar (who is now a growing prince) fallen this way, instead of attacking the warlike Swedes, and equally improved himself in the art of war, as they say he has done; and if none of the powers of Europe had envied or interrupted him, he might by this time have been Emperor of China, instead of being beaten by the King of Sweden at Narva, when the latter was not one to six in number.

As their strength and their grandeur, so their navigation, commerce, and husbandry are very imperfect, compared to the same things in Europe; also, in their knowledge, their learning, and in their skill in the sciences, they are either very awkward or defective, though they have globes or spheres, and a smattering of the mathematics, and think they know more than all the world besides. But they know little of the motions of the heavenly bodies; and so grossly and absurdly ignorant are their common people, that when the sun is eclipsed, they think a great dragon has assaulted it, and is going to run away with it; and they fall a clattering with all the drums and kettles in the country, to fright the monster away, just as we do to hive a swarm of bees!

As this is the only excursion of the kind which I have made in all the accounts I have given of my travels, so I shall make no more such. It is none of my business, nor any part of my design; but to give an account of my own adventures through a life of inimitable wanderings, and a long variety of changes, which, perhaps, few that come after me will have heard the like of: I shall, therefore, say very little of all the mighty places, desert countries, and numerous people I have yet to pass through, more than relates to my own story, and which my concern among them will make necessary.

I was now, as near as I can compute, in the heart of China, about thirty degrees north of the line, for we were returned from Nankin. I had indeed a mind to see the city of Pekin, which I had heard so much of, and Father Simon importuned me daily to do it. At length his time of going away being set, and the other missionary who was to go with him being arrived from Macao, it was necessary that we should resolve either to go or not; so I referred it to my partner, and left it wholly to his choice, who at length resolved it in the affirmative, and we prepared for our journey. We set out with very good advantage as to finding the way; for we got leave to travel in the retinue of one of their mandarins, a kind of viceroy or principal magistrate in the province where they reside, and who take great state upon them, travelling with great attendance, and great homage from the people, who are sometimes greatly impoverished by them, being obliged to furnish provisions for them and all their attendants in their journeys. I particularly observed in our travelling with his baggage, that though we received sufficient provisions both for ourselves and our horses from the country, as belonging to the mandarin, yet we were obliged to pay for everything we had, after the market price of the country, and the mandarin's steward collected it duly from us. Thus our travelling in the retinue of the mandarin, though it was a great act of kindness, was not such a mighty favour to us, but was a great advantage to him, considering there were above thirty other people travelled in the same manner besides us, under the protection of his retinue; for the country furnished all the provisions for nothing to him, and yet he took our money for them.

We were twenty-five days travelling to Pekin, through a country exceeding populous, but I think badly cultivated; the husbandry, the economy, and the way of living miserable, though they boast so much of the industry of the people: I say miserable, if compared with our own, but not so to these poor wretches, who know no other. The pride of the poor people is infinitely great, and exceeded by nothing but their poverty, in some parts, which adds to that which I call their misery; and I must needs think the savages of America live much more happy than the poorer sort of these, because as they have nothing, so they desire nothing; whereas these are proud and insolent and in the main are in many parts mere beggars and drudges. Their ostentation is inexpressible; and, if they can, they love to keep multitudes of servants or slaves, which is to the last degree ridiculous, as well as their contempt of all the world but themselves.

I must confess I travelled more pleasantly afterwards in the deserts and vast wildernesses of Grand Tartary than here, and yet the roads here are well paved and well kept, and very convenient for travellers; but nothing was more awkward to me than to see such a haughty, imperious, insolent people, in the midst of the grossest simplicity and ignorance; and my friend Father Simon and I used to be very merry upon these occasions, to see their beggarly pride. For example, coming by the house of a country gentleman, as Father Simon called him, about ten leagues off the city of Nankin, we had first of all the honour to ride with the master of the house about two miles; the state he rode in was a perfect Don Quixotism, being a mixture of pomp and poverty. His habit was very proper for a merry-andrew, being a dirty calico, with hanging sleeves, tassels, and cuts and slashes almost on every side: it covered a taffety vest, so greasy as to testify that his honour must be a most exquisite sloven. His horse was a poor, starved, hobbling creature, and two slaves followed him on foot to drive the poor creature along; he had a whip in his hand, and he belaboured the beast as fast about the head as his slaves did about the tail; and thus he rode by us, with about ten or twelve servants, going from the city to his country seat, about half a league before us. We travelled on gently, but this figure of a gentleman rode away before us; and as we stopped at a village about an hour to refresh us, when we came by the country seat of this great man, we saw him in a little place before his door, eating a repast. It was a kind of garden, but he was easy to be seen; and we were given to understand that the more we looked at him the better he would be pleased. He sat under a tree, something like the palmetto, which effectually shaded him over the head, and on the south side; but under the tree was placed a large umbrella, which made that part look well enough. He sat lolling back in a great elbow-chair, being a heavy corpulent man, and had his meat brought him by two women slaves. He had two more, one of whom fed the squire with a spoon, and the other held the dish with one hand, and scraped off what he let fall upon his worship's beard and taffety vest.

Leaving the poor wretch to please himself with our looking at him, as if we admired his idle pomp, we pursued our journey. Father Simon had the curiosity to stay to inform himself what dainties the country justice had to feed on in all his state, which he had the honour to taste of, and which was, I think, a mess of boiled rice, with a great piece of garlic in it, and a little bag filled with green pepper, and another plant which they have there, something like our ginger, but smelling like musk, and tasting like mustard; all this was put together, and a small piece of lean mutton boiled in it, and this was his worship's repast. Four or five servants more attended at a distance, who we supposed were to eat of the same after their master. As for our mandarin with whom we travelled, he was respected as a king, surrounded always with his gentlemen, and attended in all his appearances with such pomp, that I saw little of him but at a distance. I observed that there was not a horse in his retinue but that our carrier's packhorses in England seemed to me to look much better; though it was hard to judge rightly, for they were so covered with equipage, mantles, trappings, &c., that we could scarce see anything but their feet and their heads as they went along.

I was now light-hearted, and all my late trouble and perplexity being over, I had no anxious thoughts about me, which made this journey the pleasanter to me; in which no ill accident attended me, only in passing or fording a small river, my horse fell and made me free of the country, as they call it—that is to say, threw me in. The place was not deep, but it wetted me all over. I mention it because it spoiled my pocket-book, wherein I had set down the names of several people and places which I had occasion to remember, and which not taking due care of, the leaves rotted, and the words were never after to be read.

At length we arrived at Pekin. I had nobody with me but the youth whom my nephew had given me to attend me as a servant and who proved very trusty and diligent; and my partner had nobody with him but one servant, who was a kinsman. As for the Portuguese pilot, he being desirous to see the court, we bore his charges for his company, and for our use of him as an interpreter, for he understood the language of the country, and spoke good French and a little English. Indeed, this old man was most useful to us everywhere; for we had not been above a week at Pekin, when he came laughing. "Ah, Seignior Inglese," says he, "I have something to tell will make your heart glad."—"My heart glad," says I; "what can that be? I don't know anything in this country can either give me joy or grief to any great degree."—"Yes, yes," said the old man, in broken English, "make you glad, me sorry."—"Why," said I, "will it make you sorry?"—"Because," said he, "you have brought me here twenty-five days' journey, and will leave me to go back alone; and which way shall I get to my port afterwards, without a ship, without a horse, without *pecune*?" so he called money, being his broken Latin, of which he had abundance to make us merry with. In short, he told us there was a great caravan of Muscovite and Polish merchants in the city, preparing to set out on their journey by land to Muscovy, within four or five weeks; and he was sure we would take the opportunity to go with them, and leave him behind, to go back alone.

I confess I was greatly surprised with this good news, and had scarce power to speak to him for some time; but at last I said to him, "How do you know this? are you sure it is true?"—"Yes," says he; "I met this morning in the street an old acquaintance of mine, an Armenian, who is among them. He came last from Astrakhan, and was designed to go to Tonquin, where I formerly knew him, but has altered his mind, and is now resolved to go with the caravan to Moscow, and so down the river Volga to Astrakhan."—"Well, Seignior," says I, "do not be uneasy about being left to go back alone; if this be a method for my return to England, it shall be your fault if you go back to Macao at all." We then went to consult together what was to be done; and I asked my partner what he thought of the pilot's news, and whether it would suit with his affairs? He told me he would do just as I would; for he had settled all his affairs so well at Bengal, and left his effects in such good hands, that as we had made a good voyage, if he could invest it in China silks, wrought and raw, he would be content to go to England, and then make a voyage back to Bengal by the Company's ships.

Having resolved upon this, we agreed that if our Portuguese pilot would go with us, we would bear his charges to Moscow, or to England, if he pleased; nor, indeed, were we to be esteemed over-generous in that either, if we had not rewarded him further, the service he had done us being really worth more than that; for he had not only been a pilot to us at sea, but he had been like a broker for us on shore; and his procuring for us a Japan merchant was some hundreds of pounds in our pockets. So, being willing to gratify him, which was but doing him justice, and very willing also to have him with us besides, for he was a most necessary man on all occasions, we agreed to give him a quantity of coined gold, which, as I computed it, was worth one hundred and seventy-five pounds sterling, between us, and to bear all his charges, both for himself and horse, except only a horse to carry his goods. Having settled this between ourselves, we called him to let him know what we had resolved. I told him he had complained of our being willing to let him go back alone, and I was now about to tell him we designed he should not go back at all. That as we had resolved to go to Europe with the caravan, we were very willing he should go with us; and that we called him to know his mind. He shook his head and said it was a long journey, and that he had no *pecune* to carry him thither, or to subsist himself when he came there. We told him we believed it was so, and therefore we had resolved to do something for him that should let him see how sensible we were of the service he had done us, and also how agreeable he was to us: and then I told him what we had resolved to give him here, which he might lay out as we would do our own; and that as for his charges, if he would go with us we would set him safe on shore (life and casualties excepted), either in Muscovy or England, as he would choose, at our own charge, except only the carriage of his goods. He received the proposal like a man transported, and told us he would go with us over all the whole world; and so we all prepared for our journey. However, as it was with us, so it was with the other merchants: they had many things to do, and instead of being ready in five weeks, it was four months and some days before all things were got together.

Chapter XIV—ATTACKED BY TARTARS

It was the beginning of February, new style, when we set out from Pekin. My partner and the old pilot had gone express back to the port where we had first put in, to dispose of some goods which we had left there; and I, with a Chinese merchant whom I had some knowledge of at Nankin, and who came to Pekin on his own affairs, went to Nankin, where I bought ninety pieces of fine damasks, with about two hundred pieces of other very fine silk of several sorts, some mixed with gold, and had all these brought to Pekin against my partner's return. Besides this, we bought a large quantity of raw silk, and some other goods, our cargo amounting, in these goods only, to about three thousand five hundred pounds sterling; which, together with tea and some fine calicoes, and three camels' loads of nutmegs and cloves, loaded in all eighteen camels for our share, besides those we rode upon; these, with two or three spare horses, and two horses loaded with provisions, made together twenty-six camels and horses in our retinue.

The company was very great, and, as near as I can remember, made between three and four hundred horses, and upwards of one hundred and twenty men, very well armed and provided for all events; for as the Eastern caravans are subject to be attacked by the Arabs, so are these by the Tartars. The company consisted of people of several nations, but there were above sixty of them merchants or inhabitants of Moscow, though of them some were Livonians; and to our particular satisfaction, five of them were Scots, who appeared also to be men of great experience in business, and of very good substance.

When we had travelled one day's journey, the guides, who were five in number, called all the passengers, except the servants, to a great council, as they called it. At this council every one deposited a certain quantity of money to a common stock, for the necessary expense of buying forage on the way, where it was not otherwise to be had, and for satisfying the guides, getting horses, and the like. Here, too, they constituted the journey, as they call it, viz. they named captains and officers to draw us all up, and give the word of command, in case of an attack, and give every one their turn of command; nor was this forming us into order any more than what we afterwards found needful on the way.

The road all on this side of the country is very populous, and is full of potters and earth-makers—that is to say, people, that temper the earth for the China ware. As I was coming along, our Portuguese pilot, who had always something or other to say to make us merry, told me he would show me the greatest rarity in all the country, and that I should have this to say of China, after all the ill-humoured things that I had said of it, that I had seen one thing which was not to be seen in all the world beside. I was very importunate to know what it was; at last he told me it was a gentleman's house built with China ware. "Well," says I, "are not the materials of their buildings the products of their own country, and so it is all China ware, is it not?"—"No, no," says he, "I mean it is a house all made of China ware, such as you call it in England, or as it is called in our country, porcelain."—"Well," says I, "such a thing may be; how big is it? Can we carry it in a box upon a camel? If we can we will buy it."—"Upon a camel!" says the old pilot, holding up both his hands; "why, there is a family of thirty people lives in it."

I was then curious, indeed, to see it; and when I came to it, it was nothing but this: it was a timber house, or a house built, as we call it in England, with lath and plaster, but all this plastering was really China ware—that is to say, it was plastered with the earth that makes China ware. The outside, which the sun shone hot upon, was glazed, and looked very well, perfectly white, and painted with blue figures, as the large China ware in England is painted, and hard as if it had been burnt. As to the inside, all the walls, instead of wainscot, were lined with hardened and painted tiles, like the little square tiles we call galley-tiles in England, all made of the finest china, and the figures exceeding fine indeed, with extraordinary variety of colours, mixed with gold, many tiles making but one figure, but joined so artificially, the mortar being made of the same earth, that it was very hard to see where the tiles met. The floors of the rooms were of the same composition, and as hard as the earthen floors we have in use in several parts of England; as hard as stone, and smooth, but not burnt and painted, except some smaller rooms, like closets, which were all, as it were, paved with the same tile; the ceiling and all the plastering work in the whole house were of the same earth; and, after all, the roof was covered with tiles of the same, but of a deep shining black. This was a China warehouse indeed, truly and literally to be called so, and had I not been upon the journey, I could have stayed some days to see and examine the particulars of it. They told me there were fountains and fishponds in the garden, all paved on the bottom and sides with the same; and fine statues set up in rows on the walks, entirely formed of the porcelain earth, burnt whole.

As this is one of the singularities of China, so they may be allowed to excel in it; but I am very sure they excel in their accounts of it; for they told me such incredible things of their performance in crockery-ware, for such it is, that I care not to relate, as knowing it could not be true. They told me, in particular, of one workman that made a ship with all its tackle and masts and sails in earthenware, big enough to carry fifty men. If they had told me he launched it, and made a voyage to Japan in it, I might have said something to it indeed; but as it was, I knew the whole of the story, which was, in short, that the fellow lied: so I smiled, and said nothing to it. This odd sight kept me two hours behind the caravan, for which the leader of it for the day fined me about the value of three shillings; and told me if it had been three days' journey without the wall, as it was three days' within, he must have fined me four times as much, and made me ask pardon the next council-day. I promised to be more orderly; and, indeed, I found afterwards the orders made for keeping all together were absolutely necessary for our common safety.

In two days more we passed the great China wall, made for a fortification against the Tartars: and a very great work it is, going over hills and mountains in an endless track, where the rocks are impassable, and the precipices such as no enemy could possibly enter, or indeed climb up, or where, if they did, no wall could hinder them. They tell us its length is near a thousand English miles, but that the country is five hundred in a straight measured line, which the wall bounds without measuring the windings and turnings it takes; it is about four fathoms high, and as many thick in some places.

I stood still an hour or thereabouts without trespassing on our orders (for so long the caravan was in passing the gate), to look at it on every side, near and far off; I mean what was within my view: and the guide, who had been extolling it for the wonder of the world, was mighty eager to hear my opinion of it. I told him it was a most excellent thing to keep out the Tartars; which he happened not to understand as I meant it and so took it for a compliment; but the old pilot laughed! "Oh, Seignior Inglese," says he, "you speak in colours."—"In colours!" said I; "what do you mean by that?"—"Why, you speak what looks white this way and black that way—gay one way and dull another. You tell him it is a good wall to keep out Tartars; you tell me by that it is good for nothing but to keep out Tartars. I understand you, Seignior Inglese, I understand you; but Seignior Chinese understood you his own way."—"Well," says I, "do you think it would stand out an army of our country people, with a good train of artillery; or our engineers, with two companies of miners? Would not they batter it down in ten days, that an army might enter in battalia; or blow it up in the air, foundation and all, that there should be no sign of it left?"—"Ay, ay," says he, "I know that." The Chinese wanted mightily to know what I said to the pilot, and I gave him leave to tell him a few days after, for we were then almost out of their country, and he was to leave us a little time after this; but when he knew what I said, he was dumb all the rest of the way, and we heard no more of his fine story of the Chinese power and greatness while he stayed.

After we passed this mighty nothing, called a wall, something like the Picts' walls so famous in Northumberland, built by the Romans, we began to find the country thinly inhabited, and the people rather confined to live in fortified towns, as being subject to the inroads and depredations of the Tartars, who rob in great armies, and therefore are not to be resisted by the naked inhabitants of an open country. And here I began to find the necessity of keeping together in a caravan as we travelled, for we saw several troops of Tartars roving about; but when I came to see them distinctly, I wondered more that the Chinese empire could be conquered by such contemptible fellows; for they are a mere horde of wild fellows, keeping no order and understanding no discipline or manner of it. Their horses are poor lean creatures, taught nothing, and fit for nothing; and this we found the first day we saw them, which was after we entered the wilder part of the country. Our leader for the day gave leave for about sixteen of us to go a hunting as they call it; and what was this but a hunting of sheep!—however, it may be called hunting too, for these creatures are the wildest and swiftest of foot that ever I saw of their kind! only they will not run a great way, and you are sure of sport when you begin the chase, for they appear generally thirty or forty in a flock, and, like true sheep, always keep together when they fly.

In pursuit of this odd sort of game it was our hap to meet with about forty Tartars: whether they were hunting mutton, as we were, or whether they looked for another kind of prey, we know not; but as soon as they saw us, one of them blew a hideous blast on a kind of horn. This was to call their friends about them, and in less than ten minutes a troop of forty or fifty more appeared, at about a mile distance; but our work was over first, as it happened.

One of the Scots merchants of Moscow happened to be amongst us; and as soon as he heard the horn, he told us that we had nothing to do but to charge them without loss of time; and drawing us up in a line, he asked if we were resolved. We told him we were ready to follow him; so he rode directly towards them. They stood gazing at us like a mere crowd, drawn up in no sort of order at all; but as soon as they saw us advance, they let fly their arrows, which missed us, very happily. Not that they mistook their aim, but their distance; for their arrows all fell a little short of us, but with so true an aim, that had we been about twenty yards nearer we must have had several men wounded, if not killed.

Immediately we halted, and though it was at a great distance, we fired, and sent them leaden bullets for wooden arrows, following our shot full gallop, to fall in among them sword in hand—for so our bold Scot that led us directed. He was, indeed, but a merchant, but he behaved with such vigour and bravery on this occasion, and yet with such cool courage too, that I never saw any man in action fitter for command. As soon as we came up to them we fired our pistols in their faces and then drew; but they fled in the greatest confusion imaginable. The only stand any of them made was on our right, where three of them stood, and, by signs, called the rest to come back to them, having a kind of scimitar in their hands, and their bows hanging to their backs. Our brave commander, without asking anybody to follow him, gallops up close to them, and with his fusee knocks one of them off his horse, killed the second with his pistol, and the third ran away. Thus ended our fight; but we had this misfortune attending it, that all our mutton we had in chase got away. We had not a man killed or hurt; as for the Tartars, there were about five of them killed—how many were wounded we knew not; but this we knew, that the other party were so frightened with the noise of our guns that they fled, and never made any attempt upon us.

We were all this while in the Chinese dominions, and therefore the Tartars were not so bold as afterwards; but in about five days we entered a vast wild desert, which held us three days' and nights' march; and we were obliged to carry our water with us in great leathern bottles, and to encamp all night, just as I have heard they do in the desert of Arabia. I asked our guides whose dominion this was in, and they told me this was a kind of border that might be called no man's land, being a part of Great Karakathy, or Grand Tartary: that, however, it was all reckoned as belonging to China, but that there was no care taken here to preserve it from the inroads of thieves, and therefore it was reckoned the worst desert in the whole march, though we were to go over some much larger.

In passing this frightful wilderness we saw, two or three times, little parties of the Tartars, but they seemed to be upon their own affairs, and to have no design upon us; and so, like the man who met the devil, if they had nothing to say to us, we had nothing to say to them: we let them go. Once, however, a party of them came so near as to stand and gaze at us. Whether it was to consider if they should attack us or not, we knew not; but when we had passed at some distance by them, we made a rear-guard of forty men, and stood ready for them, letting the caravan pass half a mile or thereabouts before us. After a while they marched off, but they saluted us with five arrows at their parting, which wounded a horse so that it disabled him, and we left him the next day, poor creature, in great need of a good farrier. We saw no more arrows or Tartars that time.

We travelled near a month after this, the ways not being so good as at first, though still in the dominions of the Emperor of China, but lay for the most part in the villages, some of which were fortified, because of the incursions of the Tartars. When we were come to one of these towns (about two days and a half's journey before we came to the city of Naum), I wanted to buy a camel, of which there are plenty to be sold all the way upon that road, and horses also, such as they are, because, so many caravans coming that way, they are often wanted. The person that I spoke to to get me a camel would have gone and fetched one for me; but I, like a fool, must be officious, and go myself along with him; the place was about two miles out of the village, where it seems they kept the camels and horses feeding under a guard.

I walked it on foot, with my old pilot and a Chinese, being very desirous of a little variety. When we came to the place it was a low, marshy ground, walled round with stones, piled up dry, without mortar or earth among them, like a park, with a little guard of Chinese soldiers at the door. Having bought a camel, and agreed for the price, I came away, and the Chinese that went with me led the camel, when on a sudden came up five Tartars on horseback. Two of them seized the fellow and took the camel from him, while the other three stepped up to me and my old pilot, seeing us, as it were, unarmed, for I had no weapon about me but my sword, which could but ill defend me against three horsemen. The first that came up stopped short upon my drawing my sword, for they are arrant cowards; but a second, coming upon my left, gave me a blow on the head, which I never felt till afterwards, and wondered, when I came to myself, what was the matter, and where I was, for he laid me flat on the ground; but my never-failing old pilot, the Portuguese, had a pistol in his pocket, which I knew nothing of, nor the Tartars either: if they had, I suppose they would not have attacked us, for cowards are always boldest when there is no danger. The old man seeing me down, with a bold heart stepped up to the fellow that had struck me, and laying hold of his arm with one hand, and pulling him down by main force a little towards him, with the other shot him into the head, and laid him dead upon the spot. He then immediately stepped up to him who had stopped us, as I said, and before he could come forward again, made a blow at him with a scimitar, which he always wore, but missing the man, struck his horse in the side of his head, cut one of the ears off by the root, and a great slice down by the side of his face. The poor beast, enraged with the wound, was no more to be governed by his rider, though the fellow sat well enough too, but away he flew, and carried him quite out of the pilot's reach; and at some distance, rising upon his hind legs, threw down the Tartar, and fell upon him.

In this interval the poor Chinese came in who had lost the camel, but he had no weapon; however, seeing the Tartar down, and his horse fallen upon him, away he runs to him, and seizing upon an ugly weapon he had by his side, something like a pole-axe, he wrenched it from him, and made shift to knock his Tartarian brains out with it. But my old man had the third Tartar to deal with still; and seeing he did not fly, as he expected, nor come on to fight him, as he apprehended, but stood stock still, the old man stood still too, and fell to work with his tackle to charge his pistol again: but as soon as the Tartar saw the pistol away he scoured, and left my pilot, my champion I called him afterwards, a complete victory.

By this time I was a little recovered. I thought, when I first began to wake, that I had been in a sweet sleep; but, as I said above, I wondered where I was, how I came upon the ground, and what was the matter. A few moments after, as sense returned, I felt pain, though I did not know where; so I clapped my hand to my head, and took it away bloody; then I felt my head ache: and in a moment memory returned, and everything was present to me again. I jumped upon my feet instantly, and got hold of my sword, but no enemies were in view: I found a Tartar lying dead, and his horse standing very quietly by him; and, looking further, I saw my deliverer, who had been to see what the Chinese had done, coming back with his hanger in his hand. The old man, seeing me on my feet, came running to me, and joyfully embraced me, being afraid before that I had been killed. Seeing me bloody, he would see how I was hurt; but it was not much, only what we call a broken head; neither did I afterwards find any great inconvenience from the blow, for it was well again in two or three days.

We made no great gain, however, by this victory, for we lost a camel and gained a horse. I paid for the lost camel, and sent for another; but I did not go to fetch it myself: I had had enough of that.

The city of Naum, which we were approaching, is a frontier of the Chinese empire, and is fortified in their fashion. We wanted, as I have said, above two days' journey of this city when messengers were sent express to every part of the road to tell all travellers and caravans to halt till they had a guard sent for them;

for that an unusual body of Tartars, making ten thousand in all, had appeared in the way, about thirty miles beyond the city.

This was very bad news to travellers: however, it was carefully done of the governor, and we were very glad to hear we should have a guard. Accordingly, two days after, we had two hundred soldiers sent us from a garrison of the Chinese on our left, and three hundred more from the city of Naum, and with these we advanced boldly. The three hundred soldiers from Naum marched in our front, the two hundred in our rear, and our men on each side of our camels, with our baggage and the whole caravan in the centre; in this order, and well prepared for battle, we thought ourselves a match for the whole ten thousand Mogul Tartars, if they had appeared; but the next day, when they did appear, it was quite another thing.

Chapter XV—DESCRIPTION OF AN IDOL, WHICH THEY DESTROY

Early in the morning, when marching from a little town called Changu, we had a river to pass, which we were obliged to ferry; and, had the Tartars had any intelligence, then had been the time to have attacked us, when the caravan being over, the rear-guard was behind; but they did not appear there. About three hours after, when we were entered upon a desert of about fifteen or sixteen miles over, we knew by a cloud of dust they raised, that the enemy was at hand, and presently they came on upon the spur.

Our Chinese guards in the front, who had talked so big the day before, began to stagger; and the soldiers frequently looked behind them, a certain sign in a soldier that he is just ready to run away. My old pilot was of my mind; and being near me, called out, "Seignior Inglese, these fellows must be encouraged, or they will ruin us all; for if the Tartars come on they will never stand it."—"If am of your mind," said I; "but what must be done?"—"Done?" says he, "let fifty of our men advance, and flank them on each wing, and encourage them. They will fight like brave fellows in brave company; but without this they will every man turn his back." Immediately I rode up to our leader and told him, who was exactly of our mind; accordingly, fifty of us marched to the right wing, and fifty to the left, and the rest made a line of rescue; and so we marched, leaving the last two hundred men to make a body of themselves, and to guard the camels; only that, if need were, they should send a hundred men to assist the last fifty.

At last the Tartars came on, and an innumerable company they were; how many we could not tell, but ten thousand, we thought, at the least. A party of them came on first, and viewed our posture, traversing the ground in the front of our line; and, as we found them within gunshot, our leader ordered the two wings to advance swiftly, and give them a salvo on each wing with their shot, which was done. They then went off, I suppose to give an account of the reception they were like to meet with; indeed, that salute cloyed their stomachs, for they immediately halted, stood a while to consider of it, and wheeling off to the left, they gave over their design for that time, which was very agreeable to our circumstances.

Chapter XV—DESCRIPTION OF AN IDOL, WHICH THEY DESTROY

Two days after we came to the city of Naun, or Naum; we thanked the governor for his care of us, and collected to the value of a hundred crowns, or thereabouts, which we gave to the soldiers sent to guard us; and here we rested one day. This is a garrison indeed, and there were nine hundred soldiers kept here; but the reason of it was, that formerly the Muscovite frontiers lay nearer to them than they now do, the Muscovites having abandoned that part of the country, which lies from this city west for about two hundred miles, as desolate and unfit for use; and more especially being so very remote, and so difficult to send troops thither for its defence; for we were yet above two thousand miles from Muscovy properly so called. After this we passed several great rivers, and two dreadful deserts; one of which we were sixteen days passing over; and on the 13th of April we came to the frontiers of the Muscovite dominions. I think the first town or fortress, whichever it may he called, that belonged to the Czar, was called Arguna, being on the west side of the river Arguna.

I could not but feel great satisfaction that I was arrived in a country governed by Christians; for though the Muscovites do, in my opinion, but just deserve the name of Christians, yet such they pretend to be, and are very devout in their way. It would certainly occur to any reflecting man who travels the world as I have done, what a blessing it is to be brought into the world where the name of God and a Redeemer is known, adored, and worshipped; and not where the people, given up to strong delusions, worship the devil, and prostrate themselves to monsters, elements, horrid-shaped animals, and monstrous images. Not a town or city we passed through but had their pagodas, their idols, and their temples, and ignorant people worshipping even the works of their own hands. Now we came where, at least, a face of the Christian worship appeared; where the knee was bowed to Jesus: and whether ignorantly or not, yet the Christian religion was owned, and the name of the true God was called upon and adored; and it made my soul rejoice to see it. I saluted the brave Scots merchant with my first acknowledgment of this; and taking him by the hand, I said to him, "Blessed be God, we are once again amongst Christians." He smiled, and answered, "Do not rejoice too soon, countryman; these Muscovites are but an odd sort of Christians; and but for the name of it you may see very little of the substance for some months further of our journey."—"Well," says I, "but still it is better than paganism, and worshipping of devils."—"Why, I will tell you," says he; "except the Russian soldiers in the garrisons, and a few of the inhabitants of the cities upon the road, all the rest of this country, for above a thousand miles farther, is inhabited by the worst and most ignorant of pagans." And so, indeed, we found it.

We now launched into the greatest piece of solid earth that is to be found in any part of the world; we had, at least, twelve thousand miles to the sea eastward; two thousand to the bottom of the Baltic Sea westward; and above three thousand, if we left that sea, and went on west, to the British and French channels: we had full five thousand miles to the Indian or Persian Sea south; and about eight hundred to the Frozen Sea north.

We advanced from the river Arguna by easy and moderate journeys, and were very visibly obliged to the care the Czar has taken to have cities and towns built in as many places as it is possible to place them, where his soldiers keep garrison, something like the stationary soldiers placed by the Romans in the remotest countries of their empire; some of which I had read of were placed in Britain, for the security of commerce, and for the lodging of travellers. Thus it was here; for wherever we came, though at these towns and stations the garrisons and governors were Russians, and professed Christians, yet the inhabitants were mere pagans, sacrificing to idols, and worshipping the sun, moon, and stars, or all the host of heaven; and not only so, but were, of all the heathens and pagans that ever I met with, the most barbarous, except only that they did not eat men's flesh.

Some instances of this we met with in the country between Arguna, where we enter the Muscovite dominions, and a city of Tartars and Russians together, called Nortziousky, in which is a continued desert or forest, which cost us twenty days to travel over. In a village near the last of these places I had the curiosity to go and see their way of living, which is most brutish and unsufferable. They had, I suppose, a great sacrifice that day; for there stood out, upon an old stump of a tree, a diabolical kind of idol made of wood; it was dressed up, too, in the most filthy manner; its upper garment was of sheepskins, with the wool outward; a great Tartar bonnet on the head, with two horns growing through it; it was about eight feet high, yet had no feet or legs, nor any other proportion of parts.

This scarecrow was set up at the outer side of the village; and when I came near to it there were sixteen or seventeen creatures all lying flat upon the ground round this hideous block of wood; I saw no motion among them, any more than if they had been all logs, like the idol, and at first I really thought they had been so; but, when I came a little nearer, they started up upon their feet, and raised a howl, as if it had been so many deep-mouthed hounds, and walked away, as if they were displeased at our disturbing them. A little way off from the idol, and at the door of a hut, made of sheep and cow skins dried, stood three men with long knives in their hands; and in the middle of the tent appeared three sheep killed, and one young bullock. These, it seems, were sacrifices to that senseless log of an idol; the three men were priests belonging to it, and the seventeen prostrated wretches were the people who brought the offering, and were offering their prayers to that stock.

I confess I was more moved at their stupidity and brutish worship of a hobgoblin than ever I was at anything in my life, and, overcome with rage, I rode up to the hideous idol, and with my sword made a stroke at the bonnet that was on its head, and cut it in two; and one of our men that was with me, taking hold of the sheepskin that covered it, pulled at it, when, behold, a most hideous outcry ran through the village, and two or three hundred people came about my ears, so that I was glad to scour for it, for some had bows and arrows; but I resolved from that moment to visit them again. Our caravan rested three nights at the town, which was about four miles off, in order to provide some horses which they wanted, several of the horses having been lamed and jaded with the long march over the last desert; so we had some leisure here to put my design in execution. I communicated it to the Scots merchant, of whose courage I had sufficient testimony; I told him what I had seen, and with what indignation I had since thought that human nature could be so degenerate; I told him if I could get but four or five men well armed to go with me, I was resolved to go and destroy that vile, abominable idol, and let them see that it had no power to help itself, and consequently could not be an object of worship, or to be prayed to, much less help them that offered sacrifices to it.

He at first objected to my plan as useless, seeing that, owing to the gross ignorance of the people, they could not be brought to profit by the lesson I meant to teach them; and added that, from his knowledge of the country and its customs, he feared we should fall into great peril by giving offence to these brutal idol worshippers. This somewhat stayed my purpose, but I was still uneasy all that day to put my project in execution; and that evening, meeting the Scots merchant in our walk about the town, I again called upon him to aid me in it. When he found me resolute he said that, on further thoughts, he could not but applaud the design, and told me I should not go alone, but he would go with me; but he would go first and bring a stout fellow, one of his countrymen, to go also with us; "and one," said he, "as famous for his zeal as you can desire any one to be against such devilish things as these." So we agreed to go, only we three and my man-servant, and resolved to put it in execution the following night about midnight, with all possible secrecy.

We thought it better to delay it till the next night, because the caravan being to set forward in the morning, we suppose the governor could not pretend to give them any satisfaction upon us when we were out of his power. The Scots merchant, as steady in his resolution for the enterprise as bold in executing, brought me a Tartar's robe or gown of sheepskins, and a bonnet, with a bow and arrows, and had provided the same for himself and his countryman, that the people, if they saw us, should not determine who we were. All the first night we spent in mixing up some combustible matter, with aqua vitae, gunpowder, and such other materials as we could get; and having a good quantity of tar in a little pot, about an hour after night we set out upon our expedition.

We came to the place about eleven o'clock at night, and found that the people had not the least suspicion of danger attending their idol. The night was cloudy: yet the moon gave us light enough to see that the idol stood just in the same posture and place that it did before. The people seemed to be all at their rest; only that in the great hut, where we saw the three priests, we saw a light, and going up close to the door, we heard people talking as if there were five or six of them; we concluded, therefore, that if we set wildfire to the idol, those men would come out immediately, and run up to the place to rescue it from destruction; and what to do with them we knew not. Once we thought of carrying it away, and setting fire to it at a distance; but when we came to handle it, we found it too bulky for our carriage, so we were at a loss again. The second Scotsman was for setting fire to the hut, and knocking the creatures that were there on the head when they came out; but I could not join with that; I was against killing them, if it were possible to avoid it. "Well, then," said the Scots merchant, "I will tell you what we will do: we will try to make them prisoners, tie their hands, and make them stand and see their idol destroyed."

As it happened, we had twine or packthread enough about us, which we used to tie our firelocks together with; so we resolved to attack these people first, and with as little noise as we could. The first thing we did, we knocked at the door, when one of the priests coming to it, we immediately seized upon him, stopped his mouth, and tied his hands behind him, and led him to the idol, where we gagged him that he might not make a noise, tied his feet also together, and left him on the ground.

Two of us then waited at the door, expecting that another would come out to see what the matter was; but we waited so long till the third man came back to us; and then nobody coming out, we knocked again gently, and immediately out came two more, and we served them just in the same manner, but were obliged to go all with them, and lay them down by the idol some distance from one another; when, going back, we found two more were come out of the door, and a third stood behind them within the door. We seized the two, and immediately tied them, when the third, stepping back and crying out, my Scots merchant went in after them, and taking out a composition we had made that would only smoke and stink, he set fire to it, and threw it in among them. By that time the other Scotsman and my man, taking charge of the two men already bound, and tied together also by the arm, led them away to the idol, and left them there, to see if their idol would relieve them, making haste back to us.

When the fuze we had thrown in had filled the hut with so much smoke that they were almost suffocated, we threw in a small leather bag of another kind, which flamed like a candle, and, following it in, we found there were but four people, who, as we supposed, had been about some of their diabolical sacrifices. They appeared, in short, frightened to death, at least so as to sit trembling and stupid, and not able to speak either, for the smoke.

We quickly took them from the hut, where the smoke soon drove us out, bound them as we had done the other, and all without any noise. Then we carried them all together to the idol; when we came there, we fell to work with him. First, we daubed him all over, and his robes also, with tar, and tallow mixed with brimstone; then we stopped his eyes and ears and mouth full of gunpowder, and wrapped up a great piece of wildfire in his bonnet; then sticking all the combustibles we had brought with us upon him, we looked about to see if we could find anything else to help to burn him; when my Scotsman remembered that by the hut, where the men were, there lay a heap of dry forage; away he and the other Scotsman ran and fetched their arms full of that. When we had done this, we took all our prisoners, and brought them, having untied their feet and ungagged their mouths, and made them stand up, and set them before their monstrous idol, and then set fire to the whole.

We stayed by it a quarter of an hour or thereabouts, till the powder in the eyes and mouth and ears of the idol blew up, and, as we could perceive, had split altogether; and in a word, till we saw it burned so that it would soon be quite consumed. We then began to think of going away; but the Scotsman said, "No, we must not go, for these poor deluded wretches will all throw themselves into the fire, and burn themselves with the idol." So we resolved to stay till the forage has burned down too, and then came away and left them. After the feat was performed, we appeared in the morning among our fellow-travellers, exceedingly busy in getting ready for our journey; nor could any man suppose that we had been anywhere but in our beds.

But the affair did not end so; the next day came a great number of the country people to the town gates, and in a most outrageous manner demanded satisfaction of the Russian governor for the insulting their priests and burning their great Cham Chi-Thaungu. The people of Nertsinkay were at first in a great consternation, for they said the Tartars were already no less than thirty thousand strong. The Russian governor sent out messengers to appease them, assuring them that he knew nothing of it, and that there had not a soul in his garrison been abroad, so that it could not be from anybody there: but if they could let him know who did it, they should be exemplarily punished. They returned haughtily, that all the country reverenced the great Cham Chi-Thaungu, who dwelt in the sun, and no mortal would have dared to offer violence to his image but some Christian miscreant; and they therefore resolved to denounce war against him and all the Russians, who, they said, were miscreants and Christians.

The governor, unwilling to make a breach, or to have any cause of war alleged to be given by him, the Czar having strictly charged him to treat the conquered country with gentleness, gave them all the good words he could. At last he told them there was a caravan gone towards Russia that morning, and perhaps it was some of them who had done them this injury; and that if they would be satisfied with that, he would send after them to inquire into it. This seemed to appease them a little; and accordingly the governor sent after us, and gave us a particular account how the thing was; intimating withal, that if any in our caravan had done it they should make their escape; but that whether we had done it or no, we should make all the haste forward that was possible: and that, in the meantime, he would keep them in play as long as he could.

This was very friendly in the governor; however, when it came to the caravan, there was nobody knew anything of the matter; and as for us that were guilty, we were least of all suspected. However, the captain of the caravan for the time took the hint that the governor gave us, and we travelled two days and two nights without any considerable stop, and then we lay at a village called Plothus: nor did we make any long stop here, but hastened on towards Jarawena, another Muscovite colony, and where we expected we should be safe. But upon the second day's march from Plothus, by the clouds of dust behind us at a great distance, it was plain we were pursued. We had entered a vast desert, and had passed by a great lake called Schanks Oser, when we perceived a large body of horse appear on the other side of the lake, to the north, we travelling west. We observed they went away west, as we did, but had supposed we would have taken that side of the lake, whereas we very happily took the south side; and in two days more they disappeared again: for they, believing we were still before them, pushed on till they came to the Udda, a very great river when it passes farther north, but when we came to it we found it narrow and fordable.

The third day they had either found their mistake, or had intelligence of us, and came pouring in upon us towards dusk. We had, to our great satisfaction, just pitched upon a convenient place for our camp; for as we had just entered upon a desert above five hundred miles over, where we had no towns to lodge at, and, indeed, expected none but the city Jarawena, which we had yet two days' march to; the desert, however, had some few woods in it on this side, and little rivers, which ran all into the great river Udda; it was in a narrow strait, between little but very thick woods, that we pitched our camp that night, expecting to be attacked before morning. As it was usual for the Mogul Tartars to go about in troops in that desert, so the caravans always fortify themselves every night against them, as against armies of robbers; and it was, therefore, no new thing to be pursued. But we had this night a most advantageous camp: for as we lay between two woods, with a little rivulet running just before our front, we could not be surrounded, or attacked any way but in our front or rear. We took care also to make our front as strong as we could, by placing our packs, with the camels and horses, all in a line, on the inside of the river, and felling some trees in our rear.

In this posture we encamped for the night; but the enemy was upon us before we had finished. They did not come on like thieves, as we expected, but sent three messengers to us, to demand the men to be delivered to them that had abused their priests and burned their idol, that they might burn them with fire; and upon this, they said, they would go away, and do us no further harm, otherwise they would destroy us all. Our men looked very blank at this message, and began to stare at one another to see who looked with the most guilt in their faces; but nobody was the word—nobody did it. The leader of the caravan sent word he was well assured that it was not done by any of our camp; that we were peaceful merchants, travelling on our business; that we had done no harm to them or to any one else; and that, therefore, they must look further for the enemies who had injured them, for we were not the people; so they desired them not to disturb us, for if they did we should defend ourselves.

They were far from being satisfied with this for an answer: and a great crowd of them came running down in the morning, by break of day, to our camp; but seeing us so well posted, they durst come no farther than the brook in our front, where they stood in such number as to terrify us very much; indeed, some spoke of ten thousand. Here they stood and looked at us a while, and then, setting up a great howl, let fly a crowd of arrows among us; but we were well enough sheltered under our baggage, and I do not remember that one of us was hurt.

Some time after this we saw them move a little to our right, and expected them on the rear: when a cunning fellow, a Cossack of Jarawena, calling to the leader of the caravan, said to him, "I will send all these people away to Sibeilka." This was a city four or five days' journey at least to the right, and rather behind us. So he takes his bow and arrows, and getting on horseback, he rides away from our rear directly, as it were back to Nertsinskay; after this he takes a great circuit about, and comes directly on the army of the Tartars as if he had been sent express to tell them a long story that the people who had burned the Cham Chi-Thaungu were gone to Sibeilka, with a caravan of miscreants, as he called them—that is to say, Christians; and that they had resolved to burn the god Scal-Isar, belonging to the Tonguses. As this fellow was himself a Tartar, and perfectly spoke their language, he counterfeited so well that they all believed him, and away they drove in a violent hurry to Sibeilka. In less than three hours they were entirely out of our sight, and we never heard any more of them, nor whether they went to Sibeilka or no. So we passed away safely on to Jarawena, where there was a Russian garrison, and there we rested five days.

From this city we had a frightful desert, which held us twenty-three days' march. We furnished ourselves with some tents here, for the better accommodating ourselves in the night; and the leader of the caravan procured sixteen waggons of the country, for carrying our water or provisions, and these carriages were our defence every night round our little camp; so that had the Tartars appeared, unless they had been very numerous indeed, they would not have been able to hurt us. We may well be supposed to have wanted rest again after this long journey; for in this desert we neither saw house nor tree, and scarce a bush; though we saw abundance of the sable-hunters, who are all Tartars of Mogul Tartary; of which this country is a part; and they frequently attack small caravans, but we saw no numbers of them together.

After we had passed this desert we came into a country pretty well inhabited—that is to say, we found towns and castles, settled by the Czar with garrisons of stationary soldiers, to protect the caravans and defend the country against the Tartars, who would otherwise make it very dangerous travelling; and his czarish majesty has given such strict orders for the well guarding the caravans, that, if there are any Tartars heard of in the country, detachments of the garrison are always sent to see the travellers safe from station to station. Thus the governor of Adinskoy, whom I had an opportunity to make a visit to, by means of the Scots merchant, who was acquainted with him, offered us a guard of fifty men, if we thought there was any danger, to the next station.

I thought, long before this, that as we came nearer to Europe we should find the country better inhabited, and the people more civilised; but I found myself mistaken in both: for we had yet the nation of the Tonguses to pass through, where we saw the same tokens of paganism and barbarity as before; only, as they were conquered by the Muscovites, they were not so dangerous, but for rudeness of manners and idolatry no people in the world ever went beyond them. They are all clothed in skins of beasts, and their houses are built of the same; you know not a man from a woman, neither by the ruggedness of their countenances nor their clothes; and in the winter, when the ground is covered with snow, they live underground in vaults, which have cavities going from one to another. If the Tartars had their Cham Chi-Thaungu for a whole village or country, these had idols in every hut and every cave. This country, I reckon, was, from the desert I spoke of last, at least four hundred miles, half of it being another desert, which took us up twelve days' severe travelling, without house or tree; and we were obliged again to carry our own provisions, as well water as bread. After we were out of this desert and had travelled two days, we came to Janezay, a Muscovite city or station, on the great river Janezay, which, they told us there, parted Europe from Asia.

All the country between the river Oby and the river Janezay is as entirely pagan, and the people as barbarous, as the remotest of the Tartars. I also found, which I observed to the Muscovite governors whom I had an opportunity to converse with, that the poor pagans are not much wiser, or nearer Christianity, for being under the Muscovite government, which they acknowledged was true enough—but that, as they said, was none of their business; that if the Czar expected to convert his Siberian, Tonguse, or Tartar subjects, it should be done by sending clergymen among them, not soldiers; and they added, with more sincerity than I expected, that it was not so much the concern of their monarch to make the people Christians as to make them subjects.

From this river to the Oby we crossed a wild uncultivated country, barren of people and good management, otherwise it is in itself a pleasant, fruitful, and agreeable country. What inhabitants we found in it are all pagans, except such as are sent among them from Russia; for this is the country—I mean on both sides the river Oby—whither the Muscovite criminals that are not put to death are banished, and from whence it is next to impossible they should ever get away. I have nothing material to say of my particular affairs till I came to Tobolski, the capital city of Siberia, where I continued some time on the following account.

We had now been almost seven months on our journey, and winter began to come on apace; whereupon my partner and I called a council about our particular affairs, in which we found it proper, as we were bound for England, to consider how to dispose of ourselves. They told us of sledges and reindeer to carry us over the snow in the winter time, by which means, indeed, the Russians travel more in winter than they can in summer, as in these sledges they are able to run night and day: the snow, being frozen, is one universal covering to nature, by which the hills, vales, rivers, and lakes are all smooth and hard is a stone, and they run upon the surface, without any regard to what is underneath.

But I had no occasion to urge a winter journey of this kind. I was bound to England, not to Moscow, and my route lay two ways: either I must go on as the caravan went, till I came to Jarislaw, and then go off west for Narva and the Gulf of Finland, and so on to Dantzic, where I might possibly sell my China cargo to good advantage; or I must leave the caravan at a little town on the Dwina, from whence I had but six days by water to Archangel, and from thence might be sure of shipping either to England, Holland, or Hamburg.

Now, to go any one of these journeys in the winter would have been preposterous; for as to Dantzic, the Baltic would have been frozen up and I could not get passage; and to go by land in those countries was far less safe than among the Mogul Tartars; likewise, as to Archangel in October, all the ships would be gone from thence, and even the merchants who dwell there in summer retire south to Moscow in the winter, when the ships are gone; so that I could have nothing but extremity of cold to encounter, with a scarcity of provisions, and must lie in an empty town all the winter. Therefore, upon the whole, I thought it much my better way to let the caravan go, and make provision to winter where I was, at Tobolski, in Siberia, in the latitude of about sixty degrees, where I was sure of three things to wear out a cold winter with, viz. plenty of provisions, such as the country afforded, a warm house, with fuel enough, and excellent company.

I was now in quite a different climate from my beloved island, where I never felt cold, except when I had my ague; on the contrary, I had much to do to bear any clothes on my back, and never made any fire but without doors, which was necessary for dressing my food, &c. Now I had three good vests, with large robes or gowns over them, to hang down to the feet, and button close to the wrists; and all these lined with furs, to make them sufficiently warm. As to a warm house, I must confess I greatly dislike our way in England of making fires in every room of the house in open chimneys, which, when the fire is out, always keeps the air in the room cold as the climate. So I took an apartment in a good house in the town, and ordered a chimney to be built like a furnace, in the centre of six several rooms, like a stove; the funnel to carry the smoke went up one way, the door to come at the fire went in another, and all the rooms were kept equally warm, but no fire seen, just as they heat baths in England. By this means we had always the same climate in all the rooms, and an equal heat was preserved, and yet we saw no fire, nor were ever incommoded with smoke.

The most wonderful thing of all was, that it should be possible to meet with good company here, in a country so barbarous as this—one of the most northerly parts of Europe. But this being the country where the state criminals of Muscovy, as I observed before, are all banished, the city was full of Russian noblemen, gentlemen, soldiers, and courtiers. Here was the famous Prince Galitzin, the old German Robostiski, and several other persons of note, and some ladies. By means of my Scotch merchant, whom, nevertheless, I parted with here, I made an acquaintance with several of these gentlemen; and from these, in the long winter nights in which I stayed here, I received several very agreeable visits.

Chapter XVI—SAFE ARRIVAL IN ENGLAND

It was talking one night with a certain prince, one of the banished ministers of state belonging to the Czar, that the discourse of my particular case began. He had been telling me abundance of fine things of the greatness, the magnificence, the dominions, and the absolute power of the Emperor of the Russians: I interrupted him, and told him I was a greater and more powerful prince than ever the Czar was, though my dominion were not so large, or my people so many. The Russian grandee looked a little surprised, and, fixing his eyes steadily upon me, began to wonder what I meant. I said his wonder would cease when I had explained myself, and told him the story at large of my living in the island; and then how I managed both myself and the people that were under me, just as I have since minuted it down. They were exceedingly taken with the story, and especially the prince, who told me, with a sigh, that the true greatness of life was to be masters of ourselves; that he would not have exchanged such a state of life as mine to be Czar of Muscovy; and that he found more felicity in the retirement he seemed to be banished to there, than ever he found in the highest authority he enjoyed in the court of his master the Czar; that the height of human wisdom was to bring our tempers down to our circumstances, and to make a calm within, under the weight of the greatest storms without. When he came first hither, he said, he used to tear the hair from his head, and the clothes from his back, as others had done before him; but a little time and consideration had made him look into himself, as well as round him to things without; that he found the mind of man, if it was but once brought to reflect upon the state of universal life, and how little this world was concerned in its true felicity, was perfectly capable of making a felicity for itself, fully satisfying to itself, and suitable to its own best ends and desires, with but very little assistance from the world. That being now deprived of all the fancied felicity which he enjoyed in the full exercise of worldly pleasures, he said he was at leisure to look upon the dark side of them, where he found all manner of deformity; and was now convinced that virtue only makes a man truly wise, rich, and great, and preserves him in the way to a superior happiness in a future state; and in this, he said, they were more happy in their banishment than all their enemies were, who had the full possession of all the wealth and power they had left behind them. "Nor, sir," says he, "do I bring my mind to this politically, from the necessity of my circumstances, which some call miserable; but, if I know anything of myself, I would not now go back, though the Czar my master should call me, and reinstate me in all my former grandeur."

He spoke this with so much warmth in his temper, so much earnestness and motion of his spirits, that it was evident it was the true sense of his soul; there was no room to doubt his sincerity. I told him I once thought myself a kind of monarch in my old station, of which I had given him an account; but that I thought he was not only a monarch, but a great conqueror; for he that had got a victory over his own exorbitant desires, and the absolute dominion over himself, he whose reason entirely governs his will, is certainly greater than he that conquers a city.

I had been here eight months, and a dark, dreadful winter I thought it; the cold so intense that I could not so much as look abroad without being wrapped in furs, and a kind of mask of fur before my face, with only a hole for breath, and two for sight: the little daylight we had was for three months not above five hours a day, and six at most; only that the snow lying on the ground continually, and the weather being clear, it was never quite dark. Our horses were kept, or rather starved, underground; and as for our servants, whom we hired here to look after ourselves and horses, we had, every now and then, their fingers and toes to thaw and take care of, lest they should mortify and fall off.

It is true, within doors we were warm, the houses being close, the walls thick, the windows small, and the glass all double. Our food was chiefly the flesh of deer, dried and cured in the season; bread good enough, but baked as biscuits; dried fish of several sorts, and some flesh of mutton, and of buffaloes, which is pretty good meat. All the stores of provisions for the winter are laid up in the summer, and well cured: our drink was water, mixed with aqua vitae instead of brandy; and for a treat, mead instead of wine, which, however, they have very good. The hunters, who venture abroad all weathers, frequently brought us in fine venison, and sometimes bear's flesh, but we did not much care for the last. We had a good stock of tea, with which we treated our friends, and we lived cheerfully and well, all things considered.

It was now March, the days grown considerably longer, and the weather at least tolerable; so the other travellers began to prepare sledges to carry them over the snow, and to get things ready to be going; but my measures being fixed, as I have said, for Archangel, and not for Muscovy or the Baltic, I made no motion; knowing very well that the ships from the south do not set out for that part of the world till May or June, and that if I was there by the beginning of August, it would be as soon as any ships would be ready to sail. Therefore I made no haste to be gone, as others did: in a word, I saw a great many people, nay, all the travellers, go away before me. It seems every year they go from thence to Muscovy, for trade, to carry furs, and buy necessaries, which they bring back with them to furnish their shops: also others went on the same errand to Archangel.

In the month of May I began to make all ready to pack up; and, as I was doing this, it occurred to me that, seeing all these people were banished by the Czar to Siberia, and yet, when they came there, were left at liberty to go whither they would, why they did not then go away to any part of the world, wherever they thought fit: and I began to examine what should hinder them from making such an attempt. But my wonder was over when I entered upon that subject with the person I have mentioned, who answered me thus: "Consider, first, sir," said he, "the place where we are; and, secondly, the condition we are in; especially the generality of the people who are banished thither. We are surrounded with stronger things than bars or bolts; on the north side, an unnavigable ocean, where ship never sailed, and boat never swam; every other way we have above a thousand miles to pass through the Czar's own dominion, and by ways utterly impassable, except by the roads made by the government, and through the towns garrisoned by his troops; in short, we could neither pass undiscovered by the road, nor subsist any other way, so that it is in vain to attempt it."

I was silenced at once, and found that they were in a prison every jot as secure as if they had been locked up in the castle at Moscow: however, it came into my thoughts that I might certainly be made an instrument to procure the escape of this excellent person; and that, whatever hazard I ran, I would certainly try if I could carry him off. Upon this, I took an occasion one evening to tell him my thoughts. I represented to him that it was very easy for me to carry him away, there being no guard over him in the country; and as I was not going to Moscow, but to Archangel, and that I went in the retinue of a caravan, by which I was not obliged to lie in the stationary towns in the desert, but could encamp every night where I would, we might easily pass uninterrupted to Archangel, where I would immediately secure him on board an English ship, and carry him safe along with me; and as to his subsistence and other particulars, it should be my care till he could better supply himself.

He heard me very attentively, and looked earnestly on me all the while I spoke; nay, I could see in his very face that what I said put his spirits into an exceeding ferment; his colour frequently changed, his eyes looked red, and his heart fluttered, till it might be even perceived in his countenance; nor could he immediately answer me when I had done, and, as it were, hesitated what he would say to it; but after he had paused a little, he embraced me, and said, "How unhappy are we, unguarded creatures as we are, that even our greatest acts of friendship are made snares unto us, and we are made tempters of one another!" He then heartily thanked me for my offers of service, but withstood resolutely the arguments I used to urge him to set himself free. He declared, in earnest terms, that he was fully bent on remaining where he was rather than seek to return to his former miserable greatness, as he called it: where the seeds of pride, ambition, avarice, and luxury might revive, take root, and again overwhelm him. "Let me remain, dear sir," he said, in conclusion—"let me remain in this blessed confinement, banished from the crimes of life, rather than purchase a show of freedom at the expense of the liberty of my reason, and at the future happiness which I now have in my view, but should then, I fear, quickly lose sight of; for I am but flesh; a man, a mere man; and have passions and affections as likely to possess and overthrow me as any man: Oh, be not my friend and tempter both together!"

If I was surprised before, I was quite dumb now, and stood silent, looking at him, and, indeed, admiring what I saw. The struggle in his soul was so great that, though the weather was extremely cold, it put him into a most violent heat; so I said a word or two, that I would leave him to consider of it, and wait on him again, and then I withdrew to my own apartment.

About two hours after I heard somebody at or near the door of my room, and I was going to open the door, but he had opened it and come in. "My dear friend," says he, "you had almost overset me, but I am recovered. Do not take it ill that I do not close with your offer. I assure you it is not for want of sense of the kindness of it in you; and I came to make the most sincere acknowledgment of it to you; but I hope I have got the victory over myself."—"My lord," said I, "I hope you are fully satisfied that you do not resist the call of Heaven."—"Sir," said he, "if it had been from Heaven, the same power would have influenced me to have accepted it; but I hope, and am fully satisfied, that it is from Heaven that I decline it, and I have infinite satisfaction in the parting, that you shall leave me an honest man still, though not a free man."

I had nothing to do but to acquiesce, and make professions to him of my having no end in it but a sincere desire to serve him. He embraced me very passionately, and assured me he was sensible of that, and should always acknowledge it; and with that he offered me a very fine present of sables—too much, indeed, for me to accept from a man in his circumstances, and I would have avoided them, but he would not be refused. The next morning I sent my servant to his lordship with a small present of tea, and two pieces of China damask, and four little wedges of Japan gold, which did not all weigh above six ounces or thereabouts, but were far short of the value of his sables, which, when I came to England, I found worth near two hundred pounds. He accepted the tea, and one piece of the damask, and one of the pieces of gold, which had a fine stamp upon it, of the Japan coinage, which I found he took for the rarity of it, but would not take any more: and he sent word by my servant that he desired to speak with me.

When I came to him he told me I knew what had passed between us, and hoped I would not move him any more in that affair; but that, since I had made such a generous offer to him, he asked me if I had kindness enough to offer the same to another person that he would name to me, in whom he had a great share of concern. In a word, he told me it was his only son; who, though I had not seen him, was in the same condition with himself, and above two hundred miles from him, on the other side of the Oby; but that, if I consented, he would send for him.

I made no hesitation, but told him I would do it. I made some ceremony in letting him understand that it was wholly on his account; and that, seeing I could not prevail on him, I would show my respect to him by my concern for his son. He sent the next day for his son; and in about twenty days he came back with the messenger, bringing six or seven horses, loaded with very rich furs, which, in the whole, amounted to a very great value. His servants brought the horses into the town, but left the young lord at a distance till night, when he came incognito into our apartment, and his father presented him to me; and, in short, we concerted the manner of our travelling, and everything proper for the journey.

I had bought a considerable quantity of sables, black fox-skins, fine ermines, and such other furs as are very rich in that city, in exchange for some of the goods I had brought from China; in particular for the cloves and nutmegs, of which I sold the greatest part here, and the rest afterwards at Archangel, for a much better price than I could have got at London; and my partner, who was sensible of the profit, and whose business, more particularly than mine, was merchandise, was mightily pleased with our stay, on account of the traffic we made here.

It was the beginning of June when I left this remote place. We were now reduced to a very small caravan, having only thirty-two horses and camels in all, which passed for mine, though my new guest was proprietor of eleven of them. It was natural also that I should take more servants with me than I had before; and the young lord passed for my steward; what great man I passed for myself I know not, neither did it concern me to inquire. We had here the worst and the largest desert to pass over that we met with in our whole journey; I call it the worst, because the way was very deep in some places, and very uneven in others; the best we had to say for it was, that we thought we had no troops of Tartars or robbers to fear, as they never came on this side of the river Oby, or at least very seldom; but we found it otherwise.

My young lord had a faithful Siberian servant, who was perfectly acquainted with the country, and led us by private roads, so that we avoided coming into the principal towns and cities upon the great road, such as Tumen, Soloy Kamaskoy, and several others; because the Muscovite garrisons which are kept there are very curious and strict in their observation upon travellers, and searching lest any of the banished persons of note should make their escape that way into Muscovy; but, by this means, as we were kept out of the cities, so our whole journey was a desert, and we were obliged to encamp and lie in our tents, when we might have had very good accommodation in the cities on the way; this the young lord was so sensible of, that he would not allow us to lie abroad when we came to several cities on the way, but lay abroad himself, with his servant, in the woods, and met us always at the appointed places.

We had just entered Europe, having passed the river Kama, which in these parts is the boundary between Europe and Asia, and the first city on the European side was called Soloy Kamaskoy, that is, the great city on the river Kama. And here we thought to see some evident alteration in the people; but we were mistaken, for as we had a vast desert to pass, which is near seven hundred miles long in some places, but not above two hundred miles over where we passed it, so, till we came past that horrible place, we found very little difference between that country and Mogul Tartary. The people are mostly pagans; their houses and towns full of idols; and their way of living wholly barbarous, except in the cities and villages near them, where they are Christians, as they call themselves, of the

Greek Church: but have their religion mingled with so many relics of superstition, that it is scarce to be known in some places from mere sorcery and witchcraft.

In passing this forest (after all our dangers were, to our imagination, escaped), I thought, indeed, we must have been plundered and robbed, and perhaps murdered, by a troop of thieves: of what country they were I am yet at a loss to know; but they were all on horseback, carried bows and arrows, and were at first about forty-five in number. They came so near to us as to be within two musket-shot, and, asking no questions, surrounded us with their horses, and looked very earnestly upon us twice; at length, they placed themselves just in our way; upon which we drew up in a little line, before our camels, being not above sixteen men in all. Thus drawn up, we halted, and sent out the Siberian servant, who attended his lord, to see who they were; his master was the more willing to let him go, because he was not a little apprehensive that they were a Siberian troop sent out after him. The man came up near them with a flag of truce, and called to them; but though he spoke several of their languages, or dialects of languages rather, he could not understand a word they said; however, after some signs to him not to come near them at his peril, the fellow came back no wiser than he went; only that by their dress, he said, he believed them to be some Tartars of Kalmuck, or of the Circassian hordes, and that there must be more of them upon the great desert, though he never heard that any of them were seen so far north before.

This was small comfort to us; however, we had no remedy: there was on our left hand, at about a quarter of a mile distance, a little grove, and very near the road. I immediately resolved we should advance to those trees, and fortify ourselves as well as we could there; for, first, I considered that the trees would in a great measure cover us from their arrows; and, in the next place, they could not come to charge us in a body: it was, indeed, my old Portuguese pilot who proposed it, and who had this excellency attending him, that he was always readiest and most apt to direct and encourage us in cases of the most danger. We advanced immediately, with what speed we could, and gained that little wood; the Tartars, or thieves, for we knew not what to call them, keeping their stand, and not attempting to hinder us. When we came thither, we found, to our great satisfaction, that it was a swampy piece of ground, and on the one side a very great spring of water, which, running out in a little brook, was a little farther joined by another of the like size; and was, in short, the source of a considerable river, called afterwards the Wirtska; the trees which grew about this spring were not above two hundred, but very large, and stood pretty thick, so that as soon as we got in, we saw ourselves perfectly safe from the enemy unless they attacked us on foot.

While we stayed here waiting the motion of the enemy some hours, without perceiving that they made any movement, our Portuguese, with some help, cut several arms of trees half off, and laid them hanging across from one tree to another, and in a manner fenced us in. About two hours before night they came down directly upon us; and though we had not perceived it, we found they had been joined by some more, so that they were near fourscore horse; whereof, however, we fancied some were women. They came on till they were within half-shot of our

little wood, when we fired one musket without ball, and called to them in the Russian tongue to know what they wanted, and bade them keep off; but they came on with a double fury up to the wood-side, not imagining we were so barricaded that they could not easily break in. Our old pilot was our captain as well as our engineer, and desired us not to fire upon them till they came within pistol-shot, that we might be sure to kill, and that when we did fire we should be sure to take good aim; we bade him give the word of command, which he delayed so long that they were some of them within two pikes' length of us when we let fly. We aimed so true that we killed fourteen of them, and wounded several others, as also several of their horses; for we had all of us loaded our pieces with two or three bullets apiece at least.

They were terribly surprised with our fire, and retreated immediately about one hundred rods from us; in which time we loaded our pieces again, and seeing them keep that distance, we sallied out, and caught four or five of their horses, whose riders we supposed were killed; and coming up to the dead, we judged they were Tartars, but knew not how they came to make an excursion such an unusual length.

About an hour after they again made a motion to attack us, and rode round our little wood to see where they might break in; but finding us always ready to face them, they went off again; and we resolved not to stir for that night.

We slept little, but spent the most part of the night in strengthening our situation, and barricading the entrances into the wood, and keeping a strict watch. We waited for daylight, and when it came, it gave us a very unwelcome discovery indeed; for the enemy, who we thought were discouraged with the reception they met with, were now greatly increased, and had set up eleven or twelve huts or tents, as if they were resolved to besiege us; and this little camp they had pitched upon the open plain, about three-quarters of a mile from us. I confess I now gave myself over for lost, and all that I had; the loss of my effects did not lie so near me, though very considerable, as the thoughts of falling into the hands of such barbarians at the latter end of my journey, after so many difficulties and hazards as I had gone through, and even in sight of our port, where we expected safety and deliverance. As to my partner, he was raging, and declared that to lose his goods would be his ruin, and that he would rather die than be starved, and he was for fighting to the last drop.

The young lord, a most gallant youth, was for fighting to the last also; and my old pilot was of opinion that we were able to resist them all in the situation we were then in. Thus we spent the day in debates of what we should do; but towards evening we found that the number of our enemies still increased, and we did not know but by the morning they might still be a greater number: so I began to inquire of those people we had brought from Tobolski if there were no private ways by which we might avoid them in the night, and perhaps retreat to some town, or get help to guard us over the desert. The young lord's Siberian servant told us, if we designed to avoid them, and not fight, he would engage to carry us off in the night, to a way that went north, towards the river Petruz, by which he made no question but we might get away, and the Tartars never discover it; but, he said, his lord had told him he would not retreat, but would rather choose to fight. I told him he mistook his lord: for that he was too wise a man to love fighting for the sake of it; that I knew he was brave enough by what he had showed already; but that he knew better than to desire seventeen or eighteen men to fight five hundred, unless an unavoidable necessity forced them to it; and that if he thought it possible for us to escape in the night, we had nothing else to do but to attempt it. He answered, if his lordship gave him such orders, he would lose his life if he did not perform it; we soon brought his lord to give that order, though privately, and we immediately prepared for putting it in practice.

And first, as soon as it began to be dark, we kindled a fire in our little camp, which we kept burning, and prepared so as to make it burn all night, that the Tartars might conclude we were still there; but as soon as it was dark, and we could see the stars (for our guide would not stir before), having all our horses and camels ready loaded, we followed our new guide, who I soon found steered himself by the north star, the country being level for a long way.

After we had travelled two hours very hard, it began to be lighter still; not that it was dark all night, but the moon began to rise, so that, in short, it was rather lighter than we wished it to be; but by six o'clock the next morning we had got above thirty miles, having almost spoiled our horses. Here we found a Russian village, named Kermazinskoy, where we rested, and heard nothing of the Kalmuck Tartars that day. About two hours before night we set out again, and travelled till eight the next morning, though not quite so hard as before; and about seven o'clock we passed a little river, called Kirtza, and came to a good large town inhabited by Russians, called Ozomys; there we heard that several troops of Kalmucks had been abroad upon the desert, but that we were now completely out of danger of them, which was to our great satisfaction. Here we were obliged to get some fresh horses, and having need enough of rest, we stayed five days; and my partner and I agreed to give the honest Siberian who conducted us thither the value of ten pistoles.

In five days more we came to Veussima, upon the river Witzogda, and running into the Dwina: we were there, very happily, near the end of our travels by land, that river being navigable, in seven days' passage, to Archangel. From hence we came to Lawremskoy, the 3rd of July; and providing ourselves with two luggage boats, and a barge for our own convenience, we embarked the 7th, and arrived all safe at Archangel the 18th; having been a year, five months, and three days on the journey, including our stay of about eight months at Tobolski.

We were obliged to stay at this place six weeks for the arrival of the ships, and must have tarried longer, had not a Hamburgher come in above a month sooner than any of the English ships; when, after some consideration that the city of Hamburgh might happen to be as good a market for our goods as London, we all took freight with him; and, having put our goods on board, it was most natural for me to put my steward on board to take care of them; by which means my young lord had a sufficient opportunity to conceal himself, never coming on shore again all the time we stayed there; and this he did that he might not be seen in the city, where some of the Moscow merchants would certainly have seen and discovered him.

We then set sail from Archangel the 20th of August, the same year; and, after no extraordinary bad voyage, arrived safe in the Elbe the 18th of September. Here my partner and I found a very good sale for our goods, as well those of China as the sables, &c., of Siberia: and, dividing the produce, my share amounted to £3475, 17s 3d., including about six hundred pounds' worth of diamonds, which I purchased at Bengal.

Here the young lord took his leave of us, and went up the Elbe, in order to go to the court of Vienna, where he resolved to seek protection and could correspond with those of his father's friends who were left alive. He did not part without testimonials of gratitude for the service I had done him, and for my kindness to the prince, his father.

To conclude: having stayed near four months in Hamburgh, I came from thence by land to the Hague, where I embarked in the packet, and arrived in London the 10th of January 1705, having been absent from England ten years and nine months. And here, resolving to harass myself no more, I am preparing for a longer journey than all these, having lived seventy-two years a life of infinite variety, and learned sufficiently to know the value of retirement, and the blessing of ending our days in peace.

THE FORTUNES & MISFORTUNES OF THE FAMOUS MOLL FLANDERS

Who was Born in Newgate, and during a Life of continu'd Variety for Three-score Years, besides her Childhood, was Twelve Year a Whore, five times a Wife (whereof once to her own Brother), Twelve Year a Thief, Eight Year a Transported Felon in Virginia, at last grew Rich, liv'd Honest, and dies a Penitent. Written from her own Memorandums …

THE AUTHOR'S PREFACE

The world is so taken up of late with novels and romances, that it will be hard for a private history to be taken for genuine, where the names and other circumstances of the person are concealed, and on this account we must be content to leave the reader to pass his own opinion upon the ensuing sheet, and take it just as he pleases.

The author is here supposed to be writing her own history, and in the very beginning of her account she gives the reasons why she thinks fit to conceal her true name, after which there is no occasion to say any more about that.

It is true that the original of this story is put into new words, and the style of the famous lady we here speak of is a little altered; particularly she is made to tell her own tale in modester words that she told it at first, the copy which came first to hand having been written in language more like one still in Newgate than one grown penitent and humble, as she afterwards pretends to be.

The pen employed in finishing her story, and making it what you now see it to be, has had no little difficulty to put it into a dress fit to be seen, and to make it speak language fit to be read. When a woman debauched from her youth, nay, even being the offspring of debauchery and vice, comes to give an account of all her vicious practices, and even to descend to the particular occasions and circumstances by which she ran through in threescore years, an author must be hard put to it wrap it up so clean as not to give room, especially for vicious readers, to turn it to his disadvantage.

All possible care, however, has been taken to give no lewd ideas, no immodest turns in the new dressing up of this story; no, not to the worst parts of her expressions. To this purpose some of the vicious part of her life, which could not be modestly told, is quite left out, and several other parts are very much shortened. What is left 'tis hoped will not offend the chastest reader or the modest hearer; and as the best use is made even of the worst story, the moral 'tis hoped will keep the reader serious, even where the story might incline him to be otherwise. To give the history of a wicked life repented of, necessarily requires that the wicked part should be make as wicked as the real history of it will bear, to illustrate and give a beauty to the penitent part, which is certainly the best and brightest, if related with equal spirit and life.

It is suggested there cannot be the same life, the same brightness and beauty, in relating the penitent part as is in the criminal part. If there is any truth in that suggestion, I must be allowed to say 'tis because there is not the same taste and relish in the reading, and indeed it is to true that the difference lies not in the real worth of the subject so much as in the gust and palate of the reader.

But as this work is chiefly recommended to those who know how to read it, and how to make the good uses of it which the story all along recommends to them, so it is to be hoped that such readers will be more leased with the moral than the fable, with the application than with the relation, and with the end of the writer than with the life of the person written of.

There is in this story abundance of delightful incidents, and all of them usefully applied. There is an agreeable turn artfully given them in the relating, that naturally instructs the reader, either one way or other. The first part of her lewd life with the young gentleman at Colchester has so many happy turns given it to expose the crime, and warn all whose circumstances are adapted to it, of the ruinous end of such things, and the foolish, thoughtless, and abhorred conduct of both the parties, that it abundantly atones for all the lively description she gives of her folly and wickedness.

The repentance of her lover at the Bath, and how brought by the just alarm of his fit of sickness to abandon her; the just caution given there against even the lawful intimacies of the dearest friends, and how unable they are to preserve the most solemn resolutions of virtue without divine assistance; these are parts which, to a just discernment, will appear to have more real beauty in them all the amorous chain of story which introduces it.

In a word, as the whole relation is carefully garbled of all the levity and looseness that was in it, so it all applied, and with the utmost care, to virtuous and religious uses. None can, without being guilty of manifest injustice, cast any reproach upon it, or upon our design in publishing it.

The advocates for the stage have, in all ages, made this the great argument to persuade people that their plays are useful, and that they ought to be allowed in the most civilised and in the most religious government; namely, that they are applied to virtuous purposes, and that by the most lively representations, they fail not to recommend virtue and generous principles, and to discourage and expose all sorts of vice and corruption of manners; and were it true that they did so, and that they constantly adhered to that rule, as the test of their acting on the theatre, much might be said in their favour.

Throughout the infinite variety of this book, this fundamental is most strictly adhered to; there is not a wicked action in any part of it, but is first and last rendered unhappy and unfortunate; there is not a superlative villain brought upon the stage, but either he is brought to an unhappy end, or brought to be a penitent; there is not an ill thing mentioned but it is condemned, even in the relation, nor a virtuous, just thing but it carries its praise along with it. What can more exactly answer the rule laid down, to recommend even those representations of things which have so many other just objections leaving against them? namely, of example, of bad company, obscene language, and the like.

Upon this foundation this book is recommended to the reader as a work from every part of which something may be learned, and some just and religious inference is drawn, by which the reader will have something of instruction, if he pleases to make use of it.

All the exploits of this lady of fame, in her depredations upon mankind, stand as so many warnings to honest people to beware of them, intimating to them by what methods innocent people are drawn in, plundered and robbed, and by consequence how to avoid them. Her robbing a little innocent child, dressed fine by the vanity of the mother, to go to the dancing-school, is a good memento to such people hereafter, as is likewise her picking the gold watch from the young lady's side in the Park.

Her getting a parcel from a hare-brained wench at the coaches in St. John Street; her booty made at the fire, and again at Harwich, all give us excellent warnings in such cases to be more present to ourselves in sudden surprises of every sort.

Her application to a sober life and industrious management at last in Virginia, with her transported spouse, is a story fruitful of instruction to all the unfortunate creatures who are obliged to seek their re-establishment abroad, whether by the misery of transportation or other disaster; letting them know that diligence and application have their due encouragement, even in the remotest parts of the world, and that no case can be so low, so despicable, or so empty of prospect, but that an unwearied industry will go a great way to deliver us from it, will in time raise the meanest creature to appear again the world, and give him a new case for his life.

There are a few of the serious inferences which we are led by the hand to in this book, and these are fully sufficient to justify any man in recommending it to the world, and much more to justify the publication of it.

There are two of the most beautiful parts still behind, which this story gives some idea of, and lets us into the parts of them, but they are either of them too long to be brought into the same volume, and indeed are, as I may call them, whole volumes of themselves, viz.: 1. The life of her governess, as she calls her, who had run through, it seems, in a few years, all the eminent degrees of a gentlewoman, a whore, and a bawd; a midwife and a midwife-keeper, as they are called; a pawnbroker, a childtaker, a receiver of thieves, and of thieves' purchase, that is to say, of stolen goods; and in a word, herself a thief, a breeder up of thieves and the like, and yet at last a penitent.

The second is the life of her transported husband, a highwayman, who it seems, lived a twelve years' life of successful villainy upon the road, and even at last came off so well as to be a volunteer transport, not a convict; and in whose life there is an incredible variety.

But, as I have said, these are things too long to bring in here, so neither can I make a promise of the coming out by themselves.

We cannot say, indeed, that this history is carried on quite to the end of the life of this famous Moll Flanders, as she calls herself, for nobody can write their own life to the full end of it, unless they can write it after they are dead. But her husband's life, being written by a third hand, gives a full account of them both, how long they lived together in that country, and how they both came to England again, after about eight years, in which time they were grown very rich, and where she lived, it seems, to be very old, but was not so extraordinary a penitent as she was at first; it seems only that indeed she always spoke with abhorrence of her former life, and of every part of it.

In her last scene, at Maryland and Virginia, many pleasant things happened, which makes that part of her life very agreeable, but they are not told with the same elegancy as those accounted for by herself; so it is still to the more advantage that we break off here.

MOLL FLANDERS

My true name is so well known in the records or registers at Newgate, and in the Old Bailey, and there are some things of such consequence still depending there, relating to my particular conduct, that it is not be expected I should set my name or the account of my family to this work; perhaps, after my death, it may be better known; at present it would not be proper, no not though a general pardon should be issued, even without exceptions and reserve of persons or crimes.

It is enough to tell you, that as some of my worst comrades, who are out of the way of doing me harm (having gone out of the world by the steps and the string, as I often expected to go), knew me by the name of Moll Flanders, so you may give me leave to speak of myself under that name till I dare own who I have been, as well as who I am.

I have been told that in one of neighbour nations, whether it be in France or where else I know not, they have an order from the king, that when any criminal is condemned, either to die, or to the galleys, or to be transported, if they leave any children, as such are generally unprovided for, by the poverty or forfeiture of their parents, so they are immediately taken into the care of the Government, and put into a hospital called the House of Orphans, where they are bred up, clothed, fed, taught, and when fit to go out, are placed out to trades or to services, so as to be well able to provide for themselves by an honest, industrious behaviour.

Had this been the custom in our country, I had not been left a poor desolate girl without friends, without clothes, without help or helper in the world, as was my fate; and by which I was not only exposed to very great distresses, even before I was capable either of understanding my case or how to amend it, but brought into a course of life which was not only scandalous in itself, but which in its ordinary course tended to the swift destruction both of soul and body.

But the case was otherwise here. My mother was convicted of felony for a certain petty theft scarce worth naming, viz. having an opportunity of borrowing three pieces of fine holland of a certain draper in Cheapside. The circumstances are too long to repeat, and I have heard them related so many ways, that I can scarce be certain which is the right account.

However it was, this they all agree in, that my mother pleaded her belly, and being found quick with child, she was respited for about seven months; in which time having brought me into the world, and being about again, she was called down, as they term it, to her former judgment, but obtained the favour of being transported to the plantations, and left me about half a year old; and in bad hands, you may be sure.

This is too near the first hours of my life for me to relate anything of myself but by hearsay; it is enough to mention, that as I was born in such an unhappy place, I had no parish to have recourse to for my nourishment in my infancy; nor can I give the least account how I was kept alive, other than that, as I have been told, some relation of my mother's took me away for a while as a nurse, but at whose expense, or by whose direction, I know nothing at all of it.

The first account that I can recollect, or could ever learn of myself, was that I had wandered among a crew of those people they call gypsies, or Egyptians; but I believe it was but a very little while that I had been among them, for I had not had my skin discoloured or blackened, as they do very young to all the children they carry about with them; nor can I tell how I came among them, or how I got from them.

It was at Colchester, in Essex, that those people left me; and I have a notion in my head that I left them there (that is, that I hid myself and would not go any farther with them), but I am not able to be particular in that account; only this I remember, that being taken up by some of the parish officers of Colchester, I gave an account that I came into the town with the gypsies, but that I would not go any farther with them, and that so they had left me, but whither they were gone that I knew not, nor could they expect it of me; for though they send round the country to inquire after them, it seems they could not be found.

I was now in a way to be provided for; for though I was not a parish charge upon this or that part of the town by law, yet as my case came to be known, and that I was too young to do any work, being not above three years old, compassion moved the magistrates of the town to order some care to be taken of me, and I became one of their own as much as if I had been born in the place.

In the provision they made for me, it was my good hap to be put to nurse, as they call it, to a woman who was indeed poor but had been in better circumstances, and who got a little livelihood by taking such as I was supposed to be, and keeping them with all necessaries, till they were at a certain age, in which it might be supposed they might go to service or get their own bread.

This woman had also had a little school, which she kept to teach children to read and to work; and having, as I have said, lived before that in good fashion, she bred up the children she took with a great deal of art, as well as with a great deal of care.

But that which was worth all the rest, she bred them up very religiously, being herself a very sober, pious woman, very house-wifely and clean, and very mannerly, and with good behaviour. So that in a word, expecting a plain diet, coarse lodging, and mean clothes, we were brought up as mannerly and as genteelly as if we had been at the dancing-school.

I was continued here till I was eight years old, when I was terrified with news that the magistrates (as I think they called them) had ordered that I should go to service. I was able to do but very little service wherever I was to go, except it was to run of errands and be a drudge to some cookmaid, and this they told me often, which put me into a great fright; for I had a thorough aversion to going to service, as they called it (that is, to be a servant), though I was so young; and I told my nurse, as we called her, that I believed I could get my living without going to service, if she pleased to let me; for she had taught me to work with my needle, and spin worsted, which is the chief trade of that city, and I told her that if she would keep me, I would work for her, and I would work very hard.

I talked to her almost every day of working hard; and, in short, I did nothing but work and cry all day, which grieved the good, kind woman so much, that at last she began to be concerned for me, for she loved me very well.

One day after this, as she came into the room where all we poor children were at work, she sat down just over against me, not in her usual place as mistress, but as if she set herself on purpose to observe me and see me work. I was doing something she had set me to; as I remember, it was marking some shirts which she had taken to make, and after a while she began to talk to me. 'Thou foolish child,' says she, 'thou art always crying (for I was crying then); 'prithee, what dost cry for?' 'Because they will take me away,' says I, 'and put me to service, and I can't work housework.' 'Well, child,' says she, 'but though you can't work housework, as you call it, you will learn it in time, and they won't put you to hard things at first.' 'Yes, they will,' says I, 'and if I can't do it they will beat me, and the maids will beat me to make me do great work, and I am but a little girl and I can't do it'; and then I cried again, till I could not speak any more to her.

This moved my good motherly nurse, so that she from that time resolved I should not go to service yet; so she bid me not cry, and she would speak to Mr. Mayor, and I should not go to service till I was bigger.

Well, this did not satisfy me, for to think of going to service was such a frightful thing to me, that if she had assured me I should not have gone till I was twenty years old, it would have been the same to me; I should have cried, I believe, all the time, with the very apprehension of its being to be so at last.

When she saw that I was not pacified yet, she began to be angry with me. 'And what would you have?' says she; 'don't I tell you that you shall not go to service till your are bigger?' 'Ay,' said I, 'but then I must go at last.' 'Why, what?' said she; 'is the girl mad? What would you be—a gentlewoman?' 'Yes,' says I, and cried heartily till I roared out again.

This set the old gentlewoman a-laughing at me, as you may be sure it would. 'Well, madam, forsooth,' says she, gibing at me, 'you would be a gentlewoman; and pray how will you come to be a gentlewoman? What! will you do it by your fingers' end?'

'Yes,' says I again, very innocently.

'Why, what can you earn?' says she; 'what can you get at your work?'

'Threepence,' said I, 'when I spin, and fourpence when I work plain work.'

'Alas! poor gentlewoman,' said she again, laughing, 'what will that do for thee?'

'It will keep me,' says I, 'if you will let me live with you.' And this I said in such a poor petitioning tone, that it made the poor woman's heart yearn to me, as she told me afterwards.

'But,' says she, 'that will not keep you and buy you clothes too; and who must buy the little gentlewoman clothes?' says she, and smiled all the while at me.

'I will work harder, then,' says I, 'and you shall have it all.'

'Poor child! it won't keep you,' says she; 'it will hardly keep you in victuals.'

'Then I will have no victuals,' says I, again very innocently; 'let me but live with you.'

'Why, can you live without victuals?' says she.

'Yes,' again says I, very much like a child, you may be sure, and still I cried heartily.

I had no policy in all this; you may easily see it was all nature; but it was joined with so much innocence and so much passion that, in short, it set the good motherly creature a-weeping too, and she cried at last as fast as I did, and then took me and led me out of the teaching-room. 'Come,' says she, 'you shan't go to service; you shall live with me'; and this pacified me for the present.

Some time after this, she going to wait on the Mayor, and talking of such things as belonged to her business, at last my story came up, and my good nurse told Mr. Mayor the whole tale. He was so pleased with it, that he would call his lady and his two daughters to hear it, and it made mirth enough among them, you may be sure.

However, not a week had passed over, but on a sudden comes Mrs. Mayoress and her two daughters to the house to see my old nurse, and to see her school and the children. When they had looked about them a little, 'Well, Mrs. ——,' says the Mayoress to my nurse, 'and pray which is the little lass that intends to be a gentlewoman?' I heard her, and I was terribly frighted at first, though I did not know why neither; but Mrs. Mayoress comes up to me. 'Well, miss,' says she, 'and what are you at work upon?' The word miss was a language that had hardly been heard of in our school, and I wondered what sad name it was she called me. However, I stood up, made a curtsy, and she took my work out of my hand, looked on it, and said it was very well; then she took up one of the hands. 'Nay,' says she, 'the child may come to be a gentlewoman for aught anybody knows; she has a gentlewoman's hand,' says she. This pleased me mightily, you may be sure; but Mrs. Mayoress did not stop there, but giving me my work again, she put her hand in her pocket, gave me a shilling, and bid me mind my work, and learn to work well, and I might be a gentlewoman for aught she knew.

Now all this while my good old nurse, Mrs. Mayoress, and all the rest of them did not understand me at all, for they meant one sort of thing by the word gentlewoman, and I meant quite another; for alas! all I understood by being a gentlewoman was to be able to work for myself, and get enough to keep me without that terrible bugbear going to service, whereas they meant to live great, rich and high, and I know not what.

Well, after Mrs. Mayoress was gone, her two daughters came in, and they called for the gentlewoman too, and they talked a long while to me, and I answered them in my innocent way; but always, if they asked me whether I resolved to be a gentlewoman, I answered Yes. At last one of them asked me what a gentlewoman was? That puzzled me much; but, however, I explained myself negatively, that it was one that did not go to service, to do housework. They were pleased to be familiar with me, and like my little prattle to them, which, it seems, was agreeable enough to them, and they gave me money too.

As for my money, I gave it all to my mistress-nurse, as I called her, and told her she should have all I got for myself when I was a gentlewoman, as well as now. By this and some other of my talk, my old tutoress began to understand me about what I meant by being a gentlewoman, and that I understood by it no more than to be able to get my bread by my own work; and at last she asked me whether it was not so.

I told her, yes, and insisted on it, that to do so was to be a gentlewoman; 'for,' says I, 'there is such a one,' naming a woman that mended lace and washed the ladies' laced-heads; 'she,' says I, 'is a gentlewoman, and they call her madam.'

'Poor child,' says my good old nurse, 'you may soon be such a gentlewoman as that, for she is a person of ill fame, and has had two or three bastards.'

I did not understand anything of that; but I answered, 'I am sure they call her madam, and she does not go to service nor do housework'; and therefore I insisted that she was a gentlewoman, and I would be such a gentlewoman as that.

The ladies were told all this again, to be sure, and they made themselves merry with it, and every now and then the young ladies, Mr. Mayor's daughters, would come and see me, and ask where the little gentlewoman was, which made me not a little proud of myself.

This held a great while, and I was often visited by these young ladies, and sometimes they brought others with them; so that I was known by it almost all over the town.

I was now about ten years old, and began to look a little womanish, for I was mighty grave and humble, very mannerly, and as I had often heard the ladies say I was pretty, and would be a very handsome woman, so you may be sure that hearing them say so made me not a little proud. However, that pride had no ill effect upon me yet; only, as they often gave me money, and I gave it to my old nurse, she, honest woman, was so just to me as to lay it all out again for me, and gave me head-dresses, and linen, and gloves, and ribbons, and I went very neat, and always clean; for that I would do, and if I had rags on, I would always be clean, or else I would dabble them in water myself; but, I say, my good nurse, when I had money given me, very honestly laid it out for me, and would always tell the ladies this or that was bought with their money; and this made them oftentimes give me more, till at last I was indeed called upon by the magistrates, as I understood it, to go out to service; but then I was come to be so good a workwoman myself, and the ladies were so kind to me, that it was plain I could maintain myself—that is to say, I could earn as much for my nurse as she was able by it to keep me—so she told them that if they would give her leave, she would keep the gentlewoman, as she called me, to be her assistant and teach the children, which I was very well able to do; for I was very nimble at my work, and had a good hand with my needle, though I was yet very young.

But the kindness of the ladies of the town did not end here, for when they came to understand that I was no more maintained by the public allowance as before, they gave me money oftener than formerly; and as I grew up they brought me work to do for them, such as linen to make, and laces to mend, and heads to dress up, and not only paid me for doing them, but even taught me how to do them; so that now I was a gentlewoman indeed, as I understood that word, I not only found myself clothes and paid my nurse for my keeping, but got money in my pocket too beforehand.

The ladies also gave me clothes frequently of their own or their children's; some stockings, some petticoats, some gowns, some one thing, some another, and these my old woman managed for me like a mere mother, and kept them for me, obliged me to mend them, and turn them and twist them to the best advantage, for she was a rare housewife.

At last one of the ladies took so much fancy to me that she would have me home to her house, for a month, she said, to be among her daughters.

Now, though this was exceeding kind in her, yet, as my old good woman said to her, unless she resolved to keep me for good and all, she would do the little gentlewoman more harm than good. 'Well,' says the lady, 'that's true; and therefore I'll only take her home for a week, then, that I may see how my daughters and she agree together, and how I like her temper, and then I'll tell you more; and in the meantime, if anybody comes to see her as they used to do, you may only tell them you have sent her out to my house.'

This was prudently managed enough, and I went to the lady's house; but I was so pleased there with the young ladies, and they so pleased with me, that I had enough to do to come away, and they were as unwilling to part with me.

However, I did come away, and lived almost a year more with my honest old woman, and began now to be very helpful to her; for I was almost fourteen years old, was tall of my age, and looked a little womanish; but I had such a taste of genteel living at the lady's house that I was not so easy in my old quarters as I used to be, and I thought it was fine to be a gentlewoman indeed, for I had quite other notions of a gentlewoman now than I had before; and as I thought, I say, that it was fine to be a gentlewoman, so I loved to be among gentlewomen, and therefore I longed to be there again.

About the time that I was fourteen years and a quarter old, my good nurse, mother I rather to call her, fell sick and died. I was then in a sad condition indeed, for as there is no great bustle in putting an end to a poor body's family when once they are carried to the grave, so the poor good woman being buried, the parish children she kept were immediately removed by the church-wardens; the school was at an end, and the children of it had no more to do but just stay at home till they were sent somewhere else; and as for what she left, her daughter, a married woman with six or seven children, came and swept it all away at once, and removing the goods, they had no more to say to me than to jest with me, and tell me that the little gentlewoman might set up for herself if she pleased.

I was frighted out of my wits almost, and knew not what to do, for I was, as it were, turned out of doors to the wide world, and that which was still worse, the old honest woman had two-and-twenty shillings of mine in her hand, which was all the estate the little gentlewoman had in the world; and when I asked the daughter for it, she huffed me and laughed at me, and told me she had nothing to do with it.

It was true the good, poor woman had told her daughter of it, and that it lay in such a place, that it was the child's money, and had called once or twice for me to give it me, but I was, unhappily, out of the way somewhere or other, and when I came back she was past being in a condition to speak of it. However, the daughter was so honest afterwards as to give it me, though at first she used me cruelly about it.

Now was I a poor gentlewoman indeed, and I was just that very night to be turned into the wide world; for the daughter removed all the goods, and I had not so much as a lodging to go to, or a bit of bread to eat. But it seems some of the neighbours, who had known my circumstances, took so much compassion of me as to acquaint the lady in whose family I had been a week, as I mentioned above; and immediately she sent her maid to fetch me away, and two of her daughters came with the maid though unsent. So I went with them, bag and baggage, and with a glad heart, you may be sure. The fright of my condition had made such an impression upon me, that I did not want now to be a gentlewoman, but was very willing to be a servant, and that any kind of servant they thought fit to have me be.

But my new generous mistress, for she exceeded the good woman I was with before, in everything, as well as in the matter of estate; I say, in everything except honesty; and for that, though this was a lady most exactly just, yet I must not forget to say on all occasions, that the first, though poor, was as uprightly honest as it was possible for any one to be.

I was no sooner carried away, as I have said, by this good gentlewoman, but the first lady, that is to say, the Mayoress that was, sent her two daughters to take care of me; and another family which had taken notice of me when I was the little gentlewoman, and had given me work to do, sent for me after her, so that I was mightily made of, as we say; nay, and they were not a little angry, especially madam the Mayoress, that her friend had taken me away from her, as she called it; for, as she said, I was hers by right, she having been the first that took any notice of me. But they that had me would not part with me; and as for me, though I should have been very well treated with any of the others, yet I could not be better than where I was.

Here I continued till I was between seventeen and eighteen years old, and here I had all the advantages for my education that could be imagined; the lady had masters home to the house to teach her daughters to dance, and to speak French, and to write, and other to teach them music; and I was always with them, I learned as fast as they; and though the masters were not appointed to teach me, yet I learned by imitation and inquiry all that they learned by instruction and direction; so that, in short, I learned to dance and speak French as well as any of them, and to sing much better, for I had a better voice than any of them. I could not so readily come at playing on the harpsichord or spinet, because I had no instrument of my own to practice on, and could only come at theirs in the intervals when they left it, which was uncertain; but yet I learned tolerably well too, and the young ladies at length got two instruments, that is to say, a harpsichord and a spinet too, and then they taught me themselves. But as to dancing, they could hardly help my learning country-dances, because they always wanted me to make up even number; and, on the other hand, they were as heartily willing to learn me everything that they had been taught themselves, as I could be to take the learning.

By this means I had, as I have said above, all the advantages of education that I could have had if I had been as much a gentlewoman as they were with whom I lived; and in some things I had the advantage of my ladies, though they were my superiors; but they were all the gifts of nature, and which all their fortunes could not furnish. First, I was apparently handsomer than any of them; secondly, I was better shaped; and, thirdly, I sang better, by which I mean I had a better voice; in all which you will, I hope, allow me to say, I do not speak my own conceit of myself, but the opinion of all that knew the family.

I had with all these the common vanity of my sex, viz. that being really taken for very handsome, or, if you please, for a great beauty, I very well knew it, and had as good an opinion of myself as anybody else could have of me; and particularly I loved to hear anybody speak of it, which could not but happen to me sometimes, and was a great satisfaction to me.

Thus far I have had a smooth story to tell of myself, and in all this part of my life I not only had the reputation of living in a very good family, and a family noted and respected everywhere for virtue and sobriety, and for every valuable thing; but I had the character too of a very sober, modest, and virtuous young woman, and such I had always been; neither had I yet any occasion to think of anything else, or to know what a temptation to wickedness meant.

But that which I was too vain of was my ruin, or rather my vanity was the cause of it. The lady in the house where I was had two sons, young gentlemen of very promising parts and of extraordinary behaviour, and it was my misfortune to be very well with them both, but they managed themselves with me in a quite different manner.

The eldest, a gay gentleman that knew the town as well as the country, and though he had levity enough to do an ill-natured thing, yet had too much judgment of things to pay too dear for his pleasures; he began with the unhappy snare to all women, viz. taking notice upon all occasions how pretty I was, as he called it, how agreeable, how well-carriaged, and the like; and this he contrived so subtly, as if he had known as well how to catch a woman in his net as a partridge when he went a-setting; for he would contrive to be talking this to his sisters when, though I was not by, yet when he knew I was not far off but that I should be sure to hear him. His sisters would return softly to him, 'Hush, brother, she will hear you; she is but in the next room.' Then he would put it off and talk softlier, as if he had not know it, and begin to acknowledge he was wrong; and then, as if he had forgot himself, he would speak aloud again, and I, that was so well pleased to hear it, was sure to listen for it upon all occasions.

After he had thus baited his hook, and found easily enough the method how to lay it in my way, he played an opener game; and one day, going by his sister's chamber when I was there, doing something about dressing her, he comes in with an air of gaiety. 'Oh, Mrs. Betty,' said he to me, 'how do you do, Mrs. Betty? Don't your cheeks burn, Mrs. Betty?' I made a curtsy and blushed, but said nothing. 'What makes you talk so, brother?' says the lady. 'Why,' says he, 'we have been talking of her below-stairs this half-hour.' 'Well,' says his sister, 'you can say no harm of her, that I am sure, so 'tis no matter what you have been talking about.' 'Nay,' says he, "tis so far from talking harm of her, that we have been talking a great deal of good, and a great many fine things have been said of Mrs. Betty, I assure you; and particularly, that she is the handsomest young woman in Colchester; and, in short, they begin to toast her health in the town.'

'I wonder at you, brother,' says the sister. 'Betty wants but one thing, but she had as good want everything, for the market is against our sex just now; and if a young woman have beauty, birth, breeding, wit, sense, manners, modesty, and all these to an extreme, yet if she have not money, she's nobody, she had as good want them all for nothing but money now recommends a woman; the men play the game all into their own hands.'

Her younger brother, who was by, cried, 'Hold, sister, you run too fast; I am an exception to your rule. I assure you, if I find a woman so accomplished as you talk of, I say, I assure you, I would not trouble myself about the money.'

'Oh,' says the sister, 'but you will take care not to fancy one, then, without the money.'

'You don't know that neither,' says the brother.

'But why, sister,' says the elder brother, 'why do you exclaim so at the men for aiming so much at the fortune? You are none of them that want a fortune, whatever else you want.'

'I understand you, brother,' replies the lady very smartly; 'you suppose I have the money, and want the beauty; but as times go now, the first will do without the last, so I have the better of my neighbours.'

'Well,' says the younger brother, 'but your neighbours, as you call them, may be even with you, for beauty will steal a husband sometimes in spite of money, and when the maid chances to be handsomer than the mistress, she oftentimes makes as good a market, and rides in a coach before her.'

I thought it was time for me to withdraw and leave them, and I did so, but not so far but that I heard all their discourse, in which I heard abundance of the fine things said of myself, which served to prompt my vanity, but, as I soon found, was not the way to increase my interest in the family, for the sister and the younger brother fell grievously out about it; and as he said some very disobliging things to her upon my account, so I could easily see that she resented them by her future conduct to me, which indeed was very unjust to me, for I had never had the least thought of what she suspected as to her younger brother; indeed, the elder brother, in his distant, remote way, had said a great many things as in jest, which I had the folly to believe were in earnest, or to flatter myself with the hopes of what I ought to have supposed he never intended, and perhaps never thought of.

It happened one day that he came running upstairs, towards the room where his sisters used to sit and work, as he often used to do; and calling to them before he came in, as was his way too, I, being there alone, stepped to the door, and said, 'Sir, the ladies are not here, they are walked down the garden.' As I stepped forward to say this, towards the door, he was just got to the door, and clasping me in his arms, as if it had been by chance, 'Oh, Mrs. Betty,' says he, 'are you here? That's better still; I want to speak with you more than I do with them'; and then, having me in his arms, he kissed me three or four times.

I struggled to get away, and yet did it but faintly neither, and he held me fast, and still kissed me, till he was almost out of breath, and then, sitting down, says, 'Dear Betty, I am in love with you.'

His words, I must confess, fired my blood; all my spirits flew about my heart and put me into disorder enough, which he might easily have seen in my face. He repeated it afterwards several times, that he was in love with me, and my heart spoke as plain as a voice, that I liked it; nay, whenever he said, 'I am in love with you,' my blushes plainly replied, 'Would you were, sir.'

However, nothing else passed at that time; it was but a surprise, and when he was gone I soon recovered myself again. He had stayed longer with me, but he happened to look out at the window and see his sisters coming up the garden, so he took his leave, kissed me again, told me he was very serious, and I should hear more of him very quickly, and away he went, leaving me infinitely pleased, though surprised; and had there not been one misfortune in it, I had been in the right, but the mistake lay here, that Mrs. Betty was in earnest and the gentleman was not.

From this time my head ran upon strange things, and I may truly say I was not myself; to have such a gentleman talk to me of being in love with me, and of my being such a charming creature, as he told me I was; these were things I knew not how to bear, my vanity was elevated to the last degree. It is true I had my head full of pride, but, knowing nothing of the wickedness of the times, I had not one thought of my own safety or of my virtue about me; and had my young master offered it at first sight, he might have taken any liberty he thought fit with me; but he did not see his advantage, which was my happiness for that time.

After this attack it was not long but he found an opportunity to catch me again, and almost in the same posture; indeed, it had more of design in it on his part, though not on my part. It was thus: the young ladies were all gone a-visiting with their mother; his brother was out of town; and as for his father, he had been in

London for a week before. He had so well watched me that he knew where I was, though I did not so much as know that he was in the house; and he briskly comes up the stairs and, seeing me at work, comes into the room to me directly, and began just as he did before, with taking me in his arms, and kissing me for almost a quarter of an hour together.

It was his younger sister's chamber that I was in, and as there was nobody in the house but the maids below-stairs, he was, it may be, the ruder; in short, he began to be in earnest with me indeed. Perhaps he found me a little too easy, for God knows I made no resistance to him while he only held me in his arms and kissed me; indeed, I was too well pleased with it to resist him much.

However, as it were, tired with that kind of work, we sat down, and there he talked with me a great while; he said he was charmed with me, and that he could not rest night or day till he had told me how he was in love with me, and, if I was able to love him again, and would make him happy, I should be the saving of his life, and many such fine things. I said little to him again, but easily discovered that I was a fool, and that I did not in the least perceive what he meant.

Then he walked about the room, and taking me by the hand, I walked with him; and by and by, taking his advantage, he threw me down upon the bed, and kissed me there most violently; but, to give him his due, offered no manner of rudeness to me, only kissed a great while. After this he thought he had heard somebody come upstairs, so got off from the bed, lifted me up, professing a great deal of love for me, but told me it was all an honest affection, and that he meant no ill to me; and with that he put five guineas into my hand, and went away downstairs.

I was more confounded with the money than I was before with the love, and began to be so elevated that I scarce knew the ground I stood on. I am the more particular in this part, that if my story comes to be read by any innocent young body, they may learn from it to guard themselves against the mischiefs which attend an early knowledge of their own beauty. If a young woman once thinks herself handsome, she never doubts the truth of any man that tells her he is in love with her; for if she believes herself charming enough to captivate him, 'tis natural to expect the effects of it.

This young gentleman had fired his inclination as much as he had my vanity, and, as if he had found that he had an opportunity and was sorry he did not take hold of it, he comes up again in half an hour or thereabouts, and falls to work with me again as before, only with a little less introduction.

And first, when he entered the room, he turned about and shut the door. 'Mrs. Betty,' said he, 'I fancied before somebody was coming upstairs, but it was not so; however,' adds he, 'if they find me in the room with you, they shan't catch me a-kissing of you.' I told him I did not know who should be coming upstairs, for I believed there was nobody in the house but the cook and the other maid, and they never came up those stairs. 'Well, my dear,' says he, "tis good to be sure, however'; and so he sits down, and we began to talk. And now, though I was still all on fire with his first visit, and said little, he did as it were put words in my mouth, telling me how passionately he loved me, and that though he could not mention such a thing till he came to this estate, yet he was resolved to make me happy then, and himself too; that is to say, to marry me, and abundance of such fine things, which I, poor fool, did not understand the drift of, but acted as if there was no such thing as any kind of love but that which tended to matrimony; and if he had spoke of that, I had no room, as well as no power, to have said no; but we were not come that length yet.

We had not sat long, but he got up, and, stopping my very breath with kisses, threw me upon the bed again; but then being both well warmed, he went farther with me than decency permits me to mention, nor had it been in my power to have denied him at that moment, had he offered much more than he did.

However, though he took these freedoms with me, it did not go to that which they call the last favour, which, to do him justice, he did not attempt; and he made that self-denial of his a plea for all his freedoms with me upon other occasions after this. When this was over, he stayed but a little while, but he put almost a handful of gold in my hand, and left me, making a thousand protestations of his passion for me, and of his loving me above all the women in the world.

It will not be strange if I now began to think, but alas! it was but with very little solid reflection. I had a most unbounded stock of vanity and pride, and but a very little stock of virtue. I did indeed case sometimes with myself what young master aimed at, but thought of nothing but the fine words and the gold; whether he intended to marry me, or not to marry me, seemed a matter of no great consequence to me; nor did my thoughts so much as suggest to me the necessity of making any capitulation for myself, till he came to make a kind of formal proposal to me, as you shall hear presently.

Thus I gave up myself to a readiness of being ruined without the least concern and am a fair memento to all young women whose vanity prevails over their virtue. Nothing was ever so stupid on both sides. Had I acted as became me, and resisted as virtue and honour require, this gentleman had either desisted his attacks, finding no room to expect the accomplishment of his design, or had made fair and honourable proposals of marriage; in which case, whoever had blamed him, nobody could have blamed me. In short, if he had known me, and how easy the trifle he aimed at was to be had, he would have troubled his head no farther, but have given me four or five guineas, and have lain with me the next time he had come at me. And if I had known his thoughts, and how hard he thought I would be to be gained, I might have made my own terms with him; and if I had not capitulated for an immediate marriage, I might for a maintenance till marriage, and might have had what I would; for he was already rich to excess, besides what he had in expectation; but I seemed wholly to have abandoned all such thoughts as these, and was taken up only with the pride of my beauty, and of being beloved by such a gentleman. As for the gold, I spent whole hours in looking upon it; I told the guineas over and over a thousand times a day. Never poor vain creature was so wrapt up with every part of the story as I was, not considering what was before me, and how near my ruin was at the door; indeed, I think I rather wished for that ruin than studied to avoid it.

In the meantime, however, I was cunning enough not to give the least room to any in the family to suspect me, or to imagine that I had the least correspondence with this young gentleman. I scarce ever looked towards him in public, or answered if he spoke to me when anybody was near us; but for all that, we had every now and then a little encounter, where we had room for a word or two, an now and then a kiss, but no fair opportunity for the mischief intended; and especially considering that he made more circumlocution than, if he had known by thoughts, he had occasion for; and the work appearing difficult to him, he really made it so.

But as the devil is an unwearied tempter, so he never fails to find opportunity for that wickedness he invites to. It was one evening that I was in the garden, with his two younger sisters and himself, and all very innocently merry, when he found means to convey a note into my hand, by which he directed me to understand that he would to-morrow desire me publicly to go of an errand for him into the town, and that I should see him somewhere by the way.

Accordingly, after dinner, he very gravely says to me, his sisters being all by, 'Mrs. Betty, I must ask a favour of you.' 'What's that?' says his second sister. 'Nay, sister,' says he very gravely, 'if you can't spare Mrs. Betty to-day, any other time will do.' Yes, they said, they could spare her well enough, and the sister begged pardon for asking, which they did but of mere course, without any meaning. 'Well, but, brother,' says the eldest sister, 'you must tell Mrs. Betty what it is; if it be any private business that we must not hear, you may call her out. There she is.' 'Why, sister,' says the gentleman very gravely, 'what do you mean? I only desire her to go into the High Street' (and then he pulls out a turnover), 'to such a shop'; and then he tells them a long story of two fine neckcloths he had bid money for, and he wanted to have me go and make an errand to buy a neck to the turnover that he showed, to see if they would take my money for the neckcloths; to bid a shilling more, and haggle with them; and then he made more errands, and so continued to have such petty business to do, that I should be sure to stay a good while.

When he had given me my errands, he told them a long story of a visit he was going to make to a family they all knew, and where was to be such-and-such gentlemen, and how merry they were to be, and very formally asks his sisters to go with him, and they as formally excused themselves, because of company that they had notice was to come and visit them that afternoon; which, by the way, he had contrived on purpose.

He had scarce done speaking to them, and giving me my errand, but his man came up to tell him that Sir W—— H——'s coach stopped at the door; so he runs down, and comes up again immediately. 'Alas!' says he aloud, 'there's all my mirth spoiled at once; sir W—— has sent his coach for me, and desires to speak with me upon some earnest business.' It seems this Sir W—— was a gentleman who lived about three miles out of town, to whom he had spoken on purpose the day before, to lend him his chariot for a particular occasion, and had appointed it to call for him, as it did, about three o'clock.

Immediately he calls for his best wig, hat, and sword, and ordering his man to go to the other place to make his excuse— that was to say, he made an excuse to send his man away—he prepares to go into the coach. As he was going, he stopped a while, and speaks mighty earnestly to me about his business, and finds an opportunity to say very softly to me, 'Come away, my dear, as soon as ever you can.' I said nothing, but made a curtsy, as if I had done so to what he said in public. In about a quarter of an hour I went out too; I had no dress other than before, except that I had a hood, a mask, a fan, and a pair of gloves in my pocket; so that there was not the least suspicion in the house. He waited for me in the coach in a back-lane, which he knew I must pass by, and had directed the coachman whither to go, which was to a certain place, called Mile End, where lived a confidant of his, where we went in, and where was all the convenience in the world to be as wicked as we pleased.

When we were together he began to talk very gravely to me, and to tell me he did not bring me there to betray me; that his passion for me would not suffer him to abuse me; that he resolved to marry me as soon as he came to his estate; that in the meantime, if I would grant his request, he would maintain me very honourably; and made me a thousand protestations of his sincerity and of his affection to me; and that he would never abandon me, and as I may say, made a thousand more preambles than he need to have done.

However, as he pressed me to speak, I told him I had no reason to question the sincerity of his love to me after so many protestations, but—and there I stopped, as if I left him to guess the rest. 'But what, my dear?' says he. 'I guess what you mean: what if you should be with child? Is not that it? Why, then,' says he, 'I'll take care of you and provide for you, and the child too; and that you may see I am not in jest,' says he, 'here's an earnest for you,' and with that he pulls out a silk purse, with an hundred guineas in it, and gave it me. 'And I'll give you such another,' says he, 'every year till I marry you.'

My colour came and went, at the sight of the purse and with the fire of his proposal together, so that I could not say a word, and he easily perceived it; so putting the purse into my bosom, I made no more resistance to him, but let him do just what he pleased, and as often as he pleased; and thus I finished my own destruction at once, for from this day, being forsaken of my virtue and my modesty, I had nothing of value left to recommend me, either to God's blessing or man's assistance.

But things did not end here. I went back to the town, did the business he publicly directed me to, and was at home before anybody thought me long. As for my gentleman, he stayed out, as he told me he would, till late at night, and there was not the least suspicion in the family either on his account or on mine.

We had, after this, frequent opportunities to repeat our crime —chiefly by his contrivance—especially at home, when his mother and the young ladies went abroad a-visiting, which he watched so narrowly as never to miss; knowing always beforehand when they went out, and then failed not to catch me all alone, and securely enough; so that we took our fill of our wicked pleasure for near half a year; and yet, which was the most to my satisfaction, I was not with child.

But before this half-year was expired, his younger brother, of whom I have made some mention in the beginning of the story, falls to work with me; and he, finding me alone in the garden one evening, begins a story of the same kind to me, made good honest professions of being in love with me, and in short, proposes fairly and honourably to marry me, and that before he made any other offer to me at all.

I was now confounded, and driven to such an extremity as the like was never known; at least not to me. I resisted the proposal with obstinacy; and now I began to arm myself with arguments. I laid before him the inequality of the match; the treatment I should meet with in the family; the ingratitude it would be to his good father and mother, who had taken me into their house upon such generous principles, and when I was in such a low condition; and, in short, I said everything to dissuade him from his design that I could imagine, except telling him the truth, which would indeed have put an end to it all, but that I durst not think of mentioning.

But here happened a circumstance that I did not expect indeed, which put me to my shifts; for this young gentleman, as he was plain and honest, so he pretended to nothing with me but what was so too; and, knowing his own innocence, he was not so careful to make his having a kindness for Mrs. Betty a secret I the house, as his brother was. And though he did not let them know that he had talked to me about it, yet he said enough to let his sisters perceive he loved me, and his mother saw it too, which, though they took no notice of it to me, yet they did to him, an immediately I found their carriage to me altered, more than ever before.

I saw the cloud, though I did not foresee the storm. It was easy, I say, to see that their carriage to me was altered, and that it grew worse and worse every day; till at last I got information among the servants that I should, in a very little while, be desired to remove.

I was not alarmed at the news, having a full satisfaction that I should be otherwise provided for; and especially considering that I had reason every day to expect I should be with child, and that then I should be obliged to remove without any pretences for it.

After some time the younger gentleman took an opportunity to tell me that the kindness he had for me had got vent in the family. He did not charge me with it, he said, for he know well enough which way it came out. He told me his plain way of talking had been the occasion of it, for that he did not make his respect for me so much a secret as he might have done, and the reason was, that he was at a point, that if I would consent to have him, he would tell them all openly that he loved me, and that he intended to marry me; that it was true his father and mother might resent it, and be unkind, but that he was now in a way to live, being bred to the law, and he did not fear maintaining me agreeable to what I should expect; and that, in short, as he believed I would not be ashamed of him, so he was resolved not to be ashamed of me, and that he scorned to be afraid to own me now, whom he resolved to own after I was his wife, and therefore I had nothing to do but to give him my hand, and he would answer for all the rest.

I was now in a dreadful condition indeed, and now I repented heartily my easiness with the eldest brother; not from any reflection of conscience, but from a view of the happiness I might have enjoyed, and had now made impossible; for though I had no great scruples of conscience, as I have said, to struggle with, yet I could not think of being a whore to one brother and a wife to the other. But then it came into my thoughts that the first brother had promised to made me his wife when he came to his estate; but I presently remembered what I had often thought of, that he had never spoken a word of having me for a wife after he had conquered me for a mistress; and indeed, till now, though I said I thought of it often, yet it gave me no disturbance at all, for as he did not seem in the least to lessen his affection to me, so neither did he lessen his bounty, though he had the discretion himself to desire me not to lay out a penny of what he gave me in clothes, or to make the least show extraordinary, because it would necessarily give jealousy in the family, since everybody know I could come at such things no manner of ordinary way, but by some private friendship, which they would presently have suspected.

But I was now in a great strait, and knew not what to do. The main difficulty was this: the younger brother not only laid close siege to me, but suffered it to be seen. He would come into his sister's room, and his mother's room, and sit down, and talk a thousand kind things of me, and to me, even before their faces, and when they were all there. This grew so public that the whole house talked of it, and his mother reproved him for it, and their carriage to me appeared quite altered. In short, his mother had let fall some speeches, as if she intended to put me out of the family; that is, in English, to turn me out of doors. Now I was sure this could not be a secret to his brother, only that he might not think, as indeed nobody else yet did, that the youngest brother had made any proposal to me about it; but as I easily could see that it would go farther, so I saw likewise there was an absolute necessity to speak of it to him, or that he would speak of it to me, and which to do first I knew not; that is, whether I should break it to him or let it alone till he should break it to me.

Upon serious consideration, for indeed now I began to consider things very seriously, and never till now; I say, upon serious consideration, I resolved to tell him of it first; and it was not long before I had an opportunity, for the very next day his brother went to London upon some business, and the family being out a-visiting, just as it had happened before, and as indeed was often the case, he came according to his custom, to spend an hour or two with Mrs. Betty.

When he came had had sat down a while, he easily perceived there was an alteration in my countenance, that I was not so free and pleasant with him as I used to be, and particularly, that I had been a-crying; he was not long before he took notice of it, and asked me in very kind terms what was the matter, and if anything troubled me. I would have put it off if I could, but it was not to be concealed; so after suffering many importunities to draw that out of me which I longed as much as possible to disclose, I told him that it was true something did trouble me, and something of such a nature that I could not conceal from him, and yet that I could not tell how to tell him of it neither; that it was a thing that not only surprised me, but greatly perplexed me, and that I knew not what course to take, unless he would direct me. He told me with great tenderness, that let it be what it would, I should not let it trouble me, for he would protect me from all the world.

I then began at a distance, and told him I was afraid the ladies had got some secret information of our correspondence; for that it was easy to see that their conduct was very much changed towards me for a great while, and that now it was come to that pass that they frequently found fault with me, and sometimes fell quite out with me, though I never gave them the least occasion; that whereas I used always to lie with the eldest sister, I was lately put to lie by myself, or with one of the maids; and that I had overheard them several times talking very unkindly about me; but that which confirmed it all was, that one of the servants had told me that she had heard I was to be turned out, and that it was not safe for the family that I should be any longer in the house.

He smiled when he herd all this, and I asked him how he could make so light of it, when he must needs know that if there was any discovery I was undone for ever, and that even it would hurt him, though not ruin him as it would me. I upbraided him, that he was like all the rest of the sex, that, when they had the character and honour of a woman at their mercy, oftentimes made it their jest, and at least looked upon it as a trifle, and counted the ruin of those they had had their will of as a thing of no value.

He saw me warm and serious, and he changed his style immediately; he told me he was sorry I should have such a thought of him; that he had never given me the least occasion for it, but had been as tender of my reputation as he could be of his own; that he was sure our correspondence had been managed with so much address, that not one creature in the family had so much as a suspicion of it; that if he smiled when I told him my thoughts, it was at the assurance he lately received, that our understanding one another was not so much as known or guessed at; and that when he had told me how much reason he had to be easy, I should smile as he did, for he was very certain it would give me a full satisfaction.

'This is a mystery I cannot understand,' says I, 'or how it should be to my satisfaction that I am to be turned out of doors; for if our correspondence is not discovered, I know not what else I have done to change the countenances of the whole family to me, or to have them treat me as they do now, who formerly used me with so much tenderness, as if I had been one of their own children.'

'Why, look you, child,' says he, 'that they are uneasy about you, that is true; but that they have the least suspicion of the case as it is, and as it respects you and I, is so far from being true, that they suspect my brother Robin; and, in short, they are fully persuaded he makes love to you; nay, the fool has put it into their heads too himself, for he is continually bantering them about it, and making a jest of himself. I confess I think he is wrong to do so, because he cannot but see it vexes them, and makes them unkind to you; but 'tis a satisfaction to me, because of the assurance it gives me, that they do not suspect me in the least, and I hope this will be to your satisfaction too.'

'So it is,' says I, 'one way; but this does not reach my case at all, nor is this the chief thing that troubles me, though I have been concerned about that too.' 'What is it, then?' says he. With which I fell to tears, and could say nothing to him at all. He strove to pacify me all he could, but began at last to be very pressing upon me to tell what it was. At last I answered that I thought I ought to tell him too, and that he had some right to know it; besides, that I wanted his direction in the case, for I was in such perplexity that I knew not what course to take, and then I related the whole affair to him. I told him how imprudently his brother had managed himself, in making himself so public; for that if he had kept it a secret, as such a thing out to have been, I could but have denied him positively, without giving any reason for it, and he would in time have ceased his solicitations; but that he had the vanity, first, to depend upon it that I would not deny him, and then had taken the freedom to tell his resolution of having me to the whole house.

I told him how far I had resisted him, and told him how sincere and honourable his offers were. 'But,' says I, 'my case will be doubly hard; for as they carry it ill to me now, because he desires to have me, they'll carry it worse when they shall find I have denied him; and they will presently say, there's something else in it, and then out it comes that I am married already to somebody else, or that I would never refuse a match so much above me as this was.'

This discourse surprised him indeed very much. He told me that it was a critical point indeed for me to manage, and he did not see which way I should get out of it; but he would consider it, and let me know next time we met, what resolution he was come to about it; and in the meantime desired I would not give my consent to his brother, nor yet give him a flat denial, but that I would hold him in suspense a while.

I seemed to start at his saying I should not give him my consent. I told him he knew very well I had no consent to give; that he had engaged himself to marry me, and that my consent was the same time engaged to him; that he had all along told me I was his wife, and I looked upon myself as effectually so as if the ceremony had passed; and that it was from his own mouth that I did so, he having all along persuaded me to call myself his wife.

'Well, my dear,' says he, 'don't be concerned at that now; if I am not your husband, I'll be as good as a husband to you; and do not let those things trouble you now, but let me look a little farther into this affair, and I shall be able to say more next time we meet.'

He pacified me as well as he could with this, but I found he was very thoughtful, and that though he was very kind to me and kissed me a thousand times, and more I believe, and gave me money too, yet he offered no more all the while we were together, which was above two hours, and which I much wondered at indeed at that time, considering how it used to be, and what opportunity we had.

His brother did not come from London for five or six days, and it was two days more before he got an opportunity to talk with him; but then getting him by himself he began to talk very close to him about it, and the same evening got an opportunity (for we had a long conference together) to repeat all their discourse to me, which, as near as I can remember, was to the purpose following. He told him he heard strange news of him since he went, viz. that he made love to Mrs. Betty. 'Well, says his brother a little angrily, 'and so I do. And what then? What has anybody to do with that?' 'Nay,' says his brother, 'don't be angry, Robin; I don't pretend to have anything to do with it; nor do I pretend to be angry with you about it. But I find they do concern themselves about it, and that they have used the poor girl ill about it, which I should take as done to myself.' 'Whom do you mean by THEY?' says Robin. 'I mean my mother and the girls,' says the elder brother. 'But hark ye,' says his brother, 'are you in earnest? Do you really love this girl? You may be free with me, you know.' 'Why, then,' says Robin, 'I will be free with you; I do love her above all the women in the world, and I will have her, let them say and do what they will. I believe the girl will not deny me.'

It struck me to the heart when he told me this, for though it was most rational to think I would not deny him, yet I knew in my own conscience I must deny him, and I saw my ruin in my being obliged to do so; but I knew it was my business to talk otherwise then, so I interrupted him in his story thus.

'Ay!' said I, 'does he think I cannot deny him? But he shall find I can deny him, for all that.'

'Well, my dear,' says he, 'but let me give you the whole story as it went on between us, and then say what you will.'

Then he went on and told me that he replied thus: 'But, brother, you know she has nothing, and you may have several ladies with good fortunes.'

''Tis no matter for that,' said Robin; 'I love the girl, and I will never please my pocket in marrying, and not please my fancy.' 'And so, my dear,' adds he, 'there is no opposing him.'

'Yes, yes,' says I, 'you shall see I can oppose him; I have learnt to say No, now though I had not learnt it before; if the best lord in the land offered me marriage now, I could very cheerfully say No to him.'

'Well, but, my dear,' says he, 'what can you say to him? You know, as you said when we talked of it before, he well ask you many questions about it, and all the house will wonder what the meaning of it should be.'

'Why,' says I, smiling, 'I can stop all their mouths at one clap by telling him, and them too, that I am married already to his elder brother.'

He smiled a little too at the word, but I could see it startled him, and he could not hide the disorder it put him into. However, he returned, 'Why, though that may be true in some sense, yet I suppose you are but in jest when you talk of giving such an answer as that; it may not be convenient on many accounts.'

'No, no,' says I pleasantly, 'I am not so fond of letting the secret come out without your consent.'

'But what, then, can you say to him, or to them,' says he, 'when they find you positive against a match which would be apparently so much to your advantage?'

'Why,' says I, 'should I be at a loss? First of all, I am not obliged to give me any reason at all; on the other hand, I may tell them I am married already, and stop there, and that will be a full stop too to him, for he can have no reason to ask one question after it.'

'Ay,' says he; 'but the whole house will tease you about that, even to father and mother, and if you deny them positively, they will be disobliged at you, and suspicious besides.'

'Why,' says I, 'what can I do? What would have me do? I was in straight enough before, and as I told you, I was in perplexity before, and acquainted you with the circumstances, that I might have your advice.'

'My dear,' says he, 'I have been considering very much upon it, you may be sure, and though it is a piece of advice that has a great many mortifications in it to me, and may at first seem strange to you, yet, all things considered, I see no better way for you than to let him go on; and if you find him hearty and in earnest, marry him.'

I gave him a look full of horror at those words, and, turning pale as death, was at the very point of sinking down out of the chair I sat in; when, giving a start, 'My dear,' says he aloud, 'what's the matter with you? Where are you a-going?' and a great many such things; and with jogging and called to me, fetched me a little to myself, though it was a good while before I fully recovered my senses, and was not able to speak for several minutes more.

When I was fully recovered he began again. 'My dear,' says he, 'what made you so surprised at what I said? I would have you consider seriously of it? You may see plainly how the family stand in this case, and they would be stark mad if it was my case, as it is my brother's; and for aught I see, it would be my ruin and yours too.'

'Ay!' says I, still speaking angrily; 'are all your protestations and vows to be shaken by the dislike of the family? Did I not always object that to you, and you made light thing of it, as what you were above, and would value; and is it come to this now?' said I. 'Is this your faith and honour, your love, and the solidity of your promises?'

He continued perfectly calm, notwithstanding all my reproaches, and I was not sparing of them at all; but he replied at last, 'My dear, I have not broken one promise with you yet; I did tell you I would marry you when I was come to my estate; but you see my father is a hale, healthy man, and may live these thirty years still, and not be older than several are round us in town; and you never proposed my marrying you sooner, because you knew it might be my ruin; and as to all the rest, I have not failed you in anything, you have wanted for nothing.'

I could not deny a word of this, and had nothing to say to it in general. 'But why, then,' says I, 'can you persuade me to such a horrid step as leaving you, since you have not left me? Will you allow no affection, no love on my side, where there has been so much on your side? Have I made you no returns? Have I given no testimony of my sincerity and of my passion? Are the sacrifices I have made of honour and modesty to you no proof of my being tied to you in bonds too strong to be broken?'

'But here, my dear,' says he, 'you may come into a safe station, and appear with honour and with splendour at once, and the remembrance of what we have done may be wrapt up in an eternal silence, as if it had never happened; you shall always have my respect, and my sincere affection, only then it shall be honest, and perfectly just to my brother; you shall be my dear sister, as now you are my dear——' and there he stopped.

'Your dear whore,' says I, 'you would have said if you had gone on, and you might as well have said it; but I understand you. However, I desire you to remember the long discourses you have had with me, and the many hours' pains you have taken to persuade me to believe myself an honest woman; that I was your wife intentionally, though not in the eyes of the world, and that it was as effectual a marriage that had passed between us as is we had been publicly wedded by the parson of the parish. You know and cannot but remember that these have been your own words to me.'

I found this was a little too close upon him, but I made it up in what follows. He stood stock-still for a while and said nothing, and I went on thus: 'You cannot,' says I, 'without the highest injustice, believe that I yielded upon all these persuasions without a love not to be questioned, not to be shaken again by anything that could happen afterward. If you have such dishonourable thoughts of me, I must ask you what foundation in any of my behaviour have I given for such a suggestion?

'If, then, I have yielded to the importunities of my affection, and if I have been persuaded to believe that I am really, and in the essence of the thing, your wife, shall I now give the lie to all those arguments and call myself your whore, or mistress, which is the same thing? And will you transfer me to your brother? Can you transfer my affection? Can you bid me cease loving you, and bid me love him? It is in my power, think you, to make such a change at demand? No, sir,' said I, 'depend upon it 'tis impossible, and whatever the change of your side may be, I will ever be true; and I had much rather, since it is come that unhappy length, be your whore than your brother's wife.'

He appeared pleased and touched with the impression of this last discourse, and told me that he stood where he did before; that he had not been unfaithful to me in any one promise he had ever made yet, but that there were so many terrible things presented themselves to his view in the affair before me, and that on my account in particular, that he had thought of the other as a remedy so effectual as nothing could come up to it. That he thought this would not be entire parting us, but we might love as friends all our days, and perhaps with more satisfaction than we should in the station we were now in, as things might happen; that he durst say, I could not apprehend anything from him as to betraying a secret, which could not but be the destruction of us both, if it came out; that he had but one question to ask of me that could lie in the way of it, and if that question was answered in the negative, he could not but think still it was the only step I could take.

I guessed at his question presently, namely, whether I was sure I was not with child? As to that, I told him he need not be concerned about it, for I was not with child. 'Why, then, my dear,' says he, 'we have no time to talk further now. Consider of it, and think closely about it; I cannot but be of the opinion still, that it will be the best course you can take.' And with this he took his leave, and the more hastily too, his mother and sisters ringing at the gate, just at the moment that he had risen up to go.

He left me in the utmost confusion of thought; and he easily perceived it the next day, and all the rest of the week, for it was but Tuesday evening when we talked; but he had no opportunity to come at me all that week, till the Sunday after, when I, being indisposed, did not go to church, and he, making some excuse for the like, stayed at home.

And now he had me an hour and a half again by myself, and we fell into the same arguments all over again, or at least so near the same, as it would be to no purpose to repeat them. At last I asked him warmly, what opinion he must have of my modesty, that he could suppose I should so much as entertain a thought of lying with two brothers, and assured him it could never be. I added, if he was to tell me that he would never see me more, than which nothing but death could be more terrible, yet I could never entertain a thought so dishonourable to myself, and so base to him; and therefore, I entreated him, if he had one grain of respect or affection left for me, that he would speak no more of it to me, or that he would pull his sword out and kill me. He appeared surprised at my obstinacy, as he called it; told me I was unkind to myself, and unkind to him in it; that it was a crisis unlooked for upon us both, and impossible for either of us to foresee, but that he did not see any other way to save us both from ruin, and therefore he thought it the more unkind; but that if he must say no more of it to me, he added with an unusual coldness, that he did not know anything else we had to talk of; and so he rose up to take his leave. I rose up too, as if with the same indifference; but when he came to give me as it were a parting kiss, I burst out into such a passion of crying, that though I would have spoke, I could not, and only pressing his hand, seemed to give him the adieu, but cried vehemently.

He was sensibly moved with this; so he sat down again, and said a great many kind things to me, to abate the excess of my passion, but still urged the necessity of what he had proposed; all the while insisting, that if I did refuse, he would notwithstanding provide for me; but letting me plainly see that he would decline me in the main point—nay, even as a mistress; making it a point of honour not to lie with the woman that, for aught he knew, might come to be his brother's wife.

The bare loss of him as a gallant was not so much my affliction as the loss of his person, whom indeed I loved to distraction; and the loss of all the expectations I had, and which I always had built my hopes upon, of having him one day for my husband. These things oppressed my mind so much, that, in short, I fell very ill;

the agonies of my mind, in a word, threw me into a high fever, and long it was, that none in the family expected my life.

I was reduced very low indeed, and was often delirious and light-headed; but nothing lay so near me as the fear that, when I was light-headed, I should say something or other to his prejudice. I was distressed in my mind also to see him, and so he was to see me, for he really loved me most passionately; but it could not be; there was not the least room to desire it on one side or other, or so much as to make it decent.

It was near five weeks that I kept my bed and though the violence of my fever abated in three weeks, yet it several times returned; and the physicians said two or three times, they could do no more for me, but that they must leave nature and the distemper to fight it out, only strengthening the first with cordials to maintain the struggle. After the end of five weeks I grew better, but was so weak, so altered, so melancholy, and recovered so slowly, that they physicians apprehended I should go into a consumption; and which vexed me most, they gave it as their opinion that my mind was oppressed, that something troubled me, and, in short, that I was in love. Upon this, the whole house was set upon me to examine me, and to press me to tell whether I was in love or not, and with whom; but as I well might, I denied my being in love at all.

They had on this occasion a squabble one day about me at table, that had like to have put the whole family in an uproar, and for some time did so. They happened to be all at table but the father; as for me, I was ill, and in my chamber. At the beginning of the talk, which was just as they had finished their dinner, the old gentlewoman, who had sent me somewhat to eat, called her maid to go up and ask me if I would have any more; but the maid brought down word I had not eaten half what she had sent me already.

'Alas, says the old lady, 'that poor girl! I am afraid she will never be well.'

'Well!' says the elder brother, 'how should Mrs. Betty be well? They say she is in love.'

'I believe nothing of it,' says the old gentlewoman.

'I don't know,' says the eldest sister, 'what to say to it; they have made such a rout about her being so handsome, and so charming, and I know not what, and that in her hearing too, that has turned the creature's head, I believe, and who knows what possessions may follow such doings? For my part, I don't know what to make of it.'

'Why, sister, you must acknowledge she is very handsome,' says the elder brother.

'Ay, and a great deal handsomer than you, sister,' says Robin, 'and that's your mortification.'

'Well, well, that is not the question,' says his sister; 'that girl is well enough, and she knows it well enough; she need not be told of it to make her vain.'

'We are not talking of her being vain,' says the elder brother, 'but of her being in love; it may be she is in love with herself; it seems my sisters think so.'

'I would she was in love with me,' says Robin; 'I'd quickly put her out of her pain.'

'What d'ye mean by that, son,' says the old lady; 'how can you talk so?'

'Why, madam,' says Robin, again, very honestly, 'do you think I'd let the poor girl die for love, and of one that is near at hand to be had, too?'

'Fie, brother!', says the second sister, 'how can you talk so? Would you take a creature that has not a groat in the world?'

'Prithee, child,' says Robin, 'beauty's a portion, and good-humour with it is a double portion; I wish thou hadst half her stock of both for thy portion.' So there was her mouth stopped.

'I find,' says the eldest sister, 'if Betty is not in love, my brother is. I wonder he has not broke his mind to Betty; I warrant she won't say No.'

'They that yield when they're asked,' says Robin, 'are one step before them that were never asked to yield, sister, and two steps before them that yield before they are asked; and that's an answer to you, sister.'

This fired the sister, and she flew into a passion, and said, things were come to that pass that it was time the wench, meaning me, was out of the family; and but that she was not fit to be turned out, she hoped her father and mother would consider of it as soon as she could be removed.

Robin replied, that was business for the master and mistress of the family, who where not to be taught by one that had so little judgment as his eldest sister.

It ran up a great deal farther; the sister scolded, Robin rallied and bantered, but poor Betty lost ground by it extremely in the family. I heard of it, and I cried heartily, and the old lady came up to me, somebody having told her that I was so much concerned about it. I complained to her, that it was very hard the doctors should pass such a censure upon me, for which they had no ground; and that it was still harder, considering the circumstances I was under in the family; that I hoped I had done nothing to lessen her esteem for me, or given any occasion for the bickering between her sons and daughters, and I had more need to think of a coffin than of being in love, and begged she would not let me suffer in her opinion for anybody's mistakes but my own.

She was sensible of the justice of what I said, but told me, since there had been such a clamour among them, and that her younger son talked after such a rattling way as he did, she desired I would be so faithful to her as to answer her but one question sincerely. I told her I would, with all my heart, and with the utmost plainness and sincerity. Why, then, the question was, whether there way anything between her son Robert and me. I told her with all the protestations of sincerity that I was able to make, and as I might well, do, that there was not, nor every had been; I told her that Mr. Robert had rattled and jested, as she knew it was his way, and that I took it always, as I supposed he meant it, to be a wild airy way of discourse that had no signification in it; and again assured her, that there was not the least tittle of what she understood by it between us; and that those who had suggested it had done me a great deal of wrong, and Mr. Robert no service at all.

The old lady was fully satisfied, and kissed me, spoke cheerfully to me, and bid me take care of my health and want for nothing, and so took her leave. But when she came down she found the brother and all his sisters together by the ears; they were angry, even to passion, at his upbraiding them with their being homely, and having never had any sweethearts, never having been asked the question, and their being so forward as almost to ask first. He rallied them upon the subject of Mrs. Betty; how pretty, how good-humoured, how she sung better then they did, and danced better, and how much handsomer she was; and in doing this he omitted no ill-natured thing that could vex them, and indeed, pushed too hard upon them. The old lady came down in the height of it, and to put a stop it to, told them all the discourse she had had with me, and how I answered, that there was nothing between Mr. Robert and I.

'She's wrong there,' says Robin, 'for if there was not a great deal between us, we should be closer together than we are. I told her I loved her hugely,' says he, 'but I could never make the jade believe I was in earnest.' 'I do not know how you should,' says his mother; 'nobody in their senses could believe you were in earnest, to talk so to a poor girl, whose circumstances you know so well.

'But prithee, son,' adds she, 'since you tell me that you could not make her believe you were in earnest, what must we believe about it? For you ramble so in your discourse, that nobody knows whether you are in earnest or in jest; but as I find the girl, by your own confession, has answered truly, I wish you would do so too, and tell me seriously, so that I may depend upon it. Is there anything in it or no? Are you in earnest or no? Are you distracted, indeed, or are you not? 'Tis a weighty question, and I wish you would make us easy about it.'

'By my faith, madam,' says Robin, "tis in vain to mince the matter or tell any more lies about it; I am in earnest, as much as a man is that's going to be hanged. If Mrs. Betty would say she loved me, and that she would marry me, I'd have her tomorrow morning fasting, and say, 'To have and to hold,' instead of eating my breakfast.'

'Well,' says the mother, 'then there's one son lost'; and she said it in a very mournful tone, as one greatly concerned at it.

'I hope not, madam,' says Robin; 'no man is lost when a good wife has found him.'

'Why, but, child,' says the old lady, 'she is a beggar.'

'Why, then, madam, she has the more need of charity,' says Robin; 'I'll take her off the hands of the parish, and she and I'll beg together.'

'It's bad jesting with such things,' says the mother.

'I don't jest, madam,' says Robin. 'We'll come and beg your pardon, madam; and your blessing, madam, and my father's.'

'This is all out of the way, son,' says the mother. 'If you are in earnest you are undone.'

'I am afraid not,' says he, 'for I am really afraid she won't have me; after all my sister's huffing and blustering, I believe I shall never be able to persuade her to it.'

'That's a fine tale, indeed; she is not so far out of her senses neither. Mrs. Betty is no fool,' says the younger sister. 'Do you think she has learnt to say No, any more than other people?'

'No, Mrs. Mirth-wit,' says Robin, 'Mrs. Betty's no fool; but Mrs. Betty may be engaged some other way, and what then?'

'Nay,' says the eldest sister, 'we can say nothing to that. Who must it be to, then? She is never out of the doors; it must be between you.'

'I have nothing to say to that,' says Robin. 'I have been examined enough; there's my brother. If it must be between us, go to work with him.'

This stung the elder brother to the quick, and he concluded that Robin had discovered something. However, he kept himself from appearing disturbed. 'Prithee,' says he, 'don't go to shame your stories off upon me; I tell you, I deal in no such ware; I have nothing to say to Mrs. Betty, nor to any of the Mrs. Bettys in the parish'; and with that he rose up and brushed off.

'No,' says the eldest sister, 'I dare answer for my brother; he knows the world better.'

Thus the discourse ended, but it left the elder brother quite confounded. He concluded his brother had made a full discovery, and he began to doubt whether I had been concerned in it or not; but with all his management he could not bring it about to get at me. At last he was so perplexed that he was quite desperate, and resolved he would come into my chamber and see me, whatever came of it. In order to do this, he contrived it so, that one day after dinner, watching his eldest sister till he could see her go upstairs, he runs after her. 'Hark ye, sister,' says he, 'where is this sick woman? May not a body see her?' 'Yes,' says the sister, 'I believe you may; but let me go first a little, and I'll tell you.' So she ran up to the door and gave me notice, and presently called to him again. 'Brother,' says she, 'you may come if you please.' So in he came, just in the same kind of rant. 'Well,' says he at the door as he came in, 'where is this sick body that's in love? How do ye do, Mrs. Betty?' I would have got up out of my chair, but was so weak I could not for a good while; and he saw it, and his sister to, and she said, 'Come, do not strive to stand up; my brother desires no ceremony, especially now you are so weak.' 'No, no, Mrs. Betty, pray sit still,' says he, and so sits himself down in a chair over against me, and appeared as if he was mighty merry.

He talked a lot of rambling stuff to his sister and to me, sometimes of one thing, sometimes of another, on purpose to amuse his sister, and every now and then would turn it upon the old story, directing it to me. 'Poor Mrs. Betty,' says he, 'it is a sad thing to be in love; why, it has reduced you sadly.' At last I spoke a little. 'I am glad to see you so merry, sir,' says I; 'but I think the doctor might have found something better to do than to make his game at his patients. If I had been ill of no other distemper, I know the proverb too well to have let him come to me.' 'What proverb?' says he, 'Oh! I remember it now. What—

"Where love is the case,
The doctor's an ass."

Is not that it, Mrs. Betty?' I smiled and said nothing. 'Nay,' says he, 'I think the effect has proved it to be love, for it seems the doctor has been able to do you but little service; you mend very slowly, they say. I doubt there's somewhat in it, Mrs. Betty; I doubt you are sick of the incurables, and that is love.' I smiled and said, 'No, indeed, sir, that's none of my distemper.'

We had a deal of such discourse, and sometimes others that signified as little. By and by he asked me to sing them a song, at which I smiled, and said my singing days were over. At last he asked me if he should play upon his flute to me; his sister said she believe it would hurt me, and that my head could not bear it. I bowed, and said, No, it would not hurt me. 'And, pray, madam.' said I, 'do not hinder it; I love the music of the flute very much.' Then his sister said, 'Well, do, then, brother.' With that he pulled out the key of his closet. 'Dear sister,' says he, 'I am very lazy; do step to my closet and fetch my flute; it lies in such a drawer,' naming a place where he was sure it was not, that she might be a little while a-looking for it.

As soon as she was gone, he related the whole story to me of the discourse his brother had about me, and of his pushing it at him, and his concern about it, which was the reason of his contriving this visit to me. I assured him I had never opened my mouth either to his brother or to anybody else. I told him the dreadful exigence I was in; that my love to him, and his offering to have me forget that affection and remove it to another, had thrown me down; and that I had a thousand times wished I might die rather than recover, and to have the same circumstances to struggle with as I had before, and that his backwardness to life had been the great reason of the slowness of my recovering. I added that I foresaw that as soon as I was well, I must quit the family, and that as for marrying his brother, I abhorred the thoughts of it after what had been my case with him, and that he might depend upon it I would never see his brother again upon that subject; that if he would break all his vows and oaths and engagements with me, be that between his conscience and his honour and himself; but he should never be able to say that I, whom he had persuaded to call myself his wife, and who had given him the liberty to use me as a wife, was not as faithful to him as a wife ought to be, whatever he might be to me.

He was going to reply, and had said that he was sorry I could not be persuaded, and was a-going to say more, but he heard his sister a-coming, and so did I; and yet I forced out these few words as a reply, that I could never be persuaded to love one brother and marry another. He shook his head and said, 'Then I am ruined,' meaning himself; and that moment his sister entered the room and told him she could not find the flute. 'Well,' says he merrily, 'this laziness won't do'; so he gets up and goes himself to go to look for it, but comes back without it too; not but that he could have found it, but because his mind was a little disturbed, and he had no mind to play; and, besides, the errand he sent his sister on was answered another way; for he only wanted an opportunity to speak to me, which he gained, though not much to his satisfaction.

I had, however, a great deal of satisfaction in having spoken my mind to him with freedom, and with such an honest plainness, as I have related; and though it did not at all work the way I desired, that is to say, to oblige the person to me the more, yet it took from him all possibility of quitting me but by a downright breach of honour, and giving up all the faith of a gentleman to me, which he had so often engaged by, never to abandon me, but to make me his wife as soon as he came to his estate.

It was not many weeks after this before I was about the house again, and began to grow well; but I continued melancholy, silent, dull, and retired, which amazed the whole family, except he that knew the reason of it; yet it was a great while before he took any notice of it, and I, as backward to speak as he, carried respectfully to him, but never offered to speak a word to him that was particular of any kind whatsoever; and this continued for sixteen or seventeen weeks; so that, as I expected every day to be dismissed the family, on account of what distaste they had taken another way, in which I had no guilt, so I expected to hear no more of this gentleman, after all his solemn vows and protestations, but to be ruined and abandoned.

At last I broke the way myself in the family for my removing; for being talking seriously with the old lady one day, about my own circumstances in the world, and how my distemper had left a heaviness upon my spirits, that I was not the same thing I was before, the old lady said, 'I am afraid, Betty, what I have said to you about my son has had some influence upon you, and that you are melancholy on his account; pray, will you let me know how the matter stands with you both, if it may not be improper? For, as for Robin, he does nothing but rally and banter when I speak of it to him.' 'Why, truly, madam,' said I 'that matter stands as I wish it did not, and I shall be very sincere with you in it, whatever befalls me for it. Mr. Robert has several times proposed marriage to me, which is what I had no reason to expect, my poor circumstances considered; but I have always resisted him, and that perhaps in terms more positive than became me, considering the regard that I ought to have for every branch of your family; but,' said I, 'madam, I could never so far forget my obligation to you and all your house, to offer to consent to a thing which I know must needs be disobliging to you, and this I have made my argument to him, and have positively told him that I would never entertain a thought of that kind unless I had your consent, and his father's also, to whom I was bound by so many invincible obligations.'

'And is this possible, Mrs. Betty?' says the old lady. 'Then you have been much juster to us than we have been to you; for we have all looked upon you as a kind of snare to my son, and I had a proposal to make to you for your removing, for fear of it; but I had not yet mentioned it to you, because I thought you were not thorough well, and I was afraid of grieving you too much, lest it should throw you down again; for we have all a respect for you still, though not so much as to have it be the ruin of my son; but if it be as you say, we have all wronged you very much.'

'As to the truth of what I say, madam,' said I, 'refer you to your son himself; if he will do me any justice, he must tell you the story just as I have told it.'

Away goes the old lady to her daughters and tells them the whole story, just as I had told it her; and they were surprised at it, you may be sure, as I believed they would be. One said she could never have thought it; another said Robin was a fool; a third said she would not believe a word of it, and she would warrant that Robin would tell the story another way. But the old gentlewoman, who was resolved to go to the bottom of it before I could have the least opportunity of acquainting her son with what had passed, resolved too that she would talk with her son immediately, and to that purpose sent for him, for he was gone but to a lawyer's house in the town, upon some petty business of his own, and upon her sending he returned immediately.

Upon his coming up to them, for they were all still together, 'Sit down, Robin,' says the old lady, 'I must have some talk with you.' 'With all my heart, madam,' says Robin, looking very merry. 'I hope it is about a good wife, for I am at a great loss in that affair.' 'How can that be?' says his mother; 'did not you say you resolved to have Mrs. Betty?' 'Ay, madam,' says Robin, 'but there is one has forbid the banns.' 'Forbid, the banns!' says his mother; 'who can that be?' 'Even Mrs. Betty herself,' says Robin. 'How so?' says his mother. 'Have you asked her the question, then?' 'Yes, indeed, madam,' says Robin. 'I have attacked her in form five times since she was sick, and am beaten off; the jade is so stout she won't capitulate nor yield upon any terms, except such as I cannot effectually grant.' 'Explain yourself,' says the mother, 'for I am surprised; I do not understand you. I hope you are not in earnest.'

'Why, madam,' says he, 'the case is plain enough upon me, it explains itself; she won't have me, she says; is not that plain enough? I think 'tis plain, and pretty rough too.' 'Well, but,' says the mother, 'you talk of conditions that you cannot grant; what does she want—a settlement? Her jointure ought to be according to her portion; but what fortune does she bring you?' 'Nay, as to fortune,' says Robin, 'she is rich enough; I am satisfied in that point; but 'tis I that am not able to come up to her terms, and she is positive she will not have me without.'

Here the sisters put in. 'Madam,' says the second sister, "tis impossible to be serious with him; he will never give a direct answer to anything; you had better let him alone, and talk no more of it to him; you know how to dispose of her out of his way if you thought there was anything in it.' Robin was a little warmed with his sister's rudeness, but he was even with her, and yet with good manners too. 'There are two sorts of people, madam,' says he, turning to his mother, 'that there is no contending with; that is, a wise body and a fool; 'tis a little hard I should engage with both of them together.'

The younger sister then put in. 'We must be fools indeed,' says she, 'in my brother's opinion, that he should think we can believe he has seriously asked Mrs. Betty to marry him, and that she has refused him.'

'Answer, and answer not, say Solomon,' replied her brother. 'When your brother had said to your mother that he had asked her no less than five times, and that it was so, that she positively denied him, methinks a younger sister need not question the truth of it when her mother did not.' 'My mother, you see, did not understand it,' says the second sister. 'There's some difference,' says Robin, 'between desiring me to explain it, and telling me she did not believe it.'

'Well, but, son,' says the old lady, 'if you are disposed to let us into the mystery of it, what were these hard conditions?' 'Yes, madam,' says Robin, 'I had done it before now, if the teasers here had not worried my by way of interruption. The conditions are, that I bring my father and you to consent to it, and without that she protests she will never see me more upon that head; and to these conditions, as I said, I suppose I shall never be able to grant. I hope my warm sisters will be answered now, and blush a little; if not, I have no more to say till I hear further.'

This answer was surprising to them all, though less to the mother, because of what I had said to her. As to the daughters, they stood mute a great while; but the mother said with some passion, 'Well, I had heard this before, but I could not believe it; but if it is so, they we have all done Betty wrong, and she has behaved better than I ever expected.' 'Nay,' says the eldest sister, 'if it be so, she has acted handsomely indeed.' 'I confess,' says the mother, 'it was none of her fault, if he was fool enough to take a fancy to her; but to give such an answer to him, shows more respect to your father and me than I can tell how to express; I shall value the girl the better for it as long as I know her.' 'But I shall not,' says Robin, 'unless you will give your consent.' 'I'll consider of that a while,' says the mother; 'I assure you, if there were not some other objections in the way, this conduct of hers would go a great way to bring me to consent.' 'I wish it would go quite through it,' says Robin; 'if you had a much thought about making me easy as you have about making me rich, you would soon consent to it.'

'Why, Robin,' says the mother again, 'are you really in earnest? Would you so fain have her as you pretend?' 'Really, madam,' says Robin, 'I think 'tis hard you should question me upon that head after all I have said. I won't say that I will have her; how can I resolve that point, when you see I cannot have her without your consent? Besides, I am not bound to marry at all. But this I will say, I am in earnest in, that I will never have anybody else if I can help it; so you may determine for me. Betty or nobody is the word, and the question which of the two shall be in your breast to decide, madam, provided only, that my good-humoured sisters here may have no vote in it.'

All this was dreadful to me, for the mother began to yield, and Robin pressed her home on it. On the other hand, she advised with the eldest son, and he used all the arguments in the world to persuade her to consent; alleging his brother's passionate love for me, and my generous regard to the family, in refusing my own advantages upon such a nice point of honour, and a thousand such things. And as to the father, he was a man in a hurry of public affairs and getting money, seldom at home, thoughtful of the main chance, but left all those things to his wife.

You may easily believe, that when the plot was thus, as they thought, broke out, and that every one thought they knew how things were carried, it was not so difficult or so dangerous for the elder brother, whom nobody suspected of anything, to have a freer access to me than before; nay, the mother, which was just as he wished, proposed it to him to talk with Mrs. Betty. 'For it may be, son,' said she, 'you may see farther into the thing than I, and see if you think she has been so positive as Robin says she has been, or no.' This was as well as he could wish, and he, as it were, yielding to talk with me at his mother's request, she brought me to him into her own chamber, told me her son had some business with me at her request, and desired me to be very sincere with him, and then she left us together, and he went and shut the door after her.

He came back to me and took me in his arms, and kissed me very tenderly; but told me he had a long discourse to hold with me, and it was not come to that crisis, that I should make myself happy or miserable as long as I lived; that the thing was now gone so far, that if I could not comply with his desire, we would both be ruined. Then he told the whole story between Robin, as he called him, and his mother and sisters and himself, as it is above. 'And now, dear child,' says he, 'consider what it will be to marry a gentleman of a good family, in good circumstances, and with the consent of the whole house, and to enjoy all that he world can give you; and what, on the other hand, to be sunk into the dark circumstances of a woman that has lost her reputation; and that though I shall be a private friend to you while I live, yet as I shall be suspected always, so you will be afraid to see me, and I shall be afraid to own you.'

He gave me no time to reply, but went on with me thus: 'What has happened between us, child, so long as we both agree to do so, may be buried and forgotten. I shall always be your sincere friend, without any inclination to nearer intimacy, when you become my sister; and we shall have all the honest part of conversation without any reproaches between us of having done amiss. I beg of you to consider it, and to not stand in the way of your own safety and prosperity; and to satisfy you that I am sincere,' added he, 'I here offer you £500 in money, to make you some amends for the freedoms I have taken with you, which we shall look upon as some of the follies of our lives, which 'tis hoped we may repent of.'

He spoke this in so much more moving terms than it is possible for me to express, and with so much greater force of argument than I can repeat, that I only recommend it to those who read the story, to suppose, that as he held me above an hour and a half in that discourse, so he answered all my objections, and fortified his discourse with all the arguments that human wit and art could devise.

I cannot say, however, that anything he said made impression enough upon me so as to give me any thought of the matter, till he told me at last very plainly, that if I refused, he was sorry to add that he could never go on with me in that station as we stood before; that though he loved me as well as ever, and that I was as agreeable to him as ever, yet sense of virtue had not so far forsaken him as to suffer him to lie with a woman that his brother courted to make his wife; and if he took his leave of me, with a denial in this affair, whatever he might do for me in the point of support, grounded on his first engagement of maintaining me, yet he would not have me be surprised that he was obliged to tell me he could not allow himself to see me any more; and that, indeed, I could not expect it of him.

I received this last part with some token of surprise and disorder, and had much ado to avoid sinking down, for indeed I loved him to an extravagance not easy to imagine; but he perceived my disorder. He entreated me to consider seriously of it; assured me that it was the only way to preserve our mutual affection; that in this station we might love as friends, with the utmost passion, and with a love of relation untainted, free from our just reproaches, and free from other people's suspicions; that he should ever acknowledge his happiness owing to me; that he would be debtor to me as long as he lived, and would be paying that debt as long as he had breath. Thus he wrought me up, in short, to a kind of hesitation in the matter; having the dangers on one side represented in lively figures, and indeed, heightened by my imagination of being turned out to the wide world a mere cast-off whore, for it was no less, and perhaps exposed as such, with little to provide for myself, with no friend, no acquaintance in the whole world, out of that town, and there I could not pretend to stay. All this terrified me to the last degree, and he took care upon all occasions to lay it home to me in the worst colours that it could be possible to be drawn in. On the other hand, he failed not to set forth the easy, prosperous life which I was going to live.

He answered all that I could object from affection, and from former engagements, with telling me the necessity that was before us of taking other measures now; and as to his promises of marriage, the nature of things, he said, had put an end to that, by the probability of my being his brother's wife, before the time to which his promises all referred.

Thus, in a word, I may say, he reasoned me out of my reason; he conquered all my arguments, and I began to see a danger that I was in, which I had not considered of before, and that was, of being dropped by both of them and left alone in the world to shift for myself.

This, and his persuasion, at length prevailed with me to consent, though with so much reluctance, that it was easy to see I should go to church like a bear to the stake. I had some little apprehensions about me, too, lest my new spouse, who, by the way, I had not the least affection for, should be skillful enough to challenge me on another account, upon our first coming to bed together. But whether he did it with design or not, I know not, but his elder brother took care to make him very much fuddled before he went to bed, so that I had the satisfaction of a drunken bedfellow the first night. How he did it I know not, but I concluded that he certainly contrived it, that his brother might be able to make no judgment of the difference between a maid and a married woman; nor did he ever entertain any notions of it, or disturb his thoughts about it.

I should go back a little here to where I left off. The elder brother having thus managed me, his next business was to manage his mother, and he never left till he had brought her to acquiesce and be passive in the thing, even without acquainting the father, other than by post letters; so that she consented to our marrying privately, and leaving her to mange the father afterwards.

Then he cajoled with his brother, and persuaded him what service he had done him, and how he had brought his mother to consent, which, though true, was not indeed done to serve him, but to serve himself; but thus diligently did he cheat him, and had the thanks of a faithful friend for shifting off his whore into his brother's arms for a wife. So certainly does interest banish all manner of affection, and so naturally do men give up honour and justice, humanity, and even Christianity, to secure themselves.

I must now come back to brother Robin, as we always called him, who having got his mother's consent, as above, came big with the news to me, and told me the whole story of it, with a sincerity so visible, that I must confess it grieved me that I must be the instrument to abuse so honest a gentleman. But there was no remedy; he would have me, and I was not obliged to tell him that I was his brother's whore, though I had no other way to put him off; so I came gradually into it, to his satisfaction, and behold we were married.

Modesty forbids me to reveal the secrets of the marriage-bed, but nothing could have happened more suitable to my circumstances than that, as above, my husband was so fuddled when he came to bed, that he could not remember in the morning whether he had had any conversation with me or no, and I was obliged to tell him he had, though in reality he had not, that I might be sure he could make to inquiry about anything else.

It concerns the story in hand very little to enter into the further particulars of the family, or of myself, for the five years that I lived with this husband, only to observe that I had two children by him, and that at the end of five years he died. He had been really a very good husband to me, and we lived very agreeably together; but as he had not received much from them, and had in the little time he lived acquired no great matters, so my circumstances were not great, nor was I much mended by the match. Indeed, I had preserved the elder brother's bonds to me, to pay £500, which he offered me for my consent to marry his brother; and this, with what I had saved of the money he formerly gave me, about as much more by my husband, left me a widow with about £1200 in my pocket.

My two children were, indeed, taken happily off my hands by my husband's father and mother, and that, by the way, was all they got by Mrs. Betty.

I confess I was not suitably affected with the loss of my husband, nor indeed can I say that I ever loved him as I ought to have done, or as was proportionable to the good usage I had from him, for he was a tender, kind, good-humoured man as any woman could desire; but his brother being so always in my sight, at least while we were in the country, was a continual snare to me, and I never was in bed with my husband but I wished myself in the arms of his brother; and though his brother never offered me the least kindness that way after our marriage, but carried it just as a brother out to do, yet it was impossible for me to do so to him; in short, I committed adultery and incest with him every day in my desires, which, without doubt, was as effectually criminal in the nature of the guilt as if I had actually done it.

Before my husband died his elder brother was married, and we, being then removed to London, were written to by the old lady to come and be at the wedding. My husband went, but I pretended indisposition, and that I could not possibly travel, so I stayed behind; for, in short, I could not bear the sight of his being given to another woman, though I knew I was never to have him myself.

I was now, as above, left loose to the world, and being still young and handsome, as everybody said of me, and I assure you I thought myself so, and with a tolerable fortune in my pocket, I put no small value upon myself. I was courted by several very considerable tradesmen, and particularly very warmly by one, a linen-draper, at whose house, after my husband's death, I took a lodging, his sister being my acquaintance. Here I had all the liberty and all the opportunity to be gay and appear in company that I could desire, my landlord's sister being one of the maddest, gayest things alive, and not so much mistress of her virtue as I thought as first she had been. She brought me into a world of wild company, and even brought home several persons, such as she liked well enough to gratify, to see her pretty widow, so she was pleased to call me, and that name I got in a little time in public. Now, as fame and fools make an assembly, I was here wonderfully caressed, had abundance of admirers, and such as called themselves lovers; but I found not one fair proposal among them all. As for their common design, that I understood too well to be drawn into any more snares of that kind. The case was altered with me: I had money in my pocket, and had nothing to say to them. I had been tricked once by that cheat called love, but the game was over; I was resolved now to be married or nothing, and to be well married or not at all.

I loved the company, indeed, of men of mirth and wit, men of gallantry and figure, and was often entertained with such, as I was also with others; but I found by just observation, that the brightest men came upon the dullest errand—that is to say, the dullest as to what I aimed at. On the other hand, those who came with the best proposals were the dullest and most disagreeable part of the world. I was not averse to a tradesman, but then I would have a tradesman, forsooth, that was something of a gentleman too; that when my husband had a mind to carry me to the court, or to the play, he might become a sword, and look as like a gentleman as another man; and not be one that had the mark of his apron-strings upon his coat, or the mark of his hat upon his periwig; that should look as if he was set on to his sword, when his sword was put on to him, and that carried his trade in his countenance.

Well, at last I found this amphibious creature, this land-water thing called a gentleman-tradesman; and as a just plague upon my folly, I was catched in the very snare which, as I might say, I laid for myself. I said for myself, for I was not trepanned, I confess, but I betrayed myself.

This was a draper, too, for though my comrade would have brought me to a bargain with her brother, yet when it came to the point, it was, it seems, for a mistress, not a wife; and I kept true to this notion, that a woman should never be kept for a mistress that had money to keep herself.

Thus my pride, not my principle, my money, not my virtue, kept me honest; though, as it proved, I found I had much better have been sold by my she-comrade to her brother, than have sold myself as I did to a tradesman that was rake, gentleman, shopkeeper, and beggar, all together.

But I was hurried on (by my fancy to a gentleman) to ruin myself in the grossest manner that every woman did; for my new husband coming to a lump of money at once, fell into such a profusion of expense, that all I had, and all he had before, if he had anything worth mentioning, would not have held it out above one year.

He was very fond of me for about a quarter of a year, and what I got by that was, that I had the pleasure of seeing a great deal of my money spent upon myself, and, as I may say, had some of the spending it too. 'Come, my dear,' says he to me one day, 'shall we go and take a turn into the country for about a week?' 'Ay, my dear,' says I, 'whither would you go?' 'I care not whither,' says he, 'but I have a mind to look like quality for a week. We'll go to Oxford,' says he. 'How,' says I, 'shall we go? I am no horsewoman, and 'tis too far for a coach.' 'Too far!' says he; 'no place is too far for a coach-and-six. If I carry you out, you shall travel like a duchess.' 'Hum,' says I, 'my dear, 'tis a frolic; but if you have a mind to it, I don't care.' Well, the time was appointed, we had a rich coach, very good horses, a coachman, postillion, and two footmen in very good liveries; a gentleman on horseback, and a page with a feather in his hat upon another horse. The servants all called him my lord, and the inn-keepers, you may be sure, did the like, and I was her honour the Countess, and thus we traveled to Oxford, and a very pleasant journey we had; for, give him his due, not a beggar alive knew better how to be a lord than my husband. We saw all the rarities at Oxford, talked with two or three Fellows of colleges about putting out a young nephew, that was left to his lordship's care, to the University, and of their being his tutors. We diverted ourselves with bantering several other poor scholars, with hopes of being at least his lordship's chaplains and putting on a scarf; and thus having lived like quality indeed, as to expense, we went away for Northampton, and, in a word, in about twelve days' ramble came home again, to the tune of about £93 expense.

Vanity is the perfection of a fop. My husband had this excellence, that he valued nothing of expense; and as his history, you may be sure, has very little weight in it, 'tis enough to tell you that in about two years and a quarter he broke, and was not so happy to get over into the Mint, but got into a sponging-house, being arrested in an action too heavy from him to give bail to, so he sent for me to come to him.

It was no surprise to me, for I had foreseen some time that all was going to wreck, and had been taking care to reserve something if I could, though it was not much, for myself. But when he sent for me, he behaved much better than I expected, and told me plainly he had played the fool, and suffered himself to be surprised, which he might have prevented; that now he foresaw he could not stand it, and therefore he would have me go home, and in the night take away everything I had in the house of any value, and secure it; and after that, he told me that if I could get away one hundred or two hundred pounds in goods out of the shop, I should do it; 'only,' says he, 'let me know nothing of it, neither what you take nor whither you carry it; for as for me,' says he, 'I am resolved to get out of this house and be gone; and if you never hear of me more, my dear,' says he, 'I wish you well; I am only sorry for the injury I have done you.' He said some very handsome things to me indeed at parting; for I told you he was a gentleman, and that was all the benefit I had of his being so; that he used me very handsomely and with good manners upon all occasions, even to the last, only spent all I had, and left me to rob the creditors for something to subsist on.

However, I did as he bade me, that you may be sure; and having thus taken my leave of him, I never saw him more, for he found means to break out of the bailiff's house that night or the next, and go over into France, and for the rest of the creditors scrambled for it as well as they could. How, I knew not, for I could come at no knowledge of anything, more than this, that he came home about three o'clock in the morning, caused the rest of his goods to be removed into the Mint, and the shop to be shut up; and having raised what money he could get together, he got over, as I said, to France, from whence I had one or two letters from him, and no more. I did not see him when he came home, for he having given me such instructions as above, and I having made the best of my time, I had no more business back again at the house, not knowing but I might have been stopped there by the creditors; for a commission of bankrupt being soon after issued, they might have stopped me by orders from the commissioners. But my husband, having so dexterously got out of the bailiff's house by letting himself down in a most desperate manner from almost the top of the house to the top of another building, and leaping from thence, which was almost two storeys, and which was enough indeed to have broken his neck, he came home and got away his goods before the creditors could come to seize; that is to say, before they could get out the commission, and be ready to send their officers to take possession.

My husband was so civil to me, for still I say he was much of a gentleman, that in the first letter he wrote me from France, he let me know where he had pawned twenty pieces of fine holland for £30, which were really worth £90, and enclosed me the token and an order for the taking them up, paying the money, which I did, and made in time above £100 of them, having leisure to cut them and sell them, some and some, to private families, as opportunity offered.

However, with all this, and all that I had secured before, I found, upon casting things up, my case was very much altered, any my fortune much lessened; for, including the hollands and a parcel of fine muslins, which I carried off before, and some plate, and other things, I found I could hardly muster up £500; and my condition was very odd, for though I had no child (I had had one by my gentleman draper, but it was buried), yet I was a widow bewitched; I had a husband and no husband, and I could not pretend to marry again, though I knew well enough my husband would never see England any more, if he lived fifty years. Thus, I say, I was limited from marriage, what offer might soever be made me; and I had not one friend to advise with in the condition I was in, least not one I durst trust the secret of my circumstances to, for if the commissioners were to have been informed where I was, I should have been fetched up and examined upon oath, and all I have saved be taken away from me.

Upon these apprehensions, the first thing I did was to go quite out of my knowledge, and go by another name. This I did effectually, for I went into the Mint too, took lodgings in a very private place, dressed up in the habit of a widow, and called myself Mrs. Flanders.

Here, however, I concealed myself, and though my new acquaintances knew nothing of me, yet I soon got a great deal of company about me; and whether it be that women are scarce among the sorts of people that generally are to be found there, or that some consolations in the miseries of the place are more requisite than on other occasions, I soon found an agreeable woman was exceedingly valuable among the sons of affliction there, and that those that wanted money to pay half a crown on the pound to their creditors, and that run in debt at the sign of the Bull for their dinners, would yet find money for a supper, if they liked the woman.

However, I kept myself safe yet, though I began, like my Lord Rochester's mistress, that loved his company, but would not admit him farther, to have the scandal of a whore, without the joy; and upon this score, tired with the place, and indeed with the company too, I began to think of removing.

It was indeed a subject of strange reflection to me to see men who were overwhelmed in perplexed circumstances, who were reduced some degrees below being ruined, whose families were objects of their own terror and other people's charity, yet while a penny lasted, nay, even beyond it, endeavouring to drown themselves, labouring to forget former things, which now it was the proper time to remember, making more work for repentance, and sinning on, as a remedy for sin past.

But it is none of my talent to preach; these men were too wicked, even for me. There was something horrid and absurd in their way of sinning, for it was all a force even upon themselves; they did not only act against conscience, but against nature; they put a rape upon their temper to drown the reflections, which their circumstances continually gave them; and nothing was more easy than to see how sighs would interrupt their songs, and paleness and anguish sit upon their brows, in spite of the forced smiles they put on; nay, sometimes it would break out at their very mouths when they had parted with their money for a lewd treat or a wicked embrace. I have heard them, turning about, fetch a deep sigh, and cry, 'What a dog am I! Well, Betty, my dear, I'll drink thy health, though'; meaning the honest wife, that perhaps had not a half-crown for herself and three or four children. The next morning they are at their penitentials again; and perhaps the poor weeping wife comes over to him, either brings him some account of what his creditors are doing, and how she and the children are turned out of doors, or some other dreadful news; and this adds to his self-reproaches; but when he has thought and pored on it till he is almost mad, having no principles to support him, nothing within him or above him to comfort him, but finding it all darkness on every side, he flies to the same relief again, viz. to drink it away, debauch it away, and falling into company of men in just the same condition with himself, he repeats the crime, and thus he goes every day one step onward of his way to destruction.

I was not wicked enough for such fellows as these yet. On the contrary, I began to consider here very seriously what I had to do; how things stood with me, and what course I ought to take. I knew I had no friends, no, not one friend or relation in the world; and that little I had left apparently wasted, which when it was gone, I saw nothing but misery and starving was before me. Upon these considerations, I say, and filled with horror at the place I was in, and the dreadful objects which I had always before me, I resolved to be gone.

I had made an acquaintance with a very sober, good sort of a woman, who was a widow too, like me, but in better circumstances. Her husband had been a captain of a merchant ship, and having had the misfortune to be cast away coming home on a voyage from the West Indies, which would have been very profitable if he had come safe, was so reduced by the loss, that though he had saved his life then, it broke his heart, and killed him afterwards; and his widow, being pursued by the creditors, was forced to take shelter in the Mint. She soon made things up with the help of friends, and was at liberty again; and finding that I rather was there to be concealed, than by any particular prosecutions and finding also that I agreed with her, or rather she with me, in a just abhorrence of the place and of the company, she invited to go home with her till I could put myself in some posture of settling in the world to my mind; withal telling me, that it was ten to one but some good captain of a ship might take a fancy to me, and court me, in that part of the town where she lived.

I accepted her offer, and was with her half a year, and should have been longer, but in that interval what she proposed to me happened to herself, and she married very much to her advantage. But whose fortune soever was upon the increase, mine seemed to be upon the wane, and I found nothing present, except two or three boatswains, or such fellows, but as for the commanders, they were generally of two sorts: 1. Such as, having good business, that is to say, a good ship, resolved not to marry but with advantage, that is, with a good fortune; 2. Such as, being out of employ, wanted a wife to help them to a ship; I mean (1) a wife who, having some money, could enable them to hold, as they call it, a good part of a ship themselves, so to encourage owners to come in; or (2) a wife who, if she had not money, had friends who were concerned in shipping, and so could help to put the young man into a good ship, which to them is as good as a portion; and neither of these was my case, so I looked like one that was to lie on hand.

This knowledge I soon learned by experience, viz. that the state of things was altered as to matrimony, and that I was not to expect at London what I had found in the country: that marriages were here the consequences of politic schemes for forming interests, and carrying on business, and that Love had no share, or but very little, in the matter.

That as my sister-in-law at Colchester had said, beauty, wit, manners, sense, good humour, good behaviour, education, virtue, piety, or any other qualification, whether of body or mind, had no power to recommend; that money only made a woman agreeable; that men chose mistresses indeed by the gust of their affection, and it was requisite to a whore to be handsome, well-shaped, have a good mien and a graceful behaviour; but that for a wife, no deformity would shock the fancy, no ill qualities the judgment; the money was the thing; the portion was neither crooked nor monstrous, but the money was always agreeable, whatever the wife was.

On the other hand, as the market ran very unhappily on the men's side, I found the women had lost the privilege of saying No; that it was a favour now for a woman to have the Question asked, and if any young lady had so much arrogance as to counterfeit a negative, she never had the opportunity given her of denying twice, much less of recovering that false step, and accepting what she had but seemed to decline. The men had such choice everywhere, that the case of the women was very unhappy; for they seemed to ply at every door, and if the man was by great chance refused at one house, he was sure to be received at the next.

Besides this, I observed that the men made no scruple to set themselves out, and to go a-fortunehunting, as they call it, when they had really no fortune themselves to demand it, or merit to deserve it; and that they carried it so high, that a woman was scarce allowed to inquire after the character or estate of the person that pretended to her. This I had an example of, in a young lady in the next house to me, and with whom I had contracted an intimacy; she was courted by a young captain, and though she had near £2000 to her fortune, she did but inquire of some of his neighbours about his character, his morals, or substance, and he took occasion at the next visit to let her know, truly, that he took it very ill, and that he should not give her the trouble of his visits any more. I heard of it, and I had begun my acquaintance with her, I went to see her upon it. She entered into a close conversation with me about it, and unbosomed herself very freely. I perceived presently that though she thought herself very ill used, yet she had no power to resent it, and was exceedingly piqued that she had lost him, and particularly that another of less fortune had gained him.

I fortified her mind against such a meanness, as I called it; I told her, that as low as I was in the world, I would have despised a man that should think I ought to take him upon his own recommendation only, without having the liberty to inform myself of his fortune and of his character; also I told her, that as she had a good fortune, she had no need to stoop to the disaster of the time; that it was enough that the men could insult us that had but little money to recommend us, but if she suffered such an affront to pass upon her without resenting it, she would be rendered low-prized upon all occasions, and would be the contempt of all the women in that part of the town; that a woman can never want an opportunity to be revenged of a man that has used her ill, and that there were ways enough to humble such a fellow as that, or else certainly women were the most unhappy creatures in the world.

I found she was very well pleased with the discourse, and she told me seriously that she would be very glad to make him sensible of her just resentment, and either to bring him on again, or have the satisfaction of her revenge being as public as possible.

I told her, that if she would take my advice, I would tell her how she should obtain her wishes in both those things, and that I would engage I would bring the man to her door again, and make him beg to be let in. She smiled at that, and soon let me see, that if he came to her door, her resentment was not so great as to give her leave to let him stand long there.

However, she listened very willingly to my offer of advice; so I told her that the first thing she ought to do was a piece of justice to herself, namely, that whereas she had been told by several people that he had reported among the ladies that he had left her, and pretended to give the advantage of the negative to himself, she should take care to have it well spread among the women—which she could not fail of an opportunity to do in a neighbourhood so addicted to family news as that she live in was—that she had inquired into his circumstances, and found he was not the man as to estate he pretended to be. 'Let them be told, madam,' said I, 'that you had been well informed that he was not the man that you expected, and that you thought it was not safe to meddle with him; that you heard he was of an ill temper, and that he boasted how he had used the women ill upon many occasions, and that particularly he was debauched in his morals', etc. The last of which, indeed, had some truth in it; but at the same time I did not find that she seemed to like him much the worse for that part.

As I had put this into her head, she came most readily into it. Immediately she went to work to find instruments, and she had very little difficulty in the search, for telling her story in general to a couple of gossips in the neighbourhood, it was the chat of the tea-table all over that part of the town, and I met with it wherever I visited; also, as it was known that I was acquainted with the young lady herself, my opinion was asked very often, and I confirmed it with all the necessary aggravations, and set out his character in the blackest colours; but then as a piece of secret intelligence, I added, as what the other gossips knew nothing of, viz. that I had heard he was in very bad circumstances; that he was under a necessity of a fortune to support his interest with the owners of the ship he commanded; that his own part was not paid for, and if it was not paid quickly, his owners would put him out of the ship, and his chief mate was likely to command it, who offered to buy that part which the captain had promised to take.

I added, for I confess I was heartily piqued at the rogue, as I called him, that I had heard a rumour, too, that he had a wife alive at Plymouth, and another in the West Indies, a thing which they all knew was not very uncommon for such kind of gentlemen.

This worked as we both desire it, for presently the young lady next door, who had a father and mother that governed both her and her fortune, was shut up, and her father forbid him the house. Also in one place more where he went, the woman had the courage, however strange it was, to say No; and he could try nowhere but he was reproached with his pride, and that he pretended not to give the women leave to inquire into his character, and the like.

Well, by this time he began to be sensible of his mistake; and having alarmed all the women on that side of the water, he went over to Ratcliff, and got access to some of the ladies there; but though the young women there too were, according to the fate of the day, pretty willing to be asked, yet such was his ill-luck, that his character followed him over the water and his good name was much the same there as it was on our side; so that though he might have had wives enough, yet it did not happen among the women that had good fortunes, which was what he wanted.

But this was not all; she very ingeniously managed another thing herself, for she got a young gentleman, who as a relation, and was indeed a married man, to come and visit her two or three times a week in a very fine chariot and good liveries, and her two agents, and I also, presently spread a report all over, that this gentleman came to court her; that he was a gentleman of a £1000 a year, and that he was fallen in love with her, and that she was going to her aunt's in the city, because it was inconvenient for the gentleman to come to her with his coach in Redriff, the streets being so narrow and difficult.

This took immediately. The captain was laughed at in all companies, and was ready to hang himself. He tried all the ways possible to come at her again, and wrote the most passionate letters to her in the world, excusing his former rashness; and in short, by great application, obtained leave to wait on her again, as he said, to clear his reputation.

At this meeting she had her full revenge of him; for she told him she wondered what he took her to be, that she should admit any man to a treaty of so much consequence as that to marriage, without inquiring very well into his circumstances; that if he thought she was to be huffed into wedlock, and that she was in the same circumstances which her neighbours might be in, viz. to take up with the first good Christian that came, he was mistaken; that, in a word, his character was really bad, or he was very ill beholden to his neighbours; and that unless he could clear up some points, in which she had justly been prejudiced, she had no more to say to him, but to do herself justice, and give him the satisfaction of knowing that she was not afraid to say No, either to him or any man else.

With that she told him what she had heard, or rather raised herself by my means, of his character; his not having paid for the part he pretended to own of the ship he commanded; of the resolution of his owners to put him out of the command, and to put his mate in his stead; and of the scandal raised on his morals; his having been reproached with such-and-such women, and having a wife at Plymouth and in the West Indies, and the like; and she asked him whether he could deny that she had good reason, if these things were not cleared up, to refuse him, and in the meantime to insist upon having satisfaction in points to significant as they were.

He was so confounded at her discourse that he could not answer a word, and she almost began to believe that all was true, by his disorder, though at the same time she knew that she had been the raiser of all those reports herself.

After some time he recovered himself a little, and from that time became the most humble, the most modest, and most importunate man alive in his courtship.

She carried her jest on a great way. She asked him, if he thought she was so at her last shift that she could or ought to bear such treatment, and if he did not see that she did not want those who thought it worth their while to come farther to her than he did; meaning the gentleman whom she had brought to visit her by way of sham.

She brought him by these tricks to submit to all possible measures to satisfy her, as well of his circumstances as of his behaviour. He brought her undeniable evidence of his having paid for his part of the ship; he brought her certificates from his owners, that the report of their intending to remove him from the command of the ship and put his chief mate in was false and groundless; in short, he was quite the reverse of what he was before.

Thus I convinced her, that if the men made their advantage of our sex in the affair of marriage, upon the supposition of there being such choice to be had, and of the women being so easy, it was only owing to this, that the women wanted courage to maintain their ground and to play their part; and that, according to my Lord Rochester,

> 'A woman's ne'er so ruined but she can
> Revenge herself on her undoer, Man.'

After these things this young lady played her part so well, that though she resolved to have him, and that indeed having him was the main bent of her design, yet she made his obtaining her be to him the most difficult thing in the world; and this she did, not by a haughty reserved carriage, but by a just policy, turning the tables upon him, and playing back upon him his own game; for as he pretended, by a kind of lofty carriage, to place himself above the occasion of a character, and to make inquiring into his character a kind of an affront to him, she broke with him upon that subject, and at the same time that she make him submit to all possible inquiry after his affairs, she apparently shut the door against his looking into her own.

It was enough to him to obtain her for a wife. As to what she had, she told him plainly, that as he knew her circumstances, it was but just she should know his; and though at the same time he had only known her circumstances by common fame, yet he had made so many protestations of his passion for her, that he could ask no more but her hand to his grand request, and the like ramble according to the custom of lovers. In short, he left himself no room to ask any more questions about her estate, and she took the advantage of it like a prudent woman, for she placed part of her fortune so in trustees, without letting him know anything of it, that it was quite out of his reach, and made him be very well content with the rest.

It is true she was pretty well besides, that is to say, she had about £1400 in money, which she gave him; and the other, after some time, she brought to light as a perquisite to herself, which he was to accept as a mighty favour, seeing though it was not to be his, it might ease him in the article of her particular expenses; and I must add, that by this conduct the gentleman himself became not only the more humble in his applications to her to obtain her, but also was much the more an obliging husband to her when he had her. I cannot but remind the ladies here how much they place themselves below the common station of a wife, which, if I may be allowed not to be partial, is low enough already; I say, they place themselves below their common station, and prepare their own mortifications, by their submitting so to be insulted by the men beforehand, which I confess I see no necessity of.

This relation may serve, therefore, to let the ladies see that the advantage is not so much on the other side as the men think it is; and though it may be true that the men have but too much choice among us, and that some women may be found who will dishonour themselves, be cheap, and easy to come at, and will scarce wait to be asked, yet if they will have women, as I may say, worth having, they may find them as uncomeatable as ever and that those that are otherwise are a sort of people that have such deficiencies, when had, as rather recommend the ladies that are difficult than encourage the men to go on with their easy courtship, and expect wives equally valuable that will come at first call.

Nothing is more certain than that the ladies always gain of the men by keeping their ground, and letting their pretended lovers see they can resent being slighted, and that they are not afraid of saying No. They, I observe, insult us mightily with telling us of the number of women; that the wars, and the sea, and trade, and other incidents have carried the men so much away, that there is no proportion between the numbers of the sexes, and therefore the women have the disadvantage; but I am far from granting that the number of women is so great, or the number of men so small; but if they will have me tell the truth, the disadvantage of the women is a terrible scandal upon the men, and it lies here, and here only; namely, that the age is so wicked, and the sex so debauched, that, in short, the number of such men as an honest woman ought to meddle with is small indeed, and it is but here and there that a man is to be found who is fit for a woman to venture upon.

But the consequence even of that too amounts to no more than this, that women ought to be the more nice; for how do we know the just character of the man that makes the offer? To say that the woman should be the more easy on this occasion, is to say we should be the forwarder to venture because of the greatness of the danger, which, in my way of reasoning, is very absurd.

On the contrary, the women have ten thousand times the more reason to be wary and backward, by how much the hazard of being betrayed is the greater; and would the ladies consider this, and act the wary part, they would discover every cheat that offered; for, in short, the lives of very few men nowadays will bear a character; and if the ladies do but make a little inquiry, they will soon be able to distinguish the men and deliver themselves. As for women that do not think their own safety worth their thought, that, impatient of their perfect state, resolve, as they call it, to take the first good Christian that comes, that run into matrimony as a horse rushes into the battle, I can say nothing to them but this, that they are a sort of ladies that are to be prayed for among the rest of distempered people, and to me they look like people that venture their whole estates in a lottery where there is a hundred thousand blanks to one prize.

No man of common-sense will value a woman the less for not giving up herself at the first attack, or for accepting his proposal without inquiring into his person or character; on the contrary, he must think her the weakest of all creatures in the world, as the rate of men now goes. In short, he must have a very contemptible opinion of her capacities, nay, every of her understanding, that, having but one case of her life, shall call that life away at once, and make matrimony, like death, be a leap in the dark.

I would fain have the conduct of my sex a little regulated in this particular, which is the thing in which, of all the parts of life, I think at this time we suffer most in; 'tis nothing but lack of courage, the fear of not being married at all, and of that frightful state of life called an old maid, of which I have a story to tell by itself. This, I say, is the woman's snare; but would the ladies once but get above that fear and manage rightly, they would more certainly avoid it by standing their ground, in a case so absolutely necessary to their felicity, that by exposing themselves as they do; and if they did not marry so soon as they may do otherwise, they would make themselves amends by marrying safer. She is always married too soon who gets a bad husband, and she is never married too late who gets a good one; in a word, there is no woman, deformity or lost reputation excepted, but if she manages well, may be married safely one time or other; but if she precipitates herself, it is ten thousand to one but she is undone.

But I come now to my own case, in which there was at this time no little nicety. The circumstances I was in made the offer of a good husband the most necessary thing in the world to me, but I found soon that to be made cheap and easy was not the way. It soon began to be found that the widow had no fortune, and to say this was to say all that was ill of me, for I began to be dropped in all the discourses of matrimony. Being well-bred, handsome, witty, modest, and agreeable; all which I had allowed to my character—whether justly or no is not the purpose—I say, all these would not do without the dross, which way now become more valuable than virtue itself. In short, the widow, they said, had no money.

I resolved, therefore, as to the state of my present circumstances, that it was absolutely necessary to change my station, and make a new appearance in some other place where I was not known, and even to pass by another name if I found occasion.

I communicated my thoughts to my intimate friend, the captain's lady, whom I had so faithfully served in her case with the captain, and who was as ready to serve me in the same kind as I could desire. I made no scruple to lay my circumstances open to her; my stock was but low, for I had made but about £540 at the close of my last affair, and I had wasted some of that; however, I had about £460 left, a great many very rich clothes, a gold watch, and some jewels, though of no extraordinary value, and about £30 or £40 left in linen not disposed of.

My dear and faithful friend, the captain's wife, was so sensible of the service I had done her in the affair above, that she was not only a steady friend to me, but, knowing my circumstances, she frequently made me presents as money came into her hands, such as fully amounted to a maintenance, so that I spent none of my own; and at last she made this unhappy proposal to me, viz. that as we had observed, as above, how the men made no scruple to set themselves out as persons meriting a woman of fortune, when they had really no fortune of their own, it was but just to deal with them in their own way and, if it was possible, to deceive the deceiver.

The captain's lady, in short, put this project into my head, and told me if I would be ruled by her I should certainly get a husband of fortune, without leaving him any room to reproach me with want of my own. I told her, as I had reason to do, that I would give up myself wholly to her directions, and that I would have neither tongue to speak nor feet to step in that affair but as she should direct me, depending that she would extricate me out of every difficulty she brought me into, which she said she would answer for.

The first step she put me upon was to call her cousin, and to to a relation's house of hers in the country, where she directed me, and where she brought her husband to visit me; and calling me cousin, she worked matters so about, that her husband and she together invited me most passionately to come to town and be with them, for they now live in a quite different place from where they were before. In the next place, she tells her husband that I had at least £1500 fortune, and that after some of my relations I was like to have a great deal more.

It was enough to tell her husband this; there needed nothing on my side. I was but to sit still and wait the event, for it presently went all over the neighbourhood that the young widow at Captain ——'s was a fortune, that she had at least £1500, and perhaps a great deal more, and that the captain said so; and if the captain was asked at any time about me, he made no scruple to affirm it, though he knew not one word of the matter, other than that his wife had told him so; and in this he thought no harm, for he really believed it to be so, because he had it from his wife: so slender a foundation will those fellows build upon, if they do but think there is a fortune in the game. With the reputation of this fortune, I presently found myself blessed with admirers enough, and that I had my choice of men, as scarce as they said they were, which, by the way, confirms what I was saying before. This being my case, I, who had a subtle game to play, had nothing now to do but to single out from them all the properest man that might be for my purpose; that is to say, the man who was most likely to depend upon the hearsay of a fortune, and not inquire too far into the particulars; and unless I did this I did nothing, for my case would not bear much inquiry.

I picked out my man without much difficulty, by the judgment I made of his way of courting me. I had let him run on with his protestations and oaths that he loved me above all the world; that if I would make him happy, that was enough; all which I knew was upon supposition, nay, it was upon a full satisfaction, that I was very rich, though I never told him a word of it myself.

This was my man; but I was to try him to the bottom, and indeed in that consisted my safety; for if he baulked, I knew I was undone, as surely as he was undone if he took me; and if I did not make some scruple about his fortune, it was the way to lead him to raise some about mine; and first, therefore, I pretended on all occasions to doubt his sincerity, and told him, perhaps he only courted me for my fortune. He stopped my mouth in that part with the thunder of his protestations, as above, but still I pretended to doubt.

One morning he pulls off his diamond ring, and writes upon the glass of the sash in my chamber this line—

'You I love, and you alone.'

I read it, and asked him to lend me his ring, with which I wrote under it, thus—

'And so in love says every one.'

He takes his ring again, and writes another line thus—

'Virtue alone is an estate.'

I borrowed it again, and I wrote under it—

'But money's virtue, gold is fate.'

He coloured as red as fire to see me turn so quick upon him, and in a kind of a rage told me he would conquer me, and writes again thus—

'I scorn your gold, and yet I love.'

I ventured all upon the last cast of poetry, as you'll see, for I wrote boldly under his last—

'I'm poor: let's see how kind you'll prove.'

This was a sad truth to me; whether he believed me or no, I could not tell; I supposed then that he did not. However, he flew to me, took me in his arms, and, kissing me very eagerly, and with the greatest passion imaginable, he held me fast till he called for a pen and ink, and then told me he could not wait the tedious writing on the glass, but, pulling out a piece of paper, he began and wrote again—

'Be mine, with all your poverty.'

I took his pen, and followed him immediately, thus—

'Yet secretly you hope I lie.'

He told me that was unkind, because it was not just, and that I put him upon contradicting me, which did not consist with good manners, any more than with his affection; and therefore, since I had insensibly drawn him into this poetical scribble, he begged I would not oblige him to break it off; so he writes again—

'Let love alone be our debate.'

I wrote again—

'She loves enough that does not hate.'

This he took for a favour, and so laid down the cudgels, that is to say, the pen; I say, he took if for a favour, and a mighty one it was, if he had known all. However, he took it as I meant it, that is, to let him think I was inclined to go on with him, as indeed I had all the reason in the world to do, for he was the best-humoured, merry sort of a fellow that I ever met with, and I often reflected on myself how doubly criminal it was to deceive such a man; but that necessity, which pressed me to a settlement suitable to my condition, was my authority for it; and certainly his affection to me, and the goodness of his temper, however they might argue against using him ill, yet they strongly argued to me that he would better take the disappointment than some fiery-tempered wretch, who might have nothing to recommend him but those passions which would serve only to make a woman miserable all her days.

Besides, though I jested with him (as he supposed it) so often about my poverty, yet, when he found it to be true, he had foreclosed all manner of objection, seeing, whether he was in jest or in earnest, he had declared he took me without any regard to my portion, and, whether I was in jest or in earnest, I had declared myself to be very poor; so that, in a word, I had him fast both ways; and though he might say afterwards he was cheated, yet he could never say that I had cheated him.

He pursued me close after this, and as I saw there was no need to fear losing him, I played the indifferent part with him longer than prudence might otherwise have dictated to me. But I considered how much this caution and indifference would give me the advantage over him, when I should come to be under the necessity of owning my own circumstances to him; and I managed it the more warily, because I found he inferred from thence, as indeed he ought to do, that I either had the more money or the more judgment, and would not venture at all.

I took the freedom one day, after we had talked pretty close to the subject, to tell him that it was true I had received the compliment of a lover from him, namely, that he would take me without inquiring into my fortune, and I would make him a suitable return in this, viz. that I would make as little inquiry into his as consisted with reason, but I hoped he would allow me to ask a few questions, which he would answer or not as he thought fit; and that I would not be offended if he did not answer me at all; one of these questions related to our manner of living, and the place where, because I had heard he had a great plantation in Virginia, and that he had talked of going to live there, and I told him I did not care to be transported.

He began from this discourse to let me voluntarily into all his affairs, and to tell me in a frank, open way all his circumstances, by which I found he was very well to pass in the world; but that great part of his estate consisted of three plantations, which he had in Virginia, which brought him in a very good income, generally speaking, to the tune of £300, a year, but that if he was to live upon them, would bring him in four times as much. 'Very well,' thought I; 'you shall carry me thither as soon as you please, though I won't tell you so beforehand.'

I jested with him extremely about the figure he would make in Virginia; but I found he would do anything I desired, though he did not seem glad to have me undervalue his plantations, so I turned my tale. I told him I had good reason not to go there to live, because if his plantations were worth so much there, I had not a fortune suitable to a gentleman of £1200 a year, as he said his estate would be.

He replied generously, he did not ask what my fortune was; he had told me from the beginning he would not, and he would be as good as his word; but whatever it was, he assured me he would never desire me to go to Virginia with him, or go thither himself without me, unless I was perfectly willing, and made it my choice.

All this, you may be sure, was as I wished, and indeed nothing could have happened more perfectly agreeable. I carried it on as far as this with a sort of indifferency that he often wondered at, more than at first, but which was the only support of his courtship; and I mention it the rather to intimate again to the ladies that nothing but want of courage for such an indifferency makes our sex so cheap, and prepares them to be ill-used as they are; would they venture the loss of a pretending fop now and then, who carries it high upon the point of his own merit, they would certainly be less slighted, and courted more. Had I discovered really and truly what my great fortune was, and that in all I had not full £500 when he expected £1500, yet I had hooked him so fast, and played him so long, that I was satisfied he would have had me in my worst circumstances; and indeed it was less a surprise to him when he learned the truth than it would have been, because having not the least blame to lay on me, who had carried it with an air of indifference to the last, he would not say one word, except that indeed he thought it had been more, but that if it had been less he did not repent his bargain; only that he should not be able to maintain me so well as he intended.

In short, we were married, and very happily married on my side, I assure you, as to the man; for he was the best-humoured man that every woman had, but his circumstances were not so good as I imagined, as, on the other hand, he had not bettered himself by marrying so much as he expected.

When we were married, I was shrewdly put to it to bring him that little stock I had, and to let him see it was no more; but there was a necessity for it, so I took my opportunity one day when we were alone, to enter into a short dialogue with him about it. 'My dear,' said I, 'we have been married a fortnight; is it not time to let you know whether you have got a wife with something or with nothing?' 'Your own time for that, my dear,' says he; 'I am satisfied that I have got the wife I love; I have not troubled you much,' says he, 'with my inquiry after it.'

'That's true,' says I, 'but I have a great difficulty upon me about it, which I scarce know how to manage.'

'What's that, m' dear?' says he.

'Why,' says I, "tis a little hard upon me, and 'tis harder upon you. I am told that Captain ——' (meaning my friend's husband) 'has told you I had a great deal more money than I ever pretended to have, and I am sure I never employed him to do so.'

'Well,' says he, 'Captain —— may have told me so, but what then? If you have not so much, that may lie at his door, but you never told me what you had, so I have no reason to blame you if you have nothing at all.'

'That's is so just,' said I, 'and so generous, that it makes my having but a little a double affliction to me.'

'The less you have, my dear,' says he, 'the worse for us both; but I hope your affliction you speak of is not caused for fear I should be unkind to you, for want of a portion. No, no, if you have nothing, tell me plainly, and at once; I may perhaps tell the captain he has cheated me, but I can never say you have cheated me, for did you not give it under your hand that you were poor? and so I ought to expect you to be.'

'Well,' said I, 'my dear, I am glad I have not been concerned in deceiving you before marriage. If I deceive you since, 'tis ne'er the worse; that I am poor is too true, but not so poor as to have nothing neither'; so I pulled out some bank bills, and gave him about £160. 'There's something, my dear,' said I, 'and not quite all neither.'

I had brought him so near to expecting nothing, by what I had said before, that the money, though the sum was small in itself, was doubly welcome to him; he owned it was more than he looked for, and that he did not question by my discourse to him, but that my fine clothes, gold watch, and a diamond ring or two, had been all my fortune.

I let him please himself with that £160 two or three days, and then, having been abroad that day, and as if I had been to fetch it, I brought him £100 more home in gold, and told him there was a little more portion for him; and, in short, in about a week more I brought him £180 more, and about £60 in linen, which I made him believe I had been obliged to take with the £100 which I gave him in gold, as a composition for a debt of £600, being little more than five shillings in the pound, and overvalued too.

'And now, my dear,' says I to him, 'I am very sorry to tell you, that there is all, and that I have given you my whole fortune.' I added, that if the person who had my £600 had not abused me, I had been worth £1000 to him, but that as it was, I had been faithful to him, and reserved nothing to myself, but if it had been more he should have had it.

He was so obliged by the manner, and so pleased with the sum, for he had been in a terrible fright lest it had been nothing at all, that he accepted it very thankfully. And thus I got over the fraud of passing for a fortune without money, and cheating a man into marrying me on pretence of a fortune; which, by the way, I take to be one of the most dangerous steps a woman can take, and in which she runs the most hazard of being ill-used afterwards.

My husband, to give him his due, was a man of infinite good nature, but he was no fool; and finding his income not suited to the manner of living which he had intended, if I had brought him what he expected, and being under a disappointment in his return of his plantations in Virginia, he discovered many times his inclination of going over to Virginia, to live upon his own; and often would be magnifying the way of living there, how cheap, how plentiful, how pleasant, and the like.

I began presently to understand this meaning, and I took him up very plainly one morning, and told him that I did so; that I found his estate turned to no account at this distance, compared to what it would do if he lived upon the spot, and that I found he had a mind to go and live there; and I added, that I was sensible he had been disappointed in a wife, and that finding his expectations not answered that way, I could do no less, to make him amends, than tell him that I was very willing to go over to Virginia with him and live there.

He said a thousand kind things to me upon the subject of my making such a proposal to him. He told me, that however he was disappointed in his expectations of a fortune, he was not disappointed in a wife, and that I was all to him that a wife could be, and he was more than satisfied on the whole when the particulars were put together, but that this offer was so kind, that it was more than he could express.

To bring the story short, we agreed to go. He told me that he had a very good house there, that it was well furnished, that his mother was alive and lived in it, and one sister, which was all the relations he had; that as soon as he came there, his mother would remove to another house, which was her own for life, and his after her decease; so that I should have all the house to myself; and I found all this to be exactly as he had said.

To make this part of the story short, we put on board the ship which we went in, a large quantity of good furniture for our house, with stores of linen and other necessaries, and a good cargo for sale, and away we went.

To give an account of the manner of our voyage, which was long and full of dangers, is out of my way; I kept no journal, neither did my husband. All that I can say is, that after a terrible passage, frighted twice with dreadful storms, and once with what was still more terrible, I mean a pirate who came on board and took away almost all our provisions; and which would have been beyond all to me, they had once taken my husband to go along with them, but by entreaties were prevailed with to leave him;—I say, after all these terrible things, we arrived in York River in Virginia, and coming to our plantation, we were received with all the demonstrations of tenderness and affection, by my husband's mother, that were possible to be expressed.

We lived here all together, my mother-in-law, at my entreaty, continuing in the house, for she was too kind a mother to be parted with; my husband likewise continued the same as at first, and I thought myself the happiest creature alive, when an odd and surprising event put an end to all that felicity in a moment, and rendered my condition the most uncomfortable, if not the most miserable, in the world.

My mother was a mighty cheerful, good-humoured old woman —I may call her old woman, for her son was above thirty; I say she was very pleasant, good company, and used to entertain me, in particular, with abundance of stories to divert me, as well of the country we were in as of the people.

Among the rest, she often told me how the greatest part of the inhabitants of the colony came thither in very indifferent circumstances from England; that, generally speaking, they were of two sorts; either, first, such as were brought over by masters of ships to be sold as servants. 'Such as we call them, my dear,' says she, 'but they are more properly called slaves.' Or, secondly, such as are transported from Newgate and other prisons, after having been found guilty of felony and other crimes punishable with death.

'When they come here,' says she, 'we make no difference; the planters buy them, and they work together in the field till their time is out. When 'tis expired,' said she, 'they have encouragement given them to plant for themselves; for they have a certain number of acres of land allotted them by the country, and they go to work to clear and cure the land, and then to plant it with tobacco and corn for their own use; and as the tradesmen and merchants will trust them with tools and clothes and other necessaries, upon the credit of their crop before it is grown, so they again plant every year a little more than the year before, and so buy whatever they want with the crop that is before them.

'Hence, child,' says she, 'man a Newgate-bird becomes a great man, and we have,' continued she, 'several justices of the peace, officers of the trained bands, and magistrates of the towns they live in, that have been burnt in the hand.'

She was going on with that part of the story, when her own part in it interrupted her, and with a great deal of good-humoured confidence she told me she was one of the second sort of inhabitants herself; that she came away openly, having ventured too far in a particular case, so that she was become a criminal. 'And here's the mark of it, child,' says she; and, pulling off her glove, 'look ye here,' says she, turning up the palm of her hand, and showed me a very fine white arm and hand, but branded in the inside of the hand, as in such cases it must be.

This story was very moving to me, but my mother, smiling, said, 'You need not think a thing strange, daughter, for as I told you, some of the best men in this country are burnt in the hand, and they are not ashamed to own it. There's Major ——,' says she, 'he was an eminent pickpocket; there's Justice Ba——r, was a shoplifter, and both of them were burnt in the hand; and I could name you several such as they are.'

We had frequent discourses of this kind, and abundance of instances she gave me of the like. After some time, as she was telling some stories of one that was transported but a few weeks ago, I began in an intimate kind of way to ask her to tell me something of her own story, which she did with the utmost plainness and sincerity; how she had fallen into very ill company in London in her young days, occasioned by her mother sending her frequently to carry victuals and other relief to a kinswoman of hers who was a prisoner in Newgate, and who lay in a miserable starving condition, was afterwards condemned to be hanged, but having got respite by pleading her belly, dies afterwards in the prison.

Here my mother-in-law ran out in a long account of the wicked practices in that dreadful place, and how it ruined more young people that all the town besides. 'And child,' says my mother, 'perhaps you may know little of it, or, it may be, have heard nothing about it; but depend upon it,' says she, 'we all know here that there are more thieves and rogues made by that one prison of Newgate than by all the clubs and societies of villains in the nation; 'tis that cursed place,' says my mother, 'that half peopled this colony.'

Here she went on with her own story so long, and in so particular a manner, that I began to be very uneasy; but coming to one particular that required telling her name, I thought I should have sunk down in the place. She perceived I was out of order, and asked me if I was not well, and what ailed me. I told her I was so affected with the melancholy story she had told, and the terrible things she had gone through, that it had overcome me, and I begged of her to talk no more of it. 'Why, my dear,' says she very kindly, 'what need these things trouble you? These passages were long before your time, and they give me no trouble at all now; nay, I look back on them with a particular satisfaction, as they have been a means to bring me to this place.' Then she went on to tell me how she very luckily fell into a good family, where, behaving herself well, and her mistress dying, her master married her, by whom she had my husband and his sister, and that by her diligence and good management after her husband's death, she had improved the plantations to such a degree as they then were, so that most of the estate was of her getting, not her husband's, for she had been a widow upwards of sixteen years.

I heard this part of they story with very little attention, because I wanted much to retire and give vent to my passions, which I did soon after; and let any one judge what must be the anguish of my mind, when I came to reflect that this was certainly no more or less than my own mother, and I had now had two children, and was big with another by my own brother, and lay with him still every night.

I was now the most unhappy of all women in the world. Oh! had the story never been told me, all had been well; it had been no crime to have lain with my husband, since as to his being my relation I had known nothing of it.

I had now such a load on my mind that it kept me perpetually waking; to reveal it, which would have been some ease to me, I could not find would be to any purpose, and yet to conceal it would be next to impossible; nay, I did not doubt but I should talk of it in my sleep, and tell my husband of it whether I would or no. If I discovered it, the least thing I could expect was to lose my husband, for he was too nice and too honest a man to have continued my husband after he had known I had been his sister; so that I was perplexed to the last degree.

I leave it to any man to judge what difficulties presented to my view. I was away from my native country, at a distance prodigious, and the return to me unpassable. I lived very well, but in a circumstance insufferable in itself. If I had discovered myself to my mother, it might be difficult to convince her of the particulars, and I had no way to prove them. On the other hand, if she had questioned or doubted me, I had been undone, for the bare suggestion would have immediately separated me from my husband, without gaining my mother or him, who would have been neither a husband nor a brother; so that between the surprise on one hand, and the uncertainty on the other, I had been sure to be undone.

In the meantime, as I was but too sure of the fact, I lived therefore in open avowed incest and whoredom, and all under the appearance of an honest wife; and though I was not much touched with the crime of it, yet the action had something in it shocking to nature, and made my husband, as he thought himself, even nauseous to me.

However, upon the most sedate consideration, I resolved that it was absolutely necessary to conceal it all and not make the least discovery of it either to mother or husband; and thus I lived with the greatest pressure imaginable for three years more, but had no more children.

During this time my mother used to be frequently telling me old stories of her former adventures, which, however, were no ways pleasant to me; for by it, though she did not tell it me in plain terms, yet I could easily understand, joined with what I had heard myself, of my first tutors, that in her younger days she had been both whore and thief; but I verily believed she had lived to repent sincerely of both, and that she was then a very pious, sober, and religious woman.

Well, let her life have been what it would then, it was certain that my life was very uneasy to me; for I lived, as I have said, but in the worst sort of whoredom, and as I could expect no good of it, so really no good issue came of it, and all my seeming prosperity wore off, and ended in misery and destruction. It was some time, indeed, before it came to this, for, but I know not by what ill fate guided, everything went wrong with us afterwards, and that which was worse, my husband grew strangely altered, forward, jealous, and unkind, and I was as impatient of bearing his carriage, as the carriage was unreasonable and unjust. These things proceeded so far, that we came at last to be in such ill terms with one another, that I claimed a promise of him, which he entered willingly into with me when I consented to come from England with him, viz. that if I found the country not to agree with me, or that I did not like to live there, I should come away to England again when I pleased, giving him a year's warning to settle his affairs.

I say, I now claimed this promise of him, and I must confess I did it not in the most obliging terms that could be in the world neither; but I insisted that he treated me ill, that I was remote from my friends, and could do myself no justice, and that he was jealous without cause, my conversation having been unblamable, and he having no pretense for it, and that to remove to England would take away all occasion from him.

I insisted so peremptorily upon it, that he could not avoid coming to a point, either to keep his word with me or to break it; and this, notwithstanding he used all the skill he was master of, and employed his mother and other agents to prevail with me to alter my resolutions; indeed, the bottom of the thing lay at my heart, and that made all his endeavours fruitless, for my heart was alienated from him as a husband. I loathed the thoughts of bedding with him, and used a thousand pretenses of illness and humour to prevent his touching me, fearing nothing more than to be with child by him, which to be sure would have prevented, or at least delayed, my going over to England.

However, at last I put him so out of humour, that he took up a rash and fatal resolution; in short, I should not go to England; and though he had promised me, yet it was an unreasonable thing for me to desire it; that it would be ruinous to his affairs, would unhinge his whole family, and be next to an undoing him in the world; that therefore I ought not to desire it of him, and that no wife in the world that valued her family and her husband's prosperity would insist upon such a thing.

This plunged me again, for when I considered the thing calmly, and took my husband as he really was, a diligent, careful man in the main work of laying up an estate for his children, and that he knew nothing of the dreadful circumstances that he was in, I could not but confess to myself that my proposal was very unreasonable, and what no wife that had the good of her family at heart would have desired.

But my discontents were of another nature; I looked upon him no longer as a husband, but as a near relation, the son of my own mother, and I resolved somehow or other to be clear of him, but which way I did not know, nor did it seem possible.

It is said by the ill-natured world, of our sex, that if we are set on a thing, it is impossible to turn us from our resolutions; in short, I never ceased poring upon the means to bring to pass my voyage, and came that length with my husband at last, as to propose going without him. This provoked him to the last degree, and he called me not only an unkind wife, but an unnatural mother, and asked me how I could entertain such a thought without horror, as that of leaving my two children (for one was dead) without a mother, and to be brought up by strangers, and never to see them more. It was true, had things been right, I should not have done it, but now it was my real desire never to see them, or him either, any more; and as to the charge of unnatural, I could easily answer it to myself, while I knew that the whole relation was unnatural in the highest degree in the world.

However, it was plain there was no bringing my husband to anything; he would neither go with me nor let me go without him, and it was quite out of my power to stir without his consent, as any one that knows the constitution of the country I was in, knows very well.

We had many family quarrels about it, and they began in time to grow up to a dangerous height; for as I was quite estranged form my husband (as he was called) in affection, so I took no heed to my words, but sometimes gave him language that was provoking; and, in short, strove all I could to bring him to a parting with me, which was what above all things in the world I desired most.

He took my carriage very ill, and indeed he might well do so, for at last I refused to bed with him, and carrying on the breach upon all occasions to extremity, he told me once he thought I was mad, and if I did not alter my conduct, he would put me under cure; that is to say, into a madhouse. I told him he should find I was far enough from mad, and that it was not in his power, or any other villain's, to murder me. I confess at the same time I was heartily frighted at his thoughts of putting me into a madhouse, which would at once have destroyed all the possibility of breaking the truth out, whatever the occasion might be; for that then no one would have given credit to a word of it.

This therefore brought me to a resolution, whatever came of it, to lay open my whole case; but which way to do it, or to whom, was an inextricable difficulty, and took me many months to resolve. In the meantime, another quarrel with my husband happened, which came up to such a mad extreme as almost pushed me on to tell it him all to his face; but though I kept it in so as not to come to the particulars, I spoke so much as put him into the utmost confusion, and in the end brought out the whole story.

He began with a calm expostulation upon my being so resolute to go to England; I defended it, and one hard word bringing on another, as is usual in all family strife, he told me I did not treat him as if he was my husband, or talk of my children as if I was a mother; and, in short, that I did not deserve to be used as a wife; that he had used all the fair means possible with me; that he had argued with all the kindness and calmness that a husband or a Christian ought to do, and that I made him such a vile return, that I treated him rather like a dog than a man, and rather like the most contemptible stranger than a husband; that he was very loth to use violence with me, but that, in short, he saw a necessity of it now, and that for the future he should be obliged to take such measures as should reduce me to my duty.

My blood was now fired to the utmost, though I knew what he had said was very true, and nothing could appear more provoked. I told him, for his fair means and his foul, they were equally contemned by me; that for my going to England, I was resolved on it, come what would; and that as to treating him not like a husband, and not showing myself a mother to my children, there might be something more in it than he understood at present; but, for his further consideration, I thought fit to tell him thus much, that he neither was my lawful husband, nor they lawful children, and that I had reason to regard neither of them more than I did.

I confess I was moved to pity him when I spoke it, for he turned pale as death, and stood mute as one thunderstruck, and once or twice I thought he would have fainted; in short, it put him in a fit something like an apoplex; he trembled, a sweat or dew ran off his face, and yet he was cold as a clod, so that I was forced to run and fetch something for him to keep life in him. When he recovered of that, he grew sick and vomited, and in a little after was put to bed, and the next morning was, as he had been indeed all night, in a violent fever.

However, it went off again, and he recovered, though but slowly, and when he came to be a little better, he told me I had given him a mortal wound with my tongue, and he had only one thing to ask before he desired an explanation. I interrupted him, and told him I was sorry I had gone so far, since I saw what disorder it put him into, but I desired him not to talk to me of explanations, for that would but make things worse.

This heightened his impatience, and, indeed, perplexed him beyond all bearing; for now he began to suspect that there was some mystery yet unfolded, but could not make the least guess at the real particulars of it; all that ran in his brain was, that I had another husband alive, which I could not say in fact might not be true, but I assured him, however, there was not the least of that in it; and indeed, as to my other husband, he was effectually dead in law to me, and had told me I should look on him as such, so I had not the least uneasiness on that score.

But now I found the thing too far gone to conceal it much longer, and my husband himself gave me an opportunity to ease myself of the secret, much to my satisfaction. He had laboured with me three or four weeks, but to no purpose, only to tell him whether I had spoken these words only as the effect of my passion, to put him in a passion, or whether there was anything of truth in the bottom of them. But I continued inflexible, and would explain nothing, unless he would first consent to my going to England, which he would never do, he said, while he lived; on the other hand, I said it was in my power to make him willing when I pleased—nay, to make him entreat me to go; and this increased his curiosity, and made him importunate to the highest degree, but it was all to no purpose.

At length he tells all this story to his mother, and sets her upon me to get the main secret out of me, and she used her utmost skill with me indeed; but I put her to a full stop at once by telling her that the reason and mystery of the whole matter lay in herself, and that it was my respect to her that had made me conceal it; and that, in short, I could go no farther, and therefore conjured her not to insist upon it.

She was struck dumb at this suggestion, and could not tell what to say or to think; but, laying aside the supposition as a policy of mine, continued her importunity on account of her son, and, if possible, to make up the breach between us two. As to that, I told her that it was indeed a good design in her, but that it was impossible to be done; and that if I should reveal to her the truth of what she desired, she would grant it to be impossible, and cease to desire it. At last I seemed to be prevailed on by her importunity, and told her I dared trust her with a secret of the greatest importance, and she would soon see that this was so, and that I would consent to lodge it in her breast, if she would engage solemnly not to acquaint her son with it without my consent.

She was long in promising this part, but rather than not come at the main secret, she agreed to that too, and after a great many other preliminaries, I began, and told her the whole story. First I told her how much she was concerned in all the unhappy breach which had happened between her son and me, by telling me her own story and her London name; and that the surprise she saw I was in was upon that occasion. The I told her my own story, and my name, and assured her, by such other tokens as she could not deny, that I was no other, nor more or less, than her own child, her daughter, born of her body in Newgate; the same that had saved her from the gallows by being in her belly, and the same that she left in such-and-such hands when she was transported.

It is impossible to express the astonishment she was in; she was not inclined to believe the story, or to remember the particulars, for she immediately foresaw the confusion that must follow in the family upon it. But everything concurred so exactly with the stories she had told me of herself, and which, if she had not told me, she would perhaps have been content to have denied, that she had stopped her own mouth, and she had nothing to do but to take me about the neck and kiss me, and cry most vehemently over me, without speaking one word for a long time together. At last she broke out: 'Unhappy child!' says she, 'what miserable chance could bring thee hither? and in the arms of my own son, too! Dreadful girl,' says she, 'why, we are all undone! Married to thy own brother! Three children, and two alive, all of the same flesh and blood! My son and my daughter lying together as husband and wife! All confusion and distraction for ever! Miserable family! what will become of us? What is to be said? What is to be done?' And thus she ran on for a great while; nor had I any power to speak, or if I had, did I know what to say, for every word wounded me to the soul. With this kind of amazement on our thoughts we parted for the first time, though my mother was more surprised than I was, because it was more news to her than to me. However, she promised again to me at parting, that she would say nothing of it to her son, till we had talked of it again.

It was not long, you may be sure, before we had a second conference upon the same subject; when, as if she had been willing to forget the story she had told me of herself, or to suppose that I had forgot some of the particulars, she began to tell them with alterations and omissions; but I refreshed her memory and set her to rights in many things which I supposed she had forgot, and then came in so opportunely with the whole history, that it was impossible for her to go from it; and then she fell into her rhapsodies again, and exclamations at the severity of her misfortunes. When these things were a little over with her, we fell into a close debate about what should be first done before we gave an account of the matter to my husband. But to what purpose could be all our consultations? We could neither of us see our way through it, nor see how it could be safe to open such a scene to him. It was impossible to make any judgment, or give any guess at what temper he would receive it in, or what measures he would take upon it; and if he should have so little government of himself as to make it public, we easily foresaw that it would be the ruin of the whole family, and expose my mother and me to the last degree; and if at last he should take the advantage the law would give him, he might put me away with disdain and leave me to sue for the little portion that I had, and perhaps waste it all in the suit, and then be a beggar; the children would be ruined too, having no legal claim to any of his effects; and thus I should see him, perhaps, in the arms of another wife in a few months, and be myself the most miserable creature alive.

My mother was as sensible of this as I; and, upon the whole, we knew not what to do. After some time we came to more sober resolutions, but then it was with this misfortune too, that my mother's opinion and mine were quite different from one another, and indeed inconsistent with one another; for my mother's opinion was, that I should bury the whole thing entirely, and continue to live with him as my husband till some other event should make the discovery of it more convenient; and that in the meantime she would endeavour to reconcile us together again, and restore our mutual comfort and family peace; that we might lie as we used to do together, and so let the whole matter remain a secret as close as death. 'For, child,' says she, 'we are both undone if it comes out.'

To encourage me to this, she promised to make me easy in my circumstances, as far as she was able, and to leave me what she could at her death, secured for me separately from my husband; so that if it should come out afterwards, I should not be left destitute, but be able to stand on my own feet and procure justice from him.

This proposal did not agree at all with my judgment of the thing, though it was very fair and kind in my mother; but my thoughts ran quite another way.

As to keeping the thing in our own breasts, and letting it all remain as it was, I told her it was impossible; and I asked her how she could think I could bear the thoughts of lying with my own brother. In the next place, I told her that her being alive was the only support of the discovery, and that while she owned me for her child, and saw reason to be satisfied that I was so, nobody else would doubt it; but that if she should die before the discovery, I should be taken for an impudent creature that had forged such a thing to go away from my husband, or should be counted crazed and distracted. Then I told her how he had threatened already to put me into a madhouse, and what concern I had been in about it, and how that was the thing that drove me to the necessity of discovering it to her as I had done.

From all which I told her, that I had, on the most serious reflections I was able to make in the case, come to this resolution, which I hoped she would like, as a medium between both, viz. that she should use her endeavours with her son to give me leave to go to England, as I had desired, and to furnish me with a sufficient sum of money, either in goods along with me, or in bills for my support there, all along suggesting that he might one time or other think it proper to come over to me.

That when I was gone, she should then, in cold blood, and after first obliging him in the solemnest manner possible to secrecy, discover the case to him, doing it gradually, and as her own discretion should guide her, so that he might not be surprised with it, and fly out into any passions and excesses on my account, or on hers; and that she should concern herself to prevent his slighting the children, or marrying again, unless he had a certain account of my being dead.

This was my scheme, and my reasons were good; I was really alienated from him in the consequences of these things; indeed, I mortally hated him as a husband, and it was impossible to remove that riveted aversion I had to him. At the same time, it being an unlawful, incestuous living, added to that aversion, and though I had no great concern about it in point of conscience, yet everything added to make cohabiting with him the most nauseous thing to me in the world; and I think verily it was come to such a height, that I could almost as willingly have embraced a dog as have let him offer anything of that kind to me, for which reason I could not bear the thoughts of coming between the sheets with him. I cannot say that I was right in point of policy in carrying it such a length, while at the same time I did not resolve to discover the thing to him; but I am giving an account of what was, not of what ought or ought not to be.

In their directly opposite opinion to one another my mother and I continued a long time, and it was impossible to reconcile our judgments; many disputes we had about it, but we could never either of us yield our own, or bring over the other.

I insisted on my aversion to lying with my own brother, and she insisted upon its being impossible to bring him to consent to my going from him to England; and in this uncertainty we continued, not differing so as to quarrel, or anything like it, but so as not to be able to resolve what we should do to make up that terrible breach that was before us.

At last I resolved on a desperate course, and told my mother my resolution, viz. that, in short, I would tell him of it myself. My mother was frighted to the last degree at the very thoughts of it; but I bid her be easy, told her I would do it gradually and softly, and with all the art and good-humour I was mistress of, and time it also as well as I could, taking him in good-humour too. I told her I did not question but, if I could be hypocrite enough to feign more affection to him than I really had, I should succeed in all my design, and we might part by consent, and with a good agreement, for I might live him well enough for a brother, though I could not for a husband.

All this while he lay at my mother to find out, if possible, what was the meaning of that dreadful expression of mine, as he called it, which I mentioned before: namely, that I was not his lawful wife, nor my children his legal children. My mother put him off, told him she could bring me to no explanations, but found there was something that disturbed me very much, and she hoped she should get it out of me in time, and in the meantime recommended to him earnestly to use me more tenderly, and win me with his usual good carriage; told him of his terrifying and affrighting me with his threats of sending me to a madhouse, and the like, and advised him not to make a woman desperate on any account whatever.

He promised her to soften his behaviour, and bid her assure me that he loved me as well as ever, and that he had so such design as that of sending me to a madhouse, whatever he might say in his passion; also he desired my mother to use the same persuasions to me too, that our affections might be renewed, and we might lie together in a good understanding as we used to do.

I found the effects of this treaty presently. My husband's conduct was immediately altered, and he was quite another man to me; nothing could be kinder and more obliging than he was to me upon all occasions; and I could do no less than make some return to it, which I did as well as I could, but it was but in an awkward manner at best, for nothing was more frightful to me than his caresses, and the apprehensions of being with child again by him was ready to throw me into fits; and this made me see that there was an absolute necessity of breaking the case to him without any more delay, which, however, I did with all the caution and reserve imaginable.

He had continued his altered carriage to me near a month, and we began to live a new kind of life with one another; and could I have satisfied myself to have gone on with it, I believe it might have continued as long as we had continued alive together. One evening, as we were sitting and talking very friendly together under a little awning, which served as an arbour at the entrance from our house into the garden, he was in a very pleasant, agreeable humour, and said abundance of kind things to me relating to the pleasure of our present good agreement, and the disorders of our past breach, and what a satisfaction it was to him that we had room to hope we should never have any more of it.

I fetched a deep sigh, and told him there was nobody in the world could be more delighted than I was in the good agreement we had always kept up, or more afflicted with the breach of it, and should be so still; but I was sorry to tell him that there was an unhappy circumstance in our case, which lay too close to my heart, and which I knew not how to break to him, that rendered my part of it very miserable, and took from me all the comfort of the rest.

He importuned me to tell him what it was. I told him I could not tell how to do it; that while it was concealed from him I alone was unhappy, but if he knew it also, we should be both so; and that, therefore, to keep him in the dark about it was the kindest thing that I could do, and it was on that account alone that I kept a secret from him, the very keeping of which, I thought, would first or last be my destruction.

It is impossible to express his surprise at this relation, and the double importunity which he used with me to discover it to him. He told me I could not be called kind to him, nay, I could not be faithful to him if I concealed it from him. I told him I thought so too, and yet I could not do it. He went back to what I had said before to him, and told me he hoped it did not relate to what I had said in my passion, and that he had resolved to forget all that as the effect of a rash, provoked spirit. I told him I wished I could forget it all too, but that it was not to be done, the impression was too deep, and I could not do it: it was impossible.

He then told me he was resolved not to differ with me in anything, and that therefore he would importune me no more about it, resolving to acquiesce in whatever I did or said; only begged I should then agree, that whatever it was, it should no more interrupt our quiet and our mutual kindness.

This was the most provoking thing he could have said to me, for I really wanted his further importunities, that I might be prevailed with to bring out that which indeed it was like death to me to conceal; so I answered him plainly that I could not say I was glad not to be importuned, thought I could not tell how to comply. 'But come, my dear,' said I, 'what conditions will you make with me upon the opening this affair to you?'

'Any conditions in the world,' said he, 'that you can in reason desire of me.' 'Well,' said I, 'come, give it me under your hand, that if you do not find I am in any fault, or that I am willingly concerned in the causes of the misfortune that is to follow, you will not blame me, use me the worse, do my any injury, or make me be the sufferer for that which is not my fault.'

'That,' says he, 'is the most reasonable demand in the world: not to blame you for that which is not your fault. Give me a pen and ink,' says he; so I ran in and fetched a pen, ink, and paper, and he wrote the condition down in the very words I had proposed it, and signed it with his name. 'Well,' says he, 'what is next, my dear?'

'Why,' says I, 'the next is, that you will not blame me for not discovering the secret of it to you before I knew it.'

'Very just again,' says he; 'with all my heart'; so he wrote down that also, and signed it.

'Well, my dear,' says I, 'then I have but one condition more to make with you, and that is, that as there is nobody concerned in it but you and I, you shall not discover it to any person in the world, except your own mother; and that in all the measures you shall take upon the discovery, as I am equally concerned in it with you, though as innocent as yourself, you shall do nothing in a passion, nothing to my prejudice or to your mother's prejudice, without my knowledge and consent.'

This a little amazed him, and he wrote down the words distinctly, but read them over and over before he signed them, hesitating at them several times, and repeating them: 'My mother's prejudice! and your prejudice! What mysterious thing can this be?' However, at last he signed it.

'Well, says I, 'my dear, I'll ask you no more under your hand; but as you are to hear the most unexpected and surprising thing that perhaps ever befell any family in the world, I beg you to promise me you will receive it with composure and a presence of mind suitable to a man of sense.'

'I'll do my utmost,' says he, 'upon condition you will keep me no longer in suspense, for you terrify me with all these preliminaries.'

'Well, then,' says I, 'it is this: as I told you before in a heat, that I was not your lawful wife, and that our children were not legal children, so I must let you know now in calmness and in kindness, but with affliction enough, that I am your own sister, and you my own brother, and that we are both the children of our mother now alive, and in the house, who is convinced of the truth of it, in a manner not to be denied or contradicted.'

I saw him turn pale and look wild; and I said, 'Now remember your promise, and receive it with presence of mind; for who could have said more to prepare you for it than I have done?' However, I called a servant, and got him a little glass of rum (which is the usual dram of that country), for he was just fainting away. When he was a little recovered, I said to him, 'This story, you may be sure, requires a long explanation, and therefore, have patience and compose your mind to hear it out, and I'll make it as short as I can'; and with this, I told him what I thought was needful of the fact, and particularly how my mother came to discover it to me, as above. 'And now, my dear,' says I, 'you will see reason for my capitulations, and that I neither have been the cause of this matter, nor could be so, and that I could know nothing of it before now.'

'I am fully satisfied of that,' says he, 'but 'tis a dreadful surprise to me; however, I know a remedy for it all, and a remedy that shall put an end to your difficulties, without your going to England.' 'That would be strange,' said I, 'as all the rest.' 'No, no,' says he, 'I'll make it easy; there's nobody in the way of it but myself.' He looked a little disordered when he said this, but I did not apprehend anything from it at that time, believing, as it used to be said, that they who do those things never talk of them, or that they who talk of such things never do them.

But things were not come to their height with him, and I observed he became pensive and melancholy; and in a word, as I thought, a little distempered in his head. I endeavoured to talk him into temper, and to reason him into a kind of scheme for our government in the affair, and sometimes he would be well, and talk with some courage about it; but the weight of it lay too heavy upon his thoughts, and, in short, it went so far that he made attempts upon himself, and in one of them had actually strangled himself and had not his mother come into the room in the very moment, he had died; but with the help of a Negro servant she cut him down and recovered him.

Things were now come to a lamentable height in the family. My pity for him now began to revive that affection which at first I really had for him, and I endeavoured sincerely, by all the kind carriage I could, to make up the breach; but, in short, it had gotten too great a head, it preyed upon his spirits, and it threw him into a long, lingering consumption, though it happened not to be mortal. In this distress I did not know what to do, as his life was apparently declining, and I might perhaps have married again there, very much to my advantage; it had been certainly my business to have stayed in the country, but my mind was restless too, and uneasy; I hankered after coming to England, and nothing would satisfy me without it.

In short, by an unwearied importunity, my husband, who was apparently decaying, as I observed, was at last prevailed with; and so my own fate pushing me on, the way was made clear for me, and my mother concurring, I obtained a very good cargo for my coming to England.

When I parted with my brother (for such I am now to call him), we agreed that after I arrived he should pretend to have an account that I was dead in England, and so might marry again when he would. He promised, and engaged to me to correspond with me as a sister, and to assist and support me as long as I lived; and that if he died before me, he would leave sufficient to his mother to take care of me still, in the name of a sister, and he was in some respects careful of me, when he heard of me; but it was so oddly managed that I felt the disappointments very sensibly afterwards, as you shall hear in its time.

I came away for England in the month of August, after I had been eight years in that country; and now a new scene of misfortunes attended me, which perhaps few women have gone through the life of.

We had an indifferent good voyage till we came just upon the coast of England, and where we arrived in two-and-thirty days, but were then ruffled with two or three storms, one of which drove us away to the coast of Ireland, and we put in at Kinsdale. We remained there about thirteen days, got some refreshment on shore, and put to sea again, though we met with very bad weather again, in which the ship sprung her mainmast, as they called it, for I knew not what they meant. But we got at last into Milford Haven, in Wales, where, though it was remote from our port, yet having my foot safe upon the firm ground of my native country, the isle of Britain, I resolved to venture it no more upon the waters, which had been so terrible to me; so getting my clothes and money on shore, with my bills of loading and other papers, I resolved to come for London, and leave the ship to get to her port as she could; the port whither she was bound was to Bristol, where my brother's chief correspondent lived.

I got to London in about three weeks, where I heard a little while after that the ship was arrived in Bristol, but at the same time had the misfortune to know that by the violent weather she had been in, and the breaking of her mainmast, she had great damage on board, and that a great part of her cargo was spoiled.

I had now a new scene of life upon my hands, and a dreadful appearance it had. I was come away with a kind of final farewell. What I brought with me was indeed considerable, had it come safe, and by the help of it, I might have married again tolerably well; but as it was, I was reduced to between two or three hundred pounds in the whole, and this without any hope of recruit. I was entirely without friends, nay, even so much as without acquaintance, for I found it was absolutely necessary not to revive former acquaintances; and as for my subtle friend that set me up formerly for a fortune, she was dead, and her husband also; as I was informed, upon sending a person unknown to inquire.

The looking after my cargo of goods soon after obliged me to take a journey to Bristol, and during my attendance upon that affair I took the diversion of going to the Bath, for as I was still far from being old, so my humour, which was always gay, continued so to an extreme; and being now, as it were, a woman of fortune though I was a woman without a fortune, I expected something or other might happen in my way that might mend my circumstances, as had been my case before.

The Bath is a place of gallantry enough; expensive, and full of snares. I went thither, indeed, in the view of taking anything that might offer, but I must do myself justice, as to protest I knew nothing amiss; I meant nothing but in an honest way, nor had I any thoughts about me at first that looked the way which afterwards I suffered them to be guided.

Here I stayed the whole latter season, as it is called there, and contracted some unhappy acquaintances, which rather prompted the follies I fell afterwards into than fortified me against them. I lived pleasantly enough, kept good company, that is to say, gay, fine company; but had the discouragement to find this way of living sunk me exceedingly, and that as I had no settled income, so spending upon the main stock was but a certain kind of bleeding to death; and this gave me many sad reflections in the interval of my other thoughts. However, I shook them off, and still flattered myself that something or other might offer for my advantage.

But I was in the wrong place for it. I was not now at Redriff, where, if I had set myself tolerably up, some honest sea captain or other might have talked with me upon the honourable terms of matrimony; but I was at the Bath, where men find a mistress sometimes, but very rarely look for a wife; and consequently all the particular acquaintances a woman can expect to make there must have some tendency that way.

I had spent the first season well enough; for though I had contracted some acquaintance with a gentleman who came to the Bath for his diversion, yet I had entered into no felonious treaty, as it might be called. I had resisted some casual offers of gallantry, and had managed that way well enough. I was not wicked enough to come into the crime for the mere vice of it, and I had no extraordinary offers made me that tempted me with the main thing which I wanted.

However, I went this length the first season, viz. I contracted an acquaintance with a woman in whose house I lodged, who, though she did not keep an ill house, as we call it, yet had none of the best principles in herself. I had on all occasions behaved myself so well as not to get the least slur upon my reputation on any account whatever, and all the men that I had conversed with were of so good reputation that I had not given the least reflection by conversing with them; nor did any of them seem to think there was room for a wicked correspondence, if they had any of them offered it; yet there was one gentleman, as above, who always singled me out for the diversion of my company, as he called it, which, as he was pleased to say, was very agreeable to him, but at that time there was no more in it.

I had many melancholy hours at the Bath after the company was gone; for though I went to Bristol sometime for the disposing my effects, and for recruits of money, yet I chose to come back to Bath for my residence, because being on good terms with the woman in whose house I lodged in the summer, I found that during the winter I lived rather cheaper there than I could do anywhere else. Here, I say, I passed the winter as heavily as I had passed the autumn cheerfully; but having contracted a nearer intimacy with the said woman in whose house I lodged, I could not avoid communicating to her something of what lay hardest upon my mind and particularly the narrowness of my circumstances, and the loss of my fortune by the damage of my goods at sea. I told her also, that I had a mother and a brother in Virginia in good circumstances; and as I had really written back to my mother in particular to represent my condition, and the great loss I had received, which indeed came to almost £500, so I did not fail to let my new friend know that I expected a supply from thence, and so indeed I did; and as the ships went from Bristol to York River, in Virginia, and back again generally in less time from London, and that my brother corresponded chiefly at Bristol, I thought it was much better for me to wait here for my returns than to go to London, where also I had not the least acquaintance.

My new friend appeared sensibly affected with my condition, and indeed was so very kind as to reduce the rate of my living with her to so low a price during the winter, that she convinced me she got nothing by me; and as for lodging, during the winter I paid nothing at all.

When the spring season came on, she continued to be as kind to me as she could, and I lodged with her for a time, till it was found necessary to do otherwise. She had some persons of character that frequently lodged in her house, and in particular the gentleman who, as I said, singled me out for his companion the winter before; and he came down again with another gentleman in his company and two servants, and lodged in the same house. I suspected that my landlady had invited him thither, letting him know that I was still with her; but she denied it, and protested to me that she did not, and he said the same.

In a word, this gentleman came down and continued to single me out for his peculiar confidence as well as conversation. He was a complete gentleman, that must be confessed, and his company was very agreeable to me, as mine, if I might believe him, was to him. He made no professions to be but of an extraordinary respect, and he had such an opinion of my virtue, that, as he often professed, he believed if he should offer anything else, I should reject him with contempt. He soon understood from me that I was a widow; that I had arrived at Bristol from Virginia by the last ships; and that I waited at Bath till the next Virginia fleet should arrive, by which I expected considerable effects. I understood by him, and by others of him, that he had a wife, but that the lady was distempered in her head, and was under the conduct of her own relations, which he consented to, to avoid any reflections that might (as was not unusual in such cases) be cast on him for mismanaging her cure; and in the meantime he came to the Bath to divert his thoughts from the disturbance of such a melancholy circumstance as that was.

My landlady, who of her own accord encouraged the correspondence on all occasions, gave me an advantageous character of him, as a man of honour and of virtue, as well as of great estate. And indeed I had a great deal of reason to say so of him too; for though we lodged both on a floor, and he had frequently come into my chamber, even when I was in bed, and I also into his when he was in bed, yet he never offered anything to me further than a kiss, or so much as solicited me to anything till long after, as you shall hear.

I frequently took notice to my landlady of his exceeding modesty, and she again used to tell me, she believed it was so from the beginning; however, she used to tell me that she thought I ought to expect some gratification from him for my company, for indeed he did, as it were, engross me, and I was seldom from him. I told her I had not given him the least occasion to think I wanted it, or that I would accept of it from him. She told me she would take that part upon her, and she did so, and managed it so dexterously, that the first time we were together alone, after she had talked with him, he began to inquire a little into my circumstances, as how I had subsisted myself since I came on shore, and whether I did not want money. I stood off very boldly. I told him that though my cargo of tobacco was damaged, yet that it was not quite lost; that the merchant I had been consigned to had so honestly managed for me that I had not wanted, and that I hoped, with frugal management, I should make it hold out till more would come, which I expected by the next fleet; that in the meantime I had retrenched my expenses, and whereas I kept a maid last season, now I lived without; and whereas I had a chamber and a dining-room then on the first floor, as he knew, I now had but one room, two pair of stairs, and the like. 'But I live,' said I, 'as well satisfied now as I did then'; adding, that his company had been a means to make me live much more cheerfully than otherwise I should have done, for which I was much obliged to him; and so I put off all room for any offer for the present. However, it was not long before he attacked me again, and told me he found that I was backward to trust him with the secret of my circumstances, which he was sorry for; assuring me that he inquired into it with no design to satisfy his own curiosity, but merely to assist me, if there was any occasion; but since I would not own myself to stand in need of any assistance, he had but one thing more to desire of me, and that was, that I would promise him that when I was any way straitened, or like to be so, I would frankly tell him of it, and that I would make use of him with the same freedom that he made the offer; adding, that I should always find I had a true friend, though perhaps I was afraid to trust him.

I omitted nothing that was fit to be said by one infinitely obliged, to let him know that I had a due sense of his kindness; and indeed from that time I did not appear so much reserved to him as I had done before, though still within the bounds of the strictest virtue on both sides; but how free soever our conversation was, I could not arrive to that sort of freedom which he desired, viz. to tell him I wanted money, though I was secretly very glad of his offer.

Some weeks passed after this, and still I never asked him for money; when my landlady, a cunning creature, who had often pressed me to it, but found that I could not do it, makes a story of her own inventing, and comes in bluntly to me when we were together. 'Oh, widow!' says she, 'I have bad news to tell you this morning.' 'What is that?' said I; 'are the Virginia ships taken by the French?'—for that was my fear. 'No, no,' says she, 'but the man you sent to Bristol yesterday for money is come back, and says he has brought none.'

Now I could by no means like her project; I though it looked too much like prompting him, which indeed he did not want, and I clearly saw that I should lose nothing by being backward to ask, so I took her up short. 'I can't image why he should say so to you,' said I, 'for I assure you he brought me all the money I sent him for, and here it is,' said I (pulling out my purse with about twelve guineas in it); and added, 'I intend you shall have most of it by and by.'

He seemed distasted a little at her talking as she did at first, as well as I, taking it, as I fancied he would, as something forward of her; but when he saw me give such an answer, he came immediately to himself again. The next morning we talked of it again, when I found he was fully satisfied, and, smiling, said he hoped I would not want money and not tell him of it, and that I had promised him otherwise. I told him I had been very much dissatisfied at my landlady's talking so publicly the day before of what she had nothing to do with; but I supposed she wanted what I owed her, which was about eight guineas, which I had resolved to give her, and had accordingly given it her the same night she talked so foolishly.

He was in a might good humour when he heard me say I had paid her, and it went off into some other discourse at that time. But the next morning, he having heard me up about my room before him, he called to me, and I answering, he asked me to come into his chamber. He was in bed when I came in, and he made me come and sit down on his bedside, for he said he had something to say to me which was of some moment. After some very kind expressions, he asked me if I would be very honest to him, and give a sincere answer to one thing he would desire of me. After some little cavil at the word 'sincere,' and asking him if I had ever given him any answers which were not sincere, I promised him I would. Why, then, his request was, he said, to let him see my purse. I immediately put my hand into my pocket, and, laughing to him, pulled it out, and there was in it three guineas and a half. Then he asked me if there was all the money I had. I told him No, laughing again, not by a great deal.

Well, then, he said, he would have me promise to go and fetch him all the money I had, every farthing. I told him I would, and I went into my chamber and fetched him a little private drawer, where I had about six guineas more, and some silver, and threw it all down upon the bed, and told him there was all my wealth, honestly to a shilling. He looked a little at it, but did not tell it, and huddled it all into the drawer again, and then reaching his pocket, pulled out a key, and bade me open a little walnut-tree box he had upon the table, and bring him such a drawer, which I did. In which drawer there was a great deal of money in gold, I believe near two hundred guineas, but I knew not how much. He took the drawer, and taking my hand, made me put it in and take a whole handful. I was backward at that, but he held my hand hard in his hand, and put it into the drawer, and made me take out as many guineas almost as I could well take up at once.

When I had done so, he made me put them into my lap, and took my little drawer, and poured out all my money among his, and bade me get me gone, and carry it all home into my own chamber.

I relate this story the more particularly because of the good-humour there was in it, and to show the temper with which we conversed. It was not long after this but he began every day to find fault with my clothes, with my laces and head-dresses, and, in a word, pressed me to buy better; which, by the way, I was willing enough to do, though I did not seem to be so, for I loved nothing in the world better than fine clothes. I told him I must housewife the money he had lent me, or else I should not be able to pay him again. He then told me, in a few words, that as he had a sincere respect for me, and knew my circumstances, he had not lent me that money, but given it me, and that he thought I had merited it from him by giving him my company so entirely as I had done. After this he made me take a maid, and keep house, and his friend that come with him to Bath being gone, he obliged me to diet him, which I did very willingly, believing, as it appeared, that I should lose nothing by it, nor did the woman of the house fail to find her account in it too.

We had lived thus near three months, when the company beginning to wear away at the Bath, he talked of going away, and fain he would have me to go to London with him. I was not very easy in that proposal, not knowing what posture I was to live in there, or how he might use me. But while this was in debate he fell very sick; he had gone out to a place in Somersetshire, called Shepton, where he had some business and was there taken very ill, and so ill that he could not travel; so he sent his man back to Bath, to beg me that I would hire a coach and come over to him. Before he went, he had left all his money and other things of value with me, and what to do with them I did not know, but I secured them as well as I could, and locked up the lodgings and went to him, where I found him very ill indeed; however, I persuaded him to be carried in a litter to the Bath, where there was more help and better advice to be had.

He consented, and I brought him to the Bath, which was about fifteen miles, as I remember. Here he continued very ill of a fever, and kept his bed five weeks, all which time I nursed him and tended him myself, as much and as carefully as if I had been his wife; indeed, if I had been his wife I could not have done more. I sat up with him so much and so often, that at last, indeed, he would not let me sit up any longer, and then I got a pallet-bed into his room, and lay in it just at his bed's feet.

I was indeed sensibly affected with his condition, and with the apprehension of losing such a friend as he was, and was like to be to me, and I used to sit and cry by him many hours together. However, at last he grew better, and gave hopes that he would recover, as indeed he did, though very slowly.

Were it otherwise than what I am going to say, I should not be backward to disclose it, as it is apparent I have done in other cases in this account; but I affirm, that through all this conversation, abating the freedom of coming into the chamber when I or he was in bed, and abating the necessary offices of attending him night and day when he was sick, there had not passed the least immodest word or action between us. Oh that it had been so to the last!

After some time he gathered strength and grew well apace, and I would have removed my pallet-bed, but he would not let me, till he was able to venture himself without anybody to sit up with him, and then I removed to my own chamber.

He took many occasions to express his sense of my tenderness and concern for him; and when he grew quite well, he made me a present of fifty guineas for my care and, as he called it, for hazarding my life to save his.

And now he made deep protestations of a sincere inviolable affection for me, but all along attested it to be with the utmost reserve for my virtue and his own. I told him I was fully satisfied of it. He carried it that length that he protested to me, that if he was naked in bed with me, he would as sacredly preserve my virtue as he would defend it if I was assaulted by a ravisher. I believed him, and told him I did so; but this did not satisfy him, he would, he said, wait for some opportunity to give me an undoubted testimony of it.

It was a great while after this that I had occasion, on my own business, to go to Bristol, upon which he hired me a coach, and would go with me, and did so; and now indeed our intimacy increased. From Bristol he carried me to Gloucester, which was merely a journey of pleasure, to take the air; and here it was our hap to have no lodging in the inn but in one large chamber with two beds in it. The master of the house going up with us to show his rooms, and coming into that room, said very frankly to him, 'Sir, it is none of my business to inquire whether the lady be your spouse or no, but if not, you may lie as honestly in these two beds as if you were in two chambers,' and with that he pulls a great curtain which drew quite across the room and effectually divided the beds. 'Well,' says my friend, very readily, 'these beds will do, and as for the rest, we are too near akin to lie together, though we may lodge near one another'; and this put an honest face on the thing too. When we came to go to bed, he decently went out of the room till I was in bed, and then went to bed in the bed on his own side of the room, but lay there talking to me a great while.

At last, repeating his usual saying, that he could lie naked in the bed with me and not offer me the least injury, he starts out of his bed. 'And now, my dear,' says he, 'you shall see how just I will be to you, and that I can keep my word,' and away he comes to my bed.

I resisted a little, but I must confess I should not have resisted him much if he had not made those promises at all; so after a little struggle, as I said, I lay still and let him come to bed. When he was there he took me in his arms, and so I lay all night with him, but he had no more to do with me, or offered anything to me, other than embracing me, as I say, in his arms, no, not the whole night, but rose up and dressed him in the morning, and left me as innocent for him as I was the day I was born.

This was a surprising thing to me, and perhaps may be so to others, who know how the laws of nature work; for he was a strong, vigorous, brisk person; nor did he act thus on a principle of religion at all, but of mere affection; insisting on it, that though I was to him to most agreeable woman in the world, yet, because he loved me, he could not injure me.

I own it was a noble principle, but as it was what I never understood before, so it was to me perfectly amazing. We traveled the rest of the journey as we did before, and came back to the Bath, where, as he had opportunity to come to me when he would, he often repeated the moderation, and I frequently lay with him, and he with me, and although all the familiarities between man and wife were common to us, yet he never once offered to go any farther, and he valued himself much upon it. I do not say that I was so wholly pleased with it as he thought I was, for I own much wickeder than he, as you shall hear presently.

We lived thus near two years, only with this exception, that he went three times to London in that time, and once he continued there four months; but, to do him justice, he always supplied me with money to subsist me very handsomely.

Had we continued thus, I confess we had had much to boast of; but as wise men say, it is ill venturing too near the brink of a command, so we found it; and here again I must do him the justice to own that the first breach was not on his part. It was one night that we were in bed together warm and merry, and having drunk, I think, a little more wine that night, both of us, than usual, although not in the least to disorder either of us, when, after some other follies which I cannot name, and being clasped close in his arms, I told him (I repeat it with shame and horror of soul) that I could find in my heart to discharge him of his engagement for one night and no more.

He took me at my word immediately, and after that there was no resisting him; neither indeed had I any mind to resist him any more, let what would come of it.

Thus the government of our virtue was broken, and I exchanged the place of friend for that unmusical, harsh-sounding title of whore. In the morning we were both at our penitentials; I cried very heartily, he expressed himself very sorry; but that was all either of us could do at that time, and the way being thus cleared, and the bars of virtue and conscience thus removed, we had the less difficult afterwards to struggle with.

It was but a dull kind of conversation that we had together for all the rest of that week; I looked on him with blushes, and every now and then started that melancholy objection, 'What if I should be with child now? What will become of me then?' He encouraged me by telling me, that as long as I was true to him, he would be so to me; and since it was gone such a length (which indeed he never intended), yet if I was with child, he would take care of that, and of me too. This hardened us both. I assured him if I was with child, I would die for want of a midwife rather than name him as the father of it; and he assured me I should never want if I should be with child. These mutual assurances hardened us in the thing, and after this we repeated the crime as often as we pleased, till at length, as I had feared, so it came to pass, and I was indeed with child.

After I was sure it was so, and I had satisfied him of it too, we began to think of taking measures for the managing it, and I proposed trusting the secret to my landlady, and asking her advice, which he agreed to. My landlady, a woman (as I found) used to such things, made light of it; she said she knew it would come to that at last, and made us very merry about it. As I said above, we found her an experienced old lady at such work; she undertook everything, engaged to procure a midwife and a nurse, to satisfy all inquiries, and bring us off with reputation, and she did so very dexterously indeed.

When I grew near my time she desired my gentleman to go away to London, or make as if he did so. When he was gone, she acquainted the parish officers that there was a lady ready to lie in at her house, but that she knew her husband very well, and gave them, as she pretended, an account of his name, which she called Sir Walter Cleve; telling them he was a very worthy gentleman, and that she would answer for all inquiries, and the like. This satisfied the parish officers presently, and I lay in with as much credit as I could have done if I had really been my Lady Cleve, and was assisted in my travail by three or four of the best citizens' wives of Bath who lived in the neighbourhood, which, however, made me a little the more expensive to him. I often expressed my concern to him about it, but he bid me not be concerned at it.

As he had furnished me very sufficiently with money for the extraordinary expenses of my lying in, I had everything very handsome about me, but did not affect to be gay or extravagant neither; besides, knowing my own circumstances, and knowing the world as I had done, and that such kind of things do not often last long, I took care to lay up as much money as I could for a wet day, as I called it; making him believe it was all spent upon the extraordinary appearance of things in my lying in.

By this means, and including what he had given me as above, I had at the end of my lying in about two hundred guineas by me, including also what was left of my own.

I was brought to bed of a fine boy indeed, and a charming child it was; and when he heard of it he wrote me a very kind, obliging letter about it, and then told me, he thought it would look better for me to come away for London as soon as I was up and well; that he had provided apartments for me at Hammersmith, as if I came thither only from London; and that after a little while I should go back to the Bath, and he would go with me.

I liked this offer very well, and accordingly hired a coach on purpose, and taking my child, and a wet-nurse to tend and suckle it, and a maid-servant with me, away I went for London.

He met me at Reading in his own chariot, and taking me into that, left the servant and the child in the hired coach, and so he brought me to my new lodgings at Hammersmith; with which I had abundance of reason to be very well pleased, for they were very handsome rooms, and I was very well accommodated.

And now I was indeed in the height of what I might call my prosperity, and I wanted nothing but to be a wife, which, however, could not be in this case, there was no room for it; and therefore on all occasions I studied to save what I could, as I have said above, against a time of scarcity, knowing well enough that such things as these do not always continue; that men that keep mistresses often change them, grow weary of them, or jealous of them, or something or other happens to make them withdraw their bounty; and sometimes the ladies that are thus well used are not careful by a prudent conduct to preserve the esteem of their persons, or the nice article of their fidelity, and then they are justly cast off with contempt.

But I was secured in this point, for as I had no inclination to change, so I had no manner of acquaintance in the whole house, and so no temptation to look any farther. I kept no company but in the family when I lodged, and with the clergyman's lady at next door; so that when he was absent I visited nobody, nor did he ever find me out of my chamber or parlour whenever he came down; if I went anywhere to take the air, it was always with him.

The living in this manner with him, and his with me, was certainly the most undesigned thing in the world; he often protested to me, that when he became first acquainted with me, and even to the very night when we first broke in upon our rules, he never had the least design of lying with me; that he always had a sincere affection for me, but not the least real inclination to do what he had done. I assured him I never suspected him; that if I had I should not so easily have yielded to the freedom which brought it on, but that it was all a surprise, and was owing to the accident of our having yielded too far to our mutual inclinations that night; and indeed I have often observed since, and leave it as a caution to the readers of this story, that we ought to be cautious of gratifying our inclinations in loose and lewd freedoms, lest we find our resolutions of virtue fail us in the junction when their assistance should be most necessary.

It is true, and I have confessed it before, that from the first hour I began to converse with him, I resolved to let him lie with me, if he offered it; but it was because I wanted his help and assistance, and I knew no other way of securing him than that. But when were that night together, and, as I have said, had gone such a length, I found my weakness; the inclination was not to be resisted, but I was obliged to yield up all even before he asked it.

However, he was so just to me that he never upbraided me with that; nor did he ever express the least dislike of my conduct on any other occasion, but always protested he was as much delighted with my company as he was the first hour we came together: I mean, came together as bedfellows.

It is true that he had no wife, that is to say, she was as no wife to him, and so I was in no danger that way, but the just reflections of conscience oftentimes snatch a man, especially a man of sense, from the arms of a mistress, as it did him at last, though on another occasion.

On the other hand, though I was not without secret reproaches of my own conscience for the life I led, and that even in the greatest height of the satisfaction I ever took, yet I had the terrible prospect of poverty and starving, which lay on me as a frightful spectre, so that there was no looking behind me. But as poverty brought me into it, so fear of poverty kept me in it, and I frequently resolved to leave it quite off, if I could but come to lay up money enough to maintain me. But these were thoughts of no weight, and whenever he came to me they vanished; for his company was so delightful, that there was no being melancholy when he was there; the reflections were all the subject of those hours when I was alone.

I lived six years in this happy but unhappy condition, in which time I brought him three children, but only the first of them lived; and though I removed twice in those six years, yet I came back the sixth year to my first lodgings at Hammersmith. Here it was that I was one morning surprised with a kind but melancholy letter from my gentleman, intimating that he was very ill, and was afraid he should have another fit of sickness, but that his wife's relations being in the house with him, it would not be practicable to have me with him, which, however, he expressed his great dissatisfaction in, and that he wished I could be allowed to tend and nurse him as I did before.

I was very much concerned at this account, and was very impatient to know how it was with him. I waited a fortnight or thereabouts, and heard nothing, which surprised me, and I began to be very uneasy indeed. I think, I may say, that for the next fortnight I was near to distracted. It was my particular difficulty that I did not know directly where he was; for I understood at first he was in the lodgings of his wife's mother; but having removed myself to London, I soon found, by the help of the direction I had for writing my letters to him, how to inquire after him, and there I found that he was at a house in Bloomsbury, whither he had, a little before he fell sick, removed his whole family; and that his wife and wife's mother were in the same house, though the wife was not suffered to know that she was in the same house with her husband.

Here I also soon understood that he was at the last extremity, which made me almost at the last extremity too, to have a true account. One night I had the curiosity to disguise myself like a servant-maid, in a round cap and straw hat, and went to the door, as sent by a lady of his neighbourhood, where he lived before, and giving master and mistress's service, I said I was sent to know how Mr. —— did, and how he had rested that night. In delivering this message I got the opportunity I desired; for, speaking with one of the maids, I held a long gossip's tale with her, and had all the particulars of his illness, which I found was a pleurisy, attended with a cough and a fever. She told me also who was in the house, and how his wife was, who, by her relation, they were in some hopes might recover her understanding; but as to the gentleman himself, in short she told me the doctors said there was very little hopes of him, that in the morning they thought he had been dying, and that he was but little better then, for they did not expect that he could live over the next night.

This was heavy news for me, and I began now to see an end of my prosperity, and to see also that it was very well I had played to good housewife, and secured or saved something while he was alive, for that now I had no view of my own living before me.

It lay very heavy upon my mind, too, that I had a son, a fine lovely boy, about five years old, and no provision made for it, at least that I knew of. With these considerations, and a sad heart, I went home that evening, and began to cast with myself how I should live, and in what manner to bestow myself, for the residue of my life.

You may be sure I could not rest without inquiring again very quickly what was become of him; and not venturing to go myself, I sent several sham messengers, till after a fortnight's waiting longer, I found that there was hopes of his life, though he was still very ill; then I abated my sending any more to the house, and in some time after I learned in the neighbourhood that he was about house, and then that he was abroad again.

I made no doubt then but that I should soon hear of him, and began to comfort myself with my circumstances being, as I thought, recovered. I waited a week, and two weeks, and with much surprise and amazement I waited near two months and heard nothing, but that, being recovered, he was gone into the country for the air, and for the better recovery after his distemper. After this it was yet two months more, and then I understood he was come to his city house again, but still I heard nothing from him.

I had written several letters for him, and directed them as usual, and found two or three of them had been called for, but not the rest. I wrote again in a more pressing manner than ever, and in one of them let him know, that I must be forced to wait on him myself, representing my circumstances, the rent of lodgings to pay, and the provision for the child wanting, and my own deplorable condition, destitute of subsistence for his most solemn engagement to take care of and provide for me. I took a copy of this letter, and finding it lay at the house near a month and was not called for, I found means to have the copy of it put into his own hands at a coffee-house, where I had by inquiry found he used to go.

This letter forced an answer from him, by which, though I found I was to be abandoned, yet I found he had sent a letter to me some time before, desiring me to go down to the Bath again. Its contents I shall come to presently.

It is true that sick-beds are the time when such correspondences as this are looked on with different countenances, and seen with other eyes than we saw them with, or than they appeared with before. My lover had been at the gates of death, and at the very brink of eternity; and, it seems, had been struck with a due remorse, and with sad reflections upon his past life of gallantry and levity; and among the rest, criminal correspondence with me, which was neither more nor less than a long-continued life of adultery, and represented itself as it really was, not as it had been formerly thought by him to be, and he looked upon it now with a just and religious abhorrence.

I cannot but observe also, and leave it for the direction of my sex in such cases of pleasure, that whenever sincere repentance succeeds such a crime as this, there never fails to attend a hatred of the object; and the more the affection might seem to be before, the hatred will be the more in proportion. It will always be so, indeed it can be no otherwise; for there cannot be a true and sincere abhorrence of the offence, and the love to the cause of it remain; there will, with an abhorrence of the sin, be found a detestation of the fellow-sinner; you can expect no other.

I found it so here, though good manners and justice in this gentleman kept him from carrying it on to any extreme but the short history of his part in this affair was thus: he perceived by my last letter, and by all the rest, which he went for after, that I was not gone to Bath, that his first letter had not come to my hand; upon which he write me this following:—

'MADAM,—I am surprised that my letter, dated the 8th of last month, did not come to your hand; I give you my word it was delivered at your lodgings, and to the hands of your maid.

'I need not acquaint you with what has been my condition for some time past; and how, having been at the edge of the grave, I am, by the unexpected and undeserved mercy of Heaven, restored again. In the condition I have been in, it cannot be strange to you that our unhappy correspondence had not been the least of the burthens which lay upon my conscience. I need say no more; those things that must be repented of, must be also reformed.

I wish you would think of going back to the Bath. I enclose you here a bill for £50 for clearing yourself at your lodgings, and carrying you down, and hope it will be no surprise to you to add, that on this account only, and not for any offence given me on your side, I can see you no more. I will take due care of the child; leave him where he is, or take him with you, as you please. I wish you the like reflections, and that they may be to your advantage.—I am,' etc.

I was struck with this letter as with a thousand wounds, such as I cannot describe; the reproaches of my own conscience were such as I cannot express, for I was not blind to my own crime; and I reflected that I might with less offence have continued with my brother, and lived with him as a wife, since there was no crime in our marriage on that score, neither of us knowing it.

But I never once reflected that I was all this while a married woman, a wife to Mr. —— the linen-draper, who, though he had left me by the necessity of his circumstances, had no power to discharge me from the marriage contract which was between us, or to give me a legal liberty to marry again; so that I had been no less than a whore and an adulteress all this while. I then reproached myself with the liberties I had taken, and how I had been a snare to this gentleman, and that indeed I was principal in the crime; that now he was mercifully snatched out of the gulf by a convincing work upon his mind, but that I was left as if I was forsaken of God's grace, and abandoned by Heaven to a continuing in my wickedness.

Under these reflections I continued very pensive and sad for near month, and did not go down to the Bath, having no inclination to be with the woman whom I was with before; lest, as I thought, she should prompt me to some wicked course of life again, as she had done; and besides, I was very loth she should know I was cast off as above.

And now I was greatly perplexed about my little boy. It was death to me to part with the child, and yet when I considered the danger of being one time or other left with him to keep without a maintenance to support him, I then resolved to leave him where he was; but then I concluded also to be near him myself too, that I then might have the satisfaction of seeing him, without the care of providing for him.

I sent my gentleman a short letter, therefore, that I had obeyed his orders in all things but that of going back to the Bath, which I could not think of for many reasons; that however parting from him was a wound to me that I could never recover, yet that I was fully satisfied his reflections were just, and would be very far from desiring to obstruct his reformation or repentance.

Then I represented my own circumstances to him in the most moving terms that I was able. I told him that those unhappy distresses which first moved him to a generous and an honest friendship for me, would, I hope, move him to a little concern for me now, though the criminal part of our correspondence, which I believed neither of us intended to fall into at the time, was broken off; that I desired to repent as sincerely as he had done, but entreated him to put me in some condition that I might not be exposed to the temptations which the devil never fails to excite us to from the frightful prospect of poverty and distress; and if he had the least apprehensions of my being troublesome to him, I begged he would put me in a posture to go back to my mother in Virginia, from when he knew I came, and that would put an end to all his fears on that account. I concluded, that if he would send me £50 more to facilitate my going away, I would send him back a general release, and would promise never to disturb him more with any importunities; unless it was to hear of the well-doing of the child, whom, if I found my mother living and my circumstances able, I would send for to come over to me, and take him also effectually off his hands.

This was indeed all a cheat thus far, viz. that I had no intention to go to Virginia, as the account of my former affairs there may convince anybody of; but the business was to get this last £50 of him, if possible, knowing well enough it would be the last penny I was ever to expect.

However, the argument I used, namely, of giving him a general release, and never troubling him any more, prevailed effectually with him, and he sent me a bill for the money by a person who brought with him a general release for me to sign, and which I frankly signed, and received the money; and thus, though full sore against my will, a final end was put to this affair.

And here I cannot but reflect upon the unhappy consequence of too great freedoms between persons stated as we were, upon the pretence of innocent intentions, love of friendship, and the like; for the flesh has generally so great a share in those friendships, that is great odds but inclination prevails at last over the most solemn resolutions; and that vice breaks in at the breaches of decency, which really innocent friendship ought to preserve with the greatest strictness. But I leave the readers of these things to their own just reflections, which they will be more able to make effectual than I, who so soon forgot myself, and am therefore but a very indifferent monitor.

I was now a single person again, as I may call myself; I was loosed from all the obligations either of wedlock or mistress-ship in the world, except my husband the linen-draper, whom, I having not now heard from in almost fifteen years, nobody could blame me for thinking myself entirely freed from; seeing also he had at his going away told me, that if I did not hear frequently from him, I should conclude he was dead, and I might freely marry again to whom I pleased.

I now began to cast up my accounts. I had by many letters and much importunity, and with the intercession of my mother too, had a second return of some goods from my brother (as I now call him) in Virginia, to make up the damage of the cargo I brought away with me, and this too was upon the condition of my sealing a general release to him, and to send it him by his correspondent at Bristol, which, though I thought hard of, yet I was obliged to promise to do. However, I managed so well in this case, that I got my goods away before the release was signed, and then I always found something or other to say to evade the thing, and to put off the signing it at all; till at length I pretended I must write to my brother, and have his answer, before I could do it.

Including this recruit, and before I got the last £50, I found my strength to amount, put all together, to about £400, so that with that I had about £450. I had saved above £100 more, but I met with a disaster with that, which was this—that a goldsmith in whose hands I had trusted it, broke, so I lost £70 of my money, the man's composition not making above £30 out of his £100. I had a little plate, but not much, and was well enough stocked with clothes and linen.

With this stock I had the world to begin again; but you are to consider that I was not now the same woman as when I lived at Redriff; for, first of all, I was near twenty years older, and did not look the better for my age, nor for my rambles to Virginia and back again; and though I omitted nothing that might set me out to advantage, except painting, for that I never stooped to, and had pride enough to think I did not want it, yet there would always be some difference seen between five-and-twenty and two-and-forty.

I cast about innumerable ways for my future state of life, and began to consider very seriously what I should do, but nothing offered. I took care to make the world take me for something more than I was, and had it given out that I was a fortune, and that my estate was in my own hands; the last of which was very true, the first of it was as above. I had no acquaintance, which was one of my worst misfortunes, and the consequence of that was, I had no adviser, at least who could assist and advise together; and above all, I had nobody to whom I could in confidence commit the secret of my circumstances to, and could depend upon for their secrecy and fidelity; and I found by experience, that to be friendless is the worst condition, next to being in want that a woman can be reduced to: I say a woman, because 'tis evident men can be their own advisers, and their own directors, and know how to work themselves out of difficulties and into business better than women; but if a woman has no friend to communicate her affairs to, and to advise and assist her, 'tis ten to one but she is undone; nay, and the more money she has, the more danger she is in of being wronged and deceived; and this was my case in the affair of the £100 which I left in the hands of the goldsmith, as above, whose credit, it seems, was upon the ebb before, but I, that had no knowledge of things and nobody to consult with, knew nothing of it, and so lost my money.

In the next place, when a woman is thus left desolate and void of counsel, she is just like a bag of money or a jewel dropped on the highway, which is a prey to the next comer; if a man of virtue and upright principles happens to find it, he will have it cried, and the owner may come to hear of it again; but how many times shall such a thing fall into hands that will make no scruple of seizing it for their own, to once that it shall come into good hands?

This was evidently my case, for I was now a loose, unguided creature, and had no help, no assistance, no guide for my conduct; I knew what I aimed at and what I wanted, but knew nothing how to pursue the end by direct means. I wanted to be placed in a settle state of living, and had I happened to meet with a sober, good husband, I should have been as faithful and true a wife to him as virtue itself could have formed. If I had been otherwise, the vice came in always at the door of necessity, not at the door of inclination; and I understood too well, by the want of it, what the value of a settled life was, to do anything to forfeit the felicity of it; nay, I should have made the better wife for all the difficulties I had passed through, by a great deal; nor did I in any of the time that I had been a wife give my husbands the least uneasiness on account of my behaviour.

But all this was nothing; I found no encouraging prospect. I waited; I lived regularly, and with as much frugality as became my circumstances, but nothing offered, nothing presented, and the main stock wasted apace. What to do I knew not; the terror of approaching poverty lay hard upon my spirits. I had some money, but where to place it I knew not, nor would the interest of it maintain me, at least not in London.

At length a new scene opened. There was in the house where I lodged a north-country woman that went for a gentlewoman, and nothing was more frequent in her discourse than her account of the cheapness of provisions, and the easy way of living in her country; how plentiful and how cheap everything was, what good company they kept, and the like; till at last I told her she almost tempted me to go and live in her country; for I that was a widow, though I had sufficient to live on, yet had no way of increasing it; and that I found I could not live here under £100 a year, unless I kept no company, no servant, made no appearance, and buried myself in privacy, as if I was obliged to it by necessity.

I should have observed, that she was always made to believe, as everybody else was, that I was a great fortune, or at least that I had three or four thousand pounds, if not more, and all in my own hands; and she was mighty sweet upon me when she thought me inclined in the least to go into her country. She said she had a sister lived near Liverpool, that her brother was a considerable gentleman there, and had a great estate also in Ireland; that she would go down there in about two months, and if I would give her my company thither, I should be as welcome as herself for a month or more as I pleased, till I should see how I liked the country; and if I thought fit to live there, she would undertake they would take care, though they did not entertain lodgers themselves, they would recommend me to some agreeable family, where I should be placed to my content.

If this woman had known my real circumstances, she would never have laid so many snares, and taken so many weary steps to catch a poor desolate creature that was good for little when it was caught; and indeed I, whose case was almost desperate, and thought I could not be much worse, was not very anxious about what might befall me, provided they did me no personal injury; so I suffered myself, though not without a great deal of invitation and great professions of sincere friendship and real kindness—I say, I suffered myself to be prevailed upon to go with her, and accordingly I packed up my baggage, and put myself in a posture for a journey, though I did not absolutely know whither I was to go.

And now I found myself in great distress; what little I had in the world was all in money, except as before, a little plate, some linen, and my clothes; as for my household stuff, I had little or none, for I had lived always in lodgings; but I had not one friend in the world with whom to trust that little I had, or to direct me how to dispose of it, and this perplexed me night and day. I thought of the bank, and of the other companies in London, but I had no friend to commit the management of it to, and keep and carry about with me bank bills, tallies, orders, and such things, I looked upon at as unsafe; that if they were lost, my money was lost, and then I was undone; and, on the other hand, I might be robbed and perhaps murdered in a strange place for them. This perplexed me strangely, and what to do I knew not.

It came in my thoughts one morning that I would go to the bank myself, where I had often been to receive the interest of some bills I had, which had interest payable on them, and where I had found a clerk, to whom I applied myself, very honest and just to me, and particularly so fair one time that when I had mistold my money, and taken less than my due, and was coming away, he set me to rights and gave me the rest, which he might have put into his own pocket.

I went to him and represented my case very plainly, and asked if he would trouble himself to be my adviser, who was a poor friendless widow, and knew not what to do. He told me, if I desired his opinion of anything within the reach of his business, he would do his endeavour that I should not be wronged, but that he would also help me to a good sober person who was a grave man of his acquaintance, who was a clerk in such business too, though not in their house, whose judgment was good, and whose honesty I might depend upon. 'For,' added he, 'I will answer for him, and for every step he takes; if he wrongs you, madam, of one farthing, it shall lie at my door, I will make it good; and he delights to assist people in such cases—he does it as an act of charity.'

I was a little at a stand in this discourse; but after some pause I told him I had rather have depended upon him, because I had found him honest, but if that could not be, I would take his recommendation sooner than any one's else. 'I dare say, madam,' says he, 'that you will be as well satisfied with my friend as with me, and he is thoroughly able to assist you, which I am not.' It seems he had his hands full of the business of the bank, and had engaged to meddle with no other business that that of his office, which I heard afterwards, but did not understand then. He added, that his friend should take nothing of me for his advice or assistance, and this indeed encouraged me very much.

He appointed the same evening, after the bank was shut and business over, for me to meet him and his friend. And indeed as soon as I saw his friend, and he began but to talk of the affair, I was fully satisfied that I had a very honest man to deal with; his countenance spoke it, and his character, as I heard afterwards, was everywhere so good, that I had no room for any more doubts upon me.

After the first meeting, in which I only said what I had said before, we parted, and he appointed me to come the next day to him, telling me I might in the meantime satisfy myself of him by inquiry, which, however, I knew not how well to do, having no acquaintance myself.

Accordingly I met him the next day, when I entered more freely with him into my case. I told him my circumstances at large: that I was a widow come over from America, perfectly desolate and friendless; that I had a little money, and but a little, and was almost distracted for fear of losing it, having no friend in the world to trust with the management of it; that I was going into the north of England to live cheap, that my stock might not waste; that I would willingly lodge my money in the bank, but that I durst not carry the bills about me, and the like, as above; and how to correspond about it, or with whom, I knew not.

He told me I might lodge the money in the bank as an account, and its being entered into the books would entitle me to the money at any time, and if I was in the north I might draw bills on the cashier and receive it when I would; but that then it would be esteemed as running cash, and the bank would give no interest for it; that I might buy stock with it, and so it would lie in store for me, but that then if I wanted to dispose if it, I must come up to town on purpose to transfer it, and even it would be with some difficulty I should receive the half-yearly dividend, unless I was here in person, or had some friend I could trust with having the stock in his name to do it for me, and that would have the same difficulty in it as before; and with that he looked hard at me and smiled a little. At last, says he, 'Why do you not get a head steward, madam, that may take you and your money together into keeping, and then you would have the trouble taken off your hands?' 'Ay, sir, and the money too, it may be,' said I; 'for truly I find the hazard that way is as much as 'tis t'other way'; but I remember I said secretly to myself, 'I wish you would ask me the question fairly, I would consider very seriously on it before I said No.'

He went on a good way with me, and I thought once or twice he was in earnest, but to my real affliction, I found at last he had a wife; but when he owned he had a wife he shook his head, and said with some concern, that indeed he had a wife, and no wife. I began to think he had been in the condition of my late lover, and that his wife had been distempered or lunatic, or some such thing. However, we had not much more discourse at that time, but he told me he was in too much hurry of business then, but that if I would come home to his house after their business was over, he would by that time consider what might be done for me, to put my affairs in a posture of security. I told him I would come, and desired to know where he lived. He gave me a direction in writing, and when he gave it me he read it to me, and said, 'There 'tis, madam, if you dare trust yourself with me.' 'Yes, sir,' said I, 'I believe I may venture to trust you with myself, for you have a wife, you say, and I don't want a husband; besides, I dare trust you with my money, which is all I have in the world, and if that were gone, I may trust myself anywhere.'

He said some things in jest that were very handsome and mannerly, and would have pleased me very well if they had been in earnest; but that passed over, I took the directions, and appointed to attend him at his house at seven o'clock the same evening.

When I came he made several proposals for my placing my money in the bank, in order to my having interest for it; but still some difficulty or other came in the way, which he objected as not safe; and I found such a sincere disinterested honesty in him, that I began to muse with myself, that I had certainly found the honest man I wanted, and that I could never put myself into better hands; so I told him with a great deal of frankness that I had never met with a man or woman yet that I could trust, or in whom I could think myself safe, but that I saw he was so disinterestedly concerned for my safety, that I said I would freely trust him with the management of that little I had, if he would accept to be steward for a poor widow that could give him no salary.

He smiled and, standing up, with great respect saluted me. He told me he could not but take it very kindly that I had so good an opinion of him; that he would not deceive me, that he would do anything in his power to serve me, and expect no salary; but that he could not by any means accept of a trust, that it might bring him to be suspected of self-interest, and that if I should die he might have disputes with my executors, which he should be very loth to encumber himself with.

I told him if those were all his objections I would soon remove them, and convince him that there was not the least room for any difficulty; for that, first, as for suspecting him, if ever I should do it, now is the time to suspect him, and not put the trust into his hands, and whenever I did suspect him, he could but throw it up then and refuse to go any further. Then, as to executors, I assured him I had no heirs, nor any relations in England, and I should alter my condition before I died, and then his trust and trouble should cease together, which, however, I had no prospect of yet; but I told him if I died as I was, it should be all his own, and he would deserve it by being so faithful to me as I was satisfied he would be.

He changed his countenance at this discourse, and asked me how I came to have so much good-will for him; and, looking very much pleased, said he might very lawfully wish he was a single man for my sake. I smiled, and told him as he was not, my offer could have no design upon him in it, and to wish, as he did, was not to be allowed, 'twas criminal to his wife.

He told me I was wrong. 'For,' says he, 'madam, as I said before, I have a wife and no wife, and 'twould be no sin to me to wish her hanged, if that were all.' 'I know nothing of your circumstances that way, sir,' said I; 'but it cannot be innocent to wish your wife dead.' 'I tell you,' says he again, 'she is a wife and no wife; you don't know what I am, or what she is.'

'That's true,' said I; 'sir, I do not know what you are, but I believe you to be an honest man, and that's the cause of all my confidence in you.'

'Well, well,' says he, 'and so I am, I hope, too. But I am something else too, madam; for,' says he, 'to be plain with you, I am a cuckold, and she is a whore.' He spoke it in a kind of jest, but it was with such an awkward smile, that I perceived it was what struck very close to him, and he looked dismally when he said it.

'That alters the case indeed, sir,' said I, 'as to that part you were speaking of; but a cuckold, you know, may be an honest man; it does not alter that case at all. Besides, I think,' said I, 'since your wife is so dishonest to you, you are too honest to her to own her for your wife; but that,' said I, 'is what I have nothing to do with.'

'Nay,' says he, 'I do not think to clear my hands of her; for, to be plain with you, madam,' added he, 'I am no contended cuckold neither: on the other hand, I assure you it provokes me the highest degree, but I can't help myself; she that will be a whore, will be a whore.'

I waived the discourse and began to talk of my business; but I found he could not have done with it, so I let him alone, and he went on to tell me all the circumstances of his case, too long to relate here; particularly, that having been out of England some time before he came to the post he was in, she had had two children in the meantime by an officer of the army; and that when he came to England and, upon her submission, took her again, and maintained her very well, yet she ran away from him with a linen-draper's apprentice, robbed him of what she could come at, and continued to live from him still. 'So that, madam,' says he, 'she is a whore not by necessity, which is the common bait of your sex, but by inclination, and for the sake of the vice.'

Well, I pitied him, and wished him well rid of her, and still would have talked of my business, but it would not do. At last he looks steadily at me. 'Look you, madam,' says he, 'you came to ask advice of me, and I will serve you as faithfully as if you were my own sister; but I must turn the tables, since you oblige me to do it, and are so friendly to me, and I think I must ask advice of you. Tell me, what must a poor abused fellow do with a whore? What can I do to do myself justice upon her?'

'Alas! sir,' says I, "tis a case too nice for me to advise in, but it seems she has run away from you, so you are rid of her fairly; what can you desire more?' 'Ay, she is gone indeed,' said he, 'but I am not clear of her for all that.'

'That's true,' says I; 'she may indeed run you into debt, but the law has furnished you with methods to prevent that also; you may cry her down, as they call it.'

'No, no,' says he, 'that is not the case neither; I have taken care of all that; 'tis not that part that I speak of, but I would be rid of her so that I might marry again.'

'Well, sir,' says I, 'then you must divorce her. If you can prove what you say, you may certainly get that done, and then, I suppose, you are free.'

'That's very tedious and expensive,' says he.

'Why,' says I, 'if you can get any woman you like to take your word, I suppose your wife would not dispute the liberty with you that she takes herself.'

'Ay,' says he, 'but 'twould be hard to bring an honest woman to do that; and for the other sort,' says he, 'I have had enough of her to meddle with any more whores.'

It occurred to me presently, 'I would have taken your word with all my heart, if you had but asked me the question'; but that was to myself. To him I replied, 'Why, you shut the door against any honest woman accepting you, for you condemn all that should venture upon you at once, and conclude, that really a woman that takes you now can't be honest.'

'Why,' says he, 'I wish you would satisfy me that an honest woman would take me; I'd venture it'; and then turns short upon me, 'Will you take me, madam?'

'That's not a fair question,' says I, 'after what you have said; however, lest you should think I wait only for a recantation of it, I shall answer you plainly, No, not I; my business is of another kind with you, and I did not expect you would have turned my serious application to you, in my own distracted case, into a comedy.'

'Why, madam,' says he, 'my case is as distracted as yours can be, and I stand in as much need of advice as you do, for I think if I have not relief somewhere, I shall be made myself, and I know not what course to take, I protest to you.'

'Why, sir,' says I, "tis easy to give advice in your case, much easier than it is in mine.' 'Speak then,' says he, 'I beg of you, for now you encourage me.'

'Why,' says I, 'if your case is so plain as you say it is, you may be legally divorced, and then you may find honest women enough to ask the question of fairly; the sex is not so scarce that you can want a wife.'

'Well, then,' said he, 'I am in earnest; I'll take your advice; but shall I ask you one question seriously beforehand?'

'Any question,' said I, 'but that you did before.'

'No, that answer will not do,' said he, 'for, in short, that is the question I shall ask.'

'You may ask what questions you please, but you have my answer to that already,' said I. 'Besides, sir,' said I, 'can you think so ill of me as that I would give any answer to such a question beforehand? Can any woman alive believe you in earnest, or think you design anything but to banter her?'

'Well, well,' says he, 'I do not banter you, I am in earnest; consider of it.'

'But, sir,' says I, a little gravely, 'I came to you about my own business; I beg of you to let me know, what you will advise me to do?'

'I will be prepared,' says he, 'against you come again.'

'Nay,' says I, 'you have forbid my coming any more.'

'Why so?' said he, and looked a little surprised.

'Because,' said I, 'you can't expect I should visit you on the account you talk of.'

'Well,' says he, 'you shall promise me to come again, however, and I will not say any more of it till I have gotten the divorce, but I desire you will prepare to be better conditioned when that's done, for you shall be the woman, or I will not be divorced at all; why, I owe it to your unlooked-for kindness, if it were to nothing else, but I have other reasons too.'

He could not have said anything in the world that pleased me better; however, I knew that the way to secure him was to stand off while the thing was so remote, as it appeared to be, and that it was time enough to accept of it when he was able to perform it; so I said very respectfully to him, it was time enough to consider of these things when he was in a condition to talk of them; in the meantime, I told him, I was going a great way from him, and he would find objects enough to please him better. We broke off here for the present, and he made me promise him to come again the next day, for his resolutions upon my own business, which after some pressing I did; though had he seen farther into me, I wanted no pressing on that account.

I came the next evening, accordingly, and brought my maid with me, to let him see that I kept a maid, but I sent her away as soon as I was gone in. He would have had me let the maid have stayed, but I would not, but ordered her aloud to come for me again about nine o'clock. But he forbade that, and told me he would see me safe home, which, by the way, I was not very well please with, supposing he might do that to know where I lived and inquire into my character and circumstances. However, I ventured that, for all that the people there or thereabout knew of me, was to my advantage; and all the character he had of me, after he had inquired, was that I was a woman of fortune, and that I was a very modest, sober body; which, whether true or not in the main, yet you may see how necessary it is for all women who expect anything in the world, to preserve the character of their virtue, even when perhaps they may have sacrificed the thing itself.

I found, and was not a little please with it, that he had provided a supper for me. I found also he lived very handsomely, and had a house very handsomely furnished; all of which I was rejoiced at indeed, for I looked upon it as all my own.

We had now a second conference upon the subject-matter of the last conference. He laid his business very home indeed; he protested his affection to me, and indeed I had no room to doubt it; he declared that it began from the first moment I talked with him, and long before I had mentioned leaving my effects with him. ''Tis no matter when it began,' thought I; 'if it will but hold, 'twill be well enough.' He then told me how much the offer I had made of trusting him with my effects, and leaving them to him, had engaged him. 'So I intended it should,' thought I, 'but then I thought you had been a single man too.' After we had supped, I observed he pressed me very hard to drink two or three glasses of wine, which, however, I declined, but drank one glass or two. He then told me he had a proposal to make to me, which I should promise him I would not take ill if I should not grant it. I told him I hoped he would make no dishonourable proposal to me, especially in his own house, and that if it was such, I desired he would not propose it, that I might not be obliged to offer any resentment to him that did not become the respect I professed for him, and the trust I had placed in him in coming to his house; and begged of him he would give me leave to go away, and accordingly began to put on my gloves and prepare to be gone, though at the same time I no more intended it than he intended to let me.

Well, he importuned me not to talk of going; he assured me he had no dishonourable thing in his thoughts about me, and was very far from offering anything to me that was dishonourable, and if I thought so, he would choose to say no more of it.

That part I did not relish at all. I told him I was ready to hear anything that he had to say, depending that he would say nothing unworthy of himself, or unfit for me to hear. Upon this, he told me his proposal was this: that I would marry him, though he had not yet obtained the divorce from the whore his wife; and to satisfy me that he meant honourably, he would promise not to desire me to live with him, or go to bed with him till the divorce was obtained. My heart said yes to this offer at first word, but it was necessary to play the hypocrite a little more with him; so I seemed to decline the motion with some warmth, and besides a little condemning the thing as unfair, told him that such a proposal could be of no signification, but to entangle us both in great difficulties; for if he should not at last obtain the divorce, yet we could not dissolve the marriage, neither could we proceed in it; so that if he was disappointed in the divorce, I left him to consider what a condition we should both be in.

In short, I carried on the argument against this so far, that I convinced him it was not a proposal that had any sense in it. Well, then he went from it to another, and that was, that I would sign and seal a contract with him, conditioning to marry him as soon as the divorce was obtained, and to be void if he could not obtain it.

I told him such a thing was more rational than the other; but as this was the first time that ever I could imagine him weak enough to be in earnest in this affair, I did not use to say Yes at first asking; I would consider of it.

I played with this lover as an angler does with a trout. I found I had him fast on the hook, so I jested with his new proposal, and put him off. I told him he knew little of me, and bade him inquire about me; I let him also go home with me to my lodging, though I would not ask him to go in, for I told him it was not decent.

In short, I ventured to avoid signing a contract of marriage, and the reason why I did it was because the lady that had invited me so earnestly to go with her into Lancashire insisted so positively upon it, and promised me such great fortunes, and such fine things there, that I was tempted to go and try. 'Perhaps,' said I, 'I may mend myself very much'; and then I made no scruple in my thoughts of quitting my honest citizen, whom I was not so much in love with as not to leave him for a richer.

In a word, I avoided a contract; but told him I would go into the north, that he should know where to write to me by the consequence of the business I had entrusted with him; that I would give him a sufficient pledge of my respect for him, for I would leave almost all I had in the world in his hands; and I would thus far give him my word, that as soon as he had sued out a divorce from his first wife, he would send me an account of it, I would come up to London, and that then we would talk seriously of the matter.

It was a base design I went with, that I must confess, though I was invited thither with a design much worse than mine was, as the sequel will discover. Well, I went with my friend, as I called her, into Lancashire. All the way we went she caressed me with the utmost appearance of a sincere, undissembled affection; treated me, except my coach-hire, all the way; and her brother brought a gentleman's coach to Warrington to receive us, and we were carried from thence to Liverpool with as much ceremony as I could desire. We were also entertained at a merchant's house in Liverpool three or four days very handsomely; I forbear to tell his name, because of what followed. Then she told me she would carry me to an uncle's house of hers, where we should be nobly entertained. She did so; her uncle, as she called him, sent a coach and four horses for us, and we were carried near forty miles I know not whither.

We came, however, to a gentleman's seat, where was a numerous family, a large park, extraordinary company indeed, and where she was called cousin. I told her if she had resolved to bring me into such company as this, she should have let me have prepared myself, and have furnished myself with better clothes. The ladies took notice of that, and told me very genteelly they did not value people in their country so much by their clothes as they did in London; that their cousin had fully informed them of my quality, and that I did not want clothes to set me off; in short, they entertained me, not like what I was, but like what they thought I had been, namely, a widow lady of a great fortune.

The first discovery I made here was, that the family were all Roman Catholics, and the cousin too, whom I called my friend; however, I must say that nobody in the world could behave better to me, and I had all the civility shown me that I could have had if I had been of their opinion. The truth is, I had not so much principle of any kind as to be nice in point of religion, and I presently learned to speak favourably of the Romish Church; particularly, I told them I saw little but the prejudice of education in all the difference that were among Christians about religion, and if it had so happened that my father had been a Roman Catholic, I doubted not but I should have been as well pleased with their religion as my own.

This obliged them in the highest degree, and as I was besieged day and night with good company and pleasant discourse, so I had two or three old ladies that lay at me upon the subject of religion too. I was so complaisant, that though I would not completely engage, yet I made no scruple to be present at their mass, and to conform to all their gestures as they showed me the pattern, but I would not come too cheap; so that I only in the main encouraged them to expect that I would turn Roman Catholic, if I was instructed in the Catholic doctrine as they called it, and so the matter rested.

I stayed here about six weeks; and then my conductor led me back to a country village, about six miles from Liverpool, where her brother (as she called him) came to visit me in his own chariot, and in a very good figure, with two footmen in a good livery; and the next thing was to make love to me. As it had happened to me, one would think I could not have been cheated, and indeed I thought so myself, having a safe card at home, which I resolved not to quit unless I could mend myself very much. However, in all appearance this brother was a match worth my listening to, and the least his estate was valued at was £1000 a year, but the sister said it was worth £1500 a year, and lay most of it in Ireland.

I that was a great fortune, and passed for such, was above being asked how much my estate was; and my false friend taking it upon a foolish hearsay, had raised it from £500 to £5000, and by the time she came into the country she called it £15,000. The Irishman, for such I understood him to be, was stark mad at this bait; in short, he courted me, made me presents, and ran in debt like a madman for the expenses of his equipage and of his courtship. He had, to give him his due, the appearance of an extraordinary fine gentleman; he was tall, well-shaped, and had an extraordinary address; talked as naturally of his park and his stables, of his horses, his gamekeepers, his woods, his tenants, and his servants, as if we had been in the mansion-house, and I had seen them all about me.

He never so much as asked me about my fortune or estate, but assured me that when we came to Dublin he would jointure me in £600 a year good land; and that we could enter into a deed of settlement or contract here for the performance of it.

This was such language indeed as I had not been used to, and I was here beaten out of all my measures; I had a she-devil in my bosom, every hour telling me how great her brother lived. One time she would come for my orders, how I would have my coaches painted, and how lined; and another time what clothes my page should wear; in short, my eyes were dazzled. I had now lost my power of saying No, and, to cut the story short, I consented to be married; but to be the more private, we were carried farther into the country, and married by a Romish clergyman, who I was assured would marry us as effectually as a Church of England parson.

I cannot say but I had some reflections in this affair upon the dishonourable forsaking my faithful citizen, who loved me sincerely, and who was endeavouring to quit himself of a scandalous whore by whom he had been indeed barbarously used, and promised himself infinite happiness in his new choice; which choice was now giving up herself to another in a manner almost as scandalous as hers could be.

But the glittering shoe of a great estate, and of fine things, which the deceived creature that was now my deceiver represented every hour to my imagination, hurried me away, and gave me no time to think of London, or of anything there, much less of the obligation I had to a person of infinitely more real merit than what was now before me.

But the thing was done; I was now in the arms of my new spouse, who appeared still the same as before; great even to magnificence, and nothing less than £1000 a year could support the ordinary equipage he appeared in.

After we had been married about a month, he began to talk of my going to West Chester in order to embark for Ireland. However, he did not hurry me, for we stayed near three weeks longer, and then he sent to Chester for a coach to meet us at the Black Rock, as they call it, over against Liverpool. Thither we went in a fine boat they call a pinnace, with six oars; his servants, and horses, and baggage going in the ferry-boat. He made his excuse to me that he had no acquaintance in Chester, but he would go before and get some handsome apartment for me at a private house. I asked him how long we should stay at Chester. He said, not at all, any longer than one night or two, but he would immediately hire a coach to go to Holyhead. Then I told him he should by no means give himself the trouble to get private lodgings for one night or two, for that Chester being a great place, I made no doubt but there would be very good inns and accommodation enough; so we lodged at an inn in the West Street, not far from the Cathedral; I forget what sign it was at.

Here my spouse, talking of my going to Ireland, asked me if I had no affairs to settle at London before we went off. I told him No, not of any great consequence, but what might be done as well by letter from Dublin. 'Madam,' says he, very respectfully, 'I suppose the greatest part of your estate, which my sister tells me is most of it in money in the Bank of England, lies secure enough, but in case it required transferring, or any way altering its property, it might be necessary to go up to London and settle those things before we went over.'

I seemed to look strange at it, and told him I knew not what he meant; that I had no effects in the Bank of England that I knew of; and I hoped he could not say that I had ever told him I had. No, he said, I had not told him so, but his sister had said the greatest part of my estate lay there. 'And I only mentioned it, me dear,' said he, 'that if there was any occasion to settle it, or order anything about it, we might not be obliged to the hazard and trouble of another voyage back again'; for he added, that he did not care to venture me too much upon the sea.

I was surprised at this talk, and began to consider very seriously what the meaning of it must be; and it presently occurred to me that my friend, who called him brother, had represented me in colours which were not my due; and I thought, since it was come to that pitch, that I would know the bottom of it before I went out of England, and before I should put myself into I knew not whose hands in a strange country.

Upon this I called his sister into my chamber the next morning, and letting her know the discourse her brother and I had been upon the evening before, I conjured her to tell me what she had said to him, and upon what foot it was that she had made this marriage. She owned that she had told him that I was a great fortune, and said that she was told so at London. 'Told so!' says I warmly; 'did I ever tell you so?' No, she said, it was true I did not tell her so, but I had said several times that what I had was in my own disposal. 'I did so,' returned I very quickly and hastily, 'but I never told you I had anything called a fortune; no, not that I had £100, or the value of £100, in the world. Any how did it consist with my being a fortune,' said I, 'that I should come here into the north of England with you, only upon the account of living cheap?' At these words, which I spoke warm and high, my husband, her brother (as she called him), came into the room, and I desired him to come and sit down, for I had something of moment to say before them both, which it was absolutely necessary he should hear.

He looked a little disturbed at the assurance with which I seemed to speak it, and came and sat down by me, having first shut the door; upon which I began, for I was very much provoked, and turning myself to him, 'I am afraid,' says I, 'my dear' (for I spoke with kindness on his side), 'that you have a very great abuse put upon you, and an injury done you never to be repaired in your marrying me, which, however, as I have had no hand in it, I desire I may be fairly acquitted of it, and that the blame may lie where it ought to lie, and nowhere else, for I wash my hands of every part of it.'

'What injury can be done me, my dear,' says he, 'in marrying you. I hope it is to my honour and advantage every way.' 'I will soon explain it to you,' says I, 'and I fear you will have no reason to think yourself well used; but I will convince you, my dear,' says I again, 'that I have had no hand in it'; and there I stopped a while.

He looked now scared and wild, and began, I believe, to suspect what followed; however, looking towards me, and saying only, 'Go on,' he sat silent, as if to hear what I had more to say; so I went on. 'I asked you last night,' said I, speaking to him, 'if ever I made any boast to you of my estate, or ever told you I had any estate in the Bank of England or anywhere else, and you owned I had not, as is most true; and I desire you will tell me here, before your sister, if ever I gave you any reason from me to think so, or that ever we had any discourse about it'; and he owned again I had not, but said I had appeared always as a woman of fortune, and he depended on it that I was so, and hoped he was not deceived. 'I am not inquiring yet whether you have been deceived or not,' said I; 'I fear you have, and I too; but I am clearing myself from the unjust charge of being concerned in deceiving you.

'I have been now asking your sister if ever I told her of any fortune or estate I had, or gave her any particulars of it; and she owns I never did. Any pray, madam,' said I, turning myself to her, 'be so just to me, before your brother, to charge me, if you can, if ever I pretended to you that I had an estate; and why, if I had, should I come down into this country with you on purpose to spare that little I had, and live cheap?' She could not deny one word, but said she had been told in London that I had a very great fortune, and that it lay in the Bank of England.

'And now, dear sir,' said I, turning myself to my new spouse again, 'be so just to me as to tell me who has abused both you and me so much as to make you believe I was a fortune, and prompt you to court me to this marriage?' He could not speak a word, but pointed to her; and, after some more pause, flew out in the most furious passion that ever I saw a man in my life, cursing her, and calling her all the whores and hard names he could think of; and that she had ruined him, declaring that she had told him I had £15,000, and that she was to have £500 of him for procuring this match for him. He then added, directing his speech to me, that she was none of his sister, but had been his whore for two years before, that she had had £100 of him in part of this bargain, and that he was utterly undone if things were as I said; and in his raving he swore he would let her heart's blood out immediately, which frightened her and me too. She cried, said she had been told so in the house where I lodged. But this aggravated him more than before, that she should put so far upon him, and run things such a length upon no other authority than a hearsay; and then, turning to me again, said very honestly, he was afraid we were both undone. 'For, to be plain, my dear, I have no estate,' says he; 'what little I had, this devil has made me run out in waiting on you and putting me into this equipage.' She took the opportunity of his being earnest in talking with me, and got out of the room, and I never saw her more.

I was confounded now as much as he, and knew not what to say. I thought many ways that I had the worst of it, but his saying he was undone, and that he had no estate neither, put me into a mere distraction. 'Why,' says I to him, 'this has been a hellish juggle, for we are married here upon the foot of a double fraud; you are undone by the disappointment, it seems; and if I had had a fortune I had been cheated too, for you say you have nothing.'

'You would indeed have been cheated, my dear,' says he, 'but you would not have been undone, for £15,000 would have maintained us both very handsomely in this country; and I assure you,' added he, 'I had resolved to have dedicated every groat of it to you; I would not have wronged you of a shilling, and the rest I would have made up in my affection to you, and tenderness of you, as long as I lived.'

This was very honest indeed, and I really believe he spoke as he intended, and that he was a man that was as well qualified to make me happy, as to his temper and behaviour, as any man ever was; but his having no estate, and being run into debt on this ridiculous account in the country, made all the prospect dismal and dreadful, and I knew not what to say, or what to think of myself.

I told him it was very unhappy that so much love, and so much good nature as I discovered in him, should be thus precipitated into misery; that I saw nothing before us but ruin; for as to me, it was my unhappiness that what little I had was not able to relieve us week, and with that I pulled out a bank bill of £20 and eleven guineas, which I told him I had saved out of my little income, and that by the account that creature had given me of the way of living in that country, I expected it would maintain me three or four years; that if it was taken from me, I was left destitute, and he knew what the condition of a woman among strangers must be, if she had no money in her pocket; however, I told him, if he would take it, there it was.

He told me with a great concern, and I thought I saw tears stand in his eyes, that he would not touch it; that he abhorred the thoughts of stripping me and make me miserable; that, on the contrary, he had fifty guineas left, which was all he had in the world, and he pulled it out and threw it down on the table, bidding me take it, though he were to starve for want of it.

I returned, with the same concern for him, that I could not bear to hear him talk so; that, on the contrary, if he could propose any probable method of living, I would do anything that became me on my part, and that I would live as close and as narrow as he could desire.

He begged of me to talk no more at that rate, for it would make him distracted; he said he was bred a gentleman, though he was reduced to a low fortune, and that there was but one way left which he could think of, and that would not do, unless I could answer him one question, which, however, he said he would not press me to. I told him I would answer it honestly; whether it would be to his satisfaction or not, that I could not tell.

'Why, then, my dear, tell me plainly,' says he, 'will the little you have keep us together in any figure, or in any station or place, or will it not?'

It was my happiness hitherto that I had not discovered myself or my circumstances at all—no, not so much as my name; and seeing these was nothing to be expected from him, however good-humoured and however honest he seemed to be, but to live on what I knew would soon be wasted, I resolved to conceal everything but the bank bill and the eleven guineas which I had owned; and I would have been very glad to have lost that and have been set down where he took me up. I had indeed another bank bill about me of £30, which was the whole of what I brought with me, as well to subsist on in the country, as not knowing what might offer; because this creature, the go-between that had thus betrayed us both, had made me believe strange things of my marrying to my advantage in the country, and I was not willing to be without money, whatever might happen. This bill I concealed, and that made me the freer of the rest, in consideration of his circumstances, for I really pitied him heartily.

But to return to his question, I told him I never willingly deceived him, and I never would. I was very sorry to tell him that the little I had would not subsist us;

that it was not sufficient to subsist me alone in the south country, and that this was the reason that made me put myself into the hands of that woman who called him brother, she having assured me that I might board very handsomely at a town called Manchester, where I had not yet been, for about £6 a year; and my whole income not being about £15 a year, I thought I might live easy upon it, and wait for better things.

He shook his head and remained silent, and a very melancholy evening we had; however, we supped together, and lay together that night, and when we had almost supped he looked a little better and more cheerful, and called for a bottle of wine. 'Come, my dear,' says he, 'though the case is bad, it is to no purpose to be dejected. Come, be as easy as you can; I will endeavour to find out some way or other to live; if you can but subsist yourself, that is better than nothing. I must try the world again; a man ought to think like a man; to be discouraged is to yield to the misfortune.' With this he filled a glass and drank to me, holding my hand and pressing it hard in his hand all the while the wine went down, and protesting afterwards his main concern was for me.

It was really a true, gallant spirit he was of, and it was the more grievous to me. 'Tis something of relief even to be undone by a man of honour, rather than by a scoundrel; but here the greatest disappointment was on his side, for he had really spent a great deal of money, deluded by this madam the procuress; and it was very remarkable on what poor terms he proceeded. First the baseness of the creature herself is to be observed, who, for the getting £100 herself, could be content to let him spend three or four more, though perhaps it was all he had in the world, and more than all; when she had not the least ground, more than a little tea-table chat, to say that I had any estate, or was a fortune, or the like. It is true the design of deluding a woman of fortune, if I had been so, was base enough; the putting the face of great things upon poor circumstances was a fraud, and bad enough; but the case a little differed too, and that in his favour, for he was not a rake that made a trade to delude women, and, as some have done, get six or seven fortunes after one another, and then rifle and run away from them; but he was really a gentleman, unfortunate and low, but had lived well; and though, if I had had a fortune, I should have been enraged at the slut for betraying me, yet really for the man, a fortune would not have been ill bestowed on him, for he was a lovely person indeed, of generous principles, good sense, and of abundance of good-humour.

We had a great deal of close conversation that night, for we neither of us slept much; he was as penitent for having put all those cheats upon me as if it had been felony, and that he was going to execution; he offered me again every shilling of the money he had about him, and said he would go into the army and seek the world for more.

I asked him why he would be so unkind to carry me into Ireland, when I might suppose he could not have subsisted me there. He took me in his arms. 'My dear,' said he, 'depend upon it, I never designed to go to Ireland at all, much less to have carried you thither, but came hither to be out of the observation of the people, who had heard what I pretended to, and withal, that nobody might ask me for money before I was furnished to supply them.'

'But where, then,' said I, 'were we to have gone next?'

'Why, my dear,' said he, 'I'll confess the whole scheme to you as I had laid it; I purposed here to ask you something about your estate, as you see I did, and when you, as I expected you would, had entered into some account with me of the particulars, I would have made an excuse to you to have put off our voyage to Ireland for some time, and to have gone first towards London.

'Then, my dear,' said he, 'I resolved to have confessed all the circumstances of my own affairs to you, and let you know I had indeed made use of these artifices to obtain your consent to marry me, but had now nothing to do but ask to your pardon, and to tell you how abundantly, as I have said above, I would endeavour to make you forget what was past, by the felicity of the days to come.'

'Truly,' said I to him, 'I find you would soon have conquered me; and it is my affliction now, that I am not in a condition to let you see how easily I should have been reconciled to you, and have passed by all the tricks you had put upon me, in recompense of so much good-humour. But, my dear,' said I, 'what can we do now? We are both undone, and what better are we for our being reconciled together, seeing we have nothing to live on?'

We proposed a great many things, but nothing could offer where there was nothing to begin with. He begged me at last to talk no more of it, for, he said, I would break his heart; so we talked of other things a little, till at last he took a husband's leave of me, and so we went to sleep.

He rose before me in the morning; and indeed, having lain awake almost all night, I was very sleepy, and lay till near eleven o'clock. In this time he took his horses and three servants, and all his linen and baggage, and away he went, leaving a short but moving letter for me on the table, as follows:—

'MY DEAR—I am a dog; I have abused you; but I have been drawn into do it by a base creature, contrary to my principle and the general practice of my life. Forgive me, my dear! I ask your pardon with the greatest sincerity; I am the most miserable of men, in having deluded you. I have been so happy to possess you, and now am so wretched as to be forced to fly from you. Forgive me, my dear; once more I say, forgive me! I am not able to see you ruined by me, and myself unable to support you. Our marriage is nothing; I shall never be able to see you again; I here discharge you from it; if you can marry to your advantage, do not decline it on my account; I here swear to you on my faith, and on the word of a man of honour, I will never disturb your repose if I should know of it, which, however, is not likely. On the other hand, if you should not marry, and if good fortune should befall me, it shall be all yours, wherever you are.

'I have put some of the stock of money I have left into your pocket; take places for yourself and your maid in the stage-coach, and go for London; I hope it will bear your charges thither, without breaking into your own. Again I sincerely ask your pardon, and will do so as often as I shall ever think of you. Adieu, my dear, for ever!—I am, your most affectionately, J.E.'

Nothing that ever befell me in my life sank so deep into my heart as this farewell. I reproached him a thousand times in my thoughts for leaving me, for I would have gone with him through the world, if I had begged my bread. I felt in my pocket, and there found ten guineas, his gold watch, and two little rings, one a small diamond ring worth only about £6, and the other a plain gold ring.

I sat me down and looked upon these things two hours together, and scarce spoke a word, till my maid interrupted me by telling me my dinner was ready. I ate but little, and after dinner I fell into a vehement fit of crying, every now and then calling him by his name, which was James. 'O Jemmy!' said I, 'come back, come back. I'll give you all I have; I'll beg, I'll starve with you.' And thus I ran raving about the room several times, and then sat down between whiles, and then walking about again, called upon him to come back, and then cried again; and thus I passed the afternoon, till about seven o'clock, when it was near dusk, in the evening, being August, when, to my unspeakable surprise, he comes back into the inn, but without a servant, and comes directly up into my chamber.

I was in the greatest confusion imaginable, and so was he too. I could not imagine what should be the occasion of it, and began to be at odds with myself whether to be glad or sorry; but my affection biassed all the rest, and it was impossible to conceal my joy, which was too great for smiles, for it burst out into tears. He was no sooner entered the room but he ran to me and took me in his arms, holding me fast, and almost stopping my breath with his kisses, but spoke not a word. At length I began. 'My dear,' said I, 'how could you go away from me?' to which he gave no answer, for it was impossible for him to speak.

When our ecstasies were a little over, he told me he was gone about fifteen miles, but it was not in his power to go any farther without coming back to see me again, and to take his leave of me once more.

I told him how I had passed my time, and how loud I had called him to come back again. He told me he heard me very plain upon Delamere Forest, at a place about twelve miles off. I smiled. 'Nay,' says he, 'do not think I am in jest, for if ever I heard your voice in my life, I heard you call me aloud, and sometimes I thought I saw you running after me.' 'Why,' said I, 'what did I say?'—for I had not named the words to him. 'You called aloud,' says he, 'and said, O Jemmy! O Jemmy! come back, come back.'

I laughed at him. 'My dear,' says he, 'do not laugh, for, depend upon it, I heard your voice as plain as you hear mine now; if you please, I'll go before a magistrate and make oath of it.' I then began to be amazed and surprised, and indeed frightened, and told him what I had really done, and how I had called after him, as above.

When we had amused ourselves a while about this, I said to him: 'Well, you shall go away from me no more; I'll go all over the world with you rather.' He told me it would be a very difficult thing for him to leave me, but since it must be, he hoped I would make it as easy to me as I could; but as for him, it would be his destruction that he foresaw.

However, he told me that he considered he had left me to travel to London alone, which was too long a journey; and that as he might as well go that way as any way else, he was resolved to see me safe thither, or near it; and if he did go away then without taking his leave, I should not take it ill of him; and this he made me promise.

He told me how he had dismissed his three servants, sold their horses, and sent the fellows away to seek their fortunes, and all in a little time, at a town on the road, I know not where. 'And,' says he, 'it cost me some tears all alone by myself, to think how much happier they were than their master, for they could go to the next gentleman's house to see for a service, whereas,' said he, 'I knew not wither to go, or what to do with myself.'

I told him I was so completely miserable in parting with him, that I could not be worse; and that now he was come again, I would not go from him, if he would take me with him, let him go whither he would, or do what he would. And in the meantime I agreed that we would go together to London; but I could not be brought to consent he should go away at last and not take his leave of me, as he proposed to do; but told him, jesting, that if he did, I would call him back again as loud as I did before. Then I pulled out his watch and gave it him back, and his two rings, and his ten guineas; but he would not take them, which made me very much suspect that he resolved to go off upon the road and leave me.

The truth is, the circumstances he was in, the passionate expressions of his letter, the kind, gentlemanly treatment I had from him in all the affair, with the concern he showed for me in it, his manner of parting with that large share which he gave me of his little stock left—all these had joined to make such impressions on me, that I really loved him most tenderly, and could not bear the thoughts of parting with him.

Two days after this we quitted Chester, I in the stage-coach, and he on horseback. I dismissed my maid at Chester. He was very much against my being without a maid, but she being a servant hired in the country, and I resolving to keep no servant at London, I told him it would have been barbarous to have taken the poor wench and have turned her away as soon as I came to town; and it would also have been a needless charge on the road, so I satisfied him, and he was easy enough on the score.

He came with me as far as Dunstable, within thirty miles of London, and then he told me fate and his own misfortunes obliged him to leave me, and that it was not convenient for him to go to London, for reasons which it was of no value to me to know, and I saw him preparing to go. The stage-coach we were in did not usually stop at Dunstable, but I desiring it but for a quart of an hour, they were content to stand at an inndoor a while, and we went into the house.

Being in the inn, I told him I had but one favour more to ask of him, and that was, that since he could not go any farther, he would give me leave to stay a week or two in the town with him, that we might in that time think of something to prevent such a ruinous thing to us both, as a final separation would be; and that I had something of moment to offer him, that I had never said yet, and which perhaps he might find practicable to our mutual advantage.

This was too reasonable a proposal to be denied, so he called the landlady of the house, and told her his wife was taken ill, and so ill that she could not think of going any farther in the stage-coach, which had tired her almost to death, and asked if she could not get us a lodging for two or three days in a private house, where I might rest me a little, for the journey had been too much for me. The landlady, a good sort of woman, well-bred and very obliging, came immediately to see me; told me she had two or three very good rooms in a part of the house quite out of the noise, and if I saw them, she did not doubt but I would like them, and I should have one of her maids, that should do nothing else but be appointed to wait on me. This was so very kind, that I could not but accept of it, and thank her; so I went to look on the rooms and liked them very well, and indeed they were extraordinarily furnished, and very pleasant lodgings; so we paid the stage-coach, took out our baggage, and resolved to stay here a while.

Here I told him I would live with him now till all my money was spent, but would not let him spend a shilling of his own. We had some kind squabble about that, but I told him it was the last time I was like to enjoy his company, and I desired he would let me be master in that thing only, and he should govern in everything else; so he acquiesced.

Here one evening, taking a walk into the fields, I told him I would now make the proposal to him I had told him of; accordingly I related to him how I had lived in Virginia, that I had a mother I believed was alive there still, though my husband was dead some years. I told him that had not my effects miscarried, which, by the way, I magnified pretty much, I might have been fortune good enough to him to have kept us from being parted in this manner. Then I entered into the manner of peoples going over to those countries to settle, how they had a quantity of land given them by the Constitution of the place; and if not, that it might be purchased at so easy a rate this it was not worth naming.

I then gave him a full and distinct account of the nature of planting; how with carrying over but two or three hundred pounds value in English goods, with some servants and tools, a man of application would presently lay a foundation for a family, and in a very few years be certain to raise an estate.

I let him into the nature of the product of the earth; how the ground was cured and prepared, and what the usual increase of it was; and demonstrated to him, that in a very few years, with such a beginning, we should be as certain of being rich as we were now certain of being poor.

He was surprised at my discourse; for we made it the whole subject of our conversation for near a week together, in which time I laid it down in black and white, as we say, that it was morally impossible, with a supposition of any reasonable good conduct, but that we must thrive there and do very well.

Then I told him what measures I would take to raise such a sum of £300 or thereabouts; and I argued with him how good a method it would be to put an end to our misfortunes and restore our circumstances in the world, to what we had both expected; and I added, that after seven years, if we lived, we might be in a posture to leave our plantations in good hands, and come over again and receive the income of it, and live here and enjoy it; and I gave him examples of some that had done so, and lived now in very good circumstances in London.

In short, I pressed him so to it, that he almost agreed to it, but still something or other broke it off again; till at last he turned the tables, and he began to talk almost to the same purpose of Ireland.

He told me that a man that could confine himself to country life, and that could find but stock to enter upon any land, should have farms there for £50 a year, as good as were here let for £200 a year; that the produce was such, and so rich the land, that if much was not laid up, we were sure to live as handsomely upon it as a gentleman of £3000 a year could do in England and that he had laid a scheme to leave me in London, and go over and try; and if he found he could lay a handsome foundation of living suitable to the respect he had for me, as he doubted not he should do, he would come over and fetch me.

I was dreadfully afraid that upon such a proposal he would have taken me at my word, viz. to sell my little income as I called it, and turn it into money, and let him carry it over into Ireland and try his experiment with it; but he was too just to desire it, or to have accepted it if I had offered it; and he anticipated me in that, for he added, that he would go and try his fortune that way, and if he found he could do anything at it to live, then, by adding mine to it when I went over, we should live like ourselves; but that he would not hazard a shilling of mine till he had made the experiment with a little, and he assured me that if he found nothing to be done in Ireland, he would then come to me and join in my project for Virginia.

He was so earnest upon his project being to be tried first, that I could not withstand him; however, he promised to let me hear from him in a very little time after his arriving there, to let me know whether his prospect answered his design, that if there was not a possibility of success, I might take the occasion to prepare for our other voyage, and then, he assured me, he would go with me to America with all his heart.

I could bring him to nothing further than this. However, those consultations entertained us near a month, during which I enjoyed his company, which indeed was the most entertaining that ever I met in my life before. In this time he let me into the whole story of his own life, which was indeed surprising, and full of an infinite variety sufficient to fill up a much brighter history, for its adventures and incidents, than any I ever say in print; but I shall have occasion to say more of him hereafter.

We parted at last, though with the utmost reluctance on my side; and indeed he took his leave very unwillingly too, but necessity obliged him, for his reasons were very good why he would not come to London, as I understood more fully some time afterwards.

I gave him a direction how to write to me, though still I reserved the grand secret, and never broke my resolution, which was not to let him ever know my true name, who I was, or where to be found; he likewise let me know how to write a letter to him, so that, he said, he would be sure to receive it.

I came to London the next day after we parted, but did not go directly to my old lodgings; but for another nameless reason took a private lodging in St. John's Street, or, as it is vulgarly called, St. Jones's, near Clerkenwell; and here, being perfectly alone, I had leisure to sit down and reflect seriously upon the last seven months' ramble I had made, for I had been abroad no less. The pleasant hours I had with my last husband I looked back on with an infinite deal of pleasure; but that pleasure was very much lessened when I found some time after that I was really with child.

This was a perplexing thing, because of the difficulty which was before me where I should get leave to lie in; it being one of the nicest things in the world at that time of day for a woman that was a stranger, and had no friends, to be entertained in that circumstance without security, which, by the way, I had not, neither could I procure any.

I had taken care all this while to preserve a correspondence with my honest friend at the bank, or rather he took care to correspond with me, for he wrote to me once a week; and though I had not spent my money so fast as to want any from him, yet I often wrote also to let him know I was alive. I had left directions in Lancashire, so that I had these letters, which he sent, conveyed to me; and during my recess at St. Jones's received a very obliging letter from him, assuring me that his process for a divorce from his wife went on with success, though he met with some difficulties in it that he did not expect.

I was not displeased with the news that his process was more tedious than he expected; for though I was in no condition to have him yet, not being so foolish to marry him when I knew myself to be with child by another man, as some I know have ventured to do, yet I was not willing to lose him, and, in a word, resolved to have him if he continued in the same mind, as soon as I was up again; for I saw apparently I should hear no more from my husband; and as he had all along pressed to marry, and had assured me he would not be at all disgusted at it, or ever offer to claim me again, so I made no scruple to resolve to do it if I could, and if my other friend stood to his bargain; and I had a great deal of reason to be assured that he would stand to it, by the letters he wrote to me, which were the kindest and most obliging that could be.

I now grew big, and the people where I lodged perceived it, and began to take notice of it to me, and, as far as civility would allow, intimated that I must think of removing. This put me to extreme perplexity, and I grew very melancholy, for indeed I knew not what course to take. I had money, but no friends, and was like to have a child upon my hands to keep, which was a difficulty I had never had upon me yet, as the particulars of my story hitherto make appear.

In the course of this affair I fell very ill, and my melancholy really increased my distemper; my illness proved at length to be only an ague, but my apprehensions were really that I should miscarry. I should not say apprehensions, for indeed I would have been glad to miscarry, but I could never be brought to entertain so much as a thought of endeavouring to miscarry, or of taking any thing to make me miscarry; I abhorred, I say, so much as the thought of it.

However, speaking of it in the house, the gentlewoman who kept the house proposed to me to send for a midwife. I scrupled it at first, but after some time consented to it, but told her I had no particular acquaintance with any midwife, and so left it to her.

It seems the mistress of the house was not so great a stranger to such cases as mine was as I thought at first she had been, as will appear presently, and she sent for a midwife of the right sort—that is to say, the right sort for me.

The woman appeared to be an experienced woman in her business, I mean as a midwife; but she had another calling too, in which she was as expert as most women if not more. My landlady had told her I was very melancholy, and that she believed that had done me harm; and once, before me, said to her, 'Mrs. B——' (meaning the midwife), 'I believe this lady's trouble is of a kind that is pretty much in your way, and therefore if you can do anything for her, pray do, for she is a very civil gentlewoman'; and so she went out of the room.

I really did not understand her, but my Mother Midnight began very seriously to explain what she mean, as soon as she was gone. 'Madam,' says she, 'you seem not to understand what your landlady means; and when you do understand it, you need not let her know at all that you do so.

'She means that you are under some circumstances that may render your lying in difficult to you, and that you are not willing to be exposed. I need say no more, but to tell you, that if you think fit to communicate so much of your case to me, if it be so, as is necessary, for I do not desire to pry into those things, I perhaps may be in a position to help you and to make you perfectly easy, and remove all your dull thoughts upon that subject.'

Every word this creature said was a cordial to me, and put new life and new spirit into my heart; my blood began to circulate immediately, and I was quite another body; I ate my victuals again, and grew better presently after it. She said a great deal more to the same purpose, and then, having pressed me to be free with her, and promised in the solemnest manner to be secret, she stopped a little, as if waiting to see what impression it made on me, and what I would say.

I was too sensible to the want I was in of such a woman, not to accept her offer; I told her my case was partly as she guessed, and partly not, for I was really married, and had a husband, though he was in such fine circumstances and so remote at that time, as that he could not appear publicly.

She took me short, and told me that was none of her business; all the ladies that came under her care were married women to her. 'Every woman,' she says, 'that is with child has a father for it,' and whether that father was a husband or no husband, was no business of hers; her business was to assist me in my present circumstances, whether I had a husband or no. 'For, madam,' says she, 'to have a husband that cannot appear, is to have no husband in the sense of the case; and, therefore, whether you are a wife or a mistress is all one to me.'

I found presently, that whether I was a whore or a wife, I was to pass for a whore here, so I let that go. I told her it was true, as she said, but that, however, if I must tell her my case, I must tell it her as it was; so I related it to her as short as I could, and I concluded it to her thus. 'I trouble you with all this, madam,' said I, 'not that, as you said before, it is much to the purpose in your affair, but this is to the purpose, namely, that I am not in any pain about being seen, or being public or concealed, for 'tis perfectly indifferent to me; but my difficulty is, that I have no acquaintance in this part of the nation.'

'I understand you, madam' says she; 'you have no security to bring to prevent the parish impertinences usual in such cases, and perhaps,' says she, 'do not know very well how to dispose of the child when it comes.' 'The last,' says I, 'is not so much my concern as the first.' 'Well, madam,' answered the midwife, 'dare you put yourself into my hands? I live in such a place; though I do not inquire after you, you may inquire after me. My name is B——; I live in such a street'—naming the street—'at the sign of the Cradle. My profession is a midwife, and I have many ladies that come to my house to lie in. I have given security to the parish in general terms to secure them from any charge from whatsoever shall come into the world under my roof. I have but one question to ask in the whole affair, madam,' says she, 'and if that be answered you shall be entirely easy for all the rest.'

I presently understood what she meant, and told her, 'Madam, I believe I understand you. I thank God, though I want friends in this part of the world, I do not want money, so far as may be necessary, though I do not abound in that neither': this I added because I would not make her expect great things. 'Well, madam,' says she, 'that is the thing indeed, without which nothing can be done in these cases; and yet,' says she, 'you shall see that I will not impose upon you, or offer anything that is unkind to you, and if you desire it, you shall know everything beforehand, that you may suit yourself to the occasion, and be neither costly or sparing as you see fit.'

I told her she seemed to be so perfectly sensible of my condition, that I had nothing to ask of her but this, that as I had told her that I had money sufficient, but not a great quantity, she would order it so that I might be at as little superfluous charge as possible.

She replied that she would bring in an account of the expenses of it in two or three shapes, and like a bill of fare, I should choose as I pleased; and I desired her to do so.

The next day she brought it, and the copy of her three bills was a follows:—

1. For three months' lodging in her house, including my diet, at 10s. a week	6£, 0s., 0d.
2. For a nurse for the month, and use of childbed linen	1£, 10s., 0d.
3. For a minister to christen the child, and to the godfathers and clerk	1£, 10s., 0d.

4. For a supper at the christening if I had five friends at it	1£, 0s., 0d.
For her fees as a midwife, and the taking off the trouble of the parish	3£, 3s., 0d.
To her maid servant attending	0£, 10s., 0d.

	13£, 13s., 0d.

This was the first bill; the second was the same terms:—

1. For three months' lodging and diet, etc., at 20s. per week	13£, 0s., 0d.
2. For a nurse for the month, and the use of linen and lace	2£, 10s., 0d.
3. For the minister to christen the child, etc., as above	2£, 0s., 0d.
4. For supper and for sweetmeats	3£, 3s., 0d.
For her fees as above	5£, 5s., 0d.
For a servant-maid	1£, 0s., 0d.

	26£, 18s., 0d.

This was the second-rate bill; the third, she said, was for a degree higher, and when the father or friends appeared:—

1. For three months' lodging and diet, having two rooms and a garret for a servant	30£, 0s., 0d.,
2. For a nurse for the month, and the finest suit of childbed linen	4£, 4s., 0d.
3. For the minister to christen the child, etc.	2£, 10s., 0d.
4. For a supper, the gentlemen to send in the wine	6£, 0s., 0d.
For my fees, etc.	10£, 10s., 0d.
The maid, besides their own maid, only	0£, 10s., 0d.

	53£, 14s., 0d.

I looked upon all three bills, and smiled, and told her I did not see but that she was very reasonable in her demands, all things considered, and for that I did not doubt but her accommodations were good.

She told me I should be judge of that when I saw them. I told her I was sorry to tell her that I feared I must be her lowest-rated customer. 'And perhaps, madam,' said I, 'you will make me the less welcome upon that account.' 'No, not at all,' said she; 'for where I have one of the third sort I have two of the second, and four to one of the first, and I get as much by them in proportion as by any; but if you doubt my care of you, I will allow any friend you have to overlook and see if you are well waited on or no.'

Then she explained the particulars of her bill. 'In the first place, madam,' said she, 'I would have you observe that here is three months' keeping; you are but ten shillings a week; I undertake to say you will not complain of my table. I suppose,' says she, 'you do not live cheaper where you are now?' 'No, indeed,' said I, 'not so cheap, for I give six shillings per week for my chamber, and find my own diet as well as I can, which costs me a great deal more.'

'Then, madam,' says she, 'if the child should not live, or should be dead-born, as you know sometimes happens, then there is the minister's article saved; and if you have no friends to come to you, you may save the expense of a supper; so that take those articles out, madam,' says she, 'your lying in will not cost you above £5, 3s. in all more than your ordinary charge of living.'

This was the most reasonable thing that I ever heard of; so I smiled, and told her I would come and be her customer; but I told her also, that as I had two months and more to do, I might perhaps be obliged to stay longer with her than three months, and desired to know if she would not be obliged to remove me before it was proper. No, she said; her house was large, and besides, she never put anybody to remove, that had lain in, till they were willing to go; and if she had more ladies offered, she was not so ill-beloved among her neighbours but she could provide accommodations for twenty, if there was occasion.

I found she was an eminent lady in her way; and, in short, I agreed to put myself into her hands, and promised her. She then talked of other things, looked about into my accommodations where I was, found fault with my wanting attendance and conveniences, and that I should not be used so at her house. I told her I was shy of speaking, for the woman of the house looked stranger, or at least I thought so, since I had been ill, because I was with child; and I was afraid she would put some affront or other upon me, supposing that I had been able to give but a slight account of myself.

'Oh dear,' said she, 'her ladyship is no stranger to these things; she has tried to entertain ladies in your condition several times, but she could not secure the parish; and besides, she is not such a nice lady as you take her to be; however, since you are a-going, you shall not meddle with her, but I'll see you are a little better looked after while you are here than I think you are, and it shall not cost you the more neither.'

I did not understand her at all; however, I thanked her, and so we parted. The next morning she sent me a chicken roasted and hot, and a pint bottle of sherry, and ordered the maid to tell me that she was to wait on me every day as long as I stayed there.

This was surprisingly good and kind, and I accepted it very willingly. At night she sent to me again, to know if I wanted anything, and how I did, and to order the maid to come to her in the morning with my dinner. The maid had orders to make me some chocolate in the morning before she came away, and did so, and at noon she brought me the sweetbread of a breast of veal, whole, and a dish of soup for my dinner; and after this manner she nursed me up at a distance, so that I was mightily well pleased, and quickly well, for indeed my dejections before were the principal part of my illness.

I expected, as is usually the case among such people, that the servant she sent me would have been some imprudent brazen wench of Drury Lane breeding, and I was very uneasy at having her with me upon that account; so I would not let her lie in that house the first night by any means, but had my eyes about me as narrowly as if she had been a public thief.

My gentlewoman guessed presently what was the matter, and sent her back with a short note, that I might depend upon the honesty of her maid; that she would be answerable for her upon all accounts; and that she took no servants into her house without very good security for their fidelity. I was then perfectly easy; and indeed the maid's behaviour spoke for itself, for a modester, quieter, soberer girl never came into anybody's family, and I found her so afterwards.

As soon as I was well enough to go abroad, I went with the maid to see the house, and to see the apartment I was to have; and everything was so handsome and so clean and well, that, in short, I had nothing to say, but was wonderfully pleased and satisfied with what I had met with, which, considering the melancholy circumstances I was in, was far beyond what I looked for.

It might be expected that I should give some account of the nature of the wicked practices of this woman, in whose hands I was now fallen; but it would be too much encouragement to the vice, to let the world see what easy measures were here taken to rid the women's unwelcome burthen of a child clandestinely gotten. This grave matron had several sorts of practice, and this was one particular, that if a child was born, though not in her house (for she had occasion to be called to many private labours), she had people at hand, who for a piece of money would take the child off their hands, and off from the hands of the parish too; and those children, as she said, were honestly provided for and taken care of. What should become of them all, considering so many, as by her account she was concerned with, I cannot conceive.

I had many times discourses upon that subject with her; but she was full of this argument, that she save the life of many an innocent lamb, as she called them, which would otherwise perhaps have been murdered; and of many women who, made desperate by the misfortune, would otherwise be tempted to destroy their children, and bring themselves to the gallows. I granted her that this was true, and a very commendable thing, provided the poor children fell into good hands afterwards, and were not abused, starved, and neglected by the nurses that bred them up. She answered, that she always took care of that, and had no nurses in her business but what were very good, honest people, and such as might be depended upon.

I could say nothing to the contrary, and so was obliged to say, 'Madam, I do not question you do your part honestly, but what those people do afterwards is the main question'; and she stopped my mouth again with saying that she took the utmost care about it.

The only thing I found in all her conversation on these subjects that gave me any distaste, was, that one time in discouraging about my being far gone with child, and the time I expected to come, she said something that looked as if she could help me off with my burthen sooner, if I was willing; or, in English, that she could give me something to make me miscarry, if I had a desire to put an end to my troubles that way; but I soon let her see that I abhorred the thoughts of it; and, to do her justice, she put it off so cleverly, that I could not say she really intended it, or whether she only mentioned the practice as a horrible thing; for she couched her words so well, and took my meaning so quickly, that she gave her negative before I could explain myself.

To bring this part into as narrow a compass as possible, I quitted my lodging at St. Jones's and went to my new governess, for so they called her in the house, and there I was indeed treated with so much courtesy, so carefully looked to, so handsomely provided, and everything so well, that I was surprised at it, and could not at first see what advantage my governess made of it; but I found afterwards that she professed to make no profit of lodgers' diet, nor indeed could she get much by it, but that her profit lay in the other articles of her management, and she made enough that way, I assure you; for 'tis scarce credible what practice she had, as well abroad as at home, and yet all upon the private account, or, in plain English, the whoring account.

While I was in her house, which was near four months, she had no less than twelve ladies of pleasure brought to bed within the doors, and I think she had two-and-thirty, or thereabouts, under her conduct without doors, whereof one, as nice as she was with me, was lodged with my old landlady at St. Jones's.

This was a strange testimony of the growing vice of the age, and such a one, that as bad as I had been myself, it shocked my very senses. I began to nauseate the place I was in and, about all, the wicked practice; and yet I must say that I never saw, or do I believe there was to be seen, the least indecency in the house the whole time I was there.

Not a man was ever seen to come upstairs, except to visit the lying-in ladies within their month, nor then without the old lady with them, who made it a piece of honour of her management that no man should touch a woman, no, not his own wife, within the month; nor would she permit any man to lie in the house upon any pretence whatever, no, not though she was sure it was with his own wife; and her general saying for it was, that she cared not how many children were born in her house, but she would have none got there if she could help it.

It might perhaps be carried further than was needful, but it was an error of the right hand if it was an error, for by this she kept up the reputation, such as it was, of her business, and obtained this character, that though she did take care of the women when they were debauched, yet she was not instrumental to their being debauched at all; and yet it was a wicked trade she drove too.

While I was there, and before I was brought to bed, I received a letter from my trustee at the bank, full of kind, obliging things, and earnestly pressing me to return to London. It was near a fortnight old when it came to me, because it had been first sent into Lancashire, and then returned to me. He concludes with telling me that he had obtained a decree, I think he called it, against his wife, and that he would be ready to make good his engagement to me, if I would accept of him, adding a great many protestations of kindness and affection, such as he would have been far from offering if he had known the circumstances I had been in, and which as it was I had been very far from deserving.

I returned an answer to his letter, and dated it at Liverpool, but sent it by messenger, alleging that it came in cover to a friend in town. I gave him joy of his deliverance, but raised some scruples at the lawfulness of his marrying again, and told him I supposed he would consider very seriously upon that point before he resolved on it, the consequence being too great for a man of his judgment to venture rashly upon a thing of that nature; so concluded, wishing him very well in whatever he resolved, without letting him into anything of my own mind, or giving any answer to his proposal of my coming to London to him, but mentioned at a distance my intention to return the latter end of the year, this being dated in April.

I was brought to bed about the middle of May and had another brave boy, and myself in as good condition as usual on such occasions. My governess did her part as a midwife with the greatest art and dexterity imaginable, and far beyond all that ever I had had any experience of before.

Her care of me in my travail, and after in my lying in, was such, that if she had been my own mother it could not have been better. Let none be encouraged in their loose practices from this dexterous lady's management, for she is gone to her place, and I dare say has left nothing behind her that can or will come up on it.

I think I had been brought to bed about twenty-two days when I received another letter from my friend at the bank, with the surprising news that he had obtained a final sentence of divorce against his wife, and had served her with it on such a day, and that he had such an answer to give to all my scruples about his marrying again, as I could not expect, and as he had no desire of; for that his wife, who had been under some remorse before for her usage of him, as soon as she had the account that he had gained his point, had very unhappily destroyed herself that same evening.

He expressed himself very handsomely as to his being concerned at her disaster, but cleared himself of having any hand in it, and that he had only done himself justice in a case in which he was notoriously injured and abused. However, he said that he was extremely afflicted at it, and had no view of any satisfaction left in his world, but only in the hope that I would come and relieve him by my company; and then he pressed me violently indeed to give him some hopes that I would at least come up to town and let him see me, when he would further enter into discourse about it.

I was exceedingly surprised at the news, and began now seriously to reflect on my present circumstances, and the inexpressible misfortune it was to me to have a child upon my hands, and what to do in it I knew not. At last I opened my case at a distance to my governess. I appeared melancholy and uneasy for several days, and she lay at me continually to know what trouble me. I could not for my life tell her that I had an offer of marriage, after I had so often told her that I had a husband, so that I really knew not what to say to her. I owned I had something which very much troubled me, but at the same time told her I could not speak of it to any one alive.

She continued importuning me several days, but it was impossible, I told her, for me to commit the secret to anybody. This, instead of being an answer to her, increased her importunities; she urged her having been trusted with the greatest secrets of this nature, that it was her business to conceal everything, and that to discover things of that nature would be her ruin. She asked me if ever I had found her tattling to me of other people's affairs, and how could I suspect her? She told me, to unfold myself to her was telling it to nobody; that she was silent as death; that it must be a very strange case indeed that she could not help me out of; but to conceal it was to deprive myself of all possible help, or means of help, and to deprive her of the opportunity of serving me. In short, she had such a bewitching eloquence, and so great a power of persuasion that there was no concealing anything from her.

So I resolved to unbosom myself to her. I told her the history of my Lancashire marriage, and how both of us had been disappointed; how we came together, and how we parted; how he absolutely discharged me, as far as lay in him, free liberty to marry again, protesting that if he knew it he would never claim me, or disturb or expose me; that I thought I was free, but was dreadfully afraid to venture, for fear of the consequences that might follow in case of a discovery.

Then I told her what a good offer I had; showed her my friend's two last letters, inviting me to come to London, and let her see with what affection and earnestness they were written, but blotted out the name, and also the story about the disaster of his wife, only that she was dead.

She fell a-laughing at my scruples about marrying, and told me the other was no marriage, but a cheat on both sides; and that, as we were parted by mutual consent, the nature of the contract was destroyed, and the obligation was mutually discharged. She had arguments for this at the tip of her tongue; and, in short, reasoned me out of my reason; not but that it was too by the help of my own inclination.

But then came the great and main difficulty, and that was the child; this, she told me in so many words, must be removed, and that so as that it should never be possible for any one to discover it. I knew there was no marrying without entirely concealing that I had had a child, for he would soon have discovered by the age of it that it was born, nay, and gotten too, since my parley with him, and that would have destroyed all the affair.

But it touched my heart so forcibly to think of parting entirely with the child, and, for aught I knew, of having it murdered, or starved by neglect and ill-usage (which was much the same), that I could not think of it without horror. I wish all those women who consent to the disposing their children out of the way, as it is called, for decency sake, would consider that 'tis only a contrived method for murder; that is to say, a-killing their children with safety.

It is manifest to all that understand anything of children, that we are born into the world helpless, and incapable either to supply our own wants or so much as make them known; and that without help we must perish; and this help requires not only an assisting hand, whether of the mother or somebody else, but there are two things necessary in that assisting hand, that is, care and skill; without both which, half the children that are born would die, nay, though they were not to be denied food; and one half more of those that remained would be cripples or fools, lose their limbs, and perhaps their sense. I question not but that these are partly the reasons why affection was placed by nature in the hearts of mothers to their children; without which they would never be able to give themselves up, as 'tis necessary they should, to the care and waking pains needful to the support of their children.

Since this care is needful to the life of children, to neglect them is to murder them; again, to give them up to be managed by those people who have none of that needful affection placed by nature in them, is to neglect them in the highest degree; nay, in some it goes farther, and is a neglect in order to their being lost; so that 'tis even an intentional murder, whether the child lives or dies.

All those things represented themselves to my view, and that is the blackest and most frightful form: and as I was very free with my governess, whom I had now learned to call mother, I represented to her all the dark thoughts which I had upon me about it, and told her what distress I was in. She seemed graver by much at this part than at the other; but as she was hardened in these things beyond all possibility of being touched with the religious part, and the scruples about the murder, so she was equally impenetrable in that part which related to affection. She asked me if she had not been careful and tender to me in my lying in, as if I had been her own child. I told her I owned she had. 'Well, my dear,' says she, 'and when you are gone, what are you to me? And what would it be to me if you were to be hanged? Do you think there are not women who, as it is their trade and they get their bread by it, value themselves upon their being as careful of children as their own mothers can be, and understand it rather better? Yes, yes, child,' says she, 'fear it not; how were we nursed ourselves? Are you sure you was nursed up by your own mother? and yet you look fat and fair, child,' says the old beldam; and with that she stroked me over the face. 'Never be concerned, child,' says she, going on in her drolling way; 'I have no murderers about me; I employ the best and the honestest nurses that can be had, and have as few children miscarry under their hands as there would if they were all nursed by mothers; we want neither care nor skill.'

She touched me to the quick when she asked if I was sure that I was nursed by my own mother; on the contrary I was sure I was not; and I trembled, and looked pale at the very expression. 'Sure,' said I to myself, 'this creature cannot be a witch, or have any conversation with a spirit, that can inform her what was done with me before I was able to know it myself'; and I looked at her as if I had been frightened; but reflecting that it could not be possible for her to know anything about me, that disorder went off, and I began to be easy, but it was not presently.

She perceived the disorder I was in, but did not know the meaning of it; so she ran on in her wild talk upon the weakness of my supposing that children were murdered because they were not all nursed by the mother, and to persuade me that the children she disposed of were as well used as if the mothers had the nursing of them themselves.

'It may be true, mother,' says I, 'for aught I know, but my doubts are very strongly grounded indeed.' 'Come, then,' says she, 'let's hear some of them.' 'Why, first,' says I, 'you give a piece of money to these people to take the child off the parent's hands, and to take care of it as long as it lives. Now we know, mother,' said I, 'that those are poor people, and their gain consists in being quit of the charge as soon as they can; how can I doubt but that, as it is best for them to have the child die, they are not over solicitous about life?'

'This is all vapours and fancy,' says the old woman; 'I tell you their credit depends upon the child's life, and they are as careful as any mother of you all.'

'O mother,' says I, 'if I was but sure my little baby would be carefully looked to, and have justice done it, I should be happy indeed; but it is impossible I can be satisfied in that point unless I saw it, and to see it would be ruin and destruction to me, as now my case stands; so what to do I know not.'

'A fine story!' says the governess. 'You would see the child, and you would not see the child; you would be concealed and discovered both together. These are things impossible, my dear; so you must e'en do as other conscientious mothers have done before you, and be contented with things as they must be, though they are not as you wish them to be.'

I understood what she meant by conscientious mothers; she would have said conscientious whores, but she was not willing to disoblige me, for really in this case I was not a whore, because legally married, the force of former marriage excepted.

However, let me be what I would, I was not come up to that pitch of hardness common to the profession; I mean, to be unnatural, and regardless of the safety of my child; and I preserved this honest affection so long, that I was upon the point of giving up my friend at the bank, who lay so hard at me to come to him and marry him, that, in short, there was hardly any room to deny him.

At last my old governess came to me, with her usual assurance. 'Come, my dear,' says she, 'I have found out a way how you shall be at a certainty that your child shall be used well, and yet the people that take care of it shall never know you, or who the mother of the child is.'

'Oh mother,' says I, 'if you can do so, you will engage me to you for ever.' 'Well,' says she, 'are you willing to be a some small annual expense, more than what we usually give to the people we contract with?' 'Ay,' says I, 'with all my heart, provided I may be concealed.' 'As to that,' says the governess, 'you shall be secure, for the nurse shall never so much as dare to inquire about you, and you shall once or twice a year go with me and see your child, and see how 'tis used, and be satisfied that it is in good hands, nobody knowing who you are.'

'Why,' said I, 'do you think, mother, that when I come to see my child, I shall be able to conceal my being the mother of it? Do you think that possible?'

'Well, well,' says my governess, 'if you discover it, the nurse shall be never the wiser; for she shall be forbid to ask any questions about you, or to take any notice. If she offers it, she shall lose the money which you are suppose to give her, and the child shall be taken from her too.'

I was very well pleased with this. So the next week a countrywoman was brought from Hertford, or thereabouts, who was to take the child off our hands entirely for £10 in money. But if I would allow £5 a year more of her, she would be obliged to bring the child to my governess's house as often as we desired, or we should come down and look at it, and see how well she used it.

The woman was very wholesome-looking, a likely woman, a cottager's wife, but she had very good clothes and linen, and everything well about her; and with a heavy heart and many a tear, I let her have my child. I had been down at Hertford, and looked at her and at her dwelling, which I liked well enough; and I promised her great things if she would be kind to the child, so she knew at first word that I was the child's mother. But she seemed to be so much out of the way, and to have no room to inquire after me, that I thought I was safe enough. So, in short, I consented to let her have the child, and I gave her £10; that is to say, I gave it to my governess, who gave it the poor woman before my face, she agreeing never to return the child back to me, or to claim anything more for its keeping or bringing up; only that I promised, if she took a great deal of care of it, I would give her something more as often as I came to see it; so that I was not bound to pay the £5, only that I promised my governess I would do it. And thus my great care was over, after a manner, which though it did not at all satisfy my mind, yet was the most convenient for me, as my affairs then stood, of any that could be thought of at that time.

I then began to write to my friend at the bank in a more kindly style, and particularly about the beginning of July I sent him a letter, that I proposed to be in town some time in August. He returned me an answer in the most passionate terms imaginable, and desired me to let him have timely notice, and he would come and meet me, two day's journey. This puzzled me scurvily, and I did not know what answer to make of it. Once I resolved to take the stage-coach to West Chester, on purpose only to have the satisfaction of coming back, that he might see me really come in the same coach; for I had a jealous thought, though I had no ground for it at all, lest he should think I was not really in the country. And it was no ill-grounded thought as you shall hear presently.

I endeavoured to reason myself out of it, but it was in vain; the impression lay so strong on my mind, that it was not to be resisted. At last it came as an addition to my new design of going into the country, that it would be an excellent blind to my old governess, and would cover entirely all my other affairs, for she did not know in the least whether my new lover lived in London or in Lancashire; and when I told her my resolution, she was fully persuaded it was in Lancashire.

Having taken my measure for this journey I let her know it, and sent the maid that tended me, from the beginning, to take a place for me in the coach. She would have had me let the maid have waited on me down to the last stage, and come up again in the waggon, but I convinced her it would not be convenient. When I went away, she told me she would enter into no measures for correspondence, for she saw evidently that my affection to my child would cause me to write to her, and to visit her too when I came to town again. I assured her it would, and so took my leave, well satisfied to have been freed from such a house, however good my accommodations there had been, as I have related above.

I took the place in the coach not to its full extent, but to a place called Stone, in Cheshire, I think it is, where I not only had no manner of business, but not so much as the least acquaintance with any person in the town or near it. But I knew that with money in the pocket one is at home anywhere; so I lodged there two or three days, till, watching my opportunity, I found room in another stage-coach, and took passage back again for London, sending a letter to my gentleman that I should be such a certain day at Stony-Stratford, where the coachman told me he was to lodge.

It happened to be a chance coach that I had taken up, which, having been hired on purpose to carry some gentlemen to West Chester who were going for Ireland, was now returning, and did not tie itself to exact times or places as the stages did; so that, having been obliged to lie still on Sunday, he had time to get himself ready to come out, which otherwise he could not have done.

However, his warning was so short, that he could not reach to Stony-Stratford time enough to be with me at night, but he met me at a place called Brickhill the next morning, as we were just coming in to tow.

I confess I was very glad to see him, for I had thought myself a little disappointed over-night, seeing I had gone so far to contrive my coming on purpose. He pleased me doubly too by the figure he came in, for he brought a very handsome (gentleman's) coach and four horses, with a servant to attend him.

He took me out of the stage-coach immediately, which stopped at an inn in Brickhill; and putting into the same inn, he set up his own coach, and bespoke his dinner. I asked him what he meant by that, for I was for going forward with the journey. He said, No, I had need of a little rest upon the road, and that was a very good sort of a house, though it was but a little town; so we would go no farther that night, whatever came of it.

I did not press him much, for since he had come so to meet me, and put himself to so much expense, it was but reasonable I should oblige him a little too; so I was easy as to that point.

After dinner we walked to see the town, to see the church, and to view the fields, and the country, as is usual for strangers to do; and our landlord was our guide in going to see the church. I observed my gentleman inquired pretty much about the parson, and I took the hint immediately that he certainly would propose to be married; and though it was a sudden thought, it followed presently, that, in short, I would not refuse him; for, to be plain, with my circumstances I was in no condition now to say No; I had no reason now to run any more such hazards.

But while these thoughts ran round in my head, which was the work but of a few moments, I observed my landlord took him aside and whispered to him, though not very softly neither, for so much I overheard: 'Sir, if you shall have occasion——' the rest I could not hear, but it seems it was to this purpose: 'Sir, if you shall have occasion for a minister, I have a friend a little way off that will serve you, and be as private as you please.' My gentleman answered loud enough for me to hear, 'Very well, I believe I shall.'

I was no sooner come back to the inn but he fell upon me with irresistible words, that since he had had the good fortune to meet me, and everything concurred, it would be hastening his felicity if I would put an end to the matter just there. 'What do you mean?' says I, colouring a little. 'What, in an inn, and upon the road! Bless us all,' said I, as if I had been surprised, 'how can you talk so?' 'Oh, I can talk so very well,' says he, 'I came a-purpose to talk so, and I'll show you that I did'; and with that he pulls out a great bundle of papers. 'You fright me,' said I; 'what are all these?' 'Don't be frighted, my dear,' said he, and kissed me. This was the first time that he had been so free to call me 'my dear'; then he repeated it, 'Don't be frighted; you shall see what it is all'; then he laid them all abroad. There was first the deed or sentence of divorce from his wife, and the full evidence of her playing the whore; then there were the certificates of the minister and churchwardens of the parish where she lived, proving that she was buried, and intimating the manner of her death; the copy of the coroner's warrant for a jury to sit upon her, and the verdict of the jury, who brought it in Non compos mentis. All this was indeed to the purpose, and to give me satisfaction, though, by the way, I was not so scrupulous, had he known all, but that I might have taken him without it. However, I looked them all over as well as I could, and told him that this was all very clear indeed, but that he need not have given himself the trouble to have brought them out with him, for it was time enough. Well, he said, it might be time enough for me, but no time but the present time was time enough for him.

There were other papers rolled up, and I asked him what they were. 'Why, ay,' says he, 'that's the question I wanted to have you ask me'; so he unrolls them and takes out a little shagreen case, and gives me out of it a very fine diamond ring. I could not refuse it, if I had a mind to do so, for he put it upon my finger; so I made him a curtsy and accepted it. Then he takes out another ring: 'And this,' says he, 'is for another occasion,' so he puts that in his pocket. 'Well, but let me see it, though,' says I, and smiled; 'I guess what it is; I think you are mad.' 'I should have been mad if I had done less,' says he, and still he did not show me, and I had a great mind to see it; so I says, 'Well, but let me see it.' 'Hold,' says he, 'first look here'; then he took up the roll again and read it, and behold! it was a licence for us to be married. 'Why,' says I, 'are you distracted? Why, you were fully satisfied that I would comply and yield at first word, or resolved to take no denial.' 'The last is certainly the case,' said he. 'But you may be mistaken,' said I. 'No, no,' says he, 'how can you think so? I must not be denied, I can't be denied'; and with that he fell to kissing me so violently, I could not get rid of him.

There was a bed in the room, and we were walking to and again, eager in the discourse; at last he takes me by surprise in his arms, and threw me on the bed and himself with me, and holding me fast in his arms, but without the least offer of any indecency, courted me to consent with such repeated entreaties and arguments, protesting his affection, and vowing he would not let me go till I had promised him, that at last I said, 'Why, you resolve not to be denied, indeed, I can't be denied.' 'Well, well,' said I, and giving him a slight kiss, 'then you shan't be denied,' said I; 'let me get up.'

He was so transported with my consent, and the kind manner of it, that I began to think once he took it for a marriage, and would not stay for the form; but I wronged him, for he gave over kissing me, and then giving me two or three kisses again, thanked me for my kind yielding to him; and was so overcome with the satisfaction and joy of it, that I saw tears stand in his eyes.

I turned from him, for it filled my eyes with tears too, and I asked him leave to retire a little to my chamber. If ever I had a grain of true repentance for a vicious and abominable life for twenty-four years past, it was then. On, what a felicity is it to mankind, said I to myself, that they cannot see into the hearts of one another! How happy had it been for me if I had been wife to a man of so much honesty, and so much affection from the beginning!

Then it occurred to me, 'What an abominable creature am I! and how is this innocent gentleman going to be abused by me! How little does he think, that having divorced a whore, he is throwing himself into the arms of another! that he is going to marry one that has lain with two brothers, and has had three children by her own brother! one that was born in Newgate, whose mother was a whore, and is now a transported thief! one that has lain with thirteen men, and has had a child since he saw me! Poor gentleman!' said I, 'what is he going to do?' After this reproaching myself was over, it following thus: 'Well, if I must be his wife, if it please God to give me grace, I'll be a true wife to him, and love him suitably to the strange excess of his passion for me; I will make him amends if possible, by what he shall see, for the cheats and abuses I put upon him, which he does not see.'

He was impatient for my coming out of my chamber, but finding me long, he went downstairs and talked with my landlord about the parson.

My landlord, an officious though well-meaning fellow, had sent away for the neighbouring clergyman; and when my gentleman began to speak of it to him, and talk of sending for him, 'Sir,' says he to him, 'my friend is in the house'; so without any more words he brought them together. When he came to the minister, he asked him if he would venture to marry a couple of strangers that were both willing. The parson said that Mr. —— had said something to him of it; that he hoped it was no clandestine business; that he seemed to be a grave gentleman, and he supposed madam was not a girl, so that the consent of friends should be wanted. 'To put you out of doubt of that,' says my gentleman, 'read this paper'; and out he pulls the license. 'I am satisfied,' says the minister; 'where is the lady?' 'You shall see her presently,' says my gentleman.

When he had said thus he comes upstairs, and I was by that time come out of my room; so he tells me the minister was below, and that he had talked with him, and that upon showing him the license, he was free to marry us with all his heart, 'but he asks to see you'; so he asked if I would let him come up.

''Tis time enough,' said I, 'in the morning, is it not?' 'Why,' said he, 'my dear, he seemed to scruple whether it was not some young girl stolen from her parents, and I assured him we were both of age to command our own consent; and that made him ask to see you.' 'Well,' said I, 'do as you please'; so up they brings the parson, and a merry, good sort of gentleman he was. He had been told, it seems, that we had met there by accident, that I came in the Chester coach, and my gentleman in his own coach to meet me; that we were to have met last night at Stony-Stratford, but that he could not reach so far. 'Well, sir,' says the parson, 'every ill turn has some good in it. The disappointment, sir,' says he to my gentleman, 'was yours, and the good turn is mine, for if you had met at Stony-Stratford I had not had the honour to marry you. Landlord, have you a Common Prayer Book?'

I started as if I had been frightened. 'Lord, sir,' says I, 'what do you mean? What, to marry in an inn, and at night too?' 'Madam,' says the minister, 'if you will have it be in the church, you shall; but I assure you your marriage will be as firm here as in the church; we are not tied by the canons to marry nowhere but in the church; and if you will have it in the church, it will be a public as a county fair; and as for the time of day, it does not at all weigh in this case; our princes are married in their chambers, and at eight or ten o'clock at night.'

I was a great while before I could be persuaded, and pretended not to be willing at all to be married but in the church. But it was all grimace; so I seemed at last to be prevailed on, and my landlord and his wife and daughter were called up. My landlord was father and clerk and all together, and we were married, and very merry we were; though I confess the self-reproaches which I had upon me before lay close to me, and extorted every now and then a deep sigh from me, which my bridegroom took notice of, and endeavoured to encourage me, thinking, poor man, that I had some little hesitations at the step I had taken so hastily.

We enjoyed ourselves that evening completely, and yet all was kept so private in the inn that not a servant in the house knew of it, for my landlady and her daughter waited on me, and would not let any of the maids come upstairs, except while we were at supper. My landlady's daughter I called my bridesmaid; and sending for a shopkeeper the next morning, I gave the young woman a good suit of knots, as good as the town would afford, and finding it was a lace-making town, I gave her mother a piece of bone-lace for a head.

One reason that my landlord was so close was, that he was unwilling the minister of the parish should hear of it; but for all that somebody heard of it, so at that we had the bells set a-ringing the next morning early, and the music, such as the town would afford, under our window; but my landlord brazened it out, that we were married before we came thither, only that, being his former guests, we would have our wedding-supper at his house.

We could not find in our hearts to stir the next day; for, in short, having been disturbed by the bells in the morning, and having perhaps not slept overmuch before, we were so sleepy afterwards that we lay in bed till almost twelve o'clock.

I begged my landlady that we might not have any more music in the town, nor ringing of bells, and she managed it so well that we were very quiet; but an odd passage interrupted all my mirth for a good while. The great room of the house looked into the street, and my new spouse being belowstairs, I had walked to the end of the room; and it being a pleasant, warm day, I had opened the window, and was standing at it for some air, when I saw three gentlemen come by on horseback and go into an inn just against us.

It was not to be concealed, nor was it so doubtful as to leave me any room to question it, but the second of the three was my Lancashire husband. I was frightened to death; I never was in such a consternation in my life; I though I should have sunk into the ground; my blood ran chill in my veins, and I trembled as if I had been in a cold fit of ague. I say, there was no room to question the truth of it; I knew his clothes, I knew his horse, and I knew his face.

The first sensible reflect I made was, that my husband was not by to see my disorder, and that I was very glad of it. The gentlemen had not been long in the house but they came to the window of their room, as is usual; but my window was shut, you may be sure. However, I could not keep from peeping at them, and there I saw him again, heard him call out to one of the servants of the house for something he wanted, and received all the terrifying confirmations of its being the same person that were possible to be had.

My next concern was to know, if possible, what was his business there; but that was impossible. Sometimes my imagination formed an idea of one frightful thing, sometimes of another; sometime I thought he had discovered me, and was come to upbraid me with ingratitude and breach of honour; and every moment I fancied he was coming up the stairs to insult me; and innumerable fancies came into my head of what was never in his head, nor ever could be, unless the devil had revealed it to him.

I remained in this fright nearly two hours, and scarce ever kept my eye from the window or door of the inn where they were. At last, hearing a great clatter in the passage of their inn, I ran to the window, and, to my great satisfaction, saw them all three go out again and travel on westward. Had they gone towards London, I should have been still in a fright, lest I should meet him on the road again, and that he should know me; but he went the contrary way, and so I was eased of that disorder.

We resolved to be going the next day, but about six o'clock at night we were alarmed with a great uproar in the street, and people riding as if they had been out of their wits; and what was it but a hue-and-cry after three highwaymen that had robbed two coaches and some other travellers near Dunstable Hill, and notice had, it seems, been given that they had been seen at Brickhill at such a house, meaning the house where those gentlemen had been.

The house was immediately beset and searched, but there were witnesses enough that the gentlemen had been gone over three hours. The crowd having gathered about, we had the news presently; and I was heartily concerned now another way. I presently told the people of the house, that I durst to say those were not the persons, for that I knew one of the gentlemen to be a very honest person, and of a good estate in Lancashire.

The constable who came with the hue-and-cry was immediately informed of this, and came over to me to be satisfied from my own mouth, and I assured him that I saw the three gentlemen as I was at the window; that I saw them afterwards at the windows of the room they dined in; that I saw them afterwards take horse, and I could assure him I knew one of them to be such a man, that he was a gentleman of a very good estate, and an undoubted character in Lancashire, from whence I was just now upon my journey.

The assurance with which I delivered this gave the mob gentry a check, and gave the constable such satisfaction, that he immediately sounded a retreat, told his people these were not the men, but that he had an account they were very honest gentlemen; and so they went all back again. What the truth of the matter was I knew not, but certain it was that the coaches were robbed at Dunstable Hill, and £560 in money taken; besides, some of the lace merchants that always travel that way had been visited too. As to the three gentlemen, that remains to be explained hereafter.

Well, this alarm stopped us another day, though my spouse was for travelling, and told me that it was always safest travelling after a robbery, for that the thieves were sure to be gone far enough off when they had alarmed the country; but I was afraid and uneasy, and indeed principally lest my old acquaintance should be upon the road still, and should chance to see me.

I never lived four pleasanter days together in my life. I was a mere bride all this while, and my new spouse strove to make me entirely easy in everything. Oh could this state of life have continued, how had all my past troubles been forgot, and my future sorrows avoided! But I had a past life of a most wretched kind to account for, some if it in this world as well as in another.

We came away the fifth day; and my landlord, because he saw me uneasy, mounted himself, his son, and three honest country fellows with good firearms, and, without telling us of it, followed the coach, and would see us safe into Dunstable. We could do no less than treat them very handsomely at Dunstable, which cost my spouse about ten or twelve shillings, and something he gave the men for their time too, but my landlord would take nothing for himself.

This was the most happy contrivance for me that could have fallen out; for had I come to London unmarried, I must either have come to him for the first night's entertainment, or have discovered to him that I had not one acquaintance in the whole city of London that could receive a poor bride for the first night's lodging with her spouse. But now, being an old married woman, I made no scruple of going directly home with him, and there I took possession at once of a house well furnished, and a husband in very good circumstances, so that I had a prospect of a very happy life, if I knew how to manage it; and I had leisure to consider of the real value of the life I was likely to live. How different it was to be from the loose ungoverned part I had acted before, and how much happier a life of virtue and sobriety is, than that which we call a life of pleasure.

Oh had this particular scene of life lasted, or had I learned from that time I enjoyed it, to have tasted the true sweetness of it, and had I not fallen into that poverty which is the sure bane of virtue, how happy had I been, not only here, but perhaps for ever! for while I lived thus, I was really a penitent for all my life past. I looked back on it with abhorrence, and might truly be said to hate myself for it. I often reflected how my lover at the Bath, struck at the hand of God, repented and abandoned me, and refused to see me any more, though he loved me to an extreme; but I, prompted by that worst of devils, poverty, returned to the vile practice, and made the advantage of what they call a handsome face to be the relief to my necessities, and beauty be a pimp to vice.

Now I seemed landed in a safe harbour, after the stormy voyage of life past was at an end, and I began to be thankful for my deliverance. I sat many an hour by myself, and wept over the remembrance of past follies, and the dreadful extravagances of a wicked life, and sometimes I flattered myself that I had sincerely repented.

But there are temptations which it is not in the power of human nature to resist, and few know what would be their case if driven to the same exigencies. As covetousness is the root of all evil, so poverty is, I believe, the worst of all snares. But I waive that discourse till I come to an experiment.

I lived with this husband with the utmost tranquillity; he was a quiet, sensible, sober man; virtuous, modest, sincere, and in his business diligent and just. His business was in a narrow compass, and his income sufficient to a plentiful way of living in the ordinary way. I do not say to keep an equipage, and make a figure, as the world calls it, nor did I expect it, or desire it; for as I abhorred the levity and extravagance of my former life, so I chose now to live retired, frugal, and within ourselves. I kept no company, made no visits; minded my family, and obliged my husband; and this kind of life became a pleasure to me.

We lived in an uninterrupted course of ease and content for five years, when a sudden blow from an almost invisible hand blasted all my happiness, and turned me out into the world in a condition the reverse of all that had been before it.

My husband having trusted one of his fellow-clerks with a sum of money, too much for our fortunes to bear the loss of, the clerk failed, and the loss fell very heavy on my husband, yet it was not so great neither but that, if he had had spirit and courage to have looked his misfortunes in the face, his credit was so good that, as I told him, he would easily recover it; for to sink under trouble is to double the weight, and he that will die in it, shall die in it.

It was in vain to speak comfortably to him; the wound had sunk too deep; it was a stab that touched the vitals; he grew melancholy and disconsolate, and from thence lethargic, and died. I foresaw the blow, and was extremely oppressed in my mind, for I saw evidently that if he died I was undone.

I had had two children by him and no more, for, to tell the truth, it began to be time for me to leave bearing children, for I was now eight-and-forty, and I suppose if he had lived I should have had no more.

I was now left in a dismal and disconsolate case indeed, and in several things worse than ever. First, it was past the flourishing time with me when I might expect to be courted for a mistress; that agreeable part had declined some time, and the ruins only appeared of what had been; and that which was worse than all this, that I was the most dejected, disconsolate creature alive. I that had encouraged my husband, and endeavoured to support his spirits under his trouble, could not support my own; I wanted that spirit in trouble which I told him was so necessary to him for bearing the burthen.

But my case was indeed deplorable, for I was left perfectly friendless and helpless, and the loss my husband had sustained had reduced his circumstances so low, that though indeed I was not in debt, yet I could easily foresee that what was left would not support me long; that while it wasted daily for subsistence, I had not way to increase it one shilling, so that it would be soon all spent, and then I saw nothing before me but the utmost distress; and this represented itself so lively to my thoughts, that it seemed as if it was come, before it was really very near; also my very apprehensions doubled the misery, for I fancied every sixpence that I paid for a loaf of bread was the last that I had in the world, and that to-morrow I was to fast, and be starved to death.

In this distress I had no assistant, no friend to comfort or advise me; I sat and cried and tormented myself night and day, wringing my hands, and sometimes raving like a distracted woman; and indeed I have often wondered it had not affected my reason, for I had the vapours to such a degree, that my understanding was sometimes quite lost in fancies and imaginations.

I lived two years in this dismal condition, wasting that little I had, weeping continually over my dismal circumstances, and, as it were, only bleeding to death, without the least hope or prospect of help from God or man; and now I had cried too long, and so often, that tears were, as I might say, exhausted, and I began to be desperate, for I grew poor apace.

For a little relief I had put off my house and took lodgings; and as I was reducing my living, so I sold off most of my goods, which put a little money in my pocket, and I lived near a year upon that, spending very sparingly, and eking things out to the utmost; but still when I looked before me, my very heart would sink within me at the inevitable approach of misery and want. Oh let none read this part without seriously reflecting on the circumstances of a desolate state, and how they would grapple with mere want of friends and want of bread; it will certainly make them think not of sparing what they have only, but of looking up to heaven for support, and of the wise man's prayer, 'Give me not poverty, lest I steal.'

Let them remember that a time of distress is a time of dreadful temptation, and all the strength to resist is taken away; poverty presses, the soul is made desperate by distress, and what can be done? It was one evening, when being brought, as I may say, to the last gasp, I think I may truly say I was distracted and raving, when prompted by I know not what spirit, and, as it were, doing I did not know what or why, I dressed me (for I had still pretty good clothes) and went out. I am very sure I had no manner of design in my head when I went out; I neither knew nor considered where to go, or on what business; but as the devil carried me out and laid his bait for me, so he brought me, to be sure, to the place, for I knew not whither I was going or what I did.

Wandering thus about, I knew not whither, I passed by an apothecary's shop in Leadenhall Street, when I saw lie on a stool just before the counter a little bundle wrapped in a white cloth; beyond it stood a maid-servant with her back to it, looking towards the top of the shop, where the apothecary's apprentice, as I suppose, was standing upon the counter, with his back also to the door, and a candle in his hand, looking and reaching up to the upper shelf for something he wanted, so that both were engaged mighty earnestly, and nobody else in the shop.

This was the bait; and the devil, who I said laid the snare, as readily prompted me as if he had spoke, for I remember, and shall never forget it, 'twas like a voice spoken to me over my shoulder, 'Take the bundle; be quick; do it this moment.' It was no sooner said but I stepped into the shop, and with my back to the wench, as if I had stood up for a cart that was going by, I put my hand behind me and took the bundle, and went off with it, the maid or the fellow not perceiving me, or any one else.

It is impossible to express the horror of my soul all the while I did it. When I went away I had no heart to run, or scarce to mend my pace. I crossed the street indeed, and went down the first turning I came to, and I think it was a street that went through into Fenchurch Street. From thence I crossed and turned through so many ways and turnings, that I could never tell which way it was, not where I went; for I felt not the ground I stepped on, and the farther I was out of danger, the faster I went, till, tired and out of breath, I was forced to sit down on a little bench at a door, and then I began to recover, and found I was got into Thames Street, near Billingsgate. I rested me a little and went on; my blood was all in a fire; my heart beat as if I was in a sudden fright. In short, I was under such a surprise that I still knew not wither I was going, or what to do.

After I had tired myself thus with walking a long way about, and so eagerly, I began to consider and make home to my lodging, where I came about nine o'clock at night.

When the bundle was made up for, or on what occasion laid where I found it, I knew not, but when I came to open it I found there was a suit of childbed-linen in it, very good and almost new, the lace very fine; there was a silver porringer of a pint, a small silver mug and six spoons, with some other linen, a good smock, and three silk handkerchiefs, and in the mug, wrapped up in a paper, 18s. 6d. in money.

All the while I was opening these things I was under such dreadful impressions of fear, and I such terror of mind, though I was perfectly safe, that I cannot express the manner of it. I sat me down, and cried most vehemently. 'Lord,' said I, 'what am I now? a thief! Why, I shall be taken next time, and be carried to Newgate and be tried for my life!' And with that I cried again a long time, and I am sure, as poor as I was, if I had durst for fear, I would certainly have carried the things back again; but that went off after a while. Well, I went to bed for that night, but slept little; the horror of the fact was upon my mind, and I knew not what I said or did all night, and all the next day. Then I was impatient to hear some news of the loss; and would fain know how it was, whether they were a poor body's goods, or a rich. 'Perhaps,' said I, 'it may be some poor widow like me, that had packed up these goods to go and sell them for a little bread for herself and a poor child, and are now starving and breaking their hearts for want of that little they would have fetched.' And this thought tormented me worse than all the rest, for three or four days' time.

But my own distresses silenced all these reflections, and the prospect of my own starving, which grew every day more frightful to me, hardened my heart by degrees. It was then particularly heavy upon my mind, that I had been reformed, and had, as I hoped, repented of all my past wickedness; that I had lived a sober, grave, retired life for several years, but now I should be driven by the dreadful necessity of my circumstances to the gates of destruction, soul and body; and two or three times I fell upon my knees, praying to God, as well as I could, for deliverance; but I cannot but say, my prayers had no hope in them. I knew not what to do; it was all fear without, and dark within; and I reflected on my past life as not sincerely repented of, that Heaven was now beginning to punish me on this side the grave, and would make me as miserable as I had been wicked.

Had I gone on here I had perhaps been a true penitent; but I had an evil counsellor within, and he was continually prompting me to relieve myself by the worst means; so one evening he tempted me again, by the same wicked impulse that had said 'Take that bundle,' to go out again and seek for what might happen.

I went out now by daylight, and wandered about I knew not whither, and in search of I knew not what, when the devil put a snare in my way of a dreadful nature indeed, and such a one as I have never had before or since. Going through Aldersgate Street, there was a pretty little child who had been at a dancing-school, and was going home, all alone; and my prompter, like a true devil, set me upon this innocent creature. I talked to it, and it prattled to me again, and I took it by the hand and led it along till I came to a paved alley that goes into Bartholomew Close, and I led it in there. The child said that was not its way home. I said, 'Yes, my dear, it is; I'll show you the way home.' The child had a little necklace on of gold beads, and I had my eye upon that, and in the dark of the alley I stooped, pretending to mend the child's clog that was loose, and took off her necklace, and the child never felt it, and so led the child on again. Here, I say, the devil put me upon killing the child in the dark alley, that it might not cry, but the very thought frighted me so that I was ready to drop down; but I turned the child about and bade it go back again, for that was not its way home. The child said, so she would, and I went through into Bartholomew Close, and then turned round to another passage that goes into St. John Street; then, crossing into Smithfield, went down Chick Lane and into Field Lane to Holborn Bridge, when, mixing with the crowd of people usually passing there, it was not possible to have been found out; and thus I enterprised my second sally into the world.

The thoughts of this booty put out all the thoughts of the first, and the reflections I had made wore quickly off; poverty, as I have said, hardened my heart, and my own necessities made me regardless of anything. The last affair left no great concern upon me, for as I did the poor child no harm, I only said to myself, I had given the parents a just reproof for their negligence in leaving the poor little lamb to come home by itself, and it would teach them to take more care of it another time.

This string of beads was worth about twelve or fourteen pounds. I suppose it might have been formerly the mother's, for it was too big for the child's wear, but that perhaps the vanity of the mother, to have her child look fine at the dancing-school, had made her let the child wear it; and no doubt the child had a maid sent to take care of it, but she, careless jade, was taken up perhaps with some fellow that had met her by the way, and so the poor baby wandered till it fell into my hands.

However, I did the child no harm; I did not so much as fright it, for I had a great many tender thoughts about me yet, and did nothing but what, as I may say, mere necessity drove me to.

I had a great many adventures after this, but I was young in the business, and did not know how to manage, otherwise than as the devil put things into my head; and indeed he was seldom backward to me. One adventure I had which was very lucky to me. I was going through Lombard Street in the dusk of the evening, just by the end of Three King court, when on a sudden comes a fellow running by me as swift as lightning, and throws a bundle that was in his hand, just behind me, as I stood up against the corner of the house at the turning into the alley. Just as he threw it in he said, 'God bless you, mistress, let it lie there a little,' and away he runs swift as the wind. After him comes two more, and immediately a young fellow without his hat, crying 'Stop thief!' and after him two or three more. They pursued the two last fellows so close, that they were forced to drop what they had got, and one of them was taken into the bargain, and other got off free.

I stood stock-still all this while, till they came back, dragging the poor fellow they had taken, and lugging the things they had found, extremely well satisfied that they had recovered the booty and taken the thief; and thus they passed by me, for I looked only like one who stood up while the crowd was gone.

Once or twice I asked what was the matter, but the people neglected answering me, and I was not very importunate; but after the crowd was wholly past, I took my opportunity to turn about and take up what was behind me and walk away. This, indeed, I did with less disturbance than I had done formerly, for these things I did not steal, but they were stolen to my hand. I got safe to my lodgings with this cargo, which was a piece of fine black lustring silk, and a piece of velvet; the latter was but part of a piece of about eleven yards; the former was a whole piece of near fifty yards. It seems it was a mercer's shop that they had rifled. I say rifled, because the goods were so considerable that they had lost; for the goods that they recovered were pretty many, and I believe came to about six or seven several pieces of silk. How they came to get so many I could not tell; but as I had only robbed the thief, I made no scruple at taking these goods, and being very glad of them too.

I had pretty good luck thus far, and I made several adventures more, though with but small purchase, yet with good success, but I went in daily dread that some mischief would befall me, and that I should certainly come to be hanged at last. The impression this made on me was too strong to be slighted, and it kept me from making attempts that, for ought I knew, might have been very safely performed; but one thing I cannot omit, which was a bait to me many a day. I walked frequently out into the villages round the town, to see if nothing would fall in my way there; and going by a house near Stepney, I saw on the window-board two rings, one a small diamond ring, and the other a gold ring, to be sure laid there by some thoughtless lady, that had more money then forecast, perhaps only till she washed her hands.

I walked several times by the window to observe if I could see whether there was anybody in the room or no, and I could see nobody, but still I was not sure. It came presently into my thoughts to rap at the glass, as if I wanted to speak with somebody, and if anybody was there they would be sure to come to the window, and then I would tell them to remove those rings, for that I had seen two suspicious fellows take notice of them. This was a ready thought. I rapped once or twice and nobody came, when, seeing the coast clear, I thrust hard against the square of the glass, and broke it with very little noise, and took out the two rings, and walked away with them very safe. The diamond ring was worth about £3, and the other about 9s.

I was now at a loss for a market for my goods, and especially for my two pieces of silk. I was very loth to dispose of them for a trifle, as the poor unhappy thieves in general do, who, after they have ventured their lives for perhaps a thing of value, are fain to sell it for a song when they have done; but I was resolved I would not do thus, whatever shift I made, unless I was driven to the last extremity. However, I did not well know what course to take. At last I resolved to go to my old governess, and acquaint myself with her again. I had punctually supplied the £5 a year to her for my little boy as long as I was able, but at last was obliged to put a stop to it. However, I had written a letter to her, wherein I had told her that my circumstances were reduced very low; that I had lost my husband, and that I was not able to do it any longer, and so begged that the poor child might not suffer too much for its mother's misfortunes.

I now made her a visit, and I found that she drove something of the old trade still, but that she was not in such flourishing circumstances as before; for she had been sued by a certain gentleman who had had his daughter stolen from him, and who, it seems, she had helped to convey away; and it was very narrowly that she escaped the gallows. The expense also had ravaged her, and she was become very poor; her house was but meanly furnished, and she was not in such repute for her practice as before; however, she stood upon her legs, as they say, and a she was a stirring, bustling woman, and had some stock left, she was turned pawnbroker, and lived pretty well.

She received me very civilly, and with her usual obliging manner told me she would not have the less respect for me for my being reduced; that she had taken care my boy was very well looked after, though I could not pay for him, and that the woman that had him was easy, so that I needed not to trouble myself about him till I might be better able to do it effectually.

I told her that I had not much money left, but that I had some things that were money's worth, if she could tell me how I might turn them into money. She asked me what it was I had. I pulled out the string of gold beads, and told her it was one of my husband's presents to me; then I showed her the two parcels of silk, which I told her I had from Ireland, and brought up to town with me; and the little diamond ring. As to the small parcel of plate and spoons, I had found means to dispose of them myself before; and as for the childbed-linen I had, she offered me to take it herself, believing it to have been my own. She told me that she was turned pawnbroker, and that she would sell those things for me as pawn to her; and so she sent presently for proper agents that bought them, being in her hands, without any scruple, and gave good prices too.

I now began to think this necessary woman might help me a little in my low condition to some business, for I would gladly have turned my hand to any honest employment if I could have got it. But here she was deficient; honest business did not come within her reach. If I had been younger, perhaps she might have helped me to a spark, but my thoughts were off that kind of livelihood, as being quite out of the way after fifty, which was my case, and so I told her.

She invited me at last to come, and be at her house till I could find something to do, and it should cost me very little, and this I gladly accepted of. And now living a little easier, I entered into some measures to have my little son by my last husband taken off; and this she made easy too, reserving a payment only of £5 a year, if I could pay it. This was such a help to me, that for a good while I left off the wicked trade that I had so newly taken up; and gladly I would have got my bread by the help of my needle if I could have got work, but that was very hard to do for one that had no manner of acquaintance in the world.

However, at last I got some quilting work for ladies' beds, petticoats, and the like; and this I liked very well, and worked very hard, and with this I began to live; but the diligent devil, who resolved I should continue in his service, continually prompted me to go out and take a walk, that is to say, to see if anything would offer in the old way.

One evening I blindly obeyed his summons, and fetched a long circuit through the streets, but met with no purchase, and came home very weary and empty; but not content with that, I went out the next evening too, when going by an alehouse

I saw the door of a little room open, next the very street, and on the table a silver tankard, things much in use in public-houses at that time. It seems some company had been drinking there, and the careless boys had forgot to take it away.

I went into the box frankly, and setting the silver tankard on the corner of the bench, I sat down before it, and knocked with my foot; a boy came presently, and I bade him fetch me a pint of warm ale, for it was cold weather; the boy ran, and I heard him go down the cellar to draw the ale. While the boy was gone, another boy came into the room, and cried, 'D' ye call?' I spoke with a melancholy air, and said, 'No, child; the boy is gone for a pint of ale for me.'

While I sat here, I heard the woman in the bar say, 'Are they all gone in the five?' which was the box I sat in, and the boy said, 'Yes.' 'Who fetched the tankard away?' says the woman. 'I did,' says another boy; 'that's it,' pointing, it seems, to another tankard, which he had fetched from another box by mistake; or else it must be, that the rogue forgot that he had not brought it in, which certainly he had not.

I heard all this, much to my satisfaction, for I found plainly that the tankard was not missed, and yet they concluded it was fetched away; so I drank my ale, called to pay, and as I went away I said, 'Take care of your plate, child,' meaning a silver pint mug, which he brought me drink in. The boy said, 'Yes, madam, very welcome,' and away I came.

I came home to my governess, and now I thought it was a time to try her, that if I might be put to the necessity of being exposed, she might offer me some assistance. When I had been at home some time, and had an opportunity of talking to her, I told her I had a secret of the greatest consequence in the world to commit to her, if she had respect enough for me to keep it a secret. She told me she had kept one of my secrets faithfully; why should I doubt her keeping another? I told her the strangest thing in the world had befallen me, and that it had made a thief of me, even without any design, and so told her the whole story of the tankard. 'And have you brought it away with you, my dear?' says she. 'To be sure I have,' says I, and showed it her. 'But what shall I do now,' says I; 'must not carry it again?'

'Carry it again!' says she. 'Ay, if you are minded to be sent to Newgate for stealing it.' 'Why,' says I, 'they can't be so base to stop me, when I carry it to them again?' 'You don't know those sort of people, child,' says she; 'they'll not only carry you to Newgate, but hang you too, without any regard to the honesty of returning it; or bring in an account of all the other tankards they have lost, for you to pay for.' 'What must I do, then?' says I. 'Nay,' says she, 'as you have played the cunning part and stole it, you must e'en keep it; there's no going back now. Besides, child,' says she, 'don't you want it more than they do? I wish you could light of such a bargain once a week.'

This gave me a new notion of my governess, and that since she was turned pawnbroker, she had a sort of people about her that were none of the honest ones that I had met with there before.

I had not been long there but I discovered it more plainly than before, for every now and then I saw hilts of swords, spoons, forks, tankards, and all such kind of ware brought in, not to be pawned, but to be sold downright; and she bought everything that came without asking any questions, but had very good bargains, as I found by her discourse.

I found also that in following this trade she always melted down the plate she bought, that it might not be challenged; and she came to me and told me one morning that she was going to melt, and if I would, she would put my tankard in, that it might not be seen by anybody. I told her, with all my heart; so she weighed it, and allowed me the full value in silver again; but I found she did not do the same to the rest of her customers.

Some time after this, as I was at work, and very melancholy, she begins to ask me what the matter was, as she was used to do. I told her my heart was heavy; I had little work, and nothing to live on, and knew not what course to take. She laughed, and told me I must go out again and try my fortune; it might be that I might meet with another piece of plate. 'O mother!' says I, 'that is a trade I have no skill in, and if I should be taken I am undone at once.' Says she, 'I could help you to a schoolmistress that shall make you as dexterous as herself.' I trembled at that proposal, for hitherto I had had no confederates, nor any acquaintance among that tribe. But she conquered all my modesty, and all my fears; and in a little time, by the help of this confederate, I grew as impudent a thief, and as dexterous as ever Moll Cutpurse was, though, if fame does not belie her, not half so handsome.

The comrade she helped me to dealt in three sorts of craft, viz. shoplifting, stealing of shop-books and pocket-books, and taking off gold watches from the ladies' sides; and this last she did so dexterously that no woman ever arrived to the performance of that art so as to do it like her. I liked the first and the last of these things very well, and I attended her some time in the practice, just as a deputy attends a midwife, without any pay.

At length she put me to practice. She had shown me her art, and I had several times unhooked a watch from her own side with great dexterity. At last she showed me a prize, and this was a young lady big with child, who had a charming watch. The thing was to be done as she came out of church. She goes on one side of the lady, and pretends, just as she came to the steps, to fall, and fell against the lady with so much violence as put her into a great fright, and both cried out terribly. In the very moment that she jostled the lady, I had hold of the watch, and holding it the right way, the start she gave drew the hook out, and she never felt it. I made off immediately, and left my schoolmistress to come out of her pretended fright gradually, and the lady too; and presently the watch was missed. 'Ay,' says my comrade, 'then it was those rogues that thrust me down, I warrant ye; I wonder the gentlewoman did not miss her watch before, then we might have taken them.'

She humoured the thing so well that nobody suspected her, and I was got home a full hour before her. This was my first adventure in company. The watch was indeed a very fine one, and had a great many trinkets about it, and my governess allowed us £20 for it, of which I had half. And thus I was entered a complete thief, hardened to the pitch above all the reflections of conscience or modesty, and to a degree which I must acknowledge I never thought possible in me.

Thus the devil, who began, by the help of an irresistible poverty, to push me into this wickedness, brought me on to a height beyond the common rate, even when my necessities were not so great, or the prospect of my misery so terrifying; for I had now got into a little vein of work, and as I was not at a loss to handle my needle, it was very probable, as acquaintance came in, I might have got my bread honestly enough.

I must say, that if such a prospect of work had presented itself at first, when I began to feel the approach of my miserable circumstances—I say, had such a prospect of getting my bread by working presented itself then, I had never fallen into this wicked trade, or into such a wicked gang as I was now embarked with; but practice had hardened me, and I grew audacious to the last degree; and the more so because I had carried it on so long, and had never been taken; for, in a word, my new partner in wickedness and I went on together so long, without being ever detected, that we not only grew bold, but we grew rich, and we had at one time one-and-twenty gold watches in our hands.

I remember that one day being a little more serious than ordinary, and finding I had so good a stock beforehand as I had, for I had near £200 in money for my share, it came strongly into my mind, no doubt from some kind spirit, if such there be, that at first poverty excited me, and my distresses drove me to these dreadful shifts; so seeing those distresses were now relieved, and I could also get something towards a maintenance by working, and had so good a bank to support me, why should I now not leave off, as they say, while I was well? that I could not expect to go always free; and if I was once surprised, and miscarried, I was undone.

This was doubtless the happy minute, when, if I had hearkened to the blessed hint, from whatsoever had it came, I had still a cast for an easy life. But my fate was otherwise determined; the busy devil that so industriously drew me in had too fast hold of me to let me go back; but as poverty brought me into the mire, so avarice kept me in, till there was no going back. As to the arguments which my reason dictated for persuading me to lay down, avarice stepped in and said, 'Go on, go on; you have had very good luck; go on till you have gotten four or five hundred pounds, and they you shall leave off, and then you may live easy without working at all.'

Thus I, that was once in the devil's clutches, was held fast there as with a charm, and had no power to go without the circle, till I was engulfed in labyrinths of trouble too great to get out at all.

However, these thoughts left some impression upon me, and made me act with some more caution than before, and more than my directors used for themselves. My comrade, as I called her, but rather she should have been called my teacher, with another of her scholars, was the first in the misfortune; for, happening to be upon the hunt for purchase, they made an attempt upon a linen-draper in Cheapside, but were snapped by a hawk's-eyed journeyman, and seized with two pieces of cambric, which were taken also upon them.

This was enough to lodge them both in Newgate, where they had the misfortune to have some of their former sins brought to remembrance. Two other indictments being brought against them, and the facts being proved upon them, they were both condemned to die. They both pleaded their bellies, and were both voted quick with child; though my tutoress was no more with child than I was.

I went frequently to see them, and condole with them, expecting that it would be my turn next; but the place gave me so much horror, reflecting that it was the place of my unhappy birth, and of my mother's misfortunes, and that I could not bear it, so I was forced to leave off going to see them.

And oh! could I have but taken warning by their disasters, I had been happy still, for I was yet free, and had nothing brought against me; but it could not be, my measure was not yet filled up.

My comrade, having the brand of an old offender, was executed; the young offender was spared, having obtained a reprieve, but lay starving a long while in prison, till at last she got her name into what they call a circuit pardon, and so came off.

This terrible example of my comrade frighted me heartily, and for a good while I made no excursions; but one night, in the neighbourhood of my governess's house, they cried 'Fire.' My governess looked out, for we were all up, and cried immediately that such a gentlewoman's house was all of a light fire atop, and so indeed it was. Here she gives me a job. 'Now, child,' says she, 'there is a rare opportunity, for the fire being so near that you may go to it before the street is blocked up with the crowd.' She presently gave me my cue. 'Go, child,' says she, 'to the house, and run in and tell the lady, or anybody you see, that you come to help them, and that you came from such a gentlewoman (that is, one of her acquaintance farther up the street).' She gave me the like cue to the next house, naming another name that was also an acquaintance of the gentlewoman of the house.

Away I went, and, coming to the house, I found them all in confusion, you may be sure. I ran in, and finding one of the maids, 'Lord! sweetheart,' says I, 'how came this dismal accident? Where is your mistress? Any how does she do? Is she safe? And where are the children? I come from Madam —— to help you.' Away runs the maid. 'Madam, madam,' says she, screaming as loud as she could yell, 'here is a gentlewoman come from Madam —— to help us.' The poor woman, half out of her wits, with a bundle under her arm, an two little children, comes toward me. 'Lord! madam,' says I, 'let me carry the poor children to Madam ——,' she desires you to send them; she'll take care of the poor lambs;' and immediately I takes one of them out of her hand, and she lifts the other up into my arms. 'Ay, do, for God's sake,' says she, 'carry them to her. Oh! thank her for her kindness.' 'Have you anything else to secure, madam?' says I; 'she will take care of it.' 'Oh dear! ay,' says she, 'God bless her, and thank her. Take this bundle of plate and carry it to her too. Oh, she is a good woman. Oh Lord! we are utterly ruined, utterly undone!' And away she runs from me out of her wits, and the maids after her; and away comes I with the two children and the bundle.

I was no sooner got into the street but I saw another woman come to me. 'Oh!' says she, 'mistress,' in a piteous tone, 'you will let fall the child. Come, this is a sad time; let me help you'; and immediately lays hold of my bundle to carry it for me. 'No,' says I; 'if you will help me, take the child by the hand, and lead it for me but to the upper end of the street; I'll go with you and satisfy you for your pains.'

She could not avoid going, after what I said; but the creature, in short, was one of the same business with me, and wanted nothing but the bundle; however, she went with me to the door, for she could not help it. When we were come there I whispered her, 'Go, child,' said I, 'I understand your trade; you may meet with purchase enough.'

She understood me and walked off. I thundered at the door with the children, and as the people were raised before by the noise of the fire, I was soon let in, and I said, 'Is madam awake? Pray tell her Mrs. —— desires the favour of her to take the two children in; poor lady, she will be undone, their house is all of a flame,' They took the children in very civilly, pitied the family in distress, and away came I with my bundle. One of the maids asked me if I was not to leave the bundle too. I said, 'No, sweetheart, 'tis to go to another place; it does not belong to them.'

I was a great way out of the hurry now, and so I went on, clear of anybody's inquiry, and brought the bundle of plate, which was very considerable, straight home, and gave it to my old governess. She told me she would not look into it, but bade me go out again to look for more.

She gave me the like cue to the gentlewoman of the next house to that which was on fire, and I did my endeavour to go, but by this time the alarm of fire was so great, and so many engines playing, and the street so thronged with people, that I could not get near the house whatever I would do; so I came back again to my governess's, and taking the bundle up into my chamber, I began to examine it. It is with horror that I tell what a treasure I found there; 'tis enough to say, that besides most of the family plate, which was considerable, I found a gold chain, an old-fashioned thing, the locket of which was broken, so that I suppose it had not been used some years, but the gold was not the worse for that; also a little box of burying-rings, the lady's wedding-ring, and some broken bits of old lockets of gold, a gold watch, and a purse with about £24 value in old pieces of gold coin, and several other things of value.

This was the greatest and the worst prize that ever I was concerned in; for indeed, though, as I have said above, I was hardened now beyond the power of all reflection in other cases, yet it really touched me to the very soul when I looked into this treasure, to think of the poor disconsolate gentlewoman who had lost so much by the fire besides; and who would think, to be sure, that she had saved her plate and best things; how she would be surprised and afflicted when she should find that she had been deceived, and should find that the person that took her children and her goods, had not come, as was pretended, from the gentlewoman in the next street, but that the children had been put upon her without her own knowledge.

I say, I confess the inhumanity of this action moved me very much, and made me relent exceedingly, and tears stood in my eyes upon that subject; but with all my sense of its being cruel and inhuman, I could never find in my heart to make any restitution. The reflection wore off, and I began quickly to forget the circumstances that attended the taking them.

Nor was this all; for though by this job I was become considerably richer than before, yet the resolution I had formerly taken, of leaving off this horrid trade when I had gotten a little more, did not return, but I must still get farther, and more; and the avarice joined so with the success, that I had no more thought of coming to a timely alteration of life, though without it I could expect no safety, no tranquillity in the possession of what I had so wickedly gained; but a little more, and a little more, was the case still.

At length, yielding to the importunities of my crime, I cast off all remorse and repentance, and all the reflections on that head turned to no more than this, that I might perhaps come to have one booty more that might complete my desires; but though I certainly had that one booty, yet every hit looked towards another, and was so encouraging to me to go on with the trade, that I had no gust to the thought of laying it down.

In this condition, hardened by success, and resolving to go on, I fell into the snare in which I was appointed to meet with my last reward for this kind of life. But even this was not yet, for I met with several successful adventures more in this way of being undone.

I remained still with my governess, who was for a while really concerned for the misfortune of my comrade that had been hanged, and who, it seems, knew enough of my governess to have sent her the same way, and which made her very uneasy; indeed, she was in a very great fright.

It is true that when she was gone, and had not opened mouth to tell what she knew, my governess was easy as to that point, and perhaps glad she was hanged, for it was in her power to have obtained a pardon at the expense of her friends; but on the other hand, the loss of her, and the sense of her kindness in not making her market of what she knew, moved my governess to mourn very sincerely for her. I comforted her as well as I could, and she in return hardened me to merit more completely the same fate.

However, as I have said, it made me the more wary, and particularly I was very shy of shoplifting, especially among the mercers and drapers, who are a set of fellows that have their eyes very much about them. I made a venture or two among the lace folks and the milliners, and particularly at one shop where I got notice of two young women who were newly set up, and had not been bred to the trade. There I think I carried off a piece of bone-lace, worth six or seven pounds, and a paper of thread. But this was but once; it was a trick that would not serve again.

It was always reckoned a safe job when we heard of a new shop, and especially when the people were such as were not bred to shops. Such may depend upon it that they will be visited once or twice at their beginning, and they must be very sharp indeed if they can prevent it.

I made another adventure or two, but they were but trifles too, though sufficient to live on. After this nothing considerable offering for a good while, I began to think that I must give over the trade in earnest; but my governess, who was not willing to lose me, and expected great things of me, brought me one day into company with a young woman and a fellow that went for her husband, though as it appeared afterwards, she was not his wife, but they were partners, it seems, in the trade they carried on, and partners in something else. In short, they robbed together, lay together, were taken together, and at last were hanged together.

I came into a kind of league with these two by the help of my governess, and they carried me out into three or four adventures, where I rather saw them commit some coarse and unhandy robberies, in which nothing but a great stock of impudence on their side, and gross negligence on the people's side who were robbed, could have made them successful. So I resolved from that time forward to be very cautious how I adventured upon anything with them; and indeed, when two or three unlucky projects were proposed by them, I declined the offer, and persuaded them against it. One time they particularly proposed robbing a watchmaker of three gold watches, which they had eyed in the daytime, and found the place where he laid them. One of them had so many keys of all kinds, that he made no question to open the place where the watchmaker had laid them; and so we made a kind of an appointment; but when I came to look narrowly into the thing, I found they proposed breaking open the house, and this, as a thing out of my way, I would not embark in, so they went without me. They did get into the house by main force, and broke up the locked place where the watches were, but found but one of the gold watches, and a silver one, which they took, and got out of the house again very clear. But the family, being alarmed, cried out 'Thieves,' and the man was pursued and taken; the young woman had got off too, but unhappily was stopped at a distance, and the watches found upon her. And thus I had a second escape, for they were convicted, and both hanged, being old offenders, though but young people. As I said before that they robbed together and lay together, so now they hanged together, and there ended my new partnership.

I began now to be very wary, having so narrowly escaped a scouring, and having such an example before me; but I had a new tempter, who prompted me every day—I mean my governess; and now a prize presented, which as it came by her management, so she expected a good share of the booty. There was a good quantity of Flanders lace lodged in a private house, where she had gotten intelligence of it, and Flanders lace being prohibited, it was a good booty to any custom-house officer that could come at it. I had a full account from my governess, as well of the quantity as of the very place where it was concealed, and I went to a custom-house officer, and told him I had such a discovery to make to him of such a quantity of lace, if he would assure me that I should have my due share of the reward. This was so just an offer, that nothing could be fairer; so he agreed, and taking a constable and me with him, we beset the house. As I told him I could go directly to the place, he left it to me; and the hole being very dark, I squeezed myself into it, with a candle in my hand, and so reached the pieces out to him, taking care as I gave him some so to secure as much about myself as I could conveniently dispose of. There was near £300 worth of lace in the hole, and I secured about £50 worth of it to myself. The people of the house were not owners of the lace, but a merchant who had entrusted them with it; so that they were not so surprised as I thought they would be.

I left the officer overjoyed with his prize, and fully satisfied with what he had got, and appointed to meet him at a house of his own directing, where I came after I had disposed of the cargo I had about me, of which he had not the least suspicion. When I came to him he began to capitulate with me, believing I did not understand the right I had to a share in the prize, and would fain have put me off with £20, but I let him know that I was not so ignorant as he supposed I was; and yet I was glad, too, that he offered to bring me to a certainty.

I asked £100, and he rose up to £30; I fell to £80, and he rose again to £40; in a word, he offered £50, and I consented, only demanding a piece of lace, which I though came to about £8 or £9, as if it had been for my own wear, and he agreed to it. So I got £50 in money paid me that same night, and made an end of the bargain; nor did he ever know who I was, or where to inquire for me, so that if it had been discovered that part of the goods were embezzled, he could have made no challenge upon me for it.

I very punctually divided this spoil with my governess, and I passed with her from this time for a very dexterous manager in the nicest cases. I found that this last was the best and easiest sort of work that was in my way, and I made it my business to inquire out prohibited goods, and after buying some, usually betrayed them, but none of these discoveries amounted to anything considerable, not like that I related just now; but I was willing to act safe, and was still cautious of running the great risks which I found others did, and in which they miscarried every day.

The next thing of moment was an attempt at a gentlewoman's good watch. It happened in a crowd, at a meeting-house, where I was in very great danger of being taken. I had full hold of her watch, but giving a great jostle, as if somebody had thrust me against her, and in the juncture giving the watch a fair pull, I found it would not come, so I let it go that moment, and cried out as if I had been killed, that somebody had trod upon my foot, and that there were certainly pickpockets there, for somebody or other had given a pull at my watch; for you are to observe that on these adventures we always went very well dressed, and I had very good clothes on, and a gold watch by my side, as like a lady as other fold.

I had no sooner said so, but the other gentlewoman cried out 'A pickpocket' too, for somebody, she said, had tried to pull her watch away.

When I touched her watch I was close to her, but when I cried out I stopped as it were short, and the crowd bearing her forward a little, she made a noise too, but it was at some distance from me, so that she did not in the least suspect me; but when she cried out 'A pickpocket,' somebody cried, 'Ay, and here has been another! this gentlewoman has been attempted too.'

At that very instance, a little farther in the crowd, and very luckily too, they cried out 'A pickpocket,' again, and really seized a young fellow in the very act. This, though unhappy for the wretch, was very opportunely for my case, though I had carried it off handsomely enough before; but now it was out of doubt, and all the loose part of the crowd ran that way, and the poor boy was delivered up to the rage of the street, which is a cruelty I need not describe, and which, however, they are always glad of, rather than to be sent to Newgate, where they lie often a long time, till they are almost perished, and sometimes they are hanged, and the best they can look for, if they are convicted, is to be transported.

This was a narrow escape to me, and I was so frighted that I ventured no more at gold watches a great while. There was indeed a great many concurring circumstances in this adventure which assisted to my escape; but the chief was, that the woman whose watch I had pulled at was a fool; that is to say, she was ignorant of the nature of the attempt, which one would have thought she should not have been, seeing she was wise enough to fasten her watch so that it could not be slipped up. But she was in such a fright that she had no thought about her proper for the discovery; for she, when she felt the pull, screamed out, and pushed herself forward, and put all the people about her into disorder, but said not a word of her watch, or of a pickpocket, for a least two minutes' time, which was time enough for me, and to spare. For as I had cried out behind her, as I have said, and bore myself back in the crowd as she bore forward, there were several people, at least seven or eight, the throng being still moving on, that were got between me and her in that time, and then I crying out 'A pickpocket,' rather sooner than she, or at least as soon, she might as well be the person suspected as I, and the people were confused in their inquiry; whereas, had she with a presence of mind needful on such an occasion, as soon as she felt the pull, not screamed out as she did, but turned immediately round and seized the next body that was behind her, she had infallibly taken me.

This is a direction not of the kindest sort to the fraternity, but 'tis certainly a key to the clue of a pickpocket's motions, and whoever can follow it will as certainly catch the thief as he will be sure to miss if he does not.

I had another adventure, which puts this matter out of doubt, and which may be an instruction for posterity in the case of a pickpocket. My good old governess, to give a short touch at her history, though she had left off the trade, was, as I may say, born a pickpocket, and, as I understood afterwards, had run through all the several degrees of that art, and yet had never been taken but once, when she was so grossly detected, that she was convicted and ordered to be transported; but being a woman of a rare tongue, and withal having money in her pocket, she found means, the ship putting into Ireland for provisions, to get on shore there, where she lived and practised her old trade for some years; when falling into another sort of bad company, she turned midwife and procuress, and played a hundred pranks there, which she gave me a little history of in confidence between us as we grew more intimate; and it was to this wicked creature that I owed all the art and dexterity I arrived to, in which there were few that ever went beyond me, or that practised so long without any misfortune.

It was after those adventures in Ireland, and when she was pretty well known in that country, that she left Dublin and came over to England, where, the time of her transportation being not expired, she left her former trade, for fear of falling into bad hands again, for then she was sure to have gone to wreck. Here she set up the same trade she had followed in Ireland, in which she soon, by her admirable management and good tongue, arrived to the height which I have already described, and indeed began to be rich, though her trade fell off again afterwards, as I have hinted before.

I mentioned thus much of the history of this woman here, the better to account for the concern she had in the wicked life I was now leading, into all the particulars of which she led me, as it were, by the hand, and gave me such directions, and I so well followed them, that I grew the greatest artist of my time and worked myself out of every danger with such dexterity, that when several more of my comrades ran themselves into Newgate presently, and by that time they had been half a year at the trade, I had now practised upwards of five years, and the people at Newgate did not so much as know me; they had heard much of me indeed, and often expected me there, but I always got off, though many times in the extremest danger.

One of the greatest dangers I was now in, was that I was too well known among the trade, and some of them, whose hatred was owing rather to envy than any injury I had done them, began to be angry that I should always escape when they were always catched and hurried to Newgate. These were they that gave me the name of Moll Flanders; for it was no more of affinity with my real name or with any of the name I had ever gone by, than black is of kin to white, except that once, as before, I called myself Mrs. Flanders; when I sheltered myself in the Mint; but that these rogues never knew, nor could I ever learn how they came to give me the name, or what the occasion of it was.

I was soon informed that some of these who were gotten fast into Newgate had vowed to impeach me; and as I knew that two or three of them were but too able to do it, I was under a great concern about it, and kept within doors for a good while. But my governess—whom I always made partner in my success, and who now played a sure game with me, for that she had a share of the gain and no share in the hazard—I say, my governess was something impatient of my leading such a useless, unprofitable life, as she called it; and she laid a new contrivance for my going abroad, and this was to dress me up in men's clothes, and so put me into a new kind of practice.

I was tall and personable, but a little too smooth-faced for a man; however, I seldom went abroad but in the night, it did well enough; but it was a long time before I could behave in my new clothes—I mean, as to my craft. It was impossible to be so nimble, so ready, so dexterous at these things in a dress so contrary to nature; and I did everything clumsily, so I had neither the success nor the easiness of escape that I had before, and I resolved to leave it off; but that resolution was confirmed soon after by the following accident.

As my governess disguised me like a man, so she joined me with a man, a young fellow that was nimble enough at his business, and for about three weeks we did very well together. Our principal trade was watching shopkeepers' counters, and slipping off any kind of goods we could see carelessly laid anywhere, and we made several good bargains, as we called them, at this work. And as we kept always together, so we grew very intimate, yet he never knew that I was not a man, nay, though I several times went home with him to his lodgings, according as our business directed, and four or five times lay with him all night. But our design lay another way, and it was absolutely necessary to me to conceal my sex from him, as appeared afterwards. The circumstances of our living, coming in late, and having such and such business to do as required that nobody should be trusted with the coming into our lodgings, were such as made it impossible to me to refuse lying with him, unless I would have owned my sex; and as it was, I effectually concealed myself. But his ill, and my good fortune, soon put an end to this life, which I must own I was sick of too, on several other accounts. We had made several prizes in this new way of business, but the last would be extraordinary. There was a shop in a certain street which had a warehouse behind it that looked into another street, the house making the corner of the turning.

Through the window of the warehouse we saw, lying on the counter or showboard, which was just before it, five pieces of silks, besides other stuffs, and though it was almost dark, yet the people, being busy in the fore-shop with customers, had not had time to shut up those windows, or else had forgot it.

This the young fellow was so overjoyed with, that he could not restrain himself. It lay all within his reach he said, and he swore violently to me that he would have it, if he broke down the house for it. I dissuaded him a little, but saw there was no remedy; so he ran rashly upon it, slipped out a square of the sash window dexterously enough, and without noise, and got out four pieces of the silks, and came with them towards me, but was immediately pursued with a terrible clutter and noise. We were standing together indeed, but I had not taken any of the goods out of his hand, when I said to him hastily, 'You are undone, fly, for God's sake!' He ran like lightning, and I too, but the pursuit was hotter after him because he had the goods, than after me. He dropped two of the pieces, which stopped them a little, but the crowd increased and pursued us both. They took him soon after with the other two pieces upon him, and then the rest followed me. I ran for it and got into my governess's house whither some quick-eyed people followed me to warmly as to fix me there. They did not immediately knock, at the door, by which I got time to throw off my disguise and dress me in my own clothes; besides, when they came there, my governess, who had her tale ready, kept her door shut, and called out to them and told them there was no man come in there. The people affirmed there did a man come in there, and swore they would break open the door.

My governess, not at all surprised, spoke calmly to them, told them they should very freely come and search her house, if they should bring a constable, and let in none but such as the constable would admit, for it was unreasonable to let in a whole crowd. This they could not refuse, though they were a crowd. So a constable was fetched immediately, and she very freely opened the door; the constable kept the door, and the men he appointed searched the house, my governess going with them from room to room. When she came to my room she called to me, and said aloud, 'Cousin, pray open the door; here's some gentlemen that must come and look into your room.'

I had a little girl with me, which was my governess's grandchild, as she called her; and I bade her open the door, and there sat I at work with a great litter of things about me, as if I had been at work all day, being myself quite undressed, with only night-clothes on my head, and a loose morning-gown wrapped about me. My governess made a kind of excuse for their disturbing me, telling me partly the occasion of it, and that she had no remedy but to open the doors to them, and let them satisfy themselves, for all she could say to them would not satisfy them. I sat still, and bid them search the room if they pleased, for if there was anybody in the house, I was sure they were not in my room; and as for the rest of the house, I had nothing to say to that, I did not understand what they looked for.

Everything looked so innocent and to honest about me, that they treated me civiller than I expected, but it was not till they had searched the room to a nicety, even under the bed, in the bed, and everywhere else where it was possible anything could be hid. When they had done this, and could find nothing, they asked my pardon for troubling me, and went down.

When they had thus searched the house from bottom to top, and then top to bottom, and could find nothing, they appeased the mob pretty well; but they carried my governess before the justice. Two men swore that they saw the man whom they pursued go into her house. My governess rattled and made a great noise that her house should be insulted, and that she should be used thus for nothing; that if a man did come in, he might go out again presently for aught she knew, for she was ready to make oath that no man had been within her doors all that day as she knew of (and that was very true indeed); that is might be indeed that as she was abovestairs, any fellow in a fright might find the door open and run in for shelter when he was pursued, but that she knew nothing of it; and if it had been so, he certainly went out again, perhaps at the other door, for she had another door into an alley, and so had made his escape and cheated them all.

This was indeed probable enough, and the justice satisfied himself with giving her an oath that she had not received or admitted any man into her house to conceal him, or protect or hide him from justice. This oath she might justly take, and did so, and so she was dismissed.

It is easy to judge what a fright I was in upon this occasion, and it was impossible for my governess ever to bring me to dress in that disguise again; for, as I told her, I should certainly betray myself.

My poor partner in this mischief was now in a bad case, for he was carried away before my Lord Mayor, and by his worship committed to Newgate, and the people that took him were so willing, as well as able, to prosecute him, that they offered themselves to enter into recognisances to appear at the sessions and pursue the charge against him.

However, he got his indictment deferred, upon promise to discover his accomplices, and particularly the man that was concerned with him in his robbery; and he failed not to do his endeavour, for he gave in my name, whom he called Gabriel Spencer, which was the name I went by to him; and here appeared the wisdom of my concealing my name and sex from him, which, if he had ever known I had been undone.

He did all he could to discover this Gabriel Spencer; he described me, he discovered the place where he said I lodged, and, in a word, all the particulars that he could of my dwelling; but having concealed the main circumstances of my sex from him, I had a vast advantage, and he never could hear of me. He brought two or three families into trouble by his endeavouring to find me out, but they knew nothing of me, any more than that I had a fellow with me that they had seen, but knew nothing of. And as for my governess, though she was the means of his coming to me, yet it was done at second-hand, and he knew nothing of her.

This turned to his disadvantage; for having promised discoveries, but not being able to make it good, it was looked upon as trifling with the justice of the city, and he was the more fiercely pursued by the shopkeepers who took him.

I was, however, terribly uneasy all this while, and that I might be quite out of the way, I went away from my governess's for a while; but not knowing wither to wander, I took a maid-servant with me, and took the stage-coach to Dunstable, to my old landlord and landlady, where I had lived so handsomely with my Lancashire husband. Here I told her a formal story, that I expected my husband every day from Ireland, and that I had sent a letter to him that I would meet him at Dunstable at her house, and that he would certainly land, if the wind was fair, in a few days, so that I was come to spend a few days with them till he should come, for he was either come post, or in the West Chester coach, I knew not which; but whichsoever it was, he would be sure to come to that house to meet me.

My landlady was mighty glad to see me, and my landlord made such a stir with me, that if I had been a princess I could not have been better used, and here I might have been welcome a month or two if I had thought fit.

But my business was of another nature. I was very uneasy (though so well disguised that it was scarce possible to detect me) lest this fellow should somehow or other find me out; and though he could not charge me with this robbery, having persuaded him not to venture, and having also done nothing in it myself but run away, yet he might have charged me with other things, and have bought his own life at the expense of mine.

This filled me with horrible apprehensions. I had no recourse, no friend, no confidante but my old governess, and I knew no remedy but to put my life in her hands, and so I did, for I let her know where to send to me, and had several letters from her while I stayed here. Some of them almost scared me out my wits but at last she sent me the joyful news that he was hanged, which was the best news to me that I had heard a great while.

I had stayed here five weeks, and lived very comfortably indeed (the secret anxiety of my mind excepted); but when I received this letter I looked pleasantly again, and told my landlady that I had received a letter from my spouse in Ireland, that I had the good news of his being very well, but had the bad news that his business would not permit him to come away so soon as he expected, and so I was like to go back again without him.

My landlady complimented me upon the good news however, that I had heard he was well. 'For I have observed, madam,' says she, 'you hadn't been so pleasant as you used to be; you have been over head and ears in care for him, I dare say,' says the good woman; "tis easy to be seen there's an alteration in you for the better,' says she. 'Well, I am sorry the esquire can't come yet,' says my landlord; 'I should have been heartily glad to have seen him. But I hope, when you have certain news of his coming, you'll take a step hither again, madam,' says he; 'you shall be very welcome whenever you please to come.'

With all these fine compliments we parted, and I came merry enough to London, and found my governess as well pleased as I was. And now she told me she would never recommend any partner to me again, for she always found, she said, that I had the best luck when I ventured by myself. And so indeed I had, for I was seldom in any danger when I was by myself, or if I was, I got out of it with more dexterity than when I was entangled with the dull measures of other people, who had perhaps less forecast, and were more rash and impatient than I; for though I had as much courage to venture as any of them, yet I used more caution before I undertook a thing, and had more presence of mind when I was to bring myself off.

I have often wondered even at my own hardiness another way, that when all my companions were surprised and fell so suddenly into the hand of justice, and that I so narrowly escaped, yet I could not all this while enter into one serious resolution to leave off this trade, and especially considering that I was now very far from being poor; that the temptation of necessity, which is generally the introduction of all such wickedness, was now removed; for I had near £500 by me in ready money, on which I might have lived very well, if I had thought fit to have retired; but I say, I had not so much as the least inclination to leave off; no, not so much as I had before when I had but £200 beforehand, and when I had no such frightful examples before my eyes as these were. From hence 'tis evident to me, that when once we are hardened in crime, no fear can affect us, no example give us any warning.

I had indeed one comrade whose fate went very near me for a good while, though I wore it off too in time. That case was indeed very unhappy. I had made a prize of a piece of very good damask in a mercer's shop, and went clear off myself, but had conveyed the piece to this companion of mine when we went out of the shop, and she went one way and I went another. We had not been long out of the shop but the mercer missed his piece of stuff, and sent his messengers, one one way and one another, and they presently seized her that had the piece, with the damask upon her. As for me, I had very luckily stepped into a house where there was a lace chamber, up one pair of stairs, and had the satisfaction, or the terror indeed, of looking out of the window upon the noise they made, and seeing the poor creature dragged away in triumph to the justice, who immediately committed her to Newgate.

I was careful to attempt nothing in the lace chamber, but tumbled their goods pretty much to spend time; then bought a few yards of edging and paid for it, and came away very sad-hearted indeed for the poor woman, who was in tribulation for what I only had stolen.

Here again my old caution stood me in good stead; namely, that though I often robbed with these people, yet I never let them know who I was, or where I lodged, nor could they ever find out my lodging, though they often endeavoured to watch me to it. They all knew me by the name of Moll Flanders, though even some of them rather believed I was she than knew me to be so. My name was public among them indeed, but how to find me out they knew not, nor so much as how to guess at my quarters, whether they were at the east end of the town or the west; and this wariness was my safety upon all these occasions.

I kept close a great while upon the occasion of this woman's disaster. I knew that if I should do anything that should miscarry, and should be carried to prison, she would be there and ready to witness against me, and perhaps save her life at my expense. I considered that I began to be very well known by name at the Old Bailey, though they did not know my face, and that if I should fall into their hands, I should be treated as an old offender; and for this reason I was resolved to see what this poor creature's fate should be before I stirred abroad, though several times in her distress I conveyed money to her for her relief.

At length she came to her trial. She pleaded she did not steal the thing, but that one Mrs. Flanders, as she heard her called (for she did not know her), gave the bundle to her after they came out of the shop, and bade her carry it home to her lodging. They asked her where this Mrs. Flanders was, but she could not produce her, neither could she give the least account of me; and the mercer's men swearing positively that she was in the shop when the goods were stolen, that they immediately missed them, and pursued her, and found them upon her, thereupon the jury brought her in guilty; but the Court, considering that she was really not the person that stole the goods, an inferior assistant, and that it was very possible she could not find out this Mrs. Flanders, meaning me, though it would save her life, which indeed was true—I say, considering all this, they allowed her to be transported, which was the utmost favour she could obtain, only that the Court told her that if she could in the meantime produce the said Mrs. Flanders, they would intercede for her pardon; that is to say, if she could find me out, and hand me, she should not be transported. This I took care to make impossible to her, and so she was shipped off in pursuance of her sentence a little while after.

I must repeat it again, that the fate of this poor woman troubled me exceedingly, and I began to be very pensive, knowing that I was really the instrument of her disaster; but the preservation of my own life, which was so evidently in danger, took off all my tenderness; and seeing that she was not put to death, I was very easy at her transportation, because she was then out of the way of doing me any mischief, whatever should happen.

The disaster of this woman was some months before that of the last-recited story, and was indeed partly occasion of my governess proposing to dress me up in men's clothes, that I might go about unobserved, as indeed I did; but I was soon tired of that disguise, as I have said, for indeed it exposed me to too many difficulties.

I was now easy as to all fear of witnesses against me, for all those that had either been concerned with me, or that knew me by the name of Moll Flanders, were either hanged or transported; and if I should have had the misfortune to be taken, I might call myself anything else, as well as Moll Flanders, and no old sins could be placed into my account; so I began to run a-tick again with the more freedom, and several successful adventures I made, though not such as I had made before.

We had at that time another fire happened not a great way off from the place where my governess lived, and I made an attempt there, as before, but as I was not soon enough before the crowd of people came in, and could not get to the house I aimed at, instead of a prize, I got a mischief, which had almost put a period to my life and all my wicked doings together; for the fire being very furious, and the people in a great fright in removing their goods, and throwing them out of window, a wench from out of a window threw a feather-bed just upon me. It is true, the bed being soft, it broke no bones; but as the weight was great, and made greater by the fall, it beat me down, and laid me dead for a while. Nor did the people concern themselves much to deliver me from it, or to recover me at all; but I lay like one dead and neglected a good while, till somebody going to remove the bed out of the way, helped me up. It was indeed a wonder the people in the house had not thrown other goods out after it, and which might have fallen upon it, and then I had been inevitably killed; but I was reserved for further afflictions.

This accident, however, spoiled my market for that time, and I came home to my governess very much hurt and bruised, and frighted to the last degree, and it was a good while before she could set me upon my feet again.

It was now a merry time of the year, and Bartholomew Fair was begun. I had never made any walks that way, nor was the common part of the fair of much advantage to me; but I took a turn this year into the cloisters, and among the rest I fell into one of the raffling shops. It was a thing of no great consequence to me, nor did I expect to make much of it; but there came a gentleman extremely well dressed and very rich, and as 'tis frequent to talk to everybody in those shops, he singled me out, and was very particular with me. First he told me he would put in for me to raffle, and did so; and some small matter coming to his lot, he presented it to me (I think it was a feather muff); then he continued to keep talking to me with a more than common appearance of respect, but still very civil, and much like a gentleman.

He held me in talk so long, till at last he drew me out of the raffling place to the shop-door, and then to a walk in the cloister, still talking of a thousand things cursorily without anything to the purpose. At last he told me that, without compliment, he was charmed with my company, and asked me if I durst trust myself in a coach with him; he told me he was a man of honour, and would not offer anything to me unbecoming him as such. I seemed to decline it a while, but suffered myself to be importuned a little, and then yielded.

I was at a loss in my thoughts to conclude at first what this gentleman designed; but I found afterwards he had had some drink in his head, and that he was not very unwilling to have some more. He carried me in the coach to the Spring Garden, at Knightsbridge, where we walked in the gardens, and he treated me very handsomely; but I found he drank very freely. He pressed me also to drink, but I declined it.

Hitherto he kept his word with me, and offered me nothing amiss. We came away in the coach again, and he brought me into the streets, and by this time it was near ten o'clock at night, and he stopped the coach at a house where, it seems, he was acquainted, and where they made no scruple to show us upstairs into a room with a bed in it. At first I seemed to be unwilling to go up, but after a few words I yielded to that too, being willing to see the end of it, and in hope to make something of it at last. As for the bed, etc., I was not much concerned about that part.

Here he began to be a little freer with me than he had promised; and I by little and little yielded to everything, so that, in a word, he did what he pleased with me; I need say no more. All this while he drank freely too, and about one in the morning we went into the coach again. The air and the shaking of the coach made the drink he had get more up in his head than it was before, and he grew uneasy in the coach, and was for acting over again what he had been doing before; but as I thought my game now secure, I resisted him, and brought him to be a little still, which had not lasted five minutes but he fell fast asleep.

I took this opportunity to search him to a nicety. I took a gold watch, with a silk purse of gold, his fine full-bottom periwig and silver-fringed gloves, his sword and fine snuff-box, and gently opening the coach door, stood ready to jump out while the coach was going on; but the coach stopped in the narrow street beyond Temple Bar to let another coach pass, I got softly out, fastened the door again, and gave my gentleman and the coach the slip both together, and never heard more of them.

This was an adventure indeed unlooked for, and perfectly undesigned by me; though I was not so past the merry part of life, as to forget how to behave, when a fop so blinded by his appetite should not know an old woman from a young. I did not indeed look so old as I was by ten or twelve years; yet I was not a young wench of seventeen, and it was easy enough to be distinguished. There is nothing so absurd, so surfeiting, so ridiculous, as a man heated by wine in his head, and wicked gust in his inclination together; he is in the possession of two devils at once, and can no more govern himself by his reason than a mill can grind without water; his vice tramples upon all that was in him that had any good in it, if any such thing there was; nay, his very sense is blinded by its own rage, and he acts absurdities even in his views; such a drinking more, when he is drunk already; picking up a common woman, without regard to what she is or who she is, whether sound or rotten, clean or unclean, whether ugly or handsome, whether old or young, and so blinded as not really to distinguish. Such a man is worse than a lunatic; prompted by his vicious, corrupted head, he no more knows what he is doing than this wretch of mine knew when I picked his pocket of his watch and his purse of gold.

These are the men of whom Solomon says, 'They go like an ox to the slaughter, till a dart strikes through their liver'; an admirable description, by the way, of the foul disease, which is a poisonous deadly contagion mingling with the blood, whose centre or foundation is in the liver; from whence, by the swift circulation of the whole mass, that dreadful nauseous plague strikes immediately through his liver, and his spirits are infected, his vitals stabbed through as with a dart.

It is true this poor unguarded wretch was in no danger from me, though I was greatly apprehensive at first of what danger I might be in from him; but he was really to be pitied in one respect, that he seemed to be a good sort of man in himself; a gentleman that had no harm in his design; a man of sense, and of a fine behaviour, a comely handsome person, a sober solid countenance, a charming beautiful face, and everything that could be agreeable; only had unhappily had some drink the night before, had not been in bed, as he told me when we were together; was hot, and his blood fired with wine, and in that condition his reason, as it were asleep, had given him up.

As for me, my business was his money, and what I could make of him; and after that, if I could have found out any way to have done it, I would have sent him safe home to his house and to his family, for 'twas ten to one but he had an honest, virtuous wife and innocent children, that were anxious for his safety, and would have been glad to have gotten him home, and have taken care of him till he was restored to himself. And then with what shame and regret would he look back upon himself! how would he reproach himself with associating himself with a whore! picked up in the worst of all holes, the cloister, among the dirt and filth of all the town! how would he be trembling for fear he had got the pox, for fear a dart had struck through his liver, and hate himself every time he looked back upon the madness and brutality of his debauch! how would he, if he had any principles of honour, as I verily believe he had—I say, how would he abhor the thought of giving any ill distemper, if he had it, as for aught he knew he might, to his modest and virtuous wife, and thereby sowing the contagion in the life-blood of his posterity.

Would such gentlemen but consider the contemptible thoughts which the very women they are concerned with, in such cases as these, have of them, it would be a surfeit to them. As I said above, they value not the pleasure, they are raised by no inclination to the man, the passive jade thinks of no pleasure but the money; and when he is, as it were, drunk in the ecstasies of his wicked pleasure, her hands are in his pockets searching for what she can find there, and of which he can no more be sensible in the moment of his folly that he can forethink of it when he goes about it.

I knew a woman that was so dexterous with a fellow, who indeed deserved no better usage, that while he was busy with her another way, conveyed his purse with twenty guineas in it out of his fob-pocket, where he had put it for fear of her, and put another purse with gilded counters in it into the room of it. After he had done, he says to her, 'Now han't you picked my pocket?' She jested with him, and told him she supposed he had not much to lose; he put his hand to his fob, and with his fingers felt that his purse was there, which fully satisfied him, and so she brought off his money. And this was a trade with her; she kept a sham gold watch, that is, a watch of silver gilt, and a purse of counters in her pocket to be ready on all such occasions, and I doubt not practiced it with success.

I came home with this last booty to my governess, and really when I told her the story, it so affected her that she was hardly able to forbear tears, to know how such a gentleman ran a daily risk of being undone every time a glass of wine got into his head.

But as to the purchase I got, and how entirely I stripped him, she told me it pleased her wonderfully. 'Nay child,' says she, 'the usage may, for aught I know, do more to reform him than all the sermons that ever he will hear in his life.' And if the remainder of the story be true, so it did.

I found the next day she was wonderful inquisitive about this gentleman; the description I had given her of him, his dress, his person, his face, everything concurred to make her think of a gentleman whose character she knew, and family too. She mused a while, and I going still on with the particulars, she starts up; says she, 'I'll lay £100 I know the gentleman.'

'I am sorry you do,' says I, 'for I would not have him exposed on any account in the world; he has had injury enough already by me, and I would not be instrumental to do him any more.' 'No, no,' says she, 'I will do him no injury, I assure you, but you may let me satisfy my curiosity a little, for if it is he, I warrant you I find it out.' I was a little startled at that, and told her, with an apparent concern in my face, that by the same rule he might find me out, and then I was undone. She returned warmly, 'Why, do you think I will betray you, child? No, no,' says she, 'not for all he is worth in the world. I have kept your counsel in worse things than these; sure you may trust me in this.' So I said no more at that time.

She laid her scheme another way, and without acquainting me of it, but she was resolved to find it out if possible. So she goes to a certain friend of hers who was acquainted in the family that she guessed at, and told her friend she had some extraordinary business with such a gentleman (who, by the way, was no less than a baronet, and of a very good family), and that she knew not how to come at him without somebody to introduce her. Her friend promised her very readily to do it, and accordingly goes to the house to see if the gentleman was in town.

The next day she come to my governess and tells her that Sir —— was at home, but that he had met with a disaster and was very ill, and there was no speaking with him. 'What disaster?' says my governess hastily, as if she was surprised at it. 'Why,' says her friend, 'he had been at Hampstead to visit a gentleman of his acquaintance, and as he came back again he was set upon and robbed; and having got a little drink too, as they suppose, the rogues abused him, and he is very ill.' 'Robbed!' says my governess, 'and what did they take from him?' 'Why,' says her friend, 'they took his gold watch and his gold snuff-box, his fine periwig, and what money he had in his pocket, which was considerable, to be sure, for Sir —— never goes without a purse of guineas about him.'

'Pshaw!' says my old governess, jeering, 'I warrant you he has got drunk now and got a whore, and she has picked his pocket, and so he comes home to his wife and tells her he has been robbed. That's an old sham; a thousand such tricks are put upon the poor women every day.'

'Fie!' says her friend, 'I find you don't know Sir ——; why he is as civil a gentleman, there is not a finer man, nor a soberer, graver, modester person in the whole city; he abhors such things; there's nobody that knows him will think such a thing of him.' 'Well, well,' says my governess, 'that's none of my business; if it was, I warrant I should find there was something of that kind in it; your modest men in common opinion are sometimes no better than other people, only they keep a better character, or, if you please, are the better hypocrites.'

'No, no,' says her friend, 'I can assure you Sir —— is no hypocrite, he is really an honest, sober gentleman, and he has certainly been robbed.' 'Nay,' says my governess, 'it may be he has; it is no business of mine, I tell you; I only want to speak with him; my business is of another nature.' 'But,' says her friend, 'let your business be of what nature it will, you cannot see him yet, for he is not fit to be seen, for he is very ill, and bruised very much,' 'Ay,' says my governess, 'nay, then he has fallen into bad hands, to be sure,' And then she asked gravely, 'Pray, where is he bruised?' 'Why, in the head,' says her friend, 'and one of his hands, and his face, for they used him barbarously.' 'Poor gentleman,' says my governess, 'I must wait, then, till he recovers'; and adds, 'I hope it will not be long, for I want very much to speak with him.'

Away she comes to me and tells me this story. 'I have found out your fine gentleman, and a fine gentleman he was,' says she; 'but, mercy on him, he is in a sad pickle now. I wonder what the d—l you have done to him; why, you have almost killed him.' I looked at her with disorder enough. 'I killed him!' says I; 'you must mistake the person; I am sure I did nothing to him; he was very well when I left him,' said I, 'only drunk and fast asleep.' 'I know nothing of that,' says she, 'but he is in a sad pickle now'; and so she told me all that her friend had said to her. 'Well, then,' says I, 'he fell into bad hands after I left him, for I am sure I left him safe enough.'

About ten days after, or a little more, my governess goes again to her friend, to introduce her to this gentleman; she had inquired other ways in the meantime, and found that he was about again, if not abroad again, so she got leave to speak with him.

She was a woman of a admirable address, and wanted nobody to introduce her; she told her tale much better than I shall be able to tell it for her, for she was a mistress of her tongue, as I have said already. She told him that she came, though a stranger, with a single design of doing him a service and he should find she had no other end in it; that as she came purely on so friendly an account, she begged promise from him, that if he did not accept what she should officiously propose he would not take it ill that she meddled with what was not her business. She assured him that as what she had to say was a secret that belonged to him only, so whether he accepted her offer or not, it should remain a secret to all the world, unless he exposed it himself; nor should his refusing her service in it make her so little show her respect as to do him the least injury, so that he should be entirely at liberty to act as he thought fit.

He looked very shy at first, and said he knew nothing that related to him that required much secrecy; that he had never done any man any wrong, and cared not what anybody might say of him; that it was no part of his character to be unjust to anybody, nor could he imagine in what any man could render him any service; but that if it was so disinterested a service as she said, he could not take it ill from any one that they should endeavour to serve him; and so, as it were, left her a liberty either to tell him or not to tell, as she thought fit.

She found him so perfectly indifferent, that she was almost afraid to enter into the point with him; but, however, after some other circumlocutions she told him that by a strange and unaccountable accident she came to have a particular knowledge of the late unhappy adventure he had fallen into, and that in such a manner, that there was nobody in the world but herself and him that were acquainted with it, no, not the very person that was with him.

He looked a little angrily at first. 'What adventure?' said he. 'Why,' said she, 'of your being robbed coming from Knightbr——; Hampstead, sir, I should say,' says she. 'Be not surprised, sir,' says she, 'that I am able to tell you every step you took that day from the cloister in Smithfield to the Spring Garden at Knightsbridge, and thence to the —— in the Strand, and how you were left asleep in the coach afterwards. I say, let not this surprise you, for, sir, I do not come to make a booty of you, I ask nothing of you, and I assure you the woman that was with you knows nothing who you are, and never shall; and yet perhaps I may serve you further still, for I did not come barely to let you know that I was informed of these things, as if I wanted a bribe to conceal them; assure yourself, sir,' said she, 'that whatever you think fit to do or say to me, it shall be all a secret as it is, as much as if I were in my grave.'

He was astonished at her discourse, and said gravely to her, 'Madam, you are a stranger to me, but it is very unfortunate that you should be let into the secret of the worst action of my life, and a thing that I am so justly ashamed of, that the only satisfaction of it to me was, that I thought it was known only to God and my own conscience.' 'Pray, sir,' says she, 'do not reckon the discovery of it to me to be any part of your misfortune. It was a thing, I believe, you were surprised into, and perhaps the woman used some art to prompt you to it; however, you will never find any just cause,' said she, 'to repent that I came to hear of it; nor can your own mouth be more silent in it that I have been, and ever shall be.'

'Well,' says he, 'but let me do some justice to the woman too; whoever she is, I do assure you she prompted me to nothing, she rather declined me. It was my own folly and madness that brought me into it all, ay, and brought her into it too; I must give her her due so far. As to what she took from me, I could expect no less from her in the condition I was in, and to this hour I know not whether she robbed me or the coachman; if she did it, I forgive her, and I think all gentlemen that do so should be used in the same manner; but I am more concerned for some other things that I am for all that she took from me.'

My governess now began to come into the whole matter, and he opened himself freely to her. First she said to him, in answer to what he had said about me, 'I am glad, sir, you are so just to the person that you were with; I assure you she is a gentlewoman, and no woman of the town; and however you prevailed with her so far as you did, I am sure 'tis not her practice. You ran a great venture indeed, sir; but if that be any part of your care, I am persuaded you may be perfectly easy, for I dare assure you no man has touched her, before you, since her husband, and he has been dead now almost eight years.'

It appeared that this was his grievance, and that he was in a very great fright about it; however, when my governess said this to him, he appeared very well pleased, and said, 'Well, madam, to be plain with you, if I was satisfied of that, I should not so much value what I lost; for, as to that, the temptation was great, and perhaps she was poor and wanted it.' 'If she had not been poor, sir ——,' says my governess, 'I assure you she would never have yielded to you; and as her poverty first prevailed with her to let you do as you did, so the same poverty prevailed with her to pay herself at last, when she saw you were in such a condition, that if she had not done it, perhaps the next coachman might have done it.'

'Well,' says he, 'much good may it do her. I say again, all the gentlemen that do so ought to be used in the same manner, and then they would be cautious of themselves. I have no more concern about it, but on the score which you hinted at before, madam.' Here he entered into some freedoms with her on the subject of what passed between us, which are not so proper for a woman to write, and the great terror that was upon his mind with relation to his wife, for fear he should have received any injury from me, and should communicate if farther; and asked her at last if she could not procure him an opportunity to speak with me. My governess gave him further assurances of my being a woman clear from any such thing, and that he was as entirely safe in that respect as he was with his own lady; but as for seeing me, she said it might be of dangerous consequence; but, however, that she would talk with me, and let him know my answer, using at the same time some arguments to persuade him not to desire it, and that it could be of no service to him, seeing she hoped he had no desire to renew a correspondence with me, and that on my account it was a kind of putting my life in his hands.

He told her he had a great desire to see me, that he would give her any assurances that were in his power, not to take any advantages of me, and that in the first place he would give me a general release from all demands of any kind. She insisted how it might tend to a further divulging the secret, and might in the end be injurious to him, entreating him not to press for it; so at length he desisted.

They had some discourse upon the subject of the things he had lost, and he seemed to be very desirous of his gold watch, and told her if she could procure that for him, he would willingly give as much for it as it was worth. She told him she would endeavour to procure it for him, and leave the valuing it to himself.

Accordingly the next day she carried the watch, and he gave her thirty guineas for it, which was more than I should have been able to make of it, though it seems it cost much more. He spoke something of his periwig, which it seems cost him threescore guineas, and his snuff-box, and in a few days more she carried them too; which obliged him very much, and he gave her thirty more. The next day I sent him his fine sword and cane gratis, and demanded nothing of him, but I had no mind to see him, unless it had been so that he might be satisfied I knew who he was, which he was not willing to.

Then he entered into a long talk with her of the manner how she came to know all this matter. She formed a long tale of that part; how she had it from one that I had told the whole story to, and that was to help me dispose of the goods; and this confidante brought the things to her, she being by profession a pawnbroker; and she hearing of his worship's disaster, guessed at the thing in general; that having gotten the things into her hands, she had resolved to come and try as she had done. She then gave him repeated assurances that it should never go out of her mouth, and though she knew the woman very well, yet she had not let her know, meaning me, anything of it; that is to say, who the person was, which, by the way, was false; but, however, it was not to his damage, for I never opened my mouth of it to anybody.

I had a great many thoughts in my head about my seeing him again, and was often sorry that I had refused it. I was persuaded that if I had seen him, and let him know that I knew him, I should have made some advantage of him, and perhaps have had some maintenance from him; and though it was a life wicked enough, yet it was not so full of danger as this I was engaged in. However, those thoughts wore off, and I declined seeing him again, for that time; but my governess saw him often, and he was very kind to her, giving her something almost every time he saw her. One time in particular she found him very merry, and as she thought he had some wine in his head, and he pressed her again very earnestly to let him see that woman that, as he said, had bewitched him so that night, my governess, who was from the beginning for my seeing him, told him he was so desirous of it that she could almost yield of it, if she could prevail upon me; adding that if he would please to come to her house in the evening, she would endeavour it, upon his repeated assurances of forgetting what was past.

Accordingly she came to me, and told me all the discourse; in short, she soon biassed me to consent, in a case which I had some regret in my mind for declining before; so I prepared to see him. I dressed me to all the advantage possible, I assure you, and for the first time used a little art; I say for the first time, for I had never yielded to the baseness of paint before, having always had vanity enough to believe I had no need of it.

At the hour appointed he came; and as she observed before, so it was plain still, that he had been drinking, though very far from what we call being in drink. He appeared exceeding pleased to see me, and entered into a long discourse with me upon the old affair. I begged his pardon very often for my share of it, protested I had not any such design when first I met him, that I had not gone out with him but that I took him for a very civil gentleman, and that he made me so many promises of offering no uncivility to me.

He alleged the wine he drank, and that he scarce knew what he did, and that if it had not been so, I should never have let him take the freedom with me that he had done. He protested to me that he never touched any woman but me since he was married to his wife, and it was a surprise upon him; complimented me upon being so particularly agreeable to him, and the like; and talked so much of that kind, till I found he had talked himself almost into a temper to do the same thing over again. But I took him up short. I protested I had never suffered any man to touch me since my husband died, which was near eight years. He said he believed it to be so truly; and added that madam had intimated as much to him, and that it was his opinion of that part which made his desire to see me again; and that since he had once broke in upon his virtue with me, and found no ill consequences, he could be safe in venturing there again; and so, in short, it went on to what I expected, and to what will not bear relating.

My old governess had foreseen it, as well as I, and therefore led him into a room which had not a bed in it, and yet had a chamber within it which had a bed, whither we withdrew for the rest of the night; and, in short, after some time being together, he went to bed, and lay there all night. I withdrew, but came again undressed in the morning, before it was day, and lay with him the rest of the time.

Thus, you see, having committed a crime once is a sad handle to the committing of it again; whereas all the regret and reflections wear off when the temptation renews itself. Had I not yielded to see him again, the corrupt desire in him had worn off, and 'tis very probable he had never fallen into it with anybody else, as I really believe he had not done before.

When he went away, I told him I hoped he was satisfied he had not been robbed again. He told me he was satisfied in that point, and could trust me again, and putting his hand in his pocket, gave me five guineas, which was the first money I had gained that way for many years.

I had several visits of the like kind from him, but he never came into a settled way of maintenance, which was what I would have best pleased with. Once, indeed, he asked me how I did to live. I answered him pretty quick, that I assured him I had never taken that course that I took with him, but that indeed I worked at my needle, and could just maintain myself; that sometime it was as much as I was able to do, and I shifted hard enough.

He seemed to reflect upon himself that he should be the first person to lead me into that, which he assured me he never intended to do himself; and it touched him a little, he said, that he should be the cause of his own sin and mine too. He would often make just reflections also upon the crime itself, and upon the particular circumstances of it with respect to himself; how wine introduced the inclina-inclinations how the devil led him to the place, and found out an object to tempt him, and he made the moral always himself.

When these thoughts were upon him he would go away, and perhaps not come again in a month's time or longer; but then as the serious part wore off, the lewd part would wear in, and then he came prepared for the wicked part. Thus we lived for some time; thought he did not keep, as they call it, yet he never failed doing things that were handsome, and sufficient to maintain me without working, and, which was better, without following my old trade.

But this affair had its end too; for after about a year, I found that he did not come so often as usual, and at last he left if off altogether without any dislike to bidding adieu; and so there was an end of that short scene of life, which added no great store to me, only to make more work for repentance.

However, during this interval I confined myself pretty much at home; at least, being thus provided for, I made no adventures, no, not for a quarter of a year after he left me; but then finding the fund fail, and being loth to spend upon the main stock, I began to think of my old trade, and to look abroad into the street again; and my first step was lucky enough.

I had dressed myself up in a very mean habit, for as I had several shapes to appear in, I was now in an ordinary stuff-gown, a blue apron, and a straw hat and I placed myself at the door of the Three Cups Inn in St. John Street. There were several carriers used the inn, and the stage-coaches for Barnet, for Totteridge, and other towns that way stood always in the street in the evening, when they prepared to set out, so that I was ready for anything that offered, for either one or other. The meaning was this; people come frequently with bundles and small parcels to those inns, and call for such carriers or coaches as they want, to carry them into the country; and there generally attend women, porters' wives or daughters, ready to take in such things for their respective people that employ them.

It happened very oddly that I was standing at the inn gate, and a woman that had stood there before, and which was the porter's wife belonging to the Barnet stage-coach, having observed me, asked if I waited for any of the coaches. I told her Yes, I waited for my mistress, that was coming to go to Barnet. She asked me who was my mistress, and I told her any madam's name that came next me; but as it seemed, I happened upon a name, a family of which name lived at Hadley, just beyond Barnet.

I said no more to her, or she to me, a good while; but by and by, somebody calling her at a door a little way off, she desired me that if anybody called for the Barnet coach, I would step and call her at the house, which it seems was an alehouse. I said Yes, very readily, and away she went.

She was no sooner gone but comes a wench and a child, puffing and sweating, and asks for the Barnet coach. I answered presently, 'Here.' 'Do you belong to the Barnet coach?' says she. 'Yes, sweetheart,' said I; 'what do ye want?' 'I want room for two passengers,' says she. 'Where are they, sweetheart?' said I. 'Here's this girl, pray let her go into the coach,' says she, 'and I'll go and fetch my mistress.' 'Make haste, then, sweetheart,' says I, 'for we may be full else.' The maid had a great bundle under her arm; so she put the child into the coach, and I said, 'You had best put your bundle into the coach too.' 'No,' says she, 'I am afraid somebody should slip it away from the child.' 'Give to me, then,' said I, 'and I'll take care of it.' 'Do, then,' says she, 'and be sure you take of it.' 'I'll answer for it,' said I, 'if it were for £20 value.' 'There, take it, then,' says she, and away she goes.

As soon as I had got the bundle, and the maid was out of sight, I goes on towards the alehouse, where the porter's wife was, so that if I had met her, I had then only been going to give her the bundle, and to call her to her business, as if I was going away, and could stay no longer; but as I did not meet her, I walked away, and turning into Charterhouse Lane, then crossed into Batholomew Close, so into Little Britain, and through the Bluecoat Hospital, into Newgate Street.

To prevent my being known, I pulled off my blue apron, and wrapped the bundle in it, which before was made up in a piece of painted calico, and very remarkable; I also wrapped up my straw hat in it, and so put the bundle upon my head; and it was very well that I did thus, for coming through the Bluecoat Hospital, who should I meet but the wench that had given me the bundle to hold. It seems she was going with her mistress, whom she had been gone to fetch, to the Barnet coaches.

I saw she was in haste, and I had no business to stop her; so away she went, and I brought my bundle safe home to my governess. There was no money, nor plate, or jewels in the bundle, but a very good suit of Indian damask, a gown and a petticoat, a laced-head and ruffles of very good Flanders lace, and some linen and other things, such as I knew very well the value of.

This was not indeed my own invention, but was given me by one that had practised it with success, and my governess liked it extremely; and indeed I tried it again several times, though never twice near the same place; for the next time I tried it in White Chapel, just by the corner of Petticoat Lane, where the coaches stand that go out to Stratford and Bow, and that side of the country, and another time at the Flying Horse, without Bishopgate, where the Cheston coaches then lay; and I had always the good luck to come off with some booty.

Another time I placed myself at a warehouse by the waterside, where the coasting vessels from the north come, such as from Newcastle-upon-Tyne, Sunderland, and other places. Here, the warehouses being shut, comes a young fellow with a letter; and he wanted a box and a hamper that was come from Newcastle-upon-Tyne. I asked him if he had the marks of it; so he shows me the letter, by virtue of which he was to ask for it, and which gave an account of the contents, the box being full of linen, and the hamper full of glass ware. I read the letter, and took care to see the name, and the marks, the name of the person that sent the goods, the name of the person that they were sent to; then I bade the messenger come in the morning, for that the warehouse-keeper would not be there any more that night.

Away went I, and getting materials in a public house, I wrote a letter from Mr. John Richardson of Newcastle to his dear cousin Jemmy Cole, in London, with an account that he sent by such a vessel (for I remembered all the particulars to a title), so many pieces of huckaback linen, so many ells of Dutch holland and the like, in a box, and a hamper of flint glasses from Mr. Henzill's glasshouse; and that the box was marked I. C. No. 1, and the hamper was directed by a label on the cording.

About an hour after, I came to the warehouse, found the warehouse-keeper, and had the goods delivered me without any scruple; the value of the linen being about £22.

I could fill up this whole discourse with the variety of such adventures, which daily invention directed to, and which I managed with the utmost dexterity, and always with success.

At length—as when does the pitcher come safe home that goes so very often to the well?—I fell into some small broils, which though they could not affect me fatally, yet made me known, which was the worst thing next to being found guilty that could befall me.

I had taken up the disguise of a widow's dress; it was without any real design in view, but only waiting for anything that might offer, as I often did. It happened that while I was going along the street in Covent Garden, there was a great cry of 'Stop thief! Stop thief!' some artists had, it seems, put a trick upon a shopkeeper, and being pursued, some of them fled one way, and some another; and one of them was, they said, dressed up in widow's weeds, upon which the mob gathered about me, and some said I was the person, others said no. Immediately came the mercer's journeyman, and he swore aloud I was the person, and so seized on me. However, when I was brought back by the mob to the mercer's shop, the master of the house said freely that I was not the woman that was in his shop, and would have let me go immediately; but another fellow said gravely, 'Pray stay till Mr. ——' (meaning the journeyman) 'comes back, for he knows her.' So they kept me by force near half an hour. They had called a constable, and he stood in the shop as my jailer; and in talking with the constable I inquired where he lived, and what trade he was; the man not apprehending in the least what happened afterwards, readily told me his name, and trade, and where he lived; and told me as a jest, that I might be sure to hear of his name when I came to the Old Bailey.

Some of the servants likewise used me saucily, and had much ado to keep their hands off me; the master indeed was civiller to me than they, but he would not yet let me go, though he owned he could not say I was in his shop before.

I began to be a little surly with him, and told him I hoped he would not take it ill if I made myself amends upon him in a more legal way another time; and desired I might send for friends to see me have right done me. No, he said, he could give no such liberty; I might ask it when I came before the justice of peace; and seeing I threatened him, he would take care of me in the meantime, and would lodge me safe in Newgate. I told him it was his time now, but it would be mine by and by, and governed my passion as well as I was able. However, I spoke to the constable to call me a porter, which he did, and then I called for pen, ink, and paper, but they would let me have none. I asked the porter his name, and where he lived, and the poor man told it me very willingly. I bade him observe and remember how I was treated there; that he saw I was detained there by force. I told him I should want his evidence in another place, and it should not be the worse for him to speak. The porter said he would serve me with all his heart. 'But, madam,' says he, 'let me hear them refuse to let you go, then I may be able to speak the plainer.'

With that I spoke aloud to the master of the shop, and said, 'Sir, you know in your own conscience that I am not the person you look for, and that I was not in your shop before, therefore I demand that you detain me here no longer, or tell me the reason of your stopping me.' The fellow grew surlier upon this than before, and said he would do neither till he thought fit. 'Very well,' said I to the constable and to the porter; 'you will be pleased to remember this, gentlemen, another time.' The porter said, 'Yes, madam'; and the constable began not to like it, and would have persuaded the mercer to dismiss him, and let me go, since, as he said, he owned I was not the person. 'Good, sir,' says the mercer to him tauntingly, 'are you a justice of peace or a constable? I charged you with her; pray do you do your duty.' The constable told him, a little moved, but very handsomely, 'I know my duty, and what I am, sir; I doubt you hardly know what you are doing.' They had some other hard words, and in the meantime the journeyman, impudent and unmanly to the last degree, used me barbarously, and one of them, the same that first seized upon me, pretended he would search me, and began to lay hands on me. I spit in his face, called out to the constable, and bade him to take notice of my usage. 'And pray, Mr. Constable,' said I, 'ask that villain's name,' pointing to the man. The constable reproved him decently, told him that he did not know what he did, for he knew that his master acknowledged I was not the person that was in his shop; 'and,' says the constable, 'I am afraid your master is bringing himself, and me too, into trouble, if this gentlewoman comes to prove who she is, and where she was, and it appears that she is not the woman you pretend to.' 'Damn her,' says the fellow again, with a impudent, hardened face, 'she is the lady, you may depend upon it; I'll swear she is the same body that was in the shop, and that I gave the pieces of satin that is lost into her own hand. You shall hear more of it when Mr. William and Mr. Anthony (those were other journeymen) come back; they will know her again as well as I.'

Just as the insolent rogue was talking thus to the constable, comes back Mr. William and Mr. Anthony, as he called them, and a great rabble with them, bringing along with them the true widow that I was pretended to be; and they came sweating and blowing into the shop, and with a great deal of triumph, dragging the poor creature in the most butcherly manner up towards their master, who was in the back shop, and cried out aloud, 'Here's the widow, sir; we have catcher her at last.' 'What do ye mean by that?' says the master. 'Why, we have her already; there she sits,' says he, 'and Mr. ——,' says he, 'can swear this is she.' The other man, whom they called Mr. Anthony, replied, 'Mr. —— may say what he will, and swear what he will, but this is the woman, and there's the remnant of satin she stole; I took it out of her clothes with my own hand.'

I sat still now, and began to take a better heart, but smiled and said nothing; the master looked pale; the constable turned about and looked at me. 'Let 'em alone, Mr. Constable,' said I; 'let 'em go on.' The case was plain and could not be denied, so the constable was charged with the right thief, and the mercer told me very civilly he was sorry for the mistake, and hoped I would not take it ill; that they had so many things of this nature put upon them every day, that they could not be blamed for being very sharp in doing themselves justice. 'Not take it ill, sir!' said I; 'how can I take it well! If you had dismissed me when your insolent fellow seized on me it the street, and brought me to you, and when you yourself acknowledged I was not the person, I would have put it by, and not taken it ill, because of the many ill things I believe you have put upon you daily; but your treatment of me since has been insufferable, and especially that of your servant; I must and will have reparation for that.'

Then he began to parley with me, said he would make me any reasonable satisfaction, and would fain have had me tell him what it was I expected. I told him that I should not be my own judge, the law should decide it for me; and as I was to be carried before a magistrate, I should let him hear there what I had to say. He told me there was no occasion to go before the justice now, I was at liberty to go where I pleased; and so, calling to the constable, told him he might let me go, for I was discharged. The constable said calmly to him, 'sir, you asked me just now if I knew whether I was a constable or justice, and bade me do my duty, and charged me with this gentlewoman as a prisoner. Now, sir, I find you do not understand what is my duty, for you would make me a justice indeed; but I must tell you it is not in my power. I may keep a prisoner when I am charged with him, but 'tis the law and the magistrate alone that can discharge that prisoner; therefore 'tis a mistake, sir; I must carry her before a justice now, whether you think well of it or not.' The mercer was very high with the constable at first; but the constable happening to be not a hired officer, but a good, substantial kind of man (I think he was a corn-handler), and a man of good sense, stood to his business, would not discharge me without going to a justice of the peace; and I insisted upon it too. When the mercer saw that, 'Well,' says he to the constable, 'you may carry her where you please; I have nothing to say to her.' 'But, sir,' says the constable, 'you will go with us, I hope, for 'tis you that charged me with her.' 'No, not I,' says the mercer; 'I tell you I have nothing to say to her.' 'But pray, sir, do,' says the constable; 'I desire it of you for your own sake, for the justice can do nothing without you.' 'Prithee, fellow,' says the mercer, 'go about your business; I tell you I have nothing to say to the gentlewoman. I charge you in the king's name to dismiss her.' 'Sir,' says the constable, 'I find you don't know what it is to be constable; I beg of you don't oblige me to be rude to you.' 'I think I need not; you are rude enough already,' says the mercer. 'No, sir,' says the constable, 'I am not rude; you have broken the peace in bringing an honest woman out of the street, when she was about her lawful occasion, confining her in your shop, and ill-using her here by your servants; and now can you say I am rude to you? I think I am civil to you in not commanding or charging you in the king's name to go with me, and charging every man I see that passes your door to aid and assist me in carrying you by force; this you cannot but know I have power to do, and yet I forbear it, and once more entreat you to go with me.' Well, he would not for all this, and gave the constable ill language. However, the constable kept his temper, and would not be provoked; and then I put in and said, 'Come, Mr. Constable, let him alone; I shall find ways enough to fetch him before a magistrate, I don't fear that; but there's the fellow,' says I, 'he was the man that seized on me as I was innocently going along the street, and you are a witness of the violence with me since; give me leave to charge you with him, and carry him before the justice.' 'Yes, madam,' says the constable; and turning to the fellow 'Come, young gentleman,' says he to the journeyman, 'you must go along with us; I hope you are not above the constable's power, though your master is.'

The fellow looked like a condemned thief, and hung back, then looked at his master, as if he could help him; and he, like a fool, encourage the fellow to be rude, and he truly resisted the constable, and pushed him back with a good force when he went to lay hold on him, at which the constable knocked him down, and called out for help; and immediately the shop was filled with people, and the constable seized the master and man, and all his servants.

This first ill consequence of this fray was, that the woman they had taken, who was really the thief, made off, and got clear away in the crowd; and two other that they had stopped also; whether they were really guilty or not, that I can say nothing to.

By this time some of his neighbours having come in, and, upon inquiry, seeing how things went, had endeavoured to bring the hot-brained mercer to his senses, and he began to be convinced that he was in the wrong; and so at length we went all very quietly before the justice, with a mob of about five hundred people at our heels; and all the way I went I could hear the people ask what was the matter, and other reply and say, a mercer had stopped a gentlewoman instead of a thief, and had afterwards taken the thief, and now the gentlewoman had taken the mercer, and was carrying him before the justice. This pleased the people strangely, and made the crowd increase, and they cried out as they went, 'Which is the rogue? which is the mercer?' and especially the women. Then when they saw him they cried out, 'That's he, that's he'; and every now and then came a good dab of dirt at him; and thus we marched a good while, till the mercer thought fit to desire the constable to call a coach to protect himself from the rabble; so we rode the rest of the way, the constable and I, and the mercer and his man.

When we came to the justice, which was an ancient gentleman in Bloomsbury, the constable giving first a summary account of the matter, the justice bade me speak, and tell what I had to say. And first he asked my name, which I was very loth to give, but there was no remedy, so I told him my name was Mary Flanders, that I was a widow, my husband being a sea captain, died on a voyage to Virginia; and some other circumstances I told which he could never contradict, and that I lodged at present in town with such a person, naming my governess; but that I was preparing to go over to America, where my husband's effects lay, and that I was going that day to buy some clothes to put myself into second mourning, but had not yet been in any shop, when that fellow, pointing to the mercer's journeyman, came rushing upon me with such fury as very much frighted me, and carried me back to his master's shop, where, though his master acknowledged I was not the person, yet he would not dismiss me, but charged a constable with me.

Then I proceeded to tell how the journeyman treated me; how they would not suffer me to send for any of my friends; how afterwards they found the real thief, and took the very goods they had lost upon her, and all the particulars as before.

Then the constable related his case: his dialogue with the mercer about discharging me, and at last his servant's refusing to go with him, when he had charged him with him, and his master encouraging him to do so, and at last his striking the constable, and the like, all as I have told it already.

The justice then heard the mercer and his man. The mercer indeed made a long harangue of the great loss they have daily by lifters and thieves; that it was easy for them to mistake, and that when he found it he would have dismissed me, etc., as above. As to the journeyman, he had very little to say, but that he pretended other of the servants told him that I was really the person.

Upon the whole, the justice first of all told me very courteously I was discharged; that he was very sorry that the mercer's man should in his eager pursuit have so little discretion as to take up an innocent person for a guilty person; that if he had not been so unjust as to detain me afterward, he believed I would have forgiven the first affront; that, however, it was not in his power to award me any reparation for anything, other than by openly reproving them, which he should do; but he supposed I would apply to such methods as the law directed; in the meantime he would bind him over.

But as to the breach of the peace committed by the journeyman, he told me he should give me some satisfaction for that, for he should commit him to Newgate for assaulting the constable, and for assaulting me also.

Accordingly he sent the fellow to Newgate for that assault, and his master gave bail, and so we came away; but I had the satisfaction of seeing the mob wait upon them both, as they came out, hallooing and throwing stones and dirt at the coaches they rode in; and so I came home to my governess.

After this hustle, coming home and telling my governess the story, she falls a-laughing at me. 'Why are you merry?' says I; 'the story has not so much laughing room in it as you imagine; I am sure I have had a great deal of hurry and fright too, with a pack of ugly rogues.' 'Laugh!' says my governess; 'I laugh, child, to see what a lucky creature you are; why, this job will be the best bargain to you that ever you made in your life, if you manage it well. I warrant you,' says she, 'you shall make the mercer pay you £500 for damages, besides what you shall get out of the journeyman.'

I had other thoughts of the matter than she had; and especially, because I had given in my name to the justice of peace; and I knew that my name was so well known among the people at Hick's Hall, the Old Bailey, and such places, that if this cause came to be tried openly, and my name came to be inquired into, no court would give much damages, for the reputation of a person of such a character. However, I was obliged to begin a prosecution in form, and accordingly my governess found me out a very creditable sort of a man to manage it, being an attorney of very good business, and of a good reputation, and she was certainly in the right of this; for had she employed a pettifogging hedge solicitor, or a man not known, and not in good reputation, I should have brought it to but little.

I met this attorney, and gave him all the particulars at large, as they are recited above; and he assured me it was a case, as he said, that would very well support itself, and that he did not question but that a jury would give very considerable damages on such an occasion; so taking his full instructions he began the prosecution, and the mercer being arrested, gave bail. A few days after his giving bail, he comes with his attorney to my attorney, to let him know that he desired to accommodate the matter; that it was all carried on in the heat of an unhappy passion; that his client, meaning me, had a sharp provoking tongue, that I used them ill, gibing at them, and jeering them, even while they believed me to be the very person, and that I had provoked them, and the like.

My attorney managed as well on my side; made them believe was a widow of fortune, that I was able to do myself justice,

and had great friends to stand by me too, who had all made me promise to sue to the utmost, and that if it cost me a thousand pounds I would be sure to have satisfaction, for that the affronts I had received were insufferable.

However, they brought my attorney to this, that he promised he would not blow the coals, that if I inclined to accommodation, he would not hinder me, and that he would rather persuade me to peace than to war; for which they told him he should be no loser; all which he told me very honestly, and told me that if they offered him any bribe, I should certainly know it; but upon the whole he told me very honestly that if I would take his opinion, he would advise me to make it up with them, for that as they were in a great fright, and were desirous above all things to make it up, and knew that, let it be what it would, they would be allotted to bear all the costs of the suit; he believed they would give me freely more than any jury or court of justice would give upon a trial. I asked him what he thought they would be brought to. He told me he could not tell as to that, but he would tell me more when I saw him again.

Some time after this, they came again to know if he had talked with me. He told them he had; that he found me not so averse to an accommodation as some of my friends were, who resented the disgrace offered me, and set me on; that they blowed the coals in secret, prompting me to revenge, or do myself justice, as they called it; so that he could not tell what to say to it; he told them he would do his endeavour to persuade me, but he ought to be able to tell me what proposal they made. They pretended they could not make any proposal, because it might be made use of against them; and he told them, that by the same rule he could not make any offers, for that might be pleaded in abatement of what damages a jury might be inclined to give. However, after some discourse and mutual promises that no advantage should be taken on either side, by what was transacted then or at any other of those meetings, they came to a kind of a treaty; but so remote, and so wide from one another, that nothing could be expected from it; for my attorney demanded £500 and charges, and they offered £50 without charges; so they broke off, and the mercer proposed to have a meeting with me myself; and my attorney agreed to that very readily.

My attorney gave me notice to come to this meeting in good clothes, and with some state, that the mercer might see I was something more than I seemed to be that time they had me. Accordingly I came in a new suit of second mourning, according to what I had said at the justice's. I set myself out, too, as well as a widow's dress in second mourning would admit; my governess also furnished me with a good pearl necklace, that shut in behind with a locket of diamonds, which she had in pawn; and I had a very good figure; and as I stayed till I was sure they were come, I came in a coach to the door, with my maid with me.

When I came into the room the mercer was surprised. He stood up and made his bow, which I took a little notice of, and but a little, and went and sat down where my own attorney had pointed to me to sit, for it was his house. After a little while the mercer said, he did not know me again, and began to make some compliments his way. I told him, I believed he did not know me at first, and that if he had, I believed he would not have treated me as he did.

He told me he was very sorry for what had happened, and that it was to testify the willingness he had to make all possible reparation that he had appointed this meeting; that he hoped I would not carry things to extremity, which might be not only too great a loss to him, but might be the ruin of his business and shop, in which case I might have the satisfaction of repaying an injury with an injury ten times greater; but that I would then get nothing, whereas he was willing to do me any justice that was in his power, without putting himself or me to the trouble or charge of a suit at law.

I told him I was glad to hear him talk so much more like a man of sense than he did before; that it was true, acknowledgment in most cases of affronts was counted reparation sufficient; but this had gone too far to be made up so; that I was not revengeful, nor did I seek his ruin, or any man's else, but that all my friends were unanimous not to let me so far neglect my character as to adjust a thing of this kind without a sufficient reparation of honour; that to be taken up for a thief was such an indignity as could not be put up; that my character was above being treated so by any that knew me, but because in my condition of a widow I had been for some time careless of myself, and negligent of myself, I might be taken for such a creature, but that for the particular usage I had from him afterwards,—and then I repeated all as before; it was so provoking I had scarce patience to repeat it.

Well, he acknowledged all, and was might humble indeed; he made proposals very handsome; he came up to £100 and to pay all the law charges, and added that he would make me a present of a very good suit of clothes. I came down to £300, and I demanded that I should publish an advertisement of the particulars in the common newspapers.

This was a clause he never could comply with. However, at last he came up, by good management of my attorney, to £150 and a suit of black silk clothes; and there I agree, and as it were, at my attorney's request, complied with it, he paying my attorney's bill and charges, and gave us a good supper into the bargain.

When I came to receive the money, I brought my governess with me, dressed like an old duchess, and a gentleman very well dressed, who we pretended courted me, but I called him cousin, and the lawyer was only to hint privately to him that his gentleman courted the widow.

He treated us handsomely indeed, and paid the money cheerfully enough; so that it cost him £200 in all, or rather more. At our last meeting, when all was agreed, the case of the journeyman came up, and the mercer begged very hard for him; told me he was a man that had kept a shop of his own, and been in good business, had a wife, and several children, and was very poor; that he had nothing to make satisfaction with, but he should come to beg my pardon on his knees, if I desired it, as openly as I pleased. I had no spleen at the saucy rogue, nor were his submissions anything to me, since there was nothing to be got by him, so I thought it was as good to throw that in generously as not; so I told him I did not desire the ruin of any man, and therefore at his request I would forgive the wretch; it was below me to seek any revenge.

When we were at supper he brought the poor fellow in to make acknowledgment, which he would have done with as much mean humility as his offence was with insulting haughtiness and pride, in which he was an instance of a complete baseness of spirit, impious, cruel, and relentless when uppermost and in prosperity, abject and low-spirited when down in affliction. However, I abated his cringes, told him I forgave him, and desired he might withdraw, as if I did not care for the sight of him, though I had forgiven him.

I was now in good circumstances indeed, if I could have known my time for leaving off, and my governess often said I was the richest of the trade in England; and so I believe I was, for I had £700 by me in money, besides clothes, rings, some plate, and two gold watches, and all of them stolen, for I had innumerable jobs besides these I have mentioned. Oh! had I even now had the grace of repentance, I had still leisure to have looked back upon my follies, and have made some reparation; but the satisfaction I was to make for the public mischiefs I had done was yet left behind; and I could not forbear going abroad again, as I called it now, than any more I could when my extremity really drove me out for bread.

It was not long after the affair with the mercer was made up, that I went out in an equipage quite different from any I had ever appeared in before. I dressed myself like a beggar woman, in the coarsest and most despicable rags I could get, and I walked about peering and peeping into every door and window I came near; and indeed I was in such a plight now that I knew as ill how to behave in as ever I did in any. I naturally abhorred dirt and rags; I had been bred up tight and cleanly, and could be no other, whatever condition I was in; so that this was the most uneasy disguise to me that ever I put on. I said presently to myself that this would not do, for this was a dress that everybody was shy and afraid of; and I thought everybody looked at me, as if they were afraid I should come near them, lest I should take something from them, or afraid to come near me, lest they should get something from me. I wandered about all the evening the first time I went out, and made nothing of it, but came home again wet, draggled, and tired. However, I went out again the next night, and then I met with a little adventure, which had like to have cost me dear. As I was standing near a tavern door, there comes a gentleman on horseback, and lights at the door, and wanting to go into the tavern, he calls one of the drawers to hold his horse. He stayed pretty long in the tavern, and the drawer heard his master call, and thought he would be angry with him. Seeing me stand by him, he called to me, 'Here, woman,' says he, 'hold this horse a while, till I go in; if the gentleman comes, he'll give you something.' 'Yes,' says I, and takes the horse, and walks off with him very soberly, and carried him to my governess.

This had been a booty to those that had understood it; but never was poor thief more at a loss to know what to do with anything that was stolen; for when I came home, my governess was quite confounded, and what to do with the creature, we neither of us knew. To send him to a stable was doing nothing, for it was certain that public notice would be given in the Gazette, and the horse described, so that we durst not go to fetch it again.

All the remedy we had for this unlucky adventure was to go and set up the horse at an inn, and send a note by a porter to the tavern, that the gentleman's horse that was lost such a time was left at such an inn, and that he might be had there; that the poor woman that held him, having led him about the street, not being able to lead him back again, had left him there. We might have waited till the owner had published and offered a reward, but we did not care to venture the receiving the reward.

So this was a robbery and no robbery, for little was lost by it, and nothing was got by it, and I was quite sick of going out in a beggar's dress; it did not answer at all, and besides, I thought it was ominous and threatening.

While I was in this disguise, I fell in with a parcel of folks of a worse kind than any I ever sorted with, and I saw a little into their ways too. These were coiners of money, and they made some very good offers to me, as to profit; but the part they would have had me have embarked in was the most dangerous part. I mean that of the very working the die, as they call it, which, had I been taken, had been certain death, and that at a stake—I say, to be burnt to death at a stake; so that though I was to appearance but a beggar, and they promised mountains of gold and silver to me to engage, yet it would not do. It is true, if I had been really a beggar, or had been desperate as when I began, I might perhaps have closed with it; for what care they to die that can't tell how to live? But at present this was not my condition, at least I was for no such terrible risks as those; besides, the very thoughts of being burnt at a stake struck terror into my very soul, chilled my blood, and gave me the vapours to such a degree, as I could not think of it without trembling.

This put an end to my disguise too, for as I did not like the proposal, so I did not tell them so, but seemed to relish it, and promised to meet again. But I durst see them no more; for if I had seen them, and not complied, though I had declined it with the greatest assurance of secrecy in the world, they would have gone near to have murdered me, to make sure work, and make themselves easy, as they call it. What kind of easiness that is, they may best judge that understand how easy men are that can murder people to prevent danger.

This and horse-stealing were things quite out of my way, and I might easily resolve I would have to more to say to them; my business seemed to lie another way, and though it had hazard enough in it too, yet it was more suitable to me, and what had more of art in it, and more room to escape, and more chances for a-coming off if a surprise should happen.

I had several proposals made also to me about that time, to come into a gang of house-breakers; but that was a thing I had no mind to venture at neither, any more than I had at the coining trade. I offered to go along with two men and a woman, that made it their business to get into houses by stratagem, and with them I was willing enough to venture. But there were three of them already, and they did not care to part, nor I to have too many in a gang, so I did not close with them, but declined them, and they paid dear for their next attempt.

But at length I met with a woman that had often told me what adventures she had made, and with success, at the waterside, and I closed with her, and we drove on our business pretty well. One day we came among some Dutch people at St. Catherine's, where we went on pretence to buy goods that were privately got on shore. I was two or three times in a house where we saw a good quantity of prohibited goods, and my companion once brought away three pieces of Dutch black silk that turned to good account, and I had my share of it; but in all the journeys I made by myself, I could not get an opportunity to do anything, so I laid it aside, for I had been so often, that they began to suspect something, and were so shy, that I saw nothing was to be done.

This baulked me a little, and I resolved to push at something or other, for I was not used to come back so often without purchase; so the next day I dressed myself up fine, and took a walk to the other end of the town. I passed through the Exchange in the Strand, but had no notion of finding anything to do there, when on a sudden I saw a great cluttering in the place, and all the people, shopkeepers as well as others, standing up and staring; and what should it be but some great duchess come into the Exchange, and they said the queen was coming. I set myself close up to a shop-side with my back to the counter, as if to let the crowd pass by, when keeping my eye upon a parcel of lace which the shopkeeper was showing to some ladies that stood by me, the shopkeeper and her maid were so taken up with looking to see who was coming, and what shop they would go to, that I found means to slip a paper of lace into my pocket and come clear off with it; so the lady-milliner paid dear enough for her gaping after the queen.

I went off from the shop, as if driven along by the throng, and mingling myself with the crowd, went out at the other door of the Exchange, and so got away before they missed their lace; and because I would not be followed, I called a coach and shut myself up in it. I had scarce shut the coach doors up, but I saw the milliner's maid and five or six more come running out into the street, and crying out as if they were frightened. They did not cry 'Stop thief!' because nobody ran away, but I could hear the word 'robbed,' and 'lace,' two or three times, and saw the wench wringing her hands, and run staring to and again, like one scared. The coachman that had taken me up was getting up into the box, but was not quite up, so that the horse had not begun to move; so that I was terrible uneasy, and I took the packet of lace and laid it ready to have dropped it out at the flap of the coach, which opens before, just behind the coachman; but to my great satisfaction, in less than a minute the coach began to move, that is to say, as soon as the coachman had got up and spoken to his horses; so he drove away without any interruption, and I brought off my purchase, which was work near £20.

The next day I dressed up again, but in quite different clothes, and walked the same way again, but nothing offered till I came into St. James's Park, where I saw abundance of fine ladies in the Park, walking in the Mall, and among the rest there was a little miss, a young lady of about twelve or thirteen years old, and she had a sister, as I suppose it was, with her, that might be about nine years old. I observed the biggest had a fine gold watch on, and a good necklace of pearl, and they had a footman in livery with them; but as it is not usual for the footman to go behind the ladies in the Mall, so I observed the footman stopped at their going into the Mall, and the biggest of the sisters spoke to him, which I perceived was to bid him be just there when they came back.

When I heard her dismiss the footman, I stepped up to him and asked him, what little lady that was? and held a little chat with him about what a pretty child it was with her, and how genteel and well-carriaged the lady, the eldest, would be: how womanish, and how grave; and the fool of a fellow told me presently who she was; that she was Sir Thomas ——'s eldest daughter, of Essex, and that she was a great fortune; that her mother was not come to town yet; but she was with Sir William ——'s lady, of Suffolk, at her lodging in Suffolk Street, and a great deal more; that they had a maid and a woman to wait on them, besides Sir Thomas's coach, the coachman, and himself; and that young lady was governess to the whole family, as well here as at home too; and, in short, told me abundance of things enough for my business.

I was very well dressed, and had my gold watch as well as she; so I left the footman, and I puts myself in a rank with this young lady, having stayed till she had taken one double turn in the Mall, and was going forward again; by and by I saluted her by her name, with the title of Lady Betty. I asked her when she heard from her father; when my lady her mother would be in town, and how she did.

I talked so familiarly to her of her whole family that she could not suspect but that I knew them all intimately. I asked her why she would come abroad without Mrs. Chime with her (that was the name of her woman) to take of Mrs. Judith, that was her sister. Then I entered into a long chat with her about her sister, what a fine little lady she was, and asked her if she had learned French, and a thousand such little things to entertain her, when on a sudden we saw the guards come, and the crowd ran to see the king go by to the Parliament House.

The ladies ran all to the side of the Mall, and I helped my lady to stand upon the edge of the boards on the side of the Mall, that she might be high enough to see; and took the little one and lifted her quite up; during which, I took care to convey the gold watch so clean away from the Lady Betty, that she never felt it, nor missed it, till all the crowd was gone, and she was gotten into the middle of the Mall among the other ladies.

I took my leave of her in the very crowd, and said to her, as if in haste, 'Dear Lady Betty, take care of your little sister.' And so the crowd did as it were thrust me away from her, and that I was obliged unwillingly to take my leave.

The hurry in such cases is immediately over, and the place clear as soon as the king is gone by; but as there is always a great running and clutter just as the king passes, so having dropped the two little ladies, and done my business with them without any miscarriage, I kept hurrying on among the crowd, as if I ran to see the king, and so I got before the crowd and kept so till I came to the end of the Mall, when the king going on towards the Horse Guards, I went forward to the passage, which went then through against the lower end of the Haymarket, and there I bestowed a coach upon myself, and made off, and I confess I have not yet been so good as my word, viz. to go and visit my Lady Betty.

I was once of the mind to venture staying with Lady Betty till she missed the watch, and so have made a great outcry about it with her, and have got her into the coach, and put myself in the coach with her, and have gone home with her; for she appeared so fond of me, and so perfectly deceived by my so readily talking to her of all her relations and family, that I thought it was very easy to push the thing farther, and to have got at least the necklace of pearl; but when I considered that though the child would not perhaps have suspected me, other people might, and that if I was searched I should be discovered, I thought it was best to go off with what I had got, and be satisfied.

I came accidentally afterwards to hear, that when the young lady missed her watch, she made a great outcry in the Park, and sent her footman up and down to see if he could find me out, she having described me so perfectly that he knew presently that it was the same person that had stood and talked so long with him, and asked him so many questions about them; but I gone far enough out of their reach before she could come at her footman to tell him the story.

I made another adventure after this, of a nature different from all I had been concerned in yet, and this was at a gaming-house near Covent Garden.

I saw several people go in and out; and I stood in the passage a good while with another woman with me, and seeing a gentleman go up that seemed to be of more than ordinary fashion, I said to him, 'Sir, pray don't they give women leave to go up?' 'Yes, madam,' says he, 'and to play too, if they please.' 'I mean so, sir,' said I. And with that he said he would introduce me if I had a mind; so I followed him to the door, and he looking in, 'There, madam,' says he, 'are the gamesters, if you have a mind to venture.' I looked in and said to my comrade aloud, 'Here's nothing but men; I won't venture among them.' At which one of the gentlemen cried out, 'You need not be afraid, madam, here's none but fair gamesters; you are very welcome to come and set what you please.' so I went a little nearer and looked on, and some of them brought me a chair, and I sat down and saw the box and dice go round apace; then I said to my comrade, 'The gentlemen play too high for us; come, let us go.'

The people were all very civil, and one gentleman in particular encouraged me, and said, 'Come, madam, if you please to venture, if you dare trust me, I'll answer for it you shall have nothing put upon you here.' 'No, sir,' said I, smiling, 'I hope the gentlemen would not cheat a woman.' But still I declined venturing, though I pulled out a purse with money in it, that they might see I did not want money.

After I had sat a while, one gentleman said to me, jeering, 'Come, madam, I see you are afraid to venture for yourself; I always had good luck with the ladies, you shall set for me, if you won't set for yourself.' I told him, 'sir, I should be very loth to lose your money,' though I added, 'I am pretty lucky too; but the gentlemen play so high, that I dare not indeed venture my own.'

'Well, well,' says he, 'there's ten guineas, madam; set them for me.' so I took his money and set, himself looking on. I ran out nine of the guineas by one and two at a time, and then the box coming to the next man to me, my gentleman gave me ten guineas more, and made me set five of them at once, and the gentleman who had the box threw out, so there was five guineas of his money again. He was encouraged at this, and made me take the box, which was a bold venture. However, I held the box so long that I had gained him his whole money, and had a good handful of guineas in my lap, and which was the better luck, when I threw out, I threw but at one or two of those that had set me, and so went off easy.

When I was come this length, I offered the gentleman all the gold, for it was his own; and so would have had him play for himself, pretending I did not understand the game well enough. He laughed, and said if I had but good luck, it was no matter whether I understood the game or no; but I should not leave off. However, he took out the fifteen guineas that he had put in at first, and bade me play with the rest. I would have told them to see how much I had got, but he said, 'No, no, don't tell them, I believe you are very honest, and 'tis bad luck to tell them'; so I played on.

I understood the game well enough, though I pretended I did not, and played cautiously. It was to keep a good stock in my lap, out of which I every now and then conveyed some into my pocket, but in such a manner, and at such convenient times, as I was sure he could not see it.

I played a great while, and had very good luck for him; but the last time I held the box, they set me high, and I threw boldly at all; I held the box till I gained near fourscore guineas, but lost above half of it back in the last throw; so I got up, for I was afraid I should lose it all back again, and said to him, 'Pray come, sir, now, and take it and play for yourself; I think I have done pretty well for you.' He would have had me play on, but it grew late, and I desired to be excused. When I gave it up to him, I told him I hoped he would give me leave to tell it now, that I might see what I had gained, and how lucky I had been for him; when I told them, there were threescore and three guineas. 'Ay,' says I, 'if it had not been for that unlucky throw, I had got you a hundred guineas.' So I gave him all the money, but he would not take it till I had put my hand into it, and taken some for myself, and bid me please myself. I refused it, and was positive I would not take it myself; if he had a mind to anything of that kind, it should be all his own doings.

The rest of the gentlemen seeing us striving cried, 'Give it her all'; but I absolutely refused that. Then one of them said, 'D—n ye, jack, halve it with her; don't you know you should be always upon even terms with the ladies.' So, in short, he divided it with me, and I brought away thirty guineas, besides about forty-three which I had stole privately, which I was sorry for afterward, because he was so generous.

Thus I brought home seventy-three guineas, and let my old governess see what good luck I had at play. However, it was her advice that I should not venture again, and I took her counsel, for I never went there any more; for I knew as well as she, if the itch of play came in, I might soon lose that, and all the rest of what I had got.

Fortune had smiled upon me to that degree, and I had thriven so much, and my governess too, for she always had a share with me, that really the old gentlewoman began to talk of leaving off while we were well, and being satisfied with what we had got; but, I know not what fate guided me, I was as backward to it now as she was when I proposed it to her before, and so in an ill hour we gave over the thoughts of it for the present, and, in a word, I grew more hardened and audacious than ever, and the success I had made my name as famous as any thief of my sort ever had been at Newgate, and in the Old Bailey.

I had sometime taken the liberty to play the same game over again, which is not according to practice, which however succeeded not amiss; but generally I took up new figures, and contrived to appear in new shapes every time I went abroad.

It was not a rumbling time of the year, and the gentlemen being most of them gone out of town, Tunbridge, and Epsom, and such places were full of people. But the city was thin, and I thought our trade felt it a little, as well as other; so that at the latter end of the year I joined myself with a gang who usually go every year to Stourbridge Fair, and from thence to Bury Fair, in Suffolk. We promised ourselves great things there, but when I came to see how things were, I was weary of it presently; for except mere picking of pockets, there was little worth meddling with; neither, if a booty had been made, was it so easy carrying it off, nor was there such a variety of occasion for business in our way, as in London; all that I made of the whole journey was a gold watch at Bury Fair, and a small parcel of linen at Cambridge, which gave me an occasion to take leave of the place. It was on old bite, and I thought might do with a country shopkeeper, though in London it would not.

I bought at a linen-draper's shop, not in the fair, but in the town of Cambridge, as much fine holland and other things as came to about seven pounds; when I had done, I bade them be sent to such an inn, where I had purposely taken up my being the same morning, as if I was to lodge there that night.

I ordered the draper to send them home to me, about such an hour, to the inn where I lay, and I would pay him his money. At the time appointed the draper sends the goods, and I placed one of our gang at the chamber door, and when the innkeeper's maid brought the messenger to the door, who was a young fellow, an apprentice, almost a man, she tells him her mistress was asleep, but if he would leave the things and call in about an hour, I should be awake, and he might have the money. He left the parcel very readily, and goes his way, and in about half an hour my maid and I walked off, and that very evening I hired a horse, and a man to ride before me, and went to Newmarket, and from thence got my passage in a coach that was not quite full to St. Edmund's Bury, where, as I told you, I could make but little of my trade, only at a little country opera-house made a shift to carry off a gold watch from a lady's side, who was not only intolerably merry, but, as I thought, a little fuddled, which made my work much easier.

I made off with this little booty to Ipswich, and from thence to Harwich, where I went into an inn, as if I had newly arrived from Holland, not doubting but I should make some purchase among the foreigners that came on shore there; but I found them generally empty of things of value, except what was in their portmanteaux and Dutch hampers, which were generally guarded by footmen; however, I fairly got one of their portmanteaux one evening out of the chamber where the gentleman lay, the footman being fast asleep on the bed, and I suppose very drunk.

The room in which I lodged lay next to the Dutchman's, and having dragged the heavy thing with much ado out of the chamber into mine, I went out into the street, to see if I could find any possibility of carrying it off. I walked about a great while, but could see no probability either of getting out the thing, or of conveying away the goods that were in it if I had opened it, the town being so small, and I a perfect stranger in it; so I was returning with a resolution to carry it back again, and leave it where I found it. Just in that very moment I heard a man make a noise to some people to make haste, for the boat was going to put off, and the tide would be spent. I called to the fellow, 'What boat is it, friend,' says I, 'that you belong to?' 'The Ipswich wherry, madam,' says he. 'When do you go off?' says I. 'This moment, madam,' says he; 'do you want to go thither?' 'Yes,' said I, 'if you can stay till I fetch my things.' 'Where are your things, madam?' says he. 'At such an inn,' said I. 'Well, I'll go with you, madam,' says he, very civilly, 'and bring them for you.' 'Come away, then,' says I, and takes him with me.

The people of the inn were in a great hurry, the packet-boat from Holland being just come in, and two coaches just come also with passengers from London, for another packet-boat that was going off for Holland, which coaches were to go back next day with the passengers that were just landed. In this hurry it was not much minded that I came to the bar and paid my reckoning, telling my landlady I had gotten my passage by sea in a wherry.

These wherries are large vessels, with good accommodation for carrying passengers from Harwich to London; and though they are called wherries, which is a word used in the Thames for a small boat rowed with one or two men, yet these are vessels able to carry twenty passengers, and ten or fifteen tons of goods, and fitted to bear the sea. All this I had found out by inquiring the night before into the several ways of going to London.

My landlady was very courteous, took my money for my reckoning, but was called away, all the house being in a hurry. So I left her, took the fellow up to my chamber, gave him the trunk, or portmanteau, for it was like a trunk, and wrapped it about with an old apron, and he went directly to his boat with it, and I after him, nobody asking us the least question about it; as for the drunken Dutch footman he was still asleep, and his master with other foreign gentlemen at supper, and very merry below, so I went clean off with it to Ipswich; and going in the night, the people of the house knew nothing but that I was gone to London by the Harwich wherry, as I had told my landlady.

I was plagued at Ipswich with the custom-house officers, who stopped my trunk, as I called it, and would open and search it. I was willing, I told them, they should search it, but husband had the key, and he was not yet come from Harwich; this I said, that if upon searching it thcy should find all thc things be such as properly belonged to a man rather than a woman, it should not seem strange to them. However, they being positive to open the trunk I consented to have it be broken open, that is to say, to have the lock taken off, which was not difficult.

They found nothing for their turn, for the trunk had been searched before, but they discovered several things very much to my satisfaction, as particularly a parcel of money in French pistols, and some Dutch ducatoons or rix-dollars, and the rest was chiefly two periwigs, wearing-linen, and razors, wash-balls, perfumes, and other useful things necessary for a gentleman, which all passed for my husband's, and so I was quit to them.

It was now very early in the morning, and not light, and I knew not well what course to take; for I made no doubt but I should be pursued in the morning, and perhaps be taken with the things about me; so I resolved upon taking new measures. I went publicly to an inn in the town with my trunk, as I called it, and having taken the substance out, I did not think the lumber of it worth my concern; however, I gave it the landlady of the house with a charge to take great care of it, and lay it up safe till I should come again, and away I walked in to the street.

When I was got into the town a great way from the inn, I met with an ancient woman who had just opened her door, and I fell into chat with her, and asked her a great many wild questions of things all remote to my purpose and design; but in my discourse I found by her how the town was situated, that I was in a street that went out towards Hadley, but that such a street went towards the water-side, such a street towards Colchester, and so the London road lay there.

I had soon my ends of this old woman, for I only wanted to know which was the London road, and away I walked as fast as I could; not that I intended to go on foot, either to London or to Colchester, but I wanted to get quietly away from Ipswich.

I walked about two or three miles, and then I met a plain countryman, who was busy about some husbandry work, I did not know what, and I asked him a great many questions first, not much to the purpose, but at last told him I was going for London, and the coach was full, and I could not get a passage, and asked him if he could tell me where to hire a horse that would carry double, and an honest man to ride before me to Colchester, that so I might get a place there in the coaches. The honest clown looked earnestly at me, and said nothing for above half a minute, when, scratching his poll, 'A horse, say you and to Colchester, to carry double? why yes, mistress, alack-a-day, you may have horses enough for money.' 'Well, friend,' says I, 'that I take for granted; I don't expect it without money.' 'Why, but, mistress,' says he, 'how much are you willing to give?' 'Nay,' says I again, 'friend, I don't know what your rates are in the country here, for I am a stranger; but if you can get one for me, get it as cheap as you can, and I'll give you somewhat for your pains.'

'Why, that's honestly said too,' says the countryman. 'Not so honest, neither,' said I to myself, 'if thou knewest all.' 'Why, mistress,' says he, 'I have a horse that will carry double, and I don't much care if I go myself with you,' and the like. 'Will you?' says I; 'well, I believe you are an honest man; if you will, I shall be glad of it; I'll pay you in reason.' 'Why, look ye, mistress,' says he, 'I won't be out of reason with you, then; if I carry you to Colchester, it will be worth five shillings for myself and my horse, for I shall hardly come back to-night.'

In short, I hired the honest man and his horse; but when we came to a town upon the road (I do not remember the name of it, but it stands upon a river), I pretended myself very ill, and I could go no farther that night but if he would stay there with me, because I was a stranger, I would pay him for himself and his horse with all my heart.

This I did because I knew the Dutch gentlemen and their servants would be upon the road that day, either in the stagecoaches or riding post, and I did not know but the drunken fellow, or somebody else that might have seen me at Harwich, might see me again, and so I thought that in one day's stop they would be all gone by.

We lay all that night there, and the next morning it was not very early when I set out, so that it was near ten o'clock by the time I got to Colchester. It was no little pleasure that I saw the town where I had so many pleasant days, and I made many inquiries after the good old friends I had once had there, but could make little out; they were all dead or removed. The young ladies had been all married or gone to London; the old gentleman and the old lady that had been my early benefactress all dead; and which troubled me most, the young gentleman my first lover, and afterwards my brother-in-law, was dead; but two sons, men grown, were left of him, but they too were transplanted to London.

I dismissed my old man here, and stayed incognito for three or four days in Colchester, and then took a passage in a waggon, because I would not venture being seen in the Harwich coaches. But I needed not have used so much caution, for there was nobody in Harwich but the woman of the house could have known me; nor was it rational to think that she, considering the hurry she was in, and that she never saw me but once, and that by candlelight, should have ever discovered me.

I was now returned to London, and though by the accident of the last adventure I got something considerable, yet I was not fond of any more country rambles, nor should I have ventured abroad again if I had carried the trade on to the end of my days. I gave my governess a history of my travels; she liked the Harwich journey well enough, and in discoursing of these things between ourselves she observed, that a thief being a creature that watches the advantages of other people's mistakes, 'tis impossible but that to one that is vigilant and industrious many opportunities must happen, and therefore she thought that one so exquisitely keen in the trade as I was, would scarce fail of something extraordinary wherever I went.

On the other hand, every branch of my story, if duly considered, may be useful to honest people, and afford a due caution to people of some sort or other to guard against the like surprises, and to have their eyes about them when they have to do with strangers of any kind, for 'tis very seldom that some snare or other is not in their way. The moral, indeed, of all my history is left to be gathered by the senses and judgment of the reader; I am not qualified to preach to them. Let the experience of one creature completely wicked, and completely miserable, be a storehouse of useful warning to those that read.

I am drawing now towards a new variety of the scenes of life. Upon my return, being hardened by along race of crime, and success unparalleled, at least in the reach of my own knowledge, I had, as I have said, no thoughts of laying down a trade which, if I was to judge by the example of other, must, however, end at last in misery and sorrow.

It was on the Christmas day following, in the evening, that, to finish a long train of wickedness, I went abroad to see what might offer in my way; when going by a working silversmith's in Foster Lane, I saw a tempting bait indeed, and not be resisted by one of my occupation, for the shop had nobody in it, as I could see, and a great deal of loose plate lay in the window, and at the seat of the man, who usually, as I suppose, worked at one side of the shop.

I went boldly in, and was just going to lay my hand upon a piece of plate, and might have done it, and carried it clear off, for any care that the men who belonged to the shop had taken of it; but an officious fellow in a house, not a shop, on the other side of the way, seeing me go in, and observing that there was nobody in the shop, comes running over the street, and into the shop, and without asking me what I was, or who, seizes upon me, an cries out for the people of the house.

I had not, as I said above, touched anything in the shop, and seeing a glimpse of somebody running over to the shop, I had so much presence of mind as to knock very hard with my foot on the floor of the house, and was just calling out too, when the fellow laid hands on me.

However, as I had always most courage when I was in most danger, so when the fellow laid hands on me, I stood very high upon it, that I came in to buy half a dozen of silver spoons; and to my good fortune, it was a silversmith's that sold plate, as well as worked plate for other shops. The fellow laughed at that part, and put such a value upon the service that he had done his neighbour, that he would have it be that I came not to buy, but to steal; and raising a great crowd. I said to the master of the shop, who by this time was fetched home from some neighbouring place, that it was in vain to make noise, and enter into talk there of the case; the fellow had insisted that I came to steal, and he must prove it, and I desired we might go before a magistrate without any more words; for I began to see I should be too hard for the man that had seized me.

The master and mistress of the shop were really not so violent as the man from t'other side of the way; and the man said, 'Mistress, you might come into the shop with a good design for aught I know, but it seemed a dangerous thing for you to come into such a shop as mine is, when you see nobody there; and I cannot do justice to my neighbour, who was so kind to me, as not to acknowledge he had reason on his side; though, upon the whole, I do not find you attempted to take anything, and I really know not what to do in it.' I pressed him to go before a magistrate with me, and if anything could be proved on me that was like a design of robbery, I should willingly submit, but if not, I expected reparation.

Just while we were in this debate, and a crowd of people gathered about the door, came by Sir T. B., an alderman of the city, and justice of the peace, and the goldsmith hearing of it, goes out, and entreated his worship to come in and decide the case.

Give the goldsmith his due, he told his story with a great deal of justice and moderation, and the fellow that had come over, and seized upon me, told his with as much heat and foolish passion, which did me good still, rather than harm. It came then to my turn to speak, and I told his worship that I was a stranger in London, being newly come out of the north; that I lodged in such a place, that I was passing this street, and went into the goldsmith's shop to buy half a dozen of spoons. By great luck I had an old silver spoon in my pocket, which I pulled out, and told him I had carried that spoon to match it with half a dozen of new ones, that it might match some I had in the country.

That seeing nobody I the shop, I knocked with my foot very hard to make the people hear, and had also called aloud with my voice; 'tis true, there was loose plate in the shop, but that nobody could say I had touched any of it, or gone near it; that a fellow came running into the shop out of the street, and laid hands on me in a furious manner, in the very moments while I was calling for the people of the house; that if he had really had a mind to have done his neighbour any service, he should have stood at a distance, and silently watched to see whether I had touched anything or no, and then have clapped in upon me, and taken me in the fact. 'That is very true,' says Mr. Alderman, and turning to the fellow that stopped me, he asked him if it was true that I knocked with my foot? He said, yes, I had knocked, but that might be because of his coming. 'Nay,' says the alderman, taking him short, 'now you contradict yourself, for just now you said she was in the shop with her back to you, and did not see you till you came upon her.' Now it was true that my back was partly to the street, but yet as my business was of a kind that required me to have my eyes every way, so I really had a glance of him running over, as I said before, though he did not perceive it.

After a full hearing, the alderman gave it as his opinion that his neighbour was under a mistake, and that I was innocent, and the goldsmith acquiesced in it too, and his wife, and so I was dismissed; but as I was going to depart, Mr. Alderman said, 'But hold, madam, if you were designing to buy spoons, I hope you will not let my friend here lose his customer by the mistake.' I readily answered, 'No, sir, I'll buy the spoons still, if he can match my odd spoon, which I brought for a pattern'; and the goldsmith showed me some of the very same fashion. So he weighed the spoons, and they came to five-and-thirty shillings, so I pulls out my purse to pay him, in which I had near twenty guineas, for I never went without such a sum about me, whatever might happen, and I found it of use at other times as well as now.

When Mr. Alderman saw my money, he said, 'Well, madam, now I am satisfied you were wronged, and it was for this reason that I moved you should buy the spoons, and stayed till you had bought them, for if you had not had money to pay for them, I should have suspected that you did not come into the shop with an intent to buy, for indeed the sort of people who come upon these designs that you have been charged with, are seldom troubled with much gold in their pockets, as I see you are.'

I smiled, and told his worship, that then I owed something of his favour to my money, but I hoped he saw reason also in the justice he had done me before. He said, yes, he had, but this had confirmed his opinion, and he was fully satisfied now of my having been injured. So I came off with flying colours, though from an affair in which I was at the very brink of destruction.

It was but three days after this, that not at all made cautious by my former danger, as I used to be, and still pursuing the art which I had so long been employed in, I ventured into a house where I saw the doors open, and furnished myself, as I though verily without being perceived, with two pieces of flowered silks, such as they call brocaded silk, very rich. It was not a mercer's shop, nor a warehouse of a mercer, but looked like a private dwelling-house, and was, it seems, inhabited by a man that sold goods for the weavers to the mercers, like a broker or factor.

That I may make short of this black part of this story, I was attacked by two wenches that came open-mouthed at me just as I was going out at the door, and one of them pulled me back into the room, while the other shut the door upon me. I would have given them good words, but there was no room for it, two fiery dragons could not have been more furious than they were; they tore my clothes, bullied and roared as if they would have murdered me; the mistress of the house came next, and then the master, and all outrageous, for a while especially.

I gave the master very good words, told him the door was open, and things were a temptation to me, that I was poor and distressed, and poverty was when many could not resist, and begged him with tears to have pity on me. The mistress of the house was moved with compassion, and inclined to have let me go, and had almost persuaded her husband to it also, but the saucy wenches were run, even before they were sent, and had fetched a constable, and then the master said he could not go back, I must go before a justice, and answered his wife that he might come into trouble himself if he should let me go.

The sight of the constable, indeed, struck me with terror, and I thought I should have sunk into the ground. I fell into faintings, and indeed the people themselves thought I would have died, when the woman argued again for me, and entreated her husband, seeing they had lost nothing, to let me go. I offered him to pay for the two pieces, whatever the value was, though I had not got them, and argued that as he had his goods, and had really lost nothing, it would be cruel to pursue me to death, and have my blood for the bare attempt of taking them. I put the constable in mind that I had broke no doors, nor carried anything away; and when I came to the justice, and pleaded there that I had neither broken anything to get in, nor carried anything out, the justice was inclined to have released me; but the first saucy jade that stopped me, affirming that I was going out with the goods, but that she stopped me and pulled me back as I was upon the threshold, the justice upon that point committed me, and I was carried to Newgate. That horrid place! my very blood chills at the mention of its name; the place where so many of my comrades had been locked up, and from whence they went to the fatal tree; the place where my mother suffered so deeply, where I was brought into the world, and from whence I expected no redemption but by an infamous death: to conclude, the place that had so long expected me, and which with so much art and success I had so long avoided.

I was not fixed indeed; 'tis impossible to describe the terror of my mind, when I was first brought in, and when I looked around upon all the horrors of that dismal place. I looked on myself as lost, and that I had nothing to think of but of going out of the world, and that with the utmost infamy: the hellish noise, the roaring, swearing, and clamour, the stench and nastiness, and all the dreadful crowd of afflicting things that I saw there, joined together to make the place seem an emblem of hell itself, and a kind of an entrance into it.

Now I reproached myself with the many hints I had had, as I have mentioned above, from my own reason, from the sense of my good circumstances, and of the many dangers I had escaped, to leave off while I was well, and how I had withstood them all, and hardened my thoughts against all fear. It seemed to me that I was hurried on by an inevitable and unseen fate to this day of misery, and that now I was to expiate all my offences at the gallows; that I was now to give satisfaction to justice with my blood, and that I was come to the last hour of my life and of my wickedness together. These things poured themselves in upon my thoughts in a confused manner, and left me overwhelmed with melancholy and despair.

Them I repented heartily of all my life past, but that repentance yielded me no satisfaction, no peace, no, not in the least, because, as I said to myself, it was repenting after the power of further sinning was taken away. I seemed not to mourn that I had committed such crimes, and for the fact as it was an offence against God and my neighbour, but I mourned that I was to be punished for it. I was a penitent, as I thought, not that I had sinned, but that I was to suffer, and this took away all the comfort, and even the hope of my repentance in my own thoughts.

I got no sleep for several nights or days after I came into that wretched place, and glad I would have been for some time to have died there, though I did not consider dying as it ought to be considered neither; indeed, nothing could be filled with more horror to my imagination than the very place, nothing was more odious to me than the company that was there. Oh! if I had but been sent to any place in the world, and not to Newgate, I should have thought myself happy.

In the next place, how did the hardened wretches that were there before me triumph over me! What! Mrs. Flanders come to Newgate at last? What! Mrs. Mary, Mrs. Molly, and after that plain Moll Flanders? They thought the devil had helped me, they said, that I had reigned so long; they expected me there many years ago, and was I come at last? Then they flouted me with my dejections, welcomed me to the place, wished me joy, bid me have a good heart, not to be cast down, things might not be so bad as I feared, and the like; then called for brandy, and drank to me, but put it all up to my score, for they told me I was but just come to the college, as they called it, and sure I had money in my pocket, though they had none.

I asked one of this crew how long she had been there. She said four months. I asked her how the place looked to her when she first came into it. 'Just as it did now to you,' says she, dreadful and frightful'; that she thought she was in hell; 'and I believe so still,' adds she, 'but it is natural to me now, I don't disturb myself about it.' 'I suppose,' says I, 'you are in no danger of what is to follow?' 'Nay,' says she, 'for you are mistaken there, I assure you, for I am under sentence, only I pleaded my belly, but I am no more with child than the judge that tried me, and I expect to be called down next sessions.' This 'calling down' is calling down to their former judgment, when a woman has been respited for her belly, but proves not to be with child, or if she has been with child, and has been brought to bed. 'Well,' says I, 'are you thus easy?' 'Ay,' says she, 'I can't help myself; what signifies being sad? If I am hanged, there's an end of me,' says she; and away she turns dancing, and sings as she goes the following piece of Newgate wit ——

'If I swing by the string
I shall hear the bell ring
And then there's an end of poor Jenny.'

I mention this because it would be worth the observation of any prisoner, who shall hereafter fall into the same misfortune, and come to that dreadful place of Newgate, how time, necessity, and conversing with the wretches that are there familiarizes the place to them; how at last they become reconciled to that which at first was the greatest dread upon their spirits in the world, and are as impudently cheerful and merry in their misery as they were when out of it.

I cannot say, as some do, this devil is not so black as he is painted; for indeed no colours can represent the place to the life, not any soul conceive aright of it but those who have been suffers there. But how hell should become by degree so natural, and not only tolerable, but even agreeable, is a thing unintelligible but by those who have experienced it, as I have.

The same night that I was sent to Newgate, I sent the news of it to my old governess, who was surprised at it, you may be sure, and spent the night almost as ill out of Newgate, as I did in it.

The next morning she came to see me; she did what she could to comfort me, but she saw that was to no purpose; however, as she said, to sink under the weight was but to increase the weight; she immediately applied herself to all the proper methods to prevent the effects of it, which we feared, and first she found out the two fiery jades that had surprised me. She tampered with them, offered them money, and, in a word, tried all imaginable ways to prevent a prosecution; she offered one of the wenches £100 to go away from her mistress, and not to appear against me, but she was so resolute, that though she was but a servant maid at £3 a year wages or thereabouts, she refused it, and would have refused it, as my governess said she believed, if she had offered her £500. Then she attacked the other maid; she was not so hard-hearted in appearance as the other, and sometimes seemed inclined to be merciful; but the first wench kept her up, and changed her mind, and would not so much as let my governess talk with her, but threatened to have her up for tampering with the evidence.

Then she applied to the master, that is to say, the man whose goods had been stolen, and particularly to his wife, who, as I told you, was inclined at first to have some compassion for me; she found the woman the same still, but the man alleged he was bound by the justice that committed me, to prosecute, and that he should forfeit his recognisance.

My governess offered to find friends that should get his recognisances off of the file, as they call it, and that he should not suffer; but it was not possible to convince him that could be done, or that he could be safe any way in the world but by appearing against me; so I was to have three witnesses of fact against me, the master and his two maids; that is to say, I was as certain to be cast for my life as I was certain that I was alive, and I had nothing to do but to think of dying, and prepare for it. I had but a sad foundation to build upon, as I said before, for all my repentance appeared to me to be only the effect of my fear of death, not a sincere regret for the wicked life that I had lived, and which had brought this misery upon me, for the offending my Creator, who was now suddenly to be my judge.

I lived many days here under the utmost horror of soul; I had death, as it were, in view, and thought of nothing night and day, but of gibbets and halters, evil spirits and devils; it is not to be expressed by words how I was harassed, between the dreadful apprehensions of death and the terror of my conscience reproaching me with my past horrible life.

The ordinary of Newgate came to me, and talked a little in his way, but all his divinity ran upon confessing my crime, as he called it (though he knew not what I was in for), making a full discovery, and the like, without which he told me God would never forgive me; and he said so little to the purpose, that I had no manner of consolation from him; and then to observe the poor creature preaching confession and repentance to me in the morning, and find him drunk with brandy and spirits by noon, this had something in it so shocking, that I began to nauseate the man more than his work, and his work too by degrees, for the sake of the man; so that I desired him to trouble me no more.

I know not how it was, but by the indefatigable application of my diligent governess I had no bill preferred against me the first sessions, I mean to the grand jury, at Guildhall; so I had another month or five weeks before me, and without doubt this ought to have been accepted by me, as so much time given me for reflection upon what was past, and preparation for what was to come; or, in a word, I ought to have esteemed it as a space given me for repentance, and have employed it as such, but it was not in me. I was sorry (as before) for being in Newgate, but had very few signs of repentance about me.

On the contrary, like the waters in the cavities and hollows of mountains, which petrify and turn into stone whatever they are suffered to drop on, so the continual conversing with such a crew of hell-hounds as I was, had the same common operation upon me as upon other people. I degenerated into stone; I turned first stupid and senseless, then brutish and thoughtless, and at last raving mad as any of them were; and, in short, I became as naturally pleased and easy with the place, as if indeed I had been born there.

It is scarce possible to imagine that our natures should be capable of so much degeneracy, as to make that pleasant and agreeable that in itself is the most complete misery. Here was a circumstance that I think it is scarce possible to mention a worse: I was as exquisitely miserable as, speaking of common cases, it was possible for any one to be that had life and health, and money to help them, as I had.

I had weight of guilt upon me enough to sink any creature who had the least power of reflection left, and had any sense upon them of the happiness of this life, of the misery of another; then I had at first remorse indeed, but no repentance; I had now neither remorse nor repentance. I had a crime charged on me, the punishment of which was death by our law; the proof so evident, that there was no room for me so much as to plead not guilty. I had the name of an old offender, so that I had nothing to expect but death in a few weeks' time, neither had I myself any thoughts of escaping; and yet a certain strange lethargy of soul possessed me. I had no trouble, no apprehensions, no sorrow about me, the first surprise was gone; I was, I may well say, I know not how; my senses, my reason, nay, my conscience, were all asleep; my course of life for forty years had been a horrid complication of wickedness, whoredom, adultery, incest, lying, theft; and, in a word, everything but murder and treason had been my practice from the age of eighteen, or thereabouts, to three-score; and now I was engulfed in the misery of punishment, and had an infamous death just at the door, and yet I had no sense of my condition, no thought of heaven or hell at least, that went any farther than a bare flying touch, like the stitch or pain that gives a hint and goes off. I neither had a heart to ask God's mercy, nor indeed to think of it. And in this, I think, I have given a brief description of the completest misery on earth.

All my terrifying thoughts were past, the horrors of the place were become familiar, and I felt no more uneasiness at the noise and clamours of the prison, than they did who made that noise; in a word, I was become a mere Newgate-bird, as wicked and as outrageous as any of them; nay, I scarce retained the habit and custom of good breeding and manners, which all along till now ran through my conversation; so thorough a degeneracy had possessed me, that I was no more the same thing that I had been, than if I had never been otherwise than what I was now.

In the middle of this hardened part of my life I had another sudden surprise, which called me back a little to that thing called sorrow, which indeed I began to be past the sense of before. They told me one night that there was brought into the prison late the night before three highwaymen, who had committed robbery somewhere on the road to Windsor, Hounslow Heath, I think it was, and were pursued to Uxbridge by the country, and were taken there after a gallant resistance, in which I know not how many of the country people were wounded, and some killed.

It is not to be wondered that we prisoners were all desirous enough to see these brave, topping gentlemen, that were talked up to be such as their fellows had not been known, and especially because it was said they would in the morning be removed into the press-yard, having given money to the head master of the prison, to be allowed the liberty of that better part of the prison. So we that were women placed ourselves in the way, that we would be sure to see them; but nothing could express the amazement and surprise I was in, when the very first man that came out I knew to be my Lancashire husband, the same who lived so well at Dunstable, and the same who I afterwards saw at Brickhill, when I was married to my last husband, as has been related.

I was struck dumb at the sight, and knew neither what to say nor what to do; he did not know me, and that was all the present relief I had. I quitted my company, and retired as much as that dreadful place suffers anybody to retire, and I cried vehemently for a great while. 'Dreadful creature that I am,' said I, 'how may poor people have I made miserable? How many desperate wretches have I sent to the devil?' He had told me at Chester he was ruined by that match, and that his fortunes were made desperate on my account; for that thinking I had been a fortune, he was run into debt more than he was able to pay, and that he knew not what course to take; that he would go into the army and carry a musket, or buy a horse and take a tour, as he called it; and though I never told him that I was a fortune, and so did not actually deceive him myself, yet I did encourage the having it thought that I was so, and by that means I was the occasion originally of his mischief.

The surprise of the thing only struck deeper into my thoughts, any gave me stronger reflections than all that had befallen me before. I grieved day and night for him, and the more for that they told me he was the captain of the gang, and that he had committed so many robberies, that Hind, or Whitney, or the Golden Farmer were fools to him; that he would surely be hanged if there were no more men left in the country he was born in; and that there would abundance of people come in against him.

I was overwhelmed with grief for him; my own case gave me no disturbance compared to this, and I loaded myself with reproaches on his account. I bewailed his misfortunes, and the ruin he was now come to, at such a rate, that I relished nothing now as I did before, and the first reflections I made upon the horrid, detestable life I had lived began to return upon me, and as these things returned, my abhorrence of the place I was in, and of the way of living in it, returned also; in a word, I was perfectly changed, and become another body.

While I was under these influences of sorrow for him, came notice to me that the next sessions approaching there would be a bill preferred to the grand jury against me, and that I should be certainly tried for my life at the Old Bailey. My temper was touched before, the hardened, wretched boldness of spirit which I had acquired abated, and conscious in the prison, guilt began to flow in upon my mind. In short, I began to think, and to think is one real advance from hell to heaven. All that hellish, hardened state and temper of soul, which I have said so much of before, is but a deprivation of thought; he that is restored to his power of thinking, is restored to himself.

As soon as I began, I say, to think, the first think that occurred to me broke out thus: 'Lord! what will become of me? I shall certainly die! I shall be cast, to be sure, and there is nothing beyond that but death! I have no friends; what shall I do? I shall be certainly cast! Lord, have mercy upon me! What will become of me?' This was a sad thought, you will say, to be the first, after so long a time, that had started into my soul of that kind, and yet even this was nothing but fright at what was to come; there was not a word of sincere repentance in it all. However, I was indeed dreadfully dejected, and disconsolate to the last degree; and as I had no friend in the world to communicate my distressed thoughts to, it lay so heavy upon me, that it threw me into fits and swoonings several times a day. I sent for my old governess, and she, give her her due, acted the part of a true friend. She left no stone unturned to prevent the grand jury finding the bill. She sought out one or two of the jurymen, talked with them, and endeavoured to possess them with favourable dispositions, on account that nothing was taken away, and no house broken, etc.; but all would not do, they were over-ruled by the rest; the two wenches swore home to the fact, and the jury found the bill against me for robbery and house-breaking, that is, for felony and burglary.

I sunk down when they brought me news of it, and after I came to myself again, I thought I should have died with the weight of it. My governess acted a true mother to me; she pitied me, she cried with me, and for me, but she could not help me; and to add to the terror of it, 'twas the discourse all over the house that I should die for it. I could hear them talk it among themselves very often, and see them shake their heads and say they were sorry for it, and the like, as is usual in the place. But still nobody came to tell me their thoughts, till at last one of the keepers came to me privately, and said with a sigh, 'Well, Mrs. Flanders, you will be tried on Friday' (this was but a Wednesday); 'what do you intend to do?' I turned as white as a clout, and said, 'God knows what I shall do; for my part, I know not what to do.' 'Why,' says he, 'I won't flatter you, I would have you prepare for death, for I doubt you will be cast; and as they say you are an old offender, I doubt you will find but little mercy. They say,' added he, 'your case is very plain, and that the witnesses swear so home against you, there will be no standing it.'

This was a stab into the very vitals of one under such a burthen as I was oppressed with before, and I could not speak to him a word, good or bad, for a great while; but at last I burst out into tears, and said to him, 'Lord! Mr. ——, what must I do?' 'Do!' says he, 'send for the ordinary; send for a minister and talk with him; for, indeed, Mrs. Flanders, unless you have very good friends, you are no woman for this world.'

This was plain dealing indeed, but it was very harsh to me, at least I thought it so. He left me in the greatest confusion imaginable, and all that night I lay awake. And now I began to say my prayers, which I had scarce done before since my last husband's death, or from a little while after. And truly I may well call it saying my prayers, for I was in such a confusion, and had such horror upon my mind, that though I cried, and repeated several times the ordinary expression of 'Lord, have mercy upon me!' I never brought myself to any sense of my being a miserable sinner, as indeed I was, and of confessing my sins to God, and begging pardon for the sake of Jesus Christ. I was overwhelmed with the sense of my condition, being tried for my life, and being sure to be condemned, and then I was as sure to be executed, and on this account I cried out all night, 'Lord, what will become of me? Lord! what shall I do? Lord! I shall be hanged! Lord, have mercy upon me!' and the like.

My poor afflicted governess was now as much concerned as I, and a great deal more truly penitent, though she had no prospect of being brought to trial and sentence. Not but that she deserved it as much as I, and so she said herself; but she had not done anything herself for many years, other than receiving what I and others stole, and encouraging us to steal it. But she cried, and took on like a distracted body, wringing her hands, and crying out that she was undone, that she believed there was a curse from heaven upon her, that she should be damned, that she had been the destruction of all her friends, that she had brought such a one, and such a one, and such a one to the gallows; and there she reckoned up ten or eleven people, some of which I have given account of, that came to untimely ends; and that now she was the occasion of my ruin, for she had persuaded me to go on, when I would have left off. I interrupted her there. 'No, mother, no,' said I, 'don't speak of that, for you would have had me left off when I got the mercer's money again, and when I came home from Harwich, and I would not hearken to you; therefore you have not been to blame; it is I only have ruined myself, I have brought myself to this misery'; and thus we spent many hours together.

Well, there was no remedy; the prosecution went on, and on the Thursday I was carried down to the sessions-house, where I was arraigned, as they called it, and the next day I was appointed to be tried. At the arraignment I pleaded 'Not guilty,' and well I might, for I was indicted for felony and burglary; that is, for feloniously stealing two pieces of brocaded silk, value £46, the goods of Anthony Johnson, and for breaking open his doors; whereas I knew very well they could not pretend to prove I had broken up the doors, or so much as lifted up a latch.

On the Friday I was brought to my trial. I had exhausted my spirits with crying for two or three days before, so that I slept better the Thursday night than I expected, and had more courage for my trial than indeed I thought possible for me to have.

When the trial began, the indictment was read, I would have spoke, but they told me the witnesses must be heard first, and then I should have time to be heard. The witnesses were the two wenches, a couple of hard-mouthed jades indeed, for though the thing was truth in the main, yet they aggravated it to the utmost extremity, and swore I had the goods wholly in my possession, that I had hid them among my clothes, that I was going off with them, that I had one foot over the threshold when they discovered themselves, and then I put t' other over, so that I was quite out of the house in the street with the goods before they took hold of me, and then they seized me, and brought me back again, and they took the goods upon me. The fact in general was all true, but I believe, and insisted upon it, that they stopped me before I had set my foot clear of the threshold of the house. But that did not argue much, for certain it was that I had taken the goods, and I was bringing them away, if I had not been taken.

But I pleaded that I had stole nothing, they had lost nothing, that the door was open, and I went in, seeing the goods lie there, and with design to buy. If, seeing nobody in the house, I had taken any of them up in my hand it could not be concluded that I intended to steal them, for that I never carried them farther than the door to look on them with the better light.

The Court would not allow that by any means, and made a kind of a jest of my intending to buy the goods, that being no shop for the selling of anything, and as to carrying them to the door to look at them, the maids made their impudent mocks upon that, and spent their wit upon it very much; told the Court I had looked at them sufficiently, and approved them very well, for I had packed them up under my clothes, and was a-going with them.

In short, I was found guilty of felony, but acquitted of the burglary, which was but small comfort to me, the first bringing me to a sentence of death, and the last would have done no more. The next day I was carried down to receive the dreadful sentence, and when they came to ask me what I had to say why sentence should not pass, I stood mute a while, but somebody that stood behind me prompted me aloud to speak to the judges, for that they could represent things favourably for me. This encouraged me to speak, and I told them I had nothing to say to stop the sentence, but that I had much to say to bespeak the mercy of the Court; that I hoped they would allow something in such a case for the circumstances of it; that I had broken no doors, had carried nothing off; that nobody had lost anything; that the person whose goods they were was pleased to say he desired mercy might be shown (which indeed he very honestly did); that, at the worst, it was the first offence, and that I had never been before any court of justice before; and, in a word, I spoke with more courage that I thought I could have done, and in such a moving tone, and though with tears, yet not so many tears as to obstruct my speech, that I could see it moved others to tears that heard me.

The judges sat grave and mute, gave me an easy hearing, and time to say all that I would, but, saying neither Yes nor No to it, pronounced the sentence of death upon me, a sentence that was to me like death itself, which, after it was read, confounded me. I had no more spirit left in me, I had no tongue to speak, or eyes to look up either to God or man.

My poor governess was utterly disconsolate, and she that was my comforter before, wanted comfort now herself; and sometimes mourning, sometimes raging, was as much out of herself, as to all outward appearance, as any mad woman in Bedlam. Nor was she only disconsolate as to me, but she was struck with horror at the sense of her own wicked life, and began to look back upon it with a taste quite different from mine, for she was penitent to the highest degree for her sins, as well as sorrowful for the misfortune. She sent for a minister, too, a serious, pious, good man, and applied herself with such earnestness, by his assistance, to the work of a sincere repentance, that I believe, and so did the minister too, that she was a true penitent; and, which is still more, she was not only so for the occasion, and at that juncture, but she continued so, as I was informed, to the day of her death.

It is rather to be thought of than expressed what was now my condition. I had nothing before me but present death; and as I had no friends to assist me, or to stir for me, I expected nothing but to find my name in the dead warrant, which was to come down for the execution, the Friday afterwards, of five more and myself.

In the meantime my poor distressed governess sent me a minister, who at her request first, and at my own afterwards, came to visit me. He exhorted me seriously to repent of all my sins, and to dally no longer with my soul; not flattering myself with hopes of life, which, he said, he was informed there was no room to expect, but unfeignedly to look up to God with my whole soul, and to cry for pardon in the name of Jesus Christ. He backed his discourses with proper quotations of Scripture, encouraging the greatest sinner to repent, and turn from their evil way, and when he had done, he kneeled down and prayed with me.

It was now that, for the first time, I felt any real signs of repentance. I now began to look back upon my past life with abhorrence, and having a kind of view into the other side of time, and things of life, as I believe they do with everybody at such a time, began to look with a different aspect, and quite another shape, than they did before. The greatest and best things, the views of felicity, the joy, the griefs of life, were quite other things; and I had nothing in my thoughts but what was so infinitely superior to what I had known in life, that it appeared to me to be the greatest stupidity in nature to lay any weight upon anything, though the most valuable in this world.

The word eternity represented itself with all its incomprehensible additions, and I had such extended notions of it, that I know not how to express them. Among the rest, how vile, how gross, how absurd did every pleasant thing look!—I mean, that we had counted pleasant before—especially when I reflected that these sordid trifles were the things for which we forfeited eternal felicity.

With these reflections came, of mere course, severe reproaches of my own mind for my wretched behaviour in my past life; that I had forfeited all hope of any happiness in the eternity that I was just going to enter into, and on the contrary was entitled to all that was miserable, or had been conceived of misery; and all this with the frightful addition of its being also eternal.

I am not capable of reading lectures of instruction to anybody, but I relate this in the very manner in which things then appeared to me, as far as I am able, but infinitely short of the lively impressions which they made on my soul at that time; indeed, those impressions are not to be explained by words, or if they are, I am not mistress of words enough to express them. It must be the work of every sober reader to make just reflections on them, as their own circumstances may direct; and, without question, this is what every one at some time or other may feel something of; I mean, a clearer sight into things to come than they had here, and a dark view of their own concern in them.

But I go back to my own case. The minister pressed me to tell him, as far as I though convenient, in what state I found myself as to the sight I had of things beyond life. He told me he did not come as ordinary of the place, whose business it is to extort confessions from prisoners, for private ends, or for the further detecting of other offenders; that his business was to move me to such freedom of discourse as might serve to disburthen my own mind, and furnish him to administer comfort to me as far as was in his power; and assured me, that whatever I said to him should remain with him, and be as much a secret as if it was known only to God and myself; and that he desired to know nothing of me, but as above to qualify him to apply proper advice and assistance to me, and to pray to God for me.

This honest, friendly way of treating me unlocked all the sluices of my passions. He broke into my very soul by it; and I unravelled all the wickedness of my life to him. In a word, I gave him an abridgment of this whole history; I gave him a picture of my conduct for fifty years in miniature.

I hid nothing from him, and he in return exhorted me to sincere repentance, explained to me what he meant by repentance, and then drew out such a scheme of infinite mercy, proclaimed from heaven to sinners of the greatest magnitude, that he left me nothing to say, that looked like despair, or doubting of being accepted; and in this condition he left me the first night.

He visited me again the next morning, and went on with his method of explaining the terms of divine mercy, which according to him consisted of nothing more, or more difficult, than that of being sincerely desirous of it, and willing to accept it; only a sincere regret for, and hatred of, those things I had done, which rendered me so just an object of divine vengeance. I am not able to repeat the excellent discourses of this extraordinary man; 'tis all that I am able to do, to say that he revived my heart, and brought me into such a condition that I never knew anything of in my life before. I was covered with shame and tears for things past, and yet had at the same time a secret surprising joy at the prospect of being a true penitent, and obtaining the comfort of a penitent—I mean, the hope of being forgiven; and so swift did thoughts circulate, and so high did the impressions they had made upon me run, that I thought I could freely have gone out that minute to execution, without any uneasiness at all, casting my soul entirely into the arms of infinite mercy as a penitent.

The good gentleman was so moved also in my behalf with a view of the influence which he saw these things had on me, that he blessed God he had come to visit me, and resolved not to leave me till the last moment; that is, not to leave visiting me.

It was no less than twelve days after our receiving sentence before any were ordered for execution, and then upon a Wednesday the dead warrant, as they call it, came down, and I found my name was among them. A terrible blow this was to my new resolutions; indeed my heart sank within me, and I swooned away twice, one after another, but spoke not a word. The good minister was sorely afflicted for me, and did what he could to comfort me with the same arguments, and the same moving eloquence that he did before, and left me not that evening so long as the prisonkeepers would suffer him to stay in the prison, unless he would be locked up with me all night, which he was not willing to be.

I wondered much that I did not see him all the next day, it being the day before the time appointed for execution; and I was greatly discouraged, and dejected in my mind, and indeed almost sank for want of the comfort which he had so often, and with such success, yielded me on his former visits. I waited with great impatience, and under the greatest oppressions of spirits imaginable, till about four o'clock he came to my apartment; for I had obtained the favour, by the help of money, nothing being to be done in that place without it, not to be kept in the condemned hole, as they call it, among the rest of the prisoners who were to die, but to have a little dirty chamber to myself.

My heart leaped within me for joy when I heard his voice at the door, even before I saw him; but let any one judge what kind of motion I found in my soul, when after having made a short excuse for his not coming, he showed me that his time had been employed on my account; that he had obtained a favourable report from the Recorder to the Secretary of State in my particular case, and, in short, that he had brought me a reprieve.

He used all the caution that he was able in letting me know a thing which it would have been a double cruelty to have concealed; and yet it was too much for me; for as grief had overset me before, so did joy overset me now, and I fell into a much more dangerous swooning than I did at first, and it was not without a great difficulty that I was recovered at all.

The good man having made a very Christian exhortation to me, not to let the joy of my reprieve put the remembrance of my past sorrow out of my mind, and having told me that he must leave me, to go and enter the reprieve in the books, and show it to the sheriffs, stood up just before his going away, and in a very earnest manner prayed to God for me, that my repentance might be made unfeigned and sincere; and that my coming back, as it were, into life again, might not be a returning to the follies of life which I had made such solemn resolutions to forsake, and to repent of them. I joined heartily in the petition, and must needs say I had deeper impressions upon my mind all that night, of the mercy of God in sparing my life, and a greater detestation of my past sins, from a sense of the goodness which I had tasted in this case, than I had in all my sorrow before.

This may be thought inconsistent in itself, and wide from the business of this book; particularly, I reflect that many of those who may be pleased and diverted with the relation of the wild and wicked part of my story may not relish this, which is really the best part of my life, the most advantageous to myself, and the most instructive to others. Such, however, will, I hope, allow me the liberty to make my story complete. It would be a severe satire on such to say they do not relish the repentance as much as they do the crime; and that they had rather the history were a complete tragedy, as it was very likely to have been.

But I go on with my relation. The next morning there was a sad scene indeed in the prison. The first thing I was saluted with in the morning was the tolling of the great bell at St. Sepulchre's, as they call it, which ushered in the day. As soon as it began to toll, a dismal groaning and crying was heard from the condemned hole, where there lay six poor souls who were to be executed that day, some from one crime, some for another, and two of them for murder.

This was followed by a confused clamour in the house, among the several sorts of prisoners, expressing their awkward sorrows for the poor creatures that were to die, but in a manner extremely differing one from another. Some cried for them; some huzzaed, and wished them a good journey; some damned and cursed those that had brought them to it—that is, meaning the evidence, or prosecutors—many pitying them, and some few, but very few, praying for them.

There was hardly room for so much composure of mind as was required for me to bless the merciful Providence that had, as it were, snatched me out of the jaws of this destruction. I remained, as it were, dumb and silent, overcome with the sense of it, and not able to express what I had in my heart; for the passions on such occasions as these are certainly so agitated as not to be able presently to regulate their own motions.

All the while the poor condemned creatures were preparing to their death, and the ordinary, as they call him, was busy with them, disposing them to submit to their sentence—I say, all this while I was seized with a fit of trembling, as much as I could have been if I had been in the same condition, as to be sure the day before I expected to be; I was so violently agitated by this surprising fit, that I shook as if it had been in the cold fit of an ague, so that I could not speak or look but like one distracted. As soon as they were all put into carts and gone, which, however, I had not courage enough to see—I say, as soon as they were gone, I fell into a fit of crying involuntarily, and without design, but as a mere distemper, and yet so violent, and it held me so long, that I knew not what course to take, nor could I stop, or put a check to it, no, not with all the strength and courage I had.

This fit of crying held me near two hours, and, as I believe, held me till they were all out of the world, and then a most humble, penitent, serious kind of joy succeeded; a real transport it was, or passion of joy and thankfulness, but still unable to give vent to it by words, and in this I continued most part of the day.

In the evening the good minister visited me again, and then fell to his usual good discourses. He congratulated my having a space yet allowed me for repentance, whereas the state of those six poor creatures was determined, and they were now past the offers of salvation; he earnestly pressed me to retain the same sentiments of the things of life that I had when I had a view of eternity; and at the end of all told me I should not conclude that all was over, that a reprieve was not a pardon, that he could not yet answer for the effects of it; however, I had this mercy, that I had more time given me, and that it was my business to improve that time.

This discourse, though very seasonable, left a kind of sadness on my heart, as if I might expect the affair would have a tragical issue still, which, however, he had no certainty of; and I did not indeed, at that time, question him about it, he having said that he would do his utmost to bring it to a good end, and that he hoped he might, but he would not have me be secure; and the consequence proved that he had reason for what he said.

It was about a fortnight after this that I had some just apprehensions that I should be included in the next dead warrant at the ensuing sessions; and it was not without great difficulty, and at last a humble petition for transportation, that I avoided it, so ill was I beholding to fame, and so prevailing was the fatal report of being an old offender; though in that they did not do me strict justice, for I was not in the sense of the law an old offender, whatever I was in the eye of the judge, for I had never been before them in a judicial way before; so the judges could not charge me with being an old offender, but the Recorder was pleased to represent my case as he thought fit.

I had now a certainty of life indeed, but with the hard conditions of being ordered for transportation, which indeed was hard condition in itself, but not when comparatively considered; and therefore I shall make no comments upon the sentence, nor upon the choice I was put to. We shall all choose anything rather than death, especially when 'tis attended with an uncomfortable prospect beyond it, which was my case.

The good minister, whose interest, though a stranger to me, had obtained me the reprieve, mourned sincerely for this part. He was in hopes, he said, that I should have ended my days under the influence of good instruction, that I should not have been turned loose again among such a wretched crew as they generally are, who are thus sent abroad, where, as he said, I must have more than ordinary secret assistance from the grace of God, if I did not turn as wicked again as ever.

I have not for a good while mentioned my governess, who had during most, if not all, of this part been dangerously sick, and being in as near a view of death by her disease as I was by my sentence, was a great penitent—I say, I have not mentioned her, nor indeed did I see her in all this time; but being now recovering, and just able to come abroad, she came to see me.

I told her my condition, and what a different flux and reflux of tears and hopes I had been agitated with; I told her what I had escaped, and upon what terms; and she was present when the minister expressed his fears of my relapsing into wickedness upon my falling into the wretched companies that are generally transported. Indeed I had a melancholy reflection upon it in my own mind, for I knew what a dreadful gang was always sent away together, and I said to my governess that the good minister's fears were not without cause. 'Well, well,' says she, 'but I hope you will not be tempted with such a horrid example as that.' And as soon as the minister was gone, she told me she would not have me discouraged, for perhaps ways and means might be found out to dispose of me in a particular way, by myself, of which she would talk further to me afterward.

I looked earnestly at her, and I thought she looked more cheerful than she usually had done, and I entertained immediately a thousand notions of being delivered, but could not for my life image the methods, or think of one that was in the least feasible; but I was too much concerned in it to let her go from me without explaining herself, which, though she was very loth to do, yet my importunity prevailed, and, while I was still pressing, she answered me in a few words, thus: 'Why, you have money, have you not? Did you ever know one in your life that was transported and had a hundred pounds in his pocket, I'll warrant you, child?' says she.

I understood her presently, but told her I would leave all that to her, but I saw no room to hope for anything but a strict execution of the order, and as it was a severity that was esteemed a mercy, there was no doubt but it would be strictly observed. She said no more but this: 'We will try what can be done,' and so we parted for that night.

I lay in the prison near fifteen weeks after this order for transportation was signed. What the reason of it was, I know not, but at the end of this time I was put on board of a ship in the Thames, and with me a gang of thirteen as hardened vile creatures as ever Newgate produced in my time; and it would really well take up a history longer than mine to describe the degrees of impudence and audacious villainy that those thirteen were arrived to, and the manner of their behaviour in the voyage; of which I have a very diverting account by me, which the captain of the ship who carried them over gave me the minutes of, and which he caused his mate to write down at large.

It may perhaps be thought trifling to enter here into a relation of all the little incidents which attended me in this interval of my circumstances; I mean, between the final order of my transportation and the time of my going on board the ship; and I am too near the end of my story to allow room for it; but something relating to me and my Lancashire husband I must not omit.

He had, as I have observed already, been carried from the master's side of the ordinary prison into the press-yard, with three of his comrades, for they found another to add to them after some time; here, for what reason I knew not, they were kept in custody without being brought to trial almost three months. It seems they found means to bribe or buy off some of those who were expected to come in against them, and they wanted evidence for some time to convict them. After some puzzle on this account, at first they made a shift to get proof enough against two of them to carry them off; but the other two, of which my Lancashire husband was one, lay still in suspense. They had, I think, one positive evidence against each of them, but the law strictly obliging them to have two witnesses, they could make nothing of it. Yet it seems they were resolved not to part with the men neither, not doubting but a further evidence would at last come in; and in order to this, I think publication was made, that such prisoners being taken, any one that had been robbed by them might come to the prison and see them.

I took this opportunity to satisfy my curiosity, pretending that I had been robbed in the Dunstable coach, and that I would go to see the two highwaymen. But when I came into the press-yard, I so disguised myself, and muffled my face up so, that he could see little of me, and consequently knew nothing of who I was; and when I came back, I said publicly that I knew them very well.

Immediately it was rumoured all over the prison that Moll Flanders would turn evidence against one of the highwaymen, and that I was to come off by it from the sentence of transportation.

They heard of it, and immediately my husband desired to see this Mrs. Flanders that knew him so well, and was to be an evidence against him; and accordingly I had leave given to go to him. I dressed myself up as well as the best clothes that I suffered myself ever to appear in there would allow me, and went to the press-yard, but had for some time a hood over my face. He said little to me at first, but asked me if I knew him. I told him, Yes, very well; but as I concealed my face, so I counterfeited my voice, that he had not the least guess at who I was. He asked me where I had seen him. I told him between Dunstable and Brickhill; but turning to the keeper that stood by, I asked if I might not be admitted to talk with him alone. He said Yes, yes, as much as I pleased, and so very civilly withdrew.

As soon as he was gone, I had shut the door, I threw off my hood, and bursting out into tears, 'My dear,' says I, 'do you not know me?' He turned pale, and stood speechless, like one thunderstruck, and, not able to conquer the surprise, said no more but this, 'Let me sit down'; and sitting down by a table, he laid his elbow upon the table, and leaning his head on his hand, fixed his eyes on the ground as one stupid. I cried so vehemently, on the other hand, that it was a good while ere I could speak any more; but after I had given some vent to my passion by tears, I repeated the same words, 'My dear, do you not know me?' At which he answered, Yes, and said no more a good while.

After some time continuing in the surprise, as above, he cast up his eyes towards me and said, 'How could you be so cruel?' I did not readily understand what he meant; and I answered, 'How can you call me cruel? What have I been cruel to you in?' 'To come to me,' says he, 'in such a place as this, is it not to insult me? I have not robbed you, at least not on the highway.'

I perceived by this that he knew nothing of the miserable circumstances I was in, and thought that, having got some intelligence of his being there, I had come to upbraid him with his leaving me. But I had too much to say to him to be affronted, and told him in few words, that I was far from coming to insult him, but at best I came to condole mutually; that he would be easily satisfied that I had no such view, when I should tell him that my condition was worse than his, and that many ways. He looked a little concerned at the general expression of my condition being worse than his, but, with a kind smile, looked a little wildly, and said, 'How can that be? When you see me fettered, and in Newgate, and two of my companions executed already, can you can your condition is worse than mine?'

'Come, my dear,' says I, 'we have a long piece of work to do, if I should be to relate, or you to hear, my unfortunate history; but if you are disposed to hear it, you will soon conclude with me that my condition is worse than yours.' 'How is that possible,' says he again, 'when I expect to be cast for my life the very next sessions?' 'Yes, says I, "tis very possible, when I shall tell you that I have been cast for my life three sessions ago, and am under sentence of death; is not my case worse than yours?'

Then indeed, he stood silent again, like one struck dumb, and after a while he starts up. 'Unhappy couple!' says he. 'How can this be possible?' I took him by the hand. 'Come, my dear,' said I, 'sit down, and let us compare our sorrows. I am a prisoner in this very house, and in much worse circumstances than you, and you will be satisfied I do not come to insult you, when I tell you the particulars.' Any with this we sat down together, and I told him so much of my story as I thought was convenient, bringing it at last to my being reduced to great poverty, and representing myself as fallen into some company that led me to relieve my distresses by way that I had been utterly unacquainted with, and that they making an attempt at a tradesman's house, I was seized upon for having been but just at the door, the maid-servant pulling me in; that I neither had broke any lock nor taken anything away, and that notwithstanding that, I was brought in guilty and sentenced to die; but that the judges, having been made sensible of the hardship of my circumstances, had obtained leave to remit the sentence upon my consenting to be transported.

I told him I fared the worse for being taken in the prison for one Moll Flanders, who was a famous successful thief, that all of them had heard of, but none of them had ever seen; but that, as he knew well, was none of my name. But I placed all to the account of my ill fortune, and that under this name I was dealt with as an old offender, though this was the first thing they had ever known of me. I gave him a long particular of things that had befallen me since I saw him, but I told him if I had seen him since he might think I had, and then gave him an account how I had seen him at Brickhill; how furiously he was pursued, and how, by giving an account that I knew him, and that he was a very honest gentleman, one Mr. ——, the hue-and-cry was stopped, and the high constable went back again.

He listened most attentively to all my story, and smiled at most of the particulars, being all of them petty matters, and infinitely below what he had been at the head of; but when I came to the story of Brickhill, he was surprised. 'And was it you, my dear,' said he, 'that gave the check to the mob that was at our heels there, at Brickhill?' 'Yes,' said I, 'it was I indeed.' And then I told him the particulars which I had observed him there. 'Why, then,' said he, 'it was you that saved my life at that time, and I am glad I owe my life to you, for I will pay the debt to you now, and I'll deliver you from the present condition you are in, or I will die in the attempt.'

I told him, by no means; it was a risk too great, not worth his running the hazard of, and for a life not worth his saving. 'Twas no matter for that, he said, it was a life worth all the world to him; a life that had given him a new life; 'for,' says he, 'I was never in real danger of being taken, but that time, till the last minute when I was taken.' Indeed, he told me his danger then lay in his believing he had not been pursued that way; for they had gone from Hockey quite another way, and had come over the enclosed country into Brickhill, not by the road, and were sure they had not been seen by anybody.

Here he gave me a long history of his life, which indeed would make a very strange history, and be infinitely diverting. He told me he took to the road about twelve years before he married me; that the woman which called him brother was not really his sister, or any kin to him, but one that belonged to their gang, and who, keeping correspondence with him, lived always in town, having good store of acquaintance; that she gave them a perfect intelligence of persons going out of town, and that they had made several good booties by her correspondence; that she thought she had fixed a fortune for him when she brought me to him, but happened to be disappointed, which he really could not blame her for; that if it had been his good luck that I had had the estate, which she was informed I had, he had resolved to leave off the road and live a retired, sober live but never to appear in public till some general pardon had been passed, or till he could, for money, have got his name into some particular pardon, that so he might have been perfectly easy; but that, as it had proved otherwise, he was obliged to put off his equipage and take up the old trade again.

He gave me a long account of some of his adventures, and particularly one when he robbed the West Chester coaches near Lichfield, when he got a very great booty; and after that, how he robbed five graziers, in the west, going to Burford Fair in Wiltshire to buy sheep. He told me he got so much money on those two occasions, that if he had known where to have found me, he would certainly have embraced my proposal of going with me to Virginia, or to have settled in a plantation on some other parts of the English colonies in America.

He told me he wrote two or three letters to me, directed according to my order, but heard nothing from me. This I indeed knew to be true, but the letters coming to my hand in the time of my latter husband, I could do nothing in it, and therefore chose to give no answer, that so he might rather believe they had miscarried.

Being thus disappointed, he said, he carried on the old trade ever since, though when he had gotten so much money, he said, he did not run such desperate risks as he did before. Then he gave me some account of several hard and desperate encounters which he had with gentlemen on the road, who parted too hardly with their money, and showed me some wounds he had received; and he had one or two very terrible wounds indeed, as particularly one by a pistol bullet, which broke his arm, and another with a sword, which ran him quite through the body, but that missing his vitals, he was cured again; one of his comrades having kept with him so faithfully, and so friendly, as that he assisted him in riding near eighty miles before his arm was set, and then got a surgeon in a considerable city, remote from that place where it was done, pretending they were gentlemen travelling towards Carlisle and that they had been attacked on the road by highwaymen, and that one of them had shot him into the arm and broke the bone.

This, he said, his friend managed so well, that they were not suspected at all, but lay still till he was perfectly cured. He gave me so many distinct accounts of his adventures, that it is with great reluctance that I decline the relating them; but I consider that this is my own story, not his.

I then inquired into the circumstances of his present case at that time, and what it was he expected when he came to be tried. He told me that they had no evidence against him, or but very little; for that of three robberies, which they were all charged with, it was his good fortune that he was but in one of them, and that there was but one witness to be had for that fact, which was not sufficient, but that it was expected some others would come in against him; that he thought indeed, when he first saw me, that I had been one that came of that errand; but that if somebody came in against him, he hoped he should be cleared; that he had had some intimation, that if he would submit to transport himself, he might be admitted to it without a trial, but that he could not think of it with any temper, and thought he could much easier submit to be hanged.

I blamed him for that, and told him I blamed him on two accounts; first, because if he was transported, there might be a hundred ways for him that was a gentleman, and a bold enterprising man, to find his way back again, and perhaps some ways and means to come back before he went. He smiled at that part, and said he should like the last the best of the two, for he had a kind of horror upon his mind at his being sent over to the plantations, as Romans sent condemned slaves to work in the mines; that he thought the passage into another state, let it be what it would, much more tolerable at the gallows, and that this was the general notion of all the gentlemen who were driven by the exigence of their fortunes to take the road; that at the place of execution there was at least an end of all the miseries of the present state, and as for what was to follow, a man was, in his opinion, as likely to repent sincerely in the last fortnight of his life, under the pressures and agonies of a jail and the condemned hole, as he would ever be in the woods and wilderness of America; that servitude and hard labour were things gentlemen could never stoop to; that it was but the way to force them to be their own executioners afterwards, which was much worse; and that therefore he could not have any patience when he did but think of being transported.

I used the utmost of my endeavour to persuade him, and joined that known woman's rhetoric to it—I mean, that of tears. I told him the infamy of a public execution was certainly a greater pressure upon the spirits of a gentleman than any of the mortifications that he could meet with abroad could be; that he had at least in the other a chance for his life, whereas here he had none at all; that it was the easiest thing in the world for him to manage the captain of a ship, who were, generally speaking, men of good-humour and some gallantry; and a small matter of conduct, especially if there was any money to be had, would make way for him to buy himself off when he came to Virginia.

He looked wistfully at me, and I thought I guessed at what he meant, that is to say, that he had no money; but I was mistaken, his meaning was another way. 'You hinted just now, my dear,' said he, 'that there might be a way of coming back before I went, by which I understood you that it might be possible to buy it off here. I had rather give £200 to prevent going, than £100 to be set at liberty when I came there.' 'That is, my dear,' said I, 'because you do not know the place so well as I do.' 'That may be,' said he; 'and yet I believe, as well as you know it, you would do the same, unless it is because, as you told me, you have a mother there.'

I told him, as to my mother, it was next to impossible but that she must be dead many years before; and as for any other relations that I might have there, I knew them not now; that since the misfortunes I had been under had reduced me to the condition I had been in for some years, I had not kept up any correspondence with them; and that he would easily believe, I should find but a cold reception from them if I should be put to make my first visit in the condition of a transported felon; that therefore, if I went thither, I resolved not to see them; but that I had many views in going there, if it should be my fate, which took off all the uneasy part of it; and if he found himself obliged to go also, I should easily instruct him how to manage himself, so as never to go a servant at all, especially since I found he was not destitute of money, which was the only friend in such a condition.

He smiled, and said he did not tell me he had money. I took him up short, and told him I hoped he did not understand by my speaking, that I should expect any supply from him if he had money; that, on the other hand, though I had not a great deal, yet I did not want, and while I had any I would rather add to him than weaken him in that article, seeing, whatever he had, I knew in the case of transportation he would have occasion of it all.

He expressed himself in a most tender manner upon that head. He told me what money he had was not a great deal, but that he would never hide any of it from me if I wanted it, and that he assured me he did not speak with any such apprehensions; that he was only intent upon what I had hinted to him before he went; that here he knew what to do with himself, but that there he should be the most ignorant, helpless wretch alive.

I told him he frighted and terrified himself with that which had no terror in it; that if he had money, as I was glad to hear he had, he might not only avoid the servitude supposed to be the consequence of transportation, but begin the world upon a new foundation, and that such a one as he could not fail of success in, with the common application usual in such cases; that he could not but call to mind that is was what I had recommended to him many years before and had proposed it for our mutual subsistence and restoring our fortunes in the world; and I would tell him now, that to convince him both of the certainty of it and of my being fully acquainted with the method, and also fully satisfied in the probability of success, he should first see me deliver myself from the necessity of going over at all, and then that I would go with him freely, and of my own choice, and perhaps carry enough with me to satisfy him that I did not offer it for want of being able to live without assistance from him, but that I thought our mutual misfortunes had been such as were sufficient to reconcile us both to quitting this part of the world, and living where nobody could upbraid us with what was past, or we be in any dread of a prison, and without agonies of a condemned hole to drive us to it; this where we should look back on all our past disasters with infinite satisfaction, when we should consider that our enemies should entirely forget us, and that we should live as new people in a new world, nobody having anything to say to us, or we to them.

I pressed this home to him with so many arguments, and answered all his own passionate objections so effectually that he embraced me, and told me I treated him with such sincerity and affection as overcame him; that he would take my advice, and would strive to submit to his fate in hope of having the comfort of my assistance, and of so faithful a counsellor and such a companion in his misery. But still he put me in mind of what I had mentioned before, namely, that there might be some way to get off before he went, and that it might be possible to avoid going at all, which he said would be much better. I told him he should see, and be fully satisfied, that I would do my utmost in that part too, and if it did not succeed, yet that I would make good the rest.

We parted after this long conference with such testimonies of kindness and affection as I thought were equal, if not superior, to that at our parting at Dunstable; and now I saw more plainly than before, the reason why he declined coming at that time any farther with me toward London than Dunstable, and why, when we parted there, he told me it was not convenient for him to come part of the way to London to bring me going, as he would otherwise have done. I have observed that the account of his life would have made a much more pleasing history than this of mine; and, indeed, nothing in it was more strange than this part, viz. that he carried on that desperate trade full five-and-twenty years and had never been taken, the success he had met with had been so very uncommon, and such that sometimes he had lived handsomely, and retired in place for a year or two at a time, keeping himself and a man-servant to wait on him, and had often sat in the coffee-houses and heard the very people whom he had robbed give accounts of their being robbed, and of the place and circumstances, so that he could easily remember that it was the same.

In this manner, it seems, he lived near Liverpool at the time he unluckily married me for a fortune. Had I been the fortune he expected, I verily believe, as he said, that he would have taken up and lived honestly all his days.

He had with the rest of his misfortunes the good luck not to be actually upon the spot when the robbery was done which he was committed for, and so none of the persons robbed could swear to him, or had anything to charge upon him. But it seems as he was taken with the gang, one hard-mouthed countryman swore home to him, and they were like to have others come in according to the publication they had made; so that they expected more evidence against him, and for that reason he was kept in hold.

However, the offer which was made to him of admitting him to transportation was made, as I understood, upon the intercession of some great person who pressed him hard to accept of it before a trial; and indeed, as he knew there were several that might come in against him, I thought his friend was in the right, and I lay at him night and day to delay it no longer.

At last, with much difficulty, he gave his consent; and as he was not therefore admitted to transportation in court, and on his petition, as I was, so he found himself under a difficulty to avoid embarking himself as I had said he might have done; his great friend, who was his intercessor for the favour of that grant, having given security for him that he should transport himself, and not return within the term.

This hardship broke all my measures, for the steps I took afterwards for my own deliverance were hereby rendered wholly ineffectual, unless I would abandon him, and leave him to go to America by himself; than which he protested he would much rather venture, although he were certain to go directly to the gallows.

I must now return to my case. The time of my being transported according to my sentence was near at hand; my governess, who continued my fast friend, had tried to obtain a pardon, but it could not be done unless with an expense too heavy for my purse, considering that to be left naked and empty, unless I had resolved to return to my old trade again, had been worse than my transportation, because there I knew I could live, here I could not. The good minister stood very hard on another account to prevent my being transported also; but he was answered, that indeed my life had been given me at his first solicitations, and therefore he ought to ask no more. He was sensibly grieved at my going, because, as he said, he feared I should lose the good impressions which a prospect of death had at first made on me, and which were since increased by his instructions; and the pious gentleman was exceedingly concerned about me on that account.

On the other hand, I really was not so solicitous about it as I was before, but I industriously concealed my reasons for it from the minister, and to the last he did not know but that I went with the utmost reluctance and affliction.

It was in the month of February that I was, with seven other convicts, as they called us, delivered to a merchant that traded to Virginia, on board a ship, riding, as they called it, in Deptford Reach. The officer of the prison delivered us on board, and the master of the vessel gave a discharge for us.

We were for that night clapped under hatches, and kept so close that I thought I should have been suffocated for want of air; and the next morning the ship weighed, and fell down the river to a place they call Bugby's Hole, which was done, as they told us, by the agreement of the merchant, that all opportunity of escape should be taken from us. However, when the ship came thither and cast anchor, we were allowed more liberty, and particularly were permitted to come up on the deck, but not up on the quarter-deck, that being kept particularly for the captain and for passengers.

When by the noise of the men over my head, and the motion of the ship, I perceived that they were under sail, I was at first greatly surprised, fearing we should go away directly, and that our friends would not be admitted to see us any more; but I was easy soon after, when I found they had come to an anchor again, and soon after that we had notice given by some of the men where we were, that the next morning we should have the liberty to come up on deck, and to have our friends come and see us if we had any.

All that night I lay upon the hard boards of the deck, as the passengers did, but we had afterwards the liberty of little cabins for such of us as had any bedding to lay in them, and room to stow any box or trunk for clothes and linen, if we had it (which might well be put in), for some of them had neither shirt nor shift or a rag of linen or woollen, but what was on their backs, or a farthing of money to help themselves; and yet I did not find but they fared well enough in the ship, especially the women, who got money from the seamen for washing their clothes, sufficient to purchase any common things that they wanted.

When the next morning we had the liberty to come up on the deck, I asked one of the officers of the ship, whether I might not have the liberty to send a letter on shore, to let my friends know where the ship lay, and to get some necessary things sent to me. This was, it seems, the boatswain, a very civil, courteous sort of man, who told me I should have that, or any other liberty that I desired, that he could allow me with safety. I told him I desired no other; and he answered that the ship's boat would go up to London the next tide, and he would order my letter to be carried.

Accordingly, when the boat went off, the boatswain came to me and told me the boat was going off, and that he went in it himself, and asked me if my letter was ready he would take care of it. I had prepared myself, you may be sure, pen, ink, and paper beforehand, and I had gotten a letter ready directed to my governess, and enclosed another for my fellow-prisoner, which, however, I did not let her know was my husband, not to the last. In that to my governess, I let her know where the ship lay, and pressed her earnestly to send me what things I knew she had got ready for me for my voyage.

When I gave the boatswain the letter, I gave him a shilling with it, which I told him was for the charge of a messenger or porter, which I entreated him to send with the letter as soon as he came on shore, that if possible I might have an answer brought back by the same hand, that I might know what was become of my things; 'for sir,' says I, 'if the ship should go away before I have them on board, I am undone.'

I took care, when I gave him the shilling, to let him see that I had a little better furniture about me than the ordinary prisoners, for he saw that I had a purse, and in it a pretty deal of money; and I found that the very sight of it immediately furnished me with very different treatment from what I should otherwise have met with in the ship; for though he was very courteous indeed before, in a kind of natural compassion to me, as a woman in distress, yet he was more than ordinarily so afterwards, and procured me to be better treated in the ship than, I say, I might otherwise have been; as shall appear in its place.

He very honestly had my letter delivered to my governess's own hands, and brought me back an answer from her in writing; and when he gave me the answer, gave me the shilling again. 'There,' says he, 'there's your shilling again too, for I delivered the letter myself.' I could not tell what to say, I was so surprised at the thing; but after some pause, I said, 'Sir, you are too kind; it had been but reasonable that you had paid yourself coach-hire, then.'

'No, no,' says he, 'I am overpaid. What is the gentlewoman? Your sister.'

'No, sir,' says I, 'she is no relation to me, but she is a dear friend, and all the friends I have in the world.' 'Well,' says he, 'there are few such friends in the world. Why, she cried after you like a child,' 'Ay,' says I again, 'she would give a hundred pounds, I believe, to deliver me from this dreadful condition I am in.'

'Would she so?' says he. 'For half the money I believe I could put you in a way how to deliver yourself.' But this he spoke softly, that nobody could hear.

'Alas! sir,' said I, 'but then that must be such a deliverance as, if I should be taken again, would cost me my life.' 'Nay,' said he, 'if you were once out of the ship, you must look to yourself afterwards; that I can say nothing to.' So we dropped the discourse for that time.

In the meantime, my governess, faithful to the last moment, conveyed my letter to the prison to my husband, and got an answer to it, and the next day came down herself to the ship, bringing me, in the first place, a sea-bed as they call it, and all its furniture, such as was convenient, but not to let the people think it was extraordinary. She brought with her a sea-chest—that is, a chest, such as are made for seamen, with all the conveniences in it, and filled with everything almost that I could want; and in one of the corners of the chest, where there was a private drawer, was my bank of money—this is to say, so much of it as I had resolved to carry with me; for I ordered a part of my stock to be left behind me, to be sent afterwards in such goods as I should want when I came to settle; for money in that country is not of much use where all things are brought for tobacco, much more is it a great loss to carry it from hence.

But my case was particular; it was by no means proper to me to go thither without money or goods, and for a poor convict, that was to be sold as soon as I came on shore, to carry with me a cargo of goods would be to have notice taken of it, and perhaps to have them seized by the public; so I took part of my stock with me thus, and left the other part with my governess.

My governess brought me a great many other things, but it was not proper for me to look too well provided in the ship, at least till I knew what kind of a captain we should have. When she came into the ship, I thought she would have died indeed; her heart sank at the sight of me, and at the thoughts of parting with me in that condition, and she cried so intolerably, I could not for a long time have any talk with her.

I took that time to read my fellow-prisoner's letter, which, however, greatly perplexed me. He told me was determined to go, but found it would be impossible for him to be discharged time enough for going in the same ship, and which was more than all, he began to question whether they would give him leave to go in what ship he pleased, though he did voluntarily transport himself; but that they would see him put on board such a ship as they should direct, and that he would be charged upon the captain as other convict prisoners were; so that he began to be in despair of seeing me till he came to Virginia, which made him almost desperate; seeing that, on the other hand, if I should not be there, if any accident of the sea or of mortality should take me away, he should be the most undone creature there in the world.

This was very perplexing, and I knew not what course to take. I told my governess the story of the boatswain, and she was mighty eager with me treat with him; but I had no mind to it, till I heard whether my husband, or fellow-prisoner, so she called him, could be at liberty to go with me or no. At last I was forced to let her into the whole matter, except only that of his being my husband. I told her I had made a positive bargain or agreement with him to go, if he could get the liberty of going in the same ship, and that I found he had money.

Then I read a long lecture to her of what I proposed to do when we came there, how we could plant, settle, and, in short, grow rich without any more adventures; and, as a great secret, I told her that we were to marry as soon as he came on board.

She soon agreed cheerfully to my going when she heard this, and she made it her business from that time to get him out of the prison in time, so that he might go in the same ship with me, which at last was brought to pass, though with great difficulty, and not without all the forms of a transported prisoner-convict, which he really was not yet, for he had not been tried, and which was a great mortification to him. As our fate was now determined, and we were both on board, actually bound to Virginia, in the despicable quality of transported convicts destined to be sold for slaves, I for five years, and he under bonds and security not to return to England any more, as long as he lived, he was very much dejected and cast down; the mortification of being brought on board, as he was, like a prisoner, piqued him very much, since it was first told him he should transport himself, and so that he might go as a gentleman at liberty. It is true he was not ordered to be sold when he came there, as we were, and for that reason he was obliged to pay for his passage to the captain, which we were not; as to the rest, he was as much at a loss as a child what to do with himself, or with what he had, but by directions.

Our first business was to compare our stock. He was very honest to me, and told me his stock was pretty good when he came into the prison, but the living there as he did in a figure like a gentleman, and, which was ten times as much, the making of friends, and soliciting his case, had been very expensive; and, in a word, all his stock that he had left was £108, which he had about him all in gold.

I gave him an account of my stock as faithfully, that is to say, of what I had taken to carry with me, for I was resolved, whatever should happen, to keep what I had left with my governess in reserve; that in case I should die, what I had with me was enough to give him, and that which was left in my governess's hands would be her own, which she had well deserved of me indeed.

My stock which I had with me was £246 some odd shillings; so that we had £354 between us, but a worse gotten estate was scarce ever put together to being the world with.

Our greatest misfortune as to our stock was that it was all in money, which every one knows is an unprofitable cargo to be carried to the plantations. I believe his was really all he had left in the world, as he told me it was; but I, who had between £700 and £800 in bank when this disaster befell me, and who had one of the faithfullest friends in the world to manage it for me, considering she was a woman of manner of religious principles, had still £300 left in her hand, which I reserved as above; besides, some very valuable things, as particularly two gold watches, some small pieces of plate, and some rings—all stolen goods. The plate, rings, and watches were put in my chest with the money, and with this fortune, and in the sixty-first year of my age, I launched out into a new world, as I may call it, in the condition (as to what appeared) only of a poor, naked convict, ordered to be transported in respite from the gallows. My clothes were poor and mean, but not ragged or dirty, and none knew in the whole ship that I had anything of value about me.

However, as I had a great many very good clothes and linen in abundance, which I had ordered to be packed up in two great boxes, I had them shipped on board, not as my goods, but as consigned to my real name in Virginia; and had the bills of loading signed by a captain in my pocket; and in these boxes was my plate and watches, and everything of value except my money, which I kept by itself in a private drawer in my chest, which could not be found, or opened, if found, with splitting the chest to pieces.

In this condition I lay for three weeks in the ship, not knowing whether I should have my husband with me or no, and therefore not resolving how or in what manner to receive the honest boatswain's proposal, which indeed he thought a little strange at first.

At the end of this time, behold my husband came on board. He looked with a dejected, angry countenance, his great heart was swelled with rage and disdain; to be dragged along with three keepers of Newgate, and put on board like a convict, when he had not so much as been brought to a trial. He made loud complaints of it by his friends, for it seems he had some interest; but his friends got some check in their application, and were told he had had favour enough, and that they had received such an account of him, since the last grant of his transportation, that he ought to think himself very well treated that he was not prosecuted anew. This answer quieted him at once, for he knew too much what might have happened, and what he had room to expect; and now he saw the goodness of the advice to him, which prevailed with him to accept of the offer of a voluntary transportation. And after this his chagrin at these hell-hounds, as he called them, was a little over, he looked a little composed, began to be cheerful, and as I was telling him how glad I was to have him once more out of their hands, he took me in his arms, and acknowledged with great tenderness that I had given him the best advice possible. 'My dear,' says he, 'thou has twice saved my life; from henceforward it shall be all employed for you, and I'll always take your advice.'

The ship began now to fill; several passengers came on board, who were embarked on no criminal account, and these had accommodations assigned them in the great cabin, and other parts of the ship, whereas we, as convicts, were thrust down below, I know not where. But when my husband came on board, I spoke to the boatswain, who had so early given me hints of his friendship in carrying my letter. I told him he had befriended me in many things, and I had not made any suitable return to him, and with that I put a guinea into his hand. I told him that my husband was now come on board; that though we were both under the present misfortune, yet we had been persons of a different character from the wretched crew that we came with, and desired to know of him, whether the captain might not be moved to admit us to some conveniences in the ship, for which we would make him what satisfaction he pleased, and that we would gratify him for his pains in procuring this for us. He took the guinea, as I could see, with great satisfaction, and assured me of his assistance.

Then he told us he did not doubt but that the captain, who was one of the best-humoured gentlemen in the world, would be easily brought to accommodate us as well as we could desire, and, to make me easy, told me he would go up the next tide on purpose to speak to the captain about it. The next morning, happening to sleep a little longer than ordinary, when I got up, and began to look abroad, I saw the boatswain among the men in his ordinary business. I was a little melancholy at seeing him there, and going forward to speak to him, he saw me, and came towards me, but not giving him time to speak first, I said, smiling, 'I doubt, sir, you have forgot us, for I see you are very busy.' He returned presently, 'Come along with me, and you shall see.' So he took me into the great cabin, and there sat a good sort of a gentlemanly man for a seaman, writing, and with a great many papers before him.

'Here,' says the boatswain to him that was a-writing, 'is the gentlewoman that the captain spoke to you of'; and turning to me, he said, 'I have been so far from forgetting your business, that I have been up at the captain's house, and have represented faithfully to the captain what you said, relating to you being furnished with better conveniences for yourself and your husband; and the captain has sent this gentleman, who is made of the ship, down with me, on purpose to show you everything, and to accommodate you fully to your content, and bid me assure you that you shall not be treated like what you were at first expected to be, but with the same respect as other passengers are treated.'

The mate then spoke to me, and, not giving me time to thank the boatswain for his kindness, confirmed what the boatswain had said, and added that it was the captain's delight to show himself kind and charitable, especially to those that were under any misfortunes, and with that he showed me several cabins built up, some in the great cabin, and some partitioned off, out of the steerage, but opening into the great cabin on purpose for the accommodation of passengers, and gave me leave to choose where I would. However, I chose a cabin which opened into the steerage, in which was very good conveniences to set our chest and boxes, and a table to eat on.

The mate then told me that the boatswain had given so good a character of me and my husband, as to our civil behaviour, that he had orders to tell me we should eat with him, if we thought fit, during the whole voyage, on the common terms of passengers; that we might lay in some fresh provisions, if we pleased; or if not, he should lay in his usual store, and we should have share with him. This was very reviving news to me, after so many hardships and afflictions as I had gone through of late. I thanked him, and told him the captain should make his own terms with us, and asked him leave to go and tell my husband of it, who was not very well, and was not yet out of his cabin. Accordingly I went, and my husband, whose spirits were still so much sunk with the indignity (as he understood it) offered him, that he was scare yet himself, was so revived with the account that I gave him of the reception we were like to have in the ship, that he was quite another man, and new vigour and courage appeared in his very countenance. So true is it, that the greatest of spirits, when overwhelmed by their afflictions, are subject to the greatest dejections, and are the most apt to despair and give themselves up.

After some little pause to recover himself, my husband came up with me, and gave the mate thanks for the kindness, which he had expressed to us, and sent suitable acknowledgment by him to the captain, offering to pay him by advance, whatever he demanded for our passage, and for the conveniences he had helped us to. The mate told him that the captain would be on board in the afternoon, and that he would leave all that till he came. Accordingly, in the afternoon the captain came, and we found him the same courteous, obliging man that the boatswain had represented him to be; and he was so well pleased with my husband's conversation, that, in short, he would not let us keep the cabin we had chosen, but gave us one that, as I said before, opened into the great cabin.

Nor were his conditions exorbitant, or the man craving and eager to make a prey of us, but for fifteen guineas we had our whole passage and provisions and cabin, ate at the captain's table, and were very handsomely entertained.

The captain lay himself in the other part of the great cabin, having let his round house, as they call it, to a rich planter who went over with his wife and three children, who ate by themselves. He had some other ordinary passengers, who quartered in the steerage, and as for our old fraternity, they were kept under the hatches while the ship lay there, and came very little on the deck.

I could not refrain acquainting my governess with what had happened; it was but just that she, who was so really concerned for me, should have part in my good fortune. Besides, I wanted her assistance to supply me with several necessaries, which before I was shy of letting anybody see me have, that it might not be public; but now I had a cabin and room to set things in, I ordered abundance of good things for our comfort in the voyage, as brandy, sugar, lemons, etc., to make punch, and treat our benefactor, the captain; and abundance of things for eating and drinking in the voyage; also a larger bed, and bedding proportioned to it; so that, in a word, we resolved to want for nothing in the voyage.

All this while I had provided nothing for our assistance when we should come to the place and begin to call ourselves planters; and I was far from being ignorant of what was needful on that occasion; particularly all sorts of tools for the planter's work, and for building; and all kinds of furniture for our dwelling, which, if to be bought in the country, must necessarily cost double the price.

So I discoursed that point with my governess, and she went and waited upon the captain, and told him that she hoped ways might be found out for her two unfortunate cousins, as she called us, to obtain our freedom when we came into the country, and so entered into a discourse with him about the means and terms also, of which I shall say more in its place; and after thus sounding the captain, she let him know, though we were unhappy in the circumstances that occasioned our going, yet that we were not unfurnished to set ourselves to work in the country, and we resolved to settle and live there as planters, if we might be put in a way how to do it. The captain readily offered his assistance, told her the method of entering upon such business, and how easy, nay, how certain it was for industrious people to recover their fortunes in such a manner. 'Madam,' says he, "tis no reproach to any many in that country to have been sent over in worse circumstances than I perceive your cousins are in, provided they do but apply with diligence and good judgment to the business of that place when they come there.'

She then inquired of him what things it was necessary we should carry over with us, and he, like a very honest as well as knowing man, told her thus: 'Madam, your cousins in the first place must procure somebody to buy them as servants, in conformity to the conditions of their transportation, and then, in the name of that person, they may go about what they will; they may either purchase some plantations already begun, or they may purchase land of the Government of the country, and begin where they please, and both will be done reasonably.' She bespoke his favour in the first article, which he promised to her to take upon himself, and indeed faithfully performed it, and as to the rest, he promised to recommend us to such as should give us the best advice, and not to impose upon us, which was as much as could be desired.

She then asked him if it would not be necessary to furnish us with a stock of tools and materials for the business of planting, and he said, 'Yes, by all means.' And then she begged his assistance in it. She told him she would furnish us with everything that was convenient whatever it cost her. He accordingly gave her a long particular of things necessary for a planter, which, by his account, came to about fourscore or a hundred pounds. And, in short, she went about as dexterously to buy them, as if she had been an old Virginia merchant; only that she bought, by my direction, above twice as much of everything as he had given her a list of.

These she put on board in her own name, took his bills of loading for them, and endorsed those bills of loading to my husband, insuring the cargo afterwards in her own name, by our order; so that we were provided for all events, and for all disasters.

I should have told you that my husband gave her all his whole stock of £108, which, as I have said, he had about him in gold, to lay out thus, and I gave her a good sum besides; so that I did not break into the stock which I had left in her hands at all, but after we had sorted out our whole cargo, we had yet near £200 in money, which was more than enough for our purpose.

In this condition, very cheerful, and indeed joyful at being so happily accommodated as we were, we set sail from Bugby's Hole to Gravesend, where the ship lay about ten more days, and where the captain came on board for good and all. Here the captain offered us a civility, which indeed we had no reason to expect, namely, to let us go on shore and refresh ourselves, upon giving our words in a solemn manner that we would not go from him, and that we would return peaceably on board again. This was such an evidence of his confidence in us, that it overcame my husband, who, in a mere principle of gratitude, told him, as he could not be in any capacity to make a suitable return for such a favour, so he could not think of accepting of it, nor could he be easy that the captain should run such a risk. After some mutual civilities, I gave my husband a purse, in which was eighty guineas, and he put in into the captain's hand. 'There, captain,' says he, 'there's part of a pledge for our fidelity; if we deal dishonestly with you on any account, 'tis your own.' And on this we went on shore.

Indeed, the captain had assurance enough of our resolutions to go, for that having made such provision to settle there, it did not seem rational that we would choose to remain here at the expense and peril of life, for such it must have been if we had been taken again. In a word, we went all on shore with the captain, and supped together in Gravesend, where we were very merry, stayed all night, lay at the house where we supped, and came all very honestly on board again with him in the morning. Here we bought ten dozen bottles of good beer, some wine, some fowls, and such things as we thought might be acceptable on board.

My governess was with us all this while, and went with us round into the Downs, as did also the captain's wife, with whom she went back. I was never so sorrowful at parting with my own mother as I was at parting with her, and I never saw her more. We had a fair easterly wind sprung up the third day after we came to the Downs, and we sailed from thence the 10th of April. Nor did we touch any more at any place, till, being driven on the coast of Ireland by a very hard gale of wind, the ship came to an anchor in a little bay, near the mouth of a river, whose name I remember not, but they said the river came down from Limerick, and that it was the largest river in Ireland.

Here, being detained by bad weather for some time, the captain, who continued the same kind, good-humoured man as at first, took us two on shore with him again. He did it now in kindness to my husband indeed, who bore the sea very ill, and was very sick, especially when it blew so hard. Here we bought in again a store of fresh provisions, especially beef, pork, mutton, and fowls, and the captain stayed to pickle up five or six barrels of beef to lengthen out the ship's store. We were here not above five days, when the weather turning mild, and a fair wind, we set sail again, and in two-and-forty days came safe to the coast of Virginia.

When we drew near to the shore, the captain called me to him, and told me that he found by my discourse I had some relations in the place, and that I had been there before, and so he supposed I understood the custom in their disposing the convict prisoners when they arrived. I told him I did not, and that as to what relations I had in the place, he might be sure I would make myself known to none of them while I was in the circumstances of a prisoner, and that as to the rest, we left ourselves entirely to him to assist us, as he was pleased to promise us he would do. He told me I must get somebody in the place to come and buy us as servants, and who must answer for us to the governor of the country, if he demanded us. I told him we should do as he should direct; so he brought a planter to treat with him, as it were, for the purchase of these two servants, my husband and me, and there we were formally sold to him, and went ashore with him. The captain went with us, and carried us to a certain house, whether it was to be called a tavern or not I know not, but we had a bowl of punch there made of rum, etc., and were very merry. After some time the planter gave us a certificate of discharge, and an acknowledgment of having served him faithfully, and we were free from him the next morning, to go wither we would.

For this piece of service the captain demanded of us six thousand weight of tabacco, which he said he was accountable for to his freighter, and which we immediately bought for him, and made him a present of twenty guineas besides, with which he was abundantly satisfied.

It is not proper to enter here into the particulars of what part of the colony of Virginia we settled in, for divers reasons; it may suffice to mention that we went into the great river Potomac, the ship being bound thither; and there we intended to have settled first, though afterwards we altered our minds.

The first thing I did of moment after having gotten all our goods on shore, and placed them in a storehouse, or warehouse, which, with a lodging, we hired at the small place or village where we landed—I say, the first thing was to inquire after my mother, and after my brother (that fatal person whom I married as a husband, as I have related at large). A little inquiry furnished me with information that Mrs. ——, that is, my mother, was dead; that my brother (or husband) was alive, which I confess I was not very glad to hear; but which was worse, I found he was removed from the plantation where he lived formerly, and where I lived with him, and lived with one of his sons in a plantation just by the place where we landed, and where we had hired a warehouse.

I was a little surprised at first, but as I ventured to satisfy myself that he could not know me, I was not only perfectly easy, but had a great mind to see him, if it was possible to so do without his seeing me. In order to that I found out by inquiry the plantation where he lived, and with a woman of that place whom I got to help me, like what we call a chairwoman, I rambled about towards the place as if I had only a mind to see the country and look about me. At last I came so near that I saw the dwellinghouse. I asked the woman whose plantation that was; she said it belonged to such a man, and looking out a little to our right hands, 'there,' says she, is the gentleman that owns the plantation, and his father with him.' 'What are their Christian names?' said I. 'I know not,' says she, 'what the old gentleman's name is, but the son's name is Humphrey; and I believe,' says she, 'the father's is so too.' You may guess, if you can, what a confused mixture of joy and fight possessed my thoughts upon this occasion, for I immediately knew that this was nobody else but my own son, by that father she showed me, who was my own brother. I had no mask, but I ruffled my hood so about my face, that I depended upon it that after above twenty years' absence, and withal not expecting anything of me in that part of the world, he would not be able to know anything of me. But I need not have used all that caution, for the old gentleman was grown dim-sighted by some distemper which had fallen upon his eyes, and could but just see well enough to walk about, and not run against a tree or into a ditch. The woman that was with me had told me that by a mere accident, knowing nothing of what importance it was to me. As they drew near to us, I said, 'Does he know you, Mrs. Owen?' (so they called the woman). 'Yes,' said she, 'if he hears me speak, he will know me; but he can't see well enough to know me or anybody else'; and so she told me the story of his sight, as I have related. This made me secure, and so I threw open my hoods again, and let them pass by me. It was a wretched thing for a mother thus to see her own son, a handsome, comely young gentleman in flourishing circumstances, and durst not make herself known to him, and durst not take any notice of him. Let any mother of children that reads this consider it, and but think with what anguish of mind I restrained myself; what yearnings of soul I had in me to embrace him, and weep over him; and how I thought all my entrails turned within me, that my very bowels moved, and I knew not what to do, as I now know not how to express those agonies! When he went from me I stood gazing and trembling, and looking after him as long as I could see him; then sitting down to rest me, but turned from her, and lying on my face, wept, and kissed the ground that he had set his foot on.

I could not conceal my disorder so much from the woman but that she perceived it, and thought I was not well, which I was obliged to pretend was true; upon which she pressed me to rise, the ground being damp and dangerous, which I did accordingly, and walked away.

As I was going back again, and still talking of this gentleman and his son, a new occasion of melancholy offered itself thus. The woman began, as if she would tell me a story to divert me: 'There goes,' says she, 'a very odd tale among the neighbours where this gentleman formerly live.' 'What was that?' said I. 'Why,' says she, 'that old gentleman going to England, when he was a young man, fell in love with a young lady there, one of the finest women that ever was seen, and married her, and brought her over hither to his mother who was then living. He lived here several years with her,' continued she, 'and had several children by her, of which the young gentleman that was with him now was one; but after some time, the old gentlewoman, his mother, talking to her of something relating to herself when she was in England, and of her circumstances in England, which were bad enough, the daughter-in-law began to be very much surprised and uneasy; and, in short, examining further into things, it appeared past all contradiction that the old gentlewoman was her own mother, and that consequently that son was his wife's own brother, which struck the whole family with horror, and put them into such confusion that it had almost ruined them all. The young woman would not live with him; the son, her brother and husband, for a time went distracted; and at last the young woman went away for England, and has never been heard of since.'

It is easy to believe that I was strangely affected with this story, but 'tis impossible to describe the nature of my disturbance. I seemed astonished at the story, and asked her a thousand questions about the particulars, which I found she was thoroughly acquainted with. At last I began to inquire into the circumstances of the family, how the old gentlewoman, I mean my mother, died, and how she left what she had; for my mother had promised me very solemnly, that when she died she would do something for me, and leave it so, as that, if I was living, I should one way or other come at it, without its being in the power of her son, my brother and husband, to prevent it. She told me she did not know exactly how it was ordered, but she had been told that my mother had left a sum of money, and had tied her plantation for the payment of it, to be made good to the daughter, if ever she could be heard of, either in England or elsewhere; and that the trust was left with this son, who was the person that we saw with his father.

This was news too good for me to make light of, and, you may be sure, filled my heart with a thousand thoughts, what course I should take, how, and when, and in what manner I should make myself known, or whether I should ever make myself know or no.

Here was a perplexity that I had not indeed skill to manage myself in, neither knew I what course to take. It lay heavy upon my mind night and day. I could neither sleep nor converse, so that my husband perceived it, and wondered what ailed me, strove to divert me, but it was all to no purpose. He pressed me to tell him what it was troubled me, but I put it off, till at last, importuning me continually, I was forced to form a story, which yet had a plain truth to lay it upon too. I told him I was troubled because I found we must shift our quarters and alter our scheme of settling, for that I found I should be known if I stayed in that part of the country; for that my mother being dead, several of my relations were come into that part where we then was, and that I must either discover myself to them, which in our present circumstances was not proper on many accounts, or remove; and which to do I knew not, and that this it was that made me so melancholy and so thoughtful.

He joined with me in this, that it was by no means proper for me to make myself known to anybody in the circumstances in which we then were; and therefore he told me he would be willing to remove to any other part of the country, or even to any other country if I thought fit. But now I had another difficulty, which was, that if I removed to any other colony, I put myself out of the way of ever making a due search after those effects which my mother had left. Again I could never so much as think of breaking the secret of my former marriage to my new husband; it was not a story, as I thought, that would bear telling, nor could I tell what might be the consequences of it; and it was impossible to search into the bottom of the thing without making it public all over the country, as well who I was, as what I now was also.

In this perplexity I continued a great while, and this made my spouse very uneasy; for he found me perplexed, and yet thought I was not open with him, and did not let him into every part of my grievance; and he would often say, he wondered what he had done that I would not trust him with whatever it was, especially if it was grievous and afflicting. The truth is, he ought to have been trusted with everything, for no man in the world could deserve better of a wife; but this was a thing I knew not how to open to him, and yet having nobody to disclose any part of it to, the burthen was too heavy for my mind; for let them say what they please of our sex not being able to keep a secret, my life is a plain conviction to me of the contrary; but be it our sex, or the man's sex, a secret of moment should always have a confidant, a bosom friend, to whom we may communicate the joy of it, or the grief of it, be it which it will, or it will be a double weight upon the spirits, and perhaps become even insupportable in itself; and this I appeal to all human testimony for the truth of.

And this is the cause why many times men as well as women, and men of the greatest and best qualities other ways, yet have found themselves weak in this part, and have not been able to bear the weight of a secret joy or of a secret sorrow, but have been obliged to disclose it, even for the mere giving vent to themselves, and to unbend the mind oppressed with the load and weights which attended it. Nor was this any token of folly or thoughtlessness at all, but a natural consequence of the thing; and such people, had they struggled longer with the oppression, would certainly have told it in their sleep, and disclosed the secret, let it have been of what fatal nature soever, without regard to the person to whom it might be exposed. This necessity of nature is a thing which works sometimes with such vehemence in the minds of those who are guilty of any atrocious villainy, such as secret murder in particular, that they have been obliged to discover it, though the consequence would necessarily be their own destruction. Now, though it may be true that the divine justice ought to have the glory of all those discoveries and confessions, yet 'tis as certain that Providence, which ordinarily works by the hands of nature, makes use here of the same natural causes to produce those extraordinary effects.

I could give several remarkable instances of this in my long conversation with crime and with criminals. I knew one fellow that, while I was in prison in Newgate, was one of those they called then night-fliers. I know not what other word they may have understood it by since, but he was one who by connivance was admitted to go abroad every evening, when he played his pranks, and furnished those honest people they call thief-catchers with business to find out the next day, and restore for a reward what they had stolen the evening before. This fellow was as sure to tell in his sleep all that he had done, and every step he had taken, what he had stolen, and where, as sure as if he had engaged to tell it waking, and that there was no harm or danger in it, and therefore he was obliged, after he had been out, to lock himself up, or be locked up by some of the keepers that had him in fee, that nobody should hear him; but, on the other hand, if he had told all the particulars, and given a full account of his rambles and success, to any comrade, any brother thief, or to his employers, as I may justly call them, then all was well with him, and he slept as quietly as other people.

As the publishing this account of my life is for the sake of the just moral of very part of it, and for instruction, caution, warning, and improvement to every reader, so this will not pass, I hope, for an unnecessary digression concerning some people being obliged to disclose the greatest secrets either of their own or other people's affairs.

Under the certain oppression of this weight upon my mind, I laboured in the case I have been naming; and the only relief I found for it was to let my husband into so much of it as I thought would convince him of the necessity there was for us to think of settling in some other part of the world; and the next consideration before us was, which part of the English settlements we should go to. My husband was a perfect stranger to the country, and had not yet so much as a geographical knowledge of the situation of the several places; and I, that, till I wrote this, did not know what the word geographical signified, had only a general knowledge from long conversation with people that came from or went to several places; but this I knew, that Maryland, Pennsylvania, East and West Jersey, New York, and New England lay all north of Virginia, and that they were consequently all colder climates, to which for that very reason, I had an aversion. For that as I naturally loved warm weather, so now I grew into years I had a stronger inclination to shun a cold climate. I therefore considered of going to Caroline, which is the only southern colony of the English on the continent of America, and hither I proposed to go; and the rather because I might with great ease come from thence at any time, when it might be proper to inquire after my mother's effects, and to make myself known enough to demand them.

With this resolution I proposed to my husband our going away from where we was, and carrying all our effects with us to Caroline, where we resolved to settle; for my husband readily agreed to the first part, viz. that was not at all proper to stay where we was, since I had assured him we should be known there, and the rest I effectually concealed from him.

But now I found a new difficulty upon me. The main affair grew heavy upon my mind still, and I could not think of going out of the country without somehow or other making inquiry into the grand affair of what my mother had done for me; nor could I with any patience bear the thought of going away, and not make myself known to my old husband (brother), or to my child, his son; only I would fain have had this done without my new husband having any knowledge of it, or they having any knowledge of him, or that I had such a thing as a husband.

I cast about innumerable ways in my thoughts how this might be done. I would gladly have sent my husband away to Caroline with all our goods, and have come after myself, but this was impracticable; he would never stir without me, being himself perfectly unacquainted with the country, and with the methods of settling there or anywhere else. Then I thought we would both go first with part of our goods, and that when we were settled I should come back to Virginia and fetch the remainder; but even then I knew he would never part with me, and be left there to go on alone. The case was plain; he was bred a gentleman, and by consequence was not only unacquainted, but indolent, and when we did settle, would much rather go out into the woods with his gun, which they call there hunting, and which is the ordinary work of the Indians, and which they do as servants; I say, he would rather do that than attend the natural business of his plantation.

These were therefore difficulties insurmountable, and such as I knew not what to do in. I had such strong impressions on my mind about discovering myself to my brother, formerly my husband, that I could not withstand them; and the rather, because it ran constantly in my thoughts, that if I did not do it while he lived, I might in vain endeavour to convince my son afterward that I was really the same person, and that I was his mother, and so might both lose the assistance and comfort of the relation, and the benefit of whatever it was my mother had left me; and yet, on the other hand, I could never think it proper to discover myself to them in the circumstances I was in, as well relating to the having a husband with me as to my being brought over by a legal transportation as a criminal; on both which accounts it was absolutely necessary to me to remove from the place where I was, and come again to him, as from another place and in another figure.

Upon those considerations, I went on with telling my husband the absolute necessity there was of our not settling in Potomac River, at least that we should be presently made public there; whereas if we went to any other place in the world, we should come in with as much reputation as any family that came to plant; that, as it was always agreeable to the inhabitants to have families come among them to plant, who brought substance with them, either to purchase plantations or begin new ones, so we should be sure of a kind, agreeable reception, and that without any possibility of a discovery of our circumstances.

I told him in general, too, that as I had several relations in the place where we were, and that I durst not now let myself be known to them, because they would soon come into a knowledge of the occasion and reason of my coming over, which would be to expose myself to the last degree, so I had reason to believe that my mother, who died here, had left me something, and perhaps considerable, which it might be very well worth my while to inquire after; but that this too could not be done without exposing us publicly, unless we went from hence; and then, wherever we settled, I might come, as it were, to visit and to see my brother and nephews, make myself known to them, claim and inquire after what was my due, be received with respect, and at the same time have justice done me with cheerfulness and good will; whereas, if I did it now, I could expect nothing but with trouble, such as exacting it by force, receiving it with curses and reluctance, and with all kinds of affronts, which he would not perhaps bear to see; that in case of being obliged to legal proofs of being really her daughter, I might be at loss, be obliged to have recourse to England, and it may be to fail at last, and so lose it, whatever it might be. With these arguments, and having thus acquainted my husband with the whole secret so far as was needful of him, we resolved to go and seek a settlement in some other colony, and at first thoughts, Caroline was the place we pitched upon.

In order to this we began to make inquiry for vessels going to Carolina, and in a very little while got information, that on the other side the bay, as they call it, namely, in Maryland, there was a ship which came from Carolina, laden with rice and other goods, and was going back again thither, and from thence to Jamaica, with provisions. On this news we hired a sloop to take in our goods, and taking, as it were, a final farewell of Potomac River, we went with all our cargo over to Maryland.

This was a long and unpleasant voyage, and my spouse said it was worse to him than all the voyage from England, because the weather was but indifferent, the water rough, and the vessel small and inconvenient. In the next place, we were full a hundred miles up Potomac River, in a part which they call Westmoreland County, and as that river is by far the greatest in Virginia, and I have heard say it is the greatest river in the world that falls into another river, and not directly into the sea, so we had base weather in it, and were frequently in great danger; for though we were in the middle, we could not see land on either side for many leagues together. Then we had the great river or bay of Chesapeake to cross, which is where the river Potomac falls into it, near thirty miles broad, and we entered more great vast waters whose names I know not, so that our voyage was full two hundred miles, in a poor, sorry sloop, with all our treasure, and if any accident had happened to us, we might at last have been very miserable; supposing we had lost our goods and saved our lives only, and had then been left naked and destitute, and in a wild, strange place not having one friend or acquaintance in all that part of the world. The very thought of it gives me some horror, even since the danger is past.

Well, we came to the place in five days' sailing; I think they call it Philip's Point; and behold, when we came thither, the ship bound to Carolina was loaded and gone away but three days before. This was a disappointment; but, however, I, that was to be discouraged with nothing, told my husband that since we could not get passage to Caroline, and that the country we was in was very fertile and good, we would, if he liked of it, see if we could find out anything for our tune where we was, and that if he liked things we would settle here.

We immediately went on shore, but found no conveniences just at that place, either for our being on shore or preserving our goods on shore, but was directed by a very honest Quaker, whom we found there, to go to a place about sixty miles east; that is to say, nearer the mouth of the bay, where he said he lived, and where we should be accommodated, either to plant, or to wait for any other place to plant in that might be more convenient; and he invited us with so much kindness and simple honesty, that we agreed to go, and the Quaker himself went with us.

Here we bought us two servants, viz. an English woman-servant just come on shore from a ship of Liverpool, and a Negro man-servant, things absolutely necessary for all people that pretended to settle in that country. This honest Quaker was very helpful to us, and when we came to the place that he proposed to us, found us out a convenient storehouse for our goods, and lodging for ourselves and our servants; and about two months or thereabouts afterwards, by his direction, we took up a large piece of land from the governor of that country, in order to form our plantation, and so we laid the thoughts of going to Caroline wholly aside, having been very well received here, and accommodated with a convenient lodging till we could prepare things, and have land enough cleared, and timber and materials provided for building us a house, all which we managed by the direction of the Quaker; so that in one year's time we had nearly fifty acres of land cleared, part of it enclosed, and some of it planted with tabacco, though not much; besides, we had garden ground and corn sufficient to help supply our servants with roots and herbs and bread.

And now I persuaded my husband to let me go over the bay again, and inquire after my friends. He was the willinger to consent to it now, because he had business upon his hands sufficient to employ him, besides his gun to divert him, which they call hunting there, and which he greatly delighted in; and indeed we used to look at one another, sometimes with a great deal of pleasure, reflecting how much better that was, not than Newgate only, but than the most prosperous of our circumstances in the wicked trade that we had been both carrying on.

Our affair was in a very good posture; we purchased of the proprietors of the colony as much land for £35, paid in ready money, as would make a sufficient plantation to employ between fifty and sixty servants, and which, being well improved, would be sufficient to us as long as we could either of us live; and as for children, I was past the prospect of anything of that kind.

But out good fortune did not end here. I went, as I have said, over the bay, to the place where my brother, once a husband, lived; but I did not go to the same village where I was before, but went up another great river, on the east side of the river Potomac, called Rappahannock River, and by this means came on the back of his plantation, which was large, and by the help of a navigable creek, or little river, that ran into the Rappahannock, I came very near it.

I was now fully resolved to go up point-blank to my brother (husband), and to tell him who I was; but not knowing what temper I might find him in, or how much out of temper rather, I might make him by such a rash visit, I resolved to write a letter to him first, to let him know who I was, and that I was come not to give him any trouble upon the old relation, which I hoped was entirely forgot, but that I applied to him as a sister to a brother, desiring his assistance in the case of that provision which our mother, at her decease, had left for my support, and which I did not doubt but he would do me justice in, especially considering that I was come thus far to look after it.

I said some very tender, kind things in the letter about his son, which I told him he knew to be my own child, and that as I was guilty of nothing in marrying him, any more than he was in marrying me, neither of us having then known our being at all related to one another, so I hoped he would allow me the most passionate desire of once seeing my one and only child, and of showing something of the infirmities of a mother in preserving a violent affect for him, who had never been able to retain any thought of me one way or other.

I did believe that, having received this letter, he would immediately give it to his son to read, I having understood his eyes being so dim, that he could not see to read it; but it fell out better than so, for as his sight was dim, so he had allowed his son to open all letters that came to his hand for him, and the old gentleman being from home, or out of the way when my messenger came, my letter came directly to my son's hand, and he opened and read it.

He called the messenger in, after some little stay, and asked him where the person was who gave him the letter. The messenger told him the place, which was about seven miles off, so he bid him stay, and ordering a horse to be got ready, and two servants, away he came to me with the messenger. Let any one judge the consternation I was in when my messenger came back, and told me the old gentleman was not at home, but his son was come along with him, and was just coming up to me. I was perfectly confounded, for I knew not whether it was peace or war, nor could I tell how to behave; however, I had but a very few moments to think, for my son was at the heels of the messenger, and coming up into my lodgings, asked the fellow at the door something. I suppose it was, for I did not hear it so as to understand it, which was the gentlewoman that sent him; for the messenger said, 'There she is, sir'; at which he comes directly up to me, kisses me, took me in his arms, and embraced me with so much passion that he could not speak, but I could feel his breast heave and throb like a child, that cries, but sobs, and cannot cry it out.

I can neither express nor describe the joy that touched my very soul when I found, for it was easy to discover that part, that he came not as a stranger, but as a son to a mother, and indeed as a son who had never before known what a mother of his own was; in short, we cried over one another a considerable while, when at last he broke out first. 'My dear mother,' says he, 'are you still alive? I never expected to have seen your face.' As for me, I could say nothing a great while.

After we had both recovered ourselves a little, and were able to talk, he told me how things stood. As to what I had written to his father, he told me he had not showed my letter to his father, or told him anything about it; that what his grandmother left me was in his hands, and that he would do me justice to my full satis-satisfaction; that as to his father, he was old and infirm both in body and mind; that he was very fretful and passionate, almost blind, and capable of nothing; and he questioned whether he would know how to act in an affair which was of so nice a nature as this; and that therefore he had come himself, as well to satisfy himself in seeing me, which he could not restrain himself from, as also to put it into my power to make a judgment, after I had seen how things were, whether I would discover myself to his father or no.

This was really so prudently and wisely managed, that I found my son was a man of sense, and needed no direction from me. I told him I did not wonder that his father was as he had described him, for that his head was a little touched before I went away; and principally his disturbance was because I could not be persuaded to conceal our relation and to live with him as my husband, after I knew that he was my brother; that as he knew better than I what his father's present condition was, I should readily join with him in such measure as he would direct; that I was indifferent as to seeing his father, since I had seen him first, and he could not have told me better news than to tell me that what his grandmother had left me was entrusted in his hands, who, I doubted not, now he knew who I was, would, as he said, do me justice. I inquired then how long my mother had been dead, and where she died, and told so many particulars of the family, that I left him no room to doubt the truth of my being really and truly his mother.

My son then inquired where I was, and how I had disposed myself. I told him I was on the Maryland side of the bay, at the plantation of a particular friend who came from England in the same ship with me; that as for that side of the bay where he was, I had no habitation. He told me I should go home with him, and live with him, if I pleased, as long as I lived; that as to his father, he knew nobody, and would never so much as guess at me. I considered of that a little, and told him, that though it was really no concern to me to live at a distance from him, yet I could not say it would be the most comfortable thing in the world to me to live in the house with him, and to have that unhappy object always before me, which had been such a blow to my peace before; that though I should be glad to have his company (my son), or to be as near him as possible while I stayed, yet I could not think of being in the house where I should be also under constant restraint for fear of betraying myself in my discourse, nor should I be able to refrain some expressions in my conversing with him as my son, that might discover the whole affair, which would by no means be convenient.

He acknowledged that I was right in all this. 'But then, dear mother,' says he, 'you shall be as near me as you can.' So he took me with him on horseback to a plantation next to his own, and where I was as well entertained as I could have been in his own. Having left me there he went away home, telling me we would talk of the main business the next day; and having first called me his aunt, and given a charge to the people, who it seems were his tenants, to treat me with all possible respect. About two hours after he was gone, he sent me a maid-servant and a Negro boy to wait on me, and provisions ready dressed for my supper; and thus I was as if I had been in a new world, and began secretly now to wish that I had not brought my Lancashire husband from England at all.

However, that wish was not hearty neither, for I loved my Lancashire husband entirely, as indeed I had ever done from the beginning; and he merited from me as much as it was possible for a man to do; but that by the way.

The next morning my son came to visit me again almost as soon as I was up. After a little discourse, he first of all pulled out a deerskin bag, and gave it me, with five-and-fifty Spanish pistoles in it, and told me that was to supply my expenses from England, for though it was not his business to inquire, yet he ought to think I did not bring a great deal of money out with me, it not being usual to bring much money into that country. Then he pulled out his grandmother's will, and read it over to me, whereby it appeared that she had left a small plantation, as he called it, on York River, that is, where my mother lived, to me, with the stock of servants and cattle upon it, and given it in trust to this son of mine for my use, whenever he should hear of my being alive, and to my heirs, if I had any children, and in default of heirs, to whomsoever I should by will dispose of it; but gave the income of it, till I should be heard of, or found, to my said son; and if I should not be living, then it was to him, and his heirs.

This plantation, though remote from him, he said he did not let out, but managed it by a head-clerk (steward), as he did another that was his father's, that lay hard by it, and went over himself three or four times a year to look after it. I asked him what he thought the plantation might be worth. He said, if I would let it out, he would give me about £60 a year for it; but if I would live on it, then it would be worth much more, and, he believed, would bring me in about £150 a year. But seeing I was likely either to settle on the other side of the bay, or might perhaps have a mind to go back to England again, if I would let him be my steward he would manage it for me, as he had done for himself, and that he believed he should be able to send me as much tobacco to England from it as would yield me about £100 a year, sometimes more.

This was all strange news to me, and things I had not been used to; and really my heart began to look up more seriously than I think it ever did before, and to look with great thankfulness to the hand of Providence, which had done such wonders for me, who had been myself the greatest wonder of wickedness perhaps that had been suffered to live in the world. And I must again observe, that not on this occasion only, but even on all other occasions of thankfulness, my past wicked and abominable life never looked so monstrous to me, and I never so completely abhorred it, and reproached myself with it, as when I had a sense upon me of Providence doing good to me, while I had been making those vile returns on my part.

But I leave the reader to improve these thoughts, as no doubt they will see cause, and I go on to the fact. My son's tender carriage and kind offers fetched tears from me, almost all the while he talked with me. Indeed, I could scarce discourse with him but in the intervals of my passion; however, at length I began, and expressing myself with wonder at my being so happy to have the trust of what I had left, put into the hands of my own child, I told him, that as to the inheritance of it, I had no child but him in the world, and was now past having any if I should marry, and therefore would desire him to get a writing drawn, which I was ready to execute, by which I would, after me, give it wholly to him and to his heirs. And in the meantime, smiling, I asked him what made him continue a bachelor so long. His answer was kind and ready, that Virginia did not yield any great plenty of wives, and that since I talked of going back to England, I should send him a wife from London.

This was the substance of our first day's conversation, the pleasantest day that ever passed over my head in my life, and which gave me the truest satisfaction. He came every day after this, and spent a great part of his time with me, and carried me about to several of his friends' houses, where I was entertained with great respect. Also I dined several times at his own house, when he took care always to see his half-dead father so out of the way that I never saw him, or he me. I made him one present, and it was all I had of value, and that was one of the gold watches, of which I mentioned above, that I had two in my chest, and this I happened to have with me, and I gave it him at his third visit. I told him I had nothing of any value to bestow but that, and I desired he would now and then kiss it for my sake. I did not indeed tell him that I had stole it from a gentlewoman's side, at a meeting-house in London. That's by the way.

He stood a little while hesitating, as if doubtful whether to take it or no; but I pressed it on him, and made him accept it, and it was not much less worth than his leather pouch full of Spanish gold; no, though it were to be reckoned as if at London, whereas it was worth twice as much there, where I gave it him. At length he took it, kissed it, told me the watch should be a debt upon him that he would be paying as long as I lived.

A few days after he brought the writings of gift, and the scrivener with them, and I signed them very freely, and delivered them to him with a hundred kisses; for sure nothing ever passed between a mother and a tender, dutiful child with more affection. The next day he brings me an obligation under his hand and seal, whereby he engaged himself to manage and improve the plantation for my account, and with his utmost skill, and to remit the produce to my order wherever I should be; and withal, to be obliged himself to make up the produce £100 a year to me. When he had done so, he told me that as I came to demand it before the crop was off, I had a right to produce of the current year, and so he paid me £100 in Spanish pieces of eight, and desired me to give him a receipt for it as in full for that year, ending at Christmas following; this being about the latter end of August.

I stayed here about five weeks, and indeed had much ado to get away then. Nay, he would have come over the bay with me, but I would by no means allow him to it. However, he would send me over in a sloop of his own, which was built like a yacht, and served him as well for pleasure as business. This I accepted of, and so, after the utmost expressions both of duty and affection, he let me come away, and I arrived safe in two days at my friend's the Quaker's.

I brought over with me for the use of our plantation, three horses, with harness and saddles, some hogs, two cows, and a thousand other things, the gift of the kindest and tenderest child that ever woman had. I related to my husband all the particulars of this voyage, except that I called my son my cousin; and first I told him that I had lost my watch, which he seemed to take as a misfortune; but then I told him how kind my cousin had been, that my mother had left me such a plantation, and that he had preserved it for me, in hopes some time or other he should hear from me; then I told him that I had left it to his management, that he would render me a faithful account of its produce; and then I pulled him out the £100 in silver, as the first year's produce; and then pulling out the deerskin purse with the pistoles, 'And here, my dear,' says I, 'is the gold watch.' My husband—so is Heaven's goodness sure to work the same effects in all sensible minds where mercies touch the heart—lifted up both hands, and with an ecstacy of joy, 'What is God a-doing,' says he, 'for such an ungrateful dog as I am!' Then I let him know what I had brought over in the sloop, besides all this; I mean the horses, hogs, and cows, and other stores for our plantation; all which added to his surprise, and filled his heart with thankfulness; and from this time forward I believe he was as sincere a penitent, and as thoroughly a reformed man, as ever God's goodness brought back from a profligate, a highwayman, and a robber. I could fill a larger history than this with the evidence of this truth, and but that I doubt that part of the story will not be equally diverting as the wicked part, I have had thoughts of making a volume of it by itself.

As for myself, as this is to be my own story, not my husband's, I return to that part which related to myself. We went on with our plantation, and managed it with the help and diversion of such friends as we got there by our obliging behaviour, and especially the honest Quaker, who proved a faithful, generous, and steady friend to us; and we had very good success, for having a flourishing stock to begin with, as I have said, and this being now increased by the addition of £150 sterling in money, we enlarged our number of servants, built us a very good house, and cured every year a great deal of land. The second year I wrote to my old governess, giving her part with us of the joy of our success, and order her how to lay out the money I had left with her, which was £250 as above, and to send it to us in goods, which she performed with her usual kindness and fidelity, and this arrived safe to us.

Here we had a supply of all sorts of clothes, as well for my husband as for myself; and I took especial care to buy for him all those things that I knew he delighted to have; as two good long wigs, two silver-hilted swords, three or four fine fowling-pieces, a find saddle with holsters and pistols very handsome, with a scarlet cloak; and, in a word, everything I could think of to oblige him, and to make him appear, as he really was, a very fine gentleman. I ordered a good quantity of such household stuff as we yet wanted, with linen of all sorts for us both. As for myself, I wanted very little of clothes or linen, being very well furnished before. The rest of my cargo consisted in iron-work of all sorts, harness for horses, tools, clothes for servants, and woollen cloth, stuffs, serges, stockings, shoes, hats, and the like, such as servants wear; and whole pieces also to make up for servants, all by direction of the Quaker; and all this cargo arrived safe, and in good condition, with three woman-servants, lusty wenches, which my old governess had picked for me, suitable enough to the place, and to the work we had for them to do; one of which happened to come double, having been got with child by one of the seamen in the ship, as she owned afterwards, before the ship got so far as Gravesend; so she brought us a stout boy, about seven months after her landing.

My husband, you may suppose, was a little surprised at the arriving of all this cargo from England; and talking with me after he saw the account of this particular, 'My dear,' says he, 'what is the meaning of all this? I fear you will run us too deep in debt: when shall we be able to make return for it all?' I smiled, and told him that is was all paid for; and then I told him, that what our circumstances might expose us to, I had not taken my whole stock with me, that I had reserved so much in my friend's hands, which now we were come over safe, and was settled in a way to live, I had sent for, as he might see.

He was amazed, and stood a while telling upon his fingers, but said nothing. At last he began thus: 'Hold, let's see,' says he, telling upon his fingers still, and first on his thumb; 'there's £246 in money at first, then two gold watches, diamond rings, and plate,' says he, upon the forefinger. Then upon the next finger, 'Here's a plantation on York River, £100 a year, then £150 in money, then a sloop load of horses, cows, hogs, and stores'; and so on to the thumb again. 'And now,' says he, 'a cargo cost £250 in England, and worth here twice the money.' 'Well,' says I, 'what do you make of all that?' 'Make of it?' says he; 'why, who says I was deceived when I married a wife in Lancashire? I think I have married a fortune, and a very good fortune too,' says he.

In a word, we were now in very considerable circumstances, and every year increasing; for our new plantation grew upon our hands insensibly, and in eight years which we lived upon it, we brought it to such pitch, that the produce was at least £300 sterling a year; I mean, worth so much in England.

After I had been a year at home again, I went over the bay to see my son, and to receive another year's income of my plantation; and I was surprised to hear, just at my landing there, that my old husband was dead, and had not been buried above a fortnight. This, I confess, was not disagreeable news, because now I could appear as I was, in a married condition; so I told my son before I came from him, that I believed I should marry a gentleman who had a plantation near mine; and though I was legally free to marry, as to any obligation that was on me before, yet that I was shy of it, lest the blot should some time or other be revived, and it might make a husband uneasy. My son, the same kind, dutiful, and obliging creature as ever, treated me now at his own house, paid me my hundred pounds, and sent me home again loaded with presents.

Some time after this, I let my son know I was married, and invited him over to see us, and my husband wrote a very obliging letter to him also, inviting him to come and see him; and he came accordingly some months after, and happened to be there just when my cargo from England came in, which I let him believe belonged all to my husband's estate, not to me.

It must be observed that when the old wretch my brother (husband) was dead, I then freely gave my husband an account of all that affair, and of this cousin, as I had called him before, being my own son by that mistaken unhappy match. He was perfectly easy in the account, and told me he should have been as easy if the old man, as we called him, had been alive. 'For,' said he, 'it was no fault of yours, nor of his; it was a mistake impossible to be prevented.' He only reproached him with desiring me to conceal it, and to live with him as a wife, after I knew that he was my brother; that, he said, was a vile part. Thus all these difficulties were made easy, and we lived together with the greatest kindness and comfort imaginable.

We are grown old; I am come back to England, being almost seventy years of age, husband sixty-eight, having performed much more than the limited terms of my transportation; and now, notwithstanding all the fatigues and all the miseries we have both gone through, we are both of us in good heart and health. My husband remained there some time after me to settle our affairs, and at first I had intended to go back to him, but at his desire I altered that resolution, and he is come over to England also, where we resolve to spend the remainder of our years in sincere penitence for the wicked lives we have lived.

WRITTEN IN THE YEAR 1683

A JOURNAL OF THE PLAGUE YEAR

being observations or memorials
of the most remarkable occurrences,
as well public as private, which happened in
London during the last great visitation in 1665.
Written by a Citizen who continued
all the while in London.
Never made public before

A JOURNAL OF THE PLAGUE YEAR

It was about the beginning of September, 1664, that I, among the rest of my neighbours, heard in ordinary discourse that the plague was returned again in Holland; for it had been very violent there, and particularly at Amsterdam and Rotterdam, in the year 1663, whither, they say, it was brought, some said from Italy, others from the Levant, among some goods which were brought home by their Turkey fleet; others said it was brought from Candia; others from Cyprus. It mattered not from whence it came; but all agreed it was come into Holland again.

We had no such thing as printed newspapers in those days to spread rumours and reports of things, and to improve them by the invention of men, as I have lived to see practised since. But such things as these were gathered from the letters of merchants and others who corresponded abroad, and from them was handed about by word of mouth only; so that things did not spread instantly over the whole nation, as they do now. But it seems that the Government had a true account of it, and several councils were held about ways to prevent its coming over; but all was kept very private. Hence it was that this rumour died off again, and people began to forget it as a thing we were very little concerned in, and that we hoped was not true; till the latter end of November or the beginning of December 1664 when two men, said to be Frenchmen, died of the plague in Long Acre, or rather at the upper end of Drury Lane. The family they were in endeavoured to conceal it as much as possible, but as it had gotten some vent in the discourse of the neighbourhood, the Secretaries of State got knowledge of it; and concerning themselves to inquire about it, in order to be certain of the truth, two physicians and a surgeon were ordered to go to the house and make inspection. This they did; and finding evident tokens of the sickness upon both the bodies that were dead, they gave their opinions publicly that they died of the plague. Whereupon it was given in to the parish clerk, and he also returned them to the Hall; and it was printed in the weekly bill of mortality in the usual manner, thus—

Plague, 2. Parishes infected, 1.

The people showed a great concern at this, and began to be alarmed all over the town, and the more, because in the last week in December 1664 another man died in the same house, and of the same distemper. And then we were easy again for about six weeks, when none having died with any marks of infection, it was said the distemper was gone; but after that, I think it was about the 12th of February, another died in another house, but in the same parish and in the same manner.

This turned the people's eyes pretty much towards that end of the town, and the weekly bills showing an increase of burials in St Giles's parish more than usual, it began to be suspected that the plague was among the people at that end of the town, and that many had died of it, though they had taken care to keep it as much from the knowledge of the public as possible. This possessed the heads of the people very much, and few cared to go through Drury Lane, or the other streets suspected, unless they had extraordinary business that obliged them to it

This increase of the bills stood thus: the usual number of burials in a week, in the parishes of St Giles-in-the-Fields and St Andrew's, Holborn, were from twelve to seventeen or nineteen each, few more or less; but from the time that the plague first began in St Giles's parish, it was observed that the ordinary burials increased in number considerably. For example:—

From December 27 to January 3			{ St Giles's	16
"			{ St Andrew's	17
"	January 3 " "	10	{ St Giles's	12
"			{ St Andrew's	25
"	January 10 " "	17	{ St Giles's	18
"			{ St Andrew's	28
"	January 17 " "	24	{ St Giles's	23
"			{ St Andrew's	16
"	January 24 " "	31	{ St Giles's	24
"			{ St Andrew's	15
"	January 30 " February	7	{ St Giles's	21
"			{ St Andrew's	23
"	February 7 " "	14	{ St Giles's	24

Whereof one of the plague.

The like increase of the bills was observed in the parishes of St Bride's, adjoining on one side of Holborn parish, and in the parish of St James, Clerkenwell, adjoining on the other side of Holborn; in both which parishes the usual numbers that died weekly were from four to six or eight, whereas at that time they were increased as follows:—

From December 20 to December 27			{ St Bride's	0
"			{ St James's	8
"	December 27 to January 3		{ St Bride's	6
"			{ St James's	9
"	January 3 " "	10	{ St Bride's	11
"			{ St James's	7
"	January 10 " "	17	{ St Bride's	12
"			{ St James's	9
"	January 17 " "	24	{ St Bride's	9
"			{ St James's	15

"	January 24	" " 31	{ St Bride's	8
"			{ St James's	12
"	January 31	" February 7	{ St Bride's	13
"			{ St James's	5
"	February 7	" " 14	{ St Bride's	12
"			{ St James's	6

Besides this, it was observed with great uneasiness by the people that the weekly bills in general increased very much during these weeks, although it was at a time of the year when usually the bills are very moderate.

The usual number of burials within the bills of mortality for a week was from about 240 or thereabouts to 300. The last was esteemed a pretty high bill; but after this we found the bills successively increasing as follows:—

	Buried.	Increased.
December the 20th to the 27th	291	...
" " 27th " 3rd January	349	58
January the 3rd " 10th "	394	45
" " 10th " 17th "	415	21
" " 17th " 24th "	474	59

This last bill was really frightful, being a higher number than had been known to have been buried in one week since the preceding visitation of 1656.

However, all this went off again, and the weather proving cold, and the frost, which began in December, still continuing very severe even till near the end of February, attended with sharp though moderate winds, the bills decreased again, and the city grew healthy, and everybody began to look upon the danger as good as over; only that still the burials in St Giles's continued high. From the beginning of April especially they stood at twenty-five each week, till the week from the 18th to the 25th, when there was buried in St Giles's parish thirty, whereof two of the plague and eight of the spotted-fever, which was looked upon as the same thing; likewise the number that died of the spotted-fever in the whole increased, being eight the week before, and twelve the week above-named.

This alarmed us all again, and terrible apprehensions were among the people, especially the weather being now changed and growing warm, and the summer being at hand. However, the next week there seemed to be some hopes again; the bills were low, the number of the dead in all was but 388, there was none of the plague, and but four of the spotted-fever.

But the following week it returned again, and the distemper was spread into two or three other parishes, viz., St Andrew's, Holborn; St Clement Danes; and, to the great affliction of the city, one died within the walls, in the parish of St Mary Woolchurch, that is to say, in Bearbinder Lane, near Stocks Market; in all there were nine of the plague and six of the spotted-fever. It was, however, upon inquiry found that this Frenchman who died in Bearbinder Lane was one who, having lived in Long Acre, near the infected houses, had removed for fear of the distemper, not knowing that he was already infected.

This was the beginning of May, yet the weather was temperate, variable, and cool enough, and people had still some hopes. That which encouraged them was that the city was healthy: the whole ninety-seven parishes buried but fifty-four, and we began to hope that, as it was chiefly among the people at that end of the town, it might go no farther; and the rather, because the next week, which was from the 9th of May to the 16th, there died but three, of which not one within the whole city or liberties; and St Andrew's buried but fifteen, which was very low. 'Tis true St Giles's buried two-and-thirty, but still, as there was but one of the plague, people began to be easy. The whole bill also was very low, for the week before the bill was but 347, and the week above mentioned but 343. We continued in these hopes for a few days, but it was but for a few, for the people were no more to be deceived thus; they searched the houses and found that the plague was really spread every way, and that many died of it every day. So that now all our extenuations abated, and it was no more to be concealed; nay, it quickly appeared that the infection had spread itself beyond all hopes of abatement. That in the parish of St Giles it was gotten into several streets, and several families lay all sick together; and, accordingly, in the weekly bill for the next week the thing began to show itself. There was indeed but fourteen set down of the plague, but this was all knavery and collusion, for in St Giles's parish they buried forty in all, whereof it was certain most of them died of the plague, though they were set down of other distempers; and though the number of all the burials were not increased above thirty-two, and the whole bill being but 385, yet there was fourteen of the spotted-fever, as well as fourteen of the plague; and we took it for granted upon the whole that there were fifty died that week of the plague.

The next bill was from the 23rd of May to the 30th, when the number of the plague was seventeen. But the burials in St Giles's were fifty-three—a frightful number!—of whom they set down but nine of the plague; but on an examination more strictly by the justices of peace, and at the Lord Mayor's request, it was found there were twenty more who were really dead of the plague in that parish, but had been set down of the spotted-fever or other distempers, besides others concealed.

But those were trifling things to what followed immediately after; for now the weather set in hot, and from the first week in June the infection spread in a dreadful manner, and the bills rose high; the articles of the fever, spotted-fever, and teeth began to swell; for all that could conceal their distempers did it, to prevent their neighbours shunning and refusing to converse with them, and also to prevent authority shutting up their houses; which, though it was not yet practised, yet was threatened, and people were extremely terrified at the thoughts of it.

The second week in June, the parish of St Giles, where still the weight of the infection lay, buried 120, whereof though the bills said but sixty-eight of the plague, everybody said there had been 100 at least, calculating it from the usual number of funerals in that parish, as above.

Till this week the city continued free, there having never any died, except that one Frenchman whom I mentioned before, within the whole ninety-seven parishes. Now there died four within the city, one in Wood Street, one in Fenchurch Street, and two in Crooked Lane. Southwark was entirely free, having not one yet died on that side of the water.

I lived without Aldgate, about midway between Aldgate Church and Whitechappel Bars, on the left hand or north side of the street; and as the distemper had not reached to that side of the city, our neighbourhood continued very easy. But at the other end of the town their consternation was very great: and the richer sort of people, especially the nobility and gentry from the west part of the city, thronged out of town with their families and servants in an unusual manner; and this was more particularly seen in Whitechappel; that is to say, the Broad Street where I lived; indeed, nothing was to be seen but waggons and carts, with goods, women, servants, children, &c.; coaches filled with people of the better sort and horsemen attending them, and all hurrying away; then empty waggons and carts appeared, and spare horses with servants, who, it was apparent, were returning or sent from the countries to fetch more people; besides innumerable numbers of men on horseback, some alone, others with servants, and, generally speaking, all loaded with baggage and fitted out for travelling, as anyone might perceive by their appearance.

This was a very terrible and melancholy thing to see, and as it was a sight which I could not but look on from morning to night (for indeed there was nothing else of moment to be seen), it filled me with very serious thoughts of the misery that was coming upon the city, and the unhappy condition of those that would be left in it.

This hurry of the people was such for some weeks that there was no getting at the Lord Mayor's door without exceeding difficulty; there were such pressing and crowding there to get passes and certificates of health for such as travelled abroad, for without these there was no being admitted to pass through the towns upon the road, or to lodge in any inn. Now, as there had none died in the city for all this time, my Lord Mayor gave certificates of health without any difficulty to all those who lived in the ninety-seven parishes, and to those within the liberties too for a while.

This hurry, I say, continued some weeks, that is to say, all the month of May and June, and the more because it was rumoured that an order of the Government was to be issued out to place turnpikes and barriers on the road to prevent people travelling, and that the towns on the road would not suffer people from London to pass for fear of bringing the infection along with them, though neither of these rumours had any foundation but in the imagination, especially at-first.

I now began to consider seriously with myself concerning my own case, and how I should dispose of myself; that is to say, whether I should resolve to stay in London or shut up my house and flee, as many of my neighbours did. I have set this particular down so fully, because I know not but it may be of moment to those who come after me, if they come to be brought to the same distress, and to the same manner of making their choice; and therefore I desire this account may pass with them rather for a direction to themselves to act by than a history of my actings, seeing it may not he of one farthing value to them to note what became of me.

I had two important things before me: the one was the carrying on my business and shop, which was considerable, and in which was embarked all my effects in the world; and the other was the preservation of my life in so dismal a calamity as I saw apparently was coming upon the whole city, and which, however great it was, my fears perhaps, as well as other people's, represented to be much greater than it could be.

The first consideration was of great moment to me; my trade was a saddler, and as my dealings were chiefly not by a shop or chance trade, but among the merchants trading to the English colonies in America, so my effects lay very much in the hands of such. I was a single man, 'tis true, but I had a family of servants whom I kept at my business; had a house, shop, and warehouses filled with goods; and, in short, to leave them all as things in such a case must be left (that is to say, without any overseer or person fit to be trusted with them), had been to hazard the loss not only of my trade, but of my goods, and indeed of all I had in the world.

I had an elder brother at the same time in London, and not many years before come over from Portugal: and advising with him, his answer was in three words, the same that was given in another case quite different, viz., 'Master, save thyself.' In a word, he was for my retiring into the country, as he resolved to do himself with his family; telling me what he had, it seems, heard abroad, that the best preparation for the plague was to run away from it. As to my argument of losing my trade, my goods, or debts, he quite confuted me. He told me the same thing which I argued for my staying, viz., that I would trust God with my safety and health, was the strongest repulse to my pretensions of losing my trade and my goods; 'for', says he, 'is it not as reasonable that you should trust God with the chance or risk of losing your trade, as that you should stay in so eminent a point of danger, and trust Him with your life?'

I could not argue that I was in any strait as to a place where to go, having several friends and relations in Northamptonshire, whence our family first came from; and particularly, I had an only sister in Lincolnshire, very willing to receive and entertain me.

My brother, who had already sent his wife and two children into Bedfordshire, and resolved to follow them, pressed my going very earnestly; and I had once resolved to comply with his desires, but at that time could get no horse; for though it is true all the people did not go out of the city of London, yet I may venture to say that in a manner all the horses did; for there was hardly a horse to be bought or hired in the whole city for some weeks. Once I resolved to travel on foot with one servant, and, as many did, lie at no inn, but carry a soldier's tent with us, and so lie in the fields, the weather being very warm, and no danger from taking cold. I say, as many did, because several did so at last, especially those who had been in the armies in the war which had not been many years past; and I must needs say that, speaking of second causes, had most of the people that travelled done so, the plague had not been carried into so many country towns and houses as it was, to the great damage, and indeed to the ruin, of abundance of people.

But then my servant, whom I had intended to take down with me, deceived me; and being frighted at the increase of the distemper, and not knowing when I should go, he took other measures, and left me, so I was put off for that time; and, one way or other, I always found that to appoint to go away was always crossed by some accident or other, so as to disappoint and put it off again; and this brings in a story which otherwise might be thought a needless digression, viz., about these disappointments being from Heaven.

I mention this story also as the best method I can advise any person to take in such a case, especially if he be one that makes conscience of his duty, and would be directed what to do in it, namely, that he should keep his eye upon the particular providences which occur at that time, and look upon them complexly, as they regard one another, and as all together regard the question before him: and then, I think, he may safely take them for intimations from Heaven of what is his unquestioned duty to do in such a case; I mean as to going away from or staying in the place where we dwell, when visited with an infectious distemper.

It came very warmly into my mind one morning, as I was musing on this particular thing, that as nothing attended us without the direction or permission of Divine Power, so these disappointments must have something in them extraordinary; and I ought to consider whether it did not evidently point out, or intimate to me, that it was the will of Heaven I should not go. It immediately followed in my thoughts, that if it really was from God that I should stay, He was able effectually to preserve me in the midst of all the death and danger that would surround me; and that if I attempted to secure myself by fleeing from my habitation, and acted contrary to these intimations, which I believe to be Divine, it was a kind of flying from God, and that He could cause His justice to overtake me when and where He thought fit.

These thoughts quite turned my resolutions again, and when I came to discourse with my brother again I told him that I inclined to stay and take my lot in that station in which God had placed me, and that it seemed to be made more especially my duty, on the account of what I have said.

My brother, though a very religious man himself, laughed at all I had suggested about its being an intimation from Heaven, and told me several stories of such foolhardy people, as he called them, as I was; that I ought indeed to submit to it as a work of Heaven if I had been any way disabled by distempers or diseases, and that then not being able to go, I ought to acquiesce in the direction of Him, who, having been my Maker, had an undisputed right of sovereignty in disposing of me, and that then there had been no difficulty to determine which was the call of His providence and which was not; but that I should take it as an intimation from Heaven that I should not go out of town, only because I could not hire a horse to go, or my fellow was run away that was to attend me, was ridiculous, since at the time I had my health and limbs, and other servants, and might with ease travel a day or two on foot, and having a good certificate of being in perfect health, might either hire a horse or take post on the road, as I thought fit.

Then he proceeded to tell me of the mischievous consequences which attended the presumption of the Turks and Mahometans in Asia and in other places where he had been (for my brother, being a merchant, was a few years before, as I have already observed, returned from abroad, coming last from Lisbon), and how, presuming upon their professed predestinating notions, and of every man's end being predetermined and unalterably beforehand decreed, they would go unconcerned into infected places and converse with infected persons, by which means they died at the rate of ten or fifteen thousand a week, whereas the Europeans or Christian merchants, who kept themselves retired and reserved, generally escaped the contagion.

Upon these arguments my brother changed my resolutions again, and I began to resolve to go, and accordingly made all things ready; for, in short, the infection increased round me, and the bills were risen to almost seven hundred a week, and my brother told me he would venture to stay no longer. I desired him to let me consider of it but till the next day, and I would resolve: and as I had already prepared everything as well as I could as to MY business, and whom to entrust my affairs with, I had little to do but to resolve.

I went home that evening greatly oppressed in my mind, irresolute, and not knowing what to do. I had set the evening wholly—apart to consider seriously about it, and was all alone; for already people had, as it were by a general consent, taken up the custom of not going out of doors after sunset; the reasons I shall have occasion to say more of by-and-by.

In the retirement of this evening I endeavoured to resolve, first, what was my duty to do, and I stated the arguments with which my brother had pressed me to go into the country, and I set, against them the strong impressions which I had on my mind for staying; the visible call I seemed to have from the particular circumstance of my calling, and the care due from me for the preservation of my effects, which were, as I might say, my estate; also the intimations which I thought I had from Heaven, that to me signified a kind of direction to venture; and it occurred to me that if I had what I might call a direction to stay, I ought to suppose it contained a promise of being preserved if I obeyed.

This lay close to me, and my mind seemed more and more encouraged to stay than ever, and supported with a secret satisfaction that I should be kept. Add to this, that, turning over the Bible which lay before me, and while my thoughts were more than ordinarily serious upon the question, I cried out, 'Well, I know not what to do; Lord, direct me I' and the like; and at that juncture I happened to stop turning over the book at the gist Psalm, and casting my eye on the second verse, I read on to the seventh verse exclusive, and after that included the tenth, as follows: 'I will say of the Lord, He is my refuge and my fortress: my God, in Him will I trust. Surely He shall deliver thee from the snare of the fowler, and from the noisome pestilence. He shall cover thee with His feathers, and under His wings shalt thou trust: His truth shall be thy shield and buckler. Thou shalt not be afraid for the terror by night; nor for the arrow that flieth by day; nor for the pestilence that walketh in darkness; nor for the destruction that wasteth at noonday. A thousand shall fall at thy side, and ten thousand at thy right hand; but it shall not come nigh thee. Only with thine eyes shalt thou behold and see the reward of the wicked. Because thou hast made the Lord, which is my refuge, even the most High, thy habitation; there shall no evil befall thee, neither shall any plague come nigh thy dwelling,' &C.

I scarce need tell the reader that from that moment I resolved that I would stay in the town, and casting myself entirely upon the goodness and protection of the Almighty, would not seek any other shelter whatever; and that, as my times were in His hands, He was as able to keep me in a time of the infection as in a time of health; and if He did not think fit to deliver me, still I was in His hands, and it was meet He should do with me as should seem good to Him.

With this resolution I went to bed; and I was further confirmed in it the next day by the woman being taken ill with whom I had intended to entrust my house and all my affairs. But I had a further obligation laid on me on the same side, for the next day I found myself very much out of order also, so that if I would have gone away, I could not, and I continued ill three or four days, and this entirely determined my stay; so I took my leave of my brother, who went away to Dorking, in Surrey, and afterwards fetched a round farther into Buckinghamshire or Bedfordshire, to a retreat he had found out there for his family.

It was a very ill time to be sick in, for if any one complained, it was immediately said he had the plague; and though I had indeed no symptom of that distemper, yet being very ill, both in my head and in my stomach, I was not without apprehension that I really was infected; but in about three days I grew better; the third night I rested well, sweated a little, and was much refreshed. The apprehensions of its being the infection went also quite away with my illness, and I went about my business as usual.

These things, however, put off all my thoughts of going into the country; and my brother also being gone, I had no more debate either with him or with myself on that subject.

It was now mid-July, and the plague, which had chiefly raged at the other end of the town, and, as I said before, in the parishes of St Giles, St Andrew's, Holborn, and towards Westminster, began to now come eastward towards the part where I lived. It was to be observed, indeed, that it did not come straight on towards us; for the city, that is to say, within the walls, was indifferently healthy still; nor was it got then very much over the water into Southwark; for though there died that week 1268 of all distempers, whereof it might be supposed above 600 died of the plague, yet there was but twenty-eight in the whole city, within the walls, and but nineteen in Southwark, Lambeth parish included; whereas in the parishes of St Giles and St Martin-in-the-Fields alone there died 421.

But we perceived the infection kept chiefly in the out-parishes, which being very populous, and fuller also of poor, the distemper found more to prey upon than in the city, as I shall observe afterwards. We perceived, I say, the distemper to draw our way, viz., by the parishes of Clarkenwell, Cripplegate, Shoreditch, and Bishopsgate; which last two parishes joining to Aldgate, Whitechappel, and Stepney, the infection came at length to spread its utmost rage and violence in those parts, even when it abated at the western parishes where it began.

It was very strange to observe that in this particular week, from the 4th to the 11th of July, when, as I have observed, there died near 400 of the plague in the two parishes of St Martin and St Giles-in-the-Fields only, there died in the parish of Aldgate but four, in the parish of Whitechappel three, in the parish of Stepney but one.

Likewise in the next week, from the 11th of July to the 18th, when the week's bill was 1761, yet there died no more of the plague, on the whole Southwark side of the water, than sixteen. But this face of things soon changed, and it began to thicken in Cripplegate parish especially, and in Clarkenwell; so that by the second week in August, Cripplegate parish alone buried 886, and Clarkenwell 155. Of the first, 850 might well be reckoned to die of the plague; and of the last, the bill itself said 145 were of the plague.

During the month of July, and while, as I have observed, our part of the town seemed to be spared in comparison of the west part, I went ordinarily about the streets, as my business required, and particularly went generally once in a day, or in two days, into the city, to my brother's house, which he had given me charge of, and to see if it was safe; and having the key in my pocket, I used to go into the house, and over most of the rooms, to see that all was well; for though it be something wonderful to tell, that any should have hearts so hardened in the midst of such a calamity as to rob and steal, yet certain it is that all sorts of villainies, and even levities and debaucheries, were then practised in the town as openly as ever—I will not say quite as frequently, because the numbers of people were many ways lessened.

But the city itself began now to be visited too, I mean within the walls; but the number of people there were indeed extremely lessened by so great a multitude having been gone into the country; and even all this month of July they continued to flee, though not in such multitudes as formerly. In August, indeed, they fled in such a manner that I began to think there would be really none but magistrates and servants left in the city.

As they fled now out of the city, so I should observe that the Court removed early, viz., in the month of June, and went to Oxford, where it pleased God to preserve them; and the distemper did not, as I heard of, so much as touch them, for which I cannot say that I ever saw they showed any great token of thankfulness, and hardly anything of reformation, though they did not want being told that their crying vices might without breach of charity be said to have gone far in bringing that terrible judgement upon the whole nation.

The face of London was—now indeed strangely altered: I mean the whole mass of buildings, city, liberties, suburbs, Westminster, Southwark, and altogether; for as to the particular part called the city, or within the walls, that was not yet much infected. But in the whole the face of things, I say, was much altered; sorrow and sadness sat upon every face; and though some parts were not yet overwhelmed, yet all looked deeply concerned; and, as we saw it apparently coming on, so every one looked on himself and his family as in the utmost danger. Were it possible to represent those times exactly to those that did not see them, and give the reader due ideas of the horror 'that everywhere presented itself, it must make just impressions upon their minds and fill them with surprise. London might well be said to be all in tears; the mourners did not go about the streets indeed, for nobody put on black or made a formal dress of mourning for their nearest friends; but the voice of mourners was truly heard in the streets. The shrieks of women and children at the windows and doors of their houses, where their dearest relations were perhaps dying, or just dead, were so frequent to be heard as we passed the streets, that it was enough to pierce the stoutest heart in the world to hear them. Tears and lamentations were seen almost in every house, especially in the first part of the visitation; for towards the latter end men's hearts were hardened, and death was so always before their eyes, that they did not so much concern themselves for the loss of their friends, expecting that themselves should be summoned the next hour.

Business led me out sometimes to the other end of the town, even when the sickness was chiefly there; and as the thing was new to me, as well as to everybody else, it was a most surprising thing to see those streets which were usually so thronged now grown desolate, and so few people to be seen in them, that if I had been a stranger and at a loss for my way, I might sometimes have gone the length of a whole street (I mean of the by-streets), and seen nobody to direct me except watchmen set at the doors of such houses as were shut up, of which I shall speak presently.

One day, being at that part of the town on some special business, curiosity led me to observe things more than usually, and indeed I walked a great way where I had no business. I went up Holborn, and there the street was full of people, but they walked in the middle of the great street, neither on one side or other, because, as I suppose, they would not mingle with anybody that came out of houses, or meet with smells and scent from houses that might be infected.

The Inns of Court were all shut up; nor were very many of the lawyers in the Temple, or Lincoln's Inn, or Gray's Inn, to be seen there. Everybody was at peace; there was no occasion for lawyers; besides, it being in the time of the vacation too, they were generally gone into the country. Whole rows of houses in some places were shut close up, the inhabitants all fled, and only a watchman or two left.

When I speak of rows of houses being shut up, I do not mean shut up by the magistrates, but that great numbers of persons followed the Court, by the necessity of their employments and other dependences; and as others retired, really frighted with the distemper, it was a mere desolating of some of the streets. But the fright was not yet near so great in the city, abstractly so called, and particularly because, though they were at first in a most inexpressible consternation, yet as I have observed that the distemper intermitted often at first, so they were, as it were, alarmed and unalarmed again, and this several times, till it began to be familiar to them; and that even when it appeared violent, yet seeing it did not presently spread into the city, or the east and south parts, the people began to take courage, and to be, as I may say, a little hardened. It is true a vast many people fled, as I have observed, yet they were chiefly from the west end of the town, and from that we call the heart of the city: that is to say, among the wealthiest of the people, and such people as were unencumbered with trades and business. But of the rest, the generality stayed, and seemed to abide the worst; so that in the place we calf the Liberties, and in the suburbs, in Southwark, and in the east part, such as Wapping, Ratcliff, Stepney, Rotherhithe, and the like, the people generally stayed, except here and there a few wealthy families, who, as above, did not depend upon their business.

It must not be forgot here that the city and suburbs were prodigiously full of people at the time of this visitation, I mean at the time that it began; for though I have lived to see a further increase, and mighty throngs of people settling in London more than ever, yet we had always a notion that the numbers of people which, the wars being over, the armies disbanded, and the royal family and the monarchy being restored, had flocked to London to settle in business, or to depend upon and attend the Court for rewards of services, preferments, and the like, was such that the town was computed to have in it above a hundred thousand people more than ever it held before; nay, some took upon them to say it had twice as many, because all the ruined families of the royal party flocked hither. All the old soldiers set up trades here, and abundance of families settled here. Again, the Court brought with them a great flux of pride, and new fashions. All people were grown gay and luxurious, and the joy of the Restoration had brought a vast many families to London.

I often thought that as Jerusalem was besieged by the Romans when the Jews were assembled together to celebrate the Passover—by which means an incredible number of people were surprised there who would otherwise have been in other countries—so the plague entered London when an incredible increase of people had happened occasionally, by the particular circumstances above-named. As this conflux of the people to a youthful and gay Court made a great trade in the city, especially in everything that belonged to fashion and finery, so it drew by consequence a great number of workmen, manufacturers, and the like, being mostly poor people who depended upon their labour. And I remember in particular that in a representation to my Lord Mayor of the condition of the poor, it was estimated that there were no less than an hundred thousand riband-weavers in and about the city, the chiefest number of whom lived then in the parishes of Shoreditch, Stepney, Whitechappel, and Bishopsgate, that, namely, about Spitalfields; that is to say, as Spitalfields was then, for it was not so large as now by one fifth part.

By this, however, the number of people in the whole may be judged of; and, indeed, I often wondered that, after the prodigious numbers of people that went away at first, there was yet so great a multitude left as it appeared there was.

But I must go back again to the beginning of this surprising time. While the fears of the people were young, they were increased strangely by several odd accidents which, put altogether, it was really a wonder the whole body of the people did not rise as one man and abandon their dwellings, leaving the place as a space of ground designed by Heaven for an Akeldama, doomed to be destroyed from the face of the earth, and that all that would be found in it would perish with it. I shall name but a few of these things; but sure they were so many, and so many wizards and cunning people propagating them, that I have often wondered there was any (women especially) left behind.

In the first place, a blazing star or comet appeared for several months before the plague, as there did the year after another, a little before the fire. The old women and the phlegmatic hypochondriac part of the other sex, whom I could almost call old women too, remarked (especially afterward, though not till both those judgements were over) that those two comets passed directly over the city, and that so very near the houses that it was plain they imported something peculiar to the city alone; that the comet before the pestilence was of a faint, dull, languid colour, and its motion very heavy, Solemn, and slow; but that the comet before the fire was bright and sparkling, or, as others said, flaming, and its motion swift and furious; and that, accordingly, one foretold a heavy judgement, slow but severe, terrible and frightful, as was the plague; but the other foretold a stroke, sudden, swift, and fiery as the conflagration. Nay, so particular some people were, that as they looked upon that comet preceding the fire, they fancied that they not only saw it pass swiftly and fiercely, and could perceive the motion with their eye, but even they heard it; that it made a rushing, mighty noise, fierce and terrible, though at a distance, and but just perceivable.

I saw both these stars, and, I must confess, had so much of the common notion of such things in my head, that I was apt to look upon them as the forerunners and warnings of God's judgements; and especially when, after the plague had followed the first, I yet saw another of the like kind, I could not but say God had not yet sufficiently scourged the city.

But I could not at the same time carry these things to the height that others did, knowing, too, that natural causes are assigned by the astronomers for such things, and that their motions and even their revolutions are calculated, or pretended to be calculated, so that they cannot be so perfectly called the forerunners or foretellers, much less the procurers, of such events as pestilence, war, fire, and the like.

But let my thoughts and the thoughts of the philosophers be, or have been, what they will, these things had a more than ordinary influence upon the minds of the common people, and they had almost universal melancholy apprehensions of some dreadful calamity and judgement coming upon the city; and this principally from the sight of this comet, and the little alarm that was given in December by two people dying at St Giles's, as above.

The apprehensions of the people were likewise strangely increased by the error of the times; in which, I think, the people, from what principle I cannot imagine, were more addicted to prophecies and astrological conjurations, dreams, and old wives' tales than ever they were before or since. Whether this unhappy temper was originally raised by the follies of some people who got money by it—that is to say, by printing predictions and prognostications—I know not; but certain it is, books frighted them terribly, such as Lilly's Almanack, Gadbury's Astrological Predictions, Poor Robin's Almanack, and the like; also several pretended religious books, one entitled, Come out of her, my People, lest you be Partaker of her Plagues; another called, Fair Warning; another, Britain's Remembrancer; and many such, all, or most part of which, foretold, directly or covertly, the ruin of the city. Nay, some were so enthusiastically bold as to run about the streets with their oral predictions, pretending they were sent to preach to the city; and one in particular, who, like Jonah to Nineveh, cried in the streets, 'Yet forty days, and London shall be destroyed.' I will not be positive whether he said yet forty days or yet a few days. Another ran about naked, except a pair of drawers about his waist, crying day and night, like a man that Josephus mentions, who cried, 'Woe to Jerusalem!' a little before the destruction of that city. So this poor naked creature cried, 'Oh, the great and the dreadful God!' and said no more, but repeated those words continually, with a voice and countenance full of horror, a swift pace; and nobody could ever find him to stop or rest, or take any sustenance, at least that ever I could hear of. I met this poor creature several times in the streets, and would have spoken to him, but he would not enter into speech with me or any one else, but held on his dismal cries continually.

These things terrified the people to the last degree, and especially when two or three times, as I have mentioned already, they found one or two in the bills dead of the plague at St Giles's.

Next to these public things were the dreams of old women, or, I should say, the interpretation of old women upon other people's dreams; and these put abundance of people even out of their wits. Some heard voices warning them to be gone, for that there would be such a plague in London, so that the living would not be able to bury the dead. Others saw apparitions in the air; and I must be allowed to say of both, I hope without breach of charity, that they heard voices that never spake, and saw sights that never appeared; but the imagination of the people was really turned wayward and possessed. And no wonder, if they who were poring continually at the clouds saw shapes and figures, representations and appearances, which had nothing in them but air, and vapour. Here they told us they saw a flaming sword held in a hand coming out of a cloud, with a point hanging directly over the city; there they saw hearses and coffins in the air carrying to be buried; and there again, heaps of dead bodies lying unburied, and the like, just as the imagination of the poor terrified people furnished them with matter to work upon. So hypochondriac fancies represent Ships, armies, battles in the firmament; Till steady eyes the exhalations solve, And all to its first matter, cloud, resolve.

I could fill this account with the strange relations such people gave every day of what they had seen; and every one was so positive of their having seen what they pretended to see, that there was no contradicting them without breach of friendship, or being accounted rude and unmannerly on the one hand, and profane and impenetrable on the other. One time before the plague was begun (otherwise than as I have said in St Giles's), I think it was in March, seeing a crowd of people in the street, I joined with them to satisfy my curiosity, and found them all staring up into the air to see what a woman told them appeared plain to her, which was an angel clothed in white, with a fiery sword in his hand, waving it or brandishing it over his head. She described every part of the figure to the life, showed them the motion and the form, and the poor people came into it so eagerly, and with so much readiness; 'Yes, I see it all plainly,' says one; 'there's the sword as plain as can be.' Another saw the angel. One saw his very face, and cried out what a glorious creature he was! One saw one thing, and one another. I looked as earnestly as the rest, but perhaps not with so much willingness to be imposed upon; and I said, indeed, that I could see nothing but a white cloud, bright on one side by the shining of the sun upon the other part. The woman endeavoured to show it me, but could not make me confess that I saw it, which, indeed, if I had I must have lied. But the woman, turning upon me, looked in my face, and fancied I laughed, in which her imagination deceived her too, for I really did not laugh, but was very seriously reflecting how the poor people were terrified by the force of their own imagination. However, she turned from me, called me profane fellow, and a scoffer; told me that it was a time of God's anger, and dreadful judgements were approaching, and that despisers such as I should wander and perish.

The people about her seemed disgusted as well as she; and I found there was no persuading them that I did not laugh at them, and that I should be rather mobbed by them than be able to undeceive them. So I left them; and this appearance passed for as real as the blazing star itself.

Another encounter I had in the open day also; and this was in going through a narrow passage from Petty France into Bishopsgate Churchyard, by a row of alms-houses. There are two churchyards to Bishopsgate church or parish; one we go over to pass from the place called Petty France into Bishopsgate Street, coming out just by the church door; the other is on the side of the narrow passage where the alms-houses are on the left; and a dwarf-wall with a palisado on it on the right hand, and the city wall on the other side more to the right.

In this narrow passage stands a man looking through between the palisadoes into the burying-place, and as many people as the narrowness of the passage would admit to stop, without hindering the passage of others, and he was talking mightily eagerly to them, and pointing now to one place, then to another, and affirming that he saw a ghost walking upon such a gravestone there. He described the shape, the posture, and the movement of it so exactly that it was the greatest matter of amazement to him in the world that everybody did not see it as well as he. On a sudden he would cry, 'There it is; now it comes this way.' Then, 'Tis turned back'; till at length he persuaded the people into so firm a belief of it, that one fancied he saw it, and another fancied he saw it; and thus he came every day making a strange hubbub, considering it was in so narrow a passage, till Bishopsgate clock struck eleven, and then the ghost would seem to start, and, as if he were called away, disappeared on a sudden.

I looked earnestly every way, and at the very moment that this man directed, but could not see the least appearance of anything; but so positive was this poor man, that he gave the people the vapours in abundance, and sent them away trembling and frighted, till at length few people that knew of it cared to go through that passage, and hardly anybody by night on any account whatever.

This ghost, as the poor man affirmed, made signs to the houses, and to the ground, and to the people, plainly intimating, or else they so understanding it, that abundance of the people should come to be buried in that churchyard, as indeed happened; but that he saw such aspects I must acknowledge I never believed, nor could I see anything of it myself, though I looked most earnestly to see it, if possible.

These things serve to show how far the people were really overcome with delusions; and as they had a notion of the approach of a visitation, all their predictions ran upon a most dreadful plague, which should lay the whole city, and even the kingdom, waste, and should destroy almost all the nation, both man and beast.

To this, as I said before, the astrologers added stories of the conjunctions of planets in a malignant manner and with a mischievous influence, one of which conjunctions was to happen, and did happen, in October, and the other in November; and they filled the people's heads with predictions on these signs of the heavens, intimating that those conjunctions foretold drought, famine, and pestilence. In the two first of them, however, they were entirely mistaken, for we had no droughty season, but in the beginning of the year a hard frost, which lasted from December almost to March, and after that moderate weather, rather warm than hot, with refreshing winds, and, in short, very seasonable weather, and also several very great rains.

Some endeavours were used to suppress the printing of such books as terrified the people, and to frighten the dispersers of them, some of whom were taken up; but nothing was done in it, as I am informed, the Government being unwilling to exasperate the people, who were, as I may say, all out of their wits already.

Neither can I acquit those ministers that in their sermons rather sank than lifted up the hearts of their hearers. Many of them no doubt did it for the strengthening the resolution of the people, and especially for quickening them to repentance, but it certainly answered not their end, at least not in proportion to the injury it did another way; and indeed, as God Himself through the whole Scriptures rather draws to Him by invitations and calls to turn to Him and live, than drives us by terror and amazement, so I must confess I thought the ministers should have done also, imitating our blessed Lord and Master in this, that His whole Gospel is full of declarations from heaven of God's mercy, and His readiness to receive penitents and forgive them, complaining, 'Ye will not come unto Me that ye may have life', and that therefore His Gospel is called the Gospel of Peace and the Gospel of Grace.

But we had some good men, and that of all persuasions and opinions, whose discourses were full of terror, who spoke nothing but dismal things; and as they brought the people together with a kind of horror, sent them away in tears, prophesying nothing but evil tidings, terrifying the people with the apprehensions of being utterly destroyed, not guiding them, at least not enough, to cry to heaven for mercy.

It was, indeed, a time of very unhappy breaches among us in matters of religion. Innumerable sects and divisions and separate opinions prevailed among the people. The Church of England was restored, indeed, with the restoration of the monarchy, about four years before; but the ministers and preachers of the Presbyterians and Independents, and of all the other sorts of professions, had begun to gather separate societies and erect altar against altar, and all those had their meetings for worship apart, as they have now, but not so many then, the Dissenters being not thoroughly formed into a body as they are since; and those congregations which were thus gathered together were yet but few. And even those that were, the Government did not allow, but endeavoured to suppress them and shut up their meetings.

But the visitation reconciled them again, at least for a time, and many of the best and most valuable ministers and preachers of the Dissenters were suffered to go into the churches where the incumbents were fled away, as many were, not being able to stand it; and the people flocked without distinction to hear them preach, not much inquiring who or what opinion they were of. But after the sickness was over, that spirit of charity abated; and every church being again supplied with their own ministers, or others presented where the minister was dead, things returned to their old channel again.

One mischief always introduces another. These terrors and apprehensions of the people led them into a thousand weak, foolish, and wicked things, which they wanted not a sort of people really wicked to encourage them to: and this was running about to fortune-tellers, cunning-men, and astrologers to know their fortune, or, as it is vulgarly expressed, to have their fortunes told them, their nativities calculated, and the like; and this folly presently made the town swarm with a wicked generation of pretenders to magic, to the black art, as they called it, and I know not what; nay, to a thousand worse dealings with the devil than they were really guilty of. And this trade grew so open and so generally practised that it became common to have signs and inscriptions set up at doors: 'Here lives a fortune-teller', 'Here lives an astrologer', 'Here you may have your nativity calculated', and the like; and Friar Bacon's brazen-head, which was the usual sign of these people's dwellings, was to be seen almost in every street, or else the sign of Mother Shipton, or of Merlin's head, and the like.

With what blind, absurd, and ridiculous stuff these oracles of the devil pleased and satisfied the people I really know not, but certain it is that innumerable attendants crowded about their doors every day. And if but a grave fellow in a velvet jacket, a band, and a black coat, which was the habit those quack-conjurers generally went in, was but seen in the streets the people would follow them in crowds, and ask them questions as they went along.

I need not mention what a horrid delusion this was, or what it tended to; but there was no remedy for it till the plague itself put an end to it all—and, I suppose, cleared the town of most of those calculators themselves. One mischief was, that if the poor people asked these mock astrologers whether there would be a plague or no, they all agreed in general to answer 'Yes', for that kept up their trade. And had the people not been kept in a fright about that, the wizards would presently have been rendered useless, and their craft had been at an end. But they always talked to them of such-and-such influences of the stars, of the conjunctions of such-and-such planets, which must necessarily bring sickness and distempers, and consequently the plague. And some had the assurance to tell them the plague was begun already, which was too true, though they that said so knew nothing of the matter.

The ministers, to do them justice, and preachers of most sorts that were serious and understanding persons, thundered against these and other wicked practices, and exposed the folly as well as the wickedness of them together, and the most sober and judicious people despised and abhorred them. But it was impossible to make any impression upon the middling people and the working labouring poor. Their fears were predominant over all their passions, and they threw away their money in a most distracted manner upon those whimsies. Maid-servants especially, and men-servants, were the chief of their customers, and their question generally was, after the first demand of 'Will there be a plague?' I say, the next question was, 'Oh, sir I for the Lord's sake, what will become of me? Will my mistress keep me, or will she turn me off? Will she stay here, or will she go into the country? And if she goes into the country, will she take me with her, or leave me here to be starved and undone?' And the like of menservants.

The truth is, the case of poor servants was very dismal, as I shall have occasion to mention again by-and-by, for it was apparent a prodigious number of them would be turned away, and it was so. And of them abundance perished, and particularly of those that these false prophets had flattered with hopes that they should be continued in their services, and carried with their masters and mistresses into the country; and had not public charity provided for these poor creatures, whose number was exceeding great and in all cases of this nature must be so, they would have been in the worst condition of any people in the city.

These things agitated the minds of the common people for many months, while the first apprehensions were upon them, and while the plague was not, as I may say, yet broken out. But I must also not forget that the more serious part of the inhabitants behaved after another manner. The Government encouraged their devotion, and appointed public prayers and days of fasting and humiliation, to make public confession of sin and implore the mercy of God to avert the dreadful judgement which hung over their heads; and it is not to be expressed with what alacrity the people of all persuasions embraced the occasion; how they flocked to the churches and meetings, and they were all so thronged that there was often no coming near, no, not to the very doors of the largest churches. Also there were daily prayers appointed morning and evening at several churches, and days of private praying at other places; at all which the people attended, I say, with an uncommon devotion. Several private families also, as well of one opinion as of another, kept family fasts, to which they admitted their near relations only. So that, in a word, those people who were really serious and religious applied themselves in a truly Christian manner to the proper work of repentance and humiliation, as a Christian people ought to do.

Again, the public showed that they would bear their share in these things; the very Court, which was then gay and luxurious, put on a face of just concern for the public danger. All the plays and interludes which, after the manner of the French Court, had been set up, and began to increase among us, were forbid to act; the gaming-tables, public dancing-rooms, and music-houses, which multiplied and began to debauch the manners of the people, were shut up and suppressed; and the jack-puddings, merry-andrews, puppet-shows, rope-dancers, and such-like doings, which had bewitched the poor common people, shut up their shops, finding indeed no trade; for the minds of the people were agitated with other things, and a kind of sadness and horror at these things sat upon the countenances even of the common people. Death was before their eyes, and everybody began to think of their graves, not of mirth and diversions.

But even those wholesome reflections—which, rightly managed, would have most happily led the people to fall upon their knees, make confession of their sins, and look up to their merciful Saviour for pardon, imploring His compassion on them in such a time of their distress, by which we might have been as a second Nineveh—had a quite contrary extreme in the common people, who, ignorant and stupid in their reflections as they were brutishly wicked and thoughtless before, were now led by their fright to extremes of folly; and, as I have said before, that they ran to conjurers and witches, and all sorts of deceivers, to know what should become of them (who fed their fears, and kept them always alarmed and awake on purpose to delude them and pick their pockets), so they were as mad upon their running after quacks and mountebanks, and every practising old woman, for medicines and remedies; storing themselves with such multitudes of pills, potions, and preservatives, as they were called, that they not only spent their money but even poisoned themselves beforehand for fear of the poison of the infection; and prepared their bodies for the plague, instead of preserving them against it. On the other hand it is incredible and scarce to be imagined, how the posts of houses and corners of streets were plastered over with doctors' bills and papers of ignorant fellows, quacking and tampering in physic, and inviting the people to come to them for remedies, which was generally set off with such flourishes as these, viz.: 'Infallible preventive pills against the plague.' 'Neverfailing preservatives against the infection.' 'Sovereign cordials against the corruption of the air.' 'Exact regulations for the conduct of the body in case of an infection.' 'Anti-pestilential pills.' 'Incomparable drink against the plague, never found out before.' 'An universal remedy for the plague.' 'The only true plague water.' 'The royal antidote against all kinds of infection';—and such a number more that I cannot reckon up; and if I could, would fill a book of themselves to set them down.

Others set up bills to summon people to their lodgings for directions and advice in the case of infection. These had specious titles also, such as these:—

'An eminent High Dutch physician, newly come over from Holland, where he resided during all the time of the great plague last year in Amsterdam, and cured multitudes of people that actually had the plague upon them.'

'An Italian gentlewoman just arrived from Naples, having a choice secret to prevent infection, which she found out by her great experience, and did wonderful cures with it in the late plague there, wherein there died 20,000 in one day.'

'An ancient gentlewoman, having practised with great success in the late plague in this city, anno 1636, gives her advice only to the female sex. To be spoken with,' &c.

'An experienced physician, who has long studied the doctrine of antidotes against all sorts of poison and infection, has, after forty years' practice, arrived to such skill as may, with God's blessing, direct persons how to prevent their being touched by any contagious distemper whatsoever. He directs the poor gratis.'

I take notice of these by way of specimen. I could give you two or three dozen of the like and yet have abundance left behind. 'Tis sufficient from these to apprise any one of the humour of those times, and how a set of thieves and pickpockets not only robbed and cheated the poor people of their money, but poisoned their bodies with odious and fatal preparations; some with mercury, and some with other things as bad, perfectly remote from the thing pretended to, and rather hurtful than serviceable to the body in case an infection followed.

I cannot omit a subtility of one of those quack operators, with which he gulled the poor people to crowd about him, but did nothing for them without money. He had, it seems, added to his bills, which he gave about the streets, this advertisement in capital letters, viz., 'He gives advice to the poor for nothing.'

Abundance of poor people came to him accordingly, to whom he made a great many fine speeches, examined them of the state of their health and of the constitution of their bodies, and told them many good things for them to do, which were of no great moment. But the issue and conclusion of all was, that he had a preparation which if they took such a quantity of every morning, he would pawn his life they should never have the plague; no, though they lived in the house with people that were infected. This made the people all resolve to have it; but then the price of that was so much, I think 'twas half-a-crown. 'But, sir,' says one poor woman, 'I am a poor almswoman and am kept by the parish, and your bills say you give the poor your help for nothing.' 'Ay, good woman,' says the doctor, 'so I do, as I published there. I give my advice to the poor for nothing, but not my physic.' 'Alas, sir!' says she, 'that is a snare laid for the poor, then; for you give them advice for nothing; that is to say, you advise them gratis, to buy your physic for their money; so does every shop-keeper with his wares.' Here the woman began to give him ill words, and stood at his door all that day, telling her tale to all the people that came, till the doctor finding she turned away his customers, was obliged to call her upstairs again, and give her his box of physic for nothing, which perhaps, too, was good for nothing when she had it.

But to return to the people, whose confusions fitted them to be imposed upon by all sorts of pretenders and by every mountebank. There is no doubt but these quacking sort of fellows raised great gains out of the miserable people, for we daily found the crowds that ran after them were infinitely greater, and their doors were more thronged than those of Dr Brooks, Dr Upton, Dr Hodges, Dr Berwick, or any, though the most famous men of the time. I And I was told that some of them got five pounds a day by their physic.

But there was still another madness beyond all this, which may serve to give an idea of the distracted humour of the poor people at that time: and this was their following a worse sort of deceivers than any of these; for these petty thieves only deluded them to pick their pockets and get their money, in which their wickedness, whatever it was, lay chiefly on the side of the deceivers, not upon the deceived. But in this part I am going to mention, it lay chiefly in the people deceived, or equally in both; and this was in wearing charms, philtres, exorcisms, amulets, and I know not what preparations, to fortify the body with them against the plague; as if the plague was not the hand of God, but a kind of possession of an evil spirit, and that it was to be kept off with crossings, signs of the zodiac, papers tied up with so many knots, and certain words or figures written on them, as particularly the word Abracadabra, formed in triangle or pyramid, thus:—

ABRACADABRA	
ABRACADABR	Others had the Jesuits'
ABRACADAB	mark in a cross:
ABRACADA	I H
ABRACAD	S.
ABRACA	
ABRAC	Others nothing but this
ABRA	mark, thus:
ABR	
AB	* *
A	{*}

I might spend a great deal of time in my exclamations against the follies, and indeed the wickedness, of those things, in a time of such danger, in a matter of such consequences as this, of a national infection. But my memorandums of these things relate rather to take notice only of the fact, and mention only that it was so. How the poor people found the insufficiency of those things, and how many of them were afterwards carried away in the dead-carts and thrown into the common graves of every parish with these hellish charms and trumpery hanging about their necks, remains to be spoken of as we go along.

All this was the effect of the hurry the people were in, after the first notion of the plaque being at hand was among them, and which may be said to be from about Michaelmas 1664, but more particularly after the two men died in St Giles's in the beginning of December; and again, after another alarm in February. For when the plague evidently spread itself, they soon began to see the folly of trusting to those unperforming creatures who had gulled them of their money; and then their fears worked another way, namely, to amazement and stupidity, not knowing what course to take or what to do either to help or relieve themselves. But they ran about from one neighbour's house to another, and even in the streets from one door to another, with repeated cries of, 'Lord, have mercy upon us! What shall we do?'

Indeed, the poor people were to be pitied in one particular thing in which they had little or no relief, and which I desire to mention with a serious awe and reflection, which perhaps every one that reads this may not relish; namely, that whereas death now began not, as we may say, to hover over every one's head only, but to look into their houses and chambers and stare in their faces. Though there might be some stupidity and dulness of the mind (and there was so, a great deal), yet there was a great deal of just alarm sounded into the very inmost soul, if I may so say, of others. Many consciences were awakened; many hard hearts melted into tears; many a penitent confession was made of crimes long concealed. It would wound the soul of any Christian to have heard the dying groans of many a despairing creature, and none durst come near to comfort them. Many a robbery, many a murder, was then confessed aloud, and nobody surviving to record the accounts of it. People might be heard, even into the streets as we passed along, calling upon God for mercy through Jesus Christ, and saying, 'I have been a thief, 'I have been an adulterer', 'I have been a murderer', and the like, and none durst stop to make the least inquiry into such things or to administer comfort to the poor creatures that in the anguish both of soul and body thus cried out. Some of the ministers did visit the sick at first and for a little while, but it was not to be done. It would have been present death to have gone into some houses. The very buriers of the dead, who were the hardenedest creatures in town, were sometimes beaten back and so terrified that they durst not go into houses where the whole families were swept away together, and where the circumstances were more particularly horrible, as some were; but this was, indeed, at the first heat of the distemper.

Time inured them to it all, and they ventured everywhere afterwards without hesitation, as I shall have occasion to mention at large hereafter.

I am supposing now the plague to be begun, as I have said, and that the magistrates began to take the condition of the people into their serious consideration. What they did as to the regulation of the inhabitants and of infected families, I shall speak to by itself; but as to the affair of health, it is proper to mention it here that, having seen the foolish humour of the people in running after quacks and mountebanks, wizards and fortune-tellers, which they did as above, even to madness, the Lord Mayor, a very sober and religious gentleman, appointed physicians and surgeons for relief of the poor—I mean the diseased poor and in particular ordered the College of Physicians to publish directions for cheap remedies for the poor, in all the circumstances of the distemper. This, indeed, was one of the most charitable and judicious things that could be done at that time, for this drove the people from haunting the doors of every disperser of bills, and from taking down blindly and without consideration poison for physic and death instead of life.

This direction of the physicians was done by a consultation of the whole College; and, as it was particularly calculated for the use of the poor and for cheap medicines, it was made public, so that everybody might see it, and copies were given gratis to all that desired it. But as it is public, and to be seen on all occasions, I need not give the reader of this the trouble of it.

I shall not be supposed to lessen the authority or capacity of the physicians when I say that the violence of the distemper, when it came to its extremity, was like the fire the next year. The fire, which consumed what the plague could not touch, defied all the application of remedies; the fire-engines were broken, the buckets thrown away, and the power of man was baffled and brought to an end. So the Plague defied all medicines; the very physicians were seized with it, with their preservatives in their mouths; and men went about prescribing to others and telling them what to do till the tokens were upon them, and they dropped down dead, destroyed by that very enemy they directed others to oppose. This was the case of several physicians, even some of them the most eminent, and of several of the most skilful surgeons. Abundance of quacks too died, who had the folly to trust to their own medicines, which they must needs be conscious to themselves were good for nothing, and who rather ought, like other sorts of thieves, to have run away, sensible of their guilt, from the justice that they could not but expect should punish them as they knew they had deserved.

Not that it is any derogation from the labour or application of the physicians to say they fell in the common calamity; nor is it so intended by me; it rather is to their praise that they ventured their lives so far as even to lose them in the service of mankind. They endeavoured to do good, and to save the lives of others. But we were not to expect that the physicians could stop God's judgements, or prevent a distemper eminently armed from heaven from executing the errand it was sent about.

Doubtless, the physicians assisted many by their skill, and by their prudence and applications, to the saving of their lives and restoring their health. But it is not lessening their character or their skill, to say they could not cure those that had the tokens upon them, or those who were mortally infected before the physicians were sent for, as was frequently the case.

It remains to mention now what public measures were taken by the magistrates for the general safety, and to prevent the spreading of the distemper, when it first broke out. I shall have frequent occasion to speak of the prudence of the magistrates, their charity, their vigilance for the poor, and for preserving good order, furnishing provisions, and the like, when the plague was increased, as it afterwards was. But I am now upon the order and regulations they published for the government of infected families.

I mentioned above shutting of houses up; and it is needful to say something particularly to that, for this part of the history of the plague is very melancholy, but the most grievous story must be told.

About June the Lord Mayor of London and the Court of Aldermen, as I have said, began more particularly to concern themselves for the regulation of the city.

The justices of Peace for Middlesex, by direction of the Secretary of State, had begun to shut up houses in the parishes of St Giles-in-the-Fields, St Martin, St Clement Danes, &c., and it was with good success; for in several streets where the plague broke out, upon strict guarding the houses that were infected, and taking care to bury those that died immediately after they were known to be dead, the plague ceased in those streets. It was also observed that the plague decreased sooner in those parishes after they had been visited to the full than it did in the parishes of Bishopsgate, Shoreditch, Aldgate, Whitechappel, Stepney, and others; the early care taken in that manner being a great means to the putting a check to it.

This shutting up of houses was a method first taken, as I understand, in the plague which happened in 1603, at the coming of King James the First to the crown; and the power of shutting people up in their own houses was granted by Act of Parliament, entitled, 'An Act for the charitable Relief and Ordering of Persons infected with the Plague'; on which Act of Parliament the Lord Mayor and aldermen of the city of London founded the order they made at this time, and which took place the 1st of July 1665, when the numbers infected within the city were but few, the last bill for the ninety-two parishes being but four; and some houses having been shut up in the city, and some people being removed to the pest-house beyond Bunhill Fields, in the way to Islington,—I say, by these means, when there died near one thousand a week in the whole, the number in the city was but twenty-eight, and the city was preserved more healthy in proportion than any other place all the time of the infection.

These orders of my Lord Mayor's were published, as I have said, the latter end of June, and took place from the 1st of July, and were as follows, viz.:—

ORDERS CONCEIVED AND PUBLISHED BY THE LORD MAYOR AND ALDERMEN OF THE CITY OF LONDON CONCERNING THE INFECTION OF THE PLAGUE, 1665.

'WHEREAS in the reign of our late Sovereign King James, of happy memory, an Act was made for the charitable relief and ordering of persons infected with the plague, whereby authority was given to justices of the peace, mayors, bailiffs, and other head-officers to appoint within their several limits examiners, searchers, watchmen, keepers, and buriers for the persons and places infected, and to minister unto them oaths for the performance of their offices. And the same statute did also authorise the giving of other directions, as unto them for the present necessity should seem good in their directions. It is now, upon special consideration, thought very expedient for preventing and avoiding of infection of sickness (if it shall so please Almighty God) that these officers following be appointed, and these orders hereafter duly observed.

Examiners to be appointed in every Parish.

'First, it is thought requisite, and so ordered, that in every parish there be one, two, or more persons of good sort and credit chosen and appointed by the alderman, his deputy, and common council of every ward, by the name of examiners, to continue in that office the space of two months at least. And if any fit person so appointed shall refuse to undertake the same, the said parties so refusing to be committed to prison until they shall conform themselves accordingly.

The Examiner's Office.

'That these examiners he sworn by the aldermen to inquire and learn from time to time what houses in every parish be visited, and what persons be sick, and of what diseases, as near as they can inform themselves; and upon doubt in that case, to command restraint of access until it appear what the disease shall prove. And if they find any person sick of the infection, to give order to the constable that the house be shut up; and if the constable shall be found remiss or negligent, to give present notice thereof to the alderman of the ward.

Watchmen.

'That to every infected house there be appointed two watchmen, one for every day, and the other for the night; and that these watchmen have a special care that no person go in or out of such infected houses whereof they have the charge, upon pain of severe punishment. And the said watchmen to do such further offices as the sick house shall need and require: and if the watchman be sent upon any business, to lock up the house and take the key with him; and the watchman by day to attend until ten of the clock at night, and the watchman by night until six in the morning.

Searchers.

'That there be a special care to appoint women searchers in every parish, such as are of honest reputation, and of the best sort as can be got in this kind; and these to be sworn to make due search and true report to the utmost of their knowledge whether the persons whose bodies they are appointed to search do die of the infection, or of what other diseases, as near as they can. And that the physicians who shall be appointed for cure and prevention of the infection do call before them the said searchers who are, or shall be, appointed for the several parishes under their respective cares, to the end they may consider whether they are fitly qualified for that employment, and charge them from time to time as they shall see cause, if they appear defective in their duties.

'That no searcher during this time of visitation be permitted to use any public work or employment, or keep any shop or stall, or be employed as a laundress, or in any other common employment whatsoever.

Chirurgeons.

'For better assistance of the searchers, forasmuch as there hath been heretofore great abuse in misreporting the disease, to the further spreading of the infection, it is therefore ordered that there be chosen and appointed able and discreet chirurgeons, besides those that do already belong to the pest-house, amongst whom the city and Liberties to be quartered as the places lie most apt and convenient; and every of these to have one quarter for his limit; and the said chirurgeons in every of their limits to join with the searchers for the view of the body, to the end there may be a true report made of the disease.

'And further, that the said chirurgeons shall visit and search such-like persons as shall either send for them or be named and directed unto them by the examiners of every parish, and inform themselves of the disease of the said parties.

'And forasmuch as the said chirurgeons are to be sequestered from all other cures, and kept only to this disease of the infection, it is ordered that every of the said chirurgeons shall have twelve-pence a body searched by them, to be paid out of the goods of the party searched, if he be able, or otherwise by the parish.

Nurse-keepers.

'If any nurse-keeper shall remove herself out of any infected house before twenty-eight days after the decease of any person dying of the infection, the house to which the said nurse-keeper doth so remove herself shall be shut up until the said twenty-eight days be expired.'

ORDERS CONCERNING INFECTED HOUSES AND PERSONS SICK OF THE PLAGUE.

Notice to be given of the Sickness.

'The master of every house, as soon as any one in his house complaineth, either of blotch or purple, or swelling in any part of his body, or falleth otherwise dangerously sick, without apparent cause of some other disease, shall give knowledge thereof to the examiner of health within two hours after the said sign shall appear.

Sequestration of the Sick.

'As soon as any man shall be found by this examiner, chirurgeon, or searcher to be sick of the plague, he shall the same night be sequestered in the same house; and in case he be so sequestered, then though he afterwards die not, the house wherein he sickened should be shut up for a month, after the use of the due preservatives taken by the rest.

Airing the Stuff.

'For sequestration of the goods and stuff of the infection, their bedding and apparel and hangings of chambers must be well aired with fire and such perfumes as are requisite within the infected house before they be taken again to use. This to be done by the appointment of an examiner.

Shutting up of the House.

'If any person shall have visited any man known to be infected of the plague, or entered willingly into any known infected house, being not allowed, the house wherein he inhabiteth shall be shut up for certain days by the examiner's direction.

None to be removed out of infected Houses, but, &C.

'Item, that none be removed out of the house where he falleth sick of the infection into any other house in the city (except it be to the pest-house or a tent, or unto some such house which the owner of the said visited house holdeth in his own hands and occupieth by his own servants); and so as security be given to the parish whither such remove is made, that the attendance and charge about the said visited persons shall be observed and charged in all the particularities before expressed, without any cost of that parish to which any such remove shall happen to be made, and this remove to be done by night. And it shall be lawful to any person that hath two houses to remove either his sound or his infected people to his spare house at his choice, so as, if he send away first his sound, he not after send thither his sick, nor again unto the sick the sound; and that the same which he sendeth be for one week at the least shut up and secluded from company, for fear of some infection at the first not appearing.

Burial of the Dead.

'That the burial of the dead by this visitation be at most convenient hours, always either before sun-rising or after sun-setting, with the privity of the churchwardens or constable, and not otherwise; and that no neighbours nor friends be suffered to accompany the corpse to church, or to enter the house visited, upon pain of having his house shut up or be imprisoned.

'And that no corpse dying of infection shall be buried, or remain in any church in time of common prayer, sermon, or lecture. And that no children be suffered at time of burial of any corpse in any church, churchyard, or burying-place to come near the corpse, coffin, or grave. And that all the graves shall be at least six feet deep.

'And further, all public assemblies at other burials are to be foreborne during the continuance of this visitation.

No infected Stuff to be uttered.

'That no clothes, stuff, bedding, or garments be suffered to be carried or conveyed out of any infected houses, and that the criers and carriers abroad of bedding or old apparel to be sold or pawned be utterly prohibited and restrained, and no brokers of bedding or old apparel be permitted to make any outward show, or hang forth on their stalls, shop-boards, or windows, towards any street, lane, common way, or passage, any old bedding or apparel to be sold, upon pain of imprisonment. And if any broker or other person shall buy any bedding, apparel, or other stuff out of any infected house within two months after the infection hath been there, his house shall be shut up as infected, and so shall continue shut up twenty days at the least.

No Person to be conveyed out of any infected House.

'If any person visited do fortune, by negligent looking unto, or by any other means, to come or be conveyed from a place infected to any other place, the parish from whence such party hath come or been conveyed, upon notice thereof given, shall at their charge cause the said party so visited and escaped to be carried and brought back again by night, and the parties in this case offending to be punished at the direction of the alderman of the ward, and the house of the receiver of such visited person to be shut up for twenty days.

Every visited House to be marked.

'That every house visited be marked with a red cross of a foot long in the middle of the door, evident to be seen, and with these usual printed words, that is to say, "Lord, have mercy upon us," to be set close over the same cross, there to continue until lawful opening of the same house.

Every visited House to be watched.

'That the constables see every house shut up, and to be attended with watchmen, which may keep them in, and minister necessaries unto them at their own charges, if they be able, or at the common charge, if they are unable; the shutting up to be for the space of four weeks after all be whole.

'That precise order to be taken that the searchers, chirurgeons, keepers, and buriers are not to pass the streets without holding a red rod or wand of three feet in length in their hands, open and evident to be seen, and are not to go into any other house than into their own, or into that whereunto they are directed or sent for; but to forbear and abstain from company, especially when they have been lately used in any such business or attendance.

Inmates.

'That where several inmate,-c are in one and the same house, and any person in that house happens to be infected, no other person or family of such house shall be suffered to remove him or themselves without a certificate from the examiners of health of that parish; or in default thereof, the house whither he or they so remove shall be shut up as in case of visitation.

Hackney-Coaches.

'That care be taken of hackney-coachmen, that they may not (as some of them have been observed to do after carrying of infected persons to the pest-house and other places) be admitted to common use till their coaches be well aired, and have stood unemployed by the space of five or six days after such service.'

ORDERS FOR CLEANSING AND KEEPING OF THE STREETS SWEET.

The Streets to be kept Clean.

'First, it is thought necessary, and so ordered, that every householder do cause the street to be daily prepared before his door, and so to keep it clean swept all the week long.

That Rakers take it from out the Houses.

'That the sweeping and filth of houses be daily carried away by the rakers, and that the raker shall give notice of his coming by the blowing of a horn, as hitherto hath been done.

Laystalls to be made far off from the City.

'That the laystalls be removed as far as may be out of the city and common passages, and that no nightman or other be suffered to empty a vault into any garden near about the city.

Care to be had of unwholesome Fish or Flesh, and of musty Corn.

'That special care be taken that no stinking fish, or unwholesome flesh, or musty corn, or other corrupt fruits of what sort soever, be suffered to be sold about the city, or any part of the same.

'That the brewers and tippling-houses he looked unto for musty and unwholesome casks.

'That no hogs, dogs, or cats, or tame pigeons, or conies, be suffered to be kept within any part of the city, or any swine to be or stray in the streets or lanes, but that such swine be impounded by the beadle or any other officer, and the owner punished according to Act of Common Council, and that the dogs be killed by the dog-killers appointed for that purpose.'

ORDERS CONCERNING LOOSE PERSONS AND IDLE ASSEMBLIES.

Beggars.

'Forasmuch as nothing is more complained of than the multitude of rogues and wandering beggars that swarm in every place about the city, being a great cause of the spreading of the infection, and will not be avoided, notwithstanding any orders that have been given to the contrary: It is therefore now ordered, that such constables, and others whom this matter may any way concern, take special care that no wandering beggars be suffered in the streets of this city in any fashion or manner whatsoever, upon the penalty provided by the law, to be duly and severely executed upon them.

Plays.

'That all plays, bear-baitings, games, singing of ballads, buckler-play, or such-like causes of assemblies of people be utterly prohibited, and the parties offending severely punished by every alderman in his ward.

Feasting prohibited.

'That all public feasting, and particularly by the companies of this city, and dinners at taverns, ale-houses, and other places of common entertainment, be forborne till further order and allowance; and that the money thereby spared be preserved and employed for the benefit and relief of the poor visited with the infection.

Tippling-houses.

'That disorderly tippling in taverns, ale-houses, coffee-houses, and cellars be severely looked unto, as the common sin of this time and greatest occasion of dispersing the plague. And that no company or person be suffered to remain or come into any tavern, ale-house, or coffee-house to drink after nine of the clock in the evening, according to the ancient law and custom of this city, upon the penalties ordained in that behalf.

'And for the better execution of these orders, and such other rules and directions as, upon further consideration, shall be found needful: It is ordered and enjoined that the aldermen, deputies, and common councilmen shall meet together weekly, once, twice, thrice or oftener (as cause shall require), at some one general place accustomed in their respective wards (being clear from infection of the plague), to consult how the said orders may be duly put in execution; not intending that any dwelling in or near places infected shall come to the said meeting while their coming may be doubtful. And the said aldermen, and deputies, and common councilmen in their several wards may put in execution any other good orders that by them at their said meetings shall be conceived and devised for preservation of his Majesty's subjects from the infection.

'SIR JOHN LAWRENCE, Lord Mayor.
SIR GEORGE WATERMAN
SIR CHARLES DOE, Sheriffs.'

I need not say that these orders extended only to such places as were within the Lord Mayor's jurisdiction, so it is requisite to observe that the justices of Peace within those parishes and places as were called the Hamlets and out-parts took the same method. As I remember, the orders for shutting up of houses did not take Place so soon on our side, because, as I said before, the plague did not reach to these eastern parts of the town at least, nor begin to be very violent, till the beginning of August. For example, the whole bill from the 11th to the 18th of July was 1761, yet there died but 71 of the plague in all those parishes we call the Tower Hamlets, and they were as follows:—

-		The next week was thus:	And to the 1st of Aug. thus:
Aldgate	14	34	65
Stepney	33	58	76
Whitechappel	21	48	79
St Katherine, Tower	2	4	4
Trinity, Minories	1	1	4
	—	—	—
	71	145	228

It was indeed coming on amain, for the burials that same week were in the next adjoining parishes thus:—

		The next week prodigiously increased, as:	To the 1st of Aug. thus:
St Leonard's, Shoreditch	64	84	110
St Botolph's, Bishopsgate	65	105	116
St Giles's, Cripplegate	213	421	554
	—	—	—
	342	610	780

This shutting up of houses was at first counted a very cruel and unchristian method, and the poor people so confined made bitter lamentations. Complaints of the severity of it were also daily brought to my Lord Mayor, of houses causelessly (and some maliciously) shut up. I cannot say; but upon inquiry many that complained so loudly were found in a condition to be continued; and others again, inspection being made upon the sick person, and the sickness not appearing infectious, or if uncertain, yet on his being content to be carried to the pest-house, were released.

It is true that the locking up the doors of people's houses, and setting a watchman there night and day to prevent their stirring out or any coming to them, when perhaps the sound people in the family might have escaped if they had been removed from the sick, looked very hard and cruel; and many people perished in these miserable confinements which, 'tis reasonable to believe, would not have been distempered if they had had liberty, though the plague was in the house; at which the people were very clamorous and uneasy at first, and several violences were committed and injuries offered to the men who were set to watch the houses so shut up; also several people broke out by force in many places, as I shall observe by-and-by. But it was a public good that justified the private mischief, and there was no obtaining the least mitigation by any application to magistrates or government at that time, at least not that I heard of. This put the people upon all manner of stratagem in order, if possible, to get out; and it would fill a little volume to set down the arts used by the people of such houses to shut the eyes of the watchmen who were employed, to deceive them, and to escape or break out from them, in which frequent scuffles and some mischief happened; of which by itself.

As I went along Houndsditch one morning about eight o'clock there was a great noise. It is true, indeed, there was not much crowd, because people were not very free to gather together, or to stay long together when they were there; nor did I stay long there. But the outcry was loud enough to prompt my curiosity, and I called to one that looked out of a window, and asked what was the matter.

A watchman, it seems, had been employed to keep his post at the door of a house which was infected, or said to be infected, and was shut up. He had been there all night for two nights together, as he told his story, and the day-watchman had been there one day, and was now come to relieve him. All this while no noise had been heard in the house, no light had been seen; they called for nothing, sent him of no errands, which used to be the chief business of the watchmen; neither had they given him any disturbance, as he said, from the Monday afternoon, when he heard great crying and screaming in the house, which, as he supposed, was occasioned by some of the family dying just at that time. It seems, the night before, the dead-cart, as it was called, had been stopped there, and a servant-maid had been brought down to the door dead, and the buriers or bearers, as they were called, put her into the cart, wrapt only in a green rug, and carried her away.

The watchman had knocked at the door, it seems, when he heard that noise and crying, as above, and nobody answered a great while; but at last one looked out and said with an angry, quick tone, and yet a kind of crying voice, or a voice of one that was crying, 'What d'ye want, that ye make such a knocking?' He answered, 'I am the watchman! How do you do? What is the matter?' The person answered, 'What is that to you? Stop the dead-cart.' This, it seems, was about one o'clock. Soon after, as the fellow said, he stopped the dead-cart, and then knocked again, but nobody answered. He continued knocking, and the bellman called out several times, 'Bring out your dead'; but nobody answered, till the man that drove the cart, being called to other houses, would stay no longer, and drove away.

The watchman knew not what to make of all this, so he let them alone till the morning-man or day-watchman, as they called him, came to relieve him. Giving him an account of the particulars, they knocked at the door a great while, but nobody answered; and they observed that the window or casement at which the person had looked out who had answered before continued open, being up two pair of stairs.

Upon this the two men, to satisfy their curiosity, got a long ladder, and one of them went up to the window and looked into the room, where he saw a woman lying dead upon the floor in a dismal manner, having no clothes on her but her shift. But though he called aloud, and putting in his long staff, knocked hard on the floor, yet nobody stirred or answered; neither could he hear any noise in the house.

He came down again upon this, and acquainted his fellow, who went up also; and finding it just so, they resolved to acquaint either the Lord Mayor or some other magistrate of it, but did not offer to go in at the window. The magistrate, it seems, upon the information of the two men, ordered the house to be broke open, a constable and other persons being appointed to be present, that nothing might be plundered; and accordingly it was so done, when nobody was found in the house but that young woman, who having been infected and past recovery, the rest had left her to die by herself, and were every one gone, having found some way to delude the watchman, and to get open the door, or get out at some back-door, or over the tops of the houses, so that he knew nothing of it; and as to those cries and shrieks which he heard, it was supposed they were the passionate cries of the family at the bitter parting, which, to be sure, it was to them all, this being the sister to the mistress of the family. The man of the house, his wife, several children, and servants, being all gone and fled, whether sick or sound, that I could never learn; nor, indeed, did I make much inquiry after it.

Many such escapes were made out of infected houses, as particularly when the watchman was sent of some errand; for it was his business to go of any errand that the family sent him of; that is to say, for necessaries, such as food and physic; to fetch physicians, if they would come, or surgeons, or nurses, or to order the dead-cart, and the like; but with this condition, too, that when he went he was to lock up the outer door of the house and take the key away with him, To evade this, and cheat the watchmen, people got two or three keys made to their locks, or they found ways to unscrew the locks such as were screwed on, and so take off the lock, being in the inside of the house, and while they sent away the watchman to the market, to the bakehouse, or for one trifle or another, open the door and go out as often as they pleased. But this being found out, the officers afterwards had orders to padlock up the doors on the outside, and place bolts on them as they thought fit.

At another house, as I was informed, in the street next within Aldgate, a whole family was shut up and locked in because the maid-servant was taken sick. The master of the house had complained by his friends to the next alderman and to the Lord Mayor, and had consented to have the maid carried to the pest-house, but was refused; so the door was marked with a red cross, a padlock on the outside, as above, and a watchman set to keep the door, according to public order.

After the master of the house found there was no remedy, but that he, his wife, and his children were to be locked up with this poor distempered servant, he called to the watchman, and told him he must go then and fetch a nurse for them to attend this poor girl, for that it would be certain death to them all to oblige them to nurse her; and told him plainly that if he would not do this, the maid must perish either of the distemper or be starved for want of food, for he was resolved none of his family should go near her; and she lay in the garret four storey high, where she could not cry out, or call to anybody for help.

The watchman consented to that, and went and fetched a nurse, as he was appointed, and brought her to them the same evening. During this interval the master of the house took his opportunity to break a large hole through his shop into a bulk or stall, where formerly a cobbler had sat, before or under his shop-window; but the tenant, as may be supposed at such a dismal time as that, was dead or removed, and so he had the key in his own keeping. Having made his way into this stall, which he could not have done if the man had been at the door, the noise he was obliged to make being such as would have alarmed the watchman; I say, having made his way into this stall, he sat still till the watchman returned with the nurse, and all the next day also. But the night following, having contrived to send the watchman of another trifling errand, which, as I take it, was to an apothecary's for a plaister for the maid, which he was to stay for the making up, or some other such errand that might secure his staying some time; in that time he conveyed himself and all his family out of the house, and left the nurse and the watchman to bury the poor wench—that is, throw her into the cart—and take care of the house.

I could give a great many such stories as these, diverting enough, which in the long course of that dismal year I met with—that is, heard of—and which are very certain to be true, or very near the truth; that is to say, true in the general: for no man could at such a time learn all the particulars. There was likewise violence used with the watchmen, as was reported, in abundance of places; and I believe that from the beginning of the visitation to the end, there was not less than eighteen or twenty of them killed, or so wounded as to be taken up for dead, which was supposed to be done by the people in the infected houses which were shut up, and where they attempted to come out and were opposed.

Nor, indeed, could less be expected, for here were so many prisons in the town as there were houses shut up; and as the people shut up or imprisoned so were guilty of no crime, only shut up because miserable, it was really the more intolerable to them.

It had also this difference, that every prison, as we may call it, had but one jailer, and as he had the whole house to guard, and that many houses were so situated as that they had several ways out, some more, some less, and some into several streets, it was impossible for one man so to guard all the passages as to prevent the escape of people made desperate by the fright of their circumstances, by the resentment of their usage, or by the raging of the distemper itself; so that they would talk to the watchman on one side of the house, while the family made their escape at another.

For example, in Coleman Street there are abundance of alleys, as appears still. A house was shut up in that they call White's Alley; and this house had a back-window, not a door, into a court which had a passage into Bell Alley. A watchman was set by the constable at the door of this house, and there he stood, or his comrade, night and day, while the family went all away in the evening out at that window into the court, and left the poor fellows warding and watching for near a fortnight.

Not far from the same place they blew up a watchman with gunpowder, and burned the poor fellow dreadfully; and while he made hideous cries, and nobody would venture to come near to help him, the whole family that were able to stir got out at the windows one storey high, two that were left sick calling out for help. Care was taken to give them nurses to look after them, but the persons fled were never found, till after the plague was abated they returned; but as nothing could be proved, so nothing could be done to them.

It is to be considered, too, that as these were prisons without bars and bolts, which our common prisons are furnished with, so the people let themselves down out of their windows, even in the face of the watchman, bringing swords or pistols in their hands, and threatening the poor wretch to shoot him if he stirred or called for help.

In other cases, some had gardens, and walls or pales, between them and their neighbours, or yards and back-houses; and these, by friendship and entreaties, would get leave to get over those walls or pales, and so go out at their neighbours' doors; or, by giving money to their servants, get them to let them through in the night; so that in short, the shutting up of houses was in no wise to be depended upon. Neither did it answer the end at all, serving more to make the people desperate, and drive them to such extremities as that they would break out at all adventures.

And that which was still worse, those that did thus break out spread the infection farther by their wandering about with the distemper upon them, in their desperate circumstances, than they would otherwise have done; for whoever considers all the particulars in such cases must acknowledge, and we cannot doubt but the severity of those confinements made many people desperate, and made them run out of their houses at all hazards, and with the plague visibly upon them, not knowing either whither to go or what to do, or, indeed, what they did; and many that did so were driven to dreadful exigencies and extremities, and perished in the streets or fields for mere want, or dropped down by the raging violence of the fever upon them. Others wandered into the country, and went forward any way, as their desperation guided them, not knowing whither they went or would go: till, faint and tired, and not getting any relief, the houses and villages on the road refusing to admit them to lodge whether infected or no, they have perished by the roadside or gotten into barns and died there, none daring to come to them or relieve them, though perhaps not infected, for nobody would believe them.

On the other hand, when the plague at first seized a family that is to say, when any body of the family had gone out and unwarily or otherwise catched the distemper and brought it home—it was certainly known by the family before it was known to the officers, who, as you will see by the order, were appointed to examine into the circumstances of all sick persons when they heard of their being sick.

In this interval, between their being taken sick and the examiners coming, the master of the house had leisure and liberty to remove himself or all his family, if he knew whither to go, and many did so. But the great disaster was that many did thus after they were really infected themselves, and so carried the disease into the houses of those who were so hospitable as to receive them; which, it must be confessed, was very cruel and ungrateful.

And this was in part the reason of the general notion, or scandal rather, which went about of the temper of people infected: namely, that they did not take the least care or make any scruple of infecting others, though I cannot say but there might be some truth in it too, but not so general as was reported. What natural reason could be given for so wicked a thing at a time when they might conclude themselves just going to appear at the bar of Divine justice I know not. I am very well satisfied that it cannot be reconciled to religion and principle any more than it can be to generosity and Humanity, but I may speak of that again.

I am speaking now of people made desperate by the apprehensions of their being shut up, and their breaking out by stratagem or force, either before or after they were shut up, whose misery was not lessened when they were out, but sadly increased. On the other hand, many that thus got away had retreats to go to and other houses, where they locked themselves up and kept hid till the plague was over; and many families, foreseeing the approach of the distemper, laid up stores of provisions sufficient for their whole families, and shut themselves up, and that so entirely that they were neither seen or heard of till the infection was quite ceased, and then came abroad sound and well. I might recollect several such as these, and give you the particulars of their management; for doubtless it was the most effectual secure step that could be taken for such whose circumstances would not admit them to remove, or who had not retreats abroad proper for the case; for in being thus shut up they were as if they had been a hundred miles off. Nor do I remember that any one of those families miscarried. Among these, several Dutch merchants were particularly remarkable, who kept their houses like little garrisons besieged suffering none to go in or out or come near them, particularly one in a court in Throgmorton Street whose house looked into Draper's Garden.

But I come back to the case of families infected and shut up by the magistrates. The misery of those families is not to be expressed; and it was generally in such houses that we heard the most dismal shrieks and outcries of the poor people, terrified and even frighted to death by the sight of the condition of their dearest relations, and by the terror of being imprisoned as they were.

I remember, and while I am writing this story I think I hear the very sound of it, a certain lady had an only daughter, a young maiden about nineteen years old, and who was possessed of a very considerable fortune. They were only lodgers in the house where they were. The young woman, her mother, and the maid had been abroad on some occasion, I do not remember what, for the house was not shut up; but about two hours after they came home the young lady complained she was not well; in a quarter of an hour more she vomited and had a violent pain in her head. 'Pray God', says her mother, in a terrible fright, 'my child has not the distemper!' The pain in her head increasing, her mother ordered the bed to be warmed, and resolved to put her to bed, and prepared to give her things to sweat, which was the ordinary remedy to be taken when the first apprehensions of the distemper began.

While the bed was airing the mother undressed the young woman, and just as she was laid down in the bed, she, looking upon her body with a candle, immediately discovered the fatal tokens on the inside of her thighs. Her mother, not being able to contain herself, threw down her candle and shrieked out in such a frightful manner that it was enough to place horror upon the stoutest heart in the world; nor was it one scream or one cry, but the fright having seized her spirits, she—fainted first, then recovered, then ran all over the house, up the stairs and down the stairs, like one distracted, and indeed really was distracted, and continued screeching and crying out for several hours void of all sense, or at least government of her senses, and, as I was told, never came thoroughly to herself again. As to the young maiden, she was a dead corpse from that moment, for the gangrene which occasions the spots had spread [over] her whole body, and she died in less than two hours. But still the mother continued crying out, not knowing anything more of her child, several hours after she was dead. It is so long ago that I am not certain, but I think the mother never recovered, but died in two or three weeks after.

This was an extraordinary case, and I am therefore the more particular in it, because I came so much to the knowledge of it; but there were innumerable suchlike cases, and it was seldom that the weekly bill came in but there were two or three put in, 'frighted'; that is, that may well be called frighted to death. But besides those who were so frighted as to die upon the spot, there were great numbers frighted to other extremes, some frighted out of their senses, some out of their memory, and some out of their understanding. But I return to the shutting up of houses.

As several people, I say, got out of their houses by stratagem after they were shut UP, so others got out by bribing the watchmen, and giving them money to let them go privately out in the night. I must confess I thought it at that time the most innocent corruption or bribery that any man could be guilty of, and therefore could not but pity the poor men, and think it was hard when three of those watchmen were publicly whipped through the streets for suffering people to go out of houses shut up.

But notwithstanding that severity, money prevailed with the poor men, and many families found means to make sallies out, and escape that way after they had been shut up; but these were generally such as had some places to retire to; and though there was no easy passing the roads any whither after the 1st of August, yet there were many ways of retreat, and particularly, as I hinted, some got tents and set them up in the fields, carrying beds or straw to lie on, and provisions to eat, and so lived in them as hermits in a cell, for nobody would venture to come near them; and several stories were told of such, some comical, some tragical, some who lived like wandering pilgrims in the deserts, and escaped by making themselves exiles in such a manner as is scarce to be credited, and who yet enjoyed more liberty than was to be expected in such cases.

I have by me a story of two brothers and their kinsman, who being single men, but that had stayed in the city too long to get away, and indeed not knowing where to go to have any retreat, nor having wherewith to travel far, took a course for their own preservation, which though in itself at first desperate, yet was so natural that it may be wondered that no more did so at that time. They were but of mean condition, and yet not so very poor as that they could not furnish themselves with some little conveniences such as might serve to keep life and soul together; and finding the distemper increasing in a terrible manner, they resolved to shift as well as they could, and to be gone.

One of them had been a soldier in the late wars, and before that in the Low Countries, and having been bred to no particular employment but his arms, and besides being wounded, and not able to work very hard, had for some time been employed at a baker's of sea-biscuit in Wapping.

The brother of this man was a seaman too, but somehow or other had been hurt of one leg, that he could not go to sea, but had worked for his living at a sailmaker's in Wapping, or thereabouts; and being a good husband, had laid up some money, and was the richest of the three.

The third man was a joiner or carpenter by trade, a handy fellow, and he had no wealth but his box or basket of tools, with the help of which he could at any time get his living, such a time as this excepted, wherever he went—and he lived near Shadwell.

They all lived in Stepney parish, which, as I have said, being the last that was infected, or at least violently, they stayed there till they evidently saw the plague was abating at the west part of the town, and coming towards the east, where they lived.

The story of those three men, if the reader will be content to have me give it in their own persons, without taking upon me to either vouch the particulars or answer for any mistakes, I shall give as distinctly as I can, believing the history will be a very good pattern for any poor man to follow, in case the like public desolation should happen here; and if there may be no such occasion, which God of His infinite mercy grant us, still the story may have its uses so many ways as that it will, I hope, never be said that the relating has been unprofitable.

I say all this previous to the history, having yet, for the present, much more to say before I quit my own part.

I went all the first part of the time freely about the streets, though not so freely as to run myself into apparent danger, except when they dug the great pit in the churchyard of our parish of Aldgate. A terrible pit it was, and I could not resist my curiosity to go and see it. As near as I may judge, it was about forty feet in length, and about fifteen or sixteen feet broad, and at the time I first looked at it, about nine feet deep; but it was said they dug it near twenty feet deep afterwards in one part of it, till they could go no deeper for the water; for they had, it seems, dug several large pits before this. For though the plague was long a-coming to our parish, yet, when it did come, there was no parish in or about London where it raged with such violence as in the two parishes of Aldgate and Whitechappel.

I say they had dug several pits in another ground, when the distemper began to spread in our parish, and especially when the dead-carts began to go about, which was not, in our parish, till the beginning of August. Into these pits they had put perhaps fifty or sixty bodies each; then they made larger holes wherein they buried all that the cart brought in a week, which, by the middle to the end of August, came to from 200 to 400 a week; and they could not well dig them larger, because of the order of the magistrates confining them to leave no bodies within six feet of the surface; and the water coming on at about seventeen or eighteen feet, they could not well, I say, put more in one pit. But now, at the beginning of September, the plague raging in a dreadful manner, and the number of burials in our parish increasing to more than was ever buried in any parish about London of no larger extent, they ordered this dreadful gulf to be dug—for such it was, rather than a pit.

They had supposed this pit would have supplied them for a month or more when they dug it, and some blamed the churchwardens for suffering such a frightful thing, telling them they were making preparations to bury the whole parish, and the like; but time made it appear the churchwardens knew the condition of the parish better than they did: for, the pit being finished the 4th of September, I think, they began to bury in it the 6th, and by the 20th, which was just two weeks, they had thrown into it 1114 bodies when they were obliged to fill it up, the bodies being then come to lie within six feet of the surface. I doubt not but there may be some ancient persons alive in the parish who can justify the fact of this, and are able to show even in what place of the churchyard the pit lay better than I can. The mark of it also was many years to be seen in the churchyard on the surface, lying in length parallel with the passage which goes by the west wall of the churchyard out of Houndsditch, and turns east again into Whitechappel, coming out near the Three Nuns' Inn.

It was about the 10th of September that my curiosity led, or rather drove, me to go and see this pit again, when there had been near 400 people buried in it; and I was not content to see it in the day-time, as I had done before, for then there would have been nothing to have been seen but the loose earth; for all the bodies that were thrown in were immediately covered with earth by those they called the buriers, which at other times were called bearers; but I resolved to go in the night and see some of them thrown in.

There was a strict order to prevent people coming to those pits, and that was only to prevent infection. But after some time that order was more necessary, for people that were infected and near their end, and delirious also, would run to those pits, wrapt in blankets or rugs, and throw themselves in, and, as they said, bury themselves. I cannot say that the officers suffered any willingly to lie there; but I have heard that in a great pit in Finsbury, in the parish of Cripplegate, it lying open then to the fields, for it was not then walled about, [many] came and threw themselves in, and expired there, before they threw any earth upon them; and that when they came to bury others and found them there, they were quite dead, though not cold.

This may serve a little to describe the dreadful condition of that day, though it is impossible to say anything that is able to give a true idea of it to those who did not see it, other than this, that it was indeed very, very, very dreadful, and such as no tongue can express.

I got admittance into the churchyard by being acquainted with the sexton who attended; who, though he did not refuse me at all, yet earnestly persuaded me not to go, telling me very seriously (for he was a good, religious, and sensible man) that it was indeed their business and duty to venture, and to run all hazards, and that in it they might hope to be preserved; but that I had no apparent call to it but my own curiosity, which, he said, he believed I would not pretend was sufficient to justify my running that hazard. I told him I had been pressed in my mind to go, and that perhaps it might be an instructing sight, that might not be without its uses. 'Nay,' says the good man, 'if you will venture upon that score, name of God go in; for, depend upon it, 'twill be a sermon to you, it may be, the best that ever you heard in your life. 'Tis a speaking sight,' says he, 'and has a voice with it, and a loud one, to call us all to repentance'; and with that he opened the door and said, 'Go, if you will.'

His discourse had shocked my resolution a little, and I stood wavering for a good while, but just at that interval I saw two links come over from the end of the Minories, and heard the bellman, and then appeared a dead-cart, as they called it, coming over the streets; so I could no longer resist my desire of seeing it, and went in. There was nobody, as I could perceive at first, in the churchyard, or going into it, but the buriers and the fellow that drove the cart, or rather led the horse and cart; but when they came up to the pit they saw a man go to and again, muffled up in a brown Cloak, and making motions with his hands under his cloak, as if he was in great agony, and the buriers immediately gathered about him, supposing he was one of those poor delirious or desperate creatures that used to pretend, as I have said, to bury themselves. He said nothing as he walked about, but two or three times groaned very deeply and loud, and sighed as he would break his heart.

When the buriers came up to him they soon found he was neither a person infected and desperate, as I have observed above, or a person distempered—in mind, but one oppressed with a dreadful weight of grief indeed, having his wife and several of his children all in the cart that was just come in with him, and he followed in an agony and excess of sorrow. He mourned heartily, as it was easy to see, but with a kind of masculine grief that could not give itself vent by tears; and calmly defying the buriers to let him alone, said he would only see the bodies thrown in and go away, so they left importuning him. But no sooner was the cart turned round and the bodies shot into the pit promiscuously, which was a surprise to him, for he at least expected they would have been decently laid in, though indeed he was afterwards convinced that was impracticable; I say, no sooner did he see the sight but he cried out aloud, unable to contain himself. I could not hear what he said, but he went backward two or three steps and fell down in a swoon. The buriers ran to him and took him up, and in a little while he came to himself, and they led him away to the Pie Tavern over against the end of Houndsditch, where, it seems, the man was known, and where they took care of him. He looked into the pit again as he went away, but the buriers had covered the bodies so immediately with throwing in earth, that though there was light enough, for there were lanterns, and candles in them, placed all night round the sides of the pit, upon heaps of earth, seven or eight, or perhaps more, yet nothing could be seen.

This was a mournful scene indeed, and affected me almost as much as the rest; but the other was awful and full of terror. The cart had in it sixteen or seventeen bodies; some were wrapt up in linen sheets, some in rags, some little other than naked, or so loose that what covering they had fell from them in the shooting out of the cart, and they fell quite naked among the rest; but the matter was not much to them, or the indecency much to any one else, seeing they were all dead, and were to be huddled together into the common grave of mankind, as we may call it, for here was no difference made, but poor and rich went together; there was no other way of burials, neither was it possible there should, for coffins were not to be had for the prodigious numbers that fell in such a calamity as this.

It was reported by way of scandal upon the buriers, that if any corpse was delivered to them decently wound up, as we called it then, in a winding-sheet tied over the head and feet, which some did, and which was generally of good linen; I say, it was reported that the buriers were so wicked as to strip them in the cart and carry them quite naked to the ground. But as I cannot easily credit anything so vile among Christians, and at a time so filled with terrors as that was, I can only relate it and leave it undetermined.

Innumerable stories also went about of the cruel behaviours and practices of nurses who tended the sick, and of their hastening on the fate of those they tended in their sickness. But I shall say more of this in its place.

I was indeed shocked with this sight; it almost overwhelmed me, and I went away with my heart most afflicted, and full of the afflicting thoughts, such as I cannot describe just at my going out of the church, and turning up the street towards my own house, I saw another cart with links, and a bellman going before, coming out of Harrow Alley in the Butcher Row, on the other side of the way, and being, as I perceived, very full of dead bodies, it went directly over the street also toward the church. I stood a while, but I had no stomach to go back again to see the same dismal scene over again, so I went directly home, where I could not but consider with thankfulness the risk I had run, believing I had gotten no injury, as indeed I had not.

Here the poor unhappy gentleman's grief came into my head again, and indeed I could not but shed tears in the reflection upon it, perhaps more than he did himself; but his case lay so heavy upon my mind that I could not prevail with myself, but that I must go out again into the street, and go to the Pie Tavern, resolving to inquire what became of him.

It was by this time one o'clock in the morning, and yet the poor gentleman was there. The truth was, the people of the house, knowing him, had entertained him, and kept him there all the night, notwithstanding the danger of being infected by him, though it appeared the man was perfectly sound himself.

It is with regret that I take notice of this tavern. The people were civil, mannerly, and an obliging sort of folks enough, and had till this time kept their house open and their trade going on, though not so very publicly as formerly: but there was a dreadful set of fellows that used their house, and who, in the middle of all this horror, met there every night, behaved with all the revelling and roaring extravagances as is usual for such people to do at other times, and, indeed, to such an offensive degree that the very master and mistress of the house grew first ashamed and then terrified at them.

They sat generally in a room next the street, and as they always kept late hours, so when the dead-cart came across the street-end to go into Houndsditch, which was in view of the tavern windows, they would frequently open the windows as soon as they heard the bell and look out at them; and as they might often hear sad lamentations of people in the streets or at their windows as the carts went along, they would make their impudent mocks and jeers at them, especially if they heard the poor people call upon God to have mercy upon them, as many would do at those times in their ordinary passing along the streets.

These gentlemen, being something disturbed with the clutter of bringing the poor gentleman into the house, as above, were first angry and very high with the master of the house for suffering such a fellow, as they called him, to be brought out of the grave into their house; but being answered that the man was a neighbour, and that he was sound, but overwhelmed with the calamity of his family, and the like, they turned their anger into ridiculing the man and his sorrow for his wife and children, taunted him with want of courage to leap into the great pit and go to heaven, as they jeeringly expressed it, along with them, adding some very profane and even blasphemous expressions.

They were at this vile work when I came back to the house, and, as far as I could see, though the man sat still, mute and disconsolate, and their affronts could not divert his sorrow, yet he was both grieved and offended at their discourse. Upon this I gently reproved them, being well enough acquainted with their characters, and not unknown in person to two of them.

They immediately fell upon me with ill language and oaths, asked me what I did out of my grave at such a time when so many honester men were carried into the churchyard, and why I was not at home saying my prayers against the dead-cart came for me, and the like.

I was indeed astonished at the impudence of the men, though not at all discomposed at their treatment of me. However, I kept my temper. I told them that though I defied them or any man in the world to tax me with any dishonesty, yet I acknowledged that in this terrible judgement of God many better than I were swept away and carried to their grave. But to answer their question directly, the case was, that I was mercifully preserved by that great God whose name they had blasphemed and taken in vain by cursing and swearing in a dreadful manner, and that I believed I was preserved in particular, among other ends of His goodness, that I might reprove them for their audacious boldness in behaving in such a manner and in such an awful time as this was, especially for their jeering and mocking at an honest gentleman and a neighbour (for some of them knew him), who, they saw, was overwhelmed with sorrow for the breaches which it had pleased God to make upon his family.

I cannot call exactly to mind the hellish, abominable raillery which was the return they made to that talk of mine: being provoked, it seems, that I was not at all afraid to be free with them; nor, if I could remember, would I fill my account with any of the words, the horrid oaths, curses, and vile expressions, such as, at that time of the day, even the worst and ordinariest people in the street would not use; for, except such hardened creatures as these, the most wicked wretches that could be found had at that time some terror upon their minds of the hand of that Power which could thus in a moment destroy them.

But that which was the worst in all their devilish language was, that they were not afraid to blaspheme God and talk atheistically, making a jest of my calling the plague the hand of God; mocking, and even laughing, at the word judgement, as if the providence of God had no concern in the inflicting such a desolating stroke; and that the people calling upon God as they saw the carts carrying away the dead bodies was all enthusiastic, absurd, and impertinent.

I made them some reply, such as I thought proper, but which I found was so far from putting a check to their horrid way of speaking that it made them rail the more, so that I confess it filled me with horror and a kind of rage, and I came away, as I told them, lest the hand of that judgement which had visited the whole city should glorify His vengeance upon them, and all that were near them.

They received all reproof with the utmost contempt, and made the greatest mockery that was possible for them to do at me, giving me all the opprobrious, insolent scoffs that they could think of for preaching to them, as they called it, which indeed grieved me, rather than angered me; and I went away, blessing God, however, in my mind that I had not spared them, though they had insulted me so much.

They continued this wretched course three or four days after this, continually mocking and jeering at all that showed themselves religious or serious, or that were any way touched with the sense of the terrible judgement of God upon us; and I was informed they flouted in the same manner at the good people who, notwithstanding the contagion, met at the church, fasted, and prayed to God to remove His hand from them.

I say, they continued this dreadful course three or four days—I think it was no more—when one of them, particularly he who asked the poor gentleman what he did out of his grave, was struck from Heaven with the plague, and died in a most deplorable manner; and, in a word, they were every one of them carried into the great pit which I have mentioned above, before it was quite filled up, which was not above a fortnight or thereabout.

These men were guilty of many extravagances, such as one would think human nature should have trembled at the thoughts of at such a time of general terror as was then upon us, and particularly scoffing and mocking at everything which they happened to see that was religious among the people, especially at their thronging zealously to the place of public worship to implore mercy from Heaven in such a time of distress; and this tavern where they held their dub being within view of the church-door, they had the more particular occasion for their atheistical profane mirth.

But this began to abate a little with them before the accident which I have related happened, for the infection increased so violently at this part of the town now, that people began to be afraid to come to the church; at least such numbers did not resort thither as was usual. Many of the clergymen likewise were dead, and others gone into the country; for it really required a steady courage and a strong faith for a man not only to venture being in town at such a time as this, but likewise to venture to come to church and perform the office of a minister to a congregation, of whom he had reason to believe many of them were actually infected with the plague, and to do this every day, or twice a day, as in some places was done.

It is true the people showed an extraordinary zeal in these religious exercises, and as the church-doors were always open, people would go in single at all times, whether the minister was officiating or no, and locking themselves into separate pews, would be praying to God with great fervency and devotion.

Others assembled at meeting-houses, every one as their different opinions in such things guided, but all were promiscuously the subject of these men's drollery, especially at the beginning of the visitation.

It seems they had been checked for their open insulting religion in this manner by several good people of every persuasion, and that, and the violent raging of the infection, I suppose, was the occasion that they had abated much of their rudeness for some time before, and were only roused by the spirit of ribaldry and atheism at the clamour which was made when the gentleman was first brought in there, and perhaps were agitated by the same devil, when I took upon me to reprove them; though I did it at first with all the calmness, temper, and good manners that I could, which for a while they insulted me the more for thinking it had been in fear of their resentment, though afterwards they found the contrary.

I went home, indeed, grieved and afflicted in my mind at the abominable wickedness of those men, not doubting, however, that they would be made dreadful examples of God's justice; for I looked upon this dismal time to be a particular season of Divine vengeance, and that God would on this occasion single out the proper objects of His displeasure in a more especial and remarkable manner than at another time; and that though I did believe that many good people would, and did, fall in the common calamity, and that it was no certain rule to judge of the eternal state of any one by their being distinguished in such a time of general destruction neither one way or other; yet, I say, it could not but seem reasonable to believe that God would not think fit to spare by His mercy such open declared enemies, that should insult His name and Being, defy His vengeance, and mock at His worship and worshippers at such a time; no, not though His mercy had thought fit to bear with and spare them at other times; that this was a day of visitation, a day of God's anger, and those words came into my thought, Jer. v. 9: 'Shall

I not visit for these things? saith the Lord: and shall not My soul be avenged of such a nation as this?'

These things, I say, lay upon my mind, and I went home very much grieved and oppressed with the horror of these men's wickedness, and to think that anything could be so vile, so hardened, and notoriously wicked as to insult God, and His servants, and His worship in such a manner, and at such a time as this was, when He had, as it were, His sword drawn in His hand on purpose to take vengeance not on them only, but on the whole nation.

I had, indeed, been in some passion at first with them—though it was really raised, not by any affront they had offered me personally, but by the horror their blaspheming tongues filled me with. However, I was doubtful in my thoughts whether the resentment I retained was not all upon my own private account, for they had given me a great deal of ill language too—I mean personally; but after some pause, and having a weight of grief upon my mind, I retired myself as soon as I came home, for I slept not that night; and giving God most humble thanks for my preservation in the eminent danger I had been in, I set my mind seriously and with the utmost earnestness to pray for those desperate wretches, that God would pardon them, open their eyes, and effectually humble them.

By this I not only did my duty, namely, to pray for those who despitefully used me, but I fully tried my own heart, to my fun satisfaction, that it was not filled with any spirit of resentment as they had offended me in particular; and I humbly recommend the method to all those that would know, or be certain, how to distinguish between their zeal for the honour of God and the effects of their private passions and resentment.

But I must go back here to the particular incidents which occur to my thoughts of the time of the visitation, and particularly to the time of their shutting up houses in the first part of their sickness; for before the sickness was come to its height people had more room to make their observations than they had afterward; but when it was in the extremity there was no such thing as communication with one another, as before.

During the shutting up of houses, as I have said, some violence was offered to the watchmen. As to soldiers, there were none to be found. The few guards which the king then had, which were nothing like the number entertained since, were dispersed, either at Oxford with the Court, or in quarters in the remoter parts of the country, small detachments excepted, who did duty at the Tower and at Whitehall, and these but very few. Neither am I positive that there was any other guard at the Tower than the warders, as they called them, who stand at the gate with gowns and caps, the same as the yeomen of the guard, except the ordinary gunners, who were twenty-four, and the officers appointed to look after the magazine, who were called armourers. As to trained bands, there was no possibility of raising any; neither, if the Lieutenancy, either of London or Middlesex, had ordered the drums to beat for the militia, would any of the companies, I believe, have drawn together, whatever risk they had run.

This made the watchmen be the less regarded, and perhaps occasioned the greater violence to be used against them. I mention it on this score to observe that the setting watchmen thus to keep the people in was, first of all, not effectual, but that the people broke out, whether by force or by stratagem, even almost as often as they pleased; and, second, that those that did thus break out were generally people infected who, in their desperation, running about from one place to another, valued not whom they injured: and which perhaps, as I have said, might give birth to report that it was natural to the infected people to desire to infect others, which report was really false.

And I know it so well, and in so many several cases, that I could give several relations of good, pious, and religious people who, when they have had the distemper, have been so far from being forward to infect others that they have forbid their own family to come near them, in hopes of their being preserved, and have even died without seeing their nearest relations lest they should be instrumental to give them the distemper, and infect or endanger them. If, then, there were cases wherein the infected people were careless of the injury they did to others, this was certainly one of them, if not the chief, namely, when people who had the distemper had broken out from houses which were so shut up, and having been driven to extremities for provision or for entertainment, had endeavoured to conceal their condition, and have been thereby instrumental involuntarily to infect others who have been ignorant and unwary.

This is one of the reasons why I believed then, and do believe still, that the shutting up houses thus by force, and restraining, or rather imprisoning, people in their own houses, as I said above, was of little or no service in the whole. Nay, I am of opinion it was rather hurtful, having forced those desperate people to wander abroad with the plague upon them, who would otherwise have died quietly in their beds.

I remember one citizen who, having thus broken out of his house in Aldersgate Street or thereabout, went along the road to Islington; he attempted to have gone in at the Angel Inn, and after that the White Horse, two inns known still by the same signs, but was refused; after which he came to the Pied Bull, an inn also still continuing the same sign. He asked them for lodging for one night only, pretending to be going into Lincolnshire, and assuring them of his being very sound and free from the infection, which also at that time had not reached much that way.

They told him they had no lodging that they could spare but one bed up in the garret, and that they could spare that bed for one night, some drovers being expected the next day with cattle; so, if he would accept of that lodging, he might have it, which he did. So a servant was sent up with a candle with him to show him the room. He was very well dressed, and looked like a person not used to lie in a garret; and when he came to the room he fetched a deep sigh, and said to the servant, 'I have seldom lain in such a lodging as this. 'However, the servant assuring him again that they had no better, 'Well,' says he, 'I must make shift; this is a dreadful time; but it is but for one night.' So he sat down upon the bedside, and bade the maid, I think it was, fetch him up a pint of warm ale. Accordingly the servant went for the ale, but some hurry in the house, which perhaps employed her other ways, put it out of her head, and she went up no more to him.

The next morning, seeing no appearance of the gentleman, somebody in the house asked the servant that had showed him upstairs what was become of him. She started. 'Alas I,' says she, 'I never thought more of him. He bade me carry him some warm ale, but I forgot.' Upon which, not the maid, but some other person was sent up to see after him, who, coming into the room, found him stark dead and almost cold, stretched out across the bed. His clothes were pulled off, his jaw fallen, his eyes open in a most frightful posture, the rug of the bed being grasped hard in one of his hands, so that it was plain he died soon after the maid left him; and 'tis probable, had she gone up with the ale, she had found him dead in a few minutes after he sat down upon the bed. The alarm was great in the house, as any-one may suppose, they having been free from the distemper till that disaster, which, bringing the infection to the house, spread it immediately to other houses round about it. I do not remember how many died in the house itself, but I think the maid-servant who went up first with him fell presently ill by the fright, and several others; for, whereas there died but two in Islington of the plague the week before, there died seventeen the week after, whereof fourteen were of the plague. This was in the week from the 11th of July to the 18th.

There was one shift that some families had, and that not a few, when their houses happened to be infected, and that was this: the families who, in the first breaking-out of the distemper, fled away into the country and had retreats among their friends, generally found some or other of their neighbours or relations to commit the charge of those houses to for the safety of the goods and the like. Some houses were, indeed, entirely locked up, the doors padlocked, the windows and doors having deal boards nailed over them, and only the inspection of them committed to the ordinary watchmen and parish officers; but these were but few.

It was thought that there were not less than 10,000 houses forsaken of the inhabitants in the city and suburbs, including what was in the out-parishes and in Surrey, or the side of the water they called Southwark. This was besides the numbers of lodgers, and of particular persons who were fled out of other families; so that in all it was computed that about 200,000 people were fled and gone. But of this I shall speak again. But I mention it here on this account, namely, that it was a rule with those who had thus two houses in their keeping or care, that if anybody was taken sick in a family, before the master of the family let the examiners or any other officer know of it, he immediately would send all the rest of his family, whether children or servants, as it fell out to be, to such other house which he had so in charge, and then giving notice of the sick person to the examiner, have a nurse or nurses appointed, and have another person to be shut up in the house with them (which many for money would do), so to take charge of the house in case the person should die.

This was, in many cases, the saving a whole family, who, if they had been shut up with the sick person, would inevitably have perished. But, on the other hand, this was another of the inconveniences of shutting up houses; for the apprehensions and terror of being shut up made many run away with the rest of the family, who, though it was not publicly known, and they were not quite sick, had yet the distemper upon them; and who, by having an uninterrupted liberty to go about, but being obliged still to conceal their circumstances, or perhaps not knowing it themselves, gave the distemper to others, and spread the infection in a dreadful manner, as I shall explain further hereafter.

And here I may be able to make an observation or two of my own, which may be of use hereafter to those into whose bands these may come, if they should ever see the like dreadful visitation. (1) The infection generally came into the houses of the citizens by the means of their servants, whom they were obliged to send up and down the streets for necessaries; that is to say, for food or physic, to bake-houses, brew-houses, shops, &c.; and who going necessarily through the streets into shops, markets, and the like, it was impossible but that they should, one way or other, meet with distempered people, who conveyed the fatal breath into them, and they brought it home to the families to which they belonged. (2) It was a great mistake that such a great city as this had but one pest-house; for had there been, instead of one pest-house—viz., beyond Bunhill Fields, where, at most, they could receive, perhaps, two hundred or three hundred people—I say, had there, instead of that one, been several pest-houses, every one able to contain a thousand people, without lying two in a bed, or two beds in a room; and had every master of a family, as soon as any servant especially had been taken sick in his house, been obliged to send them to the next pest-house, if they were willing, as many were, and had the examiners done the like among the poor people when any had been stricken with the infection; I say, had this been done where the people were willing (not otherwise), and the houses not been shut, I am persuaded, and was all the while of that opinion, that not so many, by several thousands, had died; for it was observed, and I could give several instances within the compass of my own knowledge, where a servant had been taken sick, and the family had either time to send him out or retire from the house and leave the sick person, as I have said above, they had all been preserved; whereas when, upon one or more sickening in a family, the house has been shut up, the whole family have perished, and the bearers been obliged to go in to fetch out the dead bodies, not being able to bring them to the door, and at last none left to do it.

(3) This put it out of question to me, that the calamity was spread by infection; that is to say, by some certain steams or fumes, which the physicians call effluvia, by the breath, or by the sweat, or by the stench of the sores of the sick persons, or some other way, perhaps, beyond even the reach of the physicians themselves, which effluvia affected the sound who came within certain distances of the sick, immediately penetrating the vital parts of the said sound persons, putting their blood into an immediate ferment, and agitating their spirits to that degree which it was found they were agitated; and so those newly infected persons communicated it in the same manner to others. And this I shall give some instances of, that cannot but convince those who seriously consider it; and I cannot but with some wonder find some people, now the contagion is over, talk of its being an immedi-

ate stroke from Heaven, without the agency of means, having commission to strike this and that particular person, and none other—which I look upon with contempt as the effect of manifest ignorance and enthusiasm; likewise the opinion of others, who talk of infection being carried on by the air only, by carrying with it vast numbers of insects and invisible creatures, who enter into the body with the breath, or even at the pores with the air, and there generate or emit most acute poisons, or poisonous ovae or eggs, which mingle themselves with the blood, and so infect the body: a discourse full of learned simplicity, and manifested to be so by universal experience; but I shall say more to this case in its order.

I must here take further notice that nothing was more fatal to the inhabitants of this city than the supine negligence of the people themselves, who, during the long notice or warning they had of the visitation, made no provision for it by laying in store of provisions, or of other necessaries, by which they might have lived retired and within their own houses, as I have observed others did, and who were in a great measure preserved by that caution; nor were they, after they were a little hardened to it, so shy of conversing with one another, when actually infected, as they were at first: no, though they knew it.

I acknowledge I was one of those thoughtless ones that had made so little provision that my servants were obliged to go out of doors to buy every trifle by penny and halfpenny, just as before it began, even till my experience showing me the folly, I began to be wiser so late that I had scarce time to store myself sufficient for our common subsistence for a month.

I had in family only an ancient woman that managed the house, a maid-servant, two apprentices, and myself; and the plague beginning to increase about us, I had many sad thoughts about what course I should take, and how I should act. The many dismal objects which happened everywhere as I went about the streets, had filled my mind with a great deal of horror for fear of the distemper, which was indeed very horrible in itself, and in some more than in others. The swellings, which were generally in the neck or groin, when they grew hard and would not break, grew so painful that it was equal to the most exquisite torture; and some, not able to bear the torment, threw themselves out at windows or shot themselves, or otherwise made themselves away, and I saw several dismal objects of that kind. Others, unable to contain themselves, vented their pain by incessant roarings, and such loud and lamentable cries were to be heard as we walked along the streets that would pierce the very heart to think of, especially when it was to be considered that the same dreadful scourge might be expected every moment to seize upon ourselves.

I cannot say but that now I began to faint in my resolutions; my heart failed me very much, and sorely I repented of my rashness. When I had been out, and met with such terrible things as these I have talked of, I say I repented my rashness in venturing to abide in town. I wished often that I had not taken upon me to stay, but had gone away with my brother and his family.

Terrified by those frightful objects, I would retire home sometimes and resolve to go out no more; and perhaps I would keep those resolutions for three or four days, which time I spent in the most serious thankfulness for my preservation and the preservation of my family, and the constant confession of my sins, giving myself up to God every day, and applying to Him with fasting, humiliation, and med-meditation. Such intervals as I had I employed in reading books and in writing down my memorandums of what occurred to me every day, and out of which afterwards I took most of this work, as it relates to my observations without doors. What I wrote of my private meditations I reserve for private use, and desire it may not be made public on any account whatever.

I also wrote other meditations upon divine subjects, such as occurred to me at that time and were profitable to myself, but not fit for any other view, and therefore I say no more of that.

I had a very good friend, a physician, whose name was Heath, whom I frequently visited during this dismal time, and to whose advice I was very much obliged for many things which he directed me to take, by way of preventing the infection when I went out, as he found I frequently did, and to hold in my mouth when I was in the streets. He also came very often to see me, and as he was a good Christian as well as a good physician, his agreeable conversation was a very great support to me in the worst of this terrible time.

It was now the beginning of August, and the plague grew very violent and terrible in the place where I lived, and Dr Heath coming to visit me, and finding that I ventured so often out in the streets, earnestly persuaded me to lock myself up and my family, and not to suffer any of us to go out of doors; to keep all our windows fast, shutters and curtains close, and never to open them; but first, to make a very strong smoke in the room where the window or door was to be opened, with rozen and pitch, brimstone or gunpowder and the like; and we did this for some time; but as I had not laid in a store of provision for such a retreat, it was impossible that we could keep within doors entirely. However, I attempted, though it was so very late, to do something towards it; and first, as I had convenience both for brewing and baking, I went and bought two sacks of meal, and for several weeks, having an oven, we baked all our own bread; also I bought malt, and brewed as much beer as all the casks I had would hold, and which seemed enough to serve my house for five or six weeks; also I laid in a quantity of salt butter and Cheshire cheese; but I had no flesh-meat, and the plague raged so violently among the butchers and slaughter-houses on the other side of our street, where they are known to dwell in great numbers, that it was not advisable so much as to go over the street among them.

And here I must observe again, that this necessity of going out of our houses to buy provisions was in a great measure the ruin of the whole city, for the people catched the distemper on these occasions one of another, and even the provisions themselves were often tainted; at least I have great reason to believe so; and therefore I cannot say with satisfaction what I know is repeated with great assurance, that the market-people and such as brought provisions to town were never infected. I am certain the butchers of Whitechappel, where the greatest part of the flesh-meat was killed, were dreadfully visited, and that at least to such a degree that few of their shops were kept open, and those that remained of them killed their meat at Mile End and that way, and brought it to market upon horses.

However, the poor people could not lay up provisions, and there was a necessity that they must go to market to buy, and others to send servants or their children; and as this was a necessity which renewed itself daily, it brought abundance of unsound people to the markets, and a great many that went thither sound brought death home with them.

It is true people used all possible precaution. When any one bought a joint of meat in the market they would not take it off the butcher's hand, but took it off the hooks themselves. On the other hand, the butcher would not touch the money, but have it put into a pot full of vinegar, which he kept for that purpose. The buyer carried always small money to make up any odd sum, that they might take no change. They carried bottles of scents and perfumes in their hands, and all the means that could be used were used, but then the poor could not do even these things, and they went at all hazards.

Innumerable dismal stories we heard every day on this very account. Sometimes a man or woman dropped down dead in the very markets, for many people that had the plague upon them knew nothing of it till the inward gangrene had affected their vitals, and they died in a few moments. This caused that many died frequently in that manner in the streets suddenly, without any warning; others perhaps had time to go to the next bulk or stall, or to any door-porch, and just sit down and die, as I have said before.

These objects were so frequent in the streets that when the plague came to be very raging on one side, there was scarce any passing by the streets but that several dead bodies would be lying here and there upon the ground. On the other hand, it is observable that though at first the people would stop as they went along and call to the neighbours to come out on such an occasion, yet afterward no notice was taken of them; but that if at any time we found a corpse lying, go across the way and not come near it; or, if in a narrow lane or passage, go back again and seek some other way to go on the business we were upon; and in those cases the corpse was always left till the officers had notice to come and take them away, or till night, when the bearers attending the dead-cart would take them up and carry them away. Nor did those undaunted creatures who performed these offices fail to search their pockets, and sometimes strip off their clothes if they were well dressed, as sometimes they were, and carry off what they could get.

But to return to the markets. The butchers took that care that if any person died in the market they had the officers always at band to take them up upon hand-barrows and carry them to the next churchyard; and this was so frequent that such were not entered in the weekly bill, 'Found dead in the streets or fields', as is the case now, but they went into the general articles of the great distemper.

But now the fury of the distemper increased to such a degree that even the markets were but very thinly furnished with provisions or frequented with buyers compared to what they were before; and the Lord Mayor caused the country people who brought provisions to be stopped in the streets leading into the town, and to sit down there with their goods, where they sold what they brought, and went immediately away; and this encouraged the country people greatly-to do so, for they sold their provisions at the very entrances into the town, and even in the fields, as particularly in the fields beyond Whitechappel, in Spittlefields; also in St George's Fields in Southwark, in Bunhill Fields, and in a great field called Wood's Close, near Islington. Thither the Lord Mayor, aldermen, and magistrates sent their officers and servants to buy for their families, themselves keeping within doors as much as possible, and the like did many other people; and after this method was taken the country people came with great cheerfulness, and brought provisions of all sorts, and very seldom got any harm, which, I suppose, added also to that report of their being miraculously preserved.

As for my little family, having thus, as I have said, laid in a store of bread, butter, cheese, and beer, I took my friend and physician's advice, and locked myself up, and my family, and resolved to suffer the hardship of living a few months without flesh-meat, rather than to purchase it at the hazard of our lives.

But though I confined my family, I could not prevail upon my unsatisfied curiosity to stay within entirely myself; and though I generally came frighted and terrified home, vet I could not restrain; only that indeed I did not do it so frequently as at first.

I had some little obligations, indeed, upon me to go to my brother's house, which was in Coleman Street parish and which he had left to my care, and I went at first every day, but afterwards only once or twice a week.

In these walks I had many dismal scenes before my eyes, as particularly of persons falling dead in the streets, terrible shrieks and screechings of women, who, in their agonies, would throw open their chamber windows and cry out in a dismal, surprising manner. It is impossible to describe the variety of postures in which the passions of the poor people would express themselves.

Passing through Tokenhouse Yard, in Lothbury, of a sudden a casement violently opened just over my head, and a woman gave three frightful screeches, and then cried, 'Oh! death, death, death!' in a most inimitable tone, and which struck me with horror and a chillness in my very blood. There was nobody to be seen in the whole street, neither did any other window open, for people had no curiosity now in any case, nor could anybody help one another, so I went on to pass into Bell Alley.

Just in Bell Alley, on the right hand of the passage, there was a more terrible cry than that, though it was not so directed out at the window; but the whole family was in a terrible fright, and I could hear women and children run screaming about the rooms like distracted, when a garret-window opened and somebody from a window on the other side the alley called and asked, 'What is the matter?' upon which, from the first window, it was answered, 'Oh Lord, my old master has hanged himself!' The other asked again, 'Is he quite dead?' and the first answered, 'Ay, ay, quite dead; quite dead and cold!' This person was a merchant and a deputy alderman, and very rich. I care not to mention the name, though I knew his name too, but that would be an hardship to the family, which is now flourishing again.

But this is but one; it is scarce credible what dreadful cases happened in particular families every day. People in the rage of the distemper, or in the torment of their swellings, which was indeed intolerable, running out of their own government, raving and distracted, and oftentimes laying violent hands upon themselves, throwing themselves out at their windows, shooting themselves &c.; mothers murdering their own children in their lunacy, some dying of mere grief as a passion, some of mere fright and surprise without any infection at all, others frighted into idiotism and foolish distractions, some into despair and lunacy, others into melancholy madness.

The pain of the swelling was in particular very violent, and to some intolerable; the physicians and surgeons may be said to have tortured many poor creatures even to death. The swellings in some grew hard, and they applied violent drawing-plaisters or poultices to break them, and if these did not do they cut and scarified them in a terrible manner. In some those swellings were made hard partly by the force of the distemper and partly by their being too violently drawn, and were so hard that no instrument could cut them, and then they burnt them with caustics, so that many died raving mad with the torment, and some in the very operation. In these distresses, some, for want of help to hold them down in their beds, or to look to them, laid hands upon themselves as above. Some broke out into the streets, perhaps naked, and would run directly down to the river if they were not stopped by the watchman or other officers, and plunge themselves into the water wherever they found it.

It often pierced my very soul to hear the groans and cries of those who were thus tormented, but of the two this was counted the most promising particular in the whole infection, for if these swellings could be brought to a head, and to break and run, or, as the surgeons call it, to digest, the patient generally recovered; whereas those who, like the gentlewoman's daughter, were struck with death at the beginning, and had the tokens come out upon them, often went about indifferent easy till a little before they died, and some till the moment they dropped down, as in apoplexies and epilepsies is often the case. Such would be taken suddenly very sick, and would run to a bench or bulk, or any convenient place that offered itself, or to their own houses if possible, as I mentioned before, and there sit down, grow faint, and die. This kind of dying was much the same as it was with those who die of common mortifications, who die swooning, and, as it were, go away in a dream. Such as died thus had very little notice of their being infected at all till the gangrene was spread through their whole body; nor could physicians themselves know certainly how it was with them till they opened their breasts or other parts of their body and saw the tokens.

We had at this time a great many frightful stories told us of nurses and watchmen who looked after the dying people; that is to say, hired nurses who attended infected people, using them barbarously, starving them, smothering them, or by other wicked means hastening their end, that is to say, murdering of them; and watchmen, being set to guard houses that were shut up when there has been but one person left, and perhaps that one lying sick, that they have broke in and murdered that body, and immediately thrown them out into the dead-cart! And so they have gone scarce cold to the grave.

I cannot say but that some such murders were committed, and I think two were sent to prison for it, but died before they could be tried; and I have heard that three others, at several times, were excused for murders of that kind; but I must say I believe nothing of its being so common a crime as some have since been pleased to say, nor did it seem to be so rational where the people were brought so low as not to be able to help themselves, for such seldom recovered, and there was no temptation to commit a murder, at least none equal to the fact, where they were sure persons would die in so short a time, and could not live.

That there were a great many robberies and wicked practices committed even in this dreadful time I do not deny. The power of avarice was so strong in some that they would run any hazard to steal and to plunder; and particularly in houses where all the families or inhabitants have been dead and carried out, they would break in at all hazards, and without regard to the danger of infection, take even the clothes off the dead bodies and the bed-clothes from others where they lay dead.

This, I suppose, must be the case of a family in Houndsditch, where a man and his daughter, the rest of the family being, as I suppose, carried away before by the dead-cart, were found stark naked, one in one chamber and one in another, lying dead on the floor, and the clothes of the beds, from whence 'tis supposed they were rolled off by thieves, stolen and carried quite away.

It is indeed to be observed that the women were in all this calamity the most rash, fearless, and desperate creatures, and as there were vast numbers that went about as nurses to tend those that were sick, they committed a great many petty thieveries in the houses where they were employed; and some of them were publicly whipped for it, when perhaps they ought rather to have been hanged for examples, for numbers of houses were robbed on these occasions, till at length the parish officers were sent to recommend nurses to the sick, and always took an account whom it was they sent, so as that they might call them to account if the house had been abused where they were placed.

But these robberies extended chiefly to wearing-clothes, linen, and what rings or money they could come at when the person died who was under their care, but not to a general plunder of the houses; and I could give you an account of one of these nurses, who, several years after, being on her deathbed, confessed with the utmost horror the robberies she had committed at the time of her being a nurse, and by which she had enriched herself to a great degree. But as for murders, I do not find that there was ever any proof of the facts in the manner as it has been reported, except as above.

They did tell me, indeed, of a nurse in one place that laid a wet cloth upon the face of a dying patient whom she tended, and so put an end to his life, who was just expiring before; and another that smothered a young woman she was looking to when she was in a fainting fit, and would have come to herself; some that killed them by giving them one thing, some another, and some starved them by giving them nothing at all. But these stories had two marks of suspicion that always attended them, which caused me always to slight them and to look on them as mere stories that people continually frighted one another with. First, that wherever it was that we heard it, they always placed the scene at the farther end of the town, opposite or most remote from where you were to hear it. If you heard it in Whitechappel, it had happened at St Giles's, or at Westminster, or Holborn, or that end of the town. If you heard of it at that end of the town, then it was done in Whitechappel, or the Minories, or about Cripplegate parish. If you heard of it in the city, why, then it happened in Southwark; and if you heard of it in Southwark, then it was done in the city, and the like.

In the next place, of what part soever you heard the story, the particulars were always the same, especially that of laying a wet double clout on a dying man's face, and that of smothering a young gentlewoman; so that it was apparent, at least to my judgement, that there was more of tale than of truth in those things.

However, I cannot say but it had some effect upon the people, and particularly that, as I said before, they grew more cautious whom they took into their houses, and whom they trusted their lives with, and had them always recommended if they could; and where they could not find such, for they were not very plenty, they applied to the parish officers.

But here again the misery of that time lay upon the poor who, being infected, had neither food or physic, neither physician or apothecary to assist them, or nurse to attend them. Many of those died calling for help, and even for sustenance, out at their windows in a most miserable and deplorable manner; but it must be added that whenever the cases of such persons or families were represented to my Lord Mayor they always were relieved.

It is true, in some houses where the people were not very poor, yet where they had sent perhaps their wives and children away, and if they had any servants they had been dismissed;—I say it is true that to save the expenses, many such as these shut themselves in, and not having help, died alone.

A neighbour and acquaintance of mine, having some money owing to him from a shopkeeper in Whitecross Street or thereabouts, sent his apprentice, a youth about eighteen years of age, to endeavour to get the money. He came to the door, and finding it shut, knocked pretty hard; and, as he thought, heard somebody answer within, but was not sure, so he waited, and after some stay knocked again, and then a third time, when he heard somebody coming downstairs.

At length the man of the house came to the door; he had on his breeches or drawers, and a yellow flannel waistcoat, no stockings, a pair of slipped-shoes, a white cap on his head, and, as the young man said, 'death in his face'.

When he opened the door, says he, 'What do you disturb me thus for?' The boy, though a little surprised, replied, 'I come from such a one, and my master sent me for the money which he says you know of.' 'Very well, child,' returns the living ghost; 'call as you go by at Cripplegate Church, and bid them ring the bell'; and with these words shut the door again, and went up again, and died the same day; nay, perhaps the same hour. This the young man told me himself, and I have reason to believe it. This was while the plague was not come to a height. I think it was in June, towards the latter end of the month; it must be before the dead-carts came about, and while they used the ceremony of ringing the bell for the dead, which was over for certain, in that parish at least, before the month of July, for by the 25th of July there died 550 and upwards in a week, and then they could no more bury in form, rich or poor.

I have mentioned above that notwithstanding this dreadful calamity, yet the numbers of thieves were abroad upon all occasions, where they had found any prey, and that these were generally women. It was one morning about eleven O'clock, I had walked out to my brother's house in Coleman Street parish, as I often did, to see that all was safe.

My brother's house had a little court before it, and a brick wall and a gate in it, and within that several warehouses where his goods of several sorts lay. It happened that in one of these warehouses were several packs of women's high-crowned hats, which came out of the country and were, as I suppose, for exportation: whither, I know not.

I was surprised that when I came near my brother's door, which was in a place they called Swan Alley, I met three or four women with high-crowned hats on their heads; and, as I remembered afterwards, one, if not more, had some hats likewise in their hands; but as I did not see them come out at my brother's door, and not knowing that my brother had any such goods in his warehouse, I did not offer to say anything to them, but went across the way to shun meeting them, as was usual to do at that time, for fear of the plague. But when I came nearer to the gate I met another woman with more hats come out of the gate. 'What business, mistress,' said I, 'have you had there?' 'There are more people there,' said she; 'I have had no more business there than they.' I was hasty to get to the gate then, and said no more to her, by which means she got away. But just as I came to the gate, I saw two more coming across the yard to come out with hats also on their heads and under their arms, at which I threw the gate to behind me, which having a spring lock fastened itself; and turning to the women, 'Forsooth,' said I, 'what are you doing here?' and seized upon the hats, and took them from them. One of them, who, I confess, did not look like a thief—'Indeed,' says she, 'we are wrong, but we were told they were goods that had no owner. Be pleased to take them again; and look yonder, there are more such customers as we.' She cried and looked pitifully, so I took the hats from her and opened the gate, and bade them be gone, for I pitied the women indeed; but when I looked towards the warehouse, as she directed, there were six or seven more, all women, fitting themselves with hats as unconcerned and quiet as if they had been at a hatter's shop buying for their money.

I was surprised, not at the sight of so many thieves only, but at the circumstances I was in; being now to thrust myself in among so many people, who for some weeks had been so shy of myself that if I met anybody in the street I would cross the way from them.

They were equally surprised, though on another account. They all told me they were neighbours, that they had heard anyone might take them, that they were nobody's goods, and the like. I talked big to them at first, went back to the gate and took out the key, so that they were all my prisoners, threatened to lock them all into the warehouse, and go and fetch my Lord Mayor's officers for them.

They begged heartily, protested they found the gate open, and the warehouse door open; and that it had no doubt been broken open by some who expected to find goods of greater value: which indeed was reasonable to believe, because the lock was broke, and a padlock that hung to the door on the outside also loose, and not abundance of the hats carried away.

At length I considered that this was not a time to be cruel and rigorous; and besides that, it would necessarily oblige me to go much about, to have several people come to me, and I go to several whose circumstances of health I knew nothing of; and that even at this time the plague was so high as that there died 4000 a week; so that in showing my resentment, or even in seeking justice for my brother's goods, I might lose my own life; so I contented myself with taking the names and places where some of them lived, who were really inhabitants in the neighbourhood, and threatening that my brother should call them to an account for it when he returned to his habitation.

Then I talked a little upon another foot with them, and asked them how they could do such things as these in a time of such general calamity, and, as it were, in the face of God's most dreadful judgements, when the plague was at their very doors, and, it may be, in their very houses, and they did not know but that the dead-cart might stop at their doors in a few hours to carry them to their graves.

I could not perceive that my discourse made much impression upon them all that while, till it happened that there came two men of the neighbourhood, hearing of the disturbance, and knowing my brother, for they had been both dependents upon his family, and they came to my assistance. These being, as I said, neighbours, presently knew three of the women and told me who they were and where they lived; and it seems they had given me a true account of themselves before.

This brings these two men to a further remembrance. The name of one was John Hayward, who was at that time undersexton of the parish of St Stephen, Coleman Street. By undersexton was understood at that time gravedigger and bearer of the dead. This man carried, or assisted to carry, all the dead to their graves which were buried in that large parish, and who were carried in form; and after that form of burying was stopped, went with the dead-cart and the bell to fetch the dead bodies from the houses where they lay, and fetched many of them out of the chambers and houses; for the parish was, and is still, remarkable particularly, above all the parishes in London, for a great number of alleys and thoroughfares, very long, into which no carts could come, and where they were obliged to go and fetch the bodies a very long way; which alleys now remain to witness it, such as White's Alley, Cross Key Court, Swan Alley, Bell Alley, White Horse Alley, and many more. Here they went with a kind of hand-barrow and laid the dead bodies on it, and carried them out to the carts; which work he performed and never had the distemper at all, but lived about twenty years after it, and was sexton of the parish to the time of his death. His wife at the same time was a nurse to infected people, and tended many that died in the parish, being for her honesty recommended by the parish officers; yet she never was infected neither.

He never used any preservative against the infection, other than holding garlic and rue in his mouth, and smoking tobacco. This I also had from his own mouth. And his wife's remedy was washing her head in vinegar and sprinkling her head-clothes so with vinegar as to keep them always moist, and if the smell of any of those she waited on was more than ordinary offensive, she snuffed vinegar up her nose and sprinkled vinegar upon her head-clothes, and held a handkerchief wetted with vinegar to her mouth.

It must be confessed that though the plague was chiefly among the poor, yet were the poor the most venturous and fearless of it, and went about their employment with a sort of brutal courage; I must call it so, for it was founded neither on religion nor prudence; scarce did they use any caution, but ran into any business which they could get employment in, though it was the most hazardous. Such was that of tending the sick, watching houses shut up, carrying infected persons to the pest-house, and, which was still worse, carrying the dead away to their graves.

It was under this John Hayward's care, and within his bounds, that the story of the piper, with which people have made themselves so merry, happened, and he assured me that it was true. It is said that it was a blind piper; but, as John told me, the fellow was not blind, but an ignorant, weak, poor man, and usually walked his rounds about ten o'clock at night and went piping along from door to door, and the people usually took him in at public-houses where they knew him, and would give him drink and victuals, and sometimes farthings; and he in return would pipe and sing and talk simply, which diverted the people; and thus he lived. It was but a very bad time for this diversion while things were as I have told, yet the poor fellow went about as usual, but was almost starved; and when anybody asked how he did he would answer, the dead cart had not taken him yet, but that they had promised to call for him next week.

It happened one night that this poor fellow, whether somebody had given him too much drink or no—John Hayward said he had not drink in his house, but that they had given him a little more victuals than ordinary at a public-house in Coleman Street—and the poor fellow, having not usually had a bellyful for perhaps not a good while, was laid all along upon the top of a bulk or stall, and fast asleep, at a door in the street near London Wall, towards Cripplegate-, and that upon the same bulk or stall the people of some house, in the alley of which the house was a corner, hearing a bell which they always rang before the cart came, had laid a body really dead of the plague just by him, thinking, too, that this poor fellow had been a dead body, as the other was, and laid there by some of the neighbours.

Accordingly, when John Hayward with his bell and the cart came along, finding two dead bodies lie upon the stall, they took them up with the instrument they used and threw them into the cart, and, all this while the piper slept soundly.

From hence they passed along and took in other dead bodies, till, as honest John Hayward told me, they almost buried him alive in the cart; yet all this while he slept soundly. At length the cart came to the place where the bodies were to be thrown into the ground, which, as I do remember, was at Mount Mill; and as the cart usually stopped some time before they were ready to shoot out the melancholy load they had in it, as soon as the cart stopped the fellow awaked and struggled a little to get his head out from among the dead bodies, when, raising himself up in the cart, he called out, 'Hey! where am I?' This frighted the fellow that attended about the work; but after some pause John Hayward, recovering himself, said, 'Lord, bless us! There's somebody in the cart not quite dead!' So another called to him and said, 'Who are you?' The fellow answered, 'I am the poor piper. Where am I?' 'Where are you?' says Hayward. 'Why, you are in the dead-cart, and we are going to bury you.' 'But I an't dead though, am I?' says the piper, which made them laugh a little though, as John said, they were heartily frighted at first; so they helped the poor fellow down, and he went about his business.

I know the story goes he set up his pipes in the cart and frighted the bearers and others so that they ran away; but John Hayward did not tell the story so, nor say anything of his piping at all; but that he was a poor piper, and that he was carried away as above I am fully satisfied of the truth of.

It is to be noted here that the dead-carts in the city were not confined to particular parishes, but one cart went through several parishes, according as the number of dead presented; nor were they tied to carry the dead to their respective parishes, but many of the dead taken up in the city were carried to the burying-ground in the out-parts for want of room.

I have already mentioned the surprise that this judgement was at first among the people. I must be allowed to give some of my observations on the more serious and religious part. Surely never city, at least of this bulk and magnitude, was taken in a condition so perfectly unprepared for such a dreadful visitation, whether I am to speak of the civil preparations or religious. They were, indeed, as if they had had no warning, no expectation, no apprehensions, and consequently the least provision imaginable was made for it in a public way. For example, the Lord Mayor and sheriffs had made no provision as magistrates for the regulations which were to be observed. They had gone into no measures for relief of the poor. The citizens had no public magazines or storehouses for corn or meal for the subsistence of the poor, which if they had provided themselves, as in such cases is done abroad, many miserable families who were now reduced to the utmost distress would have been relieved, and that in a better manner than now could be done.

The stock of the city's money I can say but little to. The Chamber of London was said to be exceedingly rich, and it may be concluded that they were so, by the vast of money issued from thence in the rebuilding the public edifices after the fire of London, and in building new works, such as, for the first part, the Guildhall, Blackwell Hall, part of Leadenhall, half the Exchange, the Session House, the Compter, the prisons of Ludgate, Newgate, &c., several of the wharfs and stairs and landing-places on the river; all which were either burned down or damaged by the great fire of London, the next year after the plague; and of the second sort, the Monument, Fleet Ditch with its bridges, and the Hospital of Bethlem or Bedlam, &c. But possibly the managers of the city's credit at that time made more conscience of breaking in upon the orphan's money to show charity to the distressed citizens than the managers in the following years did to beautify the city and re-edify the buildings; though, in the first case, the losers would have thought their fortunes better bestowed, and the public faith of the city have been less subjected to scandal and reproach.

It must be acknowledged that the absent citizens, who, though they were fled for safety into the country, were yet greatly interested in the welfare of those whom they left behind, forgot not to contribute liberally to the relief of the poor, and large sums were also collected among trading towns in the remotest parts of England; and, as I have heard also, the nobility and the gentry in all parts of England took the deplorable condition of the city into their consideration, and sent up large sums of money in charity to the Lord Mayor and magistrates for the relief of the poor. The king also, as I was told, ordered a thousand pounds a week to be distributed in four parts: one quarter to the city and liberty of Westminster; one quarter or part among the inhabitants of the Southwark side of the water; one quarter to the liberty and parts within of the city, exclusive of the city within the walls; and one-fourth part to the suburbs in the county of Middlesex, and the east and north parts of the city. But this latter I only speak of as a report.

Certain it is, the greatest part of the poor or families who formerly lived by their labour, or by retail trade, lived now on charity; and had there not been prodigious sums of money given by charitable, well-minded Christians for the support of such, the city could never have subsisted. There were, no question, accounts kept of their charity, and of the just distribution of it by the magistrates. But as such multitudes of those very officers died through whose hands it was distributed, and also that, as I have been told, most of the accounts of those things were lost in the great fire which happened in the very next year, and which burnt even the chamberlain's office and many of their papers, so I could never come at the particular account, which I used great endeavours to have seen.

It may, however, be a direction in case of the approach of a like visitation, which God keep the city from;—I say, it may be of use to observe that by the care of the Lord Mayor and aldermen at that time in distributing weekly great sums of money for relief of the poor, a multitude of people who would otherwise have perished, were relieved, and their lives preserved. And here let me enter into a brief state of the case of the poor at that time, and what way apprehended from them, from whence may be judged hereafter what may be expected if the like distress should come upon the city.

At the beginning of the plague, when there was now no more hope but that the whole city would be visited; when, as I have said, all that had friends or estates in the country retired with their families; and when, indeed, one would have thought the very city itself was running out of the gates, and that there would be nobody left behind; you may be sure from that hour all trade, except such as related to immediate subsistence, was, as it were, at a full stop.

This is so lively a case, and contains in it so much of the real condition of the people, that I think I cannot be too particular in it, and therefore I descend to the several arrangements or classes of people who fell into immediate distress upon this occasion. For example:

1. All master-workmen in manufactures, especially such as belonged to ornament and the less necessary parts of the people's dress, clothes, and furniture for houses, such as riband-weavers and other weavers, gold and silver lace makers, and gold and silver wire drawers, sempstresses, milliners, shoemakers, hatmakers, and glovemakers; also upholsterers, joiners, cabinet-makers, looking-glass makers, and innumerable trades which depend upon such as these;—I say, the master-workmen in such stopped their work, dismissed their journeymen and workmen, and all their dependents.

2. As merchandising was at a full stop, for very few ships ventured to come up the river and none at all went out, so all the extraordinary officers of the customs, likewise the watermen, carmen, porters, and all the poor whose labour depended upon the merchants, were at once dismissed and put out of business.

3. All the tradesmen usually employed in building or repairing of houses were at a full stop, for the people were far from wanting to build houses when so many thousand houses were at once stripped of their inhabitants; so that this one article turned all the ordinary workmen of that kind out of business, such as bricklayers, masons, carpenters, joiners, plasterers, painters, glaziers, smiths, plumbers, and all the labourers depending on such.

4. As navigation was at a stop, our ships neither coming in or going out as before, so the seamen were all out of employment, and many of them in the last and lowest degree of distress; and with the seamen were all the several tradesmen and workmen belonging to and depending upon the building and fitting out of ships, such as ship-carpenters, caulkers, ropemakers, dry coopers, sailmakers, anchor-smiths, and other smiths; blockmakers, carvers, gunsmiths, ship-chandlers, ship-carvers, and the like. The masters of those perhaps might live upon their substance, but the traders were universally at a stop, and consequently all their workmen discharged. Add to these that the river was in a manner without boats, and all or most part of the watermen, lightermen, boat-builders, and lighter-builders in like manner idle and laid by.

5. All families retrenched their living as much as possible, as well those that fled as those that stayed; so that an innumerable multitude of footmen, serving-men, shopkeepers, journeymen, merchants' bookkeepers, and such sort of people, and especially poor maid-servants, were turned off, and left friendless and helpless, without employment and without habitation, and this was really a dismal article.

I might be more particular as to this part, but it may suffice to mention in general, all trades being stopped, employment ceased: the labour, and by that the bread, of the poor were cut off; and at first indeed the cries of the poor were most lamentable to hear, though by the distribution of charity their misery that way was greatly abated. Many indeed fled into the counties, but thousands of them having stayed in London till nothing but desperation sent them away, death overtook them on the road, and they served for no better than the messengers of death; indeed, others carrying the infection along with them, spread it very unhappily into the remotest parts of the kingdom.

Many of these were the miserable objects of despair which I have mentioned before, and were removed by the destruction which followed. These might be said to perish not by the infection itself but by the consequence of it; indeed, namely, by hunger and distress and the want of all things: being without lodging, without money, without friends, without means to get their bread, or without anyone to give it them; for many of them were without what we call legal settlements, and so could not claim of the parishes, and all the support they had was by application to the magistrates for relief, which relief was (to give the magistrates their due) carefully and cheerfully administered as they found it necessary, and those that stayed behind never felt the want and distress of that kind which they felt who went away in the manner above noted.

Let any one who is acquainted with what multitudes of people get their daily bread in this city by their labour, whether artificers or mere workmen—I say, let any man consider what must be the miserable condition of this town if, on a sudden, they should be all turned out of employment, that labour should cease, and wages for work be no more.

This was the case with us at that time; and had not the sums of money contributed in charity by well-disposed people of every kind, as well abroad as at home, been prodigiously great, it had not been in the power of the Lord Mayor and sheriffs to have kept the public peace. Nor were they without apprehensions, as it was, that desperation should push the people upon tumults, and cause them to rifle the houses of rich men and plunder the markets of provisions; in which case the country people, who brought provisions very freely and boldly to town, would have been terrified from coming any more, and the town would have sunk under an unavoidable famine.

But the prudence of my Lord Mayor and the Court of Aldermen within the city, and of the justices of peace in the out-parts, was such, and they were supported with money from all parts so well, that the poor people were kept quiet, and their wants everywhere relieved, as far as was possible to be done.

Two things besides this contributed to prevent the mob doing any mischief. One was, that really the rich themselves had not laid up stores of provisions in their houses as indeed they ought to have done, and which if they had been wise enough to have done, and locked themselves entirely up, as some few did, they had perhaps escaped the disease better. But as it appeared they had not, so the mob had no notion of finding stores of provisions there if they had broken in as it is plain they were sometimes very near doing, and which: if they bad, they had finished the ruin of the whole city, for there were no regular troops to have withstood them, nor could the trained bands have been brought together to defend the city, no men being to be found to bear arms.

But the vigilance of the Lord Mayor and such magistrates as could be had (for some, even of the aldermen, were dead, and some absent) prevented this; and they did it by the most kind and gentle methods they could think of, as particularly by relieving the most desperate with money, and putting others into business, and particularly that employment of watching houses that were infected and shut up. And as the number of these were very great (for it was said there was at one time ten thousand houses shut up, and every house had two watchmen to guard it, viz., one by night and the other by day), this gave opportunity to employ a very great number of poor men at a time.

The women and servants that were turned off from their places were likewise employed as nurses to tend the sick in all places, and this took off a very great number of them.

And, which though a melancholy article in itself, yet was a deliverance in its kind: namely, the plague, which raged in a dreadful manner from the middle of August to the middle of October, carried off in that time thirty or forty thousand of these very people which, had they been left, would certainly have been an insufferable burden by their poverty; that is to say, the whole city could not have supported the expense of them, or have provided food for them; and they would in time have been even driven to the necessity of plundering either the city itself or the country adjacent, to have subsisted themselves, which would first or last have put the whole nation, as well as the city, into the utmost terror and confusion.

It was observable, then, that this calamity of the people made them very humble; for now for about nine weeks together there died near a thousand a day, one day with another, even by the account of the weekly bills, which yet, I have reason to be assured, never gave a full account, by many thousands; the confusion being such, and the carts working in the dark when they carried the dead, that in some places no account at all was kept, but they worked on, the clerks and sextons not attending for weeks together, and not knowing what number they carried. This account is verified by the following bills of mortality:—

-	Of all of the Diseases.	Plague
From August 8 to August 15	5319	3880
" " 15 " 22	5568	4237
" " 22 " 29	7496	6102
" " 29 to September 5	8252	6988
" September 5 " 12	7690	6544
" " 12 " 19	8297	7165
" " 19 " 26	6460	5533
" " 26 to October 3	5720	4979
" October 3 " 10	5068	4327
-	——	——
-	59,870	49,705

So that the gross of the people were carried off in these two months; for, as the whole number which was brought in to die of the plague was but 68,590, here is 50,000 of them, within a trifle, in two months; I say 50,000, because, as there wants 295 in the number above, so there wants two days of two months in the account of time.

Now when I say that the parish officers did not give in a full account, or were not to be depended upon for their account, let any one but consider how men could be exact in such a time of dreadful distress, and when many of them were taken sick themselves and perhaps died in the very time when their accounts were to be given in; I mean the parish clerks, besides inferior officers; for though these poor men ventured at all hazards, yet they were far from being exempt from the common calamity, especially if it be true that the parish of Stepney had, within the year, 116 sextons, gravediggers, and their assistants; that is to say, bearers, bellmen, and drivers of carts for carrying off the dead bodies.

Indeed the work was not of a nature to allow them leisure to take an exact tale of the dead bodies, which were all huddled together in the dark into a pit; which pit or trench no man could come nigh but at the utmost peril. I observed often that in the parishes of Aldgate and Cripplegate, Whitechappel and Stepney, there were five, six, seven, and eight hundred in a week in the bills; whereas if we may believe the opinion of those that lived in the city all the time as well as I, there died sometimes 2000 a week in those parishes; and I saw it under the hand of one that made as strict an examination into that part as he could, that there really died an hundred thousand people of the plague in that one year whereas in the bills, the articles of the plague, it was but 68,590.

If I may be allowed to give my opinion, by what I saw with my eyes and heard from other people that were eye-witnesses, I do verily believe the same, viz., that there died at least 100,000 of the plague only, besides other distempers and besides those which died in the fields and highways and secret Places out of the compass of the communication, as it was called, and who were not put down in the bills though they really belonged to the body of the inhabitants. It was known to us all that abundance of poor despairing creatures who had the distemper upon them, and were grown stupid or melancholy by their misery, as many were, wandered away into the fields and Woods, and into secret uncouth places almost anywhere, to creep into a bush or hedge and die.

The inhabitants of the villages adjacent would, in pity, carry them food and set it at a distance, that they might fetch it, if they were able; and sometimes they were not able, and the next time they went they should find the poor wretches lie dead and the food untouched. The number of these miserable objects were many, and I know so many that perished thus, and so exactly where, that I believe I could go to the very place and dig their bones up still; for the country people would go and dig a hole at a distance from them, and then with long poles, and hooks at the end of them, drag the bodies into these pits, and then throw the earth in from as far as they could cast it, to cover them, taking notice how the wind blew, and so coming on that side which the seamen call to windward, that the scent of the bodies might blow from them; and thus great numbers went out of the world who were never known, or any account of them taken, as well within the bills of mortality as without.

This, indeed, I had in the main only from the relation of others, for I seldom walked into the fields, except towards Bethnal Green and Hackney, or as hereafter. But when I did walk, I always saw a great many poor wanderers at a distance; but I could know little of their cases, for whether it were in the street or in the fields, if we had seen anybody coming, it was a general method to walk away; yet I believe the account is exactly true.

As this puts me upon mentioning my walking the streets and fields, I cannot omit taking notice what a desolate place the city was at that time. The great street I lived in (which is known to be one of the broadest of all the streets of London, I mean of the suburbs as well as the liberties) all the side where the butchers lived, especially without the bars, was more like a green field than a paved street, and the people generally went in the middle with the horses and carts. It is true that the farthest end towards Whitechappel Church was not all paved, but even the part that was paved was full of grass also; but this need not seem strange, since the great streets within the city, such as Leadenhall Street, Bishopsgate Street, Cornhill, and even the Exchange itself, had grass growing in them in several places; neither cart or coach were seen in the streets from morning to evening, except some country carts to bring roots and beans, or peas, hay, and straw, to the market, and those but very few compared to what was usual. As for coaches, they were scarce used but to carry sick people to the pest-house, and to other hospitals, and some few to carry physicians to such places as they thought fit to venture to visit; for really coaches were dangerous things, and people did not care to venture into them, because they did not know who might have been carried in them last, and sick, infected people were, as I have said, ordinarily carried in them to the pest-houses, and sometimes people expired in them as they went along.

It is true, when the infection came to such a height as I have now mentioned, there were very few physicians which cared to stir abroad to sick houses, and very many of the most eminent of the faculty were dead, as well as the surgeons also; for now it was indeed a dismal time, and for about a month together, not taking any notice of the bills of mortality, I believe there did not die less than 1500 or 1700 a day, one day with another.

One of the worst days we had in the whole time, as I thought, was in the beginning of September, when, indeed, good people began to think that God was resolved to make a full end of the people in this miserable city. This was at that time when the plague was fully come into the eastern parishes. The parish of Aldgate, if I may give my opinion, buried above a thousand a week for two weeks, though the bills did not say so many;—but it surrounded me at so dismal a rate that there was not a house in twenty uninfected in the Minories, in Houndsditch, and in those parts of Aldgate parish about the Butcher Row and the alleys over against me. I say, in those places death reigned in every corner. Whitechappel parish was in the same condition, and though much less than the parish I lived in, yet buried near 600 a week by the bills, and in my opinion near twice as many. Whole families, and indeed whole streets of families, were swept away together; insomuch that it was frequent for neighbours to call to the bellman to go to such-and-such houses and fetch out the people, for that they were all dead.

And, indeed, the work of removing the dead bodies by carts was now grown so very odious and dangerous that it was complained of that the bearers did not take care to dear such houses where all the inhabitants were dead, but that sometimes the bodies lay several days unburied, till the neighbouring families were offended with the stench, and consequently infected; and this neglect of the officers was such that the churchwardens and constables were summoned to look after it, and even the justices of the Hamlets were obliged to venture their lives among them to quicken and encourage them, for innumerable of the bearers died of the distemper, infected by the bodies they were obliged to come so near. And had it not been that the number of poor people who wanted employment and wanted bread (as I have said before) was so great that necessity drove them to undertake anything and venture anything, they would never have found people to be employed. And then the bodies of the dead would have lain above ground, and have perished and rotted in a dreadful manner.

But the magistrates cannot be enough commended in this, that they kept such good order for the burying of the dead, that as fast as any of these they employed to carry off and bury the dead fell sick or died, as was many times the case, they immediately supplied the places with others, which, by reason of the great number of poor that was left out of business, as above, was not hard to do. This occasioned, that notwithstanding the infinite number of people which died and were sick, almost all together, yet they were always cleared away and carried off every night, so that it was never to be said of London that the living were not able to bury the dead.

As the desolation was greater during those terrible times, so the amazement of the people increased, and a thousand unaccountable things they would do in the violence of their fright, as others did the same in the agonies of their distemper, and this part was very affecting. Some went roaring and crying and wringing their hands along the street; some would go praying and lifting up their hands to heaven, calling upon God for mercy. I cannot say, indeed, whether this was not in their distraction, but, be it so, it was still an indication of a more serious mind, when they had the use of their senses, and was much better, even as it was, than the frightful yellings and cryings that every day, and especially in the evenings, were heard in some streets. I suppose the world has heard of the famous Solomon Eagle, an enthusiast. He, though not infected at all but in his head, went about denouncing of judgement upon the city in a frightful manner, sometimes quite naked, and with a pan of burning charcoal on his head. What he said, or pretended, indeed I could not learn.

I will not say whether that clergyman was distracted or not, or whether he did it in pure zeal for the poor people, who went every evening through the streets of Whitechappel, and, with his hands lifted up, repeated that part of the Liturgy of the Church continually, 'Spare us, good Lord; spare Thy people, whom Thou has redeemed with Thy most precious blood.' I say, I cannot speak positively of these things, because these were only the dismal objects which represented themselves to me as I looked through my chamber windows (for I seldom opened the casements), while I confined myself within doors during that most violent raging of the pestilence; when, indeed, as I have said, many began to think, and even to say, that there would none escape; and indeed I began to think so too, and therefore kept within doors for about a fortnight and never stirred out. But I could not hold it. Besides, there were some people who, notwithstanding the danger, did not omit publicly to attend the worship of God, even in the most dangerous times; and though it is true that a great many clergymen did shut up their churches, and fled, as other people did, for the safety of their lives, yet all did not do so. Some ventured to officiate and to keep up the assemblies of the people by constant prayers, and sometimes sermons or brief exhortations to repentance and reformation, and this as long as any would come to hear them. And Dissenters did the like also, and even in the very churches where the parish ministers were either dead or fled; nor was there any room for making difference at such a time as this was.

It was indeed a lamentable thing to hear the miserable lamentations of poor dying creatures calling out for ministers to comfort them and pray with them, to counsel them and to direct them, calling out to God for pardon and mercy, and confessing aloud their past sins. It would make the stoutest heart bleed to hear how many warnings were then given by dying penitents to others not to put off and delay their repentance to the day of distress; that such a time of calamity as this was no time for repentance, was no time to call upon God. I wish I could repeat the very sound of those groans and of those exclamations that I heard from some poor dying creatures when in the height of their agonies and distress, and that I could make him that reads this hear, as I imagine I now hear them, for the sound seems still to ring in my ears.

If I could but tell this part in such moving accents as should alarm the very soul of the reader, I should rejoice that I recorded those things, however short and imperfect.

It pleased God that I was still spared, and very hearty and sound in health, but very impatient of being pent up within doors without air, as I had been for fourteen days or thereabouts; and I could not restrain myself, but I would go to carry a letter for my brother to the post-house. Then it was indeed that I observed a profound silence in the streets. When I came to the post-house, as I went to put in my letter I saw a man stand in one corner of the yard and talking to another at a window, and a third had opened a door belonging to the office. In the middle of the yard lay a small leather purse with two keys hanging at it, with money in it, but nobody would meddle with it. I asked how long it had lain there; the man at the window said it had lain almost an hour, but that they had not meddled with it, because they did not know but the person who dropped it might come back to look for it. I had no such need of money, nor was the sum so big that I had any inclination to meddle with it, or to get the money at the hazard it might be attended with;

so I seemed to go away, when the man who had opened the door said he would take it up, but so that if the right owner came for it he should be sure to have it. So he went in and fetched a pail of water and set it down hard by the purse, then went again and fetch some gunpowder, and cast a good deal of powder upon the purse, and then made a train from that which he had thrown loose upon the purse. The train reached about two yards. After this he goes in a third time and fetches out a pair of tongs red hot, and which he had prepared, I suppose, on purpose; and first setting fire to the train of powder, that singed the purse and also smoked the air sufficiently. But he was not content with that, but he then takes up the purse with the tongs, holding it so long till the tongs burnt through the purse, and then he shook the money out into the pail of water, so he carried it in. The money, as I remember, was about thirteen shilling and some smooth groats and brass farthings.

There might perhaps have been several poor people, as I have observed above, that would have been hardy enough to have ventured for the sake of the money; but you may easily see by what I have observed that the few people who were spared were very careful of themselves at that time when the distress was so exceeding great.

Much about the same time I walked out into the fields towards Bow; for I had a great mind to see how things were managed in the river and among the ships; and as I had some concern in shipping, I had a notion that it had been one of the best ways of securing one's self from the infection to have retired into a ship; and musing how to satisfy my curiosity in that point, I turned away over the fields from Bow to Bromley, and down to Blackwall to the stairs which are there for landing or taking water.

Here I saw a poor man walking on the bank, or sea-wall, as they call it, by himself. I walked a while also about, seeing the houses all shut up. At last I fell into some talk, at a distance, with this poor man; first I asked him how people did thereabouts. 'Alas, sir!' says he, 'almost desolate; all dead or sick. Here are very few families in this part, or in that village' (pointing at Poplar), 'where half of them are not dead already, and the rest sick.' Then he pointing to one house, 'There they are all dead', said he, 'and the house stands open; nobody dares go into it. A poor thief', says he, 'ventured in to steal something, but he paid dear for his theft, for he was carried to the churchyard too last night.' Then he pointed to several other houses. 'There', says he, 'they are all dead, the man and his wife, and five children. There', says he, 'they are shut up; you see a watchman at the door'; and so of other houses. 'Why,' says I, 'what do you here all alone?' 'Why,' says he, 'I am a poor, desolate man; it has pleased God I am not yet visited, though my family is, and one of my children dead.' 'How do you mean, then,' said I, 'that you are not visited?' 'Why,' says he, 'that's my house' (pointing to a very little, low-boarded house), 'and there my poor wife and two children live,' said he, 'if they may be said to live, for my wife and one of the children are visited, but I do not come at them.' And with that word I saw the tears run very plentifully down his face; and so they did down mine too, I assure you.

'But,' said I, 'why do you not come at them? How can you abandon your own flesh and blood?' 'Oh, sir,' says he, 'the Lord forbid! I do not abandon them; I work for them as much as I am able; and, blessed be the Lord, I keep them from want'; and with that I observed he lifted up his eyes to heaven, with a countenance that presently told me I had happened on a man that was no hypocrite, but a serious, religious, good man, and his ejaculation was an expression of thankfulness that, in such a condition as he was in, he should be able to say his family did not want. 'Well,' says I, 'honest man, that is a great mercy as things go now with the poor. But how do you live, then, and how are you kept from the dreadful calamity that is now upon us all?' 'Why, sir,' says he, 'I am a waterman, and there's my boat,' says he, 'and the boat serves me for a house. I work in it in the day, and I sleep in it in the night; and what I get I lay down upon that stone,' says he, showing me a broad stone on the other side of the street, a good way from his house; 'and then,' says he, 'I halloo, and call to them till I make them hear; and they come and fetch it.'

'Well, friend,' says I, 'but how can you get any money as a waterman? Does any body go by water these times?' 'Yes, sir,' says he, 'in the way I am employed there does. Do you see there,' says he, 'five ships lie at anchor' (pointing down the river a good way below the town), 'and do you see', says he, 'eight or ten ships lie at the chain there, and at anchor yonder?' (pointing above the town). 'All those ships have families on board, of their merchants and owners, and such-like, who have locked themselves up and live on board, close shut in, for fear of the infection; and I tend on them to fetch things for them, carry letters, and do what is absolutely necessary, that they may not be obliged to come on shore; and every night I fasten my boat on board one of the ship's boats, and there I sleep by myself, and, blessed be God, I am preserved hitherto.'

'Well,' said I, 'friend, but will they let you come on board after you have been on shore here, when this is such a terrible place, and so infected as it is?'

'Why, as to that,' said he, 'I very seldom go up the ship-side, but deliver what I bring to their boat, or lie by the side, and they hoist it on board. If I did, I think they are in no danger from me, for I never go into any house on shore, or touch anybody, no, not of my own family; but I fetch provisions for them.'

'Nay,' says I, 'but that may be worse, for you must have those provisions of somebody or other; and since all this part of the town is so infected, it is dangerous so much as to speak with anybody, for the village', said I, 'is, as it were, the beginning of London, though it be at some distance from it.'

'That is true,' added he; 'but you do not understand me right; I do not buy provisions for them here. I row up to Greenwich and buy fresh meat there, and sometimes I row down the river to Woolwich and buy there; then I go to single farm-houses on the Kentish side, where I am known, and buy fowls and eggs and butter, and bring to the ships, as they direct me, sometimes one, sometimes the other. I seldom come on shore here, and I came now only to call on my wife and hear how my family do, and give them a little money, which I received last night.'

'Poor man!' said I; 'and how much hast thou gotten for them?'

'I have gotten four shillings,' said he, 'which is a great sum, as things go now with poor men; but they have given me a bag of bread too, and a salt fish and some flesh; so all helps out.' 'Well,' said I, 'and have you given it them yet?'

'No,' said he; 'but I have called, and my wife has answered that she cannot come out yet, but in half-an-hour she hopes to come, and I am waiting for her. Poor woman!' says he, 'she is brought sadly down. She has a swelling, and it is broke, and I hope she will recover; but I fear the child will die, but it is the Lord—'

Here he stopped, and wept very much.

'Well, honest friend,' said I, 'thou hast a sure Comforter, if thou hast brought thyself to be resigned to the will of God; He is dealing with us all in judgement.'

'Oh, sir!' says he, 'it is infinite mercy if any of us are spared, and who am I to repine!'

'Sayest thou so?' said I, 'and how much less is my faith than thine?' And here my heart smote me, suggesting how much better this poor man's foundation was on which he stayed in the danger than mine; that he had nowhere to fly; that he had a family to bind him to attendance, which I had not; and mine was mere presumption, his a true dependence and a courage resting on God; and yet that he used all possible caution for his safety.

I turned a little way from the man while these thoughts engaged me, for, indeed, I could no more refrain from tears than he.

At length, after some further talk, the poor woman opened the door and called, 'Robert, Robert'. He answered, and bid her stay a few moments and he would come; so he ran down the common stairs to his boat and fetched up a sack, in which was the provisions he had brought from the ships; and when he returned he hallooed again. Then he went to the great stone which he showed me and emptied the sack, and laid all out, everything by themselves, and then retired; and his wife came with a little boy to fetch them away, and called and said such a captain had sent such a thing, and such a captain such a thing, and at the end adds, 'God has sent it all; give thanks to Him.' When the poor woman had taken up all, she was so weak she could not carry it at once in, though the weight was not much neither; so she left the biscuit, which was in a little bag, and left a little boy to watch it till she came again.

'Well, but', says I to him, 'did you leave her the four shillings too, which you said was your week's pay?'

'Yes, yes,' says he; 'you shall hear her own it.' So he calls again, 'Rachel, Rachel,' which it seems was her name, 'did you take up the money?' 'Yes,' said she. 'How much was it?' said he. 'Four shillings and a groat,' said she. 'Well, well,' says he, 'the Lord keep you all'; and so he turned to go away.

As I could not refrain contributing tears to this man's story, so neither could I refrain my charity for his assistance. So I called him, 'Hark thee, friend,' said I, 'come hither, for I believe thou art in health, that I may venture thee'; so I pulled out my hand, which was in my pocket before, 'Here,' says I, 'go and call thy Rachel once more, and give her a little more comfort from me. God will never forsake a family that trust in Him as thou dost.' So I gave him four other shillings, and bid him go lay them on the stone and call his wife.

I have not words to express the poor man's thankfulness, neither could he express it himself but by tears running down his face. He called his wife, and told her God had moved the heart of a stranger, upon hearing their condition, to give them all that money, and a great deal more such as that he said to her. The woman, too, made signs of the like thankfulness, as well to Heaven as to me, and joyfully picked it up; and I parted with no money all that year that I thought better bestowed.

I then asked the poor man if the distemper had not reached to Greenwich. He said it had not till about a fortnight before; but that then he feared it had, but that it was only at that end of the town which lay south towards Deptford Bridge; that he went only to a butcher's shop and a grocer's, where he generally bought such things as they sent him for, but was very careful.

I asked him then how it came to pass that those people who had so shut themselves up in the ships had not laid in sufficient stores of all things necessary. He said some of them had—but, on the other hand, some did not come on board till they were frighted into it and till it was too dangerous for them to go to the proper people to lay in quantities of things, and that he waited on two ships, which he showed me, that had laid in little or nothing but biscuit bread and ship beer, and that he had bought everything else almost for them. I asked him if there was any more ships that had separated themselves as those had done. He told me yes, all the way up from the point, right against Greenwich, to within the shore of Limehouse and Redriff, all the ships that could have room rid two and two in the middle of the stream, and that some of them had several families on board. I asked him if the distemper had not reached them. He said he believed it had not, except two or three ships whose people had not been so watchful to keep the seamen from going on shore as others had been, and he said it was a very fine sight to see how the ships lay up the Pool.

When he said he was going over to Greenwich as soon as the tide began to come in, I asked if he would let me go with him and bring me back, for that I had a great mind to see how the ships were ranged, as he had told me. He told me, if I would assure him on the word of a Christian and of an honest man that I had not the distemper, he would. I assured him that I had not; that it had pleased God to preserve me; that I lived in Whitechappel, but was too impatient of being so long within doors, and that I had ventured out so far for the refreshment of a little air, but that none in my house had so much as been touched with it.

Well, sir,' says he, 'as your charity has been moved to pity me and my poor family, sure you cannot have so little pity left as to put yourself into my boat if you were not sound in health which would be nothing less than killing me and ruining my whole family.' The poor man troubled me so much when he spoke of his family with such a sensible concern and in such an affectionate manner, that I could not satisfy myself at first to go at all. I told him I would lay aside my curiosity rather than make him uneasy, though I was sure, and very thankful for it, that I had no more distemper upon me than the freshest man in the world. Well, he would not have me put it off neither, but to let me see how confident he was that I was just to him, now importuned me to go; so when the tide came up to his boat I went in, and he carried me to Greenwich. While he bought the things which he had in his charge to buy, I walked up to the top of the hill under which the town stands, and on the east side of the town, to get a prospect of the river. But it was a surprising sight to see the number of ships which lay in rows, two and two, and some places two or three such lines in the breadth of the river, and this not only up quite to the town, between the houses which we call Ratcliff and Redriff, which they name the Pool, but even down the whole river as far as the head of Long Reach, which is as far as the hills give us leave to see it.

I cannot guess at the number of ships, but I think there must be several hundreds of sail; and I could not but applaud the contrivance: for ten thousand people and more who attended ship affairs were certainly sheltered here from the violence of the contagion, and lived very safe and very easy.

I returned to my own dwelling very well satisfied with my day's journey, and particularly with the poor man; also I rejoiced to see that such little sanctuaries were provided for so many families in a time of such desolation. I observed also that, as the violence of the plague had increased, so the ships which had families on board removed and went farther off, till, as I was told, some went quite away to sea, and put into such harbours and safe roads on the north coast as they could best come at.

But it was also true that all the people who thus left the land and lived on board the ships were not entirely safe from the infection, for many died and were thrown overboard into the river, some in coffins, and some, as I heard, without coffins, whose bodies were seen sometimes to drive up and down with the tide in the river.

But I believe I may venture to say that in those ships which were thus infected it either happened where the people had recourse to them too late, and did not fly to the ship till they had stayed too long on shore and had the distemper upon them (though perhaps they might not perceive it) and so the distemper did not come to them on board the ships, but they really carried it with them; or it was in these ships where the poor waterman said they had not had time to furnish themselves with provisions, but were obliged to send often on shore to buy what they had occasion for, or suffered boats to come to them from the shore. And so the distemper was brought insensibly among them.

And here I cannot but take notice that the strange temper of the people of London at that time contributed extremely to their own destruction. The plague began, as I have observed, at the other end of the town, namely, in Long Acre, Drury Lane, &c., and came on towards the city very gradually and slowly. It was felt at first in December, then again in February, then again in April, and always but a very little at a time; then it stopped till May, and even the last week in May there was but seventeen, and all at that end of the town; and all this while, even so long as till there died above 3000 a week, yet had the people in Redriff, and in Wapping and Ratcliff, on both sides of the river, and almost all Southwark side, a mighty fancy that they should not be visited, or at least that it would not be so violent among them. Some people fancied the smell of the pitch and tar, and such other things as oil and rosin and brimstone, which is so much used by all trades relating to shipping, would preserve them. Others argued it, because it was in its extreamest violence in Westminster and the parish of St Giles and St Andrew, &c., and began to abate again before it came among them—which was true indeed, in part. For example—

From the 8th to the 15th August—

-	St Giles-in-the-Fields	242
-	Cripplegate	886
-	Stepney	197
-	St Margaret, Bermondsey	24
-	Rotherhith	3
-	Total this week	4030

From the 15th to the 22nd August—

-	St Giles-in-the-Fields	175
-	Cripplegate	847
-	Stepney	273
-	St Margaret, Bermondsey	36
-	Rotherhith	2
-	Total this week	5319

N.B.—That it was observed the numbers mentioned in Stepney parish at that time were generally all on that side where Stepney parish joined to Shoreditch, which we now call Spittlefields, where the parish of Stepney comes up to the very wall of Shoreditch Churchyard, and the plague at this time was abated at St Giles-in-the-Fields, and raged most violently in Cripplegate, Bishopsgate, and Shoreditch parishes; but there was not ten people a week that died of it in all that part of Stepney parish which takes in Limehouse, Ratdiff Highway, and which are now the parishes of Shadwell and Wapping, even to St Katherine's by the Tower, till after the whole month of August was expired. But they paid for it afterwards, as I shall observe by-and-by.

This, I say, made the people of Redriff and Wapping, Ratcliff and Limehouse, so secure, and flatter themselves so much with the plague's going off without reaching them, that they took no care either to fly into the country or shut themselves up. Nay, so far were they from stirring that they rather received their friends and relations from the city into their houses, and several from other places really took sanctuary in that part of the town as a Place of safety, and as a place which they thought God would pass over, and not visit as the rest was visited.

And this was the reason that when it came upon—them they were more surprised, more unprovided, and more at a loss what to do than they were in other places; for when it came among them really and with violence, as it did indeed in

September and October, there was then no stirring out into the country, nobody would suffer a stranger to come near them, no, nor near the towns where they dwelt; and, as I have been told, several that wandered into the country on Surrey side were found starved to death in the woods and commons, that country being more open and more woody than any other part so near London, especially about Norwood and the parishes of Camberwell, Dullege, and Lusum, where, it seems, nobody durst relieve the poor distressed people for fear of the infection.

This notion having, as I said, prevailed with the people in that part of the town, was in part the occasion, as I said before, that they had recourse to ships for their retreat; and where they did this early and with prudence, furnishing themselves so with provisions that they had no need to go on shore for supplies or suffer boats to come on board to bring them,—I say, where they did so they had certainly the safest retreat of any people whatsoever; but the distress was such that people ran on board, in their fright, without bread to eat, and some into ships that had no men on board to remove them farther off, or to take the boat and go down the river to buy provisions where it might be done safely, and these often suffered and were infected on board as much as on shore.

As the richer sort got into ships, so the lower rank got into hoys, smacks, lighters, and fishing-boats; and many, especially watermen, lay in their boats; but those made sad work of it, especially the latter, for, going about for provision, and perhaps to get their subsistence, the infection got in among them and made a fearful havoc; many of the watermen died alone in their wherries as they rid at their roads, as well as above bridge as below, and were not found sometimes till they were not in condition for anybody to touch or come near them.

Indeed, the distress of the people at this seafaring end of the town was very deplorable, and deserved the greatest commiseration. But, alas I this was a time when every one's private safety lay so near them that they had no room to pity the distresses of others; for every one had death, as it were, at his door, and many even in their families, and knew not what to do or whither to fly.

This, I say, took away all compassion; self-preservation, indeed, appeared here to be the first law. For the children ran away from their parents as they languished in the utmost distress. And in some places, though not so frequent as the other, parents did the like to their children; nay, some dreadful examples there were, and particularly two in one week, of distressed mothers, raving and distracted, killing their own children; one whereof was not far off from where I dwelt, the poor lunatic creature not living herself long enough to be sensible of the sin of what she had done, much less to be punished for it.

It is not, indeed, to be wondered at: for the danger of immediate death to ourselves took away all bowels of love, all concern for one another. I speak in general, for there were many instances of immovable affection, pity, and duty in many, and some that came to my knowledge, that is to say, by hearsay; for I shall not take upon me to vouch the truth of the particulars.

To introduce one, let me first mention that one of the most deplorable cases in all the present calamity was that of women with child, who, when they came to the hour of their sorrows, and their pains come upon them, could neither have help of one kind or another; neither midwife or neighbouring women to come near them. Most of the midwives were dead, especially of such as served the poor; and many, if not all the midwives of note, were fled into the country; so that it was next to impossible for a poor woman that could not pay an immoderate price to get any midwife to come to her—and if they did, those they could get were generally unskilful and ignorant creatures; and the consequence of this was that a most unusual and incredible number of women were reduced to the utmost distress. Some were delivered and spoiled by the rashness and ignorance of those who pretended to lay them. Children without number were, I might say, murdered by the same but a more justifiable ignorance: pretending they would save the mother, whatever became of the child; and many times both mother and child were lost in the same manner; and especially where the mother had the distemper, there nobody would come near them and both sometimes perished. Sometimes the mother has died of the plague, and the infant, it may be, half born, or born but not parted from the mother. Some died in the very pains of their travail, and not delivered at all; and so many were the cases of this kind that it is hard to judge of them.

Something of it will appear in the unusual numbers which are put into the weekly bills (though I am far from allowing them to be able to give anything of a full account) under the articles of—

Child-bed.
Abortive and Still-born.
Christmas and Infants.

Take the weeks in which the plague was most violent, and compare them with the weeks before the distemper began, even in the same year. For example:—

Child-bed. Abortive. Still-born.			
From January 3 to January 10	7	1	13
" " 10 " 17	8	6	11
" " 17 " 24	9	5	15
" " 24 " 31	3	2	9
" " 31 to February 7	3	3	8
" February 7 " 14	6	2	11
" " 14 " 21	5	2	13
" " 21 " 28	2	2	10
" " 28 to March 7	5	1	10
-	—	—	—
-	48	24	100
From August 1 to August 8	25	5	11
" " 8 " 15	23	6	8
" " 15 " 22	28	4	4
" " 22 " 29	40	6	10

" " 29 to September 5	38	2	11
September 5 " 12	39	23	...
" " 12 " 19	42	5	17
" " 19 " 26	42	6	10
" " 26 to October 3	14	4	9
	291	61	80

To the disparity of these numbers it is to be considered and allowed for, that according to our usual opinion who were then upon the spot, there were not one-third of the people in the town during the months of August and September as were in the months of January and February. In a word, the usual number that used to die of these three articles, and, as I hear, did die of them the year before, was thus:—

1664.		1665.	
Child-bed	189	Child-bed	625
Abortive and still-born	458	Abortive and still-born	617
	647		1242

This inequality, I say, is exceedingly augmented when the numbers of people are considered. I pretend not to make any exact calculation of the numbers of people which were at this time in the city, but I shall make a probable conjecture at that part by-and-by. What I have said now is to explain the misery of those poor creatures above; so that it might well be said, as in the Scripture, Woe be to those who are with child, and to those which give suck in that day. For, indeed, it was a woe to them in particular.

I was not conversant in many particular families where these things happened, but the outcries of the miserable were heard afar off. As to those who were with child, we have seen some calculation made; 291 women dead in child-bed in nine weeks, out of one-third part of the number of whom there usually died in that time but eighty-four of the same disaster. Let the reader calculate the proportion.

There is no room to doubt but the misery of those that gave suck was in proportion as great. Our bills of mortality could give but little light in this, yet some it did. There were several more than usual starved at nurse, but this was nothing. The misery was where they were, first, starved for want of a nurse, the mother dying and all the family and the infants found dead by them, merely for want; and, if I may speak my opinion, I do believe that many hundreds of poor helpless infants perished in this manner. Secondly, not starved, but poisoned by the nurse. Nay, even where the mother has been nurse, and having received the infection, has poisoned, that is, infected the infant with her milk even before they knew they were infected themselves; nay, and the infant has died in such a case before the mother. I cannot but remember to leave this admonition upon record, if ever such another dreadful visitation should happen in this city, that all women that are with child or that give suck should be gone, if they have any possible means, out of the place, because their misery, if infected, will so much exceed all other people's.

I could tell here dismal stories of living infants being found sucking the breasts of their mothers, or nurses, after they have been dead of the plague. Of a mother in the parish where I lived, who, having a child that was not well, sent for an apothecary to view the child; and when he came, as the relation goes, was giving the child suck at her breast, and to all appearance was herself very well; but when the apothecary came close to her he saw the tokens upon that breast with which she was suckling the child. He was surprised enough, to be sure, but, not willing to fright the poor woman too much, he desired she would give the child into his hand; so he takes the child, and going to a cradle in the room, lays it in, and opening its cloths, found the tokens upon the child too, and both died before he could get home to send a preventive medicine to the father of the child, to whom he had told their condition. Whether the child infected the nurse-mother or the mother the child was not certain, but the last most likely. Likewise of a child brought home to the parents from a nurse that had died of the plague, yet the tender mother would not refuse to take in her child, and laid it in her bosom, by which she was infected; and died with the child in her arms dead also.

It would make the hardest heart move at the instances that were frequently found of tender mothers tending and watching with their dear children, and even dying before them, and sometimes taking the distemper from them and dying, when the child for whom the affectionate heart had been sacrificed has got over it and escaped.

The like of a tradesman in East Smithfield, whose wife was big with child of her first child, and fell in labour, having the plague upon her. He could neither get midwife to assist her or nurse to tend her, and two servants which he kept fled both from her. He ran from house to house like one distracted, but could get no help; the utmost he could get was, that a watchman, who attended at an infected house shut up, promised to send a nurse in the morning. The poor man, with his heart broke, went back, assisted his wife what he could, acted the part of the midwife, brought the child dead into the world, and his wife in about an hour died in his arms, where he held her dead body fast till the morning, when the watchman came and brought the nurse as he had promised; and coming up the stairs (for he had left the door open, or only latched), they found the man sitting with his dead wife in his arms, and so overwhelmed with grief that he died in a few hours after without any sign of the infection upon him, but merely sunk under the weight of his grief.

I have heard also of some who, on the death of their relations, have grown stupid with the insupportable sorrow; and of one, in particular, who was so absolutely overcome with the pressure upon his spirits that by degrees his head sank into his body, so between his shoulders that the crown of his head was very little seen above the bone of his shoulders; and by degrees losing both voice and sense, his face, looking forward, lay against his collarbone and could not be kept up any otherwise, unless held up by the hands of other people; and the poor man never came to himself again, but languished near a year in that condition, and died. Nor was he ever once seen to lift up his eyes or to look upon any particular object.

I cannot undertake to give any other than a summary of such passages as these, because it was not possible to come at the particulars, where sometimes the whole families where such things happened were carried off by the distemper. But there were innumerable cases of this kind which presented to the eye and the ear, even in passing along the streets, as I have hinted above. Nor is it easy to give any story of this or that family which there was not divers parallel stories to be met with of the same kind.

But as I am now talking of the time when the plague raged at the easternmost part of the town—how for a long time the people of those parts had flattered themselves that they should escape, and how they were surprised when it came upon them as it did; for, indeed, it came upon them like an armed man when it did come;—I say, this brings me back to the three poor men who wandered from Wapping, not knowing whither to go or what to do, and whom I mentioned before; one a biscuit-baker, one a sailmaker, and the other a joiner, all of Wapping, or there-abouts.

The sleepiness and security of that part, as I have observed, was such that they not only did not shift for themselves as others did, but they boasted of being safe, and of safety being with them; and many people fled out of the city, and out of the infected suburbs, to Wapping, Ratcliff, Limehouse, Poplar, and such Places, as to Places of security; and it is not at all unlikely that their doing this helped to bring the plague that way faster than it might otherwise have come. For though I am much for people flying away and emptying such a town as this upon the first appearance of a like visitation, and that all people who have any possible retreat should make use of it in time and be gone, yet I must say, when all that will fly are gone, those that are left and must stand it should stand stock-still where they are, and not shift from one end of the town or one part of the town to the other; for that is the bane and mischief of the whole, and they carry the plague from house to house in their very clothes.

Wherefore were we ordered to kill all the dogs and cats, but because as they were domestic animals, and are apt to run from house to house and from street to street, so they are capable of carrying the effluvia or infectious streams of bodies infected even in their furs and hair? And therefore it was that, in the beginning of the infection, an order was published by the Lord Mayor, and by the magistrates, according to the advice of the physicians, that all the dogs and cats should be immediately killed, and an officer was appointed for the execution.

It is incredible, if their account is to be depended upon, what a prodigious number of those creatures were destroyed. I think they talked of forty thousand dogs, and five times as many cats; few houses being without a cat, some having several, sometimes five or six in a house. All possible endeavours were used also to destroy the mice and rats, especially the latter, by laying ratsbane and other poisons for them, and a prodigious multitude of them were also destroyed.

I often reflected upon the unprovided condition that the whole body of the people were in at the first coming of this calamity upon them, and how it was for want of timely entering into measures and managements, as well public as private, that all the confusions that followed were brought upon us, and that such a prodigious number of people sank in that disaster, which, if proper steps had been taken, might, Providence concurring, have been avoided, and which, if posterity think fit, they may take a caution and warning from. But I shall come to this part again.

I come back to my three men. Their story has a moral in every part of it, and their whole conduct, and that of some whom they joined with, is a pattern for all poor men to follow, or women either, if ever such a time comes again; and if there was no other end in recording it, I think this a very just one, whether my account be exactly according to fact or no.

Two of them are said to be brothers, the one an old soldier, but now a biscuit-maker; the other a lame sailor, but now a sailmaker; the third a joiner. Says John the biscuit-maker one day to Thomas his brother, the sailmaker, 'Brother Tom, what will become of us? The plague grows hot in the city, and increases this way. What shall we do?'

'Truly,' says Thomas, 'I am at a great loss what to do, for I find if it comes down into Wapping I shall be turned out of my lodging.' And thus they began to talk of it beforehand.

John. Turned out of your lodging, Tom I If you are, I don't know who will take you in; for people are so afraid of one another now, there's no getting a lodging anywhere.

Thomas. Why, the people where I lodge are good, civil people, and have kindness enough for me too; but they say I go abroad every day to my work, and it will be dangerous; and they talk of locking themselves up and letting nobody come near them.

John. Why, they are in the right, to be sure, if they resolve to venture staying in town.

Thomas. Nay, I might even resolve to stay within doors too, for, except a suit of sails that my master has in hand, and which I am just finishing, I am like to get no more work a great while. There's no trade stirs now. Workmen and servants are turned off everywhere, so that I might be glad to be locked up too; but I do not see they will be willing to consent to that, any more than to the other.

John. Why, what will you do then, brother? And what shall I do? for I am almost as bad as you. The people where I lodge are all gone into the country but a maid, and she is to go next week, and to shut the house quite up, so that I shall be turned adrift to the wide world before you, and I am resolved to go away too, if I knew but where to go.

Thomas. We were both distracted we did not go away at first; then we might have travelled anywhere. There's no stirring now; we shall be starved if we pretend to go out of town. They won't let us have victuals, no, not for our money, nor let us come into the towns, much less into their houses.

John. And that which is almost as bad, I have but little money to help myself with neither.

Thomas. As to that, we might make shift, I have a little, though not much; but I tell you there's no stirring on the road. I know a couple of poor honest men in our street have attempted to travel, and at Barnet, or Whetstone, or thereabouts, the people offered to fire at them if they pretended to go forward, so they are come back again quite discouraged.

John. I would have ventured their fire if I had been there. If I had been denied food for my money they should have seen me take it before their faces, and if I had tendered money for it they could not have taken any course with me by law.

Thomas. You talk your old soldier's language, as if you were in the Low Countries now, but this is a serious thing. The people have good reason to keep anybody off that they are not satisfied are sound, at such a time as this, and we must not plunder them.

John. No, brother, you mistake the case, and mistake me too. I would plunder nobody; but for any town upon the road to deny me leave to pass through the town in the open highway, and deny me provisions for my money, is to say the town has a right to starve me to death, which cannot be true.

Thomas. But they do not deny you liberty to go back again from whence you came, and therefore they do not starve you.

John. But the next town behind me will, by the same rule, deny me leave to go back, and so they do starve me between them. Besides, there is no law to prohibit my travelling wherever I will on the road.

Thomas. But there will be so much difficulty in disputing with them at every town on the road that it is not for poor men to do it or undertake it, at such a time as this is especially.

John. Why, brother, our condition at this rate is worse than anybody else's, for we can neither go away nor stay here. I am of the same mind with the lepers of Samaria: 'If we stay here we are sure to die', I mean especially as you and I are stated, without a dwelling-house of our own, and without lodging in anybody else's. There is no lying in the street at such a time as this; we had as good go into the dead-cart at once. Therefore I say, if we stay here we are sure to die, and if we go away we can but die; I am resolved to be gone.

Thomas. You will go away. Whither will you go, and what can you do? I would as willingly go away as you, if I knew whither. But we have no acquaintance, no friends. Here we were born, and here we must die.

John. Look you, Tom, the whole kingdom is my native country as well as this town. You may as well say I must not go out of my house if it is on fire as that I must not go out of the town I was born in when it is infected with the plague. I was born in England, and have a right to live in it if I can.

Thomas. But you know every vagrant person may by the laws of England be taken up, and passed back to their last legal settlement.

John. But how shall they make me vagrant? I desire only to travel on, upon my lawful occasions.

Thomas. What lawful occasions can we pretend to travel, or rather wander upon? They will not be put off with words.

John. Is not flying to save our lives a lawful occasion? And do they not all know that the fact is true? We cannot be said to dissemble.

Thomas. But suppose they let us pass, whither shall we go?

John. Anywhere, to save our lives; it is time enough to consider that when we are got out of this town. If I am once out of this dreadful place, I care not where I go.

Thomas. We shall be driven to great extremities. I know not what to think of it.

John. Well, Tom, consider of it a little.

This was about the beginning of July; and though the plague was come forward in the west and north parts of the town, yet all Wapping, as I have observed before, and Redriff, and Ratdiff, and Limehouse, and Poplar, in short, Deptford and Greenwich, all both sides of the river from the Hermitage, and from over against it, quite down to Blackwall, was entirely free; there had not one person died of the plague in all Stepney parish, and not one on the south side of Whitechappel Road, no, not in any parish; and yet the weekly bill was that very week risen up to 1006.

It was a fortnight after this before the two brothers met again, and then the case was a little altered, and the' plague was exceedingly advanced and the number greatly increased; the bill was up at 2785, and prodigiously increasing, though still both sides of the river, as below, kept pretty well. But some began to die in Redriff, and about five or six in Ratdiff Highway, when the sailmaker came to his brother John express, and in some fright; for he was absolutely warned out of his lodging, and had only a week to provide himself. His brother John was in as bad a case, for he was quite out, and had only begged leave of his master, the biscuit-maker, to lodge in an outhouse belonging to his workhouse, where he only lay upon straw, with some biscuit-sacks, or bread-sacks, as they called them, laid upon it, and some of the same sacks to cover him.

Here they resolved (seeing all employment being at an end, and no work or wages to be had), they would make the best of their way to get out of the reach of the dreadful infection, and, being as good husbands as they could, would endeavour to live upon what they had as long as it would last, and then work for more if they could get work anywhere, of any kind, let it be what it would.

While they were considering to put this resolution in practice in the best manner they could, the third man, who was acquainted very well with the sailmaker, came to know of the design, and got leave to be one of the number; and thus they prepared to set out.

It happened that they had not an equal share of money; but as the sailmaker, who had the best stock, was, besides his being lame, the most unfit to expect to get anything by working in the country, so he was content that what money they had should all go into one public stock, on condition that whatever any one of them could gain more than another, it should without any grudging be all added to the public stock.

They resolved to load themselves with as little baggage as possible because they resolved at first to travel on foot, and to go a great way that they might, if possible, be effectually safe; and a great many consultations they had with themselves before they could agree about what way they should travel, which they were so far from adjusting that even to the morning they set out they were not resolved on it.

At last the seaman put in a hint that determined it. 'First,' says he, 'the weather is very hot, and therefore I am for travelling north, that we may not have the sun upon our faces and beating on our breasts, which will heat and suffocate us; and I have been told', says he, 'that it is not good to overheat our blood at a time when, for aught we know, the infection may be in the very air. In the next place,' says he, 'I am for going the way that may be contrary to the wind, as it may blow when we set out, that we may not have the wind blow the air of the city on our backs as we go.' These two cautions were approved of, if it could be brought so to hit that the wind might not be in the south when they set out to go north.

John the baker, who bad been a soldier, then put in his opinion. 'First,' says he, 'we none of us expect to get any lodging on the road, and it will be a little too hard to lie just in the open air. Though it be warm weather, yet it may be wet and damp, and we have a double reason to take care of our healths at such a time as this; and therefore,' says he, 'you, brother Tom, that are a sailmaker, might easily make us a little tent, and I will undertake to set it up every night, and take it down, and a fig for all the inns in England; if we have a good tent over our heads we shall do well enough.'

The joiner opposed this, and told them, let them leave that to him; he would undertake to build them a house every night with his hatchet and mallet, though he had no other tools, which should be fully to their satisfaction, and as good as a tent.

The soldier and the joiner disputed that point some time, but at last the soldier carried it for a tent. The only objection against it was, that it must be carried with them, and that would increase their baggage too much, the weather being hot; but the sailmaker had a piece of good hap fell in which made that easy, for his master whom he worked for, having a rope-walk as well as sailmaking trade, had a little, poor horse that he made no use of then; and being willing to assist the three honest men, he gave them the horse for the carrying their baggage; also for a small matter of three days' work that his man did for him before he went, he let him have an old top-gallant sail that was worn out, but was sufficient and more than enough to make a very good tent. The soldier showed how to shape it, and they soon by his direction made their tent, and fitted it with poles or staves for the purpose; and thus they were furnished for their journey, viz., three men, one tent, one horse, one gun—for the soldier would not go without arms, for now he said he was no more a biscuit-baker, but a trooper.

The joiner had a small bag of tools such as might be useful if he should get any work abroad, as well for their subsistence as his own. What money they had they brought all into one public stock, and thus they began their journey. It seems that in the morning when they set out the wind blew, as the sailor said, by his pocket-compass, at N.W. by W. So they directed, or rather resolved to direct, their course N.W.

But then a difficulty came in their way, that, as they set out from the hither end of Wapping, near the Hermitage, and that the plague was now very violent, especially on the north side of the city, as in Shoreditch and Cripplegate parish, they did not think it safe for them to go near those parts; so they went away east through Ratcliff Highway as far as Ratcliff Cross, and leaving Stepney Church still on their left hand, being afraid to come up from Ratcliff Cross to Mile End, because they must come just by the churchyard, and because the wind, that seemed to blow more from the west, blew directly from the side of the city where the plague was hottest. So, I say, leaving Stepney they fetched a long compass, and going to Poplar and Bromley, came into the great road just at Bow.

Here the watch placed upon Bow Bridge would have questioned them, but they, crossing the road into a narrow way that turns out of the hither end of the town of Bow to Old Ford, avoided any inquiry there, and travelled to Old Ford. The constables everywhere were upon their guard not so much, It seems, to stop people passing by as to stop them from taking up their abode in their towns, and withal because of a report that was newly raised at that time: and that, indeed, was not very improbable, viz., that the poor people in London, being distressed and starved for want of work, and by that means for want of bread, were up in arms and had raised a tumult, and that they would come out to all the towns round to plunder for bread. This, I say, was only a rumour, and it was very well it was no more. But it was not so far off from being a reality as it has been thought, for in a few weeks more the poor people became so desperate by the calamity they suffered that they were with great difficulty kept from g out into the fields and towns, and tearing all in pieces wherever they came; and, as I have observed before, nothing hindered them but that the plague raged so violently and fell in upon them so furiously that they rather went to the grave by thousands than into the fields in mobs by thousands; for, in the parts about the parishes of St Sepulcher, Clarkenwell, Cripplegate, Bishopsgate, and Shoreditch, which were the places where the mob began to threaten, the distemper came on so furiously that there died in those few parishes even then, before the plague was come to its height, no less than 5361 people in the first three weeks in August; when at the same time the parts about Wapping, Radcliffe, and Rotherhith were, as before described, hardly touched, or but very lightly; so that in a word though, as I said before, the good management of the Lord Mayor and justices did much to prevent the rage and desperation of the people from breaking out in rabbles and tumults, and in short from the poor plundering the rich,—I say, though they did much, the dead-carts did more: for as I have said that in five parishes only there died above 5000 in twenty days, so there might be probably three times that number sick all that time; for some recovered, and great numbers fell sick every day and died afterwards. Besides, I must still be allowed to say that if the bills of mortality said five thousand, I always believed it was near twice as many in reality, there being no room to believe that the account they gave was right, or that indeed they were among such confusions as I saw them in, in any condition to keep an exact account.

But to return to my travellers. Here they were only examined, and as they seemed rather coming from the country than from the city, they found the people the easier with them; that they talked to them, let them come into a public-house where the constable and his warders were, and gave them drink and some victuals which greatly refreshed and encouraged them; and here it came into their heads to say, when they should be inquired of afterwards, not that they came from London, but that they came out of Essex.

To forward this little fraud, they obtained so much favour of the constable at Old Ford as to give them a certificate of their passing from Essex through that village, and that they had not been at London; which, though false in the common acceptance of London in the county, yet was literally true, Wapping or Ratcliff being no part either of the city or liberty.

This certificate directed to the next constable that was at Homerton, one of the hamlets of the parish of Hackney, was so serviceable to them that it procured them, not a free passage there only, but a full certificate of health from a justice of the peace, who upon the constable's application granted it without much difficulty; and thus they passed through the long divided town of Hackney (for it lay then in several separated hamlets), and travelled on till they came into the great north road on the top of Stamford Hill.

By this time they began to be weary, and so in the back-road from Hackney, a little before it opened into the said great road, they resolved to set up their tent and encamp for the first night, which they did accordingly, with this addition, that finding a barn, or a building like a barn, and first searching as well as they could to be sure there was nobody in it, they set up their tent, with the head of it against the barn. This they did also because the wind blew that night very high, and they were but young at such a way of lodging, as well as at the managing their tent.

Here they went to sleep; but the joiner, a grave and sober man, and not pleased with their lying at this loose rate the first night, could not sleep, and resolved, after trying to sleep to no purpose, that he would get out, and, taking the gun in his hand, stand sentinel and guard his companions. So with the gun in his hand, he walked to and again before the barn, for that stood in the field near the road, but within the hedge. He had not been long upon the scout but he heard a noise of people coming on, as if it had been a great number, and they came on, as he thought, directly towards the barn. He did not presently awake his companions; but in a few minutes more, their noise growing louder and louder, the biscuit-baker called to him and asked him what was the matter, and quickly started out too. The other, being the lame sailmaker and most weary, lay still in the tent.

As they expected, so the people whom they had heard came on directly to the barn, when one of our travellers challenged, like soldiers upon the guard, with 'Who comes there?' The people did not answer immediately, but one of them speaking to another that was behind him, 'Alas I alas I we are all disappointed,' says he. 'Here are some people before us; the barn is taken up.'

They all stopped upon that, as under some surprise, and it seems there was about thirteen of them in all, and some women among them. They consulted together what they should do, and by their discourse our travellers soon found they were poor, distressed people too, like themselves, seeking shelter and safety; and besides, our travellers had no need to be afraid of their coming up to disturb them, for as soon as they heard the words, 'Who comes there?' these could hear the women say, as if frighted, 'Do not go near them. How do you know but they may have the plague?' And when one of the men said, 'Let us but speak to them', the women said, 'No, don't by any means. We have escaped thus far by the goodness of God; do not let us run into danger now, we beseech you.'

Our travellers found by this that they were a good, sober sort of people, and flying for their lives, as they were; and, as they were encouraged by it, so John said to the joiner, his comrade, 'Let us encourage them too as much as we can'; so he called to them, 'Hark ye, good people,' says the joiner, 'we find by your talk that you are flying from the same dreadful enemy as we are. Do not be afraid of us; we are only three poor men of us. If you are free from the distemper you shall not be hurt by us. We are not in the barn, but in a little tent here in the outside, and we will remove for you; we can set up our tent again immediately anywhere else'; and upon this a parley began between the joiner, whose name was Richard, and one of their men, who said his name was Ford.

Ford. And do you assure us that you are all sound men?

Richard. Nay, we are concerned to tell you of it, that you may not be uneasy or think yourselves in danger; but you see we do not desire you should put yourselves into any danger, and therefore I tell you that we have not made use of the barn, so we will remove from it, that you may be safe and we also.

Ford. That is very kind and charitable; but if we have reason to be satisfied that you are sound and free from the visitation, why should we make you remove now you are settled in your lodging, and, it may be, are laid down to rest? We will go into the barn, if you please, to rest ourselves a while, and we need not disturb you.

Richard. Well, but you are more than we are. I hope you will assure us that you are all of you sound too, for the danger is as great from you to us as from us to you.

Ford. Blessed be God that some do escape, though it is but few; what may be our portion still we know not, but hitherto we are preserved.

Richard. What part of the town do you come from? Was the plague come to the places where you lived?

Ford. Ay, ay, in a most frightful and terrible manner, or else we had not fled away as we do; but we believe there will be very few left alive behind us.

Richard. What part do you come from?

Ford. We are most of us of Cripplegate parish, only two or three of Clerkenwell parish, but on the hither side.

Richard. How then was it that you came away no sooner?

Ford. We have been away some time, and kept together as well as we could at the hither end of Islington, where we got leave to lie in an old uninhabited house, and had some bedding and conveniences of our own that we brought with us; but the plague is come up into Islington too, and a house next door to our poor dwelling was infected and shut up; and we are come away in a fright.

Richard. And what way are you going?

Ford. As our lot shall cast us; we know not whither, but God will guide those that look up to Him.

They parleyed no further at that time, but came all up to the barn, and with some difficulty got into it. There was nothing but hay in the barn, but it was almost full of that, and they accommodated themselves as well as they could, and went to rest; but our travellers observed that before they went to sleep an ancient man who it seems was father of one of the women, went to prayer with all the company, recommending themselves to the blessing and direction of Providence, before they went to sleep.

It was soon day at that time of the year, and as Richard the joiner had kept guard the first part of the night, so John the soldier relieved him, and he had the post in the morning, and they began to be acquainted with one another. It seems when they left Islington they intended to have gone north, away to Highgate, but were stopped at Holloway, and there they would not let them pass; so they crossed over the fields and hills to the eastward, and came out at the Boarded River, and so avoiding the towns, they left Hornsey on the left hand and Newington on the right hand, and came into the great road about Stamford Hill on that side, as the three travellers had done on the other side. And now they had thoughts of going over the river in the marshes, and make forwards to Epping Forest, where they hoped they should get leave to rest. It seems they were not poor, at least not so poor as to be in want; at least they had enough to subsist them moderately for two or three months, when, as they said, they were in hopes the cold weather would check the infection, or at least the violence of it would have spent itself, and would abate, if it were only for want of people left alive to be infected.

This was much the fate of our three travellers, only that they seemed to be the better furnished for travelling, and had it in their view to go farther off; for as to the first, they did not propose to go farther than one day's journey, that so they might have intelligence every two or three days how things were at London.

But here our travellers found themselves under an unexpected inconvenience: namely that of their horse, for by means of the horse to carry their baggage they were obliged to keep in the road, whereas the people of this other band went over the fields or roads, path or no path, way or no way, as they pleased; neither had they any occasion to pass through any town, or come near any town, other than to buy such things as they wanted for their necessary subsistence, and in that indeed they were put to much difficulty; of which in its place.

But our three travellers were obliged to keep the road, or else they must commit spoil, and do the country a great deal of damage in breaking down fences and gates to go over enclosed fields, which they were loth to do if they could help it.

Our three travellers, however, had a great mind to join themselves to this company and take their lot with them; and after some discourse they laid aside their first design which looked northward, and resolved to follow the other into Essex; so in the morning they took up their tent and loaded their horse, and away they travelled all together.

They had some difficulty in passing the ferry at the river-side, the ferryman being afraid of them; but after some parley at a distance, the ferryman was content to bring his boat to a place distant from the usual ferry, and leave it there for them to take it; so putting themselves over, he directed them to leave the boat, and he, having another boat, said he would fetch it again, which it seems, however, he did not do for above eight days.

Here, giving the ferryman money beforehand, they had a supply of victuals and drink, which he brought and left in the boat for them; but not without, as I said, having received the money beforehand. But now our travellers were at a great loss and difficulty how to get the horse over, the boat being small and not fit for it: and at last could not do it without unloading the baggage and making him swim over.

From the river they travelled towards the forest, but when they came to Walthamstow the people of that town denied to admit them, as was the case everywhere. The constables and their watchmen kept them off at a distance and parleyed with them. They gave the same account of themselves as before, but these gave no credit to what they said, giving it for a reason that two or three companies had already come that way and made the like pretences, but that they had given several people the distemper in the towns where they had passed; and had been afterwards so hardly used by the country (though with justice, too, as they had deserved) that about Brentwood, or that way, several of them perished in the fields—whether of the plague or of mere want and distress they could not tell.

This was a good reason indeed why the people of Walthamstow should be very cautious, and why they should resolve not to entertain anybody that they were not well satisfied of. But, as Richard the joiner and one of the other men who parleyed with them told them, it was no reason why they should block up the roads and refuse to let people pass through the town, and who asked nothing of them but to go through the street; that if their people were afraid of them, they might go into their houses and shut their doors; they would neither show them civility nor incivility, but go on about their business.

The constables and attendants, not to be persuaded by reason, continued obstinate, and would hearken to nothing; so the two men that talked with them went back to their fellows to consult what was to be done. It was very discouraging in the whole, and they knew not what to do for a good while; but at last John the soldier and biscuit-maker, considering a while, 'Come,' says he, 'leave the rest of the parley to me.' He had not appeared yet, so he sets the joiner, Richard, to work to cut some poles out of the trees and shape them as like guns as he could, and in a little time he had five or six fair muskets, which at a distance would not be known; and about the part where the lock of a gun is he caused them to wrap cloth and rags such as they had, as soldiers do in wet weather to preserve the locks of their pieces from rust; the rest was discoloured with clay or mud, such as they could get; and all this while the rest of them sat under the trees by his direction, in two or three bodies, where they made fires at a good distance from one another.

While this was doing he advanced himself and two or three with him, and set up their tent in the lane within sight of the barrier which the town's men had made, and set a sentinel just by it with the real gun, the only one they had, and who walked to and fro with the gun on his shoulder, so as that the people of the town might see them. Also, he tied the horse to a gate in the hedge just by, and got some dry sticks together and kindled a fire on the other side of the tent, so that the people of the town could see the fire and the smoke, but could not see what they were doing at it.

After the country people had looked upon them very earnestly a great while, and, by all that they could see, could not but suppose that they were a great many in company, they began to be uneasy, not for their going away, but for staying where they were; and above all, perceiving they had horses and arms, for they had seen one horse and one gun at the tent, and they had seen others of them walk about the field on the inside of the hedge by the side of the lane with their muskets, as they took them to be, shouldered; I say, upon such a sight as this, you may be assured they were alarmed and terribly frighted, and it seems they went to a justice of the peace to know what they should do. What the justice advised them to I know not, but towards the evening they called from the barrier, as above, to the sentinel at the tent.

'What do you want?' says John[1].

'Why, what do you intend to do?' says the constable. 'To do,' says John; 'what would you have us to do?' Constable. Why don't you be gone? What do you stay there for?

John. Why do you stop us on the king's highway, and pretend to refuse us leave to go on our way?

Constable. We are not bound to tell you our reason, though we did let you know it was because of the plague.

John. We told you we were all sound and free from the plague, which we were not bound to have satisfied you of, and yet you pretend to stop us on the highway.

---

[1] It seems John was in the tent, but hearing them call, he steps out, and taking the gun upon his shoulder, talked to them as if he had been the sentinel placed there upon the guard by some officer that was his superior.

Constable. We have a right to stop it up, and our own safety obliges us to it. Besides, this is not the king's highway; 'tis a way upon sufferance. You see here is a gate, and if we do let people pass here, we make them pay toll.

John. We have a right to seek our own safety as well as you, and you may see we are flying for our lives: and 'tis very unchristian and unjust to stop us.

Constable. You may go back from whence you came; we do not hinder you from that.

John. No; it is a stronger enemy than you that keeps us from doing that, or else we should not have come hither.

Constable. Well, you may go any other way, then.

John. No, no; I suppose you see we are able to send you going, and all the people of your parish, and come through your town when we will; but since you have stopped us here, we are content. You see we have encamped here, and here we will live. We hope you will furnish us with victuals.

Constable. We furnish you I What mean you by that?

John. Why, you would not have us starve, would you? If you stop us here, you must keep us.

Constable. You will be ill kept at our maintenance.

John. If you stint us, we shall make ourselves the better allowance.

Constable. Why, you will not pretend to quarter upon us by force, will you?

John. We have offered no violence to you yet. Why do you seem to oblige us to it? I am an old soldier, and cannot starve, and if you think that we shall be obliged to go back for want of provisions, you are mistaken.

Constable. Since you threaten us, we shall take care to be strong enough for you. I have orders to raise the county upon you.

John. It is you that threaten, not we. And since you are for mischief, you cannot blame us if we do not give you time for it; we shall begin our march in a few minutes[1].

Constable. What is it you demand of us?

John. At first we desired nothing of you but leave to go through the town; we should have offered no injury to any of you, neither would you have had any injury or loss by us. We are not thieves, but poor people in distress, and flying from the dreadful plague in London, which devours thousands every week. We wonder how you could be so unmerciful!

Constable. Self-preservation obliges us.

John. What! To shut up your compassion in a case of such distress as this?

Constable. Well, if you will pass over the fields on your left hand, and behind that part of the town, I will endeavour to have gates opened for you.

John. Our horsemen[2] cannot pass with our baggage that way; it does not lead into the road that we want to go, and why should you force us out of the road?

---

[1] This frighted the constable and the people that were with him, that they immediately changed their note.

[2] They had but one horse among them.

Besides, you have kept us here all day without any provisions but such as we brought with us. I think you ought to send us some provisions for our relief.

Constable. If you will go another way we will send you some provisions.

John. That is the way to have all the towns in the county stop up the ways against us.

Constable. If they all furnish you with food, what will you be the worse? I see you have tents; you want no lodging.

John. Well, what quantity of provisions will you send us?

Constable. How many are you?

John. Nay, we do not ask enough for all our company; we are in three companies. If you will send us bread for twenty men and about six or seven women for three days, and show us the way over the field you speak of, we desire not to put your people into any fear for us; we will go out of our way to oblige you, though we are as free from infection as you are[1].

Constable. And will you assure us that your other people shall offer us no new disturbance?

John. No, no you may depend on it.

Constable. You must oblige yourself, too, that none of your people shall come a step nearer than where the provisions we send you shall be set down.

John. I answer for it we will not.

Accordingly they sent to the place twenty loaves of bread and three or four large pieces of good beef, and opened some gates, through which they passed; but none of them had courage so much as to look out to see them go, and, as it was evening, if they had looked they could not have seen them as to know how few they were.

This was John the soldier's management. But this gave such an alarm to the county, that had they really been two or three hundred the whole county would have been raised upon them, and they would have been sent to prison, or perhaps knocked on the head.

They were soon made sensible of this, for two days afterwards they found several parties of horsemen and footmen also about, in pursuit of three companies of men, armed, as they said, with muskets, who were broke out from London and had the plague upon them, and that were not only spreading the distemper among the people, but plundering the country.

As they saw now the consequence of their case, they soon saw the danger they were in; so they resolved by the advice also of the old soldier to divide themselves again. John and his two comrades, with the horse, went away, as if towards Waltham; the other in two companies, but all a little asunder, and went towards Epping.

---

[1] Here he called to one of his men, and bade him order Captain Richard and his people to march the lower way on the side of the marches, and meet them in the forest; which was all a sham, for they had no Captain Richard, or any such company.

The first night they encamped all in the forest, and not far off of one another, but not setting up the tent, lest that should discover them. On the other hand, Richard went to work with his axe and his hatchet, and cutting down branches of trees, he built three tents or hovels, in which they all encamped with as much convenience as they could expect.

The provisions they had at Walthamstow served them very plentifully this night; and as for the next, they left it to Providence. They had fared so well with the old soldier's conduct that they now willingly made him their leader, and the first of his conduct appeared to be very good. He told them that they were now at a proper distance enough from London; that as they need not be immediately beholden to the country for relief, so they ought to be as careful the country did not infect them as that they did not infect the country; that what little money they had, they must be as frugal of as they could; that as he would not have them think of offering the country any violence, so they must endeavour to make the sense of their condition go as far with the country as it could. They all referred themselves to his direction, so they left their three houses standing, and the next day went away towards Epping. The captain also (for so they now called him), and his two fellow-travellers, laid aside their design of going to Waltham, and all went together.

When they came near Epping they halted, choosing out a proper place in the open forest, not very near the highway, but not far out of it on the north side, under a little cluster of low pollard-trees. Here they pitched their little camp—which consisted of three large tents or huts made of poles which their carpenter, and such as were his assistants, cut down and fixed in the ground in a circle, binding all the small ends together at the top and thickening the sides with boughs of trees and bushes, so that they were completely close and warm. They had, besides this, a little tent where the women lay by themselves, and a hut to put the horse in.

It happened that the next day, or next but one, was market-day at Epping, when Captain John and one of the other men went to market and bought some provisions; that is to say, bread, and some mutton and beef; and two of the women went separately, as if they had not belonged to the rest, and bought more. John took the horse to bring it home, and the sack which the carpenter carried his tools in, to put it in. The carpenter went to work and made them benches and stools to sit on, such as the wood he could get would afford, and a kind of table to dine on.

They were taken no notice of for two or three days, but after that abundance of people ran out of the town to look at them, and all the country was alarmed about them. The people at first seemed afraid to come near them; and, on the other hand, they desired the people to keep off, for there was a rumour that the plague was at Waltham, and that it had been in Epping two or three days; so John called out to them not to come to them, 'for,' says he, 'we are all whole and sound people here, and we would not have you bring the plague among us, nor pretend we brought it among you.'

After this the parish officers came up to them and parleyed with them at a distance, and desired to know who they were, and by what authority they pretended to fix their stand at that place. John answered very frankly, they were poor distressed people from London who, foreseeing the misery they should be reduced to if plague spread into the city, had fled out in time for their lives, and, having no acquaintance or relations to fly to, had first taken up at Islington; but, the plague being come into that town, were fled farther; and as they supposed that the people of Epping might have refused them coming into their town, they had pitched their tents thus in the open field and in the forest, being willing to bear all the hardships of such a disconsolate lodging rather than have any one think or be afraid that they should receive injury by them.

At first the Epping people talked roughly to them, and told them they must remove; that this was no place for them; and that they pretended to be sound and well, but that they might be infected with the plague for aught they knew, and might infect the whole country, and they could not suffer them there.

John argued very calmly with them a great while, and told them that London was the place by which they—that is, the townsmen of Epping and all the country round them—subsisted; to whom they sold the produce of their lands, and out of whom they made their rent of their farms; and to be so cruel to the inhabitants of London, or to any of those by whom they gained so much, was very hard, and they would be loth to have it remembered hereafter, and have it told how barbarous, how inhospitable, and how unkind they were to the people of London when they fled from the face of the most terrible enemy in the world; that it would be enough to make the name of an Epping man hateful through all the city, and to have the rabble stone them in the very streets whenever they came so much as to market; that they were not yet secure from being visited themselves, and that, as he heard, Waltham was already; that they would think it very hard that when any of them fled for fear before they were touched, they should be denied the liberty of lying so much as in the open fields.

The Epping men told them again, that they, indeed, said they were sound and free from the infection, but that they had no assurance of it; and that it was reported that there had been a great rabble of people at Walthamstow, who made such pretences of being sound as they did, but that they threatened to plunder the town and force their way, whether the parish officers would or no; that there were near two hundred of them, and had arms and tents like Low Country soldiers; that they extorted provisions from the town, by threatening them with living upon them at free quarter, showing their arms, and talking in the language of soldiers; and that several of them being gone away toward Rumford and Brentwood, the country had been infected by them, and the plague spread into both those large towns, so that the people durst not go to market there as usual; that it was very likely they were some of that party; and if so, they deserved to be sent to the county jail, and be secured till they had made satisfaction for the damage they had done, and for the terror and fright they had put the country into.

John answered that what other people had done was nothing to them; that they assured them they were all of one company; that they had never been more in number than they saw them at that time (which, by the way, was very true); that they came out in two separate companies, but joined by the way, their cases being the same; that they were ready to give what account of themselves anybody could desire of them, and to give in their names and places of abode, that so they might be called to an account for any disorder that they might be guilty of; that the townsmen might see they were content to live hardly, and only desired a little room to breathe in on the forest where it was wholesome; for where it was not they could not stay, and would decamp if they found it otherwise there.

'But,' said the townsmen, 'we have a great charge of poor upon our hands already, and we must take care not to increase it; we suppose you can give us no security against your being chargeable to our parish and to the inhabitants, any more than you can of being dangerous to us as to the infection.'

'Why, look you,' says John, 'as to being chargeable to you, we hope we shall not. If you will relieve us with provisions for our present necessity, we will be very thankful; as we all lived without charity when we were at home, so we will oblige ourselves fully to repay you, if God pleases to bring us back to our own families and houses in safety, and to restore health to the people of London.

'As to our dying here: we assure you, if any of us die, we that survive will bury them, and put you to no expense, except it should be that we should all die; and then, indeed, the last man not being able to bury himself, would put you to that single expense which I am persuaded', says John, 'he would leave enough behind him to pay you for the expense of.

'On the other hand,' says John, 'if you shut up all bowels of compassion, and not relieve us at all, we shall not extort anything by violence or steal from any one; but when what little we have is spent, if we perish for want, God's will be done.'

John wrought so upon the townsmen, by talking thus rationally and smoothly to them, that they went away; and though they did not give any consent to their staying there, yet they did not molest them; and the poor people continued there three or four days longer without any disturbance. In this time they had got some remote acquaintance with a victualling-house at the outskirts of the town, to whom they called at a distance to bring some little things that they wanted, and which they caused to be set down at a distance, and always paid for very honestly.

During this time the younger people of the town came frequently pretty near them, and would stand and look at them, and sometimes talk with them at some space between; and particularly it was observed that the first Sabbath-day the poor people kept retired, worshipped God together, and were heard to sing psalms.

These things, and a quiet, inoffensive behaviour, began to get them the good opinion of the country, and people began to pity them and speak very well of them; the consequence of which was, that upon the occasion of a very wet, rainy night, a certain gentleman who lived in the neighbourhood sent them a little cart with twelve trusses or bundles of straw, as well for them to lodge upon as to cover and thatch their huts and to keep them dry. The minister of a parish not far off, not knowing of the other, sent them also about two bushels of wheat and half a bushel of white peas.

They were very thankful, to be sure, for this relief, and particularly the straw was a—very great comfort to them; for though the ingenious carpenter had made frames for them to lie in like troughs, and filled them with leaves of trees, and such things as they could get, and had cut all their tent-cloth out to make them coverlids, yet they lay damp and hard and unwholesome till this straw came, which was to them like feather-beds, and, as John said, more welcome than feather-beds would have been at another time.

This gentleman and the minister having thus begun, and given an example of charity to these wanderers, others quickly followed, and they received every day some benevolence or other from the people, but chiefly from the gentlemen who dwelt in the country round them. Some sent them chairs, stools, tables, and such household things as they gave notice they wanted; some sent them blankets, rugs, and coverlids, some earthenware, and some kitchen ware for ordering their food.

Encouraged by this good usage, their carpenter in a few days built them a large shed or house with rafters, and a roof in form, and an upper floor, in which they lodged warm: for the weather began to be damp and cold in the beginning of September. But this house, being well thatched, and the sides and roof made very thick, kept out the cold well enough. He made, also, an earthen wall at one end with a chimney in it, and another of the company, with a vast deal of trouble and pains, made a funnel to the chimney to carry out the smoke.

Here they lived comfortably, though coarsely, till the beginning of September, when they had the bad news to hear, whether true or not, that the plague, which was very hot at Waltham Abbey on one side and at Rumford and Brentwood on the other side, was also coming to Epping, to Woodford, and to most of the towns upon the Forest, and which, as they said, was brought down among them chiefly by the higlers, and such people as went to and from London with provisions.

If this was true, it was an evident contradiction to that report which was afterwards spread all over England, but which, as I have said, I cannot confirm of my own knowledge: namely, that the market-people carrying provisions to the city never got the infection or carried it back into the country; both which, I have been assured, has been false.

It might be that they were preserved even beyond expectation, though not to a miracle, that abundance went and came and were not touched; and that was much for the encouragement of the poor people of London, who had been completely miserable if the people that brought provisions to the markets had not been many times wonderfully preserved, or at least more preserved than could be reasonably expected.

But now these new inmates began to be disturbed more effectually, for the towns about them were really infected, and they began to be afraid to trust one another so much as to go abroad for such things as they wanted, and this pinched them very hard, for now they had little or nothing but what the charitable gentlemen of the country supplied them with. But, for their encouragement, it happened that other gentlemen in the country who had not sent them anything before, began to hear of them and supply them, and one sent them a large pig—that is to say, a porker another two sheep, and another sent them a calf. In short, they had meat enough, and sometimes had cheese and milk, and all such things. They were chiefly put to it for bread, for when the gentlemen sent them corn they had nowhere to bake it or to grind it. This made them eat the first two bushel of wheat that was sent them in parched corn, as the Israelites of old did, without grinding or making bread of it.

At last they found means to carry their corn to a windmill near Woodford, where they had it ground, and afterwards the biscuit-maker made a hearth so hollow and dry that he could bake biscuit-cakes tolerably well; and thus they came into a condition to live without any assistance or supplies from the towns; and it was well they did, for the country was soon after fully infected, and about 120 were said to have died of the distemper in the villages near them, which was a terrible thing to them.

On this they called a new council, and now the towns had no need to be afraid they should settle near them; but, on the contrary, several families of the poorer sort of the inhabitants quitted their houses and built huts in the forest after the same manner as they had done. But it was observed that several of these poor people that had so removed had the sickness even in their huts or booths; the reason of which was plain, namely, not because they removed into the air, but, () because they did not remove time enough; that is to say, not till, by openly conversing with the other people their neighbours, they had the distemper upon them, or (as may be said) among them, and so carried it about them whither they went. Or (2) because they were not careful enough, after they were safely removed out of the towns, not to come in again and mingle with the diseased people.

But be it which of these it will, when our travellers began to perceive that the plague was not only in the towns, but even in the tents and huts on the forest near them, they began then not only to be afraid, but to think of decamping and removing; for had they stayed they would have been in manifest danger of their lives.

It is not to be wondered that they were greatly afflicted at being obliged to quit the place where they had been so kindly received, and where they had been treated with so much humanity and charity; but necessity and the hazard of life, which they came out so far to preserve, prevailed with them, and they saw no remedy. John, however, thought of a remedy for their present misfortune: namely, that he would first acquaint that gentleman who was their principal benefactor with the distress they were in, and to crave his assistance and advice.

The good, charitable gentleman encouraged them to quit the Place for fear they should be cut off from any retreat at all by the violence of the distemper; but whither they should go, that he found very hard to direct them to. At last John asked of him whether he, being a justice of the peace, would give them certificates of health to other justices whom they might come before; that so whatever might be their lot, they might not be repulsed now they had been also so long from London. This his worship immediately granted, and gave them proper letters of health, and from thence they were at liberty to travel whither they pleased.

Accordingly they had a full certificate of health, intimating that they had resided in a village in the county of Essex so long that, being examined and scrutinised sufficiently, and having been retired from all conversation for above forty days, without any appearance of sickness, they were therefore certainly concluded to be sound men, and might be safely entertained anywhere, having at last removed rather for fear of the plague which was come into such a town, rather than for having any signal of infection upon them, or upon any belonging to them.

With this certificate they removed, though with great reluctance; and John inclining not to go far from home, they moved towards the marshes on the side of Waltham. But here they found a man who, it seems, kept a weir or stop upon the river, made to raise the water for the barges which go up and down the river, and he terrified them with dismal stories of the sickness having been spread into all the towns on the river and near the river, on the side of Middlesex and Hertfordshire; that is to say, into Waltham, Waltham Cross, Enfield, and Ware, and all the towns on the road, that they were afraid to go that way; though it seems the man imposed upon them, for that the thing was not really true.

However, it terrified them, and they resolved to move across the forest towards Rumford and Brentwood; but they heard that there were numbers of people fled out of London that way, who lay up and down in the forest called Henalt Forest, reaching near Rumford, and who, having no subsistence or habitation, not only lived oddly and suffered great extremities in the woods and fields for want of relief, but were said to be made so desperate by those extremities as that they offered many violences to the county robbed and plundered, and killed cattle, and the like; that others, building huts and hovels by the roadside, begged, and that with an importunity next door to demanding relief; so that the county was very uneasy, and had been obliged to take some of them up.

This in the first place intimated to them, that they would be sure to find the charity and kindness of the county, which they had found here where they were before, hardened and shut up against them; and that, on the other hand, they would be questioned wherever they came, and would be in danger of violence from others in like cases as themselves.

Upon all these considerations John, their captain, in all their names, went back to their good friend and benefactor, who had relieved them before, and laying their case truly before him, humbly asked his advice; and he as kindly advised them to take up their old quarters again, or if not, to remove but a little farther out of the road, and directed them to a proper place for them; and as they really wanted some house rather than huts to shelter them at that time of the year, it growing on towards Michaelmas, they found an old decayed house which had been formerly some cottage or little habitation but was so out of repair as scarce habitable; and by the consent of a farmer to whose farm it belonged, they got leave to make what use of it they could.

The ingenious joiner, and all the rest, by his directions went to work with it, and in a very few days made it capable to shelter them all in case of bad weather; and in which there was an old chimney and old oven, though both lying in ruins; yet they made them both fit for use, and, raising additions, sheds, and leantos on every side, they soon made the house capable to hold them all.

They chiefly wanted boards to make window-shutters, floors, doors, and several other things; but as the gentlemen above favoured them, and the country was by that means made easy with them, and above all, that they were known to be all sound and in good health, everybody helped them with what they could spare.

Here they encamped for good and all, and resolved to remove no more. They saw plainly how terribly alarmed that county was everywhere at anybody that came from London, and that they should have no admittance anywhere but with the utmost difficulty; at least no friendly reception and assistance as they had received here.

Now, although they received great assistance and encouragement from the country gentlemen and from the people round about them, yet they were put to great straits: for the weather grew cold and wet in October and November, and they had not been used to so much hardship; so that they got colds in their limbs, and distempers, but never had the infection; and thus about December they came home to the city again.

I give this story thus at large, principally to give an account what became of the great numbers of people which immediately appeared in the city as soon as the sickness abated; for, as I have said, great numbers of those that were able and had retreats in the country fled to those retreats. So, when it was increased to such a frightful extremity as I have related, the middling people who had not friends fled to all parts of the country where they could get shelter, as well those that had money to relieve themselves as those that had not. Those that had money always fled farthest, because they were able to subsist themselves; but those who were empty suffered, as I have said, great hardships, and were often driven by necessity to relieve their wants at the expense of the country. By that means the country was made very uneasy at them, and sometimes took them up; though even then they scarce knew what to do with them, and were always very backward to punish them, but often, too, they forced them from place to place till they were obliged to come back again to London.

I have, since my knowing this story of John and his brother, inquired and found that there were a great many of the poor disconsolate people, as above, fled into the country every way; and some of them got little sheds and barns and outhouses to live in, where they could obtain so much kindness of the country, and especially where they had any the least satisfactory account to give of themselves, and particularly that they did not come out of London too late. But others, and that in great numbers, built themselves little huts and retreats in the fields and woods, and lived like hermits in holes and caves, or any place they could find, and where, we may be sure, they suffered great extremities, such that many of them were obliged to come back again whatever the danger was; and so those little huts were often found empty, and the country people supposed the inhabitants lay dead in them of the plague, and would not go near them for fear—no, not in a great while; nor is it unlikely but that some of the unhappy wanderers might die so all alone, even sometimes for want of help, as particularly in one tent or hut was found a man dead, and on the gate of a field just by was cut with his knife in uneven letters the following words, by which it may be supposed the other man escaped, or that, one dying first, the other buried him as well as he could:—

O mIsErY!
We BoTH ShaLL DyE,
WoE, WoE.

I have given an account already of what I found to have been the case down the river among the seafaring men; how the ships lay in the offing, as it's called, in rows or lines astern of one another, quite down from the Pool as far as I could see. I have been told that they lay in the same manner quite down the river as low as Gravesend, and some far beyond: even everywhere or in every place where they could ride with safety as to wind and weather; nor did I ever hear that the plague reached to any of the people on board those ships—except such as lay up in the Pool, or as high as Deptford Reach, although the people went frequently on shore to the country towns and villages and farmers' houses, to buy fresh provisions, fowls, pigs, calves, and the like for their supply.

Likewise I found that the watermen on the river above the bridge found means to convey themselves away up the river as far as they could go, and that they had, many of them, their whole families in their boats, covered with tilts and bales, as they call them, and furnished with straw within for their lodging, and that they lay thus all along by the shore in the marshes, some of them setting up little tents with their sails, and so lying under them on shore in the day, and going into their boats at night; and in this manner, as I have heard, the river-sides were lined with boats and people as long as they had anything to subsist on, or could get anything of the country; and indeed the country people, as well Gentlemen as others, on these and all other occasions, were very forward to relieve them—but they were by no means willing to receive them into their towns and houses, and for that we cannot blame them.

There was one unhappy citizen within my knowledge who had been visited in a dreadful manner, so that his wife and all his children were dead, and himself and two servants only left, with an elderly woman, a near relation, who had nursed those that were dead as well as she could. This disconsolate man goes to a village near the town, though not within the bills of mortality, and finding an empty house there, inquires out the owner, and took the house. After a few days he got a cart and loaded it with goods, and carries them down to the house; the people of the village opposed his driving the cart along; but with some arguings and some force, the men that drove the cart along got through the street up to the door of the house. There the constable resisted them again, and would not let them be brought in. The man caused the goods to be unloaden and laid at the door, and sent the cart away; upon which they carried the man before a justice of peace; that is to say, they commanded him to go, which he did. The justice ordered him to cause the cart to fetch away the goods again, which he refused to do; upon which the justice ordered the constable to pursue the carters and fetch them back, and make them reload the goods and carry them away, or to set them in the stocks till they came for further orders; and if they could not find them, nor the man would not consent to take them away, they should cause them to be drawn with hooks from the house-door and burned in the street. The poor distressed man upon this fetched the goods again, but with grievous cries and lamentations at the hardship of his case. But there was no remedy; self-preservation obliged the people to those severities which they would not otherwise have been concerned in. Whether this poor man lived or died I cannot tell, but it was reported that he had the plague upon him at that time; and perhaps the people might report that to justify their usage of him; but it was not unlikely that either he or his goods, or both, were dangerous, when his whole family had been dead of the distempers so little a while before.

I know that the inhabitants of the towns adjacent to London were much blamed for cruelty to the poor people that ran from the contagion in their distress, and many very severe things were done, as may be seen from what has been said; but I cannot but say also that, where there was room for charity and assistance to the people, without apparent danger to themselves, they were willing enough to help and relieve them. But as every town were indeed judges in their own case, so the poor people who ran abroad in their extremities were often ill-used and driven back again into the town; and this caused infinite exclamations and outcries against the country towns, and made the clamour very popular.

And yet, more or less, maugre all the caution, there was not a town of any note within ten (or, I believe, twenty) miles of the city but what was more or less infected and had some died among them. I have heard the accounts of several, such as they were reckoned up, as follows:—

In Enfield	32	In Uxbridge	117
" Hornsey	58	" Hertford	90
" Newington	17	" Ware	160
" Tottenham	42	" Hodsdon	30
" Edmonton	19	" Waltham Abbey	23
" Barnet and Hadly	19	" Epping	26
" St Albans	121	" Deptford	623
" Watford	45	" Greenwich	231
" Eltham and Lusum	85	" Kingston	122
" Croydon	61	" Stanes	82
" Brentwood	70	" Chertsey	18
" Rumford	109	" Windsor	103
" Barking Abbot	200		
" Brentford	432	Cum aliis.	

Another thing might render the country more strict with respect to the citizens, and especially with respect to the poor, and this was what I hinted at before:

namely, that there was a seeming propensity or a wicked inclination in those that were infected to infect others.

There have been great debates among our physicians as to the reason of this. Some will have it to be in the nature of the disease, and that it impresses every one that is seized upon by it with a kind of a rage, and a hatred against their own kind—as if there was a malignity not only in the distemper to communicate itself, but in the very nature of man, prompting him with evil will or an evil eye, that, as they say in the case of a mad dog, who though the gentlest creature before of any of his kind, yet then will fly upon and bite any one that comes next him, and those as soon as any who had been most observed by him before.

Others placed it to the account of the corruption of human nature, who cannot bear to see itself more miserable than others of its own species, and has a kind of involuntary wish that all men were as unhappy or in as bad a condition as itself.

Others say it was only a kind of desperation, not knowing or regarding what they did, and consequently unconcerned at the danger or safety not only of anybody near them, but even of themselves also. And indeed, when men are once come to a condition to abandon themselves, and be unconcerned for the safety or at the danger of themselves, it cannot be so much wondered that they should be careless of the safety of other people.

But I choose to give this grave debate a quite different turn, and answer it or resolve it all by saying that I do not grant the fact. On the contrary, I say that the thing is not really so, but that it was a general complaint raised by the people inhabiting the outlying villages against the citizens to justify, or at least excuse, those hardships and severities so much talked of, and in which complaints both sides may be said to have injured one another; that is to say, the citizens pressing to be received and harboured in time of distress, and with the plague upon them, complain of the cruelty and injustice of the country people in being refused entrance and forced back again with their goods and families; and the inhabitants, finding themselves so imposed upon, and the citizens breaking in as it were upon them whether they would or no, complain that when they were infected they were not only regardless of others, but even willing to infect them; neither of which were really true—that is to say, in the colours they were described in.

It is true there is something to be said for the frequent alarms which were given to the country of the resolution of the people of London to come out by force, not only for relief, but to plunder and rob; that they ran about the streets with the distemper upon them without any control; and that no care was taken to shut up houses, and confine the sick people from infecting others; whereas, to do the Londoners justice, they never practised such things, except in such particular cases as I have mentioned above, and such like. On the other hand, everything was managed with so much care, and such excellent order was observed in the whole city and suburbs by the care of the Lord Mayor and aldermen and by the justices of the peace, church-wardens, &c., in the outparts, that London may be a pattern to all the cities in the world for the good government and the excellent order that was everywhere kept, even in the time of the most violent infection, and when the people were in the utmost consternation and distress. But of this I shall speak by itself.

One thing, it is to be observed, was owing principally to the prudence of the magistrates, and ought to be mentioned to their honour: viz., the moderation which they used in the great and difficult work of shutting up of houses. It is true, as I have mentioned, that the shutting up of houses was a great subject of discontent, and I may say indeed the only subject of discontent among the people at that time; for the confining the sound in the same house with the sick was counted very terrible, and the complaints of people so confined were very grievous. They were heard into the very streets, and they were sometimes such that called for resentment, though oftener for compassion. They had no way to converse with any of their friends but out at their windows, where they would make such piteous lamentations as often moved the hearts of those they talked with, and of others who, passing by, heard their story; and as those complaints oftentimes reproached the severity, and sometimes the insolence, of the watchmen placed at their doors, those watchmen would answer saucily enough, and perhaps be apt to affront the people who were in the street talking to the said families; for which, or for their ill-treatment of the families, I think seven or eight of them in several places were killed; I know not whether I should say murdered or not, because I cannot enter into the particular cases. It is true the watchmen were on their duty, and acting in the post where they were placed by a lawful authority; and killing any public legal officer in the execution of his office is always, in the language of the law, called murder. But as they were not authorised by the magistrates' instructions, or by the power they acted under, to be injurious or abusive either to the people who were under their observation or to any that concerned themselves for them; so when they did so, they might be said to act themselves, not their office; to act as private persons, not as persons employed; and consequently, if they brought mischief upon themselves by such an undue behaviour, that mischief was upon their own heads; and indeed they had so much the hearty curses of the people, whether they deserved it or not, that whatever befell them nobody pitied them, and everybody was apt to say they deserved it, whatever it was. Nor do I remember that anybody was ever punished, at least to any considerable degree, for whatever was done to the watchmen that guarded their houses.

What variety of stratagems were used to escape and get out of houses thus shut up, by which the watchmen were deceived or overpowered, and that the people got away, I have taken notice of already, and shall say no more to that. But I say the magistrates did moderate and ease families upon many occasions in this case, and particularly in that of taking away, or suffering to be removed, the sick persons out of such houses when they were willing to be removed either to a pest-house or other Places; and sometimes giving the well persons in the family so shut up, leave to remove upon information given that they were well, and that they would confine themselves in such houses where they went so long as should be required of them. The concern, also, of the magistrates for the supplying such poor families as were infected—I say, supplying them with necessaries, as well physic as food—was very great, and in which they did not content themselves with giving the necessary orders to the officers appointed, but the aldermen in person, and on horseback, frequently rode to such houses and caused the people to be asked at their windows whether they were duly attended or not; also, whether they wanted anything that was necessary, and if the officers had constantly carried their messages and fetched them such things as they wanted or not. And if they answered in the affirmative, all was well; but if they complained that they were ill supplied, and that the officer did not do his duty, or did not treat them civilly, they (the officers) were generally removed, and others placed in their stead.

It is true such complaint might be unjust, and if the officer had such arguments to use as would convince the magistrate that he was right, and that the people had injured him, he was continued and they reproved. But this part could not well bear a particular inquiry, for the parties could very ill be well heard and answered in the street from the windows, as was the case then. The magistrates, therefore, generally chose to favour the people and remove the man, as what seemed to be the least wrong and of the least ill consequence; seeing if the watchman was injured, yet they could easily make him amends by giving him another post of the like nature; but if the family was injured, there was no satisfaction could be made to them, the damage perhaps being irreparable, as it concerned their lives.

A great variety of these cases frequently happened between the watchmen and the poor people shut up, besides those I formerly mentioned about escaping. Sometimes the watchmen were absent, sometimes drunk, sometimes asleep when the people wanted them, and such never failed to be punished severely, as indeed they deserved.

But after all that was or could be done in these cases, the shutting up of houses, so as to confine those that were well with those that were sick, had very great inconveniences in it, and some that were very tragical, and which merited to have been considered if there had been room for it. But it was authorised by a law, it had the public good in view as the end chiefly aimed at, and all the private injuries that were done by the putting it in execution must be put to the account of the public benefit.

It is doubtful to this day whether, in the whole, it contributed anything to the stop of the infection; and indeed I cannot say it did, for nothing could run with greater fury and rage than the infection did when it was in its chief violence, though the houses infected were shut up as exactly and as effectually as it was possible. Certain it is that if all the infected persons were effectually shut in, no sound person could have been infected by them, because they could not have come near them. But the case was this (and I shall only touch it here): namely, that the infection was propagated insensibly, and by such persons as were not visibly infected, who neither knew whom they infected or who they were infected by.

A house in Whitechappel was shut up for the sake of one infected maid, who had only spots, not the tokens come out upon her, and recovered; yet these people obtained no liberty to stir, neither for air or exercise, forty days. Want of breath, fear, anger, vexation, and all the other gifts attending such an injurious treatment cast the mistress of the family into a fever, and visitors came into the house and said it was the plague, though the physicians declared it was not. However, the family were obliged to begin their quarantine anew on the report of the visitors or examiner, though their former quarantine wanted but a few days of being finished. This oppressed them so with anger and grief, and, as before, straitened them also so much as to room, and for want of breathing and free air, that most of the family fell sick, one of one distemper, one of another, chiefly scorbutic ailments; only one, a violent colic; till, after several prolongings of their confinement, some or other of those that came in with the visitors to inspect the persons that were ill, in hopes of releasing them, brought the distemper with them and infected the whole house; and all or most of them died, not of the plague as really upon them before, but of the plague that those people brought them, who should have been careful to have protected them from it. And this was a thing which frequently happened, and was indeed one of the worst consequences of shutting houses up.

I had about this time a little hardship put upon me, which I was at first greatly afflicted at, and very much disturbed about though, as it proved, it did not expose me to any disaster; and this was being appointed by the alderman of Portsoken Ward one of the examiners of the houses in the precinct where I lived. We had a large parish, and had no less than eighteen examiners, as the order called us; the people called us visitors. I endeavoured with all my might to be excused from such an employment, and used many arguments with the alderman's deputy to be excused; particularly I alleged that I was against shutting up houses at all, and that it would be very hard to oblige me to be an instrument in that which was against my judgement, and which I did verily believe would not answer the end it was intended for; but all the abatement I could get was only, that whereas the officer was appointed by my Lord Mayor to continue two months, I should be obliged to hold it but three weeks, on condition nevertheless that I could then get some other sufficient housekeeper to serve the rest of the time for me—which was, in short, but a very small favour, it being very difficult to get any man to accept of such an employment, that was fit to be entrusted with it.

It is true that shutting up of houses had one effect, which I am sensible was of moment, namely, it confined the distempered people, who would otherwise have been both very troublesome and very dangerous in their running about streets with the distemper upon them—which, when they were delirious, they would have done in a most frightful manner, and as indeed they began to do at first very much, till they were thus restrained; nay, so very open they were that the poor would go about and beg at people's doors, and say they had the plague upon them, and beg rags for their sores, or both, or anything that delirious nature happened to think of.

A poor, unhappy gentlewoman, a substantial citizen's wife, was (if the story be true) murdered by one of these creatures in Aldersgate Street, or that way. He was going along the street, raving mad to be sure, and singing; the people only said he was drunk, but he himself said he had the plague upon him, which it seems was true; and meeting this gentlewoman, he would kiss her. She was terribly frighted, as he was only a rude fellow, and she ran from him, but the street being very thin of people, there was nobody near enough to help her. When she saw he would overtake her, she turned and gave him a thrust so forcibly, he being but weak, and pushed him down backward. But very unhappily, she being so near, he caught hold of her and pulled her down also, and getting up first, mastered her and kissed her; and which was worst of all, when he had done, told her he had the plague, and why should not she have it as well as he? She was frighted enough before, being also young with child; but when she heard him say he had the plague, she screamed out and fell down into a swoon, or in a fit, which, though she recovered a little, yet killed her in a very few days; and I never heard whether she had the plague or no.

Another infected person came and knocked at the door of a citizen's house where they knew him very well; the servant let him in, and being told the master of the house was above, he ran up and came into the room to them as the whole family was at supper. They began to rise up, a little surprised, not knowing what the matter was; but he bid them sit still, he only came to take his leave of them. They asked him, 'Why, Mr—, where are you going?' 'Going,' says he; 'I have got the sickness, and shall die tomorrow night.' 'Tis easy to believe, though not to describe, the consternation they were all in. The women and the man's daughters, which were but little girls, were frighted almost to death and got up, one running out at one door and one at another, some downstairs and some upstairs, and getting together as well as they could, locked themselves into their chambers and screamed out at the window for help, as if they had been frighted out of their wits. The master, more composed than they, though both frighted and provoked, was going to lay hands on him and throw him downstairs, being in a passion; but then, considering a little the condition of the man and the danger of touching him, horror seized his mind, and he stood still like one astonished. The poor distempered man all this while, being as well diseased in his brain as in his body, stood still like one amazed. At length he turns round: 'Ay!' says he, with all the seeming calmness imaginable, 'is it so with you all? Are you all disturbed at me? Why, then I'll e'en go home and die there.' And so he goes immediately downstairs. The servant that had let him in goes down after him with a candle, but was afraid to go past him and open the door, so he stood on the stairs to see what he would do. The man went and opened the door, and went out and flung the door after him. It was some while before the family recovered the fright, but as no ill consequence attended, they have had occasion since to speak of it (You may be sure) with great satisfaction. Though the man was gone, it was some time—nay, as I heard, some days before they recovered themselves of the hurry they were in; nor did they go up and down the house with any assurance till they had burnt a great variety of fumes and perfumes in all the rooms, and made a great many smokes of pitch, of gunpowder, and of sulphur, all separately shifted, and washed their clothes, and the like. As to the poor man, whether he lived or died I don't remember.

It is most certain that, if by the shutting up of houses the sick bad not been confined, multitudes who in the height of their fever were delirious and distracted would have been continually running up and down the streets; and even as it was a very great number did so, and offered all sorts of violence to those they met, even just as a mad dog runs on and bites at every one he meets; nor can I doubt but that, should one of those infected, diseased creatures have bitten any man or woman while the frenzy of the distemper was upon them, they, I mean the person so wounded, would as certainly have been incurably infected as one that was sick before, and had the tokens upon him.

I heard of one infected creature who, running out of his bed in his shirt in the anguish and agony of his swellings, of which he had three upon him, got his shoes on and went to put on his coat; but the nurse resisting, and snatching the coat from him, he threw her down, ran over her, ran downstairs and into the street, directly to the Thames in his shirt; the nurse running after him, and calling to the watch to stop him; but the watchman, frighted at the man, and afraid to touch him, let him go on; upon which he ran down to the Stillyard stairs, threw away his shirt, and plunged into the Thames, and, being a good swimmer, swam quite over the river; and the tide being coming in, as they call it (that is, running westward) he reached the land not till he came about the Falcon stairs, where landing, and finding no people there, it being in the night, he ran about the streets there, naked as he was, for a good while, when, it being by that time high water, he takes the river again, and swam back to the Stillyard, landed, ran up the streets again to his own house, knocking at the door, went up the stairs and into his bed again; and that this terrible experiment cured him of the plague, that is to say, that the violent motion of his arms and legs stretched the parts where the swellings he had upon him were, that is to say, under his arms and his groin, and caused them to ripen and break; and that the cold of the water abated the fever in his blood.

I have only to add that I do not relate this any more than some of the other, as a fact within my own knowledge, so as that I can vouch the truth of them, and especially that of the man being cured by the extravagant adventure, which I confess I do not think very possible; but it may serve to confirm the many desperate things which the distressed people falling into deliriums, and what we call lightheadedness, were frequently run upon at that time, and how infinitely more such there would have been if such people had not been confined by the shutting up of houses; and this I take to be the best, if not the only good thing which was performed by that severe method.

On the other hand, the complaints and the murmurings were very bitter against the thing itself. It would pierce the hearts of all that came by to hear the piteous cries of those infected people, who, being thus out of their understandings by the violence of their pain or the heat of their blood, were either shut in or perhaps tied in their beds and chairs, to prevent their doing themselves hurt—and who would make a dreadful outcry at their being confined, and at their being not permitted to die at large, as they called it, and as they would have done before.

This running of distempered people about the streets was very dismal, and the magistrates did their utmost to prevent it; but as it was generally in the night and always sudden when such attempts were made, the officers could not be at band to prevent it; and even when any got out in the day, the officers appointed did not care to meddle with them, because, as they were all grievously infected, to be sure, when they were come to that height, so they were more than ordinarily infectious, and it was one of the most dangerous things that could be to touch them. On the other hand, they generally ran on, not knowing what they did, till they dropped down stark dead, or till they had exhausted their spirits so as that they would fall and then die in perhaps half-an-hour or an hour; and, which was most piteous to hear, they were sure to come to themselves entirely in that half-hour or hour, and then to make most grievous and piercing cries and lamentations in the deep, afflicting sense of the condition they were in. This was much of it before the order for shutting up of houses was strictly put in execution, for at first the watchmen were not so vigorous and severe as they were afterward in the keeping the people in; that is to say, before they were (I mean some of them) severely punished for their neglect, failing in their duty, and letting people who were under their care slip away, or conniving at their going abroad, whether sick or well. But after they saw the officers appointed to examine into their conduct were resolved to have them do their duty or be punished for the omission, they were more exact, and the people were strictly restrained; which was a thing they took so ill and bore so impatiently that their discontents can hardly be described. But there was an absolute necessity for it, that must be confessed, unless some other measures had been timely entered upon, and it was too late for that.

Had not this particular (of the sick being restrained as above) been our case at that time, London would have been the most dreadful place that ever was in the world; there would, for aught I know, have as many people died in the streets as died in their houses; for when the distemper was at its height it generally made them raving and delirious, and when they were so they would never be persuaded to keep in their beds but by force; and many who were not tied threw themselves out of windows when they found they could not get leave to go out of their doors.

It was for want of people conversing one with another, in this time of calamity, that it was impossible any particular person could come at the knowledge of all the extraordinary cases that occurred in different families; and particularly I believe it was never known to this day how many people in their deliriums drowned themselves in the Thames, and in the river which runs from the marshes by Hackney, which we generally called Ware River, or Hackney River. As to those which were set down in the weekly bill, they were indeed few; nor could it be known of any of those whether they drowned themselves by accident or not. But I believe I might reckon up more who within the compass of my knowledge or observation really drowned themselves in that year, than are put down in the bill of all put together: for many of the bodies were never found who yet were known to be lost; and the like in other methods of self-destruction. There was also one man in or about Whitecross Street burned himself to death in his bed; some said it was done by himself, others that it was by the treachery of the nurse that attended him; but that he had the plague upon him was agreed by all.

It was a merciful disposition of Providence also, and which I have many times thought of at that time, that no fires, or no considerable ones at least, happened in the city during that year, which, if it had been otherwise, would have been very dreadful; and either the people must have let them alone unquenched, or have come together in great crowds and throngs, unconcerned at the danger of the infection, not concerned at the houses they went into, at the goods they handled, or at the persons or the people they came among. But so it was, that excepting that in Cripplegate parish, and two or three little eruptions of fires, which were presently extinguished, there was no disaster of that kind happened in the whole year. They told us a story of a house in a place called Swan Alley, passing from Goswell Street, near the end of Old Street, into St John Street, that a family was infected there in so terrible a manner that every one of the house died. The last person lay dead on the floor, and, as it is supposed, had lain herself all along to die just before the fire; the fire, it seems, had fallen from its place, being of wood, and had taken hold of the boards and the joists they lay on, and burnt as far as just to the body, but had not taken hold of the dead body (though she had little more than her shift on) and had gone out of itself, not burning the rest of the house, though it was a slight timber house. How true this might be I do not determine, but the city being to suffer severely the next year by fire, this year it felt very little of that calamity.

Indeed, considering the deliriums which the agony threw people into, and how I have mentioned in their madness, when they were alone, they did many desperate things, it was very strange there were no more disasters of that kind.

It has been frequently asked me, and I cannot say that I ever knew how to give a direct answer to it, how it came to pass that so many infected people appeared abroad in the streets at the same time that the houses which were infected were so vigilantly searched, and all of them shut up and guarded as they were.

I confess I know not what answer to give to this, unless it be this: that in so great and populous a city as this is it was impossible to discover every house that was infected as soon as it was so, or to shut up all the houses that were infected; so that people had the liberty of going about the streets, even where they Pleased, unless they were known to belong to such-and-such infected houses.

It is true that, as several physicians told my Lord Mayor, the fury of the contagion was such at some particular times, and people sickened so fast and died so soon, that it was impossible, and indeed to no purpose, to go about to inquire who was sick and who was well, or to shut them up with such exactness as the thing required, almost every house in a whole street being infected, and in many places every person in some of the houses; and that which was still worse, by the time that the houses were known to be infected, most of the persons infected would be stone dead, and the rest run away for fear of being shut up; so that it was to very small purpose to call them infected houses and shut them up, the infection having ravaged and taken its leave of the house before it was really known that the family was any way touched.

This might be sufficient to convince any reasonable person that as it was not in the power of the magistrates or of any human methods of policy, to prevent the spreading the infection, so that this way of shutting up of houses was perfectly insufficient for that end. Indeed it seemed to have no manner of public good in it, equal or proportionable to the grievous burden that it was to the particular families that were so shut up; and, as far as I was employed by the public in directing that severity, I frequently found occasion to see that it was incapable of answering the end. For example, as I was desired, as a visitor or examiner, to inquire into the particulars of several families which were infected, we scarce came to any house where the plague had visibly appeared in the family but that some of the family were fled and gone. The magistrates would resent this, and charge the examiners with being remiss in their examination or inspection. But by that means houses were long infected before it was known. Now, as I was in this dangerous office but half the appointed time, which was two months, it was long enough to inform myself that we were no way capable of coming at the knowledge of the true state of any family but by inquiring at the door or of the neighbours. As for going into every house to search, that was a part no authority would offer to impose on the inhabitants, or any citizen would undertake: for it would have been exposing us to certain infection and death, and to the ruin of our own families as well as of ourselves; nor would any citizen of probity, and that could be depended upon, have stayed in the town if they had been made liable to such a severity.

Seeing then that we could come at the certainty of things by no method but that of inquiry of the neighbours or of the family, and on that we could not justly depend, it was not possible but that the uncertainty of this matter would remain as above.

It is true masters of families were bound by the order to give notice to the examiner of the place wherein he lived, within two hours after he should discover it, of any person being sick in his house (that is to say, having signs of the infection)—but they found so many ways to evade this and excuse their negligence that they seldom gave that notice till they had taken measures to have every one escape out of the house who had a mind to escape, whether they were sick or sound; and while this was so, it is easy to see that the shutting up of houses was no way to be depended upon as a sufficient method for putting a stop to the infection because, as I have said elsewhere, many of those that so went out of those infected houses had the plague really upon them, though they might really think themselves sound. And some of these were the people that walked the streets till they fell down dead, not that they were suddenly struck with the distemper as with a bullet that killed with the stroke, but that they really had the infection in their blood long before; only, that as it preyed secretly on the vitals, it appeared not till it seized the heart with a mortal power, and the patient died in a moment, as with a sudden fainting or an apoplectic fit.

I know that some even of our physicians thought for a time that those people that so died in the streets were seized but that moment they fell, as if they had been touched by a stroke from heaven as men are killed by a flash of lightning—but they found reason to alter their opinion afterward; for upon examining the bodies of such after they were dead, they always either had tokens upon them or other evident proofs of the distemper having been longer upon them than they had otherwise expected.

This often was the reason that, as I have said, we that were examiners were not able to come at the knowledge of the infection being entered into a house till it was too late to shut it up, and sometimes not till the people that were left were all dead. In Petticoat Lane two houses together were infected, and several people sick; but the distemper was so well concealed, the examiner, who was my neighbour, got no knowledge of it till notice was sent him that the people were all dead, and that the carts should call there to fetch them away. The two heads of the families concerted their measures, and so ordered their matters as that when the examiner was in the neighbourhood they appeared generally at a time, and answered, that is, lied, for one another, or got some of the neighbourhood to say they were all in health—and perhaps knew no better—till, death making it impossible to keep it any longer as a secret, the dead-carts were called in the night to both the houses t and so it became public. But when the examiner ordered the constable to shut up the houses there was nobody left in them but three people, two in one house and one in the other, just dying, and a nurse in each house who acknowledged that they had buried five before, that the houses had been infected nine or ten days, and that for all the rest of the two families, which were many, they were gone, some sick, some well, or whether sick or well could not be known.

In like manner, at another house in the same lane, a man having his family infected but very unwilling to be shut up, when he could conceal it no longer, shut up himself; that is to say, he set the great red cross upon his door with the words, 'Lord have mercy upon us', and so deluded the examiner, who supposed it had been done by the constable by order of the other examiner, for there were two examiners to every district or precinct. By this means he had free egress and regress into his house again and out of it, as he pleased, notwithstanding it was infected, till at length his stratagem was found out; and then he, with the sound part of his servants and family, made off and escaped, so they were not shut up at all.

These things made it very hard, if not impossible, as I have said, to prevent the spreading of an infection by the shutting up of houses—unless the people would think the shutting of their houses no grievance, and be so willing to have it done as that they would give notice duly and faithfully to the magistrates of their being infected as soon as it was known by themselves; but as that cannot be expected from them, and the examiners cannot be supposed, as above, to go into their houses to visit and search, all the good of shutting up houses will be defeated, and few houses will be shut up in time, except those of the poor, who cannot conceal it, and of some people who will be discovered by the terror and consternation which the things put them into.

I got myself discharged of the dangerous office I was in as soon as I could get another admitted, whom I had obtained for a little money to accept of it; and so, instead of serving the two months, which was directed, I was not above three weeks in it; and a great while too, considering it was in the month of August, at which time the distemper began to rage with great violence at our end of the town.

In the execution of this office I could not refrain speaking my opinion among my neighbours as to this shutting up the people in their houses; in which we saw most evidently the severities that were used, though grievous in themselves, had also this particular objection against them: namely, that they did not answer the end, as I have said, but that the distempered people went day by day about the streets; and it was our united opinion that a method to have removed the sound from the sick, in case of a particular house being visited, would have been much more reasonable on many accounts, leaving nobody with the sick persons but such as should on such occasion request to stay and declare themselves content to be shut up with them.

Our scheme for removing those that were sound from those that were sick was only in such houses as were infected, and confining the sick was no confinement; those that could not stir would not complain while they were in their senses and while they had the power of judging. Indeed, when they came to be delirious and light-headed, then they would cry out of the cruelty of being confined; but for the removal of those that were well, we thought it highly reasonable and just, for their own sakes, they should be removed from the sick, and that for other people's safety they should keep retired for a while, to see that they were sound, and might not infect others; and we thought twenty or thirty days enough for this.

Now, certainly, if houses had been provided on purpose for those that were sound to perform this demi-quarantine in, they would have much less reason to think themselves injured in such a restraint than in being confined with infected people in the houses where they lived.

It is here, however, to be observed that after the funerals became so many that people could not toll the bell, mourn or weep, or wear black for one another, as they did before; no, nor so much as make coffins for those that died; so after a while the fury of the infection appeared to be so increased that, in short, they shut up no houses at all. It seemed enough that all the remedies of that kind had been used till they were found fruitless, and that the plague spread itself with an irresistible fury; so that as the fire the succeeding year spread itself, and burned with such violence that the citizens, in despair, gave over their endeavours to extinguish it, so in the plague it came at last to such violence that the people sat still looking at one another, and seemed quite abandoned to despair; whole streets seemed to be desolated, and not to be shut up only, but to be emptied of their inhabitants; doors were left open, windows stood shattering with the wind in empty houses for want of people to shut them. In a word, people began to give up themselves to their fears and to think that all regulations and methods were in vain, and that there was nothing to be hoped for but an universal desolation; and it was even in the height of this general despair that it Pleased God to stay His hand, and to slacken the fury of the contagion in such a manner as was even surprising, like its beginning, and demonstrated it to be His own particular hand, and that above, if not without the agency of means, as I shall take notice of in its proper place.

But I must still speak of the plague as in its height, raging even to desolation, and the people under the most dreadful consternation, even, as I have said, to despair. It is hardly credible to what excess the passions of men carried them in this extremity of the distemper, and this part, I think, was as moving as the rest. What could affect a man in his full power of reflection, and what could make deeper impressions on the soul, than to see a man almost naked, and got out of his house, or perhaps out of his bed, into the street, come out of Harrow Alley, a populous conjunction or collection of alleys, courts, and passages in the Butcher Row in Whitechappel,—I say, what could be more affecting than to see this poor man come out into the open street, run dancing and singing and making a thousand antic gestures, with five or six women and children running after him, crying and calling upon him for the Lord's sake to come back, and entreating the help of others to bring him back, but all in vain, nobody daring to lay a hand upon him or to come near him?

This was a most grievous and afflicting thing to me, who saw it all from my own windows; for all this while the poor afflicted man was, as I observed it, even then in the utmost agony of pain, having (as they said) two swellings upon him which could not be brought to break or to suppurate; but, by laying strong caustics on them, the surgeons had, it seems, hopes to break them—which caustics were then upon him, burning his flesh as with a hot iron. I cannot say what became of this poor man, but I think he continued roving about in that manner till he fell down and died.

No wonder the aspect of the city itself was frightful. The usual concourse of people in the streets, and which used to be supplied from our end of the town, was abated. The Exchange was not kept shut, indeed, but it was no more frequented. The fires were lost; they had been almost extinguished for some days by a very smart and hasty rain. But that was not all; some of the physicians insisted that they were not only no benefit, but injurious to the health of people. This they made a loud clamour about, and complained to the Lord Mayor about it. On the other hand, others of the same faculty, and eminent too, opposed them, and gave their reasons why the fires were, and must be, useful to assuage the violence of the distemper. I cannot give a full account of their arguments on both sides; only this I remember, that they cavilled very much with one another. Some were for fires, but that they must be made of wood and not coal, and of particular sorts of wood too, such as fir in particular, or cedar, because of the strong effluvia of turpentine; others were for coal and not wood, because of the sulphur and bitumen; and others were for neither one or other. Upon the whole, the Lord Mayor ordered no more fires, and especially on this account, namely, that the plague was so fierce that they saw evidently it defied all means, and rather seemed to increase than decrease upon any application to check and abate it; and yet this amazement of the magistrates proceeded rather from want of being able to apply any means successfully than from any unwillingness either to expose themselves or undertake the care and weight of business; for, to do them justice, they neither spared their pains nor their persons. But nothing answered; the infection raged, and the people were now frighted and terrified to the last degree: so that, as I may say, they gave themselves up, and, as I mentioned above, abandoned themselves to their despair.

But let me observe here that, when I say the people abandoned themselves to despair, I do not mean to what men call a religious despair, or a despair of their eternal state, but I mean a despair of their being able to escape the infection or to outlive the plague which they saw was so raging and so irresistible in its force that indeed few people that were touched with it in its height, about August and September, escaped; and, which is very particular, contrary to its ordinary operation in June and July, and the beginning of August, when, as I have observed, many were infected, and continued so many days, and then went off after having had the poison in their blood a long time; but now, on the contrary, most of the people who were taken during the two last weeks in August and in the three first weeks in September, generally died in two or three days at furthest, and many the very same day they were taken; whether the dog-days, or, as our astrologers pretended to express themselves, the influence of the dog-star, had that malignant effect, or all those who had the seeds of infection before in them brought it up to a maturity at that time altogether, I know not; but this was the time when it was reported that above 3000 people died in one night; and they that would have us believe they more critically observed it pretend to say that they all died within the space of two hours, viz., between the hours of one and three in the morning.

As to the suddenness of people's dying at this time, more than before, there were innumerable instances of it, and I could name several in my neighbourhood. One family without the Bars, and not far from me, were all seemingly well on the Monday, being ten in family. That evening one maid and one apprentice were taken ill and died the next morning—when the other apprentice and two children were touched, whereof one died the same evening, and the other two on Wednesday. In a word, by Saturday at noon the master, mistress, four children, and four servants were all gone, and the house left entirely empty, except an ancient woman who came in to take charge of the goods for the master of the family's brother, who lived not far off, and who had not been sick.

Many houses were then left desolate, all the people being carried away dead, and especially in an alley farther on the same side beyond the Bars, going in at the sign of Moses and Aaron, there were several houses together which, they said, had not one person left alive in them; and some that died last in several of those houses were left a little too long before they were fetched out to be buried; the reason of which was not, as some have written very untruly, that the living were not sufficient to bury the dead, but that the mortality was so great in the yard or alley that there was nobody left to give notice to the buriers or sextons that there were any dead bodies there to be buried. It was said, how true I know not, that some of those bodies were so much corrupted and so rotten that it was with difficulty they were carried; and as the carts could not come any nearer than to the Alley Gate in the High Street, it was so much the more difficult to bring them along; but I am not certain how many bodies were then left. I am sure that ordinarily it was not so.

As I have mentioned how the people were brought into a condition to despair of life and abandon themselves, so this very thing had a strange effect among us for three or four weeks; that is, it made them bold and venturous: they were no more shy of one another, or restrained within doors, but went anywhere and everywhere, and began to converse. One would say to another, 'I do not ask you how you are, or say how I am; it is certain we shall all go; so 'tis no matter who is all sick or who is sound'; and so they ran desperately into any place or any company.

As it brought the people into public company, so it was surprising how it brought them to crowd into the churches. They inquired no more into whom they sat near to or far from, what offensive smells they met with, or what condition the people seemed to be in; but, looking upon themselves all as so many dead corpses, they came to the churches without the least caution, and crowded together as if their lives were of no consequence compared to the work which they came about there. Indeed, the zeal which they showed in coming, and the earnestness and affection they showed in their attention to what they heard, made it manifest what a value people would all put upon the worship of God if they thought every day they attended at the church that it would be their last.

Nor was it without other strange effects, for it took away, all manner of prejudice at or scruple about the person whom they found in the pulpit when they came to the churches. It cannot be doubted but that many of the ministers of the parish churches were cut off, among others, in so common and dreadful a calamity; and others had not courage enough to stand it, but removed into the country as they found means for escape. As then some parish churches were quite vacant and forsaken, the people made no scruple of desiring such Dissenters as had been a few years before deprived of their livings by virtue of the Act of Parliament called the Act of Uniformity to preach in the churches; nor did the church ministers in that case make any difficulty of accepting their assistance; so that many of those whom they called silenced ministers had their mouths opened on this occasion and preached publicly to the people.

Here we may observe and I hope it will not be amiss to take notice of it that a near view of death would soon reconcile men of good principles one to another, and that it is chiefly owing to our easy situation in life and our putting these things far from us that our breaches are fomented, ill blood continued, prejudices, breach of charity and of Christian union, so much kept and so far carried on among us as it is. Another plague year would reconcile all these differences; a close conversing with death, or with diseases that threaten death, would scum off the gall from our tempers, remove the animosities among us, and bring us to see with differing eyes than those which we looked on things with before. As the people who had been used to join with the Church were reconciled at this time with the admitting the Dissenters to preach to them, so the Dissenters, who with an uncommon prejudice had broken off from the communion of the Church of England, were now content to come to their parish churches and to conform to the worship which they did not approve of before; but as the terror of the infection abated, those things all returned again to their less desirable channel and to the course they were in before.

I mention this but historically. I have no mind to enter into arguments to move either or both sides to a more charitable compliance one with another. I do not see that it is probable such a discourse would be either suitable or successful; the breaches seem rather to widen, and tend to a widening further, than to closing, and who am I that I should think myself able to influence either one side or other? But this I may repeat again, that 'tis evident death will reconcile us all; on the other side the grave we shall be all brethren again. In heaven, whither I hope we may come from all parties and persuasions, we shall find neither prejudice or scruple; there we shall be of one principle and of one opinion. Why we cannot be content to go hand in hand to the Place where we shall join heart and hand without the least hesitation, and with the most complete harmony and affection—I say, why we cannot do so here I can say nothing to, neither shall I say anything more of it but that it remains to be lamented.

I could dwell a great while upon the calamities of this dreadful time, and go on to describe the objects that appeared among us every day, the dreadful extravagancies which the distraction of sick people drove them into; how the streets began now to be fuller of frightful objects, and families to be made even a terror to themselves. But after I have told you, as I have above, that one man, being tied in his bed, and finding no other way to deliver himself, set the bed on fire with his candle, which unhappily stood within his reach, and burnt himself in his bed; and how another, by the insufferable torment he bore, danced and sung naked in the streets, not knowing one ecstasy from another; I say, after I have mentioned these things, what can be added more? What can be said to represent the misery of these times more lively to the reader, or to give him a more perfect idea of a complicated distress?

I must acknowledge that this time was terrible, that I was sometimes at the end of all my resolutions, and that I had not the courage that I had at the beginning. As the extremity brought other people abroad, it drove me home, and except having made my voyage down to Blackwall and Greenwich, as I have related, which was an excursion, I kept afterwards very much within doors, as I had for about a fortnight before. I have said already that I repented several times that I had ventured to stay in town, and had not gone away with my brother and his family, but it was too late for that now; and after I had retreated and stayed within doors a good while before my impatience led me abroad, then they called me, as I have said, to an ugly and dangerous office which brought me out again; but as that was expired while the height of the distemper lasted, I retired again, and continued close ten or twelve days more, during which many dismal spectacles represented themselves in my view out of my own windows and in our own street—as that particularly from Harrow Alley, of the poor outrageous creature which danced and sung in his agony; and many others there were. Scarce a day or night passed over but some dismal thing or other happened at the end of that Harrow Alley, which was a place full of poor people, most of them belonging to the butchers or to employments depending upon the butchery.

Sometimes heaps and throngs of people would burst out of the alley, most of them women, making a dreadful clamour, mixed or compounded of screeches, cryings, and calling one another, that we could not conceive what to make of it. Almost all the dead part of the night the dead-cart stood at the end of that alley, for if it went in it could not well turn again, and could go in but a little way. There, I say, it stood to receive dead bodies, and as the churchyard was but a little way off, if it went away full it would soon be back again. It is impossible to describe the most horrible cries and noise the poor people would make at their bringing the dead bodies of their children and friends out of the cart, and by the number one would have thought there had been none left behind, or that there were people enough for a small city living in those places. Several times they cried 'Murder', sometimes 'Fire'; but it was easy to perceive it was all distraction, and the complaints of distressed and distempered people.

I believe it was everywhere thus as that time, for the plague raged for six or seven weeks beyond all that I have expressed, and came even to such a height that, in the extremity, they began to break into that excellent order of which I have spoken so much in behalf of the magistrates; namely, that no dead bodies were seen in the street or burials in the daytime: for there was a necessity in this extremity to bear with its being otherwise for a little while.

One thing I cannot omit here, and indeed I thought it was extraordinary, at least it seemed a remarkable hand of Divine justice: viz., that all the predictors, astrologers, fortune-tellers, and what they called cunning-men, conjurers, and the like: calculators of nativities and dreamers of dream, and such people, were gone and vanished; not one of them was to be found. I am verily persuaded that a great number of them fell in the heat of the calamity, having ventured to stay upon the prospect of getting great estates; and indeed their gain was but too great for a time, through the madness and folly of the people. But now they were silent; many of them went to their long home, not able to foretell their own fate or to calculate their own nativities. Some have been critical enough to say that every one of them died. I dare not affirm that; but this I must own, that I never heard of one of them that ever appeared after the calamity was over.

But to return to my particular observations during this dreadful part of the visitation. I am now come, as I have said, to the month of September, which was the most dreadful of its kind, I believe, that ever London saw; for, by all the accounts which I have seen of the preceding visitations which have been in London, nothing has been like it, the number in the weekly bill amounting to almost 40,000 from the 22nd of August to the 26th of September, being but five weeks. The particulars of the bills are as follows, viz.:—

From August the	22nd	to the	29th	7496
" "	29th	"	5th September	8252
" September the	5th	"	12th	7690
" "	12th	"	19th	8297
" "	19th	"	26th	6460
				38,195

This was a prodigious number of itself, but if I should add the reasons which I have to believe that this account was deficient, and how deficient it was, you would, with me, make no scruple to believe that there died above ten thousand a week for all those weeks, one week with another, and a proportion for several weeks both before and after. The confusion among the people, especially within the city, at that time, was inexpressible. The terror was so great at last that the courage of the people appointed to carry away the dead began to fail them; nay, several of them died, although they had the distemper before and were recovered, and some of them dropped down when they have been carrying the bodies even at the pit side, and just ready to throw them in; and this confusion was greater in the city because they had flattered themselves with hopes of escaping, and thought the bitterness of death was past. One cart, they told us, going up Shoreditch was forsaken of the drivers, or being left to one man to drive, he died in the street; and the horses going on overthrew the cart, and left the bodies, some thrown out here, some there, in a dismal manner. Another cart was, it seems, found in the great pit in Finsbury Fields, the driver being dead, or having been gone and abandoned it, and the horses running too near it, the cart fell in and drew the horses in also. It was suggested that the driver was thrown in with it and that the cart fell upon him, by reason his whip was seen to be in the pit among the bodies; but that, I suppose, could not be certain.

In our parish of Aldgate the dead-carts were several times, as I have heard, found standing at the churchyard gate full of dead bodies, but neither bellman or driver or any one else with it; neither in these or many other cases did they know what bodies they had in their cart, for sometimes they were let down with ropes out of balconies and out of windows, and sometimes the bearers brought them to the cart, sometimes other people; nor, as the men themselves said, did they trouble themselves to keep any account of the numbers.

The vigilance of the magistrates was now put to the utmost trial—and, it must be confessed, can never be enough acknowledged on this occasion also; whatever expense or trouble they were at, two things were never neglected in the city or suburbs either:—

(1) Provisions were always to be had in full plenty, and the price not much raised neither, hardly worth speaking.

(2) No dead bodies lay unburied or uncovered; and if one walked from one end of the city to another, no funeral or sign of it was to be seen in the daytime, except a little, as I have said above, in the three first weeks in September.

This last article perhaps will hardly be believed when some accounts which others have published since that shall be seen, wherein they say that the dead lay unburied, which I am assured was utterly false; at least, if it had been anywhere so, it must have been in houses where the living were gone from the dead (having found means, as I have observed, to escape) and where no notice was given to the officers. All which amounts to nothing at all in the case in hand; for this I am positive in, having myself been employed a little in the direction of that part in the parish in which I lived, and where as great a desolation was made in proportion to the number of inhabitants as was anywhere; I say, I am sure that there were no dead bodies remained unburied; that is to say, none that the proper officers knew of; none for want of people to carry them off, and buriers to put them into the ground and cover them; and this is sufficient to the argument; for what might lie in houses and holes, as in Moses and Aaron Alley, is nothing; for it is most certain they were buried as soon as they were found. As to the first article (namely, of provisions, the scarcity or dearness), though I have mentioned it before and shall speak of it again, yet I must observe here:—

(1) The price of bread in particular was not much raised; for in the beginning of the year, viz., in the first week in March, the penny wheaten loaf was ten ounces and a half; and in the height of the contagion it was to be had at nine ounces and a half, and never dearer, no, not all that season. And about the beginning of November it was sold ten ounces and a half again; the like of which, I believe, was never heard of in any city, under so dreadful a visitation, before.

(2) Neither was there (which I wondered much at) any want of bakers or ovens kept open to supply the people with the bread; but this was indeed alleged by some families, viz., that their maidservants, going to the bakehouses with their dough to be baked, which was then the custom, sometimes came home with the sickness (that is to say the plague) upon them.

In all this dreadful visitation there were, as I have said before, but two pest-houses made use of, viz., one in the fields beyond Old Street and one in Westminster; neither was there any compulsion used in carrying people thither. Indeed there was no need of compulsion in the case, for there were thousands of poor distressed people who, having no help or conveniences or supplies but of charity, would have been very glad to have been carried thither and been taken care of; which, indeed, was the only thing that I think was wanting in the whole public management of the city, seeing nobody was here allowed to be brought to the pest-house but where money was given, or security for money, either at their introducing or upon their being cured and sent out—for very many were sent out again whole; and very good physicians were appointed to those places, so that many people did very well there, of which I shall make mention again. The principal sort of people sent thither were, as I have said, servants who got the distemper by going of errands to fetch necessaries to the families where they lived, and who in that case, if they came home sick, were removed to preserve the rest of the house; and they were so well looked after there in all the time of the visitation that there was but 156 buried in all at the London pest-house, and 159 at that of Westminster.

By having more pest-houses I am far from meaning a forcing all people into such places. Had the shutting up of houses been omitted and the sick hurried out of their dwellings to pest-houses, as some proposed, it seems, at that time as well as since, it would certainly have been much worse than it was. The very removing the sick would have been a spreading of the infection, and the rather because that removing could not effectually clear the house where the sick person was of the distemper; and the rest of the family, being then left at liberty, would certainly spread it among others.

The methods also in private families, which would have been universally used to have concealed the distemper and to have concealed the persons being sick, would have been such that the distemper would sometimes have seized a whole family before any visitors or examiners could have known of it. On the other hand, the prodigious numbers which would have been sick at a time would have exceeded all the capacity of public pest-houses to receive them, or of public officers to discover and remove them.

This was well considered in those days, and I have heard them talk of it often. The magistrates had enough to do to bring people to submit to having their houses shut up, and many ways they deceived the watchmen and got out, as I have observed. But that difficulty made it apparent that they t would have found it impracticable to have gone the other way to work, for they could never have forced the sick people out of their beds and out of their dwellings. It must not have been my Lord Mayor's officers, but an army of officers, that must have attempted it; and the people, on the other hand, would have been enraged and desperate, and would have killed those that should have offered to have meddled with them or with their children and relations, whatever had befallen them for it; so that they would have made the people, who, as it was, were in the most terrible distraction imaginable, I say, they would have made them stark mad; whereas the magistrates found it proper on several accounts to treat them with lenity and compassion, and not with violence and terror, such as dragging the sick out of their houses or obliging them to remove themselves, would have been.

This leads me again to mention the time when the plague first began; that is to say, when it became certain that it would spread over the whole town, when, as I have said, the better sort of people first took the alarm and began to hurry themselves out of town. It was true, as I observed in its place, that the throng was so great, and the coaches, horses, waggons, and carts were so many, driving and dragging the people away, that it looked as if all the city was running away; and had any regulations been published that had been terrifying at that time, especially such as would pretend to dispose of the people otherwise than they would dispose of themselves, it would have put both the city and suburbs into the utmost confusion.

But the magistrates wisely caused the people to be encouraged, made very good bye-laws for the regulating the citizens, keeping good order in the streets, and making everything as eligible as possible to all sorts of people.

In the first place, the Lord Mayor and the sheriffs, the Court of Aldermen, and a certain number of the Common Council men, or their deputies, came to a resolution and published it, viz., that they would not quit the city themselves, but that they would be always at hand for the preserving good order in every place and for the doing justice on all occasions; as also for the distributing the public charity to the poor; and, in a word, for the doing the duty and discharging the trust reposed in them by the citizens to the utmost of their power.

In pursuance of these orders, the Lord Mayor, sheriffs, &c., held councils every day, more or less, for making such dispositions as they found needful for preserving the civil peace; and though they used the people with all possible gentleness and clemency, yet all manner of presumptuous rogues such as thieves, housebreakers, plunderers of the dead or of the sick, were duly punished, and several declarations were continually published by the Lord Mayor and Court of Aldermen against such.

Also all constables and churchwardens were enjoined to stay in the city upon severe penalties, or to depute such able and sufficient housekeepers as the deputy aldermen or Common Council men of the precinct should approve, and for whom they should give security; and also security in case of mortality that they would forthwith constitute other constables in their stead.

These things re-established the minds of the people very much, especially in the first of their fright, when they talked of making so universal a flight that the city would have been in danger of being entirely deserted of its inhabitants except the poor, and the country of being plundered and laid waste by the multitude. Nor were the magistrates deficient in performing their part as boldly as they promised it; for my Lord Mayor and the sheriffs were continually in the streets and at places of the greatest danger, and though they did not care for having too great a resort of people crowding about them, yet in emergent cases they never denied the people access to them, and heard with patience all their grievances and complaints. My Lord Mayor had a low gallery built on purpose in his hall, where he stood a little removed from the crowd when any complaint came to be heard, that he might appear with as much safety as possible.

Likewise the proper officers, called my Lord Mayor's officers, constantly attended in their turns, as they were in waiting; and if any of them were sick or infected, as some of them were, others were instantly employed to fill up and officiate in their places till it was known whether the other should live or die.

In like manner the sheriffs and aldermen did in their several stations and wards, where they were placed by office, and the sheriff's officers or sergeants were appointed to receive orders from the respective aldermen in their turn, so that justice was executed in all cases without interruption. In the next place, it was one of their particular cares to see the orders for the freedom of the markets observed, and in this part either the Lord Mayor or one or both of the sheriffs were every market-day on horseback to see their orders executed and to see that the country people had all possible encouragement and freedom in their coming to the markets and going back again, and that no nuisances or frightful objects should be seen in the streets to terrify them or make them unwilling to come. Also the bakers were taken under particular order, and the Master of the Bakers' Company was, with his court of assistants, directed to see the order of my Lord Mayor for their regulation put in execution, and the due assize of bread (which was weekly appointed by my Lord Mayor) observed; and all the bakers were obliged to keep their oven going constantly, on pain of losing the privileges of a freeman of the city of London.

By this means bread was always to be had in plenty, and as cheap as usual, as I said above; and provisions were never wanting in the markets, even to such a degree that I often wondered at it, and reproached myself with being so timorous and cautious in stirring abroad, when the country people came freely and boldly to market, as if there had been no manner of infection in the city, or danger of catching it.

It. was indeed one admirable piece of conduct in the said magistrates that the streets were kept constantly dear and free from all manner of frightful objects, dead bodies, or any such things as were indecent or unpleasant—unless where anybody fell down suddenly or died in the streets, as I have said above; and these were generally covered with some cloth or blanket, or removed into the next churchyard till night. All the needful works that carried terror with them, that were both dismal and dangerous, were done in the night; if any diseased bodies were removed, or dead bodies buried, or infected clothes burnt, it was done in the night; and all the bodies which were thrown into the great pits in the several churchyards or burying-grounds, as has been observed, were so removed in the night, and everything was covered and closed before day. So that in the daytime there was not the least signal of the calamity to be seen or heard of, except what was to be observed from the emptiness of the streets, and sometimes from the passionate outcries and lamentations of the people, out at their windows, and from the numbers of houses and shops shut up.

Nor was the silence and emptiness of the streets so much in the city as in the out-parts, except just at one particular time when, as I have mentioned, the plague came east and spread over all the city. It was indeed a merciful disposition of God, that as the plague began at one end of the town first (as has been observed at large) so it proceeded progressively to other parts, and did not come on this way, or eastward, till it had spent its fury in the West part of the town; and so, as it came on one way, it abated another. For example, it began at St Giles's and the Westminster end of the town, and it was in its height in all that part by about the middle of July, viz., in St Giles-in-the-Fields, St Andrew's, Holborn, St Clement Danes, St Martin-in-the-Fields, and in Westminster. The latter end of July it decreased in those parishes; and coming east, it increased prodigiously in Cripplegate, St Sepulcher's, St James's, Clarkenwell, and St Bride's and Aldersgate. While it was in all these parishes, the city and all the parishes of the

Southwark side of the water and all Stepney, Whitechappel, Aldgate, Wapping, and Ratcliff, were very little touched; so that people went about their business unconcerned, carried on their trades, kept open their shops, and conversed freely with one another in all the city, the east and north-east suburbs, and in Southwark, almost as if the plague had not been among us.

Even when the north and north-west suburbs were fully infected, viz., Cripplegate, Clarkenwell, Bishopsgate, and Shoreditch, yet still all the rest were tolerably well. For example from 25th July to 1st August the bill stood thus of all diseases:—

St Giles, Cripplegate	554
St Sepulchers	250
Clarkenwell	103
Bishopsgate	116
Shoreditch	110
Stepney parish	127
Aldgate	92
Whitechappel	104
All the ninety-seven parishes within the walls	228
All the parishes in Southwark	205
Total	1889

So that, in short, there died more that week in the two parishes of Cripplegate and St Sepulcher by forty-eight than in all the city, all the east suburbs, and all the Southwark parishes put together. This caused the reputation of the city's health to continue all over England—and especially in the counties and markets adjacent, from whence our supply of provisions chiefly came even much longer than that health itself continued; for when the people came into the streets from the country by Shoreditch and Bishopsgate, or by Old Street and Smithfield, they would see the out-streets empty and the houses and shops shut, and the few people that were stirring there walk in the middle of the streets. But when they came within the city, there things looked better, and the markets and shops were open, and the people walking about the streets as usual, though not quite so many; and this continued till the latter end of August and the beginning of September.

But then the case altered quite; the distemper abated in the west and north-west parishes, and the weight of the infection lay on the city and the eastern suburbs, and the Southwark side, and this in a frightful manner. Then, indeed, the city began to look dismal, shops to be shut, and the streets desolate. In the High Street, indeed, necessity made people stir abroad on many occasions; and there would be in the middle of the day a pretty many people, but in the mornings and evenings scarce any to be seen, even there, no, not in Cornhill and Cheapside.

These observations of mine were abundantly confirmed by the weekly bills of mortality for those weeks, an abstract of which, as they respect the parishes which. I have mentioned and as they make the calculations I speak of very evident, take as follows.

The weekly bill, which makes out this decrease of the burials in the west and north side of the city, stands thus—

From the 12th of September to the 19th—

St Giles, Cripplegate	456
St Giles-in-the-Fields	140
Clarkenwell	77
St Sepulcher	214
St Leonard, Shoreditch	183
Stepney parish	716
Aldgate	623
Whitechappel	532
In the ninety-seven parishes within the walls	149
In the eight parishes on Southwark side	1636
Total	6060

Here is a strange change of things indeed, and a sad change it was; and had it held for two months more than it did, very few people would have been left alive. But then such, I say, was the merciful disposition of God that, when it was thus, the west and north part which had been so dreadfully visited at first, grew, as you see, much better; and as the people disappeared here, they began to look abroad again there; and the next week or two altered it still more; that is, more to the encouragement of the other part of the town. For example:—

From the 19th of September to the 26th—

St Giles, Cripplegate	277
St Giles-in-the-Fields	119
Clarkenwell	76
St Sepulchers	193
St Leonard, Shoreditch	146
Stepney parish	616
Aldgate	496
Whitechappel	346
In the ninety-seven parishes within the walls	1268
In the eight parishes on Southwark side	1390
Total	4927

From the 26th of September to the 3rd of October—

St Giles, Cripplegate	196
St Giles-in-the-Fields	95
Clarkenwell	48
St Sepulchers	137

St Leonard, Shoreditch	128
Stepney parish	674
Aldgate	372
Whitechappel	328
In the ninety-seven parishes within the walls	1149
In the eight parishes on Southwark side	1201
Total	4382

And now the misery of the city and of the said east and south parts was complete indeed; for, as you see, the weight of the distemper lay upon those parts, that is to say, the city, the eight parishes over the river, with the parishes of Aldgate, Whitechappel, and Stepney; and this was the time that the bills came up to such a monstrous height as that I mentioned before, and that eight or nine, and, as I believe, ten or twelve thousand a week, died; for it is my settled opinion that they never could come at any just account of the numbers, for the reasons which I have given already.

Nay, one of the most eminent physicians, who has since published in Latin an account of those times, and of his observations says that in one week there died twelve thousand people, and that particularly there died four thousand in one night; though I do not remember that there ever was any such particular night so remarkably fatal as that such a number died in it. However, all this confirms what I have said above of the uncertainty of the bills of mortality, &c., of which I shall say more hereafter.

And here let me take leave to enter again, though it may seem a repetition of circumstances, into a description of the miserable condition of the city itself, and of those parts where I lived at this particular time. The city and those other parts, notwithstanding the great numbers of people that were gone into the country, was vastly full of people; and perhaps the fuller because people had for a long time a strong belief that the plague would not come into the city, nor into Southwark, no, nor into Wapping or Ratcliff at all; nay, such was the assurance of the people on that head that many removed from the suburbs on the west and north sides, into those eastern and south sides as for safety; and, as I verily believe, carried the plague amongst them there perhaps sooner than they would otherwise have had it.

Here also I ought to leave a further remark for the use of posterity, concerning the manner of people's infecting one another; namely, that it was not the sick people only from whom the plague was immediately received by others that were sound, but the well. To explain myself: by the sick people I mean those who were known to be sick, had taken their beds, had been under cure, or had swellings and tumours upon them, and the like; these everybody could beware of; they were either in their beds or in such condition as could not be concealed.

By the well I mean such as had received the contagion, and had it really upon them, and in their blood, yet did not show the consequences of it in their countenances: nay, even were not sensible of it themselves, as many were not for several days. These breathed death in every place, and upon everybody who came near them; nay, their very clothes retained the infection, their hands would infect the things they touched, especially if they were warm and sweaty, and they were generally apt to sweat too.

Now it was impossible to know these people, nor did they sometimes, as I have said, know themselves to be infected. These were the people that so often dropped down and fainted in the streets; for oftentimes they would go about the streets to the last, till on a sudden they would sweat, grow faint, sit down at a door and die. It is true, finding themselves thus, they would struggle hard to get home to their own doors, or at other times would be just able to go into their houses and die instantly; other times they would go about till they had the very tokens come out upon them, and yet not know it, and would die in an hour or two after they came home, but be well as long as they were abroad. These were the dangerous people; these were the people of whom the well people ought to have been afraid; but then, on the other side, it was impossible to know them.

And this is the reason why it is impossible in a visitation to prevent the spreading of the plague by the utmost human vigilance: viz., that it is impossible to know the infected people from the sound, or that the infected people should perfectly know themselves. I knew a man who conversed freely in London all the season of the plague in 1665, and kept about him an antidote or cordial on purpose to take when he thought himself in any danger, and he had such a rule to know or have warning of the danger by as indeed I never met with before or since. How far it may be depended on I know not. He had a wound in his leg, and whenever he came among any people that were not sound, and the infection began to affect him, he said he could know it by that signal, viz., that his wound in his leg would smart, and look pale and white; so as soon as ever he felt it smart it was time for him to withdraw, or to take care of himself, taking his drink, which he always carried about him for that purpose. Now it seems he found his wound would smart many times when he was in company with such who thought themselves to be sound, and who appeared so to one another; but he would presently rise up and say publicly, 'Friends, here is somebody in the room that has the plague', and so would immediately break up the company. This was indeed a faithful monitor to all people that the plague is not to be avoided by those that converse promiscuously in a town infected, and people have it when they know it not, and that they likewise give it to others when they know not that they have it themselves; and in this case shutting up the well or removing the sick will not do it, unless they can go back and shut up all those that the sick had conversed with, even before they knew themselves to be sick, and none knows how far to carry that back, or where to stop; for none knows when or where or how they may have received the infection, or from whom.

This I take to be the reason which makes so many people talk of the air being corrupted and infected, and that they need not be cautious of whom they converse with, for that the contagion was in the air. I have seen them in strange agitations and surprises on this account. 'I have never come near any infected body', says the disturbed person; 'I have conversed with none but sound, healthy people, and yet I have gotten the distemper!' 'I am sure I am struck from Heaven', says another, and he falls to the serious part. Again, the first goes on exclaiming, 'I have come near no infection or any infected person; I am sure it is the air. We draw in death when we breathe, and therefore 'tis the hand of God; there is no withstanding it.' And this at last made many people, being hardened to the danger, grow less concerned at it; and less cautious towards the latter end of the time, and when it was come to its height, than they were at first. Then, with a kind of a Turkish predestinarianism, they would say, if it pleased God to strike them, it was all one whether they went abroad or stayed at home; they could not escape it, and therefore they went boldly about, even into infected houses and infected company; visited sick people; and, in short, lay in the beds with their wives or relations when they were infected. And what was the consequence, but the same that is the consequence in Turkey, and in those countries where they do those things—namely, that they were infected too, and died by hundreds and thousands?

I would be far from lessening the awe of the judgements of God and the reverence to His providence which ought always to be on our minds on such occasions as these. Doubtless the visitation itself is a stroke from Heaven upon a city, or country, or nation where it falls; a messenger of His vengeance, and a loud call to that nation or country or city to humiliation and repentance, according to that of the prophet Jeremiah (xviii. 7, 8): 'At what instant I shall speak concerning a nation, and concerning a kingdom, to pluck up, and to pull down, and to destroy it; if that nation against whom I have pronounced turn from their evil, I will repent of the evil that I thought to do unto them.' Now to prompt due impressions of the awe of God on the minds of men on such occasions, and not to lessen them, it is that I have left those minutes upon record.

I say, therefore, I reflect upon no man for putting the reason of those things upon the immediate hand of God, and the appointment and direction of His providence; nay, on the contrary, there were many wonderful deliverances of persons from infection, and deliverances of persons when infected, which intimate singular and remarkable providence in the particular instances to which they refer; and I esteem my own deliverance to be one next to miraculous, and do record it with thankfulness.

But when I am speaking of the plague as a distemper arising from natural causes, we must consider it as it was really propagated by natural means; nor is it at all the less a judgement for its being under the conduct of human causes and effects; for, as the Divine Power has formed the whole scheme of nature and maintains nature in its course, so the same Power thinks fit to let His own actings with men, whether of mercy or judgement, to go on in the ordinary course of natural causes; and He is pleased to act by those natural causes as the ordinary means, excepting and reserving to Himself nevertheless a power to act in a supernatural way when He sees occasion. Now 'tis evident that in the case of an infection there is no apparent extraordinary occasion for supernatural operation, but the ordinary course of things appears sufficiently armed, and made capable of all the effects that Heaven usually directs by a contagion. Among these causes and effects, this of the secret conveyance of infection, imperceptible and unavoidable, is more than sufficient to execute the fierceness of Divine vengeance, without putting it upon supernaturals and miracle.

The acute penetrating nature of the disease itself was such, and the infection was received so imperceptibly, that the most exact caution could not secure us while in the place. But I must be allowed to believe—and I have so many examples fresh in my memory to convince me of it, that I think none can resist their evidence—I say, I must be allowed to believe that no one in this whole nation ever received the sickness or infection but who received it in the ordinary way of infection from somebody, or the clothes or touch or stench of somebody that was infected before.

The manner of its coming first to London proves this also, viz., by goods brought over from Holland, and brought thither from the Levant; the first breaking of it out in a house in Long Acre where those goods were carried and first opened; its spreading from that house to other houses by the visible unwary conversing with those who were sick; and the infecting the parish officers who were employed about the persons dead, and the like. These are known authorities for this great foundation point—that it went on and proceeded from person to person and from house to house, and no otherwise. In the first house that was infected there died four persons. A neighbour, hearing the mistress of the first house was sick, went to visit her, and went home and gave the distemper to her family, and died, and all her household. A minister, called to pray with the first sick person in the second house, was said to sicken immediately and die with several more in his house. Then the physicians began to consider, for they did not at first dream of a general contagion. But the physicians being sent to inspect the bodies, they assured the people that it was neither more or less than the plague, with all its terrifying particulars, and that it threatened an universal infection, so many people having already conversed with the sick or distempered, and having, as might be supposed, received infection from them, that it would be impossible to put a stop to it.

Here the opinion of the physicians agreed with my observation afterwards, namely, that the danger was spreading insensibly, for the sick could infect none but those that came within reach of the sick person; but that one man who may have really received the infection and knows it not, but goes abroad and about as a sound person, may give the plague to a thousand people, and they to greater numbers in proportion, and neither the person giving the infection or the persons receiving it know anything of it, and perhaps not feel the effects of it for several days after.

For example, many persons in the time of this visitation never perceived that they were infected till they found to their unspeakable surprise, the tokens come out upon them; after which they seldom lived six hours; for those spots they called the tokens were really gangrene spots, or mortified flesh in small knobs as broad as a little silver penny, and hard as a piece of callus or horn; so that, when the disease was come up to that length, there was nothing could follow but certain death; and yet, as I said, they knew nothing of their being infected, nor found themselves so much as out of order, till those mortal marks were upon them. But everybody must allow that they were infected in a high degree before, And must have been so some time, and consequently their breath, their sweat, their very clothes, were contagious for many days before. This occasioned a vast variety of cases which physicians would have much more opportunity to remember than I; but some came within the compass of my observation or hearing, of which I shall name a few.

A certain citizen who had lived safe and untouched till the month of September, when the weight of the distemper lay more in the city than it had done before, was mighty cheerful, and something too bold (as I think it was) in his talk of how secure he was, how cautious he had been, and how he had never come near any sick body. Says another citizen, a neighbour of his, to him one day, 'Do not be too confident, Mr—; it is hard to say who is sick and who is well, for we see men alive and well to outward appearance one hour, and dead the next.' 'That is true', says the first man, for he was not a man presumptuously secure, but had escaped a long while—and men, as I said above, especially in the city began to be over-easy upon that score. 'That is true,' says he; 'I do not think myself secure, but I hope I have not been in company with any person that there has been any danger in.' 'No?' says his neighbour. 'Was not you at the Bull Head Tavern in Gracechurch Street with Mr—the night before last?' 'Yes,' says the first, 'I was; but there was nobody there that we had any reason to think dangerous.' Upon which his neighbour said no more, being unwilling to surprise him; but this made him more inquisitive, and as his neighbour appeared backward, he was the more impatient, and in a kind of warmth says he aloud, 'Why, he is not dead, is he?' Upon which his neighbour still was silent, but cast up his eyes and said something to himself; at which the first citizen turned pale, and said no more but this, 'Then I am a dead man too', and went home immediately and sent for a neighbouring apothecary to give him something preventive, for he had not yet found himself ill; but the apothecary, opening his breast, fetched a sigh, and said no more but this, 'Look up to God'; and the man died in a few hours.

Now let any man judge from a case like this if it is possible for the regulations of magistrates, either by shutting up the sick or removing them, to stop an infection which spreads itself from man to man even while they are perfectly well and insensible of its approach, and may be so for many days.

It may be proper to ask here how long it may be supposed men might have the seeds of the contagion in them before it discovered itself in this fatal manner, and how long they might go about seemingly whole, and yet be contagious to all those that came near them. I believe the most experienced physicians cannot answer this question directly any more than I can; and something an ordinary observer may take notice of, which may pass their observations. The opinion of physicians abroad seems to be that it may lie dormant in the spirits or in the blood-vessels a very considerable time. Why else do they exact a quarantine of those who came into their harbours and ports from suspected places? Forty days is, one would think, too long for nature to struggle with such an enemy as this, and not conquer it or yield to it. But I could not think, by my own observation, that they can be infected so as to be contagious to others above fifteen or sixteen days at furthest; and on that score it was, that when a house was shut up in the city and any one had died of the plague, but nobody appeared to be ill in the family for sixteen or eighteen days after, they were not so strict but that they would connive at their going privately abroad; nor would people be much afraid of them afterward, but rather think they were fortified the better, having not been vulnerable when the enemy was in their own house; but we sometimes found it had lain much longer concealed.

Upon the foot of all these observations I must say that though Providence seemed to direct my conduct to be otherwise, yet it is my opinion, and I must leave it as a prescription, viz., that the best physic against the plague is to run away from it. I know people encourage themselves by saying God is able to keep us in the midst of danger, and able to overtake us when we think ourselves out of danger; and this kept thousands in the town whose carcases went into the great pits by cartloads, and who, if they had fled from the danger, had, I believe, been safe from the disaster; at least 'tis probable they had been safe.

And were this very fundamental only duly considered by the people on any future occasion of this or the like nature, I am persuaded it would put them upon quite different measures for managing the people from those that they took in 1665, or than any that have been taken abroad that I have heard of. In a word, they would consider of separating the people into smaller bodies, and removing them in time farther from one another—and not let such a contagion as this, which is indeed chiefly dangerous to collected bodies of people, find a million of people in a body together, as was very near the case before, and would certainly be the case if it should ever appear again.

The plague, like a great fire, if a few houses only are contiguous where it happens, can only burn a few houses; or if it begins in a single, or, as we call it, a lone house, can only burn that lone house where it begins. But if it begins in a close-built town or city and gets a head, there its fury increases: it rages over the whole place, and consumes all it can reach.

I could propose many schemes on the foot of which the government of this city, if ever they should be under the apprehensions of such another enemy (God forbid they should), might ease themselves of the greatest part of the dangerous people that belong to them; I mean such as the begging, starving, labouring poor, and among them chiefly those who, in case of a siege, are called the useless mouths; who being then prudently and to their own advantage disposed of, and the wealthy inhabitants disposing of themselves and of their servants and children, the city and its adjacent parts would be so effectually evacuated that there would not be above a tenth part of its people left together for the disease to take hold upon. But suppose them to be a fifth part, and that two hundred and fifty thousand people were left: and if it did seize upon them, they would, by their living so much at large, be much better prepared to defend themselves against the infection, and be less liable to the effects of it than if the same number of people lived close together in one smaller city such as Dublin or Amsterdam or the like.

It is true hundreds, yea, thousands of families fled away at this last plague, but then of them, many fled too late, and not only died in their flight, but carried the distemper with them into the countries where they went and infected those whom they went among for safety; which confounded the thing, and made that be a propagation of the distemper which was the best means to prevent it; and this too is an evidence of it, and brings me back to what I only hinted at before, but must speak more fully to here, namely, that men went about apparently well many days after they had the taint of the disease in their vitals, and after their spirits were so seized as that they could never escape it, and that all the while they did so they were dangerous to others; I say, this proves that so it was; for such people infected the very towns they went through, as well as the families they went among; and it was by that means that almost all the great towns in England had the distemper among them, more or less, and always they would tell you such a Londoner or such a Londoner brought it down.

It must not be omitted that when I speak of those people who were really thus dangerous, I suppose them to be utterly ignorant of their own conditions; for if they really knew their circumstances to be such as indeed they were, they must have been a kind of wilful murtherers if they would have gone abroad among healthy people—and it would have verified indeed the suggestion which I mentioned above, and which I thought seemed untrue: viz., that the infected people were utterly careless as to giving the infection to others, and rather forward to do it than not; and I believe it was partly from this very thing that they raised that suggestion, which I hope was not really true in fact.

I confess no particular case is sufficient to prove a general, but I could name several people within the knowledge of some of their neighbours and families yet living who showed the contrary to an extreme. One man, a master of a family in my neighbourhood, having had the distemper, he thought he had it given him by a poor workman whom he employed, and whom he went to his house to see, or went for some work that he wanted to have finished; and he had some apprehensions even while he was at the poor workman's door, but did not discover it fully; but the next day it discovered itself, and he was taken very in, upon which he immediately caused himself to be carried into an outbuilding which he had in his yard, and where there was a chamber over a workhouse (the man being a brazier). Here he lay, and here he died, and would be tended by none of his neighbours, but by a nurse from abroad; and would not suffer his wife, nor children, nor servants to come up into the room, lest they should be infected—but sent them his blessing and prayers for them by the nurse, who spoke it to them at a distance, and all this for fear of giving them the distemper; and without which he knew, as they were kept up, they could not have it.

And here I must observe also that the plague, as I suppose all distempers do, operated in a different manner on differing constitutions; some were immediately overwhelmed with it, and it came to violent fevers, vomitings, insufferable headaches, pains in the back, and so up to ravings and ragings with those pains; others with swellings and tumours in the neck or groin, or armpits, which till they could be broke put them into insufferable agonies and torment; while others, as I have observed, were silently infected, the fever preying upon their spirits insensibly, and they seeing little of it till they fell into swooning, and faintings, and death without pain. I am not physician enough to enter into the particular reasons and manner of these differing effects of one and the same distemper, and of its differing operation in several bodies; nor is it my business here to record the observations which I really made, because the doctors themselves have done that part much more effectually than I can do, and because my opinion may in some things differ from theirs. I am only relating what I know, or have heard, or believe of the particular cases, and what fell within the compass of my view, and the different nature of the infection as it appeared in the particular cases which I have related; but this may be added too: that though the former sort of those cases, namely, those openly visited, were the worst for themselves as to pain—I mean those that had such fevers, vomitings, headaches, pains, and swellings, because they died in such a dreadful manner—yet the latter had the worst state of the disease; for in the former they frequently recovered, especially if the swellings broke; but the latter was inevitable death; no cure, no help, could be possible, nothing could follow but death. And it was worse also to others, because, as above, it secretly and unperceived by others or by themselves, communicated death to those they conversed with, the penetrating poison insinuating itself into their blood in a manner which it is impossible to describe, or indeed conceive.

This infecting and being infected without so much as its being known to either person is evident from two sorts of cases which frequently happened at that time; and there is hardly anybody living who was in London during the infection but must have known several of the cases of both sorts.

(1) Fathers and mothers have gone about as if they had been well, and have believed themselves to be so, till they have insensibly infected and been the destruction of their whole families, which they would have been far from doing if they had the least apprehensions of their being unsound and dangerous themselves. A family, whose story I have heard, was thus infected by the father; and the distemper began to appear upon some of them even before he found it upon himself. But searching more narrowly, it appeared he had been affected some time; and as soon as he found that his family had been poisoned by himself he went distracted, and would have laid violent hands upon himself, but was kept from that by those who looked to him, and in a few days died.

(2) The other particular is, that many people having been well to the best of their own judgement, or by the best observation which they could make of themselves for several days, and only finding a decay of appetite, or a light sickness upon their stomachs; nay, some whose appetite has been strong, and even craving, and only a light pain in their heads, have sent for physicians to know what ailed them, and have been found, to their great surprise, at the brink of death: the tokens upon them, or the plague grown up to an incurable height.

It was very sad to reflect how such a person as this last mentioned above had been a walking destroyer perhaps for a week or a fortnight before that; how he had ruined those that he would have hazarded his life to save, and had been breathing death upon them, even perhaps in his tender kissing and embracings of his own children. Yet thus certainly it was, and often has been, and I could give many particular cases where it has been so. If then the blow is thus insensibly striking—if the arrow flies thus unseen, and cannot be discovered—to what purpose are all the schemes for shutting up or removing the sick people? Those schemes cannot take place but upon those that appear to be sick, or to be infected; whereas there are among them at the same time thousands of people who seem to be well, but are all that while carrying death with them into all companies which they come into.

This frequently puzzled our physicians, and especially the apothecaries and surgeons, who knew not how to discover the sick from the sound; they all allowed that it was really so, that many people had the plague in their very blood, and preying upon their spirits, and were in themselves but walking putrefied carcases whose breath was infectious and their sweat poison, and yet were as well to look on as other people, and even knew it not themselves; I say, they all allowed that it was really true in fact, but they knew not how to propose a discovery.

My friend Dr Heath was of opinion that it might be known by the smell of their breath; but then, as he said, who durst smell to that breath for his information? since, to know it, he must draw the stench of the plague up into his own brain, in order to distinguish the smell! I have heard it was the opinion of others that it might be distinguished by the party's breathing upon a piece of glass, where, the breath condensing, there might living creatures be seen by a microscope, of strange, monstrous, and frightful shapes, such as dragons, snakes, serpents, and devils, horrible to behold. But this I very much question the truth of, and we had no microscopes at that time, as I remember, to make the experiment with.

It was the opinion also of another learned man, that the breath of such a person would poison and instantly kill a bird; not only a small bird, but even a cock or hen, and that, if it did not immediately kill the latter, it would cause them to be roupy, as they call it; particularly that if they had laid any eggs at any time, they would be all rotten. But those are opinions which I never found supported by any experiments, or heard of others that had seen it; so I leave them as I find them; only with this remark, namely, that I think the probabilities are very strong for them.

Some have proposed that such persons should breathe hard upon warm water, and that they would leave an unusual scum upon it, or upon several other things, especially such as are of a glutinous substance and are apt to receive a scum and support it.

But from the whole I found that the nature of this contagion was such that it was impossible to discover it at all, or to prevent its spreading from one to another by any human skill.

Here was indeed one difficulty which I could never thoroughly get over to this time, and which there is but one way of answering that I know of, and it is this, viz., the first person that died of the plague was on December 20, or thereabouts, 1664, and in or about long Acre; whence the first person had the infection was generally said to be from a parcel of silks imported from Holland, and first opened in that house.

But after this we heard no more of any person dying of the plague, or of the distemper being in that place, till the 9th of February, which was about seven weeks after, and then one more was buried out of the same house. Then it was hushed, and we were perfectly easy as to the public for a great while; for there were no more entered in the weekly bill to be dead of the plague till the 22nd of April, when there was two more buried, not out of the same house, but out of the same street; and, as near as I can remember, it was out of the next house to the first. This was nine weeks asunder, and after this we had no more till a fortnight, and then it broke out in several streets and spread every way. Now the question seems to lie thus: Where lay the seeds of the infection all this while? How came it to stop so long, and not stop any longer? Either the distemper did not come immediately by contagion from body to body, or, if it did, then a body may be capable to continue infected without the disease discovering itself many days, nay, weeks together; even not a quarantine of days only, but soixantine; not only forty days, but sixty days or longer.

It is true there was, as I observed at first, and is well known to many yet living, a very cold winter and a long frost which continued three months; and this, the doctors say, might check the infection; but then the learned must allow me to say that if, according to their notion, the disease was (as I may say) only frozen up, it would like a frozen river have returned to its usual force and current when it thawed—whereas the principal recess of this infection, which was from February to April, was after the frost was broken and the weather mild and warm.

But there is another way of solving all this difficulty, which I think my own remembrance of the thing will supply; and that is, the fact is not granted—namely, that there died none in those long intervals, viz., from the 20th of December to the 9th of February, and from thence to the 22nd of April. The weekly bills are the only evidence on the other side, and those bills were not of credit enough, at least with me, to support an hypothesis or determine a question of such importance as this; for it was our received opinion at that time, and I believe upon very good grounds, that the fraud lay in the parish officers, searchers, and persons appointed to give account of the dead, and what diseases they died of; and as people were very loth at first to have the neighbours believe their houses were infected, so they gave money to procure, or otherwise procured, the dead persons to be returned as dying of other distempers; and this I know was practised afterwards in many places, I believe I might say in all places where the distemper came, as will be seen by the vast increase of the numbers placed in the weekly bills under other articles of diseases during the time of the infection. For example, in the months of July and August, when the plague was coming on to its highest pitch, it was very ordinary to have from a thousand to twelve hundred, nay, to almost fifteen hundred a week of other distempers. Not that the numbers of those distempers were really increased to such a degree, but the great number of families and houses where really the infection was, obtained the favour to have their dead be returned of other distempers, to prevent the shutting up their houses. For example:—

Dead of other diseases beside the plague—

From the 18th July	to the 25th		942
"	25th July	" 1st August	1004
"	1st August	" 8th	1213
"	8th	" 15th	1439
"	15th	" 22nd	1331
"	22nd	" 29th	1394
"	29th	" 5th September	1264
"	5th September to the 12th		1056
"	12th	" 19th	1132
"	19th	" 26th	927

Now it was not doubted but the greatest part of these, or a great part of them, were dead of the plague, but the officers were prevailed with to return them as above, and the numbers of some particular articles of distempers discovered is as follows:—

-	Aug. 1 to 8	Aug. 8 to 15	Aug. 15 to 22	Aug. 22 to 29	Aug. 29 to Sept.5	Sept. 5 to 12	Sept. 12 to 19	Sept 19 to 26
Fever	314	353	348	383	364	332	309	268
Spotted Fever	174	190	166	165	157	97	101	65
Surfeit	85	87	74	99	68	45	49	36
Teeth	90	113	111	133	138	128	121	112
	663	743	699	780	727	602	580	481

There were several other articles which bore a proportion to these, and which, it is easy to perceive, were increased on the same account, as aged, consumptions, vomitings, imposthumes, gripes, and the like, many of which were not doubted to be infected people; but as it was of the utmost consequence to families not to be known to be infected, if it was possible to avoid it, so they took all the measures they could to have it not believed, and if any died in their houses, to get them returned to the examiners, and by the searchers, as having died of other distempers.

This, I say, will account for the long interval which, as I have said, was between the dying of the first persons that were returned in the bill to be dead of the plague and the time when the distemper spread openly and could not be concealed.

Besides, the weekly bills themselves at that time evidently discover the truth; for, while there was no mention of the plague, and no increase after it had been mentioned, yet it was apparent that there was an increase of those distempers which bordered nearest upon it; for example, there were eight, twelve, seventeen of the spotted fever in a week, when there were none, or but very few, of the plague; whereas before, one, three, or four were the ordinary weekly numbers of that distemper. Likewise, as I observed before, the burials increased weekly in that particular parish and the parishes adjacent more than in any other parish, although there were none set down of the plague; all which tells us, that the infection was handed on, and the succession of the distemper really preserved, though it seemed to us at that time to be ceased, and to come again in a manner surprising.

It might be, also, that the infection might remain in other parts of the same parcel of goods which at first it came in, and which might not be perhaps opened, or at least not fully, or in the clothes of the first infected person; for I cannot think that anybody could be seized with the contagion in a fatal and mortal degree for nine weeks together, and support his state of health so well as even not to discover it to themselves; yet if it were so, the argument is the stronger in favour of what I am saying: namely, that the infection is retained in bodies apparently well, and conveyed from them to those they converse with, while it is known to neither the one nor the other.

Great were the confusions at that time upon this very account, and when people began to be convinced that the infection was received in this surprising manner from persons apparently well, they began to be exceeding shy and jealous of every one that came near them. Once, on a public day, whether a Sabbath-day or not I do not remember, in Aldgate Church, in a pew full of people, on a sudden one fancied she smelt an ill smell. Immediately she fancies the plague was in the pew, whispers her notion or suspicion to the next, then rises and goes out of the pew. It immediately took with the next, and so to them all; and every one of them, and of the two or three adjoining pews, got up and went out of the church, nobody knowing what it was offended them, or from whom.

This immediately filled everybody's mouths with one preparation or other, such as the old woman directed, and some perhaps as physicians directed, in order to prevent infection by the breath of others; insomuch that if we came to go into a church when it was anything full of people, there would be such a mixture of smells at the entrance that it was much more strong, though perhaps not so wholesome, than if you were going into an apothecary's or druggist's shop. In a word, the whole church was like a smelling-bottle; in one corner it was all perfumes; in another, aromatics, balsamics, and variety of drugs and herbs; in another, salts and spirits, as every one was furnished for their own preservation. Yet I observed that after people were possessed, as I have said, with the belief, or rather assurance, of the infection being thus carried on by persons apparently in health, the churches and meeting-houses were much thinner of people than at other times before that they used to be. For this is to be said of the people of London, that during the whole time of the pestilence the churches or meetings were never wholly shut up, nor did the people decline coming out to the public worship of God, except only in some parishes when the violence of the distemper was more particularly in that parish at that time, and even then no longer than it continued to be so.

Indeed nothing was more strange than to see with what courage the people went to the public service of God, even at that time when they were afraid to stir out of their own houses upon any other occasion; this, I mean, before the time of desperation, which I have mentioned already. This was a proof of the exceeding populousness of the city at the time of the infection, notwithstanding the great numbers that were gone into the country at the first alarm, and that fled out into the forests and woods when they were further terrified with the extraordinary increase of it. For when we came to see the crowds and throngs of people which appeared on the Sabbath-days at the churches, and especially in those parts of the town where the plague was abated, or where it was not yet come to its height, it was amazing. But of this I shall speak again presently. I return in the meantime to the article of infecting one another at first, before people came to right notions of the infection, and of infecting one another. People were only shy of those that were really sick, a man with a cap upon his head, or with clothes round his neck, which was the case of those that had swellings there. Such was indeed frightful; but when we saw a gentleman dressed, with his band on and his gloves in his hand, his hat upon his head, and his hair combed, of such we bad not the least apprehensions, and people conversed a great while freely, especially with their neighbours and such as they knew. But when the physicians assured us that the danger was as well from the sound (that is, the seemingly sound) as the sick, and that those people who thought themselves entirely free were oftentimes the most fatal, and that it came to be generally understood that people were sensible of it, and of the reason of it; then, I say, they began to be jealous of everybody, and a vast number of people locked themselves up, so as not to come abroad into any company at all, nor suffer any that had been abroad in promiscuous company to come into their houses, or near them—at least not so near them as to be within the reach of their breath or of any smell from them; and when they were obliged to converse at a distance with strangers, they would always have preservatives in their mouths and about their clothes to repel and keep off the infection.

It must be acknowledged that when people began to use these cautions they were less exposed to danger, and the infection did not break into such houses so furiously as it did into others before; and thousands of families were preserved (speaking with due reserve to the direction of Divine Providence) by that means.

But it was impossible to beat anything into the heads of the poor. They went on with the usual impetuosity of their tempers, full of outcries and lamentations when taken, but madly careless of themselves, foolhardy and obstinate, while they were well. Where they could get employment they pushed into any kind of business, the most dangerous and the most liable to infection; and if they were spoken to, their answer would be, 'I must trust to God for that; if I am taken, then I am provided for, and there is an end of me', and the like. Or thus, 'Why, what must I do? I can't starve. I had as good have the plague as perish for want. I have no work; what could I do? I must do this or beg.' Suppose it was burying the dead, or attending the sick, or watching infected houses, which were all terrible hazards; but their tale was generally the same. It is true, necessity was a very justifiable, warrantable plea, and nothing could be better; but their way of talk was much the same where the necessities were not the same. This adventurous conduct of the poor was that which brought the plague among them in a most furious manner; and this, joined to the distress of their circumstances when taken, was the reason why they died so by heaps; for I cannot say I could observe one jot of better husbandry among them, I mean the labouring poor, while they were all well and getting money than there was before, but as lavish, as extravagant, and as thoughtless for tomorrow as ever; so that when they came to be taken sick they were immediately in the utmost distress, as well for want as for sickness, as well for lack of food as lack of health.

This misery of the poor I had many occasions to be an eyewitness of, and sometimes also of the charitable assistance that some pious people daily gave to such, sending them relief and supplies both of food, physic, and other help, as they found they wanted; and indeed it is a debt of justice due to the temper of the people of that day to take notice here, that not only great sums, very great sums of money were charitably sent to the Lord Mayor and aldermen for the assistance and support of the poor distempered people, but abundance of private people daily distributed large sums of money for their relief, and sent people about to inquire into the condition of particular distressed and visited families, and relieved them; nay, some pious ladies were so transported with zeal in so good a work, and so confident in the protection of Providence in discharge of the great duty of charity, that they went about in person distributing alms to the poor, and even visiting poor families, though sick and infected, in their very houses, appointing nurses to attend those that wanted attending, and ordering apothecaries and surgeons, the first to supply them with drugs or plasters, and such things as they wanted; and the last to lance and dress the swellings and tumours, where such were wanting; giving their blessing to the poor in substantial relief to them, as well as hearty prayers for them.

I will not undertake to say, as some do, that none of those charitable people were suffered to fall under the calamity itself; but this I may say, that I never knew any one of them that miscarried, which I mention for the encouragement of others in case of the like distress; and doubtless, if they that give to the poor lend to the Lord, and He will repay them, those that hazard their lives to give to the poor, and to comfort and assist the poor in such a misery as this, may hope to be protected in the work.

Nor was this charity so extraordinary eminent only in a few, but (for I cannot lightly quit this point) the charity of the rich, as well in the city and suburbs as from the country, was so great that, in a word, a prodigious number of people who must otherwise inevitably have perished for want as well as sickness were supported and subsisted by it; and though I could never, nor I believe any one else, come to a full knowledge of what was so contributed, yet I do believe that, as I heard one say that was a critical observer of that part, there was not only many thousand pounds contributed, but many hundred thousand pounds, to the relief of the poor of this distressed, afflicted city; nay, one man affirmed to me that he could reckon up above one hundred thousand pounds a week, which was distributed by the churchwardens at the several parish vestries by the Lord Mayor and aldermen in the several wards and precincts, and by the particular direction of the court and of the justices respectively in the parts where they resided, over and above the private charity distributed by pious bands in the manner I speak of; and this continued for many weeks together.

I confess this is a very great sum; but if it be true that there was distributed in the parish of Cripplegate only, 17,800 in one week to the relief of the poor, as I heard reported, and which I really believe was true, the other may not be improbable.

It was doubtless to be reckoned among the many signal good providences which attended this great city, and of which there were many other worth recording,—I say, this was a very remarkable one, that it pleased God thus to move the hearts of the people in all parts of the kingdom so cheerfully to contribute to the relief and support of the poor at London, the good consequences of which were felt many ways, and particularly in preserving the lives and recovering the health of so many thousands, and keeping so many thousands of families from perishing and starving.

And now I am talking of the merciful disposition of Providence in this time of calamity, I cannot but mention again, though I have spoken several times of it already on other accounts, I mean that of the progression of the distemper; how it began at one end of the town, and proceeded gradually and slowly from one part to another, and like a dark cloud that passes over our heads, which, as it thickens and overcasts the air at one end, dears up at the other end; so, while the plague went on raging from west to east, as it went forwards east, it abated in the west, by which means those parts of the town which were not seized, or who were left, and where it had spent its fury, were (as it were) spared to help and assist the other; whereas, had the distemper spread itself over the whole city and suburbs, at once, raging in all places alike, as it has done since in some places abroad, the whole body of the people must have been overwhelmed, and there would have died twenty thousand a day, as they say there did at Naples; nor would the people have been able to have helped or assisted one another.

For it must be observed that where the plague was in its full force, there indeed the people were very miserable, and the consternation was inexpressible. But a little before it reached even to that place, or presently after it was gone, they were quite another sort of people; and I cannot but acknowledge that there was too much of that common temper of mankind to be found among us all at that time, namely, to forget the deliverance when the danger is past. But I shall come to speak of that part again.

It must not be forgot here to take some notice of the state of trade during the time of this common calamity, and this with respect to foreign trade, as also to our home trade.

As to foreign trade, there needs little to be said. The trading nations of Europe were all afraid of us; no port of France, or Holland, or Spain, or Italy would admit our ships or correspond with us; indeed we stood on ill terms with the Dutch, and were in a furious war with them, but though in a bad condition to fight abroad, who had such dreadful enemies to struggle with at home.

Our merchants were accordingly at a full stop; their ships could go nowhere—that is to say, to no place abroad; their manufactures and merchandise—that is to say, of our growth—would not be touched abroad. They were as much afraid of our goods as they were of our people; and indeed they had reason: for our woollen manufactures are as retentive of infection as human bodies, and if packed up by persons infected, would receive the infection and be as dangerous to touch as a man would be that was infected; and therefore, when any English vessel arrived in foreign countries, if they did take the goods on shore, they always caused the bales to be opened and aired in places appointed for that purpose. But from London they would not suffer them to come into port, much less to unlade their goods, upon any terms whatever, and this strictness was especially used with them in Spain and Italy. In Turkey and the islands of the Arches indeed, as they are called, as well those belonging to the Turks as to the Venetians, they were not so very rigid. In the first there was no obstruction at all; and four ships which were then in the river loading for Italy—that is, for Leghorn and Naples—being denied product, as they call it, went on to Turkey, and were freely admitted to unlade their cargo without any difficulty; only that when they arrived there, some of their cargo was not fit for sale in that country; and other parts of it being consigned to merchants at Leghorn, the captains of the ships had no right nor any orders to dispose of the goods; so that great inconveniences followed to the merchants. But this was nothing but what the necessity of affairs required, and the merchants at Leghorn and Naples having notice given them, sent again from thence to take care of the effects which were particularly consigned to those ports, and to bring back in other ships such as were improper for the markets at Smyrna and Scanderoon.

The inconveniences in Spain and Portugal were still greater, for they would by no means suffer our ships, especially those from London, to come into any of their ports, much less to unlade. There was a report that one of our ships having by stealth delivered her cargo, among which was some bales of English cloth, cotton, kerseys, and such-like goods, the Spaniards caused all the goods to be burned, and punished the men with death who were concerned in carrying them on shore. This, I believe, was in part true, though I do not affirm it; but it is not at all unlikely, seeing the danger was really very great, the infection being so violent in London.

I heard likewise that the plague was carried into those countries by some of our ships, and particularly to the port of Faro in the kingdom of Algarve, belonging to the King of Portugal, and that several persons died of it there; but it was not confirmed.

On the other hand, though the Spaniards and Portuguese were so shy of us, it is most certain that the plague (as has been said) keeping at first much at that end of the town next Westminster, the merchandising part of the town (such as the city and the water-side) was perfectly sound till at least the beginning of July, and the ships in the river till the beginning of August; for to the 1st of July there had died but seven within the whole city, and but sixty within the liberties, but one in all the parishes of Stepney, Aldgate, and Whitechappel, and but two in the eight parishes of Southwark. But it was the same thing abroad, for the bad news was gone over the whole world that the city of London was infected with the plague, and there was no inquiring there how the infection proceeded, or at which part of the town it was begun or was reached to.

Besides, after it began to spread it increased so fast, and the bills grew so high all on a sudden, that it was to no purpose to lessen the report of it, or endeavour to make the people abroad think it better than it was; the account which the weekly bills gave in was sufficient; and that there died two thousand to three or-four thousand a week was sufficient to alarm the whole trading part of the world; and the following time, being so dreadful also in the very city itself, put the whole world, I say, upon their guard against it.

You may be sure, also, that the report of these things lost nothing in the carriage. The plague was itself very terrible, and the distress of the people very great, as you may observe of what I have said. But the rumour was infinitely greater, and it must not be wondered that our friends abroad (as my brother's correspondents in particular were told there, namely, in Portugal and Italy, where he chiefly traded) [said] that in London there died twenty thousand in a week; that the dead bodies lay unburied by heaps; that the living were not sufficient to bury the dead or the sound to look after the sick; that all the kingdom was infected likewise, so that it was an universal malady such as was never heard of in those parts of the world; and they could hardly believe us when we gave them an account how things really were, and how there was not above one-tenth part of the people dead; that there was 500,000, left that lived all the time in the town; that now the people began to walk the streets again, and those who were fled to return, there was no miss of the usual throng of people in the streets, except as every family might miss their relations and neighbours, and the like. I say they could not believe these things; and if inquiry were now to be made in Naples, or in other cities on the coast of Italy, they would tell you that there was a dreadful infection in London so many years ago, in which, as above, there died twenty thousand in a week, &c., just as we have had it reported in London that there was a plague in the city of Naples in the year 1656, in which there died 20,000 people in a day, of which I have had very good satisfaction that it was utterly false.

But these extravagant reports were very prejudicial to our trade, as well as unjust and injurious in themselves, for it was a long time after the plague was quite over before our trade could recover itself in those parts of the world; and the

Flemings and Dutch (but especially the last) made very great advantages of it, having all the market to themselves, and even buying our manufactures in several parts of England where the plague was not, and carrying them to Holland and Flanders, and from thence transporting them to Spain and to Italy as if they had been of their own making.

But they were detected sometimes and punished: that is to say, their goods confiscated and ships also; for if it was true that our manufactures as well as our people were infected, and that it was dangerous to touch or to open and receive the smell of them, then those people ran the hazard by that clandestine trade not only of carrying the contagion into their own country, but also of infecting the nations to whom they traded with those goods; which, considering how many lives might be lost in consequence of such an action, must be a trade that no men of conscience could suffer themselves to be concerned in.

I do not take upon me to say that any harm was done, I mean of that kind, by those people. But I doubt I need not make any such proviso in the case of our own country; for either by our people of London, or by the commerce which made their conversing with all sorts of people in every country and of every considerable town necessary, I say, by this means the plague was first or last spread all over the kingdom, as well in London as in all the cities and great towns, especially in the trading manufacturing towns and seaports; so that, first or last, all the considerable places in England were visited more or less, and the kingdom of Ireland in some places, but not so universally. How it fared with the people in Scotland I had no opportunity to inquire.

It is to be observed that while the plague continued so violent in London, the outports, as they are called, enjoyed a very great trade, especially to the adjacent countries and to our own plantations. For example, the towns of Colchester, Yarmouth, and Hun, on that side of England, exported to Holland and Hamburg the manufactures of the adjacent countries for several months after the trade with London was, as it were, entirely shut up; likewise the cities of Bristol and Exeter, with the port of Plymouth, had the like advantage to Spain, to the Canaries, to Guinea, and to the West Indies, and particularly to Ireland; but as the plague spread itself every way after it had been in London to such a degree as it was in August and September, so all or most of those cities and towns were infected first or last; and then trade was, as it were, under a general embargo or at a full stop—as I shall observe further when I speak of our home trade.

One thing, however, must be observed: that as to ships coming in from abroad (as many, you may be sure, did) some who were out in all parts of the world a considerable while before, and some who when they went out knew nothing of an infection, or at least of one so terrible—these came up the river boldly, and delivered their cargoes as they were obliged to do, except just in the two months of August and September, when the weight of the infection lying, as I may say, all below Bridge, nobody durst appear in business for a while. But as this continued but for a few weeks, the homeward-bound ships, especially such whose cargoes were not liable to spoil, came to an anchor for a time short of the Pool[1], or fresh-water part of the river, even as low as the river Medway, where several of them ran in; and others lay at the Nore, and in the Hope below Gravesend. So that by the latter end of October there was a very great fleet of homeward-bound ships to come up, such as the like had not been known for many years.

Two particular trades were carried on by water-carriage all the while of the infection, and that with little or no interruption, very much to the advantage and comfort of the poor distressed people of the city: and those were the coasting trade for corn and the Newcastle trade for coals.

The first of these was particularly carried on by small vessels from the port of Hull and other places on the Humber, by which great quantities of corn were brought in from Yorkshire and Lincolnshire. The other part of this corn-trade was from Lynn, in Norfolk, from Wells and Burnham, and from Yarmouth, all in the same county; and the third branch was from the river Medway, and from Milton, Feversham, Margate, and Sandwich, and all the other little places and ports round the coast of Kent and Essex.

There was also a very good trade from the coast of Suffolk with corn, butter, and cheese; these vessels kept a constant course of trade, and without interruption came up to that market known still by the name of Bear Key, where they supplied the city plentifully with corn when land-carriage began to fail, and when the people began to be sick of coming from many places in the country.

This also was much of it owing to the prudence and conduct of the Lord Mayor, who took such care to keep the masters and seamen from danger when they came up, causing their corn to be bought off at any time they wanted a market (which, however, was very seldom), and causing the corn-factors immediately to unlade and deliver the vessels loaden with corn, that they had very little occasion to come out of their ships or vessels, the money being always carried on board to them and put into a pail of vinegar before it was carried.

The second trade was that of coals from Newcastle-upon-Tyne, without which the city would have been greatly distressed; for not in the streets only, but in private houses and families, great quantities of coals were then burnt, even all the summer long and when the weather was hottest, which was done by the advice of the physicians. Some indeed opposed it, and insisted that to keep the houses and rooms hot was a means to propagate the temper, which was a fermentation and heat already in the blood; that it was known to spread and increase in hot weather and abate in cold; and therefore they alleged that all contagious distempers are the worse for heat, because the contagion was nourished and gained strength in hot weather, and was, as it were, propagated in heat.

---

[1] That part of the river where the ships lie up when they come home is called the Pool, and takes in all the river on both sides of the water, from the Tower to Cuckold's Point and Limehouse.

Others said they granted that heat in the climate might propagate infection—as sultry, hot weather fills the air with vermin and nourishes innumerable numbers and kinds of venomous creatures which breed in our food, in the plants, and even in our bodies, by the very stench of which infection may be propagated; also that heat in the air, or heat of weather, as we ordinarily call it, makes bodies relax and faint, exhausts the spirits, opens the pores, and makes us more apt to receive infection, or any evil influence, be it from noxious pestilential vapours or any other thing in the air; but that the heat of fire, and especially of coal fires kept in our houses, or near us, had a quite different operation; the heat being not of the same kind, but quick and fierce, tending not to nourish but to consume and dissipate all those noxious fumes which the other kind of heat rather exhaled and stagnated than separated and burnt up. Besides, it was alleged that the sulphurous and nitrous particles that are often found to be in the coal, with that bituminous substance which burns, are all assisting to clear and purge the air, and render it wholesome and safe to breathe in after the noxious particles, as above, are dispersed and burnt up.

The latter opinion prevailed at that time, and, as I must confess, I think with good reason; and the experience of the citizens confirmed it, many houses which had constant fires kept in the rooms having never been infected at all; and I must join my experience to it, for I found the keeping good fires kept our rooms sweet and wholesome, and I do verily believe made our whole family so, more than would otherwise have been.

But I return to the coals as a trade. It was with no little difficulty that this trade was kept open, and particularly because, as we were in an open war with I the Dutch at that time, the Dutch capers at first took a great many of our collier-ships, which made the rest cautious, and made them to stay to come in fleets together. But after some time the capers were either afraid to take them, or their masters, the States, were afraid they should, and forbade them, lest the plague should be among them, which made them fare the better.

For the security of those northern traders, the coal-ships were ordered by my Lord Mayor not to come up into the Pool above a certain number at a time, and ordered lighters and other vessels such as the woodmongers (that is, the wharf-keepers or coal-sellers) furnished, to go down and take out the coals as low as Deptford and Greenwich, and some farther down.

Others delivered great quantities of coals in particular places where the ships could come to the shore, as at Greenwich, Blackwall, and other places, in vast heaps, as if to be kept for sale; but were then fetched away after the ships which brought them were gone, so that the seamen had no communication with the river-men, nor so much as came near one another.

Yet all this caution could not effectually prevent the distemper getting among the colliery: that is to say among the ships, by which a great many seamen died of it; and that which was still worse was, that they carried it down to Ipswich and Yarmouth, to Newcastle-upon-Tyne, and other places on the coast—where, especially at Newcastle and at Sunderland, it carried off a great number of people.

The making so many fires, as above, did indeed consume an unusual quantity of coals; and that upon one or two stops of the ships coming up, whether by contrary weather or by the interruption of enemies I do not remember, but the price of coals was exceeding dear, even as high as 4 a chalder; but it soon abated when the ships came in, and as afterwards they had a freer passage, the price was very reasonable all the rest of that year.

The public fires which were made on these occasions, as I have calculated it, must necessarily have cost the city about 200 chalders of coals a week, if they had continued, which was indeed a very great quantity; but as it was thought necessary, nothing was spared. However, as some of the physicians cried them down, they were not kept alight above four or five days. The fires were ordered thus:—

One at the Custom House, one at Billingsgate, one at Queenhith, and one at the Three Cranes; one in Blackfriars, and one at the gate of Bridewell; one at the corner of Leadenhal Street and Gracechurch; one at the north and one at the south gate of the Royal Exchange; one at Guild Hall, and one at Blackwell Hall gate; one at the Lord Mayor's door in St Helen's, one at the west entrance into St Paul's, and one at the entrance into Bow Church. I do not remember whether there was any at the city gates, but one at the Bridge-foot there was, just by St Magnus Church.

I know some have quarrelled since that at the experiment, and said that there died the more people because of those fires; but I am persuaded those that say so offer no evidence to prove it, neither can I believe it on any account whatever.

It remains to give some account of the state of trade at home in England during this dreadful time, and particularly as it relates to the manufactures and the trade in the city. At the first breaking out of the infection there was, as it is easy to suppose, a very great fright among the people, and consequently a general stop of trade, except in provisions and necessaries of life; and even in those things, as there was a vast number of people fled and a very great number always sick, besides the number which died, so there could not be above two-thirds, if above one-half, of the consumption of provisions in the city as used to be.

It pleased God to send a very plentiful year of corn and fruit, but not of hay or grass—by which means bread was cheap, by reason of the plenty of corn. Flesh was cheap, by reason of the scarcity of grass; but butter and cheese were dear for the same reason, and hay in the market just beyond Whitechappel Bars was sold at 4 pound per load. But that affected not the poor. There was a most excessive plenty of all sorts of fruit, such as apples, pears, plums, cherries, grapes, and they were the cheaper because of the want of people; but this made the poor eat them to excess, and this brought them into fluxes, griping of the guts, surfeits, and the like, which often precipitated them into the plague.

But to come to matters of trade. First, foreign exportation being stopped or at least very much interrupted and rendered difficult, a general stop of all those manufactures followed of course which were usually brought for exportation; and though sometimes merchants abroad were importunate for goods, yet little was sent, the passages being so generally stopped that the English ships would not be admitted, as is said already, into their port.

This put a stop to the manufactures that were for exportation in most parts of England, except in some out-ports; and even that was soon stopped, for they all had the plague in their turn. But though this was felt all over England, yet, what was still worse, all intercourse of trade for home consumption of manufactures, especially those which usually circulated through the Londoner's hands, was stopped at once, the trade of the city being stopped.

All kinds of handicrafts in the city, &c., tradesmen and mechanics, were, as I have said before, out of employ; and this occasioned the putting-off and dismissing an innumerable number of journeymen and workmen of all sorts, seeing nothing was done relating to such trades but what might be said to be absolutely necessary.

This caused the multitude of single people in London to be unprovided for, as also families whose living depended upon the labour of the heads of those families; I say, this reduced them to extreme misery; and I must confess it is for the honour of the city of London, and will be for many ages, as long as this is to be spoken of, that they were able to supply with charitable provision the wants of so many thousands of those as afterwards fell sick and were distressed: so that it may be safely averred that nobody perished for want, at least that the magistrates had any notice given them of.

This stagnation of our manufacturing trade in the country would have put the people there to much greater difficulties, but that the master-workmen, clothiers and others, to the uttermost of their stocks and strength, kept on making their goods to keep the poor at work, believing that soon as the sickness should abate they would have a quick demand in proportion to the decay of their trade at that time. But as none but those masters that were rich could do thus, and that many were poor and not able, the manufacturing trade in England suffered greatly, and the poor were pinched all over England by the calamity of the city of London only.

It is true that the next year made them full amends by another terrible calamity upon the city; so that the city by one calamity impoverished and weakened the country, and by another calamity, even terrible too of its kind, enriched the country and made them again amends; for an infinite quantity of household Stuff, wearing apparel, and other things, besides whole warehouses filled with merchandise and manufactures such as come from all parts of England, were consumed in the fire of London the next year after this terrible visitation. It is incredible what a trade this made all over the whole kingdom, to make good the want and to supply that loss; so that, in short, all the manufacturing hands in the nation were set on work, and were little enough for several years to supply the market and answer the demands. All foreign markets also were empty of our goods by the stop which had been occasioned by the plague, and before an open trade was allowed again; and the prodigious demand at home falling in, joined to make a quick vent for all sort of goods; so that there never was known such a trade all over England for the time as was in the first seven years after the plague, and after the fire of London.

It remains now that I should say something of the merciful part of this terrible judgement. The last week in September, the plague being come to its crisis, its fury began to assuage. I remember my friend Dr Heath, coming to see me the week before, told me he was sure that the violence of it would assuage in a few days; but when I saw the weekly bill of that week, which was the highest of the whole year, being 8297 of all diseases, I upbraided him with it, and asked him what he had made his judgement from. His answer, however, was not so much to seek as I thought it would have been. 'Look you,' says he, 'by the number which are at this time sick and infected, there should have been twenty thousand dead the last week instead of eight thousand, if the inveterate mortal contagion had been as it was two weeks ago; for then it ordinarily killed in two or three days, now not under eight or ten; and then not above one in five recovered, whereas I have observed that now not above two in five miscarry. And, observe it from me, the next bill will decrease, and you will see many more people recover than used to do; for though a vast multitude are now everywhere infected, and as many every day fall sick, yet there will not so many die as there did, for the malignity of the distemper is abated';—adding that he began now to hope, nay, more than hope, that the infection had passed its crisis and was going off; and accordingly so it was, for the next week being, as I said, the last in September, the bill decreased almost two thousand.

It is true the plague was still at a frightful height, and the next bill was no less than 6460, and the next to that, 5720; but still my friend's observation was just, and it did appear the people did recover faster and more in number than they used to do; and indeed, if it had not been so, what had been the condition of the city of London? For, according to my friend, there were not fewer than 60,000 people at that time infected, whereof, as above, 20,477 died, and near 40,000 recovered; whereas, had it been as it was before, 50,000 of that number would very probably have died, if not more, and 50,000 more would have sickened; for, in a word, the whole mass of people began to sicken, and it looked as if none would escape.

But this remark of my friend's appeared more evident in a few weeks more, for the decrease went on, and another week in October it decreased 1843, so that the number dead of the plague was but 2665; and the next week it decreased 1413 more, and yet it was seen plainly that there was abundance of people sick, nay, abundance more than ordinary, and abundance fell sick every day but (as above) the malignity of the disease abated.

Such is the precipitant disposition of our people (whether it is so or not all over the world, that's none of my particular business to inquire), but I saw it apparently here, that as upon the first fright of the infection they shunned one another, and fled from one another's houses and from the city with an unaccountable and, as I thought, unnecessary fright, so now, upon this notion spreading, viz., that the distemper was not so catching as formerly, and that if it was catched it was not so mortal, and seeing abundance of people who really fell sick recover again daily, they took to such a precipitant courage, and grew so entirely regardless of themselves and of the infection, that they made no more of the plague than of an ordinary fever, nor indeed so much. They not only went boldly into company with those who had tumours and carbuncles upon them that were running, and consequently contagious, but ate and drank with them, nay, into their houses to visit them, and even, as I was told, into their very chambers where they lay sick.

This I could not see rational. My friend Dr Heath allowed, and it was plain to experience, that the distemper was as catching as ever, and as many fell sick, but only he alleged that so many of those that fell sick did not die; but I think that while many did die, and that at best the distemper itself was very terrible, the sores and swellings very tormenting, and the danger of death not left out of the circumstances of sickness, though not so frequent as before; all those things, together with the exceeding tediousness of the cure, the loathsomeness of the disease, and many other articles, were enough to deter any man living from a dangerous mixture with the sick people, and make them as anxious almost to avoid the infections as before.

Nay, there was another thing which made the mere catching of the distemper frightful, and that was the terrible burning of the caustics which the surgeons laid on the swellings to bring them to break and to run, without which the danger of death was very great, even to the last. Also, the insufferable torment of the swellings, which, though it might not make people raving and distracted, as they were before, and as I have given several instances of already, yet they put the patient to inexpressible torment; and those that fell into it, though they did escape with life, yet they made bitter complaints of those that had told them there was no danger, and sadly repented their rashness and folly in venturing to run into the reach of it.

Nor did this unwary conduct of the people end here, for a great many that thus cast off their cautions suffered more deeply still, and though many escaped, yet many died; and at least it had this public mischief attending it, that it made the decrease of burials slower than it would otherwise have been. For as this notion ran like lightning through the city, and people's heads were possessed with it, even as soon as the first great decrease in the bills appeared, we found that the two next bills did not decrease in proportion; the reason I take to be the people's running so rashly into danger, giving up all their former cautions and care, and all the shyness which they used to practise, depending that the sickness would not reach them—or that if it did, they should not die.

The physicians opposed this thoughtless humour of the people with all their might, and gave out printed directions, spreading them all over the city and suburbs, advising the people to continue reserved, and to use still the utmost caution in their ordinary conduct, notwithstanding the decrease of the distemper, terrifying them with the danger of bringing a relapse upon the whole city, and telling them how such a relapse might be more fatal and dangerous than the whole visitation that had been already; with many arguments and reasons to explain and prove that part to them, and which are too long to repeat here.

But it was all to no purpose; the audacious creatures were so possessed with the first joy and so surprised with the satisfaction of seeing a vast decrease in the weekly bills, that they were impenetrable by any new terrors, and would not be persuaded but that the bitterness of death was past; and it was to no more purpose to talk to them than to an east wind; but they opened shops, went about streets, did business, and conversed with anybody that came in their way to converse with, whether with business or without, neither inquiring of their health or so much as being apprehensive of any danger from them, though they knew them not to be sound.

This imprudent, rash conduct cost a great many their lives who had with great care and caution shut themselves up and kept retired, as it were, from all mankind, and had by that means, under God's providence, been preserved through all the heat of that infection.

This rash and foolish conduct, I say, of the people went so far that the ministers took notice to them of it at last, and laid before them both the folly and danger of it; and this checked it a little, so that they grew more cautious. But it had another effect, which they could not check; for as the first rumour had spread not over the city only, but into the country, it had the like effect: and the people were so tired with being so long from London, and so eager to come back, that they flocked to town without fear or forecast, and began to show themselves in the streets as if all the danger was over. It was indeed surprising to see it, for though there died still from 1000 to 1800 a week, yet the people flocked to town as if all had been well.

The consequence of this was, that the bills increased again 400 the very first week in November; and if I might believe the physicians, there was above 3000 fell sick that week, most of them new-comers, too.

One John Cock, a barber in St Martin's-le-Grand, was an eminent example of this; I mean of the hasty return of the people when the plague was abated. This John Cock had left the town with his whole family, and locked up his house, and was gone in the country, as many others did; and finding the plague so decreased in November that there died but 905 per week of all diseases, he ventured home again. He had in his family ten persons; that is to say, himself and wife, five children, two apprentices, and a maid-servant. He had not returned to his house above a week, and began to open his shop and carry on his trade, but the distemper broke out in his family, and within about five days they all died, except one; that is to say, himself, his wife, all his five children, and his two apprentices; and only the maid remained alive.

But the mercy of God was greater to the rest than we had reason to expect; for the malignity (as I have said) of the distemper was spent, the contagion was exhausted, and also the winter weather came on apace, and the air was clear and cold, with sharp frosts; and this increasing still, most of those that had fallen sick recovered, and the health of the city began to return. There were indeed some returns of the distemper even in the month of December, and the bills increased near a hundred; but it went off again, and so in a short while things began to return to their own channel. And wonderful it was to see how populous the city was again all on a sudden, so that a stranger could not miss the numbers that were lost. Neither was there any miss of the inhabitants as to their dwellings—few or no empty houses were to be seen, or if there were some, there was no want of tenants for them.

I wish I could say that as the city had a new face, so the manners of the people had a new appearance. I doubt not but there were many that retained a sincere sense of their deliverance, and were that heartily thankful to that Sovereign Hand that had protected them in so dangerous a time; it would be very uncharitable to judge otherwise in a city so populous, and where the people were so devout as they were here in the time of the visitation itself; but except what of this was to be found in particular families and faces, it must be acknowledged that the general practice of the people was just as it was before, and very little difference was to be seen.

Some, indeed, said things were worse; that the morals of the people declined from this very time; that the people, hardened by the danger they had been in, like seamen after a storm is over, were more wicked and more stupid, more bold and hardened, in their vices and immoralities than they were before; but I will not carry it so far neither. It would take up a history of no small length to give a particular of all the gradations by which the course of things in this city came to be restored again, and to run in their own channel as they did before.

Some parts of England were now infected as violently as London had been; the cities of Norwich, Peterborough, Lincoln, Colchester, and other places were now visited; and the magistrates of London began to set rules for our conduct as to corresponding with those cities. It is true we could not pretend to forbid their people coming to London, because it was impossible to know them asunder; so, after many consultations, the Lord Mayor and Court of Aldermen were obliged to drop it. All they could do was to warn and caution the people not to entertain in their houses or converse with any people who they knew came from such infected places.

But they might as well have talked to the air, for the people of London thought themselves so plague-free now that they were past all admonitions; they seemed to depend upon it that the air was restored, and that the air was like a man that had had the smallpox, not capable of being infected again. This revived that notion that the infection was all in the air, that there was no such thing as contagion from the sick people to the sound; and so strongly did this whimsy prevail among people that they ran all together promiscuously, sick and well. Not the Mahometans, who, prepossessed with the principle of predestination, value nothing of contagion, let it be in what it will, could be more obstinate than the people of London; they that were perfectly sound, and came out of the wholesome air, as we call it, into the city, made nothing of going into the same houses and chambers, nay, even into the same beds, with those that had the distemper upon them, and were not recovered.

Some, indeed, paid for their audacious boldness with the price of their lives; an infinite number fell sick, and the physicians had more work than ever, only with this difference, that more of their patients recovered; that is to say, they generally recovered, but certainly there were more people infected and fell sick now, when there did not die above a thousand or twelve hundred in a week, than there was when there died five or six thousand a week, so entirely negligent were the people at that time in the great and dangerous case of health and infection, and so ill were they able to take or accept of the advice of those who cautioned them for their good.

The people being thus returned, as it were, in general, it was very strange to find that in their inquiring after their friends, some whole families were so entirely swept away that there was no remembrance of them left, neither was anybody to be found to possess or show any title to that little they had left; for in such cases what was to be found was generally embezzled and purloined, some gone one way, some another.

It was said such abandoned effects came to the king, as the universal heir; upon which we are told, and I suppose it was in part true, that the king granted all such, as deodands, to the Lord Mayor and Court of Aldermen of London, to be applied to the use of the poor, of whom there were very many. For it is to be observed, that though the occasions of relief and the objects of distress were very many more in the time of the violence of the plague than now after all was over, yet the distress of the poor was more now a great deal than it was then, because all the sluices of general charity were now shut. People supposed the main occasion to be over, and so stopped their hands; whereas particular objects were still very moving, and the distress of those that were poor was very great indeed.

Though the health of the city was now very much restored, yet foreign trade did not begin to stir, neither would foreigners admit our ships into their ports for a great while. As for the Dutch, the misunderstandings between our court and them had broken out into a war the year before, so that our trade that way was wholly interrupted; but Spain and Portugal, Italy and Barbary, as also Hamburg and all the ports in the Baltic, these were all shy of us a great while, and would not restore trade with us for many months.

The distemper sweeping away such multitudes, as I have observed, many if not all the out-parishes were obliged to make new burying-grounds, besides that I have mentioned in Bunhill Fields, some of which were continued, and remain in use to this day. But others were left off, and (which I confess I mention with some reflection) being converted into other uses or built upon afterwards, the dead bodies were disturbed, abused, dug up again, some even before the flesh of them was perished from the bones, and removed like dung or rubbish to other places. Some of those which came within the reach of my observation are as follow:

(1) A piece of ground beyond Goswell Street, near Mount Mill, being some of the remains of the old lines or fortifications of the city, where abundance were buried promiscuously from the parishes of Aldersgate, Clerkenwell, and even out

of the city. This ground, as I take it, was since made a physic garden, and after that has been built upon.

(2) A piece of ground just over the Black Ditch, as it was then called, at the end of Holloway Lane, in Shoreditch parish. It has been since made a yard for keeping hogs, and for other ordinary uses, but is quite out of use as a burying-ground.

(3) The upper end of Hand Alley, in Bishopsgate Street, which was then a green field, and was taken in particularly for Bishopsgate parish, though many of the carts out of the city brought their dead thither also, particularly out of the parish of St All-hallows on the Wall. This place I cannot mention without much regret. It was, as I remember, about two or three years after the plague was ceased that Sir Robert Clayton came to be possessed of the ground. It was reported, how true I know not, that it fell to the king for want of heirs, all those who had any right to it being carried off by the pestilence, and that Sir Robert Clayton obtained a grant of it from King Charles II. But however he came by it, certain it is the ground was let out to build on, or built upon, by his order. The first house built upon it was a large fair house, still standing, which faces the street or way now called Hand Alley which, though called an alley, is as wide as a street. The houses in the same row with that house northward are built on the very same ground where the poor people were buried, and the bodies, on opening the ground for the foundations, were dug up, some of them remaining so plain to be seen that the women's skulls were distinguished by their long hair, and of others the flesh was not quite perished; so that the people began to exclaim loudly against it, and some suggested that it might endanger a return of the contagion; after which the bones and bodies, as fast as they came at them, were carried to another part of the same ground and thrown all together into a deep pit, dug on purpose, which now is to be known in that it is not built on, but is a passage to another house at the upper end of Rose Alley, just against the door of a meeting-house which has been built there many years since; and the ground is palisadoed off from the rest of the passage, in a little square; there lie the bones and remains of near two thousand bodies, carried by the dead carts to their grave in that one year.

(4) Besides this, there was a piece of ground in Moorfields; by the going into the street which is now called Old Bethlem, which was enlarged much, though not wholly taken in on the same occasion.

[N.B.—The author of this journal lies buried in that very ground, being at his own desire, his sister having been buried there a few years before.]

(5) Stepney parish, extending itself from the east part of London to the north, even to the very edge of Shoreditch Churchyard, had a piece of ground taken in to bury their dead close to the said churchyard, and which for that very reason was left open, and is since, I suppose, taken into the same churchyard. And they had also two other burying-places in Spittlefields, one where since a chapel or tabernacle has been built for ease to this great parish, and another in Petticoat Lane.

There were no less than five other grounds made use of for the parish of Stepney at that time: one where now stands the parish church of St Paul, Shadwell, and the other where now stands the parish church of St John's at Wapping, both which had not the names of parishes at that time, but were belonging to Stepney parish.

I could name many more, but these coming within my particular knowledge, the circumstance, I thought, made it of use to record them. From the whole, it may be observed that they were obliged in this time of distress to take in new burying-grounds in most of the out-parishes for laying the prodigious numbers of people which died in so short a space of time; but why care was not taken to keep those places separate from ordinary uses, that so the bodies might rest undisturbed, that I cannot answer for, and must confess I think it was wrong. Who were to blame I know not.

I should have mentioned that the Quakers had at that time also a burying-ground set apart to their use, and which they still make use of; and they had also a particular dead-cart to fetch their dead from their houses; and the famous Solomon Eagle, who, as I mentioned before, had predicted the plague as a judgement, and ran naked through the streets, telling the people that it was come upon them to punish them for their sins, had his own wife died the very next day of the plague, and was carried, one of the first in the Quakers' dead-cart, to their new burying-ground.

I might have thronged this account with many more remarkable things which occurred in the time of the infection, and particularly what passed between the Lord Mayor and the Court, which was then at Oxford, and what directions were from time to time received from the Government for their conduct on this critical occasion. But really the Court concerned themselves so little, and that little they did was of so small import, that I do not see it of much moment to mention any part of it here: except that of appointing a monthly fast in the city and the sending the royal charity to the relief of the poor, both which I have mentioned before.

Great was the reproach thrown on those physicians who left their patients during the sickness, and now they came to town again nobody cared to employ them. They were called deserters, and frequently bills were set up upon their doors and written, 'Here is a doctor to be let', so that several of those physicians were fain for a while to sit still and look about them, or at least remove their dwellings, and set up in new places and among new acquaintance. The like was the case with the clergy, whom the people were indeed very abusive to, writing verses and scandalous reflections upon them, setting upon the church-door, 'Here is a pulpit to be let', or sometimes, 'to be sold', which was worse.

It was not the least of our misfortunes that with our infection, when it ceased, there did not cease the spirit of strife and contention, slander and reproach, which was really the great troubler of the nation's peace before. It was said to be the remains of the old animosities, which had so lately involved us all in blood and disorder. But as the late Act of Indemnity had laid asleep the quarrel itself, so the Government had recommended family and personal peace upon all occasions to the whole nation.

But it could not be obtained; and particularly after the ceasing of the plague in London, when any one that had seen the condition which the people had been in, and how they caressed one another at that time, promised to have more charity for the future, and to raise no more reproaches; I say, any one that had seen them then would have thought they would have come together with another spirit at last. But, I say, it could not be obtained. The quarrel remained; the Church and the Presbyterians were incompatible. As soon as the plague was removed, the Dissenting ousted ministers who had supplied the pulpits which were deserted by the incumbents retired; they could expect no other but that they should immediately fall upon them and harass them with their penal laws, accept their preaching while they were sick, and persecute them as soon as they were recovered again; this even we that were of the Church thought was very hard, and could by no means approve of it.

But it was the Government, and we could say nothing to hinder it; we could only say it was not our doing, and we could not answer for it.

On the other hand, the Dissenters reproaching those ministers of the Church with going away and deserting their charge, abandoning the people in their danger, and when they had most need of comfort, and the like: this we could by no means approve, for all men have not the same faith and the same courage, and the Scripture commands us to judge the most favourably and according to charity.

A plague is a formidable enemy, and is armed with terrors that every man is not sufficiently fortified to resist or prepared to stand the shock against. It is very certain that a great many of the clergy who were in circumstances to do it withdrew and fled for the safety of their lives; but 'tis true also that a great many of them stayed, and many of them fell in the calamity and in the discharge of their duty.

It is true some of the Dissenting turned-out ministers stayed, and their courage is to be commended and highly valued—but these were not abundance; it cannot be said that they all stayed, and that none retired into the country, any more than it can be said of the Church clergy that they all went away. Neither did all those that went away go without substituting curates and others in their places, to do the offices needful and to visit the sick, as far as it was practicable; so that, upon the whole, an allowance of charity might have been made on both sides, and we should have considered that such a time as this of 1665 is not to be paralleled in history, and that it is not the stoutest courage that will always support men in such cases. I had not said this, but had rather chosen to record the courage and religious zeal of those of both sides, who did hazard themselves for the service of the poor people in their distress, without remembering that any failed in their duty on either side. But the want of temper among us has made the contrary to this necessary: some that stayed not only boasting too much of themselves, but reviling those that fled, branding them with cowardice, deserting their flocks, and acting the part of the hireling, and the like. I recommend it to the charity of all good people to look back and reflect duly upon the terrors of the time, and whoever does so well see that it is not an ordinary strength that could support it. It was not like appearing in the head of an army or charging a body of horse in the field, but it was charging Death itself on his pale horse; to stay was indeed to die, and it could be esteemed nothing less, especially as things appeared at the latter end of August and the beginning of September, and as there was reason to expect them at that time; for no man expected, and I dare say believed, that the distemper would take so sudden a turn as it did, and fall immediately two thousand in a week, when there was such a prodigious number of people sick at that time as it was known there was; and then it was that many shifted away that had stayed most of the time before.

Besides, if God gave strength to some more than to others, was it to boast of their ability to abide the stroke, and upbraid those that had not the same gift and support, or ought not they rather to have been humble and thankful if they were rendered more useful than their brethren?

I think it ought to be recorded to the honour of such men, as well clergy as physicians, surgeons, apothecaries, magistrates, and officers of every kind, as also all useful people who ventured their lives in discharge of their duty, as most certainly all such as stayed did to the last degree; and several of all these kinds did not only venture but lose their lives on that sad occasion.

I was once making a list of all such, I mean of all those professions and employments who thus died, as I call it, in the way of their duty; but it was impossible for a private man to come at a certainty in the particulars. I only remember that there died sixteen clergymen, two aldermen, five physicians, thirteen surgeons, within the city and liberties before the beginning of September. But this being, as I said before, the great crisis and extremity of the infection, it can be no complete list. As to inferior people, I think there died six-and-forty constables and head-boroughs in the two parishes of Stepney and Whitechappel; but I could not carry my list oil, for when the violent rage of the distemper in September came upon us, it drove us out of all measures. Men did then no more die by tale and by number. They might put out a weekly bill, and call them seven or eight thousand, or what they pleased; 'tis certain they died by heaps, and were buried by heaps, that is to say, without account. And if I might believe some people, who were more abroad and more conversant with those things than I though I was public enough for one that had no more business to do than I had,—I say, if I may believe them, there was not many less buried those first three weeks in September than 20,000 per week. However, the others aver the truth of it; yet I rather choose to keep to the public account; seven and eight thousand per week is enough to make good all that I have said of the terror of those times;—and it is much to the satisfaction of me that write, as well as those that read, to be able to say that everything is set down with moderation, and rather within compass than beyond it.

Upon all these accounts, I say, I could wish, when we were recovered, our conduct had been more distinguished for charity and kindness in remembrance of the past calamity, and not so much a valuing ourselves upon our boldness in staying, as if all men were cowards that fly from the hand of God, or that those who stay do not sometimes owe their courage to their ignorance, and despising the hand of their Maker—which is a criminal kind of desperation, and not a true courage.

I cannot but leave it upon record that the civil officers, such as constables, head-boroughs, Lord Mayor's and sheriffs'-men, as also parish officers, whose business it was to take charge of the poor, did their duties in general with as much courage as any, and perhaps with more, because their work was attended with more hazards, and lay more among the poor, who were more subject to be infected, and in the most pitiful plight when they were taken with the infection. But then it must be added, too, that a great number of them died; indeed it was scarce possible it should be otherwise.

I have not said one word here about the physic or preparations that we ordinarily made use of on this terrible occasion—I mean we that went frequently abroad and up down street, as I did; much of this was talked of in the books and bills of our quack doctors, of whom I have said enough already. It may, however, be added, that the College of Physicians were daily publishing several preparations, which they had considered of in the process of their practice, and which, being to be had in print, I avoid repeating them for that reason.

One thing I could not help observing: what befell one of the quacks, who published that he had a most excellent preservative against the plague, which whoever kept about them should never be infected or liable to infection. This man, who, we may reasonably suppose, did not go abroad without some of this excellent preservative in his pocket, yet was taken by the distemper, and carried off in two or three days.

I am not of the number of the physic-haters or physic-despisers; on the contrary, I have often mentioned the regard I had to the dictates of my particular friend Dr Heath; but yet I must acknowledge I made use of little or nothing—except, as I have observed, to keep a preparation of strong scent to have ready, in case I met with anything of offensive smells or went too near any burying-place or dead body.

Neither did I do what I know some did: keep the spirits always high and hot with cordials and wine and such things; and which, as I observed, one learned physician used himself so much to as that he could not leave them off when the infection was quite gone, and so became a sot for all his life after.

I remember my friend the doctor used to say that there was a certain set of drugs and preparations which were all certainly good and useful in the case of an infection; out of which, or with which, physicians might make an infinite variety of medicines, as the ringers of bells make several hundred different rounds of music by the changing and order or sound but in six bells, and that all these preparations shall be really very good: 'Therefore,' said he, 'I do not wonder that so vast a throng of medicines is offered in the present calamity, and almost every physician prescribes or prepares a different thing, as his judgement or experience guides him; but', says my friend, 'let all the prescriptions of all the physicians in London be examined, and it will be found that they are all compounded of the same things, with such variations only as the particular fancy of the doctor leads him to; so that', says he, 'every man, judging a little of his own constitution and manner of his living, and circumstances of his being infected, may direct his own medicines out of the ordinary drugs and preparations. Only that', says he, 'some recommend one thing as most sovereign, and some another. Some', says he, 'think that pill. ruff., which is called itself the anti-pestilential pill is the best preparation that can be made; others think that Venice treacle is sufficient of itself to resist the contagion; and I', says he, 'think as both these think, viz., that the last is good to take beforehand to prevent it, and the first, if touched, to expel it.' According to this opinion, I several times took Venice treacle, and a sound sweat upon it, and thought myself as well fortified against the infection as any one could be fortified by the power of physic.

As for quackery and mountebanks, of which the town was so full, I listened to none of them, and have observed often since, with some wonder, that for two years after the plague I scarcely saw or heard of one of them about town. Some fancied they were all swept away in the infection to a man, and were for calling it a particular mark of God's vengeance upon them for leading the poor people into the pit of destruction, merely for the lucre of a little money they got by them; but I cannot go that length neither. That abundance of them died is certain—many of them came within the reach of my own knowledge—but that all of them were swept off I much question. I believe rather they fled into the country and tried their practices upon the people there, who were in apprehension of the infection before it came among them.

This, however, is certain, not a man of them appeared for a great while in or about London. There were, indeed, several doctors who published bills recommending their several physical preparations for cleansing the body, as they call it, after the plague, and needful, as they said, for such people to take who had been visited and had been cured; whereas I must own I believe that it was the opinion of the most eminent physicians at that time that the plague was itself a sufficient purge, and that those who escaped the infection needed no physic to cleanse their bodies of any other things; the running sores, the tumours, &c., which were broke and kept open by the directions of the physicians, having sufficiently cleansed them; and that all other distempers, and causes of distempers, were effectually carried off that way; and as the physicians gave this as their opinions wherever they came, the quacks got little business.

There were, indeed, several little hurries which happened after the decrease of the plague, and which, whether they were contrived to fright and disorder the people, as some imagined, I cannot say, but sometimes we were told the plague would return by such a time; and the famous Solomon Eagle, the naked Quaker I have mentioned, prophesied evil tidings every day; and several others telling us that London had not been sufficiently scourged, and that sorer and severer strokes were yet behind. Had they stopped there, or had they descended to particulars, and told us that the city should the next year be destroyed by fire, then, indeed, when we had seen it come to pass, we should not have been to blame to have paid more than a common respect to their prophetic spirits; at least we should have wondered at them, and have been more serious in our inquiries after the meaning of it, and whence they had the foreknowledge. But as they generally told us of a relapse into the plague, we have had no concern since that about them; yet by those frequent clamours, we were all kept with some kind of apprehensions constantly upon us; and if any died suddenly, or if the spotted fevers at any time increased, we were presently alarmed; much more if the number of the plague increased, for to the end of the year there were always between 200 and 300 of the plague. On any of these occasions, I say, we were alarmed anew.

Those who remember the city of London before the fire must remember that there was then no such place as we now call Newgate Market, but that in the middle of the street which is now called Blowbladder Street, and which had its name from the butchers, who used to kill and dress their sheep there (and who, it seems, had a custom to blow up their meat with pipes to make it look thicker and fatter than it was, and were punished there for it by the Lord Mayor); I say, from the end of the street towards Newgate there stood two long rows of shambles for the selling meat.

It was in those shambles that two persons falling down dead, as they were buying meat, gave rise to a rumour that the meat was all infected; which, though it might affright the people, and spoiled the market for two or three days, yet it appeared plainly afterwards that there was nothing of truth in the suggestion. But nobody can account for the possession of fear when it takes hold of the mind.

However, it Pleased God, by the continuing of the winter weather, so to restore the health of the city that by February following we reckoned the distemper quite ceased, and then we were not so easily frighted again.

There was still a question among the learned, and at first perplexed the people a little: and that was in what manner to purge the house and goods where the plague had been, and how to render them habitable again, which had been left empty during the time of the plague. Abundance of perfumes and preparations were prescribed by physicians, some of one kind and some of another, in which the people who listened to them put themselves to a great, and indeed, in my opinion, to an unnecessary expense; and the poorer people, who only set open their windows night and day, burned brimstone, pitch, and gunpowder, and such things in their rooms, did as well as the best; nay, the eager people who, as I said above, came home in haste and at all hazards, found little or no inconvenience in their houses, nor in the goods, and did little or nothing to them.

However, in general, prudent, cautious people did enter into some measures for airing and sweetening their houses, and burned perfumes, incense, benjamin, rozin, and sulphur in their rooms close shut up, and then let the air carry it all out with a blast of gunpowder; others caused large fires to be made all day and all night for several days and nights; by the same token that two or three were pleased to set their houses on fire, and so effectually sweetened them by burning them down to the ground; as particularly one at Ratcliff, one in Holbourn, and one at Westminster; besides two or three that were set on fire, but the fire was happily got out again before it went far enough to burn down the houses; and one citizen's servant, I think it was in Thames Street, carried so much gunpowder into his master's house, for clearing it of the infection, and managed it so foolishly, that he blew up part of the roof of the house. But the time was not fully come that the city was to be purged by fire, nor was it far off; for within nine months more I saw it all lying in ashes; when, as some of our quacking philosophers pretend, the seeds of the plague were entirely destroyed, and not before; a notion too ridiculous to speak of here: since, had the seeds of the plague remained in the houses, not to be destroyed but by fire, how has it been that they have not since broken out, seeing all those buildings in the suburbs and liberties, all in the great parishes of Stepney, Whitechappel, Aldgate, Bishopsgate, Shoreditch, Cripplegate, and St Giles, where the fire never came, and where the plague raged with the greatest violence, remain still in the same condition they were in before?

But to leave these things just as I found them, it was certain that those people who were more than ordinarily cautious of their health, did take particular directions for what they called seasoning of their houses, and abundance of costly things were consumed on that account which I cannot but say not only seasoned those houses, as they desired, but filled the air with very grateful and wholesome smells which others had the share of the benefit of as well as those who were at the expenses of them.

And yet after all, though the poor came to town very precipitantly, as I have said, yet I must say the rich made no such haste. The men of business, indeed, came up, but many of them did not bring their families to town till the spring came on, and that they saw reason to depend upon it that the plague would not return.

The Court, indeed, came up soon after Christmas, but the nobility and gentry, except such as depended upon and had employment under the administration, did not come so soon.

I should have taken notice here that, notwithstanding the violence of the plague in London and in other places, yet it was very observable that it was never on board the fleet; and yet for some time there was a strange press in the river, and even in the streets, for seamen to man the fleet. But it was in the beginning of the year, when the plague was scarce begun, and not at all come down to that part of the city where they usually press for seamen; and though a war with the Dutch was not at all grateful to the people at that time, and the seamen went with a kind of reluctancy into the service, and many complained of being dragged into it by force, yet it proved in the event a happy violence to several of them, who had probably perished in the general calamity, and who, after the summer service was over, though they had cause to lament the desolation of their families—who, when they came back, were many of them in their graves—yet they had room to be thankful that they were carried out of the reach of it, though so much against their wills. We indeed had a hot war with the Dutch that year, and one very great engagement at sea in which the Dutch were worsted, but we lost a great many men and some ships. But, as I observed, the plague was not in the fleet, and when they came to lay up the ships in the river the violent part of it began to abate.

I would be glad if I could close the account of this melancholy year with some particular examples historically; I mean of the thankfulness to God, our preserver, for our being delivered from this dreadful calamity. Certainly the circumstance of the deliverance, as well as the terrible enemy we were delivered from, called upon the whole nation for it. The circumstances of the deliverance were indeed very remarkable, as I have in part mentioned already, and particularly the dreadful condition which we were all in when we were to the surprise of the whole town made joyful with the hope of a stop of the infection.

Nothing but the immediate finger of God, nothing but omnipotent power, could have done it. The contagion despised all medicine; death raged in every corner; and had it gone on as it did then, a few weeks more would have cleared the town of all, and everything that had a soul. Men everywhere began to despair; every heart failed them for fear; people were made desperate through the anguish of their souls, and the terrors of death sat in the very faces and countenances of the people.

In that very moment when we might very well say, 'Vain was the help of man',—I say, in that very moment it pleased God, with a most agreeable surprise, to cause the fury of it to abate, even of itself; and the malignity declining, as I have said, though infinite numbers were sick, yet fewer died, and the very first weeks' bill decreased 1843; a vast number indeed!

It is impossible to express the change that appeared in the very countenances of the people that Thursday morning when the weekly bill came out. It might have been perceived in their countenances that a secret surprise and smile of joy sat on everybody's face. They shook one another by the hands in the streets, who would hardly go on the same side of the way with one another before. Where the streets were not too broad they would open their windows and call from one house to another, and ask how they did, and if they had heard the good news that the plague was abated. Some would return, when they said good news, and ask, 'What good news?' and when they answered that the plague was abated and the bills decreased almost two thousand, they would cry out, 'God be praised I' and would weep aloud for joy, telling them they had heard nothing of it; and such was the joy of the people that it was, as it were, life to them from the grave. I could almost set down as many extravagant things done in the excess of their joy as of their grief; but that would be to lessen the value of it.

I must confess myself to have been very much dejected just before this happened; for the prodigious number that were taken sick the week or two before, besides those that died, was such, and the lamentations were so great everywhere, that a man must have seemed to have acted even against his reason if he had so much as expected to escape; and as there was hardly a house but mine in all my neighbourhood but was infected, so had it gone on it would not have been long that there would have been any more neighbours to be infected. Indeed it is hardly credible what dreadful havoc the last three weeks had made, for if I might believe the person whose calculations I always found very well grounded, there were not less than 30,000 people dead and near 100.000 fallen sick in the three weeks I speak of; for the number that sickened was surprising, indeed it was astonishing, and those whose courage upheld them all the time before, sank under it now.

In the middle of their distress, when the condition of the city of London was so truly calamitous, just then it pleased God—as it were by His immediate hand to disarm this enemy; the poison was taken out of the sting. It was wonderful; even the physicians themselves were surprised at it. Wherever they visited they found their patients better; either they had sweated kindly, or the tumours were broke, or the carbuncles went down and the inflammations round them changed colour, or the fever was gone, or the violent headache was assuaged, or some good symptom was in the case; so that in a few days everybody was recovering, whole families that were infected and down, that had ministers praying with them, and expected death every hour, were revived and healed, and none died at all out of them.

Nor was this by any new medicine found out, or new method of cure discovered, or by any experience in the operation which the physicians or surgeons attained to; but it was evidently from the secret invisible hand of Him that had at first sent this disease as a judgement upon us; and let the atheistic part of mankind call my saying what they please, it is no enthusiasm; it was acknowledged at that time by all mankind. The disease was enervated and its malignity spent; and let it proceed from whencesoever it will, let the philosophers search for reasons in nature to account for it by, and labour as much as they will to lessen the debt they owe to their Maker, those physicians who had the least share of religion in them were obliged to acknowledge that it was all supernatural, that it was extraordinary, and that no account could be given of it.

If I should say that this is a visible summons to us all to thankfulness, especially we that were under the terror of its increase, perhaps it may be thought by some, after the sense of the thing was over, an officious canting of religious things, preaching a sermon instead of writing a history, making myself a teacher instead of giving my observations of things; and this restrains me very much from going on here as I might otherwise do. But if ten lepers Were healed, and but one returned to give thanks, I desire to be as that one, and to be thankful for myself.

Nor will I deny but there were abundance of people who, to all appearance, were very thankful at that time; for their mouths were stopped, even the mouths of those whose hearts were not extraordinary long affected with it. But the impression was so strong at that time that it could not be resisted; no, not by the worst of the people.

It was a common thing to meet people in the street that were strangers, and that we knew nothing at all of, expressing their surprise. Going one day through Aldgate, and a pretty many people being passing and repassing, there comes a man out of the end of the Minories, and looking a little up the street and down, he throws his hands abroad, 'Lord, what an alteration is here I Why, last week I came along here, and hardly anybody was to be seen.' Another man—I heard him—adds to his words, ''Tis all wonderful; 'tis all a dream.' 'Blessed be God,' says a third man, and and let us give thanks to Him, for 'tis all His own doing, human help and human skill was at an end.' These were all strangers to one another. But such salutations as these were frequent in the street every day; and in spite of a loose behaviour, the very common people went along the streets giving God thanks for their deliverance.

It was now, as I said before, the people had cast off all apprehensions, and that too fast; indeed we were no more afraid now to pass by a man with a white cap upon his head, or with a doth wrapt round his neck, or with his leg limping, occasioned by the sores in his groin, all which were frightful to the last degree, but the week before. But now the street was full of them, and these poor recovering creatures, give them their due, appeared very sensible of their unexpected deliverance; and I should wrong them very much if I should not acknowledge that I believe many of them were really thankful. But I must own that, for the generality of the people, it might too justly be said of them as was said of the children of Israel after their being delivered from the host of Pharaoh, when they passed the Red Sea, and looked back and saw the Egyptians overwhelmed in the water: viz., that they sang His praise, but they soon forgot His works.

I can go no farther here. I should be counted censorious, and perhaps unjust, if I should enter into the unpleasing work of reflecting, whatever cause there was for it, upon the unthankfulness and return of all manner of wickedness among us, which I was so much an eye-witness of myself. I shall conclude the account of this calamitous year therefore with a coarse but sincere stanza of my own, which I placed at the end of my ordinary memorandums the same year they were written:—

A dreadful plague in London was
In the year sixty-five,
Which swept an hundred thousand souls
Away; yet I alive!

H. F.

ROXANA

The Fortunate Mistress:
or,
A History of the Life and Vast Variety of Fortunes
Of
Mademoiselle de Beleau,
afterwards call'd
The Countess de Wintselsheim, in Germany. Being the Person known by the Name of the Lady Roxana, in the Time of King Charles II.

Chapter 1

I was born, as my friends told me, at the city of Poitiers, in the province or county of Poitou in France, from whence I was brought to England by my parents, who fled for their religion about the year 1683, when the Protestants were banished from France by the cruelty of their persecutors.

I, who knew little or nothing of what I was brought over hither for, was well enough pleased with being here. London, a large and gay city, took with me mighty well, who from my being a child loved a crowd and to see a great many fine folks.

I retained nothing of France but the language. My father and mother, being people of better fashion than ordinarily the people called refugees at that time were, and having fled early while it was easy to secure their effects, had, before their coming over, remitted considerable sums of money, or, as I remember, a considerable value in French brandy, paper, and other goods; and these selling very much to advantage here, my father was in very good circumstances at his coming over, so that he was far from applying to the rest of our nation that were here for countenance and relief. On the contrary, he had his door continually thronged with miserable objects of the poor starving creatures, who at that time fled hither for shelter on account of conscience or something else.

I have indeed heard my father say that he was pestered with a great many of those who for any religion they had might e'en have stayed where they were, but who flocked over hither in droves for what they call in English a livelihood; hearing with what open arms the refugees were received in England, and how they fell readily into business, being by the charitable assistance of the people in London encouraged to work in their manufactures, in Spitalfields, Canterbury, and other places, and that they had a much better price for their work than in France and the like.

My father, I say, told me that he was more pestered with the clamours of these people than of those who were truly refugees and fled in distress merely for conscience.

I was about ten years old when I was brought over hither, where, as I have said, my father lived in very good circumstances and died in about eleven years more; in which time, as I had accomplished myself for the sociable part of the world, so I had acquainted myself with some of our English neighbours, as is the custom in London; and as, while I was young, I had picked up three or four play-fellows and companions suitable to my years, so as we grew bigger we learnt to call one another intimates and friends, and this forwarded very much the finishing me for conversation and the world.

I went to English schools, and, being young, I learnt the English tongue perfectly well, with all the customs of the English young women; so that I retained nothing of the French but the speech, nor did I so much as keep any remains of the French language tagged to my way of speaking, as most foreigners do, but spoke what we call natural English, as if I had been born here.

Being to give my own character, I must be excused to give it as impartially as possible, and as if I was speaking of another body; and the sequel will leave you to judge whether I flatter myself or no.

I was (speaking of myself as about fourteen years of age) tall and very well made, sharp as a hawk in matters of common knowledge, quick and smart in discourse, apt to be satirical, full of repartee, and a little too forward in conversation; or, as we call it in English, bold, though perfectly modest in my behaviour. Being French born, I danced, as some say, naturally, loved it extremely, and sang well also; and so well, that, as you will hear, it was afterwards some advantage to me. With all these things, I wanted neither wit, beauty, nor money. In this manner I set out into the world, having all the advantages that any young woman could desire to recommend me to others and form a prospect of happy living to myself.

At about fifteen years of age my father gave me, as he called it in French, 25,000 livres, that is to say, two thousand pounds portion, and married me to an eminent brewer in the City. Pardon me if I conceal his name, for though he was the foundation of my ruin, I cannot take so severe a revenge upon him.

With this thing called a husband I lived eight years in good fashion, and for some part of the time kept a coach; that is to say, a kind of mock coach, for all the week the horses were kept at work in the dray carts, but on Sunday I had the privilege to go abroad in my chariot, either to church or otherwise, as my husband and I could agree about it; which, by the way, was not very often. But of that hereafter.

Before I proceed in the history of the married part of my life, you must allow me to give as impartial an account of my husband as I have done of myself. He was a jolly, handsome fellow as any woman need wish for a companion, tall and well made, rather a little too large, but not so as to be ungenteel; he danced well, which I think was the first thing that brought us together. He had an old father who managed the business carefully, so that he had little of that part laid on him but now and then to appear and show himself; and he took the advantage of it, for he troubled himself very little about it, but went abroad, kept company, hunted much, and loved it exceedingly.

After I have told you that he was a handsome man and a good sportsman, I have indeed said all; and unhappy was I--like other young people of our sex, I chose him for being a handsome, jolly fellow, as I have said--for he was otherwise a weak, empty-headed, untaught creature as any woman could ever desire to be coupled with. And here I must take the liberty, whatever I have to reproach myself with in my after conduct, to turn to my fellow creatures, the young ladies of this country, and speak to them by way of precaution. If you have any regard to your future happiness, any view of living comfortably with a husband, any hope of preserving your fortunes or restoring them after any disaster, never, ladies, marry a fool. Any husband rather than a fool. With some other husbands you may be unhappy, but with a fool you will be miserable; with another husband you may, I say, be unhappy, but with a fool you must; nay, if he would, he cannot make you easy, everything he does is so awkward, everything he says is so empty, a woman of any sense cannot but be surfeited and sick of him twenty times a day. What is more shocking than for a woman to bring a handsome, comely fellow of a husband into company and then be obliged to blush for him every time she hears him speak; to hear other gentlemen talk sense and he able to say nothing, and so look like a fool; or, which is worse, hear him talk nonsense and be laughed at for a fool?

In the next place, there are so many sorts of fools, such an infinite variety of fools, and so hard it is to know the worst of the kind, that I am obliged to say, no fool, ladies, at all, no kind of fool; whether a mad fool or a sober fool, a wise fool or a silly fool, take anything but a fool; nay, be anything, be even an old maid, the worst of nature's curses, rather than take up with a fool.

But to leave this awhile, for I shall have occasion to speak of it again, my case was particularly hard, for I had a variety of foolish things complicated in this unhappy match.

First, and which I must confess is very unsufferable, he was a conceited fool, tout opiniâtre; everything he said was right, was best, and was to the purpose, whoever was in company and whatever was advanced by others, though with the greatest modesty imaginable. And yet when he came to defend what he had said by argument and reason, he would do it so weakly, so emptily, and so nothing to the purpose, that it was enough to make anybody that heard him sick and ashamed of him.

Secondly, he was positive and obstinate, and the most positive in the most simple and inconsistent things such as were intolerable to bear.

These two articles, if there had been no more, qualified him to be a most unbearable creature for a husband, and so it may be supposed at first sight what kind of life I led with him. However, I did as well as I could and held my tongue, which was the only victory I gained over him; for when he would talk after his own empty rattling way with me, and I would not answer or enter into discourse with him on the point he was upon, he would rise up in the greatest passion imaginable and go away, which was the cheapest way I had to be delivered.

I could enlarge here much upon the method I took to make my life passable and easy with the most incorrigible temper in the world, but it is too long and the articles too trifling. I shall mention some of them as the circumstances I am to relate shall necessarily bring them in.

After I had been married about four years my own father died, my mother having been dead before. He liked my match so ill, and saw so little room to be satisfied with the conduct of my husband, that though he left me 5,000 livres and more at his death, yet he left it in the hands of my elder brother, who, running on too rashly in his adventures as a merchant, failed, and lost not only what he had but what he had for me too, as you shall hear presently.

Thus I lost the last gift of my father's bounty by having a husband not fit to be trusted with it; there's one of the benefits of marrying a fool!

Within two years after my own father's death my husband's father also died, and, as I thought, left him a considerable addition to his estate; the whole trade of the brewhouse, which was a very good one, being now his own.

But this addition to his stock was his ruin, for he had no genius to business. He had no knowledge of his accounts; he bustled a little about it indeed at first, and put on a face of business, but he soon grew slack. It was below him to inspect his books, he committed all that to his clerks and book-keepers, and while he found money in cash to pay the maltman and the excise, and put some in his pocket, he was perfectly easy and indolent, let the main chance go how it would.

I foresaw the consequences of this, and attempted several times to persuade him to apply himself to his business. I put him in mind how his customers complained of the neglect of his servants on one hand, and how abundance broke in his debt, on the other hand, for want of the clerk's care to secure him, and the like; but he thrust me by, either with hard words or fraudulently with representing the cases otherwise than they were.

However, to cut short a dull story which ought not to be long, he began to find his trade sunk, his stock declined, and that, in short, he could not carry on his business; and once or twice his brewing utensils were extended for the excise, and the last time he was put to great extremities to clear them.

This alarmed him, and he resolved to lay down his trade, which indeed I was not sorry for; foreseeing that if he did not lay it down in time, he would be forced to do it another way, namely, as a bankrupt. Also, I was willing he should draw out while he had something left, lest I should come to be stripped at home and be turned out of doors with my children, for I had now five children by him: the only work (perhaps) that fools are good for.

I thought myself happy when he got another man to take his brewhouse clear off his hands; for, paying down a large sum of money, my husband found himself a clear man, all his debts paid, and with between two and three thousand pounds in his pocket. And being now obliged to remove from the brewhouse, we took a house at ----, a village about two miles out of town; and happy I thought myself, all things considered, that I was got off clear upon so good terms, and had my handsome fellow had but one capful of wit, I had been still well enough.

I proposed to him either to buy some place with the money or with part of it, and offered to join my part to it, which was then in being and might have been secured; so we might have lived tolerably, at least, during his life. But as it is the part of a fool to be void of counsel, so he neglected it, lived on as he did before, kept his horses and men, rode every day out to the forest a-hunting, and nothing was done all this while. But the money decreased apace, and I thought I saw my ruin hastening on without any possible way to prevent it.

I was not wanting with all that persuasions and entreaties could perform, but it was all fruitless; representing to him how fast our money wasted, and what would be our condition when it was gone, made no impression on him; but like one stupid he went on, not valuing all that tears and lamentations could be supposed to do, nor did he abate his figure or equipage, his horses or servants, even to the last, till he had not a hundred pounds left in the whole world.

It was not above three years that all the ready money was thus spending off; yet he spent it, as I may say, foolishly too, for he kept no valuable company neither, but generally with huntsmen and horse-coursers, and men meaner than himself, which is another consequence of a man's being a fool. Such can never take delight in men more wise and capable than themselves; and that makes them converse with scoundrels, drink belch with porters, and keep company always below themselves.

This was my wretched condition, when one morning my husband told me he was sensible he was come to a miserable condition and he would go and seek his fortune somewhere or other. He had said something to that purpose several times before that, upon my pressing him to consider his circumstances and the circumstances of his family before it should be too late. But as I found he had no meaning in anything of that kind, as indeed he had not much in anything he ever said, so I thought they were but words of course now. When he said he would be gone, I used to wish secretly, and even say in my thoughts, "I wish you would, for if you go on thus you will starve us all."

He stayed, however, at home all that day, and lay at home that night. Early the next morning he gets out of bed, goes to a window which looked out towards the stables, and sounds his French horn, as he called it, which was his usual signal to call his men to go out a-hunting.

It was about the latter end of August, and so was light yet at five o'clock, and it was about that time that I heard him and his two men go out and shut the yard gates after them. He said nothing to me more than as usual when he used to go out upon his sport; neither did I rise or say anything to him that was material, but went to sleep again after he was gone for two hours or thereabouts.

It must be a little surprising to the reader to tell him at once that after this I never saw my husband more; but to go further, I not only never saw him more, but I never heard from him or of him, neither of any or either of his two servants or of the horses, either what became of them, where or which way they went, or what they did or intended to do, no more than if the ground had opened and swallowed them all up, and nobody had known it, except as hereafter.

I was not for the first night or two at all surprised, no, nor very much the first week or two, believing that if anything evil had befallen them I should soon enough have heard of that, and also knowing that as he had two servants and three horses with him, it would be the strangest thing in the world that anything could befall them all, but that I must some time or other hear of them.

But you will easily allow that as time ran on a week, two weeks, a month, two months, and so on, I was dreadfully frighted at last, and the more when I looked into my own circumstances and considered the condition in which I was left; with five children and not one farthing subsistence for them, other than about seventy pounds in money and what few things of value I had about me, which, though considerable in themselves, were yet nothing to feed a family, and for a length of time too.

What to do I knew not, nor to whom to have recourse; to keep in the house where I was I could not, the rent being too great, and to leave it without his order, if my husband should return, I could not think of that neither; so that I continued extremely perplexed, melancholy, and discouraged to the last degree.

Chapter 2

I remained in this dejected condition near a twelve-month. My husband had two sisters, who were married and lived very well, and some other near relations that I knew of and I hoped would do something for me, and I frequently sent to these to know if they could give me any account of my vagrant creature; but they all declared to me in answer that they knew nothing about him, and, after frequent sending, began to think me troublesome, and to let me know they thought so too by their treating my maid with very slight and unhandsome returns to her enquiries.

This grated hard and added to my affliction, but I had no recourse but to my tears, for I had not a friend of my own left me in the world. I should have observed that it was about half a year before this elopement of my husband that the disaster I mentioned above befell my brother, who broke, and that in such bad circumstances that I had the mortification to hear not only that he was in prison, but that there would be little or nothing to be had by way of composition.

Misfortunes seldom come alone. This was the forerunner of my husband's flight, and as my expectations were cut off on that side, my husband gone, and my family of children on my hands and nothing to subsist them, my condition was the most deplorable that words can express.

I had some plate and some jewels, as might be supposed, my fortune and former circumstances considered, and my husband, who had never stayed to be distressed, had not been put to the necessity of rifling me, as husbands usually do in such cases. But as I had seen an end of all the ready money during the long time I had lived in a state of expectation for my husband, so I began to make away one thing after another, till those few things of value which I had began to lessen apace, and I saw nothing but misery and the utmost distress before me, even to have my children starve before my face. I leave any one that is a mother of children, and has lived in plenty and good fashion, to consider and reflect what must be my condition. As to my husband, I had now no hope or expectation of seeing him any more, and indeed, if I had, he was the man of all the men in the world the least able to help me, or to have turned his hand to the gaining one shilling towards lessening our distress. He neither had the capacity nor the inclination; he could have been no clerk, for he scarce wrote a legible hand; he was so far from being able to write sense, that he could not make sense of what others wrote; he was so far from understanding good English, that he could not spell good English. To be out of all business was his delight, and he would stand leaning against a post for half an hour together, with pipe in his mouth, with all the tranquillity in the world, smoking, like Dryden's countryman that whistled as he went, for want of thought; and this even when his family was, as it were, starving, that little he had wasting, and that we were all bleeding to death, he not knowing, and as little considering, where to get another shilling when the last was spent.

This being his temper and the extent of his capacity, I confess I did not see so much loss in his parting with me as at first I thought I did, though it was hard and cruel to the last degree in him not giving me the least notice of his design; and indeed, that which I was most astonished at was that, seeing he must certainly have intended this excursion some few moments at least before he put it in practice, yet he did not come and take what little stock of money we had left, or at least a share of it, to bear his expense for a little while; but he did not, and I am morally certain he had not five guineas with him in the world when he went away. All that I could come to the knowledge of about him was that he left his hunting horn, which he called the French horn, in the stable, and his hunting saddle, went away in a handsome furniture as they call it, which he used sometimes to travel with, having an embroidered housing, a case of pistols, and other things belonging to them; and one of his servants had another saddle with pistols, though plain, and the other a long gun; so that they did not go out as sportsmen, but rather as travellers. What part of the world they went to I never heard for many years.

As I have said, I sent to his relations, but they sent me short and surly answers; nor did any one of them offer to come to see me or to see the children, or so much as to enquire after them, well perceiving that I was in a condition that was likely to be soon troublesome to them. But it was no time now to dally with them or with the world. I left off sending to them and went myself among them, laid my circumstances open to them, told them my whole case and the condition I was reduced to, begged they would advise me what course to take, laid myself as low as they could desire, and entreated them to consider that I was not in a condition to help myself, and that without some assistance we must all inevitably perish. I told them that if I had but one child, or two children, I would have done my endeavour to have worked for them with my needle, and should only have come to them to beg them to help me to some work, that I might get our bread by my labour; but to think of one single woman not bred to work, and at a loss where to get employment, to get the bread of five children, that was not possible, some of my children being young too, and none of them big enough to help one another.

It was all one; I received not one farthing of assistance from anybody, was hardly asked to sit down at the two sisters' houses, nor offered to eat or drink at two more near relations. The fifth, an ancient gentlewoman, aunt-in-law to my husband, a widow, and the least able also of any of the rest, did indeed ask me to sit down, gave me a dinner, and refreshed me with a kinder treatment than any of the rest, but added the melancholy part, viz. that she would have helped me, but that indeed she was not able; which, however, I was satisfied was very true.

Here I relieved myself with the constant assistant of the afflicted, I mean tears; for, relating to her how I was received by the other of my husband's relations, it made me burst into tears, and I cried vehemently for a great while together, till I made the good old gentlewoman cry too several times.

However, I came home from them all without any relief, and went on at home till I was reduced to such inexpressible distress, that it is not to be described. I had been several times after this at the old aunt's, for I prevailed with her to promise me to go and talk with the other relations; at least, that if possible she could bring some of them to take off the children or to contribute something towards their maintenance; and to do her justice, she did use her endeavour with them, but all was to no purpose, they would do nothing, at least that way. I think, with much entreaty, she obtained by a kind of collection among them all, about eleven or twelve shillings in money, which, though it was a present comfort, was yet not to be named as capable to deliver me from any part of the load that lay upon me.

There was a poor woman that had been a kind of a dependent upon our family, and who I had often, among the rest of the relations, been very kind to. My maid put it into my head one morning to send to this poor woman and to see whether she might not be able to help in this dreadful case.

I must remember it here, to the praise of this poor girl, my maid, that though I was not able to give her any wages, and had told her so, nay, I was not able to pay her the wages that I was in arrears to her, yet she would not leave me; nay, and as long as she had any money when I had none, she would help me out of her own; for which, though I acknowledged her kindness and fidelity, yet it was but a bad coin that she was paid in at last, as will appear in its place.

Amy (for that was her name) put it into my thoughts to send for this poor woman to come to me, for I was now in great distress, and I resolved to do so; but just the very morning that I intended it, the old aunt, with the poor woman in her company, came to see me. The good old gentlewoman was, it seems, heartily concerned for me, and had been talking again among those people, to see what she could do for me, but to very little purpose.

You shall judge a little of my present distress by the posture she found me in. I had five little children, the eldest was under ten years old, and I had not a shilling in the house to buy them victuals, but had sent Amy out with a silver spoon to sell it and bring home something from the butcher's, and I was in a parlour, sitting on the ground with a great heap of old rags, linen, and other things about me, looking them over to see if I had anything among them that would sell or pawn for a little money, and had been crying ready to burst myself to think what I should do next.

At this juncture they knocked at the door. I thought it had been Amy, so I did not rise up, but one of the children opened the door and they came directly into the room where I was, and where they found me in that posture and crying vehemently, as above. I was surprised at their coming, you may be sure, especially seeing the person I had but just before resolved to send for. But when they saw me, how I looked, for my eyes were swelled with crying, and what a condition I was in as to the house and the heaps of things that were about me, and especially when I told them what I was doing and on what occasion, they sat down, like Job's three comforters, and said not one word to me for a great while, but both of them cried as fast and as heartily as I did.

The truth was, there was no need of much discourse in the case, the thing spoke for itself. They saw me in rags and dirt, who was but a little before riding in my coach; thin, and looking almost like one starved, who was before fat and beautiful. The house, that was before handsomely furnished with pictures and ornaments, cabinets, pier-glasses, and everything suitable, was now stripped and naked, most of the goods having been seized by the landlord for rent or sold to buy necessaries. In a word, all was misery and distress, the face of ruin was everywhere to be seen; we had eaten up almost everything, and little remained, unless, like one of the pitiful women of Jerusalem, I should eat up my very children themselves.

After these two good creatures had sat, as I say, in silence some time, and had then looked about them, my maid Amy came in and brought with her a small breast of mutton and two great bunches of turnips, which she intended to stew for our dinner. As for me, my heart was so overwhelmed at seeing these two friends, for such they were, though poor, and at their seeing me in such a condition, that I fell into another violent fit of crying; so that, in short, I could not speak to them again for a great while longer.

During my being in such an agony they went to my maid Amy at another part of the same room, and talked with her. Amy told them all my circumstances, and set them forth in such moving terms and so to the life, that I could not upon any terms have done it like her myself; and, in a word, affected them both with it in such a manner, that the old aunt came to me, and though hardly able to speak for tears, "Look ye, cousin," said she in a few words, "things must not stand thus; some course must be taken, and that forthwith. Pray, where were these children born?" I told her the parish where we lived before; that four of them were born there and one in the house where I now was, where the landlord, after having seized my goods for the rent past, not then knowing my circumstances, had now given me leave to live for a whole year more without any rent, being moved with compassion, but that this year was now almost expired.

Upon hearing this account they came to this resolution: that the children should be all carried by them to the door of one of the relations mentioned above and be set down there by the maid Amy, and that I, the mother, should remove for some days, shut up the doors, and be gone; that the people should be told that if they did not think fit to take some care of the children, they might send for the churchwardens if they thought that better, for that they were born in that parish and there they must be provided for; as for the other child which was born in the parish of ----, that was already taken care of by the parish officers there, for indeed they were so sensible of the distress of the family, that they had at first word done what was their part to do.

This was what these good women proposed, and bade me leave the rest to them. I was at first sadly afflicted at the thoughts of parting with my children, and especially at that terrible thing their being taken into the parish keeping; and then a hundred terrible things came into my thoughts, viz. of parish children being starved at nurse, of their being ruined, let grow crooked, lamed, and the like for want of being taken care of, and this sank my very heart within me.

But the misery of my own circumstances hardened my heart against my own flesh and blood, and when I considered they must inevitably be starved, and I too, if I continued to keep them about me, I began to be reconciled to parting with them all, anyhow and anywhere, that I might be freed from the dreadful necessity of seeing them all perish and perishing with them myself. So I agreed to go away out of the house and leave the management of the whole matter to my maid Amy and to them; and accordingly I did so, and the same afternoon they carried them all away to one of their aunts.

Amy, a resolute girl, knocked at the door with the children all with her, and bade the eldest, as soon as the door was open, run in, and the rest after her. She set them all down at the door before she knocked, and when she knocked she stayed till a maidservant came to the door. "Sweetheart," said she, "pray go in and tell your mistress, here are her little cousins come to see her from ----," naming the town where we lived; at which the maid offered to go back. "Here, child," says Amy, "take one of them in your hand, and I'll bring the rest." So she gives her the least, and the wench goes in mighty innocently with the little one in her hand; upon which Amy turns the rest in after her, shuts the door softly, and marches off as fast as she could.

Just in the interval of this, and even while the maid and her mistress were quarrelling, for the mistress raved and scolded at her like a mad-woman, and had ordered her to go and stop the maid Amy and turn all the children out of the doors again, but she had been at the door and Amy was gone, and the wench was out of her wits and the mistress too--I say, just at this juncture came the poor old woman, not the aunt, but the other of the two that had been with me, and knocks at the door. The aunt did not go because she had pretended to advocate for me, and they would have suspected her of some contrivance; but as for the other woman, they did not so much as know that she had kept up any correspondence with me.

Amy and she had contrived this between them, and it was well enough contrived that they did so. When she came into the house the mistress was fuming and raging like one distracted, and calling the maid all the foolish jades and sluts that she could think of, and that she would take the children and turn them all out into the streets. The good poor woman, seeing her in such a passion, turned about as if she would be gone again, and said, "Madam, I'll come another time, I see you are engaged." "No, no, Mrs. ----," says the mistress, "I am not much engaged; sit down. This senseless creature here has brought in my fool of a brother's whole house of children upon me, and tells me that a wench brought them to the door and thrust them in and bade her carry them to me; but it shall be no disturbance to me, for I have ordered them to be set in the street without the door, and so let the churchwardens take care of them, or else make this dull jade carry them back to ---- again and let her that brought them into the world look after them if she will. What does she send her brats to me for?"

"The last indeed had been the best of the two," says the poor woman, "if it had been to be done; and that brings me to tell you my errand and the occasion of my coming, for I came on purpose about this very business, and to have prevented this being put upon you if I could; but I see I am come too late."

"How do you mean too late?" says the mistress. "What, have you been concerned in this affair, then? What, have you helped bring this family slur upon us?"

"I hope you do not think such a thing of me, madam," says the poor woman; "but I went this morning to ---- to see my old mistress and benefactor, for she had been very kind to me, and when I came to the door I found all fast locked and bolted, and the house looking as if nobody was at home.

"I knocked at the door but nobody came, till at last some of the neighbours' servants called to me and said, 'There's nobody lives there, mistress, what do you knock for?' I seemed surprised at that. 'What, nobody live there!' said I; 'what d'ye mean? Does not Mrs. ---- live there?' The answer was, 'No, she is gone'; at which I parleyed with one of them and asked her what was the matter. 'Matter,' says she, 'why, 'tis matter enough; the poor gentlewoman has lived there all alone, and without anything to subsist her, a long time, and this morning the landlord turned her out of doors.'

"'Out of doors!' says I; 'what, with all her children! poor lambs, what is become of them?' 'Why, truly nothing worse,' said they, 'can come to them than staying here, for they were almost starved with hunger.' So the neighbours seeing the poor lady in such distress, for she stood crying and wringing her hands over her children like one distracted, sent for the churchwardens to take care of the children; and they when they came took the youngest, which was born in this parish, and have got it a very good nurse and taken care of it; but as for the other four, they had sent them away to some of their father's relations, who were very substantial people and who, besides that, lived in the parish where they were born.

"I was not so surprised at this as not presently to foresee that this trouble would be brought upon you or upon Mr. ----, so I came immediately to bring you word of it, that you might be prepared for it and might not be surprised, but I see they have been too nimble for me, so that I know not what to advise. The poor woman, it seems, is turned out of doors into the street, and another of the neighbours there told me that when they took her children from her she swooned away, and when they recovered her out of that she ran distracted, and is put into a madhouse by the parish, for there is nobody else to take any care of her."

This was all acted to the life by this good, kind, poor creature; for though her design was perfectly good and charitable, yet there was not one word of it true in fact; for I was not turned out of doors by the landlord, nor gone distracted. It was true indeed that at parting with my poor children I fainted, and was like one mad when I came to myself and found they were gone, but I remained in the house a good while after that, as you shall hear.

Chapter 2

While the poor woman was telling this dismal story, in came the gentlewoman's husband, and though her heart was hardened against all pity, who was really and nearly related to the children, for they were the children of her own brother, yet the good man was quite softened with the dismal relation of the circumstances of the family; and when the poor woman had done he said to his wife, "This is a dismal case, my dear, indeed, and something must be done." His wife fell a-raving at him. "What!" says she, "do you want to have four children to keep? Have we not children of our own? Would you have these brats come and eat up my children's bread? No, no, let them go to the parish, and let them take care of them; I'll take care of my own."

"Come, come, my dear," says the husband, "charity is a duty to the poor, and he that gives to the poor lends to the Lord; let us lend our heavenly Father a little of our children's bread, as you call it; it will be a store well laid up for them, and will be the best security that our children shall never come to want charity or be turned out of doors as these poor innocent creatures are."

"Don't tell me of security," says the wife; "'tis a good security for our children to keep what we have together and provide for them, and then 'tis time enough to help to keep other folks' children. Charity begins at home."

"Well, my dear," says he again, "I only talk of putting out a little money to interest; our Maker is a good borrower. Never fear making a bad debt there, child, I'll be bound for it."

"Don't banter me with your charity and your allegories," says the wife angrily; "I tell you they are my relations, not yours, and they shall not roost here, they shall go to the parish."

"All your relations are my relations now," says the good gentleman very calmly, "and I won't see your relations in distress and not pity them, any more than I would my own. Indeed, my dear, they shan't go to the parish; I assure you none of my wife's relations shall come to the parish if I can help it."

"What! will you take four children to keep?" says the wife.

"No, no, my dear," says he, "there's your sister ----, I'll go and talk with her; and your uncle ----, I'll send for him and the rest. I'll warrant you when we are all together we will find ways and means to keep four poor little creatures from beggary and starving, or else it will be very hard; we are none of us in so bad circumstances but we are able to spare a mite for the fatherless; don't shut up your bowels of compassion against your own flesh and blood. Could you hear these poor innocent children cry at your door for hunger and give them no bread?"

"Prithee, why need they cry at our door?" says she, "'tis the business of the parish to provide for them. They shan't cry at our door; if they do, I'll give them nothing." "Won't you?" says he; "but I will. Remember that dreadful Scripture is directly against us, Prov. 21. 13: 'Whoso stoppeth his ears at the cry of the poor, he also shall cry himself, but shall not be heard.'"

"Well, well," said she, "you must do what you will, because you pretend to be master; but if I had my will, I would send them where they ought to be sent, I would send them from whence they came."

Then the poor woman put in and said, "But, madam, that is sending them to starve indeed, for the parish has no obligation to take care of them, and so they would lie and perish in the street."

"Or be sent back again," says the husband, "to our parish in a cripple-cart by the Justice's warrant, and so expose us and all the relations to the last degree among our neighbours, and among those who knew the good old gentleman their grandfather, who lived and flourished in this parish so many years and was so well beloved among all people, and deserved it so well."

"I don't value that one farthing, not I," says the wife, "I'll keep none of them."

"Well, my dear," says her husband, "but I value it, for I won't have such a blot lie upon the family and upon your children; he was a worthy, ancient, and good man, and his name is respected among all his neighbours; it will be a reproach to you that are his daughter, and to our children that are his grandchildren, that we should let your brother's children perish, or come to be a charge to the public, in the very place where your family once flourished. Come, say no more, I'll see what can be done."

Upon this he sends and gathers all the relations together at a tavern hard by, and sent for the four little children that they might see them, and they all at first word agreed to have them taken care of; and because his wife was so furious that she would not suffer one of them to be kept at home, they agreed to keep them all together for a while. So they committed them to the poor woman that had managed the affair for them, and entered into obligations to one another to supply the needful sums for their maintenance; and not to have one separated from the rest, they sent for the youngest from the parish where it was taken in, and had them all brought up together.

It would take up too long a part of this story to give a particular account with what a charitable tenderness this good person, who was but uncle-in-law to them, managed that affair; how careful he was of them, went constantly to see them, and to see that they were well provided for, clothed, put to school, and at last put out in the world for their advantage; but 'tis enough to say he acted more like a father to them than an uncle-in-law, though all along much against his wife's consent, who was of a disposition not so tender and compassionate as her husband.

You may believe I heard this with the same pleasure which I now feel at the relating it again, for I was terribly frighted at the apprehensions of my children being brought to misery and distress, as these must be who have no friends but are left to parish benevolence.

Chapter 3

I was now, however, entering on a new scene of life. I had a great house upon my hands, and some furniture left in it, but I was no more able to maintain myself and my maid Amy in it than I was my five children; nor had I anything to subsist with but what I might get by working, and that was not a town where much work was to be had.

My landlord had been very kind indeed after he came to know my circumstances, though before he was acquainted with that part he had gone so far as to seize my goods, and to carry some of them off too.

But I had lived three-quarters of a year in his house after that and had paid him no rent, and, which was worse, I was in no condition to pay him any. However, I observed he came oftener to see me, looked kinder upon me, and spoke more friendly to me than he used to do; particularly the last two or three times he had been there he observed, he said, how poorly I lived, how low I was reduced, and the like, told me it grieved him for my sake; and the last time of all he was kinder still, told me he came to dine with me, and that I should give him leave to treat me. So he called my maid Amy and sent her out to buy a joint of meat; he told her what she should buy, but naming two or three things, either of which she might take. The maid, a cunning wench, and faithful to me as the skin to my back, did not buy anything outright, but brought the butcher along with her with both the things that she had chosen, for him to please himself; the one was a large very good leg of veal, the other a piece of the fore-ribs of roasting beef. He looked at them, but bade me chaffer with the butcher for him, and I did so, and came back to him and told him what the butcher demanded for either of them and what each of them came to; so he pulls out 11s. 3d., which they came to together, and bade me take them both; the rest, he said, would serve another time.

I was surprised, you may be sure, at the bounty of a man that had but a little while ago been my terror and had torn the goods out of my house like a fury; but I considered that my distresses had mollified his temper, and that he had afterwards been so compassionate as to give me leave to live rent free in the house a whole year.

But now he put on the face, not of a man of compassion only, but of a man of friendship and kindness, and this was so unexpected that it was surprising. We chatted together, and were, as I may call it, cheerful, which was more than I could say I had been for three years before. He sent for wine and beer too, for I had none; poor Amy and I had drank nothing but water for many weeks, and indeed I have often wondered at the faithful temper of the poor girl, for which I but ill requited her at last.

When Amy was come with the wine he made her fill a glass to him, and with the glass in his hand he came to me and kissed me, which I was, I confess, a little surprised at, but more at what followed; for he told me that as the sad condition which I was reduced to had made him pity me, so my conduct in it and the courage I bore it with had given him a more than ordinary respect for me, and made him very thoughtful for my good; that he was resolved for the present to do something to relieve me, and to employ his thoughts in the meantime to see if he could, for the future, put me into a way to support myself.

While he found me change colour and look surprised at his discourse, for so I did, to be sure, he turns to my maid Amy, and looking at her, he says to me "I say all this, madam, before your maid, because both she and you shall know that I have no ill design, and that I have in mere kindness resolved to do something for you if I can; and as I have been a witness of the uncommon honesty and fidelity of Mrs. Amy here to you in all your distresses, I know she may be trusted with so honest a design as mine is, for, I assure you, I bear a proportioned regard to your maid too for her affection to you."

Amy made him a curtsy, and the poor girl looked so confounded with joy that she could not speak, but her colour came and went, and every now and then she blushed as red as scarlet and the next minute looked as pale as death. Well, having said this, he sat down, made me sit down, and then drank to me and made me drink two glasses of wine together. "For," says he, "you have need of it"; and so indeed I had. When he had done so, "Come, Amy," says he, "with your mistress's leave you shall have a glass too"; so he made her drink two glasses also. And then rising up, "And now, Amy," says he, "go and get dinner; and you, madam," says he to me, "go up and dress you, and come down and smile and be merry," adding, "I'll make you easy if I can "; and in the meantime, he said, he would walk in the garden.

When he was gone, Amy changed her countenance indeed and looked as merry as ever she did in her life. "Dear madam," says she, "what does this gentleman mean." "Nay, Amy," said I, "he means to do us good, you see, don't he? I know no other meaning he can have, for he can get nothing by me." "I warrant you, madam," says she, "he'll ask you a favour by and by." "No, no, you are mistaken, Amy, I dare say," said I; "you heard what he said, didn't you?" "Ay," says Amy, "it's no matter for that; you shall see what he will do after dinner." "Well, well, Amy," says I, "you have hard thoughts of him; I cannot be of your opinion. I don't see anything in him yet that looks like it." "As to that, madam," says Amy, "I don't see anything of it yet neither; but what should move a gentleman to take pity on us as he does?" "Nay," says I, "that's a hard thing too, that we should judge a man to be wicked because he's charitable, and vicious because he's kind." "Oh, madam," says Amy, "there's abundance of charity begins in that vice, and he is not so unacquainted with things as not to know that poverty is the strongest incentive, a temptation against which no virtue is powerful enough to stand out; he knows your condition as well as you do." "Well, and what then?" "Why, then he knows too that you are young and handsome, and he has the surest bait in the world to take you with."

"Well, Amy," said I, "but he may find himself mistaken too in such a thing as that." "Why, madam," says Amy, "I hope you won't deny him if he should offer it."

"What d'ye mean by that, hussy?" said I. "No, I'd starve first."

"I hope not, madam, I hope you would be wiser; I'm sure if he will set you up, as he talks of, you ought to deny him nothing; and you will starve if you do not consent, that's certain."

"What! consent to lie with him for bread? Amy," said I, "how can you talk so?"

"Nay, madam," says Amy, "I don't think you would for anything else; it would not be lawful for anything else but for bread, madam. Why, nobody can starve; there's no bearing that, I'm sure."

"Ay," says I, "but if he would give me an estate to live on, he should not lie with me, I assure you."

"Why, look you, madam, if he would but give you enough to live easy upon, he should lie with me for it with all my heart."

"That's a token, Amy, of inimitable kindness to me," said I, "and I know how to value it; but there's more friendship than honesty in it, Amy."

"Oh, madam," says Amy, "I'd do anything to get you out of this sad condition. As to honesty, I think honesty is out of the question when starvation is the case; are not we almost starved to death?"

"I am indeed," said I, "and thou art for my sake; but to be a whore, Amy!"--and there I stopped.

"Dear madam," says Amy, "if I will starve for your sake, I will be a whore or anything for your sake; why, I would die for you if I were put to it."

"Why, that's an excess of affection, Amy," said I, "I never met with before; I wish I may be ever in condition to make some returns suitable. But, however, Amy, you shall not be a whore to him, to oblige him to be kind to me; no, Amy, nor I won't be a whore to him if he would give me much more than he is able to give me or do for me."

"Why, madam," says Amy, "I don't say I will go and ask him; but I say if he should promise to do so and so for you, and the condition was such that he would not serve you unless I would let him lie with me, he should lie with me as often as he would rather than you should not have his assistance. But this is but talk, madam, I don't see any need of such discourse, and you are of opinion that there will be no need of it."

"Indeed, so I am, Amy; but," said I, "if there was, I tell you again I'd die before I would consent, or before you should consent for my sake."

Hitherto I had not only preserved the virtue itself, but the virtuous inclination and resolution; and had I kept myself there I had been happy, though I had perished of mere hunger; for, without question, a woman ought rather to die than to prostitute her virtue and honour, let the temptation be what it will.

But to return to my story. He walked about the garden, which was indeed all in disorder and overrun with weeds, because I had not been able to hire a gardener to do anything to it, no, not so much as to dig up ground enough to sow a few turnips and carrots for family use. After he had viewed it, he came in and sent Amy to fetch a poor man, a gardener that used to help our manservant, and carried him into the garden and ordered him to do several things in it to put it into a little order; and this took him up near an hour.

By this time I had dressed me as well as I could, for though I had good linen left still, yet I had but a poor head-dress, and no knots but old fragments, no necklace, no ear-rings; all those things were gone long ago for mere bread.

However, I was tight and clean, and in better plight than he had seen me in a great while, and he looked extremely pleased to see me so, for he said I looked so disconsolate and so afflicted before, that it grieved him to see me; and he bade me pluck up a good heart, for he hoped to put me in a condition to live in the world and be beholden to nobody.

I told him that was impossible, for I must be beholden to him for it, for all the friends I had in the world would not or could not do so much for me as that he spoke of. "Well, widow," says he (so he called me, and so indeed I was in the worst sense that desolate word could be used in), "if you are beholden to me, you shall be beholden to nobody else."

By this time dinner was ready and Amy came in to lay the cloth, and indeed it was happy there was none to dine but he and I, for I had but six plates left in the house and but two dishes. However, he knew how things were, and bade me make no scruple about bringing out what I had, he hoped to see me in a better plight. He did not come, he said, to be entertained, but to entertain me and comfort and encourage me. Thus he went on, speaking so cheerfully to me and such cheerful things, that it was a cordial to my very soul to hear him speak.

Well, we went to dinner. I'm sure I had not eaten a good meal hardly in a twelvemonth, at least not of such a joint of meat as the leg of veal was. I ate indeed very heartily, and so did he, and he made me drink three or four glasses of wine, so that, in short, my spirits were lifted up to a degree I had not been used to; and I was not only cheerful but merry, and so he pressed me to be.

I told him I had a great deal of reason to be merry, seeing he had been so kind to me and had given me hopes of recovering me from the worst circumstances that ever woman of any sort of fortune was sunk into; that he could not but believe that what he had said to me was like life from the dead; that it was like recovering one sick from the brink of the grave. How I should ever make him a return any way suitable was what I had not yet had time to think of; I could only say that I should never forget it while I had life, and should be always ready to acknowledge it.

He said that was all he desired of me, that his reward would be the satisfaction of having rescued me from misery; that he found he was obliging one that knew what gratitude meant; that he would make it his business to make me completely easy, first or last, if it lay in his power; and in the meantime he bade me consider of anything that I thought he might do for me for my advantage and in order to make me perfectly easy.

After we had talked thus he bade me be cheerful. "Come," says he, "lay aside these melancholy things and let us be merry." Amy waited at the table, and she smiled and laughed and was so merry she could hardly contain it, for the girl loved me to an excess hardly to be described; and it was such an unexpected thing to hear any one talk to her mistress, that the wench was beside herself almost; and as soon as dinner was over, Amy went upstairs and put on her best clothes too, and came down dressed like a gentlewoman.

We sat together talking of a thousand things, of what had been and what was to be, all the rest of the day, and in the evening he took his leave of me with a thousand expressions of kindness and tenderness and true affection to me, but offered not the least of what my maid Amy had suggested.

At his going away he took me in his arms, protested an honest kindness to me, said a thousand kind things to me which I cannot now recollect, and, after kissing me twenty times or thereabouts, put a guinea into my hand, which he said was for my present supply, and told me that he would see me again before 'twas out; also, he gave Amy half a crown.

When he was gone, "Well, Amy," said I, "are you convinced now that he is an honest as well as a true friend, and that there has been nothing, not the least appearance of anything of what you imagined, in his behaviour?" "Yes," says Amy, "I am, but I admire at it; he is such a friend as the world sure has not abundance of to show."

"I am sure," says I, "he is such a friend as I have long wanted, and as I have as much need of as any creature in the world has or ever had" and, in short, I was so overcome with the comfort of it that I sat down and cried for joy a good while, as I had formerly cried for sorrow. Amy and I went to bed that night (for Amy lay with me) pretty early, but lay chatting almost all night about it, and the girl was so transported that she got up two or three times in the night and danced about the room in her shift; in short, the girl was half distracted with the joy of it, a testimony still of her violent affection for her mistress, in which no servant ever went beyond her.

We heard no more of him for two days, but the third day he came again; then he told me, with the same kindness, that he had ordered me a supply of household goods for the furnishing the house; that in particular he had sent me back all the goods that he had seized for rent, which consisted indeed of the best of my former furniture. "And now," says he, "I'll tell you what I have had in my head for you for your present supply, and that is," says he, "that the house being well furnished, you shall let it out to lodgings for the summer gentry," says he, "by which you will easily get a good, comfortable subsistence, especially seeing you shall pay me no rent for two years, nor after neither, unless you can afford it."

This was the first view I had of living comfortably indeed, and it was a very probable way, I must confess, seeing we had very good conveniences, six rooms on a floor, and three storeys high. While he was laying down the scheme of my management, came a cart to the door with a load of goods, and an upholsterer's man to put them up; they were chiefly the furniture of two rooms which he had carried away for his two years' rent, with two fine cabinets and some pier-glasses out of the parlour, and several other valuable things.

These were all restored to their places, and he told me he gave them as freely as a satisfaction for the cruelty he had used me with before; and the furniture of one room being finished and set up, he told me he would furnish one chamber for himself, and would come and be one of my lodgers if I would give him leave.

I told him he ought not to ask me leave, who had so much right to make himself welcome. So the house began to look in some tolerable figure and clean; the garden also in about a fortnight's work began to look something less like a wilderness than it used to do; and he ordered me to put up a bill for letting rooms, reserving one for himself to come to as he saw occasion.

When all was done to his mind, as to placing the goods, he seemed very well pleased, and we dined together again of his own providing, and the upholsterer's man gone. After dinner he took me by the hand. "Come now, madam," says he, "you must show me your house" (for he had a mind to see everything over again). "No, sir," said I, "but I'll go show you your house, if you please." So we went up through all the rooms, and in the room which was appointed for himself Amy was doing something. "Well, Amy," says he, "I intend to lie with you to-morrow night." "To-night, if you please, sir," says Amy very innocently; "your room is quite ready." "Well, Amy," says he, "I am glad you are so willing." "No," says Amy, "I mean your chamber is ready to-night"; and away she ran out of the room, ashamed enough, for the girl meant no harm, whatever she had said to me in private.

However, he said no more then; but when Amy was gone he walked about the room and looked at everything, and taking me by the hand he kissed me and spoke a great many kind, affectionate things to me indeed: as of his measures for my advantage, and what he would do to raise me again in the world; told me that my afflictions and the conduct I had shown in bearing them to such an extremity had so engaged him to me, that he valued me infinitely above all the women in the world; that though he was under such engagements that he could not marry me (his wife and he had been parted for some reasons which make too long a story to intermix with mine), yet that he would be everything else that a woman could ask in a husband. And with that he kissed me again and took me in his arms, but offered not the least uncivil action to me, and told me he hoped I would not deny him all the favours he should ask, because he resolved to ask nothing of me but what it was fit for a woman of virtue and modesty, for such he knew me to be, to yield.

Chapter 3

I confess the terrible pressure of my former misery, the memory of which lay heavy upon my mind, and the surprising kindness with which he had delivered me, and withal, the expectations of what he might still do for me, were powerful things and made me have scarce the power to deny him anything he would ask. However, I told him thus, with an air of tenderness too, that he had done so much for me that I thought I ought to deny him nothing, only I hoped and depended upon him that he would not take the advantage of the infinite obligations I was under to him, to desire anything of me the yielding to which would lay me lower in his esteem than I desired to be; that as I took him to be a man of honour, so I knew he could not like me the better for doing anything that was below a woman of honesty and good manners to do.

He told me that he had done all this for me without so much as telling me what kindness or real affection he had for me; that I might not be under any necessity of yielding to him in anything for want of bread, and he would no more oppress my gratitude now than he would my necessity before, nor ask anything, supposing he would stop his favours or withdraw his kindness, if he was denied. It was true, he said, he might tell me more freely his mind now than before, seeing I had let him see that I accepted his assistance and saw that he was sincere in his design of serving me; that he had gone thus far to show me that he was kind to me, but that now he would tell me that he loved me, and yet would demonstrate that his love was both honourable and that what he should desire was what he might honestly ask and I might honestly grant.

I answered that, within those two limitations, I was sure I ought to deny him nothing, and I should think myself not ungrateful only but very unjust if I should; so he said no more, but I observed he kissed me more and took me in his arms in a kind of familiar way more than usual, and which once or twice put me in mind of my maid Amy's words. And yet I must acknowledge I was so overcome with his goodness to me in those many kind things he had done, that I not only was easy at what he did and made no resistance, but was inclined to do the like, whatever he had offered to do. But he went no further than what I have said, nor did he offer so much as to sit down on the bedside with me, but took his leave, said he loved me tenderly and would convince me of it by such demonstrations as should be to my satisfaction. I told him I had a great deal of reason to believe him, that he was full master of the whole house and of me as far as was within the bounds we had spoken of, which I believed he would not break, and asked him if he would not lodge there that night.

He said he could not well stay that night, business requiring him in London, but added, smiling, that he would come the next day and take a night's lodging with me. I pressed him to stay that night, and told him I should be glad a friend so valuable should be under the same roof with me; and indeed I began at that time not only to be much obliged to him, but to love him too, and that in a manner that I had not been acquainted with myself.

Oh let no woman slight the temptation that being generously delivered from trouble is to any spirit furnished with gratitude and just principles. This gentleman had freely and voluntarily delivered me from misery, from poverty, and rags; he had made me what I was, and put me into a way to be even more than I ever was, namely, to live happy and pleased, and on his bounty I depended. What could I say to this gentleman when he pressed me to yield to him and argued the lawfulness of it? But of that in its place.

I pressed him again to stay that night, and told him it was the first completely happy night that I had ever had in the house in my life, and I should be very sorry to have it without his company, who was the cause and foundation of it all; that we would be innocently merry, but that it could never be without him; and, in short, I courted him so, that he said he could not deny me, but he would take his horse and go to London, do the business he had to do, which, it seems, was to pay a foreign bill that was due that night and would else be protested, and that he would come back in three hours at furthest and sup with me; but bade me get nothing there, for since I was resolved to be merry, which was what he desired above all things, he would send me something from London. "And we will make it a wedding supper, my dear," says he, and with that word took me in his arms and kissed me so vehemently that I made no question but he intended to do everything else that Amy had talked of.

I started a little at the word "wedding." "What do you mean, to call it by such a name?" says I; adding, "We will have a supper, but t'other is impossible as well on your side as mine." He laughed. "Well," says he, "you shall call it what you will, but it may be the same thing, for I shall satisfy you it is not so impossible as you make it."

"I don't understand you," said I; "have not I a husband and you a wife?"

"Well, well," says he, "we will talk of that after supper." So he rose up, gave me another kiss, and took his horse for London.

This kind of discourse had fired my blood, I confess, and I knew not what to think of it. It was plain now that he intended to lie with me, but how he would reconcile it to a legal thing like a marriage, that I could not imagine. We had both of us used Amy with so much intimacy and trusted her with everything, having such unexampled instances of her fidelity, that he made no scruple to kiss me and say all these things to me before her, nor had he cared one farthing, if I would have let him lie with me, to have had Amy there too all night. When he was gone, "Well, Amy," says I, "what will all this come to now? I am all in a sweat at him." "Come to, madam," says Amy, "I see what it will come to; I must put you to bed to-night together," "Why, you would not be so impudent, you jade you," says I, "would you?" "Yes, I would," says she, "with all my heart, and think you both as honest as ever you were in your lives."

"What ails the slut to talk so?" said I. "Honest! how can it be honest?" "Why, I'll tell you, madam." says Amy; "I sounded it as soon as I heard him speak, and it is very true too. He calls you widow, and such indeed you are, for as my master has left you so many years, he is dead to be sure--at least he is dead to you, he is no husband--you are and ought to be free to marry who you will; and his wife being gone from him and refuses to lie with him, then he is a single man again as much as ever; and though you cannot bring the laws of the land to join you together, yet one refusing to do the once of a wife, and the other of a husband, you may certainly take one another fairly."

"Nay, Amy," says I, "if I could take him fairly, you may be sure I'd take him above all the men in the world. It turned the very heart within me when I heard him say he loved me; how could it do otherwise when you know what a condition I was in before, despised and trampled on by all the world? I could have taken him in my arms and kissed him as freely as he did me, if it had not been for shame."

"Ay, and all the rest too," says Amy, "at the first word. I don't see how you can think of denying him anything. Has he not brought you out of the devil's clutches, brought you out of the blackest misery that ever poor lady was reduced to? Can a woman deny such a man anything?"

"Nay, I don't know what to do, Amy," says I. "I hope he won't desire anything of that kind of me, I hope he won't attempt it; if he does, I know not what to say to him."

"Not ask you!" says Amy; "depend upon it, he will ask you, and you will grant it, too; I'm sure my mistress is no fool. Come, pray, madam, let me go air you a clean shift; don't let him find you in foul linen the wedding night."

"But that I know you to be a very honest girl, Amy," says I, "you would make me abhor you; why, you argue for the devil, as if you were one of his privy counsellors."

"It's no matter for that, madam, I say nothing but what I think. You own you love this gentleman, and he has given you sufficient testimony of his affection to you; your conditions are alike unhappy, and he is of opinion that he may take another woman, his first wife having broke her honour, and living from him, and that, though the laws of the land will not allow him to marry formally, yet that he may take another woman into his arms, provided he keeps true to the other woman as a wife; nay, he says it is usual to do so, and allowed by the custom of the place, in several countries abroad. And I must own I'm of the same mind, else 'tis in the power of a whore, after she has jilted and abandoned her husband, to confine him from the pleasure as well as convenience of a woman all the days of his life, which would be very unreasonable and, as times go, not tolerable to all people; and the like on your side, madam."

Had I now had my senses about me, and had my reason not been overcome by the powerful attraction of so kind, so beneficent a friend, had I consulted conscience and virtue, I should have repelled this Amy, however faithful and honest to me in other things, as a viper and engine of the devil. I ought to have remembered that neither he nor I, either by the laws of God or man, could come together upon any other terms than that of notorious adultery. The ignorant jade's argument that he had brought me out of the hands of the devil, by which she meant the devil of poverty and distress, should have been a powerful motive to me not to plunge myself into the jaws of hell and into the power of the real devil, in recompense for that deliverance. I should have looked upon all the good this man had done for me to have been the particular work of the goodness of Heaven, and that goodness should have moved me to a return of duty and humble obedience. I should have received the mercy thankfully, and applied it soberly to the praise and honour of my Maker, whereas by this wicked course all the bounty and kindness of this gentleman became a snare to me, was a mere bait to the devil's hook. I received his kindness at the dear expense of body and soul, mortgaging faith, religion, conscience, and modesty for (as I may call it) a morsel of bread, or, if you will, ruined my soul from a principle of gratitude and gave myself up to the devil to show myself grateful to my benefactor. I must do the gentleman that justice as to say I verily believe that he did nothing but what he thought was lawful, and I must do that justice upon myself as to say I did what my own conscience convinced me at the very time I did it was horribly unlawful, scandalous, and abominable.

But poverty was my snare, dreadful poverty! The misery I had been in was great, such as would make the heart tremble at the apprehensions of its return, and I might appeal to any that has had any experience of the world, whether one so entirely destitute as I was, of all manner of all helps or friends either to support me or to assist me to support myself, could withstand the proposal; not that I plead this as a justification of my conduct, but that it may move the pity even of those that abhor the crime.

Besides this, I was young, handsome, and with all the mortifications I had met with, was vain, and that not a little; and as it was a new thing, so it as a pleasant thing to be courted, caressed, embraced, and high professions of affection made to me by a man so agreeable and so able to do me good.

Add to this, that if I had ventured to disoblige this gentleman, I had no friend in the world to have recourse to; I had no prospect, no, not of a bit of bread; I had nothing before me but to fall back into the same misery that I had been in before.

Amy had but too much rhetoric in this cause. She represented all those things in their proper colours; she argued them all with her utmost skill, and at last the merry jade, when she came to dress me, "Look ye, madam," said she, "if you won't consent, tell him you'll do as Rachel did to Jacob when she could have no children--put her maid to bed to him; tell him you cannot comply with him, but there's Amy, he may ask her the question, she has promised me she won't deny you."

"And would you have me say so, Amy?" said I.

"No, madam, but I would really have you do so; besides, you are undone if you do not. And if my doing it would save you from being undone, as I said before, he shall if he will; if he asks me I won't deny him, not I; hang me if I do," says Amy.

"Well, I know not what to do," says I to Amy.

"Do!" says Amy; "your choice is fair and plain. Here you may have a handsome, charming gentleman, be rich, live pleasantly and in plenty; or refuse him, and want a dinner, go in rags, live in tears; in short, beg and starve. You know this is the case, madam," says Amy; "I wonder how you can say you know not what to do."

"Well, Amy," says I, "the case is as you say, and I think verily I must yield to him; but then," said I, moved by conscience, "don't talk any more of your cant, of its being lawful that I ought to marry again and that he ought to marry again, and such stuff as that; 'tis all nonsense," says I, "Amy, there's nothing in it, let me hear no more of that; for if I yield 'tis in vain to mince the matter, I am a whore, Amy, neither better nor worse, I assure you."

"I don't think so, madam, by no means," says Amy, "I wonder how you can talk so"; and then she ran on with her argument of the unreasonableness that a woman should be obliged to live single or a man to live single in such cases, as before. "Well, Amy," said I, "come let us dispute no more, for the longer I enter into that part, the greater my scruples will be, but if I let it alone the necessity of my present circumstances is such that I believe I shall yield to him if he should importune me much about it, but I should be glad he would not do it at all but leave me as I am."

"As to that, madam, you may depend," says Amy, "he expects to have you for his bedfellow to-night. I saw it plainly in his management all day, and at last he told you so too, as plain, I think, as he could." "Well, well, Amy," said I, "I don't know what to say; if he will, he must, I think; I don't know how to resist such a man that has done so much for me." "I don't know how you should," says Amy.

Thus Amy and I canvassed the business between us. The jade prompted the crime, which I had but too much inclination to commit; that is to say, not as a crime, for I had nothing of the vice in my constitution; my spirits were far from being high, my blood had no fire in it to kindle the flame of desire, but the kindness and good humour of the man and the dread of my own circumstances concurred to bring me to the point, and I even resolved, before he asked, to give up my virtue to him whenever he should put it to the question.

In this I was a double offender, whatever he was, for I was resolved to commit the crime, knowing and owning it to be a crime. He, if it was true as he said, was fully persuaded it was lawful, and in that persuasion he took the measures and used all the circumlocutions which I am going to speak of.

About two hours after he was gone, came a Leadenhall basket-woman with a whole load of good things for the mouth (the particulars are not to the purpose), and brought orders to get supper by eight o'clock. However, I did not intend to begin to dress anything till I saw him, and he gave me time enough, for he came before seven; so that Amy, who had gotten one to help her, got everything ready in time.

We sat down to supper about eight, and were indeed very merry. Amy made us some sport, for she was a girl of spirit and wit, and with her talk she made us laugh very often, and yet the jade managed her wit with all the good manners imaginable.

But to shorten the story. After supper he took me up into his chamber, where Amy had made a good fire, and there he pulled out a great many papers and spread them upon a little table, and then took me by the hand, and after kissing me very much he entered into a discourse of his circumstances and of mine, how they agreed in several things exactly; for example, that I was abandoned of a husband in the prime of my youth and vigour, and he of a wife in his middle age; how the end of marriage was destroyed by the treatment we had either of us received, and it would be very hard that we should be tied by the formality of the contract where the essence of it was destroyed. I interrupted him, and told him there was a vast difference between our circumstances, and that in the most essential part, namely, that he was rich and I was poor, that he was above the world and I infinitely below it, that his circumstances were very easy, mine miserable, and this was an inequality the most essential that could be imagined. "As to that, my dear," says he, "I have taken such measures as shall make an equality still"; and with that he showed me a contract in writing, wherein he engaged himself to me, to cohabit constantly with me, to provide for me in all respects as a wife, and repeating in the preamble a long account of the nature and reason of our living together, and an obligation in the penalty of £7,000 never to abandon me, and at last showed me a bond for £500 to be paid to me or to my assigns within three months after his death.

He read over all these things to me, and then in a most moving, affectionate manner, and in words not to be answered, he said, "Now, my dear, is this not sufficient? Can you object anything against it? If not, as I believe you will not, then let us debate this matter no longer." With that he pulled out a silk purse which had three-score guineas in it, and threw them into my lap, and concluded all the rest of his discourse with kisses and protestations of his love, of which, indeed, I had abundant proof.

Pity human frailty, you that read of a woman reduced in her youth and prime to the utmost misery and distress, and raised again, as above, by the unexpected and surprising bounty of a stranger; I say, pity her if she was not able, after all these things, to make any more resistance.

However, I stood out a little longer still. I asked him how he could expect that I could come into a proposal of such consequence the very first time it was moved to me, and that I ought (if I consented to it) to capitulate with him that he should never upbraid me with easiness and consenting too soon. He said no, but on the contrary he would take it as a mark of the greatest kindness I could show him. Then he went on to give reasons why there was no occasion to use the ordinary ceremony of delay or to wait a reasonable time of courtship, which was only to avoid scandal, but as this was private it had nothing of that nature in it; that he had been courting me some time by the best of courtship, viz. doing acts of kindness to me, and he had given testimonies of his sincere affection to me by deeds, not by flattering trifles and the usual courtship of words, which were often found to have very little meaning; that he took me not as a mistress but as his wife, and protested it was clear to him he might lawfully do it and that I was perfectly at liberty; and assured me by all that it was possible for an honest man to say, that he would treat me as his wife as long as he lived. In a word, he conquered all the little resistance I intended to make. He protested he loved me above all the world, and begged I would for once believe him; that he had never deceived me, and never would, but would make it his study to make my life comfortable and happy and to make me forget the misery I had gone through. I stood still awhile and said nothing, but seeing him eager for my answer, I smiled, and looking up at him, "And must I, then," says I, "say yes at first asking? Must I depend upon your promise? Why, then," said I, "upon the faith of that promise, and in the sense of that inexpressible kindness you have shown me, you shall be obliged, and I will be wholly yours to the end of my life." And with that I took his hand which held me by the hand, and gave it a kiss.

Chapter 4

And thus, in gratitude for the favours I received from a man, was all sense of religion and duty to God, all regard to virtue and honour, given up at once, and we were to call one another man and wife, who in the sense of the laws both of God and our country were no more than two adulterers, in short, a whore and a rogue. Nor, as I have said above, was my conscience silent in it, though it seems his was; for I sinned with open eyes, and thereby had a double guilt upon me. As I always said, his notions were of another kind, and he either was before of the opinion, or argued himself into it now, that we were both free and might lawfully marry.

But I was quite of another side, nay, and my judgment was right, but my circumstances were my temptation; the terrors behind me looked blacker than the terrors before me, and the dreadful argument of wanting bread, and being run into the horrible distresses I was in before, mastered all my resolution, and I gave myself up, as above.

The rest of the evening we spent very agreeably to me; he was perfectly good-humoured and was at that time very merry. Then he made Amy dance with him, and I told him I would put Amy to bed to him. Amy said, with all her heart; she never had been a bride in her life. In short, he made the girl so merry, that had he not been to lie with me the same night, I believe he would have played the fool with Amy for half an hour, and the girl would no more have refused him than I intended to do. Yet before, I had always found her a very modest wench as any I ever saw in all my life, but, in short, the mirth of that night and a few more such afterwards ruined the girl's modesty for ever, as shall appear by and by in its place.

So far does fooling and toying sometimes go, that I know nothing a young woman has to be more cautious of. So far had this innocent girl gone in jesting between her and I, and in talking that she would let him lie with her if he would but be kinder to me, that at last she let him lie with her in earnest; and so empty was I now of all principle, that I encouraged the doing it almost before my face.

I say but too justly that I was empty of principle, because, as above, I had yielded to him, not as deluded to believe it lawful, but as overcome by his kindness and terrified at the fear of my own misery if he should leave me. So with my eyes open and with my conscience, as I may say, awake, I sinned, knowing it to be a sin but having no power to resist. When this had thus made a hole in my heart, and I was come to such a height as to transgress against the light of my own conscience, I was then fit for any wickedness, and conscience left off speaking where it found it could not be heard.

But to return to our story. Having consented, as above, to his proposal, we had not much more to do. He gave me my writings, and the bond for my maintenance during his life and for £500 after his death; and so far was he from abating his affection to me afterwards, that two years after we were thus, as he called it, married, he made his will and gave me £1,000 more, and all my household stuff, plate, etc., which was considerable too.

Amy put us to bed, and my new friend (I cannot call him husband) was so well pleased with Amy for her fidelity and kindness to me, that he paid her all the arrears of her wages that I owed her, and gave her five guineas over; and had it gone no further, Amy had richly deserved what she had, for never was a maid so true to a mistress in such dreadful circumstances as I was in. Nor was what followed more her own fault than mine, who led her almost into it at first and quite into it at last; and this may be a further testimony what a hardness of crime I was now arrived to, which was owing to the conviction that was from the beginning upon me, that I was a whore, not a wife, nor could I ever frame my mouth to call him husband or to say "my husband" when I was speaking of him.

We lived surely the most agreeable life, the grand exception only excepted, that ever two lived together. He was the most obliging, gentlemanly man and the most tender of me that ever woman gave herself up to; nor was there ever the least interruption to our mutual kindness, no, not to the last day of his life. But I must bring Amy's disaster in at once, that I may have done with her.

Amy was dressing me one morning, for now I had two maids, and Amy was my chamber-maid. "Dear madam," says Amy, "what! ain't you with child yet?" "No, Amy," says I, "nor any sign of it." "Law, madam," says Amy, "what have you been doings. Why, you have been married a year and a half; I warrant you master would have got me with child twice in that time." "It may be so, Amy," says I, "let him try, can't you." "No," says Amy, "you'll forbid it now; I told you he should with all my heart, but I won't now, now he's all your own." "Oh," says I, "Amy, I'll freely give you my consent, it will be nothing at all to me; nay, I'll put you to bed to him myself one night or other if you are willing." "No, madam, no," says Amy, "not now he's yours."

"Why, you fool you," says I, "don't I tell you I'll put you to bed to him myself."

"Nay, nay," says Amy, "if you put me to bed to him, that's another case; I believe I shall not rise again very soon."

"I'll venture that, Amy," says I.

After supper that night, and before we were risen from table, I said to him, Amy being by, "Hark ye, Mr. ----, do you know that you are to lie with Amy tonight?" "No, not I," says he; but turns to Amy, "Is it so, Amy?" says he. "No, sir," says she. "Nay, don't say no, you fool; did not I promise to put you to bed to him?" But the girl said no still, and it passed off.

At night, when we came to go to bed, Amy came into the chamber to undress me, and her master slipped into bed first. Then I began and told him all that Amy had said about my not being with child, and of her being with child twice in that time. "Ay, Mrs. Amy," says he, "I believe so too; come hither and we'll try." But Amy did not go. "Go, you fool," says I, "can't you; I freely give you both leave." But Amy would not go. "Nay, you whore," says I, "you said if I would put you to bed you would with all your heart "; and with that I sat her down, pulled off her stockings and shoes, and all her clothes, piece by piece, and led her to the bed to him. "Here," says I, "try what you can do with your maid Amy." She pulled back a little, would not let me pull off her clothes at first, but it was hot weather and she had not many clothes on, and particularly no stays on; and at last, when she saw I was in earnest, she let me do what I would; so I fairly stripped her, and then I threw open the bed and thrust her in.

I need say no more; this is enough to convince anybody that I did not think him my husband, and that I had cast off all principle and all modesty and had effectually stifled conscience.

Amy, I dare say, began now to repent, and would fain have got out of bed again, but he said to her, "Nay, Amy, you see your mistress has put you to bed, 'tis all her doing, you must blame her." So he held her fast, and the wench being naked in the bed with him, 'twas too late to look back, so she lay still and let him do what he would with her.

Had I looked upon myself as a wife, you cannot suppose I would have been willing to have let my husband lie with my maid, much less before my face, for I stood by all the while; but as I thought myself a whore, I cannot say but that it was something designed in my thoughts that my maid should be a whore too, and should not reproach me with it.

Amy, however, less vicious than I, was grievously out of sorts the next morning, and cried and took on most vehemently, that she was ruined and undone, and there was no pacifying her; she was a whore, a slut, and she was undone! undone! and cried almost all day. I did all I could to pacify her. "A whore!" says I; "well, and am not I a whore as well as you?" "No, no," says Amy, "no, you are not, for you are married." "Not I, Amy," says I, "I do not pretend to it; he may marry you to-morrow if he will, for anything I could do to hinder it; I am not married, I do not look upon it as anything." Well, all did not pacify Amy; she cried two or three days about it, but it wore off by degrees.

But the case differed between Amy and her master exceedingly; for Amy retained the same kind temper she always had, but on the contrary he was quite altered, for he hated her heartily, and could, I believe, have killed her after it; and he told me so, for he thought this a vile action, whereas what he and I had done he was perfectly easy in, thought it just, and esteemed me as much his wife as if we had been married from our youth and had neither of us known any other; nay, he loved me, I believe, as entirely as if I had been the wife of his youth; nay, he told me, it was true in one sense, that he had two wives, but that I was the wife of his affection, the other the wife of his aversion.

I was extremely concerned at the aversion he had taken to my maid Amy, and used my utmost skill to get it altered; for though he had indeed debauched the wench, I know that I was the principal occasion of it, and as he was the best-humoured man in the world, I never gave him over till I prevailed with him to be easy with her; and as I was now become the devil's agent to make others as wicked as myself, I brought him to lie with her again several times after that, till at last, as the poor girl said, so it happened, and she was really with child.

She was terribly concerned at it, and so was he too. "Come, my dear," says I, "when Rachel put her handmaid to bed to Jacob she took the children as her own. Don't be uneasy, I'll take the child as my own; had not I a hand in the frolic of putting her to bed to you? It was my fault as much as yours." So I called Amy and encouraged her too, and told her that I would take care of the child and her too, and added the same argument to her. "For," says I, "Amy, it was all my fault; did not I drag your clothes off your back and put you to bed to him?" Thus I, that had indeed been the cause of all the wickedness between them, encouraged them both when they had any remorse about it, and rather prompted them to go on with it than to repent of it.

When Amy grew big she went to a place I had provided for her, and the neighbours knew nothing but that Amy and I were parted. She had a fine child indeed, a daughter, and we had it nursed, and Amy came again in about half a year to live with her old mistress. But neither my gentleman nor Amy either cared for playing that game over again; for, as he said, the jade might bring him a houseful of children to keep.

We lived as merrily and as happily after this as could be expected, considering our circumstances; I mean as to the pretended marriage, etc. And as to that, my gentleman had not the least concern about him for it; but as much as I was hardened, and that was as much as I believe ever any wicked creature was, yet I could not help it; there was and would be hours of intervals and of dark reflections which came involuntarily in and thrust in sighs into the middle of all my songs, and there would be sometimes a heaviness of heart which intermingled itself with all my joy and which would often fetch a tear from my eye. And let others pretend what they will, I believe it impossible to be otherwise with anybody. There can be no substantial satisfaction in a life of known wickedness; conscience will, and does, often break in upon them at particular times, let them do what they can to prevent it.

But I am not to preach, but to relate; and whatever loose reflections were, and how often soever those dark intervals came on, I did my utmost to conceal them from him, ay, and to suppress and smother them too in myself, and to outward appearance we lived as cheerfully and as agreeably as it was possible for any couple in the world to live.

After I had thus lived with him something above two years, truly I found myself with child too. My gentleman was mightily pleased at it, and nothing could be kinder than he was in the preparations he made for me and for my lying-in, which was, however, very private, because I cared for as little company as possible, nor had I kept up my neighbourly acquaintance, so that I had nobody to invite upon such an occasion.

I was brought to bed very well (of a daughter too, as well as Amy), but the child died at about six weeks old; so all that work was to do over again, that is to say, the charge, the expense, the travel, etc.

The next year I made him amends, and brought him a son, to his great satisfaction. It was a charming child and he did very well. After this, my husband, as he called himself, came to me one evening and told me he had a very difficult thing happened to him, which he knew not what to do in or how to resolve about unless I would make him easy; this was, that his occasions required him to go over to France for about two months.

"Well, my dear," says I, "and how shall I make you easy?"

"Why, by consenting to let me go," says he; "upon which condition I'll tell you the occasion of my going, that you may judge of the necessity there is for it on my side." Then to make me easy in his going, he told me he would make his will before he went, which should be to my full satisfaction.

I told him the last part was so kind that I could not decline the first part, unless he would give me leave to add that if it was not for putting him to an extraordinary expense I would go over along with him.

He was so pleased with this offer that he told me he would give me full satisfaction for it, and accept of it too. So he took me to London with him the next day, and there he made his will, and showed it to me, sealed it before proper witnesses, and then gave it to me to keep. In this will he gave a thousand pounds to a person that we both knew very well, in trust, to pay it, with the interest from the time of his decease, to me or my assigns; then he willed the payment of my jointure, as he called it, viz. his bond of a hundred pounds, after his death, also he gave me all my household stuff, plate, etc.

This was a most engaging thing for a man to do to one under my circumstances, and it would have been hard, as I told him, to deny him anything or to refuse to go with him anywhere. So we settled everything as well as we could, left Amy in charge of the house, and for his other business, which was in jewels, he had two men he entrusted, whom he had good security for, and who managed for him and corresponded with him.

Things being thus concerted, we went away to France, arrived safe at Calais, and by easy journeys came in eight days more to Paris, where we lodged in the house of an English merchant of his acquaintance and were very courteously entertained.

My gentleman's business was with some persons of the first rank, and to whom he had sold some jewels of very good value and received a great sum of money in specie, and, as he told me privately, he gained 3,000 pistoles by his bargain, but would not suffer the most intimate friend he had there to know what he had received, for it is not so safe a thing in Paris to have a great sum of money in keeping, as it might be in London.

Chapter 4

We made this journey much longer than we intended, and my gentleman sent for one of his managers in London to come over to us to Paris with some diamonds, and sent him back to London again to fetch more. Then other business fell into his hands so unexpectedly, that I began to think we should take up our constant residence there, which I was not very averse to, it being my native country, and I spoke the language perfectly well. So we took a good house in Paris and lived very well there, and I sent for Amy to come over to me; for I lived gallantly, and my gentleman was two or three times going to keep me a coach, but I declined it, especially at Paris; but as they have those conveniences by the day there at a certain rate, I had an equipage provided for me whenever I pleased, and I lived here in a very good figure, and might have lived higher if I pleased.

But in the middle of all this felicity a dreadful disaster befell me, which entirely unhinged all my affairs and threw me back into the same state of life that I was in before; with this one happy exception, however, that whereas before I was poor even to misery, now I was not only provided for, but very rich.

My gentleman had the name in Paris for a very rich man, and indeed he was so, though not so immensely rich as people imagined; but that which was fatal to him was that he generally carried a shagreen case in his pocket, especially when he went to court or to the houses of any of the princes of the blood, in which he had jewels of very great value.

It happened one day, that being to go to Versailles to wait upon the Prince of ----, he came up into my chamber in the morning and laid out his jewel case, because he was not going to show any jewels, but to get a foreign bill accepted which he had received from Amsterdam. So when he gave me the case, he said, "My dear, I think I need not carry this with me, because it may be I may not come back till night, and it is too much to venture." I returned "Then, my dear, you shan't go." "Why?" says he. "Because as they are too much for you, so you are too much for me to venture, and you shall not go unless you will promise me not to stay, so as to come back in the night."

"I hope there's no danger," said he, "seeing I have nothing about me of any value; and therefore, lest I should, take that too," says he, and gives me his gold watch, and a rich diamond which he had in a ring and always wore on his finger.

"Well, but, my dear," says I, "you make me more uneasy now than before, for if you apprehend no danger, why do you use this caution? and if you apprehend there is danger, why do you go at all?"

"There is no danger," says he, "if I do not stay late, and I do not design to do so."

"Well, but promise me, then, that you won't," says I, "or else I cannot let you go."

"I won't indeed, my dear," says he, "unless I am obliged to it. I assure you I do not intend it, but if I should, I am not worth robbing now, for I have nothing about me but about six pistoles in my little purse, and that little ring," showing me a small diamond ring, worth about ten or twelve pistoles, which he put upon his finger in the room of the rich one he usually wore.

I still pressed him not to stay late, and he said he would not. "But if I am kept late," says he, "beyond my expectation, I'll stay all night and come next morning." This seemed a very good caution, but still my mind was very uneasy about him, and I told him so, and entreated him not to go. I told him I did not know what might be the reason, but that I had a strange terror upon my mind about his going, and that, if he did go, I was persuaded some harm would attend him. He smiled, and returned, "Well, my dear, if it should be so, you are now richly provided for; all that I have here I give to you." And with that he takes up the casket or case. "Here," says he, "hold your hand, there is a good estate for you in this case; if anything happens to me, 'tis all your own, I give it you for yourself." And with that he put the casket, the fine ring, and his gold watch all into my hands, and the key of his escritoire besides, adding, "And in my escritoire there is some money; 'tis all your own."

I stared at him as if I was frighted, for I thought all his face looked like a death's head, and then immediately I thought I perceived his head all bloody, and then his clothes looked bloody too; and immediately it all went off and he looked as he really did. Immediately I fell a-crying and hung about him. "My dear," said I, "I am frighted to death; you shall not go; depend upon it, some mischief will befall you." I did not tell him how my vapourish fancy had represented him to me; that, I thought, was not proper; besides, he would only have laughed at me, and would have gone away with a jest about it. But I pressed him seriously not to go that day, or, if he did, to promise me to come home to Paris again by daylight. He looked a little graver then than he did before, told me he was not apprehensive of the least danger; but if there was, he would either take care to come in the day or, as he had said before, would stay all night.

But all these promises came to nothing, for he was set upon in the open day and robbed by three men on horseback, masked, as he went; and one of them, who it seems rifled him while the rest stood to stop the coach, stabbed him into the body with a sword, so that he died immediately. He had a footman behind the coach whom they knocked down with the stock or butt end of a carbine. They were supposed to kill him because of the disappointment they met with in not getting his case or casket of diamonds, which they knew he carried about him; and this was supposed, because after they had killed him they made the coachman drive out of the road a long way over the heath till they came to a convenient place, where they pulled him out of the coach and searched his clothes more narrowly than they could do while he was alive.

But they found nothing but his little ring, six pistoles, and the value of about seven livres in small moneys.

This was a dreadful blow to me, though I cannot say I was so surprised as I should otherwise have been; for all the while he was gone my mind was oppressed with the weight of my own thoughts, and I was as sure that I should never see him any more, that I think nothing could be like it; the impression was so strong, that I think nothing could make so deep a wound that was imaginary, and I was so dejected and disconsolate, that when I received the news of his disaster, there was no room for any extraordinary alteration in me. I had cried all that day, ate nothing, and only waited, as I might say, to receive the dismal news, which I had brought to me about five o'clock in the afternoon.

Chapter 5

I was in a strange country, and, though I had a pretty many acquaintances, had but very few friends that I could consult on this occasion. All possible enquiry was made after the rogues that had been thus barbarous, but nothing could be heard of them; nor was it possible that the footman could make any discovery of them by his description, for they knocked him down immediately, so that he knew nothing of what was done afterwards. The coachman was the only man that could say anything, and all his account amounted to no more than this, that one of them had soldier's clothes, but he could not remember the particulars of his mounting so as to know what regiment he belonged to; and as to their faces, that he could know nothing of, because they had all of them masks on.

I had him buried as decently as the place would permit a Protestant stranger to be buried, and made some of the scruples and difficulties on that account easy by the help of money to a certain person, who went impudently to the curate of the parish St. Sulpice in Paris and told him that the gentleman that was killed was a Catholic, that the thieves had taken from him a cross of gold set with diamonds, worth 6,000 livres, that his widow was a Catholic and had sent by him sixty crowns to the Church of ---- for Masses to be said for the repose of his soul. Upon all which, though not one word of it was true, he was buried with all the ceremonies of the Roman Church.

I think I almost cried myself to death for him, for I abandoned myself to all the excesses of grief, and indeed I loved him to a degree inexpressible; and considering what kindness he had shown me at first, and how tenderly he had used me to the last, what could I do less?

Then the manner of his death was terrible and frightful to me, and, above all, the strange notices I had of it. I had never pretended to the second sight or anything of that kind, but certainly if any one ever had such a thing, I had it at this time, for I saw him as plainly in all those terrible shapes as above. First, as a skeleton, not dead only, but rotten and wasted; secondly, as killed, and his face bloody; and thirdly, his clothes bloody; and all within the space of one minute, or indeed of a very few moments.

These things amazed me, and I was a good while as one stupid. However, after some time I began to recover and look into my affairs. I had the satisfaction not to be left in distress or in danger of poverty; on the contrary, besides what he had put into my hands fairly in his lifetime, which amounted to a very considerable value, I found above seven hundred pistoles in gold in his escritoire, of which he had given me the key, and I found foreign bills accepted for about 12,000 livres; so that, in a word, I found myself possessed of almost ten thousand pounds sterling in a very few days after the disaster.

The first thing I did upon this occasion was to send a letter to my maid (as I still called her) Amy, wherein I gave her an account of my disaster; how my husband as she called him (for I never called him so), was murdered, and as I did not know how his relations or his wife's friends might act upon that occasion, I ordered her to convey away all the plate, linen, and other things of value and to secure them in a person's hands that I directed her to, and then to sell or dispose the furniture of the house if she could, and so, without acquainting anybody with the reason of her going, withdraw, sending notice to his head manager at London that the house was quitted by the tenant, and they might come and take possession of it for the executors. Amy was so dexterous, and did her work so nimbly, that she gutted the house, and sent the key to the said manager almost as soon as he had notice of the misfortune that befell their master.

Upon their receiving the surprising news of his death, the head manager came over to Paris and came to the house. I made no scruple of calling myself Madame ----, the widow of Monsieur ----, the English jeweller; and as I spoke French naturally, I did not let him know but that I was his wife, married in France, and that I had not heard that he had any wife in England, but pretended to be surprised, and exclaimed against him for so base an action; and that I had good friends in Poitou, where I was born, who would take care to have justice done me in England out of his estate.

I should have observed that as soon as the news was public of a man being murdered, and that he was a jeweller, fame did me the favour as to publish presently that he was robbed of his casket of jewels, which he always carried about with him. I confirmed this, among my daily lamentations, for his disaster, and added that he had with him a fine diamond ring which he was known to wear frequently about him, valued at 100 pistoles, a gold watch, and a great quantity of diamonds of inestimable value in his casket, which jewels he was carrying to the Prince of ----, to show some of them to him; and the Prince owned that he had spoken to him to bring some such jewels to let him see them. But I sorely repented this part afterwards, as you shall hear.

This rumour put an end to all enquiry after his jewels, his ring, or his watch; and as for the 700 pistoles, that I secured. For the bills which were in hand, I owned I had them; but that as, I said, I brought my husband 30,000 livres portion, I claimed the said bills, which came to not above 12,000 livres, for my amende; and this, with the plate and the household stuff, was the principal of all his estate which they could come at. As to the foreign bill which he was going to Versailles to get accepted, it was really lost with him; but his manager, who had remitted the bill to him by way of Amsterdam, bringing over the second bill, the money was saved, as they called it, which would otherwise have been also gone. The thieves who robbed and murdered him were, to be sure, afraid to send anybody to get the bill accepted, for that would undoubtedly have discovered them.

By this time my maid Amy was arrived, and she gave me an account of her management and how she had secured everything, and that she had quitted the house and sent the key to the head manager of his business, and let me know how much she had made of everything, very punctually and honestly.

I should have observed in the account of his dwelling with me so long at ----, that he never passed for anything there but a lodger in the house, and though he was landlord, that did not alter the case; so that at his death, Amy coming to quit the house and give them the key, there was no affinity between that and the case of their master who was newly killed.

I got good advice at Paris from an eminent lawyer, a counsellor of the parliament there, and, laying my case before him, he directed me to make a process in dower upon the estate for making good my new fortune upon matrimony, which accordingly I did; and, upon the whole, the manager went back to England well satisfied that he had gotten the unaccepted bills of exchange, which was for £2,500, with some other things, which together amounted to 17,000 livres, and thus I got rid of him.

I was visited with great civility on this sad occasion of the loss of my husband (as they thought him) by a great many ladies of quality; and the Prince of ---- to whom it was reported he was carrying the jewels, sent his gentleman with a very handsome compliment of condolence to me; and his gentleman, whether with or without order, hinted as if His Highness did intend to have visited me himself, but that some accident, which he made a long story of, had prevented him.

By the concourse of ladies and others that thus came to visit me I began to be much known, and as I did not forget to set myself out with all possible advantage, considering the dress of a widow, which in those days was a most frightful thing--I say, as I did thus from my own vanity, for I was not ignorant that I was very handsome--I say, on this account I was soon made very public, and was known by the name of La belle veuve de Poitou, or 'The pretty widow of Poitou.' As I was very well pleased to see myself thus handsomely used in my affliction, it soon dried up all my tears; and though I appeared as a widow, yet, as we say in England, it was of a widow comforted. I took care to let the ladies see that I knew how to receive them, that I was not at a loss how to behave to any of them; and, in short, I began to be very popular there. But I had an occasion afterwards which made me decline that kind of management, as you shall hear presently.

About four days after I had received the compliments of condolence from the Prince of ----, the same gentleman he had sent before came to tell me that His Highness was coming to give me a visit. I was indeed surprised at that, and perfectly at a loss how to behave. However, as there was no remedy, I prepared to receive him as well as I could. It was not many minutes after but he was at the door, and came in, introduced by his own gentleman, as above, and after by my woman Amy.

He treated me with abundance of civility, and condoled handsomely the loss of my husband and likewise the manner of it. He told me he understood he was coming to Versailles, to himself, to show him some jewels; that it was true that he had discoursed with him about jewels, but could not imagine how any villains should hear of his coming at that time with them; that he had not ordered him to attend with them at Versailles, but told him that he would come to Paris by such a day, so that he was no way accessory to the disaster. I told him gravely I knew very well that all His Highness had said of that part was true, that these villains knew his profession, and knew, no doubt, that he always carried a casket of jewels about him, and that he always wore a diamond ring on his finger worth a hundred pistoles, which report had magnified to five hundred; and that if he had been going to any other place, it would have been the same thing. After this His Highness rose up to go, and told me he had resolved, however, to make me some reparation, and with these words put a silk purse into my hand with a hundred pistoles, and told me he would make a further compliment of a small pension, which his gentleman would inform me of.

You may be sure I behaved with a due sense of so much goodness, and offered to kneel to kiss his hand, but he took me up and saluted me, and sat down again (though before he made as if he was going away), making me sit down by him.

He then began to talk with me more familiarly; told me he hoped I was not left in bad circumstances; that Mr. ---- was reputed to be very rich, and that he had gained lately great sums by some jewels; and he hoped, he said, that I had still a fortune agreeable to the condition I had lived in before.

I replied, with some tears, which I confess were a little forced, that I believed if Mr. ---- had lived we should have been out of danger of want, but that it was impossible to estimate the loss which I had sustained, besides that of the life of my husband; that by the opinion of those that knew something of his affairs and of what value the jewels were which he intended to have shown to His Highness, he could not have less about him than the value of a hundred thousand livres; that it was a fatal blow to me and to his whole family, especially that they should be lost in such a manner.

His Highness returned, with an air of concern, that he was very sorry for it, but he hoped if I settled in Paris I might find ways to restore my fortune. At the same time he complimented me upon my being very handsome, as he was pleased to call it, and that I could not fail of admirers. I stood up and humbly thanked His Highness, but told him I had no expectations of that kind; that I thought I should be obliged to go over to England to look after my husband's effects there, which I was told were considerable; but that I did not know what justice a poor stranger would get among them; and as for Paris, my fortune being so impaired, I saw nothing before me but to go back to Poitou to my friends, where some of my relations, I hoped, might do something for me, and added that one of my brothers was an Abbot at ----, near Poitiers.

He stood up and, taking me by the hand, led me to a large looking-glass which made up the pier in the front of the parlour. "Look there, madam," said he; "is it fit that face," pointing to my figure in the glass, "should go back to Poitou? No, madam," says he, "stay and make some gentleman of quality happy, that may in return make you forget all your sorrows "; and with that he took me in his arms and, kissing me twice, told me he would see me again, but with less ceremony.

Some little time after this, but the same day, his gentleman came to me again, and with great ceremony and respect delivered me a black box tied with a scarlet riband and sealed with a noble coat of arms, which I suppose was the Prince's. There was in it a grant from His Highness, or an assignment, I know not which to call it, with a warrant to his banker to pay me two thousand livres a year during my stay in Paris, as the widow of Monsieur ---- the jeweller, mentioning the horrid murder of my late husband as the occasion of it, as above.

I received it with great submission and expressions of being infinitely obliged to his master, and of my showing myself on all occasions His Highness's most obedient servant; and after giving my most humble duty to His Highness, with the utmost acknowledgments of the obligation, etc., I went to a little cabinet, and taking out some money, which made a little sound in taking it out, offered to give him five pistoles.

He drew back, but with the greatest respect, and told me he humbly thanked me, but that he durst not take a farthing; that His Highness would take it so ill of him, he was sure he would never see his face more; but that he would not fail to acquaint His Highness what respect I had offered; and added, "I assure you, madam, you are more in the good graces of my master, the Prince of ----, than you are aware of, and I believe you will hear more of him."

Now I began to understand him, and resolved, if His Highness did come again, he should see me under no disadvantages if I could help it. I told him if His Highness did me the honour to see me again, I hoped he would not let me be so surprised as I was before; that I would be glad to have some little notice of it, and would be obliged to him if he would procure it me. He told me he was very sure that when His Highness intended to visit me he should be sent before to give me notice of it, and that he would give me as much warning of it as possible.

He came several times after this on the same errand, that is, about the settlement, the grant, requiring several things yet to be done for making it payable, without going every time to the Prince again for a fresh warrant. The particulars of this part I did not understand, but as soon as it was finished, which was above two months, the gentleman came one afternoon and said His Highness designed to visit me in the evening, but desired to be admitted without ceremony.

I prepared not my rooms only but myself, and when he came in there was nobody appeared in the house but his gentleman and my maid Amy; and of her I bid the gentleman acquaint His Highness that she was an Englishwoman, that she did not understand a word of French, and that she was one also that might be trusted.

When he came into my room I fell down at his feet before he could come to salute me, and with words that I had prepared, full of duty and respect, thanked him for his bounty and goodness to a poor desolate woman, oppressed by the weight of so terrible a disaster, and refused to rise till he would allow me the honour to kiss his hand. "Levez-mous donc," says the Prince, taking me in his arms, "I design more favours for you than this trifle "; and going on, he added, "you shall, for the future, find a friend where you did not look for it, and I resolve to let you see how kind I can be to one who is to me the most agreeable creature on earth."

I was dressed in a kind of half-mourning, had turned off my weeds, and my head, though I had yet no ribands or lace, was so dressed as failed not to set me out with advantage enough, for I began to understand his meaning; and the Prince protested I was the most beautiful creature on earth. "And where have I lived," says he, "and how ill have I been served that I should never till now be shown the finest woman in France?"

This was the way, in all the world, the most likely to break in upon my virtue, if I had been mistress of any, for I was now become the vainest creature upon earth, and particularly of my beauty; which, as other people admired, so I became every day more foolishly in love with myself than before.

He said some very kind things to me after this and sat down with me for an hour or more, when, getting up and calling his gentleman by his name, he threw open the door. "Au boire," says he; upon which his gentleman immediately brought up a little table covered with a fine damask cloth, the table no bigger than he could bring in his two hands, but upon it was set two decanters, one of champagne and the other of water, six silver plates, and a service of fine sweetmeats in fine china dishes, on a set of rings standing up about twenty inches high, one above another; below was three roasted partridges and a quail. As soon as his gentleman had set it all down he ordered him to withdraw. "Now," says the Prince, "I intend to sup with you."

When he sent away his gentleman I stood up and offered to wait on His Highness while he ate, but he positively refused, and told me "No; to-morrow you shall be the widow of Monsieur ---- the jeweller, but to-night you shall be my mistress; therefore sit here," says he, "and eat with me, or I will get up and serve."

I would then have called up my woman Amy, but I thought that would not be proper neither, so I made my excuse that since His Highness would not let his own servant wait I would not presume to let my woman come up, but if he would please to let me wait, it would be my honour to fill His Highness's wine; but, as before, he would by no means allow me, so we sat and ate together.

"Now, madam," says the Prince, "give me leave to lay aside my character, let us talk together with the freedom of equals. My quality sets me at a distance from you and makes you ceremonious, your beauty exalts you to more than an equality; I must then treat you as lovers do their mistresses, but I cannot speak the language; 'tis enough to tell you how agreeable you are to me, how I am surprised at your beauty, and resolve to make you happy and to be happy with you."

I knew not what to say to him for a good while, but blushed and, looking up towards him, said I was already made happy in the favour of a person of such rank, and had nothing to ask of His Highness but that he would believe me infinitely obliged.

After he had eaten he poured the sweetmeats into my lap, and the wine being out he called his gentleman again to take away the table, who at first only took the cloth and the remains of what was to eat away, and laying another cloth, set the table on one side of the room, with a noble service of plate upon it worth at least 200 pistoles; then having set the two decanters again upon the table, filled as before, he withdrew, for I found the fellow understood his business very well, and his lord's business too.

About half an hour after, the Prince told me that I offered to wait a little before, that if I would now take the trouble he would give me leave to give him some wine. So I went to the table, filled a glass of wine, and brought it to him on a fine salver which the glasses stood on, and brought the bottle, or decanter for water, in my other hand, to mix it as he thought fit.

He smiled and bid me look on that salver, which I did, and admired it much, for it was a very fine one indeed. "You may see," says he, "I resolve to have more of your company, for my servant shall leave you that plate for my use." I told him I believed His Highness would not take it ill that I was not furnished fit to entertain a person of his rank, and that I would take great care of it, and value myself infinitely upon the honour of His Highness's visit.

It now began to grow late and he began to take notice of it. "But," says he, "I cannot leave you; have you not a spare lodging for one night?" I told him I had but a homely lodging to entertain such a guest. He said something exceedingly kind on that head, but not fit to repeat, adding that my company would make him amends.

About midnight he sent his gentleman on an errand, after telling him aloud that he intended to stay here all night. In a little time his gentleman brought him a nightgown, slippers, two caps, a neckcloth, and a shirt, which he gave me to carry into his chamber, and sent his man home; and then, turning to me, said I should do him the honour to be his chamberlain of the household, and his dresser also. I smiled, and told him I would do myself the honour to wait on him upon all occasions.

About one in the morning, while his gentleman was yet with him, I begged leave to withdraw, supposing he would go to bed; but he took the hint, and said, "I'm not going to bed yet, pray let me see you again."

I took this time to undress me and to come in a new dress, which was in a manner un déshabillé, but so fine, and all about me so clean and so agreeable, that he seemed surprised. "I thought," says he, "you could not have dressed to more advantage than you had done before; but now," says he, "you charm me a thousand times more, if that be possible."

"It is only a loose habit, my lord," said I, "that I may the better wait on Your Highness." He pulls me to him. "You are perfectly obliging," says he; and sitting on the bedside, says he, "Now you shall be a princess and know what it is to oblige the gratefullest man alive "; and with that he took me in his arms. . . . I can go no further in the particulars of what passed at that time, but it ended in this, that, in short, I lay with him all night.

Chapter 5

I have given you the whole detail of this story, to lay it down as a black scheme of the way how unhappy women are ruined by great men; for though poverty and want is an irresistible temptation to the poor, vanity and great things are as irresistible to others. To be courted by a prince, and by a prince who was first a benefactor, then an admirer, to be called handsome, the finest woman in France, and to be treated as a woman fit for the bed of a prince: these are things a woman must have no vanity in her, nay, no corruption in her, that is not overcome by it; and my case was such, that, as before, I had enough of both.

Chapter 6

I had now no poverty attending me. On the contrary, I was mistress of ten thousand pounds before the Prince did anything for me. Had I been mistress of my resolution, had I been less obliging and rejected the first attack, all had been safe; but my virtue was lost before, and the devil, who had found the way to break in upon me by one temptation, easily mastered me now by another, and I gave myself up to a person who, though a man of high dignity, was yet the most tempting and obliging that ever I met with in my life.

I had the same particular to insist upon here with the Prince that I had with my gentleman before. I hesitated much at consenting at first asking, but the Prince told me princes did not court like other men, that they brought more powerful arguments, and he very prettily added that they were sooner repulsed than other men and ought to be sooner complied with, intimating, though very genteelly, that after a woman had positively refused him once, he could not, like other men, wait with importunities and stratagems and laying long sieges; but as such men as he stormed warmly, so, if repulsed, they made no second attacks; and indeed it was but reasonable, for as it was below their rank to be long battering a woman's constancy, so they ran greater hazards in being exposed in their amours than other men did.

I took this for a satisfactory answer, and told His Highness that I had the same thoughts in respect to the manner of his attacks, for that his person and his arguments were irresistible; that a person of his rank and a munificence so unbounded could not be withstood; that no virtue was proof against him, except such as was able too to suffer martyrdom; that I thought it impossible I could be overcome, but that now I found it was impossible I should not be overcome; that so much goodness, joined with so much greatness, would have conquered a saint; and that I confessed he had the victory over me by a merit infinitely superior to the conquest he had made.

He made me a most obliging answer; told me abundance of fine things which still flattered my vanity, till at last I began to have pride enough to believe him and fancied myself a fit mistress for a prince.

As I had thus given the Prince the last favour, and he had all the freedom with me that it was possible for me to grant, so he gave me leave to use as much freedom with him another way, and that was to have everything of him I thought fit to command. And yet I did not ask of him with an air of avarice, as if I was greedily making a penny of him, but I managed him with such art that he generally anticipated my demands; he only requested of me that I would not think of taking another house, as I had intimated to His Highness that I had intended, not thinking it good enough to receive his visits in. But, he said, my house was the most convenient that could possibly be found in all Paris for an amour, especially for him, having a way out into three streets, and not overlooked by any neighbours, so that he could pass and repass without observation, for one of the back ways opened into a narrow dark alley, which alley was a thoroughfare or passage out of one street into another, and any person that went in or out by the door had no more to do but to see that there was nobody following him in the alley before he went in at the door. This request I knew was reasonable, and therefore I assured him I would not change my dwelling, seeing His Highness did not think it too mean for me to receive him in.

He also desired me that I would not take any more servants or set up any equipage, at least for the present, for that it would then be immediately concluded I had been left very rich, and then I should be thronged with the impertinence of admirers, who would be attracted by the money as well as by the beauty of a young widow, and he should be frequently interrupted in his visits; or that the world would conclude I was maintained by somebody and would be indefatigable to find out the person; so that he should have spies peeping at him every time he went out or in, which it would be impossible to disappoint, and that he should presently have it talked over all the toilets in Paris that the Prince de ---- had got the jeweller's widow for a mistress.

This was too just to oppose, and I made no scruple to tell His Highness that since he had stooped so low as to make me his own, he ought to have all the satisfaction in the world that I was all his own; that I would take all the measures he should please to direct me to avoid thc impertinent attacks of others; and that if he thought fit I would be wholly within doors, and have it given out that I was obliged to go to England to solicit my affairs there after my husband's misfortune, and that I was not expected there again for at least a year or two. This he liked very well; only, he said, that he would by no means have me confined, that it would injure my health, and that I should then take a country house in some village, a good way off from the city, where it should not be known who I was, and that I should be there sometimes, to divert me.

I made no scruple of the confinement, and told His Highness no place could be a confinement where I had such a visitor; and so I put off the country house, which would have been to remove myself further from him and have less of his company, and I made the house be, as it were, shut up. Amy indeed appeared, and when any of the neighbours and servants enquired, she answered in broken French that I was gone to England to look after my affairs, which presently went current through the streets about us. For you are to note that the people of Paris, especially the women, are the most busy and impertinent enquirers into the conduct of their neighbours, especially that of a single woman, that are in the world;

though there are no greater intriguers in the universe than themselves, and perhaps that may be the reason of it, for it is an old but a sure rule that

When deep intrigues are close and shy, The guilty are the first that spy.

Thus His Highness had the most easy and yet the most undiscoverable access to me imaginable, and he seldom failed to come two or three nights in a week, and sometimes stayed two or three nights together. Once he told me he was resolved I should be weary of his company, and that he would learn to know what it was to be a prisoner; so he gave out among his servants that he was gone to ----, where he often went a-hunting, and that he should not return under a fortnight. And that fortnight he stayed wholly with me, and never went out of my doors.

Never woman in such a station lived a fortnight in so complete a fullness of human delight. For, to have the entire possession of one of the most accomplished princes in the world, and of the politest, best-bred man, to converse with him all day and, as he professed, charm him all night, what could be more inexpressibly pleasing, and especially to a woman of a vast deal of pride as I was?

To finish the felicity of this part, I must not forget that the devil had played a new game with me, and prevailed with me to satisfy myself with this amour as a lawful thing; that a prince of such grandeur and majesty, so infinitely superior to me, and one who had made such an introduction by an unparalleled bounty, I could not resist; and therefore that it was very lawful for me to do it, being at that time perfectly single and unengaged to any other man--as I was, most certainly, by the unaccountable absence of my first husband, and the murder of my gentleman who went for my second.

It cannot be doubted but that I was the easier to persuade myself of the truth of such a doctrine as this, when it was so much for my ease and for the repose of my mind to have it be so.

In things we wish, 'tis easy to deceive; What we would have, we willingly believe.

Besides, I had no casuists to resolve this doubt. The same devil that put this into my head bade me go to any of the Romish clergy and, under the pretence of confession, state the case exactly, and I should see they would either resolve it to be no sin at all, or absolve me upon the easiest penance. This I had a strong inclination to try, but I know not what scruple put me off it, for I could never bring myself to like having to do with those priests. And though it was strange that I, who had thus prostituted my chastity and given up all sense of virtue in two such particular cases, living a life of open adultery, should scruple anything; yet so it was, I argued with myself, that I could not be a cheat in anything that was esteemed sacred, that I could not be of one opinion and then pretend myself to be of another, nor could I go to confession who knew nothing of the manner of it, and should betray myself to the priest to be a Huguenot, and then might come into trouble; but, in short, though I was a whore, yet I was a Protestant whore, and could not act as if I was Popish upon any account whatsoever.

But, I say, I satisfied myself with the surprising occasion that as it was all irresistible, so it was all lawful; for that Heaven would not suffer us to be punished for that which it was not possible for us to avoid. And with these absurdities I kept conscience from giving me any considerable disturbance in all this matter, and I was as perfectly easy as to the lawfulness of it as if I had been married to the Prince and had had no other husband. So possible is it for us to roll ourselves up in wickedness, till we grow invulnerable by conscience; and that sentinel, once dozed, sleeps fast, not to be awakened while the tide of pleasure continues to flow or till something dark and dreadful brings us to ourselves again.

I have, I confess, wondered at the stupidity that my intellectual part was under all that while, what lethargic fumes dozed the soul, and how it was possible that I, who in the case before, where the temptation was many ways more forcible and the arguments stronger and more irresistible, was yet under a continued inquietude on account of the wicked life I led, could now live in the most profound tranquillity, and with an uninterrupted peace, nay, even rising up to satisfaction and joy, and yet in a more palpable state of adultery than before; for before, my gentleman who had called me wife had the pretence of his wife, being parted from him, refusing to do the duty of her once as a wife to him. As for me, my circumstances were the same; but as for the Prince, as he had a fine and extraordinary lady, or Princess, of his own, so he had had two or three mistresses more besides me and made no scruple of it at all.

However, I say, as to my own part I enjoyed myself in perfect tranquillity, and as the Prince was the only deity I worshipped, so I was really his idol. And however it was with his Princess, I assure you his other mistresses found a sensible difference; and though they could never find me out, yet I had good intelligence that they guessed very well that their lord had got some new favourite that robbed them of his company, and perhaps of some of his usual bounty too. And now I must mention the sacrifices he made to his idol; and they were not a few, I assure you.

As he loved like a prince, so he rewarded like a prince; for though he declined my making a figure, as above, he let me see that he was above doing it for the saving the expense of it--and so he told me--and that he would make it up in other things. First of all he sent me a toilet with all the appurtenances of silver, even so much as the frame of the table, and then for the house he gave me the table or sideboard of plate I mentioned above, with all things belonging to it of massy silver; so that, in short, I could not for my life study to ask him for any thing of plate which I had not.

He could then accommodate me in nothing more but jewels and clothes, or money for clothes. He sent his gentleman to the mercers, and bought me a suit or whole piece of the finest brocaded silk, figured with gold, and another with silver, and another of crimson, so that I had three suits of clothes such as the Queen of France would not have disdained to have worn at that time. Yet I went out nowhere; but as these were for me to put on when I went out of mourning, I dressed myself in them, one after another, always when His Highness came to see me.

I had no less than five several morning dresses besides these, so that I need never be seen twice in the same dress. To these he added several parcels of fine linen and of lace, so much that I had no room to ask for more, or indeed for so much.

I took the liberty once in our freedoms to tell him he was too bountiful and that I was too chargeable to him for a mistress, and that I would be his faithful servant at less expense to him, and that he not only left me no room to ask him for anything, but that he supplied me with such a profusion of good things that I scarce could wear them or use them unless I kept a great equipage, which he knew was no way convenient for him or for me. He smiled and took me in his arms, and told me he was resolved, while I was his, I should never be able to ask him for anything, but that he would be daily asking new favours of me.

After we were up, for this conference was in bed, he desired I would dress me in the best suit of clothes I had. It was a day or two after the three suits were made and brought home. I told him, if he pleased, I would rather dress me in that suit which I knew he liked best. He asked me how I could know which he would like best before he had seen them. I told him I would presume for once to guess at his fancy by my own, so I went away and dressed me in the second suit brocaded with silver, and returned in full dress, with a suit of lace upon my head which would have been worth in England £200 sterling; and I was every way set out as well as Amy could dress me, who was a very genteel dresser too. In this figure I came to him out of my dressing-room, which opened with folding doors into his bedchamber.

He sat as one astonished a good while, looking at me without speaking a word, till I came quite up to him, knelt on one knee to him, and almost, whether he would or no, kissed his hand. He took me up, and stood up himself, but was surprised when, taking me in his arms, he perceived tears to run down my cheeks. "My dear," says he aloud, "what mean these tears?" "My lord," said I after some little check, for I could not speak presently, "I beseech you to believe me, they are not tears of sorrow but tears of joy. It is impossible for me to see myself snatched from the misery I was fallen into and at once to be in the arms of a Prince of such goodness, such immense bounty, and be treated in such a manner--'tis not possible, my lord," said I, "to contain the satisfaction of it, and it will break out in an excess in some measure proportioned to your immense bounty and to the affection which Your Highness treats me with, who am so infinitely below you."

It would look a little too much like a romance here to repeat all the kind things he said to me on that occasion, but I can't omit one passage. As he saw the tears drop down my cheek, he pulls out a fine cambric handkerchief and was going to wipe the tears off, but checked his hand as if he was afraid to deface something. I say he checked his hand, and tossed the handkerchief to me to do it myself. I took the hint immediately, and with a kind of pleasant disdain, "How! my lord," said I, "have you kissed me so often and don't you know whether I am painted or not? Pray let Your Highness satisfy yourself that you have no cheats put upon you; for once let me be vain enough to say I have not deceived you with false colours." With this I put a handkerchief into his hand and, taking his hand into mine, I made him wipe my face so hard that he was unwilling to do it for fear of hurting me.

He appeared surprised more than ever, and swore, which was the first time that I had heard him swear from my first knowing him, that he could not have believed there was any such skin, without paint, in the world. "Well, my lord," said I, "Your Highness shall have a further demonstration than this--as to that which you are pleased to accept for beauty, that it is the mere work of nature." And with that I stepped to the door, and rang a little bell for my woman Amy and bade her bring me a cupful of hot water, which she did. And when it was come I desired His Highness to feel if it was warm, which he did, and I immediately washed my face all over with it before him. This was indeed more than satisfaction, that is to say, than believing, for it was an undeniable demonstration, and he kissed my cheeks and breasts a thousand times with expressions of the greatest surprise imaginable.

Nor was I a very indifferent figure as to shape. Though I had had two children by my gentleman and five by my true husband, I say I was no despisable shape. And my Prince (I must be allowed the vanity to call him so) was taking his view of me as I walked from one end of the room to the other. At last he leads me to the darkest part of the room and, standing behind me, bade me hold up my head, when putting both his hands round my neck, as if he was spanning my neck to see how small it was, for it was long and small, he held my neck so long and so hard in his hands that I complained he hurt me a little. What he did it for I knew not, nor had I the least suspicion but that he was spanning my neck. But when I said he hurt me, he seemed to let go, and in half a minute more led me to a pier-glass, and behold I saw my neck clasped with a fine necklace of diamonds whereas I felt no more what he was doing at all than if he had really done nothing at all, nor did I suspect it in the least. If I had an ounce of blood in me that did not fly up into my face, neck, and breasts, it must be from some interruption in the vessels. I was all on fire with the sight, and began to wonder what it was that was coming to me.

However, to let him see that I was not unqualified to receive benefits, I turned about: "My lord," says I, "Your Highness is resolved to conquer by your bounty the very gratitude of your servants; you will leave no room for anything but thanks, and make those thanks useless too by their bearing no proportion to the occasion."

"I love, child," says he, "to see everything suitable: a fine gown and petticoat, a fine laced head. A fine face and neck and no necklace would not have made the object perfect. But why that blush, my dear?" says the Prince. "My lord," said I, "all your gifts call for blushes, but above all I blush to receive what I am so ill able to merit, and may become so ill also."

Thus far I am a standing mark of the weakness of great men in their vice, that value not squandering away immense wealth upon the most worthless creatures; or, to sum it up in a word, they raise the value of the object which they pretend to pitch upon by their fancy--I say, raise the value of it at their own expense, give vast presents for a ruinous favour which is so far from being equal to the price, that nothing will at last prove more absurd than the cost men are at to purchase their own destruction.

I could not, in the height of all this fine doing, I say I could not be without some just reflection, though conscience was, as I said, dumb as to any disturbance it gave me in my wickedness. My vanity was fed up to such a height that I had no room to give way to such reflections.

But I could not but sometimes look back with astonishment at the folly of men of quality, who, immense in their bounty as in their wealth, give, to a profusion and without bounds, to the most scandalous of our sex for granting them the liberty of abusing themselves and ruining both.

I that knew what this carcase of mine had been but a few years before, how overwhelmed with grief, drowned in tears, frighted with the prospect of beggary, and surrounded with rags and fatherless children; that was pawning and selling the rags that covered me, for a dinner, and sat on the ground, despairing of help and expecting to be starved, till my children were snatched from me to be kept by the parish--I that was after this a whore for bread and, abandoning conscience and virtue, lived with another woman's husband; I that was despised by all my relations and my husband's too; I that was left so entirely desolate, friendless, and helpless that I knew not how to get the least help to keep me from starving--that I should be caressed by a prince for the honour of having the scandalous use of my prostituted body, common before to his inferiors, and perhaps would not have denied one of his footmen but a little while before if I could have got my bread by it.

I say I could not but reflect upon the brutality and blindness of mankind, that, because nature had given me a good skin and some agreeable features, should suffer that beauty to be such a bait for appetite as to do such sordid, unaccountable things to obtain the possession of it.

It is for this reason that I have so largely set down the particulars of the caresses I was treated with by the jeweller, and also by this Prince; not to make the story an incentive to the vice, which I am now such a sorrowful penitent for being guilty of--God forbid any should make so vile a use of so good a design--but to draw the just picture of a man enslaved to the rage of his vicious appetite: how he defaces the image of God in his soul, dethrones his reason, causes conscience to abdicate the possession, and exalts sense into the vacant throne; how he deposes the man and exalts the brute.

Oh, could we hear now the reproaches this great man afterwards loaded himself with when he grew weary of this admired creature and became sick of his vice, how profitable would the report of them be to the reader of this story. But had he himself also known the dirty history of my actings upon the stage of life that little time I had been in the world, how much more severe would those reproaches have been upon himself. But I shall come to this again.

Chapter 7

I lived in this gay sort of retirement almost three years, in which time no amour of such a kind, sure, was ever carried up so high. The Prince knew no bounds to his munificence; he could give me nothing, either for my wearing or using, or eating or drinking, more than he had done from the beginning.

His presents were after that in gold, and very frequent and large--often a hundred pistoles, never less than fifty at a time--and I must do myself the justice that I seemed rather backward to receive than craving and encroaching. Not that I had not an avaricious temper, nor was it that I did not foresee that this was my harvest in which I was to gather up and that it would not last long, but it was that really his bounty always anticipated my expectations and even my wishes, and he gave me money so fast that he rather poured it in upon me than left me room to ask it, so that before I could spend fifty pistoles I had always a hundred to make it up.

After I had been near a year and a half in his arms, as above, or thereabouts, I proved with child. I did not take any notice of it to him till I was satisfied that I was not deceived; when one morning early, when we were in bed together, I said to him, "My lord, I doubt Your Highness never gives yourself leave to think what the case should be if I should have the honour to be with child by you." "Why, my dear," says he, "we are able to keep it if such a thing should happen. I hope you are not concerned about that." "No, my lord," said I, "I should think myself very happy if I could bring Your Highness a son; I should hope to see him a lieutenant-general of the King's armies, by the interest of his father and by his own merit."

"Assure yourself, child," says he, "if it should be so I will not refuse owning him for my son, though it be, as they call it, a natural son, and shall never slight or neglect him for the sake of his mother." Then he began to importune me to know if it was so, but I positively denied it so long till at last I was able to give him the satisfaction of knowing it himself, by the motion of the child within me.

He professed himself overjoyed at the discovery, but told me that now it was absolutely necessary for me to quit the confinement which he said I had suffered for his sake, and to take a house somewhere in the country in order for health as well as for privacy against my lying-in. This was quite out of my way, but the Prince, who was a man of pleasure, had, it seems, several retreats of this kind which he made use of, I suppose, upon like occasions. And so leaving it, as it were, to his gentleman, he provided a very convenient house about four miles south of Paris, at the village of ----, where I had very agreeable lodgings, good gardens, and all things very easy to my content. But one thing did not please me at all, viz. that an old woman was provided and put into the house, to furnish everything necessary to my lying-in and to assist at my travail.

I did not like this old woman at all. She looked so like a spy upon me, or (as sometimes I was frighted to imagine) like one set privately to dispatch me out of the world as might best suit with the circumstances of my lying-in. And when His Highness came the next time to see me, which was not many days, I expostulated a little on the subject of the old woman, and by the management of my tongue as well as by the strength of reasoning I convinced him that it would not be at all convenient, that it would be the greater risk on his side, and that first or last it would certainly expose him and me also. I assured him that my servant, being an Englishwoman, never knew to that hour who His Highness was, that I always called him the Count de Clerac, and that she knew nothing else of him, nor ever should; that if he would give me leave to choose proper persons for my use, it should be so ordered that not one of them should know who he was or perhaps ever see his face, and that for the reality of the child that should be born, His Highness, who had alone been at the first of it, should if he pleased be present in the room all the time, so that he would need no witnesses on that account.

This discourse fully satisfied him, so that he ordered his gentleman to dismiss the old woman the same day; and without any difficulty I sent my maid Amy to Calais and thence to Dover, where she got an English midwife and an English nurse to come over on purpose to attend an English lady of quality, as they styled me, for four months certain. The midwife, Amy had agreed to pay a hundred guineas to, and bear her charges to Paris and back again to Dover; the poor woman that was to be my nurse had twenty pounds, and the same terms for charges as the other.

I was very easy when Amy returned, and the more because she brought with the midwife a good motherly sort of woman who was to be her assistant and would be very helpful on occasion, and bespoke a man-midwife at Paris too, if there should be any necessity for his help. Having thus made provision for everything, the Count, for so we all called him in public, came as often to see me as I could expect, and continued exceeding kind, as he had always been. One day, conversing together upon the subject of my being with child, I told him how all things were in order, but that I had a strange apprehension that I should die with that child. He smiled. "So all the ladies say, my dear," says he, "when they are with child." "Well, however, my lord," said I, "it is but just that care should be taken that what you have bestowed in your excess of bounty upon me should not be lost." And upon this I pulled a paper out of my bosom, folded up but not sealed, and I read it to him; wherein I had left order that all the plate and jewels and fine furniture which His Highness had given me should be restored to him by my woman, and the keys be immediately delivered to his gentleman in case of disaster.

Then I recommended my woman Amy to his favour for a hundred pistoles, on condition she gave up the keys, as above, to his gentleman, and his gentleman's receipt for them. When he saw this, "My dear child," said he, and took me in his arms; "what, have you been making your will and disposing your effects? Pray whom do you make your universal heir?" "So far as to do justice to Your Highness, in case of mortality, I have, my lord," said I; "and who should I dispose the valuable things to which I have had from your hand as pledges of your favour and testimonies of your bounty, but to the giver of them? If the child should live, Your Highness will, I don't question, act like yourself in that part, and I shall have the utmost satisfaction that it will be well used by your direction."

I could see he took this very well. "I have forsaken all the ladies in Paris," says he, "for you; and I have lived every day since I knew you to see that you know how to merit all that a man of honour can do for you. Be easy, child, I hope you shall not die; and all you have is your own, to do with it what you please."

I was then within about two months of my time, and that soon wore off. When I found my time was come, it fell out very happily that he was in the house, and I entreated he would continue a few hours in the house, which he agreed to. They called His Highness to come into the room if he pleased, as I had offered, and as I desired him, and I sent word I would make as few cries as possible to prevent disturbing him. He came into the room once and called to me to be of good courage, it would soon be over, and then he withdrew again; and in about half an hour more Amy carried him the news that I was delivered and had brought him a charming boy. He gave her ten pistoles for her news, stayed till they had adjusted things about me, and then came into the room again, cheered me and spoke kindly to me, and looked on the child, then withdrew; and came again the next day to visit me.

Since this, and when I have looked back upon these things with eyes unpossessed with crime, when the wicked part has appeared in its clearer light and I have seen it in its own natural colours; when no more blinded with the glittering appearances which at that time deluded me, and, as in like cases, if I may guess at others by myself, too much possessed the mind--I say, since this I have often wondered with what pleasure or satisfaction the Prince could look upon the poor innocent infant, which, though his own, and that he might that way have some attachment in his affections to it, yet must always afterwards be a remembrancer to him of his most early crime; and, which was worse, must bear upon itself, unmerited, an eternal mark of infamy, which should be spoken of upon all occasions to its reproach, from the folly of its father and wickedness of its mother.

Great men are indeed delivered from the burden of their natural children, or bastards, as to their maintenance. This is the main affliction in other cases, where there is not substance sufficient without breaking into the fortunes of the family. In those cases either a man's legitimate children suffer, which is very unnatural, or the unfortunate mother of that illegitimate birth has a dreadful affliction either of being turned off with her child and be left to starve, etc., or of seeing the poor infant packed off with a piece of money to some of those she-butchers who take children off their hands, as 'tis called--that is to say, starve 'em and, in a word, murder 'em.

Great men, I say, are delivered from this burden, because they are always furnished to supply the expense of their out-of-the-way offspring by making little assignments upon the Bank of Lyons or the Town House of Paris, and settling those sums to be received for the maintenance of such expense as they see cause.

Thus, in the case of this child of mine, while he and I conversed there was no need to make any appointment, as an appanage or maintenance for the child or its nurse, for he supplied me more than sufficiently for all those things. But afterwards, when time and a particular circumstance put an end to our conversing together--as such things always meet with a period and generally break off abruptly--I say, after that I found he appointed the children a settled allowance, by an assignment of annual rent upon the Bank of Lyons, which was sufficient for bringing them handsomely though privately up in the world, and that not in a manner unworthy of their father's blood, though I came to be sunk and forgotten in the case; nor did the children ever know anything of their mother to this day, other than as you may have an account hereafter.

But to look back to the particular observation I was making, which I hope may be of use to those who read my story, I say it was something wonderful to me to see this person so exceedingly delighted at the birth of this child, and so pleased with it; for he would sit and look at it, and with an air of seriousness sometimes, a great while together, and particularly, I observed, he loved to look at it when it was asleep.

It was indeed a lovely, charming child, and had a certain vivacity in its countenance that is far from being common to all children so young; and he would often say to me that he believed there was something extraordinary in the child, and he did not doubt but he would come to be a great man.

I could never hear him say so, but though secretly it pleased me, yet it so closely touched me another way, that I could not refrain sighing, and sometimes tears; and one time in particular it so affected me that I could not conceal it from him. But when he saw tears run down my face there was no concealing the occasion from him, he was too importunate to be denied in a thing of that moment; so I frankly answered, "It sensibly affects me, my lord," said I, "that whatever the merit of this little creature may be, he must always have a bend on his arms; the disaster of his birth will be always not a blot only to his honour, but a bar to his fortunes in the world; our affection will be ever his affliction, and his mother's crime be the son's reproach; the blot can never be wiped out by the most glorious actions; nay, if it lives to raise a family," said I, "the infamy must descend even to its innocent posterity."

He took the thought and sometimes told me afterwards that it made a deeper impression on him than he discovered to me at that time; but for the present he put it off with telling me these things could not be helped, that they served for a spur to the spirits of brave men, inspired them with the principles of gallantry and prompted them to brave actions; that though it might be true that the mention of illegitimacy might attend the name, yet that personal virtue placed a man of honour above the reproach of his birth; that as he had no share in the offence, he would have no concern at the blot; when having by his own merit placed himself out of the reach of scandal, his fame should drown the memory of his beginning.

That as it was usual for men of quality to make such little escapes, so the number of their natural children were so great, and they generally took such good care of their education, that some of the greatest men in the world had a bend in their coat of arms, and that it was of no consequence to them, especially when their fame began to rise upon the basis of their acquired merit. And upon this he began to reckon up to me some of the greatest families in France, and in England also.

This carried off our discourse for a time; but I went further with him once, removing the discourse from the part attending our children to the reproach which those children would be apt to throw upon us their originals; and when speaking a little too feelingly on the subject, he began to receive the impression a little deeper than I wished he had done. At last he told me I had almost acted the confessor to him, that I might perhaps preach a more dangerous doctrine to him than we should either of us like, or than I was aware of. "For, my dear," says he, "if once we come to talk of repentance, we must talk of parting."

If tears were in my eyes before, they flowed too fast now to be restrained, and I gave him but too much satisfaction by my looks that I had yet no reflections upon my mind strong enough to go that length, and that I could no more think of parting than he could.

He said a great many kind things which were great, like himself, and, extenuating our crime, intimated to me that he could no more part with me than I could with him. So we both, as I may say, even against our light and against our conviction, concluded to sin on; indeed, his affection to the child was one great tie to him, for he was extremely fond of it.

This child lived to be a considerable man. He was first an officer of the Garde du Corps of France, and afterwards colonel of a regiment of dragoons in Italy, and on many extraordinary occasions showed that he was not unworthy such a father, but many ways deserving a legitimate birth and a better mother. Of which hereafter.

Chapter 8

I think I may say now that I lived indeed like a queen or if you will have me confess that my condition had still the reproach of a whore, I may say, I was sure, the queen of whores; for no woman was ever more valued or more caressed by a person of such quality, only in the station of a mistress. I had indeed one deficiency which women in such circumstances seldom are chargeable with, namely, I craved nothing of him. I never asked him for anything in my life, nor suffered myself to be made use of, as is too much the custom of mistresses, to ask favours for others. His bounty always prevented me in the first, and my strict concealing myself in the last, which was no less to my convenience than his.

The only favour I ever asked of him was for his gentleman, whom he had all along entrusted with the secret of our affair, and who had once so much offended him by some omissions in his duty, that he found it very hard to make his peace. He came and laid his case before my woman Amy and begged her to speak to me, to intercede for him, which I did, and on my account he was received again and pardoned; for which, the grateful dog requited me by getting to bed to his benefactress Amy. At which I was very angry, but Amy generously acknowledged that it was her fault as much as his, that she loved the fellow so much that she believed if he had not asked her, she should have asked him; I say this pacified me, and I only obtained of her that she should not let him know that I knew it.

I might have interspersed this part of my story with a great many pleasant parts and discourses which happened between my maid Amy and I, but I omit them on account of my own story, which has been so extraordinary. However, I must mention something as to Amy and her gentleman. I enquired of Amy upon what terms they came to be so intimate, but Amy seemed backward to explain herself. I did not care to press her upon a question of that nature, knowing that she might have answered my question with a question and have said, Why, how did I and the Prince come to be so intimate? So I left off further enquiring into it, till after some time she told it me all freely of her own accord; which, to cut it short, amounted to no more than this, that like mistress, like maid. As they had many leisure hours together below while they waited respectively when my lord and I were together above, I say they could hardly avoid the usual question one to another, namely, Why might not they do the same thing below that we did above?

On that account indeed, as I said above, I could not find in my heart to be angry with Amy. I was indeed afraid the girl would have been with cold too, but that did not happen, and so there was no hurt done; for Amy had been hanselled before as well as her mistress, and by the same party too, as you have heard.

After I was up again and my child provided with a good nurse, and, withal, winter coming on, it was proper to think of coming to Paris again, which I did. But as I had now a coach and horses, and some servants to attend me, by my lord's allowance, I took the liberty to have them come to Paris sometimes, and so to take a tour into the Garden of the Tuileries and the other pleasant places of the city. It happened one day that my Prince (if I may call him so) had a mind to give me some diversion and to take the air with me, but that he might do it and not be publicly known, he comes to me in a coach of the Count de ----, a great officer of the Court, attended by his liveries also; so that, in a word, it was impossible to guess by the equipage who I was or whom I belonged to. Also, that I might be the more effectually concealed, he ordered me to be taken up at a mantua-maker's house, where he sometimes came, whether upon other amours or not was no business of mine to enquire. I knew nothing whither he intended to carry me, but when he was in the coach with me, he told me he had ordered his servants to go to Court with me, and he would show me some of the beau-monde. I told him I cared not where I went while I had the honour to have him with me. So he carried me to the fine palace of Meudon, where the Dauphin then was, and where he had some particular intimacy with one of the Dauphin's domestics, who procured a retreat for me in his lodgings while we stayed there, which was three or four days.

While I was there the King happened to come thither from Versailles, and, making but a short stay, visited madam the Dauphiness, who was then living. The Prince was here incognito only because of his being with me, and therefore when he heard that the King was in the Gardens he kept close within the lodgings; but the gentleman in whose lodgings we were, with his lady and several others, went out to see the King, and I had the honour to be asked to go with them.

After we had seen the King, who did not stay long in the Gardens, we walked up the broad terrace and, crossing the hall towards the great staircase, I had a sight which confounded me at once, as I doubt not it would have done to any woman in the world. The Horse Guards, or what they call there the Gendarmes, had upon some occasion been either upon duty or been reviewed, or something (I did not understand that part) was the matter that occasioned their being there, I know not what; but walking in the guard-chamber, and with his jack-boots on and the whole habit of the troop as it is worn when our Horse Guards are upon duty, as they call it, at St. James's Park, I say, there, to my inexpressible confusion, I saw Mr. ----, my first husband, the brewer.

I could not be deceived. I passed so near him that I almost brushed him with my clothes, and looked him full in the face, but having my fan before my face so that he could not know me. However, I knew him perfectly well, and I heard him speak, which was a second way of knowing him. Besides being, you may be sure, astonished and surprised at such a sight, I turned about after I had passed him some steps, and pretending to ask the lady that was with me some questions, I stood as if I had viewed the great hall, the outer guard-chamber, and some other things; but I did it to take a full view of his dress, that I might further inform myself.

While I stood thus amusing the lady that was with me with questions, he walked, talking with another man of the same cloth, back again, just by me; and to my particular satisfaction, or dissatisfaction, take it which way you will, I heard him speak English, the other being, it seems, an Englishman.

I then asked the lady some other questions. "Pray, madam," says I, "what are these troopers here? Are they the King's Guards." "No," says she, "they are the Gendarmes; a small detachment of them, I suppose, attended the King to-day, but they are not His Majesty's ordinary guard." Another lady that was with her said, "No, madam, it seems that is not the case, for I heard them saying the Gendarmes were here to-day by special order, some of them being to march towards the Rhine, and these attend for orders, but they go back to-morrow to Orleans where they are expected."

This satisfied me in part, but I found means after this to enquire whose particular troop it was that the gentlemen that were here belonged to, and with that I heard they would all be at Paris the week after.

Two days after this we returned for Paris, when I took occasion to speak to my lord that I heard the Gendarmes were to be in the city the next week, and that I should be charmed with seeing them march if they came in a body. He was so obliging in such things, that I need but just name a thing of that kind and it was done; so he ordered his gentleman (I should now call him Amy's gentleman) to get me a place in a certain house, where I might see them march.

As he did not appear with me on this occasion, so I had the liberty of taking my woman Amy with me, and stood where we were very well accommodated for the observation which I was to make. I told Amy what I had seen, and she was as forward to make the discovery as I was to have her, and almost as much surprised at the thing itself. In a word, the Gendarmes entered the city, as was expected, and made a most glorious show indeed, being new clothed and armed, and being to have their standards blessed by the Archbishop of Paris. On this occasion they indeed looked very gay, and as they marched very leisurely I had time to take as critical a view and make as nice a search among them as I pleased. Here, in a particular rank eminent for one monstrous-sized man on the right, here, I say, I saw my gentleman again, and a very handsome jolly fellow he was as any in the troop, though not so monstrous large as that great one I spoke of, who it seems was, however, a gentleman of a good family in Gascony, and was called the Giant of Gascony.

It was a kind of good fortune to us, among the other circumstances of it, that something caused the troops to halt in their march a little before that particular rank came right against that window which I stood in, so that then we had occasion to take our full view of him at a small distance, and so as not to doubt of his being the same person.

Amy, who thought she might on many accounts venture with more safety to be particular than I could, asked her gentleman how a particular man whom she saw there among the Gendarmes might be enquired after and found out, she having seen an Englishman riding there which was supposed to be dead in England for several years before she came out of London, and that his wife had married again. It was a question the gentleman did not well understand how to answer, but another person that stood by told her, if she would tell him the gentleman's name, he would endeavour to find him out for her, and asked jestingly if he was her lover. Amy put that off with a laugh but still continued her enquiry, and in such a manner as the gentleman easily perceived she was in earnest; so he left bantering and asked her in what part of the troop he rode. She foolishly told him his name, which she should not have done, and pointing to the cornet that troop carried, which was not then quite out of sight, she let him easily know whereabouts he rode, only she could not name the captain. However, he gave her such directions afterwards that, in short, Amy, who was an indefatigable girl, found him out. It seems he had not changed his name, not supposing any enquiry would be made after him here; but I say Amy found him out and went boldly to his quarters, asked for him, and he came out to her immediately.

I believe I was not more confounded at my first seeing him at Meudon than he was at seeing Amy. He started, and turned pale as death; Amy believed if he had seen her at first in any convenient place for so villainous a purpose, he would have murdered her.

But he started, as I say above, and asked in English, with an admiration, "What are you?" "Sir," says she, "don't you know me?" "Yes," says he, "I knew you when you were alive, but what you are now, whether ghost or substance, I know not." "Be not afraid, sir, of that," says Amy, "I am the same Amy that I was in your service, and do not speak to you now for any hurt, but that I saw you accidentally, yesterday, ride among the soldiers, I thought you might be glad to hear from your friends at London." "Well, Amy," says he then, having a little recovered himself, "how does everybody do? What, is your mistress here?" Thus they began:--

Amy. "My mistress, sir, alas! not the mistress you meant; poor gentlewoman, you left her in a sad condition."

Gent. "Why, that's true, Amy, but it could not be helped. I was in a sad condition myself."

Amy. "I believe so indeed, sir, or else you had not gone away as you did; for it was a very terrible condition you left them all in, that I must say."

Gent. "What did they do after I was gone?"

Amy. "Do, sir! very miserably, you may be sure. How could it be otherwise?"

Gent. "Well, that's true indeed, but you may tell me, Amy, what became of them, if you please; for though I went so away, it was not because I did not love them all very well, but because I could not bear to see the poverty that was coming upon them and which it was not in my power to help. What could I do?"

Amy. "Nay, I believe so indeed, and I have heard my mistress say many times she did not doubt but your affliction was as great as hers almost, wherever you were."

Gent. "Why, did she believe I was alive, then?"

Amy. "Yes, sir, she always said she believed you were alive, because she thought she should have heard something of you if you had been dead."

Gent. "Ay, ay, my perplexity was very great indeed, or else I had never gone away."

Amy. "It was very cruel, though, to the poor lady, sir, my mistress. She almost broke her heart for you at first, for fear of what might befall you, and at last because she could not hear from you."

Gent. "Alas! Amy, what could I do? things were driven to the last extremity before I went. I could have done nothing but help starve them all if I had stayed, and besides, I could not bear to see it."

Amy. "You know, sir, I can say little to what passed before, but I am a melancholy witness to the sad distresses of my poor mistress as long as I stayed with her, and which would grieve your heart to hear them."

Here she tells my whole story to the time that the parish took off one of my children, and which she perceived very much affected him, and he shook his head and said some things very bitter when he heard of the cruelty of his own relations to me.

Gent. "Well, Amy, I have heard enough so far; what did she do afterwards?"

Amy. "I can't give you any further account, sir; my mistress would not let me stay with her any longer, she said she could neither pay me nor subsist me. I told her I would serve her without any wages; but I could not live without victuals, you know, so I was forced to leave her, poor lady, sore against my will, and I heard afterwards that the landlord seized her goods. So she was, I suppose, turned out of doors, for as I went by the door about a month after I saw the house shut up, and about a fortnight after that I found there were workmen at work fitting it up, as I suppose, for a new tenant. But none of the neighbours could tell me what was become of my poor mistress, only that they said she was so poor that it was next to begging; that some of the neighbouring gentlefolks had relieved her or that else she must have starved."

Then she went on and told him that after that they never heard any more of (me) her mistress, but that she had been seen once or twice in the city, very shabby and poor in clothes, and it was thought she worked with her needle for her bread. All this the jade said with so much cunning, and managed and humoured it so well, and wiped her eyes and cried so artificially, that he took it all as it was intended he should, and once or twice she saw tears in his eyes too. He told her it was a moving, melancholy story and it had almost broken his heart at first, but that he was driven to the last extremity and could do nothing but stay and see them all starve, which he could not bear the thoughts of, but should have pistoled himself if any such thing had happened while he was there. That he left (me) his wife all the money he had in the world but £25, which was as little as he could take with him to seek his fortune in the world; he could not doubt but that his relations, seeing they were all rich, would have taken the poor children off and not let them come to the parish; and that his wife was young and handsome and, he thought, might marry again, perhaps to her advantage, and for that very reason he never wrote to her or let her know he was alive, that she might in a reasonable term of years marry, and perhaps mend her fortunes. That he resolved never to claim her, because he should rejoice to hear that she had settled to her mind, and that he wished there had been a law made to empower a woman to marry if her husband was not heard of in so long time, which time he thought should not be above four years, which was long enough to send word in to a wife or family from any part of the world.

Amy said she could say nothing to that but this, that she was satisfied her mistress would marry nobody unless she had certain intelligence that he had been dead from somebody that saw him buried. "But, alas!" says Amy, "my mistress was reduced to such dismal circumstances that nobody would be so foolish to think of her unless it had been somebody to go a-begging with her."

Amy then, seeing him so perfectly deluded, made a long and lamentable outcry, how she had been deluded away to marry a poor footman. "For he is no worse or better," says she, "though he calls himself a lord's gentleman; and here," says Amy, "he has dragged me over into a strange country to make a beggar of me." And then she falls a-howling again and snivelling, which, by the way, was all hypocrisy, but acted so to the life as perfectly deceived him, and he gave entire credit to every word of it.

"Why, Amy," says he, "you are very well dressed, you don't look as if you were in danger of being a beggar." "Ay, hang him," says Amy, "they love to have fine clothes here if they have never a smock under them, but I love to have money in cash rather than a chest full of fine clothes; besides, sir," says she, "most of the clothes I have were given me in the last place I had when I went away from my mistress."

Upon the whole of the discourse Amy got out of him what condition he was in and how he lived, upon her promise to him that if ever she came to England and should see her old mistress, she should not let her know that he was alive. "Alas! sir," says Amy, "I may never come to see England again as long as I live, and if I should, it would be ten thousand to one whether I shall see my old mistress; for how should I know which way to look for her, or what part of England she may be in? Not I," says she, "I don't so much as know how to enquire for her; and if I should," says Amy, "ever be so happy as to see her, I would not do her so much mischief as to tell her where you were, sir, unless she was in a condition to help herself and you too." This further deluded him, and made him entirely open in his conversing with her. As to his own circumstances, he told her she saw him in the highest preferment he had arrived to or was ever like to arrive to, for having no friends or acquaintances in France, and which was worse, no money, he never expected to rise; that he could have been made a lieutenant to a troop of light horse but the week before, by the favour of an officer in the Gendarmes who was his friend, but that he must have found 8,000 livres to have paid for it to the gentleman who possessed it and had leave given him to sell. "But where could I get 8,000 livres," says he, "that have never been master of 500 livres ready money at a time since I came into France?"

"Oh dear! sir," says Amy, "I am very sorry to hear you say so. I fancy if you once got up to some preferment you would think of my old mistress again and do something for her. Poor lady," says Amy, "she wants it, to be sure." And then she falls a-crying again, "'tis a sad thing indeed," says she, "that you should be so hard put to it for money when you had got a friend to recommend you, and should lose it for want of money." "Ay, so it was, Amy, indeed," says he; "but what can a stranger do that has neither money nor friends?" Here Amy puts in again on my account. "Well," says she, "my poor mistress has had the loss, though she knows nothing of it. Oh dear! how happy it would have been, to be sure, sir, you would have helped her all you could." "Ay," says he, "Amy, so I would, with all my heart, and even as I am I would send her some relief if I thought she wanted it; only that then letting her know I was alive might do her some prejudice in case of her settling, or marrying anybody."

"Alas!" says Amy. "Marry! who will marry her in the poor condition she is in?" And so their discourse ended for that time.

All this was mere talk on both sides, and words of course, for on further enquiry Amy found that he had no such offer of a lieutenant's commission or anything like it, and that he rambled in his discourse from one thing to another. But of that in its place.

You may be sure that this discourse as Amy at first related it was moving to the last degree upon me, and I was once going to have sent him the 8,000 livres to purchase the commission he had spoken of; but as I knew his character better than anybody, I was willing to search a little further into it; and so I sent Amy to enquire of some other of the troop to see what character he had, and whether there was anything in the story of a lieutenant's commission or no.

But Amy soon came to a better understanding of him for she presently learnt that he had a most scoundrelly character, that there was nothing of weight in anything he said, but that he was, in short, a mere sharper, one that would stick at nothing to get money, and that there was no depending on anything he said; and that, more especially about the lieutenant's commission, she understood that there was nothing at all in it, but they told her how he had often made use of that sham to borrow money, and move gentlemen to pity him and lend him money in hopes to get him preferment; that he had reported that he had a wife and five children in England whom he maintained out of his pay, and by these shifts had run into debt in several places, and upon several complaints for such things he had been threatened to be turned out of the Gendarmes; and that, in short, he was not to be believed in anything he said, or trusted on any account.

Upon this information Amy began to cool in her further meddling with him, and told me it was not safe for me to attempt doing him any good, unless I resolved to put him upon suspicions and enquiries, which might be to my ruin in the condition I was now in.

I was soon confirmed in this part of his character, for the next time that Amy came to talk with him he discovered himself more effectually; for while she had put him in hopes of procuring one to advance the money for the lieutenant's commission for him upon easy conditions, he by degrees dropped the discourse, then pretended it was too late and that he could not get it, and then descended to ask poor Amy to lend him 500 pistoles.

Amy pretended poverty, that her circumstances were but mean, and that she could not raise such a sum; and this she did to try him to the utmost. He descended to 300, then to 100, then to 50, and then to a pistole, which she lent him; and he, never intending to pay it, played out of her sight as much as he could. And thus being satisfied that he was the same worthless thing he had ever been, I threw off all thoughts of him; whereas had he been a man of any sense and of any principle of honour, I had it in my thoughts to retire to England again, send over for him, and have lived honestly with him. But as a fool is the worst of husbands to do a woman good, so a fool is the worst husband a woman can do good to. I would willingly have done him good, but he was not qualified to receive it or make the best use of it. Had I sent him 10,000 crowns instead of 8,000 livres, and sent it with the express condition that he should immediately have bought himself the commission he talked of with part of the money, and have sent some of it to relieve the necessities of his poor miserable wife at London and to prevent his children to be kept by the parish, it was evident he would have been still but a private trooper, and his wife and children should still have starved at London or been kept of mere charity, as, for aught he knew, they then were.

Seeing therefore no remedy, I was obliged to withdraw my hand from him that had been my first destroyer, and reserve the assistance that I intended to have given him for another more desirable opportunity. All that I had now to do was to keep myself out of his sight, which was not very difficult for me to do considering in what station he lived.

Amy and I had several consultations then upon the main question, namely, how to be sure never to chop upon him again by chance and so be surprised into a discovery, which would have been a fatal discovery indeed. Amy proposed that we should take care always to know where the Gendarmes were quartered, and thereby effectually avoid them; and this was one way.

But this was not so as to be fully to my satisfaction. No ordinary ways of enquiring where the Gendarmes were quartered were sufficient to me, but I found out a fellow who was completely qualified for the work of a spy (for France has plenty of such people). This man I employed to be a constant and particular attendant upon his person and motions, and he was especially employed and ordered to haunt him as a ghost, that he should scarce let him be ever out of his sight. He performed this to a nicety, and failed not to give me a perfect journal of all his motions from day to day; and, whether for his pleasures or his business, was always at his heels.

This was somewhat expensive, and such a fellow merited to be well paid; but he did his business so exquisitely punctual, that this poor man scarce went out of the house without my knowing the way he went, the company he kept, when he went abroad, and when he stayed at home.

By this extraordinary conduct I made myself safe, and so went out in public or stayed at home, as I found he was or was not in a possibility of being at Paris, at Versailles, or any place I had occasion to be at. This, though it was very chargeable, yet as I found it absolutely necessary, so I took no thought about the expense of it, for I knew I could not purchase my safety too dear.

By this management I found an opportunity to see what a most insignificant, unthinking life the poor indolent wretch, who by his unactive temper had at first been my ruin, now lived; how he only rose in the morning to go to bed at night; that saving the necessary motion of the troops, which he was obliged to attend, he was a mere motionless animal, of no consequence in the world; that he seemed to be one who, though he was indeed alive, had no manner of business in life but to stay to be called out of it. He neither kept any company, minded any sport, played at any game, nor indeed did anything of moment, but, in short, sauntered about like one that it was not two livres' value whether he was dead or alive; that when he was gone would leave no remembrance behind him that ever he was here; that if he ever did anything in the world to be talked of, it was only to get five beggars and starve his wife. The journal of his life, which I had constantly sent me every week, was the least significant of anything of its kind that was ever seen. As it had really nothing of earnest in it, so it would make no jest to relate it; it was not important enough so much as to make the reader merry withal, and for that reason I omit it.

Yet this nothing-doing wretch I was obliged to watch and guard against, as against the only thing that was capable of doing me hurt in the world. I was to shun him as we would shun a spectre, or even the devil if he was actually in our way, and it cost me after the rate of 150 livres a month, and very cheap too, to have this creature constantly kept in view. That is to say, my spy undertook never to let him be out of his sight an hour but so as that he could give an account of him; which was much the easier to be done, considering his way of living, for he was sure that for whole weeks together he would be ten hours of the day half asleep on a bench at the tavern door where he quartered, or drunk within the house.

Though this wicked life he led sometimes moved me to pity him and to wonder how so ill-bred, gentlemanly a man as he once was could degenerate into such a useless thing as he now appeared, yet at the same time it gave me most contemptible thoughts of him, and made me often say I was a warning for all the ladies of Europe against marrying of fools. A man of sense falls in the world and gets up again, and a woman has some chance for herself; but with a fool, once fall and ever undone, once in the ditch and die in the ditch, once poor and sure to starve.

Chapter 8

But 'tis time to have done with him. Once I had nothing to hope for but to see him again, now my only felicity was if possible never to see him, and above all to keep him from seeing me; which, as above, I took effectual care of.

Chapter 9

I was now returned to Paris. My little son of honour, as I called him, was left at ----, where my last country seat then was, and I came to Paris at the Prince's request. Thither he came to me as soon as I arrived, and told me he came to give me joy of my return and to make his acknowledgments for that I had given him a son. I thought indeed he had been going to give me a present, and so he did the next day, but in what he said then he only jested with me. He gave me his company all the evening, supped with me about midnight, and did me the honour, as I then called it, to lodge me in his arms all the night, telling me in jest that the best thanks for a son born was giving the pledge for another.

But as I hinted, so it was. The next morning he laid me down on my toilet a purse with 300 pistoles. I saw him lay it down and understood what he meant, but I took no notice of it till I came to it (as it were) casually, then I gave a great cry out and fell a-scolding in my way, for he gave me all possible freedom of speech on such occasions. I told him he was unkind, that he would never give me an opportunity to ask him for anything, and that he forced me to blush by being too much obliged, and the like; all which I knew was very agreeable to him, for as he was bountiful beyond measure, so he was infinitely obliged by my being so backward to ask any favours; and I was even with him, for I never asked him for a farthing in my life.

Upon this rallying him he told me I had either perfectly studied the art of humour, or else what was the greatest difficulty to others was natural to me, adding that nothing could be more obliging to a man of honour than not to be soliciting and craving.

I told him nothing could be craving upon him, that he left no room for it, that I hoped he did not give merely to avoid the trouble of being importuned; I told him he might depend upon it that I should be reduced very low indeed before I offered to disturb him that way.

He said a man of honour ought always to know what he ought to do, and as he did nothing but what he knew was reasonable, he gave me leave to be free with him if I wanted anything; that he had too much value for me to deny me anything if I asked, but that it was infinitely agreeable to him to hear me say that what he did was to my satisfaction.

We strained compliments thus a great while, and as he had me in his arms most part of the time, so upon all my expressions of his bounty to me he put a stop to me with his kisses, and would admit me to go on no further.

I should in this place mention that this Prince was not a subject of France, though at that time he resided at Paris and was much at Court, where I suppose he had or expected some considerable employment. But I mention it on this account, that a few days after this he came to me and told me he was come to bring me not the most welcome news that ever I heard from him in his life. I looked at him a little surprised, but he returned, "Do not be uneasy; it is as unpleasant to me as to you, but I came to consult with you about it and see if it cannot be made a little easy to us both."

I seemed still more concerned and surprised. At last he said it was that he believed he should be obliged to go into Italy, which though otherwise it was very agreeable to him, yet his parting with me made it a very dull thing but to think of.

I sat mute as one thunderstruck for a good while, and it presently occurred to me that I was going to lose him, which indeed I could but ill bear the thoughts of, and as he told me I turned pale. "What's the matter?" said he hastily; "I have surprised you indeed "; and stepping to the sideboard fills a dram of cordial water (which was of his own bringing) and comes to me. "Be not surprised," said he, "I'll go nowhere without you," adding several other things so kind as nothing could exceed it.

I might indeed turn pale, for I was very much surprised at first, believing that this was, as it often happens in such cases, only a project to drop me and break off an amour which he had now carried on so long; and a thousand thoughts whirled about my head in the few moments while I was kept in suspense (for they were but a few)--I say I was indeed surprised, and might perhaps look pale, but I was not in any danger of fainting that I knew of.

However, it not a little pleased me to see him so concerned and anxious about me; but I stopped a little when he put the cordial to my mouth, and taking the glass in my hand, I said, "My lord, your words are infinitely more of a cordial to me than this citron, for as nothing can be a greater affliction than to lose you, so nothing can be a greater satisfaction than the assurance that I shall not have that misfortune."

He made me sit down and sat down by me, and after saying a thousand kind things to me he turns upon me with a smile. "Why, will you venture yourself to Italy with me?" says he. I stopped a while and then answered that I wondered he would ask me that question, for I would go anywhere in the world, or all over the world, wherever he should desire me and give me the felicity of his company.

Then he entered into a long account of the occasion of his journey and how the King had engaged him to go, and some other circumstances which are not proper to enter into here, it being by no means proper to say anything that might lead the reader into the least guess at the person.

But to cut short this part of the story and the history of our journey and stay abroad, which would almost fill up a volume of itself, I say we spent all that evening in cheerful consultations about the manner of our travelling, the equipage and figure he should go in, and in what manner I should go. Several ways were proposed but none seemed feasible, till at last I told him I thought it would be so troublesome, so expensive, and so public that it would be many ways inconvenient to him; and though it was a kind of death to me to lose him, yet that rather than so very much perplex his affairs I would submit to anything.

At the next visit I filled his head with the same difficulties, and then at last came over him with a proposal that I would stay in Paris or where else he should direct, and when I heard of his safe arrival would come away by myself and place myself as near him as I could.

This gave him no satisfaction at all, nor would he hear any more of it, but if I durst venture myself, as he called it, such a journey, he would not lose the satisfaction of my company; and as for the expense, that was not to be named, neither indeed was there room to name it, for I found that he travelled at the King's expense, as well for himself as for all his equipage, being upon a piece of secret service of the last importance.

But after several debates between ourselves he came to this resolution, viz. that he would travel incognito, and so he should avoid all public notice either of himself or of who went with him, and that then he should not only carry me with him, but have a perfect leisure of enjoying my agreeable company (as he was pleased to call it) all the way.

This was so obliging that nothing could be more, so upon this foot he immediately set to work to prepare things for his journey, and by his directions so did I too. But now I had a terrible difficulty upon me, and which way to get over it I knew not; and that was, in what manner to take care of what I had to leave behind me. I was rich, as I have said, very rich, and what to do with it I knew not, nor whom to leave in trust I knew not. I had nobody but Amy in the world, and to travel without Amy was very uncomfortable; or to leave all I had in the world with her, and if she miscarried, be ruined at once, was still a frightful thought, for Amy might die, and whose hands things might fall into I knew not. This gave me great uneasiness and I knew not what to do, for I could not mention it to the Prince lest he should see that I was richer than he thought I was.

But the Prince made all this easy for me, for in concerting measures for our journey he started the thing himself, and asked me merrily one evening whom I would trust with all my wealth in my absence.

"My wealth, my lord," said I, "except what I owe to your goodness, is but small; but yet that little I have, I confess, causes some thoughtfulness, because I have no acquaintance in Paris that I dare trust with it, nor anybody but my woman to leave in the house, and how to do without her upon the road I do not well know."

"As to the road, be not concerned," says the Prince, "I'll provide you servants to your mind; and as for your woman, if you can trust her, leave her here, and I'll put you in a way how to secure things as well as if you were at home." I bowed and told him I could not be put into better hands than his own, and that therefore I would govern all my measures by his directions; so we talked no more of it that night.

The next day he sent me in a great iron chest, so large that it was as much as six lusty fellows could get up the steps into the house, and in this I put indeed all my wealth. And for Amy's safety he ordered a good, honest ancient man and his wife to be in the house with her to keep her company, and a maidservant and a boy, so that there was a good family, and Amy was madam the mistress of the house.

Things being thus secured, we set out incog. as he called it, but we had two coaches and six horses, two chaises, and about eight menservants on horseback all very well armed.

Never was woman better used in this world that went upon no other account than I did. I had three women servants to wait on me, one whereof was an old Madam ----, who thoroughly understood her business and managed everything as if she had been major-domo, so I had no trouble. They had one coach to themselves and the Prince and I in the other, only that sometimes, where he knew it necessary, I went into their coach, and one particular gentleman of the retinue rode with him.

I shall say no more of the journey than that when we came to those frightful mountains the Alps, there was no travelling in our coaches, so he ordered a horse litter, but carried by mules, to be provided for me, and himself went on horseback. The coaches went some other way back to Lyons; then we had coaches hired at Turin which met us at Susa, so that we were accommodated again, and went by easy journeys afterwards to Rome, where his business whatever it was called him to stay some time, and from thence to Venice.

He was as good as his word, indeed, for I had the pleasure of his company and, in a word, engrossed his conversation almost all the way. He took delight in showing me everything that was to be seen, and particularly in telling me something of the history of everything he showed me.

What valuable pains were here thrown away upon one whom he was sure at last to abandon with regret! How below himself did a man of quality and of a thousand accomplishments behave in all this! 'Tis one of my reasons for entering into this part, which otherwise would not be worth relating. Had I been a daughter or a wife of whom it might be said that he had a just concern in their instruction or improvement, it had been an admirable step, but all this to a whore!--to one whom he carried with him upon no account that could be rationally agreeable, and none but to gratify the meanest of human frailties. This was the wonder of it.

But such is the power of a vicious inclination. Whoring was, in a word, his darling crime, the worst excursion he made, for he was otherwise one of the most excellent persons in the world. No passions, no furious excursions, no ostentatious pride, the most humble, courteous, affable person in the world, not an oath, not an indecent word or the least blemish in behaviour was to be seen in all his conversation except as before excepted. And it has given me occasion for many dark reflections since, to look back and think that I should be the snare of such a person's life, that I should influence him to so much wickedness, and that I should be the instrument in the hand of the devil to do him so much prejudice.

We were near two years upon this Grand Tour, as it may be called, during most of which I resided at Rome or at Venice, having only been twice at Florence and once at Naples. I made some very diverting and useful observations in all these places, and particularly of the conduct of the ladies, for I had opportunity to converse very much among them by the help of the old witch that travelled with us. She had been at Naples and at Venice, and had lived in the former several years, where, as I found, she had lived but a loose life, as indeed the women of Naples generally do; and, in short, I found she was fully acquainted with all the intriguing arts of that part of the world.

Here my lord bought me a little female Turkish slave, who, being taken at sea by a Maltese man-of-war, was brought in there, and of her I learnt the Turkish language, their way of dressing and dancing, and some Turkish, or rather Moorish, songs, of which I made use to my advantage on an extraordinary occasion some years after, as you shall hear in its place. I need not say I learnt Italian too, for I got pretty well mistress of that before I had been there a year, and as I had leisure enough and loved the language, I read all the Italian books I could come at.

I began to be so in love with Italy, especially with Naples and Venice, that I could have been very well satisfied to have sent for Amy and have taken up my residence there for life.

As to Rome, I did not like it at all. The swarms of ecclesiastics of all kinds on one side, and the scoundrelly rabbles of the common people on the other, make Rome the unpleasantest place in the world to live in. The innumerable number of valets, lackeys, and other servants is such that they used to say that there are very few of the common people in Rome but what have been footmen or porters or grooms to cardinals or foreign ambassadors. In a word, they have an air of sharping and cozening, quarrelling and scolding, upon their general behaviour, and when I was there the footmen made such a broil between two great families in Rome, about which of their coaches (the ladies being in the coaches on either side) should give way to the other, that there was above thirty people wounded on both sides, five or six killed outright, and both the ladies frighted almost to death.

But I have no mind to write the history of my travels on this side of the world, at least not now; it would be too full of variety.

I must not, however, omit that the Prince continued in all this journey the most kind, obliging person to me in the world, and so constant, that though we were in a country where 'tis well known all manner of liberties are taken, I am yet well assured he neither took the liberty he knew he might have, nor so much as desired it.

I have often thought of this noble person on that account. Had he been but half so true, so faithful and constant to the best lady in the world, I mean his Princess, how glorious a virtue had it been in him, and how free had he been from those just reflections which touched him in her behalf when it was too late.

We had some very agreeable conversations upon this subject, and once he told me, with a kind of more than ordinary concern upon his thoughts, that he was greatly beholden to me for taking this hazardous and difficult journey, for that I had kept him honest. I looked up in his face, and coloured as red as fire. "Well, well," says he, "do not let that surprise you; I do say you have kept me honest." "My lord," said I, "'tis not for me to explain your words, but I wish I could turn 'em my own way. I hope," says I, "and believe we are both as honest as we can be in our circumstances." "Ay, ay," says he, "and honester than I doubt I should have been if you had not been with me. I cannot say but if you had not been here I should have wandered among the gay world here in Naples, and in Venice too, for 'tis not such a crime here as 'tis in other places; but I protest," says he, "I have not touched a woman in Italy but yourself, and more than that, I have not so much as had any desire to it, so that, I say, you have kept me honest."

I was silent, and was glad that he interrupted me, or kept me from speaking, with kissing me, for really I knew not what to say. I was once going to say that if his lady the Princess had been with him she would doubtless have had the same influence upon his virtue, with infinitely more advantage to him, but I considered this might give him offence; and, besides, such things might have been dangerous to the circumstances I stood in, so it passed off. But I must confess I saw that he was quite another man as to women than I understood he had always been before, and it was a particular satisfaction to me that I was thereby convinced that what he said was true, and that he was, as I may say, all my own.

I was with child again in this journey and lay in at Venice, but was not so happy as before. I brought him another son, and a very fine boy it was, but it lived not above two months; nor, after the first touches of affection (which are usual, I believe, to all mothers) were over, was I sorry the child did not live, the necessary difficulties attending it in our travelling being considered.

After these several perambulations my lord told me his business began to close and we would think of returning to France, which I was very glad of, but principally on account of my treasure I had there, which, as you have heard, was very considerable. It is true I had letters very frequently from my maid Amy, with accounts that everything was very safe, and that was very much to my satisfaction. However, as the Prince's negotiations were at an end and he was obliged to return, I was very glad to go; so we returned from Venice to Turin, and on the way I saw the famous city of Milan. From Turin we went over the mountains again, as before, and our coaches met us at Pont-à-Voisin, between Chambéry and Lyons; and so by easy journeys we arrived safely at Paris, having been absent about two years, wanting about eleven days, as above.

I found the little family we left just as we left them and Amy cried for joy when she saw me, and I almost did the same.

The Prince took his leave of me the night before, for as he told me, he knew he should be met upon the road by several persons of quality, and perhaps by the Princess herself. So we lay at two different inns that night lest some should come quite to the place, as indeed it happened.

After this I saw him not for above twenty days, being taken up in his family and also with business, but he sent me his gentleman to tell me the reason of it, and bid me not be uneasy, and that satisfied me effectually.

Chapter 10

In all this affluence of my good fortune I did not forget that I had been rich and poor once already, alternately, and that I ought to know that the circumstances I was now in were not to be expected to last always; that I had one child and expected another, and if I bred often it would something impair me in the great article that supported my interest, I mean what he called beauty; that as that declined I might expect the fire would abate, and the warmth with which I was now so caressed would cool, and in time, like the other mistresses of great men, I might be dropped again; and that, therefore, it was my business to take care that I should fall as softly as I could.

I say I did not forget, therefore, to make as good provision for myself as if I had had nothing to have subsisted on but what I now gained, whereas I had not less than ten thousand pounds, as I said above, which I had amassed, or secured rather, out of the ruins of my faithful friend the jeweller; and which, he little thinking of what was so near him when he went out, told me, though in a kind of a jest, was all my own if he was knocked on the head, and which, upon that title, I took care to preserve.

My greatest difficulty now was how to secure my wealth and to keep what I had got, for I had greatly added to this wealth by the generous bounty of the Prince ----, and the more by the private retired manner of living, which he rather desired for privacy than parsimony, for he supplied me for a more magnificent way of life than I desired if it had been proper.

I shall cut short the history of this prosperous wickedness with telling you I brought him a third son within little more than eleven months after our return from Italy, that now I lived a little more openly, and went by a particular name which he gave me abroad, but which I must omit, viz. the Countess de ----, and had coaches and servants suitable to the quality he had given me the appearance of. And which is more than usually happens in such cases, this held eight years from the beginning, during which time, as I had been very faithful to him, so I must say, as above, that I believe he was so separated to me, that whereas he usually had two or three women which he kept privately, he had not in all that time meddled with any of them, but that I had so perfectly engrossed him that he dropped them all. Not perhaps that he saved much by it, for I was a very chargeable mistress to him, that I must acknowledge, but it was all owing to his particular affection to me, not to my extravagance; for, as I said, he never gave me leave to ask him for anything, but poured in his favours and presents faster than I expected, and so fast as I could not have the assurance to make the least mention of desiring more.

Nor do I speak this of my own guess--I mean about his constancy to me and his quitting all other women--but the old harridan, as I may call her, whom he made the guide of our travelling, and who was a strange old creature, told me a thousand stories of his gallantry, as she called it, and how, as he had no less than three mistresses at one time and, as I found, all, of her procuring, he had of a sudden dropped them all, and that he was entirely lost to both her and them, that they did believe he had fallen into some new hands, but she could never hear whom or where till he sent for her to go this journey. And then the old hag complimented me upon his choice: that she did not wonder I had so engrossed him--so much beauty, etc.--and there she stopped.

Upon the whole I found by her what was, you may be sure, to my particular satisfaction, viz. that, as above, I had him all my own.

But the highest tide has its ebb, and in all things of this kind there is a reflux which sometimes also is more impetuously violent than the first aggression. My Prince was a man of a vast fortune, though no sovereign, and therefore there was no probability that the expense of keeping a mistress could be injurious to him as to his estate. He had also several employments, both out of France as well as in it, for, as above, I say he was not a subject of France, though he lived in that Court. He had a Princess, a wife with whom he had lived several years, and a woman (so the voice of fame reported) the most valuable of her sex, of birth equal to him if not superior, and of fortune proportionable, but in beauty, wit, and a thousand good qualities superior not to most women but even to all her sex; and as to her virtue, the character, which was most justly her due, was that of not only the best of princesses but even the best of women.

They lived in the utmost harmony, as with such a Princess it was impossible to be otherwise. But yet the Princess was not insensible that her lord had his foibles, that he did make some excursions, and particularly that he had one favourite mistress which sometimes engrossed him more than she (the Princess) could wish or be easily satisfied with. However, she was so good, so generous, so truly kind a wife, that she never gave him any uneasiness on this account, except so much as must arise from his sense of her bearing the affront of it with such patience and such a profound respect for him as was in itself enough to have reformed him, and did sometimes shock his generous mind so as to keep him at home, as I may call it, a great while together; and it was not long before I not only perceived it by his absence, but really got a knowledge of the reason of it, and once or twice he even acknowledged it to me.

It was a point that lay not in me to manage. I made a kind of motion once or twice to him to leave me and keep himself to her, as he ought by the laws and rites of matrimony to do, and argued the generosity of the Princess to him to persuade him; but I was a hypocrite, for had I prevailed with him really to be honest,

I had lost him, which I could not bear the thoughts of; and he might easily see I was not in earnest. One time in particular, when I took upon me to talk at this rate, I found when I argued so much for the virtue and honour, the birth, and above all the generous usage he found in the person of the Princess with respect to his private amours, and how it should prevail upon him, etc.--I found it began to affect him, and he returned, "And do you indeed," says he, "persuade me to leave you? Would you have me think you sincere?" I looked up in his face, smiling, "Not for any other favourite, my lord," said I, "that would break my heart, but for madam the Princess!" said I; and then I could say no more. Tears followed, and I sat silent awhile. "Well," said he, "if ever I do leave you it shall be on the virtuous account; it shall be for the Princess, I assure you it shall be for no other woman." "That's enough, my lord," said I, "there I ought to submit; and while I am assured it shall be for no other mistress, I promise Your Highness I will not repine, or that, if I do, it shall be a silent grief, it shall not interrupt your felicity."

All this while I said I knew not what, and said what I was no more able to do than he was able to leave me, which, at that time, he owned he could not do, no, not for the Princess herself.

But another turn of affairs determined this matter, for the Princess was taken very ill, and in the opinion of all her physicians, very dangerously so. In her sickness she desired to speak with her lord and to take her leave of him. At this grievous parting she said so many passionate kind things to him, lamented that she had left him no children (she had had three but they were dead), hinted to him that it was one of the chief things which gave her satisfaction in death, as to this world, that she should leave him room to have heirs to his family by some princess that should supply her place; with all humility, but with a Christian earnestness, recommended to him to do justice to such princess, whoever it should be, from whom, to be sure, he would expect justice; that is to say, to keep to her singly according to the solemnest part of the marriage covenant; humbly asked His Highness's pardon if she had any way offended him, and appealing to Heaven, before whose tribunal she was to appear, that she had never violated her honour or her duty to him, and praying to Jesus and the Blessed Virgin for His Highness;--and thus, with the most moving and most passionate expressions of her affection to him, took her last leave of him and died the next day.

This discourse from a Princess so valuable in herself and so dear to him, and the loss of her following so immediately after, made such deep impressions on him that he looked back with detestation upon the former part of his life, grew melancholy and reserved, changed his society and much of the general conduct of his life, resolved on a life regulated most strictly by the rules of virtue and piety, and, in a word, was quite another man.

The first part of his reformation was a storm upon me, for about ten days after the Princess's funeral he sent a message to me by his gentleman, intimating, though in very civil terms and with a short preamble or introduction, that he desired I would not take it ill that he was obliged to let me know that he could see me no more. His gentleman told me a long story of the new regulation of life his lord had taken up, and that he had been so afflicted for the loss of his Princess, that he thought it would either shorten his life or he would retire into some religious house to end his days in solitude.

I need not direct anybody to suppose how I received the news. I was indeed exceedingly surprised at it, and had much to do to support myself when the first part of it was delivered, though the gentleman delivered his errand with great respect, and with all the regard to me that he was able and with a great deal of ceremony, also telling me how much he was concerned to bring me such a message.

But when I heard the particulars of the story at large, and especially that of the lady's discourse to the Prince a little before her death, I was fully satisfied. I knew very well he had done nothing but what any man must do that had a true sense upon him of the justice of the Princess's discourse to him, and of the necessity there was of his altering his course of life if he intended to be either a Christian or an honest man. I say, when I heard this, I was perfectly easy. I confess it was a circumstance that it might be reasonably expected should have wrought something also upon me. I that had so much to reflect upon more than the Prince, that had now no more temptation of poverty or of the powerful motive which Amy used with me--namely, comply and live, deny and starve--I say, that I that had no poverty to introduce vice, but was grown not only well supplied but rich, and not only rich but was very rich; in a word, richer than I knew how to think of: for the truth of it was that thinking of it some times almost distracted me for want of knowing how to dispose of it and for fear of losing it all again by some cheat or trick, not knowing anybody that I could commit the trust of it to.

Besides, I should add at the close of this affair that the Prince did not, as I may say, turn me off rudely and with disgust, but with all the decency and goodness peculiar to himself and that could consist with a man reformed and struck with the sense of his having abused so good a lady as his late Princess had been. Nor did he send me away empty, but did everything like himself, and in particular ordered his gentleman to pay the rent of the house and all the expense of his two sons, and to tell me how they were taken care of and where; and also that I might at all times inspect the usage they had, and if I disliked anything it should be rectified. And having thus finished everything, he retired into Lorraine or somewhere that way, where he had an estate, and I never heard of him more, I mean not as a mistress.

Chapter 11

Now I was at liberty to go to any part of the world and take care of my money myself. The first thing that I resolved to do was to go directly to England, for there I thought, being among my countryfolks (for I esteemed myself an Englishwoman though I was born in France); but there, I say, I thought I could better manage things than in France, at least that I would be in less danger of being circumvented and deceived. But how to get away with such a treasure as I had with me was a difficult point, and what I was greatly at a loss about.

There was a Dutch merchant in Paris that was a person of great reputation for a man of substance and of honesty, but I had no manner of acquaintance with him, nor did I know how to get acquainted with him so as to discover my circumstances to him; but at last I employed my maid Amy (such I must be allowed to call her, notwithstanding what has been said of her, because she was in the place of a maidservant)--I say I employed my maid Amy to go to him, and she got a recommendation to him from somebody else, I knew not who, so that she got access to him well enough.

But now was my case as bad as before; for when I came to him what could I do? I had money and jewels to a vast value, and I might leave all those with him. That I might indeed do, and so I might with several other merchants in Paris, who would give me bills for it payable at London, but then I ran a hazard of my money, and I had nobody at London to send the bills to and so to stay till I had an account that they were accepted; for I had not one friend in London that I could have recourse to, so that indeed I knew not what to do.

In this case I had no remedy but that I must trust somebody, so I sent Amy to this Dutch merchant, as I said above. He was a little surprised when Amy came to him and talked to him of remitting a sum of about 12,000 pistoles to England, and began to think she came to put some cheat upon him; but when he found that Amy was but a servant, and that I came to him myself, the case was altered presently.

When I came to him myself I presently saw such a plainness in his dealing and such honesty in his countenance, that I made no scruple to tell him my whole story, viz. that I was a widow, that I had some jewels to dispose of, and also some money which I had a mind to send to England and to follow there myself, but being but a woman, and having no correspondence in London or anywhere else, I knew not what to do or how to secure my effects.

He dealt very candidly with me, but advised me, when he knew my case so particularly, to take bills upon Amsterdam and to go that way to England; for that I might lodge my treasure in the bank there in the most secure manner in the world, and that there he could recommend me to a man who perfectly understood jewels and would deal faithfully with me in the disposing them.

I thanked him; but scrupled very much the travelling so far in a strange country, and especially with such a treasure about me, that whether known or concealed, I did not know how to venture with it. Then he told me he would try to dispose of them there, that is, at Paris, and convert them into money, and so get me bills for the whole; and in a few days he brought a Jew to me who pretended to buy the jewels.

As soon as the Jew saw the jewels, I saw my folly, and it was ten thousand to one but I had been ruined and perhaps put to death in as cruel a manner as possible; and I was put in such a fright by it that I was once upon the point of flying for my life, and leaving the jewels and money too in the hands of the Dutchman without any bills or anything else. The case was thus:

As soon as the Jew saw the jewels he falls a-jabbering in Dutch or Portuguese to the merchant, and I could presently perceive that they were in some great surprise, both of them. The Jew held up his hands, looked at me with some horror, then talked Dutch again, and put himself into a thousand shapes, twisting his body and wringing up his face this way and that way in his discourse, stamping with his feet and throwing abroad his hands, as if he was not in a rage only but in a mere fury; then he would turn and give a look at me like the devil; I thought I never saw anything so frightful in my life.

At length I put in a word. "Sir," says I to the Dutch merchant, "what is all this discourse to my business? What is this gentleman in all these passions about? I wish, if he is to treat with me, he would speak, that I may understand him; or if you have business of your own between you that is to be done first, let me withdraw and I'll come again when you are at leisure."

"No, no, madam," says the Dutchman very kindly, "you must not go, all our discourse is about you and your jewels, and you shall hear it presently; it concerns you very much, I assure you." "Concerns me," says I, "what can it concern me so much as to put this gentleman into such agonies? And what makes him give me such devil's looks as he does? Why, he looks as if he would devour me."

The Jew understood me presently, continuing in a kind of rage and speaking in French, "Yes, madam, it does concern you much, very much, very much," repeating the words, shaking his head, and then turning to the Dutchman, "Sir," says he, "pray tell her what is the case." "No," says the merchant, "not yet, let us talk a little further of it by ourselves." Upon which they withdrew into another room, where still they talked very high, but in a language I did not understand. I began to be a little surprised at what the Jew had said, you may be sure, and eager to know what he meant, and was very impatient till the Dutch merchant came back, and that so impatient that I called one of his servants to let him know I desired to speak with him. When he came in I asked his pardon for being so impatient, but told him I could not be easy till he had told me what the meaning of all this was. "Why, madam," says the Dutch merchant, "in short, the meaning is what I am surprised at too. This man is a Jew and understands jewels perfectly well, and that was the reason I sent for him, to dispose of them to him for you; but as soon as he saw them he knew the jewels very distinctly, and flying out in a passion, as you see he did, told me in short that they were the very parcel of jewels which the English jeweller had about him, who was robbed going to Versailles (about eight years ago), to show them to the Prince de ----, and that it was for these very jewels that the poor gentleman was murdered. And he is in all this agony to make me ask you how you came by them, and he says you ought to be charged with the robbery and murder, and put to the question to discover who were the persons that did it, that they might be brought to justice." While he said this the Jew came impudently back into the room without calling, which a little surprised me again.

The Dutch merchant spoke pretty good English, and he knew that the Jew did not understand English at all, so he told me the latter part, when the Jew came into the room, in English; at which I smiled, which put the Jew into his mad fit again, and shaking his head, and making his devil's faces again, he seemed to threaten me for laughing, saying in French this was an affair I should have little reason to laugh at, and the like. At this I laughed again and flouted him, letting him see that I scorned him, and turning to the Dutch merchant, "Sir," says I, "that those jewels were belonging to Mr. ---- the English jeweller," naming his name readily, "in that," says I, "this person is right, but that I should be questioned how I came to have them is a token of his ignorance, which, however, he might have managed with a little more good manners till I had told him who I am. And both he and you too will be more easy in that part when I should tell you that I am the unhappy widow of that Mr. ---- who was so barbarously murdered going to Versailles, and that he was not robbed of those jewels but of others, Mr. ---- having left those behind him with me lest he should be robbed. Had I, sir, come otherwise by them, I should not have been weak enough to have exposed them to sale here, where the thing was done, but have carried them further off."

This was an agreeable surprise to the Dutch merchant, who, being an honest man himself, believed everything I said; which indeed, being all really and literally true except the deficiency of my marriage, I spoke with such an unconcerned easiness, that it might plainly be seen that I had no guilt upon me as the Jew suggested.

The Jew was confounded when he heard that I was the jeweller's wife; but as I had raised his passion with saying he looked at me with a devil's face, he studied mischief in his heart, and answered that should not serve my turn; so called the Dutchman out again, when he told him that he resolved to prosecute this matter further.

There was one kind chance in this affair which indeed was my deliverance, and that was that the fool could not restrain his passion but must let it fly to the

Dutch merchant, to whom, when they withdrew a second time, as above, he told that he would bring a process against me for the murder, and that it should cost me dear for using him at that rate; and away he went, desiring the Dutch merchant to tell him when I would be there again. Had he suspected that the Dutchman would have communicated the particulars to me, he would never have been so foolish as to have mentioned that part to him.

But the malice of his thoughts anticipated him, and the Dutch merchant was so good as to give me an account of his design, which indeed was wicked enough in its nature; but to me it would have been worse than otherwise it would to another, for upon examination I could not have proved myself to be the wife of the jeweller, so the suspicion might have been carried on with the better face; and then I should also have brought all his relations in England upon me, who, finding by the proceedings that I was not his wife but a mistress, or in English a whore, would immediately have laid claim to the jewels, as I had owned them to be his.

This thought immediately rushed into my head as soon as the Dutch merchant had told me what wicked things were in the head of that cursed Jew; and the villain (for so I must call him) convinced the Dutch merchant that he was in earnest by an expression which showed the rest of his design, and that was a plot to get the rest of the jewels into his hand.

When first he hinted to the Dutchman that the jewels were such a man's, meaning my husband's, he made wonderful explanations on account of their having been concealed so long. Where must they have lain? and what was the woman that brought them? and that she, meaning me, ought to be immediately apprehended and put into the hands of justice; and this was the time that, as I said, he made such horrid gestures and looked at me so like a devil.

The merchant hearing him talk at that rate, and seeing him in earnest, said to him, "Hold your tongue a little, this is a thing of consequence; if it be so, let you and I go into the next room and consider of it there." And so they withdrew and left me.

Here, as before, I was uneasy and called him out, and having heard how it was, gave him that answer, that I was his wife, or widow, which the malicious Jew said should not serve my turn. And then it was that the Dutchman called him out again; and in this time of his withdrawing the merchant, finding, as above, that he was really in earnest, counterfeited a little to be of his mind and entered into proposals with him for the thing itself.

In this they agreed to go to an advocate or counsel for directions how to proceed, and to meet again the next day, against which time the merchant was to appoint me to come again with the jewels in order to sell them. "No," says the merchant, "I will go further with her than so; I will desire her to leave the jewels with me, to show to another person, in order to get the better price for them." "That's right," says the Jew, "and I'll engage she shall never be mistress of them again. They shall either be seized by us," says he, "in the King's name, or she shall be glad to give them up to us to prevent her being put to the torture."

The merchant said yes to everything he offered, and they agreed to meet the next morning about it, and I was to be persuaded to leave the jewels with him and come to them the next day at four o'clock in order to make a good bargain for them, and on these conditions they parted. But the honest Dutchman, filled with indignation at the barbarous design, came directly to me and told me the whole story. "And now, madam," says he, "you are to consider immediately what you have to do."

I told him if I was sure to have justice I would not fear all that such a rogue could do to me, but how such things were carried on in France I knew not. I told him the greatest difficulty would be to prove our marriage, for that it was done in England, and in a remote part of England too, and which was worse, it would be hard to produce authentic vouchers of it, because we were married in private. "But as to the death of your husband, madam, what can be said to that?" said he. "Nay," said I, "what can they say to it? In England," added I, "if they would offer such an injury to anyone, they must prove the fact or give just reason for their suspicions. That my husband was murdered, that everyone knows; but that he was robbed, or of what or how much, that none knows, no, not myself; and why was I not questioned for it then? I have lived in Paris ever since, lived publicly, and no man has had yet the impudence to suggest such a thing of me."

"I am fully satisfied of that," says the merchant, "but as this is a rogue who will stick at nothing, what can we say? And who knows what he may swear? Suppose he should swear that he knows your husband had those particular jewels with him the morning when he went out, and that he showed them to him to consider their value and what price he should ask the Prince de ---- for them."

"Nay, by the same rule," said I, "he may swear that I murdered my husband, if he finds it for his turn."

"That's true," said he, "and if he should, I do not see what could save you. But," he added, "I have found out his more immediate design. His design is to have you carried to the Châtelet, that the suspicion may appear just, and then to get the jewels out of your hands if possible, then at last to drop the prosecution on your consenting to quit the jewels to him; and how you will do to avoid this is the question which I would have you consider of."

"My misfortune, sir," said I, "is that I have no time to consider, and I have no person to consider with or advise about it. I find that innocence may be oppressed by such an impudent fellow as this; he that does not value a perjury has any man's life at his mercy. But, sir," said I, "is the justice such here, that while I may be in the hands of the public and under prosecution, he may get hold of my effects and get my jewels into his hands?"

"I don't know," says he, "what may be done in that case; but if not he, if the court of justice should get hold of them, I do not know but you may find it as difficult to get them out of their hands again, and at least it may cost you half as much as they are worth; so I think it would be a much better way to prevent their coming at them at all."

"But what course can I take to do that," says I, "now they have got notice that I have them? If they get me into their hands they will oblige me to produce them, or perhaps sentence me to prison till I do."

"Nay," says he, "as this brute says too, put you to the question, that is, to the torture, on pretence of making you confess who were the murderers of your husband."

"Confess!" said I; "how can I confess what I know nothing of?"

"If they come to have you to the rack," said he, "they will make you confess you did it yourself, whether you did it or no, and then you are cast."

The very word rack frighted me to death almost, and I had no spirit left in me. "Did it myself!" said I; "that's impossible!"

"No, madam," says he, "'tis far from impossible; the most innocent people in the world have been forced to confess themselves guilty of what they never heard of, much less had any hand in."

"What then must I do?" said I; "what would you advise me to?"

"Why," says he, "I would advise you to be gone. You intended to go away in four or five days, and you may as well go in two days; and if you can do so, I shall manage it so that he shall not suspect your being gone for several days after." Then he told me how the rogue would have me ordered to bring the jewels the next day for sale, and that then he would have me apprehended; how he had made the Jew believe he would join with him in his design, and that he (the merchant) would get the jewels into his hands. "Now," says the merchant, "I shall give you bills for the money you desired, immediately, and such as shall not fail of being paid. Take your jewels with you and go this very evening to St. Germain-en-Laye; I'll send a man thither with you, and from thence he shall guide you to-morrow to Rouen, where there lies a ship of mine just ready to sail for Rotterdam. You shall have your passage in that ship on my account, and I will send orders for him to sail as soon as you are on board, and a letter to my friend at Rotterdam to entertain and take care of you."

This was too kind an offer for me, as things stood, not to be accepted and be thankful for; and as to my going away, I had prepared everything for parting, so that I had little to do but to go back, take two or three boxes and bundles and such things, and my maid Amy, and be gone.

Then the merchant told me the measures he had resolved to take to delude the Jew while I made my escape, which were very well contrived indeed. "First," said he, "when he comes to-morrow, I shall tell him that I proposed to you to leave the jewels with me as we agreed, but that you said you would come and bring them in the afternoon, so that we must stay for you till four o'clock; but then at that time I will show a letter from you as if just come in, wherein you shall excuse your not coming for that some company came to visit you and prevented you, but that you desire me to take care that the gentleman be ready to buy your jewels, and that you will come to-morrow at the same hour without fail.

"When to-morrow is come we shall wait at the time, but you not appearing, I shall seem most dissatisfied and wonder what can be the reason; and so we shall agree to go the next day to get out a process against you. But the next day, in the morning, I'll send to give him notice that you have been at my house, but, he not being there, have made another appointment, and that I desire to speak with him. When he comes I'll tell him you appear perfectly blind as to your danger, and that you appeared much disappointed that he did not come, though you could not meet the night before, and obliged me to have him here to-morrow at three o'clock. When to-morrow comes," says he, "you shall send word that you are taken so ill that you cannot come out for that day, but that you will not fail the next day; and the next day you shall neither come nor send or let us ever hear any more of you, for by that time you shall be in Holland, if you please."

I could not but approve all his measures, seeing they were so well contrived and in so friendly a manner for my benefit; and as he seemed to be so very sincere, I resolved to put my life in his hands. Immediately I went to my lodgings and sent away Amy with such bundles as I had prepared for my travelling. I also sent several parcels of my fine furniture to the merchant's house to be laid up for me, and bringing the key of the lodgings with me, I came back to his house. Here we finished our matters of money, and I delivered into his hands 7,800 pistoles in bills and money, a copy of an assignment on the Town House of Paris for 4,000 pistoles at 3 per cent. interest, attested, and a procuration for receiving the interest half-yearly, but the original I kept myself.

I could have trusted all I had with him, for he was perfectly honest and had not the least view of doing me any wrong; indeed, after it was so apparent that he had, as it were, saved my life, or at least saved me from being exposed and ruined--I say, after this, how could I doubt him in anything?

When I came to him he had everything ready as I wanted and as he had proposed. As to my money, he gave me first of all an accepted bill, payable at Rotterdam, for 4,000 pistoles, and drawn from Genoa upon a merchant at Rotterdam, payable to a merchant at Paris and endorsed by him to my merchant. This he assured me would be punctually paid, and so it was, to a day; the rest I had in other bills of exchange drawn by himself upon other merchants in Holland. Having secured my jewels too, as well as I could, he sent me away the same evening in a friend's coach, which he had procured for me, to St. Germain, and the next morning to Rouen. He also sent a servant of his own on horseback with me, who provided everything for me, and who carried his orders to the captain of the ship, which lay about three miles below Rouen, in the river, and by his directions I went immediately on board. The third day after I was on board the ship went away, and we were out at sea the next day after that. And thus I took my leave of France and got clear of an ugly business, which, had it gone on, might have ruined me and sent me back as naked to England as I was a little before I left it.

Chapter 12

AND now Amy and I were at leisure to look upon the mischiefs that we had escaped; and had I had any religion, or any sense of a Supreme Power managing, directing, and governing in both causes and events in this world, such a case as this would have given anybody room to have been very thankful to the Power who had not only put such a treasure into my hand, but given me such an escape from the ruin that threatened me; but I had none of those things about me. I had indeed a grateful sense upon my mind of the generous friendship of my deliverer, the Dutch merchant, by whom I was so faithfully served, and by whom, as far as relates to second causes, I was preserved from destruction.

I say I had a grateful sense upon my mind of his kindness and faithfulness to me, and I resolved to show him some testimony of it as soon as I came to the end of my rambles, for I was yet in a state of uncertainty, and sometimes that gave me a little uneasiness too. I had paper indeed for my money, and he had showed himself very good to me in conveying me away, as above. But I had not seen the end of things yet, for unless the bills were paid I might still be a great loser by my Dutchman, and he might perhaps have contrived all that affair of the Jew to put me into a fright and get me to run away, and that as if it were to save my life; that if the bills should be refused I was cheated, with a witness, and the like. But these were but surmises, and indeed were perfectly without cause, for the honest man acted as honest men always do, with an upright and disinterested principle, and with a sincerity not often to be found in the world. What gain he made by the exchange was just, and was nothing but what was his due and was in the way of his business, but otherwise he made no advantage of me at all.

When I passed in the ship between Dover and Calais, and saw beloved England once more under my view--England, which I counted my native country, being the place I was bred up in, though not born there--a strange kind of joy possessed my mind, and I had such a longing desire to be there that I would have given the master of the ship twenty pistoles to have stood over and set me on shore in the Downs. And when he told me he could not do it, that is, that he durst not do it if I would have given him a hundred pistoles, I secretly wishful that a storm would rise that might drive the ship over to the coast of England whether they would or not, that I might be set on shore anywhere upon English ground.

Chapter 12

This wicked wish had not been out of my thoughts above two or three hours, but the master steering away to the north, as was his course to do, we lost sight of land on that side and only had the Flemish shore in view on our right hand, or, as the seamen call it, the starboard side; and then with the loss of the sight the wish for landing in England abated, and I considered how foolish it was to wish myself out of the way of my business; that if I had been on shore in England, I must go back to Holland on account of my bills, which were so considerable, and I having no correspondence there, that I could not have managed it without going myself. But we had not been out of sight of England many hours before the weather began to change; the winds whistled and made a noise, and the seamen said to one another that it would blow hard at night. It was then about two hours before sunset, and we were passed by Dunkirk and I think they said we were in sight of Ostend; but then the wind grew high and the sea swelled, and all things looked terrible, especially to us that understood nothing but just what we saw before us; in short, night came on, and very dark it was, the wind freshened and blew harder and harder, and about two hours within night it blew a terrible storm.

I was not quite a stranger to the sea, having come from Rochelle to England when I was a child, and gone from London by the River Thames to France afterward, as I have said. But I began to be alarmed a little with the terrible clamour of the men over my head, for I had never been in a storm, and so had never seen the like or heard it; and once, offering to look out at the door of the steerage, as they called it, it struck me with such horror, the darkness, the fierceness of the wind, the dreadful height of the waves, and the hurry the Dutch sailors were in, whose language I did not understand one word of, neither when they cursed nor when they prayed--I say all these things together filled me with terror, and, in short, I began to be very much frighted.

When I was come back into the great cabin, there sat Amy, who was very seasick, and I had a little before given her a sup of cordial water to help her stomach. When Amy saw me come back and sit down without speaking, for so I did, she looked two or three times up at me. At last she came running to me. "Dear madam!" says she, "what is the matter? What makes you look so pale? Why, you ain't well; what is the matter?" I said nothing still, but held up my hands two or three times. Amy doubled her importunities. Upon that I said no more but, "Step to the steerage door and look out, as I did." So she went away immediately and looked too, as I had bidden her. But the poor girl came back again in the greatest amazement and horror that ever I saw any poor creature in, wringing her hands and crying out she was undone! she was undone! she should be drowned! They were all lost! Thus she ran about the cabin like a mad thing, and as perfectly out of her senses as anyone in such a case could be supposed to be.

I was frighted myself, but when I saw the girl in such a terrible agony it brought me a little to myself, and I began to talk to her and put her in a little hope. I told her there was many a ship in a storm that was not cast away, and I hoped we should not be drowned; that it was true the storm was very dreadful, but I did not see that the seamen were so much concerned as we were. And so I talked to her as well as I could, though my heart was full enough of it as well as Amy's, and death began to stare in my face, ay, and something else too, that is to say, conscience, and my mind was very much disturbed, but I had nobody to comfort me.

But Amy being in so much worse a condition, that is to say, so much more terrified at the storm than I was, I had something to do to comfort her. She was, as I have said, like one distracted, and went raving about the cabin crying out she was undone! undone! she should be drowned! and the like; and at last the ship giving a jerk, by the force, I suppose, of some violent wave, it threw poor Amy quite down, for she was weak enough before with being seasick; and as it threw her forward the poor girl struck her head against the bulkhead, as the seamen call it, of the cabin, and laid her as dead as a stone upon the floor, or deck, that is to say, she was so to all appearance.

I cried out for help, but it had been all one to have cried out on the top of a mountain where nobody had been within five miles of me; for the seamen were so engaged and made so much noise, that nobody heard me or came near me. I opened the great cabin door and looked into the steerage to cry for help, but there, to increase my fright, were two seamen on their knees at prayers, and only one man who steered, and he made a groaning noise too, which I took to be saying his prayers, but it seems it was answering to those above when they called to him to tell him which way to steer.

Here was no help for me or for poor Amy, and there she lay so still and in such a condition, that I did not know whether she was dead or alive. In this fright I went to her and lifted her a little way up, setting her on the deck with her back to the boards of the bulkhead, and I got a little bottle out of my pocket and held it to her nose, and rubbed her temples, and what else I could do, but still Amy showed no signs of life, till I felt for her pulse but could hardly distinguish her to be alive. However, after a great while she began to revive, and in about half an hour she came to herself, but remembered nothing at first of what had happened to her for a good while more.

When she recovered more fully she asked me where she was. I told her she was in the ship yet, but God knows how long it might be. "Why, madam," says she, "is not the storm over?" "No, no," says I, "Amy." "Why, madam," says she, "it was calm just now" (meaning when she was in the swooning fit occasioned by her fall). "Calm! Amy," says I, "'tis far from calm; it may be it will be calm by and by, when we are all drowned and gone to heaven."

"Heaven! madam," says she, "what makes you talk so? Heaven! I go to heaven! No, no, if I am drowned I am damned! Don't you know what a wicked creature I have been? I have been a whore to two men, and have lived a wretched abominable life of vice and wickedness for fourteen years. Oh, madam, you know it, and God knows it; and now I am to die, to be drowned. Oh! what will become of me? I am undone for ever! Ay, madam, for ever! to all eternity! Oh, I am lost! I am lost! If I am drowned I am lost for ever!"

All these, you will easily suppose, must be so many stabs into the very soul of one in my own case. It immediately occurred to me, "Poor Amy! what art thou that I am not? What hast thou been that I have not been? Nay, I am guilty of my own sin and thine too." Then it came to my remembrance that I had not only been the same with Amy, but that I had been the devil's instrument to make her wicked; that I had stripped her and prostituted her to the very man that I had been naught with myself; that she had but followed me. I had been her wicked example, and I had led her into all, and that as we had sinned together, now we were likely to sink together.

All this repeated itself to my thoughts at that very moment, and every one of Amy's cries sounded thus in my ears. "I am the wicked cause of it all; I have been thy ruin, Amy; I have brought thee to this, and now thou art to suffer for the sin I have enticed thee to; and if thou art lost for ever, what must I be? what must be my portion?"

It is true this difference was between us, that I said all these things within myself, and sighed and mourned inwardly; but Amy, as her temper was more violent, spoke aloud and cried and called out aloud like one in an agony.

I had but small encouragement to give her, and indeed could say but very little, but I got her to compose herself a little and not let any of the people of the ship understand what she meant or what she said. But even in her greatest composure she continued to express herself with the utmost dread and terror on account of the wicked life she had lived, and crying out she should be damned and the like, which was very terrible to me who knew what condition I was in myself.

Upon these serious considerations I was very penitent too for my former sins, and cried out, though softly, two or three times, "Lord, have mercy upon me." To this I added abundance of resolutions of what a life I would live if it should please God but to spare my life but this one time; how I would live but a single and a virtuous life, and spend a great deal of what I had thus wickedly got in acts of charity and doing good.

Under these dreadful apprehensions I looked back on the life I had led with the utmost contempt and abhorrence. I blushed, and wondered at myself how I could act thus, how I could divest myself of modesty and honour and prostitute myself for gain; and I thought if ever it should please God to spare me this one time from death, it would not be possible that I should be the same creature again.

Amy went further. She prayed, she resolved, she vowed to lead a new life if God would spare her but this time. It now began to be daylight, for the storm held all night long, and it was some comfort to see the light of another day, which indeed none of us expected; but the sea went mountains high, and the noise of the water was as frightful to us as the sight of the waves; nor was any land to be seen, nor did the seamen know whereabout they were. At last, to our great joy, they made land, which was in England and on the coast of Suffolk; and the ship being in the utmost distress, they ran for the shore at all hazards, and with great difficulty got into Harwich, where they were safe as to the danger of death. But the ship was so full of water and so much damaged, that if they had not laid her on shore the same day she would have sunk before night, according to the opinion of the seamen, and of the workmen on shore too who were hired to assist them in stopping their leaks.

Amy was revived as soon as she heard they had espied land, and went out upon the deck, but she soon came in again to me. "Oh, madam," says she, "there's the land indeed to be seen; it looks like a ridge of clouds, and may be all a cloud for aught I know, but if it be land 'tis a great way off; and the sea is in such a combustion, we shall perish before we can reach it. 'Tis the dreadfullest sight to look at the waves that ever was seen; why, they are as high as mountains, we shall certainly be all swallowed up for all the land is so near."

I had conceived some hope that if they saw land we should be delivered, and I told her she did not understand things of that nature; that she might be sure if they saw land they would go directly towards it, and would make into some harbour. But it was, as Amy said, a frightful distance to it. The land looked like clouds, and the sea went as high as mountains, so that no hope appeared in the seeing the land, but we were in fear of foundering before we could reach it. This made Amy so desponding still; but as the wind, which blew from the east or that way, drove us furiously towards the land, so when about half an hour after I stepped to the steerage door and looked out I saw the land much nearer than Amy represented it, so I went in and encouraged Amy again, and indeed was encouraged myself.

In about an hour or something more we saw, to our infinite satisfaction, the open harbour of Harwich and the vessel standing directly towards it, and in a few minutes more the ship was in smooth water, to our inexpressible comfort. And thus I had, though against my will and contrary to my true interest, what I wished for, to be driven away to England, though it was by a storm.

Nor did this incident do either Amy or me much service; for, the danger being over, the fears of death vanished with it, ay, and our fear of what was beyond death also. Our sense of the life we had lived went off, and with our return to life our wicked taste of life returned, and we were both the same as before, if not worse. So certain is it that the repentance which is brought about by the mere apprehensions of death wears off as those apprehensions wear off, and death-bed repentance, or storm repentance, which is much the same, is seldom true.

However, I do not tell you that this was all at once neither. The fright we had at sea lasted a little while afterwards, at least the impression was not quite blown off as soon as the storm; especially poor Amy, as soon as she set her foot on shore, she fell flat upon the ground and kissed it, and gave God thanks for her deliverance from the sea; and turning to me when she got up, "I hope, madam," says she, "you will never go upon the sea again."

I know not what ailed me, not I; but Amy was much more penitent at sea, and much more sensible of her deliverance when she landed and was safe, than I was. I was in a kind of stupidity, I know not well what to call it. I had a mind full of horror in the time of the storm, and saw death before me as plainly as Amy, but my thoughts got no vent as Amy's did. I had a silent, sullen kind of grief which could not break out either in words or tears, and which was, therefore, much the worse to bear.

I had a terror upon me for my wicked past life, and firmly believed I was going to the bottom, launching into death, where I was to give an account of all my past actions. And in this state, and on that account, I looked back upon my wickedness with abhorrence, as I have said above. But I had no sense of repentance from the true motive of repentance; I saw nothing of the corruption of nature, the sin of my life as an offence against God, as a thing odious to the holiness of His being, as abusing His mercy and despising His goodness. In short, I had no thorough effectual repentance, no sight of my sins in their proper shape, no view of a Redeemer or hope in Him. I had only such a repentance as a criminal has at the place of execution, who is sorry, not that he has committed the crime, as it is a crime, but sorry that he is to be hanged for it.

It is true Amy's repentance wore off too as well as mine, but not so soon. However, we were both very grave for a time.

As soon as we could get a boat from the town we went on shore, and immediately went to a public-house in the town of Harwich, where we were to consider seriously what was to be done, and whether we should go up to London or stay till the ship was refitted, which they said would be a fortnight, and then go for Holland as we intended and as business required.

Reason directed that I should go to Holland, for there I had all my money to receive, and there I had persons of good reputation and character to apply to, having letters to them from the honest Dutch merchant at Paris; and they might perhaps give me a recommendation again to merchants in London, and so I should get acquaintance with some people of figure, which was what I loved, whereas now I knew not one creature in the whole city of London or anywhere else that I could go and make myself known to. Upon these considerations I resolved to go to Holland, whatever came of it.

But Amy cried and trembled and was ready to fall into fits when I did but mention going upon the sea again, and begged of me not to go; or, if I would go, that I would leave her behind, though I was to send her a-begging. The people in the inn laughed at her and jested with her, asked her if she had any sins to confess that she was ashamed should be heard of, and that she was troubled with an evil conscience; told her if she came to sea and to be in a storm, if she had lain with her master she would certainly tell her mistress of it; and that it was a common thing for poor maids to confess all the young men they had lain with. That there was once a poor girl that went over with her mistress, whose husband was a ----r in ---- in the city of London, who confessed in the terror of a storm that she had lain with her master and all the apprentices so often, and in such and such places, and made the poor mistress, when she returned to London, fly at her husband and make such a stir as was indeed the ruin of the whole family. Amy could bear all that well enough, for though she had indeed lain with her master, it was with her mistress's knowledge and consent, and, which was worse, was her mistress's own doing. I record it to the reproach of my own vice, and to expose the excesses of such wickedness as they deserve to be exposed.

I thought Amy's fear would have been over by that time the ship would be gotten ready, but I found the girl was rather worse and worse; and when I came to the point that we must go on board or lose the passage, Amy was so terrified that she fell into fits, so the ship went away without us.

But my going being absolutely necessary, as above, I was obliged to go in the packet-boat some time after and leave Amy behind at Harwich, but with directions to go to London and stay there, to receive letters and orders from me what to do. Now I was become, from a lady of pleasure, a woman of business, and of great business, too, I assure you.

I got me a servant at Harwich, to go over with me, who had been at Rotterdam, knew the place and spoke the language, which was a great help to me, and away I went. I had a very quick passage and pleasant weather, and, coming to Rotterdam, soon found out the merchant to whom I was recommended, who received me with extraordinary respect; and first he acknowledged the accepted bill for 4,000 pistoles, which he afterwards paid punctually. Other bills that I had also payable at Amsterdam he procured to be received for me, and whereas one of the bills for 1,200 crowns was protested at Amsterdam, he paid it me himself, for the honour of the endorser, as he called it, which was my friend the merchant at Paris.

There I entered into a negotiation, by his means, for my jewels, and he brought me several jewellers to look on them, and particularly one to value them and to tell me what every particular was worth. This was a man who had great skill in jewels but did not trade at that time, and he was desired by the gentleman that I was with to see that I might not be imposed upon.

All this work took me up near half a year, and by managing my business thus myself and having large sums to do with, I became as expert in it as any she-merchant of them all. I had credit in the bank for a large sum of money, and bills and notes for much more.

After I had been here about three months my maid Amy writes me word that she had received a letter from her friend, as she called him--that, by the way, was the Prince's gentleman, that had been Amy's extraordinary friend indeed, for Amy owned to me he had lain with her a hundred times; that is to say, as often as he pleased, and perhaps in the eight years which that affair lasted it might be a great deal oftener. This was what she called her friend, whom she corresponded with upon this particular subject, and among other things sent her this particular news that my extraordinary friend, my real husband who rode in the Gendarmes, was dead, that he was killed in a rencounter, as they call it, or accidental scuffle among the troopers; and so the jade congratulated me upon my being now a real free woman. "And now, madam," says she at the end of her letter, "you have nothing to do but come hither and set up a coach and a good equipage, and if beauty and a good fortune won't make you a duchess, nothing will." But I had not fixed my measures yet. I had no inclination to be a wife again; I had had such bad luck with my first husband, I hated the thoughts of it. I found that a wife is treated with indifference, a mistress with a strong passion; a wife is looked upon as but an upper servant, a mistress is a sovereign; a wife must give up all she has, have every reserve she makes for herself be thought hard of, and be upbraided with her very pin-money, whereas a mistress makes the saying true, that what a man has is hers, and what she has is her own; the wife bears a thousand insults and is forced to sit still and bear it or part and be undone, a mistress insulted helps herself immediately and takes another.

These were my wicked arguments for whoring, for I never set against them the difference another way, I may say, every other way; how that, first, a wife appears boldly and honourably with her husband, lives at home and possesses his house, his servants, his equipages, and has a right to them all and to call them her own, entertains his friends, owns his children, and has the return of duty and affection from them, as they are here her own, and claims upon his estate, by the custom of England, if he dies and leaves her a widow.

The whore skulks about in lodgings, is visited in the dark, disowned upon all occasions before God and man, is maintained indeed for a time, but is certainly condemned to be abandoned at last, and left to the miseries of fate and her own just disaster. If she has any children her endeavour is to get rid of them and not maintain them, and if she lives she is certain to see them all hate her and be ashamed of her. While the vice rages and the man is in the devil's hand, she has him, and while she has him she makes a prey of him; but if he happen to fall sick, if any disaster befall him, the cause of all lies upon her, he is sure to lay all his misfortunes at her door; and if once he comes to repentance or makes one step towards a reformation, he begins with her, leaves her, uses her as she deserves, hates her, abhors her, and sees her no more. And that with this never-failing addition, namely, that the more sincere and unfeigned his repentance is, the more earnestly he looks up, and the more effectually he looks in, the more his aversion to her increases, and he curses her from the bottom of his soul; nay, it must be from a kind of excess of charity if he so much as wishes God may forgive her.

The opposite circumstances of a wife and whore are such and so many, and I have since seen the difference with such eyes, as I could dwell upon the subject a great while, but my business is history. I had a long sense of folly yet to run over; perhaps the moral of all my story may bring me back again to this part, and if it does I shall speak of it fully.

While I continued in Holland I received several letters from my friend (so I had good reason to call him) the merchant in Paris, in which he gave me a further account of the conduct of that rogue the Jew, and how he acted after I was gone; how impatient he was while the said merchant kept him in suspense, expecting me to come again, and how he raged when he found I came no more.

It seems, after he found I did not come, he found out by his unwearied inquiry where I had lived, and that I had been kept as a mistress by some great person, but he could never learn by whom, except that he learnt the colour of his livery. In pursuit of this enquiry he guessed at the right person, but could not make it out or offer any positive proof of it; but he found out the Prince's gentleman, and talked so saucily to him of it that the gentleman treated him, as the French call it, au coup de bâton; that is to say, caned him very severely, as he deserved. And that not satisfying him or curing his insolence, he was met late one night upon the Pont Neuf in Paris by two men, who, muffling him up in a great cloak, carried him into a more private place and cut off both his ears, telling him it was for talking impudently of his superiors, adding that he should take care to govern his tongue better and behave with more manners, or the next time they would cut his tongue out of his head.

This put a check to his sauciness that way, but he comes back to the merchant and threatened to begin a process against him for corresponding with me and being accessory to the murder of the jeweller, etc.

The merchant found by his discourse that he supposed I was protected by the said Prince de ----, nay, the rogue said he was sure I was in his lodgings at Versailles--for he never had so much as the least intimation of the way I was really gone--but that I was there he was certain, and certain that the merchant was privy to it. The merchant bade him defiance. However, he gave him a great deal of trouble and put him to a great charge, and had like to have brought him in for a party to my escape; in which case he would have been obliged to have produced me, and that in the penalty of some capital sum of money.

But the merchant was too many for him another way; for he brought an information against him for a cheat, wherein laying down the whole fact, how he intended falsely to accuse the widow of the jeweller for the supposed murder of her husband, that he did it purely to get the jewels from her, and that he offered to bring him (the merchant) in, to be confederate with him and to share the jewels between them; proving also his design to get the jewels into his hands and then to have dropped the prosecution upon condition of my quitting the jewels to him. Upon this charge he got him laid by the heels; so he was sent to the Conciergerie, that is to say, to Bridewell, and the merchant cleared. He got out of jail in a little while, though not without the help of money, and continued teasing the merchant a long while; and at last threatening to assassinate and murder him, so the merchant, who having buried his wife about two months before was now a single man, and not knowing what such a villain might do, thought fit to quit Paris, and came away to Holland also.

It is most certain that, speaking of originals, I was the source and spring of all that trouble and vexation to this honest gentleman; and as it was afterwards in my power to have made him full satisfaction and did not, I cannot say but I added ingratitude to all the rest of my follies. But of that I shall give a fuller account presently.

Chapter 13

I was surprised one morning when, being at the merchant's house whom he had recommended me to in Rotterdam, and being busy in his counting-house managing my bills and preparing to write a letter to him to Paris, I heard a noise of horses at the door; which is not very common in a city where everybody passes by water; but he had, it seems, ferried over the Maas from Wilhemstad, and so came to the very door. And I, looking towards the door upon hearing the horses, saw a gentleman alight and come in at the gate. I knew nothing and expected nothing, to be sure, of the person, but, as I say was surprised, and indeed more than ordinarily surprised, when coming nearer to me I saw it was my merchant of Paris, my benefactor, and indeed my deliverer.

I confess it was an agreeable surprise to me, and I was exceeding glad to see him who was so honourable and so kind to me, and who indeed had saved my life. As soon as he saw me he ran to me, took me in his arms and kissed me with a freedom that he never offered to take with me before. "Dear Madam ----," says he, "I am glad to see you safe in this country; if you had stayed two days longer in Paris you had been undone." I was so glad to see him that I could not speak for a good while, and I burst out into tears without speaking a word for a minute; but I recovered that disorder and said, "The more, sir, is my obligation to you that saved my life"; and added, "I am glad to see you here, that I may consider how to balance an account in which I am so much your debtor."

"You and I will adjust that matter easily," says he, "now we are so near together. Pray where do you lodge?" says he.

"In a very honest good house," said I, "where that gentleman, your friend, recommended me," pointing to the merchant in whose house we then were.

"And where you may lodge too, sir," says the gentleman, "if it suits with your business and your other conveniency."

"With all my heart," says he. "Then, madam," adds he, turning to me, "I shall be near you, and have time to tell you a story, which will be very long and yet many ways very pleasant to you, how troublesome that devilish fellow the Jew has been to me on your account, and what a hellish snare he had laid for you if he could have found you."

"I shall have leisure too, sir," said I, "to tell you all my adventures since that; which have not been a few, I assure you."

In short, he took up his lodgings in the same house where I lodged, and the room he lay in opened, as he was wishing it would, just opposite to my lodging-room; so we could almost call out of bed to one another, and I was not at all shy of him on that score, for I believed him perfectly honest, and so indeed he was; and if he had not, that article was at present no part of my concern.

It was not till two or three days, and after his first hurries of business were over, that we began to enter into the history of our affairs on every side, but when we began it took up all our conversation for almost a fortnight. First I gave him a particular account of everything that happened material upon my voyage, and how we were driven into Harwich by a very terrible storm; how I had left my woman behind me, so frighted with the danger she had been in that she durst not venture to set her foot into a ship again any more; and that I had not come myself if the bills I had of him had not been payable in Holland, but that money, he might see, would make a woman go anywhere.

He seemed to laugh at all our womanish fears upon the occasion of the storm, telling me it was nothing but what was very ordinary in those seas, but that they had harbours on every coast, so near that they were seldom in danger of being lost indeed. "For," says he, "if they cannot fetch one coast, they can always stand away for another, and run afore it," as he called it, "for one side or other." But when I came to tell him what a crazy ship it was, and how, even when they got into Harwich and into smooth water, they were fain to run the ship on shore or she would have sunk in the very harbour. And when I told him that when I looked out at the cabin door I saw the Dutchmen, one upon his knees here and another there, at their prayers, then indeed he acknowledged I had reason to be alarmed. But smiling, he added, "But you, madam," says he, "are so good a lady, and so pious, you would but have gone to heaven a little the sooner, the difference had not been much to you."

I confess when he said this it made all the blood turn in my veins, and I thought I should have fainted. "Poor gentleman!" thought I, "you know little of me; what would I give to be really what you really think me to be!" He perceived the disorder, but said nothing till I spoke; when, shaking my head, "Oh, sir!" said I, "death in any shape has some terror in it, but in the frightful figure of a storm at sea and a sinking ship it comes with a double, a treble, and indeed an inexpressible horror, and if I were that saint you think me to be, which, God knows, I am not, 'tis still very dismal; I desire to die in a calm if I can." He said a great many good things, and very prettily ordered his discourse between serious reflection and compliment; but I had too much guilt to relish it as it was meant, so I turned it off to something else and talked of the necessity I had on me to come to Holland, but I wished myself safe on shore in England again.

He told me he was glad I had such an obligation upon me to come over into Holland, however, but hinted that he was so interested in my welfare, and besides had such further designs upon me, that if I had not so happily been found in Holland, he was resolved to have gone to England to see me, and that it was one of the principal reasons of his leaving Paris.

I told him I was extremely obliged to him for so far interesting himself in my affairs, but that I had been so far his debtor before, that I knew not how anything could increase the debt; for I owed my life to him already, and I could not be in debt for anything more valuable than that.

He answered in the most obliging manner possible that he would put it in my power to pay that debt, and all the obligations besides that ever he had or should be able to lay upon me.

I began to understand him now, and to see plainly that he resolved to make love to me. But I would by no means seem to take the hint, and beside I knew that he had a wife with him in Paris, and I had, just then at least, no gust to any more intriguing. However, he surprised me into a sudden notice of the thing a little while after by saying something in his discourse that he did, as he said, in his wife's days. I started at that word. "What mean you by that, sir?" said I. "Have you not a wife at Paris?" "No, madam, indeed," said he, "my wife died the beginning of September last"; which, it seems, was but a little after I came away.

We lived in the same house all this while, and as we lodged not far off of one another, opportunities were not wanting of as near an acquaintance as we might desire; nor have such opportunities the least agency in vicious minds to bring to pass even what they might not intend at first.

However, though he courted so much at a distance, yet his pretensions were very honourable; and as I had before found him a most disinterested friend and perfectly honest in his dealings, even when I trusted him with all I had, so now I found him strictly virtuous; till I made him otherwise myself, even almost whether he would or no, as you shall hear.

It was not long after our former discourse when he repeated what he had insinuated before, namely, that he had yet a design to lay before me, which, if I would agree to his proposals, would more than balance all accounts between us. I told him I could not reasonably deny him anything, and except one thing, which I hoped and believed he would not think of, I should think myself very ungrateful if I did not do everything for him that lay in my power.

He told me what he should desire of me would be fully in my power to grant, or else he should be very unfriendly to offer it, and still all this while he declined making the proposal, as he called it, and so for that time we ended our discourse, turning it off to other things. So that, in short, I began to think he might have met with some disaster in his business, and might have come away from Paris in some discredit, or had had some blow on his affairs in general. And as really I had kindness enough to have parted with a good sum to have helped him, and was in gratitude bound to have done so, he having so effectually saved to me all I had, so I resolved to make him the offer the first time I had an opportunity, which two or three days after offered itself, very much to my satisfaction.

He had told me at large, though on several occasions, the treatment he had met with from the Jew, and what expense he had put him to; how at length he had cast him, as above, and had recovered good damages of him, but that the rogue was unable to make him any considerable reparation. He had told me also how the

Prince de ----'s gentleman had resented his treatment of his master, and how he had caused him to be used upon the Pont Neuf, etc., as I have mentioned above, which I laughed at most heartily.

"It is a pity," said I, "that I should sit here and make that gentleman no amends. If you would direct me, sir," said I, "how to do it, I would make him a handsome present, and acknowledge the justice he had done to me as well as to the Prince his master." He said he would do what I directed in it, so I told him I would send him 500 crowns. "That's too much," said he, "for you are but half interested in the usage of the Jew; it was on his master's account he corrected him, not on yours." Well, however, we were obliged to do nothing in it, for neither of us knew how to direct a letter to him nor to direct anybody to him; so I told him I would leave it till I came to England, for that my woman Amy corresponded with him and that he had made love to her.

"Well, but, sir," said I, "as in requital for his generous concern of me I am careful to think of him; it is but just that what expense you have been obliged to be at, which was all on my account, should be repaid you; and therefore," said I, "let me see----" And there I paused, and began to reckon up what I had observed from his own discourse it had cost him in the several disputes and hearings which he had with that dog of a Jew, and I cast them up at something above 2,130 crowns; so I pulled out some bills which I had upon a merchant in Amsterdam and a particular account in bank, and was looking on them in order to give them to him.

When he, seeing evidently what I was going about, interrupted me with some warmth, and told me he would have nothing of me on that account, and desired I would not pull out my bills and papers on that score; that he had not told me the story on that account or with any such view; that it had been his misfortune first to bring that ugly rogue to me, which though it was with a good design, yet he would punish himself with the expense he had been at for his being so unlucky to me; that I could not think so hard of him as to suppose he would take money of me, a widow, for serving me and doing acts of kindness to me in a strange country, and in distress too. But he said he would repeat what he had said before, that he kept me for a deeper reckoning, and that, as he had told me, he would put me into a posture to even all that favour, as I called it, at once, so we should talk it over another time and balance all together.

Now I expected it would come out, but still he put it off as before, from whence I concluded it could not be a matter of love, for that those things are not usually delayed in such a manner, and therefore it must be a matter of money. Upon which thought I broke the silence and told him that as he knew I had, by obligation, more kindness for him than to deny any favour to him that I could grant, and that he seemed backward to mention his case, I begged leave of him to give me leave to ask him whether anything lay upon his mind with respect to his business and effects in the world; that if it did, he knew what I had in the world as well as I did, and that if he wanted money I would let him have any sum for his occasion as far as five or six thousand pistoles, and he should pay me as his own affairs would permit; and that if he never paid me, I would assure him that I would never give him any trouble for it.

He rose up with ceremony, and gave me thanks in terms that sufficiently told me he had been bred among people more polite and more courteous than is esteemed the ordinary usage of the Dutch; and after his compliment was over he came nearer to me, and told me that he was obliged to assure me, though with repeated acknowledgments of my kind offer, that he was not in any want of money; that he had met with no uneasiness in any of his affairs, no, not of any kind whatever, except that of the loss of his wife and one of his children, which indeed had troubled him much; but that this was no part of what he had to offer me, and by granting which I should balance all obligations. But that, in short, it was that seeing Providence had (as it were for that purpose) taken his wife from him, I would make up the loss to him; and with that he held me fast in his arms and, kissing me, would not give me leave to say no, and hardly to breathe.

At length having got room to speak, I told him that, as I had said before, I could deny him but one thing in the world; I was very sorry he should propose that thing only that I could not grant.

I could not but smile, however, to myself that he should make so many circles and roundabout motions to come at a discourse which had no such rarity at the bottom of it, if he had known all. But there was another reason why I resolved not to have him, when, at the same time, if he had courted me in a manner less honest or virtuous, I believe I should not have denied him. But I shall come to that part presently.

He was, as I have said, long a-bringing it out, but when he had brought it out he pursued it with such importunities as would admit of no denial, at least he intended they should not; but I resisted them obstinately, and yet with expressions of the utmost kindness and respect for him that could be imagined, often telling him there was nothing else in the world that I could deny him, and showing him all the respect and upon all occasions treating him with intimacy and freedom as if he had been my brother.

He tried all the ways imaginable to bring his design to pass, but I was inflexible. At last he thought of a way which, he flattered himself, would not fail; nor would he have been mistaken perhaps in any other woman in the world but me. This was to try if he could take me at an advantage and get to bed to me, and then, as was most rational to think, I should willingly enough marry him afterwards.

We were so intimate together that nothing but man and wife could, or at least ought to be, more; but still our freedoms kept within the bounds of modesty and decency. But one evening, above all the rest, we were very merry, and I fancied he pushed the mirth to watch for his advantage, and I resolved that I would, at least, feign to be as merry as he, and that, in short, if he offered anything he should have his will easily enough.

About one o'clock in the morning, for so long we sat up together, I said, "Come, 'tis one o'clock, I must go to bed." "Well," says he, "I'll go with you." "No, no," says I, "go to your own chamber." He said he would go to bed with me.

"Nay," says I, "if you will, I don't know what to say; if I can't help it, you must." However, I got from him, left him and went into my chamber, but did not shut the door; and as he could easily see that I was undressing myself, he steps to his own room, which was but on the same floor, and in a few minutes undresses himself also and returns to my door in his gown and slippers.

I thought he had been gone indeed, and so that he had been in jest; and, by the way, thought either he had no mind to the thing or that he never intended it; so I shut my door, that is, latched it, for I seldom locked or bolted it, and went to bed. I had not been in bed a minute but he comes in his gown to the door and opens it a little way, but not enough to come in or look in, and says softly, "What, are you really gone to bed?" "Yes, yes," says I, "get you gone." "No, indeed," says he, "I shall not begone, you gave me leave before to come to bed, and you shan't say get you gone now." So he comes into my room, and then turns about and fastens the door, and immediately comes to the bedside to me. I pretended to scold and struggle, and bid him begone with more warmth than before, but it was all one. He had not a rag of clothes on but his gown and slippers and shirt, so he throws off his gown and throws open the bed and came in at once.

I made a seeming resistance, but it was no more indeed; for, as above, I resolved from the beginning he should lie with me if he would, and for the rest, I left it to come after.

Well, he lay with me that night and the two next, and very merry we were all the three days between; but the third night he began to be a little more grave. "Now, my dear," says he, "though I have pushed this matter further than ever I intended, or than I believe you expected from me, who never made any pretences to you but what were very honest, yet to heal it all up and let you see how sincerely I meant at first and how honest I will ever be to you, I am ready to marry you still, and desire you to let it be done to-morrow morning; and I will give you the same fair conditions of marriage as I would have done before."

This, it must be owned, was a testimony that he was very honest and that he loved me sincerely, but I construed it quite another way, namely, that he aimed at the money. But how surprised did he look, and how was he confounded, when he found me receive his proposal with coldness and indifference and still tell him that it was the only thing I could not grant.

He was astonished. "What, not take me now!" says he, "when I have been abed with you!" I answered coldly, though respectfully still, "It is true, to my shame be it spoken," says I, "that you have taken me by surprise and have had your will of me, but I hope you will not take it ill that I cannot consent to marry, for all that; if I am with child," said I, "care must be taken to manage that as you shall direct. I hope you won't expose me for my having exposed myself to you, but I cannot go any further." And at that point I stood, and would hear of no matrimony by any means.

Now because this may seem a little odd, I shall state the matter clearly as I understood it myself. I knew that while I was a mistress, it is customary for the person kept to receive from them that keep; but if I should be a wife, all I had then was given up to the husband, and I was thenceforth to be under his authority only; and as I had money enough, and needed not fear being what they call a cast-off mistress, so I had no need to give him twenty thousand pounds to marry me, which had been buying my lodging too dear a great deal.

Thus his project of coming to bed to me was a bite upon himself, while he intended it for a bite upon me, and he was no nearer his aim of marrying me than he was before. All his arguments he could urge upon the subject of matrimony were at an end, for I positively declined marrying him; and as he had refused the thousand pistoles which I had offered him in compensation for his expenses and loss at Paris with the Jew, and had done it upon the hopes he had of marrying me, so when he found his way difficult still he was amazed, and, I had some reason to believe, repented that he had refused the money.

But thus it is when men run into wicked measures to bring their designs about. I, that was infinitely obliged to him before, began to talk to him as if I had balanced accounts with him now, and that the favour of lying with a whore was equal, not to the thousand pistoles only, but to all the debt I owed him for saving my life and all my effects.

But he drew himself into it, and though it was a dear bargain, yet it was a bargain of his own making; he could not say I had tricked him into it. But as he projected and drew me in to lie with him, depending that it was a sure game in order to a marriage, so I granted him the favour, as he called it, to balance the account of favours received from him and keep the thousand pistoles with a good grace.

He was extremely disappointed in this article and knew not how to manage for a great while, and, as I dare say, if he had not expected to have made it an earnest for marrying me, he would never have attempted me the other way; so, I believed, if it had not been for the money which he knew I had, he would never have desired to marry me after he had lain with me. For where is the man that cares to marry a whore, though of his own making? And as I knew him to be no fool, so I did him no wrong when I supposed that, but for the money, he would not have had any thoughts of me that way, especially after my yielding as I had done; in which it is to be remembered that I made no capitulation for marrying him when I yielded to him, but let him do just what he pleased, without any previous bargain.

Well, hitherto we went upon guesses at one another's designs; but as he continued to importune me to marry, though he had lain with me and still did lie with me as often as he pleased, and I continued to refuse to marry him, though I let him lie with me whenever he desired it--I say, as these two circumstances made up our conversation, it could not continue long thus but we must come to an explanation.

One morning in the middle of our unlawful freedoms, that is to say, when we were in bed together, he sighed and told me he desired my leave to ask me one question, and that I would give him an answer to it with the same ingenuous freedom and honesty that I had used to treat him with. I told him I would. Why, then, his question was, why I would not marry him seeing I allowed him all the freedoms of a husband. "Oh," says he, "my dear, since you have been so kind as to take me to your bed, why will you not make me your own and take me for good and all, that we may enjoy ourselves without any reproach to one another?"

I told him that as I confessed it was the only thing I could not comply with him in, so it was the only thing in all my actions that I could not give him a reason for; that it was true I had let him come to bed to me, which was supposed to be the greatest favour a woman could grant, but it was evident, and he might see it, that as I was sensible of the obligation I was under to him for saving me from the worst circumstance it was possible for me to be brought to, I could deny him nothing; and if I had had any greater favour to yield him I should have done it, that of matrimony only excepted, and he could not but see that I loved him to an extraordinary degree, in every part of my behaviour to him; but that as to marrying, which was giving up my liberty, it was what once he knew I had done, and he had seen how it had hurried me up and down in the world and what it had exposed me to; that I had an aversion to it, and desired he would not insist upon it; he might easily see I had no aversion to him, and that if I was with child by him, he should see a testimony of my kindness to the father, for that I would settle all I had in the world upon the child.

He was mute a good while. At last says he, "Come, my dear, you are the first woman in the world that ever lay with a man and then refused to marry him, and therefore there must be some other reason for your refusal; and I have therefore one other request, and that is, if I guess at the true reason and remove the objection, will you then yield to me?" I told him if he removed the objection I must needs comply, for I should certainly do everything that I had no objection against.

"Why then, my dear, it must be that either you are already engaged and married to some other man, or you are not willing to dispose of your money to me, and expect to advance yourself higher with your fortune. Now if it be the first of these, my mouth will be stopped, and I have no more to say; but if it be the last, I am prepared effectually to remove the objection and answer all you can say on that subject."

I took him up short at the first of these, telling him he must have base thoughts of me indeed to think that I could yield to him in such a manner as I had done, and continue it with so much freedom as he found I did, if I had a husband or were engaged to any other man; and that he might depend upon it, that was not my case, nor any part of my case.

"Why then," said he, "as to the other, I have an offer to make to you that shall take off all the objection, viz. that I will not touch one pistole of your estate more than shall be with your own voluntary consent, neither now nor at any other time, but you shall settle it as you please, for your life, and upon whom you shall please after your death." That I should see he was able to maintain me without it, and that it was not for that that he followed me from Paris.

I was indeed surprised at that part of his offer, and he might easily perceive it. It was not only what I did not expect, but it was what I knew not what answer to make to. He had indeed removed my principal objection, nay, all my objections, and it was not possible for me to give any answer; for if upon so generous an offer

I should agree with him, I then did as good as confess that it was upon the account of my money that I refused him, and that though I could give up my virtue and expose myself, yet I would not give up my money, which, though it was true, yet was really too gross for me to acknowledge, and I could not pretend to marry him upon that principle neither. Then as to having him, and make over all my estate out of his hands, so as not to give him the management of what I had, I thought it would be not only a little gothic and inhuman, but would be always a foundation of unkindness between us and render us suspected one to another. So that, upon the whole, I was obliged to give a new turn to it and talk upon a kind of an elevated strain which really was not in my thoughts at first at all; for I own, as above, the divesting myself of my estate and putting my money out of my hand was the sum of the matter that made me refuse to marry. But, I say, I gave it a new turn upon this occasion, as follows:

I told him I had perhaps differing notions of matrimony from what the received custom had given us of it; that I thought a woman was a free agent as well as a man, and was born free, and, could she manage herself suitably, might enjoy that liberty to as much purpose as the men do; that the laws of matrimony were indeed otherwise, and mankind at this time acted quite upon other principles; and those such, that a woman gave herself entirely away from herself in marriage, and capitulated only to be at best but an upper servant, and from the time she took the man she was no better or worse than the servant among the Israelites who had his ears bored, that is, nailed to the door-post, who by that act gave himself up to be a servant during life.

That the very nature of the marriage contract was, in short, nothing but giving up liberty, estate, authority, and everything to the man, and the woman was indeed a mere woman ever after, that is to say, a slave.

He replied that though in some respects it was as I had said, yet I ought to consider that as an equivalent to this the man had all the care of things devolved upon him; that the weight of business lay upon his shoulders, and as he had the trust, so he had the toil of life upon him, his was the labour, his the anxiety of living; that the woman had nothing to do but to eat the fat and drink the sweet, to sit still and look round her, be waited on and made much of, be served and loved and made easy, especially if the husband acted as became him; and that, in general, the labour of the man was appointed to make the woman live quiet and unconcerned in the world; that they had the name of subjection without the thing, and if in inferior families they had the drudgery of the house and care of the provisions upon them, yet they had indeed much the easier part. For, in general, the women had only the care of managing, that is, spending what their husbands get; and that a woman had the name of subjection indeed, but that they generally commanded not the men only, but all they had, managed all for themselves, and where the man did his duty the woman's life was all ease and tranquillity, and that she had nothing to do but to be easy and to make all that were about her both easy and merry.

I returned that while a woman was single she was a masculine in her politic capacity; that she had then the full command of what she had and the full direction of what she did; that she was a man in her separated capacity, to all intents and purposes that a man could be so to himself; that she was controlled by none because accountable to none, and was in subjection to none; so I sung these two lines of Mr. ----'s:

Oh! 'tis pleasant to be free, The sweetest miss is liberty.

I added that whoever the woman was that had an estate and would give it up to be the slave of a great man, that woman was a fool, and must be fit for nothing but a beggar; that it was my opinion a woman was as fit to govern and enjoy her own estate without a man as a man was without a woman, and that if she had a mind to gratify herself as to sexes, she might entertain a man as a man does a mistress; that while she was thus single she was her own, and if she gave away that power she merited to be as miserable as it was possible that any creature could be.

All he could say could not answer the force of this as to argument; only this, that the other way was the ordinary method that the world was guided by; that he had reason to expect I should be content with that which all the world was contented with; that he was of the opinion that a sincere affection between a man and his wife answered all the objections that I had made about the being a slave, a servant, and the like; and where there was a mutual love there could be no bondage, but that there was but one interest, one aim, one design, and all conspired to make both very happy.

"Ay," said I, "that is the thing I complain of. The pretence of affection takes from a woman everything that can be called herself; she is to have no interest, no aim, no view, but all is the interest, aim, and view of the husband. She is to be the passive creature you spoke of," said I; "she is to lead a life of perfect indolence, and living by faith (not in God, but) in her husband, she sinks or swims as he is either fool or wise man, unhappy or prosperous, and in the middle of what she thinks is her happiness and prosperity she is engulfed in misery and beggary which she had not the least notice, knowledge, or suspicion of. How often have I seen a woman living in all the splendour that a plentiful fortune ought to allow her: with her coaches and equipages, her family and rich furniture, her attendants and friends, her visitors and good company, all about her to-day, to-morrow surprised with disaster, turned out of all by a commission of bankrupt, stripped to the clothes on her back; her jointure, suppose she had it, is sacrificed to the creditors so long as her husband lived, and she turned into the street and left to live on the charity of her friends, if she has any, or follow the monarch her husband into the Mint, and live there on the wreck of his fortunes till he is forced to run away from her, even there; and then she sees her children starve, herself miserable, breaks her heart, and cries herself to death. This," says I, "is the state of many a lady that has had ten thousand pounds to her portion."

He did not know how feelingly I spoke this and what extremities I had gone through of this kind; how near I was to the very last article above, viz. crying myself to death, and how I really starved for almost two years together.

But he shook his head and said, where had I lived, and what dreadful families had I lived among that had frighted me into such terrible apprehensions of things? That these things indeed might happen where men ran into hazardous things in trade, and without prudence or due consideration launched their fortunes in a degree beyond their strength, grasping at adventures beyond their stocks, and the like; but that, as he was started in the world, if I would embark with him, he had a fortune equal with mine; that together we should have no occasion of engaging in business any more, but that in any part of the world where I had a mind to live, whether England, France, Holland, or where I would, we might settle and live as happily as the world could make any one live; that if I desired the management of our estate when put together, if I would not trust him with mine, he would trust me with his; that we would be upon one bottom, and I should steer. "Ay," says I, "you'll allow me to steer, that is, hold the helm, but you'll conn the ship, as they call it; that is, as at sea, a boy serves to stand at the helm, but he that gives him the orders is pilot."

He laughed at my simile. "No," says he, "you shall be pilot, then, you shall conn the ship." "Ay," says I, "as long as you please, but you can take the helm out of my hand when you please and bid me go spin. It is not you," says I, "that I suspect, but the law of matrimony puts the power into your hands, bids you do it, commands you to command, and binds me, forsooth, to obey. You, that are now upon even terms with me, and I with you," says I, "are the next hour set up upon the throne, and the humble wife placed at your footstool; all the rest, all that you call oneness of interest, mutual auction, and the like, is courtesy and kindness, then, and a woman is indeed infinitely obliged where she meets with it, but can't help herself where it fails."

Well, he did not give it over yet, but came to the serious part, and there he thought he should be too many for me. He first hinted that marriage was decreed by Heaven, that it was the fixed state of life which God had appointed for man's felicity and for establishing a legal posterity, that there could be no legal claim of estates by inheritance but by children born in wedlock, that all the rest was sunk under scandal and illegitimacy; and very well he talked upon that subject indeed.

But it would not do; I took him short there. "Look you, sir," said I, "you have an advantage of me there indeed, in my particular case, but it would not be generous to make use of it. I readily grant that it were better for me to have married you than to admit you to the liberty I have given you, but as I could not reconcile my judgment to marriage for the reasons above, and had kindness enough for you and obligation too much on me to resist you, I suffered your rudeness and gave up my virtue. But I have two things before me to heal up that breach of honour without that desperate one of marriage, and those are, repentance for what is past, and putting an end to it for time to come."

He seemed to be concerned to think that I should take him in that manner. He assured me that I misunderstood him; that he had more manners, as well as more kindness for me, and more justice than to reproach me with what he had been the aggressor in and had surprised me into; that what he spoke referred to my words above; that the woman, if she thought fit, might entertain a man as the man did a mistress; and that I seemed to mention that way of living as justifiable, and setting it as a lawful thing and in the place of matrimony.

Well, we strained some compliments upon those points not worth repeating, and I added I supposed when he got to bed to me he thought himself sure of me; and indeed in the ordinary course of things, after he had lain with me, he ought to think so; but that, upon the same foot of argument which I had discoursed with him upon, it was just the contrary, and when a woman had been weak enough to yield up the last point before wedlock it would be adding one weakness to another to take the man afterwards, to pin down the shame of it upon herself all the days of her life, and bind herself to live all her time with the only man that could upbraid her with it; that in yielding at first she must be a fool, but to take the man is to be sure to be called fool; that to resist a man is to act with courage and vigour and to cast off the reproach which, in the course of things, drops out of knowledge and dies. The man goes one way and the woman another, as fate and the circumstances of living direct, and if they keep one another's counsel the folly is heard no more of. "But to take the man," said I, "is the most preposterous thing in nature, and (saving your presence) is to befoul oneself and live always in the smell of it. No, no," added I, "after a man has lain with me as a mistress he ought never to lie with me as a wife; that's not only preserving the crime in memory, but it is recording it in the family. If the woman marries the man afterwards she bears the reproach of it to the last hour; if her husband is not a man of a hundred thousand he some time or other upbraids her with it; if he has children they fail not one way or other to hear of it; if the children are virtuous they do their mother the justice to hate her for it, if they are wicked they give her the mortification of doing the like, and giving her for the example. On the other hand, if the man and the woman part, there is an end of the crime, and an end of the clamour. Time wears out the memory of it, or a woman may remove but a few streets and she soon outlives it and hears no more of it."

He was confounded at this discourse and told me he could not say but I was right in the main, that as to that part relating to managing estates, it was arguing à la cavalier; it was in some sense right if the women were able to carry it on so, but that in general the sex were not capable of it, their heads were not turned for it, and they had better choose a person capable and honest, that knew how to do them justice as women as well as to love them, and that then the trouble was all taken off their hands.

I told him it was a dear way of purchasing their ease, for very often when the trouble was taken off their hands, so was their money too, and that I thought it was far safer for the sex not to be afraid of the trouble, but to be really afraid of their money; that if nobody was trusted, nobody would be deceived, and the staff in their own hands was the best security in the world.

He replied that I had started a new thing in the world; that however I might support it by subtle reasoning, yet it was a way of arguing that was contrary to the general practice, and that he confessed he was much disappointed in it; that had he known I would have made such a use of it he would never have attempted what he did, which he had no wicked design in, resolving to make me reparation, and that he was very sorry he had been so unhappy; that he was very sure he should never upbraid me with it hereafter, and had so good an opinion of me as to believe I did not suspect him; but seeing I was positive in refusing him, notwithstanding what had passed, he had nothing to do but to secure me from reproach by going back again to Paris, that so, according to my own way of arguing, it might die out of memory, and I might never meet with it again to my disadvantage.

I was not pleased with this part at all, for I had no mind to let him go neither, and yet I had no mind to give him such hold of me as he would have had; and thus I was in a kind of suspense, irresolute, and doubtful what course to take.

I was in the house with him, as I have observed, and I saw evidently that he was preparing to go back to Paris, and particularly I found he was remitting money to Paris, which was, as I understood afterwards, to pay for some wines which he had given order to have bought for him at Troyes in Champagne, and I knew not what course to take; and besides that, I was very loath to part with him. I found also that I was with child by him, which was what I had not yet told him of, and sometimes I thought not to tell him of it at all; but I was in a strange place, and had no acquaintance, though I had a great deal of substance, which indeed, having no friends there, was the more dangerous to me.

This obliged me to take him one morning, when I saw him, as I thought, a little anxious about his going and irresolute. Says I to him, "I fancy you can hardly find in your heart to leave me now." "The more unkind is it in you," said he, "severely unkind, to refuse a man that knows not how to part with you."

"I am so far from being unkind to you," said I, "that I will go all over the world with you, if you desire me, except to Paris, where you know I can't go."

"It is a pity so much love," said he, "on both sides should ever separate."

"Why then," said I, "do you go away from me?"

"Because," said he, "you won't take me."

"But if I won't take you," said I, "you may take me anywhere but to Paris."

He was very loath to go anywhere, he said, without me, but he must go to Paris or to the East Indies.

I told him I did not use to court, but I durst venture myself to the East Indies with him if there was a necessity of his going.

He told me, God be thanked, he was in no necessity of going anywhere, but that he had a tempting invitation to go to the Indies.

I answered I would say nothing to that, but that I desired he would go anywhere but to Paris, because there he knew I must not go.

He said he had no remedy but to go where I could not go, for he could not bear to see me if he must not have me.

I told him that was the unkindest thing he could say of me, and that I ought to take it very ill, seeing I knew how very well to oblige him to stay without yielding to what he knew I could not yield to.

This amazed him, and he told me I was pleased to be mysterious, but that he was sure it was in nobody's power to hinder him going if he resolved upon it, except me, who had influence enough upon him to make him do anything.

Yes, I told him, I could hinder him, because I knew he could no more do an unkind thing by me than he could do an unjust one; and to put him out of his pain, I told him I was with child.

He came to me and, taking me in his arms and kissing me a thousand times almost, said, why would I be so unkind not to tell him that before?

I told him 'twas hard that, to have him stay, I should be forced do as criminals do to avoid the gallows, plead my belly, and that I thought I had given him testimonies enough of an affection equal to that of a wife; if I had not only lain with him, been with child by him, shown myself unwilling to part with him but offered to go to the East Indies with him, and except one thing that I could not grant, what could he ask more?

He stood mute a good while, but afterwards told me he had a great deal more to say if I could assure him that I would not take ill whatever freedom he might use with me in his discourse.

I told him he might use any freedom in words with me, for a woman who had given leave to such other freedoms as I had done, had left herself no room to take anything ill, let it be what it would.

"Why then," he said, "I hope you believe, madam, I was born a Christian, and that I have some sense of sacred things upon my mind. When I first broke in upon my own virtue and assaulted yours, when I surprised and, as it were, forced you to that which neither you intended nor I designed but a few hours before, it was upon a presumption that you would certainly marry me, if once I could go at length with you, and it was with an honest resolution to make you my wife.

"But I have been surprised with such a denial that no woman in such circumstances ever gave to a man, for certainly it was never known that any woman refused to marry a man that had first lain with her, much less a man that had gotten her with child. But you go upon different notions from all the world, and though you reason upon it so strongly that a man knows hardly what to answer, yet I must own there is something in it shocking to nature, and something very unkind to yourself. But, above all, it is unkind to the child that is yet unborn, who, if we marry, will come into the world with advantage enough, but, if not, is ruined before it is born, must bear the eternal reproach of what it is not guilty of, must be branded from its cradle with a mark of infamy, be loaded with the crimes and follies of its parents, and suffer for sins that it never committed. This I take to be very hard and indeed cruel to the poor infant not yet born, whom you cannot think of with any patience, if you have the common affection of a mother, and not do that for it which should at once place it on a level with the rest of the world, and not leave it to curse its parents for what also we ought to be ashamed of. I cannot, therefore," says he, "but beg and entreat you, as you are a Christian and a mother, not to let the innocent lamb you go with be ruined before it is born, and leave it to curse and reproach us hereafter for what may be so easily avoided.

"Then, dear madam," said he with a world of tenderness (and I thought I saw tears in his eyes), "allow me to repeat it, that I am a Christian, and consequently I do not allow what I have rashly, and without due consideration, done--I say I do not approve of it as lawful; and therefore though I did, with a view I have mentioned, one unjustifiable action, I cannot say that I could satisfy myself to live in a continual practice of what in judgment we must both condemn. And though I love you above all the women in the world, and have done enough to convince you of it by resolving to marry you after what has passed between us, and by offering to quit all pretensions to any part of your estate, so that I should, as it were, take a wife after I had lain with her, and without a farthing portion, which, as my circumstances are, I need not do--I say, notwithstanding my affection to you, which is inexpressible, yet I cannot give up soul as well as body, the interest of this world, and the hopes of another; and you cannot call this my disrespect to you."

If ever any man in the world was truly valuable for the strictest honesty of intention, this was the man, and if ever woman in her senses rejected a man of merit on so trivial and frivolous a pretence, I was the woman; but surely it was the most preposterous thing that ever woman did.

He would have taken me as a wife, but would not entertain me as a whore. Was ever woman angry with any gentleman on that head? And was ever woman so stupid to choose to be a whore where she might have been an honest wife? But infatuations are next to being possessed of the devil. I was inflexible, and pretended to argue upon the point of a woman's liberty, as before, but he took me short, and with more warmth than he had yet used with me, though with the utmost respect, replied, "Dear madam, you argue for liberty at the same time that you restrain yourself from that liberty which God and Nature has directed you to take, and, to supply the deficiency, propose a vicious liberty which is neither honourable nor religious. Will you propose liberty at the expense of modesty?"

I returned that he mistook me; I did not propose it, I only said that those that could not be content without concerning the sexes in that affair might do so indeed, might entertain a man as men do a mistress if they thought fit; but he did not hear me say I would do so, and though by what had passed he might well censure me in that part, yet he should find for the future, that I should freely converse with him without any inclination that way.

He told me he could not promise that for himself, and thought he ought not to trust himself with the opportunity; for that, as he had failed already, he was loath to lead himself into the temptation of offending again, and that this was the true reason of his resolving to go back to Paris; not that he could willingly leave me, and would be very far from wanting my invitation, but if he could not stay upon terms that became him, either as an honest man or a Christian, what could he do? And he hoped, he said, I could not blame him that he was unwilling anything that was to call him father should upbraid him with leaving him in the world to be called bastard; adding that he was astonished to think how I could satisfy myself to be so cruel to an innocent infant not yet born; professed he could neither bear the thoughts of it, much less bear to see it, and hoped I would not take it ill that he could not stay to see me delivered, for that very reason.

I saw he spoke this with a disturbed mind and that it was with some difficulty that he restrained his passion, so I declined any further discourse upon it, only said I hoped he would consider of it. "Oh, madam!" says he, "do not bid me consider, 'tis for you to consider." And with that he went out of the room in a strange kind of confusion, as was easy to be seen in his countenance.

If I had not been one of the foolishest, as well as wickedest creatures upon earth, I could never have acted thus. I had one of the honestest, completest gentlemen upon earth at my hand; he had in one sense saved my life, but he had saved that life from ruin in a most remarkable manner. He loved me even to distraction, and had come from Paris to Rotterdam on purpose to seek me; he had offered me marriage even after I was with child by him, and had offered to quit all his pretensions to my estate, and give it up to my own management, having a plentiful estate of his own. Here I might have settled myself out of the reach even of disaster itself; his estate and mine would have purchased even then above two thousand pounds a year, and I might have lived like a queen, nay, far more happy than a queen; and which was above all, I had now an opportunity to have quitted a life of crime and debauchery which I had been given up to for several years, and to have sat down quiet in plenty and honour, and to have set myself apart to the great work which I have since seen so much necessity of and occasion for: I mean that of repentance.

But my measure of wickedness was not yet full. I continued obstinate against matrimony, and yet I could not bear the thoughts of his going away neither. As to the child, I was not very anxious about it; I told him I would promise him that it should never come to him to upbraid him with its being illegitimate; that if it was a boy I would breed it up like the son of a gentleman and use it well for his sake. And after a little more talk as this, and seeing him resolved to go, I retired, but could not help letting him see the tears run down my cheeks. He came to me and kissed me, entreated me, conjured me by the kindness he had shown me in my distress; by the justice he had done me in my bills and money affairs; by the respect which made him refuse a thousand pistoles from me for his expenses with that traitor the Jew; by the pledge of our misfortunes, so he called it, which I carried with me; and by all that the sincerest affection could propose to do, that I would not drive him away.

But it would not do. I was stupid and senseless, deaf to all his importunities, and continued so to the last; so we parted, only desiring me to promise that I would write him word when I was delivered, and how he might give me an answer. And this I engaged my word I would do; and upon his desiring to be informed which way I intended to dispose of myself, I told him I resolved to go directly to England and to London, where I proposed to lie in; but since he resolved to leave me, I told him I supposed it would be of no consequence to him what became of me.

He lay in his lodgings that night but went away early in the morning, leaving me a letter in which he repeated all he had said; recommended the care of the child, and desired of me that as he had remitted to me the offer of a thousand pistoles which I would have given him for the recompense of his charges and trouble with the Jew, and had given it me back, so he desired I would allow him to oblige me to set apart that thousand pistoles, with its improvement, for the child and for its education; earnestly pressing me to secure that little portion for the abandoned orphan when I should think fit, as he was sure I would, to throw away the rest upon something as worthless as my sincere friend at Paris. He concluded with moving me to reflect with the same regret as he did on our follies we had committed together, asked me forgiveness for being the aggressor in the fact, and forgave me everything, he said, but the cruelty of refusing him, which he owned he could not forgive me so heartily as he should do, because he was satisfied it was an injury to myself, would be an introduction to my ruin, and that I would seriously repent of it. He foretold some fatal things which he said he was well assured I should fall into, and that at last I would be ruined by a bad husband; bid me be the more wary, that I might render him a false prophet, but to remember that if ever I came into distress I had a fast friend at Paris, who would not upbraid me with the unkind things past, but would be always ready to return me good for evil.

This letter stunned me. I could not think it possible for anyone that had not dealt with the devil to write such a letter, for he spoke of some particular things which afterwards were to befall me with such an assurance that it frighted me beforehand; and when those things did come to pass I was persuaded he had some more than human knowledge. In a word, his advices to me to repent were very affectionate, his warnings of evil to happen to me were very kind, and his promises of assistance if I wanted him were so generous that I have seldom seen the like; and though I did not at first set much by that part, because I looked upon them as what might not happen and as what was improbable to happen at that time, yet all the rest of his letter was so moving that it left me very melancholy, and I cried four and twenty hours after, almost without ceasing, about it. And yet, even all this while, whatever it was that bewitched me, I had not one serious wish that I had taken him. I wished heartily indeed that I could have kept him with me, but I had a mortal aversion to marrying him, or indeed anybody else, but formed a thousand wild notions in my head that I was yet gay enough and young and handsome enough to please a man of quality, and that I would try my fortune at London, come of it what would.

Chapter 14

THUS blinded by my own vanity, I threw away the only opportunity I then had to have effectually settled my fortunes, and secured them for this world; and I am a memorial to all that shall read my story, a standing monument of the madness and distraction which pride and infatuations from hell run us into; how ill our passions guide us, and how dangerously we act when we follow the dictates of an ambitious mind.

I was rich, beautiful and agreeable, and not yet old. I had known something of the influence I had had upon the fancies of men, even of the highest rank; I never forgot that the Prince de ---- had said with an ecstasy that I was the finest woman in France. I knew I could make a figure at London, and how well I could grace that figure. I was not at a loss how to behave; and having already been adored by princes, I thought of nothing less than of being mistress to the King himself. But I go back to my immediate circumstances at that time.

I got over the absence of my honest merchant but slowly at first. It was with infinite regret that I let him go at all, and when I read the letter he left I was quite confounded. As soon as he was out of call and irrecoverable, I would have given half I had in the world for him back again; my notions of things changed in an instant, and I called myself a thousand fools for casting myself upon a life of scandal and hazard, when after the shipwreck of virtue, honour, and principle, and sailing at the utmost risk in the stormy seas of crime and abominable levity, I had a safe harbour presented and no heart to cast anchor in it.

His predictions terrified me; his promises of kindness if I came to distress melted me into tears, but frighted me with the apprehensions of ever coming into such distress, and filled my head with a thousand anxieties and thoughts, how it should be possible for me, who had now such a fortune, to sink again into misery.

Then the dreadful scene of my life, when I was left with my five children, etc., as I have related, represented itself again to me, and I sat considering what measures I might take to bring myself to such a state of desolation again, and how I should act to avoid it.

But these things wore off gradually. As to my friend the merchant, he was gone, and gone irrecoverably, for I durst not follow him to Paris, for the reasons mentioned above. Again, I was afraid to write to him to return lest he should have refused, as I verily believed he would. So I sat and cried intolerably for some days, nay, I may say, for some weeks; but I say it wore off gradually, and as I had a great deal of business for managing my effects, the hurry of that particular part served to divert my thoughts, and in part to wear out the impressions which had been made upon my mind.

I had sold my jewels, all but the fine diamond ring which my gentleman the jeweller used to wear, and this at proper times I wore myself, as also the diamond necklace which the Prince had given me, and a pair of extraordinary ear-rings, worth about 600 pistoles; the other, which was a fine casket, he left with me at his going to Versailles, and a small case with some rubies and emeralds, etc.--I say I sold them at The Hague for 7,600 pistoles. I had received all the bills which the merchant had helped me to at Paris, and with the money I brought with me they made up 13,900 pistoles more; so that I had in ready money, and in account in the bank at Amsterdam, above 21,000 pistoles, besides jewels; and how to get this treasure to England was my next care.

The business I had had now with a great many people for receiving such large sums and selling jewels of such considerable value gave me opportunity to know and converse with several of the best merchants of the place, so that I wanted no direction now how to get my money remitted to England. Applying therefore to several merchants, that I might neither risk it all on the credit of one merchant nor suffer any single man to know the quantity of money I had--I say, applying myself to several merchants, I got bills of exchange payable in London for all my money. The first bills I took with me, the second bills I left in trust (in case of any disaster at sea) in the hands of the first merchant, him to whom I was recommended by my friend from Paris.

Having thus spent nine months in Holland, refused the best offer ever woman in my circumstances had, parted unkindly and indeed barbarously with the best friend and honestest man in the world, got all my money in my pocket and a bastard in my belly, I took shipping at the Briel, in the packet-boat, and arrived safe at Harwich, where my woman Amy was come, by my direction, to meet me.

I would willingly have given ten thousand pounds of my money to have been rid of the burthen I had in my belly, as above; but it could not be, so I was obliged to bear with that part and get rid of it by the ordinary method of patience and a hard travail.

I was above the contemptible usage that women in my circumstances oftentimes meet with. I had considered all that beforehand; and having sent Amy beforehand and remitted her money to do it, she had taken me a very handsome house in ---- Street near Charing Cross, had hired me two maids and a footman, whom she had put in a good livery, and having hired a glass coach and four horses she came with them and the manservant to Harwich to meet me, and had been there near a week before I came. So I had nothing to do but to go away to London to my own house, where I arrived in very good health, and where I passed for a French lady by the title of ----.

My first business was to get all my bills accepted, which, to cut the story short, was all both accepted and currently paid; and I then resolved to take me a country lodging somewhere near the town to be incognito till I was brought to bed, which, appearing in such a figure and having such an equipage, I easily managed without anybody's offering the usual insults of parish enquiries. I did not appear in my new house for some time, and afterwards I thought fit, for particular reasons, to quit that house and not come to it at all, but take handsome large apartments in the Pall Mall, in a house out of which was a private door into the King's garden, by the permission of the chief gardener, who had lived in the house.

I had now all my effects secured; but my money being my great concern at that time, I found it a difficulty how to dispose of it so as to bring me in an annual interest. However, in some time I got a substantial safe mortgage for £14,000 by the assistance of the famous Sir Robert Clayton, for which I had an estate of £1,800 a year bound to me, and had £700 per annum interest for it.

This with some other securities made me a very handsome estate of above £1,000 a year, enough, one would think, to keep any woman in England from being a whore.

I lay in at ----, about four miles from London, and brought a fine boy into the world, and, according to my promise, sent an account of it to my friend at Paris, the father of it, and in the letter told him how sorry I was for his going away, and did as good as intimate that if he would come once more to see me I should use him better than I had done. He gave me a very kind and obliging answer, but took not the least notice of what I had said of his coming over, so I found my interest lost there for ever. He gave me joy of the child and hinted that he hoped I would make good what he had begged for the poor infant, as I had promised; and I sent him word again that I would fulfil his order to a tittle; and such a fool, and so weak I was in this last letter, notwithstanding what I have said of his not taking notice of my invitation as to ask his pardon almost for the usage I gave him at Rotterdam, and stooped so low as to expostulate with him for not taking notice of my inviting him to come to me again as I had done; and which was still more, went so far as to make a second sort of an offer to him, telling him almost in plain words that if he would come over now I would have him. But he never gave me the least reply to it at all, which was as absolute a denial to me as he was ever able to give. So I sat down, I cannot say contented, but vexed heartily that I had made the offer at all; for he had, as I may say, his full revenge of me, in scorning to answer, and to let me twice ask that of him which he with so much importunity begged of me before.

I was now up again, and soon came to my city lodgings in the Pall Mall, and here I began to make a figure suitable to my estate, which was very great; and I shall give you an account of my equipage in a few words, and of myself too.

I paid £60 a year for my near apartments, for I took them by the year; but then, they were handsome lodgings indeed, and very richly furnished. I kept my own servants to clean and look after them, found my own kitchen-ware and firing. My equipage was handsome, but not very great; I had a coach, a coachman, a footman, my woman Amy, whom I now dressed like a gentlewoman and made her my companion, and three maids. And thus I lived for a time. I dressed to the height of every mode, went extremely rich in clothes, and as for jewels, I wanted none. I gave a very good livery laced with silver, and as rich as anybody below the nobility could be seen with. And thus I appeared, leaving the world to guess who or what I was, without offering to put myself forward.

I walked sometimes in the Mall with my woman Amy, but I kept no company and made no acquaintances, only made as gay a show as I was able to do, and that upon all occasions. I found, however, the world was not altogether so unconcerned about me as I seemed to be about them; and first, I understood that the neighbours began to be mighty inquisitive about me, as who I was and what my circumstances were.

Amy was the only person who could answer their curiosity or give any account of me, and she, a tattling woman and a true gossip, took care to do that with all the art that she was mistress of. She let them know that I was the widow of a person of quality in France, that I was very rich, that I came over hither to look after an estate that fell to me by some of my relations who died here, that I was worth £40,000 all in my own hands, and the like.

This was all wrong in Amy, and in me too, though we did not see it at first, for this recommended me indeed to those sort of gentlemen they call fortune-hunters, and who always besieged ladies, as they called it, on purpose to take them prisoners, as I called it; that is to say, to marry the women and have the spending of their money. But if I was wrong in refusing the honourable proposals of the Dutch merchant, who offered me the disposal of my whole estate and had as much of his own to maintain me with, I was right now in refusing those offers which came generally from gentlemen of good families and good estates, but who, living to the extent of them, were always needy and necessitous, and wanted a sum of money to make themselves easy, as they call it--that is to say, to pay off incumbrances, sisters' portions, and the like--and then the woman is prisoner for life and may live as they please to give her leave. This life I had seen into clearly enough, and therefore I was not to be caught that way. However, as I said, the reputation of my money brought several of those sort of gentry about me, and they found means, by one stratagem or other, to get access to my ladyship; but, in short, I answered them all well enough, that I lived single and was happy, that as I had no occasion to change my condition for an estate, so I did not see that by the best offer that any of them could make me, I could mend my fortune; that I might be honoured with titles indeed, and in time rank on public occasions with the peeresses--I mention that because one that offered at me was the eldest son of a peer--but that I was as well without the title as long as I had the estate; and while I had £2,000 a year of my own, I was happier than I could be in being prisoner of state to a nobleman, for I took the ladies of that rank to be little better.

As I have mentioned Sir Robert Clayton, with whom I had the good fortune to become acquainted on account of the mortgage which he helped me to, it is necessary to take notice that I had much advantage in my ordinary affairs by his advice, and therefore I call it my good fortune. For as he paid me so considerable an annual income as £700 a year, so I am to acknowledge myself much a debtor, not only to the justice of his dealings with me, but to the prudence and conduct which he guided me to, by his advice, for the management of my estate; and as he found I was not inclined to marry, he frequently took occasion to hint how soon I might raise my fortune to a prodigious height, if I would but order my family economy so far within my revenue as to lay up every year something to add to the capital.

I was convinced of the truth of what he said, and agreed to the advantages of it. You are to take it as you go that Sir Robert supposed by my own discourse, and especially by my woman Amy, that I had £2,000 a year income. He judged, as he said, by my way of living, that I could not spend above £1,000; and so, he added, I might prudently lay by £1,000 every year to add to the capital, and by adding every year the additional interest or income of the money to the capital, he proved to me that in ten years I should double the £1,000 per annum that I laid by. And he drew me out a table, as he called it, of the increase, for me to judge by; and by which, he said, if the gentlemen of England would but act so, every family of them would increase their fortunes to a great degree, just as merchants do by trade; whereas now, says Sir Robert, by the humour of living up to the extent of their fortunes, and rather beyond, the gentlemen, says he, ay, and the nobility too, are, almost all of them, borrowers, and all in necessitous circumstances.

As Sir Robert frequently visited me and was (if I may say so from his own mouth) very well pleased with my way of conversing with him, for he knew nothing nor so much as guessed at what I had been--I say, as he came often to see me, so he always entertained me with this scheme of frugality. And one time he brought another paper, wherein he showed me much to the same purpose as the former, to what degree I should increase my estate if I would come into his method of contracting my expenses; and by this scheme of his, it appeared, that laying up £1,000 a year, and every year adding the interest to it, I should in twelve years' time have in bank £21,058; after which, I might lay up £2,000 a year.

I objected that I was a young woman, that I had been used to live plentifully and with a good appearance, and that I knew not how to be a miser.

He told me that if I thought I had enough, it was well, but if I desired to have more, this was the way; that in another twelve years I should be too rich, so that I should not know what to do with it.

"Ay, sir," says I, "you are contriving how to make me a rich old woman, but that won't answer my end; I had rather have £20,000 now than £60,000 when I am fifty years old."

"Then, madam," says he, "I suppose your honour has no children?"

"None, Sir Robert," said I, "but what are provided for "; so I left him in the dark as much as I found him. However, I considered his scheme very well, though I said no more to him at that time, and I resolved, though I would make a very good figure--I say, I resolved to abate a little of my expense and draw in, live closer, and save something, if not so much as he proposed to me. It was near the end of the year that Sir Robert made this proposal to me, and when the year was up I went to his house in the city, and there I told him I came to thank him for his scheme of frugality, that I had been studying much upon it, and though I had not been able to mortify myself so much as to lay up £1,000 a year, yet as I had not come to him for my interest half-yearly, as was usual, I was now come to let him know that I had resolved to lay up that £700 a year and never use a penny of it, desiring him to help me to put it out to advantage.

Sir Robert, a man thoroughly versed in arts of improving money, but thoroughly honest, said to me, "Madam, I am glad you approve of the method that I proposed to you, but you have begun wrong. You should have come for your interest at the half-year, and then you had had the money to put out; now you have lost half a year's interest of £350, which is £9," for I had but 5 per cent. on the mortgage.

"Well, well, sir," says I, "can you put this out for me now?"

"Let it lie, madam," says he, "till the next year, and then I'll put out your £1,400 together, and in the meantime I'll pay you interest for the £700." So he gave me his bill for the money, which he told me should be no less than 6 per cent.--Sir Robert Clayton's bill was what nobody would refuse--so I thanked him and let it lie, and next year I did the same, and the third year Sir Robert got me a good mortgage for £2,200 at 6 per cent. interest. So I had £132 a year added to my income, which was a very satisfying article.

But I return to my history. As I have said, I found that my measures were all wrong; the posture I set up in exposed me to innumerable visitors of the kind I have mentioned above. I was cried up for a vast fortune, and one that Sir Robert Clayton managed for; and Sir Robert Clayton was courted for me as much as I was for myself. But I had given Sir Robert his cue. I had told him my opinion of matrimony in just the same terms as I had done my merchant, and he came into it presently. He owned that my observation was just, and that if I valued my liberty, as I knew my fortune and that it was in my own hands, I was to blame if I gave it away to any one.

But Sir Robert knew nothing of my design, that I aimed at being a kept mistress and to have a handsome maintenance, and that I was still for getting money, and laying it up too, as much as he could desire me, only by a worse way.

However, Sir Robert came seriously to me one day and told me he had an offer of matrimony to make to me that was beyond all that he had heard had offered themselves, and this was a merchant. Sir Robert and I agreed exactly in our notions of a merchant. Sir Robert said, and I found it to be true, that a true-bred merchant is the best gentleman in the nation; that in knowledge, in manners, in judgment of things, the merchant outdid many of the nobility; that having once mastered the world and being above the demand of business, though no real estate, they were then superior to most gentlemen even in estate; that a merchant in flush business and a capital stock is able to spend more money than a gentleman of £5,000 a year estate; that while a merchant spent, he only spent what he got, and not that, and that he laid up great sums every year.

That an estate is a pond, but that a trade was a spring; that if the first is once mortgaged it seldom gets clear, but embarrasses the person for ever; but the merchant had his estate continually flowing; and upon this he named me merchants who lived in more real splendour and spent more money than most of the noblemen in England could singly expend, and that they still grew immensely rich.

He went on to tell me that even the tradesmen in London, speaking of the better sort of trades, could spend more money in their families and yet give better fortunes to their children than, generally speaking, the gentry of England from £1,000 a year downward could do, and yet grow rich too.

The upshot of all this was to recommend to me rather the bestowing my fortune upon some eminent merchant who lived already in the first figure of a merchant, and who, not being in want or scarcity of money, but having a flourishing business and a flowing cash, would at the first word settle all my fortune on myself and children and maintain me like a queen.

This was certainly right, and had I taken his advice I had been really happy; but my heart was bent upon an independency of fortune, and I told him I knew no state of matrimony but what was at best a state of inferiority, if not of bondage; that I had no notion of it, that I lived a life of absolute liberty now, was free as I was born, and, having a plentiful fortune, I did not understand what coherence the words Honour and Obey had with the liberty of a free woman; that I knew no reason the men had to engross the whole liberty of the race and make the women, notwithstanding any disparity of fortune, be subject to the laws of marriage of their own making; that it was my misfortune to be a woman, but I was resolved it should not be made worse by the sex, and seeing liberty seemed to be the men's property, I would be a man-woman; for as I was born free, I would die so.

Sir Robert smiled, and told me I talked a kind of amazonian language; that he found few women of my mind, or that if they were, they wanted resolution to go on with it; that notwithstanding all my notions, which he could not but say had once some weight in them, yet he understood I had broken in upon them and had been married. I answered I had so, but he did not hear me say that I had any encouragement from what was past to make a second venture; that I was got well out of the toil, and if I came in again I should have nobody to blame but myself.

Sir Robert laughed heartily at me but gave over offering any more arguments, only told me he had pointed me out for some of the best merchants in London, but since I forbade him, he would give me no disturbance of that kind. He applauded my way of managing my money, and told me I should soon be monstrous rich; but he neither knew nor mistrusted that with all this wealth I was yet a whore, and was not averse to adding to my estate at the further expense of my virtue.

Chapter 15

But to go on with my story as to my way of living. I found, as above, that my living as I did would not answer; that it only brought the fortune-hunters and bites about me, as I have said before, to make a prey of me and my money; and, in short, I was harassed with lovers, beaux, and fops of quality in abundance. But it would not do; I aimed at other things, and was possessed with so vain an opinion of my own beauty, that nothing less than the King himself was in my eye; and this vanity was raised by some words let fall by a person I conversed with, who was perhaps likely enough to have brought such a thing to pass had it been sooner, but that game began to be pretty well over at Court. However, the having mentioned such a thing, it seems, a little too publicly, it brought abundance of people about me, upon a wicked account too.

And now I began to act in a new sphere. The Court was exceeding gay and fine, though fuller of men than of women, the Queen not affecting to be very much in public. On the other hand, it is no slander upon the courtiers to say they were as wicked as anybody in reason could desire them. The King had several mistresses, who were prodigious fine, and there was a glorious show on that side indeed. If the Sovereign gave himself a loose, it could not be expected the rest of the Court should be all saints; so far was it from that, though I would not make it worse than it was, that a woman that had anything agreeable in her appearance could never want followers.

I soon found myself thronged with admirers, and I received visits from some persons of very great figure, who always introduced themselves by the help of an old lady or two who were now become my intimates; and one of them, I understood afterwards, was set to work on purpose to get into my favour, in order to introduce what followed.

The conversation we had was generally courtly but civil. At length some gentlemen proposed to play, and made what they called a party. This, it seems, was a contrivance of one of my female hangers-on, for, as I said, I had two of them, who thought this was the way to introduce people as often as she pleased, and so indeed it was. They played high and stayed late, but begged my pardon, only asked leave to make an appointment for the next night. I was as gay and as well pleased as any of them, and one night told one of the gentlemen, my Lord ----, that seeing they were doing me the honour of diverting themselves at my apartment, and desired to be there sometimes, I did not keep a gaming table, but I would give them a little ball the next day if they pleased, which they accepted very willingly.

Accordingly in the evening the gentlemen began to come, where I let them see that I understood very well what such things meant. I had a large dining-room in my apartments, with five other rooms on the same floor, all which I made drawing-rooms for the occasion, having all the beds taken down for the day. In three of these I had tables placed, covered with wine and sweetmeats; the fourth had a green table for play, and the fifth was my own room, where I sat and where I received all the company that came to pay their compliments to me. I was dressed, you may be sure, to all the advantage possible, and had all the jewels on that I was mistress of. My Lord ----, to whom I had made the invitation, sent me a set of fine music from the playhouse, and the ladies danced and we began to be very merry, when about eleven o'clock I had notice given me that there were some gentlemen coming in masquerade.

I seemed a little surprised and began to apprehend some disturbance, when my Lord ----, perceiving it, spoke to me to be easy, for that there was a party of the Guards at the door which should be ready to prevent any rudeness; and another gentleman gave me a hint as if the King was among the masks. I coloured as red as blood itself could make a face look, and expressed a great surprise. However, there was no going back, so I kept my station in my drawing-room, but with the folding-doors wide open.

A while after the masks came in and began with a dance à la comique, performing wonderfully indeed. While they were dancing I withdrew, and left a lady to answer for me that I would return immediately. In less than half an hour I returned, dressed in the habit of a Turkish princess, the habit I got at Leghorn when my foreign Prince bought me a Turkish slave, as I have said--the Maltese man-of-war had, it seems, taken a Turkish vessel going from Constantinople to Alexandria, in which were some ladies bound for Grand Cairo in Egypt, and as the ladies were made slaves, so their fine clothes were thus exposed--and with this Turkish slave I bought the rich clothes too. The dress was extraordinary fine indeed, I had bought it as a curiosity, having never seen the like; the robe was a fine Persian or Indian damask, the ground white and the flowers blue and gold, and the train held five yards; the dress under it was a vest of the same, embroidered with gold, and set with some pearls in the work and some turquoise stones; to the vest was a girdle five or six inches wide, after the Turkish mode, and on both ends where it joined or hooked was set with diamonds for eight inches either way, only they were not true diamonds, but nobody knew that but myself.

The turban or head-dress had a pinnacle on the top, but not above five inches, with a piece of loose sarcenet hanging from it, and on the front, just over the forehead, was a good jewel, which I had added to it.

This habit, as above, cost me about sixty pistoles in Italy, but cost much more in the country from whence it came; and little did I think when I bought it that I should put it to such a use as this, though I had dressed myself in it many times by the help of my little Turk, and afterwards between Amy and I, only to see how I looked in it. I had sent her up before to get it ready, and when I came up I had nothing to do but slip it on, and was down in my drawing-room in a little more than a quarter of an hour. When I came there the room was full of company, but I ordered the folding-doors to be shut for a minute or two, till I had received the compliments of the ladies that were in the room, and had given them a full view of my dress.

But my Lord ----, who happened to be in the room, slipped out at another door and brought back with him one of the masks, a tall well-shaped person, but who had no name, being all masked, nor would it have been allowed to ask any person's name on such an occasion. The person spoke in French to me that it was the finest dress he had ever seen, and asked me if he should have the honour to dance with me. I bowed, as giving my consent, but said as I had been a Mohammedan I could not dance after the manner of this country; I supposed their music would not play à la moresque. He answered merrily I had a Christian's face, and he'd venture it that I could dance like a Christian, adding that so much beauty could not be Mohammedan. Immediately the folding-doors were flung open, and he led me into the room. The company were under the greatest surprise imaginable, the very music stopped awhile to gaze; for the dress was indeed exceedingly surprising, perfectly new, very agreeable, and wonderful rich.

The gentleman, whoever he was, for I never knew, led me only a courant, and then asked me if I had a mind to dance an antic, that is to say, whether I would dance the antic as they had danced in masquerade, or anything by myself. I told him anything else rather, if he pleased; so we danced only two French dances, and he led me to the drawing-room door, when he retired to the rest of the masks. When he left me at the drawing-room door I did not go in, as he thought I would have done, but turned about and showed myself to the whole room, and, calling my woman to me, gave her some directions to the music, by which the company presently understood that I would give them a dance by myself. Immediately all the house rose up and paid me a kind of a compliment by removing back every way to make me room, for the place was exceeding full. The music did not at first hit the tune that I directed, which was a French tune, so I was forced to send my woman to them again, standing all this while at my drawing-room door; but as soon as my woman spoke to them again they played it right, and I, to let them see it was so, stepped forward to the middle of the room. Then they began it again, and I danced by myself a figure which I learnt in France when the Prince de ---- desired I would dance for his diversion. It was indeed a very fine figure, invented by a famous master at Paris, for a lady or a gentleman to dance single, but being perfectly new it pleased the company exceedingly, and they all thought it had been Turkish; nay, one gentleman had the folly to expose himself so much as to say, and I think swore too, that he had seen it danced at Constantinople; which was ridiculous enough.

At the finishing the dance the company clapped and almost shouted; and one of the gentlemen cried out, Roxana! Roxana! by ----, with an oath, upon which foolish accident I had the name of Roxana presently fixed upon me all over the Court end of town as effectually as if I had been christened Roxana. I had, it seems, the felicity of pleasing everybody that night to an extreme, and my ball, but especially my dress, was the chat of the town for that week, and so the name Roxana was the toast at and about the Court; no other health was to be named with it.

Now things began to work as I would have them, and I began to be very popular as much as I could desire. The ball held till (as well as I was pleased with the show) I was sick of the night; the gentlemen masked went off about three o'clock in the morning, the other gentlemen sat down to play; the music held it out, and some of the ladies were dancing at six in the morning.

But I was mighty eager to know who it was danced with me. Some of the lords went so far as to tell me I was very much honoured in my company. One of them spoke so broad as almost to say it was the King, but I was convinced afterwards it was not; and another replied if he had been His Majesty he should have thought it no dishonour to lead up a Roxana. But to this hour I never knew positively who it was, and by his behaviour I thought he was too young, His Majesty being at that time in an age that might be discovered from a young person even in his dancing.

Be that as it would, I had 500 guineas sent me the next morning, and the messenger was ordered to tell me that the persons who sent it desired a ball again at my lodgings on the next Tuesday, but that they would have my leave to give the entertainment themselves. I was mighty well pleased with this, to be sure, but very inquisitive to know who the money came from; but the messenger was silent as death as to that point, and, bowing always at my enquiries, begged me to ask no questions which he could not give an obliging answer to.

I forgot to mention that the gentlemen that played gave a hundred guineas to the box, as they called it, and at the end of their play they asked my gentlewoman of the bedchamber, as they called her (Mrs. Amy, forsooth), and gave it her, and gave twenty guineas more among the servants.

These magnificent doings equally both pleased and surprised me, and I hardly knew where I was; but especially that notion of the King being the person that danced with me puffed me up to that degree, that I not only did not know anybody else, but indeed was very far from knowing myself.

I had now the next Tuesday to provide for the like company, but, alas! it was all taken out of my hand. Three gentlemen, who yet were, it seems, but servants, came on the Saturday, and bringing sufficient testimonies that they were right, for one was the same who brought the 500 guineas--I say three of them came and brought bottles of all sorts of wines and hampers of sweetmeats to such a quantity, it appeared they designed to hold the trade on more than once, and that they would furnish everything to a profusion.

However, as I found a deficiency in two things, I made provision of about twelve dozen of fine damask napkins, with table-cloths of the same, sufficient to cover all the tables, with three table-cloths upon every table, and sideboards in proportion. Also, I bought a handsome quantity of plate, necessary to have served all the sideboards, but the gentlemen would not suffer any of it to be used, telling me they had brought fine china dishes and plates for the whole service, and that in such public places they could not be answerable for the plate; so it was set all up in a large glass cupboard in the room I sat in, where it made a very good show indeed.

On Tuesday there came such an appearance of gentlemen and ladies that my apartments were by no means able to receive them, and those who in particular appeared as principals gave order below to let no more company come up. The street was full of coaches with coronets, and fine glass chairs; and, in short, it was impossible to receive the company. I kept my little room, as before, and the dancers filled the great room; all the drawing-rooms also were filled, and three rooms below-stairs which were not mine.

It was very well that there was a strong party of the Guards brought to keep the door, for without that there had been such a promiscuous crowd, and some of them scandalous too, that we should have been all disorder and confusion; but the three head servants managed all that, and had a word to admit all the company by.

It was uncertain to me, and is to this day, who it was that danced with me the Wednesday before, when the ball was my own; but that the King was at this assembly was out of question with me, by circumstances that I suppose I could not be deceived in, and particularly that there were five persons who were not masked, three of them had blue garters, and they appeared not to me till I came out to dance.

This meeting was managed just as the first, though with much more magnificence because of the company. I placed myself (exceedingly rich in clothes and jewels) in the middle of my little room, as before, and made my compliments to all the company as they passed me, as I did before; but my Lord ----, who had spoken openly to me the first night, came to me and, unmasking, told me the company had ordered him to tell me they hoped they should see me in the dress I had appeared in the first day, which had been so acceptable that it had been the occasion of this new meeting. "And, madam," says he, "there are some in this assembly whom it is worth your while to oblige."

I bowed to my Lord ---- and immediately withdrew. While I was above, a-dressing in my new habit, two ladies, perfectly unknown to me, were conveyed into my apartment below, by the order of a noble person who, with his family, had been in Persia; and here indeed I thought I should have been outdone, or perhaps balked.

One of these ladies was dressed most exquisitely fine indeed, in the habit of a virgin lady of quality of Georgia, and the other in the same habit of Armenia, with each of them a woman slave to attend them.

The ladies had their petticoats short to their ankles, but pleated all round, and before them short aprons, but of the finest point that could be seen; their gowns were made with long antique sleeves hanging down behind, and a train let down; they had no jewels, but their heads and breasts were dressed up with flowers, and they both came in veiled.

Their slaves were bareheaded, but their long black hair was braided in locks hanging down behind to their waists, and tied up with ribbons; they were dressed exceedingly rich, and were as beautiful as their mistresses, for none of them had any masks on. They waited in my room till I came down, and all paid their respects to me after the Persian manner, and sat down on a safra, that is to say, almost cross-legged on a couch made up of cushions laid on the ground.

This was admirably fine, and I was indeed startled at it. They made their compliments to me in French and I replied in the same language. When the doors were opened they walked into the dancing-room, and danced such a dance as indeed nobody there had ever seen, and to an instrument like a guitar with a small low-sounding trumpet, which indeed was very fine, and which my Lord ---- had provided.

They danced three times all alone, for nobody indeed could dance with them. The novelty pleased truly, but yet there was something wild and bizarre in it, because they really acted to the life the barbarous country whence they came; but as mine had the French behaviour under the Mohammedan dress, it was every way as new, and pleased much better indeed.

As soon as they had shown their Georgian and Armenian shapes, and danced, as I have said, three times, they withdrew, paid their compliments to me (for I was Queen of the day), and went off to undress.

Some gentlemen then danced with ladies all in masks, and when they stopped nobody rose up to dance, but all called out, Roxana! Roxana! In the interval my Lord ---- had brought another masked person into my room, whom I knew not, only that I could discern it was not the same person that led me out before. This noble person (for I afterwards understood it was the Duke of ----) after a short compliment led me out into the middle of the room.

I was dressed in the same vest and girdle as before, but the robe had a mantle over it, which is usual in the Turkish habit, and it was of crimson and green, the green brocaded with gold; and my Tyhiaai, or head-dress, varied a little from that I had before, as it stood higher and had some jewels about the rising part, which made it look like a turban crowned.

I had no mask, neither did I paint, and yet I had the day of all the ladies that appeared at the ball, I mean of those that appeared with faces on; as for those masked, nothing could be said of them, no doubt there might be many finer than I was. It must be confessed that the habit was infinitely advantageous to me, and everybody looked at me with a kind of pleasure, which gave me great advantage too.

After I had danced with that noble person I did not offer to dance by myself, as I had before; but they all called out Roxana! again, and two of the gentlemen came into the drawing-room to entreat me to give them the Turkish dance, which I yielded to readily; so I came out and danced just as at first.

While I was dancing I perceived five persons standing all together, and among them one only with his hat on; it was an immediate hint to me who it was, and had at first almost put me into some disorder; but I went on, received the applause of the house, as before, and retired into my own room. When I was there the five gentlemen came across the room to my side, and coming in, followed by a throng of great persons, the person with his hat on said, "Madam Roxana, you perform to admiration." I was prepared, and offered to kneel to kiss his hand, but he declined it and saluted me, and so, passing back again through the great room, went away.

I do not say here who this was, but I say I came afterwards to know something more plainly. I would have withdrawn and disrobed, being somewhat too thin in that dress, unlaced and open-breasted as if I had been in my shift, but it could not be, and I was obliged to dance afterwards with six or eight gentlemen, most, if not all of them, of the first rank; and I was told afterwards that one of them was the D---- of M----th.

About two or three o'clock in the morning the company began to decrease, the number of women especially dropped away home, some and some at a time, and the gentlemen retired downstairs, where they unmasked and went to play.

Amy waited at the room where they played, sat up all night to attend them; and in the morning, when they broke up, they swept the box into her lap, when she counted out to me sixty-two guineas and a half; and the other servants got very well too. Amy came to me when they were all gone. "Law, madam!" says Amy with a long gaping cry, "what shall I do with all this money?" And indeed the poor creature was half mad with joy.

Chapter 16

I was now in my element. I was as much talked of as anybody could desire, and I did not doubt but some thing or other would come of it, but the report of my being so rich rather was a balk to my view than anything else; for the gentlemen, that would perhaps have been troublesome enough otherwise, seemed to be kept off, for Roxana was too high for them.

There is a scene which came in here which I must cover from human eyes or ears. For three years and about a month Roxana lived retired, having been obliged to make an excursion in a manner and with a person which duty and private vows oblige her not to reveal, at least not yet.

At the end of this time I appeared again, but I must add that as I had in this time of retreat made hay, etc., so I did not come abroad again with the same lustre or shine with so much advantage as before; for as some people had got at least a suspicion of where I had been and who had had me all the while, it began to be public that Roxana was, in short, a mere Roxana, neither better nor worse, and not that woman of honour and virtue that was at first supposed.

You are now to suppose me about seven years come to town, and that I had not only suffered the old revenue, which I hinted was managed by Sir Robert Clayton, to grow, as was mentioned before, but I had laid up an incredible wealth, the time considered. And had I yet had the least thought of reforming, I had all the opportunity to do it with advantage that ever woman had, for the common vice of all whores, I mean money, was out of the question, nay, even avarice itself seemed to be glutted; for, including what I had saved in reserving the interest of £14,000, which, as above, I had left to grow, and including some very good presents I had made to me in mere compliment upon these shining masquerading meetings, which I held up for about two years, and what I made of three years of the most glorious retreat, as I call it, that ever woman had, I had fully doubled my first substance, and had near £5,000 in money which I kept at home, besides abundance of plate and jewels which I had either given me or had bought to set myself out for public days.

In a word, I had now £35,000 estate, and as I found ways to live without wasting either principal or interest, I laid up £2,000 every year at least, out of the mere interest, adding it to the principal; and thus I went on.

Chapter 16

After the end of what I may call my retreat, and out of which I brought a great deal of money, I appeared again, but I seemed like an old piece of plate that has been hoarded up some years and comes out tarnished and discoloured. So I came out blown and looked like a cast-off mistress, nor indeed was I any better, though I was not at all impaired in beauty, except that I was a little fatter than I was formerly, and always granting that I was four years older.

However, I preserved the youth of my temper, was always bright, pleasant in company, and agreeable to everybody, or else everybody flattered me; and in this condition I came abroad to the world again; and though I was not so popular as before, and indeed did not seek it, because I knew it could not be, yet I was far from being without company, and that of the greatest quality, of subjects I mean, who frequently visited me, and sometimes we had meetings for mirth and play at my apartments, where I failed not to divert them in the most agreeable manner possible.

Nor could any of them make the least particular application to me from the notion they had of my excessive wealth, which, as they thought, placed me above the meanness of a maintenance, and so left no room to come easily about me.

But at last I was very handsomely attacked by a person of honour, and (which recommended him particularly to me) a person of a very great estate. He made a long introduction to me upon the subject of my wealth. "Ignorant creature," said I to myself, "considering him as a lord; was there ever woman in the world that could stoop to the baseness of being a whore and was above taking the reward of her vice? No, no, depend upon it, if your lordship obtains anything of me you must pay for it; and the notion of my being so rich serves only to make it cost you the dearer, seeing you cannot offer a small matter to a woman of £2,000 a year estate."

After he had harangued upon that subject a good while, and had assured me he had no design upon me, that he did not come to make a prize of me, or to pick my pocket--which, by the way, I was in no fear of, for I took too much care of my money to part with any of it that way--he then turned his discourse to the subject of love, a point so ridiculous to me without the main thing, I mean the money, that I had no patience to hear him make so long a story of it.

I received him civilly, and let him see I could bear to hear a wicked proposal without being affronted, and yet I was not to be brought into it too easily. He visited me a long while and, in short, courted me as closely and assiduously as if he had been wooing me to matrimony. He made me several valuable presents, which I suffered myself to be prevailed with to accept, but not without great difficulty.

Gradually I suffered also his other importunities, and when he made a proposal of a compliment or appointment to me for a settlement, he said that though I was rich, yet there was not the less due from him to acknowledge the favours he received, and that if I was to be his I should not live at my own expense, cost what it would. I told him I was far from being extravagant, and yet I did not live at the expense of less than £500 a year out of my own pocket; that, however, I was not covetous of settled allowances, for I looked upon that as a kind of golden chain, something like matrimony; that though I knew how to be true to a man of honour, as I knew his lordship to be, yet I had a kind of aversion to the bonds, and though I was not so rich as the world talked me up to be, yet I was not so poor as to bind myself to hardships for a pension.

He told me he expected to make my life perfectly easy, and intended it so; that he knew of no bondage there could be in a private engagement between us; that the bonds of honour, he knew, I would be tied by, and think them no burthen; and for other obligations, he scorned to expect anything from me but what he knew as a woman of honour I could grant; then as to maintenance, he told me he would soon show me that he valued me infinitely above £500 a year; and upon this foot we began.

I seemed kinder to him after this discourse, and as time and private conversation made us very intimate, we began to come nearer to the main article, namely, the £500 a year. He offered that at first word, and to acknowledge it as an infinite favour to have it be accepted of; and I, that thought it was too much by all the money, suffered myself to be mastered or prevailed with to yield, even on but a bare engagement upon parole.

When he had obtained his end that way, I told him my mind. "Now you see, my Lord," said I, "how weakly I have acted, namely, to yield to you without capitulation, or anything secured to me but that which you may cease to allow when you please; if I am the less valued for such a confidence, I shall be injured in a manner that I will endeavour not to deserve."

He told me that he would make it evident to me that he did not seek me by way of bargain, as such things were often done; that as I had treated him with a generous confidence, so I should find I was in the hands of a man of honour, and one that knew how to value the obligation. And upon this he pulled out a goldsmith's bill for £300, which, putting it into my hand, he said he gave me as a pledge that I should not be a loser by my not having made a bargain with him.

This was engaging indeed, and gave me a good idea of our future correspondence; and in short, as I could not refrain treating him with more kindness than I had done before, so one thing begetting another, I gave him several testimonies that was entirely his own, by inclination as well as by the common obligation of a mistress; and this pleased him exceedingly.

Soon after this private engagement I began to consider whether it were not more suitable to the manner of life I now led, to be a little less public, and as I told my Lord it would rid me of the importunities of others, and of continual visits from a sort of people whom he knew of, and who, by the way, having now got the notion of me which I really deserved, began to talk of the old game, love and gallantry, and to offer at what was rude enough; things as nauseous to me now as if I had been married and as virtuous as other people. The visits of these people began indeed to be uneasy to me, and particularly as they were always very tedious and impertinent; nor could my Lord ---- be pleased with them at all if they had gone on. It would be diverting to set down here in what manner I repulsed these sort of people; how in some I resented it as an affront, and told them that I was sorry they should oblige me to vindicate myself from the scandal of such suggestions by telling them that I could see them no more, and by desiring them not to give themselves the trouble of visiting me, who, though I was not unwilling to be uncivil, yet thought myself obliged never to receive any visit from any gentleman after he had made such proposals as those to me; but these things would be too tedious to bring in here. It was on this account I proposed to his lordship my taking new lodgings for privacy; besides, I considered that as I might live very handsomely and yet not so publicly, so I need not spend so much money, by a great deal, and if I made £500 a year of this generous person, it was more than I had any occasion to spend, by a great deal.

My Lord came readily into this proposal and went further than I expected, for he found out a lodging for me in a very handsome house where yet he was not known--I suppose he had employed somebody to find it out for him--and where he had a convenient way to come into the garden, by a door that opened into the park, a thing very rarely allowed in those times.

By this key he could come in at what time of night or day he pleased, and as we had also a little door in the lower part of the house, which was always left upon a lock, and his was the master-key, so if it was twelve, one, or two o'clock at night he could come directly into my bedchamber.

N.B.--I was not afraid I should be found a-bed with anybody else, for, in a word, I conversed with nobody at all.

It happened pleasantly enough one night; his lordship had stayed late, and I, not expecting him that night, had taken Amy to bed with me, and when my Lord came into the chamber we were both fast asleep; I think it was near three o'clock when he came in, and a little merry, but not at all fuddled or what they call in drink, and he came at once into the room.

Amy was frighted out of her wits and cried out. I said calmly, "Indeed, my Lord, I did not expect you to-night, and we have been a little frighted to-night with fire," "Oh!" says he, "I see you have got a bedfellow with you." I began to make an apology. "No, no," says my Lord, "you need no excuse, 'tis not a man-bedfellow I see." But then, talking merrily enough, he caught his words back. "But hark ye," says he, "now I think on't, how shall I be satisfied it is not a man-bedfellow?" "Oh," says I, "I dare say your lordship is satisfied 'tis poor Amy." "Yes," says he, "'tis Mrs. Amy, but how do I know what Amy is? It may be Mr. Amy for aught I know; I hope you'll give me leave to be satisfied." I told him, yes, by all means I would have his lordship satisfied, but I supposed he knew who she was.

Well, he fell foul of poor Amy, and indeed I thought once he would have carried the jest on before my face, as was once done in a like case. But his lordship was not so hot neither but he would know whether Amy was Mr. Amy or Mrs. Amy, and so I suppose he did; and then being satisfied in that doubtful case, he walked to the further end of the room and went into a little closet and sat down.

In the meantime Amy and I got up, and I bid her run and make the bed in another chamber for my Lord, and I gave her sheets to put into it, which she did immediately, and I put my Lord to bed there and, when I had done at his desire, went to bed to him. I was backward at first to come to bed to him, and made my excuse, because I had been in bed with Amy and had not shifted me, but he was past those niceties at that time, and as long as he was sure it was Mrs. Amy and not Mr. Amy he was very well satisfied, and so the jest passed over; but Amy appeared no more all that night or the next day, and when she did, my Lord was so merry with her upon his éclaircissement, as he called it, that Amy did not know what to do with herself.

Not that Amy was such a nice lady in the main if she had been fairly dealt with, as has appeared in the former part of this work, but now she was surprised and a little hurried, that she scarce knew where she was, and besides she was, as to his lordship, as nice a lady as any in the world, and, for anything he knew of her, she appeared as such; the rest was to us only that knew of it.

Chapter 17

I held this wicked scene of life out eight years, reckoning from my first coming to England, and though my Lord found no fault, yet I found without much examining that anyone who looked in my face might see I was above twenty years old, and yet, without flattering myself, I carried my age, which was above fifty, very well too.

I may venture to say that no woman ever lived a life like me, of six and twenty years of wickedness, without the least signals of remorse, without any signs of repentance, or without so much as a wish to put an end to it. I had so long habituated myself to a life of vice, that really it appeared to be no vice to me, I went on smooth and pleasant. I wallowed in wealth, and it flowed in upon me at such a rate, having taken the frugal measures that the good knight directed, so that I had at the end of the eight years £2,800 coming in yearly, of which I did not spend one penny, being maintained by my allowance from my Lord ----, and more than maintained, by above £200 per annum; for though he did not contract for a year, as I made dumb signs to have it be, yet he gave me money so often, and that in such large parcels, that I had seldom so little as £700 to £800 a year of him, one year with another.

I must go back here, after telling openly wicked things I did, to mention something which, however, had the face of doing good. I remembered that when I went from England, which was fifteen years before, I had left five little children, turned out, as it were, to the wide world, and to the charity of their father's relations. The eldest was not six years old, for we had not been married full seven years when their father went away.

After my coming to England I was greatly desirous to hear how things stood with them, and whether they were all alive or not, and in what manner they had been maintained; and yet I resolved not to discover myself to them in the least, or to let any of the people that had the breeding of them up know that there was such a body left in the world as their mother.

Amy was the only body I could trust with such a commission, and I sent her into Spitalfields to the old aunt, and to the poor woman that was so instrumental in disposing the relations to take some care of the children, but they were both gone, dead and buried some years. The next enquiry she made was at the house where she carried the poor children and turned them in at the door. When she came there she found the house inhabited by other people, so that she could make little or nothing of her enquiries, and came back with an answer that was indeed no answer to me, for it gave me no satisfaction at all. I sent her back to enquire in the neighbourhood what was become of the family that lived in that house, and if they were removed, where they lived and what circumstances they were in, and withal, if she could, what became of the poor children, and how they lived and where, how they had been treated, and the like.

She brought me back word upon this second going that she heard as to the family, that the husband, who though but uncle-in-law to the children had yet been kindest to them, was dead, and that the widow was left but in mean circumstances, that is to say, she did not want, but that she was not so well in the world as she was thought to be when her husband was alive.

That as to the poor children, two of them, it seems, had been kept by her, that is to say, by her husband while he lived, for that it was against her will, that we all knew; but the honest neighbours pitied the poor children, they said, heartily; for that their aunt used them barbarously and made them little better than servants in the house, to wait upon her and her children, and scarce allowed them clothes fit to wear.

These were, it seems, my eldest and third, which were daughters; the second was a son, the fourth a daughter, and the youngest a son.

To finish the melancholy part of this history of my two unhappy girls, she brought me word that as soon as they were able to go out and get any work, they went from her; and some said she had turned them out of doors, but it seems she had not done so, but she used them so cruelly that they left her, and one of them went to service to a neighbour's a little way off, who knew her, an honest, substantial weaver's wife, to whom she was chambermaid, and in a little time she took her sister out of the bridewell of her aunt's house and got her a place too.

This was all melancholy and dull. I sent her then to the weaver's house, where the eldest had lived, but found that her mistress being dead, she was gone, and nobody knew there whither she went; only that they heard she had lived with a great lady at the other end of the town, but they did not know who that lady was.

These enquiries took us up three or four weeks, and I was not one jot the better for it, for I could hear nothing to my satisfaction. I sent her next to find out the honest man who, as in the beginning of my story I observed, made them be entertained, and caused the youngest to be fetched from the town where we lived, and where the parish officers had taken care of him. This gentleman was still alive; and there she heard that my youngest daughter and eldest son were dead also, but that my youngest son was alive and was at that time about seventeen years old, and that he was put out apprentice by the kindness and charity of his uncle, but to a mean trade, and at which he was obliged to work very hard.

Amy was so curious in this part that she went immediately to see him, and found him all dirty and hard at work. She had no remembrance at all of the youth, for she had not seen him since he was about two years old, and it was evident he could have no knowledge of her.

However, she talked with him and found him a good, sensible, mannerly youth; that he knew little of the story of his father or mother, and had no view of anything but to work hard for his living; and she did not think fit to put any great things into his head, lest it should take him off his business and perhaps make him turn giddy-headed and be good for nothing; but she went and found out that kind man his benefactor who had put him out, and finding him a plain, well-meaning, honest, and kind-hearted man, she opened her tale to him the easier. She made a long story, how she had a prodigious kindness for the child because she had the same for his father and mother; told him that she was the servant-maid that brought all of them to their aunt's door and ran away and left them; that their poor mother wanted bread, and what came of her after, she would have been glad to know. She added that her circumstances had happened to mend in the world, and that as she was in condition, so she was disposed to show some kindness to the children if she could find them out.

He received her with all the civility that so kind a proposal demanded, gave her an account of what he had done for the child; how he had maintained him, fed and clothed him, put him to school, and at last put him out to a trade. She said he had indeed been a father to the child. "But, sir," says she, "'tis a very laborious, hard-working trade, and he is but a thin weak boy." "That's true," says he, "but the boy chose the trade, and I assure you I gave £20 with him, and am to find him clothes all his apprenticeship. And as to its being a hard trade," says he, "that's the fate of his circumstances, poor boy; I could not well do better for him."

"Well, sir, as you did all for him in charity." says she, "it was exceeding well; but as my resolution is to do something for him, I desire you will if possible take him away again from that place where he works so hard, for I cannot bear to see the child work so very hard for his bread, and I will do something for him that shall make him live without such hard labour."

He smiled at that. "I can indeed," says he, "take him away, but then I must lose my £20 that I gave with him."

"Well, sir," said Amy, "I'll enable you to lose that £20 immediately "; and so she puts her hand in her pocket and pulls out her purse.

He began to be a little amazed at her and looked her hard in the face, and that so very much that she took notice of it and said, "Sir, I fancy by your looking at me you think you know me, but I am assured you do not, for I never saw your face before; I think you have done enough for the child, and that you ought to be acknowledged as a father to him, but you ought not to lose by your kindness to him, more than the kindness of bringing him up obliges you to; and therefore there's the £20," added she, "and pray let him be fetched away."

"Well, madam," says he, "I will thank you for the boy, as well as for myself, but will you please to tell me what I must do with him,"

"Sir," says Amy, "as you have been so kind to keep him so many years, I beg you will take him home again one year more, and I'll bring you £100 more, which I will desire you to lay out in schooling and clothes for him, and to pay you for his board; perhaps I may put him in a condition to return your kindness."

He looked pleased, but surprised very much, and enquired of Amy, but with very great respect, what he should go to school to learn, and what trade she would please to put him out to.

Amy said he should put him to learn a little Latin, and then merchants' accounts, and to write a good hand, for she would have him be put to a Turkey merchant.

"Madam," says he, "I am glad for his sake to hear you talk so, but do you know that a Turkey merchant will not take him under four or five hundred pounds?"

"Yes, sir," says Amy, "I know it very well."

"And," says he, "that it will require as many thousands to set him up?"

"Yes, sir," says Amy, "I know that very well too"; and resolving to talk very big, she added, "I have no children of my own and I resolve to make him my heir, and if ten thousand pounds would be required to set him up, he shall not want it; I was but his mother's servant when he was born, and I mourned heartily for the disaster of the family, and I always said if ever I was worth anything in the world I would take the child for my own, and I'll be as good as my word now, though I did not then foresee that it would be with me as it has been since." And so Amy told him a long story, how she was troubled for me, and what she would give to hear whether I was dead or alive, and what circumstances I was in; that if she could but find me, if I was ever so poor, she would take care of me and make a gentlewoman of me again.

He told her, that as to the child's mother, she had been reduced to the last extremity, and was obliged (as he supposed she knew) to send the children all among her husband's friends; and if it had not been for him, they had all been sent to the parish, but that he obliged the other relations to share the charge among them; that he had taken two, whereof he had lost the eldest, who died of the smallpox, but that he had been as careful of this as of his own, and had made very little difference in their breeding up; only that when he came to put him out, he thought it was best for the boy to put him to a trade which he might set up in without a stock, for otherwise his time would be lost; and that as to his mother, he had never been able to hear one word of her, no, not though he had made the utmost enquiry after her; that there went a report that she had drowned herself, but that he could never meet anybody that could give him a certain account of it.

Amy counterfeited a cry for her poor mistress, told him she would give anything in the world to see her if she was alive, and a great deal more such-like talk they had about that; then they returned to speak of the boy.

He enquired of her why she did not seek after the child before, that he might have been brought up from a younger age suitable to what she designed to do for him.

She told him she had been out of England, and was but newly returned from the East Indies. That she had been out of England, and was but newly returned, was true, but the latter was false, and was put in to blind him and provide against further enquiries, for it was not a strange thing for young women to go away poor to the East Indies and come home vastly rich. So she went on with directions about him, and both agreed in this, that the boy should by no means be told what was intended for him, but only that he should be taken home again to his uncle's, that his uncle thought the trade too hard for him, and the like.

About three days after this Amy goes again, and carried him the hundred pounds she promised him; but then Amy made quite another figure than she did before, for she went in my coach with two footmen after her, and dressed very fine also, with jewels and a gold watch; and there was indeed no great difficulty to make Amy look like a lady, for she was a very handsome, well-shaped woman, and genteel enough; the coachman and servants were particularly ordered to show her the same respect as they would to me, and to call her Madam Collins if they were asked any questions about her.

When the gentleman saw what a figure she made, it added to the former surprise, and he entertained her in the most respectful manner possible, congratulated her advancement in fortune, and particularly rejoiced that it should fall to the poor child's lot to be so provided for contrary to all expectation.

Well, Amy talked big, but very free and familiar, told them she had no pride in her good fortune (and that was true enough, for, to give Amy her due, she was far from it, and was as good-humoured a creature as ever lived), that she was the same as ever, and that she always loved this boy and was resolved to do something extraordinary for him.

Then she pulled out her money and paid him down £120, which, she said, she paid him that he might be sure he should be no loser by taking him home again, and that she would come and see him again and talk further about things with him, that so all might be settled for him in such a manner, as the accidents, such as mortality or anything else, should make no alteration to the child's prejudice.

At this meeting the uncle brought his wife out, a good, motherly, comely, grave woman, who spoke very tenderly of the youth and, as it appeared, had been very good to him, though she had several children of her own. After a long discourse she put in a word of her own. "Madam," says she, "I am heartily glad of the good intentions you have for this poor orphan, and I rejoice sincerely in it for his sake, but, madam, you know, I suppose, that there are two sisters alive too, may we not speak a word for them? Poor girls," says she, "they have not been so kindly used as he has, and are turned out to the wide world."

"Where are they, madam?" says Amy.

"Poor creatures," says the gentlewoman, "they are out at service, nobody knows where but themselves; their case is very hard."

"Well, madam," says Amy, "though, if I could find them, I would assist them, yet my concern is for my boy, as I call him, and I will put him into a condition to take care of his sisters."

"But, madam," says the good, compassionate creature, "he may not be so charitable perhaps by his own inclination, for brothers are not fathers; and they have been cruelly used already, poor girls; we have often relieved them, both with victuals and clothes too, even while they were pretended to be kept by their barbarous aunt."

"Well, madam," says Amy, "what can I do for them? They are gone, it seems, and cannot be heard of. When I see them, 'tis time enough."

She pressed Amy then to oblige their brother, out of the plentiful fortune he was like to have, to do something for his sisters when he should be able.

Amy spoke coldly of that still, but said she would consider of it, and so they parted for that time. They had several meetings after this, for Amy went to see her adopted son, and ordered his schooling, clothes, and other things, but enjoined them not to tell the young man anything but that they thought the trade he was at too hard for him, and they would keep him at home a little longer and give him some schooling to fit him for better business; and Amy appeared to him as she did before, only as one that had known his mother and had some kindness for him.

Thus this matter passed on for near a twelvemonth, when it happened that one of my maidservants having asked Amy leave, for Amy was mistress of the servants, and took and put out such as she pleased--I say, having asked leave to go into the city to see her friends, came home crying bitterly, and in a most grievous agony she was, and continued so several days, till Amy perceiving the excess, and that the maid would certainly cry herself sick, she took an opportunity with her and examined her about it.

The maid told her a long story, that she had been to see her brother, the only brother she had in the world, and that she knew he was put out apprentice to a ----, but there had come a lady in a coach to his uncle ----, who had brought him up, and made him take him home again; and so the wench ran on with the whole story, just as 'tis told above, till she came to the part that belonged to herself. "And there," says she, "I had not let them know where I lived, and the lady would have taken me, and they say would have provided for me too as she has done for my brother, but nobody could tell where to find me, and so I have lost it all and all the hopes of being anything but a poor servant all my days "; and then the girl fell a-crying again.

Amy said, "What's all this story? Who could this lady be? It must be some trick sure?" No, she said, it was not a trick, for she had made them take her brother home from apprentice, and bought him new clothes, and put him to have more learning; and the gentlewoman said she would make him her heir.

"Her heir!" says Amy; "what does that amount to? It may be she had nothing to leave him, she might make anybody her heir."

"No, no," says the girl, "she came in a fine coach and horses, and I don't know how many footmen to attend her, and brought a great bag of gold and gave it to my uncle ----, he that brought up my brother, to buy him clothes and to pay for his schooling and board."

"He that brought up your brother!" says Amy. "Why, did not he bring you up too as well as your brother? Pray, who brought you up then?"

Here the poor girl told a melancholy story, how an aunt had brought up her and her sister, and how barbarously she had used them, as we have heard.

By this time Amy had her head full enough, and her heart too, and did not know how to hold it or what to do, for she was satisfied that this was no other than my own daughter; for she told her all the history of her father and mother, and how she was carried by their maid to her aunt's door just as is related in the beginning of my story.

Amy did not tell me this story for a great while, nor did she well know what course to take in it, but as she had authority to manage everything in the family, she took occasion some time after, without letting me know anything of it, to find some fault with the maid and turn her away.

Her reasons were good, though at first I was not pleased when I heard of it, but I was convinced afterwards that she was in the right; for if she had told me of it I should have been in great perplexity, between the difficulty of concealing myself from my own child and the inconvenience of having my way of living be known among my first husband's relations, and even to my husband himself; for as to his being dead at Paris, Amy, seeing me resolved against marrying any more, had told me that she had formed the story only to make me easy when I was in Holland, if anything should offer to my liking.

However, I was too tender a mother still, notwithstanding what I had done, to let this poor girl go about the world drudging, as it were, for bread, and slaving at the fire and in the kitchen as a cook-maid. Besides, it came into my head that she might perhaps marry some poor devil of a footman or a coachman, or some such thing, and be undone that way; or, which was worse, be drawn into lie with some of that coarse cursed kind and be with child, and be utterly ruined that way; and in the midst of all my prosperity this gave me great uneasiness.

As to sending Amy to her, there was no doing that now, for as she had been servant in the house, she knew Amy as well as Amy knew me; and no doubt, though I was much out of her sight, yet she might have had the curiosity to have peeped at me, and seen me enough to know me again if I had discovered myself to her; so that, in short, there was nothing to be done that way.

However, Amy, a diligent, indefatigable creature, found out another woman and gave her her errand, and sent her to the honest man's house in Spitalfields, whither she supposed the girl would go after she was out of her place, and bade her talk with her and tell her at a distance that as something had been done for her brother, so something would be done for her too; and that she should not be discouraged, she carried her £20 to buy her clothes, and bade her not to go to service any more but think of other things; that she should take a lodging in some good family, and that she should soon hear further.

The girl was overjoyed with this news, you may be sure, and at first a little too much elevated with it, and dressed herself very handsomely indeed, and, as soon as she had done so, came and paid a visit to Madam Amy to let her see how fine she was. Amy congratulated her and lavished it might be all as she expected, but admonished her not to be elevated with it too much; told her humility was the best ornament of a gentlewoman, and a great deal of good advice she gave her, but discovered nothing.

All this was acted in the first years of my setting up my new figure here in town, and while the masks and balls were in agitation; and Amy carried on the affair of setting out my son into the world, which we were assisted in by the sage advice of my faithful counsellor, Sir Robert Clayton, who procured us a master for him, by whom he was afterwards sent abroad to Italy, as you shall hear in its place; and Amy managed my daughter too, very well, though by a third hand.

Chapter 18

MY amour with my Lord ---- began now to draw to an end, and indeed, notwithstanding his money, it had lasted so long that I was much more sick of his lordship than he could be of me. He grew old and fretful and captious, and I must add, which made the vice itself begin to grow surfeiting and nauseous to me, he grew worse and wickeder the older he grew, and that to such degree as is not fit to write of, and made me so weary of him that upon one of his capricious humours, which he often took occasion to trouble me with, I took occasion to be much less complaisant to him than I used to be; and as I knew him to be hasty, I first took care to put him into a little passion and then to resent it, and this brought us to words, in which I told him I thought he grew sick of me; and he answered, in a heat, that truly so he was. I answered that I found his lordship was endeavouring to make me sick too, that I had met with several such rubs from him of late, and that he did not use me as he used to do, and I begged his lordship he would make himself easy. This I spoke with an air of coldness and indifference such as I knew he could not bear; but I did not downright quarrel with him and tell him I was sick of him too, and desire him to quit me, for I knew that would come of itself; besides, I had received a great deal of handsome usage from him, and I was loath to have the breach be on my side, that he might not be able to say I was ungrateful.

But he put the occasion into my hands, for he came no more to me for two months; indeed, I expected a fit of absence, for such I had had several times before, but not for above a fortnight or three weeks at most. But after I had stayed a month, which was longer than ever he kept away yet, I took a new method with him, for I was resolved now it should be in my power to continue or not as I thought fit. At the end of a month, therefore. I removed and took lodgings at Kensington Gravel Pits, and that part next to the road to Acton, and left nobody in my lodgings but Amy and a footman, with proper instructions how to behave when his lordship being come to himself should think fit to come again, which I knew he would.

About the end of two months, he came in the dusk of the evening as usual. The footman answered him, and told him his lady was not at home, but there was Mrs. Amy above; so he did not order her to be called down, but went upstairs into the dining-room, and Mrs. Amy came to him. He asked where I was. "My Lord," said she, "my mistress has been removed a good while from hence, and lives at Kensington." "Ay, Mrs. Amy! how come you to be here, then?" "My Lord," said she, "we are here till the quarter-day, because the goods are not removed, and to give answers if any comes to ask for my lady." "Well, and what answer are you to give me?" "Indeed, my Lord," says Amy, "I have no particular answer to your lordship but to tell you and everybody else where my lady lives, that they may not think she's run away." "No, Mrs. Amy," says he, "I don't think she's run away, but indeed I can't go after her so far as that." Amy said nothing to that, but made a curtsy, and said she believed I would be there again for a week or two in a little time. "How little time, Mrs. Amy?" says my Lord. "She comes next Tuesday," says Amy. "Very well," says my Lord, "I'll call and see her then "; and so he went away.

Accordingly I came on the Tuesday and stayed a fortnight, but he came not; so I went back to Kensington, and after that I had very few of his lordship's visits, which I was very glad of, and in a little time after was more glad of it than I was at first, and upon a far better account too.

For now I began not to be sick of his lordship only, but really I began to be sick of the vice; and as I had good leisure now to divert and enjoy myself in the world as much as it was possible for any woman to do that ever lived in it, so I found that my judgment began to prevail upon me to fix my delight upon nobler objects than I had formerly done, and the very beginning of this brought some just reflections upon me relating to things past and to the former manner of my living. And though there was not the least hint in all this from what may be called religion or conscience, and far from anything of repentance or anything that was akin to it, especially at first, yet the sense of things and the knowledge I had of the world, and the vast variety of scenes that I had acted my part in, began to work upon my senses, and it came so very strong upon my mind one morning when I had been lying awake some time in my bed, as if somebody had asked me the question, what was I a whore for now? It occurred naturally upon this enquiry that at first I yielded to the importunity of my circumstances, the misery of which the devil dismally aggravated, to draw me to comply; for I confess I had strong natural aversions to the crime at first, partly owing to a virtuous education, and partly to a sense of religion; but the devil, and that greater devil of poverty, prevailed, and the person who laid siege to me did it in such an obliging, and I may almost say, irresistible manner, all still managed by the evil spirit--for I must be allowed to believe that he had a share in all such things, if not the whole management of them--but I say it was carried on by that person in such an irresistible manner, that (as I said when I related the fact) there was no withstanding it. These circumstances I say the devil managed, not only to bring me to comply, but he continued them as arguments to fortify my mind against all reflection, and to keep me in that horrid course I had engaged in, as if it were honest and lawful.

But not to dwell upon that now. This was a pretence, and here was something to be said, though I acknowledge it ought not to have been sufficient to me at all, but I say to leave that, all this was out of doors; the devil himself could not form one argument or put one reason into my head now that could serve for an answer, no, not so much as a pretended answer to this question, why I should be a whore now.

It had for a while been a little kind of excuse to me that I was engaged with this wicked old lord, and that I could not in honour forsake him; but how foolish and absurd did it look to repeat the word of honour on so vile an occasion. As if a woman should prostitute her honour in point of honour--horrid inconsistency. Honour called upon me to detest the crime and the man too, and to have resisted all the attacks which from the beginning had been made upon my virtue; and honour, had it been consulted, would have preserved me honest from the beginning:

For honesty and honour are the same.

This, however, shows us with what faint excuses and with what trifles we pretend to satisfy ourselves and suppress the attempts of conscience in the pursuit of agreeable crime, and in the possessing those pleasures which we are loath to part with.

But this objection would now serve no longer, for my lord had, in some sort, broken his engagements (I won't call it honour again) with me, and had so far slighted me as fairly to justify my entire quitting of him now; and so, as the objection was fully answered, the question remained still unanswered, why am I a whore now? Nor indeed had I anything to say for myself, even to myself. I could not without blushing, as wicked as I was, answer that I loved it for the sake of the vice, and that I delighted in being a whore as such--I say I could not say this even to myself, and all alone, nor indeed would it have been true. I was never able in justice and with truth to say I was so wicked as that, but as necessity first debauched me and poverty made me a whore at the beginning, so excess of avarice for getting money and excess of vanity continued me in the crime, not being able to resist the flatteries of great persons; being called the finest woman in France, being caressed by a Prince, and afterwards, I had pride enough to expect and folly enough to believe, though indeed without ground, by a great monarch. These were my baits, these the chains by which the devil held me bound, and by which I was indeed too fast held for any reasoning that I was then mistress of to deliver me from.

But this was all over now. Avarice could have no pretence, I was out of the reach of all that Fate could be supposed to do to reduce me; now I was so far from poor or the danger of it that I had £50,000 in my pocket at least--nay, I had the income of £50,000, for I had £2,500 a year coming in upon very good land security, besides £3,000 or £4,000 in money which I kept by me for ordinary occasions, and besides jewels and plate and goods which were worth near £5,600 more. These put together, when I ruminated on it all in my thoughts, as you may be sure I did often, added weight still to the question, as above, and it sounded continually in my head, what's next? what am I a whore for now?

It is true this was, as I say, seldom out of my thoughts, but yet it made no impressions upon me of that kind which might be expected from a reflection of so important a nature, and which had so much of substance and seriousness in it.

But, however, it was not without some little consequences, even at that time, and which gave a little turn to my way of living at first, as you shall hear in its place.

But one particular thing intervened besides this, which gave me some uneasiness at this time, and made way for other things that followed. I have mentioned in several little digressions the concern I had upon me for my children, and in what manner I had directed that affair. I must go on a little with that part in order to bring the subsequent parts of my story together.

My boy, the only son I had left that I had a legal right to call son, was, as I have said, rescued from the unhappy circumstances of being apprentice to a mechanic, and was brought up upon a new foot; but though this was infinitely to his advantage, yet it put him back near three years in his coming into the world, for he had been near a year at the drudgery he was first put to, and it took up two years more to form him for what he had hopes given him he should hereafter be, so that he was full nineteen years old, or rather twenty years, before he came to be put out as I intended; at the end of which time I put him to a very flourishing Italian merchant, and he again sent him to Messina in the island of Sicily. And a little before the juncture I am now speaking of, I had letters from him, that is to say, Mrs. Amy had letters from him, intimating that he was out of his time, and that he had an opportunity to be taken into an English house there, on very good terms, if his support from hence might answer what he was bid to hope for; and so begged that what would be done for him might be so ordered that he might have it for his present advancement, referring for the particulars to his master, the merchant in London whom he had been put apprentice to here, who, to cut the story short, gave such a satisfactory account of it, and of my young man, to my steady and faithful counsellor, Sir Robert Clayton, that I made no scruple to pay £4,000, which was £1,000 more than he demanded, or rather proposed, that he might have encouragement to enter into the world better than he expected.

His master remitted the money very faithfully to him, and, finding by Sir Robert Clayton that the young gentleman, for so he called him, was well supported, wrote such letters on his account as gave him a credit at Messina equal in value to the money itself.

I could not digest it very well that I should all this while conceal myself thus from my own child, and make all this favour due, in his opinion, to a stranger, and yet I could not find in my heart to let my son know what a mother he had and what a life she lived, when at the same time that he must think himself infinitely obliged to me, he must be obliged, if he was a man of virtue, to hate his mother and abhor the way of living by which all the bounty he enjoyed was raised.

This is the reason of mentioning this part of my son's story, which is otherwise no ways concerned in my history, but as it put me upon thinking how to put an end to that wicked course I was in, that my own child, when he should afterwards come to England in a good figure and with the appearance of a merchant, should not be ashamed to own me.

But there was another difficulty which lay heavier upon me a great deal, and that was my daughter, who, as before, I had relieved by the hands of another instrument, which Amy had procured. The girl, as I have mentioned, was directed to put herself into a good garb, take lodgings, and entertain a maid to wait upon her, and to give herself some breeding, that is to say, to learn to dance and fit herself to appear as a gentlewoman, being made to hope that she should, some time or other, find that she should be put into a condition to support her character and to make herself amends for all her former troubles. She was only charged not to be drawn into matrimony till she was secured of a fortune that might assist to dispose of herself suitable not to what she then was but what she was to be.

The girl was too sensible of her circumstances not to give all possible satisfaction of that kind, and indeed she was mistress of too much understanding not to see how much she should be obliged to that part for her own interest.

It was not long after this, but being well equipped and in everything well set out, as she was directed, she came as I have related above, and paid a visit to Mrs. Amy, and to tell her of her good fortune. Amy pretended to be much surprised at the alteration, and overjoyed for her sake, and began to treat her very well, entertained her handsomely, and, when she would have gone away, pretended to ask my leave and sent my coach home with her; and in short, learning from her where she lodged, which was in the city, Amy promised to return her visit, and did so; and in a word, Amy and Susan (for she was my own name) began an intimate acquaintance together.

There was an inexpressible difficulty in the poor girl's way, or else I should not have been able to have forborne discovering myself to her, and this was her having been a servant in my particular family; and I could by no means think of ever letting the children know what a kind of creature they owed their being to, or giving them an occasion to upbraid their mother with her scandalous life, much less to justify the like practice from my example.

Thus it was with me, and thus, no doubt, considering parents always find it that their own children are a restraint to them in their worst courses, when the sense of a superior Power has not the same influence. But of that hereafter.

There happened, however, one good circumstance in the case of this poor girl which brought about a discovery sooner than otherwise it would have been, and it was thus. After she and Amy had been intimate for some time and had exchanged several visits, the girl now grown a woman, talking to Amy of the gay things that used to fall out when she was servant in my family, spoke of it with a kind of concern that she could not see (me) her lady, and at last she adds, "'Twas very strange, madam," says she to Amy, "but though I lived near two years in the house, I never saw my mistress in my life, except it was that public night when she danced in the fine Turkish habit, and then she was so disguised that I knew nothing of her afterwards."

Amy was glad to hear this; but as she was a cunning girl from the beginning, she was not to be bit, and so she laid no stress upon that at first, but gave me an account of it; and I must confess it gave me a secret joy to think that I was not known to her, and that, by virtue of that only accident, I might, when other circumstances made room for it, discover myself to her and let her know she had a mother in a condition fit to be owned.

It was a dreadful restraint to me before, and this gave me some very sad reflections and made way for the great question I have mentioned above; and by how much the circumstance was bitter to me, by so much the more agreeable it was to understand that the girl had never seen me, and consequently did not know me again if she was to be told who I was.

However, the next time she came to visit Amy, I was resolved to put it to a trial and to come into the room and let her see me, and to see by that whether she knew me or not; but Amy put me by, lest indeed, as there was reason enough to question, I should not be able to contain or forbear discovering myself to her; so it went off for that time.

But both these circumstances, and that is the reason of mentioning them, brought me to consider of the life I lived, and to resolve to put myself into some figure of life in which I might not be scandalous to my own family and be afraid to make myself known to my own children, who were my own flesh and blood.

There was another daughter I had, which, with all our enquiries, we could not hear of, high nor low, for several years after the first. But I return to my own story.

Chapter 19

Being now in part removed from my old station, I seemed to be in a fair way of retiring from my old acquaintances, and consequently from the vile abominable trade I had driven so long, so that the door seemed to be, as it were, particularly opened to my reformation if I had any mind to it in earnest. But for all that, some of my old friends, as I had used to call them, enquired me out and came to visit me at Kensington, and that more frequently than I wished they would do; but it being once known where I was, there was no avoiding it, unless I would have downright refused and affronted them, and I was not yet in earnest enough with my resolutions to go that length.

The best of it was, my old lewd favourite, whom I now heartily hated, entirely dropped me. He came once to visit me, but I caused Amy to deny me and say I was gone out. She did it so oddly too, that when his lordship went away he said coldly to her, "Well, well, Mrs. Amy, I find your mistress does not desire to be seen; tell her I won't trouble her any more," repeating the words "any more" two or three times over just at his going away.

I reflected a little on it at first, as unkind to him, having had so many considerable presents from him; but, as I have said, I was sick of him, and that on some accounts which, if I could suffer myself to publish them, would fully justify my conduct; but that part of the story will not bear telling, so I must leave it and proceed.

I had begun a little, as I have said above, to reflect upon my manner of living and to think of putting a new face upon it, and nothing moved me to it more than the consideration of my having three children who were now grown up, and yet, that while I was in that station of life, I could not converse with them or make myself known to them; and this gave me a great deal of uneasiness. At last I entered into talk on this part of it with my woman Amy.

We lived at Kensington, as I have said, and though I had done with my old wicked Lord ----, as above, yet I was frequently visited, as I said, by some others, so that, in a word, I began to be known in the town, not by my name only, but by my character too, which was worse.

It was one morning when Amy was in bed with me, and I had some of my dullest thoughts about me, that Amy, hearing me sigh pretty often, asked me if I was not well. "Yes, Amy, I am well enough," says I, "but my mind is oppressed with heavy thoughts, and has been so a good while "; and then I told her how it grieved me that I could not make myself known to my own children, or form any acquaintances in the world. "Why so?" says Amy. "Why, prithee, Amy," says I, "what will my children say to themselves, and to one another, when they find their mother, however rich she may be, is at best but a whore, a common whore? And as for acquaintance, prithee, Amy, what sober lady or what family of any character will visit or be acquainted with a whore?"

"Why, all that's true, madam," says Amy, "but how can it be remedied now?" "'Tis true, Amy," said I, "the thing cannot be remedied now, but the scandal of it, I fancy, may be thrown off."

"Truly," says Amy, "I do not see how, unless you will go abroad again and live in some other nation where nobody has known us or seen us, so that they cannot say they ever saw us before."

That very thought of Amy's put what follows into my head, and I returned, "Why, Amy," says I, "is it not possible for me to shift my being from this part of the town and go and live in another part of the country, and be as entirely concealed as if I had never been known?"

"Yes," says Amy, "I believe it might, but then you must put off all your equipages and servants, coaches and horses, change your liveries, nay, your own clothes, and, if it was possible, your very face."

"Well," says I, "and that's the way, Amy, and that I'll do, and that forthwith, for I am not able to live in this manner any longer." Amy came into this with a kind of pleasure particular to herself, that is to say, with an eagerness not to be resisted; for Amy was apt to be precipitant in her motions, and was for doing it immediately. "Well," says I, "Amy, as soon as you will, but what course must we take to do it? We cannot put off servants and coach and horses and everything, leave off housekeeping, and transform ourselves into a new shape, all in a moment; servants must have warning, and the goods must be sold off, and a thousand things"; and this began to perplex us, and in particular took us up two or three days' consideration.

At last, Amy, who was a clever manager in such cases, came to me with a scheme, as she called it. "I have found it out, madam," says she; "I have found a scheme how you shall, if you have a mind to it, begin and finish a perfect entire change of your figure and circumstances in one day, and shall be as much unknown, madam, in twenty-four hours as you would be in so many years."

"Come, Amy," says I, "let us hear it, for you please me mightily with the thoughts of it." "Why, then," says Amy, "let me go into the city this afternoon, and I'll enquire out some honest, plain, sober family, where I will take lodgings for you as for a country gentlewoman that desires to be in London for about half a year, and to board yourself and a kinswoman that is half a servant, half a companion, meaning myself, and so agree with them by the month.

"To this lodging, if I hit upon one to your mind, you may go to-morrow morning, in a hackney-coach, with nobody but me, and leave such clothes and linen as you think fit, but to be sure the plainest you have; and then you are removed at once, you need never so much as set your foot in this house again (meaning where we then were) or see anybody belonging to it. In the meantime I'll let the servants know that you are going over to Holland upon extraordinary business, and will leave off your equipages, and so I'll give them warning, or, if they will accept of it, give them a month's wages. Then I'll sell off your furniture as well as I can; as to your coach, it is but having it new painted and the lining changed, and getting new harness and hammercloths, and you may keep it still or dispose of it as you think fit. And only take care to let this lodging be in some remote part of the town, and you may be as perfectly unknown as if you had never been in England in your life."

This was Amy's scheme, and it pleased me so well that I resolved not only to let her go, but was resolved to go with her myself; but Amy put me off that, because, she said, she should have occasion to hurry up and down so long, that if I was with her it would rather hinder than further her; so I waived it.

In a word, Amy went, and was gone five long hours; but when she came back I could see by her countenance that her success had been suitable to her pains, for she came laughing and gaping. "Oh, madam!" says she, "I have pleased you to the life "; and with that she tells me how she had fixed upon a house in a court in the Minories, that she was directed to it merely by accident that it was a female family, the master of the house being gone to New England, and that the woman had four children, kept two maids, and lived very handsomely, but wanted company to divert her, and that on that very account she had agreed to take boarders.

Amy agreed for a good handsome price, because she was resolved I should be used well; so she bargained to give her £35 for the half-year and £50 if we took a maid, leaving that to my choice; and that we might be satisfied we should meet with nothing very gay; the people were Quakers, and I liked them the better.

I was so pleased that I resolved to go with Amy the next day to see the lodgings, and to see the woman of the house, and see how I liked them; but if I was pleased with the general, I was much more pleased with the particular, for the gentlewoman, I must call her so, though she was a Quaker, was a most courteous, obliging, mannerly person, perfectly well bred, and perfectly well humoured, and, in short, the most agreeable conversation that ever I met with; and which was worth all, so grave, and yet so pleasant and so merry, that 'tis scarce possible for me to express how I was pleased and delighted with her company; and particularly, I was so pleased that I would go away no more, so I e'en took up my lodging there the very first night.

In the meantime, though it took up Amy almost a month so entirely to put off all the appearances of housekeeping, as above, it need take me up no time to relate it; 'tis enough to say that Amy quitted all that part of the world and came pack and baggage to me, and here we took up our abode.

I was now in a perfect retreat indeed; remote from the eyes of all that ever had seen me, and as much out of the way of being ever seen or heard of by any of the gang that used to follow me, as if I had been among the mountains in Lancashire; for when did a blue garter or a coach-and-six come into a little narrow passage in the Minories or Goodman's Fields? And as there was no fear of them, so really I had no desire to see them, or so much as to hear from them any more as long as I lived.

I seemed in a little hurry while Amy came and went so every day, at first, but when that was over I lived here perfectly retired, and with a most pleasant and agreeable lady. I must call her so, for though a Quaker, she had a full share of good breeding sufficient to her if she had been a duchess; in a word, she was the most agreeable creature in her conversation, as I said before, that ever I met with.

I pretended, after I had been there some time, to be extremely in love with the dress of the Quakers, and this pleased her so much that she would needs dress me up one day in a suit of her own clothes, but my real design was to see whether it would pass upon me for a disguise.

Amy was struck with the novelty, though I had not mentioned my design to her, and when the Quaker was gone out of the room, says Amy, "I guess your meaning; it is a perfect disguise to you; why, you look quite another body, I should not have known you myself. Nay," says Amy, "more than that, it makes you look ten years younger than you did."

Nothing could please me better than that, and when Amy repeated it I was so fond of it that I asked my Quaker (I won't call her landlady, 'tis indeed too coarse a word for her, and she deserved a much better)--I say I asked her if she would sell it. I told her I was so fond of it that I would give her enough to buy her a better suit. She declined it at first, but I soon perceived that it was chiefly in good manners, because I should not dishonour myself, as she called it, to put on her old clothes, but if I pleased to accept of them, she would give me them for my dressing clothes, and go with me and buy a suit for me that might be better worth my wearing.

But as I conversed in a very frank, open manner with her, I bid her do the like with me; that I made no scruples of such things, but that if she would let me have them, I would satisfy her. So she let me know what they cost, and to make her amends I gave her three guineas more than they cost her.

This good (though unhappy) Quaker had the misfortune to have had a bad husband, and he was gone beyond-sea; she had a good house and well-furnished, and had some jointure of her own estate which supported her and her children, so that she did not want; but she was not at all above such a help as my being there was to her, so she was as glad of me as I was of her.

However, as I knew there was no way to fix this new acquaintance like making myself a friend to her, I began with making her some handsome presents, and the like to her children; and first, opening my bundles one day in my chamber, I heard her in another room, and called her in with a kind of familiar way; there I showed her some of my fine clothes, and having among the rest of my things a piece of very fine new holland which I had bought a little before, worth about nine shillings an ell, I pulled it out. "Here, my friend," says I, "I will make you a present if you will accept of it"; and with that I laid the piece of holland in her lap.

I could see she was surprised, and that she could hardly speak. "What dost thou mean?" says she; "indeed, I cannot have the face to accept so fine a present as this "; adding, "'tis fit for thy own use, but 'tis above my wear indeed." I thought she had meant she must not wear it so fine because she was a Quaker, so I returned, "Why, do not you Quakers wear fine linen neither?" "Yes," says she, "we wear fine linen when we can afford it, but this is too good for me." However, I made her take it, and she was very thankful too. But my end was answered another way, for by this I engaged her so that as I found her a woman of understanding and of honesty too, I might upon any occasion have a confidence in her, which was indeed what I very much wanted.

By accustoming myself to converse with her, I had not only learnt to dress like a Quaker, but so used myself to "thee" and "thou," that I talked like a Quaker too, as readily and naturally as if I had been born among them; and, in a word, I passed for a Quaker among all people that did not know me. I went but little abroad, but I had been so used to a coach that I knew not how well to go without one; besides, I thought it would be a further disguise to me, so I told my Quaker friend one day that I thought I lived too close, that I wanted air. She proposed taking a hackney-coach sometimes or a boat, but I told her I had always had a coach of my own till now and I could find in my heart to have one again.

She seemed to think it strange at first, considering how close I lived, but had nothing to say when she found that I did not value the expense; so, in short, I resolved I would have a coach. When we came to talk of equipages, she extolled the having all things plain; I said so too. So I left it to her direction, and a coachmaker was sent for, and he provided me a plain coach, no gilding or painting, lined with a light-grey cloth, and my coachman had a coat of the same, and no lace on his hat.

When all was ready I dressed myself in the dress I bought of her, and said, "Come, I'll be a Quaker to-day, and you and I'll go abroad "; which we did, and there was not a Quaker in the town looked less like a counterfeit than I did. But all this was my particular plot to be the more completely concealed, and that I might depend upon being not known and yet need not be confined like a prisoner and be always in fear; so that all the rest was grimace.

Chapter 20

WE lived here very easy and quiet, and yet I cannot say I was so in my mind. I was like a fish out of water; I was as gay and as young in my disposition as I was at five-and-twenty, and as I had always been courted, flattered, and used to love it, so I missed it in my conversation; and this put me many times upon looking back upon things past.

I had very few moments in my life which in their reflection afforded me anything but regret, but of all the foolish actions I had to look back upon in my life, none looked so preposterous and so like distraction, nor left so much melancholy on my mind, as my parting with my friend the merchant of Paris, and the refusing him upon such honourable and just conditions as he had offered; and though on his just (which I called unkind) rejecting my invitation to come to him again I had looked on him with some disgust, yet now my mind ran upon him continually, and the ridiculous conduct of my refusing him, and I could never be satisfied about him. I flattered myself that if I could but see him I could yet master him, and that he would presently forget all that had passed that might be thought unkind; but as there was no room to imagine anything like that to be possible, I threw those thoughts off again as much as I could.

However, they continually returned, and I had no rest night or day for thinking of him whom I had forgot above eleven years. I told Amy of it, and we talked it over sometimes in bed, almost whole nights together. At last Amy started a thing of her own head which put it in a way of management, though a wild one too. "You are so uneasy, madam," says she, "about this Mr. ---- the merchant at Paris; come," says she, "if you'll give me leave I'll go over and see what's become of him."

"Not for ten thousand pounds," said I; "no, nor if you met him in the street, not to offer to speak to him on my account." "No," says Amy, "I would not speak to him at all, or if I did, I warrant you it shall not look to be upon your account; I'll only enquire after him, and if he is in being, you shall hear of him; if not, you shall hear of him still, and that may be enough."

"Why," says I, "if you will promise me not to enter into anything relating to me with him, nor to begin any discourse at all unless he begins it with you, I could almost be persuaded to let you go and try."

Amy promised me all that I desired, and in a word, to cut the story short, I let her go, but tied her up to so many particulars that it was almost impossible her going could signify anything; and had she intended to observe them she might as well have stayed at home as have gone, for I charged her if she came to see him she should not so much as take notice that she knew him again, and if he spoke to her she should tell him she was come away from me a great many years ago and knew nothing what was become of me; that she had been come over to France six years ago, and was married there and lived at Calais, or to that purpose.

Amy promised me nothing indeed, for, as she said, it was impossible for her to resolve what would be fit to do or not to do till she was there upon the spot, and had found out the gentleman or heard of him, but that then, if I would trust her as I had always done, she would answer for it that she would do nothing but what should be for my interest, and what she would hope I should be very well pleased with.

With this general commission, Amy, notwithstanding she had been so frighted at the sea, ventured her carcase once more by water, and away she goes to France. She had four articles of confidence in charge to enquire after for me, and, as I found by her, she had one for herself. I say four for me, because though her first and principal errand was to inform herself of my Dutch merchant, yet I gave her in charge to enquire, secondly, after my husband, whom I left a trooper in the Gendarmes; thirdly, after that rogue of a Jew, whose very name I hated, and of whose face I had such a frightful idea, that Satan himself could not counterfeit a worse; and lastly, after my foreign Prince. And she discharged herself very well of them all, though not so successful as I wished.

Amy had a very good passage over the sea, and I had a letter from her from Calais in three days after she went from London. When she came to Paris she wrote me an account, that as to her first and most important enquiry, which was after the Dutch merchant; her account was that he had returned to Paris, lived three years there and, quitting that city, went to live at Rouen. So away goes Amy for Rouen.

But as she was going to bespeak a place in the coach to Rouen, she meets very accidentally in the street with her gentleman, as I called him, that is to say, the Prince de ----'s gentleman, who had been her favourite, as above.

You may be sure there were several other kind things happened between Amy and him, as you shall hear afterwards. But the two main things were that Amy enquired about his lord, and had a full account of him; of which presently; and in the next place, telling him whither she was going, and for what. He bade her not go yet, for that he would have a particular account of it the next day from a merchant that knew him; and accordingly he brought her word the next day that he had been for six years before that gone for Holland, and that he lived there still.

This, I say, was the first news from Amy for some time--I mean about my merchant. In the meantime, Amy, as I have said, enquired about the other persons she had in her instructions. As for the Prince, the gentleman told her he was gone into Germany, where his estate lay, and that he lived there; that he had made great enquiry after me, that he (his gentleman) had made all the search he had been able, for me, but that he could not hear of me; that he believed if his lord had known I had been in England, he would have gone over to me, but that, after long enquiry, he was obliged to give it over, but that he verily believed if he could have found me he would have married me; and that he was extremely concerned that he could hear nothing of me.

I was not at all satisfied with Amy's account but ordered her to go to Rouen herself, which she did, and there with much difficulty (the person she was directed to being dead)--I say with much difficulty, she came to be informed that my merchant had lived there two years or something more; but that having met with a very great misfortune, he had gone back to Holland, as the French merchant said, where he had stayed two years; but with this addition, viz. that he came back again to Rouen and lived in good reputation there another year, and afterwards he was gone to England, and that he lived in London. But Amy could by no means learn how to write to him there, till by great accident an old Dutch skipper who had formerly served him, coming to Rouen, Amy was told of it; and he told her that he lodged in Laurence Pountney Lane in London, but was to be seen every day upon the Exchange, in the French Walk.

This, Amy thought, it was time enough to tell me of when she came over, and besides, she did not find this Dutch skipper till she had spent four or five months, and been again at Paris and then come back to Rouen for further information. But in the meantime she wrote me from Paris, that he was not to be found by any means, that he had been gone from Paris seven or eight years, that she was told he had lived at Rouen and she was a-going thither to enquire, but that she had heard afterwards that he was gone also from thence to Holland, so she did not go.

This, I say, was Amy's first account, and I, not satisfied with it, had sent her an order to go to Rouen to enquire there also, as above.

While this was negotiating, and I received these accounts from Amy at several times, a strange adventure happened to me which I must mention just here. I had been abroad to take the air as usual, with my Quaker, as far as Epping Forest, and we were driving back towards London, when on the road between Bow and Mile End two gentlemen on horseback came riding by, having overtaken the coach and passed it, and went forward towards London.

They did not ride apace, though they passed the coach, for we went very softly, nor did they look into the coach at all, but rode side by side, earnestly talking to one another and inclining their faces sideways a little towards one another, he that went nearest the coach with his face from it, and he that was furthest from the coach with his face towards it, and passing in the very next track to the coach, I could hear them talk Dutch very distinctly. But it is impossible to describe the confusion I was in when I plainly saw that the farthest of the two, him whose face looked towards the coach, was my friend the Dutch merchant of Paris.

If it had been possible to conceal my disorder from my friend the Quaker, I would have done it, but I found she was too well acquainted with such things not to take the hint. "Dost thou understand Dutch?" said she. "Why?" said I. "Why," says she, "'tis easy to suppose that thou art a little concerned at somewhat those men say, I suppose they are talking of thee." "Indeed, my good friend," said I, "thou art mistaken this time, for I know very well what they are talking of, but 'tis all about ships and trading affairs." "Well," says she, "then one of them is a man friend of thine, or somewhat is the case, for though thy tongue will not confess it, thy face does."

I was going to have told a bold lie and said I knew nothing of them, but I found it was impossible to conceal it, so I said, "Indeed, I think I know the farthest of them, but I have neither spoken to him nor so much as seen him for above eleven years." "Well, then," says she, "thou hast seen him with more than common eyes when thou didst see him, or else seeing him now would not be such a surprise to thee." "Indeed," said I, "'tis true I am a little surprised at seeing him just now, for I thought he had been in quite another part of the world, and I can assure you I never saw him in England in my life." "Well, then, 'tis the more likely he is come over now on purpose to seek thee." "No, no," said I, "knight-errantry is over, women are not so hard to come at that men should not be able to please themselves without running from one kingdom to another." "Well, well," says she, "I would have him see thee for all that, as plainly as thou hast seen him." "No, but he shan't," says I, "for I am sure he don't know me in this dress, and I'll take care he shan't see my face if I can help it"; so I held up my fan before my face, and she saw me resolute in that, so she pressed me no further.

We had several discourses upon the subject, but still I let her know I was resolved he should not know me; but at last I confessed so much, that though I would not let him know who I was or where I lived, I did not care if I knew where he lived and how I might enquire about him. She took the hint immediately, and her servant being behind the coach, she called him to the coach side and bade him keep his eye upon that gentleman, and as soon as the coach came to the end of Whitechapel he should get down and follow him closely, so as to see where he put up his horse, and then to go into the inn and enquire, if he could, who he was and where he lived.

The fellow followed diligently to the gate of an inn in Bishopsgate Street, and seeing him go in, made no doubt but that he had him fast, but was confounded when upon enquiry he found the inn was a thoroughfare into another street, and that the two gentlemen had only rode through the inn as the way to the street where they were going, and so, in short, came back no wiser than he went.

My kind Quaker was more vexed at the disappointment, at least apparently so, than I was, and asking the fellow if he was sure he knew the gentleman again if he saw him, the fellow said he had followed him so close, and took so much notice of him in order to do his errand as it ought to be done, that he was very sure he should know him again, and that, besides, he was sure he should know his horse.

This part was indeed likely enough, and the kind Quaker, without telling me anything of the matter, caused her man to place himself just at the corner of Whitechapel Church Wall every Saturday in the afternoon, that being the day when the citizens chiefly ride abroad to take the air, and there to watch all the afternoon and look for him.

It was not till the fifth Saturday that her man came, I with a great deal of joy, and gave her an account that he had found out the gentleman; that he was a Dutchman, but a French merchant; that he came from Rouen, and his name was ----, and that he lodged at Mr. ---- on Laurence Pountney Hill. I was surprised, you may be sure, when she came and told me one evening all the particulars, except that of having set her man to watch. "I have found out thy Dutch friend," says she, "and can tell thee how to find him too." I coloured again as red as fire. "Then thou hast dealt with the Evil One, friend," said I very gravely. "No, no," says she, "I have no familiar; but I tell thee I have found him for thee," and his name is so-and-so, and he lives as above recited.

I was surprised again at this, not being able to imagine how she should come to know all this. However, to put me out of pain she told me what she had done. "Well," said I, "thou art very kind, but this is not worth thy pains; for now I know it, 'tis only to satisfy my curiosity, for I shall not send to him upon any account." "Be that as thou wilt," says she; "besides," added she, "thou art in the right to say so to me, for why should I be trusted with it? Though if I were, I assure thee, I should not betray thee." "That is very kind," said I, "and I believe thee; and assure thyself, if I do send to him, thou shalt know it, and be trusted with it too."

During this interval of five weeks I suffered a hundred thousand perplexities of mind. I was thoroughly convinced I was right as to the person, that it was the man; I knew him so well, and saw him so plain, I could not be deceived. I drove out again in the coach (on pretence of air), almost every day, in hopes of seeing him again, but was never so lucky as to see him; and now I had made the discovery, I was as far to seek what measures to take as I was before.

To send to him, or speak to him first if I should see him, so as to be known to him, that I resolved not to do if I died for it; to watch him about his lodging, that was as much below my spirit as the other; so that, in a word, I was at a perfect loss how to act or what to do.

At length came Amy's letter with the last account which she had at Rouen from the Dutch skipper, which, confirming the other, left me out of doubt that this was my man; but still no human invention could bring me to the speech of him in such a manner as would suit with my resolutions; for, after all, how did I know what his circumstances were? whether married or single? And if he had a wife, I know he was so honest a man he would not so much as converse with me, or so much as know me, if he met me in the street.

In the next place, as he had entirely neglected me, which, in short, is the worst way of slighting a woman, and had given no answer to my letters, I did not know but he might be the same man still; so I resolved that I could do nothing in it unless some fairer opportunity presented which might make my way clearer to me, for I was determined he should have no room to put any more slights upon me.

In these thoughts I passed away near three months, till at last (being impatient) I resolved to send for Amy to come over and tell her how things stood, and that I would do nothing till she came. Amy in answer sent me word she would come away with all speed, but begged of me that I would enter into no engagement with him or anybody till she arrived; but still keeping me in the dark as to the thing itself which she had to say, at which I was heartily vexed, for many reasons.

But while all these things were transacting, and letters and answers passed between Amy and I a little slower than usual, at which I was not so well pleased as I used to be with Amy's dispatch--I say in this time the following scene opened.

It was one afternoon about four o'clock, my friendly Quaker and I sitting in her chamber upstairs, and very cheerful, chatting together (for she was the best company in the world), when somebody ringing hastily at the door, and no servant just then in the way, she ran down herself to the door; when a gentleman appears with a footman attending, and making some apologies which she did not thoroughly understand, he speaking but broken English. He asked to speak with me by the very same name that I went by in her house; which, by the way, was not the name that he had known me by.

She with very civil language, in her way, brought him into a very handsome parlour below-stairs, and said she would go and see whether the person who lodged in her house owned that name, and he should hear further.

I was a little surprised even before I knew anything of who it was, my mind foreboding the thing as it happened (whence that arises, let the naturalists explain to us), but I was frighted and ready to die when my Quaker came up all gay and crowing. "There," says she, "is the Dutch French merchant come to see thee." I could not speak one word to her nor stir off my chair, but sat as motionless as a statue. She talked a thousand pleasant things to me, but they made no impression on me. At last she pulled me and teased me. "Come, come," says she, "be thyself and rouse up, I must go down again to him; what shall I say to him?" "Say," said I, "that you have no such body in the house." "That I cannot do," says she, "because it is not the truth; besides, I have owned thou art above. Come, come, go down with me." "Not for a thousand guineas," said I. "Well," says she, "I'll go and tell him thou wilt come quickly." So, without giving me time to answer her, away she goes.

A million of thoughts circulated in my head while she was gone, and what to do I could not tell. I saw no remedy but I must speak with him, but would have given £500 to have shunned it; yet, had I shunned it, perhaps then I would have given £500 again that I had seen him. Thus fluctuating and unconcluding were my thoughts, what I so earnestly desired I declined when it offered itself, and what now I pretended to decline was nothing but what I had been at the expense of £40 or £50 to send Amy to France for, and even without any view, or indeed any rational expectation, of bringing it to pass; and what for half a year before I was so uneasy about, that I could not be quiet night or day, till Amy proposed to go over to enquire after him. In short, my thoughts were all confused and in the utmost disorder. I had once refused and rejected him, and I repented it heartily; then I had taken ill his silence, and in my mind rejected him again, but had repented that too. Now I had stooped so low as to send after him into France, which if he had known, perhaps he had never come after me; and should I reject him a third time! On the other hand, he had repented too in his turn perhaps, and not knowing how I had acted, either in stooping to send in search after him or in the wickeder part of my life, was come over hither to seek me again; and I might take him perhaps with the same advantages as I might have done before, and would I now be backward to see him! Well, while I was in this hurry, my friend the Quaker comes up again, and, perceiving the confusion I was in, she runs to her closet and fetched me a little pleasant cordial, but I would not taste it. "Oh," says she, "I understand thee; be not uneasy, I'll give thee something shall take off all the smell of it; if he kisses thee a thousand times he shall be no wiser." I thought with myself, "Thou art perfectly acquainted with affairs of this nature, I think you must govern me now," so I began to incline to go down with her. Upon that I took the cordial, and she gave me a kind of spicy preserve after it, whose flavour was so strong, and yet so deliciously pleasant, that it would cheat the nicest smelling, and it left not the least taint of the cordial on the breath.

Well, after this (though with some hesitation still) I went down a pair of back-stairs with her and into a dining-room, next to the parlour in which he was, but there I halted and desired she would let me consider of it a little. "Well, do so," says she, and left me with more readiness than she did before; "do consider, and I'll come to thee again."

Though I hung back with an awkwardness that was really unfeigned, yet when she so readily left me, I thought it was not so kind, and I began to think she should have pressed me still on to it; so foolishly backward are we to the thing which of all the world we most desire, mocking ourselves with a feigned reluctance when the negative would be death to us. But she was too cunning for me, for while I, as it were, blamed her in my mind for not carrying me to him, though at the same time I appeared backward to see him, on a sudden she unlocks the folding-doors which looked into the next parlour, and throwing them open, "There," says she, ushering him in, "is the person whom I suppose thou enquireth for "; and the same moment, with a kind decency she retired, and that so swift that she would not give us leave hardly to know which way she went.

I stood up, but was confounded with a sudden enquiry in my thoughts how I should receive him, and with a resolution as swift as lightning, in answer to it, said to myself, "It shall be coldly "; so on a sudden I put on an air of stiffness and ceremony, and held it for about two minutes, but it was with great difficulty.

He restrained himself too, on the other hand, came towards me gravely, and saluted me in form; but it was, it seems, upon his supposing the Quaker was behind him, whereas she, as I said, understood things too well, and had retired as if she had vanished, that we might have full freedom. For, as she said afterwards, she supposed we had seen one another before, though it might have been a great while ago.

Whatever stiffness I had put on my behaviour to him, I was surprised in my mind and angry at his, and began to wonder what kind of a ceremonious meeting it was to be. However, after he perceived the woman was gone, he made a kind of a hesitation, looking a little round him. "Indeed," said he, "I thought the gentlewoman was not withdrawn," and with that he took me in his arms and kissed me three or four times; but I, that was prejudiced to the last degree with the coldness of his first salutes when I did not know the cause of it, could not be thoroughly cleared of the prejudice though I did know the cause, and thought that even his return and taking me in his arms did not seem to have the same ardour with which he used to receive me, and this made me behave to him awkwardly, and I know not how, for a good while. But this by the way.

He began with a kind of ecstasy upon the subject of his finding me out; how it was possible that he should have been four years in England and had used all the ways imaginable, and could never so much as have the least intimation of me or of any one like me; and that it was now above two years that he had despaired of it, and had given over all enquiry; and that now he should chop upon me, as it were, unlooked and unsought for.

I could easily have accounted for his not finding me if I had but set down the detail of my real retirement, but I gave it a new, and indeed a truly hypocritical turn. I told him that any one that knew the manner of life I led might account for his not finding me; that the retreat I had taken up would have rendered it a hundred thousand to one odds that he ever found me at all; that as I had abandoned all conversation, taken up another name, lived remote from London, and had not preserved one acquaintance in it, it was no wonder he had not met with me; that even my dress would let him see that I did not desire to be known by anybody.

Then he asked if I had not received some letters from him. I told him, no, he had not thought fit to give me the civility of an answer to the last I wrote to him, and he could not suppose I should expect a return after a silence in a case where I had laid myself so low and exposed myself in a manner I had never been used to; that indeed I had never sent for any letters after that to the place where I had ordered his to be directed; and that being so justly, as I thought, punished for my weakness, I had nothing to do but to repent of being a fool, after I had strictly adhered to a just principle before. That, however, as what I did was rather from motions of gratitude than from real weakness, however it might be construed by him, I had the satisfaction in myself of having fully discharged the debt. I added that I had not wanted occasions of all the seeming advancements which the pretended felicity of a married life was usually set off with, and might have been what I desired not to name; but that, however low I had stooped to him, I had maintained the dignity of female liberty against all the attacks either of pride or avarice, and that I had been infinitely obliged to him for giving me an opportunity to discharge the only obligation that endangered me, without subjecting me to the consequence; and that I hoped he was satisfied I had paid the debt, by offering myself to be chained, but was infinitely debtor to him another way, for letting me remain free.

He was so confounded at this discourse that he knew not what to say, and for a good while he stood mute indeed, but, recovering himself a little, he said I ran out into a discourse he hoped was over and forgotten, and he did not intend to revive it; that he knew I had not had his letters, for that when he first came to England he had been at the place to which they were directed, and found them all lying there but one, and that the people had not known how to deliver them; that he thought to have had a direction there how to find me, but had the mortification to be told that they did not so much as know who I was; that he was under a great disappointment, and that I ought to know, in answer to all my resentments, that he had done a long, and (he hoped) a sufficient penance for the slight that I had supposed he had put upon me; that it was true (and I could not suppose any other) that upon the repulse I had given him in a case so circumstanced as his was, and after such earnest entreaties and such offers as he had made me, he went away with a mind heartily grieved and full of resentment; that he had looked back on the crime he had committed, with some regret, but on the cruelty of my treatment of the poor infant I went with at that time, with the utmost detestation, and that this made him unable to send an agreeable answer to me, for which reason he had sent none at all for some time; but that in about six or seven months, those resentments wearing off by the return of his affection to me and his concern in the poor child----. There he stopped, and indeed tears stood in his eyes, while in a parenthesis he only added, and to this minute he did not know whether it was dead or alive. He then went on, those resentments wearing off; he sent me several letters, I think he said seven or eight, but received no answer; that then his business obliging him to go to Holland, he came to England, as in his way, but found as above that his letters had not been called for, but that he left them at the house after paying the postage of them, and then going back to France, he was yet uneasy and could not refrain the knight-errantry of coming to England again to seek me, though he knew neither where or of whom to enquire for me, being disappointed in all his enquiries before. That he had yet taken up his residence here, firmly believing that one time or other he should meet me or hear of me, and that some kind chance would at last throw him in my way; that he had lived thus above four years, and though his hopes were vanished, yet he had not any thoughts of removing any more in the world, unless it should be at last, as it is with other old men, he might have some inclination to go home to die in his own country, but that he had not thought of it yet; that if I would consider all these steps I would find some reasons to forget his first resentments, and to think that penance, as he called it, which he had undergone in search of me, an amende honorable in reparation of the affront given to the kindness of my letter of invitation, and that we might at last make ourselves some satisfaction on both sides for the mortifications past.

I confess I could not hear all this without being moved very much, and yet I continued a little stiff and formal too a good while. I told him that before I could give him any reply to the rest of his discourse, I ought to give him the satisfaction of telling him that his son was alive; and that indeed, since I saw him so concerned about it and mention it with such affection, I was sorry that I had not found out some way or other to let him know it sooner, but that I thought, after his slighting the mother, as above, he had summed up his affection to the child, in the letter he had wrote to me about providing for it, and that he had, as other fathers often do, looked upon it as a birth which, being out of the way, was to be forgotten, as its beginning was to be repented of; that in providing sufficiently for it, he had done more than all such fathers used to do, and might be well satisfied with it.

He answered me that he should have been very glad if I had been so good but to have given him the satisfaction of knowing the poor unfortunate creature was yet alive, and he would have taken some care of it upon himself, and particularly by owning it for a legitimate child, which, where nobody had known to the contrary, would have taken off the infamy which would otherwise cleave to it, and so the child should not itself have known anything of its own disaster; but that he feared it was now too late.

He added that I might see by all his conduct since that, what unhappy mistake drew him into the thing at first, and that he would have been very far from doing the injury to me or being instrumental to add une misérable (that was his word) to the world, if he had not been drawn into it by the hopes he had of making me his own; but that, if it was possible to rescue the child from the consequences of its unhappy birth, he hoped I would give him leave to do it, and he would let me see that he had both means and affection still to do it; and that, notwithstanding all the misfortunes that had befallen him, nothing that belonged to him, especially by a mother he had such a concern for as he had for me, should ever want what he was in a condition to do for it.

I could not hear this without being sensibly touched with it. I was ashamed that he should show that he had more real affection for the child, though he had never seen it in his life, than I that bore it, for indeed I did not love the child nor love to see it; and though I had provided for it, yet I did it by Amy's hand, and had not seen it above twice in four years, being privately resolved that when it grew up, it should not be able to call me mother.

However, I told him the child was taken care of, and that he need not be anxious about it unless he suspected that I had less affection for it than he, that had never seen it in his life; that he knew what I had promised him to do for it, namely, to give it the thousand pistoles which I had offered him, and which he had declined; that I assured him I had made my will, and that I had left it £5,000 and the interest of it till he should come of age if I died before that time; that I would still be as good as that to it, but if he had a mind to take it from me into his government I would not be against it, and to satisfy him that I would perform what I said, I would cause the child to be delivered to him and the £5,000 also for its support, depending upon it that he would show himself a father to it, by what I saw of his affection to it now.

I had observed that he had hinted two or three times in his discourse his having had misfortunes in the world, and I was a little surprised at the expression, especially at the repeating it so often, but I took no notice of that part yet.

He thanked me for my kindness to the child, with a tenderness which showed the sincerity of all he had said before, and which increased the regret with which, as I said, I looked back on the little affection I had shown to the poor child. He told me he did not desire to take him from me, but so as to introduce him into the world as his own, which he could still do, having lived absent from his other children (for he had two sons and a daughter, which were brought up at Nimeguen in Holland with a sister of his) so long, that he might very well send another son of ten years old to be bred up with them and suppose his mother to be dead or alive, as he found occasion; and that as I had resolved to do so handsomely for the child, he would add to it something considerable; though, having had some great disappointments (repeating the words), he could not do for it as he would otherwise have done.

I then thought myself obliged to take notice of his having so often mentioned his having met with disappointments. I told him I was very sorry to hear he had met with anything afflicting to him in the world; that I would not have anything belonging to me add to his loss or weaken him in what he might do for his other children; and that I would not agree to his having the child away, though the proposal was infinitely to the child's advantage, unless he would promise me that the whole expense should be mine, and that if he did not think £5,000 enough for the child, I would give it more.

We had so much discourse upon this and the old affairs, that it took up all our time at his first visit. I was a little importunate with him to tell me how he came to find me out, but he put it off for that time, and only obtaining my leave to visit me again, he went away; and indeed my heart was so full with what he had said already, that I was glad when he went away. Sometimes I was full of tenderness and affection for him, and especially when he expressed himself so earnestly and passionately about the child; other times I was crowded with doubts about his circumstances. Sometimes I was terrified with apprehensions lest if I should come into a close correspondence with him, he should any way come to hear what kind of life I had led at Pall Mall and in other places, and it might make me miserable afterwards; from which last thought I concluded that I had better repulse him again, than receive him. All these thoughts and many more crowded in so fast, I say, upon me, that I wanted to give vent to them and get rid of him, and was very glad when he was gone away.

We had several meetings after this, in which still we had so many preliminaries to go through, that we scarce ever bordered upon the main subject; once indeed he said something of it, and I put it off with a kind of a jest. "Alas!" says I, "those things are out of the question now; 'tis almost two ages since those things were talked between us," says I; "you see I am grown an old woman since that." Another time he gave a little push at it again, and I laughed again. "Why, what dost thou talk of?" said I in a formal way, "dost thou not see I am turned Quaker? I cannot speak of those things now." "Why," says he, "the Quakers marry, as well as other people, and love one another as well; besides," says he, "the Quaker's dress does not ill become you "; and so jested with me again, and so it went off for a third time. However, I began to be kind to him in process of time, as they call it, and we grew very intimate, and if the following accident had not unluckily intervened, I had certainly married him, or consented to marry him, the very next time he had asked me.

Chapter 21

I had long waited for a letter from Amy, who it seems was just at that time gone to Rouen the second time, to make her enquiries about him; and I received a letter from her at this unhappy juncture which gave me the following account of my business:

1. That for my gentleman, whom I had now, as I may say, in my arms, she said he had been gone from Paris, as I have hinted, having met with some great losses and misfortunes; that he had been in Holland on that very account, whither he had also carried his children; that he was after that settled for some time at Rouen; that she had been at Rouen, and found there (by a mere accident), from a Dutch skipper, that he was in London, had been there above three years; that he was to be found upon the Exchange, on the French Walk, and that he lodged at Laurence Pountney Lane, and the like.

So Amy said she supposed I might soon find him out, but that she doubted he was poor, and not worth looking after. This she did because of the next clause, which the jade had most mind to on many accounts.

2. That as to the Prince ----, that, as above, he was gone into Germany, where his estate lay; that he had quitted the French service, and lived retired; that she had seen his gentleman, who remained at Paris to solicit his arrears, etc.; that he had given her an account how his lord had employed him to enquire for me and find me out, as above, and told her what pains he had taken to find me; that he had understood that I was gone to England; that he once had orders to go to England to find me; that his lord had resolved, if he could have found me, to have called me a countess, and so have married me and leave carried me into Germany with him; and that his commission was still to assure me that the Prince would marry me if I would come to him; and that he would send him an account that he had found me, and did not doubt but he would have orders to come over to England to attend me, in a figure suitable to my quality.

Amy, an ambitious jade, who knew my weakest part, namely, that I loved great things and that I loved to be flattered and courted, said abundance of kind things upon this occasion which she knew were suitable to me and would prompt my vanity, and talked big of the Prince's gentleman having orders to come over to me with a procuration to marry me by proxy (as princes usually do in like cases), and to furnish me with an equipage and I know not how many fine things, but told me withal, that she had not yet let him know that she belonged to me still, or that she knew where to find me or to write to me, because she was willing to see the bottom of it, and whether it was a reality or a gasconade. She had indeed told him that if he had any such commission, she would endeavour to find me out, but no more.

3. For the Jew, she assured me that she had not been able to come at a certainty what was become of him or in what part of the world he was; but that thus much she had learned from good hands, that he had committed a crime, in being concerned in a design to rob a rich banker at Paris, and that he was fled, and had not been heard of there for above six years.

4. For that of my husband the brewer, she learned that, being commanded into the field upon an occasion of some action in Flanders, he was wounded at the battle of Mons, and died of his wounds in the hospital of the Invalides; so there was an end of my four enquiries which I sent her over to make.

This account of the Prince and the return of his affection for me, with all the flattering great things which seemed to come along with it, and especially as they came gilded and set out by my maid Amy--I say this account of the Prince came to me in a very unlucky hour, and in the very crisis of my affair.

The merchant and I had entered into close conferences upon the grand affair. I had left off talking my platonics, and of my independency and being a free woman, as before; and he having cleared up my doubts too, as to his circumstances and the misfortunes he had spoken of, I had gone so far that we had begun to consider where we should live, and in what figure, what equipage, what house, and the like.

I had made some harangues upon the delightful retirement of a country life, and how we might enjoy ourselves so effectually without the encumbrances of business and the world; but all this was grimace, and purely because I was afraid to make any public appearance in the world for fear some impertinent person of quality should chop upon again and cry out, Roxana! Roxana! by ----, with an oath, as had been done before.

My merchant, bred to business and used to converse among men of business, could hardly tell how to live without it; at least it appeared he should be like a fish out of water, uneasy and dying. But, however, he joined with me, only argued that we might live as near London as we could; that he might sometimes come to 'Change and hear how the world should go abroad, and how it fared with his friends and his children.

I answered that if he chose, still to embarrass himself with business, I supposed it would be more to his satisfaction to be in his own country, and where his family was so well known, and where his children also were.

He smiled at the thoughts of that, and let me know that he should be very willing to embrace such an offer, but that he could not expect it of me, to whom England was, to be sure, so naturalised now, as that it would be carrying me out of my native country, which he would not desire by any means, however agreeable it might be to him.

I told him he was mistaken in me; that as I had told him so much of a married state being a captivity and the family being a house of bondage, that when I married I expected to be but an upper servant, so if I did, notwithstanding, submit to it I hoped he should see I knew how to act the servant's part and do everything to oblige my master; that if I did not resolve to go with him wherever he desired to go, he might depend I would never have him. "And did I not," said I, "offer myself to go with you to the East Indies?"

All this while this was indeed but a copy of my countenance, for as my circumstances would not admit my stay in London, at least not so as to appear publicly, I resolved, if I took him, to live remote in the country or go out of England with him.

But in an evil hour just now came Amy's letter, in the very middle of all these discourses, and the fine things she had said about the Prince began to make strange work with me. The notion of being a Princess and going over to live where all that had happened here would have been quite sunk out of knowledge, as well as out of memory (conscience excepted), was mighty taking; the thoughts of being surrounded with domestics, honoured with titles, be called Her Highness and live in all the splendour of a Court, and, which was still more, in the arms of a man of such rank, and who, I knew, loved and valued me--all this, in a word, dazzled my eyes, turned my head, and I was as truly crazed and distracted for about a fortnight as most of the people in Bedlam, though perhaps not quite so far gone.

When my gentleman came to me the next time I had no notion of him; I wished I had never received him at all; in short, I resolved to have no more to say to him, so I feigned myself indisposed, and though I did come down to him and speak to him a little, yet I let him see that I was so ill that I was (as we say) no company, and that it would be kind in him to give me leave to quit him for that time.

The next morning he sent a footman to enquire how I did, and I let him know I had a violent cold and was very ill with it. Two days after, he came again, and I let him see me again, but feigned myself so hoarse that I could not speak to be heard, and that it was painful to me but to whisper; and, in a word, I held him in this suspense near three weeks.

During this time I had a strange elevation upon my mind, and the Prince, or the spirit of him, had such a possession of me that I spent most of this time in the realising all the great things of a life with the Prince, to my mind; pleasing my fancy with the grandeur I was supposing myself to enjoy, and, withal, wickedly studying in what manner to put off this gentleman and be rid of him for ever.

I cannot but say that sometimes the baseness of the action struck hard with me; the honour and sincerity with which he had always treated me, and, above all, the fidelity he had shown me at Paris, and that I owed my life to him--I say all these stared in my face, and I frequently argued with myself upon the obligation I was under to him, and how base would it be now, too, after so many obligations and engagements, to cast him off.

But the title of Highness and of a Princess, and all those fine things as they came in, weighed down all this, and the sense of gratitude vanished as if it had been a shadow.

At other times I considered the wealth I was mistress of, that I was able to live like a princess though not a princess, and that my merchant (for he had told me all the affair of his misfortune) was far from being poor, or even mean; that together we were able to make up an estate of between three and four thousand pounds a year, which was in itself equal to some princes abroad. But though this was true, yet the name of Princess and the flutter of it, in a word, the pride weighed them down, and all these arguings generally ended to the disadvantage of my merchant; so that, in short, I resolved to drop him and give him a final answer at his next coming, namely, that something had happened in my affairs which had caused me to alter my measures unexpectedly; and, in a word, to desire him to trouble himself no further.

I think, verily, this rude treatment of him was for some time the effect of a violent fermentation in my blood, for the very motion which the steady contemplation of my fancied greatness had put my spirits into had thrown me into a kind of fever, and I scarce knew what I did.

I have wondered since that it did not make me mad, nor do I now think it strange to hear of those who have been quite lunatic with their pride, that fancied themselves queens and empresses, and have made their attendants serve them upon the knee, given visitors their hands to kiss, and the like; for certainly, if pride will not turn the brain, nothing can.

However, the next time my gentleman came I had not courage enough, or not ill-nature enough, to treat him in the rude manner I had resolved to do; and it was very well I did not, for soon after I had another letter from Amy in which was the mortifying news, and indeed surprising to me, that my Prince (as I with a secret pleasure had called him) was very much hurt by a bruise he had received in hunting (and engaging with) a wild boar, a cruel and desperate sport which the noblemen of Germany, it seems, much delight in.

This alarmed me indeed, and the more because Amy wrote me word that his gentleman was gone away express to him, not without apprehensions that he should find his master was dead before his coming home, but that he (the gentleman) had promised her that as soon as he arrived he would send back the same courier to her with an account of his master's health, and of the main affair; and that he had obliged Amy to stay at Paris fourteen days for his return, she having promised him before to make it her business to go to England and to find me out for his lord if he sent her such orders; and he was to send her a bill for fifty pistoles for her journey. So Amy told me she waited for the answer.

This was a blow to me several ways; for, first, I was in a state of uncertainty as to his person, whether he was alive or dead, and I was not unconcerned in that part, I assure you; for I had an inexpressible affection remaining for his person, besides the degree to which it was revived by the view of a firmer interest in him;

but this was not all, for in losing him I for ever lost the prospect of all the gaiety and glory that had made such an impression upon my imagination.

In this state of uncertainty, I say, by Amy's letter, I was like still to remain another fortnight, and had I now continued the resolution of using my merchant in the rude manner I once intended, I had made perhaps a sorry piece of work of it indeed, and it was very well my heart failed me as it did.

However, I treated him with a great many shuffles, and feigned stories to keep him off from any closer conferences than we had already had, that I might act afterwards as occasion might offer, one way or other. But that which mortified me most was that Amy did not write, though the fourteen days were expired. At last, to my great surprise, when I was with the utmost impatience looking out at the window expecting the postman that usually brought the foreign letters--I say I was agreeably surprised to see a coach come to the yard gate where we lived, and my woman Amy alight out of it and come towards the door, having the coachman bringing several bundles after her.

I flew like lightning downstairs to speak to her, but was soon damped with her news. "Is the Prince alive or dead, Amy?" says I. She spoke coldly and slightly. "He is alive, madam," said she, "but it is not much matter, I had as lieu he had been dead." So we went upstairs again to my chamber, and there we began a serious discourse of the whole matter.

First she told me a long story of his being hurt by a wild boar, and of the condition he was reduced to, so that everyone expected he should die, the anguish of the wound having thrown him into a fever; with abundance of circumstances too long to relate here; how he recovered of that extreme danger, but continued very weak; how the gentleman had been homme de parole and had sent back the courier as punctually as if it had been to the King; that he had given a long account of his lord, and of his illness and recovery. But the sum of the matter, as to me, was, that as to the lady, his lord was turned penitent, was under some vows for his recovery, and could not think any more on that affair; and especially, the lady being gone, and that it had not been offered to her, so there was no breach of honour; but that his lord was sensible of the good offices of Mrs. Amy, and had sent her the fifty pistoles for her trouble, as if she had really gone the journey.

I was, I confess, hardly able to bear the first surprise of this disappointment. Amy saw it, and gapes out as was her way), "Lawd, madam! never be concerned at it; you see he is gotten among the priests, and I suppose they have saucily imposed some penance upon him, and, it may be, sent him off an errand barefoot to some Madonna or Nostredame or other, and he is off of his amours for the present; I'll warrant you he'll be as wicked again as ever he was when he is got thorough well and gets but out of their hands again. I hate this out-o'-season repentance; what occasion had he in his repentance to be off of taking a good wife? I should have been glad to see you have been a Princess and all that, but if it can't be, never afflict yourself, you are rich enough to be a princess to yourself; you don't want him, that's the best of it."

Well, I cried for all that, and was heartily vexed, and that a great while; but as Amy was always at my elbow and always jogging it out of my head with her mirth and her wit, it wore off again.

Then I told Amy all the story of my merchant, and how he had found me out when I was in such a concern to find him; how it was true that he lodged in Laurence Pountney Lane, and how I had had all the story of his misfortune which she had heard of, in which he had lost above £8,000 sterling, and that he had told me frankly of it before she had sent me any account of it, or at least before I had taken any notice that I had heard of it.

Amy was very joyful at that part. "Well, madam. then," says Amy, "what need you value the story of the Prince, and going I know not whither into Germany, to lay your bones in another world and learn the devil's language called High-Dutch. You are better here, by half," says Amy. "Lawd, madam." says she, "why, are not you as rich as Croesus?"

Well, it was a great while still before I could bring myself off of this fancied sovereignty, and I, that was so willing once to be mistress to a King, was now ten thousand times more fond of being wife to a Prince.

So fast a hold has pride and ambition upon our minds, that when once it gets admission, nothing is so chimerical but under this possession we can form ideas of, in our fancy, and realise to our imagination. Nothing can be so ridiculous as the simple steps we take in such cases; a man or a woman becomes a mere malade imaginaire, and, I believe, may as easily die with grief or run mad with joy (as the affair in his fancy appears right or wrong), as if all was real and actually under the management of the person.

I had indeed two assistants to deliver me from this snare, and these were, first, Amy, who knew my disease, but was able to do nothing as to the remedy; the second, the merchant, who really brought the remedy but knew nothing of the distemper.

I remember when all these disorders were upon my thoughts, in one of the visits my friend the merchant made me, he took notice that he perceived I was under some unusual disorder; he believed, he said, that my distemper, whatever it was, lay much in my head, and, it being summer weather and very hot, proposed to me to go a little way into the air.

I started at his expression. "What," says I, "do you think then that I am crazed? You should then propose a madhouse for my cure." "No, no," says he, "I do not mean anything like that, I hope the head may be distempered and not the brain." Well, I was too sensible that he was right, for I knew I had acted a strange wild kind of part with him, but he insisted upon it, and pressed me to go into the country. I took him short again. "What need you," says I, "send me out of your way? It is in your power to be less troubled with me, and with less inconvenience to us both."

He took that ill, and told me I used to have a better opinion of his sincerity, and desired to know what he had done to forfeit my charity. I mention this only to let you see how far I had gone in my measures of quitting him, that is to say, how near I was of showing him how base, ungrateful, and how vilely I could act. But I found I had carried the jest far enough, and that a little matter might have made him sick of me again as he was before, so I began by little and little to change my way of talking to him, and to come to discourse to the purpose again, as we had done before.

A while after this, when we were very merry and talking familiarly together, he called me, with an air of particular satisfaction, his princess. I coloured at the word, for it indeed touched me to the quick; but he knew nothing of the reason of my being touched with it. "What d'ye mean by that?" said I. "Nay," says he, "I mean nothing but that you are a princess to me." "Well," says I, "as to that, I am content; and yet I could tell you I might have been a princess if I would have quitted you, and believe I could be so still." "It is not in my power to make you a princess," says he, "but I can easily make you a lady here in England, and a countess too, if you will go out of it."

I heard both with a great deal of satisfaction, for my pride remained, though it had been balked, and I thought with myself that this proposal would make me some amends for the loss of the title that had so tickled my imagination another way; and I was impatient to understand what he meant, but I would not ask him by any means, so it passed off for that time.

When he was gone I told Amy what he had said, and Amy was as impatient to know the manner, how it could be, as I was; but the next time (perfectly unexpected to me) he told me that he had accidentally mentioned a thing to me last time he was with me, having not the least thought of the thing itself; but not knowing but such a thing might be of some weight to me, and that it might bring me respect among people where I might appear, he had thought since of it, and was resolved to ask me about it.

I made light of it, and told him that as he knew I had chosen a retired life, it was of no value to me to be called Lady, or Countess either; but that if he intended to drag me, as I might call it, into the world again, perhaps it might be agreeable to him; but, besides that, I could not judge of the thing, because I did not understand how either of them was to be done.

He told me that money purchased titles of honour in almost all parts of the world, though money could not give principles of honour, they must come by birth and blood; that, however, titles sometimes assist to elevate the soul and to infuse generous principles into the mind, and especially where there was a good foundation laid in the persons; that he hoped we should neither of us misbehave if we came to it, and that as we knew how to wear a title without undue elevations, so it might sit as well upon us as on another; that as to England, he had nothing to do but to get an Act of Naturalisation in his favour, and he knew where to purchase a patent for Baronet, that is to say, to have the honour and title transferred to him. But if I intended to go abroad with him, he had a nephew, the son of his elder brother, who had the title of Count, with the estate annexed, which was but small, and that he had frequently offered to make it over to him for a thousand pistoles, which was not a great deal of money, and considering it was in the family already, he would, upon my being willing, purchase it immediately.

I told him I liked the last best, but then I would not let him buy it unless he would let me pay the thousand pistoles. "No, no," says he, "I refused a thousand pistoles that I had more right to have accepted than that, and you shall not be at so much expense now." "Yes," says I, "you did refuse it, and perhaps repented it afterwards."

"I never complained," says he. "But I did," says I, "and often repented it for you." "I do not understand you," says he. "Why," says I, "I repented that I suffered you to refuse it." "Well, well," said he, "we may talk of that hereafter, when you shall resolve which part of the world you will make your settled residence in." Here he talked very handsomely to me, and for a good while together; how it had been his lot to live all his days out of his native country, and to be often shifting and changing the situation of his affairs, and that I myself had not always had a fixed abode; but that now, as neither of us was very young, he fancied I would be for taking up our abode, where, if possible, we might remove no more; that as to his part, he was of that opinion entirely, only with this exception, that the choice of the place should be mine, for that all places in the world were alike to him; only with this single addition, namely, that I was with him.

I heard him with a great deal of pleasure, as well for his being willing to give me the choice as for that I resolved to live abroad, for the reason I have mentioned already, namely, lest I should at any time be known in England, and all that story of Roxana and the balls should come out; as also I was not a little tickled with the satisfaction of being still a countess, though I could not be a Princess.

I told Amy all this story, for she was still my privy counsellor, but when I asked her opinion she made me laugh heartily. "Now, which of the two shall I take, Amy?" said I. "Shall I be a Lady, that is, a baronet's lady in England, or a Countess in Holland?" The ready-witted jade, that knew the pride of my temper too almost as well as did myself, answered without the least hesitation, "Both, madam. Which of them!" says she, repeating the words, "why not both of them? and then you will be really a Princess; for sure, to be a Lady in English and a Countess in Dutch may make a Princess in High-Dutch." Upon the whole, though Amy was in jest, she put the thought into my head, and I resolved that, in short, I would be both of them; which I managed as you shall hear.

First, I seemed to resolve that I would live and settle in England, only with this condition, namely, that I would not live in London. I pretended that it would choke me up, that I wanted breath when I was in London, but that anywhere else I would be satisfied; and then I asked him whether any seaport town in England would not suit him, because I knew, though he seemed to leave off, he would always love to be among business and conversing with men of business; and I named several places, either nearest for business with France or with Holland, as Dover or Southampton for the first, and Ipswich or Yarmouth or Hull for the last; but I took care that we would resolve upon nothing. Only by this it seemed to be certain that we should live in England.

Chapter 21

It was time now to bring things to a conclusion, and so in about six weeks' time more we settled all our preliminaries; and among the rest he let me know that he should have the Bill for his naturalisation passed time enough, so that he would be (as he called it) an Englishman before we married. That was soon perfected, the parliament being then sitting, and several other foreigners joining in the said Bill to save the expense.

It was not above three or four days after, but that, without giving me the least notice that he had so much as been about the patent for Baronet, he brought it me in a fine embroidered bag, and, saluting me by the name of my Lady ---- (joining his own surname to it), presented it to me with his picture set with diamonds, and at the same time gave me a breast jewel worth a thousand pistoles, and the next morning we were married. Thus I put an end to all the intriguing part of my life, a life full of prosperous wickedness; the reflections upon which were so much the more afflicting, as the time had been spent in the grossest crimes, which the more I looked back upon, the more black and horrid they appeared, effectually drinking up all the comfort and satisfaction which I might otherwise have taken in that part of life which was still before me.

Chapter 22

THE first satisfaction, however, that I took in the new condition I was in, was in reflecting that at length the life of crime was over, and that I was like a passenger coming back from the Indies, who having, after many years' fatigues and hurry in business, gotten a good estate with innumerable difficulties and hazards, is arrived safe at London with all his effects, and has the pleasure of saying he shall never venture upon the seas any more.

When we were married we came back immediately to my lodgings (for the church was but just by), and we were so privately married that none but Amy and my friend the Quaker were acquainted with it. As soon as we came into the house he took me in his arms, and kissing me, "Now you are my own," says he. "Oh that you had been so good to have done this eleven years ago." "Then," said I, "perhaps you would have been tired of me long ago; 'tis much better now, for now all our happy days are to come. Besides," said I, "I should not have been half so rich"; but that I said to myself, for there was no letting him into the reason of it. "Oh," says he, "I should not have been tired of you; but besides having the satisfaction of your company, it had saved me that unlucky blow at Paris, which was a dead loss to me of above 8,000 pistoles, and all the fatigues of so many years' hurry and business." And then he added, "But I'll make you pay for it all, now I have you." I started a little at the words. "Ay," said I, "do you threaten already? Pray what d'ye mean by that?" and began to look a little grave.

"I'll tell you," says he, "very plainly what I mean," and still he held me fast in his arms. "I intend from this time never to trouble myself with any more business, so I shall never get one shilling for you more than I have already; all that you will lose one way. Next, I intend not to trouble myself with any of the care or trouble of managing what either you have for me or what I have to add to it, but you shall e'en take it all upon yourself as the wives do in Holland; so you will pay for it that way too, for all the drudgery shall be yours. Thirdly, I intend to condemn you to the constant bondage of my impertinent company, for I shall tie you like a pedlar's pack, at my back, I shall scarce ever be from you; for I am sure I can take delight in nothing else in this world." "Very well," says I, "but I am pretty heavy; I hope you'll set me down sometimes when you are a-weary." "As for that," says he, "tire me if you can."

This was all jest and allegory, but it was all true in the moral of the fable, as you shall hear in its place. We were very merry the rest of the day, but without any noise or clutter, for he brought not one of his acquaintance or friends, either English or foreigner. The honest Quaker provided us a very noble dinner indeed, considering how few we were to eat it, and every day that week she did the like, and would at last have it be all at her own charge, which I was utterly averse to; first, because I knew her circumstances not to be very great, though not very low; and next, because she had been so true a friend and so cheerful a comforter to me, ay, and counsellor too, in all this affair, that I had resolved to make her a present that should be some help to her when all was over.

But to return to the circumstances of our wedding. After being very merry, as I have told you, Amy and the Quaker put us to bed, the honest Quaker little thinking we had been a-bed together eleven years before; nay, that was a secret which, as it happened, Amy herself did not know. Amy grinned and made faces as if she had been pleased, but it came out in so many words, when he was not by, the sum of her mumbling and muttering was that this should have been done ten or a dozen years before, that it would signify little now; that was to say, in short, that her mistress was pretty near fifty, and too old to have any children. I chid her; the Quaker laughed, complimented me upon my not being so old as Amy pretended, that I could not be above forty, and might have a houseful of children yet. But Amy, and I too, knew better than she how it was; for, in short, I was old enough to have done breeding, however I looked; but I made her hold her tongue.

In the morning my Quaker landlady came and visited us before we were up, and made us eat cakes and drink chocolate in bed, and then left us again and bid us take a nap upon it, which I believe we did; in short, she treated us so handsomely, and with such an agreeable cheerfulness as well as plenty, as made it appear to me that Quakers may, and that this Quaker did, understand good manners as well as any other people.

I resisted her offer, however, of treating us for the whole week, and I opposed it so long that I saw evidently that she took it ill, and would have thought herself slighted if we had not accepted it; so I said no more, but let her go on, only told her I would be even with her, and so I was. However, for that week she treated us, as she said she would, and did it so very fine and with such a profusion of all sorts of good things, that the greatest burthen to her was how to dispose of things that were left; for she never let anything, how dainty or however large, be so much as seen twice among us.

I had some servants indeed which helped her off a little, that is to say, two maids, for Amy was now a woman of business, not a servant, and ate always with us. I had also a coachman and a boy. My Quaker had a manservant too, but had but one maid, but she borrowed two more from some of her friends for the occasion, and had a man-cook for dressing the victuals.

She was only at a loss for plate, which she gave me a whisper of, and I made Amy fetch a large strong-box which I had lodged in a safe hand, in which was all the fine plate which I had provided on a worse occasion, as is mentioned before, and I put it into the Quaker's hand, obliging her not to use it as mine but as her own, for a reason I shall mention presently.

I was now my Lady ----, and I must own I was exceedingly pleased with it; 'twas so big and so great to hear myself called Her Ladyship, and Your Ladyship, and the like, that I was like the Indian king at Virginia, who, having a house built for him by the English and a lock put upon the door, would sit whole days together with the key in his hand, locking and unlocking and double-locking the door, with an unaccountable pleasure at the novelty; so I could have sat a whole day together to hear Amy talk to me and call me Your Ladyship at every word, but after a while the novelty wore off and the pride of it abated, till at last truly I wanted the other title as much as I did that of Ladyship before.

We lived this week in all the innocent mirth imaginable, and our good-humoured Quaker was so pleasant in her way, that it was particularly entertaining to us. We had no music at all or dancing, only I now and then sung a French song to divert my spouse, who desired it, and the privacy of our mirth greatly added to the pleasure of it. I did not make many clothes for my wedding, having always a great many rich clothes by me, which, with a little altering for the fashion, were perfectly new. The next day he pressed me to dress though we had no company. At last, jesting with him, I told him I believed I was able to dress me so, in one kind of dress that I had by me, that he would not know his wife when he saw her, especially if anybody else was by. No, he said, that was impossible; and he longed to see that dress. I told him I would dress me in it if he would promise me never to desire me to appear in it before company. He promised he would not, but wanted to know why too; as husbands, you know, are inquisitive creatures, and love to enquire after anything they think is kept from them; but I had an answer ready for him. "Because," said I, "it is not a decent dress in this country, and would not look modest." Neither indeed would it, for it was but one degree off from appearing in one's shift, but it was the usual wear in the country where they were used. He was satisfied with my answer, and gave me his promise never to ask me to be seen in it before company. I then withdrew, taking only Amy and the Quaker with me; and Amy dressed me in my old Turkish habit which I danced in formerly, etc., as before. The Quaker was charmed with the dress, and merrily said that if such a dress should come to be worn here, she should not know what to do; she should be tempted not to dress in the Quakers' way any more.

When all the dress was put on I loaded it with jewels, and in particular I placed the large breast jewel which he had given me, of a thousand pistoles, upon the front of the Tyhiaai, or head-dress, where it made a most glorious show indeed; I had my own diamond necklace on, and my hair was tout brillant, all glittering with jewels.

His picture set with diamonds I had placed stitched to my vest, just, as might be supposed, upon my heart (which is the compliment in such cases among the Eastern people), and all being open at the breast, there was no room for anything of a jewel there. In this figure, Amy holding the train of my robe, I came down to him. He was surprised and perfectly astonished; he knew me, to be sure, because I had prepared him and because there was nobody else there but the Quaker and Amy, but he by no means knew Amy, for she had dressed herself in the habit of a Turkish slave, being the garb of my little Turk which I had at Naples, as I have said. She had her neck and arms bare, was bareheaded, and her hair braided in a long tassel hanging down her back; but the jade could neither hold her countenance nor her chattering tongue so as to be concealed long.

Well, he was so charmed with this dress that he would have me sit and dine in it, but it was so thin and so open before, and the weather being also sharp, that I was afraid of taking cold. However, the fire being enlarged and the doors kept shut, I sat to oblige him, and he professed he never saw so fine a dress in his life. I afterwards told him that my husband (so he called the jeweller that was killed) bought it for me at Leghorn, with a young Turkish slave which I parted with at Paris, and that it was by the help of that slave that I learnt how to dress in it and how everything was to be worn, and many of the Turkish customs also, with some of their language. This story agreeing with the fact, only changing the person, was very natural, and so it went off with him. But there was good reason why I should not receive any company in this dress, that is to say, not in England; I need not repeat it, you will hear more of it.

But when I came abroad I frequently put it on, and upon two or three occasions danced in it, but always at his request.

We continued at the Quaker's lodgings for above a year; for now making as though it was difficult to determine where to settle in England to his satisfaction, unless in London, which was not to mine, I pretended to make him an offer, that to oblige him I began to incline to go and live abroad with him; that I knew nothing could be more agreeable to him, and that as to me, every place was alike; that as I had lived abroad without a husband so many years, it could be no burthen to me to live abroad again, especially with him. Then we fell to straining our courtesies upon one another. He told me he was perfectly easy at living in England, and had squared all his affairs accordingly; for that, as he told me he intended to give over all business in the world, as well the care of managing it as the concern about it, seeing we were both in condition neither to want it nor to have it be worth our while, so I might see it was his intention, by his getting himself naturalised, and getting the patent of Baronet, etc. Well, for all that, I told him I accepted his compliment, but I could not but know that his native country, where his children were breeding up, must be most agreeable to him, and that if I was of such value to him I would be there then to enhance the rate of his satisfaction; that wherever he was would be a home to me, and any place in the world would be England to me if he was with me. And thus, in short, I brought him to give me leave to oblige him with going to live abroad, when in truth I could not have been perfectly easy at living in England unless I had kept constantly within doors, lest some time or other the dissolute life I had lived here should have come to be known, and all those wicked things have been known too which I now began to be very much ashamed of.

When we closed up our wedding week, in which our Quaker had been so very handsome to us, I told him how much I thought we were obliged to her for her generous carriage to us, how she had acted the kindest part through the whole, and how faithful a friend she had been to me upon all occasions; and then letting him know a little of her family unhappinesses, I proposed that I thought I not only ought to be grateful to her, but really to do something extraordinary for her towards making her easy in her affairs; and I added that I had no hangers-on that should trouble him, that there was nobody belonged to me but what was thoroughly provided for, and that if I did something for this honest woman that was considerable, it should be the last gift I would give to anybody in the world but Amy. And as for her, we were not a-going to turn her adrift, but whenever anything offered for her we would do as we saw cause; that in the meantime Amy was not poor, that she had saved together between seven and eight hundred pounds. By the way, I did not tell him how and by what wicked ways she had got it, but that she had it; and that was enough to let him know she would never be in want of us.

My spouse was exceedingly pleased with my discourse about the Quaker, made a kind of a speech to me upon the subject of gratitude, told me it was one of the brightest parts of a gentlewoman; that it was so twisted with honesty, nay, and even with religion too, that he questioned whether either of them could be found where gratitude was not to be found; that in this act there was not only gratitude, but charity, and that to make the charity still more Christian-like, the object too had real merit to attract it. He therefore agreed to the thing with all his heart, only would have had me let him pay it out of his effects.

I told him, as for that, I did not design, whatever I had said formerly, that we should have two pockets, and that though I had talked to him of being a free woman, and an independent woman and the like, and he had offered and promised that I should keep all my own estate in my own hands, yet, that since I had taken him, I would e'en do as other honest wives did, where I thought fit to give myself, I should give what I had too; that if I reserved anything, it should be only in case of mortality, and that I might give it to his children afterwards, as my own gift; and that, in short, if he thought fit to join stocks, we would see to-morrow morning what strength we could both make up in the world, and, bringing it all together, consider before we resolved upon the place of removing, how we should dispose of what we had as well as of ourselves. This discourse was too obliging, and he too much a man of sense not to receive it as it was meant; he only answered, we would do in that as we should both agree, but the thing under our present care was to show not gratitude only, but charity and affection too, to our kind friend the Quaker; and the first word he spoke of was to settle a thousand pounds upon her, for her life, that is to say, sixty pounds a year, but in such a manner as not to be in the power of any person to reach but herself. This was a great thing, and indeed showed the generous principles of my husband, and for that reason I mention it; but I thought that a little too much, too, and particularly because I had another thing in view for her about the plate. So I told him I thought if he gave her a purse with a hundred guineas as a present first, and then made her a compliment of £40 per annum for her life, secured any such way as she should desire, it would be very handsome.

He agreed to that, and the same day, in the evening, when we were just going to bed, he took my Quaker by the hand, and with a kiss told her that we had been very kindly treated by her from the beginning of this affair, and his wife before, as she (meaning me) had informed him, and that he thought himself bound to let her see that she had obliged friends who knew how to be grateful; that for his part of the obligation, he desired she would accept of that for an acknowledgment in part only (putting the gold into her hand), and that his wife would talk with her about what further he had to say to her. And upon that, not giving her time hardly to say "Thank ye," away he went upstairs into our bedchamber, leaving her confused and not knowing what to say.

When he was gone she began to make very handsome and obliging representations of her goodwill to us both, but that it was without expectation of reward; that I had given her several valuable presents before, and so indeed I had; for besides the piece of linen which I had given her at first, I had given her a suit of damask table-linen, of the linen I bought for my balls, viz. three tablecloths and three dozen of napkins; and at another time I gave her a little necklace of gold beads, and the like, but that is by the way. But she mentioned them, I say, and how she was obliged by me on many other occasions; that she was not in condition to show her gratitude any other way, not being able to make a suitable return, and that now we took from her all opportunity to balance my former friendship, and left her more in debt than she was before. She spoke this in a very good kind of a manner, in her own way, but which was very agreeable indeed, and had as much apparent sincerity, and I verily believe as real, as was possible to be expressed; but I put a stop to it, and bid her say no more, but accept of what my spouse had given her, which was but in part, as she had heard him say. "And put it up," says I, "and come and sit down here, and give me leave to say something else to you on the same head which my spouse and I have settled between ourselves in your behalf." "What dost thee mean?" says she, and blushed and looked surprised, but did not stir. She was going to speak again, but I interrupted her and told her she should make no more apologies of any kind whatever, for I had better things than all this to talk to her of; so I went on, and told her that as she had been so friendly and kind to us on every occasion, and that her house was the lucky place where we came together, and that she knew I was from her own mouth acquainted in part with her circumstances, we were resolved she should be the better for us as long as she lived. Then I told her what we had resolved to do for her, and that she had nothing more to do but to consult with me how it should be effectually secured for her, distinct from any of the effects which were her husband's; and that if her husband did so supply her that she could live comfortably and not want it for bread or other necessaries, she should not make use of it, but lay up the income of it and add it every year to the principal, so to increase the annual payment, which in time, and perhaps before she might come to want it, might double itself; that we were very willing whatever she should so lay up should be to herself, and whoever she thought fit after her, but that the £40 a year must return to our family after her life, which we both wished might be long and happy.

Let no reader wonder at my extraordinary concern for this poor woman, or at my giving my bounty to her a place in this account. It is not, I assure you, to make a pageantry of my charity, or to value myself upon the greatness of my soul, that I should give in so profuse a manner as this, which was above my figure if my wealth had been twice as much as it was; but there was another spring from whence all flowed, and 'tis on that account I speak of it. Was it possible I could think of a poor desolate woman with four children, and her husband gone from her, and perhaps good for little if he had stayed--I say, was I, that had tasted so deep of the sorrows of such a kind of widowhood, able to look on her and think of her circumstances, and not be touched in an uncommon manner? No, no, I never looked on her and her family, though she was not left so helpless and friendless as I had been, without remembering my own condition, when Amy was sent out to pawn or sell my pair of stays to buy a breast of mutton and a bunch of turnips; nor could I look on her poor children, though not poor and perishing like mine, without tears, reflecting on the dreadful condition mine were reduced to when poor Amy sent them all into their aunt's in Spitalfields and ran away from them. These were the original springs or fountain-head from whence my affectionate thoughts were moved to assist this poor woman.

When a poor debtor, having lain long in the Compter. or Ludgate, or the King's Bench, for debt, afterwards gets out, rises again in the world, and grows rich, such a one is a certain benefactor to the prisoners there, and perhaps to every prison he passes by, as long as he lives; for he remembers the dark days of his own sorrow; and even those who never had the experience of such sorrows to stir up their minds to acts of charity, would have the same charitable good disposition, did they as sensibly remember what it is that distinguishes them from others by a more favourable and merciful Providence.

This I say was, however, the spring of my concern for this honest, friendly, and grateful Quaker, and as I had so plentiful a fortune in the world, I resolved she should taste the fruit of her kind usage to me, in a manner that she could not expect.

All the while I talked to her I saw the disorder of her mind; the sudden joy was too much for her, and she coloured, trembled, changed, and at last grew pale, and was indeed near fainting, when she hastily rang a little bell for her maid, who coming in immediately, she beckoned to her, for speak she could not, to fill her a glass of wine, but she had no breath to take it in and was almost choked with that which she took in her mouth. I saw she was ill and assisted her what I could, and with spirits and things to smell too, just kept her from fainting, when she beckoned to her maid to withdraw, and immediately burst out in crying, and that relieved her. When she recovered herself a little she flew to me, and throwing her arms about my neck, "Oh!" says she, "thou hast almost killed me." And there she hung, laying her head in my neck for half a quarter of an hour, not able to speak, but sobbing like a child that had been whipped.

I was very sorry that I did not stop a little in the middle of my discourse and make her drink a glass of wine, before it had put her spirits into such a violent motion; but it was too late, and it was ten to one odds but that it had killed her.

But she came to herself at last, and began to say some very good things in return for my kindness. I would not let her go on, but told her I had more to say to her still than all this, but that I would let it alone till another time. My meaning was about the box of plate, good part of which I gave her, and some I gave to Amy, for I had so much plate, and some so large, that I thought if I let my husband see it, he might be apt to wonder what occasion I could ever have for so much, and for plate of such a kind too; as particularly a great cistern for bottles, which cost a hundred and twenty pounds, and some large candlesticks, too big for any ordinary use. These I caused Amy to sell; in short, Amy sold above three hundred pounds' worth of plate. What I gave the Quaker was worth above sixty pounds, and I gave Amy above thirty pounds' worth, and yet I had a great deal left for my husband.

Nor did our kindness to the Quaker end with the forty pounds a year, for we were always, while we stayed with her, which was above ten months, giving her one good thing or another; and, in a word, instead of lodging with her, she boarded with us, for I kept the house, and she and all her family ate and drank with us, and yet we paid her the rent of the house too; in short, I remembered my widowhood, and I made this widow's heart glad many a day the more upon that account.

Chapter 23

AND now my spouse and I began to think of going over to Holland, where I had proposed to him to live, and in order to settle all the preliminaries of our future manner of living, I began to draw in my effects, so as to have them all at command upon whatever occasion we thought fit; after which, one morning I called my spouse up to me. "Hark ye, sir," said I to him, "I have two very weighty questions to ask of you; I don't know what answer you will give to the first, but I doubt you will be able to give but a sorry answer to the other, and yet, I assure you, it is of the last importance to yourself and towards the future part of your life, wherever it is to be."

He did not seem to be much alarmed, because he could see I was speaking in a kind of merry way. "Let's hear your questions, my dear," says he, "and I'll give the best answer I can to them." "Why, first," says I,

1. "You have married a wife here, made her a lady, and put her in expectation of being something else still when she comes abroad; pray have you examined whether you are able to supply all her extravagant demands when she comes abroad, and maintain an expensive Englishwoman in all her pride and vanity? In short, have you enquired whether you are able to keep her?"

2. "You have married a wife here and given her a great many fine things, and you maintain her like a princess, and sometimes call her so; pray what portion have you had with her? what fortune has she been to you? and where does her estate lie, that you keep her so fine? I am afraid you keep her in a figure a great deal above her estate, at least above all that you have seen of it yet; are you sure you haven't got a bite, and that you have not made a beggar a lady?"

"Well," says he, "have you any more questions to ask? Let's have them all together, perhaps they may be all answered in a few words, as well as these two." "No," says I, "these are the two grand questions, at least for the present." "Why then," says he, "I'll answer you in a few words, that I am fully master of my own circumstances, and without further enquiry can let my wife you speak of know, that as I have made her a lady, I can maintain her as a lady wherever she goes with me, and this whether I have one pistole of her portion or whether she has any portion or not. And as I have not enquired whether she has any portion or not, so she shall not have the less respect showed her from me, or be obliged to live meaner or by any ways straitened on that account; on the contrary, if she goes abroad to live with me in my own country, I will make her more than a lady, and support the expense of it too without meddling with anything she has; and this I suppose," says he, "contains an answer to both your questions together."

He spoke this with a great deal more earnestness in his countenance than I had when I proposed my questions, and said a great many kind things upon it, as the consequences of former discourses, so that I was obliged to be in earnest too. "My dear," says I, "I was but in jest in my questions, but they were proposed to introduce what I am going to say to you in earnest, namely, that if I am to go abroad, 'tis time I should let you know how things stand, and what I have to bring you with your wife; how it is to be disposed, and secured, and the like. And therefore, come," says I, "sit down, and let me show you your bargain here; I hope you will find that you have not got a wife without a fortune."

He told me then that since he found I was in earnest, he desired that I would adjourn it till to-morrow, and then we would do as the poor people do after they marry, feel in their pockets and see how much money they can bring together in the world. "Well," says I, "with all my heart "; and so we ended our talk for that time.

As this was in the morning, my spouse went out after dinner to his goldsmith's, as he said, and about three hours after, returns with a porter and two large boxes with him; and his servant brought another box, which I observed was almost as heavy as the two that the porter brought, and made the poor fellow sweat heartily. He dismissed the porter, and in a little while after went out again with his man, and returning at night, brought another porter with more boxes and bundles, and all was carried up and put into a chamber next to our bedchamber, and in the morning he called for a pretty large round table and began to unpack.

When the boxes were opened I found they were chiefly full of books and papers and parchment, I mean books of accounts and writings, and such things as were in themselves of no moment to me, because I understood them not; but I perceived he took them all out and spread them about him upon the table and chairs, and began to be very busy with them. So I withdrew and left him, and he was indeed so busy among them that he never missed me till I had been gone a good while; but when he had gone through all his papers and come to open a little box, he called for me again. "Now," says he, and called me his countess, "I am ready to answer your first question; if you will sit down till I have opened this box, we will see how it stands."

So we opened the box. There was in it indeed what I did not expect, for I thought he had sunk his estate rather than raised it; but he produced me in goldsmith's bills, and stock in the English East India Company, about £16,000 sterling; then he gave into my hands nine assignments upon the Bank of Lyons in France, and two upon the rents of the Town House in Paris, amounting in the whole to 5,800 crowns per annum, or annual rent as 'tis called there; and lastly, the sum of 30,000 rix-dollars in the Bank of Amsterdam, besides some jewels and gold in the box to the value of about £1,500 or £1,600, among which was a very good necklace of pearl of about £200 value; and that he pulled out and tied about my neck, telling me that should not be reckoned into the account.

I was equally pleased and surprised, and it was with an inexpressible joy that I saw him so rich. "You might well tell me," said I, "that you were able to make me countess and maintain me as such." In short, he was immensely rich, for besides all this he showed me, which was the reason of his being so busy among the books--I say he showed me several adventures he had abroad in the business of his merchandise; as particularly an eighth share in an East India ship then abroad, an account-current with a merchant at Cadiz in Spain, about £3,000 lent upon bottomry upon ships gone to the Indies, and a large cargo of goods in a merchant's hands for sale at Lisbon in Portugal; so that in his books there was about £12,000 more, all which put together made about £27,000 sterling, and £1,320 a year.

I stood amazed at this account, as well I might, and said nothing to him for a good while, and the rather because I saw him still busy looking over his books. After a while, as I was going to express my wonder, "Hold, my dear," says he, "this is not all neither." Then he pulled me out some old seals and small parchment rolls, which I did not understand, but he told me they were a right of reversion which he had to a paternal estate in his family, and a mortgage of 14,000 rix-dollars, which he had upon it, in the hands of the present possessor, so that was about £3,000 more.

"But now hold again," says he, "for I must pay my debts out of all this, and they are very great, I assure you." And the first, he said, was a black article of 8,000 pistoles, which he had a lawsuit about at Paris, but had it awarded against him, which was the loss he had told me of, and which made him leave Paris in disgust; that in other accounts he owed about £5,300 sterling, but after all this, upon the whole, he had still £17,000 clear stock in money, and £1,320 a year in rent.

After some pause it came to my turn to speak. "Well," says I, "'tis very hard a gentleman with such a fortune as this should come over to England and marry a wife with nothing; it shall never," says I, "be said but what I have I'll bring into the public stock "; so I began to produce.

First, I pulled out the mortgage which good Sir Robert had procured for me, the annual rent £700 per annum, the principal money £14,000.

Secondly, I pulled out another mortgage upon land, procured by the same faithful friend, which at three times had advanced £12,000.

Thirdly, I pulled him out a parcel of little securities, procured by several hands, by fee-farm rents and such petty mortgages as those times awarded, amounting to £10,800 principal money, and paying £636 a year; so that in the whole there was £2,056 a year ready money constantly coming in.

When I had shown him all these, I laid them upon the table and bade him take them, that he might be able to give me an answer to the second question, viz. what fortune he had with his wife? and laughed a little at it.

He looked at them a while and then handed them all back again to me. "I will not touch them," says he, "nor one of them, till they are all settled in trustees' hands, for your own use, and the management wholly your own."

I cannot omit what happened to me while all this was acting, though it was cheerful work in the main, yet I trembled every joint of me worse, for aught I know, than ever Belshazzar did at the handwriting on the wall, and the occasion was every way as just. "Unhappy wretch," said I to myself, "shall my ill-got wealth, the product of prosperous lust and of a vile and vicious life of whoredom and adultery, be intermingled with the honest well-gotten estate of this innocent gentleman, to be a moth and a caterpillar among it, and bring the judgments of Heaven upon him and upon what he has, for my sake? Shall my wickedness blast his comforts? Shall I be fire in his wax, and be a means to provoke Heaven to curse his blessings? God forbid! I'll keep them asunder if it be possible."

This is the true reason why I have been so particular in the account of my vast acquired stock, and how his estate, which was perhaps the product of many years' fortunate industry, and which was equal, if not superior, to mine at best, was at my request kept apart from mine, as is mentioned above.

I have told you how he gave back all my writings into my own hands again. "Well," says I, "seeing you will have it be kept apart, it shall be so upon one condition which I have to propose, and no other." "And what is the condition." says he. "Why," says I, "all the pretence I can have for the making over my own estate to me, is that in case of your mortality I may have it reserved for me if I outlive you." "Well," says he, "that is true." "But then," said I, "the annual income is always received by the husband during his life, as 'tis supposed for the mutual subsistence of the family. Now," says I, "here is £2,000 a year, which I believe is as much as we shall spend, and I desire none of it may be saved; and all the income of your own estate, the interest of the £17,000 and the £1,320 a year may be constantly laid by for the increase of your estate; and so," added I, "by joining the interest every year to the capital, you will perhaps grow as rich as you would do if you were to trade with it all, if you were obliged to keep house out of it too."

He liked the proposal very well and said it should be so, and this way I in some measure satisfied myself that I should not bring my husband under the blast of just Providence for mingling my cursed ill-gotten wealth with his honest estate. This was occasioned by the reflections which at some intervals of time came into my thoughts, of the justice of Heaven, which I had reason to expect would some time or other still fall upon me or my effects, for the dreadful life I had lived.

And let nobody conclude from the strange success I met with in all my wicked doings, and the vast estate which I had raised by it, that therefore I either was happy or easy. No, no, there was a dart struck into the liver; there was a secret hell within, even all the while when our joy was at the highest, but more especially now, after it was all over, and when according to all appearance I was one of the happiest women upon earth; all this while, I say, I had such a constant terror upon my mind as gave me every now and then very terrible shocks, and which made me expect something very frightful upon every accident of life.

In a word, it never lightened or thundered but I expected the next flash would penetrate my vitals, and melt the sword (soul) in this scabbard of flesh; it never blew a storm of wind but I expected the fall of some stack of chimneys, or some part of the house would bury me in its ruins; and so of other things.

But I shall perhaps have occasion to speak of all these things again by and by; the case before us was in a manner settled. We had full £4,000 per annum for our future subsistence, besides a vast sum in jewels and plate, and besides this I had about £8,000 reserved in money, which I kept back from him, to provide for my two daughters, of whom I have yet so much to say.

Chapter 24

With this estate settled as you have heard, and with the best husband in the world, I left England again. I had not only in human prudence and by the nature of the thing, being now married and settled in so glorious a manner--I say I had not only abandoned all the gay and wicked course which I had gone through before, but I began to look back upon it with that horror and that detestation which is the certain companion, if not the forerunner, of repentance.

Sometimes the wonders of my present circumstances would work upon me, and I should have some raptures upon my soul upon the subject of my coming so smoothly out of the arms of hell, that I was not engulfed in ruin, as most who lead such lives are, first or last; but this was a flight too high for me. I was not come to that repentance that is raised from a sense of Heaven's goodness; I repented of the crime, but it was of another and lower kind of repentance, and rather moved by my fears of vengeance than from a sense of being spared from being punished and landed safe after a storm.

The first thing which happened after our coming to The Hague (where we lodged for a while) was that my spouse saluted me one morning with the title of Countess; as he said he intended to do, by having the inheritance to which the honour was annexed made over to him. It is true it was a reversion, but it soon fell, and in the meantime, as all the brothers of a Count are called Counts, so I had the title by courtesy about three years before I had it in reality.

I was agreeably surprised at this coming so soon, and would have had my spouse to have taken the money which it cost him out of my stock, but he laughed at me and went on.

I was now in the height of my glory and prosperity, and I was called the Countess de ----, for I had obtained that, unlooked for, which I secretly aimed at, and was really the main reason of my coming abroad. I took now more servants, lived in a kind of magnificence that I had not been acquainted with, was called Your Honour at every word, and had a coronet behind my coach, though at the same time I knew little or nothing of my new pedigree.

The first thing that my spouse took upon him to manage was to declare ourselves married eleven years before our arriving in Holland, and consequently to acknowledge our little son, who was yet in England, to be legitimate, order him to be brought over and added to his family, and acknowledge him to be our own.

This was done by giving notice to his people at Nimeguen, where his children (which were two sons and a daughter) were brought up, that he was come over from England, and that he was arrived at The Hague with his wife and should reside there some time, and that he would have his two sons brought down to see him, which accordingly was done, and where I entertained them with all the kindness and tenderness that they could expect from their mother-in-law, and who pretended to be so ever since they were two or three years old.

This supposing us to have been so long married was not difficult at all in a country where we had been seen together about that time, viz. eleven years and a half before, and where we had never been seen afterwards till we now returned together; this being seen together was also openly owned, and acknowledged of course, by our friend the merchant at Rotterdam, and also by the people in the house where we both lodged, in the same city, and where our first intimacies began, and who, as it happened, were all alive; and therefore to make it the more public we made a tour to Rotterdam again, lodged in the same house, and was visited there by our friend the merchant, and afterwards invited frequently to his house, where he treated us very handsomely.

This conduct of my spouse, and which he managed very cleverly, was indeed a testimony of a wonderful degree of honesty and affection to our little son, for it was done purely for the sake of the child.

I call it an honest affection, because it was from a principle of honesty that he so earnestly concerned himself to prevent the scandal which would otherwise have fallen upon the child, who was itself innocent. And as it was from this principle of justice that he so earnestly solicited me, and conjured me by the natural affections of a mother, to marry him when it was yet young within me and unborn, that the child might not suffer for the sin of its father and mother, so though at the same time he really loved me very well, yet I had reason to believe that it was from this principle of justice to the child that he came to England again to seek me, with design to marry me and, as he called it, save the innocent lamb from an infamy worse than death.

It is with just reproach to myself that I must repeat it again, that I had not the same concern for it though it was the child of my own body, nor had I ever the hearty affectionate love to the child that he had. What the reason of it was I cannot tell, and indeed I had shown a general neglect of the child through all the gay years of my London revels, except that I sent Amy to look upon it now and then and to pay for its nursing. As for me, I scarce saw it four times in the first four years of its life, and often wished it would go quietly out of the world; whereas a son which I had by the jeweller I took a different care of, and showed a differing concern for, though I did not let him know me, for I provided very well for him, had him put out very well to school, and when he came to years fit for it, let him go over with a person of honesty and good business to the Indies; and, after he had lived there some time and began to act for himself, sent him over the value of £2,000 at several times, with which he traded and grew rich, and, as 'tis to be hoped, may at last come over again with forty or fifty thousand pounds in his pocket, as many do who have not such encouragement at their beginning.

I also sent him over a wife, a beautiful young lady, well bred, an exceeding good-natured, pleasant creature; but the nice young fellow did not like her, and had the impudence to write to me, that is, to the person I employed to correspond with him, to send him another, and promised that he would marry her I had sent him to a friend of his, who liked her better than he did; but I took it so ill that I would not send him another, and withal, stopped another article of £1,000 which I had appointed to send him. He considered of it afterwards, and offered to take her; but then truly she took so ill the first affront he put upon her, that she would not have him, and I sent him word I thought she was very much in the right. However, after courting her two years, and some friends interposing, she took him, and made him an excellent wife, as I knew she would; but I never sent him the £1,000 cargo, so that he lost that money for misusing me, and took the lady at last without it.

My new spouse and I lived a very regular, contemplative life, and in itself certainly a life filled with all human felicity. But if I looked upon my present situation with satisfaction, as I certainly did, so in proportion I on all occasions looked back on former things with detestation and with the utmost affliction; and now indeed, and not till now, those reflections began to prey upon my comforts and lessen the sweets of my other enjoyments. They might be said to have gnawed a hole in my heart before, but now they made a hole quite through it; now they ate into all my pleasant things, made bitter every sweet, and mixed my sighs with every smile.

Not all the affluence of a plentiful fortune, not a hundred thousand pounds estate (for between us we had little less), not honour and titles, attendants and equipages--in a word, not all the things we call pleasure could give me any relish or sweeten the taste of things to me, at least not so much, but I grew sad, heavy, pensive, and melancholy, slept little and ate little, dreamed continually of the most frightful and terrible things imaginable; nothing but apparitions, of devils and monsters, falling into gulfs, and off from steep and high precipices, and the like; so that in the morning, when I should rise and be refreshed with the blessing of rest, I was hag-ridden with frights and terrible things formed merely in the imagination, and was either tired and wanted sleep, or overrun with vapours, and not fit for conversing with my family or any one else.

My husband, the tenderest creature in the world, and particularly so to me, was in great concern for me, and did everything that lay in his power to comfort and restore me; strove to reason me out of it, then tried all the ways possible to divert me, but it was all to no purpose, or to but very little.

My only relief was sometimes to unbosom myself to poor Amy when she and I were alone, and she did all she could to comfort me, but all was to little effect there; for though Amy was the better penitent before, when we had been in the storm, Amy was just where she used to be, now a wild, gay, loose wretch, and not much the graver for her age; for Amy was between forty and fifty by this time too.

But to go on with my own story. As I had no comforter, so I had no counsellor; it was well, as I often thought, that I was not a Roman Catholic, for what a piece of work should I have made, to have gone to a priest with such a history as I had to tell him, and what penance would any father confessor have obliged me to perform, especially if he had been honest and true to his office?

However, as I had none of the recourse, so I had none of the absolution by which the criminal confessing goes away comforted; but I went about with a heart loaded with crime, and altogether in the dark as to what I was to do, and in this condition I languished near two years. I may well call it languishing, for if Providence had not relieved me, I should have died in little time. But of that hereafter.

Chapter 25

I must now go back to another scene and join it to this end of my story, which will complete all my concern with England, at least all that I shall bring into this account. I have hinted at large what I had done for my two sons, one at Messina and the other in the Indies.

But I have not gone through the story of my two daughters. I was so in danger of being known by one of them, that I durst not see her, so as to let her know who I was; and for the other, I could not well know how to see her and own her, and let her see me, because she must then know that I would not let her sister know me, which would look strange. So that, upon the whole, I resolved to see neither of them at all, but Amy managed all that for me; and when she had made gentlewomen of them both, by giving them a good though late education, she had like to have blown up the whole case, and herself and me too, by an unhappy discovery of herself to the last of them, that is, to her who was our cook-maid, and who, as I said before, Amy had been obliged to turn away for fear of the very discovery which now happened. I have observed already in what manner Amy managed her by a third person, and how the girl, when she was set up for a lady, as above, came and visited Amy at my lodgings; after which, Amy going as was her custom to see the girl's brother (my son), at the honest man's house in Spitalfields, both the girls were there, merely by accident, at the same time, and the other girl unawares discovered the secret, namely, that this was the lady that had done all this for them.

Amy was greatly surprised at it, but as she saw there was no remedy, she made a jest of it, and so after that conversed openly, being still satisfied that neither of them could make much of it as long as they knew nothing of me. So she took them together one time and told them the history, as she called it, of their mother, beginning at the miserable carrying them to their aunt's; she owned she was not their mother, herself, but described her to them. However, when she said she was not their mother, one of them expressed herself very much surprised, for the girl had taken up a strong fancy that Amy was really her mother, and that she had for some particular reasons concealed it from her; and therefore when she told her frankly that she was not her mother, the girl fell a-crying, and Amy had much ado to keep life in her. This was the girl who was at first my cook-maid in the Pall Mall. When Amy had brought her to again a little, and she had recovered her first disorder, Amy asked what ailed her. The poor girl hung about her and kissed her, and was in such a passion still, though she was a great wench of nineteen or twenty years old, that she could not be brought to speak a great while. At last, having recovered her speech, she said still, "But oh! do not say you ain't my mother. I'm sure you are my mother"; and then the girl cried again like to kill herself. Amy could not tell what to do with her a good while; she was loath to say again she was not her mother, because she would not throw her into a fit of crying again; but she went round about a little with her. "Why, child," says she, "why would you have me be your mother? If it be because I am so kind to you, be easy, my dear," says Amy, "I'll be as kind to you still as if I was your mother."

"Ay, but," says the girl, "I am sure you are my mother too; and what have I done that you won't own me, and that you will not be called my mother? Though I am poor, you have made me a gentlewoman," says she, "and I won't do anything to disgrace you. Besides," adds she, "I can keep a secret too, especially for my own mother, sure." Then she calls Amy her dear mother, and hung about her neck again, crying still vehemently.

This last part of the girl's words alarmed Amy, and, as she told me, frighted her terribly; nay, she was so confounded with it, that she was not able to govern herself or to conceal her disorder from the girl herself, as you shall hear. Amy was at a full stop and confused to the last degree, and the girl, a sharp jade, turned it upon her. "My dear mother," says she, "do not be uneasy about it, I know it all; but do not be uneasy, I won't let my sister know a word of it, or my brother either, without you give me leave; but don't disown me now you have found me, don't hide yourself from me any longer; I can't bear that," says she, "it will break my heart."

"I think the girl's mad," says Amy. "Why, child, I tell thee if I was thy mother I would not disown thee; don't you see I am as kind to you as if I was your mother?" Amy might as well have sung a song to a kettledrum as talk to her. "Yes," says the girl, "you are very good to me indeed," and that was enough to make anybody believe she was her mother too; but however that was not the case, she had other reasons to believe and to know that she was her mother, and it was a sad thing she would not let her call her mother, who was her own child.

Amy was so heart-full with the disturbance of it that she did not enter further with her into the enquiry, as she would otherwise have done, I mean as to what made the girl so positive, but comes away and tells me the whole story.

I was thunderstruck with the story at first, and much more afterwards, as you shall hear; but, I say, I was thunderstruck at first, and amazed, and said to Amy, "There must be something or other in it more than we know of"; but having examined further into it, I found the girl had no notion of anybody but of Amy, and glad I was that I was not concerned in the pretence and that the girl had no notion of me in it. But even this easiness did not continue long, for the next time Amy went to see her she was the same thing, and rather more violent with Amy than she was before. Amy endeavoured to pacify her by all the ways imaginable. First she told her she took it ill that she would not believe her, and told her if she would not give over such a foolish whimsy she would leave her to the wide world as she found her.

This put the girl into fits, and she cried ready to kill herself and hung about Amy again like a child. "Why," says Amy, "why can you not be easy with me then and compose yourself, and let me go on to do you good and show you kindness, as I would do, and as I intend to do? Can you think that if I was your mother I would not tell you so? What whimsy is this that possesses your mind?" says Amy. Well, the girl told her in a few words, but those few such as frighted Amy out of her wits, and me too, that she knew well enough how it was. "I know," says she, "when you left ----," naming the village, "where I lived when my father went away from us all, that you went over to France; I know that too, and who you went with," says the girl. "Did not my Lady Roxana come back again with you? I know it all well enough, though I was but a child, I have heard it all." And thus she ran on with such discourse as put Amy out of all temper again; and she raved at her like a bedlam, and told her she would never come near her any more; she might go a-begging again if she would, she'd have nothing to do with her. The girl, a passionate wench, told her she knew the worst of it, she could go to service again, and if she would not own her own child she must do as she pleased; then she fell into a passion of crying again, as if she would kill herself.

In short, this girl's conduct terrified Amy to the last degree, and me too, and was it not that we knew the girl was quite wrong in some things, she was yet so right in some other, that it gave me a great deal of perplexity. But that which put Amy the most to it, was that the girl (my daughter) told her that she (meaning me her mother) had gone away with the jeweller, and into France too--she did not call him the jeweller, but with the landlord of the house; who, after her mother fell into distress, and that Amy had taken all the children from her, made much of her, and afterwards married her.

In short, it was plain the girl had but a broken account of things, but yet that she had received some accounts that had a reality in the bottom of them; so that it seems our first measures and the amour of the jeweller were not so concealed as I thought they had been, and, it seems, came in a broken manner to my sister-in-law, whom Amy carried the children to, and she made some bustle, it seems, about it; but as good luck was, it was too late, and I was removed and gone none knew whither, or else she would have sent all the children home to me again, to be sure.

This we picked out of the girl's discourse, that is to say, Amy did, at several times; but it all consisted of broken fragments of stories such as the girl herself had heard so long ago, that she herself could make very little of it; only that in the main, that her mother had played the whore, had gone away with the gentleman that was landlord of the house, that he married her, that she went into France; and as she had learnt in my family, where she was a servant, that Mrs. Amy and her Lady Roxana had been in France together, so she put all these things together, and, joining them with the great kindness that Amy now showed her, possessed the creature that Amy was really her mother; nor was it possible for Amy to conquer it for a long time.

But this, after I had searched into it as far as by Amy's relation I could get an account of it, did not disquiet me half so much as that the young slut had got the name of Roxana by the end, and that she knew who her Lady Roxana was, and the like; though this neither did not hang together, for then she would not have fixed upon Amy for her mother. But some time after, when Amy had almost persuaded her out of it, and that the girl began to be so confounded in her discourses of it that they made neither head nor tail, at last the passionate creature flew out in a kind of rage, and said to Amy that if she was not her mother, Madam Roxana was her mother then, for one of them, she was sure, was her mother; and then, all this that Amy had done for her was by Madam Roxana's order. "And I am sure," says she, "it was my Lady Roxana's coach that brought the gentlewoman (whoever it was) to my uncle's in Spitalfields, for the coachman told me so." Amy fell a-laughing at her aloud, as was her usual way; but as Amy told me, it was but on one side of her mouth, for she was so confounded at her discourse that she was ready to sink into the ground; and so was I too, when she told it me.

However, Amy brazened her out of it all; told her, "Well, since you think you are so high-born as to be my Lady Roxana's daughter, you may go to her and claim your kindred, can't you? I suppose," says Amy, "you know where to find her?" She said she did not question to find her, for she knew where she was gone to live privately, but thought she might be removed again; "for I know how it is," says she, with a kind of a smile or a grin, "I know how it all is, well enough."

Amy was so provoked that she told me, in short, she began to think it would be absolutely necessary to murder her. That expression filled me with horror; all my blood ran chill in my veins, and a fit of trembling seized me that I could not speak a good while, At last, "What, is the devil in you, Amy." said I. "Nay, nay," says she, "let it be the devil or not the devil, if I thought she knew one tittle of your history I would dispatch her if she were my own daughter a thousand times." "And I," says I in a rage, "as well as I love you, would be the first that should put the halter about your neck and see you hanged, with more satisfaction than ever I saw you in my life. Nay," says I, "you would not live to be hanged, I believe I should cut your throat with my own hand; I am almost ready to do it," said I, "as 'tis, for your but naming the thing." With that I called her "cursed devil," and bade her get out of the room.

I think it was the first time that ever I was angry with Amy in all my life, and when all was done, though she was a devilish jade in having such a thought, yet it was all of it the effect of her excess of affection and fidelity to me.

But this thing gave me a terrible shock, for it happened just after I was married, and served to hasten my going over to Holland; for I would not have been seen, so as to be known by the name of Roxana, no, not for ten thousand pounds. It would have been enough to have ruined me to all intents and purposes with my husband, and everybody else too; I might as well have been the German Princess.

Well, I set Amy to work; and, give Amy her due, she set all her wits to work to find out which way this girl had her knowledge, but more particularly how much knowledge she had, that is to say, what she really knew, and what she did not know; for this was the main thing with me, how she could say she knew who Madam Roxana was, and what notions she had of that affair was very mysterious to me; for 'twas certain she could not have a right notion of me, because she would have it be that Amy was her mother.

I scolded heartily at Amy for letting the girl ever know her, that is to say, know her in this affair; for that she knew her, could not be hid, because she, as I might say, served Amy, or rather under Amy, in my family, as is said before; but she (Amy) talked with her at first by another person, and not by herself, and that secret came out by an accident, as I have said above.

Amy was concerned at it as well as I, but could not help it, and though it gave us great uneasiness, yet as there was no remedy we were bound to make as little noise of it as we could, that it might go no further. I bade Amy punish the girl for it, and she did so, for she parted with her in a huff, and told her she should see she was not her mother, for that she could leave her just where she found her; and seeing she could not be content to be served by the kindness of a friend, but that she would needs make a mother of her, she would for the future be neither mother nor friend; and so bid her go to service again and be a drudge as she was before.

The poor girl cried most lamentably, but would not be beaten out of it still; but that which dumbfounded Amy more than all the rest, was that when she had rated the poor girl a long time and could not beat her out of it, and had, as I have observed, threatened to leave her, the girl kept to what she said before, and put this turn to it again, that she was sure, if Amy wasn't, my Lady Roxana was her mother, and that she would go find her out; adding that she made no doubt but she could do it, for she knew where to enquire the name of her new husband.

Amy came home with this piece of news in her mouth to me. I could easily perceive when she came in that she was mad in her mind, and in a rage at something or other, and was in great pain to get it out; for when she came first in, my husband was in the room. However, Amy going up to undress her, I soon made an excuse to follow her, and coming into the room, "What the devil is the matter, Amy?" says I; "I am sure you have some bad news." "News!" says Amy aloud, "ay, so I have; I think the devil is in that young wench--she'll ruin us all and herself too, there's no quieting her." So she went on and told me all the particulars; but sure nothing was so astonished as I was when she told me that the girl knew I was married, that she knew my husband's name, and would endeavour to find me out; I thought I should have sunk down at the very words. In the middle of all my amazement Amy starts up and runs about the room like a distracted body. "I'll put an end to it, that I will; I can't bear it; I must murder her; I'll kill her, by God!" and swears by her Maker in the most serious tone in the world; and then repeated it over three or four times, walking to and again in the room; "I will," in short, "I will kill her if there was not another wench in the world."

"Prithee hold thy tongue, Amy," says I; "why, thou art mad." "Ay, so I am," says she, "stark mad, but I'll be the death of her for all that, and then I shall be sober again." "But you shan't," says I, "you shan't hurt a hair of her head; why, you ought to be hanged for what you have done already, for having resolved on it, is doing it, as to the guilt of the fact; you are a murderer already, as much as if you had done it already."

"I know that," says Amy, "and it can be no worse. I'll put you out of your pain, and her too; she shall never challenge you for her mother in this world, whatever she may in the next." "Well, well," says I, "be quiet, and do not talk thus, I can't bear it"; so she grew a little soberer after a while.

I must acknowledge, the notion of being discovered carried with it so many frightful ideas, and hurried my thoughts so much, that I was scarce myself, any more than Amy, so dreadful a thing is a load of guilt upon the mind.

And yet when Amy began the second time to talk thus abominably of killing the poor child, of murdering her, and swore by her Maker that she would, so that I began to see that she was in earnest, I was terrified a great deal, and it helped to bring me to myself again in other cases.

We laid our heads together then, to see if it was possible to discover by what means she had learnt to talk so, and how she (I mean my girl) came to know that her mother had married a husband. But it would not do, the girl would acknowledge nothing, and gave but a very imperfect account of things still, being disgusted to the last degree with Amy's leaving her so abruptly as she did.

Well, Amy went to the house where the boy was, but it was all one; there they had only heard a confused story of the Lady somebody, they knew not who, which this same wench had told them, but they gave no heed to it at all. Amy told them how foolishly the girl had acted, and how she had carried on the whimsy so far in spite of all they could say to her; that she had taken it so ill, she would see her no more, and so she might e'en go to service again if she would, for she (Amy) would have nothing to do with her unless she humbled herself and changed her note, and that quickly too.

The good old gentleman who had been the benefactor to them all was greatly concerned at it, and the good woman his wife was grieved beyond all expressing, and begged her ladyship, meaning Amy, not to resent it; they promised too they would talk with her about it, and the old gentlewoman added with some astonishment, "Sure, she cannot be such a fool but she will be prevailed with to hold her tongue, when she has it from your own mouth that you are not her mother, and sees that it disobliges your ladyship to have her insist upon it "; and so Amy came away, with some expectation that it would be stopped here.

But the girl was such a fool for all that, and persisted in it obstinately, notwithstanding all they could say to her, nay, her sister begged and entreated her not to play the fool, for that it would ruin her too, and that the lady (meaning Amy) would abandon them both.

Well, notwithstanding this, she insisted, I say, upon it, and which was worse, the longer it lasted the more she began to drop Amy's Ladyship, and would have it that the Lady Roxana was her mother, and that she had made some enquiries about it, and did not doubt but that she should find her out.

When it was come to this, and we found there was nothing to be done with the girl, but that she was so obstinately bent upon the search after me that she ventured to forfeit all she had in view--I say when I found it was come to this, I began to be more serious in my preparations of my going beyond sea, and particularly it gave me some reason to fear that there was something in it; but the following accident put me beside all my measures, and struck me into the greatest confusion that ever I was in in my life.

I was so near going abroad that my spouse and I had taken measures for our going off; and because I would be sure not to go too public, but so as to take away all possibility of being seen, I had made some exception to my spouse against going in the ordinary public passage boats. My pretence to him was the promiscuous crowds in those vessels, want of convenience, and the like; so he took the hint and found me out an English merchant ship which was bound for Rotterdam, and getting soon acquainted with the master, he hired his whole ship, that is to say, his great cabin, for I do not mean his ship for freight, that so we had all the conveniences possible for our passage. And all things being near ready, he brought home the captain one day to dinner with him, that I might see him and be acquainted a little with him. So we came after dinner to talk of the ship and the conveniences on board, and the captain pressed me earnestly to come on board and see the ship, intimating that he would treat us as well as he could; and in discourse I happened to say I hoped he had no other passengers. He said, No, he had not; but he said his wife had courted him a good while to let her go over to Holland with him, for he always used that trade, but he never could think of venturing all he had in one bottom. But if I went with him he thought to take her and her kinswoman along with him this voyage, that they might both wait upon me; and so added, that if we would do him the honour to dine on board the next day, he would bring his wife on board, the better to make us welcome.

Chapter 26

Who now could have believed the devil had any snare at the bottom of all this, or that I was in any danger on such an occasion so remote and out of the way as this was? But the event was the oddest that could be thought of. As it happened, Amy was not at home when we accepted this invitation, and so she was left out of the company; but instead of Amy we took our honest, good-humoured, never-to-be-omitted friend the Quaker, one of the best creatures that ever lived, sure, and who, besides a thousand good qualities unmixed with one bad one, was particularly excellent for being the best company in the world. Though I think I had carried Amy too if she had not been engaged in this unhappy girl's affair; for on a sudden the girl was lost and no news was to be heard of her, and Amy had hunted her to every place she could think of that it was likely to find her in, but all the news she could hear of her was that she was gone to an old comrade's house of hers which she called sister, and who was married to a master of a ship who lived at Redriff, and even this the jade never told me. It seems when this girl was directed by Amy to get her some breeding, go to the boarding-school and the like, she was recommended to a boarding-school at Camberwell, and there she contracted an acquaintance with a young lady (so they are all called) her bedfellow, that they called sisters, and promised never to break off their acquaintance.

But judge you what an unaccountable surprise I must be in when I came on board the ship and was brought into the captain's cabin, or what they call it, the great cabin of the ship, to see his lady or wife, and another young person with her, who when I came to see her near-hand was my old cook-maid in the Pall Mall, and, as appeared by the sequel of the story, was neither more nor less than my own daughter. That I knew her was out of doubt, for though she had not had opportunity to see me very often, yet I had often seen her, as I must needs, being in my own family so long.

If ever I had need of courage and a full presence of mind, it was now; it was the only valuable secret in the world to me; all depended upon this occasion. If the girl knew me, I was undone, and to discover any surprise or disorder had been to make her know me, or guess it, and discover herself.

I was once going to feign a swooning, and faint away, and so falling on the ground or floor, put them all into a hurry and fright, and by that means get an opportunity to be continually holding something to my nose to smell to, and so hold my hand or my handkerchief, or both, before my mouth, then pretend I could not bear the smell of the ship or the closeness of the cabin. But that would have been only to remove into a clearer air upon the quarter-deck, where we should with it have had a clearer light too; and if I had pretended the smell of the ship, it would have served only to have carried us all on shore to the captain's house, which was hard by; for the ship lay so close to the shore that we only walked over a plank to go on board, and over another ship which lay within her. So this not appearing feasible, and the thought not being two minutes old, there was no time, for the two ladies rose up and we saluted, so that I was bound to come so near my girl as to kiss her, which I would not have done had it been possible to have avoided it, but there was no room to escape.

I cannot but take notice here that, notwithstanding there was a secret horror upon my mind and I was ready to sink when I came close to her to salute her, yet it was a secret inconceivable pleasure to me when I kissed her, to know that I kissed my own child, my own flesh and blood, born of my body, and whom I had never kissed since I took the fatal farewell of them all, with a million of tears and a heart almost dead with grief, when Amy and the good woman took them all away and went with them to Spitalfields. No pen can describe, no words can express, I say, the strange impression which this thing made upon my spirits. I felt something shoot through my blood, my heart fluttered, my head flashed and was dizzy, and all within me, as I thought, turned about, and much ado I had not to abandon myself to an excess of passion at the first sight of her, much more when my lips touched her face. I thought I must have taken her in my arms and kissed her again a thousand times, whether I would or no.

But I roused up my judgment and shook it off, and with infinite uneasiness in my mind I sat down. You will not wonder if upon this surprise I was not conversible for some minutes, and that the disorder had almost discovered itself. I had a complication of severe things upon me; I could not conceal my disorder without the utmost difficulty, and yet upon my concealing it depended the whole of my prosperity, so I used all manner of violence with myself to prevent the mischief which was at the door.

Well, I saluted her, but as I went first forward to the captain's lady, who was at the farther end of the cabin, towards the light, I had the occasion offered to stand with my back to the light when I turned about to her, who stood more on my left hand, so that she had not a fair sight of me though I was so near her. I trembled and knew neither what I did nor said; I was in the utmost extremity between so many particular circumstances as lay upon me, for I was to conceal my disorder from everybody, at the utmost peril, and at the same time expected everybody would discern it. I was to expect she would discover that she knew me, and yet was by all means possible to prevent it; I was to conceal myself if possible, and yet had not the least room to do anything towards it; in short, there was no retreat, no shifting anything off, no avoiding or preventing her having a full sight of me; nor was there any counterfeiting my voice, for then my husband would have perceived it; in short, there was not the least circumstance that offered me any assistance or any favourable thing to help me in this exigence.

After I had been upon the rack for near half an hour, during which I appeared stiff and reserved and a little too formal, my spouse and the captain fell into discourses about the ship and the sea, and business remote from us women, and by and by the captain carried him out upon the quarter-deck and left us all by ourselves in the great cabin. Then we began to be a little freer one with another, and I began to be a little revived by a sudden fancy of my own, namely, I thought I perceived that the girl did not know me; and the chief reason of my having such a notion was, because I did not perceive the least disorder in her countenance or the least change in her carriage, no confusion, no hesitation in her discourse, nor, which I had my eye particularly upon, did I observe that she fixed her eyes much upon me; that is to say, not singling me out to look steadily at me, as I thought would have been the case, but that she rather singled out my friend the Quaker and chatted with her on several things, but I observed too that it was all about indifferent matters.

This greatly encouraged me, and I began to be a little cheerful; but I was knocked down again as with a thunder-clap when, turning to the captain's wife and discoursing of me, she said to her, "Sister, I cannot but think (my lady) to be very much like such a person." Then she named the person, and the captain's wife said she thought so too. The girl replied again she was sure she had seen me before, but she could not recollect where. I answered (though her speech was not directed to me) that I fancied she had not seen me before in England, but asked if she had lived in Holland. She said, No, no, she had never been out of England; and I added that she could not then have known me in England, unless it was very lately, for I had lived at Rotterdam a great while. This carried me out of that part of the broil pretty well; and to make it go off the better, when a little Dutch boy came into the cabin, who belonged to the captain and who I easily perceived to be Dutch, I jested and talked Dutch to him, and was merry about the boy, that is to say, as merry as the consternation I was still in would let me be.

However, I began to be thoroughly convinced by this time that the girl did not know me, which was an infinite satisfaction to me; or, at least, that though she had some notion of me, yet that she did not think anything about my being who I was, and which perhaps she would have been as glad to have known as I would have been surprised if she had; indeed, it was evident that had she suspected anything of the truth, she would not have been able to have concealed it.

Thus this meeting went off, and you may be sure I was resolved, if once I got off of it, she should never see me again to revive her fancy; but I was mistaken there too, as you shall hear. After we had been on board, the captain's lady carried us home to her house, which was but just on shore, and treated us there again very handsomely, and made us promise that we would come again and see her before we went, to concert our affairs for the voyage, and the like; for she assured us that both she and her sister went the voyage at that time for our company. And I thought to myself, "Then you'll never go the voyage at all," for I saw from that moment that it would be no way convenient for my ladyship to go with them, for that frequent conversation might bring me to her mind, and she would certainly claim her kindred to me in a few days, as indeed would have been the case.

It is hardly possible for me to conceive what would have been our part in this affair had my woman Amy gone with me on board this ship; it had certainly blown up the whole affair, and I must for ever after have been this girl's vassal, that is to say, have let her into the secret, and trusted to her keeping it too, or have been exposed and undone; the very thought filled me with horror.

But I was not so unhappy neither, as it fell out, for Amy was not with us, and that was my deliverance indeed; yet we had another chance to get over still. As I resolved to put off the voyage, so I resolved to put off the visit, you may be sure, going upon this principle, namely, that I was fixed in it that the girl had seen her last of me and should never see me more.

However, to bring myself well off, and withal to see (if I could) a little further into the matter, I sent my friend the Quaker to the captain's lady to make the visit promised, and to make my excuse that I could not possibly wait on her, for that I was very much out of order; and in the end of the discourse I bade her insinuate to them that she was afraid I should not be able to get ready to go the voyage so soon as the captain would be obliged to go, and that perhaps we might put it off to his next voyage. I did not let the Quaker into any other reason for it than that I was indisposed, and not knowing what other face to put upon that part, I made her believe that I thought I was a-breeding.

It was easy to put that into her head, and she of course hinted to the captain's lady that she found me very ill, that she was afraid I would miscarry, and then, to be sure, I could not think of going.

She went, and she managed that part very dexterously, as I knew she would, though she knew not a word of the grand reason of my indisposition; but I was all sunk and dead-hearted again when she told me she could not understand the meaning of one thing in her visit, namely, that the young woman, as she called her, that was with the captain's lady, and whom she called sister, was most impertinently inquisitive into things, as who I was, how long I had been in England, where I had lived, and the like; and that, above all the rest, she enquired if I did not live once at the other end of the town.

"I thought her enquiries so out of the way," says the honest Quaker, "that I gave her not the least satisfaction; but as I saw by thy answers on board the ship, when she talked of thee, that thou didst not incline to let her be acquainted with thee, so I was resolved that she should not be much the wiser for me; and when she asked me if thou ever livedst here or there, I always said no, but that thou wast a Dutch lady, and was going home again to thy family, and lived abroad.

I thanked her very heartily for that part, and indeed she served me in it more than I let her know she did; in a word, she thwarted the girl so cleverly, that if she had known the whole affair she could not have done it better.

But I must acknowledge all this put me upon the rack again, and I was quite discouraged, not at all doubting but that the jade had a right scent of things and that she knew and remembered my face, but had artfully concealed her knowledge of me till she might perhaps do it more to my disadvantage. I told all this to Amy, for she was all the relief I had. The poor soul (Amy) was ready to hang herself, that, as she said, she had been the occasion of it all; and that if I was ruined (which was the word I always used to her), she had ruined me; and she tormented herself about it so much, that I was sometimes fain to comfort her and myself too.

What Amy vexed herself at was chiefly that she should be surprised so by the girl, as she called her, I mean surprised into a discovery of herself to the girl, which indeed was a false step of Amy's, and so I had often told her. But 'twas to no purpose to talk of that now, the business was how to get clear of the girl's suspicions, and of the girl too, for it looked more threatening every day than another; and if I was uneasy at what Amy had told me of her rambling and rattling to her (Amy), I had a thousand times as much reason to be uneasy now when she had chopped upon me so unhappily as this, and not only had seen my face, but knew too where I lived, what name I went by, and the like.

And I am not come to the worst of it yet neither; for a few days after my friend the Quaker had made her visit and excused me on the account of indisposition, as if they had done it in over and above kindness because they had been told I was not well, they comes both directly to my lodgings to visit me; the captain's wife and my daughter (whom she called sister), and the captain to show them the place. The captain only brought them to the door, put them in, and went away upon some business.

Had not the kind Quaker in a lucky moment come running in before them, they had not only clapped in upon me in the parlour, as it had been a surprise, but, which would have been a thousand times worse, had seen Amy with me; I think if that had happened I had had no remedy but to take the girl by herself and have made myself known to her, which would have been all distraction.

But the Quaker, a lucky creature to me, happened to see them come to the door before they rang the bell, and instead of going to let them in, came running in with some confusion in her countenance, and told me who was a-coming; at which Amy ran first, and I after her, and bid the Quaker come up as soon as she had let them in.

I was going to bid her deny me, but it came into my thoughts, that having been represented so much out of order, it would have looked very odd; besides, I knew the honest Quaker, though she would do anything else for me, would not lie for me, and it would have been hard to have desired it of her.

After she had let them in and brought them into the parlour, she came up to Amy and I, who were hardly out of the fright, and yet were congratulating one another that Amy was not surprised again.

They paid their visit in form, and I received them as formally, but took occasion two or three times to hint that I was so ill that I was afraid I should not be able to go to Holland, at least not so soon as the captain must go off, and made my compliments, how sorry I was to be disappointed of the advantage of their company and assistance in the voyage; and sometimes I talked as if I thought I might stay till the captain returned, and would be ready to go again. Then the Quaker put in, that then I might be too far gone, meaning with child, that I should not venture at all; and then (as if she should be pleased with it) added, she hoped I would stay and lie in at her house; so as this carried its own face with it, 'twas well enough.

But it was now high time to talk of this to my husband, which, however, was not the greatest difficulty before me. For after this and other chat had taken up some time, the young fool began her tattle again, and two or three times she brought it in that I was so like a lady that she had the honour to know at the other end of the town, that she could not put that lady out of her mind when I was by; and once or twice I fancied the girl was ready to cry. By and by she was at it again, and at last I plainly saw tears in her eyes, upon which I asked her if the lady was dead, because she seemed to be in some concern for her. She made me much easier by her answer than ever she did before; she said she did not really know, but she believed she was dead.

This, I say, a little relieved my thoughts, but I was soon down again; for after some time the jade began to grow talkative, and as it was plain that she had told all that her head could retain of Roxana and the days of joy which I had spent at that part of the town, another accident had like to have blown us all up again.

I was in a kind of déshabillé when they came, having on a loose robe like a morning-gown, but much after the Italian way, and I had not altered it when I went up, only dressed my head a little, and as I had been represented as having been lately very ill, so the dress was becoming enough for a chamber.

This morning-vest or robe, call it as you please, was more shaped to the body than we wear them, since showing the body in its true shape, and perhaps a little too plainly if it had been to be worn where any men were to come, but among ourselves it was well enough, especially for hot weather; the colour was green, figured, and the stuff a French damask, very rich.

This gown or vest put the girl's tongue a-running again, and her sister, as she called her, prompted it; for as they both admired my vest and were taken up much about the beauty of the dress, the charming damask, the noble trimming, and the like, my girl puts in a word to the sister (captain's wife). "This is just such a thing as I told you," says she, "the lady danced in." "What!" says the captain's wife, "the Lady Roxana that you told me of? Oh! that's a charming story," says she; "tell it my lady." I could not avoid saying so too, though from my soul I wished her in heaven for but naming it; nay, I won't say but if she had been carried t'other way, it had been much at one to me, if I could but have been rid of her and her story too. For when she came to describe the Turkish dress, it was impossible but the Quaker, who was a sharp, penetrating creature, should receive the impression in a more dangerous manner than the girl; only that indeed she was not so dangerous a person, for if she had known it all I could more freely have trusted her than I could the girl, by a great deal; nay, I should have been perfectly easy in her.

However, as I have said, her talk made me dreadfully uneasy, and the more when the captain's wife mentioned but the name of Roxana. What my face might do towards betraying me I knew not, because I could not see myself, but my heart beat as if it would have jumped out of my mouth, and my passion was so great, that for want of vent I thought I should have burst. In a word, I was in a kind of a silent rage, for the force I was under of restraining my passion was such as I never felt the like of. I had no vent, nobody to open myself to or to make a complaint to for my relief; I durst not leave the room by any means, for then she would have told all the story in my absence, and I should have been perpetually uneasy to know what she had said or had not said; so that, in a word, I was obliged to sit and hear her tell all the story of Roxana, that is to say, of myself, and not know at the same time whether she was in earnest or in jest; whether she knew me or no, or, in short, whether I was to be exposed or not exposed.

She began only in general with telling where she lived; what a place she had of it, how gallant a company her lady had always had in the house, how they used to sit up all night in the house gaming and dancing, what a fine lady her mistress was, and what a vast deal of money the upper servants got. As for her, she said, her whole business was in the next house, so that she got but little; except one night that there was twenty guineas given to be divided among the servants, when, she said, she got two guineas and a half for her share.

She went on, and told them how many servants there was and how they were ordered; but, she said, there was one Mrs. Amy, who was over them all, and that she, being the lady's favourite, got a great deal. She did not know, she said, whether Amy was her Christian name or her surname, but she supposed it was her surname; that they were told she got threescore pieces of gold at one time, being the same night that the rest of the servants had the twenty guineas divided among them.

I put in at that word and said 'twas a vast deal to give away. "Why," says I, "'twas a portion for a servant." "Oh, madam!" says she, "it was nothing to what she got afterwards; we that were servants hated her heartily for it, that is to say, we wished it had been our lot in her stead." Then I said again, "Why, it was enough to get her a good husband and settle her for the world, if she had sense to manage it." "So it might, to be sure, madam," says she, "for we were told she laid up above £500. But I suppose Mrs. Amy was too sensible that her character would require a good portion to put her off."

"Oh," said I, "if that was the case, 'twas another thing."

"Nay," says she, "I don't know, but they talked very much of a young lord that was very great with her."

"And pray what came of her at last?" said I; for I was willing to hear a little (seeing she would talk of it) what she had to say, as well of Amy as of myself.

"I don't know, madam," said she, "I never heard of her for several years till t'other day I happened to see her."

"Did you indeed!" says I, and made mighty strange of it; "what, and in rags, it may be," said I; "that's often the end of such creatures."

"Just the contrary, madam," says she, "she came to visit an acquaintance of mine, little thinking, I suppose, to see me, and I assure you she came in her coach."

"In her coach!" said I; "upon my word, she had made her market then. I suppose she made hay while the sun shone; was she married, pray?"

"I believe she had been married, madam," says she, "but it seems she had been at the East Indies, and if she was married, it was there, to be sure. I think she said she had good luck in the Indies."

"That is, I suppose," said I, "had buried her husband there."

"I understand it so, madam," says she, "and that she had got his estate."

"Was that her good luck?" said I. It might be good to her as to the money indeed, but it was but the part of a jade to call it good luck.

Thus far our discourse of Mrs. Amy went, and no further, for she knew no more of her; but then the Quaker unhappily, though undesignedly, put in a question, which the honest, good-humoured creature would have been far from doing if she had known that I had carried on the discourse of Amy on purpose to drop Roxana out of the conversation.

But I was not to be made easy too soon. The Quaker put in, "But I think thou saidst something was behind of thy mistress; what didst thou call her: Roxana, was it not? Pray what became of her?"

"Ay, ay, Roxana," says the captain's wife; "pray, sister, let's hear the story of Roxana; it will divert my lady, I'm sure."

"That's a damned lie," said I to myself; "if you knew how little 'twould divert me, you would have too much advantage over me." Well, I saw no remedy but the story must come on, so I prepared to hear the worst of it.

"Roxana!" says she, "I know not what to say of her; she was so much above us, and so seldom seen, that we could know little of her but by report, but we did sometimes see her too; she was a charming woman indeed, and the footmen used to say that she was to be sent for to Court."

"To Court!" said I, "why, she was at Court, wasn't she? The Pall Mall is not far from Whitehall."

"Yes, madam," says she, "but I mean another way."

"I understand thee," says the Quaker. "Thou meanest, I suppose, to be mistress to the King."

"Yes, madam," says she.

I cannot help confessing what a reserve of pride still was left in me; and though I dreaded the sequel of the story, yet when she talked how handsome and how fine a lady this Roxana was, I could not help being pleased and tickled with it, and put in questions two or three times of how handsome she was, and was she really so fine a woman as they talked of, and the like, on purpose to hear her repeat what the people's opinion of me was and how I had behaved.

"Indeed," says she at last, "she was a most beautiful creature as ever I saw in my life." "But then," said I, "you never had the opportunity to see her but when she was set out to the best advantage."

"Yes, yes, madam," says she, "I have seen her several times in her déshabillé, and I can assure you she was a very fine woman; and that which was more still, everybody said she did not paint."

This was still agreeable to me one way, but there was a devilish sting in the tail of it all, and this last article was one, wherein she said she had seen me several times in my déshabillé. This put me in mind that then she must certainly know me, and it would come out at last, which was death to me but to think of.

"Well, but, sister," says the captain's wife, "tell my lady about the ball, that's the best of all the story, and of Roxana's dancing in a fine outlandish dress."

"That's one of the brightest parts of her story indeed," says the girl; "the case was this. We had balls and meetings in her ladyship's apartments every week almost, but one time my lady invited all the nobles to come such a time and she would give them a ball; and there was a vast crowd indeed," says she.

"I think you said the King was there, sister, didn't you?"

"No, madam," says she, "that was the second time, when they said the King had heard how finely the Turkish lady danced, and that he was there to see her; but the King, if His Majesty was there, came disguised."

"That is what they call incog.," says my friend the Quaker; "thou canst not think the King would disguise himself." "Yes," says the girl, "it was so; he did not come in public with his Guards, but we all knew which was the King, well enough; that is to say, which they said was the King."

"Well," says the captain's wife, "about the Turkish dress; pray let us hear that." "Why," says she, "my lady sat in a fine little drawing-room, which opened into the great room, and where she received the compliments of the company; and when the dancing began, a great lord," says she, "I forget who they called him (but he was a very great lord or duke, I don't know which), took her out and danced with her; but after a while my lady on a sudden shut the drawing-room and ran upstairs with her woman Mrs. Amy, and though she did not stay long (for I suppose she had contrived it all beforehand), she came down dressed in the strangest figure that ever I saw in my life, but it was exceeding fine."

Here she went on to describe the dress as I have done already, but did it so exactly that I was surprised at the manner of her telling it; there was not a circumstance of it left out.

I was now under a new perplexity, for this young slut gave so complete an account of everything in the dress, that my friend the Quaker coloured at it, and looked two or three times at me to see if I did not do so too; for (as she told me afterwards) she immediately perceived it was the same dress that she had seen me have on, as I have said before. However, as she saw I took no notice of it, she kept her thoughts private to herself, and I did so too as well as I could.

I put it two or three times, that she had a good memory that could be so particular in every part of such a thing.

"Oh, madam!" says she, "we that were servants stood by ourselves in a corner, but so as we could see more than some strangers; besides," says she, "it was all our conversation for several days in the family, and what one did not observe, another did." "Why," says I to her, "this was no Persian dress; only, I suppose, your lady was some French comedian, that is to say, a stage Amazon, that put on a counterfeit dress to please the company, such as they used in the play of Tamerlane at Paris, or some such."

"No, indeed, madam," says she, "I assure you my lady was no actress; she was a fine, modest lady, fit to be a princess; everybody said if she was a mistress, she was fit to be a mistress to none but the King, and they talked her up for the King as if it had really been so. Besides, madam," says she, "my lady danced a Turkish dance, all the lords and gentry said it was so, and one of them swore he had seen it danced in Turkey himself; so that it could not come from the theatre at Paris; and then the name Roxana," says she, "was a Turkish name."

"Well," said I, "but that was not your lady's name, I suppose."

"No, no, madam," said she, "I know that; I know my lady's name and family very well. Roxana was not her name, that's true indeed."

Here she ran me aground again, for I durst not ask her what was Roxana's real name, lest she had really dealt with the devil and had boldly given my own name in for answer. So that I was still more and more afraid that the girl had really gotten the secret somewhere or other, though I could not imagine neither how that could be.

In a word, I was sick of the discourse, and endeavoured many ways to put an end to it, but it was impossible, for the captain's wife, who called her sister, prompted her and pressed her to tell it, most ignorantly thinking that it would be a pleasant tale to all of us.

Two or three times the Quaker put in that this Lady Roxana had a good stock of assurance, and that 'twas likely if she had been in Turkey, she had lived with or been kept by some great Bassa there. But still she would break in upon all such discourse, and fly out into the most extravagant praises of her mistress, the famed Roxana. I ran her down as some scandalous woman, that it was not possible to be otherwise, but she would not hear of it; her lady was a person of such and such qualifications that nothing but an angel was like her, to be sure. And yet, after all she could say, her own account brought her down to this, that, in short, her lady kept little less than a gaming-ordinary, or, as it would be called in the times since that, an assembly for gallantry and play.

All this while I was very uneasy, as I said before, and yet the whole story went off again without any discovery, only that I seemed a little concerned that she should liken me to this gay lady whose character I pretended to run down very much, even upon the foot of her own relation.

But I was not at the end of my mortifications yet neither, for now my innocent Quaker threw out an unhappy expression which put me upon the tenters again. Says she to me, "This lady's habit, I fancy, is just such a one as thine, by the description of it"; and then turning to the captain's wife, says she, "I fancy my friend has a finer Turkish or Persian dress, a great deal." "Oh!" says the girl, "'tis impossible to be finer; my lady's," says she, "was all covered with gold and diamonds;

her hair and head-dress, I forgot the name they gave it," says she, "shone like the stars, there was so many jewels in it."

I never wished my good friend the Quaker out of my company before now, but indeed I would have given some guineas to have been rid of her just now; for beginning to be curious in the comparing the two dresses, she innocently began a description of mine, and nothing terrified me so much as the apprehension lest she should importune me to show it, which I was resolved I would never agree to.

But before it came to this she pressed my girl to describe the Tyhiaai or head-dress, which she did so cleverly that the Quaker could not help saying mine was just such a one; and after several other similitudes, all very vexatious to me, out comes the kind of motion to me to let the ladies see my dress, and they joined their eager desires of it, even to importunity.

I desired to be excused, though I had little to say at first why I declined it; but at last it came into my head to say it was packed up with my other clothes that I had least occasion for, in order to be sent on board the captain's ship, but that if we lived to come to Holland together (which, by the way, I resolved should never happen), then, I told them, at unpacking my clothes they should see me dressed in it; but they must not expect I should dance in it, like the Lady Roxana in all her fine things.

This carried it off pretty well, and getting over this got over most of the rest, and I began to be easy again; and, in a word, that I may dismiss the story too as soon as may be, I got rid at last of my visitors, whom I had wished gone two hours sooner than they intended it.

Chapter 27

As soon as they were gone I ran up to Amy, and gave vent to my passions by telling her the whole story and letting her see what mischiefs one false step of hers had like, unluckily, to have involved us all in, more perhaps than we could ever have lived to get through. Amy was sensible of it enough, and was just giving her wrath a vent another way, viz. by calling the poor girl all the damned jades and fools (and sometimes worse names) that she could think of; in the middle of which up comes my honest, good Quaker and puts an end to our discourse. The Quaker came in smiling (for she was always soberly cheerful). "Well," says she, "thou art delivered at last, I come to joy thee of it; I perceived thou wert tired grievously of thy visitors."

"Indeed," says I, "so I was; that foolish young girl held us all in a Canterbury story, I thought she would never have done with it." "Why, truly I thought she was very careful to let thee know she was but a cook-maid." "Ay," says I, "and at a gaming-house, or gaming-ordinary, and at t'other end of the town too; all which (by the way) she might know, would add very little to her good name among us citizens."

"I can't think," says the Quaker, "but she had some other drift in that long discourse; there's something else in her head," says she, "I am satisfied of that." Thought I, "Are you satisfied of it? I am sure I am the less satisfied for that; at least 'tis but small satisfaction to me to hear you say so. What can this be?" says I; "and when will my uneasiness have an end?" But this was silent, and to myself, you may be sure. But in answer to my friend the Quaker, I returned by asking her a question or two about it; as what she thought was in it, and why she thought there was anything in it; "for," says I, "she can have nothing in it relating to me."

"Nay," says the kind Quaker, "if she had any view towards thee, that's no business of mine, and I should be far from desiring thee to inform me."

This alarmed me again; not that I feared trusting the good-humoured creature with it if there had been anything of just suspicion in her, but this affair was a secret I cared not to communicate to anybody. However, I say, this alarmed me a little, for as I had concealed everything from her, I was willing to do so still; but as she could not but gather up abundance of things from the girl's discourse which looked towards me, so she was too penetrating to be put off with such answers as might stop another's mouth. Only there was this double felicity in it: first, that she was not inquisitive to know or find anything out, and not dangerous if she had known the whole story. But, as I say, she could not but gather up several circumstances from the girl's discourse, as particularly the name of Amy, and the several descriptions of the Turkish dress which my friend the Quaker had seen and taken so much notice of, as I have said above.

As for that, I might have turned it off by jesting with Amy and asking her who she lived with before she came to live with me; but that would not do, for we had unhappily anticipated that way of talking by having often talked how long Amy had lived with me, and which was still worse, by having owned formerly that I had had lodgings in the Pall Mall; so that all those things corresponded too well. There was only one thing that helped me out with the Quaker, and that was the girl's having reported how rich Mrs. Amy was grown, and that she kept her coach. Now as there might be many more Mrs. Amy's besides mine, so it was not likely to be my Amy, because she was far from such a figure as keeping her coach; and this carried it off from the suspicions which the good, friendly Quaker might have in her head.

But as to what she imagined the girl had in her head, there lay more real difficulty in that part a great deal, and I was alarmed at it very much; for my friend the Quaker told me she observed that the girl was in a great passion when she talked of the habit, and more when I had been importuned to show her mine but declined it. She said she several times perceived her to be in disorder and to restrain herself with great difficulty, and once or twice she muttered to herself that she had found it out or that she would find it out, she could not tell whether, and that she often saw tears in her eyes; that when I said my suit of Turkish clothes was put up, but that she should see it when we arrived in Holland, she heard her say softly she would go over on purpose then.

After she had ended her observations, I added I observed too that the girl talked and looked oddly, and that she was mighty inquisitive, but I could not imagine what it was she aimed at. "Aimed at!" says the Quaker, "'tis plain to me what she aims at; she believes thou art the same Lady Roxana that danced in the Turkish vest, but she is not certain." "Does she believe so?" says I; "if I had thought that, I would have put her out of her pain." "Believe so!" says the Quaker, "yes, and I began to believe so too, and should have believed so still if thou hadst not satisfied me to the contrary by thy taking no notice of it and by what thou hast said since." "Should you have believed so?" said I warmly, "I am very sorry for that; why, would you have taken me for an actress or a French stage-player?" "No," says the good, kind creature, "thou carry'st it too far; as soon as thou mad'st thy reflections upon her I knew it could not be; but who could think any other when she described the Turkish dress which thou hast here, with the head-tire and jewels, and when she named thy maid Amy too, and several other circumstances concurring? I should certainly have believed it," said she, "if thou hadst not contradicted it, but as soon as I heard thee speak I concluded it was otherwise." "That was very kind," said I, "and I am obliged to you for doing me so much justice; 'tis more, it seems, than that young talking creature does." "Nay," says the Quaker, "indeed she does not do thee justice, for she as certainly believes it still as ever she did." "Does she?" said I. "Ay," says the Quaker, "and I warrant thee she'll make thee another visit about it." "Will she?" says I; "then I believe I shall downright affront her." "No, thou shalt not affront her," says she (full of her good humour and temper), "I'll take that part off thy hands, for I'll affront her for thee, and not let her see thee." I thought that was a very kind offer, but was at a loss how she would be able to do it; and the thought of seeing her there again distracted me, not knowing what temper she would come in, much less what manner to receive her in. But my fast friend and constant comforter the Quaker said she perceived the girl was impertinent, and that I had no inclination to converse with her, and she was resolved I should not be troubled with her. But I shall have occasion to say more of this presently, for this girl went further yet than I thought she had.

It was now time, as I said before, to take measures with my husband in order to put off my voyage; so I fell into talk with him one morning as he was dressing, and while I was in bed. I pretended I was very ill, and as I had but too easy a way to impose upon him, because he so absolutely believed everything I said, so I managed my discourse so as that he should understand by it I was a-breeding, though I did not tell him so.

However, I brought it about so handsomely, that before he went out of the room he came and sat down by my bedside, and began to talk very seriously to me upon the subject of my being so every-day ill; and that as he hoped I was with child, he would have me consider well of it whether I had not best alter my thoughts of the voyage to Holland, for that being seasick, and which was worse, if a storm should happen, might be very dangerous to me. And after saying abundance of the kindest things that the kindest of husbands in the world could say, he concluded that it was his request to me that I would not think any more of going till after all should be over, but that I would, on the contrary, prepare to lie in where I was, and where I knew, as well as he, I could be very well provided and very well assisted.

This was just what I wanted, for I had, as you have heard, a thousand good reasons why I should put off the voyage, especially with that creature in company; but I had a mind the putting it off should be at his motion, not my own, and he came into it of himself, just as I would have had it. This gave me an opportunity to hang back a little, and to seem as if I was unwilling. I told him I could not abide to put him to difficulties and perplexities in his business; that now he had hired the great cabin in the ship, and perhaps paid some of the money, and, it may be, taken freight for goods, and to make him break it all off again would be a needless charge to him, or perhaps a damage to the captain.

As to that, he said it was not to be named, and he would not allow it to be any consideration at all; that he could easily pacify the captain of the ship by telling him the reason of it, and that if he did make him some satisfaction for the disappointment, it should not be much.

"But, my dear," says I, "you haven't heard me say I am with child, neither can I say so, and if it should not be so at last, then I shall have made a fine piece of work of it indeed. Besides," says I, "the two ladies, the captain's wife and her sister, they depend upon our going over, and have made great preparations, and all in compliment to me; what must I say to them?"

"Well, my dear," says he, "if you should not be with child, though I hope you are, yet there is no harm done; the staying three or four months longer in England will be no damage to me, and we can go when we please, when we are sure you are not with child, or when it appearing that you are with child, you shall be down and up again. And as for the captain's wife and sister, leave that part to me, I'll answer for it there shall be no quarrel raised upon that subject; I'll make your excuse to them by the captain himself, so all will be well enough there, I'll warrant you."

This was as much as I could desire, and thus it rested for a while. I had indeed some anxious thoughts about this impertinent girl, but believed that putting off the voyage would have put an end to it all; so I began to be pretty easy. But I found myself mistaken, for I was brought to the point of destruction by her again, and that in the most unaccountable manner imaginable.

My husband, as he and I had agreed, meeting the captain of the ship, took the freedom to tell him that he was afraid he must disappoint him, for that something had fallen out which had obliged him to alter his measures, and that his family could not be ready to go time enough for him.

"I know the occasion, sir," says the captain. "I hear your lady has got a daughter more than she expected; I give you joy of it." "What do you mean by that?" says my spouse. "Nay, nothing," says the captain, "but what I hear the women tattle over the tea-table; I know nothing but that you don't go the voyage upon it, which I am sorry for. But you know your own affairs," added the captain, "that's no business of mine."

"Well, but," says my husband, "I must make you some satisfaction for the disappointment," and so pulls out his money. "No, no," says the captain, and so they fell to straining their compliments one upon another. But, in short, my spouse gave him three or four guineas, and made him take it, and so the first discourse went off again and they had no more of it.

But it did not go off so easily with me; for now, in a word, the clouds began to thicken about me and I had alarms on every side. My husband told me what the captain had said, but very happily took it that the captain had brought a tale by halves, and, having heard it one way, had told it another; and that neither could he understand the captain, neither did the captain understand himself; so he contented himself to tell me, he said, word for word, as the captain delivered it.

How I kept my husband from discovering my disorder, you shall hear presently; but let it suffice to say just now that if my husband did not understand the captain, nor the captain understand himself, yet I understood them both very well; and to tell the truth, it was a worse shock than ever I had had yet. Invention supplied me indeed with a sudden motion to avoid showing my surprise, for as my spouse and I were sitting by a little table near the fire, I reached out my hand, as if I had intended to take a spoon which lay on the other side, and threw one of the candles off of the table, and then, snatching it up, started up upon my feet, and stooped to the lap of my gown and took it in my hand. "Oh!" says I, "my gown's spoiled; the candle has greased it prodigiously." This furnished me with an excuse to my spouse to break off the discourse for the present and call Amy down. And Amy not coming presently, I said to him, "My dear, I must run upstairs and put it off and let Amy clean it a little." So my husband rose up too, and went into a closet where he kept his papers and books, and fetched a book out and sat down by himself to read.

Glad I was that I had got away, and up I ran to Amy, who, as it happened, was alone. "Oh, Amy!" says I, "we are all utterly undone "; and with that I burst out a-crying, and could not speak a word for a great while.

I cannot help saying that some very good reflections offered themselves upon this head; it presently occurred, what a glorious testimony it is to the justice of Providence, and to the concern Providence has in guiding all the affairs of men (even the least as well as the greatest), that the most secret crimes are, by the most unforeseen accidents, brought to light and discovered.

Another reflection was, how just it is that sin and shame follow one another so constantly at the heels, that they are not like attendants only, but like cause and consequence, necessarily connected one with another; that the crime going before, the scandal is certain to follow, and that 'tis not in the power of human nature to conceal the first or avoid the last.

"What shall I do, Amy?" said I as soon as I could speak, "and what will become of me?" And then I cried again so vehemently, that I could say no more a great while. Amy was frighted almost out of her wits, but knew nothing what the matter was; but she begged to know, and persuaded me to compose myself and not cry so. "Why, madam, if my master should come up now," says she, "he will see what a disorder you are in; he will know you have been crying, and then he will want to know the cause of it." With that I broke out again. "Oh! he knows it already, Amy," says I; "he knows all! 'tis all discovered! and we are undone!" Amy was thunderstruck now indeed. "Nay," says Amy, "if that be true we are undone indeed; but that can never be, that's impossible, I'm sure."

"No, no," says I, "'tis far from impossible, for I tell you 'tis so." And by this time being a little recovered, I told her what discourse my husband and the captain had had together, and what the captain had said. This put Amy into such a hurry that she cried, she raved, she swore and cursed like a mad thing; then she upbraided me that I would not let her kill the girl when she would have done it; and that it was all my own doing, and the like. Well, however, I was not for killing the girl yet, I could not bear the thoughts of that neither.

We spent half an hour in these extravagances, and brought nothing out of them neither; for indeed we could do nothing or say nothing that was to the purpose, for if anything was to come out-of-the-way, there was no hindering it nor help for it. So after thus giving a vent to myself by crying, I began to reflect how I had left my spouse below, and what I had pretended to come up for; so I changed my gown that I pretended the candle fell upon, and put on another and went down.

When I had been down a good while, and found my spouse did not fall into the story again as I expected, I took heart and called for it. "My dear," said I, "the fall of the candle put you out of your history; won't you go on with it?" "What history?" says he. "Why," says I, "about the captain." "Oh!" says he, "I had done with it; I know no more than that the captain told a broken piece of news that he had heard by halves, and told more by halves than he heard it; namely, of your being with child, and that you could not go the voyage."

I perceived my husband entered not into the thing at all, but took it for a story, which, being told two or three times over, was puzzled and come to nothing; and that all that was meant by it was what he knew or thought he knew already, viz. that I was with child, which he wished might be true.

His ignorance was cordial to my soul, and I cursed them in my thoughts that should ever undeceive him; and as I saw him willing to have the story end there, as not worth being further mentioned, I closed it too, and said I supposed the captain had it from his wife, she might have found somebody else to make her remarks upon; and so it passed off with my husband well enough, and I was still safe there where I thought myself in most danger. But I had two uneasinesses still: the first was, lest the captain and my spouse should meet again and enter into further discourse about it; and the second was, lest the busy, impertinent girl should come again, and when she came, how to prevent her seeing Amy, which was an article as material as any of the rest; for seeing Amy would have been as fatal to me as her knowing all the rest.

As to the first of these, I knew the captain could not stay in town above a week, but that his ship being already full of goods, and fallen down the river, he must soon follow; so I contrived to carry my husband somewhere out of town for a few days, that they might be sure not to meet.

My greatest concern was, where we should go. At last I fixed upon Northall; not, I said, that I would drink the waters, but that I thought the air was good, and might be for my advantage. He, who did everything upon the foundation of obliging me, readily came into it, and the coach was appointed to be ready the next morning; but as we were settling matters he put in an ugly word that thwarted all my design. And that was, that he had rather I would stay till afternoon, for that he should speak to the captain next morning if he could, to give him some letters, which he could do and be back again about twelve o'clock.

I said, "Ay, by all means"; but it was but a cheat on him, and my voice and my heart differed, for I resolved, if possible, he should not come near the captain nor see him, whatever came of it.

In the evening therefore, a little before we went to bed, I pretended to have altered my mind, and that I would not go to Northall, but I had a mind to go another way, but I told him I was afraid his business would not permit him; he wanted to know where it was. I told him, smiling, I would not tell him, lest it should oblige him to hinder his business. He answered, with the same temper but with infinitely more sincerity, that he had no business of so much consequence as to hinder him going with me anywhere that I had a mind to go. "Yes," says I, "you want to speak with the captain before he goes away." "Why, that's true," says he, "so I do," and paused a while; and then added, "But I'll write a note to a man that does business for me, to go to him; 'tis only to get some bills of loading signed, and he can do it." When I saw I had gained my point I seemed to hang back a little. "My dear," says I, "don't hinder an hour's business for me; I can put it off for a week or two, rather than you shall do yourself any prejudice." "No, no," says he, "you shall not put it of an hour for me, for I can do my business by proxy with anybody but my wife "; and then he took me in his arms and kissed me. How did my blood flush up into my face when I reflected how sincerely, how affectionately this good-humoured gentleman embraced the most cursed piece of hypocrisy that ever came into the arms of an honest man! His was all tenderness, all kindness, and the utmost sincerity; mine all grimace and deceit, a piece of mere manage and framed conduct to conceal a past life of wickedness and prevent his discovering that he had in his arms a she-devil, whose whole conversation for twenty-five years had been black as hell, a complication of crime, and for which, had he been let into it, he must have abhorred me and the very mention of my name. But there was no help for me in it, all I had to satisfy myself was that it was my business to be what I was and conceal what I had been; that all the satisfaction I could make him was to live virtuously for the time to come, not being able to retrieve what had been in time past; and this I resolved upon, though had the great temptation offered, as it did afterwards, I had reason to question my stability. But of that hereafter.

After my husband had kindly thus given up his measures to mine, we resolved to set out in the morning early. I told him that my project, if he liked it, was to go to Tunbridge; and he, being entirely passive in the thing, agreed to it with the greatest willingness, but said if I had not named Tunbridge, he would have named Newmarket (there being a great Court there, and abundance of fine things to be seen). I offered him another piece of hypocrisy here, for I pretended to be willing to go thither, as the place of his choice, but indeed I would not have gone for a thousand pounds; for the Court being there at that time, I durst not run the hazard of being known at a place where there were so many eyes that had seen me before. So that, after some time, I told my husband that I thought Newmarket was so full of people at that time, that we should get no accommodation; that seeing the Court and the crowd was no entertainment at all to me, unless as it might be so to him, that if he thought fit, we would rather put it off to another time; and that if when we went to Holland, we should go by Harwich, we might take a round by Newmarket and Bury, and so come down to Ipswich, and go from thence to the seaside. He was easily put off from this, as he was from anything else that I did not approve; and so with all imaginable facility he appointed to be ready early in the morning, to go with me for Tunbridge.

I had a double design in this, viz. first, to get away my spouse from seeing the captain any more; and secondly, to be out of the way myself, in case this impertinent girl, who was now my plague, should offer to come again, as my friend the Quaker believed she would; and as indeed happened within two or three days afterwards.

Chapter 28

Having thus secured my going away the next day, I had nothing to do but to furnish my faithful agent the Quaker with some instructions what to say to this tormentor (for such she proved afterwards), and how to manage her if she made any more visits than ordinary.

I had a great mind to leave Amy behind too, as an assistant, because she understood so perfectly well what to advise upon any emergence; and Amy importuned me to do so. But I know not what secret impulse prevailed over my thoughts against it, I could not do it for fear the wicked jade should make her away, which my very soul abhorred the thoughts of; which, however, Amy found means to bring to pass afterwards, as I may in time relate more particularly.

It is true I wanted as much to be delivered from her as ever a sick man did from a third-day ague, and had she dropped into the grave by any fair way, as I may call it--I mean had she died by any ordinary distemper--I should have shed but very few tears for her. But I was not arrived to such a pitch of obstinate wickedness as to commit murder, especially such as to murder my own child, or so much as to harbour a thought so barbarous in my mind. But, as I said, Amy effected all afterwards without my knowledge, for which I gave her my hearty curse, though I could do little more; for to have fallen upon Amy had been to have murdered myself. But this tragedy requires a longer story than I have room for here. I return to my journey.

My dear friend the Quaker was kind, and yet honest, and would do anything that was just and upright to serve me, but nothing wicked or dishonourable. That she might be able to say boldly to the creature, if she came, she did not know where I was gone, she desired I would not let her know; and to make her ignorance the more absolutely safe to herself, and likewise to me, I allowed her to say that she heard us talk of going to Newmarket, etc. She liked that part, and I left all the rest to her, to act as she thought fit, only charged her that if the girl entered into the story of the Pall Mall, she should not entertain much talk about it, but let her understand that we all thought she spoke of it a little too particularly, and that the lady (meaning me) took it a little ill to be so likened to a public mistress or a stage-player, and the like; and so bring her, if possible, to say no more of it. However, though I did not tell my friend the Quaker how to write to me or where I was, yet I left a sealed paper with her maid to give her, in which I gave her a direction how to write to Amy, and so in effect to myself.

It was but a few days after I was gone, but the impatient girl came to my lodgings on pretence to see how I did, and to hear if I intended to go the voyage, and the like. My trusty agent was at home, and received her coldly at the door, but told her that the lady which she supposed she meant was gone from her house.

This was a full stop to all she could say for a good while; but as she stood musing some time at the door, considering what to begin a talk upon, she perceived my friend the Quaker looked a little uneasy, as if she wanted to go in and shut the door, which stung her to the quick; and the wary Quaker had not so much as asked her to come in; for seeing her alone, she expected she would be very impertinent, and concluded that I did not care how coldly she received her.

But she was not to be put off so. She said if the Lady ---- was not to be spoken with, she desired to speak two or three words with her, meaning my friend the Quaker. Upon that the Quaker civilly but coldly asked her to walk in, which was what she wanted. Note, she did not carry her into her best parlour as formerly, but into a little outer room where the servants usually waited.

By the first of her discourse she did not stick to insinuate as if she believed I was in the house but was unwilling to be seen, and pressed earnestly that she might speak but two words with me; to which she added earnest entreaties, and at last tears.

"I am sorry," says my good creature the Quaker, "thou hast so ill an opinion of me as to think I would tell thee an untruth, and say that the Lady ---- was gone from my house if she was not. I assure thee I do not use any such method, nor does the Lady ---- desire any such kind of service from me as I know of. If she had been in the house, I should have told thee so."

She said little to that, but said it was business of the utmost importance that she desired to speak with me about; and then cried again very much.

"Thou seem'st to be sorely afflicted," says the Quaker, "I wish I could give thee any relief; but if nothing will comfort thee but seeing the Lady ----, it is not in my power."

"I hope it is," says she again; "to be sure it is of great consequence to me, so much that I am undone without it."

"Thou troublest me very much to hear thee say so," says the Quaker; "but why then didst thou not speak to her apart when thou wast here before?"

"I had no opportunity," says she, "to speak to her alone, and I could not do it in company; if I could have spoken but two words to her alone, I would have throw'n myself at her foot and asked her blessing."

"I am surprised at thee; I do not understand thee," says the Quaker.

"Oh!" says she, "stand my friend, if you have any charity, or if you have any compassion for the miserable, for I am utterly undone!"

"Thou terrifiest me," says the Quaker, "with such passionate expressions, for verily I cannot comprehend thee."

"Oh!" says she, "she is my mother; she is my mother, and she does not own me."

"Thy mother!" says the Quaker, and began to be greatly moved indeed; "I am astonished at thee; what dost thou mean?"

"I mean nothing but what I say," says she, "I say again she is my mother! and will not own me "; and with that she stopped with a flood of tears.

"Not own thee!" says the Quaker; and the tender, good creature wept too. "Why, she says she does not know thee, and never saw thee before."

"No," says the girl, "I believe she does not know me, but I know her, and I know that she is my mother."

"It's impossible! Thou talkest mystery," says the Quaker; "wilt thou explain thyself a little to me?"

"Yes, yes," says she, "I can explain it well enough; I am sure she is my mother, and I have broken my heart to search for her; and now to lose her again, when I was so sure I had found her, will break my heart more effectually."

"Well, but if she be thy mother," says the Quaker, "how can it be that she should not know thee?"

"Alas!" says she, "I have been lost to her ever since I was a child. She has never seen me."

"And hast thou never seen her?" says the Quaker.

"Yes," says she, "I have seen her, often enough I saw her, for when she was the Lady Roxana I was her housemaid, being a servant, but I did not know her then, nor she me, but it has all come out since; has she not a maid named Amy?" (Note, the honest Quaker was nonplussed, and greatly surprised at that question.) "Truly," says she, "the Lady ---- has several women-servants, but I do not know all their names."

"But her woman, her favourite," adds the girl; "is not her name Amy?"

"Why, truly," says the Quaker with a very happy turn of wit, "I do not like to be examined; but lest thou shouldst take up any mistakes by reason of my backwardness to speak, I will answer thee for once that what her woman's name is I know not, but they call her Cherry."

N.B.--My husband gave her that name in jest on our wedding day, and we had called her by it ever since, so that she spoke literally true at that time.

The girl replied very modestly that she was sorry if she gave her any offence in asking, that she did not design to be rude to her or pretend to examine her, but that she was in such an agony at this disaster, that she knew not what she did or said; and that she should be very sorry to disoblige her, but begged of her again, as she was a Christian and a woman, and had been a mother of children, that she would take pity on her, and if possible assist her, so that she might come to me and speak a few words to me.

The tender-hearted Quaker told me the girl spoke this with such moving eloquence that it forced tears from her, but she was obliged to say that she neither knew where I was gone nor how to write to me, but that if she did ever see me again she would not fail to give me an account of all she had said to her or that she should yet think fit to say, and to take my answer to it if I thought fit to give any.

Then the Quaker took the freedom to ask a few particulars about this wonderful story, as she called it; at which, the girl beginning at the first distresses of my life, and indeed of her own, went through all the history of her miserable education, her service under the Lady Roxana, as she called me, and her relief by Mrs. Amy; with the reasons she had to believe that as Amy owned herself to be the same that lived with her mother, and especially that Amy was the Lady Roxana's maid too and came out of France with her, she was by those circumstances, and several others in her conversation, as fully convinced that the Lady Roxana was her mother, as she was that the Lady ---- at her house (the Quaker's) was the very same Roxana that she had been servant to.

My good friend the Quaker, though terribly shocked at the story, and not well knowing what to say, yet was too much my friend to seem convinced in a thing which she did not know to be true, and which, if it was true, she could see plainly I had a mind should not be known; so she turned her discourse to argue the girl out of it. She insisted upon the slender evidence she had of the fact itself, and the rudeness of claiming so near a relation of one so much above her, and of whose concern in it she had no knowledge, at least not sufficient proof; that as the lady at her house was a person above any disguises, so she could not believe that she would deny her being her daughter if she was really her mother; that she was able sufficiently to have provided for her if she had not a mind to have her known; and therefore, seeing she had heard all she had said of the Lady Roxana, and was so far from owning herself to be the person, so she had censured that sham lady, as a cheat and a common woman; and that 'Twas certain she could never be brought to own a name and character she had so justly exposed.

Besides, she told her that her lodger (meaning me) was not a sham lady, but the real wife of a knight baronet, and that she knew her to be honestly such, and far above such a person as she had described. She then added that she had another reason why it was not very possible to be true; "and that is," says she, "thy age is in the way; for thou acknowledgest that thou art four-and-twenty years old, and that thou wast the youngest of three of thy mother's children, so that by thy account thy mother must be extremely young, or this lady cannot be thy mother; for thou seest," says she, "and any one may see, she is but a young woman now, and cannot be supposed to be above forty years old, if she is so much, and is now big with child at her going into the country. So that I cannot give any credit to thy notion of her being thy mother; and if I might counsel thee, it should be to give over that thought as an improbable story that does but serve to disorder thee and disturb thy head; for," added she, "I perceive thou art much disturbed indeed."

But this was all nothing. She could be satisfied with nothing but seeing me; but the Quaker defended herself very well, and insisted on it that she could not give her any account of me. And finding her still importunate, she affected at last being a little disgusted that she should not believe her, and added that indeed if she had known where I was gone, she would not have given anyone an account of it unless I had given her orders to do so. "But seeing she has not acquainted me," says she, "where she is gone, 'tis an intimation to me she was not desirous it should be publicly known." And with this she rose up, which was as plain a desiring her to rise up too and be gone as could be expressed, except the downright showing her the door.

Well, the girl rejected all this, and told her she could not indeed expect that she (the Quaker) should be affected with the story she had told her, however moving, or that she should take any pity on her. That it was her misfortune that when she was at the house before, and in the room with me, she did not beg to speak a word with me in private, or throw herself upon the floor at my feet and claim what the affection of a mother would have done for her; but since she had slipped her opportunity, she would wait for another. That she found by her (the Quaker's) talk that she had not quite left her lodgings, but was gone into the country, she supposed, for the air; and she was resolved she would take so much knight-errantry upon her, that she would visit all the airing places in the nation, and even all the kingdom over, ay, and Holland too, but she would find me; for she was satisfied she could so convince me that she was my own child, that I would not deny it, and she was sure I was so tender and compassionate, I would not let her perish after I was convinced that she was my own flesh and blood. And in saying she would visit all the airing-places in England, she reckoned them all up by name, and began with Tunbridge, the very place I was gone to; then reckoning up Epsom, Northall, Barnet, Newmarket, Bury, and at last the Bath. And with this she took her leave.

Chapter 29

My faithful agent the Quaker failed not to write to me immediately, but as she was a cunning as well as an honest woman, it presently occurred to her that this was a story which, whether true or false, was not very fit to come to my husband's knowledge; that as she did not know what I might have been, or might have been called in former times, and how far there might have been something or nothing in it, so she thought if it was a secret I ought to have the telling of it myself, and if it was not, it might as well be public afterwards as now; and that, at least, she ought to leave it where she found it, and not hand it forwards to anybody without my consent. These prudent measures were inexpressibly kind as well as seasonable, for it had been likely enough that her letter might have come publicly to me, and though my husband would not have opened it, yet it would have looked a little odd that I should conceal its contents from him when I had pretended so much to communicate all my affairs.

In consequence of this wise caution my good friend only wrote me in a few words that the impertinent young woman had been with her, as she expected she would, and that she thought it would be very convenient that, if I could spare Cherry, I would send her up (meaning Amy), because she found there might be some occasion for her.

As it happened, this letter was enclosed to Amy herself, and not sent by the way I had at first ordered, but it came safe to my hands; and though I was alarmed a little at it, yet I was not acquainted with the danger I was in of an immediate visit from this teasing creature till afterwards; and I ran a greater risk indeed than ordinary, in that I did not send Amy up under thirteen or fourteen days, believing myself as much concealed at Tunbridge as if I had been at Vienna.

But the concern my faithful spy (for such my Quaker was now, upon the mere foot of her own sagacity)--I say her concern for me was my safety in this exigence, when I was, as it were, keeping no guard for myself; for finding Amy not come up, and that she did not know how soon this wild thing might put her designed ramble in practice, she sent a messenger to the captain's wife's house, where she lodged, to tell her that she wanted to speak with her. She was at the heels of the messenger, and came eager for some news, and hoped, she said, the lady (meaning me) had been come to town.

The Quaker, with as much caution as she was mistress of, not to tell a downright lie, made her believe she expected to hear of me very quickly; and frequently, by the by, speaking of being abroad to take the air, talked of the country about Bury, how pleasant it was, how wholesome, and how fine the air, how the downs about Newmarket were exceeding fine, and what a vast deal of company there was, now the Court was there; till at last the girl began to conclude that my ladyship was gone thither; for, she said, she knew I loved to see a great deal of company.

"Nay," says my friend, "thou takest me wrong; I did not suggest," says she, "that the person thou enquirest after is gone thither, neither do I believe she is, I assure you." Well, the girl smiled, and let her know that she believed it for all that; so, to clinch it fast, "Verily," says she with great seriousness, "thou dost not do well, for thou suspectest everything and believest nothing. I speak solemnly to thee that I do not believe they are gone that way; so if thou givest thyself the trouble to go that way, and art disappointed, do not say that I have deceived thee." She knew well enough that if this did abate her suspicion, it would not remove it, and that it would do little more than amuse her; but by this she kept her in suspense till Amy came up, and that was enough.

When Amy came up she was quite confounded to hear the relation which the Quaker gave her, and found means to acquaint me of it, only letting me know, to my great satisfaction, that she would not come to Tunbridge first, but that she would certainly go to Newmarket or Bury first.

However, it gave me very great uneasiness, for as she resolved to ramble in search after me over the whole country, I was safe nowhere, no, not in Holland itself; so indeed I did not know what to do with her. And thus I had a bitter in all my sweet, for I was continually perplexed with this hussy and thought she haunted me like an evil spirit.

In the meantime Amy was next door to stark mad about her; she durst not see her at my lodgings, for her life, and she went days without number to Spitalfields, where she used to come, and to her former lodging, and could never meet with her. At length she took up a mad resolution that she would go directly to the captain's house in Redriff and speak with her; it was a mad step, that's true, but as Amy said she was mad, so nothing she could do could be otherwise. For if Amy had found her at Redriff, she (the girl) would have concluded presently that the Quaker had given her notice, and so that we were all of a knot, and that, in short, all she had said was right. But as it happened, things came to hit better than we expected; for that Amy, going out of a coach to take water at Tower Wharf, meets the girl just come on shore, having crossed the water from Redriff. Amy made as if she would have passed by her, though they met so full that she did not pretend she did not see her, for she looked fairly upon her first; but then, turning her head away. with a slight, offered to go from her, but the girl stopped and spoke first, and made some manners to her.

Amy spoke coldly to her and a little angry, and after some words, standing in the street or passage, the girl saying she seemed to be angry, and would not have spoken to her, "Why," says Amy, "how can you expect I should have any more to say to you, after I had done so much for you and you have behaved so to me?" The girl seemed to take no notice of that now, but answered, "I was going to wait on you now." "Wait on me!" says Amy; "what do you mean by that?" "Why," says she again, with a kind of familiarity, "I was going to your lodgings."

Amy was provoked to the last degree at her, and yet she thought it was not her time to resent, because she had a more fatal and wicked design in her head against her; which indeed I never knew till after it was executed, nor durst Amy ever communicate it to me, for as I had always expressed myself vehemently against hurting a hair of her head, so she was resolved to take her own measures without consulting me any more.

In order to this Amy gave her good words, and concealed her resentment as much as she could; and when she talked of going to her lodging, Amy smiled and said nothing, but called for a pair of oars to go to Greenwich, and asked her, seeing she said she was going to her lodging, to go along with her, for she was going home and was all alone.

Amy did this with such a stock of assurance that the girl was confounded and knew not what to say; but the more she hesitated the more Amy pressed her to go, and, talking very kindly to her, told her if she did not go to see her lodgings, she might go to keep her company, and she would pay a boat to bring her back again; so, in a word, Amy prevailed on her to go into the boat with her, and carried her down to Greenwich. 'tis certain that Amy had no more business at Greenwich than I had, nor was she going thither; but we were all hampered to the last degree with the impertinence of this creature, and in particular I was horribly perplexed with it.

As they were in the boat Amy began to reproach her with ingratitude in treating her so rudely, who had done so much for her and been so kind to her, and to ask her what she had got by it or what she expected to get. Then came in my share, the Lady Roxana; Amy jested with that, and bantered her a little and asked her if she had found her yet.

But Amy was both surprised and enraged when the girl told her roundly that she thanked her for what she had done for her, but that she would not have her think she was so ignorant as not to know that what she (Amy) had done was by her mother's order, and who she was beholden to for it. That she could never make instruments pass for principals, and pay the debt to the agent, when the obligation was all to the original. That she knew well enough who she was, and who she was employed by. That she knew the Lady ---- very well (naming the name that I now went by), which was my husband's true name, and by which she might know whether she had found out her mother or no.

Amy wished her at the bottom of the Thames; and had there been no watermen in the boat and nobody in sight, she swore to me she would have thrown her into the river. I was horribly disturbed when she told me this story, and began to think this would at last all end in my ruin; but when Amy spoke of throwing her into the river and drowning her, I was so provoked at her, that all my rage turned against

Amy and I fell thoroughly out with her. I had now kept Amy almost thirty years, and found her on all occasions the faithfulest creature to me that ever woman had; I say faithful to me, for however wicked she was, still she was true to me; and even this rage of hers was all upon my account, and for fear any mischief should befall me.

But be that how it would, I could not bear the mention of her murdering the poor girl, and it put me so beside myself that I rose up in a rage and bade her get out of my sight and out of my house; told her I had kept her too long, and that I would never see her face more. I had before told her that she was a murderer and a bloody-minded creature, that she could not but know that I could not bear the thought of it, much less the mention of it, and that it was the impudentest thing that ever was known, to make such a proposal to me, when she knew that I was really the mother of this girl, and that she was my own child; that it was wicked enough in her, but that she must conclude I was ten times wickeder than herself if I could come into it; that the girl was in the right, and I had nothing to blame her for, but that it was owing to the wickedness of my life that made it necessary for me to keep her from a discovery, but that I would not murder my child though I was otherwise to be ruined by it. Amy replied somewhat rough and short, would I not, but she would, she said, if she had an opportunity. And upon these words it was that I bade her get out of my sight and out of my house; and it went so far that Amy packed up her alls and marched off, and was gone for almost good and all. But of that in its order; I must go back to her relation of the voyage which they made to Greenwich together.

They held on the wrangle all the way by water; the girl insisted upon her knowing that I was her mother, and told her all the history of my life in the Pall Mall, as well after her being turned away, as before, and of my marriage since; and which was worse, not only who my present husband was, but where he had lived, viz. at Rouen in France; she knew nothing of Paris or of where we were going to live, namely, at Nimeguen, but told her in so many words that if she could not find me here, she would go to Holland after me.

They landed at Greenwich and Amy carried her into the Park with her, and they walked above two hours there in the farthest and remotest walks; which Amy did because as they talked with great heat, it was apparent they were quarrelling, and the people took notice of it.

They walked till they came almost to the wilderness at the south side of the Park, but the girl, perceiving Amy offered to go in there among the woods and trees, stopped short there and would go no further, but said she would not go in there.

Amy smiled and asked her what was the matter. She replied short, she did not know where she was nor where she was going to carry her, and she would go no further, and without any more ceremony turns back and walks apace away from her. Amy owned she was surprised, and came back too and called to her, upon which the girl stopped, and Amy coming up to her, asked her what she meant.

The girl boldly replied she did not know but she might murder her, and that, in short, she would not trust herself with her, and never would come into her company again alone.

It was very provoking; but, however, Amy kept her temper with much difficulty, and bore it, knowing that much might depend upon it; so she mocked her foolish jealousy and told her she need not be uneasy for her, she would do her no harm, and would have done her good if she would have let her; but since she was of such a refractory humour, she should not trouble herself, for she should never come into her company again, and that neither she nor her brother or sister should ever hear from her or see her any more; and so she should have the satisfaction of being the ruin of her brother and sister, as well as of herself.

The girl seemed a little mollified at that, and said, that for herself she knew the worst of it, she could seek her fortune, but 'twas hard her brother and sister should suffer on her score, and said something that was tender and well enough on that account. But Amy told her it was for her to take that into consideration, for she would let her see that it was all her own; that she would have done them all good, but that having been used thus, she would do no more for any of them; and that she should not need to be afraid to come into her company again, for she would never give her occasion for it any more; by the way, was false in the girl too, for she did venture into Amy's company again after that, once too much, as I shall relate by itself.

They grew cooler, however, afterwards, and Amy carried her into a house at Greenwich where she was acquainted, and took an occasion to leave the girl in a room awhile, to speak to the people in the house, and so prepare them to own her as a lodger in the house; and then going in to her again, told her there she lodged if she had a mind to find her out, or if anybody else had anything to say to her. And so Amy dismissed her and got rid of her again, and finding an empty hackney-coach in the town, came away by land to London, and the girl going down to the waterside, came by boat.

This conversation did not answer Amy's end at all, because it did not secure the girl from pursuing her design of hunting me out; and though my indefatigable friend the Quaker amused her three or four days, yet I had such notice of it at last, that I thought fit to come away from Tunbridge upon it, and where to go I knew not; but, in short, I went to a little village upon Epping Forest, called Woodford, and took lodgings in a private house, where I lived retired about six weeks, till I thought she might be tired of her search and have given me over.

Here I received an account from my trusty Quaker that the wench had really been at Tunbridge, had found out my lodgings, and had told her tale there in a most dismal tone; that she had followed us as she thought, to London, but the Quaker had answered her that she knew nothing of it, which was indeed true, and had admonished her to be easy and not hunt after people of such fashion as we were, as if we were thieves; that she might be assured that since I was not willing to see her, I would not be forced to it, and treating me thus would effectually disoblige me. And with such discourses as these she quieted her; and she (the Quaker) added that she hoped I should not be troubled much more with her.

It was in this time that Amy gave me the history of her Greenwich voyage, when she spoke of drowning and killing the girl, in so serious a manner, and with such an apparent resolution of doing it, that, as I said, put me in a rage with her, so that I effectually turned her away from me, as I have said above; and she was gone, nor did she so much as tell me whither or which way she was gone; on the other hand, when I came to reflect on it, that now I had neither assistant nor confidante to speak to or receive the least information, my friend the Quaker excepted, it made me very uneasy.

I waited and expected, and wondered from day to day, still thinking Amy would one time or other think a little and come again, or at least let me hear of her, but for ten days together I heard nothing of her. I was so impatient that I got neither rest by day nor sleep by night, and what to do I knew not. I durst not go to town to the Quaker's, for fear of meeting that vexatious creature my girl, and I could get no intelligence, where I was; so I got my spouse, upon pretence of wanting her company, to take the coach one day and fetch my good Quaker to me.

When I had her I durst ask her no questions, nor hardly knew which end of the business to begin to talk of; but of her own accord she told me that the girl had been three or four times haunting her for news from me, and that she had been so troublesome that she had been obliged to show herself a little angry with her, and at last told her plainly that she need give herself no trouble in searching after me by her means, for she (the Quaker) would not tell her if she knew; upon which she refrained awhile. But on the other hand, she told me, it was not safe for me to send my own coach for her to come in, for she had some reason to believe that she (my daughter) watched her door night and day, nay, and watched her too every time she went in and out; for she was so bent upon a discovery that she spared no pains, and she believed she had taken a lodging very near their house for that purpose.

I could hardly give her a hearing of all this for my eagerness to ask for Amy, but I was confounded when she told me she had heard nothing of her. 'Tis impossible to express the anxious thoughts that rolled about in my mind and continually perplexed me about her; particularly I reproached myself with my rashness in turning away so faithful a creature, that for so many years had not only been a servant but an agent, and not only an agent but a friend, and a faithful friend too.

Then I considered too that Amy knew all the secret history of my life, had been in all the intrigues of it, and been a party in both evil and good, and at best there was no policy in it; that as it was very ungenerous and unkind to run things to such an extremity with her, and for an occasion too in which all the fault she was guilty of was owing to her excess of care for my safety, so it must be only her steady kindness to me, and an excess of generous friendship for me, that should keep her from ill-using me in return for it, which ill-using me was enough in her power and might be my utter undoing.

Chapter 29

These thoughts perplexed me exceedingly, and what course to take I really did not know. I began indeed to give Amy quite over, for she had now been gone above a fortnight, and as she had taken away all her clothes and her money too, which was not a little, and so had no occasion of that kind to come any more, so she had not left any word where she was gone, or to which part of the world I might send to hear of her.

And I was troubled on another account too, viz. that my spouse and I too had resolved to do very handsomely for Amy, without considering what she might have got another way at all; but we had said nothing of it to her, and so I thought as she had not known what was likely to fall in her way, she had not the influence of that expectation to make her come back.

Upon the whole, the perplexity of this girl who hunted me, as if, like a hound, she had had a hot scent but was now at a fault--I say that perplexity, and this other part of Amy being gone, issued in this, I resolved to be gone, and go over to Holland; there I believed I should be at rest. So I took occasion one day to tell my spouse that I was afraid he might take it ill that I had amused him thus long, and that at last I doubted I was not with child, and that since it was so, our things being packed up and all in order for going to Holland, I would go away now when he pleased.

My spouse, who was perfectly easy whether in going or staying, left it all entirely to me; so I considered of it and began to prepare again for my voyage. But, alas! I was irresolute to the last degree; I was, for want of Amy, destitute. I had lost my right hand; she was my steward, gathered in my rents, I mean my interest money, and kept any accounts, and, in a word, did all my business; and without her indeed I knew not how to go away nor how to stay. But an accident thrust itself in here, and that even in Amy's conduct too, which frighted me away, and without her too, in the utmost horror and confusion.

I have related how my faithful friend the Quaker was come to me, and what account she gave me of her being continually haunted by my daughter, and that, as she said, she watched her very door night and day. The truth was she had set a spy to watch so effectually that she (the Quaker) neither went in nor out but she had notice of it.

This was too evident when, the next morning after she came to me (for I kept her all night), to my unspeakable surprise I saw a hackney-coach stop at the door where I lodged, and saw her (my daughter) in the coach all alone. It was a very good chance in the middle of a bad one that my husband had taken out the coach that very morning and was gone to London; as for me, I had neither life nor soul left in me, I was so confounded I knew not what to do or to say.

My happy visitor had more presence of mind than I, and asked me if I had made no acquaintance among the neighbours. I told her, Yes, there was a lady lodged two doors off, that I was very intimate with. "But hast thou no way out backward to go to her?" says she. Now it happened there was a back door in the garden, by which we usually went and came to and from the house, so I told her of it. "Well, well," says she, "go out and make a visit then, and leave the rest to me." Away I ran, told the lady (for I was very free there) that I was a widow to-day, my spouse being gone to London, so I came not to visit her but to dwell with her that day, because also our landlady had got strangers come from London. So having framed this orderly lie, I pulled some work out of my pocket, and added, "I did not come to be idle."

As I went out one way, my friend the Quaker went the other to receive this unwelcome guest. The girl made but little ceremony, but, having bid the coachman ring at the gate, gets down out of the coach and comes to the door, a country girl going to the door (belonging to the house), for the Quaker forbade any of my maids going. Madam asked for my Quaker by name, and the girl asked her to walk in.

Upon this, my Quaker, seeing there was no hanging back, goes to her immediately, but put on all the gravity upon her countenance that she was mistress of, and that was not a little indeed.

When she (the Quaker) came into the room (for they had shown my daughter into a little parlour), she kept her grave countenance but said not a word, nor did my daughter speak a good while. But after some time my girl began and said, "I suppose you know me, madam?"

"Yes," said the Quaker, "I know thee"; and so the dialogue went on.

Girl. "Then you know my business too."

Quaker. "No, verily, I do not know any business thou canst have here with me."

Girl. "Indeed, my business is not chiefly with you."

Quaker. "Why then dost thou come after me thus far?"

Girl. "You know who I seek." (And with that she cried.)

Quaker. "But why shouldst thou follow me for her, since thou knowest that I assured thee more than once that I knew not where she was?"

Girl. "But I hoped you could."

Quaker. "Then thou must hope that I did not speak truth, which would be very wicked."

Girl. "I doubt not but she is in this house."

Quaker. "If those be thy thoughts, thou may'st enquire in the house; so thou hast no more business with me. Farewell." (Offers to go.)

Girl. "I would not be uncivil; I beg you to let me see her."

Quaker. "I am here to visit some of my friends, and I think thou art very uncivil in following me hither."

Girl. "I came in hopes of a discovery in my great affair, which you know of."

Quaker. "Thou cam'st wildly indeed. I counsel thee to go back again and be easy. I shall keep my word with thee that I would not meddle in it or give thee any account, if I knew it, unless I had her orders."

Girl. "If you knew my distress, you could not be so cruel."

Quaker. "Thou hast told me all thy story, and I think it might be more cruelty to tell thee than not to tell thee; for I understand she is resolved not to see thee, and declares she is not thy mother. Willst thou be owned where thou hast no relation?"

Girl. "Oh! if I could but speak to her, I would prove my relation to her so that she could not deny it any longer."

Quaker. "Well, but thou canst not come to speak with her, it seems."

Girl. "I hope you will tell me if she is here; I had a good account that you were come out to see her, and that she sent for you."

Quaker. "I much wonder how thou couldst have such an account; if I had come out to see her, thou hast happened to miss the house, for I assure thee she is not to be found in this house."

Here the girl importuned her again with the utmost earnestness, and cried bitterly, insomuch that my poor Quaker was softened with it, and began to persuade me to consider of it, and if it might consist with my affairs to see her and hear what she had to say; but this was afterwards. I return to the discourse.

The Quaker was perplexed with her a long time; she talked of sending back the coach and lying in the town all night. This my friend knew would be very uneasy to me, but she durst not speak a word against it; but on a sudden thought she offered a bold stroke, which, though dangerous if it happened wrong, had its desired effect.

She told her, that as for dismissing her coach, that was as she pleased; she believed she would not easily get a lodging in the town, but that as she was in a strange place, she would so much befriend her that she would speak to the people of the house, that if they had a room she might have a lodging there for one night, rather than be forced back to London before she was free to go.

This was a cunning though a dangerous step, and it succeeded accordingly, for it amused the creature entirely, and she presently concluded that really I could not be there, then; otherwise she would never have asked her to lie in the house. So she grew cold again presently as to her lodging there, and said, No, since it was so, she would go back that afternoon, but she would come again in two or three days, and search that and all the towns round in an effectual manner, if she stayed a week or two to do it; for, in short, if I was in England or Holland, she would find me.

"In truth," says the Quaker, "thou wilt make me very hurtful to thee, then." "Why so?" says she. "Because wherever I go thou wilt put thyself to great expense, and the country to a great deal of unnecessary trouble." "Not unnecessary," says she. "Yes, truly," says the Quaker, "it must be unnecessary, because 'twill be to no purpose. I think I must abide in my own house, to save thee that charge and trouble."

She said little to that, except that she said she would give her as little trouble as possible, but she was afraid she should sometimes be uneasy to her, which she hoped she would excuse. My Quaker told her she would much rather excuse her if she would forbear; for that, if she would believe her, she would assure her she should never get any intelligence of me by her.

That set her into tears again; but after a while recovering herself, she told her perhaps she might be mistaken, and she (the Quaker) should watch herself very narrowly, or she might one time or other get some intelligence from her whether she would or no; and she was satisfied she had gained some of her by this journey, for that if I was not in the house I was not far off, and if I did not remove very quickly she would find me out. "Very well," says my Quaker, "then if the lady is not willing to see thee, thou givest me notice to tell her that she may get out of thy way."

She flew out in a rage at that, and told my friend that if she did, a curse would follow her and her children after her, and denounced such horrid things upon her as frighted the poor tender-hearted Quaker strangely, and put her more out of temper than ever I saw her before; so that she resolved to go home the next morning, and I, that was ten times more uneasy than she, resolved to follow her and go to London too; which however, upon second thoughts, I did not, but took effectual measures not to be seen or owned if she came any more; but I heard no more of her for some time.

Chapter 30

I stayed there about a fortnight, and in all that time I heard no more of her or of my Quaker about her. But after about two days more I had a letter from my Quaker, intimating that she had something of moment to say that she could not communicate by a letter, but wished I would give myself the trouble to come up; directing me to come with the coach into Goodman's Fields and then walk to her back door on foot, which being left open on purpose, the watchful lady, if she had any spies, could not well see me.

My thoughts had for so long time been kept, as it were, waking, that almost everything gave me the alarm, and this especially, so that I was very uneasy; but I could not bring matters to bear to make my coming to London so clear to my husband as I would have done, for he liked the place and had a mind, he said, to stay a little longer, if it was not against my inclination. So I wrote my friend the Quaker word that I could not come to town yet, and that besides I could not think of being there under spies and afraid to look out of doors; and so, in short, I put off going for near a fortnight more.

At the end of that time she wrote again, in which she told me that she had not lately seen the impertinent visitor which had been so troublesome, but that she had seen my trusty agent Amy, who told her she had cried for six weeks without intermission; that Amy had given her an account how troublesome the creature had been, and to what straits and perplexities I was driven by her hunting after and following me from place to place. Upon which Amy had said, that notwithstanding I was angry with her and had used her so hardly for saying something about her of the same kind, yet there was an absolute necessity of securing her and removing her out of the way; and that, in short, without asking my leave or anybody's leave, she would take care she should trouble her mistress (meaning me) no more, and that after Amy had said so, she had indeed never heard any more of the girl; so that she supposed Amy had managed it so well as to put an end to it.

The innocent well-meaning creature, my Quaker, who was all kindness and goodness in herself, and particularly to me, saw nothing in this but she thought Amy had found some way to persuade her to be quiet and easy and to give over teasing and following me, and rejoiced in it for my sake; as she thought nothing of any evil herself, so she suspected none in anybody else, and was exceeding glad of having such good news to write to me. But my thoughts of it ran otherwise.

I was struck as with a blast from Heaven at the reading her letter. I fell into a fit of trembling from head to foot, and I ran raving about the room like a madwoman. I had nobody to speak a word to, to give vent to my passion, nor did I speak a word for a good while, till after it had almost overcome me. I threw myself on the bed and cried out, "Lord, be merciful to me, she has murdered my child "; and with that a flood of tears burst out, and I cried vehemently for above an hour.

My husband was very happily gone out a-hunting, so that I had every opportunity of being alone, and to give my passions some vent, by which I a little recovered myself. But after my crying was over, then I fell in a new rage at Amy. I called her a thousand devils and monsters and hard-hearted tigers; I reproached her with her knowing that I abhorred it, and had let her know it sufficiently, in that I had, as it were, kicked her out of doors, after so many years' friendship and service, only for naming it to me.

Well, after some time my spouse came in from his sport, and I put on the best looks I could to deceive him; but he did not take so little notice of me as not to see I had been crying and that something troubled me, and he pressed me to tell him. I seemed to bring it out with reluctance, but told him my backwardness was more because I was ashamed that such a trifle should have any effect upon me, than for any weight that was in it. So I told him I had been vexing myself about my woman Amy not coming again, that she might have known me better than not to believe I should have been friends with her again, and the like; and that, in short, I had lost the best servant by my rashness that ever woman had.

"Well, well," says he, "if that be all your grief, I hope you will soon shake it off; I'll warrant you in a little while we shall hear of Mrs. Amy again "; and so it went off for that time. But it did not go off with me, for I was uneasy and terrified to the last degree, and wanted to get some further account of the thing. So I went away to my sure and certain comforter the Quaker, and there I had the whole story of it; and the good innocent Quaker gave me joy of my being rid of such an unsufferable tormentor.

"Rid of her! Ay," says I, "if I was rid of her fairly and honourably; but I don't know what Amy may have done; sure she hasn't made her away?" "Oh, fie!" says my Quaker, "how canst thou entertain such a notion? No, no, made her away! Amy didn't talk like that; I dare say thou may'st be easy in that, Amy has nothing of that in her head, I dare say," says she; and so threw it, as it were, out of my thoughts.

But it would not do; it ran in my head continually, night and day I could think of nothing else; and it fixed such a horror of the fact upon my spirits, and such a detestation of Amy, who I looked upon as the murderer, that, as for her, I believe if I could have seen her, I should certainly have sent her to Newgate, or to a worse place, upon suspicion; indeed I think I could have killed her with my own hands.

As for the poor girl herself, she was ever before my eyes. I saw her by night and by day; she haunted my imagination, if she did not haunt the house; my fancy showed her me in a hundred shapes and postures; sleeping or waking, she was with me. Sometimes I thought I saw her with her throat cut, sometimes with her head cut and her brains knocked out, other times hanged up upon a beam, another time drowned in the great pond at Camberwell. And all these appearances were terrifying to the last degree; and that which was still worse, I could really hear nothing of her. I sent to the captain's wife in Redriff, and she answered me she was gone to her relations in Spitalfields. I sent thither, and they said she was there about three weeks ago, but that she went out in a coach with the gentlewoman that used to be so kind to her, but whither she was gone they knew not, for she had not been there since. I sent back the messenger for a description of the woman she went out with, and they described her so perfectly that I knew it to be Amy, and none but Amy.

I sent word again that Mrs. Amy, who she went out with, left her in two or three hours, and that they should search for her, for I had reason to fear she was murdered. This frighted them all intolerably. They believed Amy had carried her to pay her a sum of money, and that somebody had watched her after her having received it, and had robbed and murdered her.

I believed nothing of that part; but I believed as it was, that whatever was done, Amy had done it, and that, in short, Amy had made her away; and I believed it the more because Amy came no more near me, but confirmed her guilt by her absence.

Upon the whole, I mourned thus for her for above a month, but finding Amy still come not near me, and that I must put my affairs in a posture that I might go to Holland, I opened all my affairs to my dear trusty friend the Quaker, and placed her, in matters of trust, in the room of Amy, and with a heavy, bleeding heart for my poor girl, I embarked with my spouse, and all our equipage and goods, on board another Holland trader, not a packet-boat, and went over to Holland, where I arrived as I have said.

I must put in a caution, however, here, that you must not understand me as if I let my friend the Quaker into any part of the secret history of my former life; nor did I commit the grand reserved article of all to her, viz. that I was really the girl's mother, and the Lady Roxana. There was no need of that part being exposed, and it was always a maxim with me that secrets should never be opened without evident utility. It could be of no manner of use to me or her to communicate that part to her; besides, she was too honest herself, to make it safe to me. For though she loved me very sincerely, and it was plain by many circumstances that she did so, yet she would not lie for me upon occasion, as Amy would, and therefore it was not advisable on any terms to communicate that part; for if the girl, or anyone else, should have come to her afterwards and put it home to her, whether she knew that I was the girl's mother or not, or was the same as the Lady Roxana or not, she either would not have denied it or would have done it with so ill a grace, such blushing, such hesitations, and falterings in her answers, as would have put the matter out of doubt, and betrayed herself and the secret too.

For this reason, I say, I did not discover anything of that kind to her; but I placed her, as I have said, in Amy's stead, in the other affairs of receiving money, interests, rents, and the like, and she was as faithful as Amy could be, and as diligent.

But there fell out a great difficulty here which I knew not how to get over, and this was, how to convey the usual supply or provision and money to the uncle and the other sister, who depended, especially the sister, upon the said supply for her support; and indeed, though Amy had said rashly that she would not take any more notice of the sister, and would leave her to perish, as above, yet it was neither in my nature nor Amy's either, much less was it in my design, and therefore I resolved to leave the management of what I had reserved for that work with my faithful Quaker, but how to direct her to manage them was the great difficulty.

Amy had told them in so many words that she was not their mother, but that she was the maid Amy that carried them to their aunt's; that she and their mother went over to the East Indies to seek their fortune, and that there good things had befallen them, and that their mother was very rich and happy; that she (Amy) had married in the Indies, but being now a widow, and resolving to come over to England, their mother had obliged her to enquire them out and do for them as she had done, and that now she was resolved to go back to the Indies again; but that she had orders from their mother to do very handsomely by them, and, in a word, told them she had £2,000 apiece for them upon condition that they proved sober, and married suitably to themselves, and did not throw themselves away upon scoundrels.

The good family in whose care they had been, I had resolved to take more than ordinary notice of; and Amy, by my order, had acquainted them with it and obliged my daughters to promise to submit to their government as formerly, and to be ruled by the honest man as by a father and counsellor, and engaged him to treat them as his children; and to oblige him effectually to take care of them, and to make his old age comfortable both to him and his wife, who had been so good to the orphans, I had ordered her to settle the other £2,000, that is to say, the interest of it, which was £120 a year, upon them, to be theirs for both their lives, but to come to my two daughters after them. This was so just, and was so prudently managed by Amy, that nothing she ever did for me pleased me better. And in this posture, leaving my two daughters with their ancient friend, and so coming away to me (as they thought to the East Indies) she had prepared everything in order to her going over with me to Holland; and in this posture that matter stood when that unhappy girl whom I have said so much of broke in upon all our measures, as you have heard; and by an obstinacy never to be conquered or pacified, either with threats or persuasions, pursued her search after me (her mother) as I have said, till she brought me even to the brink of destruction, and would in all probability have traced me out at last, if Amy had not by the violence of her passion, and by a way which I had no knowledge of, and indeed abhorred, put a stop to her, of which I cannot enter into the particulars here.

However, notwithstanding this, I could not think of going away and leaving this work so unfinished as Amy had threatened to do, and for the folly of one child, to leave the other to starve, or to stop my determined bounty to the good family I have mentioned. So, in a word, I committed the finishing it all to my faithful friend the Quaker, to whom I communicated as much of the old story as was needful to empower her to perform what Amy had promised, and to make her talk so much to the purpose, as one employed more remotely than Amy had been, needed to do.

To this purpose she had first of all a full possession of the money, and went first to the honest man and his wife and settled all the matter with them. When she talked of Mrs. Amy she talked of her as one that had been empowered by the mother of the girls in the Indies, but was obliged to go back to the Indies, and had settled all sooner if she had not been hindered by the obstinate humour of the other daughter; that she had left instructions with her for the rest, but that the other had affronted her so much that she was gone away without doing anything for her; and that now, if anything was done, it must be by fresh orders from the East Indies.

I need not say how punctually my new agent acted; but which was more, she brought the old man and his wife, and my other daughter, several times to her house, by which I had an opportunity, being there only as a lodger and a stranger, to see my other girl, which I had never done before since she was a little child.

The day I contrived to see them I was dressed up in a Quaker's habit, and looked so like a Quaker that it was impossible for them, who had never seen me before, to suppose I had ever been anything else; also my way of talking was suitable enough to it, for I had learned that long before.

I have not time here to take notice what a surprise it was to me to see my child; how it worked upon my affections; with what infinite struggle I mastered a strong inclination that I had to discover myself to her; how the girl was the very counterpart of myself, only much handsomer, and how sweetly and modestly she behaved; how on that occasion I resolved to do more for her than I had appointed by Amy, and the like.

'Tis enough to mention here that as the settling this affair made way for my going on board, notwithstanding the absence of my old agent Amy, so however I left some hints for Amy too, for I did not yet despair of my hearing from her; and that if my good Quaker should ever see her again, she should let her see them; wherein particularly ordering her to leave the affair of Spitalfields just as I had done, in the hands of my friend, she should come away to me, upon this condition nevertheless, that she gave full satisfaction to my friend the Quaker that she had not murdered my child; for if she had, I told her, I would never see her face more; how, notwithstanding this, she came over afterwards without giving my friend any of that satisfaction or any account that she intended to come over.

I can say no more now, but that, as above, being arrived in Holland with my spouse and his son, formerly mentioned, I appeared there with all the splendour and equipage suitable to our new prospect, as I have already observed.

Here, after some few years of flourishing and outwardly happy circumstances, I fell into a dreadful course of calamities, and Amy also; the very reverse of our former good days. The blast of Heaven seemed to follow the injury done the poor girl by us both, and I was brought so low again that my repentance seemed to be only the consequence of my misery, as my misery was of my crime.

THE END

The Scarlet Pimpernel Omnibus - Unabridged - The Scarlet Pimpernel, I Will Repay, Eldorado, Sir Percy Hits Back
Baroness Orczy
Oxford City Press, 2012
824 pages
ISBN: 978-1-78139-228-7

Available from www.amazon.com, www.amazon.co.uk

The Scarlet Pimpernel appears in a play and a series of novels and short stories by Baroness Emmuska Orczy. They are set at the start of the French Revolution, Pimpernel being a master of disguise and a precursor to other heroes such as Zorro and Batman. The play and the tales brought Orczy international acclaim, being translated into sixteen languages. This omnibus edition includes the following unabridged stories: The Scarlet Pimpernel, I Will Repay, Eldorado, and Sir Percy Hits Back

The Complete Captain Blood and other Famous Sabatini Novels (unabridged) - Captain Blood, Captain Blood Returns (or The Chronicles of Captain Blood), The Fortunes of Captain Blood, Scaramouche and The Sea-Hawk
Rafael Sabatini
Oxford City Press, 2012
1064 pages
ISBN: 978-1-78139-251-5

Available from www.amazon.com,
www.amazon.co.uk

This volume contains the Captain Blood novel, plus the series of short stories - Captain Blood Returns (or the Chronicles of Captain Blood) and The Fortunes of Captain Blood, plus the novels Scaramouche and The Sea-Hawk. Rafael Sabatini is a master storyteller, his stories full of action and intrigue. The Daily Telegraph described him thus: 'One wonders if there is another storyteller so adroit at filling his pages with intrigue and counter-intrigue, with danger threaded with romance, with a background of lavish colour, of silks and velvets, of swords and jewels'. This book is a must-have for fans of action-packed swashbuckling stories.

Anthony Hope Omnibus, containing Dolly Dialogues,The Prisoner of Zenda, Rupert of Hentzau, Simon Dale, The King's Mirror and Quisanté (all unabridged)
Anthony Hope
Benediction Classics, 2012
1032 pages
ISBN: 978-1-78139-255-3

Available from www.amazon.com, www.amazon.co.uk

Anthony Hope (1863 - 1933), more fully Sir Anthony Hope Hawkins was an English novelist and playwright. He was a prolific writer of adventure novels and his stories "The Prisoner of Zenda" and "Rupert of Hentzau" are minor classics of English Literature, inspiring many adaptations. These books offer the greatest swashbuckling of all time with cliffhanging chapters, romance, swordfights and foreign intrigue. In addition, Hope's other works - "Dolly Dialogues" which gave him his first major literary success - A.E.W. Mason deemed these conversations "so truly set in the London of their day that the social historian would be unwise to neglect them" and said they were written with "delicate wit [and] a shade of sadness." Then "Simon Dale" is an historical novel involving the actress and courtesan Nell Gwyn. Hope considered "The King's Mirror" to be one of his best works and he was elected chairman of the committee of the Society of Authors after he published Quisanté.

The Complete Richard Hannay - 39 Steps, Greenmantle, Mr Steadfast, Three Hostages, Island of Sheep.
John Buchan
Benediction Classics, 2012
908 pages
ISBN: 978-1-78139-203-4

Available from www.amazon.com, www.amazon.co.uk

The Complete Richard Hannay includes the five John Buchan novels that feature the hero: 39 Steps, Greenmantle, Mr Steadfast, Three Hostages, Island of Sheep. Richard Hannay was one of the first modern spy thriller heroes and has shaped the genre. Hannay is strong and silent, combining the Scottish dourness with the English "stiff upper lip". He is tough and shrewd, courageous and resourceful. However, unlike later spy thrillers he has a greater breadth of emotion. He is philosophical and refuses to demonise his enemies, he falls in love, he is dependent upon his friends and he is religious. These books are exciting, with Richard Hannay being chased over moor and glen, they are page turning thrillers.

Also from Benediction Books ...
Wandering Between Two Worlds: Essays on Faith and Art
Anita Mathias
Benediction Books, 2007
152 pages
ISBN: 0955373700

Available from www.amazon.com, www.amazon.co.uk

In these wide-ranging lyrical essays, Anita Mathias writes, in lush, lovely prose, of her naughty Catholic childhood in Jamshedpur, India; her large, eccentric family in Mangalore, a sea-coast town converted by the Portuguese in the sixteenth century; her rebellion and atheism as a teenager in her Himalayan boarding school, run by German missionary nuns, St. Mary's Convent, Nainital; and her abrupt religious conversion after which she entered Mother Teresa's convent in Calcutta as a novice. Later rich, elegant essays explore the dualities of her life as a writer, mother, and Christian in the United States-- Domesticity and Art, Writing and Prayer, and the experience of being "an alien and stranger" as an immigrant in America, sensing the need for roots.

About the Author

Anita Mathias is the author of *Wandering Between Two Worlds: Essays on Faith and Art*. She has a B.A. and M.A. in English from Somerville College, Oxford University, and an M.A. in Creative Writing from the Ohio State University, USA. Anita won a National Endowment of the Arts fellowship in Creative Non-fiction in 1997. She lives in Oxford, England with her husband, Roy, and her daughters, Zoe and Irene.

Anita's website:
http://www.anitamathias.com, and
Anita's blog Dreaming Beneath the Spires:
http://dreamingbeneaththespires.blogspot.com

The Church That Had Too Much
Anita Mathias
Benediction Books, 2010
52 pages
ISBN: 9781849026567

Available from www.amazon.com, www.amazon.co.uk

The Church That Had Too Much was very well-intentioned. She wanted to love God, she wanted to love people, but she was both hampered by her muchness and the abundance of her possessions, and beset by ambition, power struggles and snobbery. Read about the surprising way The Church That Had Too Much began to resolve her problems in this deceptively simple and enchanting fable.

About the Author

Anita Mathias is the author of *Wandering Between Two Worlds: Essays on Faith and Art*. She has a B.A. and M.A. in English from Somerville College, Oxford University, and an M.A. in Creative Writing from the Ohio State University, USA. Anita won a National Endowment of the Arts fellowship in Creative Non-fiction in 1997. She lives in Oxford, England with her husband, Roy, and her daughters, Zoe and Irene.

Anita's website:
http://www.anitamathias.com, and
Anita's blog Dreaming Beneath the Spires:
http://dreamingbeneaththespires.blogspot.com

www.ingramcontent.com/pod-product-compliance
Lightning Source LLC
Chambersburg PA
CBHW081129300726
48982CB00005B/897
9781781393277